WARHAMMER®
CHRONICLES

KNIGHTS OF THE
EMPIRE

DAN ABNETT
NIK VINCENT
JAMES WALLIS
RICHARD WILLIAMS
JOSH REYNOLDS

BLACK LIBRARY

A BLACK LIBRARY PUBLICATION

Hammers of Ulric first published in 2000.
Reiksguard first published in 2009.
Knight of the Blazing Sun first published in 2012.
Dead Calm first published in 2011
Stromfel's Teeth first published in 2012
Lords of the Marsh first published in 2012
Dead Man's Party first published in 2012
Bernheimer's Gun first published in 2014
This edition published in Great Britain in 2019 by
Black Library,
Games Workshop Ltd.,
Willow Road,
Nottingham, NG7 2WS, UK.

10 9 8 7 6 5 4 3 2 1

Produced by Games Workshop in Nottingham.
Cover illustration by Dave Gallagher.
Map by Nuala Kinrade.

A CIP record for this book is available from the British Library.

ISBN 13: 978 1 78496 893 9

This is a dark age, a bloody age, an age of daemons
and of sorcery. It is an age of battle and death, and of the
world's ending. Amidst all of the fire, flame and fury
it is a time, too, of mighty heroes, of bold deeds
and great courage.

At the heart of the Old World sprawls the Empire, the
largest and most powerful of the human realms. Known
for its engineers, sorcerers, traders and soldiers, it is
a land of great mountains, mighty rivers, dark forests
and vast cities. And from his throne in Altdorf reigns
the Emperor Karl Franz, sacred descendant of the
founder of these lands, Sigmar, and wielder
of his magical warhammer.

But these are far from civilised times. Across the
length and breadth of the Old World, from the knightly
palaces of Bretonnia to ice-bound Kislev in the far north,
come rumblings of war. In the towering Worlds Edge
Mountains, the orc tribes are gathering for another assault.
Bandits and renegades harry the wild southern lands of
the Border Princes. There are rumours of rat-things, the
skaven, emerging from the sewers and swamps across the
land. And from the northern wildernesses there is the
ever-present threat of Chaos, of daemons and beastmen
corrupted by the foul powers of the Dark Gods.
As the time of battle draws ever nearer,
the Empire needs heroes
like never before.

CONTENTS

HAMMERS OF ULRIC

Dan Abnett, Nik Vincent & James Wallis

JAHRDRUNG

A COMPANY OF WOLVES

It was, to no one's great surprise, raining in Middenheim that day.

Spring rain, fresh as ice needles, spattered down on that vast old city which sat brooding atop its granite crag, gazing down across the dismal forests around it. Another long winter season was slowly thawing, and the city, and everyone in it, was cold and wet and miserable to the bone.

In a puddled yard behind the Spread Eagle tavern, Morgenstern carefully adjusted a line of plump turnips he had arranged along the flagstones, each one sat on an upturned pail. Then he walked to the end of the yard, belched delicately with a hand to his mouth and little finger cocked, then spat on his meaty palms and hefted up the great warhammer leaning against the slimy bricks.

He began to spin it, crossing his grip deftly, looping the mighty head back and forth in a figure of eight around his shoulders. *Whooooff! Whooooff! Whooooff!* it hissed as it circled. But Morgenstern was standing a little too close to the back wall and, after another circuit, the hammerhead struck against the stonework. Several bricks shattered and dropped out, and the warhammer bounced to the ground.

Morgenstern swore colourfully, and wobbled slightly as he stooped to retrieve his weapon, rainwater dripping from his vast shaggy beard. Then he wobbled some more as he stooped to retrieve his tankard. He straightened up and supped from it. Then he tried unsuccessfully to replace the bits of brick, fussing as if somehow no one would notice the dent if he smoothed it over. Several more bricks fell out.

Giving up, Morgenstern turned back to his row of buckets and started to spin the hammer again, this time checking he had swinging room.

'Is this going to take much longer?' Aric asked from the tavern doorway. He stood leaning against the doorjamb: a tall, powerfully built young man not yet twenty-two, with a mane of black hair and bright blue eyes. He carried the gold-edged plate armour and the snowy pelt of the White Wolf Templars well.

'Hush!' said the older knight, concentrating on his swing and not looking round. Morgenstern adjusted the fall of his own wolf-pelt so it did not constrict the movement of his armoured limbs. 'Behold, my young friend, how a master of the warhammer displays his skill. See! Before me, the heads of my foes!'

'The turnips on the buckets?'

'Quite so. That is indeed what they represent.'

'These foes are what? Lying down? Buried up to the neck?'

Morgenstern smiled patiently. 'They are large and able-bodied warriors, Aric. I, however, am on a horse.'

'Of course you are.'

'For the purposes of this demonstration, imagine I am on a horse.'

Still spinning the hammer, Morgenstern began to prance back and forth on the spot like a hobbyhorse mummer in a mystery play. He made clip-clop noises with his tongue and occasionally admonished 'Steady there! Whoa, girl!'

Aric closed his eyes.

'Yah-hah!' Morgenstern barked suddenly and lurched forward, head back, as his imaginary horse bolted.

His great, thundering, armoured mass, with the hammer swooping about him in a vast circle, drummed down the yard, spraying up water and dislodging flagstones as he charged the buckets. His initial swing smashed the turnip on the first bucket, then, without breaking stride, he galloped in and out of the remaining buckets, decapitating each turnip in turn, slaloming between the rows, swooping and crossing the hammer with astonishing precision.

Aric by then had reopened his eyes. For all the pantomime idiocy, for all the drunkenness, for all the fact that Morgenstern was at the wrong end of his fifties and two hundred pounds too heavy, Aric was still impressed by the big man's weapon skill.

With a bellowing flourish, Morgenstern elegantly took out the last of his foes, bucket and all, crushing both with a blow that lofted them over the gable end. Then his boot slipped on the sheened cobbles, he stumbled at full pelt and went headfirst into the stables. Through a door he hadn't opened first.

Aric winced. He turned and went back inside. It was going to be a long day.

Inside the Spread Eagle, he rejoined Anspach, Gruber and von Glick at the small table in the corner.

'Did he do it?' Gruber asked.

Aric nodded. 'All of them.'

Anspach chuckled his dirty, melodic chuckle. He was a handsome man in his late thirties, with devilish eyes and a smile that could charm chastity belts into spontaneous release. 'That's six shillings from each of you, I fancy.'

'By the Wolf, Anspach!' von Glick grunted. 'Is there nothing you won't wager on?'

Anspach accepted his winnings. 'Actually, no. In fact, that reminds me, I have a bag of gold riding on a certain goathead going the distance at the Bernabau this afternoon.'

Von Glick shook his head in dismay. A veteran Wolf of the old school, von Glick was a slender, angular man of sixty years. His grizzled hair was long and straggly, and his chin was shaven to pepper stubble. He was stiff and disapproving about all things. Aric wondered if there was anything von Glick couldn't complain about. He somehow doubted the prim old man had ever had the passion to be a noble warrior.

'So where's Morgenstern now?' Gruber asked, toying with his tankard.

'Having a lie down,' answered Aric. 'You know, I think... he drinks too much.'

The other three snorted.

'Brother Templar,' Anspach said, 'you're too recent an addition to this noble order to have witnessed it, but our Morgenstern is famous for the prodigious scale of his imbibing! Some of his greatest victories on the field of combat... like those orc-scum he took at the Battle of Kern's Gate... such feats have been fired by Ulric, and fuelled by ale!'

'Maybe,' Aric said doubtfully, 'but I think it's getting to him. His reflexes. His co-ordination...'

'He killed the turnips, didn't he?' von Glick asked.

'And the stable door,' Aric said darkly.

They fell silent.

'Still, our Morgenstern...' Anspach began, 'I'll wager he could–'

'Oh, shut up!' growled von Glick.

Aric sat back and gazed around the smoky tavern. He could see Ganz, their new, young company commander, sitting in a booth side, with the hot-blooded Vandam talking eagerly at him.

'What's that about?' he asked Gruber. The white-haired Gruber was deep in thought and snapped up with a start as Aric addressed him.

He looked almost scared just then, Aric thought. *That's not the first time I've caught him lost in thoughts he doesn't like.*

Gruber was the most respected of the Company's men, a veteran like Morgenstern and von Glick, who had served with old Jurgen from the beginning. His hair was thin, his eyes pale, his papery skin almost translucent with age, but Aric knew there was a power, a terrible force inside that warrior.

Except now... now, for the first time since he joined the Company eighteen months before, Aric sensed that Gruber's power was waning. Was it age? Was it... Jurgen? Was it something else?

Aric gestured again over at Vandam and Ganz. 'What's Vandam bending our commander's ear about?'

'I hear Vandam wants to transfer,' von Glick said quietly. 'He's a glory-hound. He wants promotion. Word is, he sees our company as a dead end. He wants to move to another mob. Red Company, maybe.'

The four of them grunted their disapproval and all took a drink.

'Don't think Ganz will let him. Ganz has barely had time to make his mark in command since the... since that business. He won't want to lose a man before he's had a chance to prove something.' Gruber looked thoughtful. 'If they ever let us prove anything again.'

'It's not long till Mitterfruhl,' Anspach said. 'Then the campaign season really starts. We'll get something... a good raid into the Drak. I bet you.'

Aric was silent. Something had to happen soon, or this particular brave company of White Wolves was going to lose its heart entirely.

The Great Temple of Ulric was almost empty. The air was still and cold and smelled of candle smoke.

Ganz walked in, and reverently placed his gloves and warhammer in the reliquary in the entrance hall.

The acoustics in the vast, vaulted chamber were superb, and Ganz could hear the precise intonations of four knights who were whispering prayers on the other side of the high altar, kneeling, heads down. He could also hear the faint squeak of lint as a Temple adept polished the brass finials of the lectern. The great statue of Ulric himself rose up like a thundercloud to block the light from the high windows.

Ganz bowed his head and made his observance, then crossed the chamber and knelt before the Sacred Flame.

He was kneeling there when he felt the hand on his shoulder. Ganz looked up into the face of Ar-Ulric, the High Priest himself, his craggy, bearded features catching the flame light.

'We should talk, Ganz. I'm glad you came by. Walk with me to the Regimental Chapel.'

Ganz got up and fell into step beside the venerable warrior. He saw the four knights were leaving, casting curious glances in his direction.

'I came to seek... guidance, High One,' Ganz began. 'This season will be my first as a commander of men, and already, I–'

'Do you lack confidence, Ganz?'

'No, lord. But I lack experience. And the men are... listless.'

They walked down a short flight of steps and reached an iron cage door where a Templar of Grey Company stood watch. He saluted the High Priest respectfully, and undid the padlock so that the cage door could swing open. Ganz followed Ar-Ulric through and they entered the smaller, warmer interior of the temple's regimental chapel, decorated with standards, banners, trophies and the honour roll of memorial slabs.

Both men bowed briefly to the great wolfskin pelt on the wall, and to the snarling, silver-inlaid treasure on a raised plinth beneath it. The Jaws of the Wolf, the Temple's most precious icon.

The High Priest bent before it for a moment, murmured a blessing to Ulric and to Artur, then rose and turned to Ganz. His eyes twinkled like the first frost of a hard Jahrdrung. 'Your company is more than listless, Ganz. There was a time when White Company was the finest and best this Temple could field, performing deeds that the riders of other Wolf Companies like Red or Grey could only dream of. But now it is weak – it has lost its way. This whole winter they have idled here in the city, wasting their health and money and time. Several have become noted drunkards. Especially Morgenstern.'

'It is easy to exaggerate–'

'He relieved himself in the font in the Temple of Verena,' the High Priest said with great and sad certainty. 'During High Mass. And then he suggested to the priests that the Goddess herself was a "piece of all right" who could really do with a good... what was it again?'

Ganz sighed. 'Man in her life, High Priest.'

The High Priest nodded. It seemed to Ganz he was almost smiling but that could not be so and his tone confirmed it. 'Morgenstern is a disgrace. And Anspach. You know about his gambling? He owes a large amount to the stadium brokers and to various less-official wager-takers. And I have had audiences with that hotblood Vandam twice now to hear him petition me for a transfer to Red Company. Or Gold. Or anywhere.'

Ganz hung his head.

'There are others with problems too... each to his own. I don't pretend your job is easy, Ganz, taking command of a demoralised mob like this. And I know everything stems from that one incident last summer in the Drakwald. That beastpack got the better of you. They were strong. Sometimes, Ulric save us, the evil ones do win. It was a tragedy White Company lost so many good men. And to lose Jurgen. It can't be easy for you to take his place.'

'What can I do, High Priest? I don't command the respect Jurgen did. How can I rally White Company?'

The High Priest crossed to the far wall and lifted down the standard of Vess. It was old and tattered and stained with ancient, noble blood. It was one of the oldest and most revered battle standards of the Wolf Companies, carried at some of the Templars' greatest victories.

'You will take your company out, into the forests, beneath this old and venerable standard, and you will destroy the beastpack that broke your honour.'

Ganz took the shaft of the standard with amazement. He looked up and met the steely gaze of his old commander, Jurgen, the newest of the graven memorials on the wall. For a long while, Ganz stared into that marble face, remembering the long white beard, the hawkish look, the famous studded eye-patch. Ganz knew the High Priest was right. It was the only way.

* * *

It was a cold dawn, and raining once again. The fourteen brothers of White Company assembled in the stable block behind the Temple, adjusting the harnesses of their warsteeds, grumbling in low voices, their breath steaming the air.

'A raiding party? Before Mitterfruhl?' Morgenstern complained, swigging from a flask in his saddlebags as he pretended to check them.

'A drink? Before breakfast?' von Glick sneered quietly.

Morgenstern laughed at this, booming and hard, but Aric knew it was sham good-humour. He could see the pale strain in Morgenstern's pallid face, see the way his great hands shook.

Aric looked about. Vandam was resplendent, his face flushed with determination. His white wolf pelt hung just so across the shoulders of his gold-chased plate armour. Gruber looked far away, distant and preoccupied as he fumbled with the harness straps of his stamping steed. Einholt, the old, bald warrior with the facial scar and the milky eye, looked tired, as if he hadn't slept well. Aric felt sure some old dream chased the veteran each and every night without fail.

Anspach laughed and joked with his fellows. Von Glick scowled at him. Ganz looked grim and quiet. The others began to mount up, exchanging jokes and slurs – haggard Krieber, stocky Schiffer, the blond giant Bruckner, red-maned Kaspen, the whipcord Schell, and Dorff, whistling another of his tuneless refrains.

'Aric!' Ganz called, and Aric crossed the yard. As the youngest of the company, it was his privilege to carry the standard. He was amazed when Ganz placed the precious Standard of Vess into his mailed hand. Everyone in the yard fell silent.

'By the decree of the High Priest himself, we ride under the banner of Vess, and we ride for revenge,' Ganz said simply and swung into the saddle.

He turned his steed about and the company fell into step behind him, riding out of the yard into the streets and the rain beyond.

They came down the western viaduct out of the city, in the shadow of the great Fauschlag Rock. High above them, the craggy walls and towers of Middenheim pushed their way up into the cold, friendless skies, as they had done for two thousand years.

They left the smoke and stench and clamour of the city behind, moving past trains of laden handcarts bound for the Altmarkt markets: strings of cattle from Salzenmund, the piled wagons of textile merchants from Marienburg. All pulled themselves to the sides of the sixty-foot wide viaduct to let the Wolf Company pass. When a party of Ulric's best rode out, only a fool got in their way.

White Company left the viaduct and joined the Altdorf road, cantering into the damp woodlands, and followed the forest track for six hours before stopping to water their horses and eat at a village by the way. In the afternoon, the sun came up to glint off their grey and gold plate mail. The heat drew mist out of the wet trees, and they rode as if through smoke. In each village they passed, the locals came out to see a brave and feared band of Templars, singing a low battle hymn as they rode along.

They slept the night in a village longhall above a waterfall, and they rode at dawn into the darker paths, the long tracks of black mud that ran down into the oily darkness of the Drakwald Forest, a region that lay across the land like the fallen cloak of some black-hearted god.

It was noon, but a pale, weak noon, and chill rain pattered down through the naked branches of black elms and twisted maple. The ground beneath them was coated in a stinking, matted slime of dead leaves that had fallen the autumn before and now lay rotting back into the dark soil. Spring would be a long time coming here.

There seemed no sign of life except for the fourteen riders. Occasionally a woodpecker would hammer in the distance, or some loon or other bird would whoop. Aric saw cobwebs in low branches hung with rainwater like diamond chokers.

'Smoke!' von Glick called suddenly, and they reined up, sniffing the air.

'He's right!' Vandam said eagerly, sliding the long haft of his warhammer out of his saddle loop.

Ganz held up a hand. 'Steady, Vandam! If we move, we move as a company or not at all. Aric, raise the standard.'

Aric edged alongside the leader and pulled the old banner upright.

With a nod, Ganz led off and the column moved two abreast through the trees in the direction of the smoke, hooves splashing through the leaf slush and rot.

The clearing was wide and open – trees had been cleared for it and now the wood was being burnt on a stone slab set before a crude statue. Five shambling, hairy forms were worshipping at the fire.

'For Ulric! Wolves! Ride!' Ganz yelled and they broke into a gallop, tearing down the slope into the clearing itself, exploding water from the marshy ground with their heavy hooves.

The beastmen at the shrine looked round in horror, baying and breaking for cover.

At the back of the file, Morgenstern turned from the charge and looked to Gruber, who had reached a dead stop.

'What's the matter?' he bellowed. 'We're missing the fun!'

'I think my steed has thrown a shoe,' growled Gruber. 'Go on, you old fool! Ride on!'

Morgenstern turned again after the main charge and took a deep pull from his saddle bottle. Then with a huge cry he charged down the slope after the main party.

The low branch took him clean out of his saddle.

The rest thundered out across the clearing, Aric bellowing as he held the banner high. Three of the beastmen broke and fled. Two snatched up pikes and turned to face the charge, shrieking in a deep, inhuman way.

Vandam was by now leading the charge. His swinging mallet-head destroyed the skull of one of the defenders, smacking the goat-headed aberration back into the ground.

Ganz, just behind him, overshot the other and tried to wheel around. His horse lost its footing on the wet leaves and slid over, spilling him off.

The beast turned to capitalise on this but in a moment Aric and Krieber had run it down between their horses, smashing its bones.

Anspach galloped past the shrine after one of the escapees, whirling his hammer. Von Glick was close on his hind.

'Ten shillings says I make this kill!' laughed Anspach.

Von Glick cursed and tried to pull level, but Anspach hurled his hammer and it went spinning off after the fleeing creature. It decapitated a sapling and missed the beast by ten yards. Anspach swore and reined in his charge.

'Gods help you that you ever win a wager!' von Glick cried as he carried on and caught up with the beast at the tree line. He swung two blows which both missed, but the creature doubled back and was driven into the aim of Dorff, who crushed its brain.

The other two fled into the trees. Vandam, without breaking stride, galloped after them.

'Back! Vandam! Back here!' bellowed Ganz as he got up and righted his shaken horse.

Vandam paid no attention. They could hear his whoops echoing into the forest.

'Schell! Von Glick! Go and round that idiot up!' Ganz ordered and the two riders obeyed. Everyone else had galloped to a standstill around the shrine. Ganz looked back and saw that Gruber had dismounted at the edge of the clearing and was helping to prop Morgenstern against a tree. Morgenstern's horse was trotting around, with its reins trailing.

Ganz shook his head and spat an oath.

He strode up to the shrine and gazed for a moment at the crude statue. Then he swung his hammer and smashed it into splinters.

Ganz turned back and looked at his men. 'Now they know we're here. Now they will come looking for us and our job will be easier!'

'Vandam? Where are you, you idiot?' bawled von Glick as he rode slowly through the dark glades beyond the clearing. Dark meres stood stagnant between the filthy trees, and brackish water trickled down the slate outcrops. Through the trees and the mist, von Glick could make out Schell, riding a parallel course, yelling out 'Vandam! Come around the back or we'll leave you out here!'

Von Glick heard movement in the trees nearby and raised his hammer ready. Vandam rode out of the trees.

'Trust you to come looking for me, von Glick!' he snorted. 'You mother-hen the whole company! You're so stiff you wouldn't know valour if it came knocking!'

Von Glick shook his head wearily. He knew too well his own reputation with the younger members of White Company: stiff, inflexible, an old bore who nagged and complained. Jurgen had once told him he was the backbone of the company, but von Glick had a suspicion the commander had been trying to make light of von Glick's attitudes. Von Glick hated himself for it, but he couldn't help himself. There was no discipline these days. The young Templars were reckless bravos, and Vandam the very worst of them.

'Ganz ordered me to find you,' von Glick said sharply, trying to hold his anger. 'What sense is it to ride off alone like that? There's no glory in it!'

'Isn't there now?' Vandam smirked. 'I ran one to ground, broke his back. The other slipped away though.'

That was the worst of it... Vandam's arrogance was matched only by his skill as a warrior. Damn his eyes! thought von Glick.

'We'll ride back. Now!' he instructed Vandam, who shrugged mildly and turned his horse around. 'Schell!' von Glick called. 'I found him! Schell!'

Von Glick could still make out the other rider, but the mist and trees were deadening his voice.

'Go on,' von Glick told Vandam. 'I'll fetch him.'

He spurred up along the edge of a mere in the direction of Schell who saw him at last and began to ride over. Von Glick turned his horse back.

The beastman came out of the bushes with a feral scream. Driven, hounded by Vandam, it had hidden, but von Glick had passed close by its hiding place and panic had galvanised it into fierce action. The iron barb of the spear took the old Wolf through the right hip. He bellowed in pain and the horse reared. The beastman clung on, shaking his weapon, which was wedged fast in the bone and meat and armour. Von Glick screamed, hooked like a fish, pushed back in the saddle by the spear so far he couldn't reach his warhammer.

Schell bellowed in dismay and galloped in.

Vandam, hearing the commotion, turned and looked in horror.

'Ulric's bloody fists!' he gasped. 'Oh lord, no!'

The spear broke. Freed, von Glick tumbled from the saddle and landed in the shallows of the mere. The beastman lunged forward.

Schell's horse leapt the mere at the narrowest point and the warrior swung the hammer spike down on the creature, killing it instantly.

He leaped off his horse and ran to von Glick, who lay on his side in the pool, his face pale with pain. It looked like his red and gold armour was leaking into the black water.

Vandam raced up.

Schell looked up at him with fierce, angry eyes that blazed from his lean face. 'He's alive,' he hissed.

Ganz strode across the shrine clearing to where Morgenstern was picking himself up.

'Let's talk,' he said. 'Away from the others. I'm sure you don't want them hearing what I'm going to say to you.'

Morgenstern, who had twenty years more service to the Temple than Ganz, looked sour, but he did not disobey. Talking low, they moved away across the clearing.

Aric joined Gruber, who sat to one side on a fallen log.

'You okay?' he asked.

'My horse was wrong-footed. Thrown a shoe, I thought.'

'Looks fine to me,' said Aric.

Gruber looked up at the young man, his lean, lined face hard but not angry. 'What's that supposed to mean?'

Aric shrugged. With his long dark hair and trimmed black goatee, he reminded Gruber of the young Jurgen himself. 'Anything you want it to mean,' he said.

Gruber steepled his hands and thought for a moment. Aric had something, a quality. One day he would be a leader, a lot more effortlessly than poor Ganz, who tried so hard and was liked so little. Aric had natural command. He would be a great warrior for the Temple in time.

'I...' Gruber began. 'I seem to lack the fire I once had. At Jurgen's side, courage was easy...'

Aric sat next to him. 'You're the most respected man in the troop, Gruber. Everyone acknowledges that, even bluff old warhorses like Morgenstern and von Glick. You were Jurgen's right-hand man. You know, after Jurgen's death, I'll never understand why you didn't take the command when it was offered you. Why did you hand it on to Ganz?'

'Ganz is a good man... solid, unimaginative, but a good man. He'd paid his dues. I'm just a veteran. I'd be a poor commander.'

'I don't think so,' Aric said with a shake of his head.

Gruber sighed. 'What if I said it was because Jurgen was dead? How could I take the place of that man, my sworn commander, my friend? The man I failed?'

'Failed?' Aric repeated in surprise.

'That dreadful day last summer, when the beastpack fell on us out of nowhere. We stood together as a company or we fell, each man watching the other's back.'

'It was hell, all right.'

'I was right by Jurgen, fighting at his right hand. I saw the bull-man swing in with the axe. I could have blocked it, taken the blow myself, but I froze.'

'You weren't to blame!'

'I was! I hesitated and Jurgen died. If it hadn't been for me, he'd be here today.'

'No,' Aric said firmly. 'It was bad luck and Ulric called him to his hall.'

Gruber looked into the younger man's face. 'My nerve's gone, Aric. I can't tell the others... I certainly can't tell Ganz... but as we rode in to the charge, I felt my courage melt. What if I freeze again? What if it's Ganz who pays the price this time? You? I'm a coward and no use to this company.'

'You are no such thing,' Aric said. He tried to compose an argument to snap the veteran out of his grim mindset, but they were interrupted by shouting. Morgenstern strode back into the clearing, bellowing, with a stern-faced Ganz in his wake. The big ox reached his horse, pulled three bottles from his saddle bags and hurled them at a nearby tree, smashing them one by one.

'Satisfied?' he bawled at Ganz.

'Not yet,' Ganz replied stoically.

'Ganz! Ganz!' the shout echoed round the clearing. Schell led von Glick's horse back to them, the old warrior slumped in the saddle with Vandam riding alongside to support him.

'Oh great God of the Wolf!' Gruber cried leaping up.

'Von Glick!' shouted Morgenstern, pushing past the dismayed Ganz.

They lowered the wounded man down and the company stood around as Kaspen, who had studied with a barber-surgeon and an apothecary, treated the ugly wound.

'He needs a proper surgeon,' said the thick-set, flame-haired man, wiping blood from his hands. 'Wound's deep and filthy and he's lost blood.'

Ganz looked up at the sky. Evening was slipping down on them. 'We'll return to Middenheim tomorrow. First light. The fastest will ride ahead to fetch a surgeon and a cart. We–'

'We will not,' von Glick said, his voice thin and bitter. 'We will not go back on my account. This mission, this undertaking, is a holy cause to refound the strength of this company and avenge our fallen leader. We will not abandon that task! I will not let you abandon this!'

'But–'

Von Glick pulled himself up to a sitting position, wincing. 'Promise me, Ganz! Promise me we'll go on!'

Ganz faltered. He did not know what to say. He wheeled on Vandam, who stood to one side. 'You bloody fool! This is your fault! If you hadn't been so impetuous, you'd never have led von Glick into that!'

'I–' Vandam began.

'Shut up! The company stands together or it falls! You betrayed the very foundation of this brotherhood!'

'He's not to blame,' von Glick said. His eyes were glittering with strength born out of pain. 'Oh, he shouldn't have broken from the pack and ridden off alone, but I did this to myself. I should have been wary, I should have been looking. I dropped my guard, like any old fool, and paid the price.'

Silence. Ganz looked from one man to another. Most looked uncomfortable, awkward, disconcerted. The company spirit had never seemed so deflated, not even after Jurgen's death. At least then there was anger. Now, there was just disillusion, a loss of faith and comradeship.

'We'll make camp here,' Ganz said finally. 'With luck, the beasts will come for us tonight – and we can finish this.'

Dawn came, cold and pale. The last shift of watchmen – Schell, Aric and Bruckner – roused the others. Morgenstern poked the fire into life and Kaspen redressed von Glick's wound. The old warrior was as pale and cold as the morning, shivering with pain. 'Don't tell Ganz how bad I am!' he hissed to Kaspen. 'On your life, swear it!'

Anspach was going to water the horses when he found Krieber. At some time in the night, a black-fletched arrow had skewered his neck where he lay sleeping. The Templar was dead.

They stood around in silent mourning, more sombre than ever before. Ganz boiled with rage. He strode away from the group.

At the tree line, Gruber joined him. 'It is bad luck, Ganz. Bad luck on us, bad luck on poor Krieber, Ulric take his soul. We didn't deserve it, and he deserved a better end than this.'

Ganz wheeled round. 'What do I have to do, Gruber? For Ulric's sake! How can I lead this company to glory if we don't get a chance? I destroyed their shrine to bring them to us, to make them angry and drive them into a frontal attack. A pitched battle where we would shine! But no! They come back all right, and with typical beast cunning, they harry us and kill us as we sleep!'

'So we change our tactics,' Gruber said.

Ganz shrugged. 'I don't know how! I don't know what to suggest! I keep thinking about Jurgen, and how he kept command. I keep trying to think the way he did, to remember all the tricks and inspiration. And you know? *I can't remember a thing*! All those great victories we shared, and I can't recall the plan behind a single one of them!'

'Calm down and think, Ganz,' Gruber said, sighing. 'What about Kern's Gate? Remember? The winning stroke there was to swing around behind the orcs.'

'Yes, I remember it. Sound tactics.'

'Exactly!' Gruber said. 'But that was Morgenstern's idea, wasn't it? Not Jurgen's!'

'You're right,' Ganz said, his face brightening. 'And it was the same with the siege at Aldobard... there it was von Glick who suggested a two-pronged attack.'

'Yes,' Gruber agreed. 'Jurgen was a good leader all right. He knew a good idea when he heard it. He knew how to listen to his men. The company is strength, Ganz. We stand together or we fall. And if one of us has a good plan, a good leader knows not to be too proud to adopt it.'

'So?' Ganz said, trying to sound lighter than he felt. 'Any ideas?'

Late winter wind sighed through the elms. The company coughed and shuffled.

'I bet I know–' Anspach began.

There was a general groan.

'Let's hear him out,' Ganz said, hoping he was doing the right thing.

'Well, myself, I like a wager,' Anspach said as if this were news, getting up to address them. 'So do many folk – the chance to win something, something important and valuable, something more than you normally get a chance at. These beastmen are no different. They want revenge for the smashed shrine, but not so much they're going to risk their stinking hides in a frontal assault on armoured cavalry. Who would give them good odds on that? They'd rather live. But if we tempted them with something more – something they might feel was worth risking their necks for – we could lure them out. That's my plan, a tempting wager for them. And I'll bet it works.'

There was some nodding, a few sneers. Dorff whistled aimlessly. Morgenstern turned a belch into an approving chuckle.

Ganz smiled. For the first time there seemed to be a slight sense of union, of all their minds working as one.

'But what do we offer them?' Kaspen asked.

Anspach shrugged. 'I'm working on that. We carry gold and silver, between us probably quite a lot. Maybe a pot of coins...'

Vandam laughed. 'You think they'd care? The beasts don't value gold much.'

'Well, what else have we got?' asked Schell, scratching his sinewy cheek thoughtfully.

'We have this,' Aric said and lifted the standard of Vess.

'You're mad!' cried Einholt. A quiet, reserved warrior, he seldom said anything. This outburst startled them all. Aric wavered, looking into Einholt's scarred face, wishing he could read anything except scorn in the man's one good eye.

'Think! Think of the prestige, the glory they would achieve amidst their foul kind to capture this. Think of the victory it would represent,' Aric said at last.

'Think of the disgrace if we lose the bloody thing!' scoffed Vandam.

'We won't,' Aric said. 'That's the point. It's precious enough to lure them out en masse...'

'And precious enough to make damn sure we fight to the last to keep it,' von Glick finished for him. 'A good plan.'

Ganz nodded.

'So,' Dorff asked, 'do we just... leave it out in the open for them?'

'Too obvious,' Ganz said.

'And I won't leave it,' Aric said flatly. 'It's my duty. I cannot abandon the standard.'

Ganz paced the circle of men. 'So Aric stays with the standard. The rest of us lie in cover ready to strike.'

'Aric can't stand alone,' Gruber began.

'It'd still look too obvious,' Anspach added. 'Someone has to stay with him.'

'I'll do it,' Vandam said. There was ferocity in his eyes. Ganz knew the young warrior was eager to make amends for his earlier rashness.

He was about to nod when von Glick spoke up. 'A brave offer, Vandam. But you're too good in the charge to waste. Let me stay, Ganz. We'll stay with Krieber's corpse and it'll look like the standard bearer has been left to watch the dead and the dying.'

'That would be more convincing,' Anspach said.

'I'll stay too,' Gruber said. 'They'd expect at least two men. And my horse has thrown a shoe.'

Ganz looked around at them all. 'Agreed! Let's do it! For the glory of Ulric and the memory of Jurgen!'

The ten riders mounted up and thundered off across the clearing to disappear into the dark woods. Ganz paused before he rode. 'May the wolf run beside you,' he said to Aric, Gruber and von Glick.

Aric and Gruber made von Glick comfortable by the shrine. They covered Krieber with a saddle cloth, tied the horses off to the west, and lit a fire. Then Aric planted the standard in the clay soil.

'You needn't have stayed too,' he told Gruber.

'Yes, I did,' Gruber said simply. 'I need to do this very much.'

Evening sloped down on them, speckling the heavy sky with dark twists of cloud. Rain lanced down, slantwise, and a wind picked up, lifting the ragged hem of the old standard and swishing through the miserable forest.

The four remained by the fire – the two living warriors, the dead man and the man halfway between.

Von Glick's eyes were clouded as dark as the heavens. 'Ulric,' he murmured, gazing up at the cold sky. 'Let them come.'

Gruber reached out and pulled at Aric's arm. This message needed no words. Stiff from the cold, the two men lifted their warhammers and rose, standing by the guttering ashes of the fire, looking across the clearing.

'By the sacred flame, Aric my brother,' said Gruber, 'now we'll see a fight.'

The beastmen attacked.

There were perhaps four score of them, more than Aric remembered from the pitched battle the previous season when the beastmen had caught them by surprise and Jurgen fell. The misshapen monsters were clad in reeking pelts, their animalistic heads crowned by all manner of horns and tusks and antlers, their skins scaled and haired and furred, bald and muscular, diseased and slack. They bellowed as they charged in from the eastern tree-line, their foul collective breath gusting before them, eyes wild like insane cattle, wet, drooling mouths agape to expose ulcerated gums, black teeth and hooked fangs. The ground shook.

Aric and Gruber leapt onto their horses and galloped around to stand between the charge and the lonely standard.

'For Ulric!' yelled Aric, his hammer beginning its swing.

'By the hammers of the Wolf!' raged Gruber, holding his horse steady.

'For the Temple! *For the Temple*!' came a third voice. The riders glanced back. Hammer in hand, von Glick stood beside the standard, supporting his weight against the haft.

'For the Temple!' he screamed at them again.

Their battle roars as feral as the beasts, Aric and Gruber leapt their horses into the front of the pack as it came to them, giving themselves momentum and meeting the charge head on. The hammers swung and flew. Blood and spittle sprayed from cracked skulls. The hooves of the warhorses tore into flaccid flesh. Spears and blades thrust at them. The war cry of the two wolves echoed above all. Aric rejoiced. He had almost forgotten the ecstasy of combat, of the raging melee. Gruber laughed out loud. He had just remembered.

Von Glick stood his ground by the standard, despite the blood that leaked down his armour from the broken wound, and slew the first beast that charged him. The second fell, its skull cloven. The third rocked back, its ribs cracked. Now there were three, four around him, five. He was as deep in the fight as Aric and Gruber.

Aric struck left and right, blood painting across his grey armour, foam flecking back from the frenzied mouth of his steed. He saw Gruber laughing, striking...

Falling.

A lance thrust took down his mount. Gruber fell amongst the howling beasts, his hammer swinging in furious denial of the end.

They heard the thunder.

Above, in the sky as the storm broke.

Below, on the ground as the Company of Wolves charged in behind the beastpack.

Inside, in their hearts, as Ulric bayed the name of Jurgen.

The Knights of the White Company charged in line abreast, with Ganz at the centre, flanked by Vandam and Anspach.

'God's teeth, but I need a drink!' shouted Morgenstern as they swept in.

'No, you don't! You need this kind of courage instead!' rallied Ganz.

They hit the beastpack as it turned in confusion to meet them, ploughing over ranks of the fierce creatures, toppling and trampling, warhammers raining down as furiously as the downpour from above. Lightning flashed on the grotesque mayhem. Blood and rainwater sprayed into the air. The baying creatures turned from their original targets and swept into the fight with the cavalry force. Aric rode forward across the corpse-strewn ground and helped Gruber to his feet. The older warrior was speckled with blood, but alive.

'See to von Glick and watch the standard. Give me your horse,' Gruber said to Aric. Aric dismounted and returned to the banner of Vess as Gruber galloped back into the brutal fray.

Von Glick lay by the standard, which was still stuck upright in the earth. The bodies of almost a dozen beastmen lay around him.

'L-let me see...' von Glick breathed. Aric knelt beside him, and raised his head. 'So, Anspach's bold plan worked...' breathed the veteran warrior. 'He's pleased, I'll wager.'

Aric started to laugh but stopped. The old man was dead.

In the thick of the combat, Morgenstern wielded his warhammer and drove his horse through the press of bodies, swinging left and right, destroying the enemy as easily as if they had been a row of turnips on upturned pails. He laughed his raucous laugh and set about himself. Nearby, Anspach saw his display and joined the laughter, smashing down with his own hammer.

At the heart of the fight, Vandam, the fiercest of all, glory singing in his veins, destroyed beast after beast, three times the number of any of them. He was still slaughtering the monsters as their spears cut him down.

In the tumult, Ganz saw the great bull-man, the pack leader, the beast that had slain Jurgen. He charged forward, but his hammer was dragged down by the weight of creatures on him. The bull-man swung to strike at him.

The haft of Gruber's hammer blocked the axe. Gruber, yelling the war cry, rode in on his commander's right hand, guarding his flank. Ganz pulled his weapon clear and, before the massive bull-head could swing again, drove its snout back into its skull in an explosion of blood.

'In the name of Ulric!' Ganz screamed, rejoicing. The heavens thundered their applause.

Smoke rose from the storm-swept field, smoke and the steam from the blood. The Wolf Templars dismounted one by one amidst the carnage and kneeled in the mud to offer thanks to the raging sky. Fierce rain washed the blood off their armour as prayer cleansed their spirits. Of the beastman horde, not one had survived.

Ganz walked quietly to view the fallen.

Von Glick, at Aric's feet. Ganz was sure Aric was guarding the old man's body more than he was guarding the fluttering banner.

Vandam, skewered four times with crude lances, twisted at the top of a mound of dead.

'He has found his glory,' Morgenstern said. 'He's transferred to that better company. Ulric's own.'

'May the wolves guard his brave soul,' said Ganz.

Across the bloody, torn-up field, Dorff began to whistle a tune that resembled a battle hymn. Anspach caught it up and began to sing, making a shape and melody out of Dorff's notes. Einholt joined him, soft and low. It was a mourning song, of victory and loss, one of old Jurgen's favourites. Within three bars of it, all the other voices had joined the song.

They came back into Middenheim three days later. It was raining then too.

Mitterfruhl was almost on them all, but the High Priest came away from the preparations at the Temple, drawn by the excited whispers. He and his entourage were waiting for them in the Temple Square as White Company rode in, eleven riders, proud behind the fluttering banner of Vess, three noble dead lashed to their steeds.

Ranked in honour behind the motionless priest, Red, Grey, Gold and Silver Companies, the fighting packs who, with White, made up the Templar force, raised their voices in a throaty cheer.

Ganz, tall on his horse, gazed down at the High Priest.

'White Company has returned to the Temple, lord,' he said, 'and the heart has returned to White Company.'

THE DEAD AMONG US

The God of Death stared down on me as I prepared the corpse for burial. His hooded eyes were not visible but I could feel his gaze on my hands as they moved over the cold body before me, and he saw that the work was good. The atmosphere in the vaulted room beneath the temple was quiet and damp, smelling faintly of mildew, ashes and of the thousands of the dead of Middenheim who had passed through here on their last journey.

I chanted the words of the ritual under my breath, my mind aware of nothing but their rhythm and the power they held, my hands moving in the sacred patterns of the ceremony. I had done this many times before. The body before me was nothing but a carcass, its soul already blessed and freed and fled to the afterlife. My job now was to seal the corpse, to make sure that no other entity could move in and take possession of this empty shell.

A footfall on the stone steps intruded upon my concentration and broke the spell. Morr was no longer watching; the carving of the patron deity above the altar was just a carving again. The footsteps stopped for a moment, then came on down into the Factorum. The tall, well-aged frame of Brother Gilbertus blocked out the faint light for a moment as he passed through the doorway. I knew it would be him.

'I'm not disturbing you, am I?' he asked.

'Yes,' I said plainly. 'You are. That's the third Funeral Rite incantation you've interrupted this month, brother, and as penance you will take my place to perform it. This body goes out to be buried in the forest at noon today, so I suggest you start the ritual as soon as you've finished telling me why you're here.'

He didn't protest. Instead he said, 'They've found a body.'

'If you hadn't noticed, brother, this is the temple of Morr, who is the God of Death. We are priests of Morr. Bodies are what we deal with. One more corpse is hardly a reason to barge into the Factorum while another priest is performing a ceremony. Clearly your apprenticeship in Talabheim has taught you little. I may have to give you more lessons.'

He stared at me blankly, my sarcastic tone unnoticed or not understood.

I stared back at his greying forelock and the furrows of age around his eyes, and thought for a moment how old he was to be a new priest. But then I had joined the temple late in life as well. Many did.

'It's a woman,' he said. 'Murdered. I thought you'd want to know.'

I blinked. 'Where?'

'Through the heart. With a knife.'

'Where in the city, dolt?'

'Oh. The alleyway behind the Drowned Rat, in the Ostwald.'

'I'm going out.' I pulled off my ritual robes and flung them into the corner of the room. 'Start that Funeral Rite now and you will be finished by the time I get back.'

A cold Jahrdrung wind whistled over the slated rooftops and between the bleak stone buildings of Middenheim. If there had been any leaves on the few trees that grew on the heights of this rock, the pinnacle in the air that men called the City of the White Wolf, they would have been ripped off and hurled into the sky. But it was the last days of winter, the festival of Mitterfruhl was not passed, and the spring buds were not yet beginning to show. There would be no new life here for some time.

The wind cut through my thin robe as I strode up across Morrspark, the frosted grass crunching under my feet, and out into the streets, which grew narrower and less well-kept as they led south-west into the Ostwald district, crowded with early morning bustle. It was bitterly cold. I cursed myself for not putting on a cloak before leaving the temple, but haste was more important than my comfort. Rumours and falsehoods spread fast in a city as compact and tight-knit as Middenheim, and where an unexplained death was concerned, anybody speaking ill of the dead would only hinder my work.

The alley behind the Drowned Rat was narrow and sloping, stinking and crowded. A couple of members of the city watch were trying to keep onlookers away and not doing a good job of it, but the gawpers drew back slightly as I approached. The dark robes of a priest of Morr will do that, and it's not out of respect. Nobody likes being reminded of their own mortality.

As the crowd moved apart to let me pass, I saw the bald pate of Watch Captain Schtutt standing beside the corpse. He looked up, saw me and smiled in recognition, his face creased by middle-age and good living. We'd known each other for years, but I didn't smile back. He started to say something by way of a greeting, but I had already crouched down by the body.

It was a woman – or it had been. Probably turned twenty; probably beautiful. Dark brown hair with a wave to it. Something about her face said she had Norse blood, although with one eye and most of a cheek missing it was hard to tell for sure. She had the most delicate ears. Her clothes, gaudy but cheap, had been slashed all ways with a blade of some kind – a hunting knife or dagger, I guessed – before the fatal blow had slipped between

her ribs and into her heart. This had been a competent murder, and someone had tried hard to make it look like something less polished. Her left
arm was missing, and someone had thrown a rough b⸍own blanket over
an object a couple of feet from her. Blood from the cobbles had begun to
seep into its fabric.

She wasn't Filomena. Filomena had been blonde.

I remembered where I was, and looked up at Schtutt. 'What's under the
blanket?'

He muttered, 'Don't lift it,' and there was something nervous in his voice.
Then he turned to the pack of vultures and gossip-seekers and spoke loudly:
'All right, bugger off, the lot of you. Nothing more to see. Constable, get
them out of here. Give the priest of Morr room to do his magic.'

I wasn't planning any magic but the suggestion of it, together with the
taint of death in this narrow place, was enough to clear most of the crowd
away quickly. Good old Schtutt.

He looked down at me for a second, his expression filled with some stress
I couldn't identify, then bent down and raised one corner of the blanket.
Underneath was something not human: a limb, maybe four feet long. It
had no hand or bones, but large cup-like suckers along the underside. It
smelled of decay and something bitter and sharp, like wormwood and
stale wine.

It startled me. I felt Schtutt's gaze on my back, and that of the other
watchmen too. Were they looking at the thing under the blanket, or watching to see how I'd react to it? I realised I was breathing fast, and steadied
myself. Deep breath. Priests of Morr don't panic. They must not. They cannot be seen to.

'Right,' I said, and stood up. Be firm. Decisive. 'We need a cart to get all
this back to the temple. High-sided if possible.'

'I saw a soil-collector's wagon on the way here,' one of the watch
suggested.

'That'll suit. Go and fetch it.' I waited until he had gone, then gestured
down at the blanket. 'How many saw this?'

'Two or three.'

'Make sure they don't talk about it. Harass them, put the fear of Ulric in
them, anything short of cutting out their tongues. The last thing we need
is a panic about a mutant in the city.'

'Mutant,' Schtutt said. His voice was flat, like an echo. It was as if he hadn't
dared to use the word until I'd spoken it out loud, confirming his worst
fears. A tentacled limb? Well, it hadn't been hacked from a bog-octopus
or a kraken from the Sea of Claws, not in an alley in the Ostwald. But now
he'd said the word, I had to stop him saying it again where people might
hear him.

'There'll need to be a full investigation. A dissection. If it is a... well, we'll burn it quietly. For the sake of Ulric, don't go talking about mutants around the city. Even among the watch. Keep it to yourselves. But circulate the girl's description: age, height, dress, everything except the arm.' I rubbed my hands; they were freezing. 'We've got to get the body back to the temple so I can start. Where's that bloody wagon?'

It arrived, and the body was loaded unceremoniously into the cart, the soil-collectors not too happy about having their work interrupted. Nobody wanted to touch the thing under the blanket. Eventually I bundled it up in its covering and dropped it beside the corpse, in the back of the stinking wagon, then stood back so I could wipe my hands on my thin robe where Schtutt wouldn't see me do it.

The drayman flicked his whip, the elderly horse strained at the traces and the cart rumbled slowly down the filthy cobbles of the slum-streets towards the open space of Morrspark and the temple at its centre. Schtutt and I walked behind it.

'Any idea who she was?' I said.

'Apart from being–' Schtutt caught my glare. 'No, we don't. She was dressed like a tavern wench or maybe a night-girl, but she couldn't have got work with an arm like that. Although maybe she disguised it with magic. She could have lured someone into the alley, dropped the disguise, and then he killed her out of horror.

'Or maybe it was a cult killing. They say there's powerful cults of Chaos-worshippers in the city. We do find sacrifices. Cats, mostly.' He shivered. 'If I thought there was going to be trouble with Chaos, I'd take my family and leave Middenheim. Go north. My brother has an estate about thirty miles away. Would thirty miles be far enough, you think? To escape the Dark?'

I didn't reply. I was following my own thoughts. Schtutt seemed happy to continue talking without a reply.

'We shouldn't have to wait for them to act. We should track them down and burn them. Burn their homes too. To the ground,' he said, and there was a certain relish in his voice. 'Get some witch hunters to come and investigate. Remember those two who came up from Altdorf? Seventeen Chaos-worshippers found and burnt in three days. That's the sort of men we need. Eh? Dieter?'

That broke my concentration. Nobody called me Dieter these days – not in eight years, not since I'd entered the Temple. I looked across at him, meeting his gaze in silence. After a moment he looked away.

'Ulric's beard,' he muttered. 'You're not the man you were. What have they done to you in that temple of ghouls?'

I could think of a hundred replies but none of them fitted the moment, so I said nothing. Silence is the first thing a priest of Morr learns. I had learnt that lesson well. A wordless void stretched between us, until Schtutt filled it.

'Why do you do it?' he asked. 'That's what I don't understand. I remember when you were one of the best merchants in Middenheim. Everyone came to you for everything. You weren't just rich, you were–'

'I was loved.' Schtutt went silent. I continued, 'Loved by my wife and son, who vanished. You know that. Everyone knows. They were never found. I spent hundreds of crowns, thousands, looking for them. And I neglected my trading, and my business failed so I gave it away, and I joined the Temple of Morr and became a priest.'

'But why, Dieter?' That name again. Not mine, not now. 'You can't find them there.'

'I will,' I said. 'Sooner or later their souls will come to Morr, and be received by his hands, and I will know it. It's the only certainty I have any more. It was the not knowing that was killing me.'

'Is that why you do it?' he asked. 'Investigating the unexplained deaths? In case it's them?'

'No,' I said. 'No, it just passes the time.'

But I knew I was lying.

The cart trundled across the hard earth of Morrspark, still too solid for burials, and stopped outside the temple. The dark stone of the building and the bare branches of the high trees around it were silhouetted against a sky that was grey and heavy with snow yet to come, like outstretched hands offering a closed box to an unseen god.

Schtutt and his deputy carried the body down the stone steps into the vaulted gloom of the Factorum while I followed, the blanket and its unpleasant contents in my arms. There was no sign of Gilbertus, or the corpse he had been preparing for burial. Good.

The girl's body was laid on one of the grey granite slabs, and I placed the tentacle next to it, still wrapped in its blanket. The stench of the soil-wagon clung to the corpse's clothes, but there was another odour, bitter and unpleasant.

In the quiet and the semi-darkness she could almost have been any beautiful woman lying asleep. I stared at her still form. Who was she? Why had she been killed so deliberately, so coldly, and the deed disguised to look like something else? Did she have a powerful enemy, or was she dead for another reason? Was she more important dead than alive? The arm...

Schtutt shuffled his feet and coughed. I could sense his uneasiness. The bodies on the other slabs could have had something to do with it.

'We'd best be going,' he said.

'Yes,' I said abruptly. I wanted to be alone with the body, to try to get some feel for who or what had killed her. It's not that I like dead people. I don't. I just prefer them to the living.

'We'll need an official report,' he said. 'If it's mutant business the Graf will have to be told. You'll dissect her today?'

'No,' I said. 'First we do the rituals to rest her soul.'

No, not 'we'. I would do the rituals personally.

'Then we do the dissection – for the records, and for the Graf's precious paperwork. Then, if we can't find a next of kin, she gets a pauper's funeral.'

'Off the Cliff of Sighs?' Schtutt asked, shock in his voice. 'But surely mutants must be burnt? To cleanse them?'

'Did I say she was a mutant?' I asked.

'What?'

I grasped the section of tentacle that had lain beside the corpse, and shoved it at him. It felt cold and rubbery in my hand, and damp. Schtutt recoiled like a slapped dog.

'Smell it,' I said.

'What!'

'Smell it.' He sniffed at it, cautiously, then looked at me.

'Well?' I asked.

'It's... sour. Bitter. Like something stale.'

'Vinegar.' I put down the unclean flesh. 'I don't know where that came from, but I do know it wasn't attached to anyone who was alive this morning. The damn thing's been pickled.'

Schtutt and his man went eventually, promising that they'd try to find out who the girl had been. I almost asked them not to. The last way you're going to learn anything about a death in the Ostwald, with its twisting alleys and shadowy deals, is to have heavy-booted watchmen asking questions with all the subtlety of an unwashed ogre. Even if they got an answer it wouldn't do any good. I still wanted to find out who the girl was, but the more I thought about this, the more I suspected that it was her death, not herself, that was important. Someone had wanted to convince people that there were mutants in the city, and they would have managed it if the investigation had been left to the likes of Schtutt.

He wasn't a bad man, I reflected as I prepared the ritual. We'd known each other quite well in the days before I joined the temple: he'd been a young merchant trying to muscle in on trade franchises held by families much older and more powerful than his. He hadn't done well, but he hadn't given up, I'll say that for him. Then the Sparsam family had framed him for evading taxes, and part of his punishment had been a month with the city watch. And that was that: he found his niche in life there, and he was a much better watch captain than he'd been a merchant. Which didn't mean he was much of a watch captain.

I lit the last of the candles around the body, sprinkled some blessed water over the body with the appropriate ritual gestures, breathed deeply, and began the deep, slow chant of the Nameless Rite. Inside, I was waiting. The spirit of Morr moved over me and through me, within the patterns I had created with my hands and my mind, and flowed out from me to encompass the body of the woman before me, to bless it and protect it from evil.

And stopped. Something was resisting.

The energy of the Lord of Death hovered in me, waiting for me to use it. But I felt as if I was trying to force two lodestones together: the harder I pushed, the closer I came to the body, the greater was the repulsion. I kept chanting, drawing more of Morr's energy to me, trying to spread it out over the corpse, but it slipped away like rain off oiled leather. Something was wrong, very wrong. But I wasn't going to give up. I chanted on, summoning all my force, pushing Morr's power out over the corpse. The nameless resistance pushed back. I couldn't break it. Impasse.

One of the candles guttered and snuffed out, burnt down to its stub. It had been three, maybe four inches long when I'd started the ritual. Hours must have passed. I let my chanting cease and the divine power slipped away, taking the last of my energy with it. My knees felt like green twigs, and I felt myself swaying with exhaustion. Alone in the shadows, I stared at the body. The Factorum was absolutely quiet except for my own faint panting, absolutely still – but not tranquil. It was tense, as if waiting for something. The chill of the spring and the cold stones stuck needles through my robe and I shivered. For an instant I felt what the normal people must feel in here: the terror of being surrounded by the dead. The terror of not understanding.

I snuffed out the remaining candles between my fingers and hurried away, upstairs, to the comparative warmth of the main body of the temple, and felt my momentary fear fade as I did. For a moment I considered visiting the main hall and praying for a while, but instead I slipped in through the side entrance that led to the priests' private chambers, headed down the narrow stone corridor, and knocked on the door to Father Zimmerman's room. I felt uneasy about having to do this, but sometimes the only way to deal with a problem is to kick it upstairs.

There was a shuffling from within the room, a muffled voice, and then the door opened part-way from the other side and Brother Gilbertus squeezed out. I was reminded of a cat moving through a small space, or a snake. He smiled his bland smile at me and disappeared off towards the refectory. I pushed the door fully open and entered. Father Zimmerman was sitting at his writing desk. It looked as if he had been drafting a letter. Ink stained his fingers, and there were broken quills on the floor. He turned around and I saw there was ink on his white beard too.

'What is it?' he said. There was irritation in his voice: not, I guessed, from having his meeting interrupted. It probably had more to do with the fact that he didn't like me. That was fine by me. I didn't like him either.

'There's a new body in the Factorum, father.'

'Bodies are our stock in trade, brother. You may have observed that in the years you have been working here.' I thought of my words to Gilbertus earlier that day, and cursed the Talabheimer. He'd been here, telling tales of my disrespect for the dead, no doubt.

'I've been trying to bless it for burial,' I said. 'The blessing won't... won't take. It's as if something is resisting it.'

'This would be the mutant girl?'

Bugger the Talabheimer, and bugger him again. 'Yes, but she's not–'

'You waste too much time with street-scum and the dregs of life, brother. It's not a good attitude for a temple such as ours, with a certain standing in the community. You should think of other things, and spend more of your time on the good works that I have suggested you pursue.'

'I don't work for you. I work for Morr.'

'Perhaps you would be happier working for him with a solo ministry? We have been asked to establish a shrine in one of the Wasteland towns to deal with their plague victims, you know. I could recommend you for the post.'

He gestured to the writing desk. Obviously matters of transfer and administration were on his mind, but then he'd always been a petty status-minded pen-pusher, more concerned with appearances than with the real business of Morr's work. I hated him, but I realised that I wasn't going to get what I needed without an apology, so I gritted my teeth and backtracked.

'I'm sorry.' A breath. 'But we have a corpse down in the Factorum which I can't cleanse and prepare for burial. I don't know if it's enchanted or what else, but I thought you might know, and I thought you'd want to be told about it.'

'And you thought that I, being an older, more experienced and more powerful priest, might perform a Purification Rite on it for you? You did.'

I did, so I nodded – and saw his expression change, and instantly knew I'd made a mistake. It was the answer he'd wanted. He glowered at me. I could feel his dislike now, and I'd given him an excuse to vent it.

'You thought,' he hissed, 'that the senior priest of the temple of Morr in Middenheim has time to sully his hands blessing the corpse of some street tart?'

'I didn't–'

'You presume to ask me to waste my time with one of your low-lifes, and a mutant to boot? You dare to come in here and insult...'

I lowered my head and let the words wash over me. It was nothing I hadn't heard before. The antipathy between Father Albrecht Zimmerman and me was the main reason I was still only a second-tier priest after eight years in the temple, and was unlikely to rise higher. I'd accepted that. The father might be close to retirement but I knew his place would go to someone who acted like he did, thought like he did and disliked me as much as he did. Probably Gilbertus, who might be new but who seemed to be doing a lot of wheel-greasing recently. Ambitious, that Gilbertus. That letter on the father's desk was probably about him.

Eventually the words slowed and stopped. A new paragraph was about to begin, so I started paying attention again.

'As penance, I want you to go to the Cliff of Sighs, where you will find

Brother Ralf, who is due to officiate at a funeral. You will take over for him. Then come back here and pray to Saint Heinrich that your good intentions do not overcome your common sense. Pray hard, brother. Pray until the tenth bell. That is all.'

I left.

It was night. I lay awake on my hard, narrow bed and stared at the pattern of the moonlight as it fell on the stone wall of the tiny window of my tiny cell, the harsh brightness of Morrslieb's aura slowly eclipsing the warmer glow of Mannslieb. My body was completely exhausted, drained from the energy of the ritual I had performed that day, but I knew I would get no sleep tonight. It was too cold for a start, spring or no spring, and my single blanket did a bad job of keeping me warm enough to get comfortable. Besides, my mind was filled with the dead girl.

Who had she been? Where had she come from, to die so ignominiously on the streets of Middenheim? Had her death got anything to do with who she was, or had she simply been in the wrong tavern, with a kind word for the wrong man, who had led her into a dark back alley as dawn approached and stuck her over and over again with a short knife, carefully angling his blades to make the attack look frenzied. And then cut off her arm, to replace it with something inhuman, hiding her real one – he must have had a bag with him, probably a big one, watertight perhaps – and sneak away.

I could visualise the sort of man he must be, but right now I wasn't interested in him. I wanted to picture her.

She had been beautiful once. Perhaps she had been beautiful last night: what was left of her complexion hadn't had the blowsy gin-blossoms of an old street-walker. Laugh lines had creased the fresh skin around her mouth and eyes, and she wore no cosmetics. This was not a woman who had relied on her physical charms to earn a living. Not for long, anyway.

What had brought her, this Norse beauty, to Middenheim? The Norse were too pragmatic and down-to-earth to believe the old stories of the cliff-top city with its streets paved with the gold dug from the mountain below. Something other than dreams of foreign places and easy fortunes brought her here. It was probably the arm of a merchant or traveller – possibly Norse but probably not: they were loyal to their own, particularly abroad – who had abandoned her when she made eyes at another man or got pregnant, or any of the thousand other reasons that men break their promises to women.

How long had it been since the stability and love she had thought were hers had been revealed as a hollow joke? Her clothes had seemed quite new and probably too expensive for the sort of woman who drank in the Drowned Rat, so she probably hadn't been on the streets too long. Unless she had robbed someone recently. No; people can disguise themselves in life, but a dead face reveals the true character behind it, and I had seen nothing of the petty criminal in what remained of her features. There was nothing of the ground-down, hardened street-walker there either. She'd been new to the idea of having to rely on her charms and a low-cut dress to earn a living. Or new enough that she didn't yet know how to spot the sort who would be good to her, and the sort who hated her kind and wanted nothing but ill for them.

Someone in the city had to know who she was, and I wanted to bless her with her real name when I buried her. Someone knew. It might be the person who had killed her, and that meant I had to find him. Nobody at the Drowned Rat would admit to remembering a thing about last night – it was that kind of a place, and not even the fear of Morr would persuade them to talk.

There was a faint sound, a sudden vibration that seemed to run through the temple building. It came again a few seconds later. Then a pause, and a third. From somewhere further down the corridor came a scrape of wood, and the thud of a thrown-open door. Running footsteps. I thought briefly about getting up to investigate, decided that I was still too tired from the failed ritual, and rolled over. Let Zimmerman sort it out. If he was so protective of his status as head of the temple, let him take some of the responsibility that came with the position. I went back to my thoughts.

That arm – the arm that wasn't hers. It all came down to that. There are easier ways to spread the fear of Chaos and mutation around a city like Middenheim than faking the murder of a mutant in an alley. So why? The only other reason I could think of was that a dead mutant would spark an official enquiry. Lots of paperwork. Probably a promotion for someone in the Watch. Maybe a witch-hunt, and a couple of old women burnt. And the temple would be involved, because we'd have to dissect the body and make the official report. Which meant that the first place the corpse would be brought was here. But why? And why the corpse of a tall, fair-skinned Norse beauty, as nameless as me, instead of some local good-time girl?

There was a scream, and I jolted to full consciousness. – I must have dozed off. Someone pelted down the corridor outside my room, shouting something. There was a distant crash.

Trouble. I dashed outside, tugging on my robe as I went. It was dark and I couldn't see anyone in the faint moonlight, but there was a lot of noise coming from the main hall of the temple so I headed that way. Unsteady light and shouting told me I was going in the right direction. The connecting door was open – no, it was ripped off its hinges and lying on the floor. I jumped over it and arrived in the main hall.

It was mayhem. A tempest had been here. Everything was smashed. The Flames Eternal had gone out again, but in the faint light from the night-lamps on the pillars I could see three priests, two with makeshift weapons – a broom, a rod of office – circling but keeping well back from someone. It was her.

* * *

It was her. The face I'd been imagining as I lay in bed smiled dully, deadly. She looked like hell, as you would if you had been murdered a day ago. Her movements were jerky, abrupt, and there seemed to be no sight in her eyes or expression on her face except a blank grin. With her one arm she clasped the torso of Brother Rickard. The rest of him lay a few yards away. As I watched, she dropped the body and began to cast her head from side to side, as if trying to feel for something with some strange inhuman sense. It was like... I didn't know what it was like.

'Stay back!' It was Father Zimmerman. I doubted that any of us had any intention of getting any closer. He struck a stance and began to chant. From the sound of his syllables it was a ritual, but not one I recognised. The dead woman's head snapped upright, as if she had found what she was searching for. Then she took a slow, stiff step towards him.

'Father! Move!' I yelled as I looked desperately for a weapon to defend myself. The cult of Morr has never been big on armaments, and its temples aren't exactly prepared for battle. The corpse took another step towards the father. He kept chanting, faster now, and there was panic on his face. I could have run in to pull him to safety but I didn't; instead I ran away, up towards the high altar. The flattened disc of the great bowl lay there, its gold plate and the heavy liquid in it gleaming slickly in the low light. Behind me there was a scream, high like an old woman.

I reached around the rim of the bowl and lifted it with both hands. It was heavy with the liquid, which sloshed between the shallow rims. As I turned with it, I heard the snap, and an instant too late saw Father Zimmerman die, his spine broken like an autumn twig. The dead woman dropped his body and it hit the floor, twitching.

I took measured paces across the marbled tiles. The liquid slopped in the great bowl, a little spilling out with each step. The puppet-corpse was casting its head around, looking for a target as I drew closer to it. The other two priests backed away from us both. She was fifteen feet away. Ten. Her head turned in my direction, and her slashed face bared its teeth at me in a dead smile.

I flung the great bowl at her, its contents flying outwards in a wild shower. Not holy water but oil, blessed for the anointing of mourners. It covered her, soaking the remains of her once-fancy clothes. The bowl hit the floor edge-on with a clang and spun away. I leapt backwards, grabbed a night-lamp from its niche on the nearest pillar and flung it at the sodden abomination.

It was like a flower blossoming, or the sun breaking through clouds. The temple was filled with the light from the burning woman. She blazed. Something in her must have sensed what was happening as she slowly began to flail against the flames. She fell over. Her body crackled. There was a smell of roasting.

The other two priests – Ralf, I could see now, and Pieter – stood in shock and watched as the body and the temple burned. I didn't have time for that; I headed for the main doors and outside into the fierce chill of the night, my mind working furiously as I went. Dead Norse women. Missing arms. Animated corpses. On the steps I saw Gilbertus coming up.

'Where are you going?' he said.

'To raise the alarm.'

'I've done that. What was it?'

'An animated corpse. Someone was controlling it. The father is dead.'

'Ah.' He didn't seem surprised. 'Are you coming back inside?'

'No,' I said. 'For one thing it's on fire, and for another I know who killed that girl.'

'Oh. Who?'

'A necromancer,' I said. 'A necromancer with a grudge.'

If you want to know about grudges, you have to talk to a dwarf. I didn't relish the idea of having to go and see this particular dwarf at this time of night, not because he'd be in bed – I knew he wouldn't – but because of where he'd be. The Altquartier area was unpleasant enough during the day, but past midnight it was at its worst: the cheapest tarts, the pettiest criminals and the most desperate people. And at its heart lay the Breton-nian House.

Lit by harsh moonlight, the place looked just as tattered as I remembered it: an old, small tavern, its front black-painted, with cracked panes of glass in the windows and the stale smell of boiled cabbage seeping from the cheap eating room above. It looked closed but I knew it wasn't; places like this were never closed, if the patron or a regular owed you a favour. In years gone by I'd had some good evenings, some useful tip-offs and two fights in here. I hoped that the latter wouldn't be repeated tonight.

I knocked on the door, and after a few seconds it opened a crack. 'Who's there?'

'I'm looking for Alfric Half-nose,' I said.

'Who wants him?'

'Tell him...' I paused. 'Tell him it's the man who was Dieter Brossmann.'

The door closed. I could imagine the conversation that was happening on the other side. After a long minute it opened, to reveal a short, scrubby man with a pudding-bowl haircut. 'Enter,' he said.

I did. There's a trick with long robes and dresses that all high-born ladies know and all priests should learn: keep your steps light and short and silent, and if you do it right it looks like you're gliding, not walking. With the black robes of a Morr worshipper, it can look very eerie. The place had fallen silent as I came in, and the quiet lay over it like a blanket of cold dew as I moved across the small room. There were maybe ten people in, from cheap hoodlums drinking cheap beer to the less disreputable with glasses of wine or absinthe in front of them.

A man in a flat black Bretonnian hat, seated at the bar, nodded and raised a glass to me. His face was cracked with age and hard living like an old painting, and his eyes looked like bloodshot poached eggs. I recognised him from the old days, but couldn't remember his name. He probably had several.

There was a sound from one of the booths at the far end of the room. Nobody looked that way, so I knew it was what I was after and glided over to it. The great bulk of Alfric was squeezed in there, with one of his henchmen and a fat human in opulent robes sat opposite. The table was covered with empty tankards on the dwarfs' side, and gold coins. Alfric looked up. There was more grey in his beard than I remembered, and the scars around his ruined nose were a flaming red: a sure sign he'd been drinking heavily. But it would be unwise for me to assume he'd be drunk, or unobservant.

'Good evening, brother,' he said. 'Sit down. How may I be of service to the Temple of Morr this evening?'

I didn't sit. Instead I said, 'Alfric Half-nose, whose family name is Anvilbreaker, I am here to restore the balance of honour between our families.'

'Oh yes?' Alfric didn't look as if he was interested. The fat man was sweating, I noticed. He wasn't a merchant, or at least not a good one: he clearly didn't have the nerve for negotiating tricky deals. Idly I wondered who he was, and what had made him so desperate he'd come to see Alfric after the second bell of the night. He looked worried, but his problems were his own. I had mine to deal with.

'Five years ago,' I started. 'I... Oh sod it, I'll cut the formalities. You owe me a favour from the time I burnt the body of that storekeeper your grandson shot. I'm calling it in.'

'So I do, so you can.' Alfric took a swig from his tankard. 'You always were impatient. Always wanted things done your way. Your name and your taste in clothes, are they the only things you've changed since your family disappeared?' I said nothing. 'You haven't found them yet, then? Well, if you need some help, you know where to come.'

I knew he was trying to needle me, to show how displeased he was that I'd interrupted his business, so I didn't answer him. Instead I said, 'The temple was attacked this night. Someone animated a corpse against us. It looked like it was sent to kill people, not do damage, but it did a lot anyway. And Father Zimmerman is dead.' It was the second time I'd said that, but the first time I understood it. Suddenly I felt very tired. There was a spare place on the bench next to the merchant, and I sat down.

Alfric watched me, his dark eyes glinting like wet stones in the faint lamplight. 'Sounds like a necromancer's work.'

'I thought so.' A pause. 'Are there any of... such a calling in the city?'

'None that I know of. And that means probably not.' He paused for another swig. I trusted his word: Alfric's eyes and ears were everywhere in Middenheim. The dwarfs had built the place and their tunnels still pervaded it, like woodworm in a rotten cabinet. Alfric and his informants knew them all, and from listening at their secret entrances and watching at their spy-holes, he knew all the city's comings and goings. Best inform-ant and biggest blackmailer in town, Alfric Half-nose.

'So who could have done this? Do you know of anyone with a grudge against the temple?' I asked.

Alfric swilled the beer around his mouth and swallowed. 'Shut up. I'm thinking about necromancers.' He took another slow mouthful and savoured it thoughtfully.

Necromancy, I thought. If it was a necromancer then asking about grudges was pointless. Necromancers hated priests of Morr as much as we hated them. Both sides dealt in death, but we saw it as a passing, a stage in a pro-cess. They saw it as a tool. We were interested in freeing souls; they wanted to enslave them with their dark, unholy magics. Of course they'd have a grudge against us. Of course any ambitious necromancer would want to destroy the power of the local Temple of Morr, and if that meant killing its priests – well, like us, bodies were their stock in trade. But there was something about the way the girl's corpse had moved, something about the way it had sought out Father Zimmerman... I grasped for the idea, but couldn't catch it.

Alfric's voice broke my thoughts. 'One of your own corpses, was it? Corpse in the temple?'

'Yes,' I said. 'And there was something–'

'I'll know how that's happened, brother,' and he leant on that last word. 'That new priest of yours, the one from Talabheim...'

'Gilbertus.'

'Gilbertus. He's sloppy. Doesn't do the blessings properly. In too much of a hurry, like you. You should watch him at the Cliff of Sighs sometime. Goes through the motions all right, enough to fool the mourners anyway. But mark my words, those bodies are going over the cliff unblessed. Care-less. Dangerous too, if there's a necromancer around: unblessed corpses, ready to be raised. Now if there is a necromancer in town – and I'm not saying there is, mind – then be careful. Nasty, necromancers. My grand-sire tangled with one. They're fast. If they start to chant at you, count to five, he said. You'll never reach six. You'll be dead by then.'

Something, some idea about necromancers and the Temple, was form-ing itself in my mind, trying to push its way through the day's exhaustion. I stood up. The thoughts would take a while to clarify and it'd be morn-ing before I'd know if I had heard the answer I needed, but the long cold walk back to the temple would help. 'Thanks, Alfric. The debt is cleared. I'll leave you to your business.'

He looked surprised for a moment, but it took more than that to ruffle his scarred composure. 'Good seeing you again, Dieter,' he said, and turned back to his sweating customer without another word.

I walked to the door and out into the cold night. It had started to snow, and I pulled my robe closely around myself. It was only as I turned the corner away from the Bretonnian House that I realised he'd called me Dieter, and that I had forgotten to ask him anything about the dead girl. A brief image of her burning face with its dead smile flickered in my mind. Somehow her identity didn't seem so important now.

The Cliff of Sighs is a place where contradictions meet. From its edge you can see the whole of the Middenland stretching away as far as the Middle Mountains: hills, tiny towns and the vast green carpet of the Drakwald Forest with the Talabheim road winding its way through it. In the days when I could still appreciate beauty, I thought it the most romantic and lovely place in the city. Step closer to the edge, look down and you see the shattered ruins of the coffins, the shrouded bodies spread across the rocks or hanging in the branches of the trees after being dropped, and sometimes the unconsecrated corpse of a suicide or murder victim as well.

Or you could have done if it wasn't snowing so damned hard. I wrapped my cloak more tightly around me, and watched the mid-morning funeral party. Gilbertus's voice was muffled by the snow but I knew the sombre incantation he was chanting so well that I would have noticed the slightest error. So far he hadn't put a syllable wrong. Around him, the mourners huddled to protect themselves against the cold, and against their mutual grief and the fear of death. The bare pine coffin sat on its bier at the edge of the cliff. This was not an opulent affair.

Gilbertus turned slightly and I pulled my head back out of sight around the corner of the building. It was bloody cold and the sharp wind was turning my feet and fingers numb, but to move too much would give away my presence. Instead I stood, a silent shivering statue, and listened to the chant.

There.

He'd missed something. Nothing as obvious as a dropped word or missing line: just a subtle change to the rhythm of the incantation. Two lines later: again, and quickly again. Then a whole section I didn't recognise.

This wasn't some misremembered lesson. He was changing things. I didn't understand the language of the sacred chants – almost nobody did, we just learned them by rote – but I could tell that there was something wrong here. Fear crawled slowly up my spine, and I would have sweated if it wasn't for the cold.

A final blessing was said, the bier was pushed to the edge of the rock and tipped, the coffin slid off it and into space, and the mourners were ushered away from the cliffside before the crash echoed up from below. They didn't hang around, the party dispersing quickly, eager to get away from this place of death, into the warm, to console each other and start on the funeral meats, I guessed. Gilbertus lingered a moment, and I stepped out to meet him.

'Well met, brother,' I said.

'Aye, brother. Cold.' He stamped his feet. 'Are you here for a funeral?'

'In a way,' I said. 'But I want to talk to you about the attack last night.'

'Yes,' he said. 'Unpleasant affair. You've been told there's a meeting after supper to discuss who's to be acting head of the temple?' Something in his tone, his whole stance, had changed. His voice wasn't the voice of an apprentice any more. Yesterday he had spoken to me with respect. Today it was arrogance. He paused and turned away, and I wondered if he didn't want me to see his face as he spoke again:

'Last night you said you thought you knew who was behind the attack. Do you still know?'

'I was wrong last night,' I said.

'Oh yes?'

'Yes,' I said. 'I thought it was a necromancer with a grudge. It's not: it's a necromancer with ambition. Do you feel ambitious, brother?'

'When it's cold, I feel cold,' he said. A new tone, halfway between fear and aggression, had entered his voice. 'Why don't we find somewhere warm to discuss this?'

'I'm happy here,' I said. 'This won't take long. I've only got four questions. First, if you'd gone to raise the alarm last night, why didn't I see your footprints across the frost in the park?'

'Because I went a different way to you, clearly. What's the second question?'

'How did you know the dead girl had been stabbed through the heart?'

'A watchman told me. Next?'

'Where did you get the tentacle?'

He whirled to face me and I thought he was about to cast a spell. I did nothing. For a moment he paused, then let his arms drop slowly to his side. He was frightened, I could tell. Frightened but still confident.

'What do you know?' he asked.

'That you're not going to leave this cliff without killing me.'

I stepped towards him, my hands slightly raised, palms and wrists exposed. Merchant's trick. Makes you look vulnerable, unthreatening. He didn't react, or at least he didn't try to move away, which was good.

Instead he said, 'Apart from that.'

'You arrived here six months ago, disguised as a junior priest from Talabheim,' I said. 'We were expecting a Brother Gilbertus to come from there, so I imagine you killed him and took his place. You've spent six months making sure that there are a lot of unblessed corpses buried around the city which you could use your magic to reanimate later.

'Yesterday morning you killed a girl behind the Drowned Rat, enchanted the corpse, and then made it look like a mutant so it would have to be brought back to the temple for an investigation, and so there wouldn't be too much surprise when I couldn't perform the ceremony of Nameless Rite on it. You also persuaded Father Zimmerman that I was wasting the temple's time, so the corpse would lie in the Factorum all night, unblessed, ready for you to reanimate. When I met you outside the temple, you'd been there all along, controlling the dead thing.'

'You know all that?' he said.

I moved closer to him. Only a few feet separated us. Behind him, the edge of the cliff dropped away into eternity.

'It's mostly guesswork,' I admitted.

'So much guessing... for a ruined merchant still obsessed by the loss of his family. I am impressed.' The disguise had dropped completely now: he wasn't Gilbertus any more. He'd never been Gilbertus at all, except in the minds of some too-trusting priests. If any of them had been around, they wouldn't have recognised this sarcastic arrogant who dared to taunt me with my grief.

But there was no one else: the Cliff of Sighs was deserted. Just us and the swirling snow: he with his plan and his magic, I with a new-kindled memory of Filomena, and the sadness and anger that it brought.

He smiled again. 'So, brother, why would a priest of Morr – or even a necromancer – do what you've described?'

'Because,' I said, and I didn't try to keep the bile out of my voice, 'because you're ambitious. Because there would be no more powerful position for a necromancer than leading a temple of Morr. All the corpses you need, brought to your doorstep by the good citizens of Middenheim. You probably have some scheme for taking over the city in a couple of years.'

'Perhaps.' He was close to me now, and he wasn't smiling any more. His face was set cold and hard against me. Snowflakes whirled in the space between us. 'And your last question?'

'I was going to ask who the girl was,' I said. 'But it's not important any more.'

'She was young. Strong. Susceptible to my magic. A potential tool. We're alike, you and I, brother. I had no interest in the girl when she was alive, and neither did you. All the suffering, all the pain in this city, and you only have use for them when they're dead. We could work together. We could learn a lot from each other. And I could use a man like you. What say you? Join me. Come back to the temple. I'll tell you about the girl there.'

'I said it wasn't important.' But his suggestion had thrown me off-guard. Were we similar? Had I the seed of necromancy in me? Then he started to chant: high-pitched and fast, and my fate suddenly became a lot more short-term.

Count to five, Alfric had said. Five seconds to survive.

One. I moved forward two paces.

Two, and I was in front of him, the dagger drawn out from under my cloak.

Three. I plunged it deep into his stomach. Blood gushed onto my hand, hot over my numbed fingers. I raised my face to his, and our gazes met. His eyes were full of horror.

Four. A long second passed. He didn't stop chanting.

Five. I twisted the knife hard, my fingers slipping against the blood. Gilbertus gave a pain cry. The chant was broken, his spell useless. He paused for an instant, then launched himself at me. The snow-covered ground slid under my feet and I went down.

He landed on top of me, grasping at my neck. I tried to roll away, but he pinned me to the ground. He was bleeding to death, but he was still larger and stronger than me: at the very least he could take me with him.

His fingers found my neck and squeezed, twisting my head to one side. Snow covered my face, filling my eyes and nose with gritty cold. I could feel the warmth of his blood on my stomach, and the hilt of the knife in his wound pressed itself hard against my kidneys. My mind fogged with pain and darkness.

I felt like a dying man. Images formed in my head: faces. Father Zimmerman, his face contorted in death-agony. Brother Rickard, torn in half. Schtutt. My wife, Filomena, and my son Karl, smiling, the last morning I had ever seen them. And the half-face of a dead Norse girl whose name and story I would never know.

No. My job here was not finished. I had Morr's work to do.

Something poured a last burst of strength into my tired limbs. My arms found his, breaking his grip around my neck and pushing him off from me, so he rolled away across the whiteness of the burial site.

I rolled over to follow him. He was crouching, trying to get to his feet, one hand groping to pull the knife out. I kept rolling, crashing into him. I felt him fall sideways and slip, and then he grabbed my cloak and hung on. For a moment I couldn't understand why, then I felt his weight pulling at me and I knew the truth: we were at the edge of the cliff, and he was part-way over.

I didn't know if he was trying to pull himself back or wanting to take me down with him, but it didn't matter. I was sliding across the snow, being pulled over the edge of the cliff. I flung out my arms and legs, trying to get any kind of grip. All I found was soft snow. I slid further towards death.

My left hand found a small crevice in the rock, and I held onto it for dear life. I could see over the edge now. Below me, Gilbertus – the man I'd called Gilbertus – dangled. One of his hands was wrapped in my cloak, the other grasped desperately at the sheer stone of the cliff. The wind caught his garments, whipping them around him. Below us, an infinity of snow whirled and blew, obscuring everything else.

Gilbertus raised his head and stared into my eyes. His were pools of glistening darkness, like gazing into an ancient well. Even at this moment I could read nothing there. His face was as white as ice. Below, blood still spurted from his wound, spiralling away to the blizzard below.

'Pull me up,' he said. There was weakness in his voice.

'No,' I said. I wanted to batter away at his hands, to make him let go, but I was afraid that the slightest movement would make me slip further over the edge.

'Pull me up,' he said again, 'and I will take you to your wife and child.'

'You're lying,' I said, and at that moment there was a tearing, rending sound as my cloak ripped across. The necromancer swung sideways across the cliff face, held suspended in the air for a moment by the thicker fabric of the hem, and then it also parted and he dropped.

His body plunged down, fading, blown away among the blizzard, and disappeared into the whiteness. There was no scream or sound of impact. Possibly it was muffled by the snow.

I lay there for a while. Blood hammered in my temples, and my hands reflexively gripped onto whatever they could find. The snow and the rock were cold against my face. It reminded me I was alive.

Eventually I pushed myself back a yard, slowly, and stood up. Blood stained the area, but flurries of snow were already covering the pools and strands of crimson, and the footprints and marks of the recent scuffle.

My ribs ached. I looked around. The area was still deserted. No signs, no evidence, no witnesses, no complications. I whispered thanks to Morr.

For an instant I saw Gilbertus's face again, felt the weight of him suspended from his fist in my cloak, and heard his last words. He hadn't known anything. He couldn't have known anything. He would have said anything to save himself. No. He had been lying. He must have been.

His spirit had gone to Morr now. Even necromancers had to make their peace with the god of death eventually. It occurred to me that although I still thought of him as Gilbertus, I didn't know his real name.

I turned away, to walk back to the temple. Now Gilbertus was dead his spell should be broken and I should be able to lay the dead girl's soul to rest. I'd say a blessing for his spirit as well, and if anyone asked me what I had done today, I would say that I had given peace to two unquiet souls.

I wondered if I would ever do the same for my own.

CATCH AS CATCH CAN

The invisible boy had been in the city for a whole year now, and he was celebrating that triumph. He still had no job, nor any prospect of one, and his meagre supply of ready cash was reaching its limits again. But by nightfall he would have a good meal and a few glasses of beer inside him, never the less.

He had been called Wheezer, back when there were people who spoke to him or knew him, back before the city. Now he was nobody. But he was happy.

The smell of the city had burned at his nostrils and throat for a while when he had first arrived, and the stench had made him feel ill, but gradually he had come to ignore it. He was especially happy because he hadn't sneezed or wheezed once during the entire time he had lived in the city.

Back in the old good country air, he had suffered all year round from a nose that ran constantly. Through the spring and summer, he never stopped sneezing and his eyes never stopped streaming. And during harvest, he wheezed. That was how he'd come by his name. He was Wheezer.

Now he saw the funny side of all those years spent breathing good, pure country air. Bless the city's filthy, smoggy atmosphere, where, summer or winter, he felt better and better! His old nickname was now a kind of private joke. If he ever found anyone to ask him his name of course. It had been a year and no one had spoken to him. No one noticed him. No one even seemed to see him.

The weather was cold, wet, dark and miserable. Never mind winter, the change to spring was by far the worst part of the year.

Kruza sneezed heavily into a beautiful linen handkerchief that he had, only minutes before, lifted out of the pocket of some local gentleman. He wouldn't be able to sell it now, but he needed a good nose-wipe at this time of the year, and with all his other work the loss of the fence's price of one handkerchief was a trifle.

Kruza didn't feel much like work. He begrudged going out in this awful slanting drizzle, and the wind was the kind that went through you instead of round you. But it was his day tomorrow and he still had the small matter of his quota to fill. He would have finished days ago if it hadn't been for the fact that he'd found a new and very accommodating fence, and had decided to sell one or two of his better items on the outside. Just so long as the master didn't get wind of it.

'Wind, damnable wind,' Kruza muttered to himself as he passed out of the Altquartier and made his way down the steps to the Great Park. Even on a day like today there would be people trading there, which meant there would be other people with full purses. And aside from sitting in a nice little tavern somewhere drinking a long glass of ale, or better yet a hot toddy, the market gave the best shelter of anywhere in Middenheim. The stalls' awnings almost touched in places, shielding the people as well as the produce from the worst of the wind and rain.

Kruza mooched around for a while, strolling between the stalls, taking his time to pick out a likely victim. A little care spent choosing his mark now cut down on the number of targets he needed, and in the long run would give him more time in that tavern later in the day.

Wheezer followed the old cut-purse into the market in the big park. He loved the market. Mostly he stole what he needed, and of course that included money, but he took great delight in robbing the market stalls to fill his larder and make the derelict hovel he called home as pleasant as possible.

During his first year in the city, he had successfully filched enough cooking utensils, bed linens and other household items to furnish a warm and friendly nest, albeit one he enjoyed entirely alone. He'd stolen his entire wardrobe, and he'd even managed to pinch a series of small mirrors, including one in a gilt frame. He loved the mirrors and stood or hung them indiscriminately around the single room he lived in.

Today though, Wheezer needed cash. He had to eat and while his own larder (the outside sill of his single high window at this time of year) was all but full, he was celebrating his first anniversary in the city tonight and had decided to eat in style at one of the better taverns. He might even find himself a girl, he thought, and that would certainly mean hard cash.

Wheezer had his mark in sight. He usually chose the older cut-purses, although he knew, to his cost, of one or two who were still as quick of eye and fleet of foot as he was. This old coot with his one patched eye looked safe enough, though. Wheezer kept close to the old thief, feeling no need to slink or skulk about. He watched as the old man made his move.

Wheezer stood by as the old man lifted a tiny gold sundial from the pocket of an equally aged butler out doing the daily provisioning.

No good, thought Wheezer. *Who needs another timepiece? Next time.*

He followed the man on a little further, up a short cobbled slope, and round the side of a tiny handcart selling illicit liquor. Wheezer pocketed a bottle as he sidled past, just for good measure. After all, he was supposed to be celebrating today.

The old cut-purse's next target was a fat, bossy middle-aged woman. She had stopped to reprimand the man with her, surely her scolded and erstwhile cuckolded husband. Wheezer was mesmerised for a moment, the woman might well be as big as a barge and well past the prime of her life, but she was also very feminine.

Yes, a wench tonight, I think, Wheezer said to himself as he passed the woman and the cut-purse, doffing his cap to one or other of them, or perhaps to both. Neither one of them saw him, and he didn't expect them to. Putting his cap back on his head at an angle, Wheezer watched the old cut-purse snatch the little bag of money from the fat woman's waist. It was done in a moment, without anyone noticing, and the purse looked satisfyingly heavy to Wheezer. He loitered for a moment at a stall, picking up a couple of bars of rough soap and casually pocketing them while the owner's back was turned, before following the old thief onward.

Kruza stood by a stall, fingering a woman's silk shawl, when he saw Strauss. The old cut-purse had been the best in his time, and had earned himself the right to work solo in Middenheim. After twenty years of toiling for the likes of his Low King, not to mention training three generations of cut-purses, including Kruza, Strauss was in his retirement. He visited the market once a fortnight or so, just to keep his hand in, and always liked the dullest days and the oldest marks.

Kruza was not surprised to see him today and greeted him with as much cheer as he could muster, given the cold and his reddening nose.

'Well met, master,' he called as the near-blind old thief drew level with him.

'Is that you, Kruza, my boy?' the man returned, beaming his toothless grin from ear to ear. 'How goes it with you?'

'It's too cold and too damp and I have a quota to meet,' answered Kruza, trying to make it all sound like a joke and failing.

'You young pups of today,' Strauss remonstrated, 'never happy in your work. Still giving the master his pound of flesh then, are we? Only another fifteen years and a couple of hundred recruits and perhaps he'll let you off his hook.' He laughed.

'Only if he or I live that long,' Kruza said.

Wheezer watched as the old man, with his pocket full of another woman's money, stopped to speak with the tall, broad-shouldered fellow, who was apparently examining women's clothing. An odd occupation for such a strong, confident-looking man.

Now's your chance, Wheezer, old son, he thought to himself. He cleared his mind and moved in a little closer.

What is the old man blathering on about, he wondered as he slid two long, slender fingers into the side pocket of the old coat that hung from the blind old man's shoulders. He was walking away slowly and very calmly when he heard the words 'Stop! Thief!' begin to ring out – and then stop short very suddenly.

Kruza, astonished at the brazen outrage, wanted to cry out to stop the young chancer robbing his old friend. But since the purse had originally belonged to someone else, he realised it would do no good, and the words 'Stop! Thief!' came out strangled and barely loud enough to be heard by the old man standing next to him.

'I'll get him!' he said firmly, but very quietly to Strauss, and walked away purposefully toward the young man in the cap. He wondered why he couldn't remember what the boy looked like, except for the vaguest impression of a teenage kid with fair hair. Kruza prided himself that he never forgot a face, not the face of a mark, not the face of a fellow cut-purse and especially not the face of an enemy. There was something odd about this one. He realised at once that he would have to stay close to the boy; if he let him out of his sight, he would not know him again.

Wheezer left the park by the north-east gate and worked his way up the winding steps and slopes towards the north part of the Altquartier. He had made his home in a derelict building in the far north of the quarter where life was rough, but not so bad as it was further south in the heart of the district. He had stumbled upon the place, back then little more than tile-patched rafters open to the sky with rotting attic boards, late one night only a few days after he had arrived in the city. It had been cold and wet then, as it was now, and he had needed to find shelter fast.

It had taken Wheezer only a matter of days in the city to get the lay of the land, even though some of Middenheim's native citizens knew only the streets and byways of their own local quarters despite a lifetime of city dwelling. It had taken him a little longer to find a permanent place to sleep, but not too long.

Wheezer's room was the only occupied part of the ramshackle old building and was towards the top, on the third floor. His one window looked down into a narrow courtyard and the windowless backs of other buildings, so no one overlooked him. The front of the building was barred and boarded, but there was a cellar window at the side that served as a convenient front door where Wheezer could not be seen entering. The room was as solitary and isolated as he was himself, but it suited him well, and he had no desire to spread himself out among the other rooms that must exist in the building, but which Wheezer had never explored.

There was honour among thieves, even in Middenheim, and so if it took Kruza all afternoon to track down the brazen knave who had robbed venerable Strauss he would do it.

Discreetly Kruza followed the cocky young cut-purse out of the Great Park and watched him as he climbed in through the cellar window of the tall, narrow, crumbling building. Two minutes later, as the clatter of shod feet on old wooden stairs died away, Kruza slid his body, shoulder first, through the cellar window and looked around to get his bearings. In no time, he had found new scuff marks on the dusty floor and followed the ragged footprints up three flights of rickety, creaking stairs. He took his time, moving silently, as he didn't want to warn the young thug of his arrival.

Five minutes later, Kruza was leaning nonchalantly in the doorframe of a cluttered, low-lit room, watching the scrawny kid take off his cap and coat, utterly oblivious to the fact Kruza was there. Kruza gently ran his thumb down the length of his short-sword, reassuring himself of its cutting edge.

He looked on as the small, slender boy took soap and liquor from where he had secreted them in his pockets along with the heavy purse that Strauss had lifted. Then Kruza began to take in the room properly for the first time. It was extraordinary. The floor was thick with rugs and carpets, and there was a low couch covered in a colourful array of fabrics and cushions. Clean clothes and spare shoes were neatly arranged in one corner, half shielded from the room by an elegant, foreign-looking screen of pale wood. There was a deep bowl and ornate pitcher of eastern design gracing a low oval table and a large sheet of thick coarse material hung on a hook nearby. Then there were the mirrors. Kruza didn't believe he had ever encountered so many mirrors in one room, nor so much opulence in the room of a petty scoundrel. Yet despite the mirrors, the young thief was obviously used to being alone, since he had still not noticed his intruder.

Kruza had planned to surprise him. He had wanted the young thief to turn and catch him standing in the doorway, preferably running his thumb along the blade of his short-sword. But the boy just hadn't noticed him, though Kruza had held the relaxed menacing pose and repeated the gesture several times. Kruza began to feel rather silly repeating the theatrical threat.

Eventually, bored with looking into the remarkable room, Kruza was beginning to want to take a seat on that inviting couch. Then the tickle started and he knew that introductions were imminent. He had no choice in the matter, so he raised his short-sword in an aggressive stance. The sneeze came in a torrent of wet snot and doubled Kruza over with its force, his sword hand still pointing the gleaming weapon at the thief's back.

The young man, standing in the middle of the room with his back to the door, clutched his chest suddenly and fell to his knees.

Kruza thought for a moment that he'd killed his foe without even waving his sword, and cautiously entered the room to assess the situation. The lad was white, dark circles of fright ringing his wide grey eyes. Kruza realised that the thief was little more than a child and he almost felt sorry for him. Kruza didn't want to kill him like this; he didn't want the lad to die without knowing what he'd done. He tucked his sword in the back of his belt for easy access and knelt on one knee beside Wheezer, pulling him up.

'Don't faint on me, you little runt,' Kruza said. 'I don't plan to have to carry you over to that couch. I'd sooner kill you right here.'

'You already scared me half to death,' replied the pale-faced, quivering youth.

'It was just a sneeze,' Kruza said. 'Be thankful. At least it saved you from a full frontal short-sword attack.'

Wheezer flopped down on the couch. Kruza stood over him, his hands on his hips, leaning in so that he was looking down directly into Wheezer's face.

'Now listen to me,' he began, putting one hand squarely on the pommel of his sword, ready to draw it at any moment. 'What do you mean by stealing from old Strauss? There's honour amongst thieves in this city! Has your boss never told you the rules?'

'Strauss? Boss? I have no idea what you're talking about!'

'Strauss,' Kruza explained impatiently, 'is the name of the man you robbed this afternoon in the market.'

'But he was a thief,' Wheezer said, matter of fact. His voice had an unusual inflection, almost as if he was not used to talking. 'You can't steal from a thief, when what you're taking doesn't belong to him.'

'What about the stall holders on the market? You stole from them.'

'Hardly,' Wheezer said, 'When one man has more soap or liquor than he can use or sell, that's not stealing either. I never take from an empty stall or a busy one.'

Kruza looked down at him quizzically. 'Did your boss teach you nothing?'

'What boss?' Wheezer asked innocently.

'Ulric take me! You know,' Kruza was becoming impatient. 'The man you work for. The man you sell merchandise to.'

'I don't have a boss,' Wheezer answered.

'Then who do you sell your stolen goods to? Who's your fence?'

Wheezer shook his head, as if the street thief was suddenly speaking Bretonnian. 'Do you want a drink?' he asked suddenly.

'I– what?'

'A drink. I'm celebrating today. And you know, you're the first visitor I've had here, so it's only right.'

Kruza blinked. Had he missed something? The kid was... strange.

'Look, who do you sell your merchandise to?' he repeated, slowly and carefully.

'No one,' Wheezer said, beginning to catch on. 'I don't sell anything. I just take what I need or sometimes what I want. Why would I want to sell anything to anyone?'

Kruza didn't know whether to pity or laugh at this lost, lonely boy with such strange, innocent ways. There seemed to be nothing immoral about him, nothing memorable about him, almost nothing real about him at all. He did what he did and that was an end of it.

But then how, wondered Kruza, had he become so good at the stealth-craft, without a teacher. The kid must have the gift. The kid must be a natural. Kruza smiled suddenly. A thought had occurred to him.

'Perhaps I will have a drink with you after all,' he said at last, taking his hand off his sword hilt and sitting down again.

'Good, because as I said: I'm celebrating!' Wheezer announced, selecting two rather elegant, if mismatched, goblets and the bottle of pear brandy he had liberated that afternoon.

Wheezer was so excited to finally have an audience that he talked non-stop for a very long time. But Kruza didn't mind. He needed to put the lad at ease. Besides, the liquor was warming and the room was extremely comfortable. Wheezer got up, still talking, and lit a fire in the small grate just before dark. It burned gently, bringing warmth and light to the room, making it seem even more exotic than it had when Kruza had first beheld it.

'I arrived here a year ago to the day,' Wheezer was saying, 'come to collect my inheritance, or rather to be recognised by my illustrious parent.

'I turned twenty and left the forest for the city, my real home. You see, my mother lived here when I was born. She was the most beautiful artiste of her era, treading the boards of all the great theatres in all the great cities. She came to Middenheim once a year to perform, and it was on her last visit here that she met and fell in love with my father. He was young, of course, and impetuous and fell for my mother at first sight! Back then, who wouldn't have? Now, his great and noble family weren't too impressed with him, and had the gall to try and buy my mother off with cheap trinkets and idle promises, not to mention a great deal of money.

'Naturally, she declined and stayed in the city to have me, so that my father would have to recognise me. Great plan, but of course things never work out the way we expect and she died. A horrible death really. She died three days after I was born. She bled to death.

'So, off I went. Actually, I didn't go away, I was taken away by an old wet-nurse who worked for my grandfather. She was paid to take me into the forest and well, you know, kill me. She didn't have the heart to do it, of course. Instead she stayed with me and then her sister came to live with us too. Wonderful women, we never wanted for anything. They're both dead now and I wonder if they were witches, 'cause though we never went without, neither of them did anything practical. We didn't raise pigs or keep a garden, but there was always meat and greens and good bread...'

Kruza let the story wash over him as it rattled on. He was beginning to feel that the story and the kid were just part of some elaborate fever-dream brought on by his infernal ague.

'So I became a man, and before she died, my "aunt", who must have been over seventy before she took to her deathbed, told me everything. After I buried her and her sister – they died right there in the same bed on the same day – I set out to the city from the forest that had been my home my whole life. And that's it, well most of it. I can't mention my father's name, of course, not before he recognises me, officially, so to speak, but I can tell you he runs a great city, lives in a great palace and doesn't live a million miles from here. In fact, on a clear night I can see the top of his palace roofs from my little window.'

Kruza's head was floating about the room with all the good strong liquor he had drunk, but he knew when he was listening to an outrageous fairytale, or several woven together. Still, it was no business of his. He wanted the boy to relax and trust him.

Kruza left late. Remembering he still had a quota to fill, he secreted a little gilt mirror as he left, sliding it beneath his jacket.

'It's all right,' Wheezer said, having noticed. 'You have it. I took it from a thief. It doesn't belong to anyone now, so take it by all means.'

Kruza felt guilty for the first time since he was a child. 'Look, what's your name?' he asked.

'Oh, I don't have one,' the lad replied cheerily, 'being a bastard and everything. And my mother didn't live long enough to give me a name. When I was big enough to need a name my aunts called me "Wheezer". You can call me that.'

'Okay,' said Kruza. 'My name's Kruza.'

'Funny,' said Wheezer, 'I thought your name must be "Sneezer",' and he laughed at his joke. 'Did you hear that?' he asked rhetorically, 'Wheezer and Sneezer!'

Kruza blinked again, forced a grin. 'I'll see you around,' he said, and left.

A natural, that's what the boy was. The gift in his fingers, his tread, in his sheer anonymity. It was rare. There were a lot of good thieves in Middenheim, Kruza amongst them, but there was only a handful of true naturals. If the boy proved to be what Kruza thought he was, then Kruza was duty bound to begin recruiting him for his Low King.

Or keeping him for myself, Kruza wondered. The thought kept coming back to him. How easy would it be to fill his quota then, to get the Low King off his back, to finally start getting ahead, getting somewhere on his own?

But recruiting the boy wasn't going to be that easy either way. Wheezer had all sorts of crazy rules about whom he would steal from and what he would take. He saw no reason to steal for the sake of selling goods on at less than their value. He stole only to live.

But he was so good at it, and Kruza hated to see such raw talent wasted. He left it two days, and then the next morning shadowed the sleepy alley where Wheezer lived until he saw the boy emerge from his ruin. Kruza strode from the shadows, as if he was just passing, a chance encounter.

'Oh. You again,' he said.

The boy's face lit up. *He is so unaccustomed to being spoke to, Kruza thought with a touch of pity.* Just a touch; there wasn't room for much except business in Kruza's heart.

'Where are you going?'

'To work,' Kruza said, sniffing. It was another cold and wet day.

'Can I come?' Wheezer asked.

And that was how the games began. That simple.

The two of them strolled down to the Great Park, Kruza hunched over with the cold and sticking close under the awnings that would keep the wind and rain off. Wheezer almost strutted through the park, throwing out his puny chest and taking deep breaths of the freezing, damp air. He appeared to be in his element. Kruza led him to a stall crammed with all manner of household goods and they watched as a local gentlewoman, escorted by her houseman, fondled bolts of cloth on a stall nearby. Kruza almost gasped as Wheezer picked up a package of spills and half a dozen tallow candles from the stall, tucking them into his jacket. But no one else seemed to notice.

A natural, by Ulric. Kruza smiled. He nodded to his brazen companion. 'Bet you can't lift madam's money pouch,'

'Where?' Wheezer asked, looking about him.

'There,' Kruza answered, 'with the snooty-looking houseman in the short grey cloak.'

'No problem,' Wheezer said, a cock-eyed smile across his face. He walked off past the affluent woman with the heavy pouch at her waist and nipped it off without even touching her. Kruza watched, only feet away, amazed at the speed and skill with which Wheezer performed the dare. He had been ready to step in and cause a little confusion to cover Wheezer when he got caught, which had seemed inevitable with the houseman standing guard.

But it never happened. Wheezer walked around the next stall and came back behind Kruza.

'Good, good...' Kruza murmured as they walked on together. 'Where is it then?'

'Where's what?' Wheezer asked innocently.

'The pouch, you dolt,' Kruza replied. 'How much was in it?'

'No idea,' Wheezer said, 'but it was heavy enough. You can check it if you like. It's in your jerkin pocket.'

Kruza looked wide-eyed at Wheezer and slid two fingers into the pocket, drawing out the full pouch. His bottom jaw dropped so far, so fast, he almost dislocated it. He hadn't felt a thing and he was one of the best. The kid was amazing. Invisible.

Wheezer seemed to like the game, and would take any dare. As the day went on, Kruza became more and more intrigued by what the young, untrained cut-purse could do. Kruza didn't need to recruit Wheezer. The kid would give him anything and do anything for him so long as it was prefixed with 'I bet you can't...' Kruza was looking at a meal ticket.

Wheezer stole lunch for them from a stall-holder while having a conversation with him at the same time. They sat and ate the fresh sausage, a small earthenware jar of pickles and two small loaves of good bread, sitting on an empty, covered handcart behind one of the clothing stalls. Kruza's tall, athletic frame perched next to Wheezer's small compact one. Kruza was a grown man of twenty-four. Only a few years older than the other. But sitting next to him, Wheezer looked like a child from the slums.

Kruza's mood had improved dramatically. It was worth coming out in the cold and wet to watch Wheezer at work, especially when Wheezer was working for him.

During the afternoon the lad lifted two time-pieces from the inside pockets of gentlemen whose outerwear looked completely impenetrable, and completed the hat-trick by removing a barely visible necklace from a middle-aged gentlewoman whose cloak was buttoned high to her throat. Together, the conspirators then liberated a total of seven items from one young dandy who they tripped and then 'saved' from an undignified fall down a steeply stepped lane. While dusting the man down, Wheezer managed to empty three of his outer pockets and two that were concealed beneath. He had also taken the short dagger that the dandy kept in the top of one of his long boots. He was a marvel.

As evening fell, Kruza and Wheezer retired to the Drowned Rat in the Ostwald district. Kruza opened the door from the grubby street with its lengthening shadows, and they all but fell into the tavern. Pockets full, a good day's work done, and coins to spend on beer and a good supper.

Several of Kruza's friends and colleagues were crowded into the small bar, and introductions were made all round, but no one could remember Wheezer's name and very soon they forgot he was there at all. Wheezer thought them all fine fellows, apart from that chap with the flat hair, Arkady, who seemed a little churlish. Idly he found himself wondering if he had been Kruza's last best friend.

Soon the drink was flowing and the food forgotten as Kruza exchanged stories and information with his colleagues. They talked constantly of the 'Boss', although sometimes they called him 'The Man' or 'The King', complaining about him, cursing him and generally displaying their hatred for him.

Some time later a fight started. Good-natured at first, just a few fists flying to prove a point, then someone pulled a dagger and chaos broke out. Wheezer had no idea what they were fighting over, and slid down

off his stool and sheltered between the barrels that held up either end of
the bar. He stayed there with his arms wrapped round his knees, watching the mayhem.

Kruza threw himself with gusto into the melee. There was nothing like
a good brawl to end a good evening. Eventually, the fight broke up when
the landlord began arbitrarily swinging a club around his bar, screaming that enough damage had been done and he would call the guard.
Four men had sustained gashes and one had had his earlobe bitten
off. The others had slashed clothes, and bruises were rising up on their
faces and bodies from the blows of fists and hilt-pommels jabbed hard
against flesh during the closer, hand-to-hand bouts where there was no
room to use a blade.

Wheezer was astounded to see them all on good terms when they were
kicked out of the tavern, united now in cursing the pot-man, as they had
been in cursing the Low King.

A week later Kruza and Wheezer were meandering back to Wheezer's room.
The place was more comfortable and private than Kruza's, and he had
begun to adopt it as his own. Wheezer could not have been more happy.
He had company at last.

They turned east, and cut across the Wynd and up into the south side
of the Altquartier. From there they turned north toward the crumbling old
building where they now both lived. It had been a goodly walk and Kruza
decided there was time for one more drink. The single pale light outside
the Cocky Dame shone to him like a beacon and he was about to enter
the sleazy one-room tavern with its cabbage smell when Wheezer stopped
him by grasping his forearm.

'I've seen that before,' Wheezer began, pointing out a covered handcart
steered down the sloping street by a sombre man in a long cloth cape.
'What is it?'

'The dead,' Kruza said plainly. 'No one's concern but the priests of Morr.'

'They carry them off the streets?' Wheezer asked, 'Where do they take
them?'

'That one'll no doubt end up turning over and over in the air until it
lands at the bottom of the Cliff of Sighs, more broken than it is already.'

'The old priest who tended people back in the forest always came to their
homes. Bodies weren't moved, and if a homeless body was found in a field
then that was where it was buried. Don't the people here bury their own
people on their own land?' Wheezer asked.

'Huh!' Kruza snorted, raising his hands and turning his body in a gesture that encompassed the entire city. 'What land? The wealthy find a
resting-place in Morrspark, but even they are buried one above the other,
five or six deep. The rest tumble over the cliff. The priests seal the bodies and bless them and for all but the most destitute there are mourners.

But this city has little sentiment. It goes about its business, and leaves the priests to go about their's.'

'What of their belongings?' Wheezer was full of questions tonight and Kruza was still only three parts full of good ale.

'They are priests – they have few belongings...'

Wheezer interrupted. 'Not the priests!' he exclaimed. 'The dead!'

Kruza pushed through the tavern door, dragging Wheezer behind him. 'You're far too ghoulish for my liking. Come and have a drink with me and let's have an end to this talk of corpses.'

But the talk of corpses did not end. It began again later that night, when Kruza was settled on the couch in Wheezer's room, and Wheezer himself was lying on a pile of cushions on the floor. Kruza was now full of ale and more tolerant of Wheezer's questions – up to a point.

'The dead people,' began Wheezer, 'where do their possessions go?'

'I don't know,' Kruza said. 'Some are robbed before they're cold. Those who die quietly among their families are relieved of their possessions by their loved ones.'

'And the rest?' the other asked, innocently.

'The rest?' Kruza replied. 'I suppose the priests of Morr collect their belongings and return them to their mourners. Perhaps if there is no one to pass the possessions on to then they go into the coffers of the Temple, or perhaps to the Graf himself.'

'Or should I say your "illustrious parent"?' he added, and laughed so much he had to stagger off his couch and take a leak out of the room's single window. When he returned to the couch, he was asleep and snoring a ragged drunken snore before Wheezer could form his next question.

In the morning, however, Kruza remembered enough of the previous night's conversation to give Wheezer a word of warning.

'If you are thinking of robbing the dead, think again!' he said firmly. 'The dead are respected by all but the lowest of the low-scum in this city, which has its share of grave-robbers. Friendless, perverted men.'

'Sure,' Wheezer said.

'Friendless, Wheezer,' Kruza reiterated. 'If I get wind that you have robbed a corpse, I shall cut you off and I'm sure you don't want that!'

Wheezer looked at his feet. 'It's just that a corpse can't own any–' he began, but was interrupted with a glare.

'Friendless, Wheezer!' Kruza said between gritted teeth, holding the much shorter man by the front of his jerkin and lifting him to his toe tips. 'Friendless!'

Kruza continued his work, and his manipulation of Wheezer's talents continued to make him prosper. It had been a very good month. Two or three days out of every week the two would pair up and visit the markets and crowded areas of the city. By night they would eat and drink in various seedy taverns. One night Kruza took Wheezer to the Baiting Pit, but the youth didn't like it much and they left.

'I saw bears in the forest, where I lived with my aunts,' Wheezer explained. 'They were beasts of the wild and harmless enough if you respected them.'

Kruza shook his head. The kid was from another world.

Wheezer had promised Kruza that he would not rob the dead, even though he didn't understand how it could be called stealing at all, let alone the lowest of low crimes.

He wasn't going to rob the corpses, of that he was convinced, but he had become fascinated by the biers and carts that were wheeled around the streets with their dead cargo. Sometimes he would see an important-looking man in temple robes, calming the bereaved or asking questions or leaning over biers. Often the biers were steered through the streets wheeled by one man, or sometimes two, in long drab cloaks. Other times he saw corpses being tossed onto any available vehicle and being driven off by one of the city watch, and once he saw a body being removed by a White Wolf Templar, splendid in his plate armour.

Wheezer became quite fond of a good funeral, witnessing grand burials in Morrspark and simple ones at the Cliff of Sighs. No one seemed to mind him being there. In fact, no one ever noticed that he was there – except for one time.

He had climbed up to the Cliff about a fortnight after his conversation with Kruza and watched a lone priest performing a ceremony. The priest had stood over a rough plank coffin going through the necessary rituals and chanting the prayers that were almost familiar to Wheezer by now. Wheezer expected nothing, and was ready to turn away and make his way back into the city, when the strangest thing happened.

The priest stopped and spoke to him. Just briefly, pitying his loss, saying something about the corpse being at peace.

Wheezer didn't hear the actual words. This was only the second person to speak to him voluntarily since his arrival in the city more than a year before. Kruza had been the first.

'The dead of Middenheim,' Wheezer began out of nowhere, one night as they made their way to a tavern. 'They're not all taken away by priests, are they?'

'No, not all,' Kruza said. 'Since the Temple of Morr burnt down there aren't really enough of them to do all the burial work, without having to go out to collect every single body in the city.'

'I saw they were working on the temple,' Wheezer said. 'So, can anyone take a body away?'

'There are the men in long grey cloaks,' Kruza answered, 'I don't know who they are, but the priests use them a lot to carry bodies. They also ask the City Watch or anyone else who is considered more or less trustworthy.'

'Like the White Wolf I saw?' Wheezer asked rhetorically. 'You said before that the bodies were taken to the temple, Morrspark and the Cliff of Sighs, but what about the other place?'

'What other place?' Kruza asked. 'Where else would they take them?' He was becoming impatient now, Wheezer could tell, and he didn't want to make his mentor angry, so he said no more. But there was another place.

Hungover and groaning on the couch the next morning, Kruza didn't notice Wheezer sneaking out, or if he did, he didn't care. Wheezer rose early and went into the city to watch for carts. He was almost obsessed by the bodies and their resting places now, and if Kruza couldn't tell him what the 'other place' was then he would find out for himself.

Wheezer quickly spotted his first body of the day, some old man who had died in the night – perhaps violently, since this was the Altquartier – but maybe just quietly in his bed. His body was carried the short distance between where he had died and the nearest place the vehicle could get to the corpse: across a courtyard and down a short alley. Then it was heaved onto one of the narrow handcarts and wheeled away by a guard who had recently been relieved from his night watch. The middle-aged, thickset man was disgruntled at having been given the task when he was due home for his breakfast, and he manhandled the body as though it were a sack of grain. Wheezer followed the guard and his cargo until he realised they were heading toward the Temple and not that 'other place'. He let them go and began to look around for the next body.

Leaving the Altquartier and following the Garten Ring round the eastern side of the park, Wheezer detected a commotion on the other side of the wall. A cut-purse had been careless and was being attacked by his mark. The cut-purse, a man who reminded Wheezer of Kruza, what with his height and square shoulders and casual style of dress, won the fight shortly after producing a dagger from his boot. And a woman was now lamenting the loss of the bold, stout man in his thirties who that day had decided not to be a victim of robbery and was now lying on the mossy slope, a victim of murder.

Wheezer stayed close as first the City Watch and then the priest of Morr appeared. It was half an hour before a pair of constables was dispatched with the body and it was soon apparent to Wheezer that they, too, were heading for the Temple of Morr.

It was almost noon and Wheezer was prepared to give up his corpse-chasing for the day when a tall man in a long, drab cloak crossed in front of him, hauling a long body-shaped barrow with two large wheels at its centre. A second man, similarly dressed, brought up the rear of the vehicle, clutching a pair of handles on the back of the makeshift bier and following his colleague. Wheezer decided he would try one last time to follow a corpse to the 'other place'.

Wheezer followed the cart without much expectation of success. He had already failed twice today. He was delighted when the cart's course turned west and then north. Wheezer had been in this part of the city before, with its wide streets and grand houses. He had dressed carefully that morning in clean, anonymous clothes so that he could walk about unmolested by the city watch, who never seemed happier than when they were ousting some wretch or urchin from the better parts of the city. Wheezer had thrown a tatty old cloak over his neat ensemble for his walk through the poorer regions but discarded it now, as the cloaked men with their cart turned left at the Temple of Shallya. Wheezer could hear the orphans inside chanting prayers by rote, accompanied by the sporadic coughs and pained cries of the patients in the infirmary next door. He had gone there once himself when he had torn his hand open, fortunate to have the money to pay for his treatment. The physician who had attended him there had neither looked at nor spoken to Wheezer while he cleaned and dressed the wound.

Now Wheezer was in the Nordgarten district, amongst the homes of merchants and gentlemen. He did not hide in the shadows or skulk in doorways. He thrust his shoulders back and marched down wide, cobbled streets within sight of his quarry. He passed errand boys and visiting shopkeepers in the street, but it was a damp day, and cold, and the local residents were happy enough to stay in the warmth and comfort of their opulent homes.

Wheezer began to get excited. He would find out something that Kruza did not know, perhaps something new about the dead and their belongings. The 'other place'.

Wheezer saw the house ahead. It was taller and narrower than those around, giving it an imposing air. He did not know what it might once have been, but it didn't look much like the other houses in the area. Perhaps it had been a minor temple once. It was a tall, slender tower with narrow windows and a strangely curvaceous spire, which rose up in soft waves to a tiny dome at its crown. Under the base of the spire was a deep gallery of arrow slits. A second circular tower was fixed to the side of the main building, the breadth of perhaps two men passing, but with its own tiny dome and more of the unusual slits for windows.

Wheezer drew level with the makeshift bier as the two men worked it between the pair of narrow doors on the alley side of the building. It was darker in the alley, and these doors could not be seen from the street. Standing to one side of the double doors, slightly in view of the cloaked men, if they had cared to see him, Wheezer casually slid a hand out and lifted the rough, ragged-edged tarpaulin that covered the wagon. He lifted it a little higher as the two men continued to struggle with the bier, which was almost as wide as the doors.

His first glimpse suggested to Wheezer that this was no body, and his second, longer look confirmed it. On the wagon were all manner of objects, most of which Wheezer did not recognise at all, although he suspected that some of the odd-shaped glass vessels had come from an alchemist's shop. There were other things which he did recognise and, since there was no corpse to be robbed, he thrust his hand at the nearest shiny, metallic object under the tarpaulin. He pulled it out and tucked it into his jerkin. Then he stepped out entirely from behind the doorpost, doffed his cap at the cloaked men, who still did not seem to see him, and walked out of the alleyway and back towards the Temple of Shallya where he had left his cloak.

Having retrieved it, Wheezer wanted to get back and confront the sceptical, dismissive Kruza with his findings. But there was something else he needed to do first.

Wheezer crossed back into the Great Park by its south-west gate and headed toward the herbalist and apothecary stands that huddled together in their own tiny enclave, shielded on one side by a bank and on the other by the east wall of the park itself. Trade in this part of the market was thin, but Wheezer had no problem picking up the bits and pieces he wanted and he was soon on his way home. In his pockets he now carried a small, scented beeswax candle; two bundles of herbs; and a couple of rough crystals hewn from different types of rock. He wasn't quite sure what all the things under the tarpaulin had been, but it couldn't hurt to take a few simple precautions.

'Kruza!' he called, almost before he had reached the third flight of stairs, and ran up them stretching his legs to make them climb two stairs at a time. 'Kruza?'

He found the cut-purse sitting on the edge of the couch in only his shirt, which spilled to his knees. His head was in his hands and almost between his knees as he leant forward, the weight of his head almost unbearable with its attendant hangover.

'Shhh!' exclaimed Kruza and winced.

Wheezer wanted to laugh, but instead he crossed to the small, segmented wooden box that sat in a corner, where the gilt mirror had once lived. He lifted the lid and drew out a clutch of dried herbs. He took the ever-simmering kettle from its frame high over the fire, lest it dry up, and made a tea from the twigs and dry leaves. He handed it to Kruza, who balked at the smell of it, but downed it when pressed.

Wheezer left Kruza alone for half an hour, but the older cut-purse felt better surprisingly quickly and no sooner felt ravenously hungry than Wheezer had provided him with a plate of cold meat, pickles and bread.

'Now that you feel better,' Wheezer said, excited, 'I have something for you.' He lifted the object that he had stolen from under the tarpaulin, taking it out of his jerkin at the collar button and holding it out at arm's length in front of him. It swung in small circles before their eyes.

The thing Wheezer had stolen was quite beautiful and both of them gazed at it with equal hypnotic wonder. It was a chain made up of large, flat, square sections joined by fat gold links at the corners. Every square section was engraved like an elaborate belt buckle, each bearing a different motif or scene. In the centre of the chain, which was long enough to hang around a broad man's shoulders, was a larger ornament.

'Like the chain of office the Graf wears on feast-days,' murmured Kruza in a husky undertone.

'It's trying to eat itself,' Wheezer said, mesmerised.

The ornament consisted of a great dragon or snake forming an eternal circle by feasting on its own tail. Every scale of its armour-plated body was etched into the solid gold from which it was crafted. Its eyes were domed orbs of sightless ivory.

'It's beautiful!' breathed Kruza.

'Take it, then,' Wheezer said, thrusting it at arm's length, closer to Kruza's face. 'And when you get tired of it, perhaps it can help with your quota.'

'The quota!' Kruza cried, leaping off the couch as if a fire, lit long ago under the offending piece of furniture, had finally penetrated its solid base and was now biting at Kruza's backside.

'It's my day and I haven't filled my quota! Sigmar's blood!' He snatched up the heavy trinket and thrust it into his shirt. Then he pulled on breeches and boots and his short leather coat and hurried out of the room, snatching up the cloth sack holding his other acquisitions before slamming the door behind him without another word to the youth.

'Cursed thing!' Kruza yelled, storming back into the room with no regard for disturbing Wheezer. He threw the trinket onto the couch. 'He wanted nothing to do with it. The Man, who will sell anything and deal in anything, wouldn't touch it... and so my quota was lacking.'

'Oh.'

'Do you know what my penalty is for being short of my quota?' Kruza yelled, his voice still hoarse from the previous night's revelries. 'Take your trinket and may it bring you good fortune!'

Wheezer thought Kruza would leave, but instead of turning for the door, the cut-purse slumped down on the couch. Wheezer had failed, as the month had gone on, to realise that Kruza needed him more and more with every day that passed. While the cut-purse used the skills of the young, invisible thief, his own stealth-craft had become dull with lack of use and too much good living. He slouched on the couch, fingering the flat square plates of the unacceptable ornament, trying to read the story etched and carved there.

'Where did you get this, anyway? It must be tainted or horribly important for the master to turn it down flat with such an odd expression on his face. Come to think of it, I don't think my quota was doubled for any reason other than the insult of offering him this particular piece of merchandise.'

'I got it from the "other place",' Wheezer said, disinterested now, trying to work out how he could repay Kruza for his faux pas.

'What other place?' Kruza asked. And then recognition dawned. 'Ulric damn you if you stole this from a corpse!'

'No! No!' Wheezer exclaimed, backing away. He didn't care to feel the tip of that short-sword at his throat again. 'That's just the point! There was no body on the bier that went to the other place.'

'Don't talk in riddles, boy,' Kruza returned. His mood was dark and furious, and he felt like lashing out.

'I followed a corpse barrow… well, more of a covered handcart really. Anyway, I followed it to the "other place", the place I told you about. The place where the cloaked men take the bodies when they don't take them to the Temple of Morr. Only they don't take bodies at all. I lifted the cover on the wagon. There were so many things there. I snatched that thing off it,' he said, pointing to the chain. 'But I swear I wasn't robbing a body. There was no body!'

'Smugglers,' Kruza said to himself.

'What?' Wheezer asked.

'It has to be smugglers. They dress like servants of the priests of Morr, so that they can move merchandise around Middenheim. The only people never stopped by citizens or the Watch in this city are the dead. And bearers of the dead.'

Realising at last what his companion had said, Kruza leapt off the couch and grabbed Wheezer by the arm.

'Take me there!' he said. 'Now!'

Wheezer managed to persuade Kruza to wash and shave and tidy up his dress before taking him into the Nordgarten, a district that Kruza seldom visited. The pickings might be rich, but the risks were high. The Watch would be on him quicker than Altquartier rats on a dog's corpse if they suspected the smallest misdemeanour.

Kruza had little confidence walking the broad, curving streets of the better districts of Middenheim, and he unconsciously copied Wheezer's upright stance and confident gait as they passed the Temple of Shallya. The orphans were still chanting.

Wheezer walked straight up to the strange tower-building and around into the adjoining alley. He was ready to enter, without a qualm, but Kruza was more cautious.

'Let's take a look about first,' he suggested. 'There may be people. The cloaked smugglers you saw before.'

But inside himself, Kruza was itching to get on. He could smell riches in there. Riches that his Low King would accept. One swift robbery, with his silent partner in tow, could shorten his working week by several days and lengthen his leisure time by the same.

They exited the alley, back out onto the main street, and followed the building round to the tall, slender, curved tower on its other side. The tower was sheathed in gloom and shadow and Kruza began to feel rather more at home. There was no effort involved in finding the squat door in the side of the tower below a line of glassless, slit windows. It was low and black and smelled oddly of pitch.

Wheezer opened the door and Kruza took a deep breath before ducking his head and shoulders to follow the lad in. They stood together on the small square landing that signalled the ground floor level and looked up and then down at the winding, spiral staircase. Looking directly up through the shaft of the stairs, they could see shafts of light coming in through the west-facing windows. Looking directly down, they could see nothing.

'Down,' hissed Kruza, turning from the lit upper floors. Unlike Wheezer, he was only invisible in the dark. Wheezer trotted happily down the stairs, looking back to his comrade, who took every step slowly and carefully so as to make as little noise as possible. He realised for the first time that Wheezer could be as soundless as he was invisible. Kruza's own careful steps made a sloppy 'tak' sound, while Wheezer's footfalls were like a whisper.

'Keep looking down,' hissed Kruza, anxious that Wheezer might walk into something and have them both killed before they had even seen a foe. They continued down the stairs, one flight and then, just for good measure, a second. Wheezer looked to where they were going and the slow and nervous Kruza looked to where they had been.

At the second floor below ground, Wheezer stepped out onto a wider, arched landing that led to only two or three shallow, curved steps and then, as far as he could see, nothing. He had reached the bottom. Thirty seconds later Kruza joined him, almost knocking him down the last few steps as he continued to keep watch behind them.

There was still no light. There was a slight smell of spoiled milk, which Kruza didn't notice, but which Wheezer thought odd in a room two storeys below ground level. The air was very still and slightly chill and while the steps down had been damp, the floor of the cellar room was perfectly dry, even dusty underfoot.

Wheezer steadied Kruza, whose widening eyes shone out stark and white in the gloom. Then he reached into his pocket and took out the beeswax candle, which he lit, filling the air with the pungent scent of spices, casting a pool of light around himself and Kruza and making shadows in the underground place.

The cellar was a kind of circular lobby and Wheezer walked around it from one vaulted arch to the next. He stopped at each, examining the posts either side that made the doorways and then moved on, completing the circle and not crossing the centre of the floor. Kruza had stayed resolutely where he was, looking back up the steps every few seconds as if he had a nervous tick.

'This is just an entrance hall,' Wheezer said, 'but there are more rooms beyond those arches.'

He undid the top two buttons of his jerkin and pulled out a large pouch, tied around his neck with a cord. He took something from it that Kruza couldn't see.

'What are you doing?' Kruza asked, before jerking his gaze anxiously back up the stairwell.

'It's all right,' Wheezer answered, beginning to work his way back around the circle of arches, slowly. 'Someone's scrawled glyphs all over the doorways. But a little country magic will soon cancel them out.'

'Glyphs!' Kruza exclaimed as loudly as he dared, his voice still little more than a hoarse whisper. 'Magic! Right, this is all starting to spook me out! Bodies! Jewels that even a filthy fence won't buy – and now glyphs!'

What had seemed like such a good idea now was rapidly turning sour.

'What are you doing? What do you mean by "country magic"?' he hissed as Wheezer began to brush an arch support with a bundle of dry old leaves and twigs, holding his candle up to each glyph in turn and murmuring what sounded like old rhymes.

'You know the kind of thing: herbs, spider webs, rabbit droppings, all good fodder for simple country magic, just as good as your fancy town stuff any time. And these glyphs are pretty basic,' Wheezer said, moving to the next arch support.

Is there no end to this kid's weirdness, thought Kruza, *or was he really raised by witches?* Down here, the half-remembered details of that nonsense story seemed so much more believable.

It began to get lighter as Wheezer entered each side-room for just long enough to light a lamp and then on to the next.

Somehow it didn't seem quite so cold to Kruza now, or so menacing, so when Wheezer reached the fourth archway, Kruza crossed the floor to watch him weave his little bit of country magic, kicking up dust as he went.

Wheezer heard him and turned, seeing what Kruza had not.

The tall, athletic cut-purse ordinarily had a long stride, but now he was creeping and cautious. Any other time Kruza would have stepped over the thing on the floor. Now he shuffled through it.

'DDDDOOOOO...!' Wheezer started to scream out, but it was too late.

Kruza looked up at the scream, standing squarely in the confusion of sandy dust around his feet. He saw Wheezer's mouth, wide, in full scream and he felt the tension in the kid's body.

Ulric damn me, he thought very quietly to himself.

Wheezer's candle went out and the soft glow the oil lamps were giving out turned to a hard white light. More white light filled all the rooms around the lobby and for a moment Kruza thought he saw the glyphs on the arch supports whirling and dancing. Kruza could not move or speak and Wheezer's frozen face with its half-finished warning cry was locked in its strange and terrified expression. The moment seemed to last forever.

Don't let it end, Kruza thought, knowing that it must.

'...OOON'T!' Wheezer's cry finished as eight tall, grey-cloaked figures emerged from the eight archways. The man in the fourth arch from the left, standing right behind Wheezer, was lifting his arms. Kruza could see bone-pale, wasted forearms and gnarled, taloned hands emerging from the cloak. He could see nothing of the face beneath the hood. Wheezer stepped neatly to one side and stood against one of the tall columns that separated the arches, but the man kept coming. Straight for Kruza.

Kruza wanted to run. He wanted to run very badly. He could not.

He looked at Wheezer. The lad seemed to be shrugging.

He looked at his feet.

For the first time Kruza saw what he had stepped in to: the remains of an elaborate sand painting, criss-crossed with lines of black ash and swirls of cobalt and purple crystalline sand that Kruza did not recognise. He recognised only that this was a trap and he was caught in it.

Why are they taking so long? Kruza wondered, looking again at Wheezer. There was something flying through the air between them.

Kruza caught and snatched open the pouch Wheezer had thrown to him. Seeing what it was he dropped it onto the sand in disgust. An unlit scented beeswax candle, and a bunch of dried twigs and leaves, fell out of the pouch.

Kruza laid his right hand on the pommel of the short-sword which stuck out of his belt, under the back of his jacket. He took hold of the hilt and pulled it free, high over his head. His left hand came to join his right and he stood with his feet shoulder-width apart, knees slightly bent, four-square in front of the cloaked man who was still walking towards him.

I have all the time in the world, he thought as he bent his arms, bringing the short-sword up, at an angle, to shoulder height. Attack, his mind told him. He waited just a moment.

Kruza brought his sword down at the very moment the cloaked figure reached his hands out as if to strangle Kruza. The sound the sword made as it sliced into the side of the cloaked figure's neck was one of a blunt knife through a sheaf of dry paper. Nevertheless, there was blood. It gouted out of the wound in short, thick spurts, bright red in the white light, almost purple against the grey cloak.

Stunned, Kruza lifted his sword to strike again. Adjusting his stance, he realised that he had taken a step outside the sand trap. He was free of it. The bleeding man stood, his arms still in front of him, apparently unaware of the deep wide slash that had taken his head half off his body and ripped partway down into his torso. Then he sank slowly to his knees and his hands came down toward the sand.

'KKKRRRUUUZZZAAA!' Wheezer screamed.

Kruza looked up at the lad, who was pointing to the single foot that remained inside the edge of the sand painting. Kruza skipped to one side as the bleeding figure's taloned hands landed in the sand and it began to whirl with colour, coming to rest in its original pattern. The body of the cloaked figure was gone. So was the pouch and its spilled contents.

Seven remained.

The remaining cloaked men began to emerge from their archways in a kind of staggered formation. None of them saw Wheezer. They all saw Kruza.

He stepped forward again, looked once at Wheezer who remained pressed against the pillar, and once at his short-sword. The blood was gone, but the blade gleamed a promise to Kruza. The cut-purse didn't know if time had really slowed or whether it was the strange vitality in his body; whichever it was, it seemed to be working in his favour for the moment.

With the next two swings, one high and sloping, the second low and slicing, he took out two more of the grey men. He heard the paper sound again, but this time the blood remained on his sword. There was a path now between the men emerging from the right and left. Wheezer was standing right in front of him, flanked by two empty archways. Kruza looked once behind him, but the circle of men was too complete. They could not get out the way they had come. Facing front, he made a break for it, catching hold of Wheezer's arm as he went and spinning him into one of the antechambers.

Bathed for a moment in bright white light, the pair were confused. Then Wheezer saw another archway and they ran off through a series of underground chambers, which must have covered a large area beneath this part of the city.

'We need to get out of here!' Kruza managed to speak with confidence and at full volume for the first time since entering the cellar. 'We need to get back to the steps.' But Wheezer had already sprinted on, down a long, wide corridor with a high vaulted ceiling. It could almost have been a room if it wasn't for the fact that every few yards a wide archway or sometimes a door led in to other places that dwarfed the connecting corridor.

Wheezer stopped, eyes wide, looking into a great, circular room, isolated on one side of the corridor. There were no other doorways and no windows in the large open space, but there was much more. A series of small carts and stretcher-wagons littered the room, some covered in tarpaulins, some brimming over with their contents spilling and scattering randomly across the room. There was also a large pile of clothes, some ragged and worn, but others quite respectable and even elegant. If these people were smugglers they were smuggling a very strange array and variety of goods.

Kruza had not thought for a long time that they might be smugglers. Something much bigger was going on here. Kruza did not know what it was and Wheezer seemed completely oblivious.

The youth was working his way over the piles, picking out the things he could carry easily, mostly jewellery, of which there was a great deal, and smaller household items that he could tuck into various pockets in his clothes. Wheezer began to pull the tarpaulins off the carts, first one at a time and then, in a great flurry of activity, he went round the whole lot, tearing covers dramatically from carts to reveal all manner of riches beneath. Kruza stood and stared, impressed that the kid could be so single-minded, so confident or perhaps just terminally oblivious to his situation. Then Kruza remembered the cellar lobby and the cloaked men that had attacked him there and realised the fact that essentially Wheezer was invisible and that, consequently Wheezer was safe. He, on the other hand, was not.

'Wheezer! Come on! We have to get out of here!'

'Look at all this stuff!' The other exclaimed eagerly. 'There's weeks' worth of quota here and we may not get the chance to come back!'

Kruza thought he would never come back even if he ever did get the chance. This had turned into a dangerous fool's errand and one he swore he would never repeat.

'Come on, Kruza! It's there to be taken!'

Wheezer turned and lifted the last tarpaulin from the last pile of goods. The biggest pile, wider and higher than a man, closest to the doorway on the opposite side. Kruza, who only stood in the doorway and watched, could not see this corner. The tarpaulin slid off in a fluid motion like silk on highly polished wood. It had no right to do that. The tarpaulin almost rippled as it fell to the floor with a whisper. It had no right, Kruza thought afterwards.

Wheezer stood back from the smugglers' great pile of goods, so that Kruza could see the look on his face. It had never looked whiter. His eyes were great grey, vacant orbs. Kruza strode across, grasping Wheezer by the elbow for fear the lad would faint, and looked to the corner where the tarpaulin lay. On the floor was a pile of bodies, strewn into a corner, stacked as a farmer might stack hay with a pitchfork. To begin with Kruza did not know what he was looking at. Then he began to make out arms and legs and torsos and one or two swollen heads. The bodies had no natural angles; they were so broken that they had no form. The pile might have been old clothes filled with sawdust that had spilled out. No one was left in these bodies. No life. They were like scarecrows. But they had been alive once. Wheezer saw it, but Kruza felt it.

Some little thing caught Kruza's eye and he moved gingerly toward the mountain of human debris. Grasped in the hand of a dead arm that appeared not to be attached to any other dead thing in the heap, was a long, broad chain made up of flat sections joined together with links at the corners. Hanging from the chain, which was big enough to go around a broad man's shoulders, was a talisman. A great scaled snake or dragon, eating its own tail.

Kruza could not bear to look at it. He turned the mesmerised Wheezer around by the arm and began to march him away from this place. He would rather walk back the way they had come and confront the grey cloaked figures than stay for a moment longer in this place.

They strode back up the arterial tunnel, both taking firm steps, feigning the confidence that Kruza knew he for one, did not feel. If he felt his fear now he was dead for sure. He could not feel it and he could not show it.

There was nothing to hear, but the cool slightly damp air of below ground had given way to the spoiled milk smell that wafted freely from chamber to chamber, becoming stronger as they neared the entrance.

Kruza felt sure they must come upon some of the grey cloaked men, but they did not. They walked solemnly, half scared, back to the place where they had come in. Wheezer's sense of direction was unerring, just as it was when he was above ground in the city. They were soon back in the white-lit chamber that they had run from. Kruza had been waiting all the time for the grey cloaked figures to follow them, but they had not. Wheezer stepped out into the archway, which led back into the entrance cellar, Kruza close behind him.

Before them they saw eight grey cloaked figures all standing with their backs to the central sand-painting that was whirling and coalescing. The sand was spinning like a small typhoon, rising up in spirals of cobalt, purple and black among the yellowish grey of the dust. All eight figures had their hands raised in a similar gesture to that of the first grey man that Kruza had killed. They could see eight pairs of withered arms and gnarled hands, taloned but old and lifeless. These were not smugglers. Kruza believed now that these were not even men. He had thrust his short-sword into them, three of them, and killed each one. One had disappeared before his eyes. All three had now been replaced. Wheezer began to walk around the circle as the sand began to swirl more slowly, and losing height, but not shape, the whirlwind laid itself out in another intricate pattern on the floor.

As Kruza followed Wheezer, his mind whirling with panic and unanswerable questions, he saw the weapons. Each grey man was now armed with a pair of blades: a long, elegant sword with a narrow edge and heavily caged hilt and a shorter, slender dagger with a viciously curved hilt that would do serious damage to any blade it might encounter. Kruza's hand flew to the pommel of his own short-sword. He was never afraid of a brawl, but fighting off eight unknown entities with a total of sixteen blades was nothing short of madness. He would pull his own weapon only if attacked, otherwise he did not wish to provoke – only to leave.

Wheezer tried to shield Kruza from the cloaked men. He had become confident in his ability to remain so anonymous that he was virtually invisible. But Kruza was nervous, his adrenaline was pumping and he smelled of fear. Wheezer didn't know how long he could protect his friend and mentor, but he had got him into this.

The circle that was formed by the grey men began to change formation, always facing outward. The circle divided at the furthest point from Wheezer and Kruza and the figures at the two ends swung around, forming an arc that threatened to cut them off from their escape route.

Wheezer stood very still. Beads of sweat formed on Kruza's forehead, despite the chill that had fallen over the room, and he could feel his hair pasted to his head in sweat. It trickled down his back and dripped down his sides and the insides of his thighs. Kruza knew he had to wait for the attack, but felt panic rising with the gorge in his throat.

White light from the surrounding rooms glowed more strongly and the pattern at the centre of the room appeared to be giving off its own multi-coloured light, like a rainbow, rising straight and vertical from the floor.

The grey men had completed their arc. They lifted their arms away from their sides, straight out, parallel to the floor. When their blade tips touched they took a small step backward, widening the arc. Then all sixteen blades came forward together, pointing straight at Kruza.

He knew they could not all attack at once, not without killing each other, although perhaps that did not matter to them. The room was silent except for the sound of Kruza's breathing and the cold swish of blades in the air. He did not know whether his own body smell was worse, more acrid, than the smell of old, spoiled milk that was so intense now that it burned in his nostrils. His senses were heightened. He could feel every dink and dent in the pommel of his old short-sword. He moved his hand down and felt the cold hilt of the weapon. It was rough and beginning to flake, but it fit his hand now like nothing else could.

Wheezer stepped forward. They did not see him. He was not armed.

Kruza took one small sideways step, his back firmly against the wall. A grey-cloaked figure took a step toward him. Kruza had unsheathed his sword and swung it round, sending sparks from the wall behind him as the tip of the blade came into contact with stone. The sparks held in the air, vermilion for a moment, and then died. Swung hard, the short-sword disarmed the first assailant of his longer blade, leaving only the dagger. The grey cloaked figure chopped at the air, hoping to catch the blade of the short-sword and twist it, break it off.

Kruza thought he had never moved so fast. The short-sword came swinging low, below the line of the dagger. Its superior reach sliced, superficially, across his bizarre attacker's midriff, baring the flesh under the cloak, which stood out pale and unreal against the blood which oozed from it. Startled, the grey man looked down as Kruza swept his blade up through the figure from navel to sternum and beyond. The dagger dropped and the figure crawled away, his place taken instantly by another.

Kruza killed three of the men in grey. They were like automata, cold-blooded, thoughtless of the risk, and they fought with one style. Kruza began to catch the rhythm of their attack and was more confident, dispatching the third villain with a single, shoulder-high side-swipe. It was the only blow in the bout and it was deadly. Kruza heard the torn-paper sound and turned to rebut a new onslaught.

Wheezer watched the battle, unarmed and unregarded. Kruza forgot he was there.

The next three grey men, seeing their colleagues fall at the hand of the intruder, attacked together. Six blades moved close, weaving between each other, thrusting, parrying and rallying to attack again. Kruza fought hard and fast, his short-sword in three places at once, but he knew he was defeated. First came the long slash down his arm, his blood pouring down his sleeve and onto his free hand. He held the arm across his body, lest it become a weak point, and thrust with renewed vigour. Then came the slash to his head, curving down in an arc over his face, missing his eye, which was soon filling with blood from the long gash.

Wheezer looked on. No longer silent, he was shouting instructions and warnings to his friend and stamping in the sand.

Kruza was blind on one side and still he hadn't harmed any of his current assailants. He thrashed harder and stronger, turning to his blind side and fighting on, but the grey men were advancing and were close to ending the fray. The blow came soon and was almost welcome. He was struck in the shoulder. A long blade, thrust high and straight, made its way into his body through his leather jerkin – and out again through the back. There was little blood. The sword was steaming hot and cauterised the wound as it was withdrawn.

Kruza fell to his knees, his short-sword still gripped in his hand. His grasp had locked around it when his shoulder was opened and he could not let it go. He dropped his head, waiting for the fatal blow.

Wheezer stamped and screamed, but the five remaining figures did not flinch or turn. The youth let out a huge roar, ready to launch himself at the nearest grey man. But something made him look round. They took no notice of Wheezer. They didn't see him. But there was something they would take notice of.

Wheezer took half a dozen fast strides, almost running, to the centre of the cellar. Then he slid down onto his knees through the multi-coloured dust ornament that adorned the floor and which, until Kruza had dropped to the ground had, been giving off its eerie light.

Dust and sand flew everywhere and Wheezer found himself in the middle of the sand-painting on both knees, unable to move. He held his hands together, high in front of him, like he was praying, and, filling his lungs, he let out a blood curdling cry the like of which Kruza had never heard and hoped never to hear again.

'KKKKKRRRRUUUUZZAAAA!'

The scream hung in the room, echoing in circles around the vaulted ceiling, as though it would never escape.

The grey figures were turning away from him as Kruza heard the second cry.

'RRRRRRRUUUUUUNNNNNN!'

He did not think. He should have been dead and he had no idea if he could even stand, but he had no choice. Wheezer's screams compelled him.

Kruza stood, his arms crossed over his body. He staggered slightly. The sword still in his grasp made him look like some iconic statue of a great warrior-thief. He looked once at the backs of the grey men as they descended on the sand-painting. He did not see Wheezer. He turned and ran.

He ran up the stairs, out through the pitch-covered door and into the alley beyond. He ran out of the Nordgarten and didn't stop running until he reached the tall derelict house in the north of the Altquartier. All the time he ran he believed that Wheezer was right behind him. The lad had played bait, given himself the job of decoy so that Kruza could escape.

But the lad was invisible and he would escape, more easily than I, Kruza thought. *Wouldn't he?*

Kruza waited for Wheezer. He slumped onto the couch in the attic room, and waited. When he awoke it was fully daylight and Wheezer had not come.

When he awoke the second time it was dark. The blood of his open wounds had dried and was flaking off onto the couch below him and Wheezer had still not come.

When he awoke a third time he found the energy to wash in the cold water on the washstand. He ate from Wheezer's windowsill larder. The bread was stale. The youth had not come.

Kruza did not know how long he had been in that room, but his wounds were scabbed and the food on the windowsill was gone or spoiled. Wheezer had still not come.

When it came light again, Kruza pulled himself off the couch and straightened the cushions. He emptied the cold, bloody water out of the wash bowl.

After an hour or so, Kruza left Wheezer's room, closing the door firmly behind him. On the stairs down he noticed that there were no footsteps showing in the thick layer of fresh dust. He slid out of the window, wounded shoulder first and closed it firmly behind him.

Kruza walked away. He knew, as surely as he had known the lad was a natural thief, that Wheezer wasn't coming back.

MITTERFRUHL

A WOLF IN THE FOLD

It was the milk-girl who saw them first.

On a late spring evening, one month past Mitterfruhl, the sky was a dark marble blue and the stars were out. Thousands of them, polished and glinting in the heavens.

The Ganmark family had ruled the border town of Linz, a cattle-market hub at the edge of the Drakwald, for sixteen generations. Two hundred years before, the serving Margrave had established the manor at the edge of the long lake, three miles from the town. The manor house itself was a fine dwelling, with farmlands adjoining, a park and splendid prospects across to the dark stands of the Drakwald to the east.

Lenya, the milk-girl, liked working there. The work was as hard as it had been on her father's little farm, but to work at the manor house, to live in the manor house, it was almost like living at the Graf's palace in far Middenheim. It felt like she was advancing herself. Her father had always said it would be one of her many older brothers who made something of himself but here she was, the last child, the only daughter, working at the Margrave's hall, thank you very much.

She had a straw bed in the servants' wing, and the food was always plentiful. She was only seventeen, but they were good to her – cook, the chamberlain, all the senior staff. Even the Margrave had smiled at her once. Her duties were simple: in the morning, collect the eggs, at night, perform the evening milking. In the meantime, polish, clean, scrub, peel or chop anything you were told to.

She liked the evening milking, especially at this time of year. The spring sky was so clear, and the stars were, well, perfect. Her mother had always told her to count the stars when you had the chance. To make sure they were all there. If an old star went out, bad luck was sure to follow.

As she crossed the stable yard to the dairy, she noticed there seemed to be more stars out that night than usual. Like the speckles on an egg, or the twinkling bubbles on the lip of the milk pail. So many. And that beautiful blue one down by the horizon...

New stars. A good sign, surely?

Then she saw the other new stars, stars in the tree-line above the manor house. Burning, hot stars, like eyes, like–

Lenya dropped the pail.

She realised they were torches, flaming torches held aloft in the black, armoured fists of three dozen sinister horseback warriors.

Even as she realised this, the raiders broke into a charge, thundering down on the manor house. They seemed to move like part of the darkness, as if the night was blurring, as if they were made of smoke. There was a strong scent in the night air, sweet but dusty-dry.

She cried out a little, in surprise and confusion.

Then she saw the other, smaller stars... the fires that were burning behind the matt-black visors and in the sockets of the flaring, infernal horses.

Lenya Dunst cried out again. Fiercely, lustily, she cried out for her life.

'In the name of Ulric, now we'll see some fine sport!' Morgenstern announced, bellowing a laugh. Around him, in the stable block of the Temple compound, his fellow knights of White Company joined his laugh, and playful comments flew back and forth. Thirteen powerful steeds were saddled and near readiness for action. There was power in the straw-floored stone chamber, the bridled power of great horses and potent fighting men.

'Ten shillings, I'll wager you,' Anspach said with a chuckle, 'I'll have badged my armour with the blood of the enemy by the first night! Yes, I will!' he roared at the hearty gainsayers all around.

'I'll take that,' Gruber said quietly.

There was a stunned silence. Gruber was the oldest and most worthy of the company, and everyone knew how he disapproved of rakish Anspach's wagering habits. But there had been a new spring in his step, a new fire in his eyes, since their great victory in the Drakwald before Mitterfruhl. Jurgen, their dear, lost leader, had been avenged, and honour had been returned to them. Of them all, Gruber most personified the reanimation of their spirits.

'Well?' Gruber asked the dumbstruck Anspach, a wry grin on his old, lined face.

Anspach roared and stuck out a mailed fist. 'Done!' he cried.

'And done!' Gruber agreed with a more mirthful laugh.

'Now that's the spirit of the company I like to see!' howled the huge warrior Morgenstern and clapped his hands together.

Off to his right, the company's young standard bearer, Aric, smiled and made a final check of his mount's saddle. Straightening up amidst the hubbub, he caught the eye of youthful Drakken. Drakken was barely twenty, just a wolf cub really, transferred into their company to replace one of the brave souls they had lost in the Drakwald raid. He was a short, yet powerful, stocky young man, and Aric had seen his skill with the horse and hammer in practice, but he was completely inexperienced, and was certainly overawed by the boisterous, oathing company.

Aric crossed to him.

'All ready?' he asked, good-naturedly. Drakken quickly set to his saddle again, trying to look efficient.

'Relax,' said Aric. 'It was only yesterday I was like you: a virgin to war, and to the company of Wolves like these. Go with it, and you'll find your place.'

Drakken gave him a nervous grin. 'Thanks. I just feel like an outsider in this... this family.'

Aric smirked and nodded. 'Yes, this is a family. A family who lives and dies together. Trust us, and we'll trust you back.'

He cast a glance round the room, and picked out a few of the rowdy company for Drakken's benefit. Each of the warriors wore the gold-edged grey plate armour and white wolf pelt of the Temple. 'Morgenstern there. He's a prize-winning ox, and he'll drink you under any table anywhere. But he's got a good heart and heavy hammer. Gruber... stick close by him; no one has the experience or sheer courage of that man. Anspach... never trust his judgement or take his wagers, but trust his right arm. A fury on the field. Kaspen, the red-headed fellow there – he's our surgeon too. He'll see to any wounds you collect. Einholt and Schell, why they're the best trackers we have. Schiffer, Bruckner, Dorff – great horsemen all.'

He paused.

'And remember you're not alone in being new. Lowenhertz also transferred in, same time as you.'

Their eyes wandered across to the last knight, who was alone in the stable corner, checking his horse's shoeing.

Lowenhertz was a tall, regal-looking man, handsome and aquiline. It was said he had noble blood, though Morgenstern had sworn this was a bastard heritage. He was quiet and aloof, almost as quiet and reserved as Einholt, if that was possible. Ten years he'd served in the White Wolves, first in Red Company, then Grey. It seemed he had never found a place to suit him, or one that wanted him perhaps. No one knew why he had come to them, though Anspach wagered it was because he was biding his time until a command came up. Gruber thought so too, and that was enough for all of them.

'Lowenhertz?' murmured Drakken. 'He's not new blood like me. He's had time in the companies, and he... he has an air to him. He frightens me.'

Aric thought about this and nodded. 'Me too.'

Their conversation was shut off by the slamming open of the stable door. Ganz, the young company commander, resplendent in full plate and wolf-skin, strode in.

'This is it...' Kaspen murmured.

'Moment of truth,' Schell agreed, his whipcord face tense with anticipation. Dorff broke off from a wavering, tuneless whistle.

'Well, sir?' Anspach asked.

Ganz faced them. 'We ride for Linz at once–'

He had to wave down their cheering. 'Enough! Enough! Lads, it's not the glory we were hungry for. I've just had our orders conveyed by the High Priest himself.'

'And? What does the old fart have to say?' Morgenstern asked raucously.

'Respect, please, Morgenstern!' Gruber yelled.

'My apologies, old friend! I should have said what does *his highness* the old fart have to say?'

Ganz looked sad and tired. He sighed. 'Three companies of Knights Panther have been sent out to Linz to hunt down these raiders and make sure no harm befalls the town itself. We must go to provide... escort.'

'Escort?' Gruber said.

The silence which followed was total.

'The Margrave, his family and many of his household staff escaped the raid that burned his manor. As you know, Linz owes fealty to the Graf here in Middenheim, and his excellency the Graf is most concerned for his cousin the Margrave's safety. A long story cut short, we are to escort the Margrave's entourage back here to the city to keep him and his safe.'

There was an audible, collective groan.

'So the Panthers get the glory?' Anspach mused. 'They get to hunt down and battle these raiding jackals while we get nurse maid duty?'

Ganz could do nothing but shrug. 'Technically, it's an honour...' he began.

Morgenstern said something both uncomplimentary and physically challenging about 'honour'.

'All right, old friend,' Ganz said, unamused. 'Let's just do the job we've been asked to. Mount up. White Company rides with me.'

It was two days' hard ride to Linz. Late spring rain, brisk and horizontal, washed across the meadows and trackways as they rode. Then the pale sun came out again.

They could see the ruins of the Ganmark manor from several miles away, and smell it even before that. Dark, almost oily smoke hung in the air like a sinuous raincloud against the spring afternoon and there was a curious smell, like sweetmeats and spices mixed with the ash from a funeral urn.

Riding beside Ganz, Gruber wrinkled his nose. The young commander looked over at him.

'Gruber? What is it?'

Gruber cleared his throat and spat sideways as if to rid his mouth of the smell on the breeze. 'No idea. Like nothing I've ever smelt.'

'Not in this part of the land,' said a voice from beside them. Ganz and Gruber looked over to see the chiselled profile of Lowenhertz. The tall knight rode in beside them, skilled and coolly measured.

'What do you mean, brother?' asked Gruber.

Lowenhertz smiled a not entirely friendly smile. 'My great grandfather was a Knight Panther. Went on two crusades into those hellish distant lands of heat and dust. When I was a child, he used to tell stories of the ancient tombs and mausoleums, the dry, deathless things that haunted the nights. He told me stories. I remember them clearly, stood in his old solar, where he kept his books and mementoes, the old armour, the banners and gonfalons. There was always a smell in that old room – mortuary dust, dry bones, and the sweet pungent stench of the grave spices. He always told me it was the smell of death from the far-off tombs of Araby.'

He shrugged. 'I can smell it once more. And so much stronger than I did in my great grandfather's solar in childhood.'

Ganz was silent as their horses jogged on through the open meadow. Small, green butterflies, early risers in the fresh spring, whirled in formation across their path. Ganz looked ahead, down the sweep of the valley, to the blackened timber skeleton which was all that remained of Ganmark manor. Smoke still curled up, like dark fingers clawing the air.

'I'd take it as a personal favour, Lowenhertz, if you didn't share such observations with the rest of the men.'

Lowenhertz nodded curtly. 'Of course, commander.' With that he spurred his mount forward and rode ahead of them down the winding track.

At the gates of Linz, an honour-guard squadron of Panther Knights rode out to meet them, haughty and resplendent in their decorative, high-crested helms and armour. Their captain saluted Ganz stiffly and the White Wolf returned the greeting. There was little love lost between the Templars of Ulric and the regal warriors of the Graf's household bodyguard.

'Sigmar bring you safe! Captain von Volk, Knights Panther, Graf's First Royal Household.'

'Ulric look to you! Ganz, Commander, White Company.'

'Welcome to Linz, Commander, I stand relieved.'

The Panther captain fell in beside Ganz and his men rode around in a precision display until they were perfectly flanking the Wolf formation as an escort. The Panthers were in precise line, and even the light hoofbeats of their graceful steeds was in perfect time, compared to the powerful, tired syncopation of the straggled and dusty Wolves. Ganz felt someone was showing off.

'Glad you're finally here, Commander Ganz,' von Volk said curtly. 'We've been chafing to get off after these creatures, but of course we couldn't leave the Margrave and his entourage undefended.'

Ganz nodded. 'You've sent scouting parties out?'

'Of course. Four field groups. They've had no success, but I feel confident that once I field my entire force I'll have these raiding scum good and proper.'

From behind them, Gruber snorted with quiet derision.

Von Volk turned in his saddle. He was a tall, thin, fierce man with bright, flitting eyes. They lustred behind the golden grille of his ceremonial visor. 'What's that, soldier? Oh, I'm sorry, old man... were you just talking in your sleep?'

Gruber did not rise to it. 'Nothing, sir. Just clearing my throat.'

Von Volk turned away without a care. The silk draperies of his helmet's crest fluttered out behind him. 'Commander Ganz, the Margrave awaits you in the Guild Hall. I'd like you to have him and his party away by dusk.'

'And travel at night?' Ganz was all reason and charm. 'We'll leave at dawn, captain. Even a raw recruit knows that is the best time to embark on an escort drill.'

Von Volk scowled.

'Mobilise your men and get on your way,' Ganz added. 'We'll take it from here. Good hunting.'

'My dear, dear fellow!' the Margrave of Linz said, pumping Ganz's hand. 'My dear, dear fellow! How we've waited for you!'

'Sir,' Ganz managed. The vast panelled chamber of the Guild Hall was full of baggage crates and rolled carpets. Around it hung the twenty or so servants and staff who had escaped the raid on the manor.

And presumably carried this stuff to safety, Ganz mused. *How in the name of Ulric do you roll a carpet during an attack?*

The Margrave, a portly, pale aristocrat in his late thirties, had put on his best robes to greet the Wolves, but sticking-out tufts of hair and an overwhelming scent of clove oil told that he hadn't seen decent sanitation since the attack.

'I asked for Wolves, most particularly,' said the Margrave. 'In my letter to my dearest cousin, the Graf, I requested Wolves above all, a company of Wolves. Oh, let the gaudy Panthers do the hunting work, but give me Wolves to see me and my family home.'

'The Panthers are fine warriors. They'll find your attackers,' Ganz said smoothly, not believing it for a moment. 'But, assuredly, we'll get you home. Now how many are you?'

The Margrave ushered him around. 'We fill three coaches and four baggage carts. Sixteen servants, the luggage, plus myself and my children, and their nurse...'

He pointed to a pair of ghastly, knickerbockered five year olds who were thumping each other ferociously on a pile of rugs. An elderly and emaciated black-robed nurse watched over them.

'Hanz and Hartz!' sighed the Margrave, clasping his palms together. 'Aren't they adorable?'

'Unbearably,' Ganz said.

'And then, of course, there's my wife...' the Margrave added.

Ganz looked round as indicated. Her ladyship was pouring drinks for the thirsty Wolves herself, from pitchers her servants carried.

She was tall, shapely and hypnotically beautiful. Her dark, ringletted, luxuriant hair ran all the way down to the extraordinary curve her hips made in her sheer silk gown. Her skin was pale, her eyes dark and deep like pools. Her lips were full and red and–

Ganz turned back to look at the ugly children very quickly.

'They're not hers, of course,' the Margrave continued. 'Their dear, dear mother died in childbirth. Gudrun and I married last year.'

Gudrun, thought Ganz. *Ulric! Heaven has a name!*

'Wine for you, brave knight?' she asked softly.

Gruber took the beaker and gazed at the vision before him. 'Thank you, lady,' he said. She was amazing. Quite the most beautiful woman he had ever seen; dark, exotic, mysterious... yet here she was serving all these dirty, stinking warriors wine. Serving them by hand herself.

'You are our salvation, sir,' she said to him, perhaps noticing his puzzled look. 'After our nights of terror and pain, this is the least I can do.'

'She's amazing...' Anspach breathed, clutching his untouched goblet as she moved on.

'If I was thirty years younger and a hundredweight lighter...' Morgenstern began.

'You'd still be a fat old wastrel with no chance!' Einholt finished.

'Lord Ulric above us,' Drakken murmured to Aric. 'She's quite lovely...'

Aric couldn't take his eyes off the Margrave's wife, and he nodded before realising Drakken wasn't looking at her at all.

'Drakken?'

'Her, Aric.' Drakken smiled and pointed to a young girl huddled amid the servants. She was barely eighteen by Aric's guess, short and trim, but dirty and soiled from the adventures that had overtaken her, and dressed in a milk-maid's smock. She was... pretty, he had to admit.

'Drakken!' Aric hissed. 'First rule of Wolfhood... if a goddess gives you wine, you don't drool after her cherubs.'

'What goddess?' asked Drakken, staring at the milk-girl.

Aric smiled and shook his head.

They left Linz at dawn. The carts and coaches rolled out in line, flanked by the thirteen Wolf Knights, into the rich dawn mist.

At the head of the column, Ganz called Gruber, Anspach and Lowenhertz to him.

'Ride ahead. Scout the woods,' he told them. They spurred away.

Aric, the standard of the company held aloft, moved up beside Ganz.

'Drakken needs some purpose to settle his nerve, sir,' Aric said.

Ganz thought for a moment. 'You're right,' he said at last and called back for the youngest knight. Drakken rode forward eagerly.

'Join the scouts,' Ganz said. 'They could use an extra hand.'

Smiling fit to split his face, Drakken charged forward at a gallop off into the smoky woodland.

Anspach reined up sharply. For a moment, he had almost lost his bearings in the mist. The sun was up, but there was barely any light amidst the swirling vapour and dark trees.

'What was that?' he said to Gruber, just a few yards away.

'Probably Lowenhertz,' said Gruber. 'He went off to the left.'

'No!' said Anspach sharply, heeling down his prick-spurs deep to turn his horse hard. 'With me, Gruber! Now!'

The two warriors plunged through the woodland, kicking up dirt and wafting the mist. They caught a sweet and dry smell of ash. Anspach freed his hammer from its clasp.

They found Drakken in a clearing. His horse was dead, and so was one of the black knights who had ambushed him. Drakken's grey plate armour was ripped open and his shoulder was gashed, but still he screamed fiercely, swirling his warhammer to crack another head as he had the skull of the man who brought him down.

He was surrounded.

There were four more dark warriors, each clad in strangely angular black plate armour with spike-pointed, almost bulbous helmets. They swung dark blue, serrated swords that hooked into fang-like curves, and a fine mesh of chainmails rattled around their waists. Their horses were huge and black, and, like the knights themselves, their eyes glowed with an internal fire. There was something almost insubstantial about the edges of them, about the hem of their swirling cloaks, as if they were solidifying out of the mist and darkness itself. The smell of sweet spice and ash was intense.

Drakken ducked a swing that severed a young tree behind him. Anspach and Gruber leapt their horses forward to avoid the crashing timbers and branches.

Gruber swung his hammer round and came about. The nearest of these almost ghostly raiders filled Gruber's nose with the dry, dead stink and swung forward with his sword.

Anspach and his horse exploded into the gap between them and he crushed the enemy's head with a downward blow of his warhammer. The matt-black spiked helmet shattered and dark fumes billowed out as the glowing eyes went dark.

Gruber found another two on him hard, slashing with their venomous hookswords, relentless.

'Ulric curse you!' he spat, battling for a break.

Lowenhertz blasted out of the mist and undergrowth, his horse at full leap.

His whizzing hammer smashed the first warrior out of his saddle, and then with a skilled and powerful reverse turn, Lowenhertz broke the chest of Gruber's second attacker.

The remaining dark warrior spurred forward with a raucous, unintelligible curse, his red eyes blazing from behind his visor slit, his vile horse wretched and stinking.

Anspach swung his hammer round sideways over his shoulder and destroyed the last warrior outright.

For a moment, the impact resounded around the deadened clearing.

Anspach leapt down and helped the shaken Drakken up.

'Well done, youth! You're a Wolf now, no mistake.'

Gruber turned to Lowenhertz.

'Thanks go to you. You saved my life,' he said.

'Think nothing of it,' said Lowenhertz. He gazed down at the bodies of the foes. Inside the rent-open armour of the nearest, nothing but powdery bones could be seen, flaking away like ash in the breeze.

There was a long, chill silence.

'In the name of Ulric!' Gruber hissed, fear clawing deep. 'Let's get back to the convoy!'

'The dead don't lie still,' Gruber murmured to Ganz as they rejoined the halted train. Anspach was helping the injured Drakken to a cart, and Kaspen had dismounted to tend the young man's injury. Lowenhertz rode in silently, a way behind Gruber. A hush had fallen when the four warriors had returned, the bloody Drakken sharing Anspach's horse, all of them flecked with dark smudges of blood. Ganz was dreadfully aware of the way the Margrave's people stared at his men in fixed horror and silent alarm.

'Don't riddle, report!' he hissed.

Gruber shook his head, fear still shaking him, easing off his mailed gauntlets. 'We met a bevy of dark... things – Ulric save our souls! They were not... mortal! No doubt the very same abominations who took down the Ganmark Manor. Caught Drakken but by Ulric's teeth he gave them what for. We did the rest, Lowenhertz, the lion's share. But they're out there. Ulric help us, commander! These things are spectres!'

'You mean ghosts?' asked Ganz, in a tight whisper.

'I do not know what I mean! I have never met their like before!'

Ganz cursed. 'Hundreds of miles of forest and farmland, Knights Panther hunting for them, and they stumble on us! What are the chances?'

'What are the chances?' cut in Lowenhertz quietly but significantly. He seemed to appreciate the commander's urge to keep the talk out of civilian earshot. 'They raid the manor, then they find us...' He trailed off.

'What do you mean?' Aric asked, easing his grip on the lofty standard.

'I mean: maybe they're after something. Something that was in the manor, something that's here with us now!'

There was a long silence. Horses whinnied and shook off flies.

Ganz wiped his fist across his mouth. 'You seem to be remarkably well-informed, Master Lowenhertz,' he said finally.

'What do you mean?' answered the knight, his eyes hooded.

'You seem to know much of the ways of darkness,' said Ganz frankly.

Lowenhertz laughed out loud. There was little humour in it, but it shook the clearing and made everyone look.

'It is merely logic, commander... these creatures have wit. They are not brute beastfolk, not savage greenskins from the rockslopes. They move with a purpose; they have a meaning and a task to all they do. This is not a random chance.'

'Then we'll be careful,' said Ganz, simply.

'We should try to discern the nature of their purpose, sir. Perhaps by–'

Ganz cut Lowenhertz short. 'We will be careful,' he repeated more firmly. 'Aric, go check and see Drakken is comfortable and ready to move. We will ride on.'

He looked down as the Margrave hurried up on foot from his carriage. He was attended by two servants who scrambled after him and his face was not happy.

'Are we in danger, sir knight?' he asked breathlessly.

'You are in the company of Wolves, noble sir,' Ganz said gracefully. 'You requested us, I seem to recall, and knew we would see you safe...'

'Aye, indeed! I don't mean to doubt... But still... Are they still out there?'

'On my honour, Margrave, on the honour of my men and in the name of Ulric who guides us, we will be safe.'

By his side, Gruber sat back in the saddle. He was still shaking from the combat, his pulse thundering. *Too much, too hard for an old man*, he thought. His eyes scanned the carriage train as they made ready to move out.

In the door window of the Margrave's wagon, he caught sight of the nobleman's wife. She gazed out from the shadows, a wicked smile on her lips.

Gruber looked away. He wished to dear heaven he had not seen her look.

Aric rode back to the cart where Drakken was being minded. It carried several of the kitchen staff and the elderly nurse of the noble children. Drakken did not seem to notice. The milk-maid, Lenya, was vigorously helping Kaspen dress his wounds.

'Keep them clean and dry, and watch for infection,' Kaspen told her.

'I know what to do, Red-hair,' she nodded curtly, obediently.

Lenya stared aggressively down into Drakken's eyes as Kaspen got down off the wagon and balled up a cloth from the bowl of water to wring it out.

'I'll look after you, Wolf. Don't worry. I've tended to my brothers' wounds and scrapes often enough, many worse than this,' she said.

'I... I thank you,' said Drakken, a foolish smile on his face.

Aric watched them, chuckled and rode back to Ganz.

'Drakken's as happy as a cub,' he told the commander.

'Then we ride. Move on!' cried Ganz. 'Move on!'

At nightfall, they camped on a rocky slope overlooking a bend in a nameless stream. The Wolves built watch-fires all around the perimeter and stood in guard shifts all through the night.

At midnight, Ganz did his round of the duty. He passed a few moments with Einholt and the hulking Bruckner at their posts as the rest of the party settled down for sleep.

Crossing to check on Aric, Ganz saw a dark shape out beyond the edge of the firelight.

He stiffened and crept out into the darkness, his hand sliding his hunting knife from its sheath.

'Lowenhertz!' he hissed.

The knight turned in surprise, lowering a beautiful brass astrolabe through which he had been sighting the heavens.

'Commander?'

'What in the name of the Wolf are you doing out here?'

'It is difficult to take accurate readings close to the firelight,' Lowenhertz began.

'Readings?'

'Of the stars, commander. To see if any strange patterns or manifestations could be discerned. My great-grandfather taught me that celestial signs and augurs accompanied the machinations of the deathless ones...'

Ganz cut him off, angry and snarling. 'I now see why you have never made command yourself! They don't trust you, do they? Our Temple elders don't trust you with the lives of men because you are too far gone, too close to the darkness itself!'

Lowenhertz paused and frowned. 'Oh!' he said at last. 'I see. Commander, you think it's me, don't you? You think I'm a part of this danger?'

'I–' began Ganz, wrong-footed.

Lowenhertz laughed as if at a truly rich joke. 'Forgive me, sir. I am just what I seem to be: a loyal servant of Ulric whose mind sometimes asks too many questions! My father was a Knight Panther. He died at Antler Hill, torn open by the hounds of Chaos. I have always sought to be one step ahead, to know more of my foe than they know of me, to serve the Temple as best as my body – and mind – are able. I would not have you distrust me! But if I can serve you and you can trust me...'

There was a long silence. Ganz extended his hand for the astrolabe. 'So have you found anything?' he said quietly.

Drakken curled up in the rolls of carpet behind the wagon and relaxed in the firelight. A shadow fell over him and he blinked up out of his half slumber. Lenya was there, her smile luminous in the shadows.

'Are you thirsty, knight?' she asked.

'My name is Drakken,' he said. 'Krieg Drakken. I wish you would call me that.'

'I will, Krieg. On two conditions. One, if you tell me you're thirsty and two if you call me Lenya.'

'I am thirsty, Lenya,' he said softly.

She snorted and turned away to fetch a drink.

Drakken settled back and closed his eyes. His shoulder ached, but all in all this was turning out to be a fine debut as a White Wolf.

A shadow fell across him again.

'I hope the water is cool...' he began, then tailed off when he realised it wasn't the returning Lenya. The old nurse crouched down by him.

'Calm now, my little pet,' she said warmly. 'Oh, but I know I'm not so handsome as yon milk-maid, but I care as much for the well-being of my guardians. And you have had a long day.'

Drakken relaxed and smiled. Her tone was so reassuring and calm. No wonder she made her life as the custodian of children.

'I only stopped by to bless you, my lamb,' she said and reached into the neck of her smock. 'I have a lucky charm, given me by my mother years ago. I would have you take it in your hand to speed you to health.'

The nurse held out a glittering amulet attached to a long cord around her neck. Its mount was pewter, but the thing itself was a curve of glass, shaped like a claw, a fragment perhaps of something else, something very old.

'Always brought me luck and health,' she said.

He smiled and took it in his hand. It felt warm.

'Now blessing be on you, my poor wounded knight. The blessing of all the gods.'

'Thank you, lady,' Drakken said. He felt warmer, safer, more whole.

'Now Lenya returns with a cup of water,' said the nurse, taking back the charm and getting up. 'You'll have no more time with an old fool like me. Be safe, knight.'

'Again, thank you,' said Drakken.

Then Lenya was at his side again, offering the cup to his lips.

'Old Maris fussing over you again?' she said with a grin. 'She's so kind. The children dote on her. The Margrave was lucky to find her last year when he needed a wetnurse.'

'She's a fine old lady, and very caring,' said Drakken between sips. 'But I know who I would wish to have care for me...'

'Do you make a habit of spying on women?' asked the Margrave's wife with a delicious curl to her lips.

Gruber stopped in his tracks and fumbled for the right words. 'I was patrolling the camp, my lady.'

'And that brought you back behind my carriage as I was dressing for bed?' she returned.

Gruber turned away, too conscious of the fact he was in the company of a woman who wore little more than a satin shroud.

'I apologise, lady. I–'

'Oh hush, knight!' she said with a chiming laugh. 'I'm flattered a man as worthy and distinguished as you would blush in my company. I appreciate your efforts. We are all in your care.'

Gruber shifted awkwardly and then turned to go.

'What is your name, knight?'

'Wilhelm Gruber,' he said, turning back. He felt suddenly bold. 'Who are you, lady?'

'The wife of the Margrave of Linz, unless that had passed you by,' she replied, laughing again.

'Is that all?' he asked sharply.

She said nothing in return. There was a long silence.

'You'd best return to your patrol, Gruber,' she said at last. 'I don't know what you think I am, but I'm not happy at the implications.'

'Neither am I, lady,' Gruber said as he strode away. 'We'll see.'

Ganz watched the stars through the polished lenses of Lowenhertz's astrolabe. He was about to ask the name of another constellation when Lowenhertz gripped his arm hard.

'What?'

'Quiet!' hissed Lowenhertz. 'You smell that?'

Ganz inhaled. The sweet, ashy flavour of death was unmistakable.

They ducked low, and saw the glowing eye slits of warriors moving down in the vale by the stream.

'I have nothing but my knife!' whispered Ganz.

Lowenhertz tossed him his warhammer and pulled a long war-axe from his saddlebag.

'Give the word, commander. They've come back for us.'

It was a dark blur of night and firelight. Ganz thought he counted fifteen of the foe as they charged the camp from the east on foot. They were silent, the shades of the dead.

Ganz was not silent. He bellowed his warning as loud as his lungs could bear, and he and Lowenhertz leapt across the stream-side rocks to meet the silent charge.

The camp came to life. Hallowing answers came from the sentries, and roars from the sleeping men as they roused. Screams and cries rose from the terrified civilians.

Einholt met the first of the attackers, blocking and whirling his warhammer as he bayed out a call to his wolf brothers. In five seconds,

Bruckner and Aric, the other two sentries on duty, were by his side, blocking the passage between the crackling watch fires against the red-eyed ghouls that swept out of the night.

Ganz and Lowenhertz were with them a few seconds later.

There were at least twenty of the attackers now, Ganz was certain, but it was so hard to disentangle their dank shapes from the night, or their flashing eyes from the blazing fires. It was as if they were made out of the night itself.

A gleaming jet blade whistled past his head and Ganz swung back to guard himself. In doing so, his feet slipped on the earth and he half stumbled. The dark one rose up over him, blade poised. Morgenstern, only half-armoured and bedraggled from slumber, burst through the darkness and laid the creature low with a two-handed hammerblow of huge force. Ganz leapt up and called his thanks to the man-mountain, who was already driving on into the press.

He saw Aric fall, gashed in the shoulder. Einholt and Lowenhertz leapt to block him, standing their ground as he pulled himself up again. Lowenhertz's axe whistled in the cold air.

With wolf-fire in his blood, Ganz spun his borrowed hammer, used the haft to block a hard sword swing, and then slew his attacker with a sideways smash of the hammerhead.

'For the Temple! For Ulric! White Company!' he bellowed.

Across in the camp: pandemonium. Hammer held tight, Gruber tried to marshal the chaos.

'Kaspen! Anspach! Get the Margrave and his people into cover by the wagons! The rest of you forward to fight!'

Screaming servants and crying children ran in every direction. Cook pots and fire hearths were upset and kicked over.

'Damn it!' Gruber cursed.

He saw Drakken limping into the centre of the camp as fast as he could manage. 'My weapon! Any weapon!' cried the young man hoarsely.

'You're more use to me here!' Gruber shouted. 'Get the children in a wagon. Keep their heads down!'

There was another scream, more piercing than before. Gruber wheeled and saw two dark warriors had burst into the encampment from the opposite direction to the main attack, a sneak pincer to get round the cordon. They charged in towards the wagons.

It was the Margrave's wife who had screamed. She was in the open, trying to catch hold of her two terrified children. The nurse was by her side, trying to scoop the boys into her arms. The warriors bore down on them, swords raised.

Gruber raced forward, lashing out a one-handed hammer swing that shattered armour and knocked one of them to the earth. The other he met and blocked, glancing his hammer haft against the slashing blade once, twice, three times to ward off the deadly swings. By then, the first dark warrior was back on his feet.

Gruber dented the helm of the second one and sent him sprawling in time to meet the renewed attack of the first. He stared into the red-lit slits and met the furious assault, swinging a blow that smashed its shield. Then he stabbed hard with the butt of the haft, connecting with jaw. The foe went down and this time a well-placed blow ensured it would not rise again.

The second one was upright again now, intent on the Margrave's wife once more.

With a roar, Gruber hurled his hammer. The great, spinning weapon swooshed across the clearing in flickering circles and broke the creature's back.

Gruber crossed to the Margrave's wife and helped her up. The nurse gathered up the children.

'Get to the wagons!' he hissed.

'Th-thank you...' she stammered.

'They were hell-bent on getting to you,' Gruber snarled, fixing her eyes with his. 'What is it about you? Are you the jinx who brings this darkness down?'

'No!' she implored, horrified, 'No!'

There was no time for debate. Gruber recovered his hammer and rejoined the fight.

'They're retreating!' Anspach announced at last.

'Thank the Wolf!' murmured Ganz. The fight had been intense, and too close for comfort. Several of his men were wounded, and there were seven dark warriors twisted, skeletal and dead on the ground. The others, like the wraiths of fairy tales, melted away into the trees.

'Regroup!' Ganz told his men, 'Let's get inside the camp and build up the firewall. There's a long time till dawn.'

'Commander!' Gruber was calling.

Ganz joined him. The warrior whose back Gruber had snapped was still alive, twitching and hissing like a reptile on the ground. The civilians stood round in a wide, fascinated horrified circle.

'Clear these people aside!' Ganz snapped to Dorff and Schiffer. He turned to Gruber. 'I'm beginning to think Lowenhertz is right. We have something or someone these creatures want – that's why they took the manor and now hound us.'

'I agree. This was not a raid, this was a mission to retrieve. They were too direct, putting themselves at risk to get into the camp rather than harry us from a distance.' Gruber took a deep breath. 'I believe it's part of the Margrave's household, and I think I know what...'

'You think it's me,' said a voice from behind them. It was the Margrave's wife, clutching one of the sobbing children. 'I don't know what I've done to earn your mistrust, Sir Gruber. I can only imagine that you are threatened by me. All my life, my dark looks and lively manner have made men imagine me some she-devil, some brazen thing to be feared. Can I help my looks, or my appetite for life? Can I help the way I was made? I am no daemon. On my life – on the lives of my children, sirs! – I am not the root of this!'

Ganz looked over at his second-in-command. The older, white-haired man dropped his gaze to the earth.

'Seems both of us have jumped to conclusions today, old man. Both of us wrong.'

'You too?' Gruber asked.

Ganz nodded. 'Milady, take the children to cover in the wagons. We will finish this. Lowenhertz!'

The noble knight arrived. His chest plate and shoulder armour had been badly damaged in the fight and so he was stripped to his woollen pourpoint now.

'Commander?'

'You have learning, Lowenhertz... or so you like to tell me. How do we get information from our guest here?'

Lowenhertz looked down at the crippled dark one and sank to his haunches. He listened for a moment and shuddered. 'I can make little out from its rasping... the language... perhaps it is the tongue of far Araby. There is one word it repeats...' Lowenhertz thickly repeated the word back to the creature with distaste. It stirred and hissed and yelped. The White Wolf then muttered the low, guttural word again.

Ganz turned. 'We're getting nowhere...'

Lowenhertz tried the sentence again until the creature replied at last with a guttural response of his own.

'I don't understand him. The words are too strange.' Lowenhertz tried harder, repeating the word. It was no good.

Then the creature reached out and with a bony hand drew a curved symbol in the dust.

'What is that?' asked Ganz.

'I wish I knew,' said Lowenhertz. 'I cannot understand him. That picture makes no sense. What is that? A harvest moon? A crescent?'

'It's a claw,' said Drakken suddenly, from behind them. 'And I know where it is.'

The old nurse, Maris, backed away against the wagon, terror in her eyes and her hands clutched tight to the throat of her dress.

'No!' she said. 'No! You shan't have it!'

Ganz looked round at Drakken and Lowenhertz at his side.

'She's just the wetnurse,' he said.

'She has the amulet, shaped like a claw. She blessed me with it,' Drakken said.

'If it is what these creatures of darkness seek, lady, you must give it up for all our sakes,' Lowenhertz firmly said.

'This trinket my old dam gave me?' stammered the old woman. 'It's always brought me luck.'

Gruber joined them. 'This makes sense of it. Those warriors I fought... I thought they were after the Lady and her children, but they were after the nurse.'

The Margrave and his wife approached.

'Please, sir!' the old woman cried. 'Make them stop this nonsense.'

'Dear Maris,' the lady pleaded, 'you have always been kind to my children, so I will defend you from harm, but this is too important. Let us prove this. Give me the charm.'

Wizened hands shaking, the old woman produced the claw talisman and handed it to the Margrave's wife. She turned and marched across to the stricken foe. Ganz made to stop her, but Gruber held him back.

'She knows what she's doing, that one,' he told his commander.

'Lenya told me the nurse had only been with them for a while. Her predecessor had fallen ill and she was brought in from far away,' said Drakken.

Lowenhertz nodded. 'If this malign charm has been in her family for some time they may have known nothing of its power. But it has brought them after her every step of the way. They have caught her scent – or the scent of the thing she owns.'

'But what is it?' asked Aric.

'The talon of some dark daemon they worship? The shed nail of a god?' Lowenhertz shrugged. 'Who knows? Who wants to know?'

'A man of learning like you?' Ganz asked.

Lowenhertz shook his head. 'There are some things better left unknown, commander.'

The Margrave's wife showed the charm to the broken creature and then jumped back as it reared up, snarling and mewling, clawing at her.

Gruber slew it with a quick, deft blow.

'There's our proof,' he stated.

Everyone froze as a keening sounded through the forest around them. The grave-smell of spice and dry bone wafted around them again.

'They have the scent again, fresher than ever,' said Lowenhertz. 'They're coming back.'

'To arms!' Gruber cried, rallying the men.

Ganz held up his hand. 'We'd never take them. They have superior numbers and the night on their side. We barely drove them back before. There is only one way.'

The White Company and their civilian charges drew into a huddle at the centre of the firelight. Beyond the ring of flame, they saw the dark riders approach and heard their hooves. Dozens of red eyes glowed against the blackness, like infernal stars.

Ganz counted the dark shapes out beyond the fire. Once again, there were twenty, despite the number the Wolves had killed. He swore softly. 'They will always return at full strength,' he whispered to Gruber. 'We will never wear them down. We cannot fight because they will overwhelm us. We cannot run because they will outstrip us. They are driven beings of the dark who will not stop until they have what they want.'

The foe stood beyond the flames, a ring of evil forms that circled the camp entirely. The sweet ashen smell was wretched.

'Then what do we do? Fight to the last? Die in the name of Ulric?' Gruber whispered.

'That... or deny them,' said Ganz. 'Perhaps this is the only chance for survival we have...'

He took the charm and stepped forward so that the dark riders could surely see him. Then, before they could react, he set it on a rock, and swung Lowenhertz's warhammer up and round in a powerful over-shoulder swing.

The riders screamed in horror with a single voice. The hammerhead crushed the talisman. There was a burst of light and a flash of green, eldritch flame. The blast knocked Ganz backwards and vaporised the head of the hammer.

The talisman was gone.

Red lightning, like electric blood, speared around the clearing horizontally, and there was a fierce hot wind. The wraith-like creatures shrieked as one, twisting, swirling in the air like flapping black rags until they were at last whisked up into the darkness of the night and were gone.

Four days' gruelling drive brought them back to Middenheim. White Company escorted the Margrave's party right to the Graf's palace where they were to be cared for and tended. There were many partings now. As the Margrave effusively thanked Ganz time and again, Ganz found his eyes wandering the courtyard. He saw Drakken, sheepish and clumsy, kiss the feisty servant girl, Lenya, goodbye. Not for the last time, Ganz was sure. He saw Morgenstern and Anspach horseplaying with the children, and Aric consoling the frightened old woman Maris. And Gruber stood with the Lady Margrave.

'Forgive me, lady,' Gruber was saying softly. 'I mistrusted you, and that is my shame.'

'You saved my life, Sir Gruber. I'd say we're even.' She smiled and his heart winced again.

'If only you were younger and I was free,' she murmured, saying what he was thinking. Their eyes met, fierce for a second, then they both laughed aloud and said farewell.

* * *

In the great darkness of the Temple, the Wolf Choirs were singing low, heartfelt hymns of thanks. The voices hung in the still, cool air.

Lowenhertz was knelt in prayer in front of the main altar. He looked up as he heard the footsteps come up behind him.

Ganz looked down at him. In his hands, he held an object wrapped in an old wolf pelt.

'The Panthers will be most aggrieved we stole their thunder,' Lowenhertz said as he rose.

Ganz nodded. 'They'll live. And to think we thought we were going to miss the action.'

There was a long pause. Ganz fixed him with a gaze. 'I suppose you'll be transferring again now.'

Lowenhertz shrugged. 'Not if you'll let me stay, commander. I have looked for my place for a long time. Perhaps it is here in this company of Wolves.'

'Then welcome to White Company, warrior,' Ganz said. 'I will be proud to have you in my command.'

'I must see the priest-armourers,' Lowenhertz said. 'I need a new hammer consecrated.'

Ganz held out the pelt bundle. 'No need. Ar-Ulric himself allowed me to take this from the Temple reliquary.'

The old warhammer in the pelt was magnificent and covered in a patina of age and use. 'It belonged to a Wolf called von Glick. One of the bravest, a fellow and a friend, sorely missed. It would please him for his hammer to be carried by a Wolf again, rather than tarnish in an old relic chest.'

Lowenhertz took the venerable weapon and tested its weight and balance. 'It will be an honour,' he said.

Around them, the song of the Wolf Choir rose up and soared, out of the great temple and beyond into the skies above Middenheim like smoke.

THE BRETONNIAN CONNECTION

It was one of the workmen who told us, running over from the charred shell of the Temple of Morr where he had been working. The news must have been all over Middenheim by the time we heard it, retold from marketplace to coffee house, from inn to slum, shouted from window to window high above the twisted streets and steep alleys. It would be on everyone's lips by now. We stopped digging, rested on our spades and pickaxes, and stood in the half-finished grave as we contemplated what we had learned. It was the start of a spring day in the City of the White Wolf, and death was in the air.

Spring comes late to Middenheim. The ground in Morrspark stays frozen for months. Digging graves is hard and we welcomed the rest, although there would be more work soon. Countess Sophia of Altdorf, courtier and Imperial Plenipotentate to the Graf of Middenheim, former wife of the Dauphin of Bretonnia, beauty, socialite, diplomat, patroness of orphans and the diseased, had been murdered in her bed. We felt more than sorrow at the death. We were priests of Morr, God of Death. This would be a busy week for us.

We looked at each other, placed our tools on the ground and walked through the gravestones towards the Temple of Morr where it stood at the centre of the park, swathed in scaffolding as if wrapped in bandages and splints. There were people crossing the park, hundreds of them in ones and twos, heading towards it as well. Some of them were crying.

The recent fire had burned the temple almost to the ground, but the underground Factorum and the catacombs, where the wealthy dead rested, were intact and in use. All of Morr's priests in Middenheim – four of us, plus one from the Temple of Shallya assisting while the priests who had died in the fire were replaced – gathered in the darkness of the Factorum, the ritual room where the dead are prepared for burial, cremation or the long drop off the Cliff of Sighs to the rocks far below. Corpses lay on two of the granite slabs and the doorway to the burial vaults stood, black and forbidding, like the mouth of the underworld. The room was filled with the smells of death, embalming oils and tension.

Father Ralf came slowly down the steps into the Factorum, clearing his throat noisily. The High Priest's chain of office hung heavily around his neck, and he fingered it as he looked at us. Approaching sixty and with bad arthritis, he had never expected to rise as high as this job and didn't particularly welcome it, but there had been nobody else. All the other priests were too young, too inexperienced, or me. He didn't like me. That was fine: nobody liked me. Many days, I didn't like myself either.

'I'll keep this short,' he started. 'I'm sure we're all shocked by the death of Countess Sophia. But the job of the Temple is to provide moral and spiritual reassurance at a time like this. We must be strong, and be seen to be strong.' He broke off for a fit of coughing, then resumed: 'I myself will see to the late Countess's funeral arrangements. Pieter, Wolmar and Olaf, you stay in the temple. There will be many mourners, and they will need your presence and counsel. The rest of you will attend to normal business.'

'The rest of us,' I said, 'is two of us.' I gestured at myself and Brother Jakob. 'And the Countess's murder won't stop ordinary people from dying.'

Father Ralf glowered at me with his rheumy eyes. 'These are exceptional times, brother. If you had not burned down the temple, then perhaps your workload would be lighter.'

I thought about reminding him that I'd burnt it down partly to save his life, but it wasn't a good idea. Not today, not with this mood in the air. Ralf might be inexperienced at running things, but he was keen to make his authority felt, and prone to over-react. Best to let it go. 'So,' I asked, 'should Brother Jakob and I return to grave-digging, or is there more pressing business for us?'

'Jakob will finish the grave. As for you, a flophouse in the Altquartier, Sargant's, has sent word that a drunk beggar has died there. You seem to have a fondness for such people: deal with the body. And brother, don't make a mountain out of it. We have more important things to worry about.'

I waited while the others left, filing up the stairs into the daylight and the crowd of mourners outside. Jakob hung back as well. I felt sorry for him. He'd only been at the temple a few months, and the upheavals which had followed the death of Father Zimmerman had unnerved him. Now there was something really big happening, and instead of being allowed to help he had been sent to dig graves.

'Why us?' he asked, and there was bitterness in his voice.

'Because you're young and I'm not liked, and neither of us would do a good job of comforting the mourners,' I said. 'You'd best get on with that grave while the sun's thawing the ground.'

He looked at me with curiosity in his eyes. 'What did Father Ralf mean when he said you had a fondness for beggars?'

'Go and dig,' I said.

* * *

I thought about Jakob's question as I walked through the ancient city's winding streets to the Altquartier. Was it beggars I cared about? No. But anyone who died alone and unmourned, whose death nobody cared about: those were my people. Somebody should care for them, and if no one was willing to do it before they died, then I would do it afterwards. People often showed their best side in death, losing their unappealing habits, becoming calm and serene. It was much easier not to hate them in that state; and besides, it was my job. If that job sometimes brought me unexplained deaths, then I regarded it as my duty to find out what I could about them. Besides, as I told my few friends, it passed the time.

The town was awash with news and gossip about the death of the Countess. People saw my robes and stopped me in the street to pour out their grief, and it seemed that everyone had something to say: some testament to her goodness, some anecdote about her legendary love-affairs, or just sobs and moans. I noticed that it was only the humans who seemed to be so carried away. The elves, dwarfs and halflings seemed to be more reserved, but they have always been few in Middenheim. The marketplaces were still busy but the street-entertainers were absent: no jugglers, no dwarf wrestlers, no illusionists making bursts of pretty lights with their petty magics. The city was more alive than at any time since the last carnival, but its life was strangely subdued.

All the talk on the streets was of the killing: was it murder or assassination – and if the latter, who was to blame? Most of the people with theories seemed to believe the Bretonnians were behind it somehow. The Countess's death would not only allow the Dauphin to remarry, but she was still well-loved in her own country. Tensions had been high between the Empire and Bretonnia for the last few months, and there are few better ways to spur an invading army than the murder of a national treasure, particularly one in a foreign country who might be embarrassing if left alive. Other theories blamed beastmen, probably remembering a few months back to when the Templar's Arms was attacked by mutants, or mythical skaven creeping up from the long-abandoned tunnels under the city. I heard all these ideas and more, and I let them wash over me like spring rain over the city's granite walls. It was just a death, no more important to me than any other.

The twisting streets narrowed and became darker, lost in shadows from the high buildings, as I entered the Altquartier. Buildings come and go here but its slum-like feel never changes. Sargant's flophouse was a new name to me but looking at its exterior, a former merchant's warehouse off a typically steep Middenheim alley, I knew what it would be like inside: infested with lice, fleas and vermin, with straw mattresses on the bare floors of long dormitories, and the smell of boiled cabbage, dirt and desperation. Like every other flophouse in the city, it stank of wretchedness. Shapeless men in rags, some with crutches or terrible scars, stood outside and passed a skin of cheap wine between them. As I approached the door they moved aside, respectful of the robes of a Morr worshipper. Even those with nothing to live for are still afraid of death.

A big, bald man, muscle gone mostly to fat, was waiting just inside. His clothes were mock-opulent, cheap copies of the latest fashions, and he wore a short, business-like knife on his belt. I didn't expect him to be worried by my appearance, and I was right.

'You're Sargant,' I said.

He didn't move, but stared at me for a long moment.

'Didn't you used to be Dieter Brossmann?' he said, an edge to his voice. I met his gaze.

'That was my name a long time ago,' I said slowly. 'For eight years I have been a humble priest of Morr. Now, the body.'

'Aye. Follow me then.'

I accompanied him down dark corridors, hoping he would ask no further questions about the man I had once been, and waited as he unlocked a thin pine door. The room beyond was small and windowless, and Sargant didn't follow me in. I saw a bed with a body on it, and one chair nearby. A small oil lamp stood on it, illuminating the face of the corpse.

It was Reinhold. Morr take me, but it was Reinhold! He looked old and worn and tired and dirty, but he hadn't changed so much from ten years ago, when I ran the largest family firm in Middenheim and he was my eyes and ears. Little Reinhold, who knew every watchman and warehouse guard in the city, who could pick any lock in half a minute, and who even knew at least a part of the ancient dwarf tunnels under the city. Reinhold, who had taught me so much. What had brought him to this end, I wondered, and then thought, I did. Partly, at least, when I closed down the firm and became a priest.

But there would be time for such thoughts later. I had a job to do. Grateful that Sargant had left me alone, and guessing that he couldn't have known the link between Reinhold and my former self, I placed my fingers on the body's forehead – the skin felt greasy and cold – and began to chant the Blessing of Protection, to seal it against the influence of the dark forces that prey on corpses. Reinhold's soul was already with Morr and beyond my help. I'd light a candle for him when I returned to the Temple.

In the candlelight, Reinhold's face looked old and solid, as if carved from the pine-wood of the Drakwald. I moved my fingers slowly over his face and downwards as I intoned the ancient words of the prayer. I reached his throat – and stopped. There was a mark, an indentation about the size of a gold crown, pressed deep into the flesh around his Adam's apple.

I'd heard of this trick. You wrap a coin or a stone in a piece of cloth. Then you loop it around your victim's throat and pull hard. The coin cuts off the windpipe – or the main vein, I was never sure which – and death comes a little quieter and less obvious. Reinhold had been murdered.

His pockets. Sargant would almost certainly have been through them, but there might still be something there that could tell me a little. Reinhold's clothes had the hard, clammy feel of grease, dirt and sweat that comes from being worn day after day for months, and with a smell to match, and I felt unclean handling them. More than that, it felt like I was invading my dead friend's privacy. But that didn't stop me.

A handkerchief, filthy. A grubby copy of a small Sigmarite prayer-book. Five bent strands of wire, which I recognised as improvised lock-picks. Bits of gravel. No money. The right pocket was even clammier than the left one, and contained only a small clasp-knife, very blunt and rusty. I pulled out the blade, and was not too surprised to see it had reasonably fresh blood on it. That was the Reinhold I'd known.

I sat in the semi-darkness and thought for a moment, then resumed the Blessing of Protection. There was little I could do for Reinhold now. Part of me knew that Reinhold's last journey was destined to be the long drop off the Cliff of Sighs, the pauper's exit from life and the city, but that was inevitable. He had no family vault under the Temple, nor the money to pay for a grave-site in Morrspark where the more wealthy dead already lay four, sometimes five deep. The best I could do for him was to find out why he had died. I wasn't looking for revenge: that's not what being a priest of Morr is about. It would be enough to find out the reason.

As I finished the blessing the door opened and Sargant came in. 'Done?' he asked.

'Almost.' I stood up and moved to the door, heading back towards the street. No point in letting him know what I knew. 'I'll send a cart for the body. Did he die in that room?'

'Aye. Most nights he was in the dormitory wi' others, but last night he came up late with money and asked for a room for hisself. He smelled of drink and he had sausage and a skin of wine for his friend. They drank past eleven bells, then he went asleep. This morning, there he was, stiff as a board. "Eat, drink an' be merry," he said t'me yestiddy, "for tomorrer we die." An' he were right.'

I stared at him. Did Reinhold know he was going to die – that someone was planning to kill him? And if so, why did he go quietly to it instead of fighting? Had life on the street really ground him down so far that he wouldn't even defend himself against assassination? Or was there another reason? I needed to know more about Reinhold's recent life, and I knew I wouldn't get the information from Sargant.

'This friend of Reinhold's,' I asked. 'Can you give me a name?'

'Louise,' he said. 'Little Bretonnian rat, she is. Here most evenings. They were courtin'. Wanted to spend last night together, but I won't be havin' that kind o' behaviour, not in my house.'

No, of course not. You'd take money from people with nothing for a night's shelter in this squalor, but you'll forbid them anything that might give them a moment's comfort, even something as little as the warmth of another person's care. I knew too many men like Sargant: Middenheim was full of them. We were almost back at the flophouse's front door when I noticed something that surprised me. 'You're wearing a black armband,' I said. 'Are you in mourning?'

The big man looked down at his arm, as if momentarily surprised. 'Aye,' he said.

'For Reinhold?' I asked.

He stared back at me. 'Not that old drunk,' he sneered. 'The Countess.'

He turned and was gone, back into the sordid darkness of his domain. I watched him go, then looked over at the group of beggars who still stood around the door. One of them glanced up at me and I caught his eye. He twitched like a mouse trapped by an owl. 'Don't run away,' I said. 'I'm looking for Louise.'

It took a couple of coins and two hours of being guided through the city's many back-alleys to cheap inns and beggars' hideaways in old cisterns and abandoned cellars, but eventually we found her: a bag of rags and bones huddled near a brazier down near the watch-post beside the ruins of the South Gate. She looked up as we approached, recognising my guide. Her face was bloody and bruised. I crouched down in front of her.

'Who did this to you?' I asked.

'Men.' The word sounded thick and blurred, although whether it was from her Bretonnian accent or her torn lip was hard to say. I realised I had no idea how old she was – twenty, thirty, fifty even. Street people age fast, and rain, frost and cheap wine hadn't been kind to her.

'What men?'

'Men who hear my voice, who say I am spy, I kill the Countess. Stupid men, Lady take them!' she said. 'Who are you to ask such things?'

She gazed at me with grey eyes, and I remembered another woman. But she had been blonde, and her face had been filled with life and joy. Filomena had been her name and I had loved her... and not seen her for eight years. There was a silence. I remembered Louise had asked me a question.

'I was a friend of Reinhold,' I said and she turned away, her shoulders hunched. I didn't move to comfort her: she had so little left in her life, I felt I should let her keep her grief. At least I didn't have to tell her the news. After a long minute she turned back to me, tears streaking the filth on her face.

'You are priest, you bury him, yes?' she said.

'I will attend to him in death.' The reply seemed to satisfy her. 'Louise... was there anyone who hated Reinhold?'

'Hated?' She looked blank. I tried another tack.

'What did Reinhold do yesterday? Was he working?'

Louise wiped her face on a filthy sleeve. 'Didn't get work. He went looking but didn't get.'

'So what did he do?'

'Morning, Wendenbahn for begging.' I nodded: the street was popular with merchants, who gave charity to beggars for luck. 'Came back at two bells, scared.'

'Scared?'

'Saw a man. Reiner said man looked for him. No friend. Then he take his... he go out again and he.... He come back late,' she finished lamely. No, that wasn't it. She was hiding something from me, something important, because she was nervous of me. I knew how to deal with that: move to a safe subject, build up her confidence, and come back to the secret later.

'Louise,' I asked, 'do you know who this man was? Did Reinhold tell you anything about him?'

A long pause as she tried to remember. 'From the west. From Marien-burg. From past days, Reiner said. Called him "Grubworm".'

Grubworm: Claus Grubheimer. I remembered. Strange, however much we try to escape our pasts, it's always there, waiting behind us to tap our shoulder or slip a blade into our back. Ten or eleven years ago, a fresh-faced merchant with an Empire name and a Bretonnian accent had arrived in Middenheim, bringing big ideas and a permit to trade herbs from Loren. While I shook his hand and talked to him of partnership and assistance, Reinhold had picked his locks, copied his paperwork and stolen his samples. Then we planted some Black Lotus on him and tipped off the Watch what he was trading. I'd had a five-crown bet with Reinhold that they'd have his head on a pole before he could flee the city. Reinhold had won, and that was the last time either of us had seen Grubheimer. Until yesterday.

But had Grubheimer killed Reinhold? And if he had, was he looking for me? And what about Yan the Norse and Three-Fingered Kaspar, who'd also worked for me then? I hadn't seen them in years. Perhaps they were dead too. Fingers of cold panic gripped my shoulders. Be calm, I told myself, be calm. And yet my old instincts, long buried under my life as a priest, were screaming that if Grubheimer was in town, it was for one reason: revenge. I needed time to think, but if Reinhold was already dead then time was the one thing I didn't have.

'I have to go back to the Temple,' I said and stood. Louise's eyes followed me.

'Money?' she asked, in her voice the only sound of hope I'd heard from her. I looked down at her pitiful form.

'Reinhold gave you nothing at all?' I asked. She said nothing, but her eyes broke away from mine. There was something she didn't want to tell me: that hidden detail again. It could wait. I turned away, to begin the walk back through the maze of cold streets filled with sorrowful people. Something in me was crystallising, hard and sharp. I knew I'd find out what it was in a moment.

'Wait! The Countess–' she said behind me.

'No. Don't talk to me about the Countess,' I said, and walked away.

The hard thing inside me was steely-cold with fear, and something else. I knew that if Grubheimer was back in the city, he was here to kill me: he might be a citizen of Marienburg but his blood was Bretonnian, and they were not a people to forgive their enemies. I had forgiven mine eight years ago, when I became a priest and tried to forget all of the many bad things I had done. I regretted none of those things, but when I joined the Temple of Morr I knew I would never do anything like that again. Now, eight years later, a priest would be an easy target for Grubheimer to kill.

Ever since my wife and child had disappeared, a part of me had wanted to die but it was a very small part, and as I passed through the narrow streets I could feel the hardness in me building, to fight against it. Grubheimer was a desperate man, a man who would garrotte a beggar in his bed for a ten year-old revenge. If the priest I now was was to survive this, then I would need to be hard. I would need to become once more the man I had left behind: to think about life in a way I had tried to forget for eight years. It was not an appealing prospect.

But even as I wondered about it, I felt the coldness in me swell and grow, filling me with dead emotions, covering the mind of the priest of Morr and replacing them with old thoughts, old behaviours. Was the life I had led for eight years really so easily overcome? Had the past I had fought so hard to bury really risen so close to the surface? And having let the wolf out from the cage, could I ever get it back in there again?

Part of me felt panicked and sick, but I looked down at my right hand. My fist was clenched; not in anger, I realised, but in resolution. And then I looked up at an alley I was passing, and I knew what needed to be done. I walked into the gloom I used to know well, knocked hard on the door of the Black Horse tavern, and entered.

Its decor had not improved. The noontime drinkers were fewer and more subdued than I remembered, and I didn't recognise the young man in the apron who moved towards me as I crossed the threshold. He opened his mouth.

'Stop,' I said. 'Is Grizzly Bruno here?'

He chewed his lip, which is what you'd do if you're new in your job and a priest comes into a hole like the Black Horse and asks for a man with a reputation like Grizzly Bruno's. But his eyes flicked to the ceiling. I thought they would; I'd been watching for it.

'He's upstairs,' I said.

'He's asleep.'

'No I'm not,' came a heavy voice and there was Bruno, as huge and bear-like as ever. We stood awkwardly, unsure of how to greet each other. Finally he said, 'Father,' and I, grateful to escape one of his hugs, said, 'Bruno.'

'Been a long time,' he said.

'It has.'

'I take it this isn't social.'

'It isn't.'

'Well, father,' and he put weight on the word. 'What business can I help you with on a day like today?'

'Bruno, do you remember a Bretonnian herb trader called Grubheimer? About ten years ago? Got himself chased out of town for smuggling Black Lotus?'

'Can't say I do, father. It's been a long time.' But he looked interested.

'Some associates of mine,' I said carefully, 'were not unacquainted with the bag of weed that the Watch found on him. Now he's back in town, and from what I hear he's not happy. *Very* not happy.'

'I thought you'd put things like that behind you. When your wife and boy went missing.'

There was a pause. It came from me. 'I did,' I said, 'but it looks like he didn't. And I do not care to be reminded of it.'

'So – what? You want him warned away? Out of the city? Dealt with?'

'I need to know where he's staying. That'll suffice for the time.'

'A shame,' Bruno said, 'but I'll get someone on it. Can I offer you a glass of brandy and the warmth of my hearth? I'd appreciate your advice on a piece of tricky business.'

'I'm sorry, Bruno,' I said. 'I don't do that any more.'

'But you still ask for favours from old friends. I understand.' I started to say something but he held up one slab-like hand. 'No. Today I forgive you. With such a big death in the city, Morr's people must have much to do.'

'All deaths are the same size,' I said. 'It's only the living who think different.'

He looked at me for a moment, then shrugged. 'Whatever you say. You're the priest. I'll send a messenger to the Temple if I hear of your Grubheimer.'

'Thanks, Bruno,' I said. 'And any time you or your boys need advice on death, you know where to find me.'

He chuckled. 'Maybe I'll do that. But when it comes to death we have more experience than you, I think.'

A recent memory filled my head: a man plunging down into blizzard-whipped snow from the Cliff of Sighs, his blood still warm on my hands. 'Oh,' I said, 'you might be surprised.'

There was no need to bring Reinhold's body back to the Temple. A pauper's body should be flung from the Cliff of Sighs with the briefest of blessings. But however he might have died, Reinhold had lived as more than a pauper. Besides, with Father Ralf and the others occupied with the death of the Countess, nobody was going to notice, and preparing the body would give me time to think.

On my way back to the Temple, crossing from the hubbub of the streets into the relative solitude of the frozen Morrspark, I heard the sound of a spade ringing against the unyielding ground. Brother Jakob was still digging. He was standing in the grave, and the sight of him there sent an unexplained shiver down my back. I walked over, and he looked up, his face pale with cold.

'I don't suppose you're here to help,' he said bitterly.

'No, brother,' I said. 'I have other business.'

He put down the spade, rubbed his hands to get the blood back into them, and looked at me.

'You told me you're not liked around here, brother?' he asked.

'It's true enough,' I said.

'So why do you stay?'

I looked down at him. 'Why? Don't assume that "being hated" is the same as "hating", brother. I have devoted my life to Morr. I work in his temple, and I tolerate the pettiness of those whose dedication is less than my own.' I paused to stamp my feet; they were going numb. My words sounded hollow, even to me. 'But that's not what you meant to ask. You want to know why you should stay.'

He stared at me as if I had just told him his innermost secret. He paused. 'I hate it here.'

'I know.'

'I want to run away.'

'What do you want to do?'

'I want to be a knight, fight for the Empire, live and die a hero. But without my father's help I'd never get a rank or a command.'

Ah, his father, some minor noble with three sons in the army and the youngest sent into the priesthood to pray for them. 'Run away. Join a band of mercenaries,' I suggested.

He looked at me with disdain. 'There's no honour in that,' he said. 'And mostly they're Tilean too.' He spat on the cold earth.

'But it would be better than being a priest, eh?' I said. 'Life's what you make of it. If you do not make your own way, a way will be made for you. You must choose, brother, you must choose.'

He didn't reply. As I walked away I heard the ring of the shovel against the earth, striking out like a slowly tolling bell.

The half-rebuilt Temple was crowded with mourners, its normally quiet spaces filled with noise and jostling. Father Ralf's coffers would be doing well and he would be revelling in the attention which was being paid to him. The throng of people, normally obedient to one wearing the robes of Morr, seemed not to notice me and I had to shove my way between them as I made my way towards the entrance to the priests' quarters in the far wall, and my cell which lay beyond.

I didn't get there. A wailing woman tugged at my robe, begging for a blessing, and then a man in rich clothes wanted to know what the Countess's death augured for the spring rains, and I was trapped by the crowd, speaking words of comfort and saying short prayers for someone I didn't care for to people I hated. Then Father Ralf stood beside me, at my shoulder.

'Is the soul of our departed brother flying to Morr?' he asked, using the Temple's code to ask if I'd tipped the corpse from the Cliff of Sighs. I shook my head.

'Sadly, his passing was swift but not welcomed,' I said, meaning he was killed. Father Ralf looked exasperated.

'I sorrow. I must learn more of this. Be in the Factorum in five minutes.' He turned away to minister to the needs of some well-dressed goodwife. I left: I'd been heading to the Factorum anyway. The Watch would be bringing Reinhold's body there soon.

The Factorum was cold and smelled of death. I sat on one of the scrubbed marble slabs, thinking, waiting for the corpse, and trying to piece together what I knew. Reinhold had failed to find work yesterday, but he had come back with money all the same: money, and the news that Grubheimer was back in town. He returned late, got drunk, took a room alone, and there he was killed. Killed by an assassin, killed almost as if expecting it, almost as if he offered no resistance. Almost as if he felt he should die. That's a rare thought for Middenheimers, who cling as tenaciously to life as their ancient city clings to its rocky mountaintop.

Yet the more I thought about the way Reinhold had looked, the more I believed he had been prepared to die. He hadn't put up a fight. People reach that state for many reasons but desperation is not one of them: it may be a reason to take one's own life, but not to lie back quietly and let it be taken. Drugs, perhaps his wine was drugged? No; if they wanted Reinhold dead, they could have poisoned the wine. There was something more here. I'd seen it before: the sense of something completed, finished, over. A man who was determined to leave on a high note, so when people looked at his life they'd say, 'What did he accomplish? He accomplished this.'

But Reinhold had been a down-and-out, unable to find a day's work to pay for a night's lodging. The thought of imminent death can drive one to incredible ends, but only to escape it – not to welcome it. What had happened to him?

I knew I didn't have the secret of this yet but, looking at the facts, I thought I knew where it had to be hidden. I needed to find where Reinhold had got the money, and I needed to know whether he had got it before or after he saw Grubheimer in Wendenbahn. This wasn't some penny-pamphlet tale of intrigue: I was already certain that my friend had been killed by Grubheimer or someone hired by him. And I knew that meant Grubheimer would come after me. Possibly he wanted to kill my old associates first, working his way through what was left of my organisation, knowing that I'd know he was coming for me. That was good. It might give me some time.

There was a sharp knock at the door and Father Ralf entered without waiting for permission. He glared at me. I stood up, my knee-joints cracking.

'I told you to deal with this matter quickly,' he said, 'and you start a murder enquiry out of a flop-house stabbing.'

'It was more than that,' I said. 'I sense it. The dead man was a friend of mine.' My voice sounded false to me. It was my old self, Dieter, playing the role of a priest of Morr. It made me uneasy.

Father Ralf glared at me in exasperation. 'Friendship has no place in the life of a priest of Morr, brother. Besides, I did not think you cultivated friends.'

'He was a friend in my former life.'

No answer. Even Father Ralf knew of my past and my old reputation, and therefore what sort of man the deceased must have been. There was a long pause. Our breaths formed white mist, swirling in the cold lamp-lit air.

'Well,' he said, then stopped a moment. 'And another thing. I've learned you spent the afternoon walking around the city with beggars, refusing to listen to mourners who tried to speak to you. This is not behaviour becoming of a priest of our order, brother. It makes us look haughty at a time when we must be at our most open and approachable. Ar-Ulric himself mentioned the matter to me.'

I said nothing. I didn't remember ignoring anyone on the street but that didn't mean it hadn't happened. But I doubted that Ar-Ulric, the highest priest of Ulric in the whole Empire, had taken any interest in the matter. Father Ralf was trying to intimidate me and make himself look important at the same time. It might have worked if I cared about either him or Ar-Ulric. But I didn't.

'At six bells we are holding the mass ritual of mourning and remembrance for the Countess,' he continued, 'to be led by myself and Ar-Ulric. You will take part prominently because it is important that you are seen there. And you will be seen to weep for the Countess. Am I clear?'

'Yes, father,' I said plainly. Disagreeing would only have started an argument, and I needed to get rid of him so I could think. He seemed to want an argument anyway, but we were interrupted by another knock at the door. I opened it, and in a blast of cold air there was Schtutt.

'Help me get this dead bugger inside, father,' he said, gesturing to a lump lying on a cart behind him. 'I'd have brought one of the lads but everyone is over at the Nordgarten, minding the mourners at Countess Sophia's townhouse.' Then he noticed Father Ralf behind me and dropped into an embarrassed silence.

Ralf made for the door, turning back to me as he reached it. 'Six bells, brother. Do not be late,' he said, and left.

Together Schtutt and I lifted the body – the rigor mortis was wearing off and Reinhold felt like a sack of logs – and carried it down the steps, dumping it on one of the marble slabs. Schtutt was panting.

'I'm not as fit as I used to be in the old days, eh?' He wiped his brow. 'But none of us are. He certainly isn't.' He gestured at the body. He seemed to be in a mood to chat but I, aware of the passing of time and the presence of Grubheimer somewhere in the city, wasn't. Still, a thought pricked me.

'Schtutt, do you remember a Marienburger named Grubheimer? Tall, greasy black hair, Bretonnian accent, got run out of the city for smuggling Black Lotus? About ten years back?'

'Can't say I do. But if he sounds Bretonnian he wants to watch out. The city's too hot for them at the moment, with the rumours about them killing the Countess and all. There've been two stabbed in brawls already, and another one fell from a high window and broke his neck.'

'Unfortunate,' I said nervously, feeling panicky and distracted. The notion struck me that if Grubheimer had learned which flop-house Reinhold was staying in, he must know by now that I had become a priest, and if I stayed around the Temple I would be an easy victim. I needed to move. 'But I should–'

'Though,' Schtutt said, warming to his theme, 'I've heard from the best authority that the Countess was not assassinated.'

'No?' I feigned interest.

'No. More like a robbery, they reckon. There's an old dwarf tunnel as comes out in the Countess's cellar. Nobody knew it was there, but the murderer got in that way. And a stack of her jewels was missing, including the Dauphin of Bretonnia's engagement ring. Money gone too. She must have come across the robber, and–'

So the dwarfs were likely to pick up the blame for the killing. They didn't do well in Middenheim. 'A tragedy, truly,' I said. 'We are all the poorer for her loss. Now, there is much I must do.'

'Aye. I'll be off.' He looked discomforted at having his chat cut short, but left anyway.

I sat on the cold slab next to Reinhold and stared down at the body of my friend. How did his death piece together? And why were my instincts telling me that it was important to work out why Reinhold had lain down to die, when there was a man in the city trying to kill me? When I had allowed myself to think like my old self once more, I had expected a surge of ruthlessness, of sudden thought and decisive action, but there had been none of that. Perhaps the thing I had feared, the part of me I had buried eight years ago when I joined Morr's temple, had lost its edge in time, as I had hoped. Perhaps I had succeeded in destroying my dark half. Perhaps that success would lead to my own destruction.

I still needed to know where Reinhold had got his money. If I was honest, other than running and hiding, I could think of nothing better to do. The old Dieter had never run or hidden, and I wasn't going to start now. I needed to talk to Louise again.

* * *

The sun had set by the time I left the Factorum and the wind had picked up. Down by South Gate it chilled my marrow and blew the embers of the guards' brazier into fierce redness. I gazed out over the long, twisting bridge, lit by torches, as it curved down from the cliff's edge to the ground hundreds of feet below. Workmen were still busy with ladders and ropes, lanterns and stone and mortar, toiling to repair the huge breach in the viaduct that the magics of the traitor-wizard Karl-Heinz Wasmeier had caused, as he fled from the city after the last carnival. It would take weeks more to finish the job.

Behind me, in the glow of the brazier, Louise finished the pie I had bought her with the appetite of a woman who has not eaten all day. Now she would be more inclined to talk. She knew I had been Reinhold's friend, but I would still be asking hard questions. Better to start with softer ones, to make it sound as if I cared.

'How did you come to Middenheim?' I asked. She glanced at me in that way that horses do if they're nervous and about to shy. I smiled at her, my face feeling odd at the unaccustomed gesture.

She said, 'Back home, in Bretonnia, I worked for a woman. She was with a noble, brought me here when that was... when she left him. She was wild, fierce, but much money. I serve for six years. Then she throw me in the street with nothing. For no reason.' She stopped. I had expected anger or rage, but she must have told this story so many times that its emotion had all drained away. Yet I could tell there was still deep, black pain, far below. But was there resentment? Hatred? I didn't know.

I looked at her for a moment while I groped for the right thing to say. Then it came to me, all of it, in a sudden rush like a spring flood, and I said, 'You're talking about the Countess! You said her name this afternoon. You were trying to tell me something.'

Louise didn't speak but her eyes said I was right.

'Louise, what are you afraid of?'

She said nothing.

'Did Reinhold give you something last night?'

She nodded, despite herself. Tears were beginning to streak her cheeks. With frightening speed, skeins of logic were weaving themselves together in my mind.

'Reinhold knew how much you hated the Countess, didn't he? And you're afraid that he had something to do with her death. You're scared, because you realise now that you don't really want her dead, and because you don't want to believe Reinhold could do something like that... and because if he did kill her, then people might think you're involved too.'

She shook her head. For a moment I was confused.

'Louise, do you mean that's not what you believe, or,' and the realisation hit me hard and sudden, 'or because it's what you know?'

She nodded, a little nod, her silent weeping unabated.

'Did he give you some jewellery last night?'

A tiny nod.

'And you recognised it.'

Another, tinier.

'Because it was the Countess's.'

She didn't need to nod. I already knew I had the truth. I took a deep breath. This wasn't going to be easy.

'Louise, you have to trust me. The jewellery was the Countess's, but Reinhold didn't get it from her. He stole it from the man who killed her – that Bretonnian he saw earlier that day.'

'The Grubworm,' she said in a small voice.

'Yes, Grubworm. And then Grubworm went to the flop-house and killed Reinhold to get it back, but he'd already given it to you.' I paused. She said nothing. I had no idea if she believed me. 'Louise, it is my duty as a priest of Morr to understand death. We commune with death, we speak to it. We live our lives surrounded by it, and we comprehend things about it that most people could never understand. We know who killed the Countess. He will be arrested soon. Reinhold had nothing to do with it.'

I paused to let my words sink in. She still said nothing, her head buried in her hands. The cold wind blew between us, the thin flames of the brazier warming nothing at all.

'But you must give me the jewellery,' I said.

At last she looked up and met my eye. A long moment passed, and then she scrabbled amongst her dirty rags, and I knew I had won. She held out a balled fist, and I reached out to receive what lay within. As I did, she grabbed my arm with her other hand, and held hard.

'I have your word for the truth?' she hissed.

'You have my solemn word as a priest of Morr,' I lied.

A jewelled ring fell into my hand: heavy, with the soft warmth that only solid gold has. I cradled it, thinking. I didn't know what I was going to do with it, but I knew that at least I now had the truth of yesterday evening in my grasp.

Because Reinhold *had* killed the Countess. He knew the old dwarf tunnels under the city better than anyone except a dwarf. He could pick the locks, there had been blood on his pocket-knife, and he'd given Louise that ring. More importantly, I'd known Reinhold for long enough to understand what he was capable of doing. He believed that the ends justified the means, and his means were ruthless. I'd never asked him to kill anyone, but he had killed while working for me, more than once.

So he'd seen Grubheimer in town. Maybe Grubheimer had spied him and threatened him. Or maybe Reinhold had simply heard that the man was back and asking dangerous questions. Anyway, he'd realised his days were numbered, and so he looked for a grand gesture, a last stab at posthumous fame, on which to die. And given that his lover had reason to hate her, what better than the murder of the beloved Countess Sophia?

He'd stolen some of her jewellery to make it look like a burglary, fenced most of it cheaply before the murder was discovered, drunk or gave away most of the money and used the rest to buy a squalid room for the night. He gave his girlfriend her ex-employer's famed engagement ring. Then he died. Maybe he died happy. I hoped there had been a tiny shred of contentment in his mind as Grubheimer's garrotte had throttled the life from him.

But Reinhold wasn't stupid. He knew – he must have known – that the jewellery he had stolen, fenced or given to Louise would be traced back to him, and his name would resound around the city: Reinhold the Knife, the man who killed Countess Sophia. A black legend, but for some people infamy is better than anonymity. Particularly if you're dead. I guessed – no, knew – that he had wanted that to be his epitaph.

Louise coughed, a long, racking cough, and I remembered where I was. There was still the business with Grubheimer to be concluded. The ring in my hand could come in useful, though at that moment I didn't know how.

'I must go,' I said, and turned away. Louise grabbed my arm again.

'One thing more,' she said. 'You say you Reinhold's friend, but he never mentioned priest. What friend were you, to let him live like this?'

I turned back slowly. 'When Reinhold knew me,' I said quietly, 'my name was Dieter Brossmann.'

Louise dropped my arm, staring wildly. She made a strange sound, half gasp, half scream.

'You!' she spat. 'You betrayed him! You let him sink in life, to the dregs! You – you are no friend! He should have killed you! You should die! You are evil! Evil! Give me my ring!' She made a lunge for me. '*Give me my ring!*'

Two Watchmen began to hurry towards us. A Bretonnian beggar-woman screaming at a priest – they would know who to arrest. I turned away, leaving them to it, and walked swiftly back up the steep streets towards Morrspark and the Temple.

Half the city must have been crowded into the park. It was full: nobles, knights and rich merchants jostled by shoemakers, peddlers and servants. They were all packed into the cold, dark expanse, lit by occasional torches on high poles. People were even standing on the graves to get a better view of the ceremony on the Temple's steps. And yet there was no sound from any of them. As I pushed my way through the silent masses I could hear Ar-Ulric's great voice booming out over the park, interspersed with the higher, weaker tones of Father Ralf. I didn't bother to listen to what they were saying. All that mattered was that I had missed the start. There would be trouble later. If I lived that long.

I shouldered my way between the gathered ranks, heading for the Temple and the small door at its rear. I needed to be alone, and to hide the

Countess's ring, and my cell would be the best place for both. As Father Ralf and Ar-Ulric were on the steps at the front of the temple, the press was less great at the back and as I approached the door I could see it was ajar.

As I put my hand on the ornate handle, a voice behind me said, 'Dieter.'

I whirled around. There, a few paces away, was a figure I knew: medium height, greased hair greying at the temples, and a nose that spoke of aristocracy and brawling. He was larger these days, fatter or more heavily muscled. I didn't want to find out which. Instead I leapt through the door and slammed it behind me.

Grubheimer! Grubheimer was here. He had spoken to me. He had wanted me to see him. He hadn't tried to kill me. Which meant... which meant... he must have set a trap for me. And I had almost certainly jumped into it.

He had called me Dieter, and I had answered to that name for the first time in eight years. I did feel more like my old self now: calmer, more confident, more ruthless. And part of me, the priest, felt appalled and scared by that, but I ignored it. For now I had to be Dieter, or die.

I ran to my cell. It was pitifully obvious that someone had moved the thin mattress since I had been here. I lifted it, and underneath lay a small leather pouch. I pulled it open and stared at the fine grey dust inside. I didn't have to smell it to recognise it: Black Lotus powder. A foul substance. Fatal to its owners, in more ways than one. Grubheimer had put this here. He was framing me the way I'd framed him ten years ago.

Then I heard footsteps, fast and light, in the corridor. They stopped outside. I tucked the pouch in my robes, grabbed a chair as a weapon, and yanked the door open. In the corridor stood Brother Jakob.

'I saw you come in,' he said. 'Father Ralf is furious. I thought I'd better tell you.'

If he'd thought that might worry me, he was wrong. I moved forward, into the corridor, grasping him by the arm. 'There are bigger things in the air tonight. Come with me.' The implications of the Black Lotus were still flooding through my mind. Grubheimer must have known I'd find the drug. He must want me to be caught with it in person, and that meant he'd act as soon as he could. I had to dispose of the powder immediately. One hiding place came to mind and I acted without thinking of the consequences. Like Dieter.

'Take this for safekeeping,' I said, thrusting the pouch into Jakob's hands before he could protest.

'What is it?'

'Something many men would kill for. If you see trouble, stick close to me.'

I unbolted the door and we stepped outside. The massed mourners were singing the last verse of a funeral hymn, filling the world with the music of sorrow and regret. At any other time I would have been deeply moved by it, but right now it was a distraction. Almost dragging Jakob by the arm, I made my way around to the front of the Temple.

We didn't get far. A knot of Watch uniforms was moving roughly through the crowd towards us, carrying flaming torches to light their path. At their centre was Grubheimer. He pointed to me. 'This is the man,' he said. 'He is the one who offered to sell me Black Lotus this afternoon.'

'Officer, this man lies,' I said, not to Grubheimer but to the Watch Captain with him, a man I didn't know. 'I am nothing but a priest of Morr.' My voice sounded loud: the hymn had ended and from the front of the Temple Father Ralf was proclaiming a prayer. I knew its words well. The crowd around us were silent, their attention on us.

'Search him,' Grubheimer said, his voice gruff, his accent strong. 'A brown leather pouch.'

Jakob stared at me, suddenly trying to pull free of my grasp. I didn't let him go. And with a lurch I realised that I still had the Countess's ring in my closed hand. If they searched me, Grubheimer would have been more triumphant than he could possibly have dreamed.

'I have no such pouch,' I said. Jakob pulled harder. From the temple steps, I could hear Father Ralf nearing the end of the prayer to Morr.

'Maybe his catamite has it,' Grubheimer said. I drew myself up, aware of the aura my priestly robes would give me, and knowing how little they matched my terrified thoughts. And suddenly I remembered a cool, calm voice – not mine, not Dieter's, but Reinhold's – and I knew what to do.

'You accuse me of this crime,' I said slowly and with emphasis, 'because I know who you killed last night.' Grubheimer's face showed surprise, but not worry. I took a quick step forward. Before he could react I had dipped my hand into Grubheimer's waistcoat pocket and a moment later held up a heavy gold ring to the Watchmen's eyes. A simple sleight-of-hand. Reinhold had taught his friend Dieter how to do it, too many years ago.

'The Countess's engagement ring,' I said, measuring my voice carefully against the last words of Father Ralf's prayer. 'This is the assassin who killed her.'

The prayer ended. Silence spread across the park.

'This Bretonnian,' I proclaimed with a voice like the wrath of the gods, 'is the man who killed the Countess!'

Scared realisation broke across Grubheimer's face like a crack of thunder. There was a murmuring of voices. Hundreds of people had turned to look at us. How must it seem to them? Two priests, members of the Watch, and one accused man. Grubheimer knew he was caught: I saw it in his face. I grasped Brother Jakob's arm more tightly and watched as Grubheimer did what I'd expected: he panicked. But not the way I'd hoped. He didn't run. He pulled a knife and lunged at me.

Without thinking, I spun away, dragging Brother Jakob around in front of me as I went. His feet slipped on the cold, hard ground, and he screamed as he began to fall. Grubheimer's knife met his chest, slicing through the thin black robes. Blood sprayed across the crowd. I lost my balance and fell.

Someone shouted, 'Murderer!' and people began to run.

I hit the earth hard, smashing my nose against the frozen ground and knocking the wind out of myself. Grubheimer stood fixedly above me, staring down, knife in hand. He looked so startled. Something had emerged from his breast. It was six inches of sword-blade. Over the Bretonnian's shoulder, I could see the man who had stabbed him: tall, bearded, scarred. He seemed familiar. In an instant he had pulled out his sword and disappeared into the milling crowd. Grubheimer crumpled slowly to the ground like a puppet, and died there. He didn't take his eyes off me for a moment.

There was movement: people were milling about, and there were cries of terror and sorrow. A rush of noise, of whispered words, swept across the park. The solemnity of the service was broken and lost.

Beside me on the ground lay Jakob. With one hand he was trying to staunch the bleeding from the slash across his stomach, but he wasn't succeeding. The light in his eyes was fading but he stared at me as if to say: You did this.

I reached over to him and placed my hand on his breast, over his heart, and tried to think of some farewell that would make sense, to either of us. I felt his heartbeat flutter and cease, and I realised there was only one thing I could say. I knelt beside him, placed my other hand on his forehead, and began the Ritual of Final Parting, willing his soul into the arms of Morr.

That was the last touch. It was done. I was safe. Overwhelming relief and tiredness swept through me and I slumped, lying beside Jakob, my face level with his dead eyes. You, I thought: a life among the dead was no place for a man like you. You said you wanted to die a hero's death. Well, you did. The man who gave his life to stop the Countess's assassin from escaping. And perhaps you died happy.

I doubted it, but it didn't matter. What mattered was that I would be the person who attended to his corpse, and that would let me dispose of the Black Lotus.

I would need a story to explain how I had discovered Grubheimer's guilt and the ring, but that could wait. The people of Middenheim had their assassin. With the murderer revealed as a Bretonnian, the diplomatic crisis would get worse and there might even be a war, but if that happened it would be far away. Father Ralf would be furious I had spoiled his service of remembrance, but I would live with the consequences of that tomorrow.

And what of Louise? She had lost the man who made her grubby life worth living. And Reinhold: I had stolen his triumph, his posthumous glory, the infamy that would have kept his name alive long after his body had been devoured by worms, and I had given it to the man who killed him. But I had saved Louise from the knowledge that her lover had killed her mistress. Maybe that was a good thing. I didn't know, and I wasn't sure if I cared.

But it had worked. It had all come together. I had survived. Only one innocent had died. Reinhold was avenged. It felt good. I almost grinned.

A voice I recognised said, 'Father.' Above me, Grizzly Bruno offered me his hand, and I took it and climbed to my feet. Somehow I knew that his presence was no accident. People had gathered around us, pushing and shoving, trying to get a glimpse of the two bodies, and the Watch were attempting to keep order. The mood of mourning had been shattered; everyone was talking excitedly about the assassin. I could just hear Ar-Ulric's strident voice battling against the noise, but nobody was listening any more.

I turned to the man who had helped me. 'Thank you, Bruno.'

'More thanks than you know, father,' he said in a low voice. 'The man who stuck your Bretonnian? One of mine.'

'You had me followed?'

'And with good reason,' he smiled. 'You didn't notice?'

'No.' I forced a smile. 'The priestly life slows the instincts.'

'Not too much I hope, father. You owe me a favour, and I'd still appreciate your advice on that business I mentioned this afternoon. Right up your old street, it is.'

'My old street,' I repeated, a strange thoughtfulness in my voice. This afternoon I had wondered if I would be able to cage the wolf of my old memories and instincts once I had dealt with Grubworm. I had forgotten to ask myself if I would want to. I had forgotten how good victory tasted. I had forgotten so many things.

Bruno looked at me. 'How about it, father?'

I smiled and reached out to shake his hand.

'Call me Dieter,' I said.

MY BROTHER'S KEEPER

They could smell the city long before they could see it.

As that last day of their journey wore to a close, a pungent scent began to reach the caravan, carried on the cold, wet, spring air. A smell of industry: tanneries, blacksmithies, breweries, wood-fires, charcoal burners. A cloying combination of metal tang, ash, chimney-soot, and the sweetness of malting hops.

In the jolting confines of the staff carriage, Franckl oathed his distaste and emptied his insulted nostrils noisily into a lace kerchief. Curled in a corner seat, surrounded by piled strong boxes and chests that threatened to topple onto her, Lenya Dunst looked away in mild revulsion. Franckl was the Margrave's houseman, a fussy, prissy pustular wretch in his late forties, too in love with cross-gartered breeches and stiffly-laced doublets to realise they made him look like a bloated spatchcock ready for the griddle.

'That awful reek,' he moaned, wiping his pendulous nose on a corner of lace. 'What manner of place are these Wolves taking us to? Is this salvation? I think not!'

The other members of the Ganmark household crammed into the lurching carriage had no answer for him. The undercook was asleep and snoring wetly, the two chambermaids were pale and dumb with fear and fatigue, and the pot-boy had received too many claps to the back of his head from Franckl in his life to start conversing with him now. Maris, the old wetnurse, was lost in her own dreams. Or nightmares, perhaps. Since Commander Ganz had destroyed her trinket and saved them all, she had been distant and listless.

Lenya caught Franckl's eye.

'I thought a man as... worldly as you would have visited Middenheim before, Master Franckl,' she said sweetly.

Franckl harrumphed, and then realised that the lowly milkmaid was his only audience. He dabbed his nose. After all, she was a pretty little thing, almost comely in a wildcat sort of way.

'Oh, long ago, my pet, long ago... As a younger man, I journeyed far and wide, visiting many of the great cities in the Empire. Ah yes, the adventures I've had... Hmm. It's just that the sweet woodland airs of Linz had quite stolen the stench of Middenheim from my memories.'

'Indeed,' Lenya smiled.

Franckl leaned forward conspiratorially and smiled loathsomely into Lenya's face. He put a hand on her knee. It was still clutching the snorted-on kerchief.

'My dear young pet, I was quite forgetting that such a place would be new to one such as you, a lithe, healthy damsel reared in the free pastures of the country. Hmmm. It must be an overwhelming prospect.'

'I'm looking forward to it,' she said through a gritted smile.

'So young, so brave!'

So eager to get there! thought Lenya. Despite all she had been through, this was an opportunity she relished. To go to the city! To Middenheim! To move in high circles, to advance herself! As it was, she relished the stink Franckl made such a show of loathing. To Lenya, it smelled of nothing more wonderful than the future.

Franckl squeezed her knee.

'Now, you mustn't be afraid, my pet. Middenheim will be frightening to you. So many people, such a great wealth of experiences and... and odours. You must always remember, when it gets too much for you, that you have a stout and true friend to turn to. Are you afraid, Leanna?'

'That's Lenya, actually. No, I'm not.' She tensed her leg under his hand, so he could feel the tight, lean thigh muscles bulge and twist. 'Are you?'

He took his hand away sharply and looked for something else to do. He slapped the pot-boy's head for a start.

Lenya leaned over and pulled back the window drapes on the carriage to peer out. Rain fell outside. The distant perfume of Middenheim was stronger. The escorted caravan was just now clattering onto metalled cobbles from a dirt track. Lenya started back as a White Wolf cantered up alongside her carriage and glanced in at her. His smiling eyes found hers.

'Everything all right, milady?' the darkly handsome Wolf asked, majestic in his gold-edged plate mail and white pelt.

Lenya nodded. What was the Wolf's name? She hunted her memory. Anspach, that was it, Anspach.

'Everything is fine. Where are we?'

Anspach gestured ahead. 'We're just reaching the western viaduct into the city. Another half hour, and we'll be home.'

Lenya leaned out and looked down the cobbled pavement ahead. The long slow slope of the viaduct which led to Middenheim seemed to go on forever. The city itself was invisible in the drizzle.

The household carriage was one of the last in the now bedraggled caravan. The two smarter carriages ahead carried the Margrave and his family,

followed by a series of four or five farm carts. A flatbed, carrying household essentials and covered in oilcloths, brought up the rear.

Franckl suddenly pushed past Lenya and stuck his head out to speak
to the Wolf. Through the drizzle, he got his first glimpse of the city of
Middenheim.

'By Sigmar!' he exclaimed as he caught sight of the vast rock for the first
time. 'Look at it!' he cried. 'It's like a monster rising out of the ground!'
Lenya and one of the chambermaids struggled to get a look too.

Lenya gasped despite herself. It was true. Middenheim was a huge, black
monster. One she was dying to meet.

On a clear day, Middenheim could be seen from miles away, a great black
monolith penetrating the sky. Now, in the thick wet of spring, they came
upon it almost by surprise. The smell of the city grew stronger. The industrial
odours mixed with those of people going about their business, thousands of
people. Smells of food and clothes, house-dust and bodies came together
in the air and drifted into every crevice of the wagon where Lenya sat with
the houseman, the nurse and the rest of the staff.

As they advanced up the titanic western viaduct, the gloom melted
away. With the clouds parting and a huge orange sun setting behind it,
the Fauschlag stood stark and craggy against the gauzy sky. The jutting
rock was indivisible from the great city that grew around its slopes and
rose above it in a series of hard spikes and steeples.

As the convoy neared the city, traffic on the viaduct grew denser and the
low rumble of the noisy city began to separate into a rich weave of individual voices. The caravan's progress was impeded by all manner of vehicles:
hay-wains, wagons, trains of oxen, noble carriages, straggles of pilgrims,
peddlers with handcarts, outrider messengers with miles to go, surly details
of city militia. Motley clad people were leaving the city for their homes on
the outskirts or entering it to ply their trade.

'Keep the caravan tight,' Ganz called to his men and they all moved a little closer in formation. He could see the increasing mass of people ahead.
Some were no doubt trying to sneak in or out of the city, past the guards, for
reasons of their own, and Ganz didn't want any trouble now. They edged
round a milliner's heavily-laden wagon with a broken axle that was imped-
ing the flow. Morgenstern and Aric rode smartly ahead to hold back the
oncoming traffic so that the noble convoy could pass. Morgenstern cursed
at a Sigmarite devotee who tried to interest him in a lead pilgrim's keep-
sake of his god. They pressed on, up the slow curve of the viaduct towards
the snarling city above.

Lenya sat by the window of her carriage and gazed out in awe, breathing it all in. Even when they were forced to run close to the low wall of the
viaduct to pass the broken cart, she did not flinch from the yawning drop
below, the travertine supports of the ancient viaduct which reached away

into the depths of the misty chasm. Franckl glimpsed the drop and fell back into his seat, looking green.

Lenya leaned out further to look ahead. Heavily-laden carts and oxen-rigs made slow progress cheek by jowl with grand vehicles and gilt landaus, urchins banging the wheels with sticks and running away, giggling at their own audacity.

The caravan managed to stay together as dusk fell and a heavy purple sky settled over Middenheim. There were no clouds, and the stars and the rising pair of moons made the forty foot high wood and stone keeps, either side of the city southgate, appear even grander than they would have by daylight.

'Well, we've arrived at last,' Franckl said. As he pointedly pulled closed the window curtain for the last time before entering the city, Lenya saw walls the height of four tall men and three times as thick as a guardsman's torso growing proudly out of the seamless rock face below. The rock had been hewn into a great city wall by hundreds of dwarf masons, but they had done more than tame the rock; they had given it hard lines and a form that only appeared to add strength and longevity to the stones.

Passing through the south gate, there was light once more, the light of thousands of braziers and lamps burning for the folk of Middenheim. A soft yellow glow to light their way and to keep them safe from the city's human parasites, who stalked the unwary to rob them of their possessions or their lives.

Lenya pulled the window drapes open again and pegged them up to let in the light. It let in noise too: the noise of thousands of people hawking their wares, screaming at each other or calling out at them from street corners. And all the smells that had collected and built during the last stage of the journey now came together in a wave that took Lenya's breath away and apparently scorched the hairs in the houseman's nostrils.

'Sigmar save me!' Franckl gasped. 'Too much, too, too much!'

Nothing like enough, thought Lenya.

She looked across at Maris. The wetnurse had almost stopped breathing altogether as she sat huddled in the corner of the wagon.

'I don't think I can bear the noise a minute longer,' she moaned.

'Or the stink,' Franckl added. 'Haven't these heathens heard of latrines?'

'You can't crap in a field when you live on a rock, so you'd better get used to it,' Lenya said, coarse and unsympathetic as she drank in the sights inside the city walls. The caravan was crawling now, thanks to the press of people around them. Lenya was stunned by the relentless grey stone of a myriad disparate buildings. 'This is what they've brought us to and there's no getting out of it now. But it must be nothing new to a travelled man like you, Master Franckl.'

Franckl fell glumly silent.

Others in the Ganmark convoy looked out in wonder. Most of White

Company's charges were new to Middenheim. Some had never seen any city before, much less one so large or so grand. While the Wolves marched them steadily onwards and upwards past the Square of Martials and then the Konigsgarten on their way to the Middenplatz, the eyes of amazed passengers took in the awesome uniformity of barrack buildings and the Parade Square. This was the only truly flat land on the rock, used by the militia for drilling and military parades, but now it was empty, save for the central fountain spitting silvery water up from its heart.

Franckl was the first to catch sight of the Graf's palace itself, their destination.

'By all that's holy!' he exclaimed. 'Did you ever see such a place?'

'I thought you said you had?' Lenya snapped, pushing him aside to get a look.

Maris the wetnurse huddled tighter into her corner. Her hands over her abused ears and a wide kerchief folded and tied around the lower half of her face, she looked like a frightened bandit.

Lenya leaned out of her window to see a series of great stone buildings surrounded by tall, iron railings ending in spear tips, as much for security as for decoration. Beyond the railings, the private quarters were faced with beautiful carvings which softened their lines and bulk, while adding exquisite ornamentation. The tall, scrolled marble pillars made the Graf's home unique among the buildings of Middenheim. No dwarf hand had wrought such decoration. The pillars and facade of the inner palace were the work of legendary artisans, brought in from Tilea and Bretonnia, and sent away again richly rewarded for their efforts.

They passed in through the Great Gate and down the flags of the entrance drive into the yard of the Inner Palace. The caravan came to a halt. Lenya heard Ganz shouting out orders to dismount and stand attendance. She pushed open the carriage door and was down before the houseman could move. The palace yard was wide and cold. She gazed up at the buildings, quite the most beautiful structures she had ever seen, even in her dreams. Franckl almost fell out of the carriage behind her, slapping at the pot-boy's head and sending him after their luggage.

The undercook woke at last and climbed down. The chambermaids cowered together beside the horses. Maris took a long time to emerge.

Lenya saw the Wolf commander with the Margrave, shaking hands, her master effusive and excited. Nearby she saw handsome Anspach and the huge Wolf, Morgenstern, chasing the royal children in play around the yard, whooping and laughing. She saw the old warrior Gruber in quiet conversation with her lady. The tall young knight named Aric appeared behind her, taking Maris by the arm to look after her. Lenya turned again amid the activity, and found Drakken in front of her. He was smiling his sleepy, winning smile.

'I–' she began.

He kissed her.

'I'll look for you later, Krieg,' she finished.

He smiled again, then he was gone and the Wolves were departing under curt orders from their commander.

Pages and servants in pink silk livery were emerging from the palace to take in the Margrave's luggage. They were flanked by others who held torches and lamps. A tall, emaciated man in a regal, black, high-collared jacket and lace choker strode out to meet them all, pacing the ground with a silver-knobbed cane. He wore a white, ringletted and ribboned wig of the latest fashion and his skin was aristocratically powdered white.

'I am Breugal, chamberlain to the Graf,' he said in a strangled, haughty voice. 'Follow me and I will show you to your quarters.'

'Sir, I greet you!' Franckl started, striding forward, hand outstretched to take the chamberlain's. 'As one houseman to another, I rejoice in the welcome you–'

Breugal ignored the hand and turned aside. He jerked his silver-topped cane at his waiting pages. 'Get them inside! The night is chill and I have better things to do.'

The pages scurried forward, snatching up luggage. Franckl remained with his hand outstretched and untaken, amazed.

Lenya felt real sorrow for him then, sorrow and shame. Breugal strode away on clacking high heels, cane-end ticking rhythmically on the flags. Franckl and the undercook picked up their few personal belongings and followed a disdainful page into the palace.

'I shan't stay,' Lenya heard the wetnurse muttering to the Templar, Aric, as he escorted her inside.

Lenya followed them into an inner courtyard. She lifted her eyes to look at the buildings around the small cobbled space. They were shockingly spare, dank and plain compared to the great courtyard, but some of the windows were lit and Lenya could hear people moving around inside, looking out, invisible to her. As she got used to the sounds, she began to pick out voices.

'By Ulric, that old nursemaid won't last five minutes,' she heard a half-broken voice laugh. 'And the old houseman ain't fit for overmuch either,' it continued.

Lenya realised she was alone and began to walk across the courtyard to the open door.

'Look at the poor, lost, little milkmaid,' the voice came again, joined in laughter by another youthful cackle. 'We can share that one if you like... but I get first go!' Lenya picked up her ragged skirts and, scared now, hurried toward the safety of the archway and her travelling companions.

This was Middenheim. Palace life. Not what she had dreamed of. Not at all.

* * *

The first week at the palace was tough enough, but Lenya knew it would get tougher. It was a friendless place. She seldom saw the other servants she had arrived with, and the palace staff treated her like horse flop. Less than horse flop. She found herself craving the company of Franckl or the pot-boy. At least they knew who she was. The palace staff, the haughty ladies, Chamberlain Breugal, even the lowliest of the low, like the grate sweepers and the spit-boy, treated her with utter contempt. And there was a particular page, a rat-arse called Spitz. Spitz was the page that she had heard slurring her when she arrived. She despised him, but he was not her only problem. Endlessly, she found herself lost in the bowels of the palace. No matter what, she still couldn't find her way around. For all its fancy stonework, the palace was a dark labyrinth.

The Margrave and his entourage had been invited, albeit briefly, into the staterooms the evening they arrived. Lenya had been impressed by how grand they were, but soon realised she was unlikely to see them again. The Margrave received little more than political charity from the Graf, and his entire household were second-class citizens taking up space. Their given rooms were damp, and many of them were dark and windowless. They were oddly shaped and unaccommodating and Lenya, who could scout her way successfully across any heavy woodland, still could not find her way from one dingy room to another without becoming hopelessly lost.

At the end of the first miserable week, Maris left. The wetnurse, who had spent the entire time locked away, refusing to eat or drink and virtually unable to perform her natural functions, just upped and left. With the house at Linz completely gone, the nurse still preferred to live in a barn rather than endure the horrors of city life a day longer. She wandered away out of the north gate one nightfall, her bag in her hand.

With the nurse gone, Lenya became the constant companion of Gudrun, the beautiful Lady Margrave, who plunged herself into self-imposed isolation in the palace and dragged Lenya with her. The lowliest servants of the palace saw fit to scold, abuse and beat Lenya for a week or two. But it wasn't long before she was fighting back.

It was mid-afternoon, although Lenya could hardly tell time in the windowless recesses of the palace. She had been sent on an errand to the main kitchen. Returning, cross and spiteful after a particularly prolonged tirade from the larder man, she felt a hand land squarely on her behind, causing her to drop the jug of warm water that she had been sent to beg. Loud laughter behind her made Lenya turn.

'You'll have to beg for another, now!' screeched the barely grown voice of the adolescent page who stood behind her. It was Spitz. He was short and wiry with thin hair, a pallid face and large teeth, and he'd been following Lenya around since he'd seen her standing alone in the courtyard on the night she had arrived. All he wanted from his wretched little life was to become the next Breugal. He was a loathsome creature, full of his own importance, and he took Lenya for an appealing, easy target. Most of the ladies of the house, even the serving women, were completely inaccessible to him, but this was one pretty girl who had no status and, better yet, no defences.

Leering at her, spittle spilling from the corners of his lips, Spitz pushed his hand hard against Lenya's thigh and squeezed.

'Take your filthy hand off me,' Lenya growled. 'Or take the beating of your life!'

Spitz laughed again. 'Who's going to defend your honour then, my little milking cow?' His other hand came to meet the front of her dress, low on her belly.

Lenya's arms came up and under the page's hands, thrusting them off her body. Then she took his greasy head between her hands and held it firmly, as he looked at her in shocked wonder.

'You want me?' Lenya asked sweetly and then pushed his head down as hard as she could. She folded the page in half, cupping her forearm under his neck and lifting him into a tight stranglehold. Then she thrust his head between her skirt knees, squeezing until his face went a greyish puce and he passed out. She let go, dropping him to the floor. She made a wiping motion with her hands and began to walk away.

She turned to the slumped body as the page began to come round, clutching his head.

'That's the last time *any* of you touches me,' she said.

Those first weeks that Lenya spent at the palace felt like months. No, like an eternity. Lenya was not given to sentiment; she only knew that life in the country had been better than this, but she suspected that the city could be better than anything. Unfortunately, the Lady Margrave had decided that Middenheim was far too dangerous a place for any of her servants to explore unescorted, and with no friends in the palace and enough enemies among the staff to last her a lifetime, Lenya's opportunities for recreation were limited.

One afternoon, she stood with her elbows on the wall of a balcony, her hands under her chin, looking again at the view, as she remembered events of the last month and tried to put them behind her. From her vantage point Lenya could see clear across Middenheim. She could hear the buzz of a thousand voices, accented with the louder cries of a multitude of street traders. She could see down into the wider streets and avenues in the north of the city. South and east the streets became narrow in a tightly packed grey maze that she could never follow. In some places the roofs were so close together that all she could see was a narrow strip of darkness. She could only guess at what might happen in those dark, grimy, intimate places. She knew there were thieves and beggars and people of strange races, and she knew that her only hope of some kind of happiness was to escape into that city and become part of it.

Lenya had her back to the balcony door and did not hear the footsteps coming up behind her. She didn't know she had company until a pair of thick, solid hands came over her head to cover her eyes. With the shift in her light, Lenya swung round, one tight, hard fist jabbing into the silhouette of a face right behind her.

'Lenya! Ow!' Drakken cried. 'It's me.'

'Krieg! Gods, never surprise me!'

'Rest assured, I won't,' Drakken replied, wiping his bloodied nose against his sleeve. 'Jaws of Ulric, it was supposed to be a nice surprise.' He looked meekly down at the tiny, fearsome, tight little woman who sometimes cradled his heart and once or twice had bloodied his face.

'Call yourself a Wolf?' she snarled at him, watching his heart sink in his eyes. Then, hating herself for hurting him, she repented. 'I'm sorry, Krieg,' she said. 'It's just... I need to get out of here!'

'So let me take you for a walk in the Konigsgarten.'

The safety of the formal garden close to the palace was not quite what Lenya had in mind. She had taken numerous walks there with Drakken. He was a White Wolf, of course, and she had seen his bravery in battle. She wished he would be strong like that with her. Instead he was as strong as dishwater, as passionate as the well-laid, over-clipped, mossy pathways of the Konigsgarten. Oh yes, there were trees and grass and flowers, but they were forced to grow where few plants would choose to grow naturally. The rock yielded only lichens and tiny faded rock-plants. There was no soil. To Lenya, there was no nature in the garden, the plants were either forced or non-existent, and green was supplied by mosses rather than grass and twisted, stunted trees that could find nowhere to root and consequently grew only sparse dark leaves or brittle needles. There was as much spontaneity and liberty in those tight clumps of faded petals and blocks of spongy moss as there was in Lenya's life. And she hated it. She sighed.

'Not today,' she said. 'Go and wipe your nose – and stop being such a lap dog!'

Drakken turned away, hurt and puzzled.

Lenya listened to his footsteps retreating in the quiet. She looked out towards the uniform grey of the buildings of Middenheim, and then turned fast on her heels. Fearing he was gone, she called Drakken's name.

'Krieg? Krieg!' She could see him before she heard his footfall. 'You could take me out!' she said. The idea suddenly felt real to her and she smiled at him. 'Wolf Drakken,' she began again, 'would you do me the honour of escorting me into the city?'

Her smile made his heart tumble all over again. Nobody had ordered him not to take Lenya out of the palace and grounds, yet he knew that the Lady Margrave insisted Lenya be close at hand at all times.

'Lenya,' he began, hating himself for disappointing her. He could see it in her face now, a mixture of petulance and defiance and a kind of bravado. A face he could love, but feared he might never understand.

'Don't tell me,' she said. 'I know. The Lady Margrave *wouldn't approve*.' That last she said in a haughty, crabby voice that, to herself at least, exactly mimicked her ladyship. 'Then I shall go alone!' she insisted, spinning on her heels and folding her arms. Lenya had developed the skill of flouncing by practising on her father. He had sired a series of strong, lively boys before producing his only, cherished daughter. She wondered if perhaps she'd gone too far with Drakken, given him the chance to see through her little tantrum. Drakken could at least get her out of the palace.

'All right,' Drakken said, quietly. Then, realising the opportunity to escort and protect and be alone with this wonderful girl, he brightened. 'Lenya, I'd be proud to escort you into the great city of Middenheim,' he said and her broad, bewitching smile quenched any last doubts he had as to the wisdom of the venture.

Drakken and Lenya left the palace grounds without incident. Those Panther guards who recognised the young Wolf of White Company acknowledged them with a nod; those who did not merely allowed the short, powerful man in uniform and his tiny companion to pass unmolested. Drakken was proud of Lenya and she of him, although their relationship caused constant comment amongst the staff at the palace and no small amount of envy in the unmarried women there.

Drakken decided he first wanted to show Lenya his spiritual home, the Temple of Ulric.

'I've had quite enough of grey rock buildings and cold, dead places,' Lenya complained. 'I want to see people! Life! Excitement! There must be somewhere in the city where people go for their leisure, away from the dark streets and grey houses. There must be life here somewhere.'

Drakken grabbed Lenya's hand in his great paw and hurried her away, south, down a steep avenue of grand houses. They were weaving in and out of the throngs of people that Lenya had been watching from above for the past month. This was more like it.

'So, where are you taking me?' Lenya asked.

'To the Black Pool, a famous landmark,' Drakken answered. 'And if we take this road, I can still show you the Temple.'

Lenya was not pleased. She did not want to see a temple at all and the Black Pool didn't sound very lively either, but Drakken had grasped her hand so tightly and seemed so excited that there was nothing left for her to say. As they hurried down the avenue, tripping up and down short flights of steps and around steep slopes, Lenya tried to look about her at the rich houses, and the merchants and gentlemen and women who were visiting them. For so long she had seen nothing of the city and now she was being whisked through it too fast for her to take any of it in.

They turned a corner. Ahead, she caught sight of a tall, slender building and wanted to ask what it was. Drakken said something she couldn't hear and bustled her onwards.

Enough, she thought. She picked up just enough speed to come level with Drakken and jabbed her foot in front of his, an old trick she'd developed for use on her brothers. The Wolf lunged forward, arms splaying, his feet feeling for the stone pavement. Two, three mid-air steps and he managed to level his head, which he felt sure would plunge into the slabs and knock him unconscious in an instant. He found his feet and straightened. Behind him, Lenya had her hand to her face, ready for horror or hilarity, depending on the outcome of her lover's trip. As he turned, red in the face, she giggled.

'Let's slow down before we have an accident, shall we?'

Grudgingly, Drakken began a slower guided tour. Lenya caught sight of a mass of people congregating behind the low wall across the street. She could hear snippets of conversation and the low buzz that signalled excitement.

'What's that?' she asked.

'The Great Park,' he replied.

'Can we get in there? I want to see.'

'There's no gate nearby. We'll follow the ring around.'

They went on, but Lenya glanced at the activity over the park wall at regular intervals. There were people here; maybe some of them would be her kind of people. She might even begin her search, the secret purpose she had kept from everyone. At the very least she could be herself. At the palace she was invisible to the gentry and despised by the servants.

Drakken led Lenya around the Garten Ring, towards the nearest park gate. He was happy enough to do this because the route naturally took them past the Temple of Ulric, his place of worship, and also, since it housed the barracks of the White Wolves, his home. He looked at the massive structure with proud eyes.

'What do you think?' he asked. She didn't answer. He looked round to find her striding on without him for an entrance to the park.

Drakken cursed. He was about to run after her when a voice called out from the Temple atrium. It was Ganz, his commander. Drakken was torn. He couldn't ignore his commander's summons, but Lenya was almost lost in the crowds of the Garten Ring already.

'Wait there!' he yelled to Lenya. 'I'll only be a moment! Wait!' He wasn't sure if she'd heard him. Ganz called him again.

Lenya was so taken with the hubbub of the street-life, she didn't really concern herself with Drakken's absence He'd catch up, she thought. She hunted for an entrance to the park.

Following the Garten Ring, south, down more steep and winding paths, Lenya quickly found the west gate into the Great Park. The gate, swung open on its posts, was made of that same dark timber used everywhere in Middenheim, and the walls were cut from the same grey rock, but what beckoned from within seemed more alive than anything she'd ever seen.

Lenya raised her head slightly as she passed a soldier from the City Watch at the gate. Dressed, as she was, in borrowed finery, the lady-in-waiting's cast-offs that her mistress had insisted she wear, she had some vestige of confidence. But the country girl within her made Lenya certain she would have to endure some quizzing at the hands of this authority figure and she wanted to make herself look as important as possible. She had nothing to fear. The Watchman merely nodded a slight bow in her direction, before going about his business.

The Great Park wasn't a park at all. It was a labyrinth of paths which wound between a ragged collection of stalls; open carts with burners selling hot snacks, which smelled of rancid grease, and tall, narrow stands with racks of foodstuffs, old clothes and household goods. Loud men waved their arms, demonstrating wares that they sold suspiciously cheaply and in huge numbers.

Lenya was mesmerised. There were people everywhere: buyers, sellers, browsers, barterers, families, couples, household staff from noble homes on provisioning errands, urchins dashed between adult legs causing their own particular brand of chaos. Lenya forgot that she was alone and began to walk around, listening to snippets of conversation, examining the goods for sale and taking it all in. She had never seen so many people in one place, clad in so many styles of dress, nor heard so many different dialects. Ahead of her a noisy crowd was gathering around a narrow handcart. She could just see the top of the tousled straw-coloured head which belonged to the man standing on the cart.

'Miladies and gentlemen!' bawled the voice, sing-song. 'Don't just stand there gawping – put your hands in your pockets for this once-in-a-lifetime purchasing opportunity!' A pair of long arms flailed above the tousled head and Lenya saw a huge showman's grimace. The crowd laughed, heckled and some began to move away. Lenya smiled to herself, pushing in to get a better look.

She felt a movement behind her rather than heard it and was only mildly surprised when she felt the brush of a hand against the side of her waist. She'd been expecting lightfooted Drakken to catch up with her sooner or later, though she'd warned him not to surprise her. His mistake. She didn't think twice: she rammed her elbow hard behind her, following it with a straight forearm and balled fist. It wouldn't hurt Drakken, not a big tough Wolf in armour like him. But instead of connecting with the broad solid torso of the White Wolf, Lenya's elbow and then her fist connected with a soft, bony, unfamiliar target.

'Whhooff!' a small voice choked from behind her. Lenya heard a slight body fall heavily. The crowd around her fell silent and began to turn in the direction of the sound. Lenya felt a dozen pairs of eyes on her as she turned to look at what or whom she'd hit.

Sitting on the ground behind her, clutching at his stomach, legs splayed out to either side, was a gangly young man, tidily dressed with flat black hair and a wounded expression. He was all arms and legs and Lenya had to step over one protruding knee to take a good look at him.

'By all that's wise!' she exclaimed. 'What have I done?'

The crowd returned their gaze to the salesman, who'd begun his banter again, dismissing the sort of scene they saw every day in the city. The man on the ground looked quizzically at Lenya and then let out a huge, bellowing laugh.

'I'm terribly sorry, sir!' breathed a stunned Lenya, grasping the youth by the elbow and trying to help him to his feet. He laughed again.

'Don't worry,' he answered. 'Truth is, I was due a rousting anytime about now. Just caught me unawares that's all.' He clutched his stomach again as he tried to laugh through the ache that Lenya had planted there with her tight fist. His humour was infectious and Lenya began to laugh with him, not knowing what he was laughing at, but enjoying the freedom. She hadn't laughed properly out loud in weeks.

Back on his feet, the young man gently took Lenya's arm and led her to a narrow set of winding steps with tall walls either side. She felt no apprehension. When they were alone, he began to talk to her.

'So, what's a country girl like you doing walking around in city finery?'

'And what's a city boy like you doing grabbing at young ladies in public?'

'Touché,' the youth answered, bellowing his startling laugh once more.

The pair sat on the stone steps, aware only of each other and the hum of the crowd that spilled over the walls surrounding them. For the second time, an opportunistic young man had seen Lenya as an easy target. This time the man had been after her purse.

The gangly youth with the flat hair introduced himself as Arkady, petty villain, pick-pocket and general scammer. He had no reason not to be honest. He might not be quite what he seemed, but then neither was this milkmaid dressed in all the finery of court. He'd expected the rich purse of a dolt who wouldn't even notice it was missing until she tried to pay for something, and when she found her money gone would probably have a swooning fit. Instead he had got an elbow in the stomach and a fist in the solar plexus and serve him right.

Lenya found herself telling him about the farm near Linz where she'd been raised, about her brothers – and how she'd come to Middenheim. She spoke of the revolting page and the dark damp rooms she was forced to live in. She talked of the palace, but not how she had come to be at liberty in the Great Park. She was talking to a criminal after all and didn't want to confuse things by telling him about her White Wolf. She had another thing to talk about. Her secret.

'My brother came here,' she said, finally. 'It must have been a year ago now. Came to make his fortune. I never thought I'd reach Middenheim, but now I'm here, I want to find him.'

'In a city this size?' Arkady laughed again – then stopped abruptly, realising this wasn't funny to the naïve but feisty country girl. 'Look, if he came from the country,' he began, 'he's probably back in the country by now.'

'And if not?' Lenya asked.

Arkady looked at his scuffed shoes. He didn't want to hurt the girl, but she had to know the facts of life. 'If he's still here, he's probably joined one of the less... recognised guilds. One of the local lords of the underworld may have recruited him to "run errands".'

Lenya looked dismayed. 'He's honest! He'd find honest work first!'

Arkady snorted. 'There's no honest work in Middenheim for outsiders. The roads aren't paved with gold and the guilds have business tied up tighter than a houseman's codpiece. It's all nepotism and dead men's shoes. Why else do you think there's so much "free enterprise" in Middenheim? Yon market trader on his handcart – the mouthy sod with the straw hair – shunts carts in and out of the city every week. Most of them are hijacked somewhere on the other side of the wall...' Arkady's story tailed off.

'So my brother's a criminal?' asked an indignant Lenya.

Or *dead*, Arkady thought, but instead said, 'He's probably back in the country by now.'

Lenya thought for a moment, then took a deep breath. 'If he's here, I still want to find him,' she said, determined. 'Where do I find one of these "lords" to talk to? Someone has to know where he is.'

Arkady was doubtful. This girl hadn't been anywhere except the palace and this was her first visit to the streets. She knew nothing yet of the filth, squalor, and poverty, not to mention the ruthlessness of the people who populated the poorer quarters of the city. On the other hand, she had taken him out single-handed with her elbow and one puny fist when she shouldn't even have heard him.

'You're going to take me to one of these knowledgeable gentlemen!' she told him fiercely, seeing the reluctance in his open face.

'Whoa! No way! Look, there are better methods. I know someone, a rogue, but with a good heart. I'm small beans, girl... I don't have contact with any of the "Low Kings". Too dangerous for a sprat like me. But he does. He carries a little more weight. And you'll be safe with him. He'll look after you and he just might be able to find something out about that long-lost brother of yours.'

Arkady got ready to leave. 'Meet me here, day after tomorrow. Can you find this place again?'

'I think so,' Lenya answered. 'But can't you take me now?'

Arkady looked over the wall. The sky was darkening to its familiar purple hue and the Great Park was becoming quieter. He was safe enough, but Lenya wouldn't be safe for long in this place at this hour of the day.

'It's late. You might be missed. Go home, girl, straight home. Come and find me the day after tomorrow.' And with that he started to jog down the steps two at a time. In half a dozen steps he had turned a corner. Lenya watched the top of his head bobbing up and down above the height of the wall and in a few more seconds he was gone. She stood and looked around her. It was getting dark, but she could find her way back. Then she remembered Drakken.

'Sigmar! Krieg!' she exclaimed under her breath and hurried up the steps and around the wall. She'd just have to find her way back to his beloved temple and hope he was still there.

Night fell fast in Middenheim and by the time Lenya retraced her way to the great Temple of Ulric, it was dusk and the yellow evening lamps of the city were being lit. Cross at herself and at Drakken, she paced about outside the Temple for a few minutes and was ready to find her own way back to the palace when she realised just how difficult that might be.

Lenya was not known at the palace, not by anyone outside the Margrave's entourage or the domestic staff. If she tried to enter the palace grounds at any time, let alone at nightfall, she would receive short shrift from the guard. Her day's adventure was fast wearing thin. Now she realised she had to find Drakken if she was to return to the palace at all tonight. She had no very strong desire to go back to the foetid rooms she was required to call home, at least for now, but she also had no choice. Arkady had gone and she was alone in a city that, while it enthralled her, began to look sinister in the low meagre light. Silhouettes of buildings around her loomed black, hard and spiky against the sky. Pools of yellow light gave the grey stones a sickly colour. The stones seemed to absorb light, sucking it into their surfaces and draining it to small, murky pools. Shadows were long and forbidding and seemed to bear no relations to their owners. Darkness masked the uneven ground beneath Lenya's feet, making steps and slopes even more treacherous than they were by day.

Don't panic! Lenya told herself. *This is Drakken's home, he must be here. And if he isn't someone will be.*

Lenya was ready to knock on the great door of the Temple and even open it if needs be. She threw back her shoulders and lifted her fist. Putting what she hoped was a confident smile on her lips, she knocked on the door. There was no answer.

Lenya squared up to the door again and then jumped wholesale out of her skin when she heard the voice behind her.

'Can I help you, my lady?' asked the voice. A voice full of confidence and ease mixed with authority and power. Lenya turned slowly and stared at the man behind her, seeing only as high as his slender, powerful chest. She didn't need to answer.

'What are you doing out of the palace precinct?' Gruber asked as he recognised the brave farm girl from the Margrave's entourage. 'This won't do. I'll escort you back. If young Drakken knew you were missing, he'd be sending out a search party.'

Lenya lifted her eyes slowly to meet the concerned look of the veteran soldier. Drakken did know she was missing. He'd never take her out again. She wanted to cry with anger and frustration. She'd be locked up in the palace for good now.

Back in the comparative safety of the palace, Lenya spent a day and night working out what to do. She thought about her next meeting with Arkady as she bathed in cold water from the dish on her bed-stand that grew mould overnight. She thought about it as she tended her pale, frightened mistress in the sloping, windowless room that she never left; and she thought about it as she ate the cold leftovers, congealed on grubby plates, that had become the chief part of her diet.

She was grateful that Drakken had decided to keep away. He wouldn't take her out again and she didn't want to hear about how worried he was and how concerned he had been for her safety. She could rely on herself and she wouldn't have anyone suggesting otherwise.

Gruber had treated her well and kindly. Returning her to the palace via one of the more discreet side-gates, he had stopped and spoken to men from the City Watch on duty there. He introduced her to them as a girl under the direct protection of the Temple. The sentries nodded solemnly. None of them wished to get on the wrong side of the White Wolves. Now there were several of the gate guards who would recognise her if she needed them to. If any of these men were on duty, she could get in or out of the palace grounds without any trouble. If not it was a short walk to the Temple and she guessed that if Gruber had recognised her so easily then others would too. She would never be short of a trusty escort back to the palace.

Two days later therefore, Lenya left the Graf's palace, walked south towards the Great Park and found again the entrance she had used before. It was around the same time of day and the place was thronged with people again. The rocky paths were slick with the light rain and when clumps of people diverted her path onto the mossy terraces, the dark, spongy surface was almost greasy underfoot. She kept her eye on the milling people, but they all had business of their own to attend to and ignored her. She was also wary of the rougher-looking element and even crossed one path and joined another to avoid a bawdily drunken clutch of youths ready to leer at anything in a skirt.

It took her two or three attempts to find the flight of narrow steps where she had sat with Arkady only days before, and when she did find them she stumbled upon them by accident. She sat three or four steps down from the top, out of sight. After half an hour or so, Lenya began to wonder if they were the right steps after all. Then, suddenly, she looked up sharply, without knowing why. She hadn't heard anything new above the hum of the crowd, but as she fixed her gaze she caught sight of a head with flat black hair and stood, sighing with relief, to greet Arkady.

He came within a few steps of her, keeping low so as not to be seen over the wall, and beckoned her to follow him. As the steps led downward, turning sharply left and right as they went, Lenya realised why they had not encountered anyone else on the staircase. As they dropped steeper and narrower, the walls rose higher around them, becoming a low arch that dripped slightly with the thick black liquid of rotting vegetation. The steps went from being damp to being dark and wet and covered in old, slippery moss. The hem of Lenya's dress became heavy with brackish water and her tall boots began to leak.

She stopped. 'Where are we going?' she asked, apprehensive for the first time. She was with a complete stranger. Trusting him with her life in a strange city and he seemed to be leading her underground into silence and darkness.

He caught the tone in her voice. 'Trust me,' he said, and laughed. 'Honestly, it's all right. See, no one uses the old stairs much anymore, but they're safe and they'll get us to where we want to be.'

She looked at him in the gloom. 'Soon,' he said. 'I promise.'

Within a matter of minutes, the steps came to an abrupt end and Lenya followed Arkady across a tiny closed courtyard where facing roofs almost touched overhead. From there, she entered the back room of what she thought must be a private home, but was, in fact, one of the many one-room drinking holes that littered the alleys of the south-east corner of Middenheim.

'Now!' Arkady exclaimed. 'What in all the gods' names are we going to do about that awful garb?'

Lenya looked down at her dress. She'd never liked it and she already knew she couldn't wear it and walk safely through this district of the city. She needed no more than her instincts to tell her that.

'Can you get me a pair of breeches and a knife?' she asked Arkady, tugging at her dress sleeves. He looked at her, puzzled, then handed her the short knife he kept in the back of his own breeches. She had not noticed it before.

'I'll be back with the other in a moment,' he said, turning and leaving the way they had come.

Lenya took the knife and cut the sleeves off her dress at the armhole, showing the plain sleeves of her shift underneath. Then she cut the bottom four inches from her skirt; they were sodden now and smelled of standing water. Tossing the cloth into the fire, along with her petticoats,

Lenya had another idea. She poked the dwindling black log on the grate until it flared and spat ashes through the grill. She spread the ashes with a twisted shovel from the hearth and rubbed them into her hands. Then she massaged the soot into the bodice of her dress and began on the panels of her skirt. When Arkady returned she was well on her way to looking like a common woman. He held out the breeches to her.

Lenya turned her back and cut right through the front of her skirt, from a little below the waist right down to the hem. Then she cut several inches from the bottom of the breeches and put them on. She turned to Arkady and held her hands up in a dramatic gesture, waiting for his approval. He smiled and reached out to her hair, which he tousled mercilessly until it sat in a lopsided mass on her head, dripping down onto her brow and neck. He stepped back and bellowed his great laugh.

'Almost there,' he said. 'See, those milkmaid arms are a dead give away, but I think I've got just the thing.' Ducking out again, Arkady returned a moment later with a short, battered leather jerkin. It belonged to the pot-boy and Arkady had whipped it off the hook behind the door. He held it open for Lenya to shrug into. It fit well enough, and completed her reinvention. Lenya could pass anonymously through the darker streets of the city now, could pass for anyone or no one. She was ready to meet this rogue that Arkady was so proud of knowing.

Kruza sat hunched over a pot of ale in the single public room of the seedy establishment that incongruously called itself a tavern. He was partial to a pot of ale, but this weak, rancid mixture was turning his stomach and he belched loudly as Arkady and Lenya entered through the pot-door behind the plank-and-barrel structure which served for a bar. Arkady laughed his trademark laugh and Kruza lifted his head without any movement in his sloping shoulders.

Seeing the small, comely girl in clothes that were coming apart along several promising seams, Kruza straightened up. He smartened the front of his jerkin self-consciously and smiled.

'I thought you were bringing some rough and tumble farm girl!' he murmured to Arkady. 'This creature doesn't look like she belongs anywhere near a cow.'

'Wait till she opens her mouth,' Arkady grinned and Lenya, gritting her teeth, kicked him hard in the shin. 'I guess I'll leave you to it then,' he said, winking at the girl before retreating out of the door behind him.

Lenya sat next to Kruza, searching his green eyes for anything that might help her understand why she felt so drawn to him. Something there made her a little afraid and then he smiled again and her body relaxed.

'Arkady tells me you're looking for someone,' Kruza began.

'My brother, Stefan. Older than me by two years. A little taller. Fair-haired. Eyes like mine. He left Linz for Middenheim a year ago. Arkady said he was probably working as an errand boy for one of the... what did he call them? Low Kings?'

'More likely dead,' said Kruza, looking down into the fuzzy ale that he was never going to drink. 'And if he isn't, there must be a thousand men in Middenheim who fit his description.'

'But there's only one Stefan!' Lenya exclaimed. 'If you won't help, then I'll find these Low Kings for myself.'

Kruza looked again at the girl. Arkady had told him how she had fought him off in the market, but she didn't look nearly as tough as she talked. And he was sure she didn't have the money to pay him for his services. He sighed.

'Very well,' he said, 'I'll help you. But we're not going to the Low Kings. The last thing you want to do is tangle with men like Bleyden. We begin with the priest.'

Lenya was ready to protest. What use was a priest to her? But Kruza had already taken her hand and before she knew where she was, they had left the tavern and begun to walk along the narrow, dim and filthy street. This, she guessed, was the Altquartier, the roughest, poorest, most depraved part of the city. Lenya had only seen it at a distance, from her balcony in the palace. The narrow, winding thoroughfares were full of bustling, dirty people. Women shrieked at barefoot urchins and threw their waste indiscriminately onto the streets. There was almost no light: the sky was a series of thin, grey, jagged stripes above her, largely blocked out by the low roofs of leaning buildings. Ragged dogs growled and barked and slunk away when kicked by the indolent men who sat on narrow steps on the street. There was no order here, only bad smells, bad light and too much noise. Lenya stayed close to Kruza, as they became invisible among the ragged people of the slums.

Lenya soon realised she couldn't remember where she had come from. Her sense of direction was utterly blind down here. This was the steepest part of Middenheim, with more twists and turns and more slopes and steps. Alleys seemed to end in front of her and then would shift in a new, unseen direction at the last minute. She felt like she was in a maze with no clear way out, yet she knew the palace lay only a few minutes' walk away.

They hurried through the rat-runs of the Old Quarter for several minutes before Kruza began to slow down. Then he came to a stop, leaning against a wall and putting his fingers to his lips, suggesting to Lenya that she follow suit, although she felt that this would only draw attention to them. The alleys and byways of this part of Middenheim were by no means deserted. Several seconds later and Lenya began to feel bored and fidgety, until she realised that there was something going on and began to listen to the voices beyond the wall.

'Hans, oh my poor Hans!' a woman wailed, obviously deeply distressed.

A low voice, indistinct, some snuffles. Then, 'Don't touch him! Don't touch him!' The wail turned to a shriek.

The calm, low voice answered, seeming to cajole the fretful woman, but concentrate as she did, Lenya could not hear his words, only his soothing, monotone.

Kruza turned and beamed at Lenya. 'That's our man,' he said, satisfied, and Lenya began to peel her back off the mossy damp wall. But Kruza made no move, so she settled back impatiently against the wall. She watched for a sign from her guide. For the second time in one day, she was putting herself in the hands of a complete stranger.

Waiting, she looked about her, but the alleyway had drained of people. She watched fascinated as a rat worked its way through a miserable and spreading pile of detritus. Pickings were slim in these parts. They smashed bones for the marrow and then crushed the bones to thicken their soups. Here, people ate the whole fruit – pips, cores, skins and all – and the same with vegetables. And when people in this quarter ate meat, they ate the whole animal, saving blood for sausages and chewing the gristles and sinews until they were soft enough to swallow. The only waste here was human waste. The people here were ragged-looking creatures with missing hair and teeth. The scrawny, balding rat with only half its share of fangs reminded Lenya of the people. Feeling something between pathos and horror, she realised just how low the inhabitants of the Altquartier had been brought. Rats prospered everywhere – but here even the rats struggled to survive.

When the voices from the other side of the wall began to subside and people began to trickle back into the alleyway, Kruza made his move. Taking two steps he turned to look at Lenya and watched her for a moment watching the rat. Then he took her by the wrist and led her out into the tiny courtyard beyond the wall. A narrow handcart with an awkward wheel was being pulled out of the courtyard by two men dressed in drab, full-length cloth capes. A third man stood for a moment, as if in contemplation, and then followed. As the handcart swung hard round a corner Lenya saw its cargo roll and sway before a hand fell from beneath the old weatherproof skin that covered it. She tugged at Kruza's sleeve.

'There's a body on that cart!' she exclaimed in horror and surprise.

'We had to wait for it to leave,' Kruza explained 'before we could speak to the priest. He has work to do and a little respect for the dead is always welcome.' Lenya wanted to ask more questions. She did not understand what was going on and she didn't like it.

Kruza and Lenya followed the men for two or three more streets, by which time the cart with its gruesome cargo had pulled away from the man that Lenya had supposed to be the third member of the party. She was relieved to see the handcart disappear out of sight as Kruza stepped up to speak to the fellow.

The man turned, a benign, almost vacant look on his face. She didn't know what she had expected, but it was not the elderly, haggard gentleman that she now beheld.

'A word, sir, if we may,' Kruza started. 'My companion is looking for a relation in the city... We hope you won't be able to help us, but...'

'I hope so too,' the man answered in his calm tones. 'Come, we will sit and talk. If the news is bad it should not be given in the street.'

Lenya and Kruza followed the man, Lenya pulling Kruza a few steps behind.

'Who is he?' hissed Lenya. 'What bad news?'

'He is a priest of Morr,' Kruza answered. 'He deals with the dead of Middenheim and sometimes uncovers their secrets.'

'And if Stefan is not dead?' Lenya asked in a panicked whisper.

'If Stefan is not dead then the priest of Morr will not know him.' With that Kruza quickened his step to catch up with the priest as he entered a hostelry a few streets north of the courtyard where the man Hans had died.

Kruza had missed his afternoon pot of ale and gladly furnished himself and his companions with a rather better class of beverage than had been available so far that day.

'And what is your brother's name?' the priest asked as Kruza returned from the barrel.

'Stefan Dunst. He left the country over a year ago. I haven't heard of him since,' Lenya replied.

'I have attended no one of that name,' the priest answered. 'Describe him to me.'

'He was small for a man,' Lenya said, her voice shaking slightly. She cleared her throat. 'Short and slender, but strong. His skin and hair were very fair, his eyes were pale grey and large, like mine.'

'And perhaps they still are,' said the priest. 'I have not attended any soul of that description whose name I did not know.'

Lenya relaxed with relief. 'Are you sure?' she asked.

'Quite sure,' the priest said as he stood, and left without another word. His glass of ale stood untouched on the table.

'Well, that's that!' Kruza exclaimed, draining his glass of ale and smacking his lips. But Lenya was not going to be put off.

'Not quite,' she said. 'He's alive. Now all we have to do is find him. And I think you know what that means.'

Kruza knew exactly what it meant and he didn't like it. He was just like a great many petty thieves and con-men in the city, perhaps a little more successful than most, but really just the same. Kruza worked for someone. He took fewer orders than the bulk of the low-grade parasites that worked in the city, he wasn't quite the errand boy that most of them were. And he commanded at least some respect; after all, he was useful. But the bottom line was that Kruza had a boss. It went with the territory.

And that territory was his and not a safe place for a girl like Lenya.

'There's nothing more we can do today,' Kruza said as he looked at Lenya. 'It will be getting dark soon and you should get back to the palace.'

'But you said you'd help me!' Lenya yelped.

'I can help you again another day,' Kruza said, trying hard to put the girl off.

'No!' Lenya said, her tone urgent. 'Today!'

'Besides,' she changed her tack, 'I can't go back to the palace until I can find something decent to wear. You don't think I arrived in the Altquartier dressed like this, do you?'

Lenya found herself caught in a cleft stick again. The last time she had ventured into the city she had almost got herself locked out of the palace and this time the change in her appearance would exclude her for certain. Or, at the very least, someone would want to know why she looked so dreadful. What had happened to her? Who had attacked her? Questions that she was not ready to face today, or any other day for that matter. Ruining her clothes had seemed like a good idea at the time, the only sensible thing to do. Now Lenya was horrified at the prospect of returning to the palace in such a sorry state of dress.

'I'm perfectly attired for street life in this city, especially after dark,' she said. 'What better opportunity will I have to find my brother?'

Kruza wanted to laugh, partly because she was right, but more because she was standing with her feet apart and her hands on her hips, looking for all the world like a cross between a common tart and a female street-brawler. Her tone was as demanding and petulant as a dissatisfied new bride's. Taken all in all, this particular picture of Lenya was too persuasive to deny. Kruza decided he would simply have to look after her.

'All right,' he said, 'we'll try. But, I make no promises and I know a fine seamstress, who will provide you with a new suit of clothes before the night is out. And when she does, you will return to the palace.'

Lenya grinned. 'Good!' she said. 'Let's get started.'

'Not yet,' Kruza said holding her arm and gently drawing her back into her seat. 'First we must eat and there are things you need to know about the people we will be meeting tonight.' Kruza waved at the woman who sat on a stool beside the barrel, smoking a clay pipe with a long stem. Lenya felt like she was being fobbed off, but she didn't mind. She suddenly realised how hungry she was.

The sullen woman, the pipe still hanging between her lips, brought them a meal of fatty, meatless chops, black bread and preserved cabbage. While they ate, Kruza talked about the Low Kings and, in particular, his own boss, although for now he remained nameless.

'The Low Kings are aptly named. The monarchs of the underworld, the absolute rulers of the streets. Some are the lowest of the low: users, parasites, loan sharks. They run all the organised crime in this city and almost all cut-purses, scammers and petty thieves owe some allegiance to the lords of the dark. And only a handful of these Low Kings run the city of Midden-heim. The Graf thinks he runs the city, so do the guilds. But the men who run the real city, the men who control the streets, run the whores, traf-fic drugs, fund the gaming houses, are very few. They hide behind their thugs and streetwalkers, and use bumpkins and out of city runaways as cannon-fodder. They never get caught and anyone who works for them in any capacity is dispensable. Do you understand?'

Kruza looked at Lenya, noting her expression. *She's scared*, he thought. *Good!*

The Altquartier didn't look quite so awful in the semi-darkness that awaited Lenya and Kruza as they left the tavern. The pale yellow-grey light was incapable of picking up the worst details of street-life and the small braziers which stood on innumerable street corners dissipated some of the smells that gathered in the damp warmth of the daylight hours. The narrow alleys were still full of people, but they seemed less harried in the gloom. Or perhaps Lenya was simply getting used to the environment.

The two of them walked together, without hurry, down a series of streets and alleys, turning this way and that. Then Kruza stopped and turned to her.

'Do you know where you are?' he asked Lenya.

'No,' she said. 'This place is a worse labyrinth than the palace.'

Good, thought Kruza again. He didn't want her to be able to find her own way here if she should be dissatisfied with his efforts at finding her brother.

The dark was almost complete when Kruza led Lenya into the West Weg. Crowds of people were collecting and she could hear the beating of drums and raucous pipe music pounding through the air. Turning a corner, the crowds now gathering in force and laughing and screeching with antici-pated pleasure, Lenya looked up for the first time, her mouth falling open in wonder.

The building in front of her stood out like a squat stone drum, squeezed between lopsided buildings, its belly spilling out into the street as though it were pushing outward from its jostling companions. Large braziers out-side the building sent long, flickering shadows and tall bright flames up the sides of the building, giving the impression that it was throbbing. Above the cries of the crowds pushing to get into the building, Lenya could hear other sounds, like animals in cages being poked and tormented. Faint roars of frustration and fear rose to her ears.

Kruza was impatient to move on and drew Lenya away from the crowd as more people came up, pressing behind them.

'What is this place?' she asked, having to shout above the fast increas-ing volume of the crowds.

'This is the Baiting Pit,' Kruza said with a tone that sounded a little like disdain or maybe resignation.

'Why are we here?' Lenya asked.

'You wanted access to one of the Low Kings of Middenheim. The man who runs this place, and others like it, knows more about the criminal workings of Middenheim than any other man I know or have heard of. He should do: he's the greatest, most successful, perhaps I should say lowest of the Low Kings.'

The quality of Kruza's voice made Lenya anxious. She had been so sure that she wanted to meet this man, so sure that he could help her find Stefan. But Kruza was obviously afraid of him, and looked and sounded like he would rather be anywhere than here.

'I couldn't bring you here by daylight,' Kruza said carefully, 'Too dangerous with only the boss and his henchmen around. We're safer now with the crowds and noise. If anything happens to upset or disturb you, anything at all, get in among the crowd, sit out the show and then leave with them. And when you leave, find someone safe to stay near. A city guard even, if you have to.'

'If we have to go in there, why aren't we going in with the crowd?' Lenya asked.

'There's another way in. Bleyden runs this place, I know my way around.'

'Bleyden?' Lenya asked. 'How do you know him?

'I work for him,' Kruza answered, something like shame in his voice.

'The gods save us, Kruza, surely you couldn't work for such a man? You talk as if you despise him.'

'All who work for him despise him. All who owe him money despise him. He is a man with a great deal of money and power and no friends.'

Lenya saw the narrowest of alleys between the Baiting Pit and its neighbour, closed off with a tall ironwork gate. Kruza looked around him and then, opening the gate a bare few inches he sidled in, taking Lenya with him. She almost tripped on a top step that she could not see in the gloom. She steadied herself by grabbing at the gate behind her, making it clang shut heavily. Kruza's head whipped round, his green eyes glaring at her through the dusty darkness, but no one seemed to have heard them.

'Come on!' he hissed.

Two nights before, on the day of his walk into Middenheim with Lenya, Drakken had returned to his barrack dormitory very late. Morgenstern had laughed about the boy having a heavy date with his pretty country girlfriend.

'He's lost his virginity on the battlefield. Perhaps tonight's the night he'll lose it in a bed!' the veteran Wolf laughed, his voice thick with drink.

'Or against the wall of a palace courtyard,' Anspach cut in and they all laughed. Gruber sat on his cot, thinking about Lenya safely back in the castle and wondering just where young Drakken might actually be, when the man burst into the dormitory hot and cross.

Drakken threw off his pelt and the pieces of his armour, sat on his bed and put his head in his hands. Gruber crossed over to him, waving a discreet hand at the others to get on with their own business and leave Drakken alone.

As Gruber sat down next to Drakken the thickset young man dropped his hands to his lap and looked up.

'I lost her,' he said quietly. 'I lost Lenya in the city. I – I couldn't find her again. Ulric's teeth, Gruber; what will become of her alone in the city at night?'

'Don't take on, lad,' Gruber smiled a reassuring smile. 'I found her outside the temple hours ago, safe and sound. I took her back to the palace. She's probably been sleeping for hours by now.'

For one awful moment Gruber thought Drakken was going to hug him, the poor boy looked so relieved. But Drakken simply stood up and then abruptly sat again, anger and frustration showing clearly in his broad face.

After a good night's sleep, Drakken's anger had subsided and all he wanted was to make sure that Lenya was safe. He had almost decided to go to her, but he could already hear her telling him nothing was wrong and chiding him for wanting to control her. So he didn't visit his sweetheart.

Instead he watched her. Drakken spent the whole of that day monitoring Lenya's movements. To his relief, she didn't leave the palace at all. Perhaps she'd been frightened by her day in Middenheim and decided the palace was a much safer bet. Drakken doubted it.

On the afternoon of the next day, he followed Lenya when she slipped out into the city. He watched as she made her way around the Garten Ring and into the Great Park, and he stood back as she wove her way through the crowds there. He saw her disappear down the steps where she had arranged to meet Arkady for the second time.

Drakken was deeply puzzled that she should know about the steps – and very worried that she had used them. He didn't know that she had merely taken a seat and was waiting. Drakken hurried out of the Great Park. He would have to move fast if he was to get to the bottom of the steps and keep up with Lenya. They led directly to the Altquartier and his own route, on foot, was much more circuitous. Less than ten minutes later, Drakken was hiding, panting, in the shadows of a tiny courtyard at the bottom of the Great Park steps. He was sure he had missed Lenya, but he didn't know what else to do except wait.

Half an hour later, Drakken was trying to formulate a new plan when he heard footfalls on the steps and plunged himself silently back into the shadows. A stab of jealousy lurched through him as he saw Lenya with Arkady, crossing the courtyard in front of him. What was his girl doing with this young cut-purse?

Drakken was there too when Lenya met the priest of Morr. He spoke to the priest himself after he had left Lenya and a second unknown cut-purse in the tavern. Drakken couldn't fathom what was going on. There had been two strange men, the priest of Morr and, to top it all, Lenya had done something awful to her dress. What the priest of Morr told the young Wolf made no sense to him either. Lenya had never mentioned any lost brother.

Now Drakken stood outside the Baiting Pit of the West Weg, wondering why anyone would bring Lenya to such a place, when he heard the clang of the side gate closing. He watched, only feet away, as Lenya and the unknown man descended the steps into the bowels of the Pit. Drakken had a terrible feeling of foreboding. He knew at once that he would have to save Lenya. He just wasn't sure from what.

'You can't come in here!' a blunt voice came out of the shadows and noise as Lenya and Kruza crossed the threshold at the bottom of the steps. 'We're closed!'

Lenya didn't like the sound of the voice that seemed to force itself out past a mouthful of food. She didn't like the smell of frightened animals and adrenaline-choked sweat which filled the air.

'Kled?' Kruza called out as the dwarf appeared. Lenya had never seen his like before. He was as broad as he was tall and heavy, hard muscle stood out on his thick torso and short neck. He was naked above the waist and hairless. His short, solid hand made a fist around something that he was tearing lumps from with his sparse and irregular teeth.

'Kruza!' Kled the dwarf exclaimed. 'We're closed! It's not your day.' Then the short man, who oddly reminded Lenya of a cruel parody of Drakken, looked past Kruza and grinned broadly, showing the contents of his mouth.

'Been recruiting, Kruza? Give her one yourself, have you?' Kled leered shamelessly, walking round Lenya in a tight little circle, leaving a ring around her where he had disturbed the newly raked sawdust of the Baiting Pit.

'No!' The single word that Kruza uttered sounded like a threat. Kled laughed, throwing back his head before filling his mouth once more.

'I want some information,' Kruza continued. 'Information about a young man, a country boy.'

'Probably dead,' Kled said.

Lenya had had enough of this beast. He didn't scare her! At least, she told herself he didn't. Lenya stepped past Kruza.

'The priest of Morr says not,' she said and swallowed the hard lump in her throat that was making her voice sound cracked. 'Take me to Bleyden. I need to talk with him.'

'Take you to Bleyden?' repeated the dwarf, his face pressed so close to hers that Lenya wanted to step back. 'Speak not so freely of my master, trollop, or you will regret it.'

'I have to find Stefan Dunst,' Lenya said, barely able to hold her ground. 'Your master may know where he is.'

'And the price he will ask may be too great,' Kled said, his voice all threat.

Kruza stood behind Lenya in consternation. He'd promised himself he'd look after her, but she wasn't helping.

'Kled,' he began, 'I don't see any reason to disturb Master Bleyden. Perhaps you could find out if Stefan Dunst has worked for him?'

'Not a chance,' said Kled. Behind him some invisible beast lurched against the grille of its cage, roaring a hysterical sound and making the pit echo with the clang of a huge weight throwing itself against metal bars. Kled spun around, picking up a club and moving to scold the animal.

Lenya saw her opportunity. Taking Kruza's hand, she moved away from Kled toward a low door in the wall opposite. She could see light spilling from around the door's poor seal and guessed it might lead her to the Low King they called Bleyden.

From his vantage point, crouched at the top of the narrow stairwell, Drakken listened intently. He was hunched sideways on the steps, unable to sit squarely in the space that was somewhat narrower than his body. Listening and concentrating hard, he managed to hear every word of Kled's welcome. He waited, hoping that would be the end of the encounter. But when the animal roared and tried to tear its cage apart, the White Wolf heard only danger and careered down the flight of steps, as fast, but as noiselessly as he could.

Lenya pulled at the door handle, but it wouldn't open. Behind her, Kruza, beginning to sweat, moved her aside. He saw that there was no going back from this now. He took hold of the door handle and pulled. Then, in his frustration and near panic, he pushed, putting the weight of his shoulder against the door.

It flew open and Kruza fell heavily inwards, taking Lenya with him. As the door opened the sound of hundreds of excited, expectant voices rose to greet the pair. This was followed by a sudden lull, which was broken by a slow, solitary handclap of dissatisfaction. Lenya pulled herself up and began to brush sawdust from her skirt. Kruza, still on the floor on his hands and knees, raised his head, looking for all the world like a dog sniffing the air. He was not ready for what he beheld.

Kled beat the cage of the frightened creature with his club and turned back to oust Kruza and his feisty tart once and for all. But they were gone, and the pit door stood open. Kled heaved it shut before animals could get loose into the undercrofts.

Something was wrong. The audience above had gone quiet and then began to clap out a slow, strange rhythm that the dwarf had never heard in all his years at the Baiting Pit. Kled dropped his club, took his jacket from its hook and was shrugging his great shoulders into it as he raced up the winding staircase that would take him to the trainers' viewing stand.

Drakken stood at the bottom of the stairs, looking into the cellar beyond. He saw nothing, but heard the beating of a cage and the low murmur of the audience. Then clapping. And then a huge cheer.

Kneeling in the sawdust, Kruza looked into the snarling muzzle of a stocky, barrel-chested dog with a square head and tiny, glinting eyes. The spittle on the bull terrier's gleaming fangs dripped and the wound on its side leaked a yellowish liquid. In less time than it took to take one shallow, frightened breath, Kruza was on his feet, jumping over the dog. A huge cheer rose from the astounded audience.

As Kruza rose and leapt, Lenya got her first view of her surroundings. Behind Kruza, a tall thick pole stood in the centre of the packed arena. Chained to it was a massive, howling, dirty brown beast. From the huge, studded collar around its neck hung several feet of heavy link chain. The great paws that stamped the sawdust floor were manacled together, restricting its movement.

Around the massive rearing bear several more bull terriers lurched and snapped, their crazed eyes desperate for a piece of the action. Lenya turned to run. But the door they had come through was closed.

Standing at the edge of the trainer's platform, Kled put his fingers in his mouth and whistled a high pitched sound that cut across the raucous noise of the arena and made the bull terriers turn their heads for an instant. But only an instant.

Kled waved a curt message at the four brawny men who had risen from their seats in the frenzied crowd at the sound of the whistle, and were making their way down the tight tiers of seats that made up the auditorium. Planting their feet firmly on the bench seats, they worked their way effortlessly through the crowd. Soon four huge bodies, clad in leather armour and pulling on horned helmets, made their way to the tall wall which surrounded the arena stage and vaulted down.

'Get them out of there!' Kled yelled at them. 'Get them out!'

There was already chaos. The crowd were running mad with excitement. Kled's men moved in.

One of the four dropped down right behind Lenya and tried to lift her up. He hadn't reckoned on the small woman being quite so fast. She ducked under his arm and slid between his legs. As he turned to see where she had gone he felt a hot, sharp pain in his calf. The dog that Kruza had come face to face with had lost his first target and now homed in on the thug's leg as his next good meal.

The remaining thugs armed themselves with the spears that stood around the arena walls, in case of emergencies, and began to stab at the dogs. Their job was to control the situation and get the intruders out of the arena as fast as possible, before the whole show turned into a farce. Kled watched anxiously from his vantage point.

Kruza landed within feet of the bear. Crouching down on his haunches, he held out a calming hand to the frantic animal. It raged, great jaws frothing, pulling at its chains, desperate to get at its tormentors after months of repeated abuse. Dogs snarled and circled around it. In another moment, one of the thugs was closing in on Kruza, jabbing dogs ahead of him with his spear. He was a huge man with dark tattoos showing on the parts of him that were not covered in shiny, black leather armour. His nicked steel helmet with its horn ornaments and low forehead was imposing enough, but the massive, square jaw and wide red mouth with its gruesome harelip were positively terrifying.

Still looking up, Kruza lowered his hand to the floor and then lunged forward with his shoulders, grabbing the fearsome gladiator around his impressive calves. Black leather hit the sawdust amidst a spray of dust. Kruza sat on his torso and started tearing at his helmet, one hand grasping each of the bone horns and swinging from side to side, half-throttling the man inside with the tautly-twisted chin strap.

There was a roar of laughter from the crowd. Prize fights were one thing, but this comic-tragic battle was something else. They'd certainly got their money's worth.

Kled put his head in his hands. Things were going from bad to worse. He would be out of a job tomorrow for sure. He looked up as he heard the rabble rising to their feet, stamping and cheering and clapping their hands above their heads. He looked out into the arena.

In the entrance to the arena, in front of the bait door, stood a figure. Kled looked again. A huge, masked man filled the doorway. He was naked to the waist and already slick with sweat. He carried a huge mallet in one hand, with a long haft and a heavy iron head. In the other he carried a crude wooden cudgel, tipped with a series of sturdy iron spikes. Not weapons, but tools, the tools of Kled's trade, taken from the cellar by this awesome gladiator. The man stood for what seemed like an age, long enough for Kled and the audience to take in his leather breeches and knee boots, the bands wrapped tight around his wrists and his glistening torso. The man was shorter than average, but what he lacked in height he surely made up for in breadth. Over his head the man wore a crude mask, a small sack with holes cut for his eyes.

An instant later, the mallet was being swung above his head as the gladiator worked his hand down its haft. He had seen something that everyone else had missed. They had been watching him – but he had been watching the bear.

The noise of the crowd and the unfamiliarity of the number of human bodies cavorting around the arena had brought the bear to a point beyond panic. It threw itself against the post with all its weight and then lunged away from it, falling to all fours. The top of the post had splintered with the force and the chain came away. The bear was loose.

The dogs around it were too slow to react. It savaged one, mauling it with teeth and claws, and then ripped another up into the air, its back snapped, howling. The remaining dogs scurried back, fearful at this change in the odds. The bear, berserk now, sprayed dog-blood from its muzzle as it shook it and lumbered forward at the human targets around. The crowd were howling.

Standing his ground, the masked gladiator swung his mallet hard, the end of the haft now clasped firmly in his grip. He let go. Swinging high into the air, the mallet turned twice, echoing the spin that the gladiator had used, and landed with a crashing thud against the side of the bear's skull. It moaned once and collapsed to the floor, burying two of the terriers, whining, beneath its immense bulk.

The crowd roared again, and Kruza leapt off the torso of his half-choked opponent, looking to avoid the next confrontation when it came.

Lenya turned, distracted, to look at the gladiator, and someone picked her up from behind. She looked around: it was the thug with the chewed leg. He was bleeding, but still strong and upright. Lenya struggled and kicked and the audience laughed.

Their laughter ended in another great roar of approval as the mysterious gladiator swung his cudgel, two-handed, into the thug's armoured back, making him drop Lenya and stagger back. The man turned, pulling a long knife from his belt. A thrust, another slicing attempt to sink the blade into the masked gladiator's chest. The gladiator replied with a second swing of the cudgel, which left the thug lying face down on the floor, blood and gore mixing with sawdust to form a thick, dark stain.

Kled looked on in awe. Two of his best men had been taken out by Kruza the cut-purse and this mysterious fighter. Not to mention the bear, his trusted ally and performer for more than two years now, and not easily replaced. Then Kled heard the chant from the auditorium of Masked Man! Masked Man! He smiled to himself. Perhaps he had stumbled upon something after all. Perhaps this masked man could use a job.

The gladiator picked up Lenya and the crowd booed. She looked over at Kruza as he tried to drag her away and she protested, kicking and screaming and shouting.

'Kruza!' she called.

'This is no place for you, lady!' the gladiator said.

Beating the masked man's chest, she hurled abuse. 'You bastard! Let me go! I have to help Kruza!'

To her surprise, he let her go.

The remaining dogs in the arena had turned away from the action when they realised that the bear was down and a meal awaited. The last two thugs, who had been trying to keep the dogs under control with their long spears, now turned on Kruza. The audience waited with bated breath as the leather-clad fighting machines circled the cut-purse, their spears low to the ground and threatening.

Someone in the audience shouted 'Kill!' Other voices joined in until the whole auditorium was filled with the rhythm of hundreds of slowly stamping feet, measuring out each rising call of the word. 'Kill!' 'Kill!' 'Kill!' 'Kill!'

Kruza shuffled his feet in the sawdust of the arena floor, preparing himself. The first spear came in to tangle his legs, but Kruza leapt at just the right moment and it missed him. The second spear tip came in higher, shoulder height, and as soon as his leap was over, Kruza was forced into a low squat, letting the spear blade whistle close over the top of his head. The jabbing spears came in thick and fast, but Kruza was quick on his feet. The audience were almost silent, watching the three men go through this curious dance.

Lenya threw herself on the back of the thug nearest to her, the way she'd fearlessly tackle her brothers in pretend fights back home. She'd had to jump just to get her hands over his shoulders and haul herself up; Kruza's assailant was taller than Lenya by almost two heads. She put her arm around his neck, so that her elbow nestled against his throat. Then she locked her wrists together with opposite hands and threw the entire weight of her body back and down. Her feet dangled in mid-air for a moment, but she could feel him going. She lifted her knees into the small of his back and kicked out again, throwing herself clear as she brought him down on his back, retching and coughing from her choke-hold.

The masked gladiator sidled around the fight, one eye on the feeding dogs, and picked his mallet up from the floor. Then he went for the remaining thug. His first swing matched exactly with the low forward lunge of the leather-clad fighter. Both missed, but the masked man's balance never wavered, and he brought the mallet round in another long arc. This time it connected. The double horned helmet flew off the thug's head and sailed way up into the auditorium, grasping hands rising up to catch the souvenir. Long before his helmet was caught, the thug was lying on the ground, his legs twisted in an awkward direction with the momentum of the blow, his head bloody and gaping.

Kled stood stolidly in the stand, counting his losses. Two useful armed fighters, at least a couple of dogs (and the rest would be useless for at least a fortnight after their vast meal), and his favourite baiting bear. And his gains? Well the masked man would counter any losses if he could be persuaded to fight again.

The thugs Kruza and Lenya had disabled were getting back to their feet, but neither looked like they wanted a rematch. The crowd were making a noise fit to raise the dead.

The masked gladiator turned to Lenya and Kruza. 'We're leaving. Now,' he told them, shouting over the din.

'The bait door's closed – ' Lenya began.

The gladiator raised his mallet. 'Not for long.'

Kled scrambled back down the winding stairs to the cellar, desperate to catch up with his new find before he disappeared into the night. Wild applause still rang in his ears, soon to be followed by cries of 'More!' and 'Masked Man! Masked Man!'

On their way out of the cellar, the gladiator, the sackcloth mask still firmly over his head, lifted a bundle over his shoulder and led the dishevelled pair away from their unexpected adventure. Lenya noticed that the bundle appeared to be wrapped in some kind of skin or fur.

The strange trio hurried away from the deserted exterior of the Baiting Pit and down a series of empty alleys. They stopped in a tiny square between the backs of tall buildings. There was barely room for the three of them, but there were no windows and they could not be overlooked. The masked man knelt down to his furry bundle and began to untie it. Then, impatiently, the masked fighter tore off his sackcloth hood, leaving his hair glued firmly down with sweat to his glistening forehead.

'Krieg!' Lenya exclaimed in a tight, breathy squeak. 'Krieg... But how....? What...?' She was so surprised she couldn't catch her breath and her fingers began to tingle. She thought she was going to throw up.

'You know him?' Kruza asked. Then the cut-purse saw what the half-naked man was taking from his bundle. He thought for a moment about running, but there was a look in the other's eyes that told him not to chance it.

Once dressed again in his pelt and breastplate the White Wolf, Krieg Drakken, led Lenya and Kruza to a nearby hostelry. Kruza did not know what to say, so busied himself at the barrel, furnishing all three with tall pots of good ale. He didn't like mixing with such a powerful authority figure, not one bit. But he didn't feel like leaving Lenya after what they'd been through.

'I could have helped you find your brother,' Drakken was saying in a stern tone. 'Why didn't you trust me? I nearly brought disgrace to my Temple, having to go into the pit to rescue you! If any had recognised me...'

'I'm sorry,' she said. She wondered why she had not confided in him. Was it simply that she owed him so much already? She didn't want to think about it.

'No one's going to find him now!' she murmured in a hollow voice. 'After all this...'

Lenya had never felt such hopeless futility. All the leads had been false, all the trails cold, all the risks not worth the taking. She had fought against it as valiantly as she could, but at last the great bulk of Middenheim had overwhelmed her will and her strength.

'Oh Stefan!' she exclaimed. 'Why did you have to come to this place! Brave little Wheezer, out to make his fortune!' Her hands came to her face and tears began to fall.

'What did you say?' Kruza asked sharply. 'You said his name was Stefan.'

'Yes,' she sniffed, 'but when we were children his nickname was Wheezer...'

'Wheezer...' Kruza repeated, barely audible over Lenya's sobs. 'Ulric damn me!' he exclaimed. He stood up in alarm, his chair crashing down behind him.

'Your brother was Wheezer?'

MITTHERBST

WOLF'S BANE

The night was old and dry. The lemon-rinded moons of high summer hung sullenly in a sky of soft purple. Moths beat against lit windows and masked lanterns. In the dim precincts of the Great Temple of Ulric, a warm silence filled the long hallways and cloisters. It was past midnight, and still the heat of the day had not subsided. Cooler than the streets in daylight, the great stones of the Temple building now radiated the heat they had absorbed, sweating warmth out of the walls and pillars.

Aric, the White Company's standard bearer, crossed the shadowy atrium of the mighty shrine, by the light of two hundred smoking candles. Sweat beaded his broad, young brow. Custom and observance forced him to wear the grey-gold plate mail and white wolf pelt of the Templar uniform, but he dearly wished he could strip it all off.

Guard duty. White Company had the vigilia watch, patrolling the palace of Ulric until first light and the chime of matins. Aric longed for the fresh chill and mist which he hoped the pre-dawn would bring to signal the end of their duty.

By the arched door of a side chapel dedicated to fallen sons of Ar-Ulric, Aric saw Lowenhertz. The tall Wolf had leant his warhammer against the jamb, and was standing, peering out across the city from an unglazed lancet. At the sound of Aric's approach, he spun like lightning and raised the hammer.

'Stand down, brother,' Aric said with a smile.

'Aric...' Lowenhertz muttered, lowering his hammer.

'How goes the night?'

'Stifling. Smell the air.'

They stood together on the narrow parapet under the arch and breathed in. Sweat; woodsmoke; corrupting sanitation.

'Ah, Middenheim,' Aric murmured.

'Middenheim in high summer,' Lowenhertz returned. 'Damn its rocky heart.'

Somewhere down below in Altmarkt, hand bells were chiming furiously and there was a distant fuzz of orange. Another fire in the tinder-dry streets.

There had been a dozen or more that week alone. And beyond the city, brush-blazes, sparked by summer lightning, had regularly lit portions of the forest at night. Wells were drying up, latrines were stinking, brawls were flaring, disease was rife, and clove oil sales were booming. A hot, smoky summer by any standards and for Middenheim an exceptional season.

'Hottest summer in eighty years,' said Lowenhertz, who knew such things.

'Hottest I've ever known,' Aric answered. He paused, significantly.

'What?' Lowenhertz asked, looking round.

Aric shrugged. 'I... Nothing.'

'What?'

'I half expected you to tell me why. With your learning and all. I half expected you to tell me that a summer season as stifling as this was a sure sign of some disaster.'

Lowenhertz looked faintly angry, as if mocked.

'I'm sorry,' Aric said. 'I should continue with my rounds.'

As he walked away, Lowenhertz called out. 'Brother Aric?'

'Lowenhertz?'

'You're right, you know. A summer like this... not from any learning of mine, or signs, or portents. But heat like this gets to men's minds. Bakes them, twists them. Before autumn, there will be trouble.'

Aric nodded solemnly and walked away. He liked Lowenhertz, but there was nothing the man couldn't see the bad side of.

'Then take it off!' Morgenstern snapped. The sweltering night had done nothing for his demeanour and his huge bulk was rank with sweat. He had shed his wolf-pelt and his armour, and was sitting by the font in the main chapel, dressed in his undershirt, pressing his face and neck against the cool stone of the water-filled basin. Above him, the great statue of Ulric rose into the gloom, silent, immense.

And probably sweating too, Morgenstern decided.

'It's against the rules!' protested Drakken, the youngest of the Wolves and the newest recruit, who had drawn this duty to share with the great, ox-like veteran.

'Ulric eat the rules!' Morgenstern spat, with a sideways nod of respect to the vast statue. 'If you're as hot as me you'll ditch that armour and sweat it out! Name of the Wolf, you're hot blooded enough to be courting that fiery maid from the Margrave's court! You must be curdling in there!'

Drakken shook his head wearily and pulled his pelt around his powerful, stocky form as if to defy the heat.

Short, surly, thick-set, stubborn, Morgenstern thought. *Our boy Drakken undoubtedly has dwarf blood in his ancestry. His bastard forefathers surely dug this city out of the rock itself.*

He got to his feet, aware that Drakken was trying not to watch him. Morgenstern reached into the font.

'What are you doing?' Drakken hissed.

The old veteran pulled a corked bottle of ale out of the holy water. 'Cooling down,' he said. He unpopped the flask and poured the chilled liquid down his throat. He could almost hear Drakken choking on his own saliva and envy.

Drakken spun round and strode across to the big man. 'For Ulric's sake, give me some of that!'

'*Some of what?*'

Aric advanced down the centre file of the great chamber, the thousands of candle flames rippling at the sudden breeze of his billowing pelt.

Drakken froze. There was a fluid plop as the bottle dropped out of sight into the font from Morgenstern's chubby fingers.

'Morgenstern?'

The huge Wolf turned soberly and dipped his cupped hands into the font water, raising them to baptise his face in a cascading splash of dancing silver.

'Holy water, Brother Aric,' Morgenstern said, shaking out his sodden locks like a hound. He saw how Aric stared at his unarmoured bulk. 'At late hours like this, I like to chasten myself with the watery blessing of Ulric, so that I may be fresh for duty.'

'Is that so?'

'Oh yes,' said Morgenstern, splashing his face and torso again. 'Why, I'm surprised an earnest young devotee of the Wolf like you doesn't know the ritual. Why else would I have stripped off my armour? I'm absolving my sins, you see? Before Ulric. Absolving, oh yes. It's chastening. Very chastening.'

'Very chastening,' agreed Drakken.

Morgenstern knew the young Templar was a heartbeat away from laughing. He grabbed Drakken by the neck and plunged him face down into the water of the font.

'See? Young Drakken is willing! He thirsts for chastening! Can I oblige you with a nocturnal baptism too?'

Aric shook his head. 'Forgive me for intruding upon your observances, Brother Morgenstern. I had no idea you were so... devout.'

'I am a Brother of Wolves, Aric. It wounds me to think you would believe me to be tardy in such details. A lesson to you. You imagine us veterans to be a slack lot, more interested in wine and song and womanly comfort.' Morgenstern held Drakken's struggling head under. 'The likes of me shame you younger Wolves! Why, I have half a mind to go outside right now and beat my naked back with bitter withy twigs to scourge my soul for Ulric's sake! When was the last time you did that?'

'I forget. Again, forgive me,' Aric said, turning away to continue with his rounds. 'I stand humbled before your strict devotion.'

'Don't mention it.'

'You might want to let Drakken up before he drowns, though,' Aric added as he walked away, smirking.

'What? Oh, yes...'

'You bastard! I nearly drowned!' Drakken said as he came up. Or that's what he would have said, had he not been trying to vomit up a lung. He lay gasping and retching on the tiles by the font for a good two minutes after Aric had gone.

Morgenstern kicked him playfully in the ribs. 'See the trouble you'd get me into, boy?' Morgenstern asked. He dipped into the font and pulled a second cooled bottle out.

A moth knocked repeatedly against the lamp. Anspach thought to swat it, but it was a good bet a warhammer didn't make for an effective moth-swatter. He was just considering what odds he'd take to swat a moth with a warhammer when Aric appeared.

'How goes the night, Brother Anspach?'

'Hot and lousy, Brother Aric.'

They stood together at the foot of the steps under the corbel-vaulted ceiling of the entrance to the regimental trophy chapel. Beyond the cage door, on the wall, bas-reliefs and frescoes showed Wulcan, the smiting of Blitzbeil, the commemoration of the Fauschlag Rock and a score of other images from the long history of Middenheim.

'The patrol?' Anspach asked, obviously bored.

'Nothing. Lowenhertz watches the Chapel of the Fallen. Drakken and Morgenstern are clowning in the main hall. Kaspen and Einholt are falling asleep in the weaponarium annexe. Gruber paces the high turret solemnly. A quiet night.'

Anspach nodded, and pulled out a flask from under his pelt. 'Something to cool you down?' he suggested.

Aric hesitated and then accepted the offering. 'Tastes good,' he began appreciatively.

He handed the flask back and turned away. His toe kicked against something on the flags, something that skittered away. Searching for it, Aric picked it up.

A padlock.

'How long has this been lying there?'

Anspach shrugged, coming over. 'I have no idea...'

They both turned to look at the portico of the trophy chapel. The iron cage door was ajar.

'Oh no! Oh, curse me, Ulric!' Anspach spat leaping forward. Aric was beside him. They shoved the loose cage door open and thundered inside. Aric held up a lamp, and moths battered and wove around him.

The plinth in the corner of the shrine, under the great wolf-skin, was empty. The Jaws of Ulric, a silver inlaid relic made from the fangs of a great forest wolf in olden times, the greatest of their treasures, was missing.

Aric and Anspach backed away in horror.

'I'm in trouble,' Anspach breathed.

'You're in trouble? Anspach, we're all in trouble.'

Matins. Dawn came, hot, branding, intense. In a private annexe deep inside the oven heat of the Temple, Ganz listened attentively to Ar-Ulric, the High Priest. Every now and then he murmured 'Yes, High Priest,' or 'No, High Priest' or 'Obviously, High Priest.'

'The Teeth of Ulric,' the High Priest was saying, his breath exhausting itself in the hot air. 'Of all relics, our most prized!'

'Yes, High Priest,' Ganz said, obligingly.

'It must be returned.'

'Obviously, High Priest.'

Flies and beetles pattered against the window grills.

'If we were to admit we had lost the relic, Middenheim itself would lose heart. The city folk would round on us, and despair. An ill omen. The worst.'

'Yes, High Priest.'

'I can give you two days' grace.'

'Sir?'

'Two days to find and recover the relic before I have to go public and bring shame and torment on us all – especially the White Company who were on guard duty when it was stolen.'

'I see, High Priest.'

'Two days, Ganz. Do not fail the Temple.'

He would not. Not. *Not.*

But for the life of him, he didn't know where to begin. Stalking back from the High Priest's chambers, through chapter gardens where feeble mists baked off the beds, Ganz cursed himself over and again. He had no choice. He had to... to... enlist them all to his trust...

Even Morgenstern – and Anspach.

'Well, sir,' Anspach said, looking suitably solemn. 'I think our best bet–'

'Silence!' Ganz barked. The room held the silence for a second and then sound thundered again as Ganz slammed the door on his way out. The remaining members of the Wolf Company looked at each other. Aric sighed. Dorff began to whistle, nervously and tunelessly. Morgenstern slowly and belatedly lowered his legs from the table he had been resting them on. Gruber skulked darkly at the back of the room. The others shuffled.

'I only said–' Anspach began.

'Oh, shut up,' Aric muttered. 'We've disgraced him. Disgraced our order. Our Temple, our city.'

'Is it really that bad?' Drakken asked quietly and suddenly wished he hadn't.

'The Teeth of Ulric were cut from the muzzle of the great White Wolf of Holzbeck by Artur himself, bless his fine spirit. They are holy of all holies. And on our watch, we let them be stolen.' Lowenhertz moved into the centre of the room as he spoke, his voice low, like the intonation of a funeral bell in the Temple of Morr. 'Disgrace barely covers it.'

Anspach rose to his feet. 'I know what you're all thinking. It was me. I was watching the reliquary. I was the one who failed.'

'I was with you when we found the broken lock–' began Aric.

Anspach shushed him back. 'After the event, I'm sure. It was me, Aric. And you all think I must have been drunk or stupid or distracted...'

'Were you?' asked Gruber, a stiletto voice from the back of the room.

Anspach shook his head. 'No, Gruber, not that anyone would believe me. Fact is, I thought I was performing my duties with particular vigilance.'

'I was drunk,' Morgenstern said suddenly. They all looked at him. 'On the way, at least,' he qualified. 'Drakken was in no state to stand a good watch either, thanks to me. I'm as much to blame...'

'I was covering the vigilia watch. For Ganz. It was my duty,' Aric said quietly. 'I saw Morgenstern's clowning. I saw Anspach ready at the gate. I saw Einholt and Kaspen dozing in the weapon hall.'

Einholt and Kaspen looked down.

'I saw us all! Neglecting our duties or performing them, one and the same. It was a quiet night and nothing was wrong. I should have charged you all with the spirit of Ulric so that none shirked. I did not. This is down to me.'

'Well,' Gruber said, walking into the light and igniting his pipe with a soft kiss of flame from the spindle. 'Aric may be right. Maybe it is his fault...'

'I was drunk!' Morgenstern exclaimed.

'Sleeping!' cut across Einholt.

'Distracted!' Lowenhertz snapped.

'Unwary!' Anspach cried.

'Enough! Enough!' Gruber cried, holding up his hand. 'All of us to blame... None of us? That's the whole thing, isn't it? The company failed, not any individual. And let's think about this carefully. I've seen Morgenstern drunk as a lord and still notice a goblin sneak by. Anspach may gamble his life away, but still his nose is sharper than any in the company. He would not have missed a theft like that. Lowenhertz, the sternest of us all; he would not have passed over some clue or hint that treachery was in progress. Einholt, not he, not even sleeping, Kaspen likewise. Drakken, with his eager eyes and sense of duty... Do you not see?'

'See what?' asked Aric.

'Magic, Aric! Magic stole the Jaws of Ulric! Despite our failings, only magic could have snuck in and robbed us of the prize. If we'd all been sober and studious and alert... still it would be gone! Go and fetch Ganz back. We have work to do.'

It felt strange... wrong, somehow, to be out in the streets of Middenheim without the familiar weight of the armour and wolf pelt. Aric scratched inside the chafing collar of a light linen cape that he hadn't worn since he had first been admitted into the Company as a petitioner.

But this was how Morgenstern and Anspach had said it should go, and for all their manifold failings, they knew such things. If White Company was going to scour the city of Middenheim for the Teeth of Ulric, shake down every tavern, question every fence, prise up and examine the underside of every cobble, they could not do so as Wolf Templars.

So here they were, as the sun rose to mid-morning above the raked roofs, here they were scrubbed and shaved and heavy-headed after the long night, wearing ill-assorted tunics, capes and robes, most of which had festered in long-boxes and chests in the cellars of the chapter house for months and years. Morgenstern, in fact, had been forced to send Drakken out for new clothes. Since he had last worn his civilian garb, he had added many pounds and many more inches. Morgenstern had also appropriated a large-brimmed hat which he imagined gave him a dashing, mysterious air. It in fact made him look like a bulbous forest toadstool on the wilt, but Aric said nothing.

They all looked so odd, so unlike themselves. Gruber in a faintly genteel, faded robe and tunic that seemed a decade or two old-fashioned; Schell in a surprisingly rich velvet cape that smelled of pomanders; Lowenhertz in rough breeches and a leather tunic, like a woodsman. Even the ones who looked normal seemed odd. Aric wasn't used to seeing any of them like this.

Except Anspach, in his tailored coat, polished boots and suavely draped cloak. Though they all spent off-duty hours in the city's stews and taverns, only Anspach habitually dressed out of armour or company colours. Where Morgenstern could carouse until dawn in full armour in the Man o'War, the gaming halls, arenas and dice parlours that were Anspach's particular vice demanded a more refined mode of dress.

They assembled in the street, new men to each other, not speaking for several minutes in the warming glare of the strengthening Mittherbst sun. The air was yet clear and cool, the sky porcelain blue.

Finally Ganz joined them, almost unrecognisable in a serge doublet and hooded woollen over-robe. He said nothing, for there was no need for words, not many at least. Gruber, Anspach and Morgenstern had convinced Ganz of the correct course of action left open to them, and the labour ahead of them had been divided. Now as Ganz came out, he gave a nod acknowledged by all his men, and the party broke into smaller groups, heading away from each other into different quarters of the ancient town.

'Let me do the talking,' Anspach told Ganz and Aric as they approached the south doors of the Baiting Pit off West Weg. At night, on those times he'd passed it, this squat stone drum of a theatre had seemed to Aric like a mouth of hell, with its flaming braziers, hooting pipe music, drums, the pounding and cheering and roaring. The roaring of men and animals.

In daylight, in the unforgiving brightness of the summer light, it was a miserable, flaking place: worn, soiled and stained by all manner of unwholesome deposits. Hand-bills fluttered and shredded along the travertine walls between the daubings of less than sober or less than literate citizens. The blackened metal braziers were extinguished and dead. Two men were sweeping the gateway, pushing all manner of trampled trash out of the steps into the gutter trench. Another was pumping water from the street spigot into a row of buckets. All looked sour and half awake.

'It would have been better if we'd come tonight,' hissed Anspach, 'when the place is open. There would be activity to cover our–'

'There's no time,' returned Ganz. 'Now, if you so want to do the talking, do it to someone other than me!'

They entered, passing through the suddenly freezing shadow of the gateway into the tall-sided, circular pit, where tiers of wooden galleries overlooked a deep stone well, at the bottom of which was dirty sand and a few deep-set posts with manacle points. Caged grills in the pit wall at arena level led off into the place's dingy undercrofts. Down in the pit, another man was scattering sand on dark brown stains. The air smelled of mingled sweat and smoke, an overwhelming odour.

'We're closed,' said a blunt voice from their left. The trio swung around. A hefty dwarf, stripped to the waist and hugely muscled, tipped forward and got up off the stool where he had been sitting, chewing on bread and sausage.

'Where's Bleyden?' Anspach asked.

'We're. Closed,' repeated the dwarf. He took an unfeasibly large bite off the sausage and chewed, staring at them.

'Kled,' said Anspach with a soothing cock of his head and a shrug. 'Kled, you know me.'

'I know nothing.'

'You know you're closed,' Anspach corrected.

The dwarf frowned. He put the sausage to his mouth to bite again, then the bread, and then the sausage, undecided. His eyes never left Anspach.

'What do you want?' he asked, adding, 'we're closed,' again in case any had missed it, and to show that by enquiring what was wanted, he was making a huge exception.

'You know I've had a run of... ill fortune. Bleyden's been good enough to extend me a line of credit, but he insisted on me making some interim repayments as soon as possible. Well, here I am!' Anspach beamed.

The dwarf, Kled, thought for a moment more, his cheeks and lips bulging unpleasantly as his tongue chased lumps of meat out of the sides of his gums. Then he beckoned with the gnawed end of his sausage.

Anspach nodded to Ganz and Aric to follow smartly. Ganz was glowering, his face as dark as Mondstille.

'I hope you both have money,' Anspach said in a hushed voice.

'If this is some con to get me to settle your gambling debts–' began Ganz, choking on the words.

They were passing into a sequence of smelly, stuffy wooden rooms under the seating. Boxes of junk lined the walls, rows of empty bottles, buckets, the occasional dirty billhook. The dwarf stomped ahead, passing neatly under every low doorway where each of the Templars had to duck.

'Bleyden owns this place, and four like it,' Anspach said. 'He runs all the girls in Altmarkt, and has a lot of other business... dealings. He knows a lot about the fate of, shall we say "purloined" goods? But he won't talk to us unless he's got a good reason. And my outstanding ninety crowns is a very good reason.'

'*Ninety*?' Ganz barked, the word almost becoming a squeak as they ducked under another low beam.

'My dear Anspach,' a soft voice said from the smoky gloom ahead of them. 'What a *delightful* surprise.'

'Look there,' Morgenstern whispered from under his preposterous floppy brim. 'Ah! Ah! Ah! Not so obviously, boy!'

Drakken adjusted his stare to look at something on the ground by Einholt's feet.

'You see them? By the fountain, pretending they're not watching?' continued Morgenstern, looking studiously the other way.

'No–' Drakken began.

'I do,' Einholt said. Jagbald Einholt was the quiet man of the company, tall and broad and bald with a jagged beard and a long scar across his eye, cheek and throat. With his milky eye, it was often hard to tell which way he was looking. Now, with a furtive measure as practised as Morgenstern, he was assessing the watchers by the fountain while apparently regarding the weather cock on the Merchant Chandlers.

'Big bruisers. Four of them. Been with us since the Cocky Dame.' Morgenstern stretched as if he hadn't a care in the world.

Drakken dropped to his knees to adjust the strapping of his boot and got a good look from behind the cover of Morgenstern's voluminous cape.

'You were asking a lot of questions,' he said, straightening up and whispering to Morgenstern. 'Five taverns we've been in now, and in each one you've bent the ear of the barman with vague questions about something lost.'

'We've got someone's interest and no mistake,' Einholt mused.

'Let them make the move,' Morgenstern said, heading off. 'We'll try the Tardy Ass next. It's past midday. We can take an ale there too.'

'This isn't an excuse for a tavern crawl,' Drakken began.

Morgenstern looked hurt. 'My boy, I'm taking this all too seriously. What other morning would I have gone through five taverns before noon and still not had a jar?'

They moved west down the rolling cobbles of Scrivener's Passage, dodging between the pack carts coming up from the markets. A hundred yards behind, the four men left the fountain and followed.

The Guildhall of the Apothecaries on Ostwald Hill had a noxious, yellow pallor to it. It was a rotting, half-timbered building of great age and veneration that sagged as if poison was in the wood and stones. Gruber and Lowenhertz entered into the close air of the audience hall through an unattended archway, and gazed around at the stained glass fronts of the many workshops and apothecums.

'You know this place?' Gruber asked, wrinkling his nose. The air was dry, with an oxidised reek.

'I come here from time to time,' replied Lowenhertz, as if such visits were as natural for a soldier like him as a trip to the armour smiths. The response made Gruber smile, a thin grin cracking his old, lined face. The tall and darkly handsome Lowenhertz had been an enigma since he transferred to White Company in the spring. It had taken a while for them to trust him past his overbearing intellect and strange, wide learning. But he had proved himself, proved himself loyal, proved himself in the field of combat. Now they looked at his odd, educated ways with gentle good humour, and none in the company denied he was an asset. A man with the learning to think his way around a thousand subjects and still fight like a pack-sire wolf when the blood was up.

'Stay here a moment,' Lowenhertz said, moving away into the dimmer reaches of the Guildhall, under a stained and alarmingly singed Guild banner. Gruber loosened his cloak, checked the dagger in his waistband and leant against a wall. He thought of the others, in twos and threes, scouting the city just now. Aric and their commander, Ganz, following Anspach's lucky-charm ways into the gaming places and the wager-pits; Schell, Kaspen and Schiffer in the markets; Bruckner and Dorff checking with their drinking friends in the Watch and the Militia; Morgenstern, Drakken and Einholt doing the rounds of the taverns. He didn't know what alarmed him most – that Anspach's cavalier attitude might provoke untold trouble from the criminal underclass, that Bruckner or Dorff might say too much to their cronies, that Schell and his party might get inveigled into the clutches of the merchant class, or that Morgenstern was visiting taverns. No, that was it. Morgenstern was visiting taverns. Gruber sighed. He prayed to Ulric that between them, steady old Einholt and earnest young Drakken would have the strength to keep Morgenstern's thirst reined in.

As for them: it had fallen for Gruber to go with Lowenhertz to pursue the latter's lead. Lowenhertz had suggested that the Teeth of Ulric might have been taken for some mystical purpose, and in these alchemical work-places that answer might be found. It had been Gruber's suggestion, after all, that magic had played a part in the theft.

He felt uneasy. Science didn't agree with him, and he was disarmed by the notion of men who spent their days mixing vials and philtres and potions. It was a short step from that to sinister black what-not in Gruber's book.

Lowenhertz reappeared under the Guild awning and beckoned. Gruber went over.

'Ebn Al-Azir will see us.'

'Who?'

Lowenhertz frowned at him. 'The chief alchemist. I've known him for years. He is from foreign parts, far away, but his work is excellent. Be appropriately humble.'

'Very well,' Gruber said, 'but it may kill me.' Gruber had precious little time for the outland types with their strange skins, odd scents and bewildering ways.

'Remove your boots,' Lowenhertz said, stopping him on the threshold of a narrow doorway.

'My what?'

'A mark of respect. Do it.' Gruber saw that Lowenhertz's feet were now bare. He cursed quietly as he yanked off his kid-skin riders.

The narrow door let onto a narrower staircase that circled up into the gloomy reaches of the Guildhall. Above, they ducked through a lancet archway and into a long, high attic room. The air seemed golden here. Sunlight streamed down thickly, like honey, through angled skylights of pumice glass, and was caught and suspended in rich hangings of silk and net. The room was carpeted in a rug of elaborate design, the hues and weaving astonishing and vibrant. Intricately wrought lamps and jewelled censers of gold filigree smoked around the room illuminating, in addition to the slow sunlight, a cluttered space of books and scrolls, chests and wall-hangings, charts and articulated skeletons – birds, beasts, and things akin to men. Stove fires cooked blue-hot under sculptural glass vessels in which liquids of vivid colours hissed and steamed and gave off oily vapours. A bell was chiming. The air smelled of rich, cloying sweetnesses. Gruber tried to breathe, but the air was too close. Perfume clogged his senses for a moment, perfume and incense.

On a rounded foot-table nearby, on the ivory inlaid top, lay a puppet, a glaring man in clown's pantaloons with jewelled joints and a belled cap. The puppet lay discarded, strings loose, in a rictus of death, like so many figures Gruber had seen on the field of war. That's how we all look when our strings go slack, he thought. The snarling stare of the puppet glared up at him out of a white porcelain face. Gruber looked away. He laughed humourlessly to himself. A sixty year-old veteran like him, afraid of a puppet a foot high!

A figure rose in the gloom, parted hanging nets and stepped out to meet them. He was small, dressed in a high-throated blue gown with embroidery at the neck and wide cuffs. His face was waxy and sallow, and there was a look of great age in his hollow eyes. Age, or perhaps...

'My old friend Heart-of-a-Lion!' he said. His accent was melodious and heavy.

Lowenhertz bowed his head, 'Master Al-Azir! How go your stars?'

The little man put his hands together. Long-nailed and dark, they emerged from his cuffs like the recessed blades from some mechanical weapon. Gruber had never seen so many rings: spirals, signets, loops, circles.

'My stars travel with me and I follow them. For now, my house is benign and it smiles on me the gift of heaven.'

'For that I am happy,' Lowenhertz said. He glanced a look at Gruber.

'Huh? Oh... as am I, sir.'

'Your friend?' asked Al-Azir with a flash of white teeth, inclining his head and circling a hand towards Gruber.

He moves like a puppet, thought Gruber, like a damn puppet on strings, all grace and motion lent by the hand of a trained puppeteer.

'This is my worthy comrade, Gruber,' said Lowenhertz. 'What trust you give to me must also go to him. We are brothers of the Wolf.'

Al-Azir nodded. 'Refreshment?' he asked.

No, it wasn't a question. It was an obligation, Gruber decided. Al-Azir made a brief hissing sound through his teeth and a huge man came out from behind the nets; bald, monumentally muscled and naked except for a breech-clout. His eyes were shadowed and unforthcoming, and he carried an ornate tray on which sat three tiny silver cups, a silver spouted pot and a bowl of jagged brown crystals with a pair of clawed tongs resting in them.

The vast servant set the tray down on the foot-table and retreated, taking the puppet with him. Al-Azir ushered them to sit on bolsters and satin cushions around the foot-table. He poured steaming oil-black fluid from the pot into the three cups with attentive care, each move slow and graceful.

Gruber watched Lowenhertz for a cue. Lowenhertz lifted the cup nearest him – it looked like a silver thimble in his hands –and dropped a cluster of the crystals into it with the tongs, which he then used to stir the thick fluid. He muttered something and nodded before sipping.

Lowenhertz didn't die choking and frothing, which Gruber took to be a good sign. He mimicked the process, lifting the cup and stirring the crystals in with the clawed tongs. Then he murmured, 'Ulric preserve me' and nodded. But there was no way he was going to sip.

He suddenly became aware of Lowenhertz glaring at him fiercely.

Gruber took a sip, licked his lips and smiled. Keeping that sip down was the hardest battle he had ever fought. It tasted like tar; smoked tar; smoked, boiled tar. With a bitter taste of mildew and a syrupy flavour of corruption.

'Very good,' he said finally, when at last he was certain opening his mouth wouldn't result in the reproduction of his last meal.

'Something troubles you,' said Al-Azir.

'No, it's quite nice really–' began Gruber, and then shut up.

'Something is lost,' went on Al-Azir, melodious and soft. 'Something precious. Eh! Precious.'

'You know this, master?'

'The stars tell me, Heart-of-a-Lion. There is pain in the ruling house of Xerxes, and both Tiamut and Darios, Sons of the Morning, draw hooked blades against each other. Eh! It is seen and written in water.'

'Your learning astounds me as ever, master. The heavens convolute and you read the signs. Tell me what you know.'

'I know nothing and everything,' replied Al-Azir, sipping slowly, head bowed.

Then cut to the latter, Gruber cursed inwardly. *Enough with this stars stuff!*

'What has been taken, Heart-of-a-Lion?' asked Al-Azir gently.

Lowenhertz was about to speak when Gruber cut in.

'Why don't–' He saw Lowenhertz's angry snarl and held up a hand for calm.

'Forgive my bluntness, Master Al-Azir,' Gruber corrected himself, 'but this is a matter of delicacy. We would appreciate knowing what you know before we unburden ourselves fully.'

He glanced at Lowenhertz, who nodded cautious approval, his lips pursed.

'For such help,' Gruber went on, 'my Lord Ulric may surely shine his thanks upon you. I am sure his light lurks somewhere in your firmament.'

'I'm sure it does,' Al-Azir replied with an ivory-white smile. 'Somewhere.'

'My friend is in earnest, Master Al-Azir,' Lowenhertz said. 'Can you tell us what you know?'

Al-Azir set his cup down and folded his hands so they each disappeared up the opposite sleeve. He stared down at the intricate inlay of the table-top. 'The Jaws of the Wolf, so the stars say.'

Gruber felt his guts clench. He leaned forward to catch every soft, curling word.

'Jaws of the Wolf, precious jaws, bone bright. They are precious and they have been taken.'

'By who? For what purpose?' Lowenhertz asked.

'By darkness, Heart-of-a-Lion. Foul darkness. They cannot be recovered. Eh! I have seen woe on this rock-city! Pain! Pestilence! Eh! I have seen misery and weeping and lamentation!'

'Cannot be recovered?' Lowenhertz's voice seemed suddenly frail. 'Why not, master? What is the darkness you speak of?'

'Night. But not a night of the stars to read and learn from. A night without stars. That is when the Jaws of the Wolf will bite the living heart from Middenheim rock-city. Eh!'

Gruber looked up. Lowenhertz seemed on the point of leaving, as if he'd heard enough.

'What can we do?' Gruber asked directly.

'That's it,' said Lowenhertz. 'Master Al-Azir has said his piece. We must go now!'

'I'm not going anywhere!' snapped Gruber, shaking off Lowenhertz's hand. 'Master Al-Azir, if you know this much, you must know more! I beg you, tell us! What can we do?'

'Enough, Gruber!'

'No! Sit down, Lowenhertz! Now!'

Al-Azir made gentle shushing motions with his hands and Lowenhertz sat again. 'It is as I said. They cannot be recovered. They are lost to you forever.'

Gruber leant across the table to face Al-Azir. 'Your pardon, sir. I am a White Wolf, of White Company, beloved of Ulric. I know when a battle is lost and when it is won, but I will still stay the course. The Jaws of Ulric may be gone from us and beyond recovery, but I will fight on... fight on, I say! A Wolf fights to the death even when the battle is lost! So tell me this at least: who is the enemy I am losing to? What are his signs?'

The huge servant emerged from behind the nets, flanking his master. His sword was splayed and curved and almost as tall as Gruber.

Gruber didn't back off. He had a hand on the pommel of the blade in his waistband and his nose right in the face of the tiny, old alchemist. 'Tell me! It may not do me any good in your eyes, but tell me anyway!'

Al-Azir waved a hand and the servant and his sword departed. 'Gruber of the Wolf, I pity you. But I admire your courage. Eh! Even though you will lose what is dear to you. Look for the Black Door. Look for the north of seven bells. Look for the lost smoke.'

Gruber sat back on his bolster. He felt stunned. 'Look for–'

'You heard him,' Lowenhertz said from the doorway.

Gruber looked up into the eyes of Al-Azir, which fixed upon him for the first time. Gruber was amazed at the clarity and humour of the brown eyes in those sallow hoods.

Without thinking, he took up his cup and drained it. Then he reached his hand forward and clasped Al-Azir's as it was extended. 'If you've helped me, my thanks,' he said.

Al-Azir smiled. A genuine smile. 'You cannot win, Gruber. But make a good job of losing. Eh! It has been interesting talking with you.'

Out in the courtyard, Gruber was smiling as he pulled on his boots. Lowenhertz growled, 'What do you think you were doing in there? There are ways, customs, protocols!'

'Aw, shut up. He liked me... Heart-of-a-Lion.'

'I thought you were going to attack him.'

'So did I,' Gruber said cheerfully, leading the way to the exit gate. 'But you know what? I think he liked me better than you. You've been round there so long with your yes master, no master, and here I am, an ignorant Wolf, and he tells me what's what.'

'Maybe... but what have we got?'

'A lead, Lowenhertz – or weren't you listening? We've got a lead.'

'But he said we'd lose any–'

'Who cares? Come on!'

Bleyden was a small, slight man, little taller than the dwarf Kled, but rake thin. He wore an immaculate silk doublet and curious gloves of black hide. He perched in an upholstered throne chair that was set up on boxes to give him commanding height. Aric thought it just drew attention to his diminutive stature. He couldn't help smiling at the way Bleyden's clerical desk was similarly raised on boxes so he could reach it from the chair.

The little man took the bag of coins that Ganz handed him. Aric saw ice in Ganz's look as he handed over the bag. *He may kill Anspach for this,* Aric decided.

Bleyden opened the draw-string of the bag and peeked inside like a child with a bag of sweets. A delighted look flashed across his small, drawn features. *He must be eighty, judging from his thin silver hair and tight waxy skin,* thought Aric, *and no bigger than a stable lad from the Wolf Barrack. And this man is the Low King who rules the crime syndicates of the eastern city?*

Bleyden began to count off coins from the bag onto his desk top. His nimble, gloved fingers made neat, ten-coin piles in a row, each pile meticulously straightened and flushed. It took all of three minutes, three silent minutes where the only sound was Kled chewing the last of the sausage and scribing marks in the old doorframe with a large, rusty knife he had suddenly produced.

'Forty-seven crowns,' beamed Bleyden, looking up from the neat stacks and handing the folded purse back to Ganz. The commander took it wordlessly.

'A down-payment on my debt. Satisfactory, I trust?' Anspach said.

'Quite satisfactory,' the tiny man replied. He slid a red-bound ledger from a shelf under the desk, opened it carefully and made a deliberate mark in ink with his quill. He looked up. 'I am impressed with the fraternal loyalty of the Knight Templars,' he said, his voice oozing like treacle. 'To stand payment for a colleague.'

'We Wolves stand together,' Ganz replied without a trace of irony. Or emotion.

We'll stand together all right, Aric thought, *and watch as Ganz beats Anspach to death in the stable block tonight.* There was a smile that was battling to get out and stretch on Aric's face. He bit his cheek hard.

'Was there anything else?' Bleyden asked. 'I am busy. And we are closed, as I'm quite sure Kled informed you.'

'Information,' Ganz said. The word was hard and solid, like a splinter of the Fauschlag Rock. 'Anspach tells me you know things. About the circulation of... goods in the city.'

Bleyden raised his eyebrows at Anspach. 'Does he? I'm surprised at you, Anspach. You know what loose tongues do.'

'Fall out,' Kled said ominously from behind them.

Bleyden chuckled. 'What is your name, friend of Anspach?'

'Ganz.'

'Commander of White Company! Well, I'm honoured!' Bleyden chuckled again. 'I had no idea I was in the presence of such greatness. Commander Ganz... well, well, well. A stranger to my establishments. Why is that?'

'Unlike Anspach, I find no need to take risks or see death when I'm off-duty. My working life is amply full of such activities.'

'And the fact that you are standing before me alive implies that the death you speak of is the kind you deal out. My, my, Commander Ganz. That's about as close to a threat as anything I've heard in years.'

'You should get out more,' Ganz said.

Great Ulric, but he's pushing him! thought Aric. He suddenly wondered where the dwarf and his rusty knife were. Behind them still. Should he risk settling a hand on the haft of the dagger in his belt, or was that going to give Kled all the excuse he needed? Aric swallowed. *Careful, commander,* he willed.

Bleyden was still smiling. 'Information comes at a price, Commander Ganz. All you've done is diminish Anspach's tally. I've seen nothing today that suggests to me I should volunteer information.'

'What would?' Ganz asked.

'Settling Anspach's debt might make me reconsider. Settling it with interest.'

'But I've given you all my–'

Bleyden pursed his lips and shook his little head. 'Coins are coins. If you're out of them, there are other ways to pay. A favour, perhaps? I would value greatly the idea that I could call upon a commander of a Templar Company when I needed it. Consider it a down-payment of trust.'

Aric could see how Ganz's shoulders tightened. Anspach looked worried. Aric knew the last thing he had intended was for their commander to pollute his hands by making an honour-promise to a beast like Bleyden. This was not going well.

But there was the honour of the Temple too, of the Wolves as a whole. Aric suddenly realised in his heart that Ganz would be prepared to take the offer, to corrupt himself and leave himself honour-bound to this scum if that was what it took.

Ganz was about to speak when Aric pushed forward and dropped his own purse on the desk. Bleyden looked at it as if it was a bird-dropping.

'My own coins. Fifty-eight crowns. Count it. That, with my commander, pays Anspach's dues... with interest.'

Bleyden sucked at his teeth.

'As I said, I am impressed with the fraternal loyalty of the Knight Templars. Ask away.'

Anspach cleared his throat. 'Has anything of... singular value passed into the secret trade this morning? Something that might fetch an impossible price?'

Bleyden tapped his teeth with his gloved finger tips. 'Have you Wolves lost something?'

'Answer!' Ganz hissed.

'No. Nothing. On my honour, however you value it.'

There was a long silence. For all that effort, nothing! Aric felt like striking the grinning child-man. He certainly knew how to string along his dopes for extra revenue.

'Let me out of here!' Ganz barked and turned to go. Kled stood aside from the door and made an 'after you' gesture that any chamberlain in the Graf's palace would have been proud of.

'Don't go away angry, Commander Ganz,' Bleyden said suddenly. 'I am a vicious and conniving businessman, but I am still a businessman. I understand the mechanisms of trade and I know when a customer should feel he's got his money's worth. Listen to me now...'

Ganz turned back.

'I don't know what you've lost, Wolf, and I don't care. If it comes into my hands, I'll get the best price for it and you'll get first refusal. All I can offer now is this... you're not the only ones.'

'What do you mean?'

'Last night, many noble bodies in this city were deprived of valuable things. You're not the first to come here today asking questions. Not the last either, I'll warrant. Everyone knows of Bleyden's skill in disposal of valuables. There is a word on the street too.'

'And?' said Anspach.

'Your money's worth, if it will help. Last night, the Merchants' Guild was robbed of the stamped gold scales that stand in their Guildhall, the symbol of their trade. Last night, something of great symbolic worth was taken from the chapter house of the Knights Panther. Last night, the ceremonial pledging cup of the City Militia went missing. Last night, the Alembic of Crucifal was taken from its locked cabinet in the chancel of the Alchemists' Guildhall. Last night, the Temple of Shallya was robbed of the Unimpeachable Veil. Is this picture clear to you? Is it worth your down-payment? Those are all I know of, but you can wager there are others. Last night, someone systematically robbed all the great institutions of this town of their most hallowed icons.'

Ganz breathed a long sigh. It was worse than he had feared.

'I don't know what's going on in Middenheim,' Bleyden said. 'This isn't a crime spree. This is a conspiracy.'

Ganz motioned the others to follow him. He paused at the door. And turned. 'My thanks, Bleyden. However you value it.'

'Immeasurably, Commander Ganz. And I ask you a favour.'

Ganz paused. 'What?'

'When you find out what's going on, tell *me*. Frankly, it's all rather worrying.'

They left the Tardy Ass by the back door and stood in a shadowed alley while Morgenstern relieved himself against a wall.

'One ale, you said,' Drakken remarked.

'We kept him to three; be thankful,' Einholt said wearily.

'And yet something!' said Morgenstern triumphantly, rearranging his clothes. 'I told you nothing happens in this city without the innkeepers knowing it first!'

Drakken frowned and shot a look at Einholt. Had he been in a different tavern, listening to a different conversation?

'What something?' asked Einholt.

'Didn't you see how dreary and dull it was in there? Didn't you see what was missing?'

'I'm not quite the expert you are in the details of Middenheim's hostelries,' Einholt said sourly.

'Pretend we didn't notice and tell us before we die of old age,' Drakken added.

'The Cup of Cheer! *The Cup of Cheer*! It was obvious!'

They shot him wounding looks of incomprehension.

As if he was explaining it patiently to babies, Morgenstern began. 'The Cup of Cheer is the mascot icon of the Guild of Vittalers. Every year they compete for it and the winning tavern sets it in pride of place above the bar, the stamp that marks them as the best ale-house in town. The Tardy Ass won it last Mitterfruhl and where was it? Aha! Under the cloth draped over the alcove above the bar? I think not! It's gone too!'

'Let me get this straight,' Einholt said. 'You're suggesting we compare the loss of the Teeth of Ulric to the theft of some battered chalice that innkeepers hold dear?'

'We each have our own treasures,' Morgenstern said. He was probably going to explain further when the four long shadows passed across them.

The four men from the fountain. They approached down the alley, two from either end, faces fixed and grim.

'Time for some fun,' Morgenstern remarked. And charged them.

His huge bulk felled the pair advancing from the western end, smashing one aside into a stagnant pool of horse urine and slamming the other against the wall. The other two were on Drakken and Einholt in a second.

Drakken dropped and swung low, punching the ribs of his attacker and then throwing him over his head, propelled by his own charge. Einholt was locked with his man, grappling and thrashing, overturning crates of empty bottles and refuse.

Morgenstern was busy slamming the head of his assailant back into the mouldy alley wall. He seemed intent on finding a space between the bricks that it would fit. His other attacker was now back on his feet. A glimmer of steel lit in his hands.

Drakken cried out. Ducking the renewed assault of the man he had sent flying, he dodged two, three, four punches before planting one of his own, which laid the man out on the cobbles, his jaw lolling. Einholt broke his man's grip with a knee to his softer parts and smacked him to the ground with an open hand. The man's flailing legs came round and ripped Einholt's feet out from under him. They went down into the muck and sewage, clawing and biting.

Drakken sprang down the alley past Morgenstern and his sagging victim, and tackled the man with the knife. He looped his hand in low, catching the wrist, and threw the man against the wall. A slam of the wrist, then another, and at last the knife flew loose.

Down the alley, Einholt finally got the better of his opponent and left him stewing unconscious in the drain ditch.

Drakken was locked in fury with the last one, hands around his throat. Morgenstern suddenly leaned over them, holding the fallen knife by the blade.

'Drakken! Boy! See the hilt? See the markings? These men are Knights Panther. I think we should talk to them, don't you?'

A hot, dull caul of evening hung around the city, and surly strands of twilight filtered into the window spaces and archways of the Templars' barracks. In the long, suffocatingly hot Temple eating hall, ranged around in the fluttered candlelight, sat White Company in their motley garb, and four others – the rather battered individuals encountered by Morgenstern's party. Ganz leaned down into the face of their leader, who was dabbing a bloody lip with a fold of cloth.

'When you're ready, von Volk of the Panthers.'

'I'm ready, Ganz of the Wolves.' The man looked up at him. The last time they had exchanged such grim looks, they had been on horseback at the gates of Linz in the spring.

Von Volk patted his swollen lip again and cast an angry look across at Morgenstern, who smiled broadly. 'Last night, at the chime of compline, the regimental shrine of the Knights Panther at the palace was robbed.'

'What was taken?' Ganz asked.

'Does it matter? We were out to retrieve our loss when we came upon a group of rascals asking questions and seeking information. It... it seemed to us that they knew something about our loss, so we tracked them and intercepted them.'

'Oh, that's what it was! Interception!' Morgenstern chuckled. 'And I thought it was a sound trouncing!'

Two of the Panthers sprang to their feet, eyes blazing and fists clenched, but Ganz shouted them into place.

He looked at von Volk a minute more and then sank onto the bench beside him, their eyes fixed. 'Panther, we too were robbed. And, as far as we can be certain, so was every other great institution of the city.'

Von Volk seemed surprised at Ganz's candour. He turned away, thoughtful. 'A conspiracy, then?' he murmured.

'And one we have a lead on,' Gruber said, stepping forward.

Ganz and von Volk looked at him.

'Ah, not a good one,' Gruber was forced to admit, grilled by the stern looks of the company commanders. 'But a lead nonetheless...'

As vespers struck and twilight dropped across Middenheim like a damask curtain in a theatre pit, they spread out again. Wolves and Panthers together, splitting into parties to search the city even more thoroughly than before. Von Volk had summoned ten more Panthers from the Royal Barracks and they had arrived, clad in plain clothing, to be apportioned off into the working groups.

Aric was with the third group: Lowenhertz, Gruber, Einholt, von Volk himself and two arrogant, silent Panther knights named by their commander as Machan and Hadrick. They passed out into the streets, under the gently swinging lamps. Sultry evening swaddled around them. Now they were all shrouded in heavy capes to disguise their weapons and partial armour.

Gruber paused to look up at the sullen sky with its haze of ruddy, cloudy light. 'A night without stars...' he murmured.

'The stars are there!' Lowenhertz snapped. 'It's early yet, and the twilight haze and cook-smoke of the city are obscuring the heavens. But it will be a clear night. Not a night without stars.'

'Maybe,' Gruber returned, unconvinced.

They were on Tannery Hill, pacing the steep cobbles up to the crest of the city. To either side of them, taverns shook with laughter, music and carousing.

Eight o'clock struck. The bells of the city chimed irregularly, and mismatched. Aric listened to them. Bells, he thought. Just as Gruber had spoken of in his cryptic clues. The first, a delicate plink-plinking note down in Altmarkt. The second a dull bong from Temple Square. The third a triple chime, emptied by distance and the wind, from Ostmark. Then the fourth, a tinny strike from the small church in Sudgarten.

A pause, then the fifth, sixth and seventh came together, overlapping. The last peals drifted away from the College Chapels on the upper slope of the Palast District.

Then a long break, and afterwards the slender tower of the Milliner's struck eight. To the north of them, by several hundred yards.

'Is it just me...?' Aric began. He looked round to see both Gruber and Lowenhertz, transfixed by the staggered sounds and positions of the chimes.

Gruber stroked his lean chin and glanced at Lowenhertz.

'Well, Heart-of-a-Lion?'

'Just... just a coincidence. What are the chances? We happen to be standing where we can hear seven peals to the south and then one to the north. Al-Azir couldn't have–'

Gruber turned to face Lowenhertz fully. His face was expressionless, but Aric could hear real anger in his tone. The Panther Knights and Einholt looked on, uneasy.

'You bemuse me, Lowenhertz,' Gruber hissed. 'You seem to know more about the mystical and esoteric world than all of us, you bother to chase leads from strange foreigners who would bewilder us with their customs, you urge us to look for secrets in the fabric of the earth... and you deny this? Why? Ulric take me, I'm a blind old heathen next to you, but even I can imagine that your Al-Azir, if he has the skills and knowledge you reckon of him, would have given a portent-clue, particular to us!'

Lowenhertz sighed. 'You're right, old man. You don't understand the delicate ways of enlightened souls such as Al-Azir. Ulric! I don't even pretend to! There was more to his meaning than this! His intellect and understanding is refined far beyond our capacity! He–'

'Would have given us a clue we could understand if we were sharp enough?' cut in Aric smartly. 'How would you explain the complex tactics of a cavalry formation to one untutored in the arts of horse-war? Simply? In words a simpleton could understand? I think so!'

'Aric's right,' growled Einholt. 'I respect you as a battle-brother, Lowenhertz, and respect your learning, but I think you're thinking too hard.'

Gruber smiled. 'Well put, Jagbald, old friend. Lowenhertz, you know your foreign friend was trying to help me, not you. I was the one that asked – a dumb soldier, not a man of learning like you. Wouldn't he have couched his meaning in a way I could understand? And do you not doubt his powers, to know ahead of time we – I – would be in the right place to understand that meaning?'

Lowenhertz was a silent shadow in the gathering dark.

'North of seven bells, he said,' Gruber went on. 'Could it hurt to test that? Could it hurt to believe he has a vision beyond ours? Wasn't that why you took me to him in the first place? And made me take off my damn boots and drink that foul tar?'

Lowenhertz sighed and nodded. He turned and strode uphill, north towards the thin spike of the Milliner's clock tower.

They checked the streets and alleyways around the Milliner's Hall for the best part of an hour. As the clocks chimed again, true dark was settling over the Fauschlag. The hot clouds of sunset had wilted away. The dark bowl of heaven was black-purple and starless.

Von Volk took Aric's sleeve suddenly and gestured upwards. 'Look for lost smoke, Wolf. Wasn't that the damn riddle?'

Aric nodded. He looked where the Panthers' commander was indicating. The night air above the street was hazed by chimney smoke from the homes and taverns around them. The smoke was almost invisible, but it dimpled and blurred the cold solidity of the darkness.

'Then where's that coming from?' asked von Volk.

Aric looked, and realised the Panther's eyes were keen. One column of faint haze seemed to have no source, no obvious flue or chimney to emit it. It simply vented from a space between stacked roof-slopes, ghostly and slow.

'Ar-Ulric seal my lips!' Aric began. He turned and looked at von Volk fiercely.

'Lost smoke?' the Panther asked with a predatory grin.

Aric called the others in to join them and together, the seven men prowled down Chute Lane towards the complex clump of ancient dwellings that the smoke was exuding from.

'Gods!' Einholt spat. 'Where's its source?'

'Nowhere...' murmured the Panther Machan dangerously, his hand inside his cloak, clutching the hilt of his sword.

Gruber stopped them all with a wave of his hand. They were edging into a dark alley, having to stoop low because of the way the buildings on either side leaned in, making a tunnel of relaxed, sooty brick. The alley was full of refuse, mire and a trickle of water. Rats chittered and darted around their feet. Einholt, Hadrick and von Volk filled hand-lamps with oil from a flask and lit them from the same taper, holding the pottery dishes up above their stooped heads as they led the way in.

Fifteen yards down the gently turning alley, probing deeper than anyone but rats or fleeing cut-purses had been in years, they saw it.

'Ulric damn me!' Gruber said, almost voicelessly.

A door. Lower than a man, more of a hatch, built into the brick wall of the alleyway tunnel. Timber-built and strong. And black with pitch.

'Look for the black door,' Gruber said.

'The lost smoke, the north of seven bells...' added Aric.

'On a night without stars,' Lowenhertz finished.

Lowenhertz pulled out his warhammer from under his cape and smashed the black door in off its hinges.

Darkness beckoned them.

Within, a narrow stairway led down below street level. They had to stoop and hunch, knocking scalps and elbows against the confines.

'Dwarf-made?' Aric wondered.

'As old as the Fauschlag itself,' agreed Einholt, ominously.

From what little they could see around them, by the flickering lamp-flames, the steps were hewn from the rock and turned gently to the right. The walls were travertine brick for as long as the old foundations of the buildings over the alley descended, and then became smooth, tooled stone. They'd gone down at least thirty feet. Leading the way by his lamp, von Volk touched the rock wall and his fingers came away with sticky black-ness on their tips.

'Caulked with pitch, like the door. Like a boat's keel.'

'And fresh too,' Lowenhertz muttered, also touching the walls. 'This place is well-tended and maintained.'

'But why the pitch?' Machan asked. 'To keep the damp out?'

'Or to keep something in,' Lowenhertz finished.

The steps levelled out and they found themselves in an underground tunnel tall enough for them to stand up in, but so narrow they could only move in single file.

'Which way?' Hadrick asked.

'North,' Gruber replied with great and awful certainty.

They moved north. After a hundred yards, they came upon another flight of steps down and they descended. The air began to smell of damp antiq-uity, the sweat of the old rock that now surrounded them and on which Middenheim was raised.

Von Volk's lamp sputtered out and Einholt refilled it from his oil-flask. Once the lamp was reignited, Einholt tossed the empty flask away. 'That's almost it for light,' he told them all. 'I have a little more oil left,' Aric said. 'But maybe we won't need it,' he added, sliding past von Volk, scraping his back on the tarry rock wall. He edged ahead, his feet silent on the smooth, cold, damp of the stone. 'Look. Am I imagining that?'

He wasn't. Light. Cold, fretful light, ahead and below them. With Aric in the lead, they followed it, extinguishing their lamps to save oil as the light grew.

After another hundred yards and another descending stairway, they came out into a wide tunnel of rough rock, like a mine. Threads of tiny sil-ver lamps were looped on wire along each wall as far as they could see in each direction. The rough rock wall was rich with scintillating shards that caught the light and made it seem as if they were walking amongst stars.

'Glass specks... crystal...' murmured Gruber, stroking the rough wall with his fingers.

'Or gems, precious gems,' returned von Volk, looking more closely at the shards. 'This is the spur of an old dwarf mine, or I'm a Bretonnian! An old place, dug long before the city was raised.'

'I fear you're right,' Lowenhertz said. 'This is an ancient, forgotten place.'

'Not forgotten, Heart-of-a-Lion,' Gruber said quietly. 'Who lit the lamps?'

Aric and Einholt both paused to inspect the silver lamps. They were intricate metal trinkets with compact glass chimneys. Their wicks burned with an intense white light, sucking fuel from the reservoirs beneath them.

'They're not burning oil,' Einholt said.

'Indeed not. I've never seen anything like this!' Aric muttered, amazed. Lowenhertz joined him to look. He sucked in a short, startled breath as he studied the lamp.

'Alchemy!' he said, turning to the others. 'These lamps are fired by an alchemical mix, a contact reaction... Gods! The best I know, Al-Azir included, could perhaps have wrought one such lamp in a month of industry!'

'And there are hundreds of them... ranged as far as we can see.' Gruber's voice seemed deflated of strength at the wonder of it.

They paced on down the lit tunnel, two abreast now, gazing about themselves. Gruber and von Volk took the lead, with Hadrick and Einholt behind them, then Aric and Machan, and Lowenhertz bringing up the rear. By now, all had drawn weapons: warhammers in the hands of the Wolves, swords in the hands of the Panthers. Hadrick also carried a crossbow, which he had wound to tension and let swing around his shoulder on a leather strap.

A crossway now, as the mine tunnel they traced intersected with another. The one they followed was lit with lamps and the other dark. There seemed no doubt as to the route they should take. Aric felt beads of perspiration gather on his scalp, despite the musty chill of the rock around him. He had lost all sense of time since they had come down here.

The passage widened and let out into a long, low cavern similarly draped with alchemical lamps. The walls seemed to be made of solid quartz and glowed like ice in the lamp-light. They advanced across the uneven floor.

'I'd be careful, if I were you,' said a voice from nowhere.

The Panthers and Wolves froze, looking about themselves, mystified.

Three figures approached from a side chamber none had seen was there. The Wolves and Panthers swung their weapons up ready. 'Make yourselves known!' cried von Volk.

The three figures stepped into the light of the lamps: a tall man in a long green cloak flanked by two Tilean mercenaries in leather hauberks and quilted leggings, their longswords drawn and their faces dark and stern behind the grilles of basket-helms. The green-cloaked man, whose face was long and clean-shaven, smiled a chilling smile which creased his pale, smooth skin. His eyes were hooded and deeply shadowed by dark skin.

'I am Master Shorack. My full title is longer and more burdensome, so you may know me as that. This pair are Guldo and Lorcha. They have no longer or more burdensome titles than that. They are, however, experienced and terrifying killers. So let's know you without delay.'

Von Volk and Gruber were about to move forward aggressively, but Lowenhertz stayed them both and pushed between them to face the cloaked man. Instantly, the two Tileans swung the tips of their long, gleaming blades to the point at his throat.

'Master Shorack, well met,' Lowenhertz said calmly, as if the swords weren't there.

'Is that you, Lowenhertz of the Wolves?' the cloaked man asked, squinting into the light. He made a subtle gesture and the Tileans smartly withdrew their blades, falling back behind him. He stepped forward. 'My, my, Lowenhertz. Who is this with you?'

'A mixed pack of Wolves and Panthers, master. Seeking the same as you, if I'm any judge.'

'Really? I'm very impressed. Everyone in the city running hither and yon to find their lost treasures, and you... Wolves and Panthers... get as close as me.'

'Who in Ulric's name is this, Lowenhertz?' Gruber spat indignantly.

'Master Shorack, Master Magician Shorack, of the Magicians' Conclave,' Aric said from behind. He'd never met the man, but he recognised the name.

'In person,' smiled Shorack. 'Humour me, Temple-Knights... what led you here?'

'A hunch,' Aric said.

'Determination...' von Volk said.

'Lowenhertz,' said Gruber, stepping forward. 'Or rather, me. From devious clues left by another of your stripe, Ebn Al-Azir.'

Shorack scoffed loudly. 'That charlatan? My dear sir, he's an alchemist, a tinkerer with the world's elements, a child in the realms of creation! I, sir, am a magician. A master of my art! There is no comparison!'

'I happened to like old Al-Azir, as a matter of fact,' Gruber said reflectively, realising he was voicing his thoughts. He paused, then continued anyway, turning to look into Shorack's dark eyes. 'Which is rare for me. Ordinarily, I'd have no truck with such people. In my experience, there are men who walk bravely in the light of goodness, and there are creatures who haunt the darkness and play with magic. There... is no comparison.'

Shorack cleared his throat, looking at Gruber intently. 'Was that some kind of threat, old warrior? An insult?'

'Just a statement of fact.'

'Assuming we're here for the same purpose,' Aric said softly from behind Gruber, 'maybe we should skip the insults entirely and work together.'

'Unless Master Shorack here is behind the injustice we seek to rectify,' von Volk said coldly.

Gruber grunted in agreement. He had been the first to ascribe the thefts to magic, and nothing he had seen so far had disabused him of the notion. Now an actual magician crossed their path, damn his hide...

'Sir! If I was your enemy, you would not be alive to conduct this charming bar-room spat!' Shorack's teeth gleamed in the light. 'Indeed, did I not first cry out a warning?'

'Warning?' Lowenhertz asked, clearly uncomfortable at the confrontation.

'Take it as a gesture of good faith. The hallway you were about to venture down is warded.' The Wolves and Panthers turned to look down the rough-hewn, glowing quartz chamber.

'Magic awaits the unwary and the unprepared here. Guarding magic. Simple stuff, so very much beneath my powers, but it would surely have caught you had you advanced.'

'And done what?' von Volk asked the magician.

Shorack smiled. 'Have you ever been drunk, soldier?'

Von Volk shrugged. 'On occasions. At feast days. What of it?'

Shorack laughed gently. 'Think how it feels to be drunk – if you are a tankard of ale.'

He turned and strode down the uneven floor, raising his hands wide, muttering a few high-pitched words that made Aric think for a moment of fingernails on glass. The sound made him catch his breath slightly. There was a smell too, a distant odour of decomposition, like a drain had been cracked open somewhere nearby.

'It is safe now,' Shorack said, turning back. 'The ward of guarding has been dispelled. We may all continue safely.'

'I stand in awe of your work, Master Shorack,' Gruber said, apparently with great humility. 'You speak baby-talk, break wind and tell us your invisible magic has saved us from a sorcerous trap we couldn't see.'

Shorack paced right up to Gruber till they were face to face. The magician was smiling again. 'Your scorn delights me. It is so refreshing to be disrespected. What is your name?'

'Gruber, of the Wolves.'

Shorack leaned forward until he was nose to nose with the old Wolf. His smile disappeared and was replaced by an expression as cold and hard and threatening as a drawn dagger. Gruber didn't even blink. 'Be thankful, Gruber of the Wolves, that you do not see. Be thankful that the magical world is invisible to your dull eyes, or you would claw out those eyes and die screaming in terror.'

'I'll remember to mention you to Ulric in my prayers,' Gruber replied tonelessly.

'Enough!' barked Aric, losing patience. 'If we're going on together, let's go on! Why don't you tell us what you're here for, Master Shorack?'

'You know already,' Shorack said, turning courteously to Aric.

'We know the Magician's Conclave must have lost something precious, as we have, a treasure as you put it. What?'

'It cannot be named. A charm. Priceless. To describe its properties and purpose would rob you of sanity.'

They all turned as Einholt chuckled. 'Invisible this, unspeakable that! Gruber's right – isn't it funny that we've only got this fellow's word for everything, and that he keeps sparing our sensitive ears from the actual truth. You should work the theatres, Master Shorack! You're a fine melodramatist!'

Shorack looked at him. Aric saw a strange look cloud the magician's face. It seemed like recognition... and pity.

'Einholt,' Shorack said flatly, at last.

'You know me, sir?' Einholt asked.

'Your name just came to me. The invisible world you mock spoke it to me. Einholt. You are a brave man. Stay out of the shadows.'

'Stay – what?'

Shorack had looked away, as if he found the sight of Einholt's face uncomfortable. *No*, thought Aric, *not uncomfortable. Unendurable. As if it... terrified him.*

'Shall we continue, Wolves and Panthers?' asked the magician brightly. Too brightly, in Aric's opinion. Shorack led the party down the quartz hall, his bodyguards at his heels.

'What did he mean?' Einholt hissed at Lowenhertz. 'What was that about?'

Lowenhertz shrugged. 'I don't know, Brother Wolf. But I know this: do as he says. Stay out of the shadows.'

More steps, a lamp-lit stairwell descending from the rear end of the quartz hall. As far as Gruber could judge, the steps brought them another hundred feet down into the rock, along a wide, sweeping staircase. Three times, Shorack had them stop so he could perform more pantomime and save them from invisible traps.

Enough theatrics! Gruber heard himself think. But there was no denying the cold chill of the nonsense words Shorack used for those pantomimes. Gruber caught Aric watching carefully and with concern. He saw, too, the black worry on Einholt's tense face.

Gruber edged down the steps until he was descending beside Shorack.

'You're a man of esoteric learning, Master Shorack. Have you any explanation for the troubles we find ourselves in? Why the thefts? Why something from each of the city's great institutions?'

'Do you know how to place a charm on a person, Gruber? A love charm, a luck-knot, a curse?' Shorack answered.

'No. I'm a soldier, as you know.'

'Any charm, from the simplest to the most abstract, requires a signifier. Something belonging to the individual you wish to charm. For a love-potion, a hank of hair; for luck, some coins from his purse or a favourite ring; for a curse... well, a drop of blood is the most efficacious. The signifier becomes the basis for the charm, the heart of the ritual that sets it.'

The stairs turned to the left and descended again steeply. The air was getting colder, damper, and now there was a taste of smoke.

'Imagine now you wished to place a charm upon something larger than a man – a city, let's say. A hank of hair won't do. You need signifiers of a different kind.' Shorack glanced at Gruber, one eyebrow raised to enquire if he was making sense.

'The items we've lost, those are the signifiers?'

'Indeed. Oh, I cannot be sure. We may be on the trail of some deranged trophy collector. But I doubt it. I believe someone is setting out to place a conjuration upon the entire city of Middenheim.'

Gruber sucked in his breath. In fairness, he had already begun to imagine such a thing, before he'd even conversed with the prim magician. From the battlefields of his career, he had seen the way the unholy enemy treasured marks of their foe for their mystical potency. They would go to great lengths to take standards, weapons, scalps, skulls. Gruber said nothing more, and led them down the steps.

The stairs brought them out, at last, into a huge chamber that Aric would think of ever afterwards as the cellar. Paved with violet tiles, it was as vast as the drill field of the Wolves' Temple barracks, but broken into sections by rows of pillars that flared upwards into corbel vaults. Aric imagined that once this place had been a huge larder, a wine-storehouse, a provisionary, crammed with racked flasks of dwarf brew, shelves of jarred root vegetables, muslin-wrapped cheeses and pickled fruit, and hung with salted meats. Now it was empty, the walls and pillars pitched black, strung with white lights. A stronger light source emanated from the far end, two hundred feet away, the glow criss-crossed by the back-lit shadows of the pillars. There was a low, sucking, rasping sound, as if the stones around them were taking long, slow breaths. And there was a smell of spoiled milk.

And another sound: a chanting. A murmur of priestly voices intoning something very far away. The sound came from the direction of the distant glow, and was given its rhythm by the beat of a bass tambour. The party spread out low, silently, hugging the pillars for cover. Gruber edged left with Einholt, Machan and von Volk. Aric took the right, with Hadrick and the Tilean, Guldo. Centrally, Lowenhertz advanced with Shorack and the other mercenary, Lorcha. They fluttered from pillar cover to pillar cover, darting between shadows, weapons drawn, moving towards the glow.

Lowenhertz settled into hiding behind a pillar. That sound – not the chanting, the seismic panting – filled his mind with fear. Shorack scurried up next to him, dabbing at the edges of his mouth with a silk handkerchief. There was blood on the cloth.

'Master Shorack?' whispered Lowenhertz.

'Nothing, my old friend,' the magician coughed back. Lowenhertz could smell the metallic stink of blood on his breath. 'Nothing. There are spirits loose in the air here – dead, vile things. The scent of them burns my throat.'

From his position in cover, Aric looked over at the source of the light. A wood fire, kindled in the stone basin of an ancient stone salting bath. The flames licked up, blazing the bundles of fragrant wood spindles incandescently, spilling off the sour stench. The smoke rose, as if pulled, up and out through a flue in the cellar's roof. *Now, at last, the source of the lost smoke becomes clear*, he thought.

Around the fire, stone blocks had been set like shoeing anvils or stools. They had been ranged around the central furnace in a peculiar, apparently random manner. On each one sat a priceless trophy: a glittering pledging cup, a crystal bottle, a gauzy fold of linen, a gold chalice, a beaded and pearled bracelet of panther claws, a mayoral badge, a sceptre, a silver timepiece, a furled dagger, a small silken bag... other items he couldn't make out. And one final one he could: the Jaws of Ulric, gaping, glittering in the firelight.

Aric could also see the twenty hooded figures kneeling amongst the blocks, facing the fire. They were the source of the chanting. One of them struck upon a drum.

At the heart of it all, his back to the fire so he faced the worshippers, stood a thin figure. Emaciated, wrapped in dark wadding, the figure seemed to jerk and move stiffly, like a puppet. It twitched in time to the beat. Aric could not see any detail, but he knew it was the most loathsome thing he had ever seen. He wished to be anywhere else now; fighting beast-packs in the Drakwald would be a holiday next to this horror.

Crouched behind the pillar next to Shorack, Lowenhertz realised how pale and perspiring the man had become.

'Shorack?' Lowenhertz whispered in concern.

Shorack settled his back to the pillar for a moment, trying to slow his breathing. His face was damp and pasty. 'This is... bad, Lowenhertz,' he murmured. 'Crown of Stars! I spend my life flexing my powers in the invisible world, and the gods know sometimes I tinker with the darker excesses. Their lure is great. But this... this is ritual magic so dark, so foul I – I have never seen or felt its like. Lowenhertz, I never even dreamed such abomination existed! This place is Death's place now!'

Lowenhertz looked at the magician in the dim light. The sense of him as a haughty, capable figure was all gone now, all his confidence and theatrical airs wasted away. Lowenhertz knew Shorack was powerful for an urban magician, among the best of his kind in the city. His skills had been enough to get them this far. But he was just a man now; a frightened man, way out of his depth. Lowenhertz felt immeasurable pity for the magician. And immeasurable fear for them all. If the great Shorack was scared...

From his vantage point, Gruber laid low on his belly and took in the scene. There were the lost treasures, and he had no doubt that they were being used, as Shorack had described, as signifiers in some great charm. *No*, he reconsidered, *curse is probably a far more appropriate word*. His flesh crawled. That panting, breathing sound around them, as if the walls were sighing. That beat, that chanting. And worst of all, that jerking puppet shape by the fire. Gruber wished Ulric had been merciful and spared him from ever having to see such a thing.

Von Volk was beside him. Fear made von Volk's eyes black, unblinking pits. 'What do we do, Wolf?' he whispered.

'Is there a choice, Panther?' Gruber mouthed. 'A great and stifling darkness is being born here that will overwhelm the city we guard with our lives. We must do what we were trained to do and pray it is enough.'

Von Volk nodded, took a deep breath, readied his blade and then looked across the cellar to Aric's group on the far side. The Panther commander caught Hadrick's eye and made a curt, chopping motion with his fist. Hadrick raised his crossbow.

The beat slapped. The chanting continued. The stones panted around them, sucking for breath. The fire cracked. The reek of death and decay choked the air. The puppet figure twitched.

Hadrick fired.

The crossbow bolt hit the twitching puppet in the chest and smashed it backwards into the fire. It shrieked – a ghastly, not-human noise – and clawed at the barb impaling it, floundering in the flames that licked into its filthy swaddling.

The hooded worshippers stopped mid-chant, jumped up and began to turn. A second later, the Wolves, Panthers, and Shorack's mercenaries were on them.

Aric charged the firelight, hammer whirling in his hand. It all became a blur. Lorcha was beside him, his longsword hissing through the air.

The puppet thing, ablaze like a torch, was still shrieking and trying to pull itself out of the fire.

The hooded chanters spun to meet them, throwing aside black velvet capes to reveal fierce men in mail-armour, brandishing swords and war-axes. Their screaming faces and their armour were plastered with blood and daubed markings.

Aric's whirring hammer smashed through the face of the first enemy he came upon. The hammerhead tore out the lower jaw, sending the pink, glistening hunk away like a blood-tailed comet, winking with exposed white bone. The next one was on him, and he blocked with his hammer-haft, stopping the axe-blow. Kicking low and hard, Aric dropped the attacker and then rolled in to crush his head flat between hammer and violet tiles.

Gruber waded in, breaking a neck out of true with his hammer, then spinning to face the next sword that came at him. Einholt was beside him, cleaving a ribcage with a sidewards strike. Von Volk broke his sword on his first clash with an enemy blade, and then savagely ripped the life out of his aggressor with the broken length, before throwing him aside and snatching up his axe. In von Volk's practised hands, it dug deep into the skull of the next foe within arm-reach.

Lowenhertz smashed a chanter backwards off his feet with a deft underswing that splintered a snarling face.

Machan struck at them, his sword whispering. Blood sprayed from the wounds he cut. Then he was scissored by two enemy blades. He dropped, screaming, in two, blood-venting pieces.

Hadrick had, by then, enough time to reload, and he slammed his bolt into the forehead of one of Machan's killers. A second later, he was carried back, shrieking, and pinned to a pillar by a foe whose lance had impaled him. Guldo decapitated the foe and pulled the lance out, allowing Hadrick to fall. But he was already dead.

Aric was nearly at the sacred jaws, but then he took a rip across the shoulder and went down on one knee. Gruber and Lowenhertz were hemmed in by fierce hand-to-hand on all sides. The top of Guldo's head was axed off and he fell, stone dead. Von Volk swung his axe up between the legs of a foe-man and split him to the sternum. But his captured axe was wedged and he tried in vain to pull it free.

Shorack raised his hand and with a gesture, at once slight yet full of unknowable power, wilted one of the chanters into fatty, smoking residue. The sounds and stinks of burning metal and flesh choked the air. The sorcerer shook slightly and took one step back as if to steady himself. Then he spun and destroyed the cultist closing on Gruber with nothing more than the clenching of his hand in the air. For a moment, Lowenhertz noted through the ferocious melee, the old Shorack was back with them, imposing, confident, capable, chilling.

Aric broke an opponent's hip and a ribcage. He turned. He saw. The burning, shrieking thing in the fire was getting up again, blackened and smouldering and tarry.

It looked at them through cindered eye-slits. It fixed its gaze on Shorack. It spoke through a mouth thick with fat blisters and crackling flesh.

'Die,' it said, its voice that of a dead thing.

Shorack screamed as if his insides were boiling. Gruber reached for him, but the magician was wrenched into the air by things none of them could see but all could feel. Cold forces of air, eddies of icy wind. Einholt smashed an axe-man aside and reached out to grab Shorack's trailing cloak. He realised with fear that he was seeing the effects of Shorack's invisible world for real now.

The magician spun up, away, out of his reach, thrashing and bedevilled by the harsh grip of unseen things. His green cloak, his clothes, one boot, all shredded off him and fluttered away. Weals and bloody rips scourged his flesh. Almost stripped bare, drenched in blood, half-butchered, Shorack slammed up into the vaulted roof. Bones snapped. It looked as if he had fallen upwards and hit the ceiling as if it was the ground. An immense, invisible force pressed him there, spread-eagled on his back. Blood pooled across the roof around him instead of pouring to the actual floor.

His ruined face, a mask of blood, glared down at Gruber and Einholt looking up from below. It was all the other Wolves, the Panthers and the remaining Tilean, Lorcha, could do to keep their attentions and eyes on the battle at hand. There was something mesmerising about Shorack's gruesome, inexorable demise.

Shorack looked down into the frantic face of Gruber. A moment before his eyes burst and his skull collapsed against the roof, he spoke. Eight words, forced out of a blood-filled mouth, the last act of his life, a monumental act of will power.

'Break. The. Charm. Without. The. Signifiers. It. Cannot.'

Eight words. A ninth, maybe a tenth, would have completed the whole, but the meaning was enough for Gruber.

An invisible force exploded Shorack's carcass across the roof in a shower of blood and meat. It coated the ceiling for a moment and then rained down on them all, leaving a pungent mist of blood vapour in the air.

Gruber was already moving, his hammer raised. Coated in Shorack's blood, he found two of the enemy turning to block him, axes raised. Gruber swung the warhammer round in a complete, whickering circle, both hands gripping the leather loop at the end of the haft, twisting his body-weight to counterbalance the swing. Two skulls broke like earthenware before the swing was done.

Then he was clear, amongst the stone blocks set around the fireplace, each one bearing its precious icon. He knew he was within the weave of a great dark sorcery now, something invisible that laced itself between the signifiers. His skin prickled with static, his hair stood on end, and there was a smell that clawed at his sinuses. A smell of sweet corruption, like a week-old corpse. Magic, he knew, and would never forget. Black magic. *Death magic.*

He thought of Ganz, on the dangerous ride back from Linz, how he had driven the wraith-things back by destroying their precious talon. He knew he had to do the same... again... now... here. A signifier must be destroyed to break the charm. And he knew, clearly and coldly at last, what Al-Azir had really meant.

They cannot be recovered. They are lost to you for ever. Gruber of the Wolf, I pity you. But I admire your courage. Eh! Even though you will lose what is dear to you.

There was no choice. It was set, Gruber was sure, in the intricate and unchangeable workings of the stars. He had time for one blow and he knew, as a Wolf of the Temple of Ulric, where, in fairness, that blow should fall.

The Jaws of the Wolf, so holy, so precious, cut by Artur himself, glittered on the block before him.

He raised his hammer.

Something ripped into his back and agony lanced through him. Gruber screamed. Talons raked down his back from shoulders to waist, shredding off cloak, hauberk and undershirt and slicing deep cuts in his flesh. He stumbled to his knees. The blackened puppet-thing rose up behind him, its curled, skeletal fingers like hooks, red with his blood. It twitched, deathless eyes glittering, and smashed Gruber to the floor with a sideswipe. Blood poured down the side of Gruber's head where the swipe had struck.

For the rest of his life, his left ear would be a rag of flesh, like a flower with the petals torn off.

Gasping, Gruber looked up at the monster that lurched and jiggled over him. Its long, angular limbs twitched and spasmed like a badly-worked marionette. *Or no*, thought Gruber, his pain lending his mind frightening clarity. *Like something half-finished. Like a mockery of a man, a skeleton that remembers how to move but hasn't the flesh or the sinew or the practice to do it well.* Backlit by the firelight, that was all it seemed to be: a large human skeleton, clad in shreds of tomb-dry skin and scraps of burnt bandage, twitching and jerking as it tried to behave like a man again. Tried to be a man again.

Only the eyes were whole: coral-pink fires of livid fury. It gazed down at him. Its bare, sooty teeth clacked open, tearing the dry, blistered flesh of its long-withered mouth.

'Die,' it said.

'Die yourself!' snarled Einholt, storming in from the side and smashing the dreadful thing into the air with an expert swing of his hammer. Twisting, the puppet-thing tumbled away into the darkness beyond the fire.

Einholt glanced down at Gruber once, but he didn't hesitate. It seemed the veteran Wolf had wit enough to arrive at the same conclusions as Gruber. Einholt swung around, hammer lifted over the block, resembling for all who saw, the great god who first wrought the Fauschlag. Then the Jaws of the Wolf, the precious icon of the Wolf Order, disintegrated into a million flying fragments under his hammerhead.

And then... nothing.

There was no great explosion, no fiery flash, no sound, no fury. The cellar just went cold. The walls stopped breathing. The reek of magic vanished and the static charge in the air dissolved. The fire went out.

Blackness. Cold. Damp. The smell of blood, and of death.

Flints scraped together and a small light pierced the gloom. A lamp was lit. Carrying it, Lorcha moved into the circle of blocks, retrieved the small velvet pouch and put it in his jerkin.

'It is made right,' he said to the others in the darkness around him, his accent thick with Tilean vowels. 'I will inform the Conclave.'

A moment later, and he and his lamp were gone.

Aric lit a taper from his pack and raised its small yellow light aloft. Lowenhertz did the same, lighting the last of the lamp-oil he carried. Faint light filtered into the gore-soaked chamber. Urgently, they took kindling from a stack behind the fireplace and made torches. Einholt helped Gruber from the floor.

'Ulric love you, Brother Einholt,' Gruber said, embracing him.

'May Ulric forgive me too,' Einholt replied.

By the kindling light, they gathered the trophies into sacks, Aric reverently handing the panther claw bracelet to von Volk.

The Panther took it and nodded to Aric. 'Ulric watch over you for what you have done here. Your sacrifice will be known to all of my order.'

'And perhaps our orders may not be such rivals from this time,' Gruber suggested as he limped over. 'Panther blood has been spilled to achieve this too.'

He and von Volk clasped hands silently.

'We have everything,' Einholt said. He and Aric carried sacking full of the most precious things in the city. 'I suggest it's time to get out of here. Our light won't last long and there are citizens of Middenheim who will be relieved to get these trinkets back.'

Lowenhertz loomed behind them, a torch raised. His face was pale and determined in the half-light. 'There's... there's no sign of it. The thing Einholt struck. It's destroyed or–'

'Escaped,' Gruber finished.

CONFESSION

The air above Middenheim was cold and still. Below, winds found their way in and out of every byway and alley, whining through gaps in the stones and sucking over damp cobbles. Autumn had come.

The street braziers were built higher, their flames licking against the stone walls, making their black surfaces matt with soot, their fires burning till dawn. Dusk came early now and for many the working day was foreshortened. Citizens were keeping shorter hours, preparing for the harshness of the winter to come, when many would die of the cold and the numerous winter ills and ailments that befell the towering city's population year in and year out.

But for some, the autumn season simply meant they began and ended their working days in darkness. One such was Kruza. He went about his work sleekly, picking his final mark of the day. The last of the merchants were leaving the city in torch-bearing gaggles, among them a rotund middle-aged man with a florid flare of red across his high, round cheeks and magnificent bulbous nose. His pockets looked heavy and, tucked half into the breast of a long, embroidered coat which would not fasten across the fatty mound of his chest, the strings and clasp of a pouch were clearly visible. Kruza spotted him coming out of one of the better alehouses at the edge of Freiburg and followed him into the north end of the Altquartier slums.

Kruza strode easily on past his mark, whose own rolling gait and small steps made slower progress down the steep cobbles. The cut-purse paused for a moment and then turned back the way he had come, checking the position of the purse in the merchant's coat as he passed him, very close. The mark took no heed.

Kruza had marked his target and was ready to make his move when he saw something ahead of him. He flicked his eyes up and away from his intended victim, just in time to see the hem of a long, grey cloak disappear into the doorway of a tavern on the opposite side of the narrow street.

Kruza paused, then took a few more hesitant steps. When he turned back to his mark, the man was disappearing down and round into a sloping side-way. Kruza began to follow the merchant again, trying to concentrate, reminding himself of his quota.

But he could feel the hunting eyes behind him now.

He turned sharply on his heels and this time the pair of cloaked figures, for there were two of them now, barely had time to duck out of sight.

In an instant, Kruza forgot his mark and ducked into the shadows himself. He held the cold palms of his hands flat together before his face, as if in prayer – to Ranald, maybe, the trickster thief-god. No, to any god who would listen. His hands were suddenly clammy with sweat. He felt a bead form on his forehead and find the groove of the long scar down the side of his face. It trickled down the scar to his jaw. It hung there for a moment, then it was joined by another droplet of sweat. The two fell as one from his chin.

He had watched for this moment for months, prepared for it over and over, but now it had finally come, he was not ready. He could never be ready for the return of the grey men who bore the gleaming tail-eating snake sigil. They had got Wheezer and now they would get him.

Kruza stepped out into the middle of the narrow street, looking about him, not for a place to hide, nor for support from others, but to get the lay of the land. He had a sick feeling that there was justice in them coming for him. They had taken Wheezer, and he had been an innocent. His soul wasn't soiled like Kruza's. Of course they would come for him, a hundred times as fierce.

There was only one way to deal with this. He had run before and Wheezer had paid the price. This time he would stand and fight. And if he died, then he would no longer have the boy's doom on his conscience. His hand on the pommel of his short-sword, Kruza stood with his feet braced on the cobble-ridges and his shoulders thrown back. He let out a huge shout – of challenge, of remorse, of warning. Those who heard it could not tell what it meant, only that they should stay away. Kruza heard doors bang and the shutters close on windows all around. Then silence.

The men in grey cloaks heard the cry too as they stood in the next alley, shielded from sight.

'A brave boy, this cut-purse of yours,' the taller, leaner figure said in a low, sardonic voice. 'He means to come to us!'

The shorter, heavily-built second figure turned lightly on his feet and stepped into the deserted street, pulling his companion after him. They stood, thirty paces from the braced figure of the cornered cut-purse, whose scream was still echoing around the close buildings and losing itself in the labyrinth of the Altquartier's streets and alleys.

The taller of the grey figures put a hand beneath his cloak, reaching for his weapon. His heavier companion raised his hands to the hood which cloaked his face in cloth and shadow, and opened his mouth to call out.

But Kruza flew across the thirty paces between himself and the grey men before any had a chance to speak. His short-sword was raised above him in a two-handed grip. He meant to bring it down hard, and fight to the death, even if it was his own. His bloodshot eyes, with their lids peeled well back, showed white all round the black holes of his massively dilated pupils. Another yell began to find its way past his gritted teeth.

Then came the impact.

Kruza barely held on to his short-sword as it bounced and twitched in his hands from the hammer blow which had swung from nowhere to knock it from his grasp.

He swung again in a crude, wobbling arc which was parried hard by a deft hammer-haft, sending tiny shards of steel and wood flying with the intensity of the blow.

Kruza's next swing came in low, but not deep enough. It tore a huge rent in the flowing grey of the taller figure's cloak.

The figure jerked away and threw his head back, freeing it from the shadowy cowl of the cloak's hood. Kruza saw a face with pink-flushed skin and dark eyes that gleamed back at him. There was no sign of the papery skin and pallid thinness of the other grey men. This man was flesh and blood – and ready to fight for all he was worth.

A hammer came in again, swung by the shorter grey man. Kruza blocked it ferociously and sliced in with his sword. The shorter man dodged it. He, too, had removed his hood and had shrugged off half of the cloak. Around his body, Kruza could see the pelt.

He had seen that skin before. His mind raced as he swung his sword again at the fur-wrapped torso. As he cut deeply through the hide, missing the man beneath, Kruza thought of that other man. Weeks back, at the Baiting Pit! The man with his parcel of armour wrapped in a hide, just like this one. The masked gladiator!

Kruza looked into Drakken's face, confused. *The White Wolf. Lenya's White Wolf! Was he one of the grey men?*

Kruza's nostrils flared wide as he sucked in air to control his panic. Spittle coated his lips and his teeth were clenched, allowing no more sounds to escape his body. There were two hammers whooshing through the air around him in a show of Wolf Temple strength. Or was it the strength of the grey men? He did not know.

His short-sword found only air with its next strike. Then, turning and striking again, he felt flesh rip at the end of his sword. Before he could savour it, he was on the ground, doubled over, shocked and winded by a solid blow to the centre of his chest.

Why... why was he not dead? Why had the blow not killed him? Why had he been allowed to live when he was prepared to die?

Kruza let out a soft moan as he lay on the ground.

* * *

Anspach rubbed a fist against the flesh wound to his shoulder, as Drakken knelt down by Kruza's sprawled form, tentatively reaching out a hand to grab the broken thief.

Anspach was thoroughly enjoying himself. Drakken had spoken to him of a cut-purse whom he needed to find – some personal feud, so it seemed, one he wanted to keep quiet. The young Templar had enlisted Anspach's help to do it. It wasn't so difficult for a man with Anspach's knowledge of the city's underbelly, and the little battle in the quiet street of the Altquartier was a positive bonus. Something to warm the cockles on this cold autumn night. Drakken had not told him the young thief had so much spirit, or such a strong sword arm. No harm done. A light flesh wound to the shoulder that would heal in no time, and the indignity, for Drakken, of having his pelt rent into two pieces, neither of which would be big enough to cover the huge young Wolf's torso now.

Explain that to Ganz, Anspach thought to himself. He smirked down at the strange picture of a bedraggled Wolf, offering his hand to a young street thug. He felt almost nostalgic.

On the north side of Middenheim, a giant, blond Wolf Templar strode down the wide avenues just south of the Palace. Alongside him was a tiny woman, her feet skittering in a half-run, half-skip to keep up with him.

'But why did Krieg send you? And where are you taking me?' Lenya gasped, breathing hard and trying to hold her skirts and cloak up out of the thin rime that was beginning to glisten across the even cobbles.

Bruckner stopped in his tracks. Lenya almost overtook him, and then passed and leaned forward, holding her side.

'I have a stitch. Can't we go a little slower?' she asked.

'A little, perhaps,' Bruckner said, not really looking at her. 'Drakken asked me to escort you, for your own safety. He will tell you himself why he needs to see you.' He still did not look at his companion, possibly because he would have to stoop a long way to look her in the face – or perhaps simply because he had a job to do, a favour to perform for a colleague, one that held no interest for him.

Bruckner strode on southward, checking himself after a few of his long strides and slowing down just enough for Lenya to keep up with him. If she ran every other step.

Drakken and Anspach half frog-marched and half carried Kruza out of the street and into an adjoining alley, where he could recover for a moment away from the people who had heard the fight and were now coming out to see what had happened.

The cut-purse sat, his back to a mossy wall. He coughed and spat onto the dark, earthy ground between his jutting knees. He seemed meek enough now as Anspach stood facing him, leaning against the opposite wall. There was only just room for the two of them. Drakken stood to one side, waiting for the cut-purse to recover so that he could continue the business of the evening. He had expected Kruza to come quietly, expected him to be a coward, like all street scum. He felt grudging admiration for the bravery Kruza had shown in fighting them, however ill-conceived it might have been.

Kruza looked up briefly at Anspach. In a single flicker of his eye, he took in the stature of the man: the slight injury he had suffered, the position of his warhammer, his elegant, relaxed stance. Kruza had the eyes of a thief and he used them now. He marked every detail. Then he leaned forward in another loud, convulsing coughing fit. His head bent, his hand darted out, the elbow still resting against his knee.

Drakken did not know what was happening. Suddenly Kruza was on his feet, the point of a short dagger pressed into Drakken's neck, with Anspach crying out and stumbling back, caught, off-guard and unsuspecting for one fleeting moment. But only for a moment.

Anspach brought his hammer round low at little more than half-tilt and took Kruza out at the knees. The cut-purse fell on his rump, hard on the earth floor of the alley, and dropped the knife that he had taken out of Anspach's boot during his dramatic coughing fit. Kruza raised his hands, knowing, at last, that he was beaten.

'It's over. Use me, as you will. Or kill me,' he said. And Anspach smiled again. This was turning into quite an evening of entertainment. That young cut-purse had taken his knife without him feeling it! *Ulric, but he was good!*

Anspach gave his hand to Kruza. The cut-purse thought he saw the Templar grin as he pulled Kruza to his feet. But their gaze had met for only the briefest moment, and Drakken was pushing in to take charge of the situation again.

'Behave! There's someone I want you to talk to,' Drakken said. 'Follow me. Anspach, watch our backs.'

Lenya and Bruckner continued south at a slightly more leisurely pace, but try as she might, the serving girl could not draw the Wolf into any kind of conversation.

'You must at least be able to tell me where we are going?' she asked.

'You'll see,' was his only answer.

'How far is it?' she tried again.

'Not far,' he said curtly.

Down another sloping street, along the north wall of the Great Park, and then south again. He said nothing more and Lenya did not know what else to ask. She watched her feet traverse the cobbles, first smooth and broad and flat, then, in the poorer quarters, ragged, chipped, uneven. Here, the stones were smaller and arranged in swirls and mosaics that bore no resemblance to the even brickwork to the north. So... at least she knew that they were heading toward the Altquartier.

* * *

Kruza followed Drakken, with his even stride, while listening to the relaxed, light tread of the one called Anspach behind him. They didn't have far to go. Turning north and west in the cold air, through almost empty lanes, they stopped outside the great double doors of the quarter's ostlers.

The ostler did a poor trade here. His stables were only full when the city was brimming with rich visitors. Sometimes the overspill from the more respectable handlers to the north would find its way here. But this establishment's richest customers were still only moderately comfortable merchants who left the city for their country dwellings by dusk and only needed somewhere to keep their horses during the hours of trade. It was not such a bad life for the ostler and his sons, and not a bad living. The stables were always empty at night, so the bedding straws were changed only with the turn of the moons, and the horses, who ate in their country stables at dawn and dusk, demanded little feed during daylight hours.

Drakken swung one of the doors open, just wide enough for the three to file in. There was the light of a single torch, resting in its rusty sconce against the courtyard wall. The yard opened into a series of narrow stalls, with stable half-doors. The place smelled of stale bedding-straw and age-old horse dung.

Kruza had never been near a horse. There were few in the Altquartier, and those he met with in other parts of the city he gave a wide berth to. But there was no noise here, no snort or trample, and the cut-purse relaxed slightly when he realised all the stalls were empty.

But he did not relax for long. Drakken rounded on him as soon as they were off the street, pushed him back against the coarse boarding of a stall panel. He stood with his face tilted up to meet Kruza's. Their noses were almost touching.

Drakken had a deep frown on his face and Kruza tensed all over again. His body felt like a series of taut cables and blocks of unyielding rock, like the pulleys and counterweights of the lifts that served the Fauschlag, yanking and stretching at themselves as they hoisted impossible burdens.

His chest felt so tight and hard he wondered how he would breathe. With Drakken right in his face, he wondered how much longer he would be allowed to breathe. Kruza looked slyly at Anspach, who stood guard by the great, black door, which hung on its hinges, just ajar. No ally there. Kruza knew the Wolves would stick together.

'She'll be here soon,' Drakken began.

She? thought Kruza and then realisation dawned. *Lenya! I must account to Lenya for Wheezer's death. That is why they have brought me here. And then this Drakken will kill me!*

'After the fight at the Baiting Pit, you took flight. I suppose I can't blame you. I scared you off, calling you a thief and a liar and a murderer. And mayhap that's what you are. But if you are, then Lenya deserves to hear it from your own mouth. She will not listen to me.'

'Lenya needs to know what happened to Wheezer. She sought him out. She talks of nothing but her brother, of the dead ends she followed. She talks of you knowing him. If you really know what happened to her brother, then you must tell it plainly and put her mind at ease once and for all. And if you killed him, then you will answer to the Watch,' Drakken finished grimly

What can I say to her, Kruza wondered? The moment when he could have told her everything was long gone. Gone with that last meeting, the night they were saved from the Baiting Pit by this same White Wolf. When he realised, with true shock, that her brother was the same boy he'd tried to forget. *I don't want to tell her any of it. I don't understand it. All these months I have tried not to think of it!*

But with this pair of White Wolves watching him, he knew that he would have to tell Lenya something. He decided in that moment that he would rather have paid with his life in the street where the three of them had done battle, than face Lenya with his story.

There was no more time for thought. Lenya was backing into the stable courtyard through the narrow door. She was talking to someone who must have been on the other side.

'Why would you bring me here? This can't be right!' she exclaimed and then, turning, saw them. Her eyes locked onto Kruza, who bowed his head and said nothing. Then she was running towards Drakken. She put her hands on his broad torso and he took her elbows gently, one in each hand.

'Lenya,' he said, 'I brought you here to talk to the cut-purse. Ask him what you like about your brother. He will answer your questions.' This last he said with his eyes locked on Kruza. It was a warning.

Lenya turned, Drakken still holding her gently,

'You knew Stefan?'

'No... I knew Wheezer...' Kruza realised they were repeating the last words they had spoken that night after the fight in the Baiting Pit.

'Leave us, Krieg,' she waved an arm at her Templar-lover, her intent gaze not leaving Kruza's face.

'What power the milk-maid has,' Anspach said wryly to Drakken as they stood together in the street with Bruckner, outside the ostlers. Drakken looked at him.

'Power over the Wolf and the cut-purse both,' Anspach finished, amused. Drakken glanced down, a deep flush of anger and embarrassment climbing up from his neck, over his face and deep into his brow. It was followed by a frown that furrowed into the flush on his crimson forehead, leaving purple and white lines.

'I knew Wheezer,' Kruza began by repeating himself. 'I knew him by no other name. He said he had no name. The bastard child of a nobleman and a mother who died in childbirth. I couldn't know he was your brother.'

I called him "brother", but I never even knew that for sure. No one really knew him, Lenya thought. *Mostly we barely noticed him. But she said nothing.* Kruza was talking and she thought if she interrupted him, he would stop. She wanted to hear it, whatever it was he had to say.

'He didn't look like you.'

He didn't look like anyone, she thought.

'You said he was honest, do you remember?' Kruza asked, but he didn't wait for an answer. 'He was, in a strange way. I caught him stealing from an old cut-purse, a teacher of mine. But he only stole what didn't belong to anyone, or what was surplus or excess. I was his first visitor. His first friend in Middenheim. I hope I was his friend.'

If you were his friend, you were the only friend he ever had, thought Lenya, and the memory pained her. *People were cruel to him, if they saw him at all. In the end no one even seemed to see him.*

'I've never known anyone who could steal like he could. Silently, without being seen. I... I used him.' He hung his head. 'I'm not proud of it, but at least I didn't recruit him and let Bleyden get hold of him and use him worse. We were friends.' It was as if he was talking solely to himself.

You couldn't use Wheezer. He had his own kind of freedom, his own ways, thought Lenya, but said nothing. She knew truth when she heard it.

There was a long pause, and she realised that they were still standing in the middle of the stable courtyard. It was open to the stars and the night was turning purple and cold. Grey and black clouds the colour of the Fauschlag Rock were scudding across the sky, obliterating the twin moons, and she felt the deepening chill. Kruza stood stock-still in front of her, as he had been standing when she first entered the courtyard. Lenya put her hand out to Kruza, who shrugged it off before it even met his sleeve.

'Don't! You won't like me after you've heard this. I used him... he stole to help me fill my quota. I would dare him. It was a game,' he said, not looking at Lenya.

Just don't try playing hide and seek with him, Lenya thought.

'He stole for me and I listened to his tales. He had the most extraordinary room, full of beautiful things. We drank together and I would fall asleep on his couch, half-listening to his stories. I knew I was using him, using his skills as a thief, but I meant him no real harm. He liked to play the game and then go back to talk about the witches that brought him up. Nonsense like that. No one else saw him, you see.'

Mother's little foundling, she thought, *and now I'll never know why she called him that, and why we all laughed, my father, my brothers, even my mother, sadness in her eyes. Maybe he didn't belong to us at all. Maybe he never belonged to anyone.*

'I think he died, Lenya. I'm sorry. I think he's dead.' Kruza had thought it for a long time, but he'd never said it before.

Dead! Before I could find him or understand him. Why did he have to die? The moan that was in her heart never found its way to her lips. She felt slightly faint.

'He was invisible, he should have been safe... but he didn't come out. He never came out.' Kruza's voice was low and he was surprised by how calm he sounded. He knew what to tell her now. 'I thought it was just a trick, or luck, that no one ever saw him. But it wasn't.'

'He stumbled on a smuggling scam, a big one.' Kruza paused, looking at Lenya for the first time. She looked pale. The girl shivered.

Lenya was cold and afraid. She turned about in confusion, looking for somewhere to go, somewhere to feel safe and warm. There were only the empty stables around them, but surely they would yield some heat. She turned her back on Kruza and walked toward the half-door on the nearest stall. She placed her hand on the old blackened latch. It was well-greased and moved easily under her hand. She turned again to Kruza. He realised she was waiting for him and walked toward her. She turned into the dark stable, which smelled much like the stables back in Linz. It reminded her of the horses she sometimes tended and the cows she often milked there. Kruza remained standing, slumped a little against the half-door. He was tired and heart-sore. Even though he had survived the ordeal with the Wolves, he felt the worst was yet to come.

'There were smugglers. Wheezer knew. He followed the bodies, told me the story,' he began again once Lenya was settled in a pile of old hay.

No one ever saw Wheezer. That's how he could disappear for days at a time. 'Off with his folk!' mother would say. Now, I don't think she was being fanciful. We never knew where he was or what he was doing, but I was always happy to see him return from the woods. I loved him and I loved his stories. Lenya took a breath when she remembered again that Stefan was dead, her memories of him tumbling over and over in her head.

Kruza went on, halting. 'Only they weren't bodies. And the grey men weren't from Morr's Temple. They were smugglers, bringing all manner of things into the city. Ah, I don't even know why I'm talking to you. Wheezer's gone.'

There was a part of Lenya that wanted to ask about the smugglers, who they were, where Wheezer had followed them to. But she knew if she asked, Kruza might not want to talk to her at all. She felt a chill that she hadn't expected in the warm, close air of the old stable.

Kruza made small circles in the hay dust on the floor with the point of one of his boots.

'Wheezer took me to the smugglers' place. I didn't want to go in there at first,' Kruza said, looking at Lenya in a way that prevented her asking the question he dreaded: Where did Wheezer die?

She sat still and Kruza continued to make the small circles with his foot. His head was bowed and she could barely hear him. 'Wheezer was excited. There was so much there, he said. "It's there to be taken," I remember his words. It seemed... it seemed like an easy job.' His voice dropped yet further.

Lenya leaned up onto her knees, closer to him, wanting to hear it all, whatever was left of his reminiscences. Kruza lurched back from her unhappily, as if he didn't want to be any closer.

'The smugglers were there, dozens of them. They saw us. I tried...' he blurted, unconsciously running his hand down the narrow scar on the side of his face, almost hidden by his hair. Lenya had not seen it before.

He got that scar trying to save Wheezer. He was Wheezer's friend, she thought. *Why does he doubt it?*

'I got out and I waited. I waited in his room. I don't know how long. I waited until there was fresh dust on the stairs, but Wheezer didn't come back.'

Kruza paused for a moment, then suddenly turned on his heels and left the stall. He crossed towards the door that led out onto the street, which was open just a crack. A moment later, it swung wider out on its hinges and Drakken stepped in out of the shadows.

'Well?' he asked.

Lenya, emerging after Kruza, was about to answer when she realised that Drakken was talking to the cut-purse. Kruza looked like he had seen a ghost. He had that same look he had when Lenya had first said the name Wheezer all those months ago.

'It's okay,' Lenya told Drakken, on Kruza's behalf. She took the lad's arm. 'Thank you,' she said, not knowing what else she could say. This man had tried to save Wheezer's life. He had a scar. There was nothing left. She had mourned Wheezer for too long already.

'Now do what you will with me,' Kruza said as Drakken stood before him. 'I will die peacefully, if die I must.'

'No!' Lenya cried, firm and unafraid. 'Let him go, Drakken. He has done no wrong. He was Wheezer's friend and he did him no harm.'

Lenya allowed Drakken to take her in his arms.

'And thank you, Krieg,' she said. 'I can let Stefan rest now.'

They parted. Kruza strode away from the place as fast as he could, trying to lose himself in the dark streets. He thought that he had put Lenya's mind at rest. Maybe...

He wondered if Wheezer was at rest. He wondered if his own mind would ever be at rest.

He had told the story. He had told what had happened to Wheezer. Well, so he had left some things out, things his mind had long sinced tried to blank. There were things in this city that you didn't speak of, that you forgot as quickly as you could. Like the grey-cloaked men and their hideous place.

Lenya knew quite enough. Now she could mourn and sleep easy. As for himself, he would forget. Forget it all. He would go to the Drowned Rat and wash it all out of his mind. Lenya, Wheezer, the damn Wolf... even the grey men.

LONE WOLF

The magician was looking at him, intently, fiercely, as if he recognised him.

'Einholt,' said Shorack flatly, at last.

'You know me, sir?' he asked, surprised.

'Your name just came to me. The invisible world you mock spoke it to me. Einholt. You are a brave man. Stay out of the shadows.'

Einholt sat up on his cot in the darkness. His mouth was dry and his skin was wet. The dream had changed. For the first time in twenty winters, the dream had changed, melted away, been replaced by another.

Perhaps he should be pleased, but he wasn't.

The dormitory around him was quiet and lit only by pre-dawn starlight shafting from the clerestory windows. His brothers in White Company snored or coughed under rumpled blankets on the rows of cots set against the white-lathe walls.

Naked except for his knee-length undershirt, Einholt swung out of his bed and put his bare feet flat on the cold stone floor. He murmured a hoarse day-break prayer to Ulric, breathing deeply. Then he pulled his wolf-pelt around his shoulders and crept down the length of the dormitory, half-blind, his night vision still weak.

He pulled the heavy dormitory door closed behind him quietly and stepped out into the cloister yard. Hooded candles burned with pale light around the square, set on plinths next to the entrance of each of the Wolf Company dormitories. The sky was lightless yet, and the air was cold and grey with the dawn light. Not yet matins, Einholt thought. By the candle-plinth next to the entrance to White Company's sleeping hall, there was a jug of water and a pewter cup. Einholt took a long draft of the icy liquid, but his mouth remained dry.

'Your name just came to me. The invisible world you mock spoke it to me. Einholt. You are a brave man. Stay out of the shadows.'

He tried to shake the thought out of his head, but it was stuck as fast as a flint under a warsteed's shoe. Just theatrics, he chided himself. He'd said as much before, to the man's face, in fact. That haughty magician had been an actor, full of dramatic flourishes that meant nothing. He'd just been trying to scare him.

But Shorack had known his name. And there had been nothing theatrical about the way he'd died, crushed against that pitchy cellar roof.

Einholt paced his way through the sleeping precinct of the Temple, along cold halls and through vestries with rough matting floors.

Stay out of the shadows.

He murmured the prayer of protection they had all learned by rote on admission to the Order, over and over to himself. Torches that had burned through the night fluttered as they began to die in wall sconces. Dead smoke drifted through the cool air. Outside, far outside, early cockerels began to crow. Something rumbled. Distant, autumnal thunder, the cold sky rubbing icily against itself.

Einholt tried to remember his dream. Not the dream of the harsh night, not Master Shorack and his warnings. The original dream. The one that had lasted twenty winters. His scar twitched. Funny, it had been with him for so long, haunted him for so many years, and now it was hard to remember even a scrap of it. The new dream had usurped it completely.

Your name just came to me. The invisible world you mock spoke it to me.

He entered the Temple via the west porch, under the great barrel-vaults of the vestibule. Two Wolf Templars stood guard, warming their hands at a brazier set on a brass tripod. Fulgar and Voorms, of Grey Company.

'You rise early, Einholt of the White,' the latter said, with a smile, as he approached them.

'And dress informally,' Fulgar smirked.

'Ulric calls me, brothers,' Einholt said simply. 'Would you delay answering him by stopping to dress?'

'Ulric watch you,' they intoned reverently, almost as one voice, letting him pass.

The Temple opened to him. Ulric, a vast shadow in the dome, loomed over him.

Einholt knelt before the altar, the multitude of candles flickering around him. A long moment's contemplation, and he at last snagged the old dream, as one would catch the sleeve of an acquaintance passing on a busy street.

Hagen, twenty winters past. How could he have forgotten that? The Red, the Gold and the White Companies together, great Jurgen in overall command of the field. The phalanxes of green-pigs down in the vale at the edge of the brook, raucous and whooping. Four hundred of them, more besides, shambling, heavy-set, shaking spears and axes into the winter noon.

'Now we'll see glory,' von Glick had said with a gleeful laugh that they all joined. Von Glick. Younger then, firm and thick with muscled middle age, hair dark and wild.

Gruber too, the great unswaying oak of the company, at Jurgen's right hand. Morgenstern, a trimmer man then, the company rogue, throwing witty jibes down the slope at the greenskin beasts. That was a time long before drink had coarsened and slackened his bulk, before Anspach had joined them and taken Morgenstern's crown as company joker, before he had become nothing but company drunkard.

Kaspen was there, of course, a red-headed youth, his first time on the field. Reicher as well, bless his arm. And long-mourned Vigor, Lutz and the boy, Drago, the young pup Einholt had been given to personally train, recently and heroically baptised in action and now hungry for more. Vigor would see another three seasons, Lutz another decade in the service of Ulric. Drago would not see another daybreak.

Jurgen rose in the saddle and beheld the foe. Grave behind his studded eye-patch, he turned to the Temple companies. He told them battle was drawn.

That's wrong, Einholt told himself. Dreams do that, they play with the facts. Jurgen lost his eye at Holtzdale, years later. But this was the great Jurgen as he remembered him best, branded into his memory. And Reicher. Hadn't he fallen at Klostin, years before the fight at Hagen?

Twenty long winters turning the events of that day over in his sleep. No wonder the details weren't right anymore. Hadn't there been one awful night, years back, just after the battle, when he dreamed that he and only he, Jagbald Einholt, had sat on the rise, facing the green-pig horde alone?

Kneeling before the altar, Einholt sighed. He leaned forward, resting on his splayed hands now as well as his knees, as the memories, both true and false, swirled up around him like flames. As they had done, every night for twenty years. Until tonight.

The massed charge down the slope. That was true. Jurgen's booming order, the wailing cry of the Templars, the thunder of hooves.

Dawn thunder rolled outside the Temple, outside his dream. *Hooves*, he thought.

He could smell the mashed sap of the torn grasses, the roped spittle of chargers, the stinking adrenaline sweat of the men around him. He was moving, making his own thunder as he came down the slope outside Hagen, horse and Wolf fused into one fighting being.

They caught the enemy at the brook, riding them down despite their superior numbers. More of the foe died from trampling than hammer-blows that day.

His steed hit the water in a wall of spray, breaking two squealing pigs under its lashing hooves. Kaspen was next to him, rejoicing in the glory of battle, his youthful fears forgotten. How many times had Einholt seen that transformation since then? Aric, on his first venture... Drakken at Linz... a wonder to behold. A wonder in honour of the Temple. Wolf-cubs, thrown into the fire and coming through unburned and jubilant. Like Drago.

Had he ever been that young? Had he ever been baptised in battle that way? Surely, but so very long ago.

For the glory of Ulric now, in the brook-bed, water thrown up, blasting all around them, drenching them. Blood drenching them. Scything hammers cutting the spray, shattering fanged snouts. Broken, exploded green carcasses, floating in the water around their steeds. On the far side, chasing down the stragglers, Wolves urging their mounts up into the bulrushes. Thick stems snapping and whipping on either side. Screams from behind. His hammerhaft slick in his hand.

Young Drago, galloping past, yelling out, 'With me, Einholt!' Drago turning to the left into a spinney of willows. Full of the wolf-spirit, over-confident.

Not that way. Not that way. He was bolting after Drago now, bending low under the slashing fronds of the weeping trees. Not that way.

Cut right, no, *left*! Where in Ulric's name was Drago?

Every time. Every night. The same fierce effort to change the facts.

Not that way. Not into the willow stand. Not this time...

Drago was screaming suddenly. A scream choked in blood. Too late! Always too late! Drago, down in the rushes, his dead steed on its back nearby, hooves curled up towards the weeping branches overhead. Blood-steam in the air from its ripped belly. Pig things, crowding round Drago, hacking down at him again and again and–

Einholt's curse was white-hot. He ploughed into them, his hammer whirling. Bones snapped and things squealed. A greenskin reeled away, blood fountaining from its cloven skull. Drago! *Drago*!

Dismounting, running to him, blind to the danger.

You are a brave man. Stay out of the shadows.

Drago! There! Crumpled in the rushes, like a fledgling in a nest. Alive, praise Ulric please, alive! Struggling through the bulrushes to Drago, the shadows of the willows falling across him.

Stay out of the shadows.

Drago...

Dead. Unmistakably dead. Torn. Ruptured. Butchered. His splintered hammer still clutched in hacked-off fingers.

Rising, turning, raging.

You are a brave man.

A green thing right behind him. Foul breath. Snorting rage. A reek of animal sweat. An axe, flint-bladed, vast, already sweeping down.

Now, oh yes, now the point of the dream. The moment that always woke him, dry-mouthed and wet-skinned. Every night for twenty winters.

The impact.

Einholt swung back onto his haunches in front of the altar, realising he had cried out. His hand went to his face, an involuntary gesture, tracing the line of the livid scar with shaking fingers. From the brow, down through the eye, down the meat of the cheek to the line of the jaw. Einholt closed his good eye and let blackness wipe the world away.

'Ulric watch over me...' he murmured. A tear of pain trickled from his good eye. His bad eye hadn't wept for twenty years.

'He is always there to watch over you, brother. Ulric does not forget his chosen ones.'

Einholt switched round to see who had spoken. By the glow of the candles, he saw a hooded priest of the Temple standing behind him. He couldn't see the man's face under the fold of the hood, but the priest radiated kindness and calm.

'Father,' Einholt breathed, recovering his scattered wits. 'I'm sorry... a dream, a bad dream...'

'A waking dream, it looked to me.' The priest approached, holding out thin, pale hands in a gesture of calming. He seemed to limp, unsteady. *He is old*, Einholt thought. *One of the frail, ancient masters of the Temple. This is an honour.*

'I have been troubled by my dreams for a... a long time. Now I am troubled by the change in them.' Einholt breathed deeply to clear his mind. What he'd just said already seemed stupid to him.

The priest knelt beside him so they were both facing the high altar. His movements were slow and shaky, as if old, rheumatic bones might shatter if he moved too swiftly. The hooded cleric made the sign of Ulric and uttered a small blessing. Then, without looking round at the Templar, he spoke again.

'The way of the Temple Knight is never peaceful. You are raised and bred to take part in the bloodiest of wars. I have seen enough Templars come through this place to know none are ever untroubled. Violence perturbs the soul, even holy violence in the name of our beloved god. I can't count the nights I've listened to the complaints and fears of Wolves who come to this high altar for succour.'

'I have never shirked from battle, father. I know what it is. I have seen a share of it.'

'I'm not doubting your courage. But I understand your pain.' The priest shuffled his position, as if making his fragile old form more comfortable.

'Your dream of twenty years. It scars you?'

Einholt managed a thin laugh. 'I was too late to save a good friend's life, my pupil's life. And I paid the price. I wear my scars, father.'

'So you do.' The priest seemed not to look at him, but Einholt could not tell how the unseen head moved inside that cowl.

'This has troubled your dreams for years. I understand. But Ulric burns such things into our dreams for a purpose.'

'I know that, father.' Einholt wiped a hand across his sweat-drenched, bald scalp. 'The memory focuses my thoughts, reminds me of the duty and the dues we owe to the Great Wolf. I have never complained before.

I have lived with it and it has lived with me. A badge of honour I wear when I sleep.'

The priest was silent for a moment. 'Yet tonight, for the first time in years, it brings you here, makes you cry out.'

'No,' said Einholt simply, then turned to look at the cowled shape beside him. 'I came because the dream has gone. For the first time, it didn't come to me.'

'And what did?'

'Another dream. The first new dream I've had since the Battle of Hagen.'

'And was it so terrible?'

'It was nothing. A memory.'

'Of something recent?'

'I was one of the brothers who destroyed the curse below the city just days ago. I smashed the Teeth of Ulric so that the magic would founder.'

The priest tried to rise, but faltered. Einholt reached out a brawny arm to support him, and felt how thin and skeletal the arms of the old man were beneath the robes. He helped the priest rise. Stiffly, unsteadily, the old priest nodded his thanks, the cowl barely moving, and shuffled round behind the kneeling Wolf.

'Einholt,' he said at last.

'You know me, sir?' Einholt asked, surprised. He felt a terrible sense of déjà vu. As if it was Shorack beneath the cowl, Shorack repeating the strange act of recognition he had made in the quartz tunnel under the Fauschlag.

'Ar-Ulric himself has praised your action,' the priest said. 'The commanders of the Knights Panther have sent letters of commendation. Other institutions in the city, on recovery of their trophies, have honoured your name. Of course I know you.'

'Will Ulric forgive me for my crime?'

'There was no crime.'

'I broke the Jaws of the Wolf of Holtzbeck. Our holiest of holies. With my Temple-blessed hammer, I smashed them apart.'

'And saved Middenheim, perhaps. You are a brave man.'

Stay out of the shadows.

'I–' Einholt began to rise.

'Ulric forgives you a thousandfold. You knew when to place valour above possession. When to put the city before the Temple. Your sacrifice makes you most beloved of Ulric. You have nothing to repent.'

'But the dream–'

'Your conscience belabours the act. It is understandable. You feel guilty for simply being part of such a momentous undertaking. But your soul is clean. Sleep well, Einholt. The memory will fade. The dreams will flicker and die.'

Einholt rose fully, turning to face the stick-thin figure in the cowled robe. 'That... that is not what I dream of, father. I know that breaking the Jaws was the right thing to do. If I hadn't done it, Gruber would have, Aric, Lowen-hertz. We all knew it must be done. I do not repent the act. I would do it again, if events were repeated.'

'I'm glad to hear it.'

'Father... I dream of a magician. He was part of our fight. He died. The invisible world where Ulric dwells, that realm alien to me... tore him and broke him. Magic, father. I don't know anything about that.'

'Go on.'

'Just before we fought, he spoke to me. He knew none of the others, but he knew me. He said–'

'*Einholt,*'

'*You know me, sir?*'

'*Your name just came to me. The invisible world you mock spoke it to me. Einholt. You are a brave man. Stay out of the shadows.*'

Einholt realised he had paused.

'What did he say?' prompted the old man.

'He said the invisible world knew me too. It had told him my name. He warned me to... to stay out of the shadows.'

'Magicians are fools,' the priest said, jerking as he shuffled around to turn away. 'All my life, and believe me it's been a long one, I've mistrusted their words. He meant to scare you. Magicians do that. It's part of their power, to be theatrical and play upon honest men's fears.'

As I thought, Einholt realised, relieved.

'Einholt... brother... there are shadows all around you,' the old priest said, holding up a palsied, frail hand to gesture at the many sidelong shadows that were cast by the altar, the candles, the lancet windows in the gathering dawn, the statue of Ulric himself.

'You cannot stay out of shadows. Don't try. Middenheim is full of them. Ignore the magician's foolish prattle. You can do that, can't you? You're a brave man.'

'I am. Thank you, father. I take your words with gratitude.'

Outside, matins struck. Behind it, came a rumble of... hooves. No, Einholt reassured himself. Dawn thunder. An early winter storm chasing the edges of the Drakwald. That was it.

He turned back to speak to the Temple father again, but the old priest was gone.

He had been in the Temple balneary for almost an hour when Kaspen found him.

'Einholt?' Kaspen's call broke the steamy quiet. There had been nothing louder than the slosh of water and the sound of Temple servants pumping fresh water into the heating barrels in the adjacent furnace chamber since he had first come into the bath-house.

Einholt pulled himself up to a sitting position in one of the great stone tubs, wiping water from his goatee and looking across at his red-haired Wolf brother.

'Kas?'

Kaspen was dressed in his Temple workshirt, breeches and boots. His thick mane of fire-red hair was pulled back in a leather clasp behind his skull.

'Your cot was empty when we rose, and when you didn't join us to break your fast, Ganz sent me to find you. Some of Grey Company said they'd seen you in the Temple at dawn.'

'I'm all right,' Einholt replied, answering his friend's unspoken question, but he felt stupid. The pads of his fingers were wrinkled like dried fruit. The water in the stone basin around him was tepid. *Ulric, it didn't take a man an hour to wash night-sweat from his body!*

But some things took more effort to wash away.

Einholt pulled himself out of the water and Kaspen threw him a scrub-cloth and his undershirt. Einholt stood dripping on the flags beside the basin, rubbing water and dead skin off his body vigorously with the rough cloth.

'So... you're all right.' Kaspen turned and helped himself to oat-cakes and watered honey from the bench table by the door. Einholt knew that tone. He and Kaspen had been particular friends since the younger man had joined the company. That was... *twenty years since*. Einholt had been in his prime then, twenty-five years old, and the teenaged Kaspen had been one of the pups given to his charge to train. A red-haired youth, still clumsy and long-limbed, joining the other young cub already in his charge.

Drago.

Einholt pulled on his undershirt, wrapping the scrub-cloth round the back of his neck. 'What's on your mind, Kas?'

'What's on yours? Is it the dream again?'

Einholt flinched. Kaspen was the only other member of the company he had confided his troubled sleep to.

'Yes. No.'

'Riddles? Which?'

'I slept badly. I can't remember why.'

Kaspen looked hard at him, as if waiting for more. When no more came, he shrugged. 'Rested enough for weapons drill?' he asked.

The hours between terce and sext were given to weapons drill each weekday for every Templar, no matter his level of experience. In the sparring yard, Gruber, Drakken, Lowenhertz and Bruckner were already at work, along with Wolves from Red Company. The other members of White Company were on a watch rotation at the Temple.

Einholt and Kaspen strode down the yard steps in full armour, pelts slung away from their hammer-arms ready for practice. The morning was damp and cool, though the dawn thunder had gone. The autumn light was glassy and sidelong, and threw long shadows off the canopies along the eastern side of the yard. Gruber and the other men of White were working at the row of pels in the shade, refining techniques against the wooden practice posts with double-weight weapons to develop their strength. The men of Red were wrestling on a straw mat, or putting stone shot to build their throwing power.

Einholt felt no inclination to join them. He stopped in the middle of the yard, in the clear light. Out of the shadows.

'Let's allow Ulric to guide us, Kas,' Einholt said, as he did from time to time in the yard.

Kaspen made no comment. He knew what that meant, had known it from the day Jagbald Einholt, his friend and one time mentor, first led him out into the practice square. He stopped beside him, facing the same way into the morning sun, placing himself carefully so that he was two hammer-and-arm lengths from his comrade.

Wordlessly, they began. Perfectly matched, perfectly synchronised, they raised their hammers and began to swing them. Round to the left, back to the right, high to the left, low to the right, two-handed holds, grips flexing expertly as they nursed the centrifugal pull of the heavy-headed hafts.

Then, smartly, full circles to the left ending in hard stops, hammers raised; a drop that allowed the hammer-heads to begin to fall before they used that descent to power into underswings to the right.

Round again, the other way, hammers hissing in the air. Faster now, switching to a one-handed grip on the haft-loop; up right, figure-eight, switch hands. Down left, figure-eight, switch back. Straight to the right and around, arresting the swing and switching hands again. Straight to the left and round, feet gently pivoting as they urged their weapons through the air, barely moving anything else but their arms from the shoulders.

Faster still, like a murderous, silent dance whose rhythm was struck out by the rush of their weapons, as only two master warriors who have practised together for years can manage.

Now the increasing force and speed with which they moved their weapon-weights around moved them too. Wide swings round to the rear in their right hands, causing them both to jump-step smartly to stop the hammers tearing away. A mirror repeat, reverse step.

Then back to twin-palm grips, this time with the right at the base of the haft, left at the head, spinning the hammers before them like staves, practising the use of the haft for blocking. With each return, a grunt and a stamp forward. Block right, hilt upright. Block forward, haft cross-ways. Block left, haft upright. Repeat. Repeat faster. Repeat, repeat, repeat.

In the far shadows, Bruckner stopped his work and nodded his companions over to look. They all stopped, even the Wolves from Red Company. Though the most novice Wolf was an expert with the warhammer, few Templars in any of the noble companies could put on an exhibition drill of such perfect matched-timing as Einholt and Kaspen. It was always a pleasure to watch.

'Ulric's name!' Drakken murmured in awe. He'd seen the two Wolves practise many times, but never like this. Never with such flawless grace, never with such speed.

Gruber frowned, though he had seen it on occasions before. *They're pushing themselves. Like they have something to get out of their systems. Or one of them has, at least.*

'Watch them closely, and learn,' he told Drakken, who needed no encouragement. 'I know you can handle a hammer well enough, but there's no end to the mastery. See the way they switch hands? There's barely any grip there. They're letting the hammers do the work, using the force of the spin to carry them where they want them.'

'Like a horse,' Lowenhertz said beside him, clearly impressed. 'You don't force it, you guide its strength and weight.'

'Well said, Heart-of-a-Lion,' Gruber remarked, knowing there was little any could teach the saturnine Wolf about hammer-use. 'There's more skill in the controlled use of a warhammer than in a dozen sword-masters with their feints and nimble wrists and fancy prancing.'

Drakken smiled. Then his expression ebbed. 'What are they doing?' he asked, nervously. 'They're moving closer to each other!'

'Krieg, my lad,' Bruckner chuckled, 'you'll love this bit...'

Einholt and Kaspen now moved well into hammer-reach of each other, head on, their circling weapons and arms just blurs. The pace of the practice was marked out by the whistling chop of the weapons as they punched through the air. Each side-swing precisely missed the swing of the other, so that Einholt and Kaspen were like a pair of hurricane-driven windmills face to face, the sails of one slicing deftly in between those of the other.

There were impressed murmurs from the Red Company men behind them. *Now the switch,* Gruber thought, waiting for it.

Breaking his rhythmic swing out from the cross-swirling hammers, Einholt went low and swung at Kaspen's legs, as the red-head leapt over it and swung high through the empty space where Einholt's head had been. Without breaking speed, they reversed and repeated, Einholt leaping and Kaspen ducking. Neither was stinting on strength. If either faltered, if either connected, the blows were full-force killing blows. Mirrors, they swung at each other, each side-stepping to dodge the other's circling weapon, Kaspen left, Einholt right, then back again, across and repeat.

'Madness!' Drakken gasped.

'Want to try it?' Bruckner joked to the stocky young Wolf.

Drakken didn't reply. He was all but hypnotised by the dancing warriors and their whirling, deadly hammers. He wanted to rush out there and then and tell Lenya all about the incredible show he'd seen, though for the life of him, he didn't know how he'd describe it or make her believe it.

Left. Right. Under. Above.

Whooff! Whooff! Whooff! Whooff!

Drakken looked to Gruber as if he was about to applaud.

Above. Left. Under. Right.

Whooff! Whooff! Whooff! Whooff!

The hammer-spinning fighters circled each other, moving around, advancing towards the watchers under the awning.

Right. Above. Left. Under.

Whooff! Whooff! Whooff! Whooff!

Their turning bodies edged into the shadow of the canopy.

Lowenhertz suddenly grabbed Gruber's arm. 'Something's–'

Under. Left. Right. Right–

The hurtling hammers crossed together and struck. The powerful crack resounded across the yard. Einholt and Kaspen were flung backwards from each other by the impact, Einholt's hammer-haft splintering.

Curses and oaths broke the suddenly still air as the Wolves of White Company ran forward to their two sprawled comrades, the men of Red close behind.

Einholt was sitting up, clutching his armoured right forearm. His right hand was bruised and swelling. Kaspen lay on his back, unmoving, his left temple torn open, blood leaking down onto the flags.

'Kas! Kaspen! *Aghh!*' Einholt struggled to rise, the pain of his sprained arm knocking him back down again.

'He's all right! He's all right!' barked Lowenhertz, stooping by Kaspen, pressing the end folds of his wolf pelt into the head wound to staunch the blood. Kaspen stirred and groaned.

'Just a graze,' Lowenhertz insisted. He flashed a reassuring look back across to Einholt, as Bruckner and Gruber got the bald Wolf onto his feet.

Nursing his arm, Einholt pushed past his comrades to reach Kaspen. His face was as dark as Mondstille.

'Ulric damn me,' he murmured.

Kaspen was sitting up now, grinning ruefully, dabbing at his head and wincing.

'I must be getting slack, Jag. You caught me a good one.'

'Get Kaspen to the infirmary!' Gruber snapped, as men of Red Company helped Bruckner and Drakken carry the bleeding Wolf out of the yard. Gruber glanced round. Einholt was looking down at his broken hammer. He chafed at his swelling, purple wrist and hand.

'You too, Einholt!' Gruber snarled.

'Just a sprain...' Einholt murmured.

'Now!'

Einholt wheeled on the veteran Wolf. 'It's just a sprain! Some cold dressing and a herbal balm and it'll be fine!'

Gruber stepped back involuntarily. Einholt, quiet, self-mastered Einholt, had never spoken to him or anyone else like that Not ever.

'Brother,' he said, forcing calmness into his voice. 'You're a brave man–'

'And I'll stay out of the shadows!' Einholt spat, and strode away across the yard.

Lowenhertz edged quietly into the regimental chapel of the Wolves. The air was thick with incense, the rich perfume hanging heavy in the cold autumn air.

Einholt was kneeling before the empty plinth that for years had been the resting place of the Teeth of Ulric. His wounded forearm, stripped of its vambrace, the leather under-sleeve pulled back, was clutched to his chest, the flesh puffy and black.

'Einholt?' he breathed.

'You know me, sir?'

'Like a brother, I hope.' Lowenhertz was glad when Einholt looked up, the fury gone from his eyes.

'It was the shadow, wasn't it?'

'What?'

'The shadow of the canopy. It made you hesitate for a moment, made you mis-swing.'

'Maybe.'

'Maybe nothing. You know I was there. I heard what Shorack said to you.'

Einholt got to his feet and turned to face Lowenhertz. 'And I recall your advice. "Do as he says. Stay out of the shadows." Wasn't that it, Heart-of-a-Lion?'

Lowenhertz looked away. 'I know what I said. Ulric save me, I didn't know what else to say.'

'You're not like the others. Not like me. You take magicians and their kind seriously.'

Lowenhertz shrugged. 'Sometimes, maybe. I know they can often be right when they seem wrong. But Master Shorack was always a showman foremost in my experience. Full of cheap tricks. You shouldn't take his words so seriously.'

Einholt sighed. He looked away from Lowenhertz. 'I know what he said. I know what I dream.'

Lowenhertz was silent for a moment. 'You need help, brother Wolf. More help than I can offer. Stay here. Here, I say. I'll find Ar-Ulric. He will calm your mind.'

Lowenhertz turned to go.

'Kas is all right, isn't he?' Einholt asked, quietly.

'He'll not forget the lesson today, but yes. He'll be fine.'

'Been a long time since I taught him anything,' Einholt said sourly, looking back at the great Wolf Pelt on the wall. 'Twenty winters...' He coughed. 'Two pupils I've let down now.'

'Two?'

'Drago. Before your time with us.'

'Kaspen's no pupil any more,' said Lowenhertz. 'He knew what he was doing today. Practice accidents happen. I once broke a thumb in...'

Einholt wasn't hearing him.

Lowenhertz paused in the cage-door of the chapel. 'Brother, you're not alone, you know.'

'My hammer,' Einholt said quietly. 'I broke it. Funny, I've been wanting to ever since I used it to smash the Jaws. Didn't think it should be used for anything after that.'

'The weaponsmiths will bless you a new one.'

'Yes... that'd be good. The old one was... used up.'

'Stay here, Jagbald. I'll find the High Priest.'

Lowenhertz was gone and Einholt sank down in front of the Great Pelt again. His fingers twitched. His scar ached. His mind was flushed with images of Hagen Field over and again.

The greenskins, their tusks so white and sharp... the willows... Drago screaming. The impact. The shadows of the trees.

Stay out of the shadows.

'You are still not at peace, Wolf.'

The old voice crackled through the air behind him.

Einholt looked up. It was the ancient, cowled priest from the dawn before.

'Father?'

Einholt supposed Lowenhertz must have sent the old man to sit with him while he sought out Ar-Ulric. The fragile figure stalked towards him, one claw hand out to steady itself against the chapel wall. The thin form cast a long, brittle shadow in the candle light.

'Einholt. You broke the spell. You smashed the Jaws. Ulric is pleased with you.'

Einholt paused, looking down at his knees. 'So you say... but there's something in your voice... as if you are not, father.'

'This world has taught man that he must make sacrifices. For those sacrifices to be truly potent, that which is sacrificed must be valuable too. Things, lives, men. The same for all. I believe the most valuable Temple Wolf of all now is the one that shattered the Jaws of Ulric and dismayed the darkness. That's you, isn't it, Einholt?'

Einholt got to his feet. The throbbing pain in his wrenched forearm was terrible.

'Yes, that's me, father. What of it? Do you mean that somehow I have become more than I was before? That my action has bestowed some particular significance upon me?' Einholt fought to keep fear from his voice, but true fear was what he felt. Nothing in the holy shrine reassured him. The old priest's words disquieted him in ways he could not even begin to explain. 'You talk as if I am now invested with some power...'

'The history of our Temple, our Empire – even the world itself – is full of men who have become more than men by their deeds. Champions, saviours, heroes. Few choose such roles. Fewer still are ready to deal with what it really means. Your actions have made you a hero. That is your destiny. The blood of heroes is more holy than that of mortal men. In the invisible world, such men are luminous.'

Einholt opened his mouth to speak, but his voice died. He shivered, his breath shallow and fast. 'I-invisible world? Just this dawn past, in the Temple, I told you what the magician had said to me, told you he said the invisible world knew me too. Said it had told him my name. You told me to forget it. To dismiss it as nonsense. Now you... echo his words.'

'You misunderstood me, Templar–'

'I don't think I did! What is this, father? What game are you playing?'

'Calm yourself. There is no game.'

'In the name of Ulric, father, what are you saying to me?'

'You simply need to understand your destiny. More than most men. Seek that, and your mind will find peace.'

'How?'

The old priest paused. 'Ulric always amazes me, brother. To some he gives the question, while to others he gives the answer.'

'What does that mean?' Einholt barked, yet louder and angrier than before.

The old man in his cowled gown held up his arms in a calming gesture. His limbs quaked and shook, so very frail. 'Ulric has given the question to you. He has left the answer to others.'

Einholt grabbed the priest by the front of his tunic and held him tight so that the old man gasped inside his cowl. His breath stank of age and putrescence. Einholt tried to look into the darkness of the cowl, but light seemed to refuse to enter.

'*Which others*?'

'You're hurting me, wolf brother! My old bones!'

'Which others!'

'Morgenstern. Morgenstern knows.'

Einholt cast the old priest aside and rushed out of the chapel. Those Panthers, Wolves and worshippers of Ulric present in the Temple were perplexed to see a Wolf Templar, rushing from the regimental chapel and out towards the door, evading each pool of shadow and following the lances of sunlight shining in through the western windows.

Einholt almost collided with Aric on the steps of the temple.

'Morgenstern! Where is he?'

'Einholt?'

'Morgenstern, Aric! Where is he?'

'Off duty, old friend. You know what that means...'

Einholt spun away from Aric, almost throwing the younger knight to the floor as he raced away.

There was no sign of him in the Split Veil, or the Coppershiners. The Swan in Sail had last seen him a week Tuesday, and he had a tab to pay. The surly staff in the Drowned Rat said he'd been in early, supped a few, and then heaved his bulk out, saying he was heading down to the stews in Altquartier.

Altquartier, with vespers approaching and the sun heaving sideways in the sky. Einholt descended the steep streets and curling, mossy steps of Middenheim, past late-goers chasing homewards or barwards as the sun set. It became increasingly difficult for him to dodge the shadows. He hugged the eastern side of every curving street and alley, hungrily keeping to the last shafts of sunlight shafting over the roofs opposite. He avoided three streets completely because evening shadow had blanketed them entirely. But he kept on.

You are a brave man. Stay out of the shadows.

The Cut Purse. Its beckoning lamps shining. Early yet, late sunlight splashing the edges of the street. He kept to the light, a fever in his brain now, bursting in through the bar-doors so sharply that all present looked round at him.

'Morgenstern?'

'Here an hour since, now off to the Cocky Dame,' said a bar-girl who knew her employer didn't want any trouble with the Temple.

Einholt was running now, running like a lone wolf hunted by a pack of hounds. The pain in his dangling arm was forgotten, or blanked at least. He eked out every thread of sunlight in his path, skirting round the rapidly growing shadows of the early autumn evening.

Thunder, in the distant sky. Like hooves.

He hurtled into the Cocky Dame, lower on the city slopes, deeper in Altquartier. Einholt smashed two drinkers off their bench as he slammed in through the curtain door. He picked them up, tossing coins from his purse into cursing, scabby faces which bit off their snarls in alarm when they saw who had unseated them.

'The Wolf Morgenstern. Is he here?'

The chief barmaid was a powdered, dissolute sow with several black teeth, a stained balloon cap and a scent of week-old sweat not even a whole bottle of perfume could mask, though that's how much she'd clearly applied. She grinned a lascivious domino grin and propped her low-cut bosom up under her arms and pushed it out at him. 'No, my fine wolf, but there are more interesting things in the – *ow*!'

He had pushed her and her pallid frontage aside. 'Where's Morgenstern?' he snarled into the face of the barman, grabbing the startled bruiser by the collar of his patched jerkin. Einholt yanked the man off his feet and over the bar-top towards him on his chest, scattering earthenware jugs and pewter cups.

'Gone! Not here!' The barman stammered, trying to wrestle free from this mad Wolf, gazing up in true fear. The tavern all around fell silent. Brawls were common, but to see a Temple Wolf, in full armour and pelt, blood-mad – that was a frightening novelty.

'Where?'

'Some n-new place down in the old quarter! Opened just a few days ago! I heard him say he wanted to try it out!'

'What new place?'

'I forget–'

'*Remember*, Ulric damn you!'

'The Destiny! That's what they call it! The Destiny! Used to be something else! Now it's the Destiny!'

Einholt threw himself out of the Cocky Dame, and skidded to a halt. He had grabbed at the barman with his wounded arm, unthinking. Now renewed pain coursed in his limb like fire. He should have been calmer, taken Gruber's advice, had it seen to. There would have been time enough for this madness on the morrow. Time – and safety. Now the sun was done. Vespers had just struck.

The shadows were everywhere. Long shadows of evening. Black smudges of twilight. Dark stains of night. Daylight was a vague, departing twinkle above the glowering, blind roofline, far out of his reach even if his arm had been sound.

Einholt turned, panting hard. He reached up to grab one of the lamps hanging outside the Cocky Dame, then winced and pulled back with a curse. Spitting to clear his mouth, he reached out again more gingerly, now with his good arm, folding his damaged limb against his breastplate. He lifted the lamp off its hook and held it above him. Light surrounded him. He cast just the smallest shadow, a little pool under his feet. Raising the lamp high, he hurried down the Altquartier street, pulse throbbing, arm aching, mind tumbling.

After a while, he yearned to change hands with the lantern, but his bruised forearm was worse than useless. Sweat pricked his skin as he maintained the effort of keeping the lamp aloft. It was brass and lead glass, as heavy as a hammer. Twice he had to set it down on the cobbles and crouch into its light, resting his over-stressed arm.

By the twitching light, round the next steep corner, he saw the newly-painted sign: the Destiny. One of the festering, one-room stews in the grimmest Altquartier slums, changing hands and identities almost from day to day. *Destiny*. He chuckled at the irony despite himself. He had found his destiny, all right.

Einholt pushed in through the drape doors.

'Morgenstern! Morgenstern of the Temple!' he barked, swinging the lamp around. In the flickering gloom, various drinkers slid away from him and removed themselves from the attention of his questing light.

He pushed further into the stink, half-stumbling over a discarded wooden board in the gloom. The old sign board of the inn, its previous identity, taken down when the new management took over.

He was at the bar now, a row of lacquered barrels with a teak plank on the top. He slammed the lamp down on the teak, smashing a bowl.

'Morgenstern?' he gasped, out of breath, into the faces of the staff.

'No Morgenstern here, Templar... but if your name is Einholt, there's a fellow yonder waiting for you.'

Waving the lamp like his own personal totem, Einholt glanced around. At the end of the bar he saw–

The old priest. How in the name of Ulric had the old, lame man got here ahead of him? How had he known?

'Father? What is this, father?'

'An end to things, Einholt.'

'What?'

'Want a drink?' asked the barman, convivially, moving close. Einholt pushed him away roughly.

'What do you mean, father?'

The old priest's voice rose out of his robes, pungent and sallow. 'You were the Wolf that destroyed the spell. Broke the Teeth of Ulric. Saved your city.'

'Yes, father.'

'Good. It can be only you. You are the most... *guilty.*'

'What?'

'You are my truest foe. I could not touch you in the Temple, but now I have chased you out into the shadows where you are vulnerable at last.'

The skeletal priest slowly turned towards Einholt. The cowl flopped back. Einholt was appalled by what was revealed beneath. He was a Wolf Templar and a servant of Ulric, who had fought beastmen and things of the Darkness – and still he had never seen anything so monstrous.

Einholt backed away.

'Look,' said the unliving thing that had masqueraded as the priest. It gestured with a claw at the discarded sign board Einholt had stumbled over.

He saw what it said.

You are a brave man. Stay out of the shadows.

Einholt started to cry out, but the rake-thin creature under the cowl suddenly moved so very fast. A blur. Einholt knew what was coming. It was like... the moment. Like the point of the old dream. The moment that had always woken him, dry-mouthed and wet-skinned. Every night for twenty winters.

The impact.

Einholt saw his own blood spray the dark, dirty bartop beside him. He heard thunder outside, hooves of the riders come to carry him away to the invisible world where lost souls like Drago and Shorack had found their miserable destinies.

Einholt, life spilling out of him like water from a shattered flask, fell across the old sign board. His blood, hero's blood, more holy than that of mortal men, gushed across the faded lettering he had read: 'Welcome to The Shadows Drinking House.'

Stay out of the shadows.

The thing stood over him, blood dripping from its ancient, soot-blackened, sharpened finger-bones. The figures in the dim bar around it, patrons and bar staff alike, collapsed as one, like puppets with their strings cut. They had all been dead for hours now anyway.

Its eyes glowed once, twice... *coral pink.*

MONDSTILLE

HAMMERS OF ULRIC

It seems to me now, looking back on that fiercely hard winter, that the evil which swarmed over us was a long, long time coming. A destiny, for Middenheim perhaps. Destiny can be that cruel. I have seen the hand-marks of Destiny on the poor frames of countless men and women who have come into my care. Angry stab wounds, mindless battery, jealous beatings. In the service of Morr, I have been witness to the manifold unkindnesses of Destiny.

It has dealt me poorly too, back when I was a merchant, before I took the way of the dead. Death is cruel, but life is crueller. Hard, cold, unforgiving, like a bleak Mondstille at its most savage.

There are those that fight against it. Ganz, worthy Ganz, and his valiant crew. The servant girl, Lenya. The street-thief Kruza. Morr look to them, Ulric too. Sigmar. Shallya. Hell, any of them. Any of those feeble gods, high up in their invisible world, who claim to watch over us but who simply watch us.

Watch us. Watch our pain. Watch our discomfort. Watch our ends. Like the crowd in the Bear Pit on West Weg, cheering us to our tormented doom.

I've had my fill of gods and the invisible world. I've had my fill of this life and any other. I am a man of death. I stand at the brink of it all, watching like the gods. And the daemons.

They all cheer, you know. Gods and daemons alike. They all cheer.

— from the papers of Dieter Brossmann, priest of Morr

Winter armed the city for war. Frost, as thick as a dagger's blade, coated every surface and icicles as sharp as swords hung from every eave and awning. Snow, like fleece under-armour, swaddled the rooftops tightly, under the plate-mail of ice.

War was coming. Far to the west, along the borders, the noble armies of Bretonnia were chafing for the spring, anxious to assault the Empire, the recent loss of Countess Sophia of Altdorf a perfect excuse. Though rounds of ambassadors shuttled back and forth, no one really doubted that come next spring, nations would be in conflict. News had also drifted in that beast-packs were rising in the ice forests of the Drakwald, making huge numbers, stinking the air with their scent, harrying settlements and townships. They'd never risen in Mondstille before. It was as if something, something huge and dark and redolent with the reek of evil, was drawing them out of their woodland haunts.

Armoured for war, shivering, nervous, Middenheim crouched on top of the aching cold of the Fauschlag Rock and waited for its suffering.

Only a very few, rare souls knew that the real war would be fought within.

Watch Captain Schtutt was warming his numb hands at a feeble brazier in the guard post on Burgen Bahn when he heard distant wailing trickling down through the frosty Osstor district. It was past midnight.

'Sigmar spank me! Not now!' he hissed. Pfalz, Blegel and Fich, his companions on the late watch, looked round at him unenthusiastically.

'Pfalz, come with me. You two: stay in here,' he told them. Blegel and Fich looked relieved. Yes, like they wanted to go outside.

Schtutt pulled on his mittens, placed his leather cap on his bald scalp and took up his pole-arm and his lamp. He thought about adding his barbute, but the idea of the cold cheek-guards against his face was intolerable. 'Come on, Pfalz! What are you buggering about at?'

Pfalz got his gloves on and picked up his pike. 'Coming, captain.'

'We won't be but a moment,' Schtutt told Blegel and Fich.

Like they cared.

He opened the door. The fierce cold of Mondstille cut down into him like a glass portcullis. He gasped. He heard Pfalz groan beside him.

The night air was clear and crystal-hard. Schtutt pulled the watch post door closed behind them and they shuffled out to meet the winter darkness.

The captain stopped for a moment and listened to the cold, hoping desperately that whatever the trouble was, it had died down, or had been his imagination, or had at any rate frozen solid. But there it was once more, the wailing – the fear.

'Come on! Let's see to it!' Schtutt said to his lieutenant, and they clumped off over the frosty cobbles and crisp patches of lying snow, leaving the only sets of tracks. They followed the sounds to the next turn in the road, where the street to the left dropped away steeply down a stairway flanked by snow-flecked, overhanging houses. There, the shivering sounds ebbed away for a moment.

'Up there?' Pfalz suggested, gesturing with his pike to the right. He wiped his watering nose on the back of his glove.

Schtutt shook his head. 'No... down there... down towards the college.'

They hurried down the steps as best they could, going gingerly because of the rime-ice under the snow. Last thing Schtutt wanted was to brain himself going arse-over-end on the Ostweg stairs in the middle of the night.

Ahead, in the slit of sky visible between the steep townhouses on either side, they could begin to see the noble, grey dome of the Royal College of Music, iced with snow that reflected the moonlight, so that it glowed like a small half-moon itself. The shriek came again, from an alley hard to the left of the foot of the stairs. Needles of ice hung from the low-arched gate of the alleyway.

'That came from the Wolf-Hole,' Schtutt said. There was a small street-shrine dedicated to Ulric a little further in that direction. The alley brought them into a small crossroads square, where five alleys met. In the centre sat the Wolf-Hole shrine, a font-like bowl of black stone, with a small graven image of a wolf's head raised on a plinth in the middle. Traders and local householders would leave lit candles, coins or votive offerings of flowers and herbs on the lip of the shrine as they went about their daily lives.

Tonight, in the coldest hour of darkness, someone had left another kind of offering altogether. Blood, dark as wine, spattered the snow around the Wolf-Hole.

The first body, a middle-aged man in his night shirt, was draped over the font so that his head, arms and shoulders were under the water level inside the bowl. Whether he had drowned before the back of his torso had been ripped away was not clear.

The second, a woman in a torn brocade surcoat, lay at his feet. She was twisted into a posture even the contortionists in the Mummer's Company would have found impossible to mimic.

The third, another man in the black doublet and hose of a merchant, lay on his back a few yards from the Wolf-Hole. He had no face left to be known by.

The snow was speckled in all directions with blood, and with bloody scuff-marks where heavy feet had moved and churned.

Schtutt and Pfalz stood together, speechless, viewing the scene.

The captain shivered, but for the first time that night it wasn't from cold. He forced his mind to think, his body to move. He was City Watch, damn it, he had a job to do!

'Left! Left!' he hissed at Pfalz with a curt swing of the lantern, as he himself stalked around the right hand side of the Wolf-Hole, pole-arm held out straight and ready in his left hand.

This was recently done. Steam rose from the wounds. Schtutt saw that the blood had been... used. Markings had been daubed on the font-bowl and on the statue of Ulric. Letters. Words. Others had been marked on the walls surrounding the little cross-yard.

Murder. Desecration. Schtutt swallowed hard. He thought about sending

Pfalz back to the guard post to rouse the others so that they could investigate in well-armed numbers. A good thought, but that would mean being left here alone, which was a truly bad one.

Pfalz pointed. A trail of blood led down one of the adjacent alleys. They followed it, boots crunching on the frost. Another moan, a half-shriek, from up ahead.

'Gods!' Schtutt snarled and plunged down the alley at a trot, Pfalz at his heels. The doors of a house to the right, a well-appointed respectable townhouse, had been kicked in and splintered. More bloody words daubed the walls and wood. Inside, firelight, loose and spreading, danced. Someone was shrieking.

They pushed inside. The hall had been ransacked and defaced. Two more bodies, hacked beyond the point of recognition, were piled inside the door, spreading a lake of cherry-bright blood across the floorboards. A lamp had been smashed, and flames were taking hold of the newlpost and lower risers of the staircase and the tapestries along one wall. The air was full of acrid ash-smoke, and the firelight flared and flickered in Schtutt's vision. He didn't even think to notice how nice the warmth was.

A woman, her clothing ripped and bloody, was cowering on the floor by a door beneath the stairs. She shuddered and moaned and, every now and then, rasped out a thin shriek of pain and fear.

Schtutt ran to her, bending low. She was bruised and had a cut to her arm, but he could make out no greater injury than that. As he leant by her, she glanced up in surprise, and flinched in terror, pulling back from his touch.

'Easy! Easy! You're safe now! I'm a captain of the Watch. Who did this? Is he still here?'

Her pale, bruised, tear-stained face regarded him almost blankly. Her lips quivered. 'Ergin. Where's Ergin?' she asked suddenly, tremulously.

'Ergin?'

'M-my husband... where is he? Ergin? Ergin?' Her voice began to rise into a panicked wail.

Schtutt tried to calm her. Her screams were piercing his nerves. He glanced around, saw where Pfalz had set aside his pike and was trying to beat down the flames with a length of the tapestry he had pulled down.

Schtutt was about to call to him, and tell him to send out for the firewatch, when he saw the figure on the stairs, creeping down towards them. A man, or at least a shape of a man, covered in darkness and crouched like a wild beast. There were only three bright things about him, three things which flashed in the flamelight. His wide, white, staring eyes, and the steel hand-axe in his grip.

'Pfalz!' Schtutt bawled as the figure pounced, throwing itself off the lower landing of the staircase, down onto the fire-beating watchman. The woman shrieked, louder and more hysterically than before, probably prompted as much by the volume of Schtutt's roar as anything she had seen.

Pfalz looked up in time enough to raise his arms in defence. The figure flew into him and they both smashed over onto the floor. The slicing axe skidded off the mail-shirt of the cursing, struggling watchman. Pfalz fought to get the daemon off him, but both were now wrestling in the lake of blood from the corpses that covered the floor, and they slipped and thrashed, unable to get purchase, spraying red droplets into the air.

Schtutt charged in, his boots also slipping on the gore. As he closed, he realised why the figure seemed so dark. It was drenched from head to toe in blood. It soaked the clothes, matted the hair, stained the skin. *Not his own*, Schtutt thought.

He didn't dare risk a thrust with his pole-arm for fear of striking Pfalz. Instead, Schtutt brought the haft of it down like a flail across the attacker's back. The pole broke loudly, and the bestial figure convulsed with an animal yelp and tumbled off Pfalz. But it still had the axe.

Pfalz had taken a gouge to his ribs, and was clutching it as he looked round and yelled, 'Kill it! Kill it, in the name of Sigmar, captain!'

Schtutt had two feet of pole with the blade-head still attached. He faced the creature, low and set. The figure had turned its entire malevolent attention onto him.

'Put it down... put the cleaver down,' Schtutt ordered, in a practised, bass tone that had ended a good few tavern brawls before the body-count could escalate into double figures. He could hear Pfalz's pain-inspired urgings, but he still felt he had to try. A hand-to-hand fight with a maniac was the last thing anyone needed at this hour of the night.

'Put it down. Now.'

If the blood-soaked thing had any intention of putting the axe down, it was down through Schtutt's head. It leapt right at him, axe raised, howling a noise Schtutt would never forget.

'You idiot!' he managed to spit, just before the figure cannoned into him and knocked his breath out. The flailing axe smacked into Schtutt's temple and spun his head round as they went over. Simultaneously, the blade-head of Schtutt's pole-arm punched right through the killer's torso, driven as much by the figure's momentum as by Schtutt's muscle-power.

Schtutt landed on his back, the impaled killer thrashing out its death throes on top of him, wild and frenzied, like someone suffering a brain-fit.

Schtutt felt the body go limp at last. He felt the blood from his pain-wrenched head pouring down into his eyes.

Fine night to go leaving your barbute in the guard post, he thought, and passed out.

Kruza was huddled in a corner of the Drowned Rat, wrapped in his velvet cloak. When frost actually began to form on his glass, he realised it was late enough. He tossed coins onto the table and shambled out into the painfully cold street.

The moons were up, winter moons, curled like claws. There was something about this winter that chilled him beyond the weather. Everywhere, talk was of bad omens and ill portents, of gathering war and rising darkness. The same talk as every day, every year, actually, but now it seemed different. It was no longer the doom-mongering of the gloomy drunks at the crowded bars, the nerve-jangled alarmists in the gaming-dens, or the crafty soothsayers working their business. It was... real. It was an ill time, and Kruza didn't like the feel of it at all.

There were stories doing the rounds, from the stews of Altquartier to the exclusive drinking halls of the Nordgarten. Spook stories: stories of vile murder, lunacy and strange phantoms in the snow. It was said a respectable butcher in the Altmarkt had run mad with a skinning knife the day before, killing two of his employees and three of his fellow traders before the Watch had cut him down. A novice sister at the Temple of Shallya had hanged herself from the hands of the water-clock in Sudgarten, stopping the mechanism forever at the hour of midnight. In the stables of the coach-runners on Neumarket, the animals had gone into frenzies the night before the first snows, and ripped and bitten at each other in the narrow barns; two had died and four more had been destroyed.

Moreover, luminous balls and arcs of green fire, like trapped lightning, had played around the towers of the Temple of Myrmidia for half an hour two sunsets past. People said shades had been seen to walk in Morrspark. A terrible smell of charnel corruption had invaded the Office of the City Clerics and driven the staff out, pale and bilious. Grotesque faces had been seen, for an instant, pressed to windows, or in household mirrors. In the Cut-Purse Tavern, a water-stain in the shape of a howling face had seeped into the plaster wall of the pot room, and no amount of scrubbing could wash it out. Three men known personally to Kruza had seen old relatives, long dead, standing over their beds when they woke, misty and screaming silently, before vanishing. Some even said there was plague in the Altquartier.

Certainly, winter-ague and influenza was rife. It was winter, after all. But plague? That bred in the hot seasons, in the stink and the flies. The cold was its enemy, surely? And death? Common currency in Middenheim. But even by the city's wretched standards, murder and violence was alarmingly common.

An ill time indeed. Kruza looked up into the darkness, at the twinkling, ominous stars. He wished sometimes he could read the wisdom others told him was indelibly written there. Even without such skills, he saw only threat in the faraway lights. Perhaps he should consult a star-reader. But did he really want to know what was coming?

He moved off, down the icy lane. Almost at once, although he had been sure he was alone in the side-street, he felt there was a presence beside him, a panting exuberance.

He looked round, his hand on his dagger-grip.

No one. His mind playing tricks. Too many scare-stories, too much imagination and far too little wine.

But... it was still there. Unmistakable. A breath. An invisibility that shadowed his movements, just unseen, always behind him.

It reminded him of–

Now that was just stupid. It was only because the boy had been on his mind of late.

But–

The breath again, just at his heels. He whipped around, suddenly very sober, his dagger drawn.

Wheezer?

'Come on, Kruza! It's there to be taken!'

Kruza started, but there really was no one there.

Just a winter wind, hissing through the arches and doorways around him.

He shuddered and headed for his bed.

At the Graf's Palace, high on the rock, ceremonial banners fluttered stiffly, weighed down with frost. Large black iron braziers burned at the Great Gate and lined the length of the entrance drive. Two horsemen on war-steeds rattled past the guards without breaking stride and flew down that line of fire.

Inside the palace, Lenya was kneeling in a passageway near the main hall, warming her hands illicitly on a back-grate of the main kitchen chimney flue. She was resting, secretly, for a moment. The chief domestics had forced the staff to work flat out all evening for some important, unnamed event.

She froze in the gloom as she heard a tik-tak tik-tak coming down the stone passage, and pulled herself into hiding behind a chilly suit of display armour. The chamberlain, Breugal, limped past her, not noticing the lowly servant girl far away from her business and area of the palace.

Breugal strode into the wide, cold space of the main entrance, his silver-headed cane chipping time in rhythm with his steps. He stopped. He thinks no one can see him, grinned Lenya from hiding. She had to stifle her laughter as she saw him adjust his ribboned wig and exhale onto a palm in front of his face to test his breath.

The riders drew up outside. One stayed with the horses; the other strode in, slamming open the great doors of the hallway.

Ganz, commander of White Company, paused for a moment on the threshold and kicked the ice off his sabatons, rowel spurs and grieves against the doorjamb.

Breugal observed this disdainfully, watching the ice-hunks skitter away from the Knight Templar's leg armour across the polished marble floor.

'Someone will have to clear that up,' he said snidely to Ganz as he paced forward, his cane-end clicking.

'I'm sure,' Ganz said, not really listening.

'The palace is honoured by a visit from the worthy Temple, but I'm afraid the Graf has retired for the night. He is expecting important guests early tomorrow and he needs his rest. You must return tomorrow... later tomorrow.' Breugal steepled his fingers together, his cane tucked under his armpit, bowing gravely.

'I'm not here to see His Highness. I was sent for. Find me von Volk.'

There was a pause. Breugal looked stiffly at the expectant Ganz.

'Find... you...'

Ganz stepped forward towards the chamberlain. 'Yes? Wasn't it clear enough? Find me von Volk.'

Breugal backed away from the huge knight. He looked like he was choking on something utterly distasteful.

'My dear... sir. You can't come in here at the dead of night and demand such things of the Royal Chamberlain. Even if you are a Knight of Ulric.'

Breugal smiled his most courtly smile, the smile that said he was the true master here. A smile that had broken courtly love matches, ruined careers and terrified three generations of household staff.

Ganz seemed stunned for a moment. He turned away. Then he snapped back, fixing the chamberlain with a stare as hot as the sun itself.

'I'll tell you what I can do. I am charged with the power of the exalted Ar-Ulric to serve the Temple and Ulric and the Graf. I'll come in here any time I damn well please and all the Royal Chamberlains will scurry hither and yon until my will is done!

'Understand?' he added, for good measure.

Breugal's astonished mouth made several unsuccessful vowel sounds as he stepped back.

From her cover, Lenya grinned a triumphant smile. *I do believe Herr Breugal is going to wet his britches*, she thought. *This is priceless!*

'He understands all right, Wolf!' a voice rang out from the far side of the hall. Von Volk, flanked by two other Knights Panther, strode out across the marble to greet Ganz. Von Volk had his ornamental crested helm under his arm, his head bare, while the other two were regally adorned with full close-helms rising a foot above their scalps into gilded panther icons and crenelated fans.

Ganz and von Volk met in the middle of the hall, armour clashing as they smacked gauntlets. Their smiles were genuine.

'Von Volk! It is good to meet you again under better circumstances! Gruber has spoken well of you.'

'Ganz of the White! And I have spoken well of Gruber!'

They turned together and both looked darkly at the waiting Chamberlain.

'Was there something?' asked von Volk.

'N-no, sir Knight Panther,' Breugal began.

Von Volk leaned into his face and snarled like a big cat. 'Then go!'

Breugal went. *Tik-tak tik-tak*, as fast as his cane could pace.

'I apologise for that self-important arse,' von Volk said.

'None needed. I've known many of his type. Now, why the summons?'

Von Volk breezed his waiting men away with a flick of his hand. They backed off. Lenya craned to hear.

'The ambassadors from Bretonnia are arriving in the next few hours. His Highness the Graf wants their visit to be as secure as possible.'

'None of us wants war with Bretonnia,' Ganz noted dourly.

'There's the point of it. There's sickness in the Panther barracks. An ague, a phlegmy fever. I've seventeen men down, bed-ridden. How's your Temple?'

'Healthy as yet. What would you have us do?'

'Support us. When the ambassadors arrive, security will be our foremost need. I haven't the men. I'm hoping the Temple Wolves will reinforce us.'

'Ar-Ulric has told me to provide you with everything you need, Panther. Consider it a pledge of strength.'

Lenya almost spilled out of her hiding place as she leaned to hear the last of this. *This is terrible*, she thought. *This is truly terrible. Plague, disease, foreign invaders...*

'I'll go and marshal my men,' Ganz said to von Volk, and saluted as the three Panthers exited. Ganz stood alone in the middle of the hall for a moment, then looked directly at Lenya's hiding place.

'I can see you, milk-maid. Don't worry, Drakken will be amongst the troops I send. Try not to distract him.'

Ganz turned and left through the main doors to his waiting horse.

Lenya sighed. *How the hell does he do that?*

By the torchlight, Gruber looked down at the Wolf-Hole shrine. Abruptly he knelt and, head bowed, uttered a prayer of blessing in its direction.

'I didn't know what to do, sir,' said the Watch captain with the bandaged head, from behind him. 'I didn't know if I should clean it off...'

Gruber stood and turned, his gold-edged grey armour gleaming in the torch light. 'You did right, captain. And valiantly.'

'Just did my job,' Schtutt said.

'In exemplary fashion,' Gruber smiled. But the smile was hollow, Schtutt noticed.

'Schell! Kaspen! Hold that crowd back!' Gruber called sharply to the Wolves who edged the small yard of the Wolf-Hole, facing the gathering, anxious crowds. Gruber followed the bald Watch captain down the alley to the invaded townhouse.

'This is where you killed it?' he asked mildly.

'With my broken pole, sir!' Schtutt replied, holding his gore-caked weapon up.

'Very nice.'

'There is a matter of-'

'Of what?' asked Gruber,

'Of... jurisdiction.'

'A shrine of Ulric has been abominably desecrated. Can there be a question?'

Schtutt thought about the words, and then about how big and armoured the Wolves were, and then about how he'd had quite enough of fighting this night.

'All yours,' he said to the wiry veteran Gruber, and took a pace back.

Gruber stepped into the townhouse. He cast a quick glance at the mashed corpses in their lake of blood. The fire had been put out, and neighbours were consoling the weeping woman. The murderer lay in the middle of the floor, the hole Schtutt's weapon had made horribly visible.

'Ergin, my Ergin...' murmured the woman, inconsolably.

'Your husband?' Gruber asked, moving forward.

'Y-yes...'

'Where is he?' Gruber asked.

The woman pointed to the ruined killer's corpse in the middle of the floor. 'There.'

Her husband... did this? Gruber was amazed and appalled. The rumours of madness in Middenheim had seeped back to the Temple quarters of late: rumours of killing and insanity and shades. He hadn't believed a word of them until now.

A robe-shrouded figure entered the room behind him. Gruber was about to cast a question when he recognised the man's office and simply bowed instead.

'Gruber, of Ulric.'

'Dieter Brossmann, of Morr. I was about to ask the circumstances of Morr's work here, but I see it plainly, Wolf.'

Gruber moved close to the hooded priest. 'Father, I want to know everything about this act, all the details you can learn before you bury the shreds.'

'I will supply them. Come to me before nones and I will have searched out the facts, such as they are.'

Gruber nodded. 'These markings, the words daubed here and on the Wolf-Hole basin. They mean nothing to me, but I sense their evil.'

'And I too,' said the priest of Morr. 'I don't know what they mean either, but words written in fresh blood can hardly be good, can they?'

Just before dawn, the snow began to fall again, coating the city with a powder two or three inches thick. Up on the Palast Rock, the entire household staff had been working through the small hours. Already ovens were lit and water-barrels heating. Housemen in pink silk liveries were out with shovels, clearing the main approach drive and laying rock salt. Amongst them, Franckl paused, cursing at the starchy high collar of his new livery. All of the Margrave's staff had been seconded to serve the Graf during this critical visit by the Bretonnian ambassador. Like the Royal Bodyguard, too many of the palace staff were sick with the wretched winter ague.

Throughout the palace, servants were at work, changing linen, scrubbing floors, polishing cutler-ware, laying fires and wiping frost off the insides of the guest apartment window panes.

The staff had all been wondering what was afoot since the moment Breugal set them to work suddenly in the late evening as if it was early morning. A visit, that much was certain. When Lenya overheard Ganz and von Volk talking in the main hall, she became the only member of the domestic staff of a rank lower than chamberlain to know the details. And she had no one to tell. Even now she was working as part of the house-staff, she was alone and friendless.

In the palace, that was. As she hurried down the west gallery with two buckets of warm water to replenish the girls working on the main staircase with hog-brushes, she saw the snow out of the windows, settling down in the light of the braziers down the drive, and wondered how Kruza was faring on a night like this.

Just before the chime of vigiliae, a detachment of Wolf Templars rode up Palast Hill and in through the Great Gate, whipped by flakes, their thunderous hooves muffled by the snow. Aric led them, the Bannerole of Ulric held high in his left hand. Behind him, Morgenstern, Drakken, Anspach, Bruckner and Dorff in a tight pack, and then a dozen more Templars, six each from Red and Grey Companies. A Panther knight at the Gatehouse hailed them, and directed them around the inner courtyard to the Royal Guardhouse.

They reined up in the stone square before the guardhouse, the breath of their chargers steaming the air. The horses trod uncomfortably on the unfamiliar depth of the snowcover. Uniformed pages, their cold faces as flushed pink as their silk coats, scurried out to grasp reins.

Aric dismounted smartly and, flanked by Bruckner, Olric from the Grey and Bertolf from the Red, marched across the doorway where a squad of Knights Panther in full armour, torches raised high, waited for them under the portico. Aric saluted the lead Panther.

'Aric, of the White, Bearer of the Standard. The Great Wolf watch you, brother. Ar-Ulric, bless his name, has given me command of this reinforcement detail.'

The lead Panther had raised his ornate gold visor. His face was stern and dark, and his flesh looked pasty and ill next to the rich gold and reds of his steepled crest.

'I am Vogel, Captain, Graf's Second Own Household. Sigmar bless you, Temple Knight. Herr Captain von Volk told me to expect you.'

Aric sensed tension. The man seemed ill, and unlike von Volk, he still seemed to harbour some of the stiff rivalry that had become tradition between the Templars and the Bodyguard. Relations between the Wolves and Panthers may have thawed in von Volk's eyes, mused Aric, but the old prejudices are deep rooted.

'We appreciate the assistance of the Temple in this fragile hour,' Vogel went on, sounding anything but appreciative. 'Border scouts report the ambassador's party is just a few hours away, despite the snows. And the brotherhood of Panthers is... unmanned. Many of us are bedridden with the fever.'

'We will say deliverance litanies for them. They are strong, robust men. They will survive.' Aric sounded confident, but Vogel seemed unsteady as he turned to lead them in. The Wolf leader could see dark tracks of sweat on the Panther's exposed, pallid cheek. And there was a smell. A smell of rank, sickly sweat, of illness, half-cloaked in the pomander scent of the courtly knights. Vogel was not the only Panther here who was sick.

Ulric protect us too, Aric thought. It smells the way the city air does when the plague visits. And hadn't Anspach reported some loose rumour about plague in the stews and slums?

The Panther honour guard fell in behind Aric and Vogel, and the Wolves followed en masse. They marched down a marble colonnade into the draughty main halls of the palace, where candles and – such luxury! – oil lamps burned in wall sconces, for mile after mile, it seemed to Aric, in every direction down the tapestry- and mirror-lined promenades.

'Just tell us what you'd have us do, and we'll get to it,' Aric said. 'What duties would you have us perform?'

'I don't expect you Wolves to have a working knowledge of this labyrinthine palace. The layout can be disconcerting to strangers.' Vogel seemed to enjoy the word 'strangers', as it emphasised the fact the noble Wolves were on Panther turf now. 'Don't stray, or you'll get lost. We need patrols to sweep the palace, so I'll draw them up from the Panther companies. You Templars would do us a service if you agreed to stand watch on the guest apartments.'

'It will be an honour to serve,' Aric said. 'Show us the area and the places to watch.'

Vogel nodded. He waved up two of his knights. Their visors were shut and they seemed like automatons to Aric. He had never realised before how much he appreciated the Wolf custom of going to battle helm-less, hair flying. Faces and expressions communicated a lot, particularly in the heat of war.

'Krass! Guingol! Show the Wolves the layout of the guest quarters.'

'Aye, sir!' said Guingol. Or Krass. *Who in Ulric's name could tell behind those golden grilles?*

Vogel turned to Aric. 'Stand firm, Wolf. All of you. The watch-word is "Northwind".'

'Northwind.'

'Repeat it only to your men. If any you meet can't provide it, detain them. Or slay them. No exceptions.'

'I understand,' Aric said.

Vogel saluted.

'May the day pass well,' he said. 'May none be found wanting.'

'As you say,' smiled Aric courteously.

Vogel and his men turned and clanked away down the gallery, armour jingling. Aric turned to Guingol and Krass. 'Let's get on, shall we?' he asked.

They nodded and strode forward. The Wolves followed.

'This place smells bad,' whispered Bertolf of the Red.

'Like sickness,' Bruckner agreed.

'Like plague,' Olric said dourly.

Behind them, in the ranks, Drakken glanced uneasily at Morgenstern. 'The Grey Wolf is right, isn't he? Plague?'

Morgenstern chuckled deeply, richly, stroking his vast, cuirassed belly as he stomped down the hallway. 'Boy, you're too much the pessimist. Plague? In this cold snap? Never!'

'Ague, maybe,' Dorff said sullenly from behind them, his directionless whistling drying up for once.

'Oh, ague! Yes, ague! Perhaps that!' Morgenstern chortled. 'Since when did anyone ever die of the sneezes?'

'Apart from the dozens who died last Jahrdrung?' Dorff asked.

'Oh, shut up and whistle something cheerful!' snapped Morgenstern. Sometimes morale was just too difficult to build.

'What's the betting,' said Anspach, who had been silent up until then, 'what's the betting that this is the worst mess we ever got into?'

The Wolf Templars slammed to a halt, the White Company men bottling the Red and Grey behind them. Aric, with his Panther escort, had gone on a few more paces before he realised they had all stopped behind him, squabbling and confrontational.

'I was only saying!' Anspach said.

'Keep it to yourself!' one of the Red Company snarled.

'He's right!' a Grey Templar snapped. 'Doom is coming to the Fauschlag!' Others murmured agreement.

'Plague... it's true...' Drakken said, wondering.

'I've heard that!' said another Red Wolf. 'Thick and rife in the Altquartier stews!'

More agreement.

'We're on the brink of disaster!' said Olric, shaking his head.

Bertolf was beginning to explain something about ghosts walking the streets when Aric pushed past the bemused Panther escort and rounded on the gaggle of Templars.

'Enough! Enough! This kind of talk defeats us all before we've even begun!'

Aric had thought his voice was fierce and commanding. This was his first duty as a commander, and he intended to prosecute it with all the firmness and vigour of Ganz. No, of Jurgen. He was going to prove himself a fine leader of men. But he found himself shouted down by the arguing Wolves, comments blasting back and forth quicker than he could counter them. A boiling hubbub of voices filled the passageway. Aric had anticipated some trouble from the men of the other companies put under his command, but he had expected the men of White to follow him. Now there was nothing but mayhem, fierce conversation, disruption. And no discipline.

'Enough!' said a deep voice next to the increasingly frantic standard bearer. Silence fell, hard as an executioner's axe.

All eyes turned to Morgenstern. Very softly, he said, 'There's no plague. There's a touch of fever, but it will pass. And since when have we been afraid of rumours? Eh? Eh? This great rock-city has stood for two thousand years! Will such a place fall in one night? I think not! Doom on all our heads? Never! Not when we have armour on our backs, weapons in our hands and the spirit of Ulric to lift us!'

The silence was broken now as men of all Wolf Companies voiced their agreement with the great White Company ox.

'Let's do what we have to do and make the morrow safe for all good souls! And the morrow after that! For the Graf, for Ar-Ulric, for every man and woman in this beloved city!'

Morgenstern's throaty voice rose above the men's murmurings. Like the holler of a hero of old.

'Wolves of Ulric! Hammers of Ulric! Do we stand together, or do we waste the night with dispiriting rumour? Eh?'

They cheered. They all cheered. *Ulric take me,* Aric sighed. *I have a lot to learn.*

Guingol and Krass showed them the layout of the guest block. Aric appointed duties to all of the seventeen Templars in his command. He remembered, at a nudge from Morgenstern, to tell them the watchword.

He was left at the main doors of the guest apartments with the portly soldier.

'Thank you,' he hissed, a full three minutes after he was sure they were alone.

'Aric, Aric, never thank me.' Morgenstern turned to look at him, compassion in his huge, bearded face. 'I did as much for Jurgen when he was young.'

Aric looked at him.

'In panic, no one listens to a commander. They listen to those in the ranks beside them. They know the truth comes from the common man. It's a trick. I'm glad I could help.'

'I'll remember this.'

'Good. I remember when old Vulse used it, back when I was a pup. Who knows, in years to come, you'll be the old ranking veteran who can do the same for another generation of scared cubs.'

They both smiled. Morgenstern pulled a hip-flask out from under his pelt. 'Shall we bless the night?' he asked.

Aric paused, then took the filled cap Morgenstern offered. They drank a shot together, Aric from the cap and Morgenstern from the flask, clinking both together before sipping.

'Ulric love you, Morgenstern,' Aric whispered, wiping his mouth and handing the cap back to the big Wolf. 'I'll do a circuit of the men, make sure they're all in place.'

Morgenstern nodded. Aric slid away down the passageway.

As soon as the standard bearer was gone, Morgenstern sank back against the door jamb and knocked back a deep swallow from the flask.

His hands were trembling.

Plague, yes. Doom, yes, Death to them all, certainly. It had taken all his strength to speak out. To keep Aric's position as leader.

But in his great heart, he knew. He knew.

This was the end of everything.

Kruza awoke in the last hours of the night. His low, spare attic was cold as hell. His scar itched damnably.

He tried to remember what had woken him. A dream.

Wheezer.

He had been telling Kruza something. Wheezer had been standing next to the Graf and the Graf hadn't seen him.

Something about... the serpent, the self-biting monster. The world-eater.

Kruza shook so hard he had to crawl across the attic boards and pour a drink from the flask on the table. It was chilly, almost icy. Only the lead-weight of the liquor had kept it from freezing. He swilled it down, and the heat of the drink hit the back of his gullet.

Wheezer... what were you trying to tell me? What were you trying to tell me?

Nothing. Silence. Yet something was there.

The trinket? Was that it? The ceremonial necklace? Or something else?

Mist floated around him. His limbs felt hard and rigid with the cold. He took another drink. It warmed everything above his throat and everything else was rigid and dead.

Lenya. He remembered now. *Lenya. You want me to watch for your sister! She's in danger!*

That was no problem. Defending Lenya was something he didn't feel was an arduous task. Ranald take that Wolf of hers... Lenya...

Then he realised – or remembered, or simply imagined – what Wheezer had really been trying to tell him from the quiet world of phantoms. It wasn't just Lenya, though she was important.

It was everyone. It was Middenheim. It was the whole city.

He got up, pulling on his leather breeches and jerkin. His face was troubled, but he was not shaking any more.

First light came, pale and clear, the sky a translucent blue. Snow lay a foot thick on the countryside and the city. Only the sheer black sides of the rock were free of it.

A train of gilt carriages and emblemed outriders churned up the southern viaduct, now just recently repaired, and flew in through the gate, puffing up sheets of snow. Holding the regal pennants of Bretonnia high, the vanguard of knights stormed up through the empty streets, leading the convoy of coaches towards the palace.

At the Great Gate, an honour guard of Panther Knights was mounted, and they turned to ride in with the speeding coaches. As the hurtling procession reached the entry yard, and pink-clad pages with torches ran out to form a fan of fire to greet the honoured visitors, housemen rolled out a velvet carpet to the foot-rest of the ambassador's carriage.

Nones was yet to strike as Gruber led Ganz in through the porch of the Temple of Morr. They looked up at the burned sections of the eerie temple, and the stretches that artisans were beginning to rebuild, many covered in tarpaulins against the weather. The day was clear and very cold, snow threatening again. Behind them, the escort detail of Schell, Schiffer, Kaspen and Lowenhertz.

Brother Olaf admitted them into the Factorum. The chamber was a cold, dank place, vaulted, smelling fiercely of astringent lavender-water and embalming fluids. Under the swinging ceiling lamps, Father Dieter looked up from the body on the cold slab as the Wolf Knights entered, rowel spurs clinking on the hard steps.

Gruber led them down the steps into the dark chamber. Even he was unnerved by the plinth slabs and the cold air. And the shrouded corpses laid out on those blocks. He had seen Father Dieter once before, in Osstor Street by the Wolf-Hole. Now Gruber saw him un-hooded. A tall, grim man, tonsure-headed, his eyes clear and cold, as if driven by some great, old regret.

Dieter looked up. 'Wolf Brother Gruber.'

'Father. This is Ganz, my commander.'

Ganz approached the priest of Morr and made a brief, respectful bow.

'What can you show us of this horror, father?' he asked simply.

Dieter led them across to the slab in the centre of the room where a male corpse lay, naked. The only distinguishing mark, as Ganz could see, was the wound through the white chest.

'The Wolf-Hole killer,' the priest said quietly, his hand flowing out to indicate the body. 'He was covered from head to foot in the blood of others when he came in. I have washed the corpse.'

'What has it told you?' Gruber asked.

'Look here.' The priest ushered Ganz and Gruber closer, indicating the sunken features of the dead man. 'When all the blood was gone, and despite the rigor, I saw a sallowness, a pale, sweaty pain.'

'Meaning?'

'This man was sick. Very sick. Out of his mind.'

'How can you be so sure?' asked Ganz.

'Because he's not the first like it I've had in here. Or the last. He was sick, brother Ganz, death-sick. Madness was in him.'

'And is that why he attacked and murdered?' Gruber asked.

'Most likely.'

'And the desecrations? On the Wolf-Hole and the house?' asked Gruber.

The priest of Morr opened a small chapbook. 'Like you, I didn't recognise them, but I took them down carefully. I have since compared them to writings in our Librarium.'

'And?'

'They are names. The script is antique, and thus curious to our eyes, but the names are... common. The names of people. Citizens. Amongst them, the name of our killer here, Ergin. Also the names of his brother, his brother's wife, his neighbour, and three others who lived in the quarter nearby.

'A roll-call of the dead,' breathed Lowenhertz quietly.

'Indeed,' the priest said, looking up sharply, as if surprised by the Wolf's insight. 'Or a roll of those that would be dead, if we assume they were written by the killer. A list then, almost a celebration of the sacred murder.'

Ganz frowned. 'Sacred? What was sacred about that act?'

The priest smiled slightly, though it reminded Ganz of the way a dog smiles before it bites. 'Not in our terms, commander. I meant no blasphemy. But can you not see how this was a ritual thing? A ritual crafted by madness. The setting, for instance. It was more than chance that the murders desecrated a shrine holy to the patron deity of this city.'

'Have you seen this before?' Ganz asked.

'Yes, twice now. Twice in the last two days. A butcher ran amok in the Altmarkt, exhibiting similar signs of fever-madness. He had gouged the names of his five victims and himself in a side of meat hanging from his awning. Also, a scrivener in Freiburg, at the start of the week, just before the snows. Three dead there, stabbed with a quill-knife before the man threw himself from a window. Again, the fever-madness. Again, the names... the killer and his three victims, entered into a ledger the scrivener was working on, in a delicate copperplate hand.'

'Again the ritual,' Lowenhertz said, uneasy.

'Quite so. However, the incident at the Wolf-Hole last night was a little different in one respect. There were more names on the walls than victims at the scene.'

'You checked this?'

'I made... enquiries.'

'A priest with the instincts of an inquisitor,' mused Gruber, almost smiling.

'I can't be sure,' Father Dieter said, apparently ignoring the remark, 'if it was simply that Ergin was stopped by the valiant watch before he could reach his... quota. Or if the madness is causing the afflicted to enscribe other names down.'

'Other names?' asked Lowenhertz.

'A roll-call of the dead, you called it yourself. Who can say when the killing might stop?'

Ganz was pacing now, his hand to his brow in thought. 'Slow down, father. Let me try and take this in. Something you just said fills me with great alarm.'

'Has anything I have just said not?' asked the priest mildly.

Ganz turned to face him, pointing a finger as he locked onto the specific thought. 'You said if the madness is causing the afflicted to do this. I am no doctor of physic, but I know enough to realise a disease, an ague, doesn't direct purpose! That there is a brain-fever in Middenheim, so dire it can drive men to bestial rages, I can accept – but one that guides them on a particular course? Sets their agenda, their ritual, as you call it? Makes them perform the same way, makes them use the same old script? It beggars belief! No ague does that!'

'Quite so, Brother Ganz. But I never said it was a natural ague.'

The Factorum was quiet for a moment as this sunk in. The priest and the Wolves were as silent and unmoving as the dead around them. Gruber broke the still air at last with a low curse. 'Ulric damn me! Magic!'

Father Dieter nodded, pulling a shroud over the body of Ergin.

'I've had my fill of that this year already,' Gruber added.

'Have you?' the priest asked, suddenly and sharply interested. 'You're not alone. A dark undertow of the foulest sorcery has pervaded this city since Jahrdrung last. I have experienced it personally. And that is one of the clues for me. Another of the names, daubed on the wall near the Ulric shrine: Gilbertus. In the early year, just before Mitterfruhl, I had... dealings with one who called himself that. He was trying to pervert this holy Temple in the service of the darkest magic of all.'

'Where is he now?' Schell asked, not really wanting to know.

'Dead. Appropriately, as his name appeared in Ergin's list.'

'And the others?' asked Lowenhertz.

The priest consulted his chap-book again. 'Common names, as I said: Beltzmann, Ruger, Aufgang, Farber – I know a Farber, and he still lives, but it may not be him – Vogel, Dunst, Gorhaff, and another, curious, as it was written twice. That name is Einholt.'

All the Wolves froze. Ganz felt a trickle of ice-sweat bead down his brow. Lowenhertz made a warding sign and looked away.

'Does that mean anything to you? I see it does.'

'Commander!' the agitated Kaspen gasped, his face shockingly pale under his mane of red. 'We–'

Ganz silenced him with a raised hand. 'What else?' Ganz asked, stepping towards the priest and trying to master his own nerves. He wanted to stay circumspect until he had got the measure of this dour funeral cleric.

'Two more besides. Another name, but not a local one – Barakos. Anything?'

The Wolves shook their heads.

'And a symbol, or an indication of a symbol at least. The word "Ouroboros", in the antique script again.'

'Ouroboros?' Ganz asked.

Gruber looked round at Lowenhertz, knowing in his stewing gut that he would know.

'The wyrm that eats itself,' said Lowenhertz darkly. 'Its tail in its mouth, the universe consuming all that it is and all that has come before.'

'My, my,' Father Dieter said. 'I had no idea the Templars were so learned.'

'We are what we are,' Ganz stated flatly. 'Is that what you think this symbol means, father?'

The priest of Morr shrugged, closing his chap-book and binding it shut with a black ribbon. 'I am no expert,' he said, self-deprecatingly and inaccurately. 'The Ouroboros is an ancient sign. It means destruction.'

'No, more than that,' Lowenhertz said, moving forward. 'It means death defied. Undeath. Life beyond the grave.'

'Yes, it does,' said the priest of death, his voice hard. 'It is the symbol of necromancy, and that was the self-same vile sin Gilbertus was guilty of. I thought that menace had vanished with Gilbertus when he pitched off the Cliff of Sighs. I was wrong. Gilbertus may have just been the start.'

'What do we do?' Ganz asked.

'Fleeing the city might be a good option,' the priest said phlegmatically.

'And those of us who can't? Those of us who are needed here? What do we do?'

'Fight,' said the priest of Morr, without hesitation.

It was nearly midday, but the streets of the Altquartier were mournfully empty and thick with snow. No more had yet fallen and the air was glassy, but the sheer cold kept the population inside, around their hearths, desperate for warmth.

As he stalked down Low File Walk, wrapped in his cloak, Kruza wondered if other forces were keeping the streets quiet. Those rumours of plague. He couldn't believe them still, but there was a sickly smell in the cold, windless air. Of corruption, And of spoiled milk.

The thought hooked him, the memory. That smell, down in the pits of the tower house in the Nordgarten. The place he had last seen Wheezer alive.

It had been months since he'd last visited Wheezer's lonely home. In fact, Kruza thought, hadn't the final time been just after he'd last smelled that stink of spoiled milk?

He found his way up the dark stairs of the ruinous place, lighting a candle from his tinder box as much for the warmth it afforded his fingers as for light. Snow had blown in through empty window cases and drifted on the steps, and ice crusted the walls, like sheets of pearl.

He opened the door. It took a kick of his boot to free the ice around the jamb. Miraculously, almost painfully, the room was precisely as he had last seen it. No one had been here. Frost caked every surface, sheening the many mirrors and making the carpets and hangings crisp and rigid. It was as frozen as it was in his memory.

Kruza crunched across the rug, glancing around. He set the candle down on the low table, where the flame-heat melted the covering frost into great, wobbling beads. Kruza realised he had his short-sword drawn. Just like when he had burst in the first time, the very first time. His sword... drawn. *When had he done that? What instinct had made him unsheath his weapon?*

He looked around. *Now, where would it be?* He closed his eyes, trying to remember. Wheezer was in his mind. Wheezer laughing. Wheezer pulling a sack of bread and cheeses from the gable window ledge where he left them to stay fresh. Wheezer sitting by the fire, making up his tortuous, fairy-tale autobiography.

Kruza opened his eyes and looked again. He remembered taking a gilt mirror from the corner by the door at the end of his first visit. To make up his quota for Bleyden. The segmented wooden box where Wheezer kept his herbs sat there now. Kruza crossed to it. He reached out to open the lid and paused.

Here?

There was a noise behind him. Kruza spun like a cornered fox, blade out. Wheezer was there, nodding, smiling. *That's the place, Kruza, that's the place.*

But it wasn't Wheezer. It wasn't anybody. The candle stub Kruza had put on the table had slid off onto the floor, carried by the thawing drips of frost.

Kruza stamped out the feeble flames which were licking into the carpet where the candle lay.

'Don't do that, Wheez–' he said to the empty room, and caught himself doing it. Like he still believed Wheezer was with him.

Kruza went back to the herb-box and pulled open the lid. The scents from within were frail and thin in the cold. He rummaged inside with his numb fingers until he found the trinket and pulled it out.

The segmented metal band, the world-eater ornament with its sightless, ivory eyes. It was – damn it all – warm.

Kruza tucked the thing inside his jerkin and headed for the door. Ice crunched under his boots. He took one last look back at the frozen room. As sure as he was of anything, that Wheezer was a natural, that Wheezer was dead, as sure as he was even of his own name, he knew he wasn't coming back here. Ever.

He reached the street and hurried up the hill through the snow, slipping occasionally on the ice under the powder-cover. There was no one around, but somehow Kruza felt more guilty than he'd ever done in his life before. He, master of ten thousand thefts, all of them guilt-free, now felt the sting of shame for stealing a dead boy's trinket. *Stealing from the dead, Kruza!*

Worst of it was, he was sure Wheezer would have wanted him to have it. Or was the guilt in his mind because he was sure Wheezer would have rather Kruza never touched the sinister ornament again?

Before he could consider, he heard sobbing from his left; a side-lane. A woman, crying hard. Involuntarily, he went that way, into a jumble of ruins where a long burned-out stew-house stood. Snow clung to the blackened beams, and icicles hung like infernal defences.

There was something written on the sooty stone wall nearby. Words that he couldn't read. They were fresh, written in a dark liquid. *Tar? What is this?* And then as quickly, he thought, *What am I doing here?*

He saw the woman, a slum-mother, curled in a crotch of fire-black beams, sobbing. She was covered with blood. Kruza stopped abruptly. He could see a pair of feet, a man's, poking out from behind a heap of snow. The snow around the feet was dark red.

Enough. Not your business. Time to go, he thought, just as the man with the sword came out of the ruins behind him, shrieking from a foam-flecked mouth, death in his hideous, blazing eyes.

A midday feast was underway at the palace. Having rested briefly through the early part of the morning and then bathed in more warm water than the palace would usually raise for a week, the foreign ambassadors were being entertained by the Graf in the main hall. The air was thick with cooking smells from the kitchen, and delicious aromas from the platters the page-boys paraded out into the hall in series under Breugal's watchful eyes. Music, made by a bass-viol, a crumhorn, a psaltery, a tambour and a sackbut in the hands of the Graf's court players, filled the air.

'Quickly! Quickly now!' Breugal hissed in the side passage giving into the main hall, scurrying the platter-laden pages along. He tapped time with his cane and his eyes were as bright as ice. He had put on his finest two-horned periwig and an embroidered, broken-sleeve doublet under his houseman's coat, and his chisel face was extra powdered, white as the snow, or as the faces of the dead.

He cuffed a passing page as the boy made slow progress, and then clapped his hands again. He had heard many tales of the opulence of the Bretonnian court, and he would not have his own house found wanting in the eyes of these visitors.

Breugal stopped another page and sampled the goose-liver stuffed hog-trotters to make sure the cook was performing his duties. Excellent. Too much salt, but excellent all the same. *Let the haughty Bretonnians put on a feast as fine as this!*

Lenya was serving in the kitchen, one of several house-maids helping the undercooks decant mead and wine into the table jugs. The great low-vaulted kitchens, with their steaming pots, roaring fires and bellowing men, were all but overwhelming. She thought she'd welcome the heat after the aching cold of the weather, but here it was too much. She was sweating, shaking, flushed, and her throat was burning and hoarse. Wiping her hands on her apron front, she looked round as she heard someone call her name.

'Lenya! Lenya, girl!'

In the shadows of the back-doorway of the kitchen block, she saw Franckl. He was beckoning to her, pale and sweaty, his doublet front pulled open to expose a waxy, sweaty chest. His pink-silk livery-coat was dark under the armpits, big half-moons of sweat.

Glancing round to make sure she wasn't being watched, she crossed to him.

'Franckl?' The hierarchy of the Graf's palace had long since made them equals in status.

The Margrave's old houseman was mopping his pale brow, He looked as if his heart would seize and burst in another minute.

'Damn Breugal's had me shovelling snow since midnight,' Franckl gasped.

'You don't look well, sir,' she admitted.

'A drink is all I ask. Something cool but warming, if you understand me.'

She nodded and slunk back into the kitchen, dodging scurrying pages with armfuls of serving dishes.

She sneaked a stopped bottle of ale from a cooling bucket by the winery door and hurried back.

'Here. Don't say I never did anything for you. And don't let anyone see.'

He nodded, too busy breaking the stopper and choking down the cold ale. His face went pink with relief and delight. His eyes watered.

'What is this?' came a voice.

They both looked around. Franckl coughed out his last mouthful of ale in a spray. Leaning on his cane, Breugal stood over them, utterly disdainful and menacing, utterly composed... except for the trickle of sweat oozing out from under his wig and blotting the powder on his brow. Even he wasn't immune to the baking heat and chaos of the kitchen.

Neither Lenya nor Franckl spoke or even moved.

Breugal raised his cane and pointed the silver tip at Franckl. 'You, I will have whipped for this. And you...' The cane point moved slowly across at Lenya. Breugal smiled suddenly; a little, repellent, rat-like grin as an idea occurred to him. 'You I will have whipped also.'

'Is there trouble here?' asked a voice.

They all glanced round. A Wolf Templar stood, framed in the outer doorway, his hulking armoured form black against the snow outside.

Breugal frowned. 'Just a household matter, good Sir Wolf. I am dealing with it.'

Drakken stepped out of the door shadow. 'When you've so much to do? Sir, you're the Master of Ceremonies, the fulcrum on which this entire feast depends. You haven't time to waste chastising the indolent.'

Breugal paused. He had just been flattered, he knew he had. But it was not like any flattery he had experienced before.

'Captain von Volk of the Panthers has commanded my Templars to patrol the palace. Discipline and security are our duties. Charming the ambassador from Bretonnia is yours.'

'Quite so, but–'

'No buts,' Drakken said sharply. His commanding presence reminded Lenya of a hooded gladiator she had once seen dominate the action of the Baiting Pit.

Drakken leaned down and casually took the ale-flask from the speechless Franckl. 'I will take this man into the yard and break this bottle across his wretched skull. The girl I will beat with my fist until she knows correction. Will that serve you?'

Breugal smiled, without much fun in his eyes. 'Yes, Sir Templar, but I assure you I can easily deal with this infraction of–'

'You have work to do,' Drakken said, stepping towards the chamberlain. His spur chinked on the kitchen step. 'And so have I. All interlopers and malingerers are the guards' duty to punish.'

'No, this isn't right at all!' said Breugal, suddenly. 'You have the watch, of course, but–'

'Captain von Volk was very clear. All interlopers are the business of the guard. The watchword is Northwind, as I'm sure you know. We Templars prosecute that duty with a force fiercer than any north wind.'

Breugal knew he was out-ranked. He backed away. 'I am in your hands. Sigmar invest you with radiance.'

The chamberlain tik-takked on his cane away across the kitchen, cuffing pages and ordering staff about viciously to make up for his disappointment,

'And Ulric bite your bony arse,' Drakken muttered as the bewigged man departed.

He pushed Franckl and Lenya out into the snowy yard and closed the door. Lenya was laughing out loud and even Franckl was smirking. Drakken held the ale-flask out to the houseman, who flinched briefly, expecting the worst, and then accepted it.

'Leave some for me,' Drakken smiled and Franckl nodded, taking it and hurrying away towards the shelter of the timber store.

Lenya grabbed her Templar gleefully, ignoring the cold, hard bulk of his plate mail under her hands and forearms.

'You found me, Krieg!' she cried, delightedly.

He smiled and kissed her mouth roughly.

'Of course,' he murmured as their lips parted.

'Ganz said you would be here.'

'My commander is right in all things.'

Lenya frowned, leaning away from him, her arms still about him. 'But how did you find me?'

'I sneaked away.'

'From?'

'From my patrol. They won't miss me.'

'Are you sure?' she asked curiously. She had a bad feeling Drakken was taking a big risk.

He kissed her again. And again. He knew he was sure.

They had been interrupted by a convoy of biers which had arrived at the porch of Morr's Temple from the Wynd district. Father Dieter went down to assist the watchmen and the other initiates of Morr as they unloaded the miserable burden.

The Wolf Templars went outside and stood together by their tethered horses, waiting.

'Why don't you tell him, sir?' Kaspen asked.

'Tell him?'

'About Einholt! Ulric's breath! He said his name was writ in blood!'

'I heard him,' Ganz said, his voice low.

'I agree with Kaspen here,' said Lowenhertz, his voice slow with considered thought. He looked up at Ganz. 'This priest of Morr is an ally, I'm sure. Gods, he knows what he's talking about! Tell him about Einholt. Fit the pieces together... the puzzle pieces you and he hold separately!'

'Perhaps,' Ganz said.

Gruber took the commander to one side. 'Lowenhertz is right. I think we should trust this man.'

'Do you trust him, Wilhelm?'

Gruber looked away, then right back at Ganz, straight in the eyes. 'No. But I know when a risk's worth taking. And I know it's now. You weren't with us in the tunnels under the Fauschlag. You didn't see what I saw, what Aric and Lowenhertz saw. You didn't see what Einholt did.'

'You've told me. That's enough.'

'Is it? Ganz, there was an evil down there like nothing I have felt before, or hope to do again. There was a... thing. It escaped. Ulric take me if this isn't part of this curse falling on our city. And from what the priest there says, he knows about it too!'

Ganz spun away, silent. His thoughts were broken by the priest re-emerging from the Temple. The man was wiping blood from his hands with a scrap of winding sheet. Ganz crossed to him. They stood face to face in the snow at the foot of the Temple steps.

'It's happened again,' the father said. 'Freiburg now. A wealthy merchant disembowelled his entire family and staff and then hanged himself. Twelve dead. Two hundred and eighteen names on the wall.'

'What?'

'You heard,' Dieter growled. He plucked a scroll of parchment from his belt and opened it out. 'My friends in the Watch wrote the names down. I haven't begun to cross-check them yet. But you can see the way it's building, can't you? With each act of murder, the list becomes longer. How many more before it numbers everyone in the city. You, me, the Graf...' His voice trailed off.

'Einholt was a beloved member of White Company. Three months ago, he was singular in valour and... saved this city. There is no other way to describe it. He saved it from some skulking darkness in the tunnels below. Then, a week later, he vanished. We haven't seen him since.'

'He is dead.'

'So we suppose,' Ganz said – and then realised it wasn't a suggestion.

'I know it to be true. It was a simple thing to check the records of the city and find the missing Einholt.'

Ganz glared at the priest, who held up calming hands.

'Forgive me that I knew. I have no doubt Einholt was the bravest of you. My... sources told me what he did.'

'What kind of priest are you?'

The priest of Morr looked darkly at Ganz. 'The best kind: one who cares. And one who knows.'

'What do we do?' asked Ganz, sighing in admission.

'Let's consider the facts. A force of dark necromancy threatens this city...'

'Agreed.'

'We have seen its mark. As I can conjecture, it has been with us at least a year. It has had time to take a firm toe-hold. To plan. To scheme. To build.'

'Again, agreed.'

The priest paused for a moment, his breath wiping the air with steam. Ganz realised for the first time how frightened the priest was behind his confident bearing.

'We have seen its sign too, the tail-eating snake, as I said. It inflicts upon Middenheim a distemper, a magic-fever that corrupts minds and makes them do its bidding, for some fell cause we are yet ignorant of.'

'Are we?'

'Maybe. Its curse is on us now, though, wouldn't you say? Its ritual menace is all around us.'

'Yes.' Ganz was grim. 'Do you know why?'

Father Dieter was silent for a moment. He looked down at his feet, half-buried in the snow. 'The last act? The finale? It's making ritual lists of the dead. Unless I'm a fool, those lists will soon number every soul in Midden-heim. Necromancy is death magic. The greater the death, the greater the magic. It works, as I understand it – and believe me, Temple commander, I have made no great study of its vile aberrations – by sacrifice. A single death allows it to work some unholiness. A multiple death will work greater magic. The blood-sacrifice of a city–'

'Ulric take me! Could it be that much?' gasped Ganz.

'That much? That little! Ten thousand souls sacrificed here is nothing to the hundreds of thousands rendered up to the Dark Ones if Breton-nia goes to war with the Empire. Isn't that the point? This city-state hangs upon the cusp of conflict. What greater sacrifice to the foul hells of necro-mancy could there be than the heaps of the slain, murdered in open war?'

Ganz turned away from the priest. He felt as if he wanted to be sick, but choked it back. That would be unseemly in front of his men, in front of outsiders.

'You said we should fight?' he said, his voice thin, glancing back at the priest. 'Where do you suggest we make our stand?'

'Where is Bretonnia? What place is most vulnerable? Where does the *power* live?'

'Mount up!' Ganz bellowed at his men, running forward through the snow. 'Make for the Palast Hill! Now!'

'I'm coming with you,' Father Brossmann said. Ganz wasn't listening.

'Ganz!'

On his charger, Ganz cantered around in the snowy yard and saw the priest of Morr racing up behind him.

He held out his hand and yanked the man up behind him.

'I hope you know how to ride!' he spat.

'In another life, yes,' said the priest grimly.

They galloped out of the temple yard, kicking up divots of snow, head-ing for the palace.

Kruza ducked the scything blade. The man was mad, that was clear enough from his eyes. It reminded Kruza of the intense determination behind a public executioner's hood. The sword whickered into a soot-flaking cross-beam and stuck. Kruza ripped round with his short-sword but missed his frenzied attacker.

The man was plague-sick, Kruza could see that. His skin was pallid and sweaty, cold and white with fever. He ripped his sword out from the beam and attacked again. The sword was a long, rusty broadsword, far longer in reach than Kruza's short blade. The sword whipped around again, trying to find Kruza's throat. He ducked and came up behind the swing, jabbing with his own blade.

The blade bit into ribs, through ribs, into organs and wetness.

The fever-driven man went down, screaming and convulsing.

'Kruza! Kruza! Kruza!' The man ranted as he died.

Kruza was already running for the palace hill.

The snow that had choked the sky's gullet all day began to fall heavily as the daylight faded. It was only mid-afternoon, but the snow-clouds added their bulk to the sky and made it like early night. Thick snow, at first, then as the temperature dropped, sleet and freezing rain came, driving hard across the city, fusing into the laying snow as it fell. Wilting slush became rigid and unbroken snow-cover began to glow like glass as it transformed into ice.

Lenya had escaped the kitchen after her meeting with Drakken. Her lips still tingling, she found shelter in the timber store where Franckl and a dozen other housemen, pages and domestic girls had escaped out of the rain. Someone had lit a small fire and Franckl's bottle obviously wasn't the only one stolen that day. Lenya slipped into the musty gloom, the rain pattering off the tiles like slingshots, and found a place beside Franckl, accepting a swig from his bottle.

'That's a good man you've found there,' he said.

'It is.' Lenya wasn't comfortable in this throng. She wanted to get back inside, but she was sure she'd be frozen alive by the time she reached the kitchen arch across the yard. Winter thunder rolled, hard and heavy above the city rock, like the hooves of god-steeds.

She crawled up a stack of timber until she could see out of the window-slit towards the main gates, blurry through the hail. Distantly, she could see watchfires, steaming out, Panthers pulling the braziers into cover, sliding the gates closed. Their decorative plumes wilted and sagged on their helmets.

She jumped as something banged off the roof. Then again, and again. Like fists. Outside, she saw hail the size of cannon-lead smacking down into the snow, puffing it up and fracturing the ice crust with their weight. A murder storm. The most lethal a winter in the Empire could unleash. In a moment, the banging got louder and more hasty as the strikes over-lapped. Hail was lobbing down now, and thunder barked again. Through the pelt, she saw a Panther at the gate struck squarely by a stone and go down, his comrades running to him. Another dropped immediately, hit, his helmet torn off.

Lenya gasped. She'd seen storms of all force out in Linz, on the farm. Never like this. Never this fury.

Ganz pulled his riders in under the sloping side-roof of a coaching inn as the deadly hail fell. Riding on into this would be madness. Behind him, on the saddle-back, the priest whispered, 'Just the start...'

Ganz made no answer. The palace gates were only two streets away. In this elemental assault, an impossible distance.

* * *

Kruza reached the palace walls. He was cold through to the bones in the icy downpour and at least one hail-stone had smashed into his shoulder, leaving an aching bruise. Another ricocheted off the stones by his face, filling his eyes with ice-chips.

He ducked and sank down. The gates were shut. He had no idea how he was going to get inside.

In the palace, the guests were retiring. The feast had been a rousing success and now the ambassadors from Bretonnia asked for rest before the night's festivities. The Graf and his nobles were also returning to their quarters for a while. Hail drummed on the roof and thunder twisted the air.

Patrolling the guest apartments, Aric watched as Knights Panther and torch-bearing pages ushered the visiting dignitaries to their rooms. Already he could smell the kitchens as they stoked up the next round of entertainment. *Sleep well*, he thought. *You'll need all your strengths replenished come compline chime.*

He crossed into the corridor where Drakken was supposed to be on guard. Aric was standing by the doors into the guest rooms when the young, stocky knight appeared.

'Where have you been?' he asked.

'On duty–' Drakken began.

Aric's eyes quested into the young man's face. 'Indeed? Here?'

'I left for a moment...'

'How long a moment?'

Drakken paused. 'I suppose... half an hour...' he began.

'Ulric damn you!' Aric spat, and wheeled towards the doors. Thunder rolled outside, and a gust of wind breathed down the corridor, extinguishing all the lamps. 'How long did half an hour give them?'

'Who?'

'Whoever wanted to get inside!', Aric snarled, his hammer raised, kicking in the door.

Drakken ran after the Wolf, down a velvet-lined antechamber and into the first apartment. The carpet was on fire here from a spilled lantern. Two servants, in the tunics of Bretonnia, were dead on the floor. Words – names – had been daubed on the walls in their blood.

There was a scream from the adjoining room.

Aric burst through. A maid in waiting was pressed to the wall, on her haunches, shrieking. A hulking shape, almost a black shadow, backlit by the fireplace, had the Bretonnian ambassador held in the air by his throat. Blood dripped down. The ambassador was gasping out his last.

The hulking shape turned and looked at the sudden intrusion. It dropped the half-dead ambassador onto the ornamental rug.

Its one good eye glowed coral pink.

In a voice as low as the underworld, as dull as hoof-beats and as thick as tar, it said two clear words.

'Hello, Aric.'

The bombardment of hail was even fiercer than before. Under the stable lip, the Temple warhorses skipped and shuddered.

'We cannot wait. Not now,' said the priest, a shadow behind Ganz.

'But–'

'Now, or all is lost.'

Ganz turned towards the dimly lit faces of his men.

'Ride! In the name of Ulric! Ride!' he shouted.

Exploding out of cover, ice-chips shattering around their hooves, the thunder breaking above them, they rode.

Kruza was half-buried in a snow-drift, his hands still flat against the aching cold of the stone wall, when the firelight throbbed over him.

He blinked and glanced up at the three Knights Panther standing around him.

'No weather for lazing out here,' said one.

'Not when the Graf is waiting to hear the sound of your voice,' said another.

'W-what?' Kruza asked, numb in almost every way.

Lenya oozed in between two of the Panthers.

'I was telling them that the great minstrel singer was late, and the Graf would be most displeased if he didn't arrive in time for the feast,' she said.

'Of course...'

'Come on!' she pulled him up. 'I saw you at the gate,' she hissed into his ear. 'What are you doing here?'

'Protecting you,' he murmured. He was sure there were icicles on the underside of his tongue.

'Great job you're doing!' she said.

The Panthers helped her into the gates with him as hail belted down around them.

There was a sound of thunder outside, like hooves.

'He thwarted me, so I chose him. He made me weaker than ever, so it was right I should take his form as my own.'

The thing with the pink eye was speaking, though Aric wasn't really listening.

'A thousand years, alone and buried within the Fauschlag. Can you imagine that, Aric? A thousand years. No, of course you can't, you're too far gone with fear.'

The impossible hulking shape paced around the candle and firelit chamber, circling the Templar.

'I took the form anyway. A good strong form. There was justice in it.'

'What are you?' asked Aric. 'You look like–'

'Einholt?' the thing sneered at him. 'I do, don't I? I borrowed his corpse. It was so full of zest and vigour.'

Einholt looked back at Aric with a blazing pink eye. The other was milky and dead, bisected by the scar, just as Aric remembered it. Einholt, pale, armoured, speaking, moving, alive. But not Einholt. No, that look. That penetrating, burning look...

'I am Einholt. He is me. It's amazing how his memories are preserved in this brain. Like inlay work on a good sword. My, these memories are mother-of-pearl! So bright! So hard! That's how I know you, Aric wolf-son. I know what you did. Not so great a crime as this Einholt, but party to it.'

'You have the face of my friend, but I know you are evil,' Aric said, raising his hammer hesitantly.

'Then go on! Crush this!' Einholt said, grinning and pointing at his own face. 'I dare you! Kill your long-lost comrade forever!'

Aric lowered his hammer. He sank to his knees.

'I wanted life again. Form, volume, bulk. You cheated me of that, just as the priest cheated me last Jahrdrung. But now, I am returned, renewed! Eager! Salivating for life!'

Einholt smiled down at the kneeling, weeping Aric. A warhammer was in his left hand, and he brought it up.

Drakken's flying hammer slammed him back across the room.

Einholt, or the thing that had once been Einholt, crashed into a side-table and shattered it under its falling bulk. It let out a raging snarl of anger that was entirely inhuman as it pulled itself upright. Drakken's fierce blow had dented its upper left breast-plating and torn the shoulder pauldron clean off.

Its one good eye throbbed like pink fire in time to its roar. Einholt's hammer was still in its hand.

Drakken pulled Aric up. The young Wolf yanked his dagger from his belt, his hammer too far away to retrieve.

'Come on!' he yelled.

'The pup has more spirit than you, Aric. Young Drakken has fewer qualms about striking his old comrade Einholt.'

Or a terrible guilt of dereliction to make up for, thought Drakken. We wouldn't be here... the ambassador wouldn't be vomiting blood on the floor, if it hadn't been for me...

Aric rose. It was as if Drakken's abrupt intervention had galvanised him anew, given him confidence. He looped his hammer through the air, circling the pink-eyed shade.

'Go!' he said to Drakken.

'But–'

'Go!' Aric repeated, his eyes never leaving the enemy before him. 'Get the ambassador out of this place. Sound the alarm! Go! Go!'

Covered by Aric and his looping weapon, Drakken dragged the gasping, semi-alive Bretonnian dignitary onto his shoulder and stumbled to the door. As soon as he was outside in the hall, he began to bellow at the top of his voice. By then, the maid had already run screaming from the suite. Cries and alarms filled the palace halls.

Aric and the thing circled.

'Shall we try it, Aric wolf-son?' asked Einholt-that-was, his hammer slowly whickering the air as it made lazy figure of eights.

'Try what?' Aric replied stiffly, his hammer held in a more defensive guard.

'Man to man, you and me...'

'You're no man.'

The thing laughed. The bottom edge of Einholt's laugh was stained with the inhuman rumble. Like thunder.

'Maybe. But I am still Einholt. One of the best hammer-arms in the Temple. Remember the displays I used to put on, me and Kaspen? What was it Jurgen said? "The art of the hammer lives in its best form as long as Jagbald Einholt is alive"? Guess what, little pup Aric –little starched-front, duty-bound Aric – Jagbald Einholt lives, and more immeasurably now than you could ever imagine!'

'No!'

'Oh yes, boy!' the thing hissed, its pink eye pulsing as it circled again, the hammer loops increasing in speed. 'Did you never think how it would be to face one of your own? Did you never idly suppose who in White Company could master who? Could you beat Drakken? Possibly, but the pup has fury. Gruber? Maybe with your youthful power. Ganz? Not him. Lowenhertz? Not him either. And... Einholt?'

It paused. It winked its dead, milky eye, slow and chilling.

'You don't stand a chance.'

Einholt's hammer snapped out deftly, hard, breaking the steady flow of Aric's returns, knocking the standard bearer's weapon out of true. Aric cried sharply as the snagged haft-loop tore into his fingers as he tried to arrest the knock. The pink-eyed thing smacked him in the chest with the butt of his hammer-head a second later.

Aric recoiled. His breastplate was dented and his breath was gone. He struggled to bring his own hammer round to deflect the next blow, but once-Einholt was already there, leering, circling round with a blow that shattered the upper vambrace of Aric's left arm and broke the bone.

Pain sparked like white stars, like snowflakes, across his vision. Aric kept the grip on the hammer with his remaining hand, pushing backwards, crashing into furniture.

'*You're not Einholt!*' he bellowed.

'I am!'

'No! What are you? What are you? The thing from the cellar?'

The shade's next blow took Aric in the right hip and spun him to his knees on the fire hearth.

Aric gagged. His vision already failing, his left arm dangling broken at his side, grinding agonisingly with every move. He struggled to stay conscious.

'The thing from the cellar?' said the monstrosity, the lowest register of its so-familiar voice twisted again by the thick, thunderous undernotes. 'I am all this city fears and more. I am the power that will blot Middenheim from the map and bleed the stars dry. I am Barakos.'

'Well met!' Aric snapped, smashing his hammer upwards in his one good hand.

The blow knocked the thing several yards back across the room, blood spraying from its broken jaw. It destroyed a lampstand and writing desk as it fell.

'Jagbald Einholt trained me well,' Aric gasped, and collapsed onto the rug, consciousness fleeing his pain-assaulted mind.

Drakken slid the ambassador off his shoulder at a turn in the hallway, laying him down on an ornamental chaise. He couldn't get his bearings. There was shouting and confusion in the palace all around. He cupped his hands to his mouth and yelled 'Here! Here! To me! Send a surgeon!'

Two page boys appeared, side by side, took a look at the blood-flecked, comatose Bretonnian on the couch and fled, screaming.

'Drakken?' The young Templar look around. It was Olric of the Grey, racing up, sweaty and pale.

'What in the name of Ulric is going on?' he stammered.

'Murder! Evil! Magic! Here in the palace! Quick, Wolf brother! We must get him to a surgeon!'

Olric looked down at the crumpled man in his regal robes.

'Faraway gods! That's one of the foreign nobles! Come on, grab his feet. No, the end of the chaise, as a stretcher.'

They took the ambassador up, on the chaise, each gripping the stunted legs of the piece of furniture. Olric, his hammer slung over his back, led the way, backing down the hall under the twitching lamp light.

'Panthers! *Panthers*!' he cried. 'Show yourselves! Show us to the infirmary!'

Struggling with the other end of the chaise, Drakken wanted to explain, wanted to tell Olric what he had seen back in the royal apartments. But the words choked in his mouth. How could he begin to tell this fellow Templar that Einholt, one of the White, was the assassin?

He was struggling with his words when six Panther Knights appeared, hurrying down the hall to them. Vogel, his visor raised, led them. The others, hidden behind their gilt face-plates, could all be Krass and Guingol, over and again, for all Drakken could tell.

Olric turned, fighting with the weight of the chaise. 'Vogel! Good! Look to us, man! Foul murder has been done!'

The Panthers paused, and Vogel slammed down his visor. He paced forward, and punched his broadsword through Olric's torso. Olric bellowed, his mouth bubbling blood as he went down, his end of the chaise smashing to the marble floor. The Bretonnian noble slumped off the makeshift stretcher and rolled limply across the floor.

Vogel pulled his sword out of Olric, ripping the backplate of the Wolf's armour away. Olric dropped on his face hard, falling into a lake of his own blood. The Panthers, Vogel at the lead, moved in on Drakken.

The young Wolf could smell the sickness smell again, riper and fuller than before. Spoiled milk. The smell of madness and the magic of the dead.

Vogel flew at him but Drakken was ready. He ducked under the sword arm and deflected the swinging blow with a lash of his armoured left arm. At the same time, he pulled out his dagger and slammed the blade deep into Vogel's neck, punching it up through the throat armour and through the madman's spine. Blood jetted out through the multiple joints of the Panther's gleaming, segmented helm. Vogel fell, pulling Drakken's buried knife away with him.

Unarmed now, as five more closed, swords ready.

A shockwave of stone on metal rang down the hall as Morgenstern and Anspach came in on the Panthers from the rear. Anspach sent his first foe face-down, the back of the ornate Panther armour splintered and bloody. Morgenstern decapitated another as easily as hoisting a turnip off a bucket-top. The helmeted head thukked off the ceiling and went clattering away.

The three remaining Panthers turned to face the onslaught.

Drakken could hear Morgenstern and Anspach yelling out the battle cry of White Company, and repeating the war-chant, 'Hammers of Ulric! Hammers of Ulric!'

Drakken snatched up Vogel's fallen sword and waded in, swinging the unfamiliar weapon like a hammer. A Panther was in his face, slicing hard with expertise.

Drakken blocked the strike as he would have done with a hammer haft, and sparks flew from the blades. He came around again, circling the sword around his head two-handed, as a hammer-man would turn his weapon, and cut the Panther through the shoulder, down to the belly. The sharp sword cut armour plate like a hot-iron through ice.

Morgenstern slammed a Panther into the hallway wall with his bulk, and killed him with repeated blows from his circling hammer. Anspach clove in the plumed helm of the last. They grouped, back to back, defending the fallen body of the ambassador, as dozens of other Knights Panther charged down at them from both sides.

The hail ceased. An oppressive stillness settled over the city and the night. The sky was an ice-haze of cold, smoky fumes, making the stars glint pink and bloodshot. Thunder moaned in the stillness, like distant packs of cavalry, turning far away for the next assault.

The palace gates were locked shut.

'Open!' Ganz bellowed, his steed bucking. The priest clung tight to the armoured warrior to remain seated.

'The palace is closed!' yelled a Panther Knight back from the gateway, behind the bars. 'Alarm has been sounded! No one may enter!'

Steadying his horse, Ganz looked further, and saw the lamps flashing in the windows of the great palace, heard the cries and bells and screams.

'Let us in!' he repeated, his voice a thunder all of its own.

'Go back!' returned the gate-guards.

Gruber slung his horse in around Ganz, and came up to the gates side-long, hammer whirling. With celebrated precision, he smashed the padlock off the gate-bolt. Then he reared his horse and the front hooves crashed the gates open as they came down.

The six Wolves bolted down the main entrance yard through the gates as the Panthers rushed out to waylay them. The hurtling fury of Ulric's Temple Men at full charge. What could they do against that? Better they tried to stop a storm, a north wind, a thunderbolt. It was over in seconds.

Ganz's Wolves threw themselves off their steeds at the palace entrance, letting their chargers run free. With Gruber and the priest of Morr at their head, they crashed into the main hall, and had to stand aside as a gaggle of court musicians and domestics fled past them out into the night. Kaspen caught one by the throat, a lute player who clutched his instrument to his belly to protect it.

'Murder! Madness! Murder!' the man gagged, trying to tear free.

'Go!' snapped Kaspen, throwing the man out of the door. The six knights and the priest advanced across the great space off the hallway. The vast building beyond rang with screams and yells and incessant hand-bell alarms.

'We're too late,' said Ganz.

'We're never too late,' snapped Dieter of Morr. 'This way.'

'Where are we going?'

'The guest apartments.'

'And how do you know where they are?' Ganz asked.

'Research,' the priest of Morr smiled back at him. It was the coldest smile Ganz had ever seen in his entire life.

Backed into a corner, sweeping at anything that came in range, the three great White Templars stood in a line, side by side: Morgenstern, Anspach, Drakken. Two hammers and one novice sword against twenty fever-maddened Knights Panther who bottled them in a back end of the corridor. Already, four more Panthers lay dead or dying. It was all the three Wolves could do to fend off the attacks now, to keep the weapons away.

Through the press, Drakken could see von Volk and a dozen more Panthers charging down from the end of the hall. This is it, he thought. *This is where the sheer weight of numbers–*

Von Volk cut a Panther knight down with a swing of his sword. Then another. He and his men hacked into the back of the insane press that had cornered the Wolves.

That first blow had been historic, unprecedented. The first time a holy Panther Knight had slain another of his kind. It didn't remain unprecedented for long. Drakken knew what he was witnessing was extraordinary. Panther against Panther. He thought of Einholt. *Had a Wolf ever killed a Wolf?*

He thought of Aric. The thought was too painful to keep in his head.

Morgenstern bellowed, and urged Anspach and Drakken up with him to crush the mad Panthers against von Volk and his relieving force.

Three fierce minutes, and nearly twenty-five noble Knights Panther lay dead or broken on the hallway floor. Von Volk pulled off his helmet and sank to his knees in horror, his helm crashing out of his loose grip and rolling away across the ground. His other, loyal knights also sank down, or turned away, horrified at what they had done. What they had been forced to do.

'In the Graf's name...' gasped von Volk, tears in his eyes. 'What in all of creation have we had to do here tonight? My men... my...'

Morgenstern knelt down in front of von Volk and grabbed the knight's clenched hands between his mighty paws. 'You have done your duty and may Ulric – and Sigmar – thank you. There is rank insanity in the Palace of Middenheim tonight, and you have kept your duty well and seen it off. Mourn these poor souls, yes. I will join you in that. But they were turned, von Volk. They were not the men you knew. Evil had taken them. You did what was right.'

Von Volk looked up into the face of the obese White Wolf. 'You say. They were not your own.'

'Still enough, you did right. Our loyalty is to our kind, but when evil strikes, our truest loyalty is to the Crown.'

Morgenstern pulled out his flask and von Volk slugged greedily from the offered bottle.

'It's only the start of the horrors we may have to face now,' Anspach advised, helping von Volk up.

The Knights Panther captain nodded, wiped his mouth and took another slug of the fire-water.

'Sigmar look to all those who have done this here tonight. For I will show them no mercy.'

They found Aric face down in front of the guest room fireplace, blood matting his hair and seeping out of his armour joints. Dorff and Kaspen lifted him up and laid him on the bed, stripping off his armour. There was no surgeon to call, as the palace doctor was attending to the Bretonnian ambassador. The priest of Morr pushed in.

'I usually tend the dead, but I know about medicine, a thing or two at least.' With the help of Kaspen, who had been trained as White Company's bone-setter and wound-binder for the battlefield, Dieter began to dress the young knight's injuries.

'A madness befell my men,' von Volk was saying.

'A madness befalls this city,' Lowenhertz returned. 'We have learned that foul necromancy permeates this place, seeking its own ends. The fever is part of it. It is not a true plague, it is magic-born, bred to infect us all with insanity and killing glee. Is that not so, priest?'

Father Dieter looked up from his work splinting Aric's shattered left arm.

'Quite so, Lowenhertz. The sickness that afflicts Middenheim is magical in nature. A madness. You've seen the signs, von Volk. You've read the words on the walls.'

'A madness that makes those touched kill and kill again for the glory of blood-letting,' Ganz said, without life or spark in his voice. 'At any time, it could afflict us. It is spreading, pestilential, all around us.'

Drakken stepped forward. 'I know the evil,' he said.

'What'

'The thing you said you fought in the cellar,' Drakken said to Gruber. 'The thing with the pink eyes. It was here. But it wasn't a stick-form, a flimsy thing, it was...'

He couldn't say the name.

'What?' Lowenhertz snarled impatiently.

Gruber held him back from the pale young Wolf, who was still about to speak.

But it was the priest of Morr who finished the sentence. 'Einholt.'

They all looked around and then back at Drakken.

'Was it?' asked Ganz.

Drakken nodded. 'It said it was him, but it wasn't. It had borrowed his body like you might borrow a cloak. It wore him. It wasn't Einholt, but it looked like him.'

'And... fought like him.' Aric eased up onto his good elbow and looked at them all. 'It was Einholt's flesh, Einholt's blood, Einholt's skill and memories. But it was a hollow, evil thing inside. The thing said it had taken Einholt for revenge, because Einholt had somehow stopped it... in the cellar, I suppose. It wanted a body. It chose Einholt.'

Father Dieter had finished dressing Aric's injuries. He pulled Ganz to one side.

'I fear,' he said reluctantly, 'that we are not simply dealing with a necromancer here.'

Ganz looked round at him, feeling the ice-sweat trickle down his back.

'To possess a form, as your man Aric relates... this is something more.'

'It said its name was Barakos,' Aric said, leaning forward, listening to them from the bed.

'Barakos?' Dieter mused, his eyes lifted. 'Why, then, it's true.'

Ganz grabbed the priest of Morr by the front of his robes and slammed him into the hardwood panels of the stateroom. The Wolves and Panthers looked on in shock.

'You know? You knew?'

'Let me go, Ganz.'

'YOU KNEW!?'

'Let me go!'

Ganz released his grip and Father Dieter slid down so his feet were on the floor. He rubbed his throat.

'Barakos. The name appeared on the walls at Wolf-hole. I asked you all if you knew it – you did not. I cast it aside myself, hoping that it was just a coincidence. The name of some Araby merchant now in town who would fall victim to the plague-murders.'

'And what is it really?'

'Nothing. Everything,' the priest said. 'In the old books, it is written "Babrakkos", an ancient name even when Middenheim was founded. A dark power, deathless, necromantic. Also known as Brabaka, and in the nursery rhyme: Ba ba Barak, come see thee tarry! You know it?'

'I know it.'

'All those references refer to a pestilential liche-thing that threatened Middenheim in the earliest of days. Babrakkos. Barakos now, perhaps. I think it's back. I think it's living again. I think it wants the city of Middenheim dead so as to conjure enough death-magic force to make it a god. An unclean god, but a god never the less, as we would understand it, Ganz of the White.'

'A liche...' Even Ganz's voice was pale. 'How do we fight such a thing?'

Father Dieter shrugged. 'It has clearly already begun upon its work. Tonight is its hour. We have the men, but not the time. If we could find the foe, we might be able to thwart it, but–'

'I know where it is,' a voice from the door said.

The Wolves and the Panthers looked round. Lenya smiled at them as Drakken, humbly, led her in.

'Not me, actually. My friend here.' Lenya dragged the shabby figure of Kruza into the light behind her and Drakken. She held up the ornament, the world-eater, the biting snake. Lamp-light flickered off it.

'This is Kruza. My friend. My brother's friend. He knows where the monster dwells.'

Snow, in icy pellets, had begun to fall out of the frosty pink night again. It was like riding down into Hell.

The dark cityscape was dotted with dozens of fires; numerous buildings blazed from Ostwald to the Wynd. Screaming and wailing and clamour rolled down the streets all around, where fever-maddened citizens brawled or fought in packs like wild beasts. Bodies littered the cold streets, the falling snow forming crusty shrouds over those that had lain longest. Names, written in blood, wax, ink and ice covered the street walls and the sides of buildings. The cold air smelled of spoiled milk.

The company rode out through the broken gates of the palace and down the steep Gafsmund streets into Nordgarten. Ganz led them, with Gruber at his side, carrying the standard. Kruza and the priest rode on stubborn palfreys taken from the palace stables, close at the lead knights' heels. Kruza had never been on a horse before in his life. But then again, every single thing that had happened to him tonight was new – and none of it was welcome.

Behind the lead four, Morgenstern, Kaspen, Anspach, Bruckner and Dorff, then Lowenhertz, Schell, Schiffer and Drakken. Next, in a close formation, the vengeful von Volk and six of his best Panthers, all men who had yet shown no signs of the fever. Bertolf, of Red Company, had ridden hard for the Temple, to raise the companies there in support. Aric, by necessity of his wounds, had been left at the palace, where von Volk's trusted Lieutenant Ulgrind was trying to re-establish calm.

Packs of feral citizens howled at them as they passed, some hurling stones, some even running out to dare the Templars in their insanity.

At the top of one of the sloping residential avenues, Ganz stopped them and looked round at the shivering cut-purse. The company leader mused for a moment that the fate of them all, the fate of the city itself, depended upon the sort of street-filth who would normally be invisible to him. The young man didn't seem much, rangy and lean in ragged clothes, his expression clearly showing he wished to be elsewhere. Any elsewhere. But he had come to them, so Drakken's girl had said. Come to the palace, braving the deadly storm, fired by some need to serve even he couldn't explain. Somehow, Ganz thought, in a moment of wonderful clarity, it seemed just. The foulness threatened them all. It was only right that the city stood to face it together, from the highest to the lowliest.

'Well, Kruza?' Ganz asked, making sure he remembered and used the ruffian's name. He wanted the young man to know he was an important part of the enterprise.

Kruza thought and then pointed down the hill. 'Down, and then the second turn to the left.'

'Are you sure, Kruza?'

'Sure as I can be,' the cut-purse replied. Why did the big warrior keep using his name like that? He was scared enough – by the night, and the evil, and the simple fact of being here amongst this company of Wolves. Somehow, hearing his name on the lips of a warrior of Ulric was most terrible of all. He shouldn't be here. It was wrong.

'Come on, Kruza! It's there to be taken!' the priest muttered encouragingly, beside him.

Kruza looked round. 'What? What did you say?'

'I said, come on. Show us the place,' replied the priest, frowning. He could see the fear in Kruza's eyes. 'What is it?'

'Just ghosts, father, voices of the dead – but I guess you know all about that.'

'Too much, lad, too much.'

Ganz led them on, at a canter now. Kruza was having trouble staying in his saddle, but the big, elderly Wolf – Morgenschell, was it? – spurred forward and came alongside him, taking the palfrey's reins.

'Just hold on. I'll lead you,' he said, his voice rich and deep and encouraging. The big Wolf winked at him and it made Kruza smile. It made the armoured giant seem human somehow, like the sort of man he would happily sit and sup with at the Drowned Rat. More than anything else, that wink steadied his nerve. But for it, he might have fled, leaving them all to their heroic doom. It was the wink that made him stay with them. Kruza grasped the saddle-front and clung on as the great Wolf dragged his steed down the slope into a gallop.

Rocks and abuse rained on them from a group of shadows at the street bend as they tore by. A house had been sacked and was ablaze. Bodies curled in the stained snow. One had been nailed upside down to a wall, and bowls set under it to collect the blood for more inscriptions.

'So,' Anspach considered out loud to those around him. 'What are the odds tonight, you reckon? I have a bag of gold pieces says we can take this monster down, even if it does look like one of our own! I'll give three to one! That's better than the Low Kings would give you!'

'And who'll be around to collect if you lose?' Bruckner asked sourly.

'He's right,' Kruza cried, turning to look back. 'You sell the wager sweetly, but those odds are just the sort of deal Bleyden would offer!'

The Wolves around laughed loudly. Ganz heard it and it cheered him that they could keep their spirits so.

'You know Bleyden?' Anspach asked, spurring forward, genuinely interested.

'Doesn't everyone?' the priest asked dryly.

'This is not for your ears,' Anspach said. He looked at Kruza. 'You know him?'

'He's like a father to me,' Kruza said, and even above the noise of the hooves, the Wolves could hear the acid irony in his tone. They laughed again.

'There's a matter of a tally,' Anspach went on, ignoring the jibes. 'If you could have a word...'

'You mean, if we live through this night?' Kruza asked, mildly, jolted by his steed.

'Oh, I'll make sure you live through this night,' Anspach told him seriously.

'There, lad!' said Morgenstern. 'You've Anspach as your guardian angel! You shouldn't have a fear in the world now!'

More laughter; more jibes and taunts. Ganz let them have their jokes.

He wanted them ready when the time came. Full of jubilation, confidence, full of the strength of Ulric.

They turned into the next street. It was deserted, and the falling snow clung to every horizontal like a pelt. Ganz slowed his horse to a walk, and the others made double file behind.

'Kruza?'

Kruza looked around, though he knew exactly where it was. The tall, narrow, peculiar townhouse was just as he remembered it. It was fixed in his mind. The lean, slender tower with narrow windows and that strangely curvaceous spire, which rose up in soft waves to a tiny dome at its crown. The gallery of arrow slits under the base of the spire. The second circular tower fixed to the side of the main building, the breadth of perhaps two men passing, but with its own tiny dome and more of the strange slits for windows.

A place branded on his mind. A place of horror and foul magic and death.

He raised his hand. He pointed.

'*There*, Wolf,' he said.

He woke, hearing distant fighting. Pain washed back into his body, like a tide. But it was softer now, as if he was floating.

Aric looked up from the bed. His broken arm throbbed. *Like the single pink eye had throbbed.*

In the flickering grate-light of the guest chamber, he saw the girl, Lenya, taking a glass of hot, brown liquid from a silver tray carried by a cadaverous old man in brocade, periwig and powder.

'Will there be anything else? The knight looks pale.'

'That will do, Breugal,' Lenya said, and the chamberlain nodded and left the room.

'You have no idea how much fun this is!' she laughed. 'The palace staff, even stuffed-rump Breugal, are falling all over themselves to help me as I tend the poor, brave knight who saved the ambassador's life!'

'S-so he's alive?'

Lenya started, almost dropping the glass. 'You're awake?'

Aric crawled up into a sitting position on the satin bolsters. 'Yes. Why, who were you talking to?'

'Um. Myself.'

'He's alive, the Bretonnian?'

'Yes... here, drink this.' She held out the glass and helped him sip. It was pungent and full of spices.

'What is it?'

'A tonic. From a recipe my brother taught me. The High Chamberlain prepared it by hand himself, if you don't mind!'

Aric smiled at her infectious good humour. The warmth of the balm was seeping into him. He felt better already.

'Your brother knows a good recipe.'

'Knew,' she corrected.

'He was this Wheezer, the boy the cut-purse was talking about?'

'His name was Stefan. But yes, he was Wheezer.'

'I will thank him when I see him.'

'But–'

'I know, I know. The cut-purse says he's dead. But for his courage, Ulric has surely taken him to his hall. I will thank him there, when I arrive.'

She thought about this for a moment, and then nodded. Her smile returned.

Aric was glad of it. He could see why Drakken loved the girl. She was so full of spirit and energy, it sometimes obscured her beauty. But that beauty was there. Her vivid, ice-light eyes, her hair so very dark.

'I heard fighting,' he said.

'The Panther, Ulgrind, is driving out the last of the fever-mad. It's got to the staff now. The chef attacked some pages, and a matron-lady stabbed a houseman with her embroidery needles.'

'Is the Graf safe? His family?'

'Sequestered by Ulgrind in the east wing.' Lenya looked down at him, holding out the glass for him to drink again. 'They say the city is running mad. Wild creatures, murdering in the streets. I never wanted to come here, and now I wish I never had.'

'You liked it back in Linz?'

'I miss the open country. The pastures and the woods. I miss my father and my mother. I visited their farm every week when I was serving at the Margrave's hall. I write to them each month, and put the missel on the Linz coach.'

'Has your father written back?'

'Of course not. He can't write.'

She paused. 'But he sent me this.' She showed him a cheap, tarnished silver locket that held a twist of hair, hair as dark as hers.

'It was his mother's. The clip is from my own mother's locks. He got the local priest to write my name and place on the wrapper. It was enough to let me know he had received my letters.'

'You're a long way from home, Lenya.'

'And you?'

'My home is down the hill, at the Temple of Ulric,' Aric replied quietly, sipping the warm tonic.

'Before that, I mean.' Lenya sat on a high-backed chair by the posted bed.

'There was no before that. I was a foundling, left at on the steps of the Temple just hours after my birth. The Temple life is all I've ever known.'

She thought about this. 'Do all Wolves join the Temple that way?'

He pulled up straighter, laughing, minding his splinted arm. 'No, of course not. Some are proposed as children, the sons of good families, or soldier lines. Your Drakken, he joined at eighteen, after serving in the Watch. So did Bruckner, though a little younger, I think. Lowenhertz was the son of a Panther. He came to White Company late in life. It took him a time to find his right place. Anspach was a cut-purse, a street boy, without connections, when Jurgen himself recruited him. There's a story there that Jurgen never told and Anspach refuses to relate. Dorff, Schell, Schiffer – they were all soldiers in the Empire's ranks and were sent to us on the vouchsafe of their commanders. Others, men like Gruber and Ganz, they are the sons of Wolves, following their fathers.'

'Are you the son of a Wolf?'

'I often think so. I like to think so. I believe that's why I was left on the Temple steps.'

Lenya was silent for a while. Then she said. 'What about the big one, Morgenstern?'

'Son of a merchant, who proposed him for admission when his father saw how strong he was. He's been with us since his teenage years.'

'So you are all different? From different places?'

'Levelled as one by Ulric, in his holy service.'

She paused. 'What about Einholt?'

He was silent for a while, as if wrestling with thoughts. 'He was the son of a Wolf, serving in the Temple since childhood. Old Guard... like Jurgen. He recruited and trained; Kaspen, for one. Myself, when the time came. There were others.'

'Others?'

'The fallen, the slain. Brotherhood has its price, Lenya of Linz.'

She smiled and held up a finger to silence him. 'Hush now, you make me sound like some high lady.'

'In Drakken's eyes you are. You should cherish that.'

'I fear for him,' she said suddenly. 'There was something in his face when he left. Like he had wronged and wanted to make amends.'

'Krieg has nothing to prove.'

She stood, looking away from Aric into the fire-glow. 'It was because he was with me, wasn't it? He came to me, did me a service, in fact. He left his post, didn't he? That's why you're hurt.'

Aric swung his legs off the bed and paused for a moment, fighting the pain in his arm. 'No!' he spat. 'No – he was true. True to the company over and again. Whatever he thinks he did, whatever wrong, I absolve him of it. He saved me.'

'Will he save the city too?' Lenya asked, gazing into the embers of the fireplace.

'I trust him to.'

She looked round at him suddenly, horrified. 'What are you doing? Lie down again, Aric! Your arm–'

'Hurts a lot, but it's splinted. Find me my armour.'

'Your armour?'

Aric smiled up at her, trying to keep the pain from his face. 'I can't let them have all the glory, can I?'

'Then I'm coming too!'

'No.'

'Yes!'

'Lenya–'

She grabbed him by the shoulders so hard he winced and then shrunk back, apologising. 'I need to be with Drakken. I need to find him. If you're going – and you shouldn't with your wounds – if you're going, I'm coming with you!'

'I don't think–'

'You want your armour? That's the deal!'

Aric stood up, swayed, and found his balance. 'Yes, I want my armour. Get it and we'll go.'

They waited outside for a moment, their horses in a wide semicircle in the street facing the main arched doors. The moment was long enough for snow to begin to settle on their shoulders and scalps. Around them, the howls of the city rolled. Above them, snow-thunder, like the grinding of mountains on the move, shook the air.

'There was a small door to the rear,' said Kruza out of nowhere. 'That was where Wheezer and I got in...'

'It's long past time for sneaking, my friend,' Ganz said, looking round at him. He pulled his hammer from the saddle-loop and turned it once, loosening his arm.

'Hammers of Ulric! Knights of the Panther! Are you with me?'

The rousing 'Aye!' was half-drowned by the thunder of his hooves. Ganz crashed his horse forward and took the doors in with a massive up-swing of his hammer. Wood splintered and caved. Checking his steed's step for a second, Ganz ducked and rode right in through the front arch of the townhouse.

His horse stamped into a paved hall tall enough for him to rise upright again. Lamps in the wall brackets guttered in the sudden wash of air. Snow fluttered in around him. The chamber was bathed in yellowish light, and the stink of spoiled milk was unmistakable here. Gruber and Schell ducked in on their horses behind him. Ganz had dismounted, looking around.

'Kruza!' he yelled.

The thief appeared in the door, on foot, rubbing his sore rump, his short-sword in his hand.

Ganz gestured around. An arch led off the hall onto the stair-tower. Two other doors were next to each other in the left wall.

'The stairs,' Kruza gestured with his sword-point. 'We went down, two flights.'

Gruber had checked the other doors in turn by then, kicking them in. Empty rooms, cold and dark and layered with dust.

Ganz moved towards the stair-tower. The other Wolves and Panthers had entered on foot now.

'No welcoming party?' von Volk asked dryly, his blade glinting in the lamp-light.

'I don't think they were expecting us,' Morgenstern said.

'I don't think they were expecting anyone,' Lowenhertz corrected.

'Let's go and tell them we're here,' Ganz said, but a voice halted him.

The priest of Morr, cowled and stern, stood in the centre of the hallway, his hand raised.

'A moment more, Ganz of the White. If I can do anything tonight, any little thing, perhaps it is to bless those bound for war.'

The warriors all turned to face him, eyes averted from his gaze. He made a sign in the air with one elegant hand. His other, by his side, clutched the symbol of his god.

'Your own gods will look to you, the gods of the city you come to fight for. Ulric will be in your hearts to inspire you to courage and strength. Sigmar will burn in your minds with the righteousness of this undertaking.' He paused a moment and made another sign.

'My own lord is a dark shadow next to such awesome forces of the invisible world. He does not smite, he does not punish, nor even judge. He just is. An inevitable fact. We come to find glory, but we each may find death. It is Morr who will find you then. So in his name above all, I bless you. Ulric for the heart, Sigmar for the mind – and Morr for the soul. The God of Death is with you tonight, with you as you destroy that thing which perverts death.'

'For Ulric! Sigmar! And Morr!' Ganz growled, and the others caught it and repeated fiercely.

Anspach saw how Kruza stood back, saying nothing, his eyes dark with fear.

'And for Ranald, Lord of Thieves!' the Wolf said aloud. 'He has no Temple in Middenheim, no high priest, but he is worshipped well enough and he'll miss the place if it goes. Besides, he's played his part tonight too.'

Kruza blinked as eleven Templars of Ulric, seven Knights Panther and a priest of Morr volleyed the name of the thieves' dark trickster-spirit into the close air.

Then Ganz and von Volk led the party off down the stairwell, brisk and determined.

'Ranald was my lord for a long while, brother,' Anspach hissed to Kruza as he swept past, pulling him on. 'I know he relishes every little bit of worship he can get.'

The stairs swept down. Weapons ready, the pack descended. Intricate lamps shedding a white alchemical glow were looped down the walls.

Gruber pointed them out to Ganz. 'Just as in the cellar where we bested it last.'

'He's right,' put in von Volk. 'It was the same.'

The lower basement, circular, arched and dust-floored, was lit with the same white light from dozens of lamps. The walls were blank. Kruza looked around in confusion.

'This... this is not as it was. There were doorways, lots of them, and... it's changed. How can it have changed? It's only been... three seasons!'

Kruza crossed to the walls as the warriors fanned out. His trembling fingers traced the seamless stone. 'There were doors!' he repeated, as if angry with himself. 'All around! They can't have been bricked up – there would be some sign!'

'It's uniform and smooth,' Drakken noted, checking the far side. 'Are you sure this is the same place, thief?'

Kruza whirled angrily, but the steady haft of Anspach's hammer kept his short-sword from coming up.

'Kruza knows what he's talking about,' Anspach said calmly.

'We know magic is at work,' said Father Dieter from behind. 'Magic has done things here. You can smell it. Like rancid milk.'

Lowenhertz nodded to himself. Or like grave spices, sweetmeats, ash, bone-dust and death all wrapped up together. Just as he had smelled at the Margrave's hall in Linz, and in his great grandfather's solar, all those years ago. Had the wraiths they had fought this spring in the woodlands above Linz been part of this too? The priest had said the evil was old and great and had been planning for a while. And it was after power, strength, that much was also clear from everything he had heard. The old wetnurse's amulet, the one Ganz had destroyed. Had that been a piece of this puzzle as well? A trophy, a powerful talisman their fell enemy had been trying to recover? Had they already thwarted it once before this year, without knowing it?

The irony made him smile. 'We've beaten you at every turn, even when we didn't realise it,' he murmured. 'We'll beat you now.'

'What did you say?' asked Ganz.

'Thinking out loud, commander,' said Lowenhertz, hurriedly. He glanced at the priest of Morr. The father had said something about defeating a necromancer called Gilbertus in the youngest part of the year; another part of it. Lowenhertz knew he would enjoy discussing this with the priest when all was done, putting the scraps together into a patchwork of sense.

Sharply, Lowenhertz realised he was imagining a time when it was over and they were all alive. *That was good*, he decided.

Kruza was busy searching the walls, fingertip by fingertip. His hair was dripping with sweat and melting snow. He would find it, he would. They had believed in him. He would not fail now.

Simply, unbelievably, the answer was there. Square ahead of the door from the stairs. Kruza didn't know where the other doors had gone, and he believed the priest when he spoke of magic. But here it was. Not magic at all.

'Ganz!' he called, in his eagerness, not caring about respect or rank. The Wolf commander crossed to him, apparently past caring either.

Kruza pointed to the wall, to the solid stones that matched the walls around, and pulled them aside.

Ganz started despite himself.

A drape of canvas, like a tapestry, painted perfectly to match the stones around, completely masking the archway beyond.

'We go to war, but the skills of a cut-purse show us where the war is,' chuckled Morgenstern.

Beyond the painted drape, a dark passageway, unlit and thick with warmth and smoke, led off into the unknown. Ganz marched through as confidently as he would through the doors of the Temple. The others followed.

Drakken was at the rear of the file. Kruza, holding the drape, caught him by the arm and glared into his face.

'You wanted me to look a fool in the eyes of your mighty comrades, Wolf?' he hissed.

Drakken shrugged off the arm. 'I didn't need to. You were doing well enough on your own.'

'She doesn't love you, Templar,' Kruza blurted suddenly.

Drakken turned back. 'And you'd know?'

'I know how she looks at me.'

Drakken shrugged.

'And I know you don't love her,' added Kruza, pushing his luck.

'We're here to save the city, and you think of her?'

Kruza grinned, almost triumphantly. 'You don't. That's why I know you don't love her.'

'There will be time for this later,' Drakken said, disconcerted, and passed under the arch.

Kruza let the drape drop back behind Drakken. Alone, he walked to the centre of the room and knelt in the dust, running the fingers of his left hand through the soft soil. This was the place. The place he'd last seen Wheezer. The place where Wheezer had–

Come on, Kruza! It's there to be taken!

Kruza started. There was no one there. Of course not. Wheezer wasn't outside him, he never had been. Kruza knew the ghost haunted secret spaces inside his mind.

'I'm coming,' he said, raising his sword and pushing in through the drape.

In the driving snow, Aric's horse reared on the steps of the Temple of Ulric, and the Templar felt the girl behind him on the saddle hold tight as he fought the reins with his one good arm.

'What are we doing?' she gasped into his ear as the horse righted itself.

'Nordgarten, Kruza said! The place was in Nordgarten! You're as bad as Drakken, wanting to show me the Temple of the Wolf all the damn time!'

Aric dismounted. 'This is important. Come with me. I need your help.'

They strode in through the great atrium. Commotion filled the air. Bertolf had raised the alarm, and the stationed companies, Red, Grey, Gold and Silver, were martialling to support their White Company brothers.

With Lenya supporting him, Aric limped down the main aisle towards the great statue of Ulric. The cold air was rank with incense. The Wolf-choir was singing a hymn of deliverance into the night. Thousands of candle-flames shuddered as they passed.

Lenya was silent, looking around. She had never been in this great, pious place, and now realised why Drakken had wanted to show it to her. In a way beyond words, she understood what the Temple meant, what the Wolves meant. She was struck dumb, and surprised to find herself truly humbled.

They approached the great shrine of the Eternal Flame. Aric pulled off his wolf-pelt and began to wrap it around his hammer-head. With his one functioning hand, he made poor work of it. He glanced round. 'Give me strips off your skirt.'

'What?'

'Tear them off! Now!'

Lenya sat on the cold floor and began to shred strips of cloth from her skirt hem.

Aric had found a relic-bag and shocked Lenya by emptying out the dusty contents so he could pull free the leather thong. With the thong and the strips she gave him, the Wolf tied the pelt tightly around the head of his warhammer, using his teeth to brace against his one useable hand. She moved in, helping him to tie the bindings.

'What are we doing, Aric?' she asked.

Aric dipped the pelt-wrapped hammer into the Eternal Flame. The pale fire licked into it and Aric raised a torch of incandescent flame.

'Now? Now we're going to find the others,' he told her.

Kruza joined Ganz and von Volk in the vanguard as the party pressed down the dark passageway. There was a dim light ahead, like a promise of dawn.

'This is not as it was before,' he told Ganz. 'It's utterly changed. I guess magic does that.'

'I guess it does,' said Ganz.

They reached the light and the passage opened out.

The chamber they looked out on was vast. Impossible. Immeasurable. The cold, craggy black rock of the Fauschlag arched up over them, lit by a thousand naked fires.

'Ulric's name! It's bigger than the stadium!' Anspach gasped.

'How could this be down here and we not know it?' breathed Bruckner.

'Magic,' said the priest of Morr. It seemed to be his answer to everything.

Ganz gazed down into the vast black bowl of the chamber, where flames flickered from hundreds of braziers, the firelight mingling with the white gleam of the thousands upon thousands of alchemical lamps roped along the rugged walls. There were hundreds of worshippers down there, robed, kneeling, wailing out a turgid prayer, the words of which punctured his soul in a dozen, evil places. The air was rich with the smell of decay and death.

At the far end, before the assembled worshippers, a raised dais, an altar.

On it, a throne of rock, carved from the Fauschlag itself. On that, a cowled figure, soaking up the adoration.

Volcanic fire-mud belched and spurted in a pit behind the dais, and sulphur-smoke gathered in the upper spaces of the cavern. To the left of the chamber stood a great cage or box, as large as a Nordgarten mansion, shrouded in tar-treated canvas. It rocked and trembled.

'What... do we do?' Kruza stammered, knowing he wasn't going to like the answer.

'We kill as many as we can,' growled von Volk.

Ganz stayed his hand. 'A good plan, but I'd like to polish up the details.' He pointed his warhammer at the figure on the throne, far away.

'He is our enemy. Kill as many as necessary to reach him. Then kill him.' Von Volk nodded.

Kruza shook his head. 'Your plan sounds no better than the Panther's! I thought you warriors were clever! Tactical!'

'This is war,' von Volk snarled back at him. 'If you've no stomach for it, go! Your job is done!'

'Aye,' sneered Drakken from behind. 'We'll call on you when we've done the work.'

'Ulric eat you whole!' Kruza spat back into Drakken's face. 'I finish what I start!'

'Then we're agreed,' Ganz said. 'The liche-thing is the target. Cut your way to it, by whatever means you can. Kill it. The rest is inconsequential.'

Ganz raised his hammer.

'Now!' he yelled.

But Kruza was already leading the charge, short-sword raised, bellowing a battle-cry from the seat of his lungs. The Wolves and Panthers followed him, bellowing too, weapons swinging.

The priest of Morr caught Lowenhertz by the arm.

'Father?'

'Could I trouble you for a weapon?'

Lowenhertz blinked and pulled his dagger out, handing it handle first to the priest. 'I didn't think you–'

'Neither did I,' said Dieter Brossmann and turned to follow the charge.

They fell upon the worshippers of undeath from behind, slaughtering many before they could rise from prayer. Blood sprayed the dusty floor of the rock-chamber.

Three prongs: Ganz with Drakken, Gruber, Lowenhertz, Dorff, and Kaspen; von Volk with his Knights Panther, and Schell and Schiffer; Kruza with Anspach, the priest, Morgenstern and Bruckner. They trampled the unholy congregation, chopping and hacking with their hammers and blades. The multitude rose and turned on them. Men and women and other, bestial things, throwing off their cloaks and hoods, raising weapons and raucous howls against the attackers. Kruza saw that each one wore a world-eater talisman round its neck, each identical to the one Wheezer had taken, the one now in his belt-pouch.

Von Volk's assault foundered as the enemy rose up around them, thickly, fiercely. A Panther fell, decapitated. Another spun back, gutted. Von Volk took a wound to his left arm and continued to hack away through the bodies that rose to meet him.

The thing on the throne stood up. It looked down in quiet wonder at the carnage below.

It tipped its head back up and rejoiced. Its unholy laugh thundered. *Death! More Death! Death unnumbered!*

Kruza's party meshed into heavy fighting on the right side of the cavern. Cultists were all around them. Kruza stabbed out with his sword, ripping and turning. He had never known anything like this. The turmoil, the heat, the blood mist in the air, the noise. This was warfare, something he had never thought he'd experience, in his wildest dreams. A cut-purse, like him... waging war! At his side, Anspach, Bruckner and Morgenstern belted into the frenzied mob with their hammers.

A bestial, robed thing with ashen hide, glassy eyes and the snout of a goat, reared up at him. Kruza, his blade stuck solid in his last foe, flinched. A dagger tore out the thing's neck.

The priest of Morr looked down at the bloody blade in his hand. 'Morr is with me,' he repeated softly to himself. 'Morr is with me.'

Kruza spun and impaled a rabid woman with an axe who was about to shorten the priest by a head-span.

Morgenstern crunched a face nearby, chuckling. 'This reminds me of the fight at Kern's Gate.'

'Everything reminds you of the fight at Kern's Gate!' snarled the huge blond warrior, Bruckner, as he swung his hammer in the tight, stinking press.

'That's because he's senile!' Anspach barked, whistling his hammer down and over into a skull that flattened obligingly.

'I am not!' Morgenstern grumbled, rattling his hammer left and right, destroying bodies.

'No, he's–' Bruckner faltered. His mouth moved to finish the sentence, but only blood came out. A lance-head as long as a sword blade had impaled him from behind. He looked down at the steel jutting from his breastplate, blood jetting out around it. More blood found its way out of his mouth, foaming. He fell.

'Bruckner!' Morgenstern raged. Bruckner seemed to fall slowly in Morgenstern's mind, the long blond hair lank with gore as he struck the ground. White anger seared Morgenstern's brain. Like a bear, he shrugged off the cultists clawing at him, throwing them aside. One actually flew six or seven feet up into the air from the force of the Wolf's arms. Screaming as if insane, the Wolf flew into the thickets of the enemy. He was berserk. The dense enemy numbers recoiled and broke under his assault, smashed apart as they failed to get clear of him. Blood, meat and bone-shards flew out around his reckless frenzy.

Kruza looked down at the slain Bruckner in horror. He realised he had believed these Wolves to be invulnerable, man-gods who strode the battle fields of the world, denying danger. Despite everything, he had felt safe with them, as if the immortality was catching.

But Bruckner was dead. Just a dead man, not a wolf-god at all. They could all die. They were all only men. A very few men, surrounded by feral foe who outnumbered them five to one or more.

A hand grabbed him from behind, pushing him to the floor. Anspach blocked and killed two more cultists that Kruza, in his shocked daze, had been wide open to.

'Get up! Fight!' Anspach bawled. Kruza was shaking as he got to his feet. Robed creatures, stinking and yowling, were all around them. Kruza raised his sword and covered Anspach's back.

'I– I was lost there for a minute,' Kruza said, clashing blades with a cultist.

'Shock, fear, hesitation – they'll kill you quicker than any blade! Bruckner's dead! Dead! Hate them for it! Use the hate!' screamed Anspach. He said something else, but he was incoherent now. Tears of rage boiled down his blood-splashed face.

Kruza saw it, then, and the world turned upside down. Commotion and panic had pulled the canvas shrouds off the trembling cage close to them. The frenzied creature revealed inside the cage was an impossibility to Kruza. His mind refused to accept it.

A cultist pulled the cage open and the great snaking dragon streamed out to devour them all, and then the world, and then itself.

Von Volk's blade splintered in a cracking chest and he dropped it. Three of his Panthers were dead, crushed under the frenzy. Schell, the Wolf, howled out and threw him a captured sword. It spun end over end above the press. Von Volk caught it cleanly and laid in again.

Behind him, in a mob of bellowing and thrashing bodies, Schiffer was brought down, stabbed and pummelled into the dust by dozens of the enemy. His last act was to howl the name of his god up into the faces of the beasts that hacked and jabbed at him. A spear-point thrust directly into his screaming mouth silenced his oaths for all time.

Von Volk saw the lean Templar, Schell, turn back to drive the whooping carrion from Schiffer's smashed corpse.

He grabbed him. 'No! No, Schell! He's gone! We must fight onwards, to the throne! We must!'

'Hammers of Ulric!' Schell cried with fury as he turned back with the Panther leader to fight on. 'Drown them in blood! Drown them in blood!'

They fought on together, the other Panther Knights at their flank, cutting a swathe through the hectic mass.

Ganz broke from the mass first and charged the dais. Lowenhertz was behind him, with Drakken and Gruber. Kaspen was still caught in the vicious melee.

Dorff was dead. Kaspen had seen him fall a moment before, cut apart by frenzied cultists. His tuneless whistling would never haunt White Company again. Kaspen stood his ground, red mane drenched in blood, howling like a forest wolf, hammer whirling. He held ground and faced the rushing mob, partly to give his commander and the others time to reach the throne, and partly to make the bastards pay for Dorff's life, one by one.

Ganz reached the stone steps of the dais. Above him the hooded figure threw off its robes and laughed down at him. Volcanic flame-light from behind made the Templar armour it wore glow as if it were red hot. One pink eye gleamed.

'Einholt!' gasped Ganz. He had known what he was going to face, but still it fazed him. *Einholt, Einholt... Ulric spare my soul...*

'Oh, we're all friends here,' wheezed the one-eyed thing, beckoning to Ganz.

The commander of White Company saw how the Wolf armour it wore was rusting and beginning to moulder. The flesh of Einholt's grinning face was greenish and starting to stretch. It stank of decay, of the grave. It held out its hand to him. 'Call me by my real name, Ganz. Call me Barakos.'

Ganz didn't reply. He flew at the monstrosity, hammer swinging in a wide, sidelong arc. But the decaying thing was faster – terrifyingly fast. It smashed Ganz aside with a fierce blow of Einholt's warhammer. Ganz fell hard, clutching at his dented breastplate and the cracked ribs beneath. He tried to rise but he had no breath. His lungs refused to draw. His vision went bright and hazy, and there was a coppery taste in his mouth.

Barakos took a step towards him.

Lowenhertz and Drakken leapt up the last few steps and ploughed in to attack the liche.

Lowenhertz was first and fastest, but the undead thing somehow dodged his first strike, blocked the return and then sent Lowenhertz flying clean off the dais with a hammerblow that took him in the belly.

Sweeping around, not even looking, as if it knew precisely where everything and everyone was, it reversed the swing and snapped Drakken's collarbone as the young Wolf came at him. Drakken shrieked out and dropped to the stone.

Barakos stood over the writhing Templar, as if wondering how best to finish him. It chuckled dreamily, its voice like syrup. Then it looked up.

At the top of the steps, Gruber stood facing him.

'You again, old knight.' said the thing with the face of his old friend.

'I should have killed you in the cellar.'

'You can't kill what has no life.' The liche's voice was hoarse and dry, but there was a depth to it, an inhuman grumble that curled the edges of the words, like age-mould curling the edges of old parchment.

Hammers whirled. Gruber met the liche's attack with unbridled fury. Two smacks, three, hafts and head spinning and counter-striking.

Gruber feinted left and landed a glancing blow at the thing's hip, but it seemed not even to flinch. It blocked Gruber's next swing with the centre of its haft, then kicked at the Wolf under the locked weapons. Gruber staggered backwards and the liche rattled round with a wide, devastating blow that slammed the warrior away down the steps. The old knight bounced once off the stone, his armour denting and rattling, and crumpled at the base of the flight.

The thing was laughing down at Gruber when Ganz's blow smashed it back across the dais. Rotting straps tore and the left cuisse flopped away. The mail beneath was rusty and oozing with oily black decay from the corpse beneath.

Ganz sallied in again, before the creature could right itself. It managed to raise an arm to ward off the next strike, but Ganz's weapon smashed into the hand, tearing off the tarnished gauntlet. Several fingers came off in a spray of stagnant fluid and shattered mail-rings.

Ganz roared, like a pack-sire wolf, bringing his weapon around. He could taste victory now, taste it like–

The thing recovered, unsteady but ferocious, lashing out with a poorly executed, frantic blow.

The flat-side of the hammer-head struck Ganz across the neck and ear. He felt his cheek crack. His head snapped round with the blow and he lurched away, taking two steps before falling onto his hands and knees. Blood drooled out of his mouth onto the stone between his hands. The world spun upside down, voices and fighting booming in his rushing head as if heard from underwater.

His face white with pain, Drakken pulled at Ganz with his one working arm, shrieking aloud as the effort ground his shattered collar-bone.

'Move! Move!' he gasped. Ganz was a dead weight, barely supporting himself on his hands. The liche moved towards them. It was not laughing now. Pink fury throbbed in the one seeing eye. It opened its mouth and pus-yellow fluid dribbled out around shrivelled gums and blackened teeth. It flexed its two-handed grip on the hammer, ignoring the missing fingers.

Lowenhertz was suddenly between it and the two wounded Templars. He was breathing hard, raggedly, and the armour on his belly was badly buckled. Blood ran down the armour on his legs at the front.

'You... will... be... denied...' Lowenhertz said, dragging the words out one by one.

'I will destroy you all,' the thing returned, thunder back in the edges of its voice. As it spoke the words, two maggots fell from its mouth and adhered to the front of its cuirass.

'Make... sure you... do,' Lowenhertz gasped. 'For... as long as... only one of us... survives... . you will be... denied.'

Lowenhertz swung at the thing, which dodged deftly, but the knight reversed the swing abruptly with a display of arm-strength that one in his state should not have been capable of. The reverse hit the liche in the side. Rusty armour broke and straps snapped. Ribs cracked like twigs, and brown, viscous matter spurted out, more maggots amongst it.

It faltered, setting the head of Einholt's hammer down and leaning on the weapon to support itself. Lowenhertz almost gagged at the stink coming out of it. It was the old smell, the death smell, rich with spices and decay, from his great grandfather's solar, from the hideous tombs of the far southlands. But a hundred, a thousand times worse.

Lowenhertz took a step forward to swing the hammer again, but the creature knocked him away with a backward smack of its free hand.

Kaspen screamed as he charged in, reaching the top of the dais at last, a trail of slaughtered cultists in his wake. His red hair streamed out behind him. He was drenched from head to foot in blood, as red as his mane.

'Einholt!' he bawled, wanting to bring his hammer down, wanting to slay the foul thing. But it was Einholt still, his old friend, 'For the love of all we have shared, comrades of the Wolf, sons of Ulric, please, Jagbald, pl–'

Kaspen's old friend killed him with a single blow.

The dragon, the great serpent, the Ouroboros, slashed out into the cavern below, death incarnate. Its long neck, as thick as a warhorse's girth and armoured in livid scales each the size of a knight's shield, curling back in a swan-throated S-shape as it coiled to strike. Its beaked, wedge-shaped skull with back-flared horns, was the size of a hay-cart. Its eyes were fathomless dark pearls, a mirror only of unknowable terror. Where it had come from could not be divined; all that was true was that it lived, writhing in its foul undeath. And it raged, screeching its eternal anger at all life.

Kruza stumbled backwards and fell over one of the countless corpses that littered the floor. 'No, no... impossible...' he stammered.

Hooked talons, each as big as a man's thigh, dug into the rock as the vast thing found purchase. Its tail, so very long and slender, sliced around, throwing screaming cultists high into the air or breaking them like corn stalks. The wyrm made a noise, deep in its vast throat, high and keening, like a blizzard wind. Its scaled flesh was gold-green, like tarnished coins, but its vast head was white as bone.

The neck moved in a snap, the great curve suddenly straightening like a whip, driving the head forward and down hard as a lightning strike. The beak clashed, rending and butchering cultists. It raised its head, gnashing at the shreds of bodies and limbs in its huge maw, then slithered forward and struck again. It was wild, uncontrollable, killing everything it saw.

'How can we fight that?' Kruza gasped as Anspach grabbed him.

'We can't! We don't! Run!' replied the Templar, white-faced with fear.

Morgenstern appeared from the milling confusion and panic. He said something, but it was drowned out by another blizzard keening from the wyrm. There was a further clack of jaws, and more screaming, as it struck again.

'I! Said! Run!' Morgenstern repeated, emphatically.

'My plan exactly,' Anspach said. The trio headed for cover amid the milling enemy, heading for the rocky alcoves and depressions along the great cavern wall.

Then the world disappeared. There was no ground. Kruza was flying, looking up at the sulphur smoke gathering in the roof of the cavern.

Abruptly, the ground came back, hard under him, and pain jolted through him. He rolled over, looking around. The wyrm's great tail had scourged through the crowd, sending him and the two Templars flying. There were broken corpses and wounded cult-beasts all around. Kruza couldn't see Anspach or Morgenstern now.

The keening cry of the wyrm came again.

Kruza could smell the vast monster now, a dry, clean smell like hide-oil or grain alcohol.

He got up into a crouch, preparing to run – and realised the wyrm was upon him.

Kruza looked up into the dark, pearl eyes of the world-eater, the Ouroboros. There was nothing there, no spark of intelligence or reason or life. It seemed to fix on him, though. The swan-neck coiled backwards, ready to strike, ready to bring the huge arrow-head skull down at him, beak wide open.

In the last second left of his life, Kruza thought of Wheezer, Wheezer who had innocently brought him to this place and time and doom. *I'm going to be killed by a dragon, Wheezer! How do you like that, eh? Who'd have thought it? It's so unlikely, it's almost funny.*

It seemed right, though. He had failed Wheezer and Wheezer had died, died saving him. It was time to pay for that.

I *just wish*, Kruza thought, *I just wish that I could be as invisible as you. I never did figure out how you did that. Except that you were a natural. Invisible, like you, yeah, that's what I'd like to be.*

The wyrm keened its rage at the whole sorry world. Its neck flexed and whipped. It struck.

As if knowing its end was upon it, the ancient city of Middenheim shook. The sky stretched and broke as the storm exploded down from the ghastly magenta sky. Snow and hail bombarded the roofs, shattering some, smashed windows and tore away chimneys and weather cocks. Lightning lanced the streets, exploding houses, destroying towers. Lurid green energies, writhing like serpents, coiled around the Fauschlag. The northern viaduct buckled and collapsed into the deeps, a half-mile stretch torn clean away.

The Temple of Morr, still only half-rebuilt, burst into flames spontaneously. The fire was pink, unearthly. It made a sound like laughter as it burned.

Lightning struck the Temple of Sigmar and brought the top of the tower down through the nave roof.

The chaos and killing in the streets was now overwhelming. Fever-madness and storm-panic drove the population into frenzied rioting. The Companies of the Wolf, heading from the Temple of Ulric to assist Ganz's men, were caught in a mass riot, and found themselves fighting for their lives as lightning skewered the night, hail hurtled down, and death burned out the heart of Ulric's citadel.

Shades and spirits were everywhere. It was as if the doors of death were opened, as if the invisible world had been permitted to get loose and roam the city. Phantoms, pale, gaunt and shrieking, billowed around the streets, dozens, hundreds of them. Some spewed out of the ground in Morrspark, like venting steam. Many came crawling and shimmering, stalking back up from the depths below the Cliff of Sighs. The dead were walking, free; the living would soon be dead.

Lenya thought she would surely go mad. She clung to Aric as they rode as fast as possible through the chaos. Skeletal, emaciated things made of smoke circled them, laughing and beckoning. It was all Aric could do to keep the horse from shying. Thunder, so loud, and lightning, so bright, broke the sky into pieces.

'Lenya? Lenya!'

She realised they had stopped. Lenya slipped down onto the slushy street, soaked and bruised by the hail that still fell. She helped Aric dismount. He held the hammer-torch aloft. It blazed. Was that what was keeping the shades from touching us? Lenya wondered. She could see them all around still, flickering, darting ghosts, transparent white like ice on a window's glass.

'Where are we?' she asked over a crash of storm.

Aric gestured with the torch. There was a townhouse ahead, curious and towered. Warhorses, Temple warhorses, roamed the street around, trailing their reins, rearing at thunderflashes.

'Nordgarten,' he said. 'I can't say what we'll find in there. It may be–'

'Worse than this?' she asked, pulling him forward. 'I doubt it. Come on!'

The smoky things in the air around them were gathering, growing in numbers, lighting the street with their ghastly luminosity. Lenya tried not to look at them. She tried not to hear the whispering they made.

They reached the splintered doorway and Lenya helped Aric to limp inside.

Funny thing, thought Kruza. *I'm still alive.*

He felt his body and made sure it was still in one piece. The vast wyrm was slithering right past him now. It had struck, dismembering more squealing cultists just a few feet from him.

With this luck, I should go straight to the wager-pits right now, he thought stupidly. He turned and gazed at the huge, sinuous creature as it moved past, chomping and killing.

I'm invisible, he thought. *Ulric smile on me, I'm invisible! It can't see me!*

He stooped and picked up a sword. Not his own; that was long lost in the confusion. It was a long-bladed, basket-hilted weapon one of the beast-things had dropped.

He could see Anspach and Morgenstern, raising their hammers to confront the wyrm as the cultists scattered around them. *Brave, doomed*, he thought. *What can they hope to do against this?*

What can I do?

The thought dug into his mind. Kruza didn't know how, but he was sure he had been spared thanks to Wheezer. The dead were walking free again tonight, and somehow Wheezer had come to him, and generously shared his talent for invisibility.

No, that's not it. He's been with me all along. In my head. He was waiting to be called upon.

He tried the sword for balance and then calmly walked towards the slithering beast. Blood and body parts were strewn, steaming, in its gory wake. It showed no sign of noticing him. He got right up close to its scaled flank, close enough to hear its rasping breath, close enough to smell its rich, clean scent. It was keening again, killing. Morgenstern and Anspach would be next.

Kruza lifted his hand and placed it flat against the scaled hide of the wyrm's flank. The armoured flank was warm and dry. His fingers found a space between the scales and directed the point of the sword there. All the while the cut-purse was almost calm, as if safe within some sphere of protection, or the eye of the storm.

He put his full weight behind the pommel and drove it in.

The wyrm shrieked. The braying sound it made echoed around the room, louder even than its keening. Hot, syrupy blood gouted from the wound, smashing into Kruza. The liquid pressure knocked him over.

He was flat on his back and soaked with sticky wyrm gore when the monstrosity went into convulsions. Its vast, serpentine form spasmed and lashed, crushing cultists under it or pulping them with its jerking tail. Morgenstern and Anspach leapt into cover.

Shaking the chamber and vibrating wildly, the wyrm keened again, three times, each one louder and more shrill than the last. Its claws ripped into the rocky ground, striking sparks and sending shards of stone in all directions. Its death throes killed more of the foe than the Templars' brave assault had done. But they were death-throes. One last, bitter wail, and the wyrm collapsed. The ground shook. The tail lashed round one more time and fell dead and heavy.

I've killed a bloody dragon, thought Kruza, as he blacked out.

Drakken struggled with Ganz, who was half-conscious and far gone. Lowenhertz lay still on the rock of the dais, next to Kaspen's corpse. The liche, panting and ragged, slowly swung around to look at the youngest Wolf.

'I'll give you credit, boy...' Barakos sneered through his borrowed mouth. 'You Wolves did more than I thought you capable of. You hurt me. I'll need another body now.'

It limped towards them. Drakken tried to scramble back, tried to bring Ganz with him, but his smashed bones knotted and meshed and he passed out for a second with pain.

When he came to, Barakos was right in his face, leaning down and leering. The grave-stink of his breath was horrific.

'But it's all too late. Far too late. It's over and I have already won.' The dead thing smiled, and the expression ripped the decaying skin around its mouth. Its voice was low, resonating with that undertow of inhuman power. 'Middenheim is dead. Sacrificed upon my altar. All those lives, thousands of them, spent and spilled, feeding the great power that will grant me a measure of godhood. Not much – just enough to turn this world into a festering cinder. A thousand ages it has taken me, but I have triumphed. Death has given me eternal life. The last few moments pass now, as the city rises to murder itself. Then it will be done. I'll need a new form to inhabit.'

Barakos looked at the terrified Drakken. 'You're young, firm. With my power, I can heal that injury in a second. You'll do. A handsome boy – I've always longed for good looks.'

'N-no! In the n-name of Ulric!' Drakken gasped, reaching for a weapon that wasn't there.

'Ulric is dead, boy. It's high time you got used to your new lord.'

'Barakos,' said a voice from behind them.

The priest of Morr stood at the top of the steps. Gore soaked his robes, and he had taken a head wound that drizzled blood down his lined face. He opened his hand and the bloody dagger Lowenhertz had lent him clattered to the floor.

'Dieter. Dieter Brossmann,' Barakos said, rising and turning to face the priest. 'Father, in many ways you have been my fiercest foe. But for you, the stalwart Wolves would never have recognised my threat. And when you defeated Gilbertus, my! How I cursed your soul and name!'

'I'm flattered.'

'Don't be. You'll be dead in a few more moments. Heh! Only you saw – only you knew – dogged, relentless, hiding in your books and manuscripts, hunting out the clues.'

'An evil as old as yours is easy to find,' the priest stated dourly, stepping forward.

'And why did you hide in your books, I wonder?'

'What?' the priest paused for a second.

'Dieter Brossmann, the worthy merchant – if a little ruthless. Why did you turn to the way of Morr and forsake your life in Middenheim?'

The priest stiffened. 'This is no time for games.'

'But of course: your beloved wife and child,' the liche hissed, backnoted by the burr of distant thunder.

'They're dead.'

'No, they're not, are they? They merely left you, left you and ran away from you, because you were brutal and unscrupulous and harsh. You drove them away. They're not dead, are they? They're alive, hiding away in Altdorf, hoping never to see you again.'

'No, that's not–'

'It is the truth. In your mind, you made them dead, sent them to Morr! To avoid the bleak truth that you destroyed your own family with your cruelty and your greed. It was conscience and denial that made you pretend they were dead, made you take the path of Morr.'

Dieter Brossmann's face was as hard as the Fauschlag Rock. 'I will pay for my crimes in another life, Morr watch me. When will you pay for yours?'

The priest of Morr moved forward again, raising his hands. 'You're dead, aren't you, Barakos?' he said simply. 'Undead, passed beyond. That form you inhabit – poor Einholt of the White – he's dead too. You may be about to embrace god-like powers, but right now you're a corpse. And so you should be taken to Morr.'

Another step and the priest began to intone the funeral litany, the Nameless Rite. Dieter Brossmann began to bless the corpse that stood before him, bless it and protect it from evil and send the lost soul to Morr, the Lord of Death.

'No!' gasped the undead thing, quivering with rage. 'No! No, you shall not! You will not!'

The priest of Morr continued to chant, driving all his will and the full holiness of his duty back into the foul being before him.

Ritual, ritual as old as Middenheim, dug into the liche, slowly dislodging its being from the body it dwelt in. It convulsed, coughing, spewing brackish fluid. 'No, you bastard priest! No!' It began cursing in a babble of a thousand tongues.

It was a brave try. Looking on, clutching Ganz, Drakken believed for a moment it would succeed. But then the staggering liche reached Dieter Brossmann and, flinching, smashed him back off the dais with a vicious blow of his deathless hand.

The storm suddenly ceased. The last few pebbles of hail clattered across the streets. The pink night buckled and went dark.

A moment had come. The moment when a foul thing became a fouler god.

Every flame and candle and lamp and torch in the city went out.
Except one.

One step at a time, Lenya supporting his weight, Aric mounted the dais. At the top, he faced the cadaverous relic that had been Einholt. A glance showed him the fallen Lowenhertz and Kaspen, Drakken clutching Ganz.

So much, so hard fought...

'You – again?' rumbled Barakos. 'Aric, dear boy, you're far too late.'

Aric, using his good arm, began to swing his hammer, turning it in great whooshing circles. The flame-head traced the circles with fire. The Endless Flame, the flame of the wolf-god. The hammer whistled round, the pelt lashed to it burning with unearthly radiance.

Aric let it fly, a perfect hammer release, just as Jagbald Einholt had taught him.

The burning hammer head struck the creature in the chest, knocking it onto its back.

Aric slumped, his strength gone out.

Lenya looked at the fallen liche, saw the tiny fingers of Eternal Flame crackling over its dented, decayed chest as it struggled to rise again. The burning hammer lay on its side, guttering out as if it were their last hope fading.

The one pink eye locked onto hers, as the Barakos rose like it was lifting itself out of the grave.

'I really don't think so...' it rasped, and it was too much to be endured.

Lenya rushed forward. It took all her strength to lift Aric's pelt-wrapped hammer. It took strength she didn't know she had to swing it up and bring it down on the liche-thing.

'For Stefan!' she snarled as the burning hammer smashed the dead monstrosity back into the rock of the dais.

The thing shook and ignited, blazing from head to foot with the Eternal Flame of Ulric. It jiggled and quivered, a living torch, issuing a keening shriek even louder than the great deathless dragon-thing, the world-eater, Ouroboros. The heat of the blaze was so great Lenya fell back. Barakos was incandescent, like a twitching firework, white hot and molten.

Undeath died. A clawing shade, frosty and steaming, tried to climb out of the torching body, tried to find a new home. But the sacred flames were too intense. The spirit folded back into the fire and was gone, shrieking out its last. Barakos, the endless, had finally found his end.

Cautious, tentative daylight filtered down across the city as prime struck.

A week had passed since the night of horror. Middenheim was rebuilding, burying its numerous dead, and getting on with life.

In a canopy tent erected in Morrspark, and duly consecrated to Morr himself, Dieter Brossmann conducted a funeral rite for five Templars of

Ulric. Their names were Bruckner, Schiffer, Kaspen, Dorff and Einholt. It was unusual. Usually the High Priest Ar-Ulric would consecrate the fallen Temple men. But Ganz had insisted.

The priest spoke softly, as if he was recovering from some injury. In truth he was – the dressing on his brow showed that, but it wasn't the physical wounds that really hurt him. Dieter Brossmann would have scars inside him for a long while yet.

In the palace, healers attended Captain von Volk, the only Panther to survive the battle in Nordgarten. Bedridden, he asked the priests of Sigmar who treated him if, may they forgive him, a priest of Ulric might also attend.

In the Spread Eagle Tavern, after the solemn service in Morrspark, Morgenstern, Schell, Anspach, Gruber and Lowenhertz raised and clashed their tankards. It felt as it always did after a great battle. Victory and defeat mingled, bittersweet. They did their best to carouse and celebrate the victory and forget what had been lost. More worthy names for the walls of the Regimental Chapel. More souls gone to run with the Great Pack.

'To the fallen! May Ulric bless them all!' Morgenstern cried, chasing the tang of victory in their hearts.

'And to the new blood!' Anspach added dryly.

They clashed again.

'New blood!' they chorused.

'What new blood?' Aric asked, limping in, his arm bound.

'Haven't you heard?' asked Gruber, as if some great irony was at work. 'Anspach here has proposed a new cub for the Temple...'

She kissed his lips and then turned from his bed.

'Lenya – I love you,' Drakken said. It sounded stupid, and he felt stupid, trussed up in bandages and splints to set his collar wound.

'I know you do.' She looked away. 'I have to get back. Breugal needs the maids to draw water for the feast. I'm dead if I stay.'

'You fear Breugal still? After all that has happened!'

'No,' she said. 'But I have a job to keep.'

He shrugged, then winced, wishing dearly he hadn't. 'Ow... I know, I know... but answer – do you love me?' Drakken looked up out of the infirmary bed.

'I love... a Wolf Templar, of White Company,' she declared emphatically, and left the room to get on with her chores.

The great statue of Ulric lowered over him.

Ar-Ulric, great Ar-Ulric, finished his intonation, scent-smoke from the altar burners swirling around him, and handed the newly forged hammer to Ganz, who took it carefully, mindful of his injuries.

'In the name of Ulric, I admit you to the Temple, bring you in to White Company,' Ganz pronounced soberly, 'where you may find comradeship and glory. You have proved your bravery. May you endure the long years of training keenly, and find a purpose and meaning to your life in the service of the Temple.'

'I take this as a blessing, as I take this hammer,' came the reply.

'Ulric look to you. You are a Wolf now.'

'I know it.'

The initiate lowered the hammer. The heavy pelt and the grey and gilt plate were unfamiliar and burdensome.

'How do you move in this stuff?' he whispered to his new master.

'You'll get used to it... beast-slayer,' Ganz smiled.

Kruza flexed his armoured limbs and laughed.

In the Altquartier, down a filthy back-alleyway between stews, slum children were playing with a tight bound ball of cloth. They threw the ball back and forth against the narrow, greasy, dingy walls.

And chanted.

Ba ba Barak, come see thee tarry!
Slow not, wait not, come and harry.
Ba ba Barak come and sup,
And eat the world and sky right up!

And at the end, they all flopped down, shamming death. This time.

REIKSGUARD

Richard Williams

North of Here Lie The
Dreaded Chaos Wastes.

Here Be Trolls...

laus

Erengrad.

Praag.

middle mountains.

Kislev

Kislev.

eim.

Wolfenburg.

Talabheim

The Empire

dorf.

Karak Kad

Nuln.

Sylvania.

The
Moot.

Dracken
-hof.

Zhufbar.

Averheim.

Black
Water.

Black fire Pass.

ak
Norn.

PART ONE

'Our history teaches us that the heart of the Empire once beat in the chest of a single man. His name was Sigmar. On the day of his coronation, the creation of our Empire, he planted that heart in Reikland. Since that day, that heart has been uprooted and carried to each corner of our nation. On its long journey it has gained great victories and suffered terrible scars; it has been split into pieces and been reformed; it has learned fortitude, defiance, justice and nobility.

'Now it has returned to Reikland. Sigmar grant that it may be sustained here and its stay be so pleasing that this honour never depart.'

– Emperor Wilhelm III, Elector Count of Reikland,
Prince of Altdorf, Founder of the Reiksguard, 2429 IC

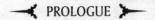 PROLOGUE

HELBORG

The Nordland coast, near Hargendorf
2502 IC
Twenty years ago

Kurt Helborg guided his horse carefully through the frozen mud up the side of the ridge where the Imperial army had set its positions. As he climbed, he risked a glance beside him, down the snow-covered slope. The land was grey, muffled under the blanket of the morning fog, which was only now, grudgingly, beginning its retreat. Helborg could see the bleak coastline starting to emerge, and the shape of the Norscan tribe's encampment that lay out near the beaches. He could not make out individual figures at this distance, but he could sense the tribe beginning to stir.

He crested the ridge. Spread out before him, the Empire's army was also making its preparations. The tents of the Nordlanders were clustered in their regiments. The state troops, their blue and yellow uniforms faded and ragged, had congregated around the cooking fires. Long lines of men had formed before the armourers, each wanting a new edge for their swords and halberds, and they traded old stories to pass the time. Their gravelly voices were loud and boisterous, even this early in the day. The militia companies were quieter; fewer of them were yet out of their tents, but those few who were awake were conscientiously sighting their bows and testing their arrows. Even for these woodsmen, levied soldiers though they were, a battle against sea-raiders was no unusual event.

'You had best bring up the rest of your brothers, preceptor, if you plan to fight the day,' a sonorous voice chided. Theoderic Gausser, the Elector Count of Nordland, had emerged impatiently from his tent half-dressed to admonish the Reiksguard knight. His page and attendants hurried out after him, garments and pieces of armour piled in their arms. Nordland ignored them, directing his belligerent stare straight at Helborg.

'Good morrow, my lord,' Helborg replied as he brought his steed to a halt. There was a moment's pause as Nordland waited pointedly. Courtly ceremony demanded that a knight dismount rather than remain at a higher

285

level than an elector count; however here on the battlefield, when the army was at such risk, Helborg was in no mood to pander to Nordland's misplaced sense of propriety. The elector count scowled.

'Good morrow, indeed. Now answer me, preceptor, will the Reiksguard stand or will they flee?'

Helborg bridled at Nordland's insinuation, but held his temper in check. He had come here for a reason.

'The Reiksguard will stand, my lord, as your shieldbearer, but not as your pallbearer.'

'What?'

'My brothers and I have ridden out already this morning to test the ground. It will not hold your attack.'

'Again with this? You had your say last night. We have heard all these words before–'

'And they have been borne out, my lord.' Helborg cut the elector count off. 'There the enemy stands exactly where I said they would. Proceed as I advised, fall back to Hargendorf. The enemy must follow for there is no other escape, their ships are sunk, there is no route west but through Laurelorn...'

'I need no aid from those of Laurelorn,' Nordland spat.

'When that sun rises...'

Nordland jammed his fist into a gauntlet and held it up at Helborg.

'Hear me well, Preceptor Helborg. You may well be ordained to become the captain of your order, you may be a favourite of your Emperor; he may even make you Reiksmarshal one day. But until that day, you do not tell me how to command an army of Nordland on Nordland soil.'

His point made, the elector count turned his back to the knight and motioned one of his attendants to fix his neck-guard.

'He is your Emperor as well, my lord,' Helborg replied firmly, and then waited for Nordland to explode at him.

Nordland's shoulders rose and his attendants backed away, but he did not turn around. Instead, he exhaled and then clipped the neck-guard in place himself.

'Karl Franz is a pup,' Nordland said, quietly but clearly. 'Elected no more than one month, he brings his cannon and his mages to save us all from these raiders. He picks his battle, burns their ships and turns the sea to blood. And then no sooner does the tide go out, than he takes his toys and his mages back to Altdorf to garner his laurels and enjoy his triumph. And while he has gone home, I am still here, to finish what he started. He is my Emperor, yes, but how long he will last we shall see. The men of Nordland have been fighting this war long before the Reikland princes took the throne, and we will be fighting here still, long after it slips through their fingers.'

Nordland finished speaking. The air around him was still. He took up his helmet from the paralysed hands of his page. Helborg had not moved, but he felt as though his body must be shaking with rage. Carefully, he unclenched his jaw.

'You will never speak of the Emperor in that manner again.'

Nordland gave a bark of laughter and then half-turned to look Helborg in the eye.

'Or what?'

Helborg held his gaze as easily as he held a sword in his hand.

'I do not say what will happen; I only say that you will never speak of the Emperor in that way again.'

Nordland pulled the helmet over his head and stomped away.

'Just be ready, Reiklander, if you are called.'

A troop of horsemen galloped into the camp, young noblemen to Helborg's eye, and Nordland hailed the lead rider and beckoned him over. The rider pulled his horse up and fair leaped out of the saddle, the frost on the ground cracking as he landed.

'My boy!' Nordland exclaimed. 'You made it in time.'

Helborg knew that there was nothing to be gained by pursuing Nordland further, and he turned his steed away.

The sun was rising and the battle had begun. The soldiers of Nordland stood ready in their disciplined regiments of halberdiers and spearmen; the woodsmen with their bows stood in groups of skirmishers down the frosted slope. The Norscan tribesmen, Skaelings he had heard they called themselves, had sorted themselves into a rough line and formed a shield wall. They had used the long beams from their wrecked dragon ship to build a crude war altar to whatever petty sea-god it was that they worshipped. Obviously, it was there that they intended to make a final stand. Some of them wore armour, a few were as completely encased in plate as a knight, many wore barely anything at all. The cold was nothing to them.

The cold was something to him, though, Helborg reflected, as he sat in the saddle in the front line of the Reiksguard knights. The interior of his helm was near frozen enough that his cheek might stick to it. Still, better too cold than too hot. He had boiled under a hot midday sun in his armour too often to resent the frost. The cold would allow him to fight all the harder.

Nordland had positioned the Reiksguard out on his right flank in the midst of a scrub of dead trees. The elector count had said that this position might conceal them, so they could ambush the foe. However, Helborg knew that such a strategy relied upon the enemy advancing close enough to be surprised. All the Skaelings need do was sit and wait for the Empire regiments to come to them, and the Reiksguard knights would be left too far from the battle to do any good. When the Emperor had returned to Altdorf, he had left Helborg and his Reiksguard knights behind deliberately to ensure that his great victory would not be reversed. How could Helborg carry out these instructions if he was not allowed into the fight?

The woodsmen began to pepper the Skaeling shield wall with arrows, and the Empire drummers took up a marching beat. Helborg looked to his side to check the front line of his knights. The young knight beside him, Griesmeyer, sensed his concern.

'Perhaps, Brother Helborg, this show is meant to entice them towards us.'

'No, Brother Griesmeyer,' Helborg sighed, 'the elector count means to win the battle without us.'

'Then, with such a commander, we are sure to fight this day indeed,' Griesmeyer responded lightly.

Helborg could not find it within himself to chuckle. Instead, he turned to the younger knight.

'I did not say so before, but I am glad you could persuade Brother Reinhardt to rejoin us.' Helborg nodded over at another knight, Heinrich von Reinhardt, who was sitting intently at the far end of the squadron.

'I am glad also,' Griesmeyer replied carefully, 'but the credit is not mine to claim.'

'You have not spoken to him of late?'

'Not since the campaign began, preceptor.'

'The two of you were very close as novices.'

'And after, preceptor.'

'Indeed. And after. A pity.' Helborg turned away. 'Perhaps you will change that after today.'

Griesmeyer paused. 'Yes, preceptor.' But Helborg had already returned to watching the battle.

The uneven slope had frozen hard during the night and the sun had yet to rise high enough to begin to melt it. Despite the steady beat of their drums, the Empire regiments advanced slowly, the officers working hard to keep the ranks in order. Even the normally sure-footed woodsmen slipped and slid on the ice-covered ground.

At the bottom, the Skaelings stood quiet behind their shield wall. They did not shout or chant as Helborg had seen before. Norscans were normally impetuous; their shield wall was an imposing defence indeed to an army without cannon or gunners, but once they had worked themselves into a frenzy, it was easy to goad them to attack and to break their line. These Skaelings, however, even with their backs to the sea, stood calm as the Empire's drums carried the regiments towards them.

The sun finally rose clear above the ridge; Helborg imagined that many of the Nordland soldiery were grateful for its warmth on the backs of their necks. They did not know, as Helborg did, that that warmth would doom their attack.

The regiments advanced and the woodsmen fell back, unable to scratch the Skaelings behind their solid shields. As they ran to the sides, a flurry of movement went through the Skaeling line. Lightly armed youngbloods, stripped to the waist to display their woad, burst through the shield wall and ran a dozen paces forwards. They skidded to a halt and hurled their weapons into the face of the tightly packed Empire regiments. Barbed jave-lins, razor-sharp axes and knives all whistled through the air. The spearmen regiments instinctively raised their shields, knocking the missiles aside. The halberdiers had no such protection and the brightly uniformed men in the front ranks fell, feebly groping at the blackened shafts of the weap-ons buried in their bodies.

Shamans, cowled in furs and feathers, flung bloated heads at the Nord-land soldiers. The heads burst apart as they hit shield or weapon, enveloping the ill-fated soldiers they struck, leaving them clawing at their throats and eyes.

The cries of the wounded and the dying rang out. The woodsmen lifted their bows and sighted the youngbloods who had abandoned their shield wall. Without that protection, the woodsmen's arrows easily found their marks. The reckless youths died where they stood, even as they reached back to throw again. Most of the survivors scampered back from the killing ground, but some, incensed by the proximity of their enemy, ran instead for the regiments, shrieking oaths to their dark gods.

The Nordlanders were unimpressed and held firm, catching the young-bloods' first wild blows and then chopping them down without breaking step. And all the while the Imperial drums marched them on.

Their advance down the hill had been painfully slow; it had taken the bet-ter part of an hour. But their discipline had held their formation together over the broken ground. The slope dipped sharply two dozen paces in front of the shield wall and then flattened out before rising slightly to the Skaelings' line. So for a moment, as they closed on the foe, the front lines of the regiments disappeared from sight as though they were swallowed by the earth. It was at that instant that the Skaelings gave a mighty roar, all together, and hauled their profane standards high.

Helborg felt a tiny jab of alarm and he could see that the elector count far to his left shifted uneasily. But then the blue and yellow banners flut-tered back into view; the regiments were on the flat. Over the last few yards, the halberdiers raised their blades high and the spearmen lowered their points. The Empire regiments struck the enemy line in a single hammer blow, and the battle proper commenced.

All down the line, weapons swung, clanging against shields and slicing into flesh. The regimental banners dipped and rose as their bearers strug-gled forwards, urging their men on. The spearmen bashed their shields against the wall and then stabbed low, impaling the legs of the Skaeling warriors and bringing them crashing to the ground, opening a gap in the wall. The halberdiers, meanwhile, were more direct and hacked down with their heavy blades, splintering apart wooden Norscan shields. The Skaelings struck back; their strongest warriors, in their heavy armour, bullied their way through the soldiers who opposed them. Spear stabs skittered off their greaves and the halberd blades merely dented their metal shields instead of smashing them to pieces. These champions fought past the soldiers' polearms and cleaved Nordlander men apart with each blow from their massive swords.

For all their efforts, though, they were too few. Gradually, inevitably, the Empire regiments were winning. The shield wall was weakening, dis-integrating, as the lightly armoured Skaelings fell and their victorious champions pushed forwards. The Skaelings were holding their line and the shield wall had not yet moved, but the famous Norscan ill-discipline was finally showing.

Helborg saw the elector count begin to relax, the satisfaction clear on his face. Nordland spurred his mount forwards, his bodyguard staying close behind, so he could be there for the victory.

Helborg would not be held back any longer, and took the elector count's advance as tacit permission for himself. He led his knights from their point-less concealment and formed them up in two lines, ready to fight. For Helborg could see, as Gausser had not yet realised, that Nordland's battle plan was about to unravel.

A halberdier, hefting his weapon around for another blow, suddenly had the frozen mud beneath his right foot slip away and he tumbled back-wards, the head of his halberd lodging itself in the shoulder of his comrade behind. A grizzled spearman brought his opponent, a tattooed brute with teeth like a boar, wailing to the ground. The spearman lunged forwards to finish the boar-man off and felt his front foot bury itself in the sludge and refuse to move. He threw his arms forwards to break his fall and looked up just in time to see the head of an axe sweep down towards his undefended face.

All down the line, the Empire soldiery had begun to stumble. The ground beneath them, which had appeared frozen solid by the night's chill, had melted under the pounding of the battle, the warmth of the capricious sun and the hot, spilt blood. Weighed down by their breastplates, shields and weapons, the soldiers' heavy tread was shattering the surface ice and trapping their legs in the shifting, treacherous bog beneath. The officers still shouted their orders, but the soldiers were no longer listening as each began to look to his own safety. The advance had stalled. With every step now, each soldier edged back towards the steeper slope behind him. The blue and yellow banners themselves began to droop as their bearers fought to keep their own footing.

In a matter of minutes, Nordland's army had gone from a half-dozen solid, well-ordered regiments to a mass of struggling individuals, fight-ing for their lives. The Skaelings, who had arranged their shield wall on firmer ground, hooted at the Nordlanders' plight. Once more, the shield wall opened and the youngbloods ran out, spinning their axes and knives at the flailing soldiers.

The horrified woodsmen, close at hand, raised their bows again. The youngbloods, dancing their way across the bodies and rocks stuck within the half-melted ice, had sprung upon the backs of the retreating Nordlanders, and there were no easy targets. The woodsmen fired. A few hit home, catching the crowing youngbloods in their throats and faces, but most flew wide, the woodsmen unwilling to risk hitting their ill-fated comrades. Even while hundreds of soldiers were still clawing their way out of the bog, the nimble youths had crossed and scrambled up the bank, joyfully cutting and slicing as they went. In the face of this, the woodsmen too stepped back.

The army was on the verge of collapse. The Nordlanders were a hardy and resilient stock, and were certainly no cowards, but in the great confusion none of them knew where to look for their orders. The veterans sought for the regimental banners, desperate for direction, but the flags had been left behind in the ice-bog, their bearers prize targets for the Skaelings' blades. No soldier who had gone to retrieve them had survived.

One banner, however, still flew. A wildly moustachioed officer, bleeding heavily from a barbed javelin in his side, had dragged himself to the foot of the bank. With the hollering Skaelings on his heels, he tried to pull himself up the steep slope. His leg gave out and he slipped back down. A young spearman above him saw his distress and turned back to aid him; with the last of his strength the officer pushed the banner up high towards the reaching arms of the spearman. He took hold and the officer sighed in relief; relief that turned to despair as a whirling axe took the top of the spearman's head off like a knife through an egg. The banner wavered. The officer, a Norscan knife between his shoulders, groaned his last and the banner sank down with him.

Though his attack had turned to disaster, the elector count was not slow to react. His army needed their leader and he would not disappoint them. He seized his personal standard and galloped forwards, urging his mount as fast as it could go down the slippery slope. He held his banner high and bellowed as he went, 'Nordland! Nordland! To me! Rally!'

His men responded and hurried towards him. The day had been lost. Nordland's advantage in numbers, which had been slight even before, had been stripped from him in the mud-pits before the shield wall. However, if the Skaelings relented, held back in their position, then Nordland could at least reorder his regiments and retreat in good order back to Hargendorf. The Skaelings, however, had no intention of allowing their foe the time they needed. Their brutal youngbloods were already running up behind the Nordlanders, slicing at exposed backs, but veering away where bands of soldiers had stopped and were making a stand. Of more concern, Helborg could see that the heavily armoured warriors were now crossing the bog and forming up on the bank. They had stripped the long ship beams from their war-altar and had laid those across the unsafe ground. Hundreds of them had already made the near side and were starting to stalk up the hill, dispatching the enemy wounded as they passed. If this juggernaut reached the Empire's line before it had reformed, Helborg doubted the shaken Nordlanders would rally a second time.

As Helborg raised his arm he knew all his brothers' eyes were upon him, waiting to be released.

'Reiksguard!' he called. 'To battle!'

As one, the Reiksguard knights spurred their mounts to a trot, heading straight at the Skaeling warriors. The line was packed so tightly that the flanks of each horse pressed against its neighbour's. Helborg had drilled them to precision, and despite the broken ground each brother adjusted his pace instinctively to keep the line unbroken. The rumble of the hooves striking dirt rolled down the slope, and each and every warrior, whether Nordlander or Skaeling, knew what was coming. The Empire soldiers who had fallen back across the Reiksguard's path needed no further prompting and scurried out of the way. The Skaelings followed suit, their lust for death and battle insufficient to face down the tonnes of man, beast and metal bearing towards them.

For a split-second, Helborg saw the warriors at the bottom of the slope hesitate, some turning to retreat behind the relative safety of the bog and their shield wall. But then one of their chieftains stepped forwards, arms encased in long bladed gauntlets shaped as the claws of a crab. He shouted for his men to hold their ground. They brought up their shields, readying another wall.

Helborg gave the order and the Reiksguard knights broke into a canter. The rumble of the hooves grew into a storm, and everyone on the battlefield who was not engaged in mortal combat turned to watch the Reiksguard's charge.

The Reiksguard's first line was aimed straight at the centre of the new shield wall. Helborg nudged his steed with his heels to turn him a degree to the left, confident that the correction would be fed up and down the line. He was not ashamed to admit that the first time he had been a part of a charge of the Reiksguard knights he had felt fear, but now he could only feel the eagerness, the excitement, the power flowing through his brothers and into him. This new Emperor Karl Franz said his dearest wish was an Empire at an honourable peace, and as the Emperor wishes so does the Reiksguard; but in Sigmar's name Kurt Helborg could not deny that he loved war.

Scant yards away, Helborg yelled his final command; the Reiksguard dropped their lance points and shot forwards into a gallop. This was the moment where they showed their enemy the fate that awaited them. The Skaelings were braced for the impact; they knew it would hurt, but their line would hold and then, once they had stopped the horses, they could bring down the knights from their saddles and slaughter them. They knew this in their minds; but as they saw the lance points lower, their spirits quailed and, on animal instinct, they leant back, off-balance.

The Reiksguard struck. The force of his lance's impact hammered Helborg back in the saddle. He twisted, held the lance for a split-second to ensure it penetrated and then released. The years of drill made his actions automatic. As his hand released the lance's grip, it went straight to his sword's hilt and pulled it from its scabbard. He drew back and high to avoid the brother beside him, then arced around and cut down like the sail of a windmill. First to his right, then to his left, catching any foe that came close. Helborg did not need to think; his body did what it had been trained to do. But Helborg's thoughts raced; while his body fought, his mind seized every sound, every sight it could to determine if their charge had been a success. How many brothers had fallen? Had the shield wall broken? Were the Reiksguard winning? Should they run? He could not tell and so his body fought on.

His steed butted forwards, burying the spikes on its champron into a howling face. Helborg stabbed down at another who was aiming a cut at his horse's unarmoured legs. Helborg felt a blow to his hip on the other side, but ignored it and stabbed down again. His armour would hold, but he would not survive if his mount was crippled. Though the Skaeling line was a hair's breadth from collapse, they had held and were pushing back. The knights had been pushed apart so that the enemy could get in between and swarm them down. Blows from maces and axes pounded on the knights' armour, chains and ropes sought to tangle the warhorses' legs. Having withstood the initial shock, barely, the enemy's numbers were beginning to tell.

And then the Reiksguard's second wave hit. Helborg was near jolted from his saddle again as his brothers slammed in, filling the spaces that had formed between the first wave and knocking the Skaelings down the hill. Within an instant, the wall broke and their warriors scrabbled down the bank still littered with Nordlander dead. Helborg called his knights to a halt. As much as he wished it, he knew he could not pursue the Skaelings into the bog. Already the main body of the Skaeling tribe were making crossings on either flank, and his knights, stood still, could not hold the centre. The day had been lost, but the Empire's honour had not been surrendered.

There was still much to do, and the Reiksguard spurred away from the top of the bank before they could be trapped there. Helborg ordered his squadrons to the left and to the right, to break up the skirmishes being fought there and allow the Nordlanders to disengage. Helborg looked up the hill. The elector count was still there, readying to lead the next assault himself. Helborg cursed.

'You cannot attack again!' he said as he rode up to the elector count. 'You must hold them at Hargendorf.'

'You've done well, Reiklander,' Nordland said, not even turning around. 'I don't deny it. You've given us our chance and now we can turn the tide.'

Helborg hastily dismounted and strode over to the man. Nordland's bodyguards closed ranks and kept the bloodied Reiksguard knight a yard back from their lord.

'If you are killed here today,' Helborg insisted, 'then it will throw the defence of the north into disarray. I cannot allow you to attack!'

'Who commands Nordland's army? Some Reiklander or–'

'Just look!' Helborg, in frustration, pointed down at the dark mass of Skaelings crawling up the slope, whooping and chanting in victory.

Nordland looked, and then gasped.

'My boy...' he whispered.

Helborg followed his gaze.

A dozen richly dressed horsemen were charging down the slope on the left at the advancing Skaeling flank. They were the young nobles that Helborg had seen early that morning, and Nordland's reaction left him without a doubt that it was the elector count's son at their head. They whooped as the first few Skaelings they encountered dived out of their way, and rode further in, searching for kills. The Skaeling flank halted when the nobles struck, almost as though bemused by the foolish valiance of such an unsupported attack. And then the Skaelings swarmed. For a moment, Helborg saw the nobles realise their predicament, rein in their mounts and try to turn back, and then the dark horde swallowed them up.

As his son's mount fell, Nordland cried again and made for his horse. Helborg held him back and this time the elector count's bodyguards did not stop him. Helborg looked for his Reiksguard brothers, but they were dispersed, struggling all across the field to keep the Skaelings back. Then one of the bodyguards shouted. Helborg looked: a single Reiksguard knight had broken away from his squadron and had plunged into the horde, carving his way through Norscan warriors surrounding the site where Nordland's son had fallen. It was one man against a hundred; it was suicide.

Then suddenly Helborg saw Griesmeyer break away and gallop towards the lone knight. As Griesmeyer charged, he called the knight's name.

'Reinhardt!'

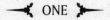

ONE

DELMAR

The Reinhardt estate, Western Reikland
Spring 2522 IC

'Reinhardt! To your right!'

Heeding the warning, Delmar von Reinhardt flattened himself in the saddle. The beastman's clumsy swing sailed over Delmar's head. The young nobleman slashed back, cutting open the beastman's head. Black blood gushed from behind its horns as it staggered and then fell into the undergrowth.

Delmar did not look back. He did not dare. Riding fast this deep into the woods, he had far greater chance of being unseated by a low-hanging branch or crashing into a bloodhedge than being struck by an enemy's weapon. He had to keep riding, keep the exhausted beastkin from escaping further into the woods. None of them could be allowed to escape.

The forest burned with the red light of the setting sun, and Delmar caught glimpses of his men amongst the trees as they chased down the survivors of the beastkin tribe. Each band blew their horns to mark their positions, but they had no breath spare to shout oaths or curses at their enemy. Delmar too was tired; his horse, Heinrich, was drenched in sweat, but Delmar urged him on all the harder. Every last one of these killers had to be brought down. If not, then other villages would pay the same price as Edenburg.

Another beastman burst from a thicket and blundered into Delmar's path. There was no chance to avoid it and Heinrich crashed forwards, knocking the creature to the ground. Delmar felt Heinrich drop away beneath him, pitching him forwards, almost out of the saddle. Delmar's heart leapt into his throat. He threw himself hard to the other side and Heinrich managed to catch his footing and stumble back up.

Delmar reined Heinrich in and instantly slid down from the saddle. His legs felt like water, but they still obeyed his commands. Sword ready, he trod carefully back over the vines and rotten logs to where the beastman had fallen. It had not moved.

This one was smaller than the rest, almost human in its looks. It was pale and thin, with sunken eyes and wispy hair. Its chest was a mass of spear-cuts. It was still alive, but only barely. Its breathing was shallow, rasping, and the blood oozed from its wounds. Death seemed close, but Delmar knew these mutant creatures were tough. With the luck of its unholy gods it might just heal, escape, and then return the stronger to slaughter again.

Delmar did not hesitate. A single blow severed the beast's head from its body. The dead eyes bulged for a moment and then were still. Delmar turned away to see the alderman of Edenburg and his hunting band riding up behind him, bloodied boar-spears in their hands.

'My thanks for your warning, alderman.' Delmar's voice remained steady, despite his fatigue. That was good.

'I would only wish I could have kept up with you better,' the alderman replied. 'You ride these woods faster than I could a level field.'

'Heinrich is a good steed,' Delmar replied, stroking his horse's neck to calm him.

The horns blew again around them. Delmar silently gritted his teeth and hauled himself back into the saddle.

'My lord,' the alderman protested, 'you have been riding a night and a day. The foe is beaten. You have done enough.'

Delmar turned back to the alderman. His blue eyes were bright with exhaustion, but the determination in his face was the only reply he needed to give. The alderman recognised the look; it was that same one his father had.

Delmar tapped Heinrich's flanks with his heels and, once more, the two of them chased after the horns.

The alderman did not see Delmar again until the next morning. At some time in the night, Delmar had returned to the remains of Edenburg and collapsed next to the village's boundary wall. The alderman would not have seen him hidden there, but Heinrich still remained over him, standing sentinel.

Delmar had not even lain himself out properly. He had slept sitting, his back against the wall, his blood-blackened sword still in his hand. The alderman thought it prudent to wake him from outside its reach. Delmar struggled back to consciousness; he instinctively tried to rise and clattered back down. The alderman handed him a gourd of water then sat down beside him.

'I've sent word back to your mother and your grandfather that you are safe.'

Delmar, still drowsy, nodded his thanks as he took the gourd.

'Sigmar be praised,' the alderman said. 'To Edenburg,' he toasted.

Delmar took a swig from the gourd, then splashed the rest over his face, slicking his brown hair back from his eyes. He blinked the water away and then stared at the burned-out houses.

'Praise Sigmar indeed,' Delmar replied wearily. The villagers of Edenburg were already awake, sifting through the remains of their homes. As hard as the battle had been the day before, they would have to work harder today if they wished to sleep beneath a roof by nightfall.

'I learnt long ago,' the alderman said 'that a village is not in its structures, but in its people. And those we have saved. You have saved, my lord.'

Before them, the bell of Edenburg's small temple of Sigmar began to ring. It tolled for the dead.

The beastman tribe had come down from the mountains in the depths of the last winter; it had been another blow to a province already reeling from the failed harvest the summer before and teetering on the brink of famine. The state troops had been called away for the war in the north, and so there were no soldiers to oppose them. The beastkin journeyed east, attacking all in their path, slaughtering the adults, carrying off children and stealing precious livestock supplies. If villagers stood they were killed, if they ran they were chased down, if they hid the tribe burned them out of their refuges. The beastmen killed for food and they killed for sport. But then they had reached Edenburg.

'We were fortunate,' Delmar replied. 'It could have been far worse.'

The beastmen had struck the night before. The villagers of Edenburg barricaded themselves within the temple of Sigmar and rang its bell to signal their distress. While some of the beastmen tried to batter their way in, the rest ran wild through the streets. They had little use for gold, but snatched food or flesh of any kind. Their favoured target was always a village's inn, for the stores it held and for the drink these degenerates craved.

They broke open the cellar of the inn of Edenburg expecting to find a few casks of mead and ale. But they were to be surprised. The cellar held whole vats of wine, racks of spirits, enough not just for a village, but for a city. The word of this discovery quickly spread amongst them and the streets emptied as more of the beastmen hurried to take their share of this treasure.

'Fortune, my lord,' the alderman gently admonished Delmar, 'had a great deal of help on this occasion.'

In the temple, the villagers had heard the battering against their barricades slow, and then stop altogether. Fearing a trap, they stayed still until the sun rose and they could make sure that the beastmen had gone.

But the beastmen had not gone. Beyond all restraint, they had drunk what they had found in a single night. The first villagers who emerged found Edenburg littered with these monsters prostrate in the streets. And in the distance, from all directions, came the militias, every able man from every neighbouring town. With them was Delmar von Reinhardt. Delmar, who had ordered every last bottle to be taken from the cellars of the Reinhardt estate and planted in Edenburg, and who had now ridden all night from village to village to bring the militias to arms.

The beastmen had awoken then and tried to stagger back to the cooling shade of their forests, their once-fearsome tribe reduced to a mewling rabble. They had been caught against the cliffs of the Grotenfel, and there they had been destroyed.

'I do not know what it cost you, my lord. But I take Verena's oath that we shall repay you.'

Had the alderman not sounded so serious, Delmar might have laughed. Those wines and spirits had been everything from his family's cellars. The collection had taken them generations to build up and, beside the estate itself, it had been quite the most valuable thing that his father had left him. It had been his reserve, his last gasp, to sustain the family should their finances grow dire. This one village alderman could not repay it.

'Save your coppers, alderman. Whatever value others placed upon it, this was its true value for me. Our villagers are safe again, for a few years at least. And what has greater value than that?'

'We shall find a way, my lord,' the alderman replied stiffly, for lord or not, no man doubted that he might make good his bond.

Suddenly, the villagers began to stir from the ashes of their homes. For a moment, Delmar thought the foe might have returned, but the villagers were excited, not fearful. He rose to follow them.

Another horseman had entered the village, but this was no town official nor messenger. It was a warrior. A knight. A knight who was robed in red and white and who wore the symbol of the skull encircled by a laurel wreath.

'Sir knight!' the alderman hailed him. 'If you come for battle then I fear you are a day too late!'

The alderman glanced at Delmar, only to see the nobleman's face wide with amazement.

'Griesmeyer!' Delmar shouted with delight.

It had been eight years since Delmar had last seen his father's old brother-in-arms. Griesmeyer appeared older now than Delmar remembered, of course. His dark red hair, kept close-cropped in the young man's fashion, was shot through with grey. The lines on his face were etched deeper. But the greatest difference was not in the knight, but in himself. He had grown from a child to a man and now was almost half a head taller than the knight who used to tower over him. It felt wrong: he should not be able to look down upon such a great man as Lord Griesmeyer.

The timing of the knight's return could be no coincidence. His grandfather, in one of his few lucid moments, had written to the order recommending Delmar to their service not two months before, and now surely Griesmeyer had brought their reply. Delmar burned with the urge to ask, but it was not his place to demand answers from a Reiksguard knight.

Griesmeyer had visited the Reinhardt estates often, though given his service to the Emperor, his arrival could never be predicted. But eight years ago his visits had ceased entirely. When he had asked his mother why, she did not reply. She could not stand even to hear Griesmeyer's name mentioned, and Delmar had acquiesced in her wishes. But he had been barely more than a child then; now he was a man. As the two of them rode into the estate's courtyard, Delmar vowed to himself that whatever his purpose, Griesmeyer would not leave so abruptly this time.

'Lance and hammer, Delmar, you are so changed, and yet your estate is exactly as it was,' Griesmeyer called over the clatter of the horse hooves on the cobblestones.

'We change nothing here. Not in the last eight years, not in the last twenty.' Delmar jumped off his horse, his fatigue forgotten.

'Come,' Delmar continued, calling for the family's manservant to attend. 'Take your ease with us. Let me take your saddle and come inside.'

Griesmeyer looked as though he was about to accept, but then glanced up over Delmar's head. 'No, my boy, I have arranged lodgings in Schroderhof. I will spend the night there and return tomorrow.'

'In Schroderhof?' Delmar was taken aback. 'We have more than enough room for old friends of my father's. You will stay here.'

Griesmeyer glanced above again and this time Delmar half-turned to see what had caught his eye. His mother stood at the nursery window, staring down at them.

Griesmeyer's tone turned serious. 'Your father, Morr allow him rest, would have advised you better than to gainsay your elders.'

The knight reached into his saddlebag, pulled out a sealed parchment and handed it to Delmar. 'Here. My mission today was solely to deliver you this. You will need the day to rest from your exertions and then say your goodbyes. And so I leave you 'til tomorrow.'

Delmar looked at the parchment; he could scarce breathe with excitement. The seal was that of the Reiksmarshal, the Captain of the Reiksguard, Kurt Helborg himself. The letter had to be what Delmar hoped; it could be nothing else.

'And there was one other matter...' Griesmeyer reached again into his saddlebag and pulled out a sword, its sheath marked with the Reiksguard colours.

'Your sword?' Delmar asked.

'Not my sword,' Griesmeyer replied, turning his horse away. 'Your father's. And now yours. Keep its edge keen, young Delmar von Reinhardt, for the Reiksguard will need it, and you, before long.'

Despite Griesmeyer's assurances, Delmar was not content that the knight felt unwelcome at the estate. Nevertheless Delmar was ultimately grateful for Griesmeyer's tactful retreat. When the household learned that the Grand Order of the Reiksguard had received his grandfather's recommendation and were willing to consider him, there was an outpouring of emotion from family, friends and servants alike that would have mortified Delmar if Griesmeyer had been there to witness it.

Much had to be done, though in truth less than Delmar expected. His mother had been readying for the day that her only son should follow his father's path for years. The estate's steward was an experienced, sensible man and well trusted in the locality. He advised Delmar to call an immediate conclave of the aldermen of the neighbouring villages. They gathered quickly and applauded Delmar's success. Many of their sons had gone away to war already. Now the threat of the beastkin was gone, they were proud that their lord would be there with them. The aldermen readily reaffirmed their oaths of loyalty to the Reinhardt family, as Delmar reaffirmed his family's oaths to them.

When Griesmeyer returned early the next morning, he found Delmar already waiting, packed, horse saddled and his duty done.

'I was surprised yesterday, my lord,' Delmar said, as they walked their horses to the Altdorf road. 'I had expected... that is, I had hoped that a messenger would come. I could never have dreamed that a knight would deliver the message personally.'

Griesmeyer rode slowly, bareheaded, enjoying the sun. Delmar watched as the knight drank in the soft countryside that they passed, the blossom on the trees, the bright spring flowers in the field.

'Lord Griesmeyer?'

The knight turned back to him. 'Apologies, Delmar. It has been a long, harsh winter. I am glad to be reminded that there are still places in the Empire of peace and beauty.'

Delmar briefly thought of the blood that had been spilt not two days before, but said nothing. What had been a great battle to him was little more than a skirmish when compared against the clash of armies in the north.

'The order would not normally send a knight on such a mission, no,' Griesmeyer continued. 'I requested it specifically. I have been looking for an excuse to travel back here for years now, but my duties have prevented it. When I learned of this though, a chance to welcome the next generation of Reinhardts into the Reiksguard, how could I pass it up?'

Delmar felt his chest swell with pride, but it did not deflect him from his purpose. 'Has it been your duties then, that have kept you from returning to us?'

'Aye,' Griesmeyer replied. 'I swear I must have travelled to every province, eaten in every town and slept in every field following our Emperor. People will say that he will slow down as he grows old, and I say to them that I believe the sun will slow in the sky before our Emperor Karl Franz!'

'I do not doubt it,' Delmar agreed.

'I was glad to see your grandfather looking so well also, I had heard he had been taken very ill last winter.'

'He is recovered now. His body at least.'

'And what of his other condition, has there been any improvement?' Griesmeyer asked.

Delmar's mind flicked back to his grandfather last evening. He had been happy then, but it had been the happiness of an infant. He had no understanding of what was happening around him; he merely watched in wonder at the celebrations. Delmar had tried to speak to him, tried to say goodbye, had hoped that his departure might raise a spark of the great man who had once lived inside that body, but he was disappointed. Delmar had nodded and smiled, and his grandfather had nodded and smiled back again. He wondered now if he would even notice that his grandson had left.

'I am afraid not, my lord. We had some hope that his mind might recover in those first few years, but now we have reconciled ourselves that he will never truly return to us.'

'A great regret,' Griesmeyer said. 'I never had the honour to fight beside him, but whenever we speak of those days, he is always spoken of in the highest regard. Just as his son is, and his grandson will be, I am sure.'

Delmar wished to ask then of his father. It had been eight years since he had last heard Griesmeyer's tales of their time together in the order. But after eight years of wanting, Delmar found himself hesitant to ask.

Instead, they rode for two days, talking of everything but. Griesmeyer asked of all the events of Delmar's life that he had missed and, in return, the knight recounted tales of eight years of the Empire's wars. It was not until they were in sight of Altdorf itself that Delmar dared ask about his father's last campaign. Griesmeyer held silent for a few moments. For the first time, Griesmeyer's contented mask slipped, and Delmar saw the look of sorrow that he wore behind.

The old knight's tone was sombre. He described it all in great detail: the argument between the elector count and Helborg, Nordland's failed assault, the Reiksguard's charge and dispersal across the slope, and then the young nobles' foolish attack. Delmar's father, Brother Reinhardt, had been the closest. Without hesitation, he had plunged into the Skaeling horde and pulled the youth from the ground. Griesmeyer had seen Reinhardt's horse run clear, Nordland's son unconscious across its saddle. He and his brother knights had cut their way through the Skaelings, trying to reach where Reinhardt still fought, but their efforts had not been enough. Reinhardt disappeared under a mass of the savage warriors and it was all the knights could do to turn about and escape themselves.

Delmar had only the faintest memories of his father. All Delmar could remember was of playing with a toy that his father had given him, and of a knight tending to his mother when she was bedridden. He would not even know his father's face if his mother had not kept a portrait. Even so, Delmar felt proud to be associated with his father's heroism, the only sadness he felt was that he had had no chance to know him.

* * *

The road to Altdorf ran to the western bank of the Reik, and from there it followed the river until it reached the great Imperial city. The river was crammed with boats, traders journeying back and forth to Marienburg, but also ferries and transports, anything that could float, stacked with people heading upriver from Altdorf. Delmar stared at them from the bank; these were not travellers by choice, they were farmers, trappers, village folk. They were refugees.

'Surely,' he said to Griesmeyer, 'the war cannot have reached so far south that the Reik is threatened?'

'I do not know,' Griesmeyer replied, echoing Delmar's concern. 'Perhaps there has been news in the last few days. The foe's great armies are on our northern border, it is true, but the Empire is riddled through with their allies and followers. The beastkin in the forests, the greenskins in the mountains, the marauder bands who may ride where they will, now our armies are distracted. It is a time that any man of sense looks for a thick wall to stand behind.'

They left the slow-moving boats behind and approached Altdorf itself. The closer they rode, the more noxious the river became. For the Altdorfers, the Reik was not only their trading lifeline, it was also their sewer, and the refuse they dumped washed up along the banks. Griesmeyer cut away from the river then, and headed for the main road leading to the western gate. An hour's travel along a track through the woods, and finally there it was.

Delmar had been to the capital before, but only as a child. He had wondered if, like Griesmeyer, the city might appear lessened now he was a man.

It did not.

The city of Altdorf rose high above the forest, as though a god had lifted the towns from an entire province and stacked them all one atop the other. A grand wall had been built about it for its defence, but the buildings inside had long since risen above the wall's height. Every scrap of land, no matter how unpromising, had been built upon, and when the land within the walls was exhausted, Altdorf had begun to build upon itself.

They approached through the western gate, solidly fortified and flanked by two stone statues of watchful griffons bearing hammers. The gate was jammed with wagons, once again some traders and some refugees who were clamouring to get into the city, but one look at Griesmeyer's insignia and uniform were enough for the guards there to wave them in. Once inside, Delmar was plunged into a greater darkness than he had experienced in the forests. The sky disappeared amongst the towering buildings. The crowds, the noise, the stench of the place were overpowering; so many people all pressed close together. The villagers around the Reinhardt estate had weathered the famine, but others had not. When the crops failed last summer, men took their families from the starving countryside into the cities to find what work they could. Altdorf, the glorious capital of the great

Empire, had become a meat barrel crammed with the desperate and the dying.

Delmar constantly soothed Heinrich as they pushed their way through the hawkers, the labourers, the vendors and the beggars. He kept as close as he could to Griesmeyer, steering his own horse calmly ahead. They were not far from the Reiksguard chapter house when a trumpet sounded ahead of them. The mass of people parted and crammed against the buildings. A squadron of Reiksguard cavalry had appeared, thundering through the streets. Delmar moved aside, but Greismeyer hailed them and their leader brought them to a a halt.

'Brother Griesmeyer,' the lead knight commanded. 'You have returned in time. The invasion has begun and the Emperor needs our swords.'

'Aye, Marshal, we will come at once.'

Marshal? Delmar nearly exclaimed. This was the Reiksmarshal! This was Kurt Helborg himself before him. Delmar stared at the knight on his fearsome grey steed. The man was powerfully built, far more so than the slighter Griesmeyer. His eyes were stern, unyielding, but the most distinctive feature of his face was his mighty moustache. It was thick as a plume and stretched nearly twice the width of his face, curled with precision to either side. Truly it was a monster that doubtless scared any opponent as much as any weapon in his hand.

'Who is this?' Helborg demanded, his deep voice stern.

'This is Delmar von Reinhardt, he will be joining our novices.'

Delmar thought he saw Helborg give a flicker of recognition when Griesmeyer said the Reinhardt name. But if it had been there, it had quickly vanished in the Marshal's scowl.

'This is a matter for the inner circle, Brother Griesmeyer. Send the novice on his way.'

'At once, my lord,' Griesmeyer replied. Helborg spurred his horse and the party was away.

'You know the chapter house?' Griesmeyer asked. Delmar nodded. 'Good. Give them your name. You are expected.'

With that, Griesmeyer rode after them and the crowds swarmed back into the middle of the gloomy street and Delmar made his way onwards.

The chapter house of the Grand Order of the Reiksguard was not hard to find. It was a separate citadel within Altdorf, encircled by its own wall and defences so that a hundred trained warriors might hold it even if the rest of the city should fall. Unlike the rest of the city, the houses around its wall had been kept low, only a couple of storeys, and none higher than the wall itself. Stringent city ordinances stipulated these restrictions, and where these ordinances were ignored the Reiksguard's own ordnance enforced them.

Delmar had found the large black gates of the chapter house imposingly barred and locked. He was challenged from above. Delmar looked up and saw a guard on duty, standing beside the ornate frieze of the coronation of Emperor Wilhelm III that arched over the gates.

'I am here with a letter. I am to join the order.'

'Are you? We'll see,' the guard replied, a snicker in his voice. 'Keep going around. You want the white gate, the next one.'

Delmar thanked him despite his rudeness, and continued on. The next gate was smaller, decorated only with a small sculpture of Shallya, but no less closed. The guard there challenged him. Delmar shouted up over the raucous bellowing of the street vendors.

'I am Delmar von Reinhardt. I am one of the novices.'

'Wait there, Lord Reinhardt,' the guard shouted back, 'someone is already coming.'

Delmar nodded and urged Heinrich to the side to move him from the middle of the street.

'You there! On the horse! Do not move!'

Delmar looked back up, but the shout had not come from the walls. He turned and there, in a knot of the crowd, he saw a pistolier, weapon drawn and pointed straight at him.

'Do not move!' the pistolier shouted again, and fired.

The bullet whipped straight over Heinrich's head and Delmar tipped back on instinct. Heinrich, spooked and sensing his rider's distress, reared back. As Heinrich went up, Delmar felt his balance begin to go and threw his weight forwards to stay in the saddle. The Altdorfers nearby backed away from the horse's flailing hooves. Heinrich landed, and before he could rear again Delmar dragged its reins to the side, forcing the horse to turn, preventing him from balancing evenly on its hind legs and rearing again. Delmar gripped the reins and jumped from the saddle, searching for his attacker.

The pistolier was still there, but he was not reloading his gun, nor even making his escape. He and the women around him were laughing!

Enraged, Delmar pulled Heinrich forwards and shoved his way through the gaggle. The women, street jades interested only in passing distraction, fell back leaving the indolent pistolier alone. Automatically, Delmar sized up his opponent. This was no petty Altdorf cut-throat: his clothes were black, but richly made, cut to show red cloth beneath. He was bareheaded, for he had given his hat as a mark of favour to the prettiest of the jades, who in turn planned to barter it for liquor as soon as she could. His thin face, more accustomed to a cockily ingratiating smile, was frowning with irritation.

'Hey!' the pistolier shouted as Delmar seized him by the neck.

'Who are you?' Delmar demanded. 'What in Sigmar's name were you doing?'

'What was I doing?' The pistolier twisted in Delmar's grip. 'What were you doing wandering into my shot?'

'Your shot?'

The pistolier pointed past Delmar's head. Delmar glanced around and saw the weathervane upon the chancery behind him still spinning from being struck by the pistolier's bullet.

'Trust me,' the pistolier spat back, 'if I had been aiming for you, you would be dead already. The only harm I cause is that which I intend...'

The pistolier wrenched himself from Delmar's grip, spun about, snatched his hat from the jade who had been sneaking away and tossed back his cloak, revealing the sword at his hip.

'...and I do not intend any to you. If you had been a better horseman you would have been perfectly safe.'

Delmar released Heinrich's reins and moved his hand to his own sword's grip. 'I will have your name, sir.'

The pistolier's hand inched closer to his rapier.

'I am Siebrecht von Matz. And if you are such a fool as to think you can beat me with a blade,' Siebrecht held up his left hand, little finger outstretched, displaying the ring bearing his family's coat of arms, 'then you can kiss my signet.'

Siebrecht gave a sharp, self-satisfied smile, but Delmar had already taken hold of his sword's hilt. Just as quickly Siebrecht gripped his own. Before they could draw, they were interrupted by a crash as the gates beside them slammed open and a second squadron of knights galloped past. The crowd ran from the horses and drove the two fighters apart. Delmar was pushed back, but then forced his way through the cram of bodies after his opponent. He caught sight of Siebrecht, but then another knight blocked his path. What remained of him, at least, for one of his eyes was covered by a patch, one of his legs was a wooden peg and his right hand had no fingers.

'Delmar von Reinhardt? Siebrecht von Matz?'

Moving their hands cautiously from their swords, Delmar and Siebrecht answered in unison, 'Aye.'

'Come inside, novices. I am Brother Verrakker. Welcome to the Reiksguard.'

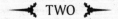

TWO

SIEBRECHT

Inside, the Reiksguard citadel was no less formidable. Unlike out in the city, where the houses and shops had grown tall haphazardly as each occupant had tried to outdo his neighbour, the home of the Reiksguard Order was commanding by design. Each building locked firmly into the next and each corner the novices turned revealed another imposing sight. Monuments and memorials were crammed in every courtyard, and statues of the heroes of the Empire stood at guard beside every entrance. The walls were decorated with the heraldry of the multitude of noble families who had served and, once their service was done, had poured money into their old order. Greater even than these were the Grand Hall of the order and the Chapel of the Warrior Sigmar, and, greater still, at the citadel's heart soared the tower of the chapter house of the Order of the Reiksguard itself, emblazoned on each side with the skull, the wreath and the cross of the order, watching over its warriors and the city beyond.

Siebrecht von Matz tried hard not to be impressed, and failed.

Less impressive, though, were Siebrecht's fellow novices. The interfering horseman, Delmar, had pointedly ignored Siebrecht after they had entered the citadel and Siebrecht had returned the favour. Reiklanders, Siebrecht muttered. He swore that their pride was more precious to them than their own lives. Siebrecht was sure of his aim; he was the best damn shot of any he knew in Nuln, and there had been no danger. No, if only that Reiklander Delmar had not overreacted, all would have been well.

The crippled knight who had come to meet them, Brother Verrakker, had forgone comment at seeing them about to draw on one another. Instead, he had merely bid them follow him inside and led them to a side-court where the rest of the novices were assembled.

No sooner had the three of them arrived than half the novices gathered around and greeted Delmar boisterously. They shook his hand and slapped his back and loudly congratulated each other for their privilege of joining the hallowed ranks of the order.

'Reiklanders,' Siebrecht muttered again, shaking his head. He could recognise them with ease; they all had the same close-cropped hair and simple but well-cut clothes in the military style that was the current Altdorf fashion. So slavishly did they follow the fashion that Siebrecht did not know how they could tell each other apart.

He had known that a greater proportion of his fellow novices would hail from the Imperial city and its surroundings. Reikland prided itself on having more of its sons in the service of the Emperor than any other province. There was no service more convenient for the offspring of the Altdorf aristocracy than a knightly order established within their very walls, and there was no order more prestigious for the status-obsessed nobles than the personal guard of the Emperor. So Siebrecht should not have been surprised that, once the novices were all together, fully half of them were Reiklanders and had ostentatiously gathered in a tight-knit group to the exclusion of the rest.

Siebrecht instead regarded the remaining novices, those left standing at the fringes of the Reiklander huddle. The 'Provincials', as the Reiklanders were already referring to them. None of them were speaking; instead, they eyed each other warily. All of them were armed, and most kept their hands near their weapons. They had all come from quite a distance.

One of them, who carried a small mallet as well as a sword, was an Ostermarker; Siebrecht could tell by the severe expression on his face as much as by the darker hue of his skin. The next was an Averlander, his clothes ribboned with the province's colours of yellow and black. Most recognisable of all was a Nordlander who stood half a head taller than even the burly Middenlander beside him. He carried not one, but three heavy blades at his belt and had a round shield strapped to his back.

So these, then, were to be his companions. Siebrecht sighed. Savages and inbreds from every backwater the Empire possessed. It had been too much to hope that he might see another from Nuln, anyone he might know already. As he searched around, though, one of the other Provincials stood out, for he was regarding the Reiklanders with exactly the same contempt that Siebrecht himself felt. A good enough place to start.

Siebrecht watched him for a moment as the novice shifted his intense stare from the Reiklanders to the others. Siebrecht caught his eye and the two warriors held each other's gaze for a moment. One of them would have to make the first move, and in such situations Siebrecht prided himself that the first move would always be his.

He crossed the distance between them. Unlike the rest, this novice's attire was more restrained, and did not scream his origins as the other novices' had, but as Siebrecht stuck out his hand he noticed the golden glint of a small talisman around the other man's neck shaped like a comet.

'Siebrecht von Matz,' Siebrecht introduced himself. 'You are from Talabheim?' he said, with confidence.

The Talabheim novice glanced down at the proffered hand and then looked back up at Siebrecht. If he had been put off by Siebrecht's hearty salutation, he did not show it.

'That's right,' the novice replied, gripping Siebrecht's hand with equal force, 'Gunther von Krieglitz.'

Krieglitz's eyes quickly flicked down Siebrecht's attire. 'How was your journey from Nuln?'

Siebrecht flashed a smile. This Krieglitz was quick.

'Not long enough to this destination,' he replied, then leaned in closer. 'After we are done here, I need to find a tavern and get a drink. You coming?'

Siebrecht waited, expressing an air of innate confidence he did not feel, while Krieglitz considered for a moment. These first encounters, the first alliances you formed within a new group, they marked you for the rest of your time. It dictated the friends you would make, the opportunities you would have, the kind of life that might be yours.

'All right,' Krieglitz replied, 'but let us get the Nordlander along as well.'

Krieglitz took Siebrecht's shoulder and guided him towards the big northerner.

'No one's going to stop us with him beside us,' Krieglitz concluded.

Siebrecht smiled again. He liked the man already.

Krieglitz in fact invited the rest of the Provincials as well.

'It's the Reiksguard way, you know. Everything in big regiments,' he told Siebrecht.

And the others, not wishing to be left with the Reiklanders, all agreed. Brother Verrakker returned to show them where their belongings might be stored, apologising as he hobbled along that the knight commander had not also been available to greet them. Commander Sternberg, he explained, had just departed to join the order on the road to the north, as had Marshal Helborg himself.

At that, one of the Reiklanders spoke up.

'If the order are heading to the war, then surely so should we. We have seen battle before.'

'Oh, you may go as soon as you wish, Novice Falkenhayn,' Verrakker replied. 'But if you wish to go as one of the Reiksguard then you will have to wait until you have proven yourself worthy of the order first.'

Siebrecht warmed to Verrakker. He was a crippled warrior whose only role now was to play nursemaid to arrogant novices, but he still had some steel to him.

Falkenhayn stayed silent in a bad humour. Siebrecht took a moment to inspect the Reiklander. "Falkenhayn", Siebrecht knew it to be the name of a powerful family, and this novice obviously enjoyed that power. He had even trimmed his sideburns sharply across his cheek to resemble the markings of a bird of prey. Siebrecht noticed that the other Reiklanders were already looking to him as their leader. All except Delmar, who did not appear at home even amongst his own kind.

Once the novices' belongings were stored, Verrakker showed them to their sleeping quarters and then left them to their own devices. As soon as he had gone, the Reiklanders left as a group to explore the citadel further. Siebrecht nodded to Krieglitz, and the Provincials went back to the white gate and brazenly strode out into the city.

The Nordlander introduced himself as Theodericsson Gausser, and Siebrecht and Krieglitz realised that they had been joined by the grandson of the current elector count. Unlike Krieglitz, who was the eldest son of a younger branch of the noble family of Talabheim, and Siebrecht himself, whose own family had little influence in Nuln's affairs, Gausser's grandfather was one of the most powerful men in the Empire. Gausser himself was reluctant to speak of his connection or much of anything else for that matter.

'Your grandfather is a great man,' Siebrecht ventured. If by great, Siebrecht considered, one meant a rapacious land-grabber for whom dominion over half the Empire would be insufficient.

Gausser merely grunted.

Siebrecht eyed their surroundings carefully again. Altdorf was not short of publicans or taverns, but Siebrecht had instinctively guided the novices away from the finer establishments and towards the poorer quarter. The tavern he had decided upon was no den, but it was rough enough to have some life to it. It reminded him of the drinking spots that his band of bored noble sons had frequented back in Nuln. In any case, Siebrecht reasoned, the swords the novices wore on their belts kept them safe from the casual violence of the tavern's other patrons. It was better than out on the street where they had been assailed by legions of beggars: men and women, aged and young, whose desperation overruled their fear.

Once they were seated, however, Siebrecht found easy banter between the novices in short supply. The Averlander, Alptraum, watched everything but had little to say of his own; and the Middenlander, Straber, and the Ostermarker, Bohdan, had gone to the bar with some complaint about the liquor. Weisshuber at least offered to buy the drinks, even if he did stare at everything as though he was a newborn.

'Are you sure we should have left?' the wide-eyed Stirlander, Weisshuber, piped up. 'No one said we could leave.'

'No one said we had to stay either,' Siebrecht blithely replied.

'If you're so concerned, Weisshuber,' Krieglitz said, 'then head back now.'

'Let's not be too hasty, Gunther,' Siebrecht intervened. 'As long as our new friend wishes to enjoy the city, and has coin and a generous spirit, then he should stay. We will not be missed before the evening service.'

'It is a wondrous city,' Weisshuber continued, 'I have never seen the capital before today. It is so alive.'

Siebrecht and Krieglitz shared a glance.

'Alive like a rat's nest.' Siebrecht made a dismissive noise. 'It is nothing to Nuln. You wish to see beauty then see Nuln, my friend. Do not forget, Nuln was the capital of the Empire for more than a century, before Altdorf.'

'And Talabheim before that,' Krieglitz said. Siebrecht raised a sceptical eyebrow at his fellow novice. 'In its own way,' Krieglitz admitted.

'Talabheim is a great city,' Siebrecht graciously conceded.

'It is strong,' Gausser stated. 'That is good.'

'Thick walls,' Alptraum murmured, staring off through the window at the spires of Altdorf, 'but full of paper and lawyers.'

Krieglitz scowled. 'At least we have law. Is there any law in Averland these days?'

'We have lawyers,' Alptraum said. 'Saw a lawyer once.'

'Only the one?'

'It would have been more... but the rest of them escaped.'

The Averlander's strange comment hung over the table for a moment.

'Taal's teeth.' Krieglitz said in disbelief. 'I would never have expected to meet someone like you here.' Siebrecht chortled, spilling some of his wine. Krieglitz continued, 'Nor one like you either, Novice Matz.' This time the touch of concern was clear in his voice.

'I tell you, my friend,' Siebrecht said, wiping the spilt wine from his face with his sleeve, 'I did not expect to meet me here either.'

'I did not expect to see you here, old friend,' Falkenhayn said to Delmar. 'How many years has it been?'

'A fair few,' Delmar replied. 'I could not come to the city...'

'...and I would never be seen in the country,' Falkenhayn laughed, and led the way on. He seemed quite familiar with the chapter house, and Delmar remembered that Falkenhayn's father had been a knight of the Reiksguard as well.

Falkenhayn had shown them the Grand Hall first, which, as its name implied, was very grand indeed. Tables long enough to seat a hundred at a time stretched down its length. Stone arches criss-crossed its ceiling. Shafts of light shone through lined windows and warmed the rich, dark, oak-panelled walls. It was also currently very empty. Aside from the novices, there were scarce half a dozen knights taking their afternoon meal.

'Wait, my brothers, 'til we see it full with the whole order,' Falkenhayn said to the others. 'It is a sight to be seen.'

Most of the knights who were present were accompanied by one of the order sergeants to aid them. Delmar was surprised to see them here, aiding the crippled, but apparently their duties extended far beyond merely protecting the chapter house's walls. The knights themselves had a great need of aid, for they had such a diverse range of injuries as to be more likely patients in Shallya's wards.

They were clustered near the far end of the hall, close to the top table where places were always reserved for the Reiksmarshal and the order's senior

officers. Behind the top table was displayed a tapestry depicting Sigmar grant-
ing the land of the Empire to the tribal chieftains who would become the first
Imperial counts. And above that were displayed the personal coats of arms of
each of the grand masters of the order who had served to date. Delmar saw
Kurt Helborg's own heraldry in the eighth position along.

At the opposite end, where the novices had filed in, there was another
display of shields. These were far smaller, though, for there were dozens,
hundreds of them. It was a wall of remembrance, Delmar realised, and
there, a foot or so above his head, hung the shield of his father.

'Come on, brother, let's move on,' Falkenhayn told Delmar in a hushed
voice, and he started to lead him outside.

'Come on, Proktor,' Falkenhayn said, louder, to the other Reiklander who
had stayed behind, staring at the wall.

Outside, Delmar released his breath. He was no stripling youth any
more, he had fought, killed, commanded others in battle. His father had
gone from his life long ago, and Delmar had thought he had reconciled
himself to that loss. Still it felt strange to be walking these corridors that
his father had walked, seeing the traces of his existence that still lingered here.

The courtyard beyond the Grand Hall opened up into a wide expanse of
empty ground. After seeing so many buildings crammed atop each other,
Delmar was surprised to see open space left untouched.

'It is the practice field,' Falkenhayn answered. 'Where the novices train,
the knights as well, when they are here.' Falkenhayn's tone was tinged with
disappointment that the order was on the march without them.

The other Reiklander novices stretched their legs around the field. The
day's events and the anticipation of the formal induction tomorrow had
got their blood up, and they began to spar with each other.

Watching with Falkenhayn from the side, Delmar saw how companion-
able the other novices were with each other.

'It seems you are all old friends already,' he said.

'We are,' Falkenhayn replied. 'We have all been serving in the pistolkorps
together this past year.'

'Of course,' Delmar said quietly.

'Proktor there, you remember Proktor,' Falkenhayn continued, indicating the slightest of the novices. 'He and I enlisted together.'

Delmar nodded. Proktor's family and Falkenhayn's were related and,
throughout their youth together, he had ever been Falkenhayn's shadow.

'Harver and Breigh were already there,' Falkenhayn said, pointing out
the two novices wrestling with each other. 'And Hardenburg came a few
months after. You don't have any sisters, do you, Reinhardt? I should keep
them away from Hardenburg if you do.'

Delmar looked at the pleasant-faced young man as he adjudicated over
the other novices' bout.

'No, no sisters or brothers.'

'Ah, Reinhardt,' Falkenhayn said, 'do not doubt that you have brothers now.' Falkenhayn looked out to the other novices, 'Doesn't he, Falcons!'

The Reiklanders looked up from their sport.

'Falcons!' they cried back.

'What's that?' Delmar asked.

'Just a name the pistolkorps called us. The others are quite fond of it.'

'Falcons?' Delmar said. 'After you?'

Falkenhayn shrugged.

'It is a shame you were not with us then. We could have used your strength. But come on, let us make up for lost time.' Falkenhayn took him over to join the others. 'And let us only hope that the war continues long enough for us to show the Empire's foes how the sons of Reikland fight!'

Siebrecht and the other Provincials made their way, slowly but steadily, back to the chapter house. Siebrecht and Krieglitz walked side by side, Bohdan and Straber supported each other, Alptraum walked on his own and Gausser carried the unconscious Weisshuber over his shoulders.

The wine had insulated Siebrecht nicely against the cool night and the human squalor in the streets around him. He was far happier now he was on the other side of the cup. He found himself singing an old nursery song, written as a learning rhyme to teach common children the provinces of the Empire. As Siebrecht recited the first line, Krieglitz and Gausser, strangers from across the Empire who had never met before that day, joined in and sang together.

A voice from a window above gave the novices a short, sharp critique of their abilities as minstrels. Siebrecht responded by launching into the second verse with all the greater gusto. Krieglitz very firmly clamped his hand over Siebrecht's mouth.

'Be quiet, you idiot. You'll get us into even more trouble.'

Siebrecht flailed but could not slip from the Talabheimer's grip.

'Talabec! Talabec!' One of the beggar women rose from the gutter and stumbled towards Krieglitz. 'You are from Talabecland?'

'What of it?' Krieglitz said, pushing Siebrecht away and moving his hand to his sword. The beggar woman saw the movement and cowered away.

'Nothing, noble lord! I did not mean any harm. Be generous and spare your fellow countryman.'

Krieglitz let his sword drop back. 'You would have been better to stay at home.'

'Our homes were burned, noble lord. The beastkin in the forests.'

Krieglitz grudgingly flicked her a coin, which she caught and hid instantly beneath her clothes. 'That is my last one. Do not send your friends after me looking for more.'

'More trouble,' Krieglitz muttered under his breath as he led the Provincials on.

'You concern yourself too much,' Siebrecht said, far more sober than he had been a few moments before. 'We will be fine.'

'I doubt that indeed.'

'I would wager it.'

'What?'

'Come, I shall prove it,' Siebrecht retorted. 'A gold crown that we have not been missed.'

'You are ridiculous, Siebrecht.'

'Think of it as simple prudence, Gunther. Would you pay a crown to guarantee there was no trouble?'

'Perhaps,' Krieglitz admitted.

'Then if we are not, you have your money's worth. And if we are, you have another crown to console you for your loss. It is prudent, I would say. Are you Talabheimers not known for your prudence?'

Krieglitz shook his head but said, 'Very well.'

'Done and done. Come on, Gausser, let us get the young Stirlander to his bed.'

'I cannot believe it, Siebrecht,' Krieglitz said. 'You have got me gambling on my very career.'

Siebrecht laughed at his friend. 'And it is only the first day. Imagine what there will be tomorrow!'

'Are you awake, Novice Matz?' Brother Verrakker said gently.

Siebrecht groggily cracked an eyelid. It was still dark. He closed it again.

'Good,' Verrakker said. 'Take him.'

Siebrecht was very much awake as the sergeants hurled him into the deep pool of black water beneath the chapter house. He gasped at the shock of the icy water and quickly surfaced, then instinctively ducked again as the struggling forms of the other Provincials were thrown in after him. All of them rose, spluttering protests.

The only one of them still dry was Gausser, who was wrestling on the side with three sergeants trying to restrain him. One of them lost their grip, and Gausser picked him up and launched him bodily into the pool. The sergeants who had been handling the other novices glanced at each other, then threw themselves onto the struggling Nordlander.

'Enough!' Verrakker said, and the sergeants carefully loosened their grip. 'Novices, you will clean this pool. You will empty the water, scrub its walls, wash them clean, then refill it.'

Siebrecht's foot strained to reach the bottom while keeping his head on the surface; he found he could stand, so long as he stayed on tip-toe. He tried to shout back at Verrakker, but his breath still had not returned.

'Novice Gausser,' Verrakker continued, and the Nordlander shrugged himself free. 'You may leave with us, or you may stand with your brothers. It is your choice.'

Gausser stood for a moment beside the pool, then, staring at Verrakker with bloody-minded defiance, he slowly lowered himself into the water.

'As I thought,' Verrakker concluded. 'We shall return when you are done. And here, something to help...'

Verrakker dragged a bucket through the water and then held it up. Water poured out through its perforated base.

'You can't leave us. We could catch our deaths in here!' Siebrecht finally managed to gasp.

'We have excellent healers, Novice Matz,' Verrakker replied as he and the sergeants filed out. The sergeant Gausser had soaked left with a pointed backwards glance.

'And if they should fail...' Verrakker continued. 'Well, you shall not be the first.'

The cold remained in their bones the rest of the day, and Siebrecht spent most of their induction around the chapter house either shivering or yawning. He had expected the other Provincials to attach a certain degree of blame to him regarding their unfortunate experience. Weisshuber took it with equanimity, though; Alptraum acted as though nothing had happened; Gausser accepted it with his usual impenetrable stoicism; and Bohdan and Straber thought it had been a great joke.

Only Krieglitz appeared to hold a grudge. Siebrecht decided to shake him from it. That evening, once the novices were sent back to their quarters, he wandered over to him and flicked him a gold coin.

Krieglitz caught it sullenly. 'You really do not care, do you?'

'That I do not.' And Siebrecht did not. The Reiksguard had been no choice of his. Throughout his childhood, his father, the old baron, had done nothing but blame the Reikland emperors for all the woes in the world. He clutched his bitterness still, his one solace, as he blindly brought the Matz family to its knees. He allowed candles to be lit only rarely, as he said he could not afford them. He detested any sounds of laughter or mirth, and so Siebrecht and his brothers and sisters crept around like mice. The baron had turned the family home into the family grave.

Of all them, only the baron's younger brother, Siebrecht's uncle, had escaped the poison of the household completely. And once he left, the baron never allowed him back. The uncle had gone into the merchant trade, and would return once every few years, laden with gifts. Even then, Siebrecht's mother had to take him and his siblings into Nuln to meet him as the baron refused to have his brother set foot upon his land.

As he grew older, Siebrecht had also kept away as best he could, gaming, drinking; he and his friends had even joined the pistolkorps when the war came and they took what excitement they could from the tedious patrols and brief alarms. Siebrecht had hoped that they might stay together and join the city regiments. He would have cut a fine figure indeed in their black uniform, and the Countess of Nuln was renowned for her fondness for having young officers entertain her at her grand dances.

Instead his family had sent him here, far from his friends and his ambitions, to protect the life of the very man they had raised him to detest. So, no, he did not care.

'Understand me, Siebrecht,' Krieglitz said, with deliberate import. 'This may not be important to you, but it is to me. To my family. So I will be your comrade, I will be your friend, but I will not let you be my undoing. Agreed?'

'Agreed,' Siebrecht said, and they shook hands on it. 'I will not be your undoing, Gunther, I would wager a crown upon it.'

'Of course, you would.' Krieglitz shook his head.

Verrakker called the novices to the practice field and had them stand in a loose semi-circle at the corner. They each wore their plain cloth tunics and had been given a sword, a wooden waster.

They were met there by several of the order's sergeants and two of the Reiksguard's fightmasters. The first fightmaster stood formally at ease, his feet a shoulder-width apart, his hands behind his back. Or, to be more precise, hand, singular, for the fightmaster's left arm ended no more than an inch below his elbow. Nevertheless, the knight held the arm at the perfect angle, as though his hands still grasped each other. The second knight stood a step directly behind him. Unlike the first, his face was downcast, his eyes were bandaged and his head was completely bald, not a hair upon it, not on his scalp, nor above his eyes, nor on his chin. He had his hand on the shoulder of the fightmaster before him.

Verrakker introduced his brother-knights: 'This is Brother Talhoffer and Brother Ott,' Verrakker said, indicating the lead knight and then the second. 'While you are novices, you will not address them as such. Until you can prove yourselves worthy and become full brothers, you will address them as Fightmaster Talhoffer and Fightmaster Ott, or simply as master.'

Verrakker bowed to the fightmasters deferentially and hobbled away. As the other novices turned their attention to the fightmasters, Siebrecht, thoughtfully, watched Verrakker go.

'We are well met, noble sons,' Fightmaster Talhoffer declared. 'I see in you the burning need to serve your Empire and I can tell you now that the Empire has great need of that service. You will have heard already that before you may become a brother of this grand order you must prove yourself in three disciplines: strength of body, strength of mind and strength of spirit. Of these three, strength of body is the most important, for without a strong body you will never protect the Emperor from those who seek to do him harm. Strength of body is what you will learn from me.'

There was a shifting amongst the novices. Some of the Provincials and the Reiklanders were not impressed. They were not children who needed to be taught basic drills.

'You have all served before,' Talhoffer continued. 'You have all fought. You all show promise, else you would never have been allowed here. Promise, though, is not enough. We do not entrust the life of our Emperor to those who merely have promise, we entrust it only to those who have proven their ability. Not simply to fight, but to fight as a knight of the Reiksguard must. We will train you to fight and we will test you. You may think you are a great warrior already, but if you cannot or will not learn what we have to teach, then there is no place for you here.'

Talhoffer drew out the pause, waiting for one of the more prideful novices to speak and knowing that none of them would. The novices stayed silent.

'We will teach you how to fight as a Reiksguarder in every circumstance, on horse, on foot, in the crush of a regiment, in a single combat, against one opponent and against many. For we must be prepared to serve in whatever manner the Emperor demands.'

Talhoffer beckoned to one of the sergeants attending him, who passed him a halberd.

'You must become adept in all the arms of the Empire as well.' Talhoffer easily hefted the heavy weapon in a single grip. 'Skill with lance and sword are not sufficient, you must be ready to use whatever weapon is to hand.

'While you will spar with each other to learn and to practise, the purpose of your training is to fight the enemies of the Empire. Not each other. Some of you, I warrant, have drawn your sword in anger against a comrade because of injury to your honour. That ends here. Duels of any kind between members of the order are strictly prohibited. For we are a brotherhood, and from this point on you must be brothers to each other.'

Siebrecht stole a glance in the direction of Delmar, but he and the rest of the Reiklanders merely looked on.

'Now, I shall call each one of you up in turn to judge what you have learnt already, or rather, how much work I will have to undo the bad habits that poor teaching has already instilled within you.'

He told the novices to sit and then called Harver forwards. Siebrecht had expected that Talhoffer himself would spar, but instead one of the sergeants squared off against him. It was a surprise: the sergeants were all common-born, and while noblemen learned to use a sword from childhood, few commoners had the money or the time.

In a few blows it was over, and Harver was flat on his back.

Siebrecht dropped his pretence of uninterest and watched the bouts closely. He had been quietly confident, for in Nuln duelling was a constant pastime for his band of libertines. He had had to defend himself not only in single combats but also in the sudden and deadly street fights that erupted between different bands over the important things in life: wagers, women and honour. But these sergeants had been taught well.

Novice after novice stepped up and, no matter what their past experience, each was defeated. Siebrecht allowed himself a small smile when Delmar had his sword knocked from his hand.

'Novice Matz, your turn to spar,' Talhoffer ordered. 'Let us see whether you Nulners are as eager with the sword as you are with your pistol.'

There was a stir amongst the Reiklanders: news of the clash between Delmar and Siebrecht on their first day had spread quickly amongst them.

As Siebrecht rose, he whispered to Krieglitz, 'A crown of mine says I mark him.'

Siebrecht stood up and walked over with his typical swagger. He took his position and settled into his guard, ready for the sergeant to attack.

'Novices!' Talhoffer interrupted before the fight could begin. 'You did not tell me that the Reiksguard had accepted a Tilean!'

It took Siebrecht a moment to realise that the fightmaster was talking about him.

'I do not follow your meaning, master, I am no Tilean.'

'If you are no Tilean, Novice Matz, then why do you stand like one?'

Confused, Siebrecht looked down at his feet.

'Take up a proper Imperial guard, novice, we shall have none of the Tilean "arts" here. They are fit only for women.'

The other novices, realising the fightmaster's joke, laughed hugely, the Reiklanders especially. Embarrassed, Siebrecht shifted to a fair approximation of the 'plough' guard that the sergeant had adopted, holding his sword at waist height, pointed at his opponent. Siebrecht cursed under his breath. All the duelling instructors of Nuln taught the Tilean style, there was no fault in it, and now he had allowed himself to be forced into a style in which he was less comfortable.

Before Siebrecht could reconsider, the sergeant took the initiative and advanced, raising his sword into a roof guard, hilt by the shoulder, blade pointing straight up as he went. Anticipating the downwards slash, Siebrecht gathered his blade in and, when the blow came, was ready to lift his own blade in reply. The sergeant's weapon crashed down upon his own with full force; Siebrecht felt his elbow give way and grabbed his hilt with his free hand to prevent his guard collapsing. On the sidelines he heard the fightmaster tut disapprovingly. Siebrecht had intended to beat the sergeant's sword away and twist his blade to respond with a cut of his own, but it was all he could do to keep his opponent from his neck. The sergeant drew back, preparing another strike, and Siebrecht took the opportunity to step quickly backwards, giving him a few precious seconds to recover.

The sergeant advanced again, but this time it was Siebrecht who attacked with a lightning thrust, not to his opponent's chest but to his thigh. This was what true swordplay was about, Siebrecht knew, not words, nor tricks, but simply being faster than any opposition, and in that he excelled. The sergeant corrected his strike, sweeping his blade down early to deflect Siebrecht's thrust away. Siebrecht was ready for it and, just before the swords made contact, he flicked his wrist and brought the point over the sergeant's hilt and up against his chest. It was a move designed for lighter, slimmer weapons than this ungainly practice sword, and his wrist muscles protested at such treatment. But the sergeant was surprised and had to throw his body back to evade the sword's tip. Siebrecht thrust forwards again to realise his advantage, but the sergeant found his feet and managed to stumble backwards, before finally knocking Siebrecht's sword away with a desperate swipe.

There was another moment's pause as both sides reassessed the other. Siebrecht could tell that his fellow novices had been impressed; none of them had managed to so much as trouble the sergeant, let alone drive him back. But he also knew that the sergeant had been too confident; he would not be caught out so readily next time. The sergeant, though, appeared to have learned nothing from the last engagement and once more advanced with a high guard, exactly as he had done the first time. It was obviously a trap, evidently the sergeant hoped for Siebrecht to draw his sword in again ready to block and allow him a chance to close the distance, perhaps even reverse his guard into a downwards thrust. Siebrecht did the opposite and threw himself forwards, thrusting straight at the sergeant's chest this time, trusting to his sheer speed to succeed without any tricks.

As Siebrecht moved, the sergeant leaped forwards, keeping his sword high but twisting to evade the novice's point. Siebrecht's blade slipped past the sergeant's side and so he hurriedly stepped back to pull away. Too late. The sergeant's free arm slammed down, pinning Siebrecht's blade between his arm and his chest. Desperate, Siebrecht tried to twist the weapon to cut its way clear, but the sergeant had already snaked his arm around Siebrecht's sword hand and locked the elbow. Dropping his own sword, the sergeant gripped Siebrecht's shoulder and dropped his weight, dragging the novice down with him. They both hit the ground, but the sergeant landed on top and still with his grip. In mere moments, Siebrecht was face down with the sergeant's knee in the small of his back.

At an order from Talhoffer, the sergeant released the lock on his arm and the pressure of the sergeant's knee lifted. Feeling humiliated, Siebrecht clambered to his feet.

'You still have your sword in your hand at least, Novice Matz, though you would find it of little use where you were.'

Aware of the mocking stares of the other novices who were enjoying his defeat, Siebrecht did not say what he wished and instead muttered something under his breath.

'What was that, Novice Matz?'

Ah, curse them, Siebrecht thought, he had a legitimate grievance.

'I thought this was sword sparring, master, not wrestling.' If he had known that he would have to defend himself against wrestling moves as well, he would not have been taken off guard.

Talhoffer considered the novice from Nuln. 'Did I ever say that this was sword sparring, Novice Matz?'

No, he hadn't, Siebrecht recalled. They had all simply assumed.

'No, master,' he admitted.

'Was it simply because you were given a sword that you thought a sword was the only weapon with which you could fight?'

Siebrecht did not speak, but gave a half-nod.

'Though it is true that you will learn sword from me, and wrestling from Master Ott, we draw no distinction between them in combat. We fight with the whole of our body, Novice Matz. Every resource at our disposal.'

◄ THREE ►

FALKENHAYN

'I am Master Lehrer,' the grey knight announced from his throne behind the solid oak desk in the depths of the order's library. 'You will have heard already that before you may become a brother of this grand order you must prove yourself in three disciplines: strength of body, strength of mind and strength of spirit. Of these three, strength of mind is the most important, for without a strong mind and the ability to reason, even the strongest body is easily outwitted or dumbfounded. This is what you will learn from me.'

'In this place,' the master continued, 'you shall learn the full meaning of knightly duty, to the Emperor, to his people and to yourself. You shall also learn judgement; for if you are to be a knight, rather than merely a soldier, you shall have to be a judge, of your own actions and the actions of others'. For there is no better judge than an honourable knight, who has truth in his words, duty in his heart and a sword in his hand.'

Beneath his shaggy beard, the old master's mouth slowly twisted into a smile. Delmar listened closely. He thought of Griesmeyer; aye, there would be a knight Delmar would trust as a judge.

'As well as that, we shall also examine the Empire's greatest victories and its greatest defeats, for our ability to reason and learn from our mistakes is what sets us apart from beasts. We shall study the Empire's most successful generals and its most terrible foes. We shall begin today with Emperor Wilhelm III.'

Behind Delmar, at the back of the novices, someone scoffed.

'Novice Matz,' Master Lehrer called, 'you wish to speak?'

Delmar turned around, as did every other novice, and stared at Siebrecht.

'No, master,' Siebrecht replied. 'A cough only.'

Delmar once again found himself growing angry at the Nulner's disrespect towards the order's masters.

But Master Lehrer, who took a degree of malicious enjoyment in hooking impertinent novices, was not to be disabused.

'Well, Novice Matz, you are called upon now. So we will sit silently until you share your thoughts with us.'

320

Delmar watched as Siebrecht paused for a moment, testing the master's pledge, but Lehrer's amused expression was impenetrable.

'My only thought, master,' Siebrecht began, 'was that there might be emperors worthy of study before more recent times.'

'You mean, before the Reikland emperors?' Lehrer replied, dryly. 'Go on then, novice, who would you suggest?'

Delmar could see Siebrecht's cockiness return to him. 'I, for one, master, have learnt much from the great Emperor Magnus the Pious,' he said, then adding, 'of Nuln.'

Master Lehrer sat satisfied. 'I take your meaning, novice. I prefer to start with Emperor Wilhelm because that is where our order's own records begin. But Emperor Magnus's reign was two centuries ago, long before our order was founded, and there are precious few contemporary accounts of his great victories.'

'Master,' Falkenhayn spoke up, giving Delmar a wink, 'I feel I must say that is greatly unfortunate. For if we are only to study the last hundred years I scarce think we will find any general of Nuln of note.'

Siebrecht scoffed again. 'Small surprise when the Reikland princes allow scant few from other provinces to command the Empire's armies.'

Falkenhayn bridled at that. 'The surprise is that any provincial might be given command, when it is Reikland that must provide half the men of the Emperor's armies and all the officers.'

'Ridiculous,' Siebrecht shot back.

'Is it? Reikland is but one province in ten, and yet we Reiklanders here are half the novices. Truly we are called the Reiksguard for a reason!' That brought a small cheer of support from the other Reikland novices, but Delmar stayed silent. He saw the look of disquiet on the faces of the Provincial novices, and pulled at Falkenhayn to try and sit him down.

'Oh, I do not dispute it,' Siebrecht countered. 'I only say that it is ridiculous that Reikland officers prefer and advance their own kind ahead of any other.'

If Siebrecht expected Falkenhayn to deny it he was mistaken.

'And why should they not?' Falkenhayn declared. The room went silent. 'Why should they not when it is Reikland blood being spilt on every border of the Empire? When it is Reikland lives that are lost defending each and every province?' Falkenhayn looked over the other novices.

'We are a nation under siege,' he continued, 'attacked not only by force of arms, but also by the worship of dark gods and the snares of foreign culture. There are wolves to the north, warmongering princes to the south, barbarians to the east...'

'I hope,' Krieglitz interrupted, standing, 'that you refer to those beyond the borders of the Empire.'

'Of course, brother,' Falkenhayn responded stiffly, 'those beyond the borders of the true Empire. And those within our borders who have thrown over our ways in favour of these others. With such danger riddled through-out our realm, can you blame a Reikland general looking first to those of his own province, men that he knows hold the interests of the Empire higher than any other...?'

The quiet library burst into uproar as the Provincial novices shot to their feet in outrage, followed just as quickly by the Reiklanders.

Master Lehrer thumped a bronze skull ornament against his desk until he could make himself heard. He shouted at them all to be seated once more, and, finally, continued to speak.

'Excellent!' he chortled, as the room simmered. 'I sense we may have potential for some lively debates here. Let us then begin, not with Wilhelm, nor with Magnus, but rather with that great victory which defined the Empire at its birth, the First Battle of Black Fire Pass, and in particular Sigmar's unification of the twelve peoples of the Empire. I trust my point will be lost on none of you.'

'I am Brother Verrakker,' Verrakker said. 'You have heard many times now that before you may become a brother of this grand order you must prove yourself in three disciplines: strength of body, strength of mind and strength of spirit. Of these three, strength of spirit is the most important, for without a strong spirit one can stray from the true path. And one's strength and one's mind can be turned to betray all you once defended. Strength of spirit is not to be learned, and I shall not be your teacher. Only your judge.'

'This is the Empire.' Talhoffer declared.

One of his sergeants stood, ready, in the middle of four of the Reiklander novices. They each carried a waster in their hand wrapped in cloth. The cloth was damp from red dye so that a blow would mark the fighter struck.

'The Empire is surrounded by its foes. All of whom, whether they admit it or not, desire to see us brought to our knees.'

The novices eyed the sergeant warily and closed in on him. So far he had done nothing but casually shift his position to keep track of his opponents. He held his sword loosely by his side. From across the circle, Delmar saw Falkenhayn gesture at him to attack. Delmar stepped forwards, swiftly lifted his blade high and cut down.

'Encircled as we are, we cannot allow our enemies the chance to strike together.'

As Delmar swung, the sergeant moved, slipping inside the arc of the blade and using the flat of his sword to guide the cut away to the side.

'And therefore we must allow ourselves to stay fixed to our guard, to hold on the defence.'

The sergeant shot forwards, maintaining the contact with Delmar's blade even as the novice instinctively drew back, keeping it off the line between them.

'Every defence must contain an attack. And every attack must contain a defence.'

The sergeant slammed his weapon down Delmar's sword arm onto his shoulder, then without pause drew it down his chest to his belly. Delmar looked down and saw the lurid red slash it had left across his body. The sergeant did not pause, but gripped Delmar with his free hand and pivoted around behind him, pushing the novice forwards. Falkenhayn's charging swing, intended to strike the sergeant down from behind, instead smacked into Delmar. Still twisting, using Delmar's body as a shield, the sergeant spun about and struck a heavy blow into Falkenhayn's side.

'Reinhardt, Falkenhayn, stand out.' Talhoffer ordered. The frustrated novices reluctantly stood aside and the sergeant squared off against the remaining pair. No one doubted the outcome.

'Attack and defence are the same. That is our overriding tenet. We fight as the Empire fights. Man and nation, there is no distinction. If an enemy should strike at us, we must first try to evade the blow. If we cannot, then we must control it so that it does not hit us with its full force. And that deflection of force must itself form a riposte to strike back. Only with such a principle can our Empire stand against the myriad foes that surround us.'

'That was preposterous,' Falkenhayn complained afterwards as he and his fellows suffered in the washing room, scrubbing the red dye from their shifts. 'In any battle, we would be wearing armour. That cut would never have got through our armour and so I should not have been stood down. It was no fair test of our martial skills.'

'It is a fairer test of your laundry skills then,' Gausser spoke up from the other pool. Falkenhayn ignored the jibe, for he never dared face the Nordlander directly.

'We will get better, brother,' Delmar said calmly.

Falkenhayn recommended, 'If we are to wear armour to fight, then we should practise in armour. That is obvious.'

'Thank you, brother. We got your wish,' Hardenburg remarked bitterly, struggling to lever himself to his feet. The novices stood in the arming room, all encased in heavy grey plate.

'It's as heavy as a Stirlander matron! Pardon my word, Weisshuber,' Hardenburg laughed.

'This isn't proper armour.' Falkenhayn was still complaining. 'These are just segments of strapped iron plate; they do not even fit together properly.'

'It is so they can be adjusted,' Delmar answered, even though Falkenhayn had not asked a question.

'It would need to be,' Siebrecht said to Krieglitz at the other end of the room, 'to fit over Falkenhayn's head.'

'He has enough spare room down there though.' Krieglitz knocked his armoured fist against his armoured crotch. The clang of metal against metal drew the Reiklanders' attention.

Hardenburg thought to join in the Provincials' banter.

'This is the one piece I'm glad for,' he said. He and the Provincials laughed together, until Falkenhayn put his hand on Hardenburg's shoulder. 'Leave them be, Tomas,' he ordered. Hardenburg looked back, but the moment's unity was gone and the old division between the novices was back.

As well as the long sword, Talhoffer demonstrated the other weapons of the Empire's armies: spears and halberds, which allowed a knight to keep a greater distance from particularly dangerous foes and, when fighting on foot, to ward away enemy horsemen; greatswords, heavy two-handed blades feared by many of the Empire's foes; maces and warhammers, which could break limbs and skulls in a single blow; even the dagger, though with such an array of weaponry at their disposal the novices could barely imagine when they should need such a short blade.

Though he had been introduced alongside Master Talhoffer, Ott had not involved himself in any of Talhoffer's sword teaching. The fightmaster was something of a mystery to the novices. He barely made any sound and certainly never went to speak. And Siebrecht had seen that he wore around his neck the symbol of peaceful Shallya, the healer, similar to that beside the white gate. It was a strange god for a warrior to venerate. In training he merely stood behind Talhoffer, eyes closed, listening. Delmar had occasionally seen him make subtle gestures to the other fightmaster, the same gestures that Delmar had once seen a village girl without hearing make in order to communicate with her parents, but Talhoffer had never made them back. He replied instead with speech.

Once the novices had been equipped with their armour, however, Ott's sessions on close-quarter fighting began in earnest. While Talhoffer never fought with the novices directly, leaving his well-trained sergeants to provide the demonstration of what he dictated, the same was not true of Fightmaster Ott. Instead, Ott practiced the reverse, he spoke only through his sergeants and fought himself, demonstrating his staggering repertoire of grapples, locks, limb-breaks, throws and strangles upon the novices personally. They fought in practice bouts, often with small blunted stakes to represent daggers. Against a fully armoured knight who was standing and mobile, a dagger presented little threat; however if that same knight could be brought to the ground or held in position then that small blade became deadly, as it could be forced between openings and joins in the armour. The novices had all wrestled as youngsters, in horseplay with their fellow youths, and now they began to see the deadly art from which their childish games had derived.

Delmar had been one of the first to face Master Ott in a practice bout. While Delmar did not expect to win, he thought that he would provide a fair showing, just as Siebrecht on the first day of duelling. Though Ott had experience, he was not very tall. Delmar had the advantage in both height and reach, and his skill at riding had given him a sure sense of balance. When Delmar had squared off against Ott, the master had barely even opened his eyes; the eyelids were raised only a crack and the eyes themselves hidden in the shadow. Delmar got his first hold on Ott easily, and just as easily Ott slipped out of it, taking Delmar's arm with him. The master twisted as he went and, for all Delmar's steady feet, he found himself forced to the ground; it was either that or have his arm ripped off at the shoulder. The master's dagger pricked him at the back of his neck and the bout was over.

Once Ott had 'assessed' the skill of each of the novices, and left them choking on the earth, his tuition began. He took the novices through the move and then paired them off to practise, ending each session with a proper practice bout.

Against the other novices, Delmar fared far better, winning most of his bouts. The novice who excelled was, of course, Gausser. Not only was he far larger and stronger than the others, but Nordland was infamous for settling disputes through trials of combat.

Despite his domination, his training did not go without incident. It was near the end of one of the sessions. Most of the novices, exhausted, preferred to rest in wrestling clinches rather than continue to try to trip or throw their opponents. In the midst of that amiable lethargy, however, a violent argument erupted.

'Can you not hear, Nordlander? Can anything penetrate that head of yours if it is not drummed upon it?'

'You did not say it, Falkenhayn. I would have heard it if you had said it.'

Ott had tapped Falkenhayn to wrestle Gausser. But before the bout was done, Falkenhayn had cried out loudly and accused Gausser of ignoring his attempts to concede the bout.

'I said it again and again and you ignored it! I swear he's broken my arm.' Falkenhayn gingerly presented the injured limb to the sergeant beside him.

Delmar and the other novices crowded around. Proktor gently took hold of Falkenhayn's arm, but Falkenhayn suddenly jerked it away with another cry of pain.

Gausser now turned to the sergeant as well; he was getting uncomfortable having to defend himself.

'If he had not been squirming so much, I would not have needed to hold on so tight.'

'You admit it then!' Falkenhayn exclaimed. 'You were holding tighter than you should to hurt me.'

'I did not mean to hurt you,' Gausser answered, but without conviction. His dislike of the Reikland novices and Falkenhayn in particular was well known.

'But you did not stop when I said relent.'

'That, I did not hear you say,' Gausser stated, his accent thickening as he grew more flustered. He was not accustomed to such duels of words.

'How convenient that you can ignore the rules when it pleases you.'

That charge, effectively calling the Nordlander a cheat, pushed Gausser over the edge.

'No, no, no,' Gausser bellowed, taking a menacing step forwards. Siebrecht and Krieglitz rushed to either side to prevent him going further, just as Delmar and Proktor pulled Falkenhayn behind them to protect him. 'No to your clever lying words. I fight fair. You did not say relent. You carry on fighting and now you complain. It is you Reiklanders who ignore rules when it pleases! You take back what you say or we fight again! Here! To prove who is right.' Gausser stomped back a few paces to free himself of his friends' grip and started to tear off the practice plate.

'You are just proving all I said. Did you not hear through your skull?' Falkenhayn called back, safe behind the other Reikland novices. 'You broke my arm! A fair fight that would be.'

'Then choose your champion,' Gausser snarled, throwing his breastplate off his shoulders. 'If you can find an honourable man who will stand in place of a worthless lying slug like you.'

'That barbarian,' Falkenhayn muttered to his fellow Reiklanders. 'He has insulted my honour. I have no choice but to fight him now.'

'No, Franz, no,' Proktor urged, 'your arm. You'll not stand a chance. Let me fight for you.'

'You are a good brother and a good cousin, Laurentz, but even with an arm broken I stand a better chance against him than you do.'

'I will do it,' Delmar said.

Falkenhayn's face lit up. 'My thanks, and my honour, are with you, Delmar.'

'Here is my champion!' Falkenhayn shouted to Gausser.

'No duels!' Weisshuber cried from the middle. 'Don't you remember, no duels.'

'This is no duel,' Siebrecht jibed back. 'This is training!'

'Novices! Stand apart!' The sergeant yelled. Obediently, they did so, edging back, but eyes still fixed on the other side.

Master Ott stepped in between them. He turned his head from one side to the other, as though inspecting the two groups of novices with his closed eyes. The sergeant stood by his side to interpret his gestures.

'Master Ott says,' the sergeant stated, 'that it is not the privilege of novices to change his rota. But if two novices wish to train, then let them train. But let them train well, in accordance with what they have been taught. Alone, without aid from any other, with plate and daggers, and with these sergeants in place to ensure the rules are followed.'

Delmar did not know how it had come to this. This did not feel like the right thing to do, and yet he was defending his comrade's honour; how could there be wrong in that? Falkenhayn had looked at him so imploringly, what could he do besides offer his aid? And yet he knew that he could not win. He had done well in practice, but Gausser was half a foot taller than he and built like a great cannon. He had trounced all the other novices, and Delmar had been no exception. Gausser would expect the first few moments to be tentative, each testing the other. If Delmar struck fast he might catch him off-guard. If he managed to knock Gausser to the ground in the first few seconds, that might be his only chance.

The sergeant gave them the signal to begin and Delmar charged, and so did Gausser. As soon as he saw the Nordlander run at him as well, Delmar tried to check his stride, side step and trip him. Gausser merely kicked the tripping leg out of the way and crashed into Delmar. Delmar managed to pivot rather than fall and spun to the other side of the circle, grasping the moment to recover. The two went at each other again, this time more warily. Delmar ran through the techniques that Ott had taught them. He dived in to try to lock Gausser's arm, but the novice held it in close and then smacked Delmar across the chest, knocking him back over the Nordlander's hip. Delmar felt his balance go and rolled himself away. Gausser came in for him, grabbing around his torso. Delmar kept low, seized Gausser's knee and then drove into his gut with all his strength. Surprised, Gausser took a half-step back to regain his footing and Delmar pushed all the harder. It was not enough, Gausser's leg was like a tree trunk and refused to shift. Delmar was suddenly crushed to the ground as Gausser intentionally collapsed forwards onto Delmar's back. They both went down on their fronts, but Gausser was on top, and after a brief scramble Delmar felt the wooden dagger push through a gap in his armour. The sergeant called the point and Gausser allowed Delmar back to his feet.

They began again. From the initial clinch, Delmar desperately tried to wrap his arm around Gausser's neck, but the Nordlander simply allowed him to get his hold and then heaved Delmar off the ground and knocked his legs out from under him. Again Delmar went down to the groans of the Reiklander novices. Another point against him.

Delmar could see that Gausser was growing confident, and he had good reason. Though Gausser did not have the technique of Master Ott, his experience, his weight and reach, were more than enough. Delmar would have to surprise him. Gausser came at him again and Delmar grabbed his arm and spun into him, ready to roll the Nordlander over his shoulder. Gausser was ready for it, had planted his feet and was about to use his strength to pull his arm back and wrap it around Delmar's throat. Delmar, however, kept spinning, under Gausser's arm and out the other side. With a twist of his hands, Delmar locked Gausser's arm and the strength went from it. Delmar went to his belt and drew his dagger, ready to hold it to the back of Gausser's neck and win the point, when the Nordlander twisted himself around, stepping into Delmar's body and punching him hard in the stomach. The metal plate protected Delmar from the worst of the blow, but the lock was broken, and Gausser lifted him high and then dropped him on the ground once more.

'Stay down this time, Reiklander,' Gausser said as he was awarded the point again. With three points against him, the result seemed conclusive. 'I win!' Gausser announced. 'The gods have found for me, Falkenhayn, they agree you are a slug too.'

Gausser turned back to be congratulated by his fellows, but they stared past him.

'My champion still stands,' Falkenhayn crowed back. Gausser turned about and there, indeed, Delmar had got back to his feet and was readying to fight.

Gausser shook his head in bewilderment. 'What are you doing, Reiklander? Have you not had enough?'

Delmar did not trust himself to be able to speak, to open his mouth and be able to form words. His legs felt like water. His head was ringing and stuffed full of fog. His balance was shaky. But he stood ready to fight and the Reiklanders gave a great cheer.

Gausser knocked him down again, with ease. Gausser held him down and whispered to him, 'I have no anger against you, Reinhardt. Relent. Your honour is not at stake here.'

'But,' Delmar gasped back, 'the honour of my brother is. And I will not relent,' was all he could say.

The sergeant called the point and Gausser backed away from him warily. He sensed that the tone of the fight had changed. The Provincials were no longer cheering his success. Instead, it was the Reiklanders who cheered, each and every time Delmar rose back to his feet. The more points he scored and the more Delmar clambered back up, the more Gausser grew frustrated. The more Gausser grew frustrated, the more the Reiklanders cheered.

'Why do you still call points? They mean nothing any longer,' Gausser berated the sergeant and threw his dagger away.

'Novice Gausser!' the sergeant warned over the hooting crowd.

'No! No! If this is how he wishes it then this is how it will be.'

Delmar could no longer speak, he could barely think. All his energy went to staying on his feet. His vision had narrowed and he could only see straight ahead. He saw Gausser come at him again and half-heartedly threw an arm out to grapple. The Nordlander easily blocked it, took his legs out from under him and brought him down to the ground again. Delmar felt himself being flipped over onto his back and then Gausser's elbow pressing down onto his throat in a strangle.

'Relent, Reinhardt. Relent!' Gausser demanded, both fearsome and fearful at the same time. Delmar struggled to breathe.

'That is enough, Novice Gausser,' the sergeant interrupted. Gausser, conscious that all eyes were upon him, broke his hold at once.

'You see,' he muttered as he got back to his feet, 'these Reiklanders, they are stubborn until the end.'

The sergeant watched Master Ott's gestures. 'Yes,' he said on the fightmaster's behalf. 'You fought well, Novice Gausser. It is a lesson to you all, that when an enemy will not relent then your only safety lies in its destruction. But we are only training today, so I will not require you to demonstrate to the fullest extent.'

Gausser nodded and then retreated back to the Provincial novices, as the Reiklanders tended to Delmar. Neither side said anything to the other, but there were many looks exchanged, and none of them of brotherhood.

From that day on Falkenhayn refused point-blank to spar with Gausser any more, and Gausser replied by refusing to spar with either Falkenhayn, Proktor or Delmar. The Reiklanders swore as a group that none of them would train with Gausser any further, and the Provincials returned the favour by refusing to train with the Reiklanders.

Ott ordered Delmar to spend a day in the order sanatorium to recover from Gausser's rough handling. Delmar spent the morning deep in thought, reflecting on the division between the novices. Falkenhayn had treated him well; he and the other Reiklanders had accepted him like a brother. It was as much as he had hoped. Nevertheless, in keeping his Falcons together, Falkenhayn had driven a wedge between the novices. A wedge, Delmar realised, that he himself had initiated. Siebrecht continued to show nothing but contempt for the Reiksguard and his instruction, but he should not have let that one novice's attitude poison his to the rest of the Provincials.

As he turned these grim thoughts over in his mind, he was happily surprised to be visited by Griesmeyer. The knight had returned from the main army with correspondence from the Reiksmarshal. He still had the dust of the road on him.

'My apologies that I was not able to see you all the way here that first day,' Griesmeyer said, taking a seat on the bed beside Delmar's.

'All was well, my lord, I was able to find my way.' Delmar winced a little at speaking, as his throat was still sore. 'How goes the war? The foe has invaded?'

'Yes, Kislev has fallen. Their armies are in the Empire, into Ostland. There are attacks from the east as well, into Ostermark. And everywhere throughout the forests there are reports of beastkin or marauder warbands on the march.'

'To where?'

'Hochland, without doubt. From there, perhaps Talabheim, perhaps Middenheim, though they would be fools to besiege either of those. Perhaps they even intend to strike here.'

'Will you be able to stop them?'

'The Emperor is pulling in our allies. We are gathering a mighty host. We will stop them.' Griesmeyer seemed confident. 'But let us not talk of it for a few moments. Instead, tell me how you have found your time with the order.'

'It has been... an honour.'

Griesmeyer looked at Delmar with a sceptical eye. 'A restrained answer for one I'd have thought would be so full of excitement.'

'I am sorry, my lord.'

'I am not interested in your apologies, I will have an answer from you,' Griesmeyer insisted.

Delmar hesitated, but could think of no other avenue than the truth. 'It is all... not quite as I expected.'

'What all is this? Come, novice, clarity of thought is what we strive for here. What did you expect?'

'Just... more! When I think of how I pictured the Reiksguard barracks before I came here...'

'Yes? How did you picture it?'

'Fuller. Full of people: knights training, hurrying back and forth to the Imperial Palace to be at the Emperor's side. Stories of old campaigns, talk of new ones, the Reiksmarshal in the chapter house convening meetings of the order where matters of the Empire's defence would be discussed and decided. To be full of life, instead of quiet like the grave. There's just us, the sergeants who keep to themselves, and the tutors...'

Delmar was embarrassed by his outburst.

'And none of those are the image you had of a Reiksguard knight, correct?'

'I apologise, my lord. I do not mean to disrespect them. I know, I have been told, that they were all formidable warriors before...'

'Before they were crippled, yes. Oh, I did not think you meant them any disrespect. I know you well enough for that.' Griesmeyer got to his feet and strode over to the sanatorium's window looking out onto the practice field. 'I understand you better than you realise. When I have visited here when the banners are away the place resembles a Shallyan infirmary more than a knightly order. But we must find a role for them all.'

Griesmeyer turned back to him. 'You must understand, Delmar, that these men have dedicated their lives to the order, many of them have nowhere else to go. Their lands have been lost, or are managed by others, relatives who they barely know perhaps, and who would have little use for a warrior who cannot fight. As they have given for the order, so must the order provide for them. Your tutors are the lucky ones in that respect; they can remain active in the martial way, others can only contribute by different means.'

'I understand, of course, my lord,' Delmar replied, his shame deepening. Griesmeyer saw the novice's contrition and changed the topic.

'What do you think of them? Your tutors?'

'Master Lehrer is a good teacher. I like him, though I sometimes find it difficult to understand how some of the matters he speaks of relate to a knight's duty. Master Talhoffer can be... hard on us at times, but there is great value in what he teaches. Master Ott...'

'Yes?'

'I do not know. It is hard to know what to make of him.'

'Hmmm... If you know Master Lehrer well, I should talk to him about Ott. You may find you understand him better. And what of Master Verrakker?'

'Master? He said he was merely a brother.'

'Did he?' Griesmeyer pondered. 'Well, who should know better than he. How have you found him?'

'I believe he has a thankless task.'

'That is true indeed. I spoke to Brother Verrakker earlier this morning. Is the peace and quiet all that is concerning you? He mentioned that there were some disputes between the novices. Are you involved in those?'

Delmar did not speak at once. Griesmeyer had been very kind to him, but if Delmar confided in him would he then take formal action? That would only deepen the divide between the two groups.

'If I am,' Delmar replied, 'then those disputes would be mine alone to resolve.'

'Ah!' Griesmeyer replied, laughing. 'The old Reinhardt pride, I remember it well from your father. Do not think, though, that the masters are blind. It was the same in my day. Even more so, for I was a novice before Karl Franz was elected. The old Emperor was failing, showing his age, and all my fellow novices could talk of was the succession.'

'I was with novices from every single province,' Griesmeyer continued, 'each of whom thought that their ruler was the only conceivable candidate. Sigmar alone knows what would have happened to the Reiksguard if another Emperor had decided to move his capital to a different city, to Middenheim or Talabheim. Can you imagine the White Wolves, the Panthers and ourselves all barracked together? You would not be able to move in the streets for knights on their warhorses.'

Delmar smiled at the image.

'As it resulted, the throne stayed in Reikland and went to Karl Franz, and he has made a good job of it, though he has faced hard enough times. The arguments though, that even we novices had at the time...'

Griesmeyer cut off the thought with a curt gesture.

'I remember when, in learning our history, I first heard of the civil wars in the Time of the Three Emperors. I remember that I could not believe that there were so many people then who honestly considered it best to tear our nation to pieces. However, as the years have passed, and I have travelled, and met hundreds of my fellow subjects... I become more and more surprised to meet those who wish to hold it together.'

Griesmeyer shook away the memory. 'I will leave your disputes to yourself, Delmar, but I will say this. Do not forget that you do not have to follow the same path as others do. It is you who are responsible for your conduct, no one else.

'And know this, Delmar, it is politicians who conquer through division. And you know what little the Reiksguard thinks of politics. No, it is leaders who unite and rule.'

Delmar thought on it. 'Is the same true of the Emperor?'

Griesmeyer gave his half-smile of amusement. 'It is not the Reiksguard's place to judge their Emperor. The elector counts are more than willing to take up that duty.'

'You have seen him?'

'The Emperor? Often. I could not call myself one of his guard if I had not.'

'What is he like?'

Griesmeyer was about to reply, but then paused. 'You will find out soon enough once he returns.'

'If he returns,' Delmar whispered. 'Not all return from the north.'

Griesmeyer's tone softened. 'I will not deceive you, Delmar. There have been times in our history when our realm has been in greater peril, but never in my lifetime. But I am only one man, and our nation has ever had its spirit tested by those who hate us. They spill our blood and we spill theirs. For centuries, for tens of centuries now. Do I like it? No. Would I give my life to banish them for ever? Without a moment's doubt. But do I fear their coming? Never. Never again.'

'I am due back to the north,' Griesmeyer said, rising from his seat upon the bed, 'and it is true, I may not return. But the Empire cannot be killed as can a single man. It will live still.'

'We should go with you,' Delmar suddenly declared. 'When you leave, we novices should ride with you. We can do no good here. Let us come and fight for the Emperor.'

Griesmeyer looked archly. 'You think your dozen swords would make the difference?'

'Perhaps,' Delmar ventured.

'Well, I do not. And neither does the Marshal. You will stay here until you are ready, though you may believe me that your tutors are pushing you as fast as you are able.'

Griesmeyer looked down upon his friend's only son. 'Do not concern yourself, Delmar, that all may be done before you may serve. There is a war being fought far greater than this single campaign, and it holds the entire Empire within its grip. Take my word, we shall not be free of it for many years.'

Delmar, once recovered, returned to the novices. The two groups were keeping their distance on the practice field: the Reiklanders were training at the pell whilst the Provincials rehearsed the close-order drills under a sergeant's supervision. Falkenhayn was attacking the wooden pell with a fury, and Harver and Breigh had looks of thunder upon their faces; Hardenburg just lay on the grass, covering his face.

'What has happened?' Delmar asked.

'There is word from the north,' Proktor supplied.

'What is it? Has Ostland fallen?'

'Ostland!' Falkenhayn shouted from the pell, in a voice loud enough for the Provincials to hear it. 'Ostland proved to be little more than a bump in the foe's path. It's Middenheim.'

'Middenheim?' Delmar was shocked. 'Middenheim has fallen?' It was impossible; the fortress-city of the White Wolf could never have been taken so quickly.

Proktor shook his head. 'It is besieged, and by such a great horde that... the army's hope for victory is slim.'

Delmar immediately thought of Griesmeyer, already riding hard back to the north. He looked over at the Provincials but could not see the novice from Middenland.

'Where is Straber?'

Proktor looked to Falkenhayn, but the other novice turned back to the pell.

'What is it?' Delmar asked.

'A messenger came for him,' Proktor said quietly. 'His estates have been burned. His father's body was found. The women were missing. It is thought they are dead as well. At least... it is hoped. Death would be a mercy to being captured by those monsters. He has ridden for home.'

'As they all will.' Falkenhayn, sweating, came across from the pell. 'It is as I always said, Reinhardt. They cannot be relied upon. It will be us Reiklanders who will carry the Empire.'

'Brother,' Delmar replied, 'Straber's home is in peril. His father is dead. That means he is the lord of those lands. Of course he must go back and defend them.'

'And when Middenheim falls and Nordland is threatened, will Gausser then go? Then Bohdan back to Ostermark, Krieglitz to Talabheim?' Falkenhayn flicked his sword as if knocking those novices away. 'Perhaps, Delmar, each man should only defend that patch of ground on which he stands? Is that how we should defend our Empire?'

'Calm yourself, brother,' Delmar said.

'No, brother, I shall not calm myself,' Falkenhayn shouted. 'You answer me, is that how we should defend our Empire?'

Delmar looked to the others, but there was no sign of support from Harver or Breigh; Hardenburg still lay there, his face covered; Proktor was the picture of misery.

'No,' Delmar conceded, 'it is not.'

'Thank you, brother,' Falkenhayn spat, and took his sword back to the pell.

* * *

It was to be a full day before Falkenhayn had calmed down sufficiently to make his peace with Delmar. It was frustrating; they all felt it. To be closed up in the chapter house whilst the Reiksguard was fighting the Empire's enemies was intolerable, but there was nothing that could be done except leave the order as Straber had, and none of the Reiklanders wished to do that. As the news of the siege of Middenheim raced around the city, it drove the masses of starving refugees to even greater desperation. If Middenheim could fall, where would be safe within the Empire? The Altdorf officials began to stockpile food in case a similar fate befell the capital. Traders, priests and storekeepers followed their example. What food had been available to the refugees in the streets was cut off. The officials proclaimed that everyone in the city had to tighten their belts. But for some their belts could be tightened no further, and their desperation drove them to greater acts of violence.

As the tension built in the streets, so too did it grow amongst the novices. To gain peace, Delmar decided to follow Griesmeyer's advice and inquire about Master Ott of Master Lehrer. Lehrer directed him to a section in the Reiksguard's annals. The passage was still relatively fresh, having been written only a few years previously.

There had been a battle, but Delmar could not tell where as, unlike the others, there was no location specified. It must have been at night, however, for there were repeated references to the dark in which the enemy had concealed themselves and in which the battle was subsequently fought. There was no specific mention of the name of the foe in this instance, merely the ambushes and traps they sprung upon the Reiksguard as they advanced. There was mention of Brother Ott, however.

During one of their attacks, a foul missile had exploded over him. He had been covered with an evil smoke which had burnt his skin and filled his lungs with its poison. It was one Brother Talhoffer who had covered himself with his cloak and dared plunge into the cloud of gas. He had emerged, dragging the unconscious Ott with one hand and still carrying his sword with the other. Talhoffer had just called for aid when one of the frenzied creatures charged at him. Both of them had struck at the same time, the knight running the creature through with his sword, the creature chopping through the knight's other arm, by which he held his brother, with a jagged glaive. At the loss of his arm, Talhoffer had apparently kicked the creature's corpse away, dropped his sword, seized Ott with his remaining hand and continued to pull him to safety until other brothers arrived.

'It is a noble tale,' Master Lehrer commented from behind his desk after Delmar had finished reading. 'Our healers went to work on them both as soon as the army emerged from the pit. Talhoffer was recovered within a few days, though of course his arm was left behind. Brother Ott, however, languished for weeks. It was not until he had been brought back here, swaddled in bandages like a newborn babe, and was treated by the High

Priestess of Shallya herself that he finally awoke. That daemon-smoke had taken his voice, and burned his eyes so that to see daylight gave him great pain; while it took time for his body to mend, so far as it could, it took longer to heal his spirit, for him to find some useful purpose again.'

'He has found that, master,' Delmar replied earnestly.

'Treat such knowledge with discretion, though, I ask you, novice. The moment of such an injury marks the end of a knight's ability to serve in battle. For proud men such as Talhoffer and Ott, it is a type of death. I believe that you should know it, though, to help you to understand. They are men of experience, and it is beholden on you novices to learn all you can from them. They are all honourable knights, each with his own story.'

'Do you have a story yourself, master?' Delmar asked. 'Is it among these shelves?'

'Aye, a short one,' Lehrer replied with mock weariness, 'but that one you will have to find yourself. I will not aid you there.'

The unrest within the chapter house was not limited to the novices. Talhoffer grew more and more critical of the novices' progress as the days of the siege progressed. He dismissed Weisshuber from their ranks with an almost casual disregard. The novices discovered his possessions gone from their quarters; it was that abrupt. It came as a regret, but no surprise; the genial Stirlander simply did not have the proficiency for the violence inherent in the knightly occupation.

Yet still Talhoffer reserved his most scathing words for his favourite target, Siebrecht von Matz.

'If you stand there with your sword stuck out, Novice Matz, waiting for it to be beaten aside, then your opponent will oblige you.'

'Guards should be moments of transition, Novice Matz, not poses for your heroic memorial. Keep moving.'

'If you insist on cutting from your wrist instead of your elbow, Novice Matz, then your arm will fall off. I guarantee it.'

'Ah, so that's what happened to you,' Siebrecht, sore and harangued, muttered bitterly. He had had enough of this.

'He's fast,' Verrakker commented, 'and skilled. You have to give Novice Matz that.'

'So he has some skill, brother,' Talhoffer said through clenched teeth, trying not to move. 'What of it?'

The two knights stood with Brother Ott upon the top of the tower of the chapter house. It was as good a place for privacy as any. All Altdorf was lain out below them; the Imperial Palace, the Great Temple, and buildings, so many buildings crammed with people.

Talhoffer had commissioned a portrait of himself and had judged this the perfect backdrop. He might have reconsidered if he had known what a hash the artist was to make in bringing his canvas and easel up the small spiral staircase.

'Please hold your pose, my lord.' The artist, already irate and behind time, tried to keep the chiding tone from his voice.

'I had hoped that you were driving Matz all the harder because you recognised his potential and wished to prevent him being complacent. Yet you dismiss that skill so easily, brother,' Verrakker said. 'Is he not one of the ablest fighters of all the novices you have tested?'

Talhoffer took his time in consideration. 'On foot, perhaps. On a horse he has little to distinguish himself from the rest.'

'Then why have you made him your whipping boy?'

Talhoffer turned to his fellow knight. The artist let out a small grunt of irritation, and Talhoffer rounded back on him.

'Oh, paint your backdrop, man, and give us a few moments' peace.'

The artist duly bent back down to his work, and Talhoffer and Verrakker crossed to the other side of the roof.

'Is there a reason you take a particular interest in this novice's well-being, brother?'

'That is the very question I am trying to ask you.'

Talhoffer ignored Verrakker's words and continued on his original line. 'You and he are both from Nuln, are you not? Some old loyalty there perhaps?'

'You tell me, brother. Is his home the reason you dislike him so?'

'Ah!' Talhoffer scoffed. 'Petty provincial prejudices are beneath one who has schooled counts and kings, brother.'

'So I would have thought.'

Irritated at Verrakker's insinuation, Talhoffer dropped his usual superior air.

'I have no cause against his skill or the city of his birth, brother. It is his attitude to which I take offence.'

'And what of that?'

'That he does not wish to be here. Even Ott can see that. The other novices, as unskilled, raw or insufferable as they may be, they all have the spirit that comes from understanding what a privilege they have been given. For Matz, the sooner he plucks up the courage to leave, the better. For all of us.'

'It is not your place to judge his spirit, brother. It is mine, of which you are well aware.'

'Oh, yes, you and Brother Purity.'

'Where did you hear that name?' Verrakker snapped, his tone so sharp that it cut Talhoffer to the quick.

Talhoffer, in surprise, stumbled over his words, then began again.

'You are not the only one to know some of the order's secrets, brother,' he said.

'That is a matter for the inner circle. And until and unless you are elevated to those ranks you shall not speak that name again. On your oath, Talhoffer.'

Talhoffer backed down and Verrakker was glad of it. He did not like having to push his authority with the fightmaster. Ever since he had been admitted to the order's inner circle and Talhoffer had not, it had been a sticking point between them. Evidently, the matter still rankled with the fightmaster.

'You and your secrets,' Talhoffer started again. 'Even your little pretence to the novices that you are some doddering invalid.'

Verrakker saw that the fightmaster was trying to salvage a little of his own dignity and adopted a more conciliatory tone.

'You learn much of a man by how he treats his lessers.'

Talhoffer gave a short bark of a laugh. 'Just like the sword, Verrakker, those who live by secrets will die by them.'

'I have enough people telling me my destiny, brother,' Verrakker said, indicating an end to their conversation. 'We should concentrate on the novices and the task in hand.'

'Very well, then,' Talhoffer declared, once more gathering up his haughtiness around him. 'I will judge Novice Matz solely on his skill, and leave the question of his spirit to you and... your judgement. Let it be on your heads,' the fightmaster chuckled at his own joke, 'as to whether this weak-willed stripling should ever be allowed to call himself a Reiksguard knight.'

'Thank you, brother,' Verrakker replied, but Talhoffer was not finished.

'So, as I have answered your question, brother, will you do me the privilege of answering mine? Why do you take a particular interest in this novice?'

'I take a particular interest in all my charges, and I do believe that we shall need the sword of every single one of them in the weeks ahead.'

'You have heard something more from the siege?'

Verrakker nodded. 'Our army is converging upon the siege lines. There is a battle, a great battle that is about to occur. Our scouts have a count of the size of the enemy. And I do not believe we will win.'

The two knights both turned and stared out over the battlements, over the city, over the maddened crowds, over the river and the forests. Though it was far too distant for them to see, they both looked to that great bastion of the north: Middenheim, where the fate of the Empire was being decided.

— FOUR —

HERR VON MATZ

The ten remaining novices marched, fully armed and armoured, in close order. At a command from Talhoffer, they halted, drew their swords and instantly began the drills that he had taught them, stabs from high, from low, and downwards swings.

Talhoffer looked the novices over with a critical eye. Only Krieglitz was performing up to the fightmaster's standards; Gausser had power behind his blows but they were too slow; Bohdan and Alptraum were slow to learn them, Bohdan especially, as he was older than the rest and more set in his habits. Siebrecht, though, was quick, of sword and wit, but he was lazy and only did the least he could to escape the fightmaster's censure.

The Reiklanders' progress, meanwhile, was far more acceptable. Talhoffer could tell that they had fought together before. They attacked in unison, covered each other and responded to Falkenhayn's orders in an instant. Harver and Breigh in particular, Talhoffer noted, fought beside each other as though they had done so their entire lives. None of the Reiklanders had the strength or innate skill of a couple of the Provincials; Proktor was too slight and Delmar's swordsmanship far too untutored, but they fought far better as a squadron and that was how they would have to fight in the Reiksguard.

If he had had enough time Talhoffer knew he could have brought the Provincials up to that standard. This could have been one of the finest novice squadrons he had taught, but Verrakker was adamant that there was not the time. Push them on, push them on, he had told Lehrer and the fightmasters, they will rise to it. They will be ready.

Well, Talhoffer would show Verrakker how ready they were not. He had given the sergeants a small mission of their own, and they were now strapping something to the pell. One of them raised his hand to show that they were finished, and Talhoffer called the novices over.

'Though we are part of the greatest realm of man, mankind exists in other nations all around us,' Talhoffer announced, 'Bretonnia and Estalia to the west, Tilea and the border lands to the south, Kislev and the tribes

338

of the Norse to the north,' Talhoffer's eyes glossed quickly past Gausser, for the Nordlanders' heritage was more intertwined with the Norse than they would ever admit, 'and the horse brigands of the east. It is our nature to march under different banners and test our strength against each other. Just as we have our knightly orders, so too do they have their champions. Here!'

The pell was dressed in a full suit of armour, so that it could almost be a man stood there. It was not Reiksguard armour though. It was crudely forged and painted black.

'The men of the north: some wear little more than furs and skins and can be fought like normal men, but others are encased within plate as thick as a Bretonnian's, even as thick as a dwarf's.' Talhoffer walked slowly around the armoured pell.

'Hammers and maces at the head. You don't need to cut the skin if you can bash their brains loose instead,' he said as he indicated the helmet. 'If you only have a sword, however, and most likely you will... Novice Reinhardt, Novice Gausser, step forwards.'

The two novices did so, and a sergeant gave them each a sharpened metal long sword. Talhoffer stepped away.

'Novice Reinhardt,' the fightmaster ordered, 'one of your strongest cuts, if you please.'

Delmar took up a roof guard with the weapon and then, after a breath, stepped forwards and drove the sword down with all his weight against the armour's shoulder pauldron. The blade struck the plate with a crashing ring and the impact nearly jarred the weapon from Delmar's hands. With the novices crowding around, Delmar stepped up to look at the damage and was disappointed to see that there was only a slight dent.

'Back. All of you,' Talhoffer chided. 'Novice Gausser, can you do better?'

Gausser stepped up and targeted the pauldron on the other side. Delmar could see the Nordlander's massive shoulder muscles knot, then release as he swung the sword down like a mallet. The ring was even louder this time, and Gausser stepped forwards with a satisfied look on his face to examine the plate. His face fell, however, when he saw that the dent he had created was only slightly deeper. It had certainly not penetrated the armour.

'Do not be disappointed, novices. It takes a blade of magical keenness for a man to slice apart full plate. No, if you only have a sword with which to strike at these armoured warriors then here is what you may do. First, the murder stroke.' A sergeant wearing armoured gauntlets stepped up, grasped Gausser's long sword in both hands by the end of the blade and then brought the hilt down on the armour's helmet. He stepped away, leaving a sizeable dent in the helmet's crown, enough to have killed the wearer.

'Come in and look now,' Talhoffer said to the novices. 'You see the cross-guard acts as a rudimentary hammer. It can also be used to hook your opponent's weapon away if you wish to wrestle him to the ground. Second, the thrust with the half-sword. Better when the foe is on the ground, but as circumstances demand. Novice Reinhardt, a thrust, but through the gap in the armour. Use your free hand to grip the blade half-way down its length and use that to hit your target. It is accuracy, not speed that matters here.'

Delmar looked for a gap and twisted the blade so that it was pointed at the join in the armpit. Up close now, he could hear a slight buzzing noise from within. With a glance at the fightmaster to ensure he should continue, Delmar slid the blade firmly through the join and into the space for the body. There was a second's resistance inside, but then the blade slipped easily through.

'Well done, Novice Reinhardt.' Talhoffer smiled a cold smile.

Suddenly, Delmar coughed and gagged. A foul stench erupted from the armour, and the other novices who had come in close to watch stumbled backwards, spluttering.

'That is the last lesson about fighting these casements,' the fightmaster warned. 'When you do break it open, you can never know what you will find inside!'

Talhoffer ripped open the helmet's visor to reveal an inhuman face, rotted through, its maw hanging open in seeming surprise. From its mouth emerged a stream of flies, disturbed from their feeding by the blow to the head. The novices scrambled back a distance.

The sergeants laughed hugely. It had not been easy to manhandle the dead pig in there at first light this morning. But it had been worth it to see their charges' faces.

Talhoffer did not laugh however. If Verrakker thought that they were ready for the test of spirit then he was sorely mistaken.

'Novices!' Talhoffer called them back to order, but his instruction was fated not to continue.

'Brother Talhoffer! Brother Ott!' a knight called from the steps of the chapter house. Talhoffer, Ott and Verrakker went over and gathered in a tight huddle, exchanged a few words, then hurried into the chapter house together.

'Do you sense it, brothers?' Krieglitz asked the others.

'No,' Siebrecht replied, 'but I see it.'

'The tension,' Alptraum spoke up, 'the concern they have. They don't count us at services; they don't care if we whisper at meals. None of them raises his voice any more. It is as if they must stay quiet so as to hear whatever may come.'

'All the better for us,' Siebrecht joked, but even he could not convince himself that he enjoyed the oppressive atmosphere. It reminded him too greatly of home, where his father was always waiting for the next disaster to befall them.

The wind picked up. Alptraum stopped and turned into it.

'It's from the north,' the Averlander stated, his eyes closed.

'There's blood on it.' Gausser's great nostrils flared, as though he were a whale dredging the sea.

Siebrecht looked at Krieglitz in bemusement at their friends' strange behaviour, but Krieglitz too was staring with them in the same direction.

Out in the city, a bell started to strike. It was one of the bells of the Great Temple and it sounded a doleful, sorrowful note. Then a second bell rang; this one with a lighter tone. Then a third chimed, and a fourth, and a fifth. And now they were ringing all across the city.

'Victory! Victory! The siege is lifted! The foe are on the run!' the cry went up from the chapter house. Victory. Victory. The word resounded in the novices' heads so loudly that they no longer heard the bells. Victory! Gausser gave a giant whoop of delight. Krieglitz clasped Siebrecht's hand and shook it with delight.

'Victory!' Delmar shouted to the Reiklanders, and even Falkenhayn could not help but smile with relief.

Delmar saw Talhoffer step out of the chapter house.

'Master!' he called out. 'The war is over!'

Talhoffer strode quickly over. 'We are done for the day,' he ordered the novices. 'Be back tomorrow at first light. We will need to make up for the time we have lost.'

'Master, is the war over?' Delmar asked.

'We have a victory, Novice Reinhardt, that is all. Tomorrow, first light, all of you.'

But the city did not share the fightmaster's dour assessment. They had endured a hungry winter and a spring of fear. The news of the great victory around Middenheim was their first glimpse of hope and they would make the most of it.

As the novices' training intensified, all they could hear for days beyond the walls of the chapter house was the city celebrating with everything it could. The beggars in the streets and the refugees from the other provinces, who had been despised as parasites dragging Altdorf down, were treated once more as fellow subjects. The Altdorfers' hatred would turn back upon them, the refugees knew, so the most hopeful of them departed the city to journey back to their homes, though none of them knew what they would find left.

In such a time of general wellbeing, Siebrecht could not resist slipping out into the city to enjoy the jubilation. He had thought he had covered his tracks well, but he had no regrets when the sergeants came for him again.

Siebrecht, prepared for the worst, was escorted to the guardhouse by the white gate. There, however, he realised that, for once, it was not him that was in trouble.

'Ah, there you are, Siebrecht,' a familiar voice greeted him. 'Be a good boy now and explain to these suspicious gentlemen that I am no spy or pilferer.'

There sat a man whom Siebrecht instantly recognised. The forehead was higher, the hair greyed, the skin sagged slightly over the distinctive cheek-bones, but the family resemblance, alas, was clear.

'You can stand testament for this man?' The sergeant asked.

'He's my uncle,' Siebrecht said.

'You sound surprised.' his uncle retored. 'Did you not receive my let-ter? I could scarcely pass through this great city without paying a visit to my dearest nephew.'

'We discovered him concealed within a goods cart,' a sergeant said, his posture stating clearly his desire to drag their captive out feet first.

'I was not concealed and I resent your implication,' Herr von Matz said, taking umbrage. 'I was inspecting the guildmarks upon the seals. My good brother, the Baron von Matz, has entrusted his eldest son into your order's care and I will report back of the dubious origin and the even more dubi-ous quality of the food you serve here. I am certain that he will apply most readily to your commander as regards your treatment of his son and your rough handling of me.'

'Uncle!' Siebrecht admonished him. 'Sergeant, my uncle's name I can stand surety for, to his nature I cannot. Do you wish to hold him further?'

'I do not wish to hold him, nor see him again.'

'Wishes, sergeant...' his uncle began, but Siebrecht shot his uncle a sharp look and he subsided.

'Come on, uncle.'

'If I may be permitted to speak, I would like to ask for my hat back.' He stared pointedly at the sergeant, who disdainfully retrieved the ridiculously plumed hat and handed it back.

'Novice Matz,' the sergeant said as he showed them out. 'Herr Matz.'

'Herr von Matz,' the uncle corrected tartly, and the sergeant closed the door on his face.

Out on the crowded street, Siebrecht saw his uncle drop his pretence of petty indignation and straighten into the role of a respectable man of means. Herr von Matz led his nephew a short way through the busy streets back to his lodgings, ignoring all of Siebrecht's attempts to question him along the way. Finally Siebrecht gave up, and followed in silence as his uncle entered an unremarkable house, nodded his greetings to the house-keeper and sat down in a private room where some food had already been laid out.

Herr von Matz produced a small wooden case, delicately inlaid with sculpted bone. He took out his knife and carving fork and sat down to eat. Seeing his chance, Siebrecht took control of the conversation.

'So, my uncle, is your purpose here solely to embarrass me before my order?'

'Embarrass you?' Herr von Matz paused mid-slice. 'I am quite certain I took considerable pains to ensure that I only embarrassed myself.'

'What?'

'You, meanwhile, played the role of the mortified and reasonable relative superbly. I can assure you that the next time those sergeants see you they will not be thinking how exceedingly arrogant you are, rather they will reflect on how great an improvement you are on the previous generation.'

Siebrecht could not believe his uncle's gall. 'Are you claiming that you provoked the entire thing in order that I would appear less annoying to some common sergeants?'

Herr von Matz waggled his fork at his nephew. 'Don't be dismissive of your lessers, my boy. An Emperor may give you titles, but he'll never clean your boots. Those sergeants there, I'm sure they have the run of the chapter house, am I right? Keys to every lock, an ear to every door? Very useful.'

Siebrecht lavished scorn in his reply. 'So you crept into a cart and hid so that I may have the opportunity to befriend them.'

'No, of course not. That was a mere fortuitous opportunity.'

'Then what were you doing?'

'Trying to see the seals, the guildmarks, as I said.'

'You truly care about the freshness of the food?'

'Why should I? I'm not going to eat it, am I? If I wanted to trade in food then I would buy it at home, or Averland, and I would send it north. Far too dangerous though, the cost of escort would be prohibitive. And so few people in the north have the money to pay these days.'

'Then what were you interested in?'

'The ore, of course. The ore, the charcoal, the cloth. Anything that can travel. You see the seal, you know the supplier.'

'You wish to supply the Reiksguard? Is that it then?'

'Perhaps. Perhaps there are some suppliers who are taking too great a profit, or have one too many middlemen that might be circumvented. The value of good ore is high now because of the war; charcoal is short because of the danger in the forests; so much cloth is needed for all the uniforms for the Emperor's armies; but when the war is done will the values stay high? Or will the wars never end?'

'Did you not hear the bells, uncle? The war has just ended.'

Herr von Matz gave a tiny short laugh, which fully encapsulated his opinion on his nephew's naïveté.

'There cannot be a new campaign,' Siebrecht said. 'Not already.'

Herr von Matz sized up his nephew carefully.

'You will find, young Siebrecht, that the beginnings and ends of wars are marked by historians. Not by those who are still fighting them long after some man of letters has declared that a victory was won. Here's a piece of information for you. See how you fare in realising its value. Have you ever heard of a dwarfen hold named Karak Angazhar?'

'No. Should I have done?'

'Not a youth in your position, whose only interest is in the next bottle, no.'

Siebrecht bit back a sharp remark. 'What about it then?'

'It has been besieged, for several months now, by the goblin tribes of the Black Mountains.'

'Dwarfs and goblins fighting. My word, uncle, what astonishing news you bring me,' Siebrecht replied, barely trying to conceal the sarcasm in his voice. 'I am truly staggered.'

Herr von Matz gave his nephew a sharp clip around the ear.

'Oh, I did forget how clever you are. Very well then, I will leave it at this. Karak Angazhar is not one of the great dwarfen strongholds, it is no equal of Karaz-a-Karak or Barak Varr, and yet before this month is out the soldiers of the Empire will march from Altdorf to go and rescue it. And, most likely, the Reiksguard will be at their head.'

'What? Why would we? The old alliance is strong of late, but we are stretched to the limit. And if it is a choice between dwarfs and our own realm, then I know which we should defend.'

'That, I will leave you to discover. And when the Reiksguard marches, you had better ensure that you are still with them. And still in a condition to give a good account of yourself.' He pointedly picked up Siebrecht's glass and placed it on the far side of the table, out of his reach. 'It would not do to have the order think ill of you.'

Siebrecht snorted. 'I would not care if they did.'

'Decide upon your opinions, Siebrecht,' his uncle taunted him. 'First, you are ashamed that I have embarrassed you before your brothers, and now you say you do not care what they think.

'Let me be sure that you rightly understand the truth of your circumstances.' Herr von Matz fixed Siebrecht with his glare. 'The Reiksguard was not so willing to consider your application, simply because of your name. Your name, our name, has little to recommend it any more. No, the Reiksguard's consideration was bought; yes, with that same coin that you so quickly squander.'

'You bribed the Reiksguard to accept me?' Siebrecht could not believe it.

Herr von Matz sighed heavily. Under his brother's indolent upbringing Siebrecht had obviously experienced much of the world, but had never thought to understand it.

'No,' he said patiently. 'I would not even try. Men of honour are simply too expensive for the worth they can provide. And as soon as they accept, they lose their one source of value. Their honour! You do not bribe men of honour. You bribe the amenable men whom the men of honour trust. You needed recommendations and there are nobles highly placed in Wissenland, all around the Empire, who are willing, nay eager, to be influenced. Some of them near ripped my hand clean off, so keen were they to grasp their gratuity.'

'For what purpose then?' Siebrecht pushed himself away from the table and stormed around the room. 'For what purpose was I sent here, away from my family, away from my friends, away from my life? To be run ragged by Reikland martinets? To have insults hurled at me by Reikland boors? To die, protecting a Reikland prince?'

Herr von Matz met his nephew's fiery outburst coolly. He continued eating without even looking up. Siebrecht felt stymied, and yet he was unwilling to give up his temper. Instead, he stomped over to the shutters and slammed them back hard. The sounds of the city burst in, and Siebrecht leaned into the street and sucked in the air.

'When you're finished,' Herr von Matz remarked between mouthfuls, 'do close those shutters and sit down.'

Siebrecht stubbornly held his post at the window for a minute more, but then did as his uncle told him.

'What do you think of Novice Gausser?' Herr von Matz asked as he sat.

'Gausser?' Siebrecht was taken off guard by the change in topic. 'Well... he's as strong as an ox and about as bright.'

'Do you think he's good to his friends?'

'I suppose.'

'He could be Emperor one day, you know.'

Siebrecht laughed at that. 'Is that another certain prediction of yours? I'll take your wager on that one for sure.'

'Why not?' Herr von Matz replied calmly. 'He is the grandson of an elector count, if he inherits that then all he need be is elected. Alptraum?'

'A loon!'

'His family hold the Averland guilds and merchants in their pocket. Falkenhayn?'

'A Mootland cesspit!'

'He will inherit whole streets here in Altdorf, indeed the one this very house is in.'

'Ranald's balls, uncle, do you know all the other novices? Have you had your spies on me ever since I arrived?'

'Spies? Who would need a spy for that? You and your fancies, Siebrecht. You think I wouldn't ask who you were training with? It's not a secret. If a family have their son in the Reiksguard they proclaim it from their rooftops.'

'Excellent, then! Now you've shown me that they are rich and I am humble, I feel a whole new joy at my internment with them.'

'The point is, Siebrecht, that they are rich and you are with them. These men whom you have so quickly dismissed, each one of them is of ten times the consequence of any of your drinking partners in Nuln. You are here so that, in years to come, when you have long quit the Reiksguard, you may enter the court of any province in the Empire and be welcomed there by its ruler as an old and dearest friend. Money has less relevance than you assume, those sergeants' treatment of me today is ample proof of that. Look at Reinhardt, you know Reinhardt?'

'Oh, I've met Novice Reinhardt.'

Herr von Matz ignored the rancour in Siebrecht's tone.

'The Reinhardts have little money beyond their estate. But his great-grandfather was one of the first Reiksguard knights. His grandfather served. His father died in battle. Do you think he had to buy the recommendations from petty nobles for the order to consider his application? No money can buy the influence his name has in the order and, through them, with half the rulers in this land. The privilege will flow to him like honey. All I want for you is to be able to taste it. This is an opportunity that you will have at no other time in your life.'

'An opportunity for you, you mean,' Siebrecht struck back, 'to say that your family has a son in the most prestigious guard of the Emperor.'

'It will get you coin if you want it. Titles, if you want those. Do not doubt that women come with both if that is your only desire. Forgive me then for a design which meets both our ambitions.'

'We have coin. We have titles. You make us sound so desperate, uncle.'

'You think there is coin in the barony?' Herr von Matz said as he poured himself another glass. 'For generations now its wealth has been ebbing away. Your father inherited the barony and then sat on it, like an addled hen that sits on a stone and waits for it to hatch. He feels his way of life slipping away but he does not know how to stop it. He's become quite solicitous to me these last few months, did you know? Why do you think that is? Brotherly love? Not a chance. It is my coin that he hosts, not his brother. No, Siebrecht, it is well you know now: there are no riches in the barony. And that means that you must either be a great Baron von Matz, or you will be the last.'

Siebrecht sat, silenced by his uncle's frank admissions.

'It is only for a few years,' Herr von Matz continued, his tone more conciliatory. 'Serve well. Make your name. Resist the urge to plunge your breast onto the enemy's sword. Then come back to your life, though I predict that you will not look on it the same as you did. You will help your father in managing the estate, and you will have the privilege to do what it will take to restore the family's fortunes.'

'For just a few years.'

'Three at most. Enough to establish yourself, to get yourself known for more than drinking, impertinence and wild gunmanship. There is no purpose in exposing you to needless risk.' Herr von Matz gave an honest smile. 'You and I, Siebrecht, we're the ones on whom the family name depends.'

Siebrecht said nothing. His head stayed downcast, his sight fixed on the grain of the wood in the table, not wishing to meet his uncle's gaze. He knew his uncle was right; he'd known for years. Something he knew but could never admit.

Herr von Matz was satisfied with the impression he had made upon his nephew. He sat back in his chair and wiped his mouth.

'Emperor Wilhelm,' he began, 'as much as any good man of Nuln should detest him, I cannot but admit that his creation of the Reiksguard was a master-stroke. Other emperors had founded knightly orders before, but none of them ever saw their true potential. Other orders...' Herr von Matz waved his hand dismissively. 'The Order of the Black Bear want the strongest, the Knights of Sigmar's Blood want the learned, even our own great Emperor Magnus, when he founded the Knights Griffon, asked only for the most devout.

'It was only Emperor Wilhelm who ever asked for the eldest. The heirs. More than any of the others, Wilhelm looked to the future; for after ten or twenty years, once their fathers were dead, the heirs were the nobles themselves. And each of them had been taught and drilled to have abso-lute loyalty to their Emperor. To leave the rule of the Empire to him. To shun politics altogether! Everyone knows that the Reiksguard have vowed to never interfere in the political world. Loyalty, first, last and always, isn't that right? And an end to civil wars as well, because it is so much harder to shed the blood of one you have called brother.'

Herr von Matz paused a moment to catch his breath, the ancient wiles of a long-dead emperor exciting him far more than any scheme of his own.

'Yes, Siebrecht. Emperor Wilhelm was a very clever man.' His meal fin-ished, he wiped his cutlery clean and replaced them in their box. 'And it behoves clever men like Wilhelm and you and I not only to know the world, but also to understand how it works. There are the spoken reasons, and then there are the unspoken reasons. And it is the unspoken reasons that are by far the most valuable.'

Herr von Matz stood, ending the interview. Siebrecht was most relieved to be away. His uncle, however, insisted on walking him back to the bar-racks. Once there, Siebrecht thought he would leave. However, he blithely strolled up to the same guardhouse from which, an hour before, he had been so roughly ejected. The sergeant was less than pleased to see him return, but Herr von Matz laid on such a spectacular display, alternating between profuse apologies for his earlier conduct and the highest praise for the close attention that the guards had taken in ensuring the safety of his nephew, that even the stoniest of them could not help but mellow a little.

When he finally took his leave, he asked both Siebrecht and the sergeant to walk him back out onto the street, where he engaged the sergeant in a few minutes more of animated, good-natured conversation, so that to any passer-by the two of them might have appeared as the warmest of acquaint-ances. Herr von Matz then bid them a friendly farewell and crossed over the square to his next interview: a timber supplier who, impressed by Herr von Matz's ostentatious connections within the prestigious Reiksguard, found himself agreeing to a far greater discount than he had originally intended.

'These, novices, are the files.'

Master Talhoffer had brought the novices in their awkward plate armour down to the far end of the practice field. Set up there were lines of thick wooden fence posts, each one six feet high, arranged in neat rows a pace or so apart. The novices had assumed the posts had been set up for building or cultivation. They were wrong.

'You have been taught how to march in formation. Some of you even manage not to fall over your own feet while you do so. You have been taught the drills to use so that you do not strike your brothers beside you. But rehearsing drills is very different to facing another man in the crush of combat.

'We could simply pack you together and let you go swing at each other, as I see you do each day with your wasters, but then we would flood the sanatorium with unconscious novices, brained by their fellows in the battle line. Therefore we have this. The files. Each one is a corridor, roughly the width of what you might have to fight in battle proper. We will begin here, and when you have all eventually mastered the art of not smacking your blade in a wooden post, you will finally have the chance to embed it in your fellow's skull.

'Split into two groups, one man at the end of each corridor. When I say begin, you will all enter your corridor; the first one out the other side is the victor. Understand?'

The novices split, once again into Reiklanders and Provincials. However this time it meant that instead of sparring between themselves as they usually did, they would face each other.

'Reinhardt,' Falkenhayn whispered to Delmar, 'come, let us stay together and fight side by side.' Falkenhayn indicated the file to his right and Delmar took up the position there. He looked down the column and realised that Falkenhayn had matched him against Gausser again. He checked the files beside him: Falkenhayn himself was facing Siebrecht, who, even aside from his cavalier behaviour that first day, had failed to impress Delmar. This training was wasted on him, he truly did not care to be here and rarely bothered to stir himself to action even when sparring. He would happily fall if it was less effort than fighting. No doubt Falkenhayn would have an easy time against him. Beyond him, Proktor faced Krieglitz. There, Delmar considered, was a proper fighter. He did his province proud, though as Falkenhayn said, a man should be judged not only by prowess but by the company he chooses, and Delmar considered that Krieglitz's friendship with Siebrecht had firmly held the Talabheimer back.

Talhoffer called on them to be ready, and Delmar concentrated once more on his own column and the hefty Nordlander at the end of it. Talhoffer ordered them to begin and the novices entered the files. Delmar saw Falkenhayn sprint forwards on his left, charging Siebrecht down. He had decided to approach Gausser more cautiously. He had charged the last time they fought and little good it had done him. Gausser was slower than he, but the plate weighed Delmar down far more than the Nordlander. The two warriors walked steadily towards each other until they met in the middle. Already Delmar heard the crunch of armoured bodies hitting each other from either side and the yells of success of those who had already emerged. He ignored them and kept his focus.

He and Gausser exchanged a few stabs, each testing the other's guard. However Delmar quickly realised that in confined quarters such light blows against an armoured opponent were insignificant. What counted was strength and weight, and in both Gausser would best him. Gausser obviously came to the same conclusion, for he reversed his wooden sword and swung the hilt in a murder stroke at Delmar's head.

Instinctively, Delmar gave ground; he would ordinarily have gone to the left or right, but in the files there was nowhere to go but back. He brought his own sword up with both hands and blocked the murder stroke. Gausser had no fear of Delmar's retaliation and no thought of relenting, so he swung again to batter his way past Delmar's guard or force him back out of the file. Delmar let the Nordlander crash against his sword once more, but on the third stroke he stepped back even further and allowed the murder stroke to knock his weapon out of his hand completely. Gausser had expected to meet solid resistance, and so for a second was left off-balance, overextended. Delmar grabbed the hilt of Gausser's sword and pulled his opponent hard, forwards and down. Gausser refused to release his own blade and so as Delmar pulled, Gausser came with it.

They stumbled back together a few steps and Delmar almost had Gausser trip, but the Nordlander twisted his body and killed his forwards momentum by slamming into a post with his shoulder. Delmar was ready for it. As Gausser reared up to steady himself, Delmar dropped low, wrapping his arms around Gausser's knees and gripped them tight in a bear hug. Gausser was solid, but in the mud even he was not strong enough to keep his stance. Delmar heaved his legs together and shoved hard against them as low as he could. Unable to bend down and grab the Reiklander without falling over himself, Gausser held tightly to the fence post, but with one final surge Delmar finally took the legs out from under him. Gausser toppled to the ground with all the majesty of an oak felled in the forest. Delmar ran for the exit and did not look back until he was out. Only then did he turn around. Gausser was still picking himself up. Delmar went to Falkenhayn beside him to congratulate him as well, but his friend had a face of thunder.

'It was a trick, Reinhardt, he won with a stupid Nulner trick,' Falkenhayn railed. Falkenhayn had charged, as Delmar had seen, and Siebrecht, ever insolent, had stepped out of his way rather than bother with the exercise. Falkenhayn had run for it; he would be out of the files before any other. But as he passed, Siebrecht had kicked out, and Falkenhayn had lost his footing and slammed the side of his head into a post.

It had been a trick, Delmar decided, but it had been a fair one, only accomplished because of Falkenhayn's own mistaken assumption. Proktor too had, predictably, lost against Krieglitz and the two victorious Provincial novices stood at the other end of the files commiserating Gausser on his comeuppance.

Delmar raised his hand in salute.

'What are you doing, Reinhardt?' Falkenhayn bristled. 'Put that hand down.'

Delmar let his friend pull his arm down. The Provincials had seen it, but did not return it.

That day was only their first at the files. They continued to train there each day, sometimes sparring with sergeants armed with long spears or pikes, sometimes packed three, five or even ten novices to each file. The novices learned how, even stuck in the rear ranks, they might aid the fighter at the front to win his combat, while those at the front learned how to maintain the pressure on the enemy, knock down their opponents and then step over them to allow those behind to finish them off. All of them learned the danger of falling in the middle of a melee, and Delmar was not the only one of them to suffer the indignity of being kicked around on the floor for several minutes before he could finally crawl clear.

In armoured combat, Gausser continued to dominate, though Delmar gave a good enough account of himself to regularly best the other novices. Where the sergeants sparred with them intentionally without armour, however, Delmar noted that it was Siebrecht, with his new determination, who began to demonstrate the greatest ability. His technique still included some remnants of his Tilean instruction, but now that he was used to the heavier weight of the Reiksguard's swords his skill became apparent. His sheer speed, in particular, led him to fare far better than the rest in exercises where a single fighter was left to face multiple opponents. Though Talhoffer did not go so far as to praise Siebrecht for his improvement, the fightmaster relented in his previous criticism.

When they weren't performing close-order drills on foot, the novices were doing so on horseback. In this, Alptraum had great proficiency. Averland was renowned for its horses and riders, and indeed most of the Reiksguard's own mounts bore Averland markings.

Delmar, though, surpassed even him. At last, Delmar prayed thankfully, after being bested in every other way, he had at least one discipline in which he could be proud. A discipline in which he could be the one to help others.

Horsemanship was inherent within the noble classes. They had all learned to ride as children, but to ride so close as to be stirrup to stirrup with your brother beside you, whilst carrying a heavy lance and shield and controlling your mount with your knees, required a higher level of experience entirely. These urban nobles who visited their horses twice a week in their stables and took them for a jaunt outside the city walls simply had not developed the same familiarity that Delmar had on a country estate where he rode Heinrich out every day between village and town and was responsible for every aspect of his horse's care.

Delmar had not been allowed to use Heinrich in the Reiksguard's training; Talhoffer had told him that a knight of the order had to be able to control any mount owned by the order, which were all specially trained to carry the weight of a man in full armour. As hard as battles were on men, they were far worse for horses and a knight might find himself changing mounts as many as half a dozen times; his control could not rely on a personal connection with his steed. Therefore a novice was given a different horse for each exercise, and he was personally liable if his mount bit or kicked at another as they walked or practised their charges. A kick, if it struck the other animal badly, had the potential to cripple the leg and render a hugely expensive warhorse useless, and so all of Delmar's friends were eager to learn the danger signs of an agitated steed and the correct preventative measures.

The danger was not only to the horses. In a close formation charge, Harver's horse misstepped. In trying to right his steed's course, Harver barrelled into Breigh beside him. Both horses fell, Harver was knocked from his saddle and was left bruised, Breigh was caught in his mount, his horse fell hard upon its side and Breigh's leg was snapped.

Breigh spent a night in agony while the order's healers worked upon him; Falkenhayn and the distraught Harver stayed with him. Breigh went home the next day, forgiving Harver with every breath, and vowing to Falkenhayn that he would return as soon as he was able to walk once more.

Once again, the sergeant stood at the ready in the middle of four novices. Delmar caught the eyes of Hardenburg, then Bohdan, then Siebrecht. They yelled and charged as one. The sergeant pulled no punches; Delmar only just caught sight of the sergeant's sword as it pierced his guard and smacked him soundly on the side of the head before moving on.

'Reinhardt out. Hardenburg out.' Talhoffer paused. 'Sergeant, you may stand down.'

The sergeant hauled himself back to his feet, his shift covered in bloody marks landed by the remaining two novices. He scowled at Delmar and stalked away.

'Killed again, Novice Reinhardt,' Talhoffer said to him afterwards.

'Yes, master.' At least this time it had been to his head and it would not take so long to wash the dye from his shift.

'Your skill with the sword is not great.'

'I will improve, master.'

'Still, I should not like to be you in battle.'

'No, master,' Delmar replied, unable to prevent the tinge of failure from colouring his voice.

He would never be a great swordsman, Talhoffer could tell. But he had nevertheless led the charge against a superior opponent, knowing what it would cost him but trusting that his brothers together would be victorious. And he had been right.

'No, Novice Reinhardt,' Talhoffer considered. 'I would not wish to be you in battle. But I would stand beside you.'

FIVE

KARL FRANZ

The novices' routine was broken one day when, after the service at the Great Temple, Verrakker did not take them back to the barracks, but rather into the grounds of the palace. The gardens themselves were not huge, as befitted a residence that had been largely carved out of the existing city, but they were beautiful. The summer had not yet reached its height and everything there was in bloom. The flowering plants were clustered around statues of heroes of the Empire, both ancient and modern, and had been carefully chosen to represent some aspect of each hero's character or achievements. Beyond the cultivated gardens, the grounds settled into a verdant lawn bordered by the cooling shade of the trees and hedgerows, which softened the sounds of the city.

Despite the beauty on offer, there were few around to enjoy it. With the Emperor on campaign with the army in the north, the palace was quiet. Without the Emperor, or the frenzy of supplicants who typically surrounded him, the staff had little to do but keep the apartments in order. Those noblemen who were officers to the Imperial court had mostly left with the Emperor, and those who stayed preferred to perform their official duties from their own residences, where they were more comfortable and could manage their personal business matters away from prying eyes. Those administrators who were left in the palace kept themselves busy enough, maintaining the flow of correspondence between the court on campaign and the court left in residence, and had little reason to trespass out of their own domains.

The one part of the palace grounds that was still frequented was the Imperial Zoo, and it was there that Verrakker was leading the novices. Delmar had seen it before, years ago; everyone who came to the capital made sure to visit and gaze in wonder at the bizarre creatures of the Emperor's menagerie. The zoo predated the return of the Imperial capital to Altdorf and it had displayed hundreds of different animals from across the Old World and beyond, though not all survived long once they were resident. But it was not the exotic animals that were the true draw of the zoo, it was rather the monsters. They were warped and terrifying, and Delmar, along with men, women and children alike, had queued patiently for the chance to be scared witless by such things as the Spawn of Hochland.

Verrakker walked them past the line of Altdorfers waiting outside the spawn's tented cage, and all the other public enclosures that radiated out from the central pavilion. He took them back into the working areas of the zoo, where the grisly tasks of feeding and cleaning the animals were kept hidden from the sight of the public behind tall hedges .

'Here we are,' Verrakker announced.

The novices had been led to a set of stables, not greatly different from the Reiksguard's own at the citadel. The horses were all fine specimens, all warhorses and mostly of Averland stock, Alptraum proudly noted, but there was nothing particularly special about them.

At the rear of them, Delmar noticed one horse that was special: a pure white charger, though Delmar could see little more than its head over the herd. Then it reared and spread a pair of giant swan-like wings.

'These are the Emperor's mounts,' Delmar whispered.

'That's right, Novice Reinhardt,' Verrakker replied.

Delmar stared, his mouth open, at the pegasus as it whinnied and bucked while its handlers tried to calm it.

'Come on, this way,' Verrakker said. 'There is more to see.'

Here, behind the stables, there were a series of other enclosures, each one containing a majestic beast: griffons, pegasi and more. In one massive, darkened enclosure they could see nothing in the shadows, yet Delmar felt a cold, ancient gaze bearing down upon him.

Delmar asked why the bars on the enclosures were only ten feet high. 'These beasts can fly,' he said, 'those bars will not keep them in. Why is there no roof?'

'The bars are not meant to keep them in,' Verrakker replied, 'these creatures are here by their own will. The bars are there to keep inquisitive fools out.'

At that moment, the Emperor's mounts all lifted their heads as one and gave an ear-splitting cry. The novices jumped away from the enclosures; even Verrakker took a step back. Then their cry was answered from above. Delmar looked up and saw a griffon in the sky, wheeling and swooping above the zoo. And on its back was a rider, whose distinctive profile was known across the land.

'The Emperor!' someone shouted, as handlers and retainers raced to the stableyard where the griffon was coming in to land. The novices ran with them.

Delmar arrived first, in time to see the fierce griffon Deathclaw slow his flight with backwards beats of his mighty wings and settle on the ground with incongruous grace. The handlers took the griffon's reins and helped the rider out of the saddle. There he was, Delmar realised, no more than a

dozen feet before him. Emperor Karl Franz, Prince of Altdorf, Grand Prince
of Reikland, Count of the West March. Delmar stared at him and, for the
merest instant, the Emperor looked back. Delmar was struck by the tiredness in his eyes. Then the Emperor was distracted by one of his attendants,
and turned back to give Deathclaw an affectionate rub behind its ears and
on its beak. Delmar found himself surprised to see this legendary figure
make such an ordinary gesture. He noticed then that the griffon was sweating and shaking with exertion. There must be some emergency for the
Emperor to come back alone, unexpected, with the army still so far distant.

Then a band of Reiksguard knights, who were on guard at the palace,
came running up and formed a crude protective circle around the Emperor.
Verrakker grabbed Delmar's shoulders and ushered him and the other
novices out of the way.

The novices were left in a state of high excitement and yet they were told
little of what had transpired to hasten the Emperor's return. Their regular training was curtailed, as the order required every able knight to stand
guard duty at the palace until the Reiksguard squadrons returned. Talhoffer, Verrakker and even Ott took up their old ceremonial guard armour and
joined the regular garrison. The novices were left to spar with each other
and run drills under the supervision of their sergeants; of their tutors only
Master Lehrer remained, and they had never seen him out of his library,
or even out from behind his desk.

Three days after the Emperor's arrival, the squadrons of the Grand Order
of the Reiksguard processed into the capital with Kurt Helborg at their
head. They were the first of the regiments from the victory at Middenheim to return to the city, and the novices joined the hundreds of citizens
of Altdorf who sweltered in the summer heat to line the route and cheer
them home. The knights, their silver armour dazzling in the sun, marched
their warhorses in close order through the streets up to the chapter house,
as stoic in the face of popular acclaim as they had been in the face of the
enemy. Delmar and the other novices, swept up in the jubilation, yelled
their praise. The great Wilhelm Gate of the chapter house opened and
received them home again.

It was Siebrecht who first spotted the second group of arrivals. They
appeared at the chapter house in covered wagons through the white gate
to the side of the barracks. That caravan carried the injured knights who
had survived, but had not been fit to ride back in with the main procession. It also carried the precious armour of the knights who had not been
so fortunate and had been buried on the battlefields of Middenland.

Delmar followed the knightly procession into the grounds of the barracks
and around the side of the chapter house through to the stables. When
he arrived the yard was full of sweating horses, irritable in the heat of the

midday sun. Stablehands hurried back and forth as fast as their dignity allowed, helping the knights out of the saddle and leading their steeds to the next empty stall.

Delmar skirted his way around the edges until he saw Griesmeyer, his red hair matted and darkened with sweat. He was still mounted, waiting patiently for a stablehand to attend him.

'Lord Griesmeyer!' Delmar cried as he squeezed his way past two warhorses.

Griesmeyer turned in his direction, and in that instant before recognition dawned, Delmar saw the tightness around his eyes and the furrows in his brow. Then his face broke out into a smile and the ghosts were gone.

'Delmar!' he said. 'I thought it would not be long until I saw you.'

Delmar respectfully took hold of the knight's reins and stroked the horse's neck. 'My lord, how went the battle?'

'Sigmar's breath, novice! I shall tell you all, but give me a moment.'

Griesmeyer was even better than his word. He went with Delmar to the novices' quarters and there sat and answered all their questions of the siege. The knight conjured up images of the ravening hordes of savage northern warriors; the horrific mutants and monsters that they held captive to unleash upon their enemies, the daemonic war engines made of metal which pulsed with life, and the dark champions that strode through the ranks, gripping ancient weapons inscribed with arcane markings that burned with power.

But then he spoke of the Empire's army, where the most famous regiments stood in a single battle line: the Carroburg Greatswords, the cannon of Nuln, the Scarlet Guard of Stirland, the Death's Head of Ostermark, huntsmen from Ostland, the Hochland rifles, and halberdiers, spearmen, swordsmen and archers from across the provinces.

The novices felt a surge of pride at that, and even more so when Griesmeyer described the Reiksguard's final charge which broke the last of the foe's resistance. None were more proud though than Delmar, for the other novices knew that the knight had visited them because of him. And he was proud also, he realised, to see his fellow novices united.

Afterwards, Griesmeyer asked Delmar to walk him back across the yard.

'Do you think they enjoyed my stories?' he asked.

'Aye, my lord,' Delmar replied, 'I think that their only regret was that they could not be there to see it themselves before it was all done.'

'Good, for the war is not done at all.'

'Pardon, my lord?' Delmar could not quite believe what the knight had said.

'This war could not be won in a single battle. Some of their warbands have scattered, but many have stayed together under one of their generals and retreated into the mountains or the forests. It is a snakebite, the fang has gone but the poison is left behind. I am sure we will march north again soon, unless the Emperor has another purpose for us, and then your friends will have their chance. Presuming you have been found worthy of joining, of course?'

'The masters have said that the testing is concluded. But they have not yet told us their decision. Have you heard that I–'

'I have not spoken to them,' Griesmeyer cut him off, 'but I am sure you have trained hard and that your dedication will be rewarded. When is your vigil to be held?' he asked.

'The night after next,' Delmar replied.

'For certain you will know before then,' the knight replied unhelpfully. 'I am glad they waited until the order could return.'

'Is that why they have delayed?' Delmar queried. 'For our testing is finished. We do not know what we should be doing.'

At that Griesmeyer stopped in his tracks. He peered into Delmar's eyes for several long seconds, as though he was searching for something there.

'Keep your guard high, novice,' Griesmeyer finally said. 'It is not finished until you take the oaths.'

'I will, my lord,' Delmar muttered, then Griesmeyer dismissed him and went on alone.

Delmar sat quietly in his small cell, trying to pray. The novices had all been moved from their dormitory for that night and each was placed in a separate cell within the chapter house. It was supposed to allow them some privacy and rest before their vigil the next night. The vigil was to be the last test they would face as novices. Should they pass, then they would be called to take their oaths to become a full brother-knight of the Reiksguard. Throughout their vigil they would pray and be prayed over.

Rumours abounded amongst the novices that the prayers the priests used were ones of exorcism and that in times past novices had had daemons discovered within them, had been driven mad, attacked their fellows or even burst spontaneously into flames. Griesmeyer had scoffed at such tall tales, though he could recall an instance where the intensity of the ceremony had been such that one novice, who had been put under great pressure by his family, burst out laughing and had to be removed and calmed down.

The purpose of the event in truth, Griesmeyer had said, was to give each novice a final chance to reconsider whether they could honestly swear the binding oaths of loyalty that would then be asked of them. The oaths of a brother-knight to the Reiksguard and to the order's rule superseded any others that a warrior might take, whether to family, province, friends or gods, short of those he took to the Emperor himself. As strange as it seemed to Delmar, Griesmeyer said that there had been occasions where it was only at the vigil itself that a novice had realised that he could not swear sole loyalty to the order and so had had to withdraw. The brother-knights who successfully completed the vigil together would, from then after, forever be witnesses to the fact that each of them had taken their oaths to the Reiks-guard with the full knowledge of what that entailed.

Delmar did not believe that this would present any difficulty for him. He knew the oaths, he had learned them by heart from his grandfather ten years before he would set foot in the chapter house as a novice. He would not baulk now at swearing them in earnest. Nevertheless, he could not settle at prayer. They had each been given an icon bearing the cross, skull and laurel wreath, the insignia of a full brother-knight, to aid them. He had felt a surge of pride as they placed the icon around his neck, but he found it of no help in prayer. It was quiet outside his cell, dark also; he could think of no reason why he should not be at peace and yet he was not. Disappointed at himself, he gave up on his prayer and instead decided that rest was what he needed. He lay down on the cot and closed his eyes. He felt his breath deepen and sleep quickly took him.

Delmar woke. There was a sharp smell in his sinuses and he sleepily rubbed the bridge of his nose with his fingertips. It was still quiet. He turned onto his side to get back to sleep. No, it wasn't quiet, it was completely silent. There were no croaks or calls from the night animals in the chapter house's grounds. No murmurs from the ever-wakeful city around its walls. Delmar opened his eyes. There was a flickering light from under his door. A lantern. Something, someone, was outside.

The door-bolt began to slide back.

Delmar shot up as though ice-water was in his veins. He dived from his bed; he did not have his sword, but his hand reached for a weapon, for any weapon. The intruder heard the noise and slammed the bolt back. The door flew open. A man stood there, silhouetted by the lantern light.

'Delmar?' the man asked. His voice deep, thick, but not harsh.

Delmar squinted at him and took a grip on one of the bed legs, readying to throw the entire piece of furniture at the assailant if need be.

'Who is that?'

The man held the lantern in front of him and its light fell upon a face that Delmar had only seen in portrait but yet knew better than his own.

'Delmar, my son.'

'Father?'

'Father?'

'Yes, son?'

'Father.' Delmar rose to his feet and took the hand held out to him. The hand gripped him back. It was flesh. It was real.

'Father,' Delmar said again and grasped the man's shoulder. It was solid.

'Yes, son?' Delmar looked into the blue eyes, greyer slightly with age.

Delmar clutched him close, expecting the body to evaporate like smoke. It did not. Delmar hugged his father tightly to him, unable to contain his joy.

'It's all right, son. It's all right,' Delmar heard him whisper in his ear.

Then, and only then, did the questions tumble out. 'What are you doing here? Where have you been? They said you were dead, Father. They told Mother you were dead.'

'They were lies, Delmar. Everything they told you was a lie. But come, quickly, I cannot be found here.'

Delmar followed him out of the cell and down through the corridors. His father wore a long travelling cloak, but beneath it his clothes were matted dark red.

'Is that blood? Are you injured?' Delmar asked.

'It is not mine,' his father replied, and Delmar saw the slumped bodies of sergeants hidden in the shadows. Delmar looked away, and his father led him out of the buildings and towards the stables.

'What has happened to you?' Delmar asked, hurrying to keep up.

'Many things, Delmar. Many things,' his father said, moving quickly between the horses' stalls. 'I have seen marvels. Experienced wonder. I have touched the edge of existence and my eyes have been opened.'

'Here,' his father said, stopping at the stall of Delmar's horse. 'Put a saddle on Heinrich and let us be gone.'

Delmar hesitated.

'What is the matter?' his father asked.

'Is this for the night? Is it for good? I... I cannot just leave.'

His father looked at him for a moment, then saddled the horse himself. 'I am leaving, Delmar. Stay if you wish, but if you do, you shall not see me again.'

'Wait! That is not fair!' Delmar exclaimed. 'Of course I wish to come with you. But I have taken oaths...'

'Then all you have done is lie to liars. Do not concern yourself with your oaths, for they do not if it does not suit their interest.'

Delmar reached into his saddlebag.

'Let me then at least leave a note for Lord Griesmeyer. I shall not mention anything, but merely say that I left of my own accord.'

His father pulled himself into the saddle.

'Leave your note then,' he said. 'But your Lord Griesmeyer will never read it.'

Delmar looked up at his father and saw again the blood on his clothes, on his hand.

'Do not judge me, Delmar,' his father said. 'He took your father from you. He took my life from me. It was quicker than he deserved.'

Delmar took a step back, then steadied himself against his horse.

'If it is any comfort,' his father continued, 'he died with honour. Such honour as he had left.'

'Give me your hand, Delmar,' his father reached out. 'Give me your hand. We must go. We must go now.'

Delmar looked up at his father. His hero. His measure of nobility. He looked at the bloodied hand held out towards him. Sigmar help him, he took it.

The white gate was unbarred and open for them. Delmar could see no sign of the sergeants that should be at posts there. Instead, as they rode through, Delmar saw the shadows shift in the corner of his eye. He turned but the movement was gone. His father paid it no heed and guided Heinrich through the quiet streets towards the tenements of the poor quarter. The houses' windows were all battened and shut, those refugees who'd stayed lay crammed in the gutters and did not look up as the lone horse walked by. A pox had begun to spread amongst the poorest of Altdorf and the word was out that the refugees were to blame.

As they rode, his father pressed Delmar for details of his life, the estates, his grandfather and mother. Delmar related all he could remember, and then asked him of how he had returned to them. His father grew quiet; he spoke softly of his time as a captive of the Skaelings, how he had been sold as a slave to another tribe further north, of his failed attempts to escape and, finally, how he had rendered such service to his master that he had been freed.

'When was this?' Delmar asked. His father appeared fit and strong, he was not fresh from a slavedriver's whip.

'Over five years past now.'

'Five years?' Delmar gasped. 'You stayed away so long.'

'I was freed, Delmar, but I was not free. I had obligations to meet and debts to repay. If I had fallen in the midst of them, well, I did not want you to have your father returned to you only to have him snatched away again.'

'But now you are done? You are free?'

'No. But I had to come back now. I had to because of you, Delmar. You have disappointed me.'

Delmar felt a hole open in his chest as he heard his father's words. 'Disappointed? How?'

'When I heard you had joined the order, when I heard that you had left your mother and your grandfather behind to pursue your own self-ish ambition.'

'What?' Delmar gasped. 'It was nothing of the kind. They wanted me to come.'

'They wanted to be left alone? Vulnerable? Eking by on what little fortune the family has left until some passing marauder takes even that from them?'

Delmar could not believe it. For all his life he had hoped for his father to return, had dreamed it, but never had he conceived that he would return for this.

'I do not understand, I thought it was my duty. I thought it was your duty, your path that I was to follow.'

'You will learn, Delmar, that you will make mistakes that you cannot correct. Only pray that your child does not make the same ones.' His father carried on riding calmly. 'I know now that my prayers were in vain.'

'Here.' His father pulled Heinrich up into a small walled courtyard amongst the tenements. 'We shall spend the rest of the night here.'

He dismounted, tied the horse up and locked the gates behind them.

'And what will we do tomorrow?' Delmar asked, following his father into the house.

'Tomorrow,' his father said, walking down the steps into the cellar, 'we take you back home. Where you belong.'

'Home?' Delmar said. 'I can't just go home. I've sworn to the order, they need me.'

'Need you? Need you more than your family?' his father replied. He looked at Delmar. 'Oh, I understand now. You thought the order was waiting, expectant, for you to arrive at their door. That they would laud you and praise you, because you were special? That they would give you some magic sword and dispatch you to Middenheim, where you would stand against the Chaotic horde beside Helborg and Karl Franz and that they would look to you to save the city? You live in a fantasy, Delmar. No, if you stayed you would serve and you would die and be little more than a footnote. Just as I was. You do not choose your fate in the Reiksguard, it is chosen for you.'

Delmar looked down, confused. Yes, he had dreams, what young man did not? But there were dreams, and there was duty. He looked back up at his father.

'If service is all the order can offer me, then it is all I require. And the only sword they gave me, Father,' Delmar reached back and drew his blade, 'is yours.'

'The only sword that is mine, Delmar, is the one I carry within me.' His father held up his bloodied hand and, with a stroke of shadow, his hand and forearm flattened and discoloured, transforming into a bloodied blade. He drew a spiral in the air with its point and, wherever it touched, it leeched the colour from the world.

'You see, Delmar, the Reiksguard is nothing. Your oaths to them are nothing. Give them up and come home with me.'

'No,' Delmar said. His father's sword-arm drew a circle at Delmar's feet and the ground burst into a grey flame.

'Do not disappoint me again,' his father ordered. He gestured again and Delmar's sword melted through his hands.

'No!' Delmar bellowed, and that sharp smell once more burst in his sinuses.

The grey glow dimmed around the illusionist and a sergeant opened the cover from around the lantern. Verrakker checked on Delmar, but the novice had already fallen back into a natural sleep.

'We are finished here,' Verrakker announced. 'Go and prepare the next.' He nodded at the sergeant, who ushered the illusionist out of the cell.

One other figure remained. A woman. A crone, doubled over. She hobbled over to the bed where Delmar lay.

'If,' the crone began, 'my last maternal feeling had not already been burnt from me, I might almost feel sorry for the boy.'

Verrakker did not reply. He did not enjoy this testing, but he knew better than anyone how necessary it was. He had overheard the novices and their talk; they had thought the test of the spirit would be one of simple courage. To face a monster, perhaps. They had had little idea of what the enemies of the Empire were capable of. The dark mages and daemons that whispered in a man's mind to plague them with their most personal terrors, or tempt them with corrupting dreams of glory. Too many strong men had been lost, not to fear, but to pride. The belief that they were greater than their oaths, that their ambition trumped the order's own. Too many had fallen and turned their swords against their homes. Truly, man's most determined foes came from his own ranks.

The crone continued her inspection. 'The father, though,' she tutted, 'so predictable. All these boys, driven by their fathers, one way or another. Never a thought for their mothers. No.'

'We are finished,' Verrakker interrupted. 'Let us move on.'

'Oh, I am in no hurry,' the crone continued. 'You let me out of my hole so little, you cannot blame me for savouring the moment.' She played her splintered nails across Delmar's sleeping face.

'Do not touch him!' Verrakker ordered and grabbed her hand away. The crone whipped about, her free hand going for his neck, and Verrakker grabbed it and held both puny wrists in a single grip.

The crone, hands pinned together, smiled up at him. Her blind eyes flickered from side to side.

'I do not need to use my talent to know this boy's fate. Testing, acceptance, service, a little glory, death, a modest memorial, then oblivion. Same as his father. Yours, however...'

The crone stretched out her smallest finger and placed it against Verrakker's wrist, below his glove. 'Your destiny is far more interesting, Master Verrakker.'

'Do not think that you may read my weakness as easily as this boy's. I am one of the inner circle and I have faced far worse than you.' Verrakker replied, his voice level, his composure like steel. 'As to my destiny, I reconciled myself to that long ago.'

The crone tried to spit at him, but nothing but dry air reached Verrakker's face. He tightened his grip around her wrists in warning.

'Break them then, if you wish,' the crone declared. 'I can do nothing to stop you. But I know you will not. For the first fate we learn to read is our own.'

Verrakker paused for a moment, then pushed the crone away. She rubbed her wrists.

'It amuses me greatly,' the crone said, as she ran her hands over her shaven scalp and retied the last vestiges of hair into a braid.

'What has?'

'That you bring me out to use the very gift for which you keep me in my cage.'

'Your "gift" was not our concern, though there are witch hunters and templars enough to burn you for that alone. I would have cared not if you had spent your life where you were, reading commoners' fates. But to try to read the fate of an emperor? To know his terrors and temptations? That I care about a great deal.'

'An emperor who died only a few years after? Do you not wonder, Verrakker, if the Reiksguard had let me read him whether he might have been saved? Do you not wonder why I did it, knowing I was destined to fail? Do not answer, I can tell you do.'

'Hence you serve your purpose, and it is that alone that has kept you alive for all these years.'

The crone chuckled. 'When you threaten the life of one who knew their fate before she could even speak, Verrakker, you sound like a fool.'

'On,' Verrakker ordered, his tone brooking no further postponement, 'you have delayed long enough. On to the next.'

'Yes, on,' the crone concurred. 'Let us see what you have next for old "Brother Purity".'

Two of the novices did not return from the trial of the spirit.

The novices were excused services and gathered in the Great Hall for the morning meal. Siebrecht was the first there. He was still shaky, but already the details of the vivid dream he had had during the night were fading. As he saw the haunted look upon the faces of the first novices who joined him, though, he knew that some machination of Verrakker's had been at work.

Siebrecht watched as Delmar, Falkenhayn, Proktor, Hardenburg, Gausser, Bohdan and finally Alptraum, entered the Great Hall and took their seats. No one could explain what had happened to them, but Siebrecht could guess. Proktor said that he had seen Harver's possessions being taken away, and there was no doubt in any of the novices' minds that whatever test they had faced, he had failed.

Siebrecht could surmise why. The accident with Breigh had affected him greatly. Carrying such guilt, a man's spirit could easily be broken. Unlike Breigh, however, Harver would never be allowed back. Harver, though, was not Siebrecht's first concern. The face that he most expected to see, most wanted to see, did not appear.

'My lord, my lord Verrakker,' Siebrecht interrupted the knight when he appeared in the Great Hall.

'Matz, what are you doing? Novices should not be speaking at meals.'

'Where is Gunther?' Siebrecht's determined expression convinced Verrakker not to try to quiet him there, within the hall that was quickly filling with hungry knights. Verrakker bustled Siebrecht outside.

'Show some courtesy,' he berated the novice as he went. 'If you cannot hold your questions for the proper time, at least have a respectful tongue in your mouth.' But Siebrecht did not care for Verrakker's censure, only the answers he might give.

'Where is Gunther?' he asked again.

'You mean Novice Krieglitz?'

'Yes, yes,' Siebrecht demanded. 'He did not return last night. He cannot have failed; I know him too well, my lord. If I have passed then he must too, for he has twice the courage that I do.'

'I cannot talk of it,' Verrakker said, but Siebrecht heard the note of hesitation in his voice.

'Please,' he asked and, in desperation, he added, 'brother?'

Verrakker relented. 'He received news last night that has meant that he has had to delay.'

'What news?'

'I cannot and I do not wish to say. And you will get no more from me.'

'But he is still here? He has not gone?'

'Yes, he is in a room in the upper corridors, but he is not to be seen or spoken with. Do you understand me, Siebrecht?'

'Perhaps next time, Novice Matz, you will recognise an order when I give it to you.'

Brother Verrakker was seriously displeased. He had been called to the guardhouse and there found the wretched novice in the corner of his cell and under the sergeants' watchful guard.

Even crammed into a corner, Siebrecht maintained his composure. 'In my defence, my lord, I did not see or speak with Novice Krieglitz.'

'Only because the sergeant saw you climb atop the antechapel and try to scale the side of the chapter house.'

'I would have succeeded as well,' Siebrecht muttered.

'Quiet!' Verrakker snapped and slammed his good hand down on the cell door. Siebrecht near jumped from his skin.

'It beggars belief, novice.' Verrakker did not shout or bawl; his voice was quiet, but no less chilling for that. 'That for all your attempts at dedication, you still carry this air about you. That your opinions, that you yourself, are somehow greater than this order. That you are more right than your superiors, and that therefore you may obey or refuse their instructions as you think fit. This order is not a pastime; it is not some indolent band of aristocrats playing at soldiers. It is a sacred duty and no one is greater than it, not you, not I, not the Reiksmarshal himself.'

'I am sorry, my lord. I truly am...' Siebrecht mumbled.

'I doubt it,' the knight interrupted. 'And it would not be enough, in any case. I realise now that you cannot help yourself saluting with one hand and biting your thumb with the other.'

Siebrecht struggled for something to say, but he could think of nothing.

Verrakker spoke again, his tone more level this time. 'Tell me this instead: why did you do it?'

Siebrecht's mind went blank for a moment, then every possible reason he could have had tumbled into his thoughts. His perverse amusement in defying the order; how if there was a secret he desperately wanted to know more about it; how he wanted Krieglitz back to help him endure the insufferable Reiklanders.

'Well, novice?'

Siebrecht scrabbled down through his own thoughts, and therein found his true reason.

'Because he is my brother,' Siebrecht said, unfolding himself and standing to his feet. 'And because a Reiksguard knight should not allow his brother to feel he has been abandoned. Not even at the last.'

Verrakker tested Siebrecht's gaze for a long moment, before finally speaking. 'Well put. Master Lehrer would be proud of you.'

'It is no rhetoric, my lord.'

'No. I realise.'

The silence stretched between them, Verrakker's knuckles twitching as he drummed his missing fingers.

'You have a day, Novice Matz, to reconsider your position within this order. Tomorrow night there is the novices' vigil and then their oaths. Until then, I do not want you in the citadel. Your uncle has agreed to take you into his custody for the duration. If you decide not to return after that time, then I will understand.'

Siebrecht nodded. Verrakker paused, deciding something for himself, and then continued. 'You caused a great deal of commotion, you realise? I would warrant that there are none within the chapter house, even those in a room along the upper corridors, who would not know of your actions or why you undertook them.'

Siebrecht understood the meaning in the knight's words. 'I thank you, my lord.'

'Thank me? You have nothing for which to thank me.'

'For a knight's judgement.'

For a moment Verrakker looked genuinely touched, then he scoffed at such flattery and left Siebrecht alone.

'If you had wanted information,' Herr von Matz scolded his nephew when he collected him, 'then I do not know why you did not simply ask me. Yes, the young Novice Krieglitz, a sad case, indeed.'

'What is?' Siebrecht asked. 'What is happening to him?'

'Not to him, rather to his father, the Baron von Krieglitz. He has been accused of consorting with dark powers.'

'What?' Siebrecht could not believe his ears.

'A rather melodramatic turn of phrase, I know, but not a charge to be taken lightly in any case.'

'Can it be true, uncle? I cannot believe that it can be true.'

'Who can say? Talabecland is rife with intrigue at present. Since their little internal coup all the noble families are manoeuvring themselves into position, each trying to undermine and outflank the other. And a scandalous legal charge has ever been a favoured weapon in the political armoury of the Talabheim families. Krieglitz's father is of little consequence himself, but his family's connections run straight up to the countess.'

'So this is just politicking. Talabheim will sort itself out and Gunther will be fine.'

'That would be true in any ordinary accusation, but this one has been endorsed by the Order of Sigmar. It is their investigation now.'

'The witch hunters?' Siebrecht gasped.

'Indeed,' Herr von Matz replied. 'Have you ever seen the witch hunters at work when they have discovered their prey? I have. A common family that I knew slightly. It was not the punishment that chilled me so, it was the hunters' dedication to it, their thoroughness. The woman was exposed as being tainted, mortally corrupted; she and her family were hounded from their home. They caught the husband there, and he refused to denounce her, so they burnt him. The witch hunters and their templars pursued the rest into the hills, but still that was not enough and they chased and chased, until finally their quarry was spent and they lay down on the cold hillside to die. I saw them bring the bodies back, the clothes cut open to reveal the marks of corruption. I remember thinking how small those marks were, and yet how significantly they were treated.

'She had asked me to stand as a witness of her character at the trial. I refused for I did not want their attention drawn to me. And I am glad I did so. That is why from that day forwards I have been careful to display my worship of Sigmar, Ulric, Taal and Rhya, Morr, Myrmidia, Manann, even though I hate the sea, Shallya and Verena. So that no matter what kind of templar may break down my door and drag me out, they will find me a model devotee of whatever god they worship.

'Fear evil men, Siebrecht, for they will take all you have and destroy all you are. But fear the good man with a righteous cause more, for they will do the same and convince you that they were right to do so.'

The dream of his father had unsettled Delmar and he had returned to Master Lehrer's library. After reading about Talhoffer and Ott, he had gone back often to learn more from the annals of the Reiksguard. He had discovered what had happened to Lehrer who, in his first campaign after taking his oaths, had lost both his legs to a scythed chariot on a campaign in the Southlands.

Delmar's favourite accounts, though, had been the ones that included his father. Searching back, Delmar had found his name mentioned in several records before Karl Franz. He had even found the listing of the knights of his father's vigil and saw his name there beside Griesmeyer's. Delmar had read of his father's first battles, but then there had been no mention of him at all for a year. Delmar thought back and realised that that was because it was the year that Delmar himself had been born. Heinrich von Reinhardt had returned to his estate to be with his wife.

A year on, there was his name again: a brief notation amongst those assigned to guard the Supreme Patriarch on some expedition to Ostermark. Then his name vanished once more. He had been injured on that expedition and had taken a long time to heal. Then there were swathes of notes from the period of Karl Franz's election. The Reiksguard prided itself on staying above political matters, but as the Emperor's guard they could not afford to remain ignorant of them, especially at such an uncertain time.

Afterwards, when Karl Franz led his first campaign against the Norse who plagued the coast of the Sea of Claws, there was Heinrich von Reinhardt. Delmar had read all he could about his father, yet there was one book which he had not yet had the courage to open.

'Ah...' Lehrer replied. 'I did wonder when you would finally ask to see it.'

Lehrer reached down below his desk and pulled out the volume. 'I have marked the passages that you will wish to read.'

It was a brief account, for the Reiksguard had not considered the battle against the survivors of the Skaeling tribe of any great significance. The war had already been won, after all; the fact that the fighting still continued was neither here nor there to the annalist. Furthermore only a few squadrons of Reiksguard knights were involved, and had only been left behind to placate Count Theoderic Gausser as the remaining regiments of the army returned home. The account merely reported the bare facts: the Count of Nordland's disastrous attack, Helborg's charge, then noted that the knights dispersed to cover the army's retreat. And then, Delmar could not believe it, it was literally a footnote: the death of Heinrich von Reinhardt was a footnote below the account of the battle.

Delmar read the line a dozen times, willing more to appear. 'Is this all?' he asked Lehrer.

'Not what you expected, is it.'

'This cannot be all there is.'

'You tell me, Novice Reinhardt. You are the one who has supposedly been paying attention when I have spoken of the internal functions of our order.'

'What else...? Wait,' Delmar realised, 'he's on the wall of remembrance.

And before a knight is added, you said there is a hearing to ensure that a knight did not pass through want of bravery.'

'That is correct. And there would have been a hearing in this instance, because of the circumstances.'

'What circumstances?'

'Brother Heinrich von Reinhardt died because he disobeyed the orders of his preceptor,' Lehrer explained. 'He broke ranks from his squadron and rode into the heart of the enemy. He did it for the noblest reasons to be sure, but to be a knight of the Reiksguard is to renounce one's own will and subject oneself to the will of another. It would have had to be deliberated. Alas...'

But Delmar was already moving through the shelves into the depths of the library. He returned a few minutes later, bearing an open document holster.

'It's empty.'

'Alas,' Lehrer continued, 'our records of those deliberations were taken from us. I was here by that time. I recall the master librarian then was quite put out by it.'

'Who took them?'

'The orders came from the inner circle. But the knight who took them was–'

'Griesmeyer.' The name jumped unbidden to Delmar's lips.

'Yes.'

Lehrer took the holster from the novice's hands and closed it. 'You should not consider it too unusual. Brother Griesmeyer was the only one who was with your father at the end. The deliberations were almost entirely his testimony. And they were great friends.'

'So I have been told.'

'I was relieved, in a way, when I heard that they were together when your father passed. I do hope that they had had a chance to put their differences behind them before the end.'

Delmar was still thinking of how he might retrieve those records when Lehrer's words sunk in.

'Put what behind them? I did not know of any argument between them. What were their differences?'

'Oh,' Lehrer remarked, placing his forefinger on his temple as if it would aid his recollection. 'Well, this was all a long time ago. I do not think I ever knew. They certainly were great friends as novices, and then after... But it was...' Lehrer rocked back thoughtfully in his chair.

'Yes, I remember, it was when your father came back from the Patriarch's expedition in Ostermark. That was the time I met you, in fact. Your grandfather brought you and your mother here. We thought that your father might heal quickly once he was back, but it was not so. Rather than keep you and your mother in lodgings in Altdorf, he decided to return to his estate for his convalescence. At that time, I am sure that he and Brother Griesmeyer were still as close as they ever were.

'When your father returned, it was after the election and so it must have been no more than a year later, but the two of them were much changed. They had previously been inseparable, but by then they were never seen in public together. There were stories of some terrible arguments between the two of them in private. I would never have spoken to them about it, but it was well known at the time. Still, when the new Emperor gave the call to march to the north, they both went. Perhaps being on campaign together again may have made the difference. I certainly hope it did.'

'Yes,' Delmar muttered.

'What of you, novice? Do you not have any memories of that time?'

'A few,' Delmar thought back. 'My mother, crying in the ursery. Over my father, I think. But then sometimes when I remember it I see him there as well, or a shape at least, of a man. A knight, most definitely a knight. So perhaps it was before he passed, but then it should not be that she was so distraught. I do not know.'

'Or perhaps they are several memories blended together,' Lehrer mused. 'Memory is an uncertain record when set against ink and parchment. I have discovered many people who will swear in all honesty that they remember as red what was blue, and as white what was black. Do not let it trouble you. Keep to your reins, Novice Reinhardt.'

The vigil began at dusk and was held in the Reiksguard's chapel, sited beside the chapter house's main chamber. The eight novices who still remained had processed in, wearing simple white shifts. They were each first interviewed by two knights, brothers that none of them had seen before, and questioned as to their beliefs, their faith, their families and whether there was any hidden infirmity or physical corruption that would prevent their serving the order. Once this was satisfactorily completed, they were reminded of the oaths that they were to swear, and of the rules and regulations of the order, and then they were left to pray.

There was little to see within the chapel. The interior was lit only by a few evenly spaced candles, and without the sun outside, the glorious scenes set in the stained-glass windows were dark and could not be seen.

Siebrecht knelt. His thoughts chased round and round his head. He told himself that though he did not know enough, there was no way he had at present of finding the answers, and so he should concentrate on being at peace. He settled his thoughts for a time, and then a minute would pass and he would notice Krieglitz's absence once more and the thoughts would chase around again.

Delmar knelt, and tried not to think. He tried not to think of how his father and Griesmeyer had knelt together in this exact same spot twenty-five years before at their own vigil. He tried not to think of his ancient memory of his mother in mourning, and yet another knight being there. He tried not to think of the chill in his mother's voice when she spoke of Griesmeyer or the look in her eyes when she saw her son with him. He tried not to think of the dream of his father and the doubts that it had placed in his mind. Above all, he tried not to think of that battle in which his father had paid his final service, and how the only witness to his last few minutes alive was Griesmeyer. Delmar tried not to think. He tried to pray, but to no avail. Either the gods did not hear him, or they had sent him these thoughts themselves.

The novices remained there until dawn when the light from the rising sun shone through the glass windows and the image of Sigmar Triumphant blossomed before them. They were led from the chapel into the chapter house where every brother of the order without duty had gathered. The novices recognised some of the knights, their tutors: Talhoffer, Ott, Verrakker, even Lehrer was there in his engineered chair, a cloak covering the stumps of his legs. In the centre sat the grand master, Reiksmarshal Kurt Helborg himself, the officers of the order by his side, and by them Delmar saw Griesmeyer, a smile of pride on his lips. Before the assembled order, the novices swore the solemn oaths of fraternity and, one by one, their names were called for the order's assent.

'Brothers of the Grand Order of the Reiksguard, here stand before us those who would join our ranks. Each one, the eldest son of a most noble family, and able to bear arms. They have proven themselves of sufficient strength in body, mind and spirit. They have sworn to uphold our duties and they have pledged themselves to our cause without doubt, without condition, without restraint. Will you call them brother?'

The eight of them, four Reiklanders, four Provincials, stood as a single squadron. Each man stepped forth when his name was called and, as the order confirmed him, the Reiksguard insignia was placed over his shoulders.

Delmar listened as the knight acclaimed each novice in turn: Alptraum of Averland, Bohdan of Ostermark, Falkenhayn, Gausser of Nordland, Hardenburg, and Siebrecht von Matz. When they reached Proktor, the knights' shout was so loud that it fair rattled the glass in the windows. Then came his turn.

'Delmar von Reinhardt?' the officer called.

'Aye!' The knights bellowed and cheered their new brothers.

And with that they became Reiksguard.

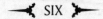

KRIEGLITZ

While the Emperor had been away, his palace had been in hibernation; once he was back it awoke with a surge of vitality. The Imperial officers returned and re-established themselves and their staffs in their appointed chambers. Servants bustled from room to room, preparing each so that no matter where the Emperor chose to walk he would find his path furnished and well fragranced against the smell of the city outside. Noblemen flocked back so that they might garner the Emperor's favour, and the Reiksguard tripled the palace guard to ensure that each of these different groups did not trespass where they should not.

'As part of the palace guard,' Verrakker briefed the new young knights, 'you must be ever vigilant, ready at a second's notice to halt an assassin or an enemy assault. What you will find, however, is that you spend most of your day telling some persistent perfumed fop of a courtier to step back and allow the Emperor his privacy.

'It is the Emperor's will when he wishes to make himself available and when he does not. It is their duty to obey, and not to substitute their own wishes for his. No matter who they are. They will all be noblemen and lords, unused to being denied. Some may even try to pull rank over you; if they try they shall not be successful.'

Delmar, Siebrecht and the other young knights laughed.

'And finally, I would remind you all: though it is rarely glorious, being a guard at the palace is one of the most solemn duties within the Reiksguard. A lapse on your part could be the means by which our Emperor is murdered, a civil war erupts and the Empire collapses in flames. So consider that. And then consider that any negligence, any dereliction, any reckless act committed whilst on this duty is considered treason. And guards have, and will continue to be, executed for that crime.'

The problem of protecting the Emperor was made all the more difficult by the Imperial Palace itself. Though the Reikland princes had only been elected to the Imperial throne a hundred years previously, the palace had been built

371

long before. Some even said that part of its structure dated back to the first
time Altdorf had been the capital of the Empire, centuries ago. The place
itself had been built and rebuilt, extended and redesigned as it had been put
to different uses over the years. This rate of expansion only increased when
the emperors took occupancy and adapted it to be the principal seat of government. Separate buildings were sited nearby for these purposes and, as
the palace grew still further, these buildings were connected and subsumed
into the whole. A past Imperial architect had described the result as, 'a residence where the differing architectural styles were not so much at odds as
in outright conflict,' and had begged the emperor of his day for the funds to
build a fresh palace anew. Those funds, once collected, instead were spent
quelling a provincial uprising, leading the architect to append to his previous comment the words, 'and therefore the palace is as fitting a symbol for
the Empire as anything.'

Architectural symbolism aside, this left the palace in some areas full of
grand reception halls and elegant apartments, in others a maze of uneven
courtyards and twisting passages, and all the more difficult to guard as a
result. Exploring the buildings, learning his way around, kept Siebrecht
from his thoughts for his first few days on guard. But as the novel quickly
became the routine, he found himself brooding again over his friend's troubles. There was little else to distract him; the courtiers, for all Verrakker's
warnings concerning their tenacity, had learned from grim experience that
arguing with the impassive Reiksguarders was at best a waste of breath,
and at worst would find them exiled from court after a short stay in the
palace's cells.

The Emperor himself had pared his schedule of public appearances to
the bone and made it plain to all that his first, last and only order of business at present was the ongoing conduct of the war, and that he would
not entertain any personal applications. Instead, his day was dominated
by meetings of the Council of State; the members of that council quickly
became familiar faces to Siebrecht and the other young knights. This merely
added to Siebrecht's frustration, however; in the next room from him the
most senior members of the government were in discussions that were
deciding the future of the Empire, and yet he was stuck outside warding
away the unwelcome. The council members themselves treated the knights
as little more than pieces of furniture and ignored Siebrecht's presence even
as he stepped smartly aside to let them pass. Siebrecht silently nursed a
grievance at such treatment; he was not a servant, he was a noble lord and
now a knight of the grandest military order. It was all yet another example
of Reiklander arrogance. Yet then he overheard something that cast such
petty thoughts from his mind.

'But if he should ask about Karak Angazhar, I would not know what to
say...'

The speaker was Baron von Stirgau, Chamberlain of the Seal and the

Emperor's diplomatic advisor. Karak Angazhar was the name of the dwarfen hold that his uncle had mentioned weeks before. Siebrecht had given it little more thought at the time, however now he found it being discussed at the highest levels. Baron von Stirgau quietened his conversation before entering the council chamber, but he had not cared about speaking before Siebrecht, standing immobile beside the entrance. Perhaps there was an advantage to being treated as part of the furniture after all. The council meetings were held in seclusion with the Emperor and even Reiksguard knights were not privy to them; however, Siebrecht could piece together much from what the councillors said privately to each other before they entered and as they left.

'...retreated to the Middle Mountains, our silver mines there are lost...'

'...still no word from Count Feuerbach, and now this scandal in a noble family, Talabheim is on the edge...'

'...last we saw them was Krudenwald, but an army such as that cannot simply disappear...'

'...a dozen more bodies hanging from trees, not that I'd mourn the loss of such scum, but better human scum than that which is replacing them...'

'...who is in power down there. Is it anyone?'

'...the Cult of Sigmar have their own problems at present, I should leave them be...'

Siebrecht absorbed it all, inferred and speculated on what he could. He was missing many of the specifics, but he could gather what desperate straits the Empire was in: three of its grand provinces devastated by the northern war; two more without clear leadership; their recent allies increasingly distracted by their own concerns; a canker was left near its heart, defeated but not destroyed; and money.

'...think the regiments will be disbanded anytime soon, you are much mistaken...'

'...he cannot afford to do it, he cannot afford not to do it...'

'...I do not believe that for a moment...'

'...but where is the money to come from?'

Money needed for the troops; money needed to rebuild walls, roads, cities, farms; and from the sour look upon the face of Chancellor Hochsvoll and the way she uneasily toyed with the rings upon her grasping fingers, it was money the Empire did not have.

But Siebrecht did not hear any further mention of Karak Angazhar until one hot night at the height of summer. Siebrecht was stationed immediately outside the council chamber; council meetings were typically formal, sedate affairs, but this time the voices were raised and Siebrecht could hear them.

'I appreciate the tremendous difficulties of our situation in the north, it only makes it all the more imperative that we secure our border to the south as well.' Siebrecht recognised the voice of Count von Walfen, the Chancellor of Reikland and, it was said, the Emperor's personal spymaster.

'I do not understand why the dwarfs cannot help themselves,' Chancellor Hochsvoll replied, her tone icy even in this heat.

Baron von Stirgau sought to explain in his distinguished intonation. 'The ambassador from the High King has been very open concerning this. Both their strongholds of Barak Varr and Karak Hirn have been besieged; the attackers have been driven off, but at such cost that they cannot send out an expedition to relieve Karak Angazhar.'

'If they do not care sufficiently to defend it, why should we?'

'Because of its location, chancellor,' Walfen repeated. 'It is at the head of the Upper Reik and no more than a few days' march from Black Fire Pass. If it should fall, it would be the perfect staging post for all manner of attacks into Averland, all our defences in the pass itself would be out-flanked and rendered useless, and we would forever be under the threat of attacks launched down the Reik river itself. The dwarfs would survive it, but we would not. Our southern lifeline could be cut.'

'You mean the trading routes would be cut,' Hochsvoll retorted. 'Do not think I am unaware of your interests in that area.'

'The Empire's interests, do you mean? Or do you consider that the main-tenance of healthy, profitable and above all, taxable trading routes to be of no interest to the Imperial coffers?'

'Future revenues are all well and good, but who is going to pay for it now?' Chancellor Hochsvoll retorted.

'It is not money which is the issue,' the bass voice of the Reiksmarshal Kurt Helborg interrupted, 'it is men. The army is still needed in the north. Despite what you might hear people say in the streets, the war is still being fought.'

'Could you not simply spare a handful of regiments?' Baron von Stir-gau asked.

'No.' The Reiksmarshal's tone brooked no refusal.

'Well, what about the mercenary armies?' Stirgau continued.

'And who would pay for those?' Hochsvoll began again.

'There are still troops in Averland, Reiksmarshal,' Walfen interceded.

'Averland's regiments marched north, Wissenland's as well.'

'I was referring to the Reikland garrisons that we have maintained in Averland these last two years. Since the unfortunate death of Elector Count Leitdorf.'

'They are with the army as well.'

'Not all of them.'

This flat refutation provoked Helborg, already hot and tired. 'Do not question my knowledge of the positioning of the Empire's troops.'

'I do not question your knowledge,' Walfen's emphasis was slight but noticeable, 'indeed, I rely upon it. I know that you have a sound strate-gic mind and therefore would not strip our southern provinces entirely of their defences. And I also know that that is where you still send their pay. So, if we may proceed on the basis that there are still men in those garrisons?'

But Kurt Helborg was not to be so easily outflanked. 'There are men left there, but very few. Only enough to ensure that when this current crisis is past, we still have defences in place to ensure we can protect that border. They are not to be frittered away on an ill-judged expedition.'

'They should not be needed to fight, Reiksmarshal, merely to help recruitment.'

'Recruitment of whom?'

'There are still men in Averland. Men able to carry a halberd and march to a drum. The state troops are with the army, that's true, but there are still men there able to fight.'

'Yes, in case of invasion. In case their towns and homes are threatened.'

'If Karak Angazhar is not relieved then that is exactly what will happen.'

'You may convince us here of that,' Helborg intoned, 'but words will not convince the aldermen of Averheim, Streissen or Heideck to allow us to raise their militias, and there is no Elector Count of Averland to aid you.'

Walfen was ready to play his hand. 'Which is why we will need to send one regiment, but only one regiment. But it must be a regiment whose mere presence will inspire the militias to form, who will convince the aldermen of the towns of Averland of the great importance of this expedition to the Empire, that the eyes of the Emperor himself are upon them. And it must be a regiment which is not needed in the north, and indeed has already returned to the city.'

His meaning was clear even to Siebrecht.

'You mean the Reiksguard,' Helborg said.

'Yes, I do.'

'They have only just returned.'

'I am sure they will not be reluctant to fulfil their duty and to march again to war.'

'Soldiers should always be reluctant to march to war, baron. It is amateurs who are eager for it.'

Siebrecht had to imagine the look of distaste and contempt Helborg gave Walfen at that moment. Then someone was talking, but they were quiet and he could not make out their voice. It must be the Emperor, he realised, giving his final verdict on the matter.

'As you command, my lord,' Helborg finally said, 'I will ensure the necessary arrangements are made as quickly as possible.'

The Graf von Falkenhayn did not care for celebratory balls; in his younger days he had used the family ballroom for fencing instruction, and to house his model recreations of the epic battles from the history of the Empire. That usage, however, changed when he married; his wife, the Gravine von

Falkenhayn, cared for balls very much. And he cared for her. So out went the swords, armour, miniatures and scenery, and the gravine set to work to make the room a suitable location for her and the graf to celebrate the events of the season. Their ballroom could not compete in size with the grand ballroom of the Imperial Palace, but that did not prevent her from challenging her rival in every other respect. The walls were festooned with golden ornaments and silver mirrors. On the ceiling was an epic mural of the founding of Altdorf, and over each arch, a gilded falcon stood with its wings outstretched. She made the room fit indeed, and this evening there were several hundred of her closest friends there to admire it. For her son, Franz, had been accepted into the Reiksguard and there was absolutely no one of her acquaintance who should not have the opportunity to attend and congratulate her personally.

Everywhere that Siebrecht looked he saw young noblemen and women talking, dancing, drinking and enjoying themselves. Everywhere except right beside him.

'I do not understand why we came.' Bohdan's disaffection caused his heavy Ostermark accent to sound all the harsher.

Beside them, Gausser grunted. His attention was fixed on the delicate wine saucer he held between his big fingers and trying not to snap it in two.

'It's a ball. We were invited,' Siebrecht reminded them cheerfully, trying to raise their spirits and failing.

'And what are we to the Gravine von Falkenhayn that she should invite us, I wonder?' Bohdan mistrusted any large gathering of nobility. There were too many Ostermarker tales of such evenings where, at the height of the festivities, the outside doors were locked and the hosts, daemons in human form, began a far bloodier feast. He had not yet spotted the wife of the Graf von Falkenhayn, but he was not going to relax his guard an instant.

'Listen,' Siebrecht explained again, 'Falkenhayn wanted his precious Falcons along, of course, but with the delegation from Averland as the guests of honour, the gravine wanted Alptraum here, and Alptraum wanted us, his fellow vigil-brothers, along so he did not have to spend the whole evening with the Reiklanders.'

Alptraum need not have worried, Siebrecht reflected, for as soon as the young knight had arrived he had been swooped upon by the Averland nobles, each eager to update him with news of the latest political manoeuvrings in the province and enrol him in their cause. Behind the scenes in the leaderless province, the families were fighting tooth and nail for every advantage and now that Alptraum was a knight of the Reiksguard, he had become a far more significant piece on their game board.

Gausser grunted again. Bohdan was staring suspiciously at an elderly baroness with pale, withered skin and sunken cheeks who was seated nearby. He glared at her hard until she, rather unsettled, got shakily to her feet and moved away.

Siebrecht rolled his eyes at his comrades' behaviour and, despite his original intention, decided that all their evenings would be best served if he and they parted company. As the next group of revellers swung past, he slipped away and made for the opposite corner of the ballroom. He sashayed around the dancers in the centre of the room, assessing the event with an experienced eye. Ostentatious simplicity was the fashion for the season, Altdorf society's acknowledgement of the deprivation that everyone else in the Empire suffered. The ladies were garbed in simple lines which were all the more expensive to tailor, while the noblemen wore military uniforms, at least all of them who could lay claim to one. The rest made do with clothes cut in a similar fashion. Despite the myriad regimentals on display, Siebrecht was pleased that his own Reiksguard uniform still caught the eye of many of the young ladies waiting for young men to ask them to dance.

Young men, his treacherous mind added, who would otherwise be present if they had not been left behind on the plains of Middenland. Siebrecht quashed the thought instantly; he had had precious few chances of enjoying such occasions since his arrival in Altdorf and he was not going to ruin this one with useless lamentation.

He took a moment's casual repose beside the sculpture of a falcon about to take flight. He had spotted the Reiklanders on his journey: Falkenhayn was holding court as usual to anyone who would listen, his faithful Proktor was by his side ready to confirm all his boasts, Delmar was looking uncomfortable and awkward, and the fair-faced Hardenburg was heavily engaged with a string of soppy-eyed girls. Hardenburg, Siebrecht decided, had the right idea and he was about to introduce himself to a promising noble daughter dallying nearby when another familiar face caused him to forget his original purpose entirely.

'Uncle?'

Herr von Matz turned, glass in hand, and exclaimed: 'Siebrecht, my boy!'

He excused himself from his conversation and unsteadily navigated a path to his nephew.

'Uncle?' Siebrecht asked. 'What are you doing here?'

Herr von Matz looked at him, slightly dazed. 'It is a festivity, is it not? So I am being festive!' he replied, taking another gulp of his drink.

'I cannot believe it. Are you drunk?'

With his free hand, his uncle grabbed him by the shoulder and leaned in close. Siebrecht, no lightweight himself, fair recoiled from the stink of wine emanating from him.

'Not at all, my dear boy,' Herr von Matz whispered, quickly and crisply, all trace of intoxication gone. 'But one finds that drinkers and sots are far more loose-tongued around their own kind than those who maintain a sober disposition, and so one must, alas, adopt all the pretence with none of the pleasure.'

'Your stench is certainly convincing,' Siebrecht muttered, trying not to breathe through his nose.

'Ah, a necessary evil, and the laundry a necessary expense. But what of you? You should be enjoying yourself, a young warrior off to war and all that.'

'You heard of that? We only learned of it today!'

'Heard of it? I predicted it, did I not? Karak Angazhar!'

'Aye, uncle, so you did,' Siebrecht acknowledged. 'Does your network of informants now extend to knowing the Emperor's own mind before he does?'

Herr von Matz chortled. 'Nothing of the kind, Siebrecht. There was some inside knowledge, yes, but the rest was merely the comprehensive application of thought and an understanding of the unspoken reasons.'

Siebrecht glanced away at that.

'Ah, I see your mind has begun to work like that as well,' Herr von Matz continued. 'It is not a pleasant path. You will find no heroes or villains upon it, merely fellow travellers like myself. So, Karak Angazhar! You will be marching the day after tomorrow, up alongside the River Reik, I imagine, riding as quickly as you can. Allowing your supplies to be brought up by boat. Recruit what militia you can along the way and then up into the mountains.'

'Taal's teeth, uncle. Did you have a spy in the chapter house today?' Every detail his uncle had told him was exactly the same as the Reiksmarshal had dictated to the assembled order earlier that day.

'Yes, of course,' he replied, bemused.

'Who?'

'You!'

Siebrecht was taken aback. 'Me? I did not tell you a thing.'

'That is because you are not a very good spy! Not yet, at least.' Herr von Matz scoffed. 'You think I need a spy in the chapter house to know the Reiksguard are preparing to leave? You can tell simply by watching the place through the gate! You think the sudden burst of feverish labour that heralds the order's departure goes unnoticed? That your suppliers can magic their goods into your store houses without sending urgent messages around the city to gather what they can?'

Another fact clicked into place in Siebrecht's mind. 'Our suppliers. The guildmarks?'

Herr von Matz smiled encouragingly at his nephew as one would at a puppy who has learnt his first trick.

'That might tell you that we were leaving, perhaps even when we would depart. But not the route we would take, nor that we would be raising troops along the way.'

'Both eminently deducible, my boy. But I will admit that I have had help besides my inference in this matter. The Reiksmarshal did tell you that you would be joined by some Averland worthies who had arrived in the city and would be accompanying you to aid in raising the troops.'

'Yes, as soon as the news went out the gravine tracked them down and made them all the guests of honour tonight,' Siebrecht replied innocently, but his thoughts were catching up with him.

'Well? You did ask what I was doing here?' Herr von Matz reached into his jacket and brought out a feather dyed yellow and black, the colours of Averland.

'You're part of the Averland delegation?' Siebrecht was astonished.

'Correct, and we were given the path of your march, I mean our march, at the same time as you were.'

'What possible reason would they have to…? You're not even from Averland.'

Herr von Matz was affronted. 'I will have you know that I am well known in Averland.'

'I imagine that you are well known in many places.' Siebrecht contained his sarcasm.

'Indeed,' his uncle replied, pleased at himself as much as his nephew. 'It will be pleasant to spend more time with you,' Herr von Matz continued. 'And now our subsequent meeting is established I will allow you to get on and enjoy the evening.'

Siebrecht merely nodded as his uncle turned away.

'One last thing,' Herr von Matz said, turning back. 'A question I perhaps should have asked you before. Karak Angazhar.'

'Yes?'

'Why are you going?'

'The Reiksmarshal said…' Siebrecht recollected, 'that it is the old alliance. They are attacked in Barak Varr and Karak Hirn, and after aiding us in the north they cannot mount an expedition of their own.'

'Hmmm… that was what you were told. Why do you think you are going?'

Siebrecht considered it. 'The trading routes. If Karak Angazhar should fall then so would Black Fire Pass and our trading routes with the High King would be cut. Trade we desperately need if we are to rebuild after this war.'

'Good… but let me ask again. Why are you going?'

Now Siebrecht knew what his uncle was driving at. 'To serve well. Make my name. So that I will have the privilege to restore our family's fortunes.'

'And…?' Herr von Matz prompted him. 'Resist the urge to plunge your breast onto the enemy's sword.'

'Aye,' Siebrecht replied with good humour.

'And do not forget it.'

Siebrecht wandered back through the white gate. The sergeants there regarded him warily, and he waved at them happily. They would not trouble him tonight, not returning from the Gravine von Falkenhayn's illustrious ball and with a campaign the day after tomorrow. Siebrecht had cheer in his heart. In spite of his uncle's appearance, he had enjoyed himself immensely, and was happily on the other side of the cup. He had sorely missed such evenings since coming to Altdorf.

He made his way into the buildings and threaded his way through the corridors for several minutes before he realised that he was heading back to the novices' dormitory. Since he and his brothers had become full brother-knights, their belongings had been taken from the novices' quarters and into the other wing. He dutifully turned around and tried to find his way to his bed.

On his travels he passed the arming room, and a light inside caught his eye. A single candle flame illuminated the figure inside. It was Krieglitz. The novice was in the middle of strapping himself into armour. It was not the ceremonial plate that they wore as sentries at the palace, it was a full suit of plate. What a Reiksguard knight wore when he went to war.

'Gunther?'

Krieglitz looked up.

'Ah, it's you. Help me on with this, Siebrecht, will you?'

'What are you doing?'

Krieglitz raised the half-fastened elbow cowter.

'What does it look like?'

His smile was there, but it was not the generous expression with which Siebrecht was familiar. It was dark. Bitter.

'Gunther,' he said again slower, 'what are you doing?'

Krieglitz caught the edge in Siebrecht's voice and stopped tying the piece of armour.

'What are you saying, Siebrecht? You can't be thinking that I would...'

'I don't know what to think,' Siebrecht snapped back, his mind quickly clear again. 'You vanish for days. No one sees you. There are all these stories...'

'Stories?' Krieglitz chuckled. 'I would have taken that big lug Gausser to be the gullible one, not you, my friend.'

'Then tell me, what is the truth?' Siebrecht took his brother's arm. 'All I hear of is accusations and trials.'

'Yes, my family are having difficulties.' Krieglitz brushed him away. 'But these allegations, they are all political. How can a son of Nuln, of all people, not recognise politics when he sees it?'

'But the witch hunters are involved, Gunther. If the witch hunters are involved, then this is above politics.'

'Ah, enough gold will turn a witch hunter's head as easily as any other man's,' he dismissed, but without conviction. 'Another one came this morning.'

'What did he say?'

'He said,' Krieglitz mocked, 'that there was evidence enough that my family... my father... has a taint.' He spat the last word.

Siebrecht felt his stomach drop. The witch hunters were strange men, rarely wanted, never liked, but they would pursue any hint of mortal corruption without restraint.

Neither of them spoke for a long moment. Krieglitz's eyes were fixed on the flame of the slowly burning candle.

'What did the constable say?' Siebrecht eventually asked.

'He told the witch hunter… that the order has jurisdiction over the order's affairs. But that as I was not yet a brother of the order…' Krieglitz trailed off. Then he looked away from the candle and straight at Siebrecht. 'I am to return home, and there to share my family's fate.'

'I'm certain you will defend your name. There can be nothing to these charges, but smoke.'

'Aye, smoke, yes.' Krieglitz drifted off again. Siebrecht saw his friend needed help.

'Shouldn't you be packing then? If you are going home?' He wanted to get Krieglitz out of this dark place.

'It's all being taken care of. They told me I need not concern myself.' Krieglitz looked at the cowter afresh. 'I came down here… I wanted to know what it was to wear it all. I wanted to feel what it was like; before I left.'

'You'll be back soon enough,' Siebrecht said, knowing he could only offer cold comfort. 'A crown of mine says you'll be back before the month is out.'

'Hah, I'll take that bet. Still, I would like to know now. Help me on with this, my friend.' Siebrecht did so, and soon Krieglitz stood in the full regalia of a Reiksguard knight.

'How does it feel?' Siebrecht asked.

'Good. It's light. The Reiklanders were right: it is lighter than the practice plate.' Krieglitz inspected himself. 'Do you remember, Siebrecht, when Master Lehrer taught us the meaning of every single piece of this armour?'

Krieglitz lifted his right shoulder pauldron an inch. 'You remember what these stood for?'

Siebrecht did. 'Brotherhood.'

'For a knight stands shoulder to shoulder with his brothers,' Krieglitz recited. 'As the pauldrons defend a knight from the gravest strokes, likewise a knight is defended by his brothers and without them is in peril of death.'

Krieglitz paused for a moment, then continued. 'How do I feel? I feel strong. I feel connected. Like a true brother.'

'I'll help you take it off,' Siebrecht offered.

'Wait, I would take a turn in it. I would like to walk a way, feel how it moves.'

Krieglitz led the way, through the corridors. Siebrecht had expected the armour to make a fearful noise, but it was quiet, so well constructed and maintained that the plates slid over each other with ease.

'Have you heard of the inner circle?' Krieglitz asked as they walked.

'I've heard the name. They are some of the older knights, no?'

'Oh, they are that. But they are much more. You know the power a sin-gle Reiksguard knight carries. Imagine the power that those who direct the actions of hundreds of knights have. Knights who serve by the Emper-or's side, who guard his rooms in the palace. Knights who campaign with every Imperial general.'

'I can well believe it. What of them?'

'I have a mission from them. I can say no more, not even to you.'

They stepped out of the building. Above them the stars and moons shone in the dark.

'I'm going to walk a little further,' Krieglitz announced.

'Gunther, no.'

'Just once around the walls.'

'Then I will come with you.'

'No, Siebrecht. It is you who drag me into mischief, remember?'

'You'll get yourself in trouble, Gunther.'

Krieglitz laughed. 'They can hardly do any more to me. Go. Go back. You cause a clamour and they'll find us both. I just need the air.'

Siebrecht hesitated; he thought to insist, but if Krieglitz resented his company then it might push him away still further. If he stayed within the walls, there was little harm he could do; and there were sentries enough to make leaving the citadel difficult even without a full suit of armour. 'You will not leave without saying farewell.'

'You have my oath as a Reiksguard knight,' Krieglitz said lightly.

'I'd rather have your wager. I think you value those greater.'

'If that were true, then I would be a sorry knight indeed.' Krieglitz held out his hand for Siebrecht to shake. 'I must prove to you the contrary, and hereby wager never to collect the crown you so rashly lost to me just now.'

Siebrecht took his hand and smiled. 'How much is the wager?'

'A crown, of course.'

'And that was the last you spoke to him.'

'Yes, constable. That was the end of it. He left and I returned to the dormitory,' Siebrecht stated again, but still the scribe wrote it down. The constable leaned back and stared at Siebrecht hard, as though he could strip away falsities and lies simply through his gaze. Siebrecht did not care how he looked at him. A few hours ago Siebrecht would have feigned courage to cover his fear, exercised his wit to prove he was not afraid, but now there was simply no fear to feel. Nothing of anything.

The search for Krieglitz had begun soon after first light, when a sergeant had gone to escort him to morning prayers and discovered that he had not returned. The constable had sent stewards down through the streets to pick up his trail. Before lunch they had returned with a ferryman who had a story to tell. By the afternoon, the order's strongest swimmers were diving into the Reik off the bridge. Before the sun went down, they had dragged poor Krieglitz's body out of the river.

They had not had to search far. The heavy Reiksguard armour had dragged Krieglitz straight down and anchored him to the muddy bottom. Once they pulled his body to the bank, the order stripped the armour off. Sergeants from the Marshal's household had collected it up and returned it to the citadel, for it to be cleaned, oiled and used again. As Siebrecht's uncle had often reminded him, a good set of armour was most expensive and not to be lightly cast aside. The body itself, however, was not returned to the chapter house. There was no place for an unquiet spirit in the Reiksguard's garden of Morr. A priest was found, who mumbled a few words over the body, and it was wrapped in a shroud for transportation.

'You saw no one else on your way back to your quarters.'

'No.'

'And there was nothing else that occurred that night, that you discussed? Think one last time please, Brother Matz.'

He had already told them everything, everything less Krieglitz's mention of the inner circle. Shattered as he was, Siebrecht could sense that such a revelation would make them redouble their questioning. He just wanted to leave, find a corner, find a drink.

He felt himself beginning to shake and saw the constable share a glance with the other knight: Griesmeyer. Siebrecht knew his name. He was the one Delmar had brought back to show off to the rest of the novices that day.

Griesmeyer leaned forwards and entered the conversation. 'We are not looking to place shame on others, Matz. Novice Krieglitz took that with him. You should not have assisted him with the armour, but you cannot blame yourself for his death.'

Siebrecht looked up at that. 'I do not blame myself! I blame the perjurers and the zealots who brought such baseless accusations, with no further cause than their own advancement. Rumours and lies, these are the weapons they wielded to kill my friend!'

Siebrecht felt the anger burn within him, and the constable and Griesmeyer shared another look. Griesmeyer nodded and then dismissed the scribe, who put down his quill and left. The constable followed him out. Griesmeyer turned back to Siebrecht.

'Rumours and lies there may have been, but the accusations were true,' Griesmeyer stated plainly. 'Baron von Krieglitz has been tried and condemned; there was unquestionable evidence of his physical corruption. Amulets imbued with dark power have been discovered in his household, to heal him they claimed. One of his stewards has been exposed as a practitioner of illegal magics and has been burned. The Countess of Talabheim has denounced that line of her family and allowed the Order of Sigmar to seize the baron's estate and possessions. The baron himself has disappeared, as has one of his sons. There can be no doubt.

This is the news that we brought Novice Krieglitz last evening before he saw you.'

Siebrecht reeled. All of Krieglitz's behaviour the night before, his protestations that there might be hope, had been pretence. Unlikely as it may have been, Siebrecht had never given up the belief that there might be some other explanation for what had happened to his friend, that there may have been some foul play or accident that had thrown him into the river. But if he had already been told that his father's taint was certain, if the inner circle already knew... In an instant, Siebrecht saw the thread that connected the discrepancies he had noted over the last day. His uncle's admonition rang in his head: understand the unspoken reasons.

'It is all a great tragedy.' Siebrecht straightened up; he found it easy to control himself now. 'But not as great a tragedy as if my unfortunate friend's shame had touched this most noble order. As you said, he has taken all that with him.'

Griesmeyer, noting the young knight's new composure, cautiously agreed. 'It is a great tragedy.'

'It is, in its own way, fortunate then that Novice Krieglitz's actions have allowed us to sever the order's ties with that family so speedily. That he was able to escape his custody last night and then that he, fully armoured, could scale our wall and slip past our keen-eyed sentries without raising the alarm. But then, can we ascribe it all to fortune? For surely there is no way to restrain a man who is determined to meet his end.'

Griesmeyer gave Siebrecht an odd look.

'Novice Krieglitz was never bound here. He was free to leave at will. As you all are. And as you say, a man who longs for death will find his way.'

Siebrecht saw a shadow fall over Griesmeyer's face for a moment, as though he were lost in remembrance. Then he stood to take his leave, but there was one more question Siebrecht wished him to answer.

'My lord Griesmeyer, if I may ask, you are a knight of the inner circle?'

'I am,' he replied. 'Your interest?'

'Just to know your lordship better.'

'There are few secrets here, Brother Matz, though active minds do wilfully perceive them where they are not. If to expunge your grief you must create your villains, then that is your concern; but do not drag your fellows down into your pit. For if you do, then it will no longer be your concern, it will be ours.'

'That is ridiculous, Siebrecht,' Gausser repeated.

'You weren't there. It was written across his face.'

They were out on the practice field, watching Bohdan conclusively trounce Hardenburg with the halberd. They stood apart from the Reiklanders, or perhaps the Reiklanders stood apart from them. It was only a day after Krieglitz's body had been found, and neither faction was eager to share company with the other.

'Was it written across this Griesmeyer's face?' Gausser asked. 'Or was it written across the inside of your eyes?'

Siebrecht was in no mood to be doubted.

'Ulric's teeth, brother, do you even remember Krieglitz? Just a few weeks ago he was standing here with us. Think back then, was there any of us less likely to take his own life? Bohdan over there is as strung as tight as a crossbow, Falkenhayn's so paranoid that he throws down a challenge at the slightest whiff of disrespect, and Reinhardt has such a morbid obsession with his dead father that he named his own horse after him!'

'That I hear, but I also hear your voice when you told me how changed our brother was when you discovered him that night.'

'But don't you see? That was after they got to him. Poured their poisons into his ear and pushed him towards a resolution designed for their own convenience.'

'Only gods may know men's souls, Siebrecht.'

'Then perhaps there are some men here who believe that they are a god's equal. Look, there he is.' Siebrecht indicated off to one side. It was Griesmeyer, riding down towards the white gate. He stopped beside the Reiklander contingent and exchanged salutes. Delmar stepped forwards and the two of them had a warm, comradely exchange, though Siebrecht could not hear the specifics.

'Of course,' Siebrecht spat. Gausser grunted without comment. Siebrecht continued, 'I can't stay confined in here this evening. I'm going over the wall. Will you come with me, brother?'

Gausser considered it for a moment and then stirred. 'Aye, if only to ensure that you come back.'

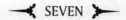

SEVEN

GAUSSER

Each month the Reiksguard squadrons were in Altdorf, they were subject to inspection. Typically this was performed by the Reiksmarshal and it was his opportunity to ensure his order was fully manned, with its arms and armour in good repair. New knights who had stood their vigil and taken their oaths in the period since the last inspection were given particular attention, a tradition dating back from when the Reiksguard's training and testing was not nearly so formal nor so strict. In more recent times, a new knight's first inspection had become a symbol of his final acceptance into the order, and for the noble families of Altdorf, it was the perfect opportunity for them to attend and bask in the reflected honour.

As the Reiksguard had just returned from the victory at Middenheim, and as it became increasingly known that they would shortly be departing again, the inspection took on a greater significance. And when, a few days before, the palace announced that the Emperor himself would take the inspection, it became a far grander event entirely.

The knights adopted the full Reiksguard battle armour, less the helm, in place of which they wore a cockaded hat bearing the badge of the order and red and white plumes, the colours of the ruling Emperor. They formed up not by the chapter house, but in the grounds of the Imperial Palace, and presented themselves there for the eye of the Emperor.

When Delmar and his brothers awoke that morning, it was clear that Siebrecht and Gausser had not returned from the night before. They eventually appeared, Gausser as upright as ever, Siebrecht ashen-faced and obviously the worse for the night's excesses. They were all full brother-knights now, not novices, and so enjoyed far greater liberty. But that did not mean that the others would make Siebrecht's life the least bit easier for him as a result. It was only Gausser who made sure that the Nulner reported with the rest at the appointed time.

Many of the families of the Reikland knights were in attendance. The Graf and Gravine von Falkenhayn, the Baron and Baroness von Proktor, and, Delmar was overjoyed to see, his mother and grandfather had made the journey to Altdorf as well. Delmar was doubly honoured that day for he had been chosen to carry the standard for the new knights' squadron. The weather proved to be scorching hot and the palace servants ran back and forth with shades and canopies for the nobler sections of the crowds. The new knights slowly boiled in their battle armour, but they would rather be toasted alive than show any sign of discomfort before the Emperor.

Karl Franz himself gave no indication that he felt the heat. He sat calmly on the back of his steed with his champion, Ludwig Schwarzhelm, by his side, as though he would be quite content to remain there for the entire day. When the Reiksguard were ready to begin, Helborg rode to the Emperor, saluted and took his position on his other flank. His eyes flicked to Schwarzhelm, and the two locked gazes for an instant before the Reiksguard began to march.

The Emperor accepted the salutes of the Reiksguard regiments, first the Reiksguard's trumpeters, mounted as cavalry, and then the rest marching on foot. When the time came for the new knights to present themselves, he dismounted and walked up their line. The knights stood at painfully strict attention, eyes forwards, but none of them could resist stealing a glance at the Emperor as he stepped before them. In that split-second, each of them believed that they had discerned some unique insight into the great man. The most mundane moment for him was, for them, a moment of the greatest significance.

As for Karl Franz, he was long accustomed to such curiosity and knew not to dishonour them by catching their eyes as they glanced. There was only a single knight of them whom he truly noticed, and that was one who had a particular look of fierce concentration carved upon his face. He was the only one whose eyes did not flicker as he passed. In truth, Siebrecht von Matz barely noticed the shadow fall across his face. He had begun the morning with a throbbing head and a tongue as dry as the desert. After hours baking in his armour, it was all he could do to endure this new type of damnation.

At length the inspection was over, the audience was duly impressed by another display of the military might of the Empire, and the Reiksguard broke up to make their way back to their chapter house in individual squadrons. The new knights were left until last; some of them were allowed to disperse to greet their families, but Delmar, as standard bearer, had to remain central, to act as their rallying point. He looked over at his own family again and saw the steward taking care of his grandfather. His mother, though, was not with them. Delmar scanned the milling crowd and caught a glimpse of her further along. She was talking with someone, and so Delmar shifted his position to be able to see her better. She was talking with none other than Griesmeyer. Delmar was surprised; he had never seen the two of them utter a word to each other in his company. What had they to talk about now?

The standard from another squadron fluttered through his line of vision as they marched away. When he could see them again Delmar realised that they were not simply talking, they were in the midst of an argument. He could not hear the words, but it was clear his mother was nearly shouting at the knight, she had one hand on her hip and with the other she was yanking a necklace around her own throat. Griesmeyer meanwhile had half-slipped back into a defensive guard, almost as though he expected to be physically attacked. Though Delmar had no idea what had happened, whether he was standard bearer or not, he could not stand apart. He made a move towards them. But then it was over, his mother stormed away leaving Griesmeyer behind.

Delmar stood in the arming room, fixed upon his thoughts. He had found his mother after the inspection; she had been too upset for him to ask what had happened between her and Griesmeyer. She had merely held him tight and implored him to return home from the campaign alive. Delmar had felt torn; the boy's heart within him was wrenched to see his mother in such a state and did not wish to leave her. Now, however, he discovered that his childhood heart was tempered by a man's spirit. For the first time the display of the emotion itself had made him feel awkward, he had wished to comfort her but found himself holding back, and was relieved when the steward had announced that they were returning to the estate immediately. His secret relief only exacerbated his feelings of guilt. How could he honour his oath to the order, knowing that in doing so he could never make any pledge as to his safety to those he loved, whose lives were rested upon his?

Worse were these new questions about his father and Griesmeyer. Delmar was not a man comfortable with secrets. Secrets, his mother had drilled him as a child, led only to lies, and lies led to damnation. In the countryside, especially as the lord's son, he lived his life in the plain sight of his neighbours, and what one of them saw or heard would inevitably make it back to his mother's ears, so there had been little purpose in trying to conceal anything. But now she was keeping secrets from him, as was Griesmeyer as well.

In the midst of his doubt and uncertainty, though, there was at least one accomplishment of which he could be proud: that he was a knight of the Reiksguard. The order's demands upon him were great, but at least they were plainly put. Even as the other pillars of his life shook, the order would stand firm.

As he brooded on such thoughts, the noise of his comrades' discussions around him began to intrude. None of them could stop talking about the events of the day; those with whom the Emperor had shared a few words repeated them endlessly to anyone who would listen, and everyone spoke of how they now had a far greater insight into the man because of the way he had looked into their eyes. As with all such events, though, there was always one speaker driven more by his personal concerns.

'Here's what I do not comprehend,' Hardenburg grumbled as he pulled his sabatons from his aching feet, 'why are we barracked so far from the palace? I swear I can see the heat shimmer from my foot. Look at this.' Hardenburg pushed his foot at Proktor who scowled and quickly retreated from the offending object. 'They should have built our chapter house right beside it. Then we would not have to trudge there and back for every occasion.'

'If you did not have to gawk at every pair of peaches on display then we could march all the faster,' Proktor snipped.

'Ah,' Hardenburg sighed, 'but how can I resist when in this heat they do swell so delightfully?'

'You're disgusting, Hardenburg.'

'For your opinions, brother, I do not give a fig.'

'I do not give a fig for what you think either,' Proktor retorted.

'Keep your fig then, I say. Though I should be heartily surprised if you ever find a lady to accept it.'

Some of the other knights laughed at that and Hardenburg bowed ostentatiously. Flustered, Proktor looked imploringly to Falkenhayn, but his friend was enjoying his embarrassment as well.

'Ya, he makes his point,' said Bohdan, stirring from the other side of the room. 'In case of sudden attack or riot, we should be close to the Emperor's side. In Ostermark, when the night closes in, a guard should be with his master. Out of sight...' Bohdan shook his head. 'One can never be sure what is out there.'

'Who can say?' Falkenhayn spoke up, resenting the Ostermarker's intrusion in their conversation. 'Most likely there was not space in the palace when the order was founded.'

'Perhaps then you do not recall the palace well, brother.' Bohdan's thick accent only added to the contempt in his voice. 'Your many absences from sentry duties must have blunted your recollection.'

Falkenhayn's anger rose at the impertinence, but Hardenburg was quicker.

'More likely the Emperor wanted distance from our stables,' he said, chortling at his own wit. He addressed Delmar, 'Brother Reinhardt will tell you what a noxious place they are, for he spends more time there than anywhere else.'

Delmar did not wish to be drawn into the conversation, but he would not shy from it. He stepped in between them to hang his breastplate upon the rack. 'It does not become you to be so discourteous, my brother,' he admonished Hardenburg lightly. Delmar turned to Bohdan: 'And your concern is proper, my friend, for the protection of the Emperor is our highest duty. What are we if we cannot protect him? But it is not so very far between here and there. We have sentries there to counter smaller threats and, in case of larger, they know to raise the alarm. The whole order then can ride, and any besieger who threatens our Emperor's life will quickly find himself surrounded. So for any such assault to succeed, the foe would have to stop up two locations instead of one, divide and weaken their forces. It is sound doctrine.'

The proud Ostermarker held Delmar's gaze for a few moments, then nodded his approval. That satisfied them all; even Hardenburg had no glib response. Falkenhayn allowed himself to be calmed, and in greater peace they set back to unfastening their armour.

'It is in case the Reiksguard ever turn on their Emperor,' Siebrecht spoke up from the corner. 'So that he will have at least some fortification between him and his guard.'

The room went deathly quiet. Falkenhayn drew breath to erupt, but Delmar stilled him with a gesture.

'Repeat what you said,' Delmar told Siebrecht.

Siebrecht looked up from his half-unfastened greave. He had said it as an off-hand comment. The thought had struck him and gone to his mouth without his mind intervening. He could take the words back easily, but then he saw the expression on Delmar's face: the intense seriousness in the broad, open features, the furrowing of his brow in disapproval. It was all Siebrecht could do not to laugh at how ridiculous he looked.

Instead he stood and readied himself. If this was to happen, then let it happen here.

'Brothers!' Verrakker shouted, appearing at the door. 'What are you all doing still half-armoured? You are all tardy. Wasting your day with talk, no doubt. I should rip your tongues out! Back to your task. In silence! Not another word from any of you. I can't cut your tongues, but I can cut your wine. Yes, Brother Matz, I thought that would catch your attention. Back to it!'

Verrakker glared at them all, his hand twitching as his drummed his non-existent fingers in impatience. The knights quickly bent themselves back to their armour, obedient Delmar amongst them. Siebrecht slowly breathed out, and relaxed his grip on the heavy metal arm-guard he was holding behind his back to knock Delmar senseless.

'Daemon's breath,' Bohdan swore as they left, 'what ever possessed you to say such a thing?'

Siebrecht shrugged. 'But am I wrong though?' Siebrecht turned to the Nordlander striding beside them, 'Am I wrong, Gausser?'

'That is not important.'

'It's important to me!'

'Matz! Matz!' The knights heard the steps of someone running up behind them. It was Proktor. He halted in front of them.

'Siebrecht von Matz,' he started formally, 'my brother Delmar von Reinhardt requires an apology from you, for the offence you have caused the order.'

'Tell me, Proktor,' Siebrecht rounded on him, 'is this Reinhardt or is this your precious Falkenhayn speaking through him?'

Proktor looked stricken for a moment and then recovered. 'I do not know what you refer to, I come from Reinhardt as one of his seconds.'

'One of his seconds?' Siebrecht replied in disbelief. 'He wishes to duel over this?'

'No duels, no duels...' Alptraum said, mimicking the long-departed Weisshuber.

Proktor ignored the Averlander. 'He does not wish to, but he is prepared to do so if you refuse.'

'Siebrecht...' Gausser began.

'Damn his blinkered arrogance then!' Siebrecht spat. 'I will not apologise for Reinhardt's propensity for self-deception! As he is so eager to style himself the order's champion then he will have to prove his ability. Tell him I will meet him outside the western city gate.'

Proktor reeled slightly from Siebrecht's fierce response.

'At what time?'

'Now!' Siebrecht growled at him. Proktor hurried away. It was too much. It was all too much. Months of training with these insufferable Reiklanders, enduring their pomposity and righteous belief in their born right to lead. Then Krieglitz and the cold calculating stare of that knight Griesmeyer, with whom Delmar had been so sickeningly proud of having an association. Now this?

'Siebrecht...' Gausser began again, with a tone of warning.

'No, Gausser,' Siebrecht defied him. 'It is enough. You may be with me, or you may walk away, but do not try to stop me. You had your crack at Reinhardt and you couldn't keep him down. But I will have a sword in my hand. Let me see him defy that.'

Duels between brothers of the order were forbidden; discipline was a cornerstone of the Reiksguard's effectiveness and discipline could not be maintained with brothers drawing their swords upon each other in anger. Instead, the order had developed a very formal process to resolve accusations. It was designed particularly to draw the heat from any disagreement and to emphasise the order's fraternity, to ensure that hundreds of proud noblemen, used to their own way, could live together in close quarters without killing each other. The weight and slow deliberation of this system, however, made it all the more attractive for hot-blooded young knights to settle their grievances quickly and physically. Though the order's jurisdiction extended to its knights wherever they were, such combats were always arranged outside the city walls to avoid interruptions and, should injuries result, they could be blamed upon a sudden attack by brigands or a beastkin warband.

'Matz has brought this all upon himself, brother,' Falkenhayn assured

Delmar as the Reiklanders pushed their way through the streets, still crowded from the Emperor's inspection earlier in the day. 'From the very beginning he has treated the order with the utmost contempt. The drinking sessions, his rudeness to our masters, and remember Krieglitz and him? As thick as thieves, and look now what we know about that family.

'Who is he anyway? He's been a Reiksguard knight a few weeks, never stood in a battle line, and he thinks it's his place to spit on the order's name and drag it through the mud. He thinks it's his place to tell us, when our families have served faithfully for generations?' Falkenhayn shook his head in exasperation. 'It is more than a quarrel, brother, it is your duty to teach this wastrel some respect before it is too late.'

Siebrecht and Gausser were waiting for them outside the gate, and the group moved a distance away from the crush of wagons trying to enter or exit the city. Once they were far enough away, Delmar nodded at Proktor.

'Brother Reinhardt gives you one last chance to apologise for your offence,' Proktor announced.

Siebrecht, in reply, held his pinky finger on which he wore his signet ring up at Delmar.

'He knows what he can do,' he smirked. 'Tell Brother Reinhardt he has one last chance to apologise for his idiocy.'

Delmar had not wished to fight before, he had merely wanted Siebrecht to take back his words, but now nothing could divert him from this course. This was not Griesmeyer, this was not his father, this was simple. He was right and Siebrecht was wrong.

They strode away from the western gate in silence until they reached the tree-line and were concealed from the road. They found a suitable clearing and the two parties retired to either side to ready themselves. At one end, Falkenhayn continued to feed Delmar gleeful encouragement: 'He's quick, don't forget, brother. He'll feint most likely; do not allow him to draw your guard. Keep pressing him back, get him close and you'll have him!'

Delmar heard him, but needed no words to inspire him. The sight of Siebrecht's face and his permanently self-satisfied expression were all the encouragement he required.

At the other end, Gausser was less supportive: 'This is truly what you wish, brother? For your family? For your name? For your life?'

'My life? My life is in no danger. It is Reinhardt's you should concern yourself with, for he can never best me with the blade.'

'That is not my meaning,' Gausser scowled.

As much as he could lie to Gausser, Siebrecht could not lie to himself. Though he felt his body energised for the upcoming fight, he could not deny that, underneath, he was exhausted. The drink from the night before, the lack of sleep, then to spend the whole day at attention, roasting in the sun. His mouth was dry, his hands were clammy; he drew his sword and held it out, and could see the blade shake in his grip. If he could not finish the fight in the first few strokes, then may the gods lend him strength, for he would have none left himself.

On the other side, Delmar drew his own sword and held it ready. He did not nervously practise a few swings, nor fearfully take up a guard before it was time. He was just ready. Watching him, Siebrecht's treacherous mind flicked back to that day before Master Ott, where Delmar had taken all that Gausser could dole out and still refused to give in; and then Siebrecht recalled the story of Delmar and his battle against the beastmen. Siebrecht had assumed that such stories were like those he told of himself, each one consisting of a grain of truth well fermented in bravado. But what if Delmar's stories had all been true? Gods, Siebrecht realised, just how far had he underestimated this Reiklander?

Proktor stepped into the middle of the clearing and asked one last time if Siebrecht would apologise. Siebrecht, focused upon Delmar, curtly shook his head. It didn't matter. It was too late now anyway.

'Then let it begin!' Proktor announced and stepped away.

Siebrecht never even saw the blow. The fist struck him in the side of his face with all the power of a cannon. His vision exploded and went black; he did not even feel himself hit the forest floor. His eyes fluttered open for a moment and he saw his attacker standing over him.

'Gausser?' he mouthed.

Gausser stepped away from him, stretching his fist. On the other side of the clearing Delmar watched, astonished, as the Nordlander then drew his sword and took up a ready stance.

'What trickery is this?' Falkenhayn cried beside him.

'No trickery,' Gausser replied. 'If a fighter cannot fight, then his second takes his place.'

Falkenhayn started to protest again, but Delmar cut him off.

'Step away, Gausser. My quarrel is not with you.'

'That cannot be done, Reinhardt.' The huge Nordlander did not move an inch.

'Our families are linked, Theodericsson. Not by blood, but by battle.'

'That I know.'

'Our fathers fought, side by side, comrades-in-arms against your foe. I ask you... on that bond... step back.'

Siebrecht clambered back to his feet. 'I will be considered no coward, who will not fight for himself. Where did my sword go? Give me that blade, Gausser. I do not need you to stand before me...'

Gausser smoothly turned around and punched him hard above the stomach. Siebrecht's eyes bulged out of their sockets and he slowly folded up into a ball on the ground, struggling for breath.

Delmar stared in disbelief. 'What are you doing? What has he done for you that you protect him so?'

Gausser slowly shook his head. 'You do not understand. Matz is my friend, yes. My brother. I would not see him hurt. But I do not do this for him. I do this for you, Reinhardt. I do this to honour your father, and to honour mine. You do not know it, what I can see. You do not know it, but you are the best of us. You are not the strongest; you are not the fastest; but you are the bravest. Before, you stood up against me for your friend, knowing you would most likely lose. You hold firm in your convictions against those who try to turn you from the true path of the knight. I have seen you with your family and you are the stone that they build themselves upon.'

'But this...' Gausser continued on, gesturing at the swords, at Siebrecht, and everything around them. 'This is not bravery. Your comrade here, your brother, is hurting. Not in his body, but in his mind, in his spirit. You can hurt him more if you wish; you can kill him, easily. But is that a brave act? Is that what a brave man does for his brother in need? I do this for you, Reinhardt. We will fight. You will vent your anger upon me, as you once allowed me to do upon you. We will fight until we drop. Then we will be friends again. And you will go forth from this place without the wound to your soul that you would inflict if you fought your poor brother here. And then, when you see in yourself what I see, you will still have the chance to become the knight you should be.'

No one spoke. No one had ever thought that Gausser could speak for so long, and with such power.

'Theodericsson Gausser,' Delmar finally began, his voice suddenly weak. 'You have shamed me. Your words have... No... I have shamed myself. I cannot fight you. And if you do not stand aside I cannot fight him either. And in this circumstance, I find my anger is now dissolved. All it leaves behind is the lesson you taught me here today.'

Delmar sheathed his sword. With his head bowed, he walked out from the woods. Falkenhayn met Gausser's steady gaze for a moment, then he ran after and Proktor after him.

'That cannot be it,' Falkenhayn exclaimed. 'The savage and the slanderer are standing there and you are just going to run away like a coward?' Falkenhayn took a hold on Delmar's shoulder to stop him.

Delmar halted. Falkenhayn, despite himself, edged away. Delmar looked deep into his eyes and said in final tones: 'Do not touch me again.'

With that he walked out from under the trees and back into the sun.

The Wilhelm Gate of the citadel opened, and once more the Grand Order of the Reiksguard processed through. There were crowds to see them go, but they were quiet, more respectful, for the knights were marching to campaign. Their route had been cleared for them and so they proceeded without interference through the city, past the Imperial Palace and down to the river. The supplies they would need had been loading aboard their boats since first light; they would travel even quicker than the knights could on land and so would be ready for them when they stopped at night.

As they crossed the bridge, Siebrecht, a welt of a bruise upon his cheek, deftly removed a gold crown from his belt and tossed it high out over the water. Gausser looked in askance at his bizarre behaviour.

'Settlement of a wager,' Siebrecht replied.

Gausser, who understood when words were needed and when words were not, decided not to inquire further. Instead, he checked his distance a fraction from the knight riding in front of him, and returned his attention to the magnificent sight of the Grand Order of the Reiksguard marching to war.

PART TWO

'On this day, I counted how long we have endured the grobi's siege, for I thought we may have reached one hundred days. I searched out our records, their runes freshly marked, but could find no date for its commencement. I spoke to the king, but he said that I should dig for the answer myself.

I stood at the guard post in the western tunnels, but the grobi launched no attack today. When my watch was done I returned to my endeavour. I found the date that Thorntoad first attacked our patrols. I found the date the last trading boat reached us unmolested. I found the date we retreated from the hold of Und Urbaz north of the pass, the date our settlers were recalled from the highland meadows, the date we closed our gates and tunnels against our foes outside. But none of these was called the start of the siege.

I went to the king before my next watch and retold what I had found. I asked him which of these dates he thought was when the siege had begun. He called his oldest counsellor forwards, who placed before him a stone engraved. It was a thousand years old, and it was a copy of records long before that. The king pointed at a single line thereon, the journal of a day when our ancient king-dom was still young. It said that on this day was the kingdom of Karak Angazhar laid siege by the tribes of the grobi.

To my father, to his counsellors, to our ancestors, that was the first day of the grobi's siege. And it will continue until the last drop of blood falls upon our stone, whether it be theirs or ours.'

– Extract from the personal ledger of
Ung Gramsson, son of Gramrik, King of Karak Angazhar

PART TWO

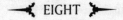

DANSIG

The foot of the Black Mountains
The Nedrigfluss, border of Averland and
the dwarf kingdom of Karak Angazhar
Autumn 2522 IC

'Gausser! Alptraum! Bohdan! Come in!' Siebrecht shouted, standing barefoot in the shallows on the bank of the Nedrigfluss. His three brothers crouched sceptically on the bank.

'Isn't that glacier water?' Alptraum asked.

'It's invigorating,' Siebrecht replied. 'What's this? Three brother-knights of the Reiksguard afraid of a little water?'

Alptraum, warily, began to take off his boots. Gausser and Bohdan stood aloft.

'He is clearly lying,' Bohdan stated flatly.

'That is certain,' Gausser replied.

Siebrecht rolled his eyes. 'How Nordland and Ostermark must be proud of their native sons, less courageous than two soft southerners.'

Gausser shrugged and shook off his boots. Bohdan followed him. The three of them slid down the bank and splashed into the water together.

'It's freezing!' Alptraum cried, shooting straight back out again and scaling the bank. Siebrecht burst out into great peals of laughter as he fled.

'How can you stand it?' Alptraum asked, sitting on the bank, rubbing his feet warm again.

'Simple! My feet are already numb,' Siebrecht replied. He pulled one of them out of the water for Alptraum to inspect and there was a definite bluish tinge.

'And people say that Averlanders are mad,' Alptraum shot back.

Siebrecht laughed again and clumsily hauled himself out. These past three weeks had been better than he had ever hoped. They rode hard the whole day long, across the magnificent plains of Averland, and at night the boats came up the Reik with food and bedding for them all.

When they had left Altdorf, Siebrecht had been sunk in a misery from which his brothers did not think he would emerge. But his mood had risen with each step he took away. By the time they passed his home of Nuln he was restored completely, and he had regaled his brothers with tales of his adventures in the city's backstreets. As they drew closer to the Black Mountains, they began to break their journey at the towns along the way so that the inhabitants might admire them and join the militias which were marching behind.

Now they had arrived at the border and here the river boats landed armour, barding, rations for both men and horses, camp equipment, even a few field cannon brought from Nuln. Everything too heavy to bring quickly by road, the Reiksmarshal had brought speedily up the river. It was incredible. Siebrecht had served as a pistolier attached to the Wissenland militia before he joined the Reiksguard; in fact he still carried that same pistol, though as a knight he was not supposed to have it. He had seen the Wissenland militia on the march. Six hundred men, trudging ten, fifteen miles a day. Never enough shelter, never enough food. But the Reiksguard, they had gone twice as fast, sometimes more, and done it in comfort. Three weeks since leaving Altdorf at the centre of the Empire, the order was gathered on the southern border, ready to fight.

The feeling returned to Siebrecht's feet and he sat to pull his boots on. Only then did he realise that Gausser and Bohdan had not followed him out of the river. The two of them were still standing in the shallows; both of them had their arms folded as though perfectly willing to stand there until the Nedrigfluss dried up.

'That Nulner says this is cold,' Bohdan scoffed. 'He has never felt the chill of rivers that run from the Worlds Edge Mountains.'

'That is true,' Gausser replied, 'but one does not know cold until one has swum in the Sea of Claws.'

'Indeed,' Bohdan conceded, 'but the Sea of Claws is nothing compared to the frozen lakes of Kislev.'

Siebrecht shook his head and left the two of them to another of their self-imposed endurance trials. They had been competing against each other ever since Altdorf, and if the results of the past were repeated there would be no quick winner.

Beside Siebrecht, Alptraum started and pointed north. 'Another militia's coming in,' he said. 'How many men do you think?'

'Let's go and take a look at them.'

Siebrecht and Alptraum wandered away from the river, back through the makeshift Empire camp. As well as the order's knights and sergeants, there were nearly a thousand militiamen who had arrived already from towns such as Heideck, Grenzstadt, Loningbruck and Streissen. This new militia, though, came from further afield.

'It's Averheim! It's Averheim!' Alptraum shouted and broke into a trot to greet them.

Siebrecht could not quite fathom it: Alptraum, who had been so

withdrawn in Altdorf, had come into his own as soon as they crossed
into Averland. In every town they stopped, he introduced himself to those
he met. When the militias arrived in camp, he did the same, as though he
could learn the name of every single militiaman who was to march with
the army. He was doing it again now, right before Siebrecht's eyes, shaking the hands of each man in the militia, asking for all the latest news from
Averheim and listening intently to what they said.

The only Averlander in the army that Alptraum had not approached was
the commander of the militias, the Graf von Leitdorf. The graf had set his
pavilion in the centre of the camp and Siebrecht had noticed that Alptraum would take a significant detour rather than walk past its entrance.
The militia captains, who all reported to the graf, also kept a wary distance
from Alptraum, as though any association with him might tar them in the
eyes of their own commander.

Siebrecht knew the Leitdorf and Alptraum families were old rivals for the
title of Elector Count of Averland. The title had been vacant for three years
already and still none of the noble families had achieved ascendancy. Siebrecht was no stranger to the political struggles in Nuln and Wissenland, but
they at least, after a few days' excitement, were resolved. These Averlanders
seemed in no rush to resolve anything, including who should be their lord.

Siebrecht, though, had his own distraction. Amongst the yellow and
black colours of the Averheim militia, he saw Herr von Matz dismounting
from his horse and, as ever, Twoswords was with him.

Herr von Matz did not join the army alone. He brought a retinue with
him. He said they were his travel guards, necessary protection on the dangerous roads. Siebrecht accepted the explanation, but did not believe it.
He had seen many bodyguards on the streets of Nuln and they all looked
alike: big, imposing men, who could deter casual ruffians with a glance.
They dressed smartly, for no noble would retain a bodyguard who looked
like a vagabond. But Herr von Matz's dishevelled rogues, to Siebrecht's eye,
looked more likely to rob a noble of his coin than defend him. Some were
short, some were slight, and all of them wore clothes that looked like they
had been dredged up from a cesspit. There was at least one dwarf amongst
their number, most likely born and raised in Nuln for he wore an ill-fitting
black tunic which aped the human fashion.

Herr von Matz never introduced any of them by name. One of them
carried a pair of blades strapped in a cross on his back so Siebrecht had
named him Twoswords, and Twoswords never left Herr von Matz's side.
He was a swarthy beast; he had a thick, black beard and a shaven head,
so that from a distance his face appeared almost upside down. Even with
his eye for detail, Siebrecht could not discern the man's origins; his features had everything from Estalia to Kislev about them, and Siebrecht had
never heard him talk so there was no accent to decipher.

Herr von Matz waved at his nephew, but did not walk over. Instead, his uncle headed straight for the graf's pavilion. Siebrecht left Alptraum, who was still engaged with the militiamen, and headed back to the river. He had seen boats being prepared to ferry the first knights across the stretch of water where the Nedrigfluss flowed into the Reik, and he did not want to miss the landing on the western bank.

The boats had just pushed off when Siebrecht arrived. The knights onboard anticipated danger, but did not wish to wear full armour in case the boat capsized. Instead they carried large shields and wore only their breastplates. The boats were also heavily manned by sergeants carrying their crossbows. Siebrecht doubted whether they could shoot accurately from a moving river boat, but they looked fierce enough. Falkenhayn and the other Reiklanders stood close to Preceptor Jungingen. Their squadron had been assigned to Jungingen's banner for the campaign, and Falkenhayn missed no chance to attend upon the preceptor. Delmar stood on his own. Siebrecht stood apart from the both of them, not wishing to be associated with either.

Delmar had annoyed Siebrecht. Not by anything he had said or done, rather by what he had not done. After the aborted duel, Falkenhayn had cut his ties to Delmar and told his two remaining Falcons to do the same. Siebrecht had hoped that Delmar would challenge him, that the Reiklanders would split between the two. Instead, Delmar had kept himself apart from his former friends, and the Reiklanders had fallen into line with Falkenhayn. Delmar was pushed away. And he had shown no interest in the Provincials. Instead, on the road from Altdorf, whatever cloud had lifted from Siebrecht had gathered over him.

Siebrecht preferred not to think on Delmar too much. He associated him, and his patron Griesmeyer, with too many ill memories. While Siebrecht was not proud of his own behaviour, he felt no desire to make amends. Instead, as Gausser, Bohdan and Alptraum arrived by his side, he turned his attention back to the boats on the river. Beyond them, the Black Mountains loomed, the closer hills covered with dense forest, the further peaks of grey stone with touches of snow. But it was not those for which the Black Mountains were so named; instead it was the dark clouds that were packed overhead. Some were formed in the shape of great anvils, others clumped and tumbled down like avalanches, a few rose as horrific beasts ready to swallow any who dared travel beneath them. The sunny pastures of Averland were behind them, and before them was no realm intended for man.

Kurt Helborg watched the first boat land safely on the western bank of the Reik and disgorge the knights it carried, then the second, then the third. Satisfied, he left the crossing to Knight Commander Sternberg and returned to his tent where the war council was gathering.

Sigmar grant him strength, but he was tired of this. Tired of marching, tired of campaigns, tired of loss. The burden of his office of the Marshal of the Empire had never been so great as it had been this year. Ever since he had returned from Middenheim, he had begun to wonder what his life would be like without the mantle of Reiksmarshal upon him. What a normal day might be if he did not hold the fates of thousands of men in his hand.

Helborg reached the entrance to his tent. There stood Griesmeyer, awaiting his return and deep in thought. For all their years of friendship, Helborg had never been able to read his comrade the way he could so many others. Perhaps that was, perversely, why he valued his advice so highly.

'How is the council today?' Helborg asked.

Griesmeyer's face relaxed. 'They will be all the better for your intervention, Marshal.'

'And the graf?'

'Better than yesterday,' Griesmeyer replied. 'He has brought a new militia captain with him.'

Helborg's face darkened. Graf von Leitdorf had tried to bring two dozen of his staff and captains to the first council and Helborg had had to have undiplomatic words with him afterwards in order to trim his retinue down.

'You may approve of this one, though,' Griesmeyer said.

'Who is he?'

'He is of no title. His name's Ludwig Voll of the bergjaegers. He has just arrived.'

Helborg's tone lifted at that. 'Does he bring men with him?'

'I do not know, Marshal.'

'Then let us find out.' Helborg quickly stroked his finger across his bushy moustache, pulled back the tent flap and led the way inside.

'Ah, Marshal Helborg...' Graf von Leitdorf declared, looking up from his cluster of staff.

Helborg waited a moment for Leitdorf to finish that sentence, to see if he would dare chide the Marshal of the Empire. Leitdorf thought better of it and stayed silent. Ever since Helborg had become Reiksmarshal, the Leitdorfs of Averland had been a constant source of difficulty. The last head of their family, Marius Leitdorf, the Elector Count of Averland, known popularly as 'the Mad', had been infamous for his erratic behaviour; his moods had been as fickle as an infant's, swinging from contentment to rage to embittered misanthropy in a heartbeat. Helborg could tolerate the existence of such individuals for the most part, so long as he was not obliged to interact with them in any way; but to have such a capricious mind in a position to raise and command armies was beyond his sufferance. It was with mixed feelings indeed that Helborg had heard of Marius's death, valiant as it had been.

Helborg had every expectation that this newly elevated scion of that family, Graf von Leitdorf, would be the same as his predecessor. For all the control that the graf displayed in his public appearance, Helborg could see in the hawkish face and those pinched eyes that same madness lurking within, waiting for its moment to emerge.

'Graf von Leitdorf,' Helborg said simply, 'my thanks for your attendance.'

Leitdorf contented himself with a simple incline of the head as acknowledgement. Helborg nodded at the officers of the order present, Sub-Marshal Zöllner and the senior preceptor, Osterna. He then looked pointedly at the one man he did not recognise.

'Would you introduce yourself, sir?'

Ludwig Voll was a small, rangy man. He wore furs and coarse cloth whilst every other at the council wore armour and silks. Helborg could see that he was somewhat cowed; he was little more than a peasant and he was in the company of lords and the great general of the Empire.

'My name is...' he began, stumbling a little over his words, 'that is, ah, I am Jaeger Ludwig Voll of the bergjaegers.'

'The bergjaegers have a great reputation, Jaeger Voll. I am pleased to see that you have responded to the Emperor's call. How many men have you brought to join us?'

'Well, there's just myself... I've none with me, your lordship,' Voll began. 'I thought it best to see how many you needed and then send for them, rather than...' The jaeger's voice trailed off as he felt the atmosphere in the tent chill. The Reiksmarshal was not impressed.

'How many can you summon?' Helborg asked.

Jaeger Voll, to his credit, did not collapse before the Reiksmarshal's fierce gaze as others had. 'Near two hundred, or thereabouts,' he replied quickly.

'Then summon them all. Have them join us by the end of tomorrow.'

'All of them?' Graf von Leitdorf interjected. 'Is that truly necessary? They are responsible for a great length of these mountains–'

'Yes.' Helborg cut him off. 'It is entirely necessary. We do not know the forces ranged against us, but they must be considerable or they would be no challenge to the dwarfs of Karak Angazhar.'

Helborg unrolled a map over the table in the centre of the tent and addressed the council.

'The cartographers of Altdorf would have us believe these mountains are part of the Empire's realm; they are nothing of the kind. Even before these goblins closed the river, Karak Angazhar has never welcomed visitors to these mountains. Even our traders have not been permitted beyond here.' Helborg pointed to a peak annotated as the Litzbach. 'And so, as you can see, our knowledge of the mountains and of the passes beyond is limited. We do not know where the goblins have their lairs, nor of any of Karak Angazhar's outposts. We must consider these lands as much enemy territory as others a thousand miles from our borders. And we must move quickly through them. The months for campaigns are done and Ulric's wintry breath will descend on us any day. This foe must be defeated before the first snows fall or, if not, we will have to rely on Karak Angazhar to save us!'

The soldiers in the tent duly registered their dismay at such a dishonour.

'We should be across the Nedrigfluss by the end of the day. Tomorrow, we march for the Litzbach. Sub-Marshal Zöllner will detail the marching order.'

'Marshal,' Leitdorf interrupted again, his voice quieter in an attempt to indicate a private aside, 'does this order include the militias?'

'Of course.' Helborg made no attempt to hush his own voice.

'I have not been consulted as to this...'

'You are being consulted now,' Helborg overrode him, watching for the madness to flicker. 'I have no doubt it will meet with your approval. Sub-marshal, continue.'

The boat creaked ominously as Siebrecht stepped aboard. Even though the other bank was secure, he felt his heart begin to pound. He had laughed and splashed in the water before, but once they were in the middle of the river, that same water would be their death should they fall in. Even if they survived the cold, his own breastplate would drag him down. Just as Krieglitz's had.

Siebrecht fiddled with the breastplate's straps.

'Keep them loose, let it just hang off your shoulders,' Delmar said beside him. 'Then if you fall in, it will come off.'

Surprised that Delmar had addressed him directly, Siebrecht could only nod his thanks.

'We should be ready to die for the Reik, not drown in it,' Delmar continued, taking his seat.

'Gausser,' Siebrecht whispered to the Nordlander as he stepped aboard. 'Something's very wrong.'

'What?' Gausser replied, seeing the panic in his brother's face.

'I think...' Siebrecht began. 'I think Reinhardt just made a joke.'

Once the council was finally concluded, Helborg strode quickly from the tent and back to the river. There, the serious Commander Sternberg was quietly supervising the crossing.

'Which banner is that?' Helborg asked, looking out to the knights in the middle of the river.

'Squadrons from Jungingen's banner,' Sternberg replied, his eyes never leaving the boats on the water.

Helborg nodded and felt his ire lessen; the crossing at least was going to plan. He noticed that Griesmeyer had appeared beside him, politely waiting for his Reiksmarshal's attention.

'You were right, brother.'

'In what way, my lord?'

'The graf was better than yesterday.'

Griesmeyer smiled at that. Helborg, however, did not. The graf would be a problem. With the wars of the last few years these noblemen had grown increasingly full of themselves. The Emperor's own armies were not enough and so he had called upon his nobles ceaselessly for military aid. They knew how much they were needed.

At some point, Helborg would have to disabuse the graf of his notion that he was in joint command, simply because his militias were half the army. Helborg should tell him that a hundred Reiksguard knights were equal to a thousand of his unruly farmhands and cattlemen. But not here, not now. Not while the militias were still within an easy march of their homes, and the salted beef they were providing to feed his knights had not yet arrived.

'I did not think highly of this jaeger,' Helborg continued, recalling Griesmeyer's recommendation. 'I have enough amateurs to deal with in these militia captains, I do not need another. Has he left to fetch his men?'

'I believe he has.'

'There is that at least.'

'Before he left, my lord, he asked me to give you this.' Griesmeyer handed Helborg the map from the meeting and unrolled it. Helborg looked at it closely: there were a slew of corrections and new annotations upon it, marking smaller peaks, passes, elevations and, most importantly, the location of the dwarfen outpost of Und Urbaz and the goblin nests around it.

'He did not say where his knowledge came from,' Griesmeyer continued, 'but he did tell me that he wished his possession of such detail should not be made known to the dwarfs. I believe that, as well as being an Averland mountain guard, Jaeger Voll has also employed himself as an illicit prospector and poacher.'

'Well, he's our poacher now,' Helborg smiled, still poring over the map, readjusting his plans. 'Ensure he attends the next council, brother.'

Griesmeyer was about to reply when there was a sudden commotion from the bank. A flight of black shapes had flown from the trees on the far side. For an instant they could almost be mistaken for birds. They were arrows, and they flew straight for the knights crammed on the boats.

The boat rocked and swayed as every knight instinctively rose to his feet.

'Shields!' someone cried, but it was far too late. The volley, aimed with time and care at the slow-moving craft, proved deadly accurate. The shafts struck, some hitting the wooden hull, some deflecting off their breastplates, and the rest piercing arms and hands, instinctively raised in protection. A chorus of pained yells rose above the boat.

'Sit down!' the boatmaster screamed as staggering knights made the craft list beyond his control. Delmar and Siebrecht obeyed, keeping their heads low behind the shields now being raised, but the knight beside them stayed standing. Delmar took a hold of the knight's breastplate to encourage him to sit, the boat swayed again and the knight leaned over the edge. Delmar glanced up at his face, and saw the frantic eyes and the hand gripping the arrow sticking out of his throat. The dying knight began to topple over the side and Delmar reached out to grab hold of him. Siebrecht saw Delmar jump up and rose himself to seize him.

'Down! Down! Down!' the boatmaster cried again as the shifting weight tipped the boat even further. Delmar felt someone pull at him and the breastplate slipped from his grip. The stricken knight splashed into the water. Delmar whipped his head back, ready to swear at whoever had held him back, when Gausser gathered both him and Siebrecht and bore all three of them down to the deck. The boat listed hugely once more, and then the boatmaster regained control and brought it back onto an even keel.

Helborg saw the face of the dead knight as another boat pulled the body from the river. It was Brother Dansig. Helborg did not know him well; he had only been in the order for a few seasons, but he had survived the war and the great charge at Middenheim only to fall here before the campaign even began.

The knights and sergeants on the other bank had reached the dense clump of trees from which the arrows had been shot, but they found nothing except a small tunnel in the earth down which the goblins had escaped. They sent back word that they were unable to follow.

Before them the forest was quiet again, and the peaks beyond remained unmoved. Beneath this veneer of peace, however, Helborg knew a bloody war was being fought.

Deep beneath a mountain, the dwarf grappled for his axe. The leering goblin held tight with one claw, whilst with the other it scratched the dwarf's plated face-mask. It hooked its nails into the mask's eye sockets and, with a screech, broke it from the helmet. It was a screech that swiftly turned into a scream as the dwarf wrested the axe away and brought it down in a final stroke.

Free for a moment, the dwarf fumbled around for his mask. It was an heirloom, it had been passed down from his grandfather, he could not lose it. But then he heard the hiss of more grobi coming down the tunnel towards him. His good sense returned and he left the armour wherever it had fallen. His grandfather would understand.

He hastened away from the grobi, not sure which way to turn. He knew that his comrades were dead. Those of his band who had not been killed outright in the grobi assault would not survive long in their hands. It would be the same for any greenskin captured by his own kind. There was no concept of mercy or surrender; the grobi were vermin, to be hunted and destroyed, though that knowledge gave him little comfort when the vermin were hunting him.

The dwarf also knew that he was trapped. The grobi had been too quick. He had seen the iron hatch close, he had heard the bars drawn across so as to prevent the attackers penetrating any deeper into the hold, even though it meant consigning him and his comrades to their fate. It was a hard choice, but then these were hard times. All his life had been hard times.

This tunnel led him away from the sounds of the grobi, but it led him away from the hold as well. The dwarf knew these tunnels, had walked them often in the years before the siege began. There was no chance to double back; he had to go on. The further he went from the hold, though, the deeper he went into the grobi's territory. The dwarf knew then that he would not be returning home.

But then a tunnel branched away to the side, and through it he heard the sound of distant thunder. He remembered where it led. It would not be pleasant, but it was the only chance remaining to him. He hurried towards the thunder as quickly as he could and, as it became deafening, he emerged out into the cavern.

It was a waterfall, part of the river that flowed from these mountains and down into the Empire of man. It would take him from the grobi, it would take him to the surface. There was danger as well, but it would be day. The grobi of the mountains were dark creatures and abhorred the light. The sounds of pursuers behind settled the dwarf's choice. He was at least young, for everyone knew that old dwarfs did not float. With the greatest reluctance, he lay down his axe, his helmet and his armour, everything about his person that might drag him down. With that, and an oath to his ancestors, he jumped forwards and dived into the water.

The dwarf awoke on the hard bank, pummelled and tenderised by the raging river, but alive. It had worked. He felt the rock beneath his hands; he felt the sun on the back of his head. With an effort he managed to raise himself to his knees and look about. He had washed up in the pass of Bar Kadrin. On each side, all about him, the giant stone heads of his ancestors looked down upon him. If he had been here a year ago, he would have been safe. But how the seams had shifted in that year. The sculptures were now defaced and he was far from home.

A shadow fell across his body. This was no goblin. He looked up, and up, at the monster that stood over him. It was not alone either, for behind it the grobi hunters stood with their nets waiting for the monster to finish with their prize. It sniggered and then brought a meaty fist down upon his head.

Barely conscious, the dwarf felt himself being dragged away in a goblin's net and all he could hear was the same name being chanted over and over again in glee.

'Thorntoad! Thorntoad! Thorntoad!'

◀ NINE ▶

THORNTOAD

The ogre known as Burakk the Craw watched as the mouth of the great stone goblin filled with its lesser, green kin. There were emissaries from each of the ten tribes of the mountains hereabouts; Burakk could see the emblems of the Black Ears, the Stinkhorns, the Splinters, the Biters and all the rest, being waved about the dark-cloaked throng. They were restless, for they did not like being out from under the earth. Even here, at night and on the side of a mountain scooped out so deep that it was never touched by the sun, they felt exposed to the endless sky. But this place was sacred to them, and they had been called here for a reason. They were here to listen to their leader speak.

On a ledge above them, the banners of Thorntoad's tribe, the Death Caps, rose. A hiss of anticipation went through the crowd. He was coming. Thorntoad was coming. Burakk stirred slightly; only two years ago, their reaction would have been very different. The Death Caps had been pariahs, perennial victims of the tribes that had encroached upon their territory on every side, pushing them to the fringes. The name of Thorntoad was unknown outside of one squig herder who kept him as a freakish pet. A year since, after one defeat too many, the Death Caps had turned upon their chieftain. In the chaos that followed, each goblin that attempted to declare himself chief had been quickly deposed, and then disposed of, by another. The other tribes readied themselves to move in, sensing the Death Caps' weakness, waiting for them to exhaust themselves fighting each other. It had been then that Thorntoad the freak had broken free from his cage and, in a night of savagery unparalleled even amongst greenskins, he had seized control. When the other tribes next awoke, it was to a newly united Death Caps. Some of the tribes attacked nevertheless, and the goblins they lost became much-needed food for Thorntoad's hungry fiends. From that day on, Thorntoad's name was known, not as the freak, but as the warlord.

'Thorntoad! Thorntoad! Thorntoad!' the thousand-strong crowd chanted, fever rising. The Great Maw was fickle, Burakk decided, the next bite was never like the last.

Then, with an explosion of excitement, Thorntoad of the Ten Tribes emerged. The goblin warlord was the most wretched specimen of flesh Burakk had ever seen. His body was deformed like a blasted sapling, his legs were thin and crooked, but his arms were powerful. He climbed up the rock with the motion of a spider. He was naked, save for a rag, for the name of Thorntoad was no colourful moniker: there were spines arrayed across the goblin's skin. His thorns, he called them, and they could not bear to be covered with the dark robes the other goblins wore. He vaulted to the top and stood there, bent over, supported as much by his hands as by his withered legs, hideous and triumphant. In this place, he was more than their warlord, he was their totem, he was their connection to their gods.

'Now, my fiends,' Thorntoad began, his screeching, reedy voice music to his goblins' ears, 'now have our starving days turned to nights of glee and gold. Now do we roam free throughout these hills while our foes cower and hide beneath the ground.'

The cloaked goblins howled with delight, shaking helms and weapons captured in battle.

'Now it is our bellies that are full and theirs which are not; our hunger spasms turned to victory dances. Now it is our claws stretched round their throats, and with each moon that rises, our grip grows tighter. Now they are desperate; now they wish they had fled.'

The horde shook their standards and drummed their spearshafts in elation.

'While we dig them out, they dig their graves. While they eat rocks, we eat their bones. Each moon brings us closer, my fiends, each one to the feast we have ahead. But for now, my gift to you all... the trophies we have won!'

At Thorntoad's signal, the Death Caps behind him stepped forwards to the ledge, dragging bundles behind, wrapped up in cloth. They threw them off the cliff, over the crowds below. As the bundles dropped they unravelled, the black cloth streaming behind, one end fastened to the ledge above. Then the cloth ran out and caught its fall. The contents of each bundle was revealed, the bloodied body of a dwarfen warrior, and they hung above the baying crowd like bait upon a fishing pole. Thorntoad revelled in the exultation for a moment more then reached for each body in turn, cut it down and launched it to be swallowed by the ravening horde.

Burakk the Craw grunted and left the greenskins to their petty feeding. Though he began to hunger himself, he knew that Thorntoad would not have dared to forget his cut. Whatever pageantry the freak performed for the benefit of his tribes, the choicest food went to Burakk and his ogres. After all, he would not be known as Thorntoad of the Ten Tribes if it had not been for Burakk. He would not be known at all.

Burakk reached the edge of the mouth of the great stone goblin, the side of a mountain that, the tribes swore, resembled a giant greenskin face shaped there by their gods. Thorntoad was still lauding himself over the sea of black and green. Yes, much had changed in two years. Two years ago, Burakk had been a shadow of his present self. Dazed, without food so long that his gut had shrunk, he had been wandering these mountains without direction when Thorntoad's Death Caps had found him. Near out of his wits, he had lumbered at them on instinct, caught one of the slower ones, but the others had entangled him with nets and kept him at a distance with their spears. Burakk had thought that was his end and he was ready to consign himself to the Great Maw. But the goblins had not eaten him, as he had assumed they would, as he would have done them. Instead, they kept him caged, started feeding him, and once the hunger-dullness had receded, Thorntoad had come to talk.

It had not been easy. It had taken a week for them to start to communicate at the basest level. Burakk, though, was in a cage and had nothing else to do, and Thorntoad concentrated all his time there. Thorntoad wanted the ogre to fight for him, and would feed him in return. He was not the first ogre to have stumbled into this area of the mountains; individuals and small groups had been spotted for months. All of them stunned, confused, many pitted with gunshot or with bones broken by cannonball. They were survivors of some crushing defeat of an ogre tyrant, somewhere in the Empire, and had been chased into the mountains by the victors. When the ogres, maddened with hunger, saw goblins, they attacked; and so the goblins had killed any who appeared. As strong as an ogre was, it could not match a hundred goblins swarming over it. Thorntoad saw in Burakk an opportunity, not simply to add a single ogre to his tribe, but dozens. All Burakk had to do, when they found another ogre, was to convince him to join their cause, by whatever means Burakk could. Burakk readily agreed and their alliance had been struck.

From that day, Thorntoad began to move against the other tribes. Whilst an ogre did not readily fit into all goblin tunnels, he could cause enough destruction on the surface for Thorntoad's Death Caps to triumph beneath the ground. Burakk himself earned his epithet of 'the Craw' after swallowing one Black Ear chieftain whole. Burakk added more ogres to the tribe as well, though not every one they encountered was willing to submit to his authority. Those that did not provided sustenance for the rest. Now, Burakk the Craw was a tyrant himself, with sixty bull-ogres at his command, who each bore a Craw marking upon his cheek. Whatever each bull's origins, they were now a tribe of their own, and Thorntoad paid them in food for lending him their might. First in goblins from the tribes they overwhelmed, and when Burakk had come to find their gristly frames sickening, with dwarfs. Yes, Burakk believed, they would have a grand supper of dwarf-flesh this night.

'This is all?' Burakk rumbled, eyeing the paltry few bundled bodies at his feet.

Thorntoad sat on his haunches above his throne-room. The throne had been carved for the chieftain of the Stinkhorn tribe, the former occupiers of the great stone goblin. Once the Death Caps had achieved dominance, however, Thorntoad had made this mountain his lair and kept this throne, though it did not suit him. Those same spines upon his body with which he had impaled the old Stinkhorn chieftain prevented him from finding any comfort on his seat. All he could do was perch upon the top of the throne back, shifting constantly, for even with his spines lowered he was never able to find a position in which he could rest.

Instead, he had stretched ropes across the ceiling and buried metal rings in the walls, so that they formed a web through which Thorntoad's wasted legs were no hindrance. It was amongst these that he lurked, looking down upon his ogre ally.

'That is all,' Thorntoad spoke. 'Yes, Burakk Craw, that is all.'

'What of this one?' Burakk stomped over to a dwarfen warrior tied securely to the wall. Thorntoad scurried from his position, sliding across the surface of his web, and landed directly above Burakk's head.

'It is mine.'

The dwarf's chest sagged a little, blood bubbles forming at its lips as it breathed out.

'It is not dead,' Burakk observed.

'What I do with what is mine, is mine to say alone,' Thorntoad warned, and the ogre stiffly turned away from the prisoner.

'My bulls hunger, they need more than this,' Burakk replied, kicking the bundles in the centre of the room.

'They need? They need? But what do they deserve, Burakk Craw? These were taken by my fiends, not your bulls. Your bulls were not even there. I cannot give the choicest cuts to those who did not fight.'

'We cannot fight in your warrens, goblin. But they hide down there because of my bulls. We stopped them walking the surface. We stopped their caravans travelling down the river. That was our doing.'

'And for which you took your reward and ate most of what was taken, while my fiends scraped their dinners off rocks. Now they have won and taken spoils; they too must be rewarded.'

Thorntoad's logic meant nothing to Burakk. An ogre tyrant commanded the loyalty of his bulls only so long as he ensured their hunger was sated. Thorntoad's goblins could survive on nothing but the fungi that grew in their tunnels; Burakk's ogres needed meat.

'We ate better when the fight was hard than we do when the fight is almost won,' he grumbled.

'Ah, Burakk Craw,' Thorntoad hissed as he climbed the ropes back to the top once more, 'the fight is not done yet.'

An object fell from the darkness around Thorntoad's voice and bounced with a clang. Burakk picked it up. It was a helmet, but this one did not have a finely wrought face-mask as was typical of dwarfen warriors; this one was plain, crudely made by comparison.

'It is from the warriors of the tribes of men. Have you heard of them, Burakk Craw?'

The ogre murmured assent. He remembered these men: the way their flimsy bodies broke, the way their swords and spears bounced off his skin; but he also remembered their guns, their cannon which roared like giants, their iron shot that smashed through gutplates and took an ogre's life from a hundred paces away.

'An army of their warriors has crossed into our mountains, marching to the dwarfs' aid. They are well fed, and they have plump animals with them too. So have patience, ogre, your next feast marches towards you.

'And in the meanwhile, the Snaggle Tooths did not attend this night; you may take your bulls and eat your fill of them.'

Burakk grunted again, then took up the bundles and dragged them away. Thorntoad watched until he had left, and then slithered down his ropes and rings to his prisoner. He pulled on a chain nearby and a goblin was dragged from a hole, the chain connected to a collar around his neck. Thorntoad could not bear to have squig-beasts in his presence; they reminded him too much of his own years of degradation, and in return they detested him, smelling his freakishness upon him. Instead, Thorntoad kept other goblins as his pets, as he had once been kept. This one had been a shaman, and had thought to call down Gork and Mork's judgement upon Thorntoad. Instead the gods had proved who they truly favoured. Thorntoad yanked the shaman's chain again and drew him over to the bound dwarf.

'Wake it up,' Thorntoad ordered.

The miserable shaman took a small pouch of spores and blew them in the dwarf's face. The warrior stirred, mouthing words in the dwarfs' secret tongue. The dwarfs protected their language closer than they protected their gold; they thought if they did so, they could conceal their secrets from their foes. That they could, if the only place their foes looked for knowledge was in their books. Thorntoad preferred to look for knowledge in people; it was far quicker, provided you could hurt them enough. And here the dwarfen language was no protection, for in their greed for wealth and trade, the dwarfs had learned another language, one which had no secrets, one which even a goblin could learn: the language of men.

'What... you... name?' Thorntoad asked the dwarf in broken Reikspiel.

The dwarf gave no reaction, and muttered another few words of his native gibberish. Thorntoad slipped a razor from the rock and held it close beside the dwarf's ear.

'I... cut off... you... beard,' Thorntoad sneered. The dwarf's eye suddenly widened, and Thorntoad grinned in delight. The convenient tribes of men had solved another problem of his. He and the dwarf could understand each other; and that was all that Thorntoad needed. That, and time.

Delmar sat at the base of a tree, the rain drumming on his helmet. The drops poured down the grooves in the metal in tiny rivers, and each time he turned his head a fresh gush of water cascaded off like a waterfall. He clutched his cloak tightly to him, though that had long since grown sodden. Ahead of him, a group of knights and bergjaegers were stepping carefully into a dry cavern, looking for any sign of goblin presence. Every cave, every crevasse, had to be checked in case of ambush.

It had been four days since they crossed the Nedrigfluss, and it had been two days since the rain began. It fell in heavy, packed downpours such as Delmar had never before encountered. The army's progress had stalled. The higher paths had been washed away in muddy slime and the lower submerged beneath the swelling Reik. On the first day they had tried to carry on and made a little progress, but by the second it was fruitless; it took no more than a few dozen horses upon a fresh track to turn it into a morass.

Around Delmar, the other knights of Jungingen's banner did what they could to keep both themselves and their equipment dry. Some sat under trees like Delmar, some even under their horses; they had stored their bright plumes, and their scarlet cloaks were so waterlogged that they were nearly black. It was a picture of misery, and Delmar felt the most miserable of all.

This campaign was not as he had hoped his first would be. He had not even seen the enemy. The goblins knew they stood little chance against the knights at close quarters and so they gave ground, harassing them from a distance. The only proof Delmar even had of their existence had been the occasional shower of black arrows from the depths of the woods and the tops of cliffs. They caused little harm to the knights in their thick armour, but each time the column was attacked, it came to a halt while the site of the attack was investigated and secured.

Delmar's investigations concerning Griesmeyer and his father were equally unsuccessful. He had spoken to every knight in his banner, but none had been with the order twenty years before. Preceptor Jungingen himself had only served for ten. He was ambitious as well, and was determined to reach one of the senior offices within the order, and so only had praise for the influential Griesmeyer.

Though Delmar was surrounded now by nearly a thousand men whom he called brother, there was not one of them whom he trusted enough to confide in. For all the talk of brotherhood during their training, of the connection that ran through each knight of the Reiksguard, here he was on campaign and he felt nothing. The older knights of the banner had drawn close during the war in the north, but he had not been a part of that. Amongst the knights of his vigil, Siebrecht, Gausser, Falkenhayn and the rest, those brothers to whom he should be closest, there was still that division.

Delmar had thought, had hoped, that the rivalry between the Reiklanders and the Provincials would have fallen away on campaign, that they would be united in the face of the common foe, but it had not happened. The distance between the two factions was still there, and Delmar no longer fit with either. He could not stand Falkenhayn's superiority and posturing, and yet there was no place for him amongst the Provincials.

For all of Gausser's words the day of the aborted duel, he and Siebrecht had never been out of each other's company, and yet Delmar could not make his peace with the knight from Nuln. Gausser had shamed Delmar into withdrawing his challenge, but Siebrecht had never withdrawn his own injurious comments. His mind may have been sick with grief at the time, but it was no longer. He therefore either meant what he had said, in which case he denigrated everything that Delmar believed in, or he did not and it was sheer pride and arrogance that prevented him apologising. If that was the case then he was just as bad as Falkenhayn, and Delmar wanted nothing to do with either of them.

A bergjaeger emerged from the cavern and declared it clear. Delmar and the knights around him wearily clambered back to their feet, brushing off the mud as best they could, and led their horses inside.

Some way ahead, Kurt Helborg led his own horse into the shelter beneath a ledge. Ahead of him a crew of a light cannon had blocked the path, struggling to lever their burden upwards. It was too wet to bring out the map, but Helborg did not need it in any case. This territory was burnt into his brain and he saw the pattern of mountains and rivers every time he closed his eyes. For all the care and attention to detail that had gone into its creation, though, the map did not tell him what he most desperately needed to know. Where, in Sigmar's name, was his enemy?

Councillors of state like Count von Walfen and the Baron von Stirgau thought they knew what war was because they read dispatches and watched it happen from a distance. Helborg had heard of a game that was becoming increasingly popular amongst the noblemen of Altdorf and the palace courtiers. They used models as fighting men, and they played on a board to represent a battlefield, standing over it as gods. They thought it taught them strategy, generalship, the qualities of a Reiksmarshal. Helborg had had Preceptor Trier sit down with him for an hour and teach him the basics of the game; Helborg had then vowed never to play it again. It was a toy, an exercise in fantasy. Nothing more. Had the players been blindfolded, kept in separate rooms, only been told once an hour of the positions of their forces and been required to feed their models each day or have them disappear, then, perhaps, they might acquire the merest inkling of command.

The army had progressed nearly five miles up the western bank of the Reik, passing the lower peak of the Litzbach and crossing another smaller tributary, known as the Sonnfluss. The vanguard of the army had reached the next tributary along, the Unkenfluss, and there it had paused; for on the other side of the Unkenfluss was Und Urbaz.

Und Urbaz was little more than an outpost, a walled watchtower and storerooms for trade. But nothing constructed by the dwarfs was ever less than sturdy and as a race they could not help but build with a touch of grandeur. Und Urbaz was as strong as any Empire fort, and its walls and towers were sculpted with the faces of dwarfen warriors and the anvil and fire totems of Karak Angazhar.

The dwarfs, though, were nowhere to be seen. The grey walls were blackened with smoke, and the lower sculptures had been attacked and chiselled away. Whether the place had been captured or whether the dwarfs had left of their own accord, Helborg could not discern. Goblins had certainly been there since, and if they hid there still then they could wreak havoc upon the army as it tried to cross the Unkenfluss.

Jaegar Voll assured Helborg that the Unkenfluss could be forded an hour or so to the west and, for once, Helborg had relented in his pursuit of speed. He sent Sub-Marshal Zöllner and Wallenrode's banner up the tributary. They were to cross where they could, then take Und Urbaz from the flank. And if they failed, Helborg had deployed the cannon ready to pound Und Urbaz to dust.

Zöllner's knights were harassed by goblin archers from the heights every step of the way, but their casualties were light, their armour protecting them from the goblins' barbs. It took them half a day, though, to reach the ford in the Unkenfluss and then circle back.

As the rain began again, Helborg watched Zöllner's assault from across the river. As he expected, Zöllner orchestrated an expert assault with his knights both mounted and on foot. They quickly surmounted the undefended walls and disappeared inside. All a general's skill, though, could not protect his men from the unknown, and Helborg waited impatiently for them to re-emerge. Half an hour passed, and Helborg watched Zöllner himself head into the outpost. Whether it meant that they had encountered the enemy or not, Helborg did not know. He did not, though, try to call over or send one of his guard to check. He had trained Zöllner, he had trained all his preceptors personally. They trusted his orders, and he trusted them to carry them out.

After an hour, Zöllner's knights re-emerged. There had been no goblins. The chambers under Und Urbaz had been cut deep and had taken time to explore. But Helborg's hope that Und Urbaz might hold some means of communicating with the dwarfs was in vain. The tunnels which stretched further into the mountains had been collapsed, deliberately.

With Zöllner's knights standing watch, the rest of the army crossed behind them. The soldiers hoping to spend a few dry days inside the outpost were to be disappointed, however. The storerooms were full to their low ceilings with the charred remains of barrels and crates, and the stench the goblins had left behind was unbearable.

Even the watchtower was no use, for its insides had been gutted and it floors broken apart. And so it was left there, unclaimed by either side, looming over the army as the rain poured down.

Und Urbaz was the gate to Karak Angazhar, keeping all the unwelcome, men included, from trespassing too deep into the dwarfen kingdom. For beyond Und Urbaz lay the great mountain bastion known as the Stadel-horn, which dipped at only one place for the route of the Reik. Voll said the dwarfs called it Bar Kadrin, but the bergjaegers called it the Dragon's Jaw.

It was there, Helborg predicted, that the goblins would attack. And it was there, he knew, that they might be destroyed.

The Dragon's Jaw, just as Und Urbaz, bore the marks of its previous own-ers. The dwarfs, in more prosperous times, had carved giant faces of their ancestors into the rocky outcrops on each side, in the hope that they would watch over the river below them and the dwarfs' enterprise. When the greenskins had taken control, they too had put their own touch upon the landscape and smashed the faces into grotesque parodies more akin to their own features.

The Jaw cut through the Stadelhorn bastion, leaving the heights to the west and the peak known as the Predigtstuhl to the east. It sides were steep and what little level ground there was at the base of the pass was filled with the raging Reik. Helborg's army would be horribly exposed as it marched through, for only three or four men could walk abreast on either bank. For all that the goblins may have abandoned Und Urbaz, they would not, they could not, leave them to travel through the pass unopposed.

Helborg sheltered against the thundering rain in the lee of the watch-tower and looked out into the Jaw. He could not simply entrust his fate to Sigmar and advance blindly into that. In the first two days since they entered the mountains, he had sent out scouting parties spread on either side of the army's line of advance to look for the enemy. They had found them. None of his scouts had managed to travel more than a mile from the main body before being attacked and driven back. If they could not ven-ture even that far without the protection of armoured knights, there was no chance that a single rider might slip past and make it all the way to Karak Angazhar. The dwarfs, Helborg assumed, must be in similar straits for if they had sent a messenger, by boat or foot, then it had not reached him.

It had been Jaeger Voll who found the solution, and on the third day he had left the army to make the arrangements. He had only just returned.

'Did you get them?' Helborg asked the smaller man.

'Aye, my lord. They're outside.'

'Good,' Helborg said. 'Where would be best for them?'

'Normally,' the bergjaeger said, 'we would use them from the Litzbach, from there they could reach Und Urbaz. But now the dwarfs are no longer here, the Litzbach will be no good.'

'Then where?'

The bergjaeger brought out his own small map, painted with black oil on calfskin and quite waterproof. 'The only place then is here.' A dirty finger pointed at a spot. Helborg peered down. The bergjaeger's finger was pointed at the Predigtstuhl.

'That mountain, jaeger, is huge, and the western face is infested with goblins. I have had more and more reports of sightings every hour.'

'Aye,' the bergjaeger muttered patiently, 'but we will not need to be at the peak. On the eastern face, there is a ridge. If we go around the Predigtstuhl and up onto that ridge, then we will reach Karak Angazhar itself.'

'Brother Sternberg?' Helborg called for the knight further down the wall.

'Yes, Marshal?'

'Who is there left to cross the Unkenfluss?'

'The sergeants' rearguard, Marshal, and Preceptor Jungingen and his banner.'

'Very well. We will divert Jungingen and his knights to the eastern bank of the Reik. You can meet them there, Jaeger Voll.'

'Aye,' the bergjaeger replied, but did not move. Above them, the rain continued to fall.

Helborg considered the man for a moment. He was often dubious about these kinds of local irregular troops: their loyalties were divided between the Empire and their home; they were unused to direct command and often proved stubbornly independent. They had no understanding of the brutal choices that war put upon commanders and their men. This wiry bergjaeger with his pointed face had proved himself motivated and ingenious, but his obedience had yet to be tested.

'I will have a message sent to Preceptor Jungingen to expect you and your men. You leave at once.'

'Aye, my lord. We will set out as soon as the storm breaks.'

Here was the moment, Helborg knew, where the true extent of the bergjaeger's loyalty would emerge.

'No, Jaeger Voll. At once. You must be in position to act as soon as the rain clears; we cannot wait and hope that it holds off long enough for you to circumvent the Predigtstuhl as well.'

The bergjaeger paused and sucked air through his teeth in thought. He knew, far better even than the great Reiksmarshal, the danger in that order, in climbing even part way up the Predigtstuhl in such weather, not knowing what forces might oppose them. But then, the Reiksmarshal knew that he knew better, and yet still it had to be done.

'Aye, Marshal,' Voll said slowly. 'At once.'

Helborg dismissed the bergjaeger with a nod. This mountain hunter was indeed proving to be quite exceptional.

As his boat approached, Siebrecht sat and eyed the eastern bank of the Reik warily. The water had risen to the forest's edge and the trees cloaked the ground in shadow. He could not help but be reminded of their crossing of the Nedrigfluss and of the arrows that had shot from the darkness to kill them. The leading elements of Jungingen's banner had already landed and cleared the bank, but still Siebrecht could not quiet his trepidation. Gausser and Bohdan behind him were speaking of their new companions, Jaeger Voll and his men. Five of them had caught the knights' attention, for instead of carrying a bow they each had a long pipe, twice the height of a man and curved and splayed at the bottom end, strapped in a harness on their backs. The tubes were wrapped up tight against the rain.

Siebrecht turned to his brothers. 'Standard bearers, do you think?'

'Amidst the woods?' Gausser shook his head.

'They look like winged lancers, down on their luck,' Bohdan remarked dryly.

Ahead of them, Delmar turned about in his seat. 'I have seen longrifles that length in the hands of hunters in Hochland.'

'Perhaps,' Siebrecht carefully replied. He felt the eyes of the other young knights upon them, watching what would happen between the two, and suddenly could not think of anything else to say.

No one else had any other suggestions to make and so Delmar turned back around.

'Ready for landing,' the boatman announced, and the knights took hold of the side of the boat with one hand and the hilt of their swords with the other.

The knights left their boat as soon as it hit the bank, and made for the cover of the trees. They had left their horses behind; they carried all they needed. The sergeants took the boats back across the river so as to leave no trace of them for a goblin scout to see.

Led by the bergjaegers, the knights cut directly away from the bank, straight into the forest. They kept to the low ground, where the tree canopy was thickest, and skirted around the lower slopes of the Predigtstuhl. The rain over the previous few days had made the forest floor treacherous; dips in the ground that had filled with water slowed their progress, but threatened no more than the dignity of any knight who slipped into them. Siebrecht was thankful that they were not fully armoured. The knights wore only partial plate, as with such a trek before them, the weight was not worth the protection. As ever, the bergjaegers led the way, searching out the driest paths, but the five pipebearers stayed in the middle of the column. The orders were that these men were there to be protected.

Siebrecht, never at home in woodland, quickly lost his bearings. There was nothing to see but the trees ahead, which looked remarkably similar to the trees behind. The grey light that filtered through the clouds and the leaves did little to help him distinguish between them. All the knights stuck close together, hemmed in by the forest on either side. At some arbitrary moment, about an hour or so into their trek, Jaeger Voll called them to a halt, then led them off again sharply to the right.

'I am glad someone has a clue where we are going,' Siebrecht muttered under his breath.

'We're to the north-east of the Predigtstuhl, we're about to climb the eastern face,' Delmar supplied.

Siebrecht had not meant his idle thought to be overheard, and felt a touch of resentment at Delmar's presumption. 'You sound pretty certain of yourself, Reinhardt.'

Delmar shrugged. 'I am.'

Sure enough, not ten minutes passed before the ground started to rise, the mud giving way to stone. The canopy began to thin and, in a gap, the knights saw the eastern side of the peak of the Predigtstuhl. Siebrecht forwent comment.

The forest of the lower slopes had been dark and gloomy, but as they climbed, the woods took on an added air of malevolence. The trees were thinner, their bark as black as cannon metal. Their lower branches had been hacked away; a few even had crude glyphs daubed upon them, though they were old and faded. Marks of their goblin owners, Siebrecht guessed, and realised for the first time how deep into enemy territory the knights had come. No one unsheathed a weapon, though, as they needed both of their hands free for the difficult path ahead. They had left the mud behind, but now the knights had to clamber up rocks, slick with the rain. The bergjaegers took turns standing watch over each obstacle, ensuring every knight made it safely up. Jaeger Voll somehow managed to be everywhere at once, climbing up and down the side of the path with the ease of one born to it.

The sound of the rain was soon drowned by the ragged breathing of the knights. Gausser, to Siebrecht's surprise, was the first of the squadron to start to lag behind. Siebrecht dropped back to help him, but the Nordlander swatted him away, ashamed of his own weakness. Siebrecht himself, though, could not maintain the pace for much longer, and he and Alptraum gradually slowed and watched Delmar obstinately pull ahead, keeping up with the leaders. Inexorably, and despite Voll's best efforts, the column began to stretch out back along its path.

Finally, Siebrecht rounded a tight corner and saw the lead knights leaning against the boulders ahead of him. He flopped down beside Delmar, chest heaving.

'Thank Shallya you stopped,' Siebrecht gasped, then realised Delmar was staring at him with urgent warning.

'What?' Siebrecht asked. Delmar urgently put his finger to his mouth. Siebrecht peered over Delmar's head. There was a deep cavern, hidden behind a great flat stone. Voll had crept towards its entrance, his pick ready in his hand, and was preparing to go inside.

'What is it?' Siebrecht whispered. 'Is it goblins?'

'We don't know,' Delmar replied. 'But the bergjaegers don't think so. There are no markings, no totems around the sides.'

'What is it then?'

'Maybe trolls, something wild for certain. Maybe it's the reason the goblins don't come here any more.' Delmar shifted so as to have easier access to his sword. 'Maybe Dragon's Jaw isn't just a name.'

'You are so great a comfort to me, Reinhardt.'

One of the knights ahead of them shot them both an angry look and they quietened. Voll disappeared into the cavern's mouth. And what if he doesn't come out again, Siebrecht found himself thinking, what then?

But Voll did come out again, his weapon stored back in his pack. He gave the knights a brief shake of the head and then led them on. The bergjaegers began to range further ahead of the knights, determined to discover any further threats before the column chanced upon them. Siebrecht kept close to the vanguard now, and saw the bergjaegers appear and disappear amongst the trees. The knights passed a few more caves, these ones clearly goblin dens, though long abandoned.

Then, the trees thinned and the knights emerged onto the crest of a ridge. The storm had finally moved on and Siebrecht could see the dark thunderhead clouds slide east in the direction of Black Fire Pass. To the south, there was the distinctive crater of a dormant volcano and beyond that a tantalising glimpse of the corner of some great lake from which the highest reaches of the River Reik flowed.

Preceptor Jungingen wasted no time admiring the view; even while the rest of the banner arrived he began addressing his knights.

'Brothers, we hold here. I cannot tell you how long, only that in the next few hours we may have every single foe upon this mountain at our throats. The Reiksmarshal himself told me that the fate of our campaign relies upon us keeping them back until we are finished. Prepare yourselves, my brothers, for today we prove our Marshal's trust.'

The other knights solemnly concurred, but Siebrecht had already begun looking past his preceptor at the pipebearers who were now carefully unwrapping their strange burdens.

'Are they horns?' Siebrecht asked, approaching the bergjaegers after Jungingen had finished speaking.

'If horns can be twelve feet long,' Gausser said, 'then that they can be.'

'Aye,' Jaeger Voll answered them. 'The sighorns of the Black Mountains they are.'

'And what can they do?' Siebrecht continued. 'Will they bring the mountains crashing down upon the goblins' heads?'

'Perhaps,' Voll replied. 'In their way.'

Like many of the devices of man, the sighorns of the Black Mountains had their origins in war. The human tribes of the region, aping their dwarfen betters, blew horns as they charged into battle to frighten their enemies. It was the Averlanders' great hero Siggurd, according to their legends at least, who fashioned a warhorn so long that he could sound the news of the great victory at Black Fire Pass to all the tribes of the mountains at once.

Other legends, however, say that the language of the sighorns came from the dwarfs of Karak Angazhar who, notorious for their isolationism, gave the mountain men a means by which messages could be passed without the need for physical meeting or revealing the location of their hold.

Whatever the truth of its creation, and though Averland soldiers now marched to the drum and the trumpet, the tradition of the sighorn messages to the dwarfs of Karak Angazhar had survived. Voll merely hoped the dwarfs would be listening.

Delmar heard the low, mournful notes of the sighorns doled out in careful measure down the slope of the Predigtstuhl, through the valley of the Upper Reik and towards the peaks where, somewhere, Karak Angazhar was hidden. Now he understood Jungingen's words. Before they reached dwarfen ears, those notes would be heard by every goblin in between. The knights were exposed there on the wrong side of the mountain, waiting for a reply, and they had just announced their presence to anyone who cared to listen.

Delmar stood on sentry, expecting for a goblin horde to surge over the peak above or burst from the trees below. He kept his hand ready by his sword, his father's sword, which would once more be wielded against the Empire's foes, and waited.

The sound of the horns reached even the great stone goblin, and the ears of the Death Caps there. They reached for their weapons, the strongest of them bearing swords and axes taken from the dwarfs, and looked to Thorntoad in anticipation. Thorntoad, however, snapped at them to stay still, and disappeared into his lair.

His prisoner was still there; the shaman had kept the dwarf alive these past days, forcing him to eat scraps of meat, stolen bread and a very specific type of toadstool of Thorntoad's own cultivation. The poisons in the toadstool were not fatal, but they attacked the mind, fuddling the senses and churning its memories. The dwarf's beard was ragged and damp with its own sweat, for it laboured within a fever-dream, not awake, not asleep, not in the present, not in the past, but somewhere in between.

Thorntoad used one of his nails to open the dwarf's eye. Its pupil was as small as a pinhead. It was ready. Thorntoad hung from a hoop, so that his lips were an inch from the dwarf's ear.

'Hear me... Gramsson...' The prisoner's name was the first thing he had discovered. 'Hear me...'

Thorntoad could see the dwarf struggling to wake, but failing.

'Eye... close... Gramsson...' Thorntoad reassured him. 'Speak...'

The dwarf began to talk in its native language once again.

'No... Man tongue... speak... man tongue...'

The dwarf's eyes opened and crossed for an instant. New beads of sweat formed above its eyebrows.

'Aye, my king,' the dwarf replied. Thorntoad nodded. For some reason his prisoner's mind had fixated upon the dwarfen king and it had addressed Thorntoad as such during their previous interrogation. Thorntoad was only too happy to encourage the drugged misconception.

'Hear... the noise... hear the horns?'

'Aye, my king.'

'It is... message... from men...'

The dwarf paused and Thorntoad feared its mind had slipped away again. But it had not, it was listening.

'Aye, they call to Karak Angazhar.' The dwarf paused again as it translated the horn's notes. 'They wish a response.'

Thorntoad's spines bristled with excitement. 'Hear... Gramsson... tell me more...'

The sighorns blew for an hour and still no goblins had been seen. Some of the knights began to relax, considering that if the goblins were to attack then they would have done so already. Others grew more concerned, believing instead that the delay gave the goblins a chance to mass together, making it all the more likely that when they did attack, Jungingen's knights would be overwhelmed.

Siebrecht, for the first time since leaving Altdorf, began to feel that old nervous buzz that meant his body was craving a drink. If he just had a single cup of wine, he would quite happily wait for these greenskins until the winter came. He glanced around at his companions. Gausser was like a boulder, solid, unmoving; Alptraum was humming along with the sighorns. Over with the Reiklanders, Hardenburg appeared to be in an even worse way than Siebrecht; and Delmar... Delmar was relaxed but alert, at rest but ready for action. It was the look of a hunter.

Voll patrolled the sentries' positions and stopped by Siebrecht. He looked up at the clouds warily. It was too early for dusk, Siebrecht knew, it was another rainstorm brewing.

'If we are here much longer,' Siebrecht said to the bergjaeger quietly, 'we shall not need the greenskins. The rain will wash us off this mountain before they will.'

'The rain is good and the rain is bad,' Voll replied. 'The goblins don't like it. While it rains, we're safe. Mostly.'

'And the bad?' Siebrecht had to ask.

'Can't use the horns. We have to keep them covered. And even if we played on, the storm would drown them out.'

'But then we will head home, won't we? We cannot be meant to stay here the night.' Siebrecht felt himself give a tiny shake. He put it down to the cold.

'It's not my place to say,' Voll said evenly. 'But I heard your leader's words. Didn't sound to me as though he planned on leaving until the job was done.'

Just then, the sighorns quietened and the players did not start the measure again. Alptraum stopped humming and started listening. From somewhere in the mountains, a dwarfen horn was replying.

TEN

GRAMRIK

'King Gramrik Thunderhead?' Kurt Helborg asked ceremonially.

'Aye,' the imposing ruler of Karak Angazhar replied in formal Reikspiel. 'We have kept our oath to answer the call of the hunters' horns, just as we have upheld our ancient oaths to defend the mouth of the great river.' The dwarfen lord planted the bottom of the long shaft of his axe-hammer firmly on the ground. 'We are glad that the sons of Sigmar have come to destroy the grobi by our side.'

The Reiksmarshal and the dwarfen king met on the lower reaches of the Achhorn, a razor-thin ridge on the far western side of the Stadelhorn Heights that stood apart from the mountains around. Helborg had had his wish granted. More than he had wished. The king himself had answered his call to meet. There had been a price, however. The dwarfs had opened up a new tunnel, outside the goblins' siege lines, one whose existence they had so far kept secret. Now they had revealed it, the tunnel would have to be collapsed lest it allow the goblins back into Karak Angazhar. Preceptor Jungingen was a capable man and he had sent a squadron of his knights ahead of the rest of the banner to bring the dwarfen message back to the army as quickly as they could. But even then it had allowed Helborg precious little time. Griesmeyer had the Reiksmarshal's personal guard to arms at once and they sent word ahead so that, as they raced west, Osterna's banner was primed to escort them.

It should be enough; Helborg knew that the unruly goblins needed time to gather their forces together. A hundred and fifty Reiksguard knights would be enough to brush aside any goblin warband that stumbled across their path. Helborg left orders for the rest of the army to ready themselves, but to remain where they were. It would not do to have dribs and drabs of men come after them, nor was he willing to weaken the main force so greatly that they might be assaulted in his absence.

They rode hard. For the first time since entering the mountains each knight gave his steed its head. They journeyed up the Unkenfluss and around the goblin tribes that inhabited the Stadelhorn Heights and up

425

onto the Achhorn. With surprise on their side, his knights had arrived at the meeting place unchallenged. Helborg doubted, though, that the journey back would be so easy.

'Now let us talk,' King Gramrik declared.

Delmar and Siebrecht held the reins of the horses of the Marshal's guard. They were most fortunate to be there: it had been the two of them who had been first to reach the Reiksmarshal with the dwarf's message and so, when his guard had mounted up, Griesmeyer had beckoned them on as well. Now, they were present when the two commanders, one human, one dwarf, met for the first time. Their two personal guards, Griesmeyer's knights and Gramrik's dwarfen veterans, stayed a few paces back; this was a meeting of equal allies, after all, and neither side wished to appear that they were imposing their will.

Delmar stared at the dwarf veterans standing rigidly behind their lord. They wore plate armour similar to the Reiksguard's; unsurprising, Delmar realised, as the order's plate was forged by dwarfen armourers in Altdorf. But the knights' armour was, for the most part, shining and new; the dwarfs' plate bore the scars and dents of hundreds of battles and skirmishes. Their axes were notched from use, yet still carried a razor-keen edge. The warriors' faces were covered with fearsome warmasks of plate and mail, and the eyes behind them glared out with an indomitable determination. These were warriors indeed.

The sky was still dark. The storm which had begun to threaten whilst they were on the Predigtstuhl still had not erupted. The clouds hung low, bulging as though filled with water and ready to burst. The wind had also picked up and maverick gusts blew up and down the slope.

'That is our position, King Thunderhead,' Helborg concluded. 'We can advance to you but the bank on either side of the river through the valley is too narrow. We cannot get through without support, not without great cost at least.'

The dwarf lord ruminated deeply and then spoke: 'We will honour our ancestors, and hope that they will provide.'

Helborg was taken aback by the curtness of the response, but then he sensed something in the king's tone. Honouring their ancestors nothing. The dwarfs of Karak Angazhar had something, some scheme or device, of which they did not wish him to know. He struggled for a moment between relief and annoyance. How could he plan effectively, form a strategy, how could he command an army if his own allies would not tell him what they were to do?

'Well, Reiksmarshal?' Gramrik prompted. The King of Karak Angazhar stamped the shaft of his axe-hammer on the rocky ground again and, as if in response, the clouds above them crashed with thunder.

'Grobi!' the alarm went up around them. A dwarf hurried up to Gramrik: 'Grobi, my king. There are grobi warbands in the heights to the east.'

'How many?' Gramrik demanded.

'Two, three hundred, coming up from the ground,' the dwarf replied.

'We are out of time, Reiksmarshal. I must return to the tunnel before my miners bring it down...'

'Goblins! Goblins! Reiksguard to your horses!' the bellicose Osterna cried as he galloped through his men.

'Osterna!' Helborg bellowed, meaning to quieten his subordinate. Gramrik was already making to leave.

'Goblins, Marshal! Goblins to the north!'

'I...' Helborg began, and then realised what Osterna had said. 'To the north?'

'Yes, Marshal.' Osterna pointed back the way the knights had come. 'A few hundred to the north, blocking our path.'

'Grobi!' the call came again, but not from the north or the east. This time it came from the south, and at that Helborg realised that surprise had never been on his side at all.

'Treachery!' Gramrik boomed, clutching his axe-hammer in both hands.

'Never!' Helborg snapped back. 'No knight of mine...'

'No dwarf would ever...'

The sky crashed again, echoing the two generals' anger. Helborg's guard and Gramrik's warriors were tense, each eyeing the other, waiting to follow their commander's lead. Preceptor Osterna, meanwhile, was organising his mounted knights into their squadrons, ready to attempt a break-out through the green horde.

'Get on your horses, manling, and run,' Gramrik boomed. 'I was a skrati to allow myself to be lured from the hold. Angazhar will stand, as it always has, alone!'

Helborg looked at the furious dwarfen king, at the readied dwarfen warriors behind him, at the goblins advancing, surrounding his knights, and came to his decision.

He drew the runefang sword from its gilded scabbard at his side. The dwarfen warriors hefted their hammers and the Reiksguard went for their weapons in reply. Helborg prepared no blow, however, instead he reversed his blade and held it out to Gramrik. Even in the grim half-light the runefang still shone brilliantly.

'King Gramrik. Do you know what this is?' He indicated the runes etched deep into the metal. 'Do you know what they mean?'

Gramrik did not need to read them. 'Aye, there's none of my kind that doesn't.'

'They were a gift; from your High King to my Emperor. A gift of thanks for when Sigmar stood beside Kurgan Ironbeard in battle at the birth of my Empire. We stood together then. We shall stand together now,' Helborg stated calmly. 'My brothers and I came to defend your hold and all within it. If you doubt me, then here, here is your gift returned. You may take it back.'

Gramrik's thunder faded, and he held up his hand to refuse the ancient sword.

'I know why you truly come, Kurt Helborg of the manling Empire, but you have spoken well nonetheless. We shall stand together then, as Sigmar and great King Kurgan did. But it matters little unless one of us survives. They have surrounded us, and if my tunnel still stands it shall not for long. Your horses though, can carry you out. I shall make my stand here and buy you the time to escape.'

'If you do not return, King Thunderhead, then none of your kin will answer my calls.'

'Aye,' Gramrik admitted.

'Then you must return to your hold, no matter what the cost. We must make for the tunnel, as fast as we can. And if that is lost, we make our stand where there is something solid which may protect our backs.'

'Then put your backs to ours, manling. For you'll find there's nothing more solid than a dwarf with an oath to keep.'

Gramrik turned to order his warriors, and Helborg called Griesmeyer over. 'Tell Osterna, forget our path back; we follow the dwarfs.' Griesmeyer nodded and went to obey, when Helborg caught his arm and brought him close.

'Find a horse yourself,' the Reiksmarshal ordered, his eyes fierce. 'Get through their lines, however you can, and bring my army back to me.'

'Delmar!' Griesmeyer shouted through the storm, riding up beside him. 'Keep your steed!'

Delmar looked about, confused; he raised his visor and a flurry of rain splashed against his face. 'My lord?'

'The Marshal needs us to gather the army and bring it here. Dump anything from your saddle that you do not need to fight,' Griesmeyer replied. 'We shall need the space, for we carry the life of our Reiksmarshal and the King of Karak Angazhar with us.'

Griesmeyer spurred his horse and Delmar followed. The two riders raced for the thinner section of the goblin encirclement. Against such determination, the few goblins in their path scurried to the side, and Delmar saw the path through was clear. But then the black arrows whistled through the air and plunged down upon them. Delmar felt their impact against his back and side and hunched over the saddle so as to protect his horse. He galloped clear, but Griesmeyer was not so fortunate. With a screeching whinny, the old knight's mount fell.

Delmar heard the sound and checked his horse to glance back.

'On! On!' Griesmeyer shouted, already on his feet from his stricken mount. 'Your duty first!'

Griesmeyer began to run from the eager goblins and their spears, and Delmar turned his horse and spurred it again.

* * *

Thorntoad squatted upon his palanquin as he watched the men and dwarfs panic before him. Seeing them squirm and struggle warmed him against the driving rain.

'See, Burakk Craw!' he said to the ogre pacing beside him. 'The horns were not a trick. They are exactly where the prisoner said they would be!' Thorntoad watched to see in which direction the dwarfs were forming. 'And now they show their path. Go to it!'

Burakk licked his lips in anticipation and loped away. Thorntoad hopped back and forth in his excitement. Even with forewarning, he had only time to gather a portion of his own Death Caps from their warrens, but the Biters in the north and the Stinkhorns to the south had been closer. He had run to death a dozen of his bearers rousting the two tribes, but it had been worth it. No matter what the dwarfs and the men did, in a few minutes they would be overwhelmed.

'My men are mounted, Marshal,' Osterna reported back.

'Good. The king is ready, you must clear his path.' Helborg pointed down the ridge to the south in the direction Gramrik was already marching. 'Charge, break through, circle back and...'

Helborg's voice trailed away. 'Marshal?' Osterna asked, but Helborg was looking past him. There, in the north, a single knight was fighting alone against the tide of goblins rising against him.

'Griesmeyer,' Helborg said.

Osterna turned and saw it too. 'I'll bring my men around, Marshal. We will save him.'

'No,' Helborg countermanded. 'Follow my orders. Protect the king.'

Helborg spurred away leaving Osterna no chance to argue.

Griesmeyer felt the goblin leap upon his back and scratch its nails across his visor, grasping for his eyes. He switched his grip on his sword and then swung it back over his shoulder as though he were a flagellant absolving himself with a whip. The sword cut through the goblin's shoulder and into its back. Its grip loosened and Griesmeyer hauled it off him with his free hand.

He heard the goblins closing behind him again; with his next step he planted his foot and twisted, whipping his sword around in a rising stroke. One grasping goblin lost an arm, the second had his face cut in two. They fell back and tripped the others behind them. Griesmeyer did not stop to see the results, but struggled on. The mud beneath his foot shifted and, off-balance, he slipped. Desperately, he caught his fall, and his knee twisted and screamed as the weight fell badly upon it.

Through the drumming of the rain upon his helmet, he heard Reiksguard trumpets sound the charge ahead. For a moment, he thought he was saved, but the thunder of their hooves receded. Wherever they were charging, it was not for him.

He took another step and his knee near collapsed beneath him. He realised he could no longer run. This was the end, then. He turned and faced the horde behind him, and the goblins crowed as their prey stood at bay. He would see how many he could take with him. A dozen sounded fair. He had a bad leg, after all.

But then the thunder rose again.

'Reiksguard!' Helborg roared as he charged in. His mighty steed barrelled into the goblin warband and sent the closest goblins flying. He swept the deadly runefang around in a great arc and ended five more greenskin lives. His horse leapt forwards, trampling more beneath its hooves, and the blade scythed down again.

With a nudge of his heel, Helborg turned his horse from the goblins as they reeled back and spurred it towards Griesmeyer.

'Brother!'

Griesmeyer reached up his hand to grasp Helborg's as he passed, but Helborg leaned out, lifted Griesmeyer bodily from the ground and swung him into the saddle.

'The army... the message...?' Helborg shouted without ceremony as they raced away.

'Delmar got through,' Griesmeyer gasped back, 'Delmar got through.'

Siebrecht roared as he rode amongst Osterna's knights. The goblins did not even stand, but broke before the knights struck. The knights followed through, stabbing at the backs of the dark-clothed goblins as they scrambled away. Gods, Siebrecht exulted, such a feeling of power! Of unstoppable force! His heart raced. He felt sick. He felt magnificent. He struck down again and another black shape collapsed with a shriek, but he could hear nothing but the pounding of his blood in his ears.

'Turn!' Osterna roared. 'Turn and reform!' Siebrecht did not even hear it until another knight smacked his helmet with the flat of his blade. Siebrecht caught himself and turned.

Behind them, in the gloom of the storm and the closing day, Siebrecht could barely make out the battle behind him. The king had led his warriors into the knights' path, but the goblins to the east were moving in too quickly. Osterna had reformed, but Siebrecht's distraction had left him far behind when the knights charged again. Siebrecht was thirty paces behind them, and so was the first to see the ogres.

Osterna's men charged, but these goblins held. The horses kicked and the knights hacked away at their foe below them. Burakk and his ogres had run around the lower level of the ridge, out of sight of the Reiksguard, and then climbed up. They held their warcry back until they were only a few paces away. Preceptor Osterna, closest to them, whirled around in his saddle just in time to see Burakk's mace smash into his face.

The blow was so powerful that it knocked Osterna's head off his shoulders and sent it spiralling into the air. The knights' armour, which had proved so invulnerable against the goblins' weapons, was little defence against the strength of an ogre. The next knight was knocked from his mount by a mallet, his ribs broken. Another dodged away from the swing of a cutlass the length of a man, only to have it decapitate his panicking horse. More knights were culled as the hefty clubs and bludgeons broke skulls and snapped necks.

'Back! Back!' the order went up amongst the knights, and their steeds needed no encouragement. The ogres launched themselves forwards and tackled their horses to the ground, sending the knights sprawling into the waiting clutches of the triumphant goblins.

Just then a single cry rose above the ogres' roars. It was Siebrecht charging in. He had not thought to hold back; he had just seen his brothers in peril and so gone to intervene. It was only when the ogres turned to look at him, that he realised he was about to die, and that it would be his own stupid fault.

He rode down the edge of the ridge, where the path was clear of Osterna's men, and held his sword out before him as though it were a lance. He picked his target, an ogre holding the severed arm of a knight dead at its feet, and aimed for above its armoured gut-plate, straight for the heart. Siebrecht's sword struck true, the impact near knocking him out of his saddle, and he plunged the blade deep into the ogre's heart.

The ogre looked down in surprise at the blade embedded in his chest. And then he started to snigger.

'Morr have mercy,' Siebrecht whispered to himself, as he reached in his saddle for his pistol. The ogre seized him with both hands and lifted him bodily from his terrified mount. The ogre's mouth opened wide, intending to bite Siebrecht's head off. Siebrecht's pistol was in his hand, but the ogre had his arm pinned by his side.

Siebrecht twisted his hand until the muzzle pointed straight up. As the ogre's mouth came down from above him, he pulled the trigger with his thumb and prayed the powder had kept dry. The ignition burnt his wrist, the bullet whipped past his face and shot through the roof of the ogre's mouth.

Siebrecht tried to break free from the ogre's grip, but even as it died, its brain shot through, it was too strong. The ogre toppled backwards, off the ridge, out into the blackness, taking Siebrecht with him.

Delmar saw the body in the grey light of the next morning.

He had ridden as hard as he could with the Reiksmarshal's message, but night had closed in before he had made half the distance back and he had to find his way back in the rain and the pitch darkness. Eventually, he had reached the camp and found Sub-Marshal Zöllner. Zöllner, though, much as the decision pained him, could not send his men out into the night, and so they had had to wait. At the first hint of light his banner had set out with Delmar riding ahead of them.

Following the route back, Delmar had spied a herd of horses in the distance, a strange sight amongst these mountains. He had ridden to them and seen the Reiksguard markings upon them. Their riders were nowhere to be seen. It was an ill omen. The Reiksguard would only loose their horses in the direst straits, where escape was no longer possible.

He had reached the site of the battle to see his worst fears confirmed. Though it was clear from the blood and broken weapons that men and goblins had fought and died in that place, there were no bodies. They had all been dragged away as food, and that meant the goblins had won.

It was then that he had looked down over the ridge's edge and seen the corpse below. It was an ogre, half-sunken into a mire. It had obviously fallen during the fight to the bottom of the slope and had then been overlooked by the goblin scavengers.

Then it moved.

Delmar looked closer in the half-light. It was definitely moving. Only a fraction, but it was enough. It was still alive. Delmar climbed down to it. His mission of rescue had been a failure. He had not been here to defend his brothers, but dispatching this one beast might bring the dead some small satisfaction.

He drew close, stepping carefully around the swampy ground, and unsheathed his sword. The ogre spasmed again, except that here, closer, Delmar could see that it was not the ogre. It was something beneath it.

'Siebrecht!' Delmar called. 'Siebrecht, can you hear me?'

Siebrecht, unconscious beneath the ogre's corpse, shifted a little. At his motion, the thick mud sucked him down further.

'Sigmar preserve us.' Delmar waded into the mud and tried to heave the ogre's body off. 'Siebrecht, wake up!'

Siebrecht did so, felt the suffocating mud all around him, felt the pressure pushing him down, and panicked. He tried to take great gulping breaths and swallowed mud instead, which made him choke and panic all the more.

'Take hold, brother.' Delmar strained as he lifted the ogre's body a fraction.

'Siebrecht!' he shouted again to get his attention. 'Take hold of me and pull yourself out.'

Siebrecht did so, grabbing Delmar and dragging himself onto firmer ground, coughing up the mud. When he was clear, Delmar collapsed and let the ogre sink.

'Siebrecht, can you talk? Did any others survive?'

Siebrecht shook his head. 'I don't know,' he gasped. 'I fell with this...' He waved a hand at the submerged ogre. 'Is it over?'

'Yes. Yes, it is.' Delmar sighed, and looked back up the slope.

'Did we win?'

'I do not think so.'

But Delmar was mistaken. Another of Zöllner's scouts had seen a section of the ridge suddenly cave in upon itself. Fearing another goblin attack, Zöllner led a squadron of knights ahead to investigate, only to discover the Reiksmarshal and the dwarfen king stepping calmly out into the dawn. Zöllner's joy at seeing Helborg alive was tempered, though, when he saw the number of his brothers laid out behind. Fully half of Osterna's men were dead, or injured so that they would never ride again. Of Osterna himself, they had only his body. His head was not recovered.

It had only been by the Reiksmarshal's own heroism that the dead had not been taken by the goblins and the ogres. Siebrecht's lone charge had bought Osterna's knights the chance to escape, but it had been the Reiksmarshal who had then ridden up and rallied them. And rather than fleeing with the dwarfs, he had led the charge back against the ogres, slaying several of them, and knocking them back long enough for his knights to gather their fallen brothers. When Gramrik saw his aim, the dwarfen king could not help but return as well and help the Reiksguard, both the living and the dead, to the safety of the tunnel.

Gramrik's miners had then collapsed the tunnel entrance behind them, and the goblins picked the battlefield clean, before they too trudged back to their warrens. The dwarfs though, had not returned to Karak Angazhar. Instead they had waited out the night with the knights beneath the ground. And when morning came, the miners dug a new tunnel to return them to the surface.

During the long night, Gramrik had revealed the truth of his scheme to aid the Empire through the Dragon's Jaw. Now, Helborg looked into the dwarf's aged face in the morning light. He saw the deep furrows in the king's brow, the scars on his cheek where his white beard no longer grew and the flint in his eyes. Helborg had spent his life fighting for the Empire, but his life was but a single season to this warrior. The success of the campaign rested upon whether these two old soldiers could trust one another.

Helborg decided they could.

'I will lead my army into the Jaw,' he said.

'Aye,' Gramrik replied solemnly. 'Be ready tomorrow morning. That'll give us time enough.'

'Time enough for you to consult your ancestors?' Helborg asked lightly.

'Aye,' Gramrik said. Helborg thought he saw the trace of a smile beneath the thick beard. 'That's about right.'

'Ten of my bulls. Ten!' Burakk the Craw waved his hands, five fingers splayed as though each one was named for one of his lost ogres.

Burakk rampaged back and forth, waiting for Thorntoad to reply. He had said nothing in front of those who had returned from the battle; to do so would have been a public challenge against Thorntoad and it was not the time to do that, not while the goblins still outnumbered Burakk's bulls three hundred to one. No, he had stayed silent out there; but in here, in private, Thorntoad owed him answers.

'Ten bulls lost,' Burakk continued, bellowing even louder. 'And what to show for it? Nothing! The Empire men, they took their fallen with them. The dwarfs the same! They left nothing. Nothing but your goblins and ten of my bulls.'

'I am certain they tasted well enough.' Thorntoad prodded Osterna's severed head with his nail, idly testing how much pressure its eyeballs could take.

'We will not win by eating our own kind, goblin. You promised me the flesh of the men and their animals. But you do not take it!' Burakk pounded the rock wall for emphasis. 'You shoot your arrows at them from afar. You snatch one or two in the night and then run when the men in armour come after you. Their army marches unchallenged. This night is the only time we have been close enough to spit upon them. When are we to attack in strength? Bring the tribes together? Drive the men back; leave their dead so we may eat? Eat!'

Thorntoad dropped from the ceiling and landed, hunched, upon the throne's back. 'Soon, Burakk Craw, soon. They are stopped already at the mouth of the valley between the mountains of the Black Ears and Biter Peak. The river runs fast, the banks are steep and narrow, and there is no path around, save that which will take them a week out of their way. We will crush their armour beneath our boulders, and when they can fight no more we will descend upon them and feed.'

'And what if the dwarfs interfere again?'

'They are captives behind our siege lines. Trapped in their hold. They cannot interfere.'

'They did so last night! What use is your siege if the dwarfs come and go at will? Give me the name of the tribe to punish and we shall feast upon them.'

'They used a secret way, and in doing so exposed it to us. We have discovered their path and the dwarfs have been forced to seal it off. They cannot use it again.' The warlord climbed the wall behind the throne and crawled, upside down, across the roof until they were so close that the ogre's rancid breath made the goblin's thorns rise. 'And as we are at war with these tribes of men, I cannot allow you to feed on the fiends I need for the fight. As you say, Burakk Craw, we will not win eating our own kind. Either of our kinds.'

Another knight that Siebrecht did not recognise shook his hand to congratulate him. Word had spread since the night before. By the time Delmar and

Siebrecht had returned to Jungingen's banner, the preceptor had heard all about Siebrecht's triumph against the ogre champion. It had been a glint of heroism in what had otherwise been a bloody night of loss.

Jungingen knew that his knights' successes reflected well upon him and so he ensured that the whole banner was turned out to give Siebrecht a worthy welcome. Siebrecht had quickly lost sight of Delmar amongst the press of his brother-knights and their commendations. As unexpected as the reception was, Siebrecht had adored it. It was just as it had been back amidst the gangs of noble youths in Nuln, where each victory over their rivals was cause for celebration. He had been the fastest blade amongst them and they had been so proud of him. Now, for the first time, the Reiksguard were proud of him as well.

Siebrecht woke that afternoon in a different humour. His brow was hot, his head was stuffed and his throat felt as though a stone were lodged within it. After the alarms of the day and night before, the Reiksmarshal had few orders for the army, but to rest and take care of the wounded and the dead, and to be ready to attack the Jaw the day after. Siebrecht could not imagine how he would be ready to fight tomorrow if he still felt as bad as this, or worse.

The sergeants had built a small cooking fire nearby for the knights' morning meal. These sergeants were strange men, Siebrecht decided. As a novice, he had thought the sergeants were little more than sentries, the tutors' muscle and, occasionally, his gaolers. But out on campaign, they were very different. They were careful, protective even, of the brother-knights. They marched all day with the army, in the evening they lit the fires and cooked, and at night they stood guard. All to ensure that when their knights went into the fray, they would fight at their best. They took their pride in carrying their knights to battle, and carrying them home again.

One of the older sergeants brought over two cups, one for Siebrecht and the other for Gausser who sat by his side. Siebrecht accepted the cup gratefully, but then smelt the horrible stench coming from it and pushed it away.

'Drink it, my lord,' the sergeant insisted.

'Damned if I will,' Siebrecht replied. 'It smells terrible. How did you make it? By washing out a cannon?'

The sergeant chuckled, and Siebrecht realised that he was not laughing with him, the sergeant was laughing at him. Siebrecht felt suddenly quite patronised. Beside him, Gausser downed his at a stroke.

'Drink it, brother,' he said. 'It is not so bad.'

Siebrecht tried to ignore the sergeant's encouraging smile and raised the cup again. He gave it a sniff in case its odour had improved. It hadn't. Instead, he held his breath as he swigged it down. As Gausser said, it did not taste as bad as it smelt. The first taste was very bitter, almost acrid, but it was quickly washed away. The sergeant nodded approvingly at him, as though he were a child who had taken his own medicine for the first time.

'You will feel better soon, my lord.'

'Will I, by the gods?' Siebrecht stared at the thick, black residue left at the bottom.

The sergeant took the cups back. 'I have served the order on campaign for nearly forty years, my lord. We know how to keep fighting men ready.'

'And how many did you poison along the way?' Siebrecht muttered, as the sergeant pottered back to the fire and to his fellows. He was being a mite uncharitable, but he was not well and the sergeants were grinning at him with patronising indulgence. Siebrecht pointedly turned away from them as another knight came over to shake his hand.

Delmar watched from the shade of the trees as Siebrecht modestly accepted another knight's compliments.

'Thinking that should have been you?' a familiar voice interrupted.

Delmar instantly stood. 'My lord Griesmeyer,' he said formally. 'How are you?'

The older knight was only half-armoured, wearing a blue doublet in place of his breastplate. He leaned casually against the tree trunk and scratched the short red beard on his chin.

'Better than when you saw me this morning. And please, Delmar, we have fought together now; surely you may call me brother.'

'Yes, my lord, I will.'

Griesmeyer laughed lightly at the young knight's intractability. 'Your brother over there, Matz, he did well yesterday.'

'Yes, he did.'

'You did well also, Delmar.'

Delmar felt his throat tighten. 'I was not the first to best an ogre. I did not pull you from the horde. I did not charge with the Reiksmarshal and defend my fallen brothers.'

'Those were not your orders. Your orders were to give the Reiksmarshal the message from Karak Angazhar, which you did. And then your orders were to bring the army, which you did as well. The Reiksmarshal trusted you with his life and those of all the rest of us; that is a far greater commendation than the ones that Brother Matz has been receiving.'

Delmar hated this. He hated that Griesmeyer was saying exactly what he wanted to hear, and yet his suspicions ensured he could take no comfort from it. He hated Griesmeyer's easy familiarity; that the knight had not even noticed the distance that had arisen between them. Most of all Delmar hated himself; that he knew Griesmeyer had lied to him, and yet he still wanted to believe.

'Yes, my lord,' he replied without emotion.

'Please, Delmar,' the older knight chided him, 'call me brother.'

'I would, my lord, if you would do the same.'

'Call you brother?' Griesmeyer said, surprised. 'I do already.'

'No, my lord, you call me Delmar,' he corrected softly. 'Would you call me Brother Reinhardt?'

Griesmeyer paused at that. He pushed himself away from the tree and regarded Delmar thoughtfully.

'You hesitate,' Delmar said, 'because that is what you called my father. Am I correct?'

Griesmeyer stroked his short beard. 'You took me off guard for a moment. That is all. Of course I shall call you Brother Reinhardt if that is your wish.'

'It is, my lord.'

'Very well then,' Griesmeyer replied, speaking slowly to emphasise his words. 'Brother Reinhardt.'

'Brother Griesmeyer.' This was it then, Delmar knew, the time to ask the question that was eating away inside him. 'Brother Griesmeyer, how did my father die?'

'Is that it, Brother Reinhardt?' the old knight said with compassion. 'Is that what has been worrying you so?'

Griesmeyer looked out over the knights encamped.

'I suppose it is only to be expected that you should think of it now, on your first campaign,' he said. 'But I have told you already of all the circumstances of that day.'

Delmar considered his words carefully.

'My mother blames you for his death, does she not? You have not told me why she does that.'

'Of course your mother blames me. She felt her world end when I brought her the news, she had to blame someone. And she knew I was his friend, that I should have kept him safe.'

'You were not friends on that day, were you? I know of the arguments you and he had. Gods, the whole order knew. Were you even speaking to him that day?'

'I would have given my life for his, if I could.' But Griesmeyer did not answer the question.

'How did my father die, Brother Griesmeyer?' Delmar demanded.

'He died...' the knight snapped back, but then checked himself. 'He died with honour.' At that, Griesmeyer turned his back on Delmar and walked away.

The morning broke gloriously over the Dragon's Jaw. The rain that had pelted down over the last few days and swollen the river, the rain that the men begrudged and the goblins despised, held off. The dark clouds had moved east to threaten the mountains around Black Fire Pass and, for once, the sky was clear. The gods, both of men and greenskins, had decreed this day for battle.

It was to be a battle where the Reiksguard would force their way through the Dragon's Jaw or their campaign would be at an end. The army would have to endure a harrowing retreat back to Averland with the goblins at their heels, and Karak Angazhar would truly have to stand alone.

The Dragon's Jaw was well named. The cliffs on either side rose sharply like the sides of that creature's mouth. The rocky outcrops that jutted out of the slope were its jagged teeth, and the fast-flowing Reik at its base, its fat, lashing tongue.

It was a landscape that threatened to close and swallow them whole.

The trumpets roused the Empire camp once the sun had risen. The bergjaegers that had been sentry pickets for the last few hours of the night gratefully yawned, their duty done. They returned to their regiment and there found a comfy piece of dirt to lie upon. The men, whether knight or militiaman or bergjaeger, arose. Their officers did not hurry them; they did not need to. The men had had the entire day before to prepare and to dwell upon the battle ahead; to reflect upon the chaos of combat, the injuries they might suffer, the killing blow they might receive. They did not rise eagerly, but at least with relief that the waiting would soon be over.

Helborg rode back towards the camp with his guard. As was his habit, he had risen as early as he could to test the ground ahead. He had given his orders for battle yesterday, and nothing that he had seen warranted their alteration. His legs and his horse's flanks were soaked through with river water, though, and he wished to dry off before the chill got to him. He had long ago learned that part of taking care of his army, was taking care of himself. He did not have to look too far back in the Empire's history to find battles that had been lost because of their general's indisposition.

He rode past the army as it assembled. Twelve hundred knights, nearly the Reiksguard's full strength, were in the field, wearing their laurel crests and plumes. There was Preceptor Wallenrode, whose knights had made their name battling the horde of the orc warlord Vorgaz Ironjaw, and wore the badge of their victory in each of their standards. There was Preceptor Trier, who commanded in his banner three more of his own name, two cousins and his own son. There was Preceptor Jungingen, whose keen mind and drive to succeed had made him invaluable despite his youth. And there, at the front, was Osterna's banner. Even though their preceptor was dead, his knights had refused to fight under any other name.

Beyond them assembled the militia. There were cattlemen from Heideck, vintners from Loningbruck, slaughtermen and their apprentices from Aver-heim, burghers from Streissen, and the citizen-guard of Grenzstadt, many of whom were dwarfs themselves. Dwarfs of the Empire, though, and distant from their cousins in Karak Angazhar, though no less keen to fight for them. They were all citizens of Averland, far from their homes, but still defending them.

Siebrecht sat, armed and armoured, waiting on his mount. He patted the animal's neck, though in truth he was trying to calm himself. He did not look at the great force of knights around him; instead his focus was on their path ahead. He had begun the day well, miraculously restored from his sickness. When he joined his squadron, all of them, Reiklander and Provincial alike, had deferred to him.

'There they are.' Gausser's voice shook Siebrecht from his reverie. A tribe of the goblins had emerged from the slope of the Predigtstuhl on the other bank of the river.

'That will not do them much good,' Bohdan said. 'They are on the wrong bank if they think to halt our march.'

'Is that all of them?' Alptraum asked. 'I see only a few hundred.'

'Of course it is not all of them,' Siebrecht bit back, harsher than he intended. 'The rest of them will be before us. Look how many of them carry bows; they are not there to stop us, they are there to bleed us as we pass.'

And with the Reik between them, only Voll and the bergjaegers could respond, the knights could not touch them.

Evidently, however, the Reiksmarshal disagreed. With the sound of a trumpet, Osterna's knights began to advance towards the goblins, heading straight towards the river.

Delmar leaned up in his saddle in order to see. This was strange indeed. Every story he had ever heard of Kurt Helborg had told of his generalship, his tactical mastery that had brought the Empire's armies victory after victory. Yet, once Delmar had seen the army's deployment as the sun rose, he could not help but wonder if the rumours of Helborg's exhaustion after his return from the north had truth behind them.

Delmar saw that Hardenburg had taken the place beside him. That was odd. As genial as the Reiklander was, he always fell in line with Falkenhayn, and had not spoken to Delmar since Altdorf.

'Are you well this morning, brother?' asked Hardenburg .

'I am vexed, Tomas.'

'Oh?' Hardenburg sounded surprised. 'In what way?'

'Our deployment, it makes no sense.'

'What do you mean?'

'Why are we mounted? Look at the valley sides, look at those cliffs. You think a horse could even walk along that incline, let alone charge? It's only flat enough for us to ride right beside the river and there only enough for us to go three or four abreast. If a few of our knights should fall at the front, the rest of us would be trapped. The goblins need only sweep down from the slopes and drive us into the river.'

Hardenburg nodded, but his mind was elsewhere.

'And now he has ordered Osterna's knights against those goblins across the river?' Delmar continued. 'What, does he think that their armour will help them swim?'

Others, too had taken an interest in their hushed conversation. 'What's that you're whispering there?' Falkenhayn called.

Hardenburg looked guilty, as though he had been discovered betraying his friend's trust.

'The line of battle makes no sense, Reinhardt says,' he replied.

'Does he? And does Brother Reinhardt think he knows better than the Reiksmarshal?' Falkenhayn snorted. 'Brothers, listen to this: Reinhardt thinks he knows better than our Reiksmarshal! Perhaps, Reinhardt, he should be submitting the order of battle for your approval, do you think?'

Falkenhayn nudged his horse forwards a step. 'Here, let us apply to the preceptor at once and get you permission to ride to him, so you can show him how grievously he has erred. For surely it is every loyal knight's duty to question his general's orders.'

Delmar felt the eyes of the squadron upon him, Reiklander and Provincial alike. Falkenhayn was baiting him, trying to make him flustered and back down. On another day, back in the sophisticated noble circles of Altdorf, Falkenhayn might have succeeded; but here, upon the field of battle, there was no chance at all.

'Put a thought in your head before you put words in my mouth, Falkenhayn,' Delmar replied, his voice calm and measured with that same tone of command that had come to him at Edenburg. 'And should you question my loyalty again, you had best be ready to draw your sword and have your second ready to return your body home.'

Delmar held Falkenhayn's stare until a short trumpet note alerted the squadron. The standards were raised; the battle was about to begin.

Had the Reiksmarshal overheard Delmar's concerns, he would not have disagreed. The floor of the valley was covered by the fast-flowing Reik, swelled with rain; the narrow banks were too steep for cavalry, and any man who climbed the slope would be easy pickings for any archers upon the cliffs. The Dragon's Jaw was no place for an army of the Empire to fight. Yet fight they must.

War was ever the reconciliation of the ideal to the real, with the difference paid in soldiers' lives. The key for any general, at least for any general who wished to command an army more than once, was to ensure that difference was as slight as victory would allow. Sometimes that required caution, sometimes that required courage, and sometimes the gods provided a weary general with a boon for his service. The gods... though today the dwarfs were ample substitute.

A cry went up from the bergjaegers, a shout picked up by the knights, then the militia and carried all the way back to the Reiksmarshal, but Helborg had already seen it. King Gramrik had provided his miracle.

The Reik had stopped flowing.

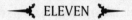

ELEVEN

DRAGON'S JAW

'It is done, my king,' the dwarfen engineer reported. 'The lower tunnels are flooding and the level of the lake has dropped enough that it is too low to flow out of the basin. The river is halted.'

'For how long?' King Gramrik asked.

'I cannot say for certain, my king. But I would judge a few hours, maybe a little more, before the tunnels fill and the river flows again.'

A few hours, Gramrik brooded; it had taken them ten years to clear those mines. Given a few more years the machinery might have been in place to make it simple to pump them clear, but now that effort had been lost and who knew if they would ever have a chance to try again.

And, as much as the manlings of the Empire had begged for his help, when word got back to their masters there would be some amongst them who would decide that they could not trust their oldest allies with such control over the river they considered their own. It was ever thus, dealing with the manlings, the memory of their fears lasted far longer than that of the favours they owed.

The Reik had drained away, but only upstream of the pass. Behind the Empire army, the Unkenfluss continued to flow into the Reik's channel, and the other, lower, tributaries merged with it downstream. As the waters had receded in the valley, the riverbed was exposed. Helborg had inspected the ground himself the day before: the Reik ran fast through the narrow pass, and any loose soil was carried further downstream. The riverbed was not mud but rather rock smoothed by the river's passage. It was not ideal, Helborg knew, but it should be enough.

As the waters dropped, Osterna's knights urged their horses from the walk to the trot and splashed down the bank into the remains of the Reik with as little trouble as they would cross a stream. Had the Snaggle Tooths made a stand upon the far bank, then they might have had a chance. They were still hundreds against only sixty. But the goblins of the wretched Snaggle Tooth tribe only stared, their red eyes wide in horror, as the barrier they had thought to protect them from harm poured away. They were transfixed by the sight of the knights approaching, the sharp swords, their iron skin, their giant warhorses with heavy hooves that would crush their bones. Only a few had the presence of mind to fire their bows, and those few shots were aimed in such fear that they spiralled harmlessly away.

Osterna's knights had not even reached the other bank before the Snaggle Tooths broke, fighting and clawing at each other in the flight to their warrens in the mountain. Then the knights climbed the bank, spurred their horses hard and raced forwards into the green panicking mass, roaring with bloodlust, as they cut down and avenged the brothers they had lost.

Delmar and his squadron cheered at the sight of Osterna's victory, but already the rest of the army was moving. Helborg had used the distraction of Osterna's charge to cover his new deployment. The Averland drummers had taken up the beat, and the militias were traversing the riverbed and were forming up in a column on the other side.

In the few minutes of Osterna's charge, the Reiksmarshal's army had gone from rest to full march. Now, Delmar saw the sense of the Reiksmarshal's plan and shook his head in wonder.

On the cliffs of the Stadelhorn Heights, Thorntoad saw it too. His scouts had kept a beady eye on the Empire army the whole day and night before, just in case they made an attempt to cross onto the eastern bank. They had not, and so Thorntoad had brought the bulk of his warriors; the Black Ears, the Splinters and his own Death Caps, onto the west side leaving only Nardy and his Snaggle Tooths there to harass from a distance. Together they would have swarmed their foe and forced them back into the river. But now the river was gone. The Snaggle Tooths had run, and the enemy had crossed to the other bank and were out of range of his archers on the western cliffs.

A column of their soldiers was already marching into the pass. It was not the armoured men, but the lesser ones, the militias. They were marching quickly down the eastern bank. The human general obviously hoped that Thorntoad had been so stunned by the attack on the Snaggle Tooths, that the militias might pass unhindered. Well, that general had much to learn of Thorntoad, if it thought that he would even blink at their loss. They were the lowest fraction of his tribes.

'Gigit!' He called to the tribe he had placed at the northern end of the pass. Warboss Gigit of the Splinters acknowledged the order and strapped the ill-fitting dwarfen helm to his head. With a cry, he ordered his warriors down the slope.

The Splinters poured down the mountainside towards the riverbed and the militia column beyond. Those in the lead chewed the fungi that made them feel fearless and strong, and the rest followed their example, emboldened by the power of the mob.

Behind them came their bosses with their whips and their prods. Thorntoad understood that, so long as a goblin feared what was behind him more than what was before him, it gave him that same kind of madness that nobler creatures called bravery, and the thousand Splinters ran down the slope, slipping, skidding, falling, whooping and shrieking in their excitement.

Helborg watched them come. The enemy's first charge, it was a sight he had seen many times before. It told him much about the opponent. For instance, here, it told him that Thorntoad had never faced an army of the Empire before, and did not know how fast his knights could ride.

He gave the order, and Wallenrode's knights raised their standards with the orc-head badge.

'Charge!'

The Splinters' attack was reduced to tatters and, their horses wearied, Wallenrode's knights reformed behind the safety of the marching militia column before trotting back, triumphantly holding their bloody blades aloft. Those goblins who had survived the charge by Wallenrode's banner milled about in confusion, some were already turning their backs, sensing the opportunity to slip away. Gigit stormed down to them, smashing heads together as he went. He loomed over them all and bellowed for order. His goblins stared, waiting for his command. Gigit opened his mouth to speak and an arrow ripped through the back of his throat.

From across the riverbed, Jaegar Voll strung another arrow to his bow. The rest of the bergjaegers fired and showed the goblin archers the true power of the bow when used at close range in the hands of men whose lives daily depended upon their ability. The bergjaegers fired and sixty goblins fell, some with two or more shafts embedded within them.

Burakk watched the remnants of the Splinters scrabble their way back up the slope. More had survived than they deserved. The knights on their horses, who had broken them so easily, could not climb the slope in pursuit. The militias, once the Splinters had fled, had blithely continued their march. Even their bowmen did not fire after them, preferring to conserve their arrows for the long battle ahead.

'Herd those together, I shall have use for them later,' Thorntoad ordered of the returning Splinters. 'Do not look so concerned, Burakk Craw.'

'It was a thousand of your creatures.'

'And I have ten thousand more.'

Delmar watched as another tribe of goblins was sent down into pass. This time, the honour went to Trier's banner. The knights charged down the riverbed, but this time the goblins were more wary. They did not strive so hard to reach the militia column on the other side; instead they braced for the knights' impact.

Trier's knights were ready and stayed in close order so as to bring the full weight of their charge upon the goblin tribe. But as they closed, breaks appeared in the goblin ranks. The prodders were shoving some of their kin to the front. These goblins laughed and bawled in delirium, their eyes rolling, their mouths frothing as they chewed their maddening mushrooms. Each one dragged behind them on a long chain an iron ball, bigger than cannon-shot.

To the charging knights' horror, these mad greenskins began to twirl and dance. Their muscles bulged with unnatural strength, and they lifted their chains and whirled them about like morning stars, as their fellow goblins unleashed them in the knights' direction and retreated away cackling with laughter.

The bergjaegers near the militia sprinted forwards, nocking arrows to their bows. They stood and fired. The nearest of these fanatics fell, shot through like pin-cushions, but not all.

The fanatics were still shrieking and spinning as the charge hit. With no room to manoeuvre, Trier's knights could only pray as the whirling balls flew at them.

Holes appeared in the knights' first line as the bone-crushing weights smacked into the flanks of horses and their riders, smashing legs, chests and heads. The first men of the battle died, and a band of sergeants and went to try and recover them. The stricken knights though, bore forwards. Even in death, they collapsed upon their foe, and the remaining fanatics were buried beneath the bodies of the horses and men that they had killed.

The rest of the charge hit home, knocking the greenskins aside once more, leaving untouched only those goblin warbands who had sheltered directly behind the fanatics. These goblins, though, had only a few seconds to count their blessings, before the second wave, guiding their horses around the carnage, struck and cut them apart.

The goblin warlord appeared unconcerned and ordered even more down from the heights.

Delmar heard his banner's trumpeter call them to form up. It was their turn at last.

'We charge in two lines,' Jungingen commanded. 'Charge. Cut free by the squadron. Reform around my standard.'

At the trumpeter's note, the knights nudged their horses to the trot. Jungingen led them down the bank onto the riverbed. Delmar and the others were in the second line, unable to see their foe clearly past the first line, and so Delmar watched the knights ahead of him, to gain forewarning of obstacles ahead.

The trumpeter blew again and the knights urged their mounts to the gallop. The danger of the uneven ground was aggravated by the slumped greenskin bodies that impeded their path; however, the experienced knights of the first line maintained their formation.

Then, at last, Jungingen raised his lance and the trumpeter blew the charge. The knights spurred their horses as one. Delmar could hear the cries of alarm from the goblins ahead. In the last few seconds, the first line lowered their lances. The charge struck and Delmar saw the lance arms of the knights ahead jolt back as the lances plunged and the knights impaled the closest goblins.

The knights dropped their spent lances and drew their swords; the line slowed, but it did not stop, and the knights held together. The greenskins in the centre were running, but those to either side were not. Delmar saw the goblins clearly for the first time, hooded in their dark cloaks against the sun, desperation in their eyes, spears and blades clutched tight.

'Second line, to the flanks!' Jungingen ordered.

'To the right!' Falkenhayn shouted to the squadron, and the knights turned to strike beside the first line, their own formation loosening. Delmar readied his lance and picked his target, one of the few goblins that stood its ground. The goblin had braced itself with a short spear, but too short, for Delmar's lance had the range. Delmar let his lance tip drop, aimed it square at the goblin's belly, braced against his stirrups and let the weight of his charge run the goblin through. With the impact, he knocked the spearhead aside with his shield, then dropped the broken lance and drew his sword.

All about him, his brothers were charging home, some equalling Delmar's success, others having less effect as their targets ran or dived to the ground between the horses' hooves.

'Cut free!' Falkenhayn ordered. The greenskins were running well now, easy kills for the knights' swords. But as the greenskins broke, a second tribe appeared behind them, carrying standards of a diseased toadstool. Their spears were ready, and pointed at Jungingen's knights whose charge was spent. In there as well, Delmar saw, were goblins carrying heavy nets, ready to launch them on the knights as soon as they ploughed through.

The fleeing goblins were halted and, for a moment, the tide flowed back against the knights. They were suddenly engulfed by panicking goblins, screeching, tearing and biting at anything in their way. The knights in the centre were boxed in, the goblins before and their brothers to either side. Out on the right, Delmar saw the chance to break out. He glanced at Falkenhayn, but the Reiklander was too busy stabbing down at the goblins cowering beneath his horse.

'Break right!' Delmar bellowed, cutting the way through. 'Break right, go around!'

Falkenhayn looked up, 'What? No! On! On!' he shouted, but the rest of the squadron was already following Delmar. First the squadron, then as the knights in the centre got space, the whole banner followed Delmar out and around the trap Thorntoad had lain for them.

* * *

This Thorntoad had never fought the Empire before, Helborg reflected, but it learned quickly, and it had no compunction in sacrificing a score of more of its own kind to bring down a single knight, herding its weaker kin to act as buffers, to slow each banner's charge, then counter with its own. And the knights were beginning to fall; no longer when the banners returned did they do so eagerly, with only their swords bloodied. The sheer numbers of Thorntoad's tribes were beginning to tell, and he had still not unleashed his ogres yet.

Siebrecht reined his horse in around the squadron's standard and tried not to let his exhaustion show. His thighs ached from controlling his mount, and his sword arm burned with the strain of constantly hacking; down at these low targets. That's all that was required, hacking; no thrusts, no parries, no finesse, just chopping down with all his might. The stains of goblin blood upon his sword and his horse's flanks were evidence of his success.

They had a moment's respite and he shakily raised his visor. He was the last of the squadron to reform again, but at least the margin was getting smaller as the other knights and horses wore out as well. Siebrecht had always considered himself a good horseman, not the best, but good enough to ride for a day without complaint. But this was something else entirely: the short bursts, the quick turns, to be watching your horse's step, watching your enemy, watching all about you as to where your brothers were going. More than once he had heard the order to cut free, only to look about and realise his brothers had already wheeled away. It was thanks only to his horse's herd instincts that he stayed with them.

He did not know how the others were doing it. Delmar and his horse, especially, moved as though they had been born together. Their squadron had charged half a dozen times in the last hour. Each time Delmar had been the first to strike, the first to the turn, the first to reform. He might as well be a bloody centaur in disguise.

The goblins were all along the riverbed now, the dead and the living. There were nearly two thousand of the creatures together, too many for the cavalry to clear away in a simple charge. A courageous squadron from Osterna's banner that had tried was swiftly bogged down amongst the mass, their horses hamstrung and the knights toppled onto the floor and swarmed.

The militia still advanced steadily, but they were still only halfway through the Dragon's Jaw, and Siebrecht could feel the momentum of the battle shifting in the goblins' favour. Few of the Empire had fallen, but if the column stalled and wavered those losses would quickly multiply.

The Reiksguard were fighting by the squadron now, each band of knights trying to contain the goblins as best they could, without getting caught in their horde.

Falkenhayn was still calling their squadron's orders, but it was Delmar's lead that the knights now followed. There had been a moment two charges before; their squadron had just reformed. 'Beware right!' Delmar had shouted: a goblin warband with nets and spears had broken from the horde, looking to snare the knights while they were resting. Falkenhayn, already irritated by Delmar pre-empting his orders, had seen the danger as well and had snapped, 'To the right!'

Some knights in the squadron had listened to Delmar and wheeled left, the others had listened to Falkenhayn and thought his words were a command and wheeled right. The moment of confusion that resulted gave the goblins their chance and they had rushed forwards, hurling their nets to entangle the horses' heads and legs.

The Reiksmarshal's own guard had been close by and had cut them free, but it had been a damned near thing.

'On! On!' Falkenhayn called to the squadron. 'The standard, take the standard!'

One of the mobs of Death Caps had finally broken and their standard was exposed. The knights could see the horrible thing, being passed frantically back to the rear of the goblin tribe. It was almost within their grasp, and they all knew the glory that went with it. Their fatigue disappeared and they spurred their horses on to charge after the running bearers, ignoring the rest of the goblins cowering to either side. A few of the greenskins who had bows had the instinct to fire an arrow at the passing knights. Most of the arrows, fired in haste, spiralled wildly; some hit Reiksguard armour and skimmed uselessly off; others flew past the knights and struck goblins on the other side. One, however, hit its mark.

Delmar's horse had just pushed off with its hind legs when the point of the arrow burst through its eye and stuck in its brain. The hind legs had pushed, but the front then simply failed to move. Delmar felt the animal beneath him die and readied himself for the fall; as the horse crashed down he was thrown over its head. He curled himself up as tight as his armour allowed and hit the ground rolling. He blinked away the dirt that had been driven through his visor into his eye and levered himself up from the ground. He had no thought but that he was in danger and he must escape.

Only two of the other knights saw his horse collapse. Falkenhayn, though, considered a single knight an acceptable loss for this chance at glory. The other knight did not even think of glory; he saw Delmar fall and, in an instant, reined his horse in to turn back.

'Delmar! Delmar!' he called. 'Give me your hand!'

Delmar looked ahead and there saw Siebrecht galloping back towards him, hand outstretched.

'No, Siebrecht,' he tried to shout. 'You can't...'

He held up his arms to ward his brother off, but instead Siebrecht grabbed one of them and heaved to swing Delmar onto the back of his saddle.

Siebrecht, though, as he quickly learned, was no Helborg, and found himself dragged from the saddle and onto the ground.

'Taal's teats, Delmar,' Siebrecht spluttered from the mud, 'you never do make anything easy for yourself.'

Delmar hauled him up, 'What kind of fool...'

'Apparently, my kind of fool, Delmar. I assure you I will berate myself...' Siebrecht trailed off. The goblins had reformed and now there were dozens of them, maybe a hundred, and they were all staring back at Siebrecht.

'Delmar,' he whispered, 'get your sword. I'll be damned if I'm going to fight here alone.'

The massed ranks of the goblins hissed and edged forwards. The odds were impossible, Siebrecht knew, but then he did not have to win, he merely had to delay the inevitable long enough for his brothers to come.

'Hear me!' he bellowed at them. 'For I am the great Siebrecht von Matz, the finest swordsman of the Empire!' He swept his blade through the air, its edge making a threatening swish. The goblins paused. Good work, Siebrecht told himself, now keep it going. 'You may feel brave because you are a multitude, but I tell you now: I may not kill you all, but I shall cut in two the first of you who approaches, and the second, and the third!'

Siebrecht paused for dramatic effect. 'So! Whichever of you wishes to be the first to die, step forwards!' He spun his deadly sword twice around his body for emphasis.

'A brilliant ploy,' Delmar muttered, standing at his back, sword in his hand.

'Thank you,' Siebrecht replied, his gaze never wavering from the beady red eyes of his adversaries.

'It might have worked as well,' Delmar replied, 'if only goblins understood a single word of our Imperial tongue.'

'Ah...' Siebrecht began, and then the goblins charged.

'Haaaaa!' Siebrecht yelled, and charged right back at them. He whipped his sword at them, moving it faster than any of them had ever seen. Sheer speed! Being faster than the rest, this was what true swordplay was about!

Siebrecht lunged at the first goblin in his path and, as it went to defend itself, he turned the lunge into a cut that took its head off. The goblin beside it blocked the blow as Siebrecht followed through, but Siebrecht spun the blade about its head and cut straight down through its shoulder. He felt something strike his side, but his armour held and Delmar, behind him, hacked the attacker down. Siebrecht flicked his point up and ran the next goblin through. He quickly pushed it back to pull his blade free, and brought it up and around like a windmill's sail and cut a greenskin behind Delmar in two.

Delmar bashed another goblin's nose in with his hilt, lifted it up bodily and threw it back upon the spearpoints of its fellows. Delmar and Siebrecht fought back to back, shoulder to shoulder, brother to brother. Siebrecht's heart raced; he glanced this way and that, looking for the next threat.

'Step back, foul fiend,' Siebrecht found himself exulting at the next goblin who approached them. Foul fiend, Siebrecht madly wondered at his own turn of phrase, where did that come from?

'I have grim news, Delmar,' Siebrecht shouted as he changed a high thrust into a low cut and took the goblin's leg. 'I'm beginning to talk like you.'

'Just shut up and fight!' Delmar snapped back as he drove his blade through a goblin's belly.

The goblin, though, was not finished. Its claws scrabbled at Delmar's visor and its fingers took grip, dragging Delmar down with it in its death throes. Siebrecht whirled his blade around to keep the goblins at bay for a moment and reached down to Delmar.

'Here,' Siebrecht ordered. 'Quick. Get up.'

'Quick! Get down!' That same hand shoved him hard and Delmar fell flat in the dirt. The sounds of charging knights thundered over their heads.

'Siebrecht!' Alptraum called from atop his steed. 'Take heart!'

'Your brothers are with you!' Bohdan cried.

'That is certain,' Gausser finished.

They and a squadron of Wallenrode's knights carved their path clear. Delmar and Siebrecht hauled themselves up, ready to stumble after, but as they did so they realised that the goblins were falling back, not in flight. Thorntoad had descended to the floor of the Dragon's Jaw and had recalled all his warriors. When they looked at the conglomeration of tribes before them, both Delmar and Siebrecht knew they could not pass.

For two hours now, the armies of the Empire and of the Ten Tribes of Thorntoad had hammered against each other in the Dragon's Jaw. The battle left a trail of its dead behind on the banks of the riverbed as it staggered onwards through the pass: mostly greenskins, but some Reiksguard as well. The sergeants had done their best to recover those fallen, but the goblins swarmed each knight that fell and so precious few still lived to be rescued. Helborg could feel his army's exhaustion, and as his brothers grew weaker so their losses would mount. Thorntoad had succeeded. The cost had been great: eleven thousand goblins began in his great horde and half of those now lay upon the field, and more had scattered, taking their chance to run into the mountains and escape both the Death Cap prods and the knights' lances. But in throwing the goblin warriors' lives into the grinder, Thorntoad had managed to wear the knights down to the point where the day was in its grasp. And now standing at the very end of the pass, in the throat of the Dragon's Jaw, he had gathered the full Black Ear tribe and, at their centre, the ogres of Burakk the Craw. The ogres roared that the battle might continue, that they might fill their bellies to bursting, and the horde advanced to drive the Reiksguard from the pass and, perhaps, wipe them from this earth.

If the circumstances had been ideal, Helborg would have retreated. Their achievements that day should have been enough for any army. But the truth of this day was that they had to pass through the Dragon's Jaw, or retreat and be harried all the way to Averland. Helborg had known retreats before; they were terrible things, far costlier in lives than the fighting itself. A generation of the Empire's eldest sons might be lost in these mountains if he turned his back upon this foe. Helborg arranged his own forces to make his stand. Most of his knights were dismounted, their horses too weak to carry them. These wearied foot-knights held the right, the militias the left, and in the centre all the cavalry that remained to him. His own guard and, perhaps, five score knights from a mix of banners.

Burakk watched as his enemy stood before him, waiting to be ended. He had seen it before many times: the foe, so exhausted that he accepts his own death. Well, Burakk would oblige. Before him, the men had placed their horses; perhaps they would have one last charge in them, but it would be slow, and once they did, his ogres were ready to take their lives.

As they closed, he heard the man general shout an order, and then suddenly the knights turned their horses around and walked back. That will not save you! Burakk thought to himself with glee.

But as the knights retreated, they stepped around something else behind them. It was a sight he had seen before, and wished he would never see again. As the knights stepped back, they revealed a line of cannon. Cannon, whose black mouths gaped like death.

'Fire!'

The cannon roared louder than any man, than any ogre could. The cannonballs whipped past Burakk and through his ranks of bulls, ripping limbs from their sockets, smashing through gut-plates. Three of his bulls died in that instant. Burakk heard Thorntoad shouting: 'On! On! Charge them down.'

But Burakk could not. The cannon fired again and this time Burakk did not even look to see how many he lost. He turned his back and ran for safety back at the Stadelhorn Heights that reminded him of his home. His ogres ran with him, and following their example, the Black Ears broke as well. Facing defeat, Thorntoad had no choice but to escape as well, though as he went he swore vengeance against the ogres who had snatched such a victory from his grasp.

The Dragon's Jaw was forced, and the flowing Reik washed away the battlefield of the day. Tired but victorious, the Reiksguard made camp on the flat beyond. The sergeants and the bergjaegers stood guard, but all knew that after such a defeat, the goblins would not attack that night.

Fires were lit against the plunging temperatures, and soldiers across the army gathered around them, trading tales of their day and alcohol with which to celebrate.

'Keep that away from me,' Alptraum said to the wineskin Bohdan offered. The other Provincials sitting around the fire voiced their dismay.

'Brother Matz,' a voice sounded from outside the circle. The conversation stopped and all the young knights turned to look at the newcomer.

'Brother Reinhardt,' Siebrecht said. 'I am glad to see you well recovered.'

Delmar tried to smile through his split lip and bruised cheek. 'A few scrapes only. I have fallen off horses enough to know how to bounce.'

The knights laughed, but then there was that silence again. Siebrecht glanced at Gausser and he could read the Nordlander's thoughts clear upon his face, but Siebrecht knew that his friend would not intervene to impose a settlement. No, Siebrecht knew, Gausser wanted he and Delmar to put the rivalry behind them themselves.

'What are you doing standing there, Delmar?' Siebrecht said. 'Come, you must help. The heroes of the Dragon's Jaw here,' Siebrecht waved his cup at his friends across the fire, 'have exhausted me with tales of their victory. I need reinforcement! Sit down. Sit down.' Delmar sat, easing his injured leg to the ground. 'Bohdan,' Siebrecht continued, 'another cup of that fine wine.'

Delmar noticed Siebrecht give the Ostermarker a sly wink.

'Oh yah,' Bohdan replied. He poured a large measure from the wineskin into a cup and handed it around the fire. Alptraum's eyes flashed with mischief and only Gausser maintained his usual solemn demeanour. Delmar took the cup and went to taste it.

'No, no, no,' Siebrecht interrupted, 'you cannot sip it. Sipping is disrespectful to the wine, and disrespectful to the one who gave it.' He nodded pointedly at Bohdan.

Bohdan took his cue and chimed in: 'Yah, most disrespectful.'

'You must be bold, Delmar,' Siebrecht continued. 'As you were in battle today, unwavering. Seize the cup and drink it bravely.'

Delmar ignored Siebrecht and instead swirled the wine thoughtfully. He did not much care for wine, and the concealed glee in Siebrecht's face told him that this brew would be especially potent or vile. He could tip it out on the ground and walk away. That's what the old Delmar would have done back in Altdorf; his mother had always told him to chart his own path and not play the games of others. But Delmar was learning that life was not so simple.

This ploy of theirs was designed to embarrass him. If it had been Falkenhayn running the scheme then Delmar would know his motivation, for Falkenhayn raised himself up by pushing others down. But Siebrecht had saved his life today, why did he now want to make him look a fool?

Delmar thought back to the day of their duel, his shock when Gausser had knocked his friend to the ground and refused to let him rise. Delmar had thought the Nordlander was saving his friend when in fact he had been saving Delmar. The truth was that only through a man's intentions can one discern the real nature of his actions. The only question he had to answer was whether he thought, after all they had been through, he could trust this knight of Nuln.

Delmar took a firm grip on the cup and then swigged the wine down. The other knights watched with baited breath. Delmar licked his lips; it had not been unpleasant, more savoury than sweet. But then he felt the inside of his mouth begin to hotten, his gums were on fire and his teeth about to melt.

'Well?' Siebrecht asked. 'What do you think?'

Delmar maintained his composure as much as he was able; he sucked in cold air but that gave him only a moment's respite from the inferno. Summoning every ounce of his self-control he answered: 'Palatable... An acquired taste perhaps,' and then collapsed into a coughing fit.

The knights around the fire fell about laughing and Siebrecht slapped Delmar heartily on the back.

'What is it?' Delmar gasped.

'Ostermark pepper wine,' Siebrecht replied. 'Dreadful gunk, but Bohdan seems to like it.'

Through his watering eyes, Delmar saw Bohdan pour himself another cup and raise it to him in salute.

'He lasted longer than you, Siebrecht,' Bohdan called.

'He is more used to having fire in his belly,' Gausser stated.

Siebrecht took mock offence. 'I am simply more accustomed to the best,' he declared grandly, and the laughter continued.

'Brothers!' A group of knights appeared around them. It was Falkenhayn, Proktor and Hardenburg. The laughter stopped. 'This is where you have been hiding.'

Falkenhayn looked around the circle at Bohdan, Alptraum and Gausser, and very deliberately ignored Delmar and Siebrecht. 'Preceptor Jungingen sent us to find you. He wants to congratulate all the brothers who carried off the Death Cap standard, all together.'

None of the Provincials moved. 'Come on,' Falkenhayn insisted, 'stand up, stand up. The preceptor's orders.'

Alptraum and Bohdan got to their feet at that. Gausser glanced at Siebrecht, but then did likewise. The Reiklanders welcomed them and Falkenhayn led them off. One of them, however, lingered at the fire.

'What wine is that you're drinking?' Hardenburg asked.

'Ostermark pepper wine,' Delmar replied. He held his cup up to his brother-knight. 'Come sit with us, Tomas, and try some.'

Hardenburg hesitated. Delmar saw the indecision in his eyes. Hardenburg was a good man, but the privilege of his birth, his handsome face and his protective elder sisters had led him to sail through life, never having to make a decision of his own. And when he had joined the pistolkorps and then the Reiksguard, he had had Falkenhayn's lead to follow.

Now, though, he was troubled. Troubled by something he could not confide to his exacting and ambitious friend. He was beginning to realise what he had been missing: true brotherhood. It was not the wine he desired, it was the confidence of another troubled spirit that he saw in Delmar. But Hardenburg found it was harder than he thought to defy the expectations of one he had followed for so long.

'Another evening, Reinhardt,' Hardenburg said, his courage failing him. 'Honour awaits.'

And so he too went.

Delmar and Siebrecht were the only ones left. It had only been seven days since the army had marched into the mountains, but Delmar felt so much had changed. Siebrecht most of all: the sly, fool-tongued wastrel that Delmar had challenged back in Altdorf was not the same man as the knight who had returned for him this day, shielding him when he was at the foe's mercy, and giving up his own chance of glory at the same time.

'I am sorry you cannot be with your friends,' Delmar said.

Siebrecht turned back and looked deep into the fire. 'It is no matter.'

'It was a great service to me, and one I will strive to repay.'

'No, no.' Siebrecht waved his finger. 'You saved me once already. I have merely repaid you.'

Delmar hesitated, but he could not accept any honour that was not rightfully his. 'I should tell you, Siebrecht. I was not searching for you that morning. In truth, I did not even think of you until I saw you there. I was searching for another.'

Siebrecht looked from the fire and stared at Delmar's downcast, penitent face.

'Yes. Griesmeyer. Of course you were,' Siebrecht said.

Delmar looked up, confused.

'Why,' Siebrecht continued, 'in Sigmar's name, would you have been searching for me? For me, more than any other knight? I was hiding under an ogre from goblins eating their dead!'

Siebrecht threw up his hands. 'But that does not impair my debt to you in the slightest. Why you were there does not matter. How you came across me does not matter. It is what you did when you found me that was your service.'

'But, brother, a knight cannot take credit for an act he did not intend–'

'Pah!' Siebrecht exclaimed. 'Intention is overrated. My uncle told me years ago, "If you reward a man for good intentions, then good intentions are all you shall ever receive." No. Reward a man for good actions. No matter your intention, your action when you saw me was to come to my aid.'

Delmar shook his head. 'I cannot accept that.'

'Very well,' Siebrecht countered, folding his arms. 'In that case, consider this if it gives you comfort. I did myself no harm today in defending you. I did not share the "glory" in taking some ragged, rotting standard, but still I hear my name mentioned.'

Siebrecht got to his feet so as to make his gestures all the grander. 'A single knight, standing above his fallen brother, defending him against every foe that approaches; to these Reiksguarders it is the greatest symbol of their noble ideals of brotherhood. Glory is one thing, any knight can gain glory. But brotherhood... that is what they hold as the true virtue of this order. Think of it this way, Delmar; that I knew I would garner far greater renown for myself defending you than I would with the others. And so, though my actions were good, you may disregard my service for my intentions were all for my own reward.'

Siebrecht bowed theatrically and stood over Delmar, willing him to agree. Agree, Delmar, he thought, compromise your precious duty and admit your own self-interest. Prove yourself no better than my uncle, no better than me.

Delmar spoke: 'I cannot think that way, brother.'

'I can,' Siebrecht flopped down again, 'but sometimes I wish I did not.'

They shared a moment's peace, broken only by the sound of their friends' revelry around the preceptor's fire.

'It sounds to me,' Delmar began, 'that your uncle has had great influence over you.'

'As much as your father has had over you.' Siebrecht flicked a rock idly into the flames.

'Perhaps that is true,' Delmar conceded.

'And we cannot escape them. I cannot escape mine because he seems to be wherever I go; and you cannot escape yours because you carry him with you. And everyone who knew him sees him in you.'

'You did not know him though,' Delmar said.

'No. But at times I feel as though I am the only one who does not. Even Gausser has stories of the Reiksguard knight who saved his father's life. And just this evening, in fact, another knight told me that my rushing to your defence reminded him of Griesmeyer galloping to your father, and that you must inspire the same devotion in your friends that your father did.'

Siebrecht gave a hollow laugh. 'It is just my luck, that it is my most noble act that inspired him to think the best of you!'

'What knight was this?' Delmar asked.

'What?'

'The knight who said I reminded him of my father.'

'I don't know his name,' Siebrecht replied, a little irked at Delmar's failure to appreciate Siebrecht's woes. 'But you know him, we saw him today. The one with the long beard and the broken nose. He was in Wallenrode's banner. Wolfsenberger, that is his name.'

'Yes, I remember.' Delmar quickly got to his feet.

'You're not retiring are you?' Siebrecht asked.

'Yes,' Delmar lied instinctively, but then reconsidered. He would not fool Siebrecht in any case. 'I mean, not yet. I am going to look for him.'

'Of course you are,' Siebrecht muttered. 'You can carry your father with you as long as wish, Delmar. But sooner or later you will have to accept that the man he was is not the man you are.'

'It is not that. It is...'

'It is what?'

No, Delmar considered, he would not tell Siebrecht of his doubts of his father and Griesmeyer. There were some things that could not be said. They could barely be thought.

'Good night, Siebrecht. Thank you for the wine.'

Siebrecht scoffed and Delmar left. Siebrecht threw another stone on the fire. The noise from around the preceptor had quietened, but there was still no sign of Gausser or the others. His thoughts returned to Delmar and his father. He simply did not understand Delmar's obsession with one who had died so long ago. Siebrecht could tell him that no matter what he learnt, he would discover nothing about himself that he did not already know.

Taal's teeth, Siebrecht swore to himself, he could tell Delmar from the bitter experience of knowing his own father that there was no insight to be had there. No, there was no one in his family to whom Siebrecht thought he bore any true resemblance. Not his father, not his younger brother or sisters, and most definitely not his uncle.

'I am encouraged to see that you are making new friends, Siebrecht.' Herr von Matz stepped into the circle around the fire.

Of course, Siebrecht sighed to himself. If you even think his name he shall appear. For once, however, his uncle was alone.

'So where is Twoswords?'

'Twoswords?'

'Your bodyguard. Your escort. Your sentinel. Your chaperone. The one with the face only fit for the circus or the zoo.'

'Yes, I understand,' Herr von Matz said, amused. 'Twoswords, you call him? How interesting.'

'Not really.' It had been a long, bloody day and Siebrecht was not in the mood for his uncle's diversions. 'What's his real name?'

'I don't know.'

Siebrecht blinked. 'You don't know his name?'

'No, you asked if I knew his real name, which I do not. I know the name by which he was introduced to me and how I think of him. But now you say it, Twoswords has a certain ring. I think I shall use it in the future.'

Siebrecht was weary. 'Whatever you wish, uncle.' He waved him away, but Herr von Matz instead took it as an invitation to sit.

'I hear you have made something of a name for yourself in the last few days. Besting an ogre single-handed.'

'I was lucky, that was all.'

Herr von Matz peered at his nephew, unimpressed.

'I am not here to praise you, Siebrecht. Risking your life for so little consequence? When I heard of your exploits I could scarce believe my ears.'

Siebrecht could scarce believe his own ears. 'What are you saying? That I should not have killed it?'

'I am saying that you should never have put yourself in a position where you had to best an ogre single-handed in the first place. What were there? Near a hundred knights with you? As many dwarfs again?' Herr von Matz shook his head in dismay at his nephew's thick-headedness. 'I told you before, resist the urge to plunge your chest upon the enemy's swords. You thought I was a fool back then, didn't you? But I know better than you think. I've seen how these knightly orders instil their doctrine within impressionable young men: the blind devotion to fraternity, the passion for self-sacrifice. That is not to be your destiny, Siebrecht.'

'If that is the case then I find it all the harder to understand why you have placed me with them.'

'Because I believe better of you than you do yourself. I believe you are sharp-witted enough to see past the fiction that entrances the rest.'

'But if I am so important to you, to the family,' Siebrecht exclaimed, giving vent to his bewilderment, 'then why expose me to such danger?'

'All life is risk and danger. If you listen to me and do as I say, but still Morr takes you, then I shall weep for you. But if you die because you have stood forwards and taken a blow meant for another, because you have been convinced that your brother's life is worth more than your own, then I shall not shed a single tear. Let those that crave honour in death seize it; do not let their example blind you as well.'

Siebrecht could not make out his uncle at all. Herr von Matz berated him with concern, bludgeoned him with kindness, to keep him safe.

'Is this all you came for, uncle?'

'No, I have something more interesting for you.' Herr von Matz smiled. All trace of his previous censure dropped away and Siebrecht felt the tendrils of his uncle's ingenious charm reach out towards him. 'It is something of great opportunity for us.'

'By which you mean, of great opportunity for yourself.'

Herr von Matz leaned in close and whispered: 'Not at all. Not at all. It is an opportunity for those who would see this campaign concluded in victory and Karak Angazhar freed. Not in weeks, but in days!'

The reflection of the fire danced in his eyes. 'Are you one of those, Siebrecht?'

'Of course. What must I do?'

'Not here. Come with me.'

Siebrecht followed his uncle to the northern edges of the camp and the pickets stationed there. Siebrecht thought that his uncle would stop there, for they were far enough out of earshot of any casual eavesdropper, but he did not.

They were challenged from the darkness. Herr von Matz identified himself and the bergjaeger emerged, greeting him like an old friend. Siebrecht saw the glint of the coin pass from his uncle to the sentry. The bergjaeger disappeared back to his hiding place and Herr von Matz beckoned him on.

'Wait, uncle. You cannot mean to go out there now.' He peered warily back down the Dragon's Jaw. The Reik had returned to its old course and the night made it as black as pitch. It had washed away much of the remnants of the day's carnage, but only the gods knew what else might be out there, picking over the remains. Only the gods, Siebrecht reflected, and maybe his uncle.

'Come on, Siebrecht. Not much further.'

He felt his uncle's urging; he should follow him as he wished. After all, he surely had Siebrecht's best interests at heart. He should just say yes and follow him.

'No,' he said. 'No, uncle, I go no further. You see I have learnt one lesson from you at least: I shall not follow any man blindly. Any man, including you.'

Herr von Matz regarded the young knight without expression; his attitude of easy geniality had evaporated. Siebrecht waited. For the first time he found that his uncle could neither fluster nor infuriate him. He felt calm, perfectly calm.

'Very well then,' Herr von Matz began, 'I shall attempt to open your eyes.'

'The truth, uncle,' Siebrecht warned.

'Yes. The truth.' Herr von Matz stepped towards his nephew. 'Ever since we entered these mountains, my guards and I have been searching for a single piece of information. One fact that will allow the Reiksguard to end this campaign at a stroke. I will not toy with you and ask you to guess what it is.'

'I do not need to guess, uncle. I know. It is the location of Thorntoad's lair.'

'That it is.' Herr von Matz was impressed. 'The Reiksguard does not face a single army of goblins; it faces ten tribes of them, far more used to battling between themselves than cooperating. It is only the sheer force of their leader's will that keeps their claws from each others' throats. Remove Thorntoad and you will not need to kill the rest, they will tear each other apart to choose a new leader. And by the time they're finished, what horde remains will not be worthy of the name and it will be years before they will threaten Karak Angazhar or the Empire again.'

'And you know where it is?' Siebrecht felt his heart pound; his uncle had not lied, this was a great opportunity indeed.

'I am close. I have the name of one who can tell me and, an hour ago, we made contact. I am to go and meet him now, though I do not know what to expect, and so I want you to come with me.'

'What of your men? Won't they protect you?'

'They will go. They are not far from here.' His uncle leaned in very close to whisper. 'But they are not what you think. They are not my protectors, they are my keepers. They serve another master, not me. I cannot be sure what their true orders are. There is no man within a hundred miles of here whom I trust more than I trust you. And so I ask you, my nephew: come with me.'

Faced with such a plea, Siebrecht did not deny him. 'I will come.'

Twoswords and the other keepers were, as his uncle had said, close by. They were hidden, quiet, amongst the talus and scree at the base of the Stadelhorn Heights, waiting and watching. Without a word, they fell into step with the knight and his uncle. They were dragging two loads behind them, wrapped in canvas. None of them carried torches or lanterns; instead their compliant dwarf led the way, the starlight more than enough for him.

They struck suddenly into a tunnel burrowed into the heights and emerged in a dry crater. One of the keepers lit a fire at the bottom. It would not be seen far. The keepers shrank away from the light. They were on edge; they knew how exposed they were here and they did not like it.

Herr von Matz, though, stood in the light and Siebrecht stayed with him, though he kept his hand near his weapon. He did not know what kind of man they were to meet out here, but he would have to be exceptional indeed to meet so close to the foe. A foul wind gusted down into the crater for a moment, and then a new range of boulders appeared above them at the crater's lip. One of them stepped forwards.

It was an ogre. Siebrecht went for his sword.

TWELVE

WOLFSENBERGER

'I do wish you hadn't done that,' Herr von Matz remarked.

The ogre thundered at them; its folds of muscled flesh, mottled and embedded with hooks and skinning knives, rippled in outrage. Its two meaty hands, each as big as a cannonball, grabbed a pair of wicked blades from the armour plate covering its gut and its huge mouth opened wider and wider as if to swallow them all. A dozen more of its kind rose from the crater's lip, as if the boulders had stood and were readying to charge.

The keepers drew an assortment of weapons as well, but Herr von Matz stepped in front of them. He stared the ogre in the eye and bawled right back in its face.

The ogre paused; it opened its mouth again and a lower rumble emerged. Herr von Matz replied in a series of grunts, smacking his fist on the ground and on his belly. He turned to his men and indicated for them to lower their weapons. He gave Siebrecht a pointed look and the knight grudgingly sheathed his sword.

Siebrecht watched his uncle and the ogre communicate. The ogre growled, making a noise like an avalanche, and Herr von Matz did the same. He made savage gestures with his hands, just like the ogre. It looked bizarre, the diminutive figure of his uncle 'speaking' the ogre's own language, but it was working. Herr von Matz was making himself understood. He waved at his men and four of them dragged up the heavy sacks. They loosened the threads and opened the canvas, revealing two dead Averland longhorn cattle, taken from the army's herd.

The ogre peered at the meat and Siebrecht could see it start to salivate. It ripped a leg off one of the cattle and tore into the dripping flesh with its teeth. The other ogres moved into the light, their bodies daubed with warpaint in a variety of different colours. They clustered in behind, sniffing the air and drooling. Their chieftain finished with the leg and threw the remains, still with a fair bit of meat on, over his shoulder, and there was a scuffle to catch it.

The ogre chieftain lifted the carcass and began to chew upon the torso.

Though its mouth was full, Herr von Matz began to speak again in that crude language. The ogre initially ignored him, its gaping maw feasting on the first longhorn, then throwing what was left to the others, before starting on the second. As Herr von Matz continued, however, the ogre began to respond. Its voice still rumbled, but it was quieter than before, its actions less violent; the beast was actually listening to what Herr von Matz was saying. The atmosphere of hostile encounter had dissipated, to be replaced by one of negotiation.

Burakk the Craw led his ogres back to their stronghold further up the heights. The human had surprised him. He had simply gone there to eat. They had eaten the scout the human had sent to find the ogres, cutting it up even as it screamed out its message. It had said that more of its kind would be at that place and so Burakk had gone to add them to his gut.

But while he had been eating the cattle, the humans' words had sunk into him. The deal was simple. Burakk liked simple. Thorntoad made things too complicated. The goblins did not understand how the world worked. Burakk was strong, his ogres were strong. They would take what they wished, and the goblins could fight over what remained.

Burakk had no desire for a dwarfen hole in the ground. That was what the goblins wanted, not he. No, it was time to set the world back to how it should be. And the human's deal was tempting indeed.

Herr von Matz and his keepers retraced their path to the camp. The sad dwarf, who, Siebrecht had noticed, had made himself scarce during the encounter with the ogres, was once more leading the way.

'You must manage your instincts better in future,' Herr von Matz chided his nephew. 'We are lucky the Craw did not think you were a real threat otherwise he would have killed us both where we stood. And then where would we be?'

'Dead?' Siebrecht glibly replied. His thoughts were still tangled in confusion and fear, and in such instances his quick tongue answered without him.

'Do not make light of such things,' his uncle warned. 'I lost two of my men just trying to get this ogre's name.'

'Burakk.' Siebrecht had heard his uncle already mention it, though he could barely conceive honouring such a monstrosity with a name of its own.

'Yes, Burakk the Craw. Aptly titled as well. I've never seen any creature eat so, but I suppose it is no stranger way of choosing their leaders than ours. I feared that even two full-grown longhorns might not keep his attention for time enough.'

'How can you speak so casually about them, uncle? They're the enemy,' Siebrecht stated.

'To mercenaries, the only difference between enemy and ally is simply who pays them the most,' Herr von Matz replied.

'They are mercenaries?' Siebrecht had seen mercenaries before, Tileans mainly, in Nuln to sell their services. They typically wore colourful uniforms with outrageous plumes and boasted of their great victories; they were a far cry from the ogres they had just left.

'They were not, but they are now.' Herr von Matz looked at Siebrecht. 'Can you work it out? Who they are? Or do I have to spoon-feed you again?'

'Who they are, uncle? They're ogres! What more is there to know?'

'What of their markings? Tell me about those, or did you spend the entire time thinking up your clever jokes?'

Siebrecht sighed and tried to remember. 'Their markings... They each had the same mark on their right cheek.'

'Yes, the Craw's own mark most likely. What of their other markings?'

'It was just warpaint, like every savage. There was no consistency to it.'

'Now what if I told you that that warpaint was their tribal markings? What could you then conclude?'

'Obviously, that none of them were of the same tribe.' It was only when he said it that Siebrecht realised how wrong that sounded. 'Why should that be the case though?'

'You tell me.'

Siebrecht was thinking now. 'Outcasts, banding together?'

'A good thought. But let me remind you of something you already know. Have you heard of a battle, about three years ago, on the River Aver where the army of Nuln fought an ogre horde, a conglomeration of tribes, and triumphed?'

'The Battle of a Hundred Cannons? I remember I thought it was a ridiculous name,' Siebrecht replied, irritated at how his uncle was dragging this out. 'Of course I've heard of it, the whole city went mad with celebration. There was a parade. When I joined the pistolkorps at Nuln they wouldn't stop talking about it.'

'Those ogres we saw were all members of tribes that fought and were destroyed at that battle.'

'They are the survivors then.'

'Yes, survivors of a battle where their tribes were destroyed by the massed cannon batteries of Nuln and the dwarfen guns of Karaz-a-Karak.'

The insight struck Siebrecht. 'Then that is why they ran at the Dragon's Jaw when the cannon fired upon them.' Siebrecht stared at his uncle. 'Was that your doing?'

Herr von Matz scoffed. 'The Reiksmarshal does not need me to tell him to point a cannon at an ogre and shoot. But he did need to have the cannon with him. Bringing cannon into the mountains does not make a great deal of sense otherwise. But once he had them given to him, he found the best way to use them.'

Then his uncle had had his hand in this campaign all along, Siebrecht thought, even the victory at the Jaw. Or alternatively, he reconsidered, none of this is true. And his uncle was concocting a story that gave him credit due to others.

Siebrecht shook his head to clear his fatigue. This was what his uncle did; this was what he always did for as long as Siebrecht could remember. When his uncle returned to the family estates for one of his visits, he filled your head with stories and fantasies, pretended to speak with authority on topics of which he knew nothing. He drew no line between fact and fiction, using either or both as he required at any one time. He had not changed. But Siebrecht had. He was not the same wide-eyed cub, suffocated at home and eager for any glimpse of the world beyond the estate wall. He was a Reiksguarder now, he had sworn his oaths to the order, and the order was here in these mountains for a purpose.

'Did you get what we were after? Did it tell you where we may trap Thorntoad?'

'Oh yes, he told me that.'

'And we're going to tell the Reiksmarshal?'

'Yes... in our own way.'

Searching through the standards and tents of the dark camp, Delmar found Wolfsenberger. He was sitting before a fire, in a chosen circle of comrades, talking of the events of the day before and the day to come. Delmar watched them for a moment before he approached and he was struck by the resemblance of this band of older knights to Siebrecht and the others, clustered around a fire. Their faces bore the lines of age, their movements were stiffer, but the easy familiarity between them was just the same. Delmar could hear the accents in their voices, from Middenland, Stirland and across the rest of the Empire. A Hochlander with a monocle and a pinched moustache was relating a story to his assembled fellows, Wolfsenberger, listening, sat on the far side of the fire. His face was long, his cheeks sunken, his skin pale; he wore a beard, but he wore it carelessly, leaving its grey hairs straggling around the sides of his face. His nose was bent below its bridge, evidence of a break that had never properly healed.

'Brother Wolfsenberger?' Delmar asked.

Wolfsenberger and his band of brothers turned to look at Delmar.

'Yah, what is it you want?' Wolfsenberger replied, the words flattened with the distinctive accent of an Ostlander. 'It is Brother Reinhardt, yah? We saw each other today.'

'That we did, brother. Brother Matz and I have much to thank you for.'

'Yah,' Wolfsenberger nodded. 'But it was our pleasure. You and your friend made quite a stand. No thanks are needed.' A murmur of agreement went around Wolfsenberger's comrades.

'Well, you have them in any case,' Delmar said. 'But I had another reason for troubling you.'

'Go on.'

'You knew my father? Heinrich von Reinhardt? You were in the order with him?'

'We all were. Our first campaign,' Wolfsenberger indicated his fellows, 'was his last.'

'I have questions. About his death.'

'Ah, then that would be for me. For I was the only one of us there,' Wolfsenberger said. 'But you should ask your questions of Brother Griesmeyer, he was senior to me; I had only just taken my oaths, and he was closest to it all.' The knight turned back to the fire, dismissing Delmar, and his comrades did the same.

'I would rather ask you, brother.'

Wolfsenberger paused for a long while. 'It was a tragedy. But it was a noble death. He saved the elector count's son, but he could not save himself. And there was nothing anyone could have done.'

'Oh,' Delmar murmured.

'You sound disappointed. Is that not what you came to hear? Is that not what Griesmeyer told you?'

'It was what he said, brother. But it is not what I came to hear, for I do not believe him.'

Wolfsenberger stared at Delmar hard and then exchanged glances with his comrades. One by one, they rose and took their conversation to another fire, leaving just Wolfsenberger there alone.

'Sit with me, Brother Reinhardt,' Wolfsenberger quietly ordered. Delmar obeyed him, his breath shallow, his chest tight in nervous excitement. He had been right, there was more to learn, but he almost feared what he might discover.

'Sit with me, Delmar, and listen to my words.' The faded knight beckoned Delmar down. 'You were right to disbelieve, for what you have been told is a lie. I was there at the end, and I have never forgotten what I saw.'

'Reinhardt!' the young Griesmeyer cried, as the knight charged against the Norscan warriors. The Skaelings had been too focused upon their prey, the young noblemen trapped in their midst, and the sounds of the battle had drowned the drumming hooves of the lone knight's charge. The first few managed to dive out of his path. Let others be the ones to use their bodies to halt the mighty warhorse, not them. The next few were slower to see Reinhardt and were slammed aside, bones broken. Reinhardt, with an expert touch, sighted his steed at the gaps as they formed within the mass of Skaeling warriors. Then he tapped his heels and the horse slowed, bunched its powerful hind legs and shot from the earth, leaping the final barrier of men that kept the knight from his goal.

The horse burst into the circle of those few Nordland nobles who still lived, surrounding the elector count's son, still dazed from his fall. Reinhardt pulled back on the reins and his steed reared on the very edge of the bank over the thawing, bloody bog. Reinhardt pulled his sword from its sheath and raised it high, so that all of his enemies could see the fate that awaited them.

Just for a moment, the Skaelings fell back, slipping down the bank where they knew the horse could not follow. The nobles took their chance and fled, leaving their lord and the knight behind. Their flight broke the Skaelings' hesitation; like hunting dogs they chased whatever ran from them. Reinhardt leant down to pull the elector count's son to his feet, but a thrown axe ended the life of Reinhardt's horse. It bucked and twisted in its death throes and Reinhardt tumbled from the saddle.

The Skaelings pounced upon their fallen foe, expecting an easy kill, only to find death themselves as his sword lashed out and cut the first attackers down.

A warrior swung down, using a captured Nordland halberd like a mallet. Reinhardt spun away and took the man's arm with a circular cut. Another threw a blow with an axe; Reinhardt caught the shaft with the flat, then ran his sword down and skinned the Skaeling's knuckles to the bone. A daubed, frenzied youth lunged, and Reinhardt trapped the seax beneath his arm, shattered the elbow and let the youth fall wailing back.

The attack paused for a moment as a Skaeling champion in black plate armour forced his way to the front and slashed at the knight. Reinhardt let the strike connect, his shoulder pauldron absorbing the blow, the wicked serrated edge designed to tear into flesh glancing uselessly off the knight's metal shell. Reinhardt smoothly reversed his sword and smashed in the side of the champion's helm with a two-handed murder stroke. The champion stumbled and did not rise again.

Then there were shouts, oaths roared in the Imperial tongue. Two knights were with him. Two of his brothers cutting a bloody path through the Skaelings towards him. The first, Reinhardt knew, was his old friend Griesmeyer. The other, that new knight who proudly wove Ostland colours into his crest wreath: Brother Wolfsenberger.

'Your father told me to take the elector count's son,' Wolfsenberger continued to Delmar. 'So I did. I hauled the frightened youth over my saddle and spurred my horse away. I was exhilarated, so young myself, my first campaign, such a daring venture and we had succeeded!

'I had thought that Griesmeyer and Reinhardt would be a few steps behind me, but when I reached the edge of the horde I saw they had not followed. I glanced back. Griesmeyer was mounted, but your father remained on foot. His sword was still inverted, the hilt high, ready for another murder stroke.

'And then I saw an act that scorched my spirit.' Wolfsenberger paused, as though the power of the old memory was still too much to bear.

'As the hilt of your father's sword swung up high, Griesmeyer reached down from his saddle and caught it in his hand. He pulled and the blade slipped from your father's fingers. He took his sword from him. He took his sword from him!' Wolfsenberger repeated in his astonishment. 'That same sword you carry at your belt.

'Griesmeyer turned his back and galloped away, leaving your father defenceless. And then those savages were on him again. Their attack redoubled in rage at being denied their victim. I could barely save myself and the elector count's son.'

Delmar could bear it no more, and he shot to his feet. 'It is beneath contempt! It is beyond excuse!'

'Sit down, brother,' Wolfsenberger said, regaining his calm. 'You will cause a scene.'

'A scene? I swear to you now, I will cause far more than that!' Delmar's hand gripped the hilt of his sword. Gods, he had known that something had been withheld. Something hidden. But he could never have guessed this! His sword was ready. He would find Griesmeyer this instant and, in the goddess Verena's name, he would have justice!

The occasions Delmar had spent with Griesmeyer, the adulation he had given him, the pride he had taken in his association with this murderer. It sickened him.

'And you,' Delmar rounded on the knight. 'You were his brother. How can you tell me this now when you stayed silent that day? How could you let this man walk free for twenty years when he deserves to hang for his crime?'

Delmar was a moment away from lashing out at Wolfsenberger himself. However, the faded knight sat unperturbed. He raised his hand to Delmar. 'Here, help me up.'

Delmar, fuming, grudgingly took hold of Wolfsenberger's hand and pulled him up. The knight got to his feet and then, in the blink of an eye, kicked Delmar's knee out from under him. Delmar landed hard and swiftly found himself pinned to the ground, Wolfsenberger's knee lodged in the small of his back.

'There!' Wolfsenberger whispered harshly. 'Now you know the feeling of being betrayed by one you trusted. You think to threaten me? You are a cub, a Reikland infant. You whine for the food the adults eat, and then you cry when you find it does not suit your taste, and blame the one who gave it you!'

'You are a knight!' Delmar replied, though the weight pressing upon his back made it hard for him to speak. 'You swore an oath and you said nothing!'

'I said nothing, yes. You think I am mad enough to charge one of the inner circle? Even then he was one of Helborg's favourites, and I was just an Ostlander, little more than a novice. They would have ruined me. If you are searching for justice within this order then you will search in vain. It was my word against his and it would have ruined me. A knight who charges another without proof puts himself at risk of the same punishment.'

'But Heinrich was your brother,' Delmar gasped.

'What do I care if one Reiklander kills another? How many years have those of Reikland eaten well and lived warm, whilst Ostlanders have gone cold and hungry in the fields? No, Delmar von Reinhardt, it is no business of mine. And I say, if you value your life or your future, then make it no business of yours.'

'I could never...'

'Then go,' Wolfsenberger interrupted him. 'And let there be one fewer Reiklander in this world.' There was an alarm running through the camp, men were waking, gathering their weapons. Even though darkness was still upon them, they were being ordered to battle. The knight released the pressure on Delmar's back and stepped away. 'Go, Delmar von Reinhardt, find your justice or find your death.'

Siebrecht, his uncle and the rest arrived back at the Empire camp at the exact same spot that they had left. The pickets ignored them as though they were ghosts. Herr von Matz's keepers dispersed on errands of their own, except for Twoswords of course, who did not let Siebrecht out of his sight. They did not march straight to the Reiksmarshal's tent as Siebrecht had assumed they would; instead Herr von Matz led them to the militia's part of the camp and the pavilion of the Graf von Leitdorf.

The capricious graf did not take kindly to being awoken at such an hour, but once he heard what news he had been brought he granted an interview at once. The graf was not a man who easily trusted others; if he had not been born naturally suspicious, then three years of political manoeuvring between the Averland nobility for the vacant title of elector count would have made him so. Despite that, Herr von Matz came to him with recommendations from high places, and he had a Reiksguard knight with him as well, which lent credence to his information.

Once he had heard what this Matz character had to say, he knew he had to inform the Reiksmarshal. That obligation, however, did not go so far as to require him to blunder out into the night half-dressed. He called for his stewards to dress him properly, and sent a man to alert the Reiksmarshal and afford him the same opportunity. The two commanders of the army would meet, but they would do so in a manner befitting their rank and position.

After half an hour, the graf was ready and attended the Reiksmarshal. This time, Siebrecht and Herr von Matz were not invited inside. Helborg was less concerned with ceremony, and within a few minutes of the graf arriving Helborg's sergeants hurried from the tent to fetch Sub-Marshal Zöllner, Knight Commander Sternberg and, at the Reiksmarshal's specific request, Jaeger Voll. Ten minutes after they entered the tent, the sergeants left again and this time brought back the five remaining preceptors. The graf, feeling a little overwhelmed, called for his own militia captains and quickly the tent became full to bursting with tired, excited officers.

The men in the camp still awake sensed their leaders' agitation and the few impromptu victory celebrations still proceeding petered out as the men watched the shadows on the canvas of the Reiksmarshal's tent. At one instant they danced back and forth in heated discussion, the next they flew as the officers strode out. Squadrons of knights were dispatched to confirm the information the graf had presented, but the Reiksmarshal's instincts told him it was true. It was time to wake the army.

The word rippled out from the centre of the camp: every man was to stand to, ready to march as soon as there was a hint of grey light. The militia, thinking that after the trials of the previous day they might be allowed a chance to rest, grumbled and groaned at being disturbed. But then they saw the Reiksguard, already armoured, quiet, disciplined, and the militia stilled their complaints. Helborg looked over his order's swift preparations with a sense of pride. All through his youth he had studied campaigns; time and again he had read tales of brilliant generals who had won battle after battle, but lost the war because their armies, even in victory, had been expended and unable to seize the advantage bought with soldiers' blood. So instead their grand armies were ground down by foes with mediocre ability but inexhaustible tenacity.

The Empire needed a force that could march and fight, die and win, and the next day do it all again, and again, until the final victory was achieved. And that force was what he had created with the Reiksguard. Watching his knights now, bloodied, exhausted, but ready to ride to battle once more on his command, he felt the connection. He felt their tirelessness flow through his brothers and into him, and the weight he had carried in his soul ever since Middenheim finally lifted.

He was their inspiration, and they were his.

The morning chill of the mountains was nothing to Delmar; his fury kept him hot. He forced his way through the crowds of men. Knights, militia, bergjaegers, all blocked his path, all kept him from the one he sought. The army was rousing, its soldiers buzzing within the confines of the camp, each one looking for food, for a weapon, for a friend, for his regiment. There was order to it; within half an hour each one would be back with his banner, waiting for his general's instructions, but right now to Delmar's eyes it was little better than chaos. The entire landscape of the camp had changed: the regimental standards that had been embedded into the ground had all been uprooted in preparation to march. Tents he had used as landmarks finding his way to Wolfsenberger were being hurriedly dismantled and packed away. The army was sweeping clear every trace of its presence on this ground. Finally, Delmar spotted a banner, the Reiksmarshal's standard, fluttering in the pre-dawn near the graf's pavilion. Delmar headed towards it. Wherever the Reiksmarshal was, Griesmeyer was never far from his side.

Delmar pushed towards it, his determination such that the soldiers around him gave him a wide berth. His hand was ready on the pommel of his sword, that same sword he had been so honoured to receive when Griesmeyer presented it to him, now only a reminder of his shame at being so completely duped. Griesmeyer had bought his devotion with the very instrument by which the knight had ensured his father's death.

The Reiksmarshal's guard were already mounted. Helborg, as ever, was eager to check the battleground ahead of the fight. Their horses shivered in the cold, snorting smoke through their nostrils as though ready to breathe fire. There his father's murderer was, Delmar saw him, sitting upon his mount, talking amiably with a sergeant beside him.

'Delmar!' Siebrecht cried, appearing beside him. 'What are you doing here?'

'Siebrecht? I...'

'Come, we must get to our banner. You will not believe the tale I have to tell you.' The excitement shone in Siebrecht's eyes. 'Come on, quickly, they'll ride out without us.'

Delmar could see the Reiksmarshal's guard readying to leave, and when they did Griesmeyer would be gone.

'Wait a moment. I have to...'

Siebrecht saw the object of his brother-knight's fixation and let him advance.

'Griesmeyer,' Delmar stated.

The knight of the inner circle turned from his conversation with the sergeant beside him and regarded Delmar calmly.

'What is the matter, Brother Reinhardt?'

'Do not call me that,' Delmar snapped. 'You have no right to say that name.'

That surprised the knight; but Delmar wanted it clear that he was not Griesmeyer's pet novice any longer. The knight turned his horse and looked down upon him.

'Be careful of your tone, Delmar. It takes liberties that I cannot believe you intend.'

'I spoke to Brother Wolfsenberger.'

The words hung in the frosty mountain air between them. For all his anger, Delmar still clutched a tiny thread of hope that Wolfsenberger had been wrong. That the faded knight had some personal vendetta against Griesmeyer and wished to slur his name. But the look Delmar saw in the older knight's face at the mention of the name was all the confirmation Delmar needed.

Delmar gripped his father's sword and tried to drag it free. He found his arm restrained, however; Siebrecht had grasped his arm and was holding tight.

'Delmar! In Sigmar's name, what do you think you are doing?'

Griesmeyer was even more outraged. 'Delmar, you dare...?'

Delmar tried to wrestle his weapon free, but Siebrecht was equally determined that he should not destroy his career and perhaps end his life. While
they struggled, the Reiksmarshal's standard was raised and a trumpet
blared. As one, the knights around them spurred their horses. Griesmeyer
had no choice but to follow.

'Brother Matz!' Griesmeyer shouted back. 'Take care of your friend; he
suffers like the last, but do not allow him the same fate. On your honour.
On your name, Matz.'

Siebrecht thought of Krieglitz's body being dragged from the water. The
Reiksmarshal's guard rode out, and Siebrecht released his grip upon his
brother. Delmar shoved him away.

'I shall kill him when I meet him again, Siebrecht. I shall kill him.'

Siebrecht took hold of him and dragged him off in the direction of their
banner. Siebrecht knew he had failed Krieglitz, but he also knew he would
not fail another.

'Kill him tomorrow, Delmar,' Siebrecht told his friend, as he pulled him
away from his insanity. 'Today, just do not kill yourself.'

THIRTEEN

REINHARDT

The clouds hung low that morning, blanketing the valley below the Karl-kopf. The Reiksguard knights had ridden ahead to surround the mountain on the south-west and east faces, leaving the militia behind.

The bergjaegers had stayed to bring them along, and the militias followed them through the mist. These ordinary men of Averland had weathered a battle, frozen during the night and had been disturbed from their sleep before the sun had risen, and yet once they were marching they did not grumble. They saw their officers' excitement; they sensed their advantage, that this time it was they who had the upper hand. They had seen the foe beaten once, and now they were going to finish them. Yesterday, they had been burghers, cattlemen, vintners and apprentices; this morning, though, they were hunters.

Helborg watched them from above as they advanced into the valley. He did not like to have militias under his command. Each man ate the same as one of his knights, yet they were worth far less in a fight. It was more than that, though. They were not soldiers. They were workers. They were the ones who would rebuild each time soldiers trampled across their lands. They produced, whereas soldiers only destroyed. They were the men that their towns could not survive without. To lose them here would devastate their communities in a way an invader could not.

And yet, as great as their worth to others, as little as their worth to him, he could not win this battle without them.

He regarded their target again. Voll had called it the Karlkopf. What he had not known, and what Helborg now knew, was that the mountain the Averlanders called the Karlkopf was also called the great stone goblin by the tribes of the Black Mountains. That was Thorntoad's lair.

The Ten Tribes of Thorntoad were so called for a reason. They were not a single force: they were ten forces, cobbled together by the iron will of a single leader. That was how these greenskin hordes functioned; Helborg had fought enough of them to know that. A strike at the head, that was the surest way to halt them. Thorntoad had had its chance to eliminate the

Reiksmarshal on the Achhorn, and the blow had been parried. The goblin warlord would find Helborg's counterstroke far harder to evade.

Thorntoad sat perched upon his palanquin as he was carried amongst his Death Caps through the tunnels behind the great stone goblin. After a defeat such as this, any warlord was vulnerable. If he locked himself away, as he might wish, then his fiends would whisper to each other. Bargains would be struck, one would rise and declare that their gods' judgement was upon their warlord, and then they would come for him. Thorntoad knew this, for it was how he had seized control of the Death Caps two years ago.

As much as he longed for the peace of his web, he had to stay out. Keep each one of his Death Caps in his eye. Have each of them know that he was watching them, and that if they stood against him, then they would stand alone.

If he held his Death Caps, he would hold the great stone goblin. If he held the great stone goblin, he would hold the Ten Tribes still. Yes, he had taken losses, but he had left five of his tribes to maintain the sieges of Karak Angazhar and those were untouched.

He would not look to meet the armoured men in battle again and fight as they wished. No, he had learned that lesson well. He was a goblin. He would fight as goblins should. Run when the enemy isstrong, hide when they search, then strike when they show weakness. He would let the men march on, if they so wished. They could parade into the dwarfen kingdom with standards unfurled for all he cared. Then he would close the path behind them and they would be trapped there by the winter, with all the more mouths to feed.

These mountains would be his again, and then he would turn his attention to those who had betrayed him. He would make himself a new throne, and there he would sit upon the skull of Burakk Craw.

Jungingen's banner rode quickly. The low cloud gave them some cover, but there was little chance goblins infesting the Karlkopf would not see them nor hear the thundering hooves. Speed then, speed was what they had. While the army of the Empire had been able to gather and move within half an hour of the orders being given, the goblin tribes had dispersed back to their warrens across the heights, the Predigtstuhl and the mountains around. And it took time for a goblin chieftain to kick and prod his warriors into action. But once they did, they would come and the Reiksguard itself would be surrounded. So, speed was the knights' weapon for now, and the knights pushed their horses as hard as they could.

Falkenhayn, carrying the squadron's banner, and his falcons rode at the head of their squadron. Delmar was behind them, speaking to no one and listening only to his daemons. At the rear Gausser and Siebrecht kept up as best they could.

Siebrecht thumped up and down in his saddle as he rode the uneven path around the mountain. Though it did his bones few favours, at least it kept him awake. The fight at the Achhorn, the hours he had spent beneath that rotting ogre corpse, his sickness, the battle at the Dragon's Jaw, his uncle's late-night escapade and now Delmar losing all sanity moments before another fight, it was too much!

Or at least, Siebrecht smirked to himself, it would be too much for a lesser man. But for Siebrecht von Matz, who had trained at the taphouses of Nuln, who had drunk and danced for two days straight without releasing his partner or his glass, who had paraded in the burning sun before the Emperor whilst his brain pooled in his boots, this was nothing!

With a kick, he spurred his horse faster up the slope. He was Siebrecht von Matz, and he would sleep when he was dead!

'That look upon Delmar's face,' Gausser said beside him. 'I have seen it before. In your face, brother.'

'And I have seen it too, in another,' Siebrecht replied. 'Are we agreed then, in our wager?'

'I do not need to gamble on a brother's life,' Gausser said. 'My oaths are enough.'

Siebrecht shook his head. 'My family does not have your honour, Theodericsson. We do not understand brotherhood. My father does not, my uncle does not, and, in my heart, I know I am the same. We are driven only by grasping self-interest, and so it must be my interest that Delmar von Reinhardt lives to see another morning.'

'Then in this case I accept.' A trace of amusement showed in the Nordlander's strong face. 'I shall owe you a crown if Delmar survives the day...'

'And I shall owe you ten thousand if he does not,' Siebrecht finished with a flourish.

Gausser smiled with a big, open grin. 'You are a strange man, Siebrecht.'

'At last, brother, you understand me!' Siebrecht cried as they rode on.

Trier's banner, crossing the valley directly to the Karlkopf's northern face, reached its positions first. The knights rode as high as they could up the slope, and then dismounted, handing their reins over to the sergeants who would stay behind and wait for the casualties. In the northern war, Trier's knights had fought together in the Middle Mountains. They knew their objective, and they knew what to do without further instruction. Reiksguard armour was strong, but so fine was its construction that its weight was no greater than that carried by a fully laden mountaineer. Trier's veterans knew that even a mountain could be conquered, with time and a steady pace.

Helborg ordered his personal guard to go with them, for this northern face would be the hardest-fought assault. It looked towards the Dragon's Jaw and it was the gentler slope, so Helborg expected Thorntoad to send every one of its Death Caps to defend it. Once Trier had broken through,

Jungingen was beyond the valley to the south-west, and Zöllner and Wallenrode were riding around to the eastern slopes, to cut off the goblins' escape in those directions. The goblins would be forced down into the depths, and there they would meet the dwarfs coming up.

Somewhere between the Reiksguard's hammer and Gramrik's anvil, Helborg prayed, Thorntoad would be caught.

And then there was the militia. Helborg had had them bring the entire supply train with them. The wagons were dragged to an exact position that he had specified to make a rudimentary fort. It was nothing like the mighty wagenburgs of Kislev or the armoured caravan trains that made the perilous journey east, but it was a barrier. It was a boundary. It said to the men of the militia, that whilst the land beyond might belong to the goblins, inside it was the Empire. Helborg looked over the ragged but proud militia regiments as they cut the draught teams loose and chained the wagons together to build their fort in between the heights and the Karlkopf. They, Helborg knew, were soon to be caught on an anvil all of their own.

'Brother-knights,' Preceptor Jungingen told his knights as they dismounted, 'goblins are cowardly creatures, but even cowards will stand and fight to protect their homes. No mercy! No prisoners! Remember, they do not take prisoners; they take food for their pets and sport for their blades. We are not here to defeat them. We are here to eradicate them. In Sigmar's name!'

The preceptor's tone shifted as he moved onto more practical matters. Jungingen knew that the Reiksmarshal did not expect much from his attack. Their slope was the steepest, his knights less experienced, but Jungingen had no intention of simply meeting the Reiksmarshal's expectations.

'There is no room for regiments, for grand manoeuvres. You cannot wait for orders; you must advance up wherever you can find purchase. You must look to the brothers in your squadron. They are your regiment, they are your banner today. Follow your standard, and if you should lose that, follow another. If you keep climbing, you will not go wrong. The dwarfs will be attacking from below, we from above; make for the summit for there we believe we shall find Thorntoad, and it is that creature's death which is our goal.'

As the banner stood ready, Siebrecht and Gausser stood close beside Delmar. Unlike the other knights who looked up the slope, Delmar stared straight ahead, unmoving, his mind a thousand miles away.

The clouds had risen and the sun had broken over the peak of Karak Angazhar to the east. The Empire army in the valley would now be in plain sight.

The Death Caps on the lower slopes squawked their alarm back up to their fellows above. Thorntoad climbed up his web and out a hole near the very peak. The men were here! Their army covered his valley; the armoured ones were already slaughtering his fiends that were too slow to get out of their way down below. They were coming straight for him! How did they know? Traitors, again. Everywhere he looked, there were traitors.

Thorntoad dropped, and swung down to the throne room's floor. He pulled his shaman from his hole. The goblin growled at him and Thorntoad smacked him twice about the head to remind him of his obedience. The warlord snapped two of the toadstools growing on the cavern wall and then climbed back up again, dragging the shaman with him. He shoved the shaman through the hole and out onto the mountain. The goblin hissed and recoiled at the early morning sun. Thorntoad twisted the chain around his neck and pulled him against the rock. The shaman yelped in pain and the warlord shoved the two toadstools in his mouth, then held him down and forced him to swallow.

The shaman kicked a little, and lay still. Then he began twisting and writhing under Thorntoad's strong arms. Thorntoad pulled him up, the shaman's eyes burning green with power.

'Call them...' Thorntoad hissed in his ear. 'Call them all!'

The shaman struggled free, body popping and spluttering with each step. Then he curled down into a ball, hugging his bony knees. The green glow expanded from his centre until it enveloped him completely. The shaman threw his body back, reaching up to the sky. The power shot upwards, keeping the goblin's shape and growing until, for an instant, a greenskin god appeared above the mountain, roaring its call, its arms outstretched and beckoning.

Within every mountain around, the goblins heard. They grabbed their weapons and obeyed.

All in the Empire army heard the greenskin god's call. The militiamen each took a step back in fear. The knights each took a step forwards; they had been shown where their enemy was.

Helborg had been expecting it ever since he had led his army into the valley. Every goblin would be on the march now. They would surround the knights on the Karlkopf and there they would trap the Reiksguard and slowly destroy them. Unless, that was, a more tempting target lay in their path.

Fourteen hundred militiamen sat in the valley, guarding the wagons and tending the herd, and lying across the path from the goblin warrens in the heights and the Predigtstuhl. Six thousand goblins and three dozen ogres would now be heading towards them.

This was the role that the militia would play, the purpose they had marched all the way from Averheim and Streissen and Loningbruck to serve. They were there to hold their ground, to stand and die, to give his knights the time to finish their task.

Helborg rode amongst them, and they cheered him as he passed. He told his gonfanonier to fly the order standard as high as he could. Helborg wanted to be seen, not only by the militiamen but also by the red eyes in the hills. He wanted to draw the goblins all into this valley and hurl themselves at the militia. And when they did, they would find Helborg waiting for them here.

Helborg wanted to be fighting alongside his brothers and conquering the Karlkopf, but they did not need him to accomplish their task. As he saw the ordinary men of Averland, far from home, look up with hope, confident that their Reiksmarshal would assure them victory, Helborg knew that this was where he was needed.

'Cover, Falcons. Falcons, take cover!' Falkenhayn shouted with the last of his breath, as he scrabbled up the steep mountain path into the safety of an overhang. Black arrows and rocks bounced harmlessly down either side of his hiding place. His Falcons, Proktor and Hardenburg, were with him, and he was sure his squadron had surged ahead of every other. He had sprinted ahead lower down, where his effort would be seen by the preceptor. Now, higher up, he could take his time to recover. The goblins had rolled a pair of boulders into the path ahead in any case, and were defending them like a barricade. He would have to find another way around.

He sat, cradling the squadron's standard, and gasped to regain his breath. The ungainly Provincials were struggling up behind him, the intolerable Delmar in the lead. Some of them still had worth, that Alptraum, maybe Bohdan as well. They had shown proper deference and appreciation at the preceptor's fire last night. Once Falkenhayn had planted the squadron's banner upon this mountain's peak, they would fall into line and join his Falcons. Even Gausser, perhaps, for though he was an ill-mannered brute, he was the grandson of an elector count, and so there must be something to him.

Gausser, though, was following Delmar and Siebrecht like their shadow. The three of them were approaching now, and Siebrecht had raised his shield to ward away the missiles from above.

'Cover! To cover!' Falkenhayn stood up and ordered them over. Delmar, the first to arrive, walked up to him. Falkenhayn pointed Delmar to a spot further down, but then Delmar strode past. He was heading straight to the rock barricade, even breaking into a run. Siebrecht was behind him.

'Hey!' Falkenhayn panted after them, outraged, but then he felt a sudden tug as the standard was plucked from his hand.

'Thank you, brother!' Gausser shouted, took a proper grip upon the standard, and then he followed the charge.

Delmar held up his arm and the hastily aimed arrow stuck his gauntlet and skittered away. The pain of the impact flashed up his shoulder, but it was not enough to block out the rage within him. A goblin standing upon the barricade heaved a rock at him, but it flew wide and bounced off Siebrecht's shield. It was not enough. He ran full-tilt at the boulders in his path; his chest burned, his legs ached. It was not enough. He drew his sword and cut the leg from that goblin even as it tried to jump away. Its blood spurted out. It was not enough. He smashed himself against the stone and heaved to shove them out of their way, straining every muscle with effort. It was not enough. His brothers were with him, Gausser pushing with him, Siebrecht protecting them both with sword and shield. They were not enough. The boulder shifted and the path was clear; the goblins ran from him, ran back up the slope towards that strange formation that resembled a greenskin face carved into the hillside. They had run from him. It was not enough.

In the dim light of the throne room, Thorntoad levered a stone from the wall. Beneath it a narrow shaft went straight down. Rungs were hammered into the sides; it had taken him days, but no goblin was ever forced into a corner from which he could not escape. He tossed a few more toadstools to the shaman, lying dripping on the ground. He would provide a useful distraction. The great Warlord Thorntoad of the Ten Tribes lowered his spines and slid down into the bowels of the great stone goblin.

Helborg's experienced eye looked across the advancing goblin horde. In the tribes' rush they had not had time to work any of their goblins up into the frothy-mouthed fanatics that had caused such carnage in the Dragon's Jaw. It was only small relief, for each of the goblins within the horde strode towards the wagon fort with an intensity of purpose that Helborg had never seen in their kind before.

Voll and the bergjaegers who had gone out to stall the horde were now running back again. Their shots were pinpricks to the goblin mass; they could not even slow them, let alone stop them.

The bergjaegers ran into the fort and climbed up to their new firing posts on the roofs of the wagons of the central enclosure. Within that central enclosure, the longhorn cattle began to stamp, smelling the approach of the goblins. If all else failed, Helborg would stampede the longhorns into the goblins to cover a retreat up the mountainside. But all else would have to fail for a general such as he to fall back upon such an erratic and unpredictable ploy.

As the horde drew closer, a ripple of unease went through the militiamen.

'Stay in your ranks. Hold your lines and you will be victorious,' Helborg reassured them. His voice echoed with confidence, and in spite of the odds it gave the men hope. It was a hope that Helborg did not share. Once the ogres reached them, the wagons would be no defence at all.

Siebrecht pulled himself over the ledge and tried not to throw up inside his helmet. In this brief moment of peace, he reflected unfavourably on his former confidence. It struck him that in the past, after he had drunk and danced for two days straight, he had tended to go and get some sleep. The one thing he did not do was try to run up a mountain after a doom-seeking madman.

Gausser, in little better shape, helped him up and the two knights struggled not to gasp at what they saw. It was a veritable city, a goblin shanty town of dens and burrows dug into the ground and roofed with moss and lichen. They bulged like spores so that the earth itself appeared diseased. The sprawling town lay concealed within the shade of the cliffs above, which arched overhead casting the dwellings in the creatures' beloved shadow. It was as though the mountainside itself was split open with a leering goblin grin, the rocks its teeth and the shanty town its wide, sickly tongue.

The remaining goblins had fled. They ran, not up the steep slopes either side of the giant mouth but instead into a wide cavern that lay at the base of the overhang: the mountain's throat. Delmar, Siebrecht and Gausser paused there, while Alptraum and Bohdan caught up behind them. The knights had been told not to enter the tunnels; they had been warned of the devious traps the foe might lay. They were tired, but their blood was high. Surely only a coward would let his enemy flee without pursuit?

Siebrecht wiped his bloodied sword blade on the roof of a goblin dirt-den, dislodging the toadstools growing there. Gausser leaned wearily on another and it moaned under his weight. Delmar just stood where he was, unmoving. Siebrecht saw Preceptor Jungingen crest the ledge. In spite of Jungingen's hunger for glory, even he regarded the deep cavern with a wary eye. He called his second to him: 'How many have we lost so far?'

The preceptor's gonfanonier picked his way through the greenskin corpses. 'Four, I think, preceptor. Some of the sergeants are carrying them down now. Three, I believe, will recover, but I fear Brother Verlutz will not.'

'The priests of Shallya will not fail him, brother,' Jungingen replied. The thought struck Siebrecht that the preceptor could have no knowledge of his brother's injuries, could not know whether the injured man would live or not; yet Jungingen's confidence was such that even the knights who had seen Verlutz's death-white face half-believed that he would survive. Now was not the time to allow men to linger over the lost.

Deep in the shadow cast by the wide overhang towering above them, Jungingen paused at the entrance to the mountain's throat and peered inside. His brother-knights closed in behind him, staring into the depths. Nearly the whole banner had reformed here, waiting for their preceptor's orders. Siebrecht could see Jungingen's mind working, weighing the decision of whether to follow the goblins and enter the mountain or stay to their original course. Siebrecht could not decide himself what the right choice was; there was simply not enough information to be sure one made the right choice, and yet if one did not then the lives of all his brothers might be forfeit. This was what it was to be a leader, Siebrecht realised: to choose without fear, and then bear the consequences without regret.

'Keep climbing, and we will not go wrong,' a knight announced.

Jungingen looked around to see who had repeated his own words back to him.

'Brother Reinhardt. You speak out of turn.' Jungingen paused for a moment. 'But you speak well. Brothers, back to your squadrons. Look for paths on either side. The summit is our goal, remember. That is what we promised our Reiksmarshal.'

The knights moved, following his orders.

'And if they should return to retake their hovels, preceptor?' the gonfanonier asked.

'Then we shall have the advantage of height over them. Or, over these stunted wretches, even greater height than we did before!'

The knights who heard raised a low chuckle at that. But that brief merriment was cut short by an inhuman screech from above their heads. The savage noise began high, piercing, but then dropped low, and Siebrecht felt it move down his chest, through his gut and lower still, until it burrowed deep into the ground at his feet. The sound became a rumble that rattled the earth then rose again over their heads as it grew louder and louder. Siebrecht looked up and saw the rocks above them shake, then drop. The heavy overhang was falling down upon them all.

The jaws of the great stone goblin of the mountainside closed shut and swallowed the knights whole.

The roar of the avalanche on the south side of the Karlkopf echoed around the armies. The militias in the valley and the knights of the other banners paused, their faces raised, fearful that the mountain would fall upon them all. Those goblin tribes advancing from the north fell back at the anger of their god and the dwarfs in their tunnels each whispered an oath. The thunder quietened and there was a moment's hush across the battlefields, then sword and spear struck out once more and the struggle recommenced.

Kurt Helborg swore by every god he knew, and then sent two of his riders to learn what had happened. He prayed for the best and prepared for the worst, for he knew his prayers were rarely answered.

One wish, though, the gods had granted him. The ogres were not to be seen.

The goblin scavenger skittered down the talus slope left by the rockfall, a curved skinning knife in his hand. The humans in their metal skin had thought themselves invulnerable to the goblin weapons, had grown complacent, but they had not counted on the power of the greenskin gods and their shaman. The scavenger grinned; he would unearth one of these humans and take himself a nice trophy, and a good meal into the bargain.

He scrambled to the edge of the scree; the humans there were less buried and easier to reach. He chose his prize and landed on its chest. He put the tip of his blade into a gap between the armour plate at the neck and made ready to take the kill.

A gauntleted fist burst up through the dirt beside him and grabbed the hand with the knife. The scavenger shrieked and jumped away, but the hand would not let go. The scavenger tried to pull himself free and, with a jerk, the knife came back up, guided by the gauntlet, straight into the goblin's chest.

Delmar threw the dying goblin to one side, pulled himself out from under the loose rocks and clambered unsteadily to his feet. The goblin's cry had alerted its kin, and a dozen more scavengers started scrabbling towards him. He looked for his sword; his scabbard had been ripped from his belt. He dug down into the dirt. The first goblin had already reached him, charging with its weapon raised. Delmar's questing hand felt a hilt, took hold and pulled hard. His sword came free and he whipped it round, slicing the top of the goblin's head clean off. The other goblins saw their comrade's fate and caught their step, wanting to be sure they could strike all together. Delmar saw them begin to gather and, without a moment's hesitation, he attacked.

He ran at them, his sword high, held double-handed, ready to smash down with a crushing blow. The first goblin hissed in defiance and raised its spear to knock the sword away. Delmar shifted his grip and instead swung his sword back and around like a windmill's sail, cutting up below the goblin's guard and embedding itself between the goblin's legs. The greenskin howled and Delmar shoved it back, cutting the blade free. He spun his sword back around again and cleaved the goblin's head straight down the middle. Without pause, he struck left and right, knocking another goblin back with the pommel and running a third through. The other goblins began to scramble away, up the slope, back towards their line of archers, unwilling to face this crazed warrior. As they turned, two more fell, their backs cut through by Delmar's sword; but his blood-rage was interrupted by the sound of shifting rock beside him. Another gauntlet broke free. Delmar stared at it for an instant, then dropped his sword, fell to his knees and dug with both hands. He pushed the rocks aside and pulled Siebrecht free.

'Brother? Brother? Can you hear me?' Delmar gasped.

Siebrecht spluttered. 'Aye.'

'Then dig!'

The distinctive form of Gausser staggered over, supported by Bohdan. The big Nordlander had taken a nasty blow and was leaning heavily on the Ostermarker.

'By my heart,' Siebrecht gasped when he looked about him. Where Jungingen's banner had been scant moments before was now just another slope upon the mountainside. Siebrecht counted three dozen knights or so who were struggling back to their feet. The rest were trapped beneath the rocks.

Beside him, Delmar uncovered Alptraum. The Averlander squirmed and pushed as Delmar pulled him clear. Alptraum struggled to his feet, breath rasping, chest heaving. He grabbed at the straps of his helmet; he had to get it off. He had to breathe.

'No, Alptraum, keep it on!'

Alptraum tore the imprisoning armour off and took a great freeing breath.

'Get down, brother!' Delmar cried, then ducked on instinct as he heard the flurry of arrows fly over. He felt a couple bounce off his plate, but all thoughts of his own safety were as naught when he heard Alptraum's scream.

'Gods! Gods! Gods!' was all Alptraum could gasp with the agony of the black-shafted arrow embedded in his cheek.

'Get your head down, I say!' Delmar ordered, and tackled the shocked knight to the ground, covering the wounded man with his own body.

'Sergeants! Sergeants!' Delmar called, but there were no sergeants to come. Those who had been digging the knights out had run into cover from the goblins' shots. Delmar dragged Alptraum into the lee of one of the hovels still standing and sat him there. Siebrecht, aiding Gausser and Bohdan, followed.

'Get it out, brother!' Alptraum shouted, but then he yanked at it himself, breaking the flimsy shaft and leaving the arrowhead embedded still. Alptraum gritted his teeth against the pain.

'Ah, Shallya's mercy,' Siebrecht said as he saw the metal barb in Alptraum's cheek.

'Cannot push it through,' Bohdan spoke dourly. 'He shall need a surgeon to dig that out.'

'You take him then,' Delmar declared, 'I shall put an end to those that did this.'

Delmar was already rising, sword ready, when Siebrecht caught him. Sigmar's breath, Siebrecht thought, he was going to charge up that slope against those goblins single-handed. He really did wish to die.

'Wait. Wait! Delmar!' Siebrecht shouted. 'Wait 'til we are all ready. Wait 'til we can go together.'

Through his visor, Siebrecht saw that his words had impact: the wild look in Delmar's eyes dimmed and he gave a curt nod of agreement.

Siebrecht relaxed a fraction. 'Finally, some sense' he muttered. 'And it only took a half a mountain to knock it back into you.'

If Delmar heard him he did not acknowledge it. Instead, he peered over the fungoid roof of the hovel. 'We go together,' Delmar repeated Siebrecht's words. 'The others are still dragging themselves out. We must clear those goblins from over our heads or we will never get the rest of our brothers free. There's a path up the rockfall to the goblins' position. It is narrow and steep, but it will serve.

'Two men in front, shields high. No swords, for we shall need the spare hand for climbing.' Delmar pulled his shield from his back; there was no doubt he would be one of the two. As to the second: 'Gausser?' Siebrecht asked the injured Nordlander. 'Are you recovered? Can you do it?'

'That is certain!' Gausser declared, swaying only slightly.

'No, Gausser, not you,' Delmar countermanded. 'Bohdan, you are with me.' The Ostermarker looked up, thick eyebrow raised. 'Gausser is too big. They will focus their fire upon us and the shield will cover you better. Siebrecht, Gausser, you follow with your swords. We shall need you right behind us or when we reach the top we shall be slaughtered. Ready?'

His brothers nodded their assent.

'Then, brothers, advance!'

Delmar smashed his shield into the goblin's face, the arrow barbs embedded within it merely adding to its potency. The goblin, its bow broken, was knocked bodily off the cliff and the black-robed creature slipped down into the waiting arms of the knights climbing below.

They had begun their charge with four knights; they had finished it with forty. Each one of Jungingen's banner who could still walk had seen them run, had heard their calls to battle and had followed.

'Your sword, Delmar! Don't forget your sword,' Siebrecht reminded him, his own blade flashing out, cutting one goblin down and sending another scrambling away. Delmar hurled his shield at a knot of the greenskins huddled together in defiance, then drew his sword and set about them with Bohdan.

'Reiksguard!' Gausser bellowed beside them, flying the squadron's banner. Ignoring his weapon, Gausser simply plunged the pole forwards with such force as to impale the evil creatures.

'Falcons!' Falkenhayn called as he, Proktor and Hardenburg struck together.

The goblins were breaking in front of them, Delmar saw, and they were not retreating up the mountain back to another defensive line. They were running left and right, fleeing to the Karlkopf's other faces in hopes of escape. Throntoad's lair had to be close.

The goblins fled, but the knights did not pursue. They had thrown back the immediate threat, and now their concern returned to their squadron-brothers still struggling from the avalanche. First, the walking wounded turned, then a few of their brothers to aid them. Then a few more to aid the sergeants desperately clearing the rubble. In the face of such disaster, the battle could wait a few moments. Their brothers needed them and their brotherhood called them back.

Thanks to their actions, sixteen more brothers were saved from the rockfall than would otherwise have been found in time. Five knights who had survived the fall had died, trapped and waiting for rescue. Twenty-nine knights were already dead, crushed in the first few seconds. Amongst their number, the banner's gonfanonier, his blood seeping from his armour and staining the banner's standard, and Preceptor Jungingen himself, his fast-rising career within the order cut short along with his life, buried under a ton of rock. Of all his knights, only one squadron obeyed his final order, to climb and keep on climbing.

It had been because of Bohdan.

'Not this way.' Bohdan said when his vigil-brothers turned to go back. 'Up. We must go up.'

'What? Why?' Delmar asked.

The Ostermarker's eyes flared. 'Evil is there.'

'Look!' Siebrecht shouted, pointing above them. Nearly hidden within the mouth of a cave above them, a robed goblin stood alone. Its head bobbed as it chanted, its voice raising to a familiar screech. It was that same noise the knights had heard before the rockfall, and now it was once again channelling its power.

'Shaman!' Bohdan blurted, and ran towards it. Monstrous green shapes were forming around its body as it readied to strike again.

Bohdan shifted his grip upon his sword and then hurled it like a javelin at the shaman. One of the green shapes became an arm, and shot from the goblin knocking the flying sword to one side. Then it formed a fist and struck Bohdan hard, lifting him from the ground, knocking him twenty feet down the slope and leaving the indentation of four bony knuckles on his helmet.

Bohdan fell, but his attack had broken the shaman's concentration. The green shapes faded, and it ran back into the darkness of the cavern. The knights followed it, Bohdan stunned but waving them on, and they stepped into the gloom.

'Look at this place,' Falkenhayn whispered, his eyes adjusting quickly. 'It's a throne room.'

Hardenburg was the first who chanced to look up. 'In Sigmar's name,' he gasped.

'What are those things?' Proktor asked.

The ceiling of the cavern went high and was criss-crossed with taut cables and rope; the sloping roof was embedded with steel rings right to the top.

'It's a web,' Delmar said.

'If that is a web, then where is the spider?' Gausser intoned, ominously.

'You just had to ask...' Siebrecht muttered, but his eyes did not stop searching for the threat. The knights slowly backed towards each other, each of them feeling the darkness bear down upon them.

'Enough! We are not here to fear the monsters. We are here for the monsters to fear us!' Delmar declared, and the oppressive moment passed.

'The shaman came in, it must be here. Search about and find it before it brings the mountain down again upon us.'

The squadron divided, but there were at least half a dozen passages leading away from the central chamber. These goblins evidently did not like to be backed into a corner. Delmar even saw light at the end of some of them and heard the echoing sounds of the assaults on the other faces of the mountain. The shaman could be hiding down any of them.

'Here, brothers! Look at this,' Hardenburg called from behind them. He motioned to Falkenhayn and Proktor to join him and peeled away the surface of lichen from the wall to reveal a pink, fleshy nose.

'It's a dwarf,' Hardenburg said. It was strung up against the wall, covered with fungi feeding off the body.

'Is it dead?' Falkenhayn asked.

Hardenburg raised his visor and held his face close to the dwarf's. He felt the wisp of breath against his cheek.

'He's alive,' he exclaimed.

Falkenhayn and Proktor used their blades to cut through the binding ropes, and Hardenburg took hold of the dwarf and eased him gently from the parasitic arbour.

As they lowered him, Siebrecht saw the shaman. It had climbed into the web, and was crouching across two of the ropes, gorging itself on the toadstools growing on that section.

'There,' he whispered to Delmar.

'Where?' Delmar replied, looking around.

'There!' Siebrecht shouted as the shaman began to glow with power once more. Siebrecht threw his sword as Bohdan had done, but the weapon went wide. The shaman turned and hissed down at them, except the hiss turned into a roar, a roar that shook the cavern, that shook the very base of the mountain.

'It's going to come down right on top of us!' Falkenhayn yelled. 'Anyone? A bow? A pistol?'

Siebrecht drew his pistol, took a moment to aim and fired. The shot flew true, heading straight between the shaman's eyes, then struck a shield of energy about the goblin and ricocheted away. Both Falkenhayn and Siebrecht swore. Delmar looked around, searching through the web of ropes illuminated by the shaman's light. One of them that the shaman stood upon was buried in the wall just above Delmar's head. He took up his sword and swept it up. The blade bit into the rope, but it cut only halfway. The rope shook and the shaman shifted off it and onto another. Delmar looked to see where the rope ran.

'Gausser!' he shouted, and pointed to the other rope's anchor. The Nordlander drew his blade in a mighty arc and cut it with a single blow. The rope whipped back at the shaman, but it leaped up and caught hold of another. This one though, its anchor loosened by the tremors rippling through the mountain, came loose in its hand. Desperately, the shaman clawed out and grasped another, dangling from it by its nails, all the while burning brighter and brighter with the power building up inside.

Delmar traced the rope back, but it was too high.

'Gausser?' he shouted in desperation. The Nordlander swiped as high as he could, but it was just out of his reach.

'Siebrecht?' Delmar called, but Siebrecht shook his head. His spare powder and shot were in his saddle.

Frustrated, Falkenhayn whipped his sword up at the rope, but it struck without effect. Then Delmar saw it.

'Gausser! Falkenhayn!' The two knights looked back as Delmar rushed over. 'Proktor,' he said, motioning up.

Proktor looked at Delmar and understood. The three knights seized him by his legs and lifted him from the ground. Gausser took the strain, while Delmar and Falkenhayn pushed the legs of the smallest of their number as high as they could. The rocks fell down around their feet, but they ignored them. Proktor swung, and cut, but not hard. He swung again and the shaman began to twist to try and swing to another rope. Proktor swung a third time, and the blade skimmed away.

'Come on, Laurentz,' Falkenhayn shouted. 'For your brothers!'

Proktor swung up and hit the spot of his first cut, shearing the rope through. It spiralled away. Proktor overbalanced and the tower of knights tumbled. The shaman dropped down and bounced upon the floor, the power dissipating through the stone.

'I have him!' Hardenburg shouted and plunged his blade twelve inches through the shaman's black heart.

The shaman burst and a cloud of red spores ripped from its body. The other knights could only watch as the red spores hung in the air for a moment, glistening with unholy magic; then they were suddenly sucked up into Hardenburg. They flew into him, slipping through every hole and chink in his finely crafted armour.

Hardenburg's eyes bulged wide. Then he clenched and twisted, and he gave a great wail of pain as the spores went to their vicious work. He collapsed, tearing at his helmet and his collar; his armour trapped the spores against the skin, their protection rather than his own.

The knights clustered around their fallen brother. Hardenburg gave another agonised cry and slipped from consciousness.

'We must get him down to the sergeants at once,' Proktor said, and this time no one disagreed. The virulent red spores gave the fair-faced Reiklander the look of having been butchered. Delmar reached to lift him.

'Proktor and I shall carry him, Reinhardt.' Falkenhayn's tone brooked no disagreement. 'You may carry the dwarf.'

But none had a chance to lift either of them, for beyond the throne they heard the commotion of more men coming down a passage. The leading knight bore the markings of one of Helborg's personal guard. It must be Griesmeyer! Delmar's hand grasped his sword. But the knight raised his visor and Delmar realised his mistake. It was not Griesmeyer, but another of the guard.

The knight looked at them and then turned to his brothers who were following behind him. 'Pass the word back, the Karlkopf has already been taken!'

Helborg felt the trembling stop and then saw the Reiksguard flag fly from the top of the Karlkopf. He felt a surge of his old excitement at a battle won. The militiamen struggling in the valley against the goblin tribes saw it too and raised a rousing cheer, just as the goblins gave a creaking moan and turned to retreat.

The ogres had never appeared.

While Gausser and Bohdan took the dwarf down the mountainside, Siebrecht followed Delmar as he passed through the tunnel and out onto the eastern face. There he found Griesmeyer amongst the rest of Helborg's personal guard.

'We should talk, you and I,' Griesmeyer said. Delmar nodded, and Griesmeyer led him by a rough path onto a plateau near the peak itself. Siebrecht reluctantly let the two knights go.

To the west Delmar saw the Stadelhorn Heights and beyond those the Achhorn ridge. To the north was the wooded Predigtstuhl stretching down to the Dragon's Jaw below. To the east were only the frosted peaks that hid Karak Angazhar from sight, and the deep blue mountain lake that fed the Reik. Although there were thousands of men all about them, on the mountain slopes and on the flats below, here they were alone. They would have privacy enough to fight.

'It is fitting enough,' Delmar decided, as he looked about.

'Fitting enough for what?' Griesmeyer asked.

'For what other reason are we here?' he said, raising his sword and taking his guard.

'Reiksguard do not fight Reiksguard,' Griesmeyer declared.

'You wish to hide behind that, do you?' Delmar had been calm, but the older knight's stubborn impenitence reignited his rage. 'Very well. Here.'

Delmar reached inside the collar of his armour. He pulled off his Reiksguard insignia and threw it to the ground. 'I hereby quit the order. There, now, let us go to it; for since Wolfsenberger told me his tale I cannot endure both our existences. One must end. And it must end now.'

'To quit the order? And seek to kill me?' Griesmeyer was angering as well. 'You've placed great belief in that knight's words.'

'Why should he lie?' Delmar challenged the older knight.

'Why should I?' Griesmeyer shot back.

The sharp exclamation hung fixed in the frozen air between them. Delmar weighed his sword in his hand, as he weighed Griesmeyer's words in his mind.

'Whether you have lied or not... you have not told me the truth,' Delmar said.

'I have told you all the truth it is safe for you to know.'

'And who are you to judge that for me?'

At last, Griesmeyer's restraint shattered completely and he thundered: 'I am a knight of the Reiksguard, ordained of the inner circle; I have faced daemons and beasts beyond your imagination, and I carry the Emperor's life as my greatest honour and my constant burden.' He sucked in a breath of the cold air. 'That is who I am. Who are you? Answer me that, Delmar, who are you?'

Delmar had never felt such anger from Griesmeyer before. The calm, tempered knight he knew was gone, replaced by a savage warrior filled with heat. His sudden rage struck Delmar like a blow.

'I am his son.' It was all Delmar could answer and Griesmeyer found he had no reply to that.

'Then listen, Heinrich's son, to what I say,' Griesmeyer began. 'For I now, here, break the oath that I once swore, never to reveal what I am to tell.'

'Take the boy!' Reinhardt ordered. The young knight, Wolfsenberger, held Nordland's son tight and spurred his horse away through the reeling Skaeling horde.

Griesmeyer cut down another too-eager northern warrior and then looked back to his brother.

'Give me your hand!' he cried. 'Brother, your hand.' Griesmeyer reached out to pull his friend up onto his horse.

'No, brother,' Reinhardt replied, calmly, hefting his sword still by its blade. 'Here I will stand. Here I will fall.'

Griesmeyer swore. 'Do not be a fool, Heinrich. Just take my hand. Think of your wife! Think of your son!'

'They have never left my thoughts.'

Griesmeyer yanked his horse around. 'I shall not tell them, Heinrich. I shall not be the one they despise, the one they shall blame for taking you from them.'

'Yes you will, brother. For you could not bear for them to hear it from another,' Reinhardt said. 'And I shall beg one more favour.'

Reinhardt raised his sword high, handle first, to his brother, and Griesmeyer instinctively caught its grip.

'Give it to Delmar. Give it to my son.'

'Gods damn you! Gods damn you!' Griesmeyer's sight began to blur with frustration.

'They have already, my brother.'

* * *

'No!' Delmar cried. 'It was not so! My father would never...'

Delmar screamed his denial, raised his sword and charged. Griesmeyer drew his own and held it straight. Delmar's cut crashed down and the old knight's guard gave way. But Griesmeyer had already stepped aside and Delmar's swing went wide. Griesmeyer's blade spun and whirled across his brow; the knight uncoiled and struck Delmar square in the back of the head.

Delmar staggered. His fingers went numb. His sword slipped from his grasp. The blow was with the flat; it had not penetrated his helmet, but it had been delivered with such force as to knock him senseless. Delmar's legs buckled and he collapsed upon the rock.

With the tip of his blade, Griesmeyer raised the young man's visor. Delmar blinked up into the cloudless sky.

'Just lie still, Delmar. Just lie still,' the old knight soothed. 'And listen to your elders.'

'It was the year before Emperor Karl Franz's election,' he continued. 'The Patriarch's expedition started badly. Heinrich had come with us, though I knew it pained him to leave you and your mother behind while you were still so young. In our first action, a champion of theirs, a sorcerer of some kind, cast a bolt of dark energy that fair tore our squadron to shreds. I was lucky. Heinrich was not, but he held tightly to his life and defied Morr at his very gates. Battered, we came home, and while I prepared to march forth once more, he returned to you and stayed there whilst he recovered.

'The year progressed. The campaign was done. And then, that winter, he called me to your home. I arrived, joyous to see him so recovered, and he had a surprise for me: your mother's belly was swelling again. She was due on any day, and he wished me there for we were family.

'The birthing came upon her suddenly, and it was most terrible. A day and a night she suffered in bed, whilst your father tormented himself with the thought of her loss. You were so small a child, but you were already brave. And it was you and I, together, who kept him sane.

'The gods, however, had already marked him down. The babe, when it came, was a hideous thing. I cannot describe its horror in mere words; it was no mortal creature, it was a darkling child of Chaos.

'Your mother, mercifully, was already collapsed in exhaustion. Your father though, was left to gaze upon it: its horns and claws and mottled skin, its limbs twisted, confused and too great in number. He took it away, into the chill night, and returned next morning with it gone.

'I had hoped, I had prayed that that would be the end of it all. A grievous shock to any family, yes, but not unknown. Your father had taken the right action, harsh, but quick. And now it was simply time to heal. Your mother improved, you made yourself her constant companion and though she hurt she never forgot what a blessing she had in you already. Heinrich, though, he slipped away, and naught that I could do would prevent it. The foe he fought was not one to be defeated with sword or lance. It was one inside him. He prayed, morning to night, to rid himself of the taint he carried; the corrupting strain with which that dark sorcerer had left him infected.

'I tried to talk to him, but he would not listen. The sermons of Sigmar's priests hold a man very strong. When he said that prayer had failed him, he journeyed back to Altdorf and I went after him. I caught him steps before he declared himself to the witch hunters. I told him that if he did, then it would not only be his life that would be forfeit but yours and your mother's as well, and he at last relented. I brought him back to the chapter house, thinking to bring him to his brothers' care. But there we argued for days on end, until all the words had been said, and we spoke to each other no more.

'And then Karl Franz was elected and he led us north to fight against the Norse harrying Nordland's coast. When I heard we were marching I feared that in my absence your father would destroy himself. Imagine my joy then, when I learned he was to come with us. Imagine my joy, then imagine what I felt when I realised that he had come north to end himself.

'I brought the news to you myself. Your mother, at first, accepted my words. To marry a Reiksguarder is to accept that such loss might befall you at a moment. But as the next years passed, and your father's face appeared in your own, I saw her feelings harden towards me each time I returned. When I did visit, it was a reminder of all she had lost. And when I told you stories of my life, and duelled with sticks as swords, she only saw the true father you had been denied, the father I should have brought her home.

'She told me then I was no longer welcome. And thus I have not been, until my oath to your father brought me back to present his sword to you.'

The old knight finished his tale. Delmar slowly picked himself up from the ground and walked to the edge of the plateau. There to the east was the mountain lake from which the Reik poured. Somewhere there was the well-spring that fed that lake, the source of the Reik, the greatest of the rivers from which the Empire drew its power. This was no place for endings, Delmar decided. It was where journeys commenced and the past was washed clean.

◄ FOURTEEN ►

HARDENBURG

Burakk the Craw looked out over the green and fertile plains of southern Averland. The army of men had been left well behind, distracted by the goblin fortress, assuming that the ogres were fleeing deeper into the mountains. Not a chance. Not when the Empire's army had left this soft province undefended, with its beasts and men fattened from their harvest. No. This was Burakk's reward from the Great Maw. Never again would he play humble before a greenskin creature. Now it was he who was their chief; the trickle of goblins who had come to give their service had become a flood once it was clear that their great stone goblin was lost. As he and his bulls had raced across the slopes that night, the goblins had sprinted after. They knew Thorntoad was lost, and their praises of him turned to curses; his plans to become goblin-king of the dwarfen hold were scattered as the dust. Instead, his goblins joined the ogres and became their willing servants.

'Tyrant!' One of his bulls approached him up the slope. He was dragging something through the dirt behind him. It looked like some hairy animal, drowned in the river.

'Found this. Washed up on the bank.' The bull held it out for Burakk to examine.

Thorntoad unravelled and came up screeching. He whipped one arm around and his spines made a dozen tiny slices in Burakk's outstretched hand. Thorntoad spun about and dug his teeth into the wrist of the bull holding one of his crippled legs. The bull shouted in pain and let go his grip as the goblin freak took a chunk from his flesh. Thorntoad, though, did not fall, he held on tight and scrambled up the bull's shoulder. He flipped himself over and sat upon the ogre's shoulders, clamping his arms around the ogre's face and letting his thorns dig in. The bull's shout turned into a strangled bellow and he blindly grabbed at the goblin on his shoulders, only to grasp handfuls of razor spines. Thorntoad was screeching again, this time in triumph, as he dug his heels into the ogre's back as though to ride him to safety.

Burakk swung his hefty club and smacked them both hard. The ogre, brained, fell to the side and Thorntoad tumbled from his shoulders. Burakk raised his club again to finish the goblin off, but the freak sprang up and raced up the cliffside out of the ogre's reach.

Thorntoad was not done. No sooner was he safe than he turned back. The struggle had been heard by the ogres and goblins alike, and now both came to see. Thorntoad looked over his goblins newly sworn to the tribe of the Craw. There were still enough, he could win them back!

'My fiends!' he called, hanging onto the rockface with one hand and reaching out to them with the other. 'My magnificent fiends! Your black hearts are in my chest. Your broken teeth within my mouth. Do not submit your fates to these betrayers who will have you serve them in the day and then will gorge themselves upon you at night. Let yours be the first blow! Seize your blades and set upon these hulks. Rend their bodies and drain their spleens. Our own great victory is still within–'

The heavy stone struck the goblin's temple. Burakk's aim had been good. Thorntoad crumpled and fell from his perch, landing in a spindly mass at the feet of his goblins below.

'Take his thorns,' Burakk ordered. The goblins' blades came out and they cut Thorntoad's spines from him. As they were cleared, the mighty Thorntoad was revealed beneath for what he truly was, a pitiful, slight freak.

Burakk lifted him by his leg above his head, and his breath roused the denuded freak to consciousness. It was too late. The mouth of the Craw opened and engulfed its victim. Burakk felt it wriggle as it slid down his gullet. He swallowed and then it went still. His bulls cheered and his goblins cackled, and he acknowledged their ovation as he strode back to the edge. Out there, upon the plains, Burakk could see a farm: both cattle and humans, plump and juicy. The Feast of Averland would begin with them. His tribe's course was set, and it would prove satisfying indeed.

The cold metal prongs of the grey instrument forced the flesh of Alptraum's cheek apart even wider and the Averlander howled in pain. His attempt at quiet stoicism had long since been abandoned.

Alptraum crouched before the sergeant who was slowly opening up the side of his face to extract the arrow's tip. He clenched his jaw against the agony for a moment, then gave up and continued in his systematic defamation of the Empire's lower pantheon.

Delmar, Siebrecht, Gausser and Bohdan watched from a few paces distant. As Alptraum's oaths progressed onto the lesser goddesses and took on a more lurid tone, Siebrecht turned to Gausser.

'Can we not get him a horse's bit to bite down on?'

'The swearing helps him, he says,' Gausser replied.

'I do not doubt it,' Siebrecht said. 'I am just not certain it's helping anyone else.'

The sergeant twisted and pulled, and Alptraum's shouts rose to new heights. With his own cry of triumph, the sergeant extracted the arrow with his pincers. Alptraum, exhausted and hoarse, collapsed onto his back as his brothers congratulated him.

As they set about bandaging the wound, the sergeant held the arrow point up to the light of the torch. 'Would you like to keep it, my lord?' he asked. 'Many of our brother-knights do. A memento of battle?'

Alptraum looked at him as though he had recommended they should fling themselves onto hot irons for fun. 'Throw the cursed thing away! I never want to see it again.'

'As you wish, my lord,' the sergeant said, slipping the arrowhead away, and passing Alptraum a draft. 'Here, drink this. It will help fight the infection.'

That it did, and it also swiftly put the young Averland knight to sleep. Delmar watched as his knotted face finally relaxed.

'I'm going to see Hardenburg,' Delmar told Siebrecht.

Siebrecht nodded and then, after Delmar had left, he stepped over to the sergeant who was putting away his surgeon's tools.

'I'll give you half a crown for the arrowhead,' Siebrecht whispered.

The sergeant almost asked why he wanted it, but then he saw the twinkle in Siebrecht's eyes and decided that the less he knew the better.

'Two crowns,' the sergeant countered.

'One.'

'One and a half.'

'One,' Siebrecht said, more firmly this time.

'Done.'

Siebrecht smiled and turned back to Gausser. 'Brother? Our wager? Delmar lives. Pay the man.'

Growling something beneath his breath, Gausser reluctantly reached for a coin.

Delmar stepped past the other convalescing knights. Most of them here would survive, cared for by the order's sergeants, who carried their knights to battle and carried them home again. The dying were kept separate; the sergeants did not want to tempt Morr when he came for the dead to take the living as well. Their last hours would be spent with the prayers of a priest, until they passed and their bodies could be moved. At least, Delmar thought sombrely, his father had been spared that slow dissolution of life.

The Reiksmarshal had confirmed all of Griesmeyer's words. At last, Delmar knew the truth of what had happened to his father. And yet, in gaining knowledge, he had lost his certainty. The order had concealed the taint of a man to allow him to keep his honour. It had deceived and sinned, broken the faith of knights like Wolfsenberger, but in pursuit of a noble goal. Griesmeyer had lied to his brother's wife and his son, but all for the purpose of protecting them from those who would consider them tainted as well.

By all the priests' teachings Delmar had ever heard, Griesmeyer was wrong, the order was wrong, dangerous, complicit even. Where there was mortal taint, there could be no exceptions made. And yet Delmar held in his heart the fervent belief that they had been right in what they had done. He could not resolve it.

But then Delmar thought back to the crippled masters of the chapter house: Verrakker, Lehrer, Talhoffer and Ott. The order cared for its own, no matter what befell them in its service. No matter if their wounds were self-evident, or hidden inside. Brotherhood – that was the order's true strength.

Hardenburg lay amongst the living. His entire body was swathed in anointed bandages that were fighting the spores that covered him. His flesh had become a tiny battlefield of its own as the infection and the medicine waged war.

'Tomas?' Delmar announced his presence.

Hardenburg's eyes looked over; his head was too bandaged to move.

'Delmar?' he croaked. 'I am glad you have come.'

'I have something for you.' Delmar was holding a piece of plate, a shoulder pauldron. 'It is from your harness.'

Hardenburg focused upon it. 'What are those markings?'

'The dwarf we freed from the goblins' lair. The one you saved.'

Hardenburg nodded a fraction.

'That dwarf,' Delmar continued, 'was King Gramrik's son.'

Hardenburg gave a hollow chuckle beneath his bandages. 'Is there a reward? Is there gold?' he joked, his voice weak.

'No, brother,' Delmar laughed. 'But in his thanks, he ordered this rune carved upon our armour. Of all our squadron.'

Delmar held the pauldron forwards so Hardenburg could see, and the injured knight peered at the markings.

'Do you know what it means?' he asked.

'No,' Delmar admitted, 'but I think it must be a mark of strength, and of courage. I thought it should travel back to Altdorf with you, not in some caravan.'

Hardenburg shakily reached out with his hand and traced the pattern lightly.

'Yes,' he decided, 'yes, you are right. Strength and courage.'

Hardenburg continued to touch the rune, but Delmar saw his eyes glass over with worry once more.

'Do you not like it?'

'No, it is not that. I am just afraid, that is all.'

'Of what, Tomas?'

'Of what people will think of me back home in Eilhart. I do not think many of my friends back there will wish to see me like this.'

'Your real friends will.'

'Maybe, then, it is I who does not want them to see me like this. Even if I heal, they shall never look at me the same again.'

Hardenburg brushed one of his bandages aside slightly and Delmar saw the virulent work of the goblin's toxic spores upon the young man's body. Hardenburg would survive, Delmar knew, but he would bear those ugly scars upon his skin forever.

But the order cared for its own. No matter what.

'Then do not go back to Eilhart just yet. The chapter house is no bad place to heal,' he said. 'You will get the finest treatment from the sisters of Shallya.' Delmar got to his feet. 'Consider it, Tomas. For when you are amongst your brothers, you have nothing to fear.'

'I know,' Hardenburg replied, replacing the bandage. 'I think I will,' he decided.

Delmar placed the pauldron down on the bed by his brother's hand.

'I will tell you, Delmar,' Hardenburg said. 'I knew this was to happen to me.'

Delmar looked back up at him. 'How so?'

'I had a dream, back in Altdorf. It was the night before our vigil. It was so vivid, so real.'

'You dreamt this?'

'Aye, I think I did. It's hard to picture it now.' His eyes closed. 'But I know it was a nightmare. I was marked, scarred, like this, and there was some bargain, I could make myself whole again.'

Hardenburg opened his eyes. 'I remember thinking when I woke up that to be so disfigured was the worst that could happen to me. Worse even than death. I wanted to talk to you about it but...'

Someone coughed behind them. It was Falkenhayn.

'If you are finished, Reinhardt,' he said, stiffly. 'Then I would appreciate some time to sit with my brother.'

Hardenburg acknowledged Falkenhayn, but then beckoned Delmar to lean down close to him.

'But now the worst has happened to me, and I have survived,' he whispered, 'and so I have nothing left to fear.'

Delmar leaned up. 'I'm glad to hear it, Tomas.'

He stood and took his leave, but as he passed Falkenhayn the other knight stopped him.

'Do not think,' Falkenhayn said quietly, 'that the order has mistaken your desperate race up that mountainside for anything more than it was. They can discern the difference between a proper leader and an ill-balanced mind, yearning for its own destruction. You and your Provincials will not take this squadron from me.'

Delmar looked closely into Falkenhayn's eyes, searching for some kind of comprehension on his part of what was truly happening.

'There are no Provincials, Franz, not any more. Nor Falcons, nor Reiklanders.' Delmar motioned to the rune both he and Falkenhayn wore on their shoulders. 'We are united. For we are brothers.'

'Oh,' Falkenhayn replied, 'do not think you can catch me that way,

Reinhardt. I am no fool. You may be the more able warrior, but you shall never best me in this.' Falkenhayn raised his voice a degree, just so it would be heard by the others nearby. 'Stay with me, Reinhardt. Sit with me over our fallen brother and let us comfort him together.'

Delmar could not believe it had taken him so long to see how small a man Falkenhayn truly was. But then they were interrupted; more pressing news had arrived at camp.

'Uncle! Uncle!' Siebrecht hurried down the slope. At the bottom, Herr von Matz watched a line of men and dwarfs loading a riverboat. 'Have you heard?'

'What is it, Siebrecht?'

Siebrecht caught his breath to answer, and then noticed that one of the men loading the riverboat was Twoswords. Then he realised that all the rest were his uncle's keepers as well. 'Wait. What is this? Where are you going?'

'Back to Nuln,' Herr von Matz replied. 'Now the goblins are broken the river is open again, and I can get my shipment safely there. I had begun to think that it might have been trapped in Karak Angazhar for good.'

'What? You already had a shipment here?'

'I admit,' Herr von Matz smiled, 'I was perhaps overly modest about my relations with the dwarfs of Karak Angazhar. We have been trading partners for some years now. But you seemed so heartened to hear that I had a trace of altruism that I did not want to disappoint you, especially going to war.'

Siebrecht stopped the next pair of men carrying a crate.

'Open it,' he ordered. They looked at Herr von Matz.

'Go ahead,' Herr von Matz said wearily.

Using a pick, they levered the crate's lid open. Siebrecht looked inside.

'It's pistol shot?' he said in disbelief. 'You came all this way for a few crates of pistol shot?'

'There is a war on, Siebrecht.' Herr von Matz waved at his men to close the crate up. 'There has never been greater demand for fine dwarfen shot. For nobility only. And perhaps I might interest the Reiksguard in some as well. They're worth a small fortune, I can tell you.'

Siebrecht had no interest in his uncle's commercial enterprises; there were events of far greater importance unfolding. 'You can't leave now, uncle. You haven't heard about the ogres.'

'What about them?'

'They didn't disperse into the mountains. They've gone down the Reik valley, and they've taken the goblins with them.'

'They are not blocking the river, I hope.'

'No, they're into Averland. They're heading for the villages.' Herr von Matz ignored his nephew and carried on supervising the loading. Siebrecht took hold of his shoulder to gain his attention. 'You don't understand. The militias are here, the villages are defenceless.'

As Siebrecht gripped his uncle, Twoswords suddenly appeared behind him. Herr von Matz gestured for his guardian to hold back and gently removed Siebrecht's hand. 'So, what would you have me do about it?'

'We can ride ahead of the army; as soon as we catch up with the ogres you can talk to Burakk again. I know it was you who convinced him to break with Thorntoad; you can convince him to return to the mountains.'

'Why would I do that?'

'Why?' Siebrecht blinked at his uncle's impenetrability. 'Burakk is going to lay waste to Averland! The army is in the north, the militia is here, there's nothing to stop him.'

'No, Siebrecht, I understand what Burakk will do. I mean, why would I go and renege on our agreement?'

Siebrecht was about to repeat himself when he realised what his uncle had said. Herr von Matz motioned to his men to hurry loading the last few crates.

'You... agreed this?'

Herr von Matz regarded him coolly. 'Of course. How do you think I convinced him to give up Thorntoad's lair? How do you think I convinced him to stand aside as the Reiksguard rooted the goblins out?'

Siebrecht was staggered, 'I thought... I thought you had given him money. Or offered him mercy, so he could escape into the mountains.'

'Money or mercy? If you had listened for a single moment when I told you about them,' Herr von Matz said, the scorn and disappointment clear in his voice, 'then you would know perfectly well that ogres have no use for either. They want food. And at this moment Averland is full of villagers, fat from the harvest. It was ideal.'

'Gods, you are a traitor.' Siebrecht's hand went to the hilt of his weapon. In a flash, Twoswords whirled and Siebrecht felt the man's two blades crossed under his chin like scissors at his throat.

'You are developing a habit, Siebrecht,' Herr von Matz said, 'of reaching for your sword at the most inopportune moments.'

Siebrecht swallowed carefully. The rest of his uncle's men were watching from the boat with interest; the dwarfs from Karak Angazhar were nowhere to be seen. He dared not turn his head to see if there was anyone behind him who might come to his aid. He released his grip on his sword and it slid back into its scabbard.

'There's a good boy.' Herr von Matz said it as though he were speaking to a child. Twoswords did not lower his blades though.

'So it was all for coin?' Siebrecht began. 'You gave up Averland for trade? For this one pathetic shipment?'

'Listen to me, Siebrecht. Truly listen for once. Burakk and his ogres will gorge themselves on cattle and villagers, they will burn a few towns, then they will get bored and move on. It is nothing that Averland has not endured before, and nothing they will not have to endure again.'

'They are going to kill hundreds of our people.'

'Yes,' Herr von Matz agreed, 'they will only kill hundreds of our people. What price is that? Karak Angazhar is safe. Black Fire Pass is safe. The Empire is safe.'

The last crate was placed aboard the boat and his men gathered up Herr von Matz's personal belongings.

'I am a patriot in my own way,' he continued. 'No one will acclaim me as they will your friend Reinhardt, no one will sing sagas about me as they will for Gausser. But everything I do is done for the good of the Empire.'

'So you are the good man, with the righteous cause.' Siebrecht spat.

Herr von Matz paused as the memory of their conversations in Altdorf clicked into place.

'Now that, my nephew, is simply impolite. That quick tongue of yours will get you into trouble wherever you go. Let us just hope that your sword stays quicker.'

'It will. It will be quicker than today.' Siebrecht scowled at Twoswords and, able to do little else to him with his blades around his neck, stuck his tongue out at him. Twoswords smiled back, and then opened his mouth and displayed where his tongue had been cut out.

'I know,' Herr von Matz said, climbing over the side of the boat, 'that's why I shall watch your future career with keen interest.'

At that, Twoswords sheathed his blades and stepped into the boat just as it pushed off from the bank. Siebrecht rubbed his neck where the sharp steel had pressed against his skin, and watched the boat row away.

'So,' Siebrecht called after his departing uncle. 'Reinhardt will have the acclaim and Gausser will have the sagas?'

'Yes?' Herr von Matz called back.

'Then what will I have?'

'You get the best of it, my lad. You will have the choice!'

Still smarting, Siebrecht traversed the base of the Karlkopf. The mountain was surrounded now with pillars of smoke: from pyres cremating the corpses of the goblins and from the fires lit by the dwarfs and the Reiksguard to flush the tunnels clean of any goblin survivors. It was a forlorn task, they all knew; the grobi, as the dwarfs called them, could never be finally defeated, they were a disease that infested these mountains. Their power in this area had been broken for a time, but it would not be long before their kind migrated once more from the west and south and took up residence again.

Snow was beginning to fall, blowing over the peaks and down the valleys with bursts of chill wind. Down on the plains, Siebrecht knew, Rhya still held sway, but up in the mountains Ulric, the god of winter, had taken residence. Two riders approached him along the bank of the river. They were Delmar and Gausser. Siebrecht raised his hand in salute.

'Brothers!' he cried, against a flurry of snow.

They reined their horses in, Delmar in the lead. 'Siebrecht, we heard that you might have left with your uncle.'

'Not a chance, brother. Not a chance.' Siebrecht looked past Delmar and nodded at Gausser. 'Where are you headed?'

'Sternberg has taken command of Osterna's and Jungingen's knights. They are to remain behind to guard the wounded and the bodies of our fallen brothers. The rest of the order is to chase after the ogres. Zöllner's banner will lead the way and we have permission to join them...'

'I am coming too,' Siebrecht stated suddenly.

'I am glad to hear it,' Delmar replied, 'for we have brought your horse for that very purpose.' Delmar looked behind him and Gausser, a look of deep satisfaction upon his face, led forwards the spare steed.

'You are good brothers indeed,' Siebrecht declared as he mounted up. 'To victory or death!'

'No, Siebrecht,' Delmar amended, his gaze fixed down the Reik valley and into the green lands beyond. 'Just to victory.'

Count von Walfen, the Chancellor of Reikland, strode briskly through the halls of the Imperial Treasury. His haste was not caused by urgency, but by eagerness. This was to be a great day for him indeed.

He arrived at his destination: a vault, unlocked and empty aside from the neat stacks of crates and a single figure. Walfen bowed deeply.

'My Imperial Majesty.'

'Let us proceed,' replied the Emperor Karl Franz.

'As you say, majesty.' Walfen stepped forwards and unbolted the nearest crate. Normally, he would not have performed such manual work himself, but he had done far worse in order to keep this secret. The bolts loosened and he opened the lid.

'Pistol shot,' the Emperor stated.

Walfen nodded. 'Who would take special interest in cases of pistol shot? But beneath the tarnish they are purest silver, majesty. The first instalment of the war loan from High King Thorgrim.'

'Ingenious.'

'This is nothing, majesty. The true ingenuity was your persuasion of the High King, that he might put his silver to work rather than add it to his hoard.'

The Emperor ignored the flattery. After two decades of rule, he did not hear it any more. 'Will it be enough?' he asked. 'Will it be enough to rebuild the walls, to replant the crops, to bandage the wounds of my broken realm and set its lifeblood flowing again?'

'It will, majesty.'

The ghost of a smile tugged at Karl Franz's lips, and a fraction of the heavy burden he always bore lifted from his shoulders.

'And who else knows?'

'A few on the High King's Council of Elders, also King Gramrik. Recent events aside, Karak Angazhar is a far better route for future payments than Black Fire Pass. It is far quicker down the Reik, and those dwarfs' preference for isolation greatly reduces the chance of discovery.'

'I believe we can rely upon the dwarfs' discretion,' the Emperor said.

'And then just you and I,' Walfen replied.

The Emperor, though, appeared thoughtful, and so Walfen continued. 'We agreed, majesty, the common citizenry is not ready to know how indebted we are to the dwarfs. As we rebuild all that has been destroyed, your citizens must believe that it is a result of the strength of our great nation, and that we are not subordinated to any others, even to our oldest allies. Should the mob prove fickle, it would imperil the safety of every dwarfen citizen of your Empire.'

'We did so agree,' the Emperor concurred. 'And none of your couriers knew what it was they were transporting? None of those sent to retrieve it after Karak Angazhar was besieged?'

Walfen's instinctive response was to agree, but then he caught the stern look in the Emperor's eye. The same look that had faced down kings and elector counts, and held the fractious Empire together throughout twenty years of strife and war.

'There is one, majesty.'

'And you trust him?'

'I have done for many years.'

'Keep a watch on him, nevertheless.'

'I will, majesty.'

'You shall have to tell Chancellor Hochsvoll, of course.'

'Of course.'

The Emperor raised an eyebrow at Walfen's quick response.

'It will be her responsibility to keep this money safe, to spend it where we need it most and, ultimately, when we are strong again, to make our repayments to the High King. She must be told. You cannot keep your secrets from all your fellow council-members. Though I know you would prefer it that way. And you might consider some reconciliation with the Reiksmarshal. This came at some cost to him.'

Walfen stood firm. 'My only desire is to serve you as best I can.'

'Yes, my councillor, yes,' Karl Franz relented. 'And you have done that today.'

'My thanks, majesty.'

'No, count. My thanks to you.'

Count von Walfen bowed again. Karl Franz took his leave, his mind already turning to other matters.

THE FEAST OF AVERLAND

The foothills of the Vaults
Early 2523 IC

The ogre once known as Burakk the Craw stumbled and fell upon the stony ground. Each time he did so he found it that much harder to rise again. The ever-present hunger within his gut maddened him. He could not think, he could not reason, all he could do was drag his emaciated body towards the mountains rising in the distance. His clothes hung off him, slack; his prized gut-plate had long since slipped off his shrinking belly. He lay face down upon the ground, mouth slowly trying to grind the dirt in his teeth. He did not have long left; starved this way, the ogre body turned to consume itself. Its last act of worship of the Great Maw.

It should not be like this. He had been a tyrant, he had had a tribe of bull-ogres of his own, and a thousand goblin servants to wait upon them. The land of men was defenceless, an open larder filled with the plumpest stock. His first days had been glorious, his ogres had run wild through the villages they reached, plucking beasts and men from within their flimsy homes with ease and gorging upon them. The Feast of Averland, they had called it, a banquet with a table the size of a province, and as many courses as there were men and beasts remaining.

Even then, though, Burakk had sensed that something was amiss. His bulls ate their fill time and again; the scraps were plentiful, though the goblins still squabbled over them as was their way; but he, no matter how much he consumed, could not quench his unnatural hunger. He ate all he could, until his jaw ached with chewing, taking what food he wished even from the mouths of his bulls. It was all for naught, for his hunger still burned.

Then those men in armour, with banners of red and white, had come after him. Mounted on their heavy horses, they charged his greenskin servants down and ran his bulls through with their lances. Some of them were killed, of course; his bulls tackled their steeds, and then crushed the fallen knights with their mauls. But the rest came on, unfearing, unwavering, relentless in their pursuit. While their number seemed without limit, each bull Burakk lost could not be replaced.

Food was no longer so plentiful. The easy meat had fled beyond their reach, and now these knights herded them even further distant. As each skirmish bought fresh losses, Burakk's hunger grew even more intense. His body began to waste away. As his proud gut diminished, his bulls began to drift away, no longer in awe of their leader. As they went, so their goblin servants went with them. These splinter tribes struck out on their own, and more than most were quickly fodder for the avenging knights.

Then Burakk had been left with only one bull-ogre to follow him. The first morning this last survivor saw Burakk was alone, he drew his carving knives and set about to make Burakk his meal. Burakk was weak, but was no birthling, and it was he who broke his challenger's bones and drank the marrow from them.

Yet even as he consumed the body, his hunger ate at him from within. He was done. He had nothing left. He set his sights upon the nearest mountains, those mountains that reminded him of his distant home, knowing he would not reach them.

And here he lay, alone on some nameless slope, no victor's sword at his throat, no cannon shot through his chest. His final foe, the betrayer he could not best, was his own body which had turned on him and judged that he must die. Why it had, Burakk did not know. The Great Maw was calling, and he would go.

As the sun dipped low, the ogre's corpse began to cool. Its blood no longer flowed, its muscles would not move. But there was motion still. A pulse, a beat, within that barrel chest. A shape that grew larger, pushing up with violent struggle.

'Ah! Freeeeee!' Thorntoad screamed, as he pulled his broken form up through the ogre's slack throat and out its lolling mouth.

'Freeee!' Thorntoad cried again, his regrown thorns still glistening with the ogre flesh to which they had clung to keep him from the ogre's stomach.

'Free...' Thorntoad said once more, before collapsing as his exhaustion took hold. He had survived, though survival was too grand a word for the baseness of his existence these last few weeks, living an inch from destruction, feeding on the masticated bola that came down the ogre's throat. It had been plentiful at least for a time, and then it had ceased. But Thorntoad's starving time was over now; his head dipped down across the ogre corpse and his razor teeth took a bite. Burakk the Craw would attend one last meal, not as the diner, but as the feast.

'Is this the place?' Delmar asked.

'No. It was a little further down,' Griesmeyer replied.

The two knights guided their steeds carefully down the snow-covered slope.

'Was it as cold as this then?' Delmar wondered.

'Worse,' Griesmeyer stated, with great bravado.

Delmar chuckled. Griesmeyer pulled his horse up and looked in each direction to check his bearings.

'This is it?'

Griesmeyer paused a moment. 'Yes, it is.'

Delmar swung himself out of his saddle, patted his horse and took the last few steps to the edge of the bank on foot. He looked down its length. It was smaller than he thought it would be. Such a small gap, and yet twenty years before, in this very place, two hundred men of Nordland had lost their lives. Two hundred men of Nordland, and one Reiksguard knight.

'Is there anything left?' Perhaps it had been a foolish wish, but he had thought, had hoped, that there might be something left; something to mark the event that once happened here.

'Perhaps, beneath the snow.' Griesmeyer knew Delmar's wishes. 'But there is nothing left of him here, Delmar. All that remains of my brother is in you.'

Delmar nodded and looked out across the endless grey of the Sea of Claws. He had wanted to see this place, wanted to gaze upon that same horizon as his father had done at his end. But Griesmeyer was correct. There was nothing of his father on this ugly coast.

'Come on, Delmar.'

The two knights crested the last hill. Arrayed before them stood the army of Nordland. The grizzled regiments of halberdiers and spearmen had covered their blue and yellow uniforms with thick coats to keep out the cold, and, in the centre of the line this time, the Reiksguard knights had swapped their scarlet cloaks for furs. Delmar broke company with Griesmeyer and returned to his brothers. He touched his gauntlet to his visor in salute as he passed his squadron's standard-bearer.

'Your errand is done?' The hulking knight handled the standard with ease.

'It is.'

'Then rejoin our squadron, Brother Reinhardt.'

'At once, Brother Gausser,' Delmar smiled.

Delmar directed his steed towards the far end of the line of knights. He nodded on his way to Bohdan and Alptraum, the Averlander's grin crinkling the scar running down his cheek. Delmar turned his horse about and stepped into formation. The knight beside him raised his visor.

'I have had a letter from home,' Siebrecht said.

'It reached you all the way here?'

'Aye, Delmar, they have civilisation beyond the borders of Reikland, you know,' his friend admonished. Siebrecht pulled off one of his gauntlets and produced a parchment. 'It is in the hand of my father, though I believe we both may guess who the true correspondent is...'

Delmar readily agreed. Herr von Matz had not reappeared since they broke the siege of Karak Angazhar, but the sight of each devastated Averlander village in their pursuit of the ogres had been reminder enough.

'My father writes,' Siebrecht continued, adopting a haughty tone, 'to posit to me that once this campaigning season is done, I might consider interrupting my time with the order for a while. Apparently, an opportunity may arise to raise the family's fortunes, should I join the service of my uncle.'

'And how have you replied?' Delmar inquired.

Siebrecht looked pointedly at Delmar, and then slowly began to tear the letter to pieces.

'I would not be so hasty if I were you,' Delmar said. 'We may need the parchment for kindling.'

The two of them laughed at that and, as if in agreement, their horses snorted underneath them. Their merriment was interrupted by another rider who drew level beside them, a rider who gripped his reins in one hand and with the other drummed upon his saddle, even though that hand had no fingers.

'Still the disrespectful tongue, Matz,' Master Verrakker said pointedly.

The two young knights turned to their master. 'How goes the training of the Nordland troops?' Siebrecht asked.

'We will see today,' Verrakker judged, 'how they will fare against a real enemy.'

'It is strangely fortuitous timing, Brother Reinhardt, is it not,' Siebrecht said archly, 'that Elector Count Theoderic should have had such a sudden change of heart on the Reiksguard to invite them to come and train his new army, just before this new threat is spotted off his shores.'

'Stranger still,' Delmar replied, 'that the Reiksguard should have agreed so readily and dispatched a whole banner commanded by Lord Griesmeyer, a banner that includes the elector count's grandson, no less, to escort the three fightmasters.'

Verrakker harrumphed without further comment.

'A suspicious man,' Siebrecht concluded, 'might be led to believe that all was not as it appeared to be in the grand province of Nordland. Would you not agree, Master Verrakker?'

Verrakker gave Siebrecht a baleful look. 'Griesmeyer was right about you, Matz. You perceive secrets and shadows, when the truth could not be more clear. Both of you!'

'Brother!' Fightmaster Talhoffer called. He and Ott were mounted, both upon the same steed. Ott sat behind his brother; his eyes were bandaged against the light, but he had a great smile upon his face as he drew deep breaths of the sea air.

Talhoffer continued, 'We are needed, brother...' Talhoffer looked to say more, but then saw the other knights listening, 'about that certain matter.'

Verrakker shook his head at Talhoffer's clumsy attempt at subterfuge, then turned his horse, and the three masters trotted off together.

A stir went through the army: some news had been received. Sails had been spied on the horizon, the foe had been spotted. Delmar and Siebrecht could see the gonfanonier preparing to raise the banner's standard. Griesmeyer rode to the head of the knight squadrons. He drew his sword and pointed it straight in the direction they would take.

'Reiksguard!' he called. 'To battle!'

KNIGHT OF THE
BLAZING SUN

Josh Reynolds

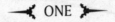

ONE

The orcs came down out of the Worlds Edge Mountains into Ostermark like a green tide, sweeping villages and towns before them in a cascade of flame and pillage. But the men of the Mark stood firm and met the orcs with pike, shot and sword. Soldiers in purple and yellow livery crashed against barbaric green-skinned savages, matching Imperial steel and age-old strategy against inhuman muscle and brute cunning. Men and orcs screamed and died as the frozen ground turned to mud and the sun swung high in the sky.

Elsewhere, horses pawed the frost-covered earth in nervous anticipation. Their breath escaped in bursts of steam which drifted haphazardly through the close-set scrub trees that surrounded them and their riders. Hector Goetz reached down and stroked his mount's muscular neck. The warhorse whinnied eagerly. 'Easy Kaspar,' he said. 'Easy. Miles to go yet.' Goetz was a tall man, and he wore the gilded armour of a knight of the Order of the Blazing Sun easily, if not entirely comfortably. He glanced down the row of similarly armoured riders that spread out to either side of him and wished he felt more confident in his chances of surviving the coming engagement.

'Just give him a thump, boy,' someone said. Goetz twisted in his saddle, meeting the cheerful gaze of his hochmeister. Tancred Berlich was a big, bluff man with a grey-streaked beard and a wide grin. Red cheeks and a splotchy nose completed the image of a man more concerned with food and drink than fighting and death. He had commanded the Kappelburg Komturie for as long as Goetz could remember. 'Horses are like soldiers... a thump or three is good for morale.'

Goetz chuckled as Berlich gave a booming laugh. His smile faded as Berlich's opposite number from the Bechafen Komturie glared at them through the open visor of his ornate helmet.

'I know that proper military discipline is difficult for you, Tancred, but I would like to remind you that this is an ambush!' the man hissed through gritted teeth. Of an age with his fellow Hochmeister, Alfonse Wiscard looked older. His face was a hatchet made of wrinkles and his eyes were like chips of ice. Those cool orbs swivelled to Goetz a moment later. 'Control your hochmeister, brother, or the orcs will be on us far sooner than we anticipate,' he said.

'Leave the boy alone, Wiscard,' Berlich said before Goetz could reply. 'He's got more experience than all of the puppies you brought along combined. Don't you boy?'

'I... have seen my share,' Goetz said, looking straight ahead. 'More than most perhaps.'

'The Talabeclander insults us!' one of Wiscard's men said.

'Quiet,' Wiscard snapped. His face was twisted into as sour an expression as Goetz had ever seen. He felt impressed despite himself. 'Quiet, all of you; we are here to fight orcs, not rehash old grudges.' The provinces of Talabecland and Ostermark had been at each other's throats for decades, for one reason or another. While the only loyalties the members of the Order were supposed to hold were to Myrmidia, the Order itself and the Emperor, in that order, occasionally the old traditional disagreements crept in.

'Besides, the boy's not really a Talabeclander; he's from Solland!' Berlich said, pounding Goetz on the shoulder.

'Solland hasn't existed for a long time. Longer than my lifetime,' Goetz protested.

'Modesty. I think he's the heir,' Berlich whispered loudly to Wiscard. 'Old Helborg owes the boy a sword, or my name isn't Tanty!'

'Sudenland is gone, hochmeister. As is its Elector,' Goetz said patiently. 'Sudenland' was how his mother had insisted on referring to the dead province, now long since absorbed by Wissenland. It was a peculiarity of the old families, and one Goetz had never been able to shake. 'And your name is Tancred. I have never heard anyone refer to you as "Tanty".'

'See? See? Only royalty talks down its nose like that! Boy'll be Emperor if he survives,' Berlich laughed.

Goetz craned his neck as a young pistolier rode up. Both horse and rider were clearly exhausted. The pistolier had sweat dripping down his youthful features, cutting tracks in the grime that otherwise covered his face. 'Milords,' he wheezed. 'The Lord Elector Hertwig requests that you see to the flank!'

'Ha! Finally!' Berlich growled, slamming a fist into his thigh.

Goetz watched the young man lead his horse away, both of them covered in sweat and reeking of a hard ride and exhaustion. It hadn't been so long ago that he himself had ridden among the ranks of the pistolkorps. They had taught him the art of riding and of the usefulness of black powder. Thinking of that last one, he wondered what he wouldn't give for a brace of pistols now. Even just one would mean one less orc to face up close. Unfortunately, while Myrmidia was a goddess of battlefield innovation, her followers were forced to follow the law of the land. Gunpowder was far too rare and unstable to be given to a force prone to reckless headlong charges into the maw of the enemy army.

Goetz sighed. He'd earned his spurs as a pistolier, against orcs then as well. Of course, the raiders he and his compatriots had put to flight then had been as nothing compared to the horde that now crawled across his field of vision, from horizon to horizon. He was suddenly quite thankful for the heavy plate he wore, with all of its dwarf-forged strength between him and the crude axes of the green-skinned savages he was even now readying himself to face. He'd seen what an orc could do to an unarmoured man – and an armoured one, come to that – and the more layers between him and that gruesome fate was well worth the inevitable sweat and chafing. Not to mention the smell.

Still, a pistol would have been nice.

'Don't look so glum, boy,' Berlich said, jostling him out of his reverie. 'Cheer up! We'll be charging any minute now!' The hochmeister grinned eagerly, and bounced slightly in his saddle like an excited urchin. 'Blood and thunder, we'll turn them into so much paste!'

Goetz turned back around, peering through the protective embrace of the thicket where they were waiting. While most of the orc army was already engaged in the swirling melee beyond, some canny boss had managed to restrain his impetuous followers. That was impressive, and slightly frightening. Orcs usually had all the restraint of a rabid hound. When one proved capable of thinking beyond putting its axe through the nearest skull, it meant trouble for anyone unlucky enough to be caught in its path. Right at that moment, the unlucky ones looked to be the eastern flank of Elector Hertwig's battered force, as a stomping, snorting, squealing flood of orcish BoarRiders hurtled towards the purple-and-gold lines. Goetz tightened his grip on his reins and took hold of his lance, jerking it up from where he'd stabbed it into the ground.

'Thunder and lightning, that's how it'll be!' Berlich said, lifting his own lance. Goetz took a deep breath and set his shield. He caught Wiscard's eye, and the hochmeister nodded briskly.

'We go where we are needed,' Wiscard said, intoning the first part of the Order's creed.

'We do what must be done,' Goetz replied along with all the rest.

'And Myrmidia have mercy on those green buggers because I'll have none!' Berlich roared, standing up in his saddle. 'Let's have at them! Hyah!' Then, with a slow rumble that built to a thunderous crescendo, the Order of the Blazing Sun rode to war. They brushed aside the thicket with the force of their passage and the Order's specially-bred warhorses bugled bloodthirsty cries as they launched forwards.

Seconds later, wood met flesh with a thunderous roar, and the ground trembled at the point of impact. Lances cracked and splintered as they tore through the orc lines, shoving bodies back atop bodies and creating eddies in the green tide. Goetz's teeth rattled inside his helmet as his lance was reduced to a jagged stump of brightly painted wood. He tossed it aside and drew his sword, wheeling his horse around even as the broken weapon struck the ground. Goetz lashed out as a green shape crashed against him in the press of combat.

The orc's mouth gaped wide, its foul breath spilling out from between a gate of yellowed tusks as the sword passed between its bulbous head and its sloped shoulders. The head, still mouthing now-silent curses, tumbled forward, striking Goetz's shield and springing away into the depths of the melee.

The body, its neck-stump spurting blood, was carried in the opposite direction by the snorting, kicking boar its legs were still clamped around. Goetz hauled on his horse's reins, forcing the trained destrier to sidestep the grunting beast. The horse bucked and kicked at the fleeing pig and then swung around at Goetz's signal, lunging towards the next opponent with a savage whinny.

Goetz's sword chopped down left and right until his arm began to ache from the strain. The orcs kept coming, treading on the bodies of their dead or dying fellows in their excitement as they fought to get to grips with the men who had crashed into their flank.

It had been a bold move, and a necessary one, but Goetz wasn't so sure that it had been a smart one. Fifty men, even fifty fully-armoured knights of the Order of the Blazing Sun, could not stand against the full weight of an orc horde, no matter how righteous their cause or how strong their sword-arms. Now, with their task accomplished, they found themselves surrounded by an army of angry berserkers as the rest of the Elector's forces attempted to reach them. It was not a position that Goetz enjoyed being in.

A crude spear crashed against his thigh and skittered off his armour, leaving a trail of sparks in its wake. Goetz swung his horse around and iron-shod hooves snapped out, pulping a malformed green skull with deadly efficiency. He brought his shield up instinctively as a swift movement caught his eye. Arrows sprouted from the already battered face of the shield and Goetz chopped his sword down, slicing through the hafts as he whispered a quiet prayer to Myrmidia.

'Hear me, Lady of Battle; keep me from harm and kill my enemy, if you please,' he said as he took a moment to catch his breath. He looked around. The battle had devolved into a chaotic melee, with ranks and order forgotten in the heat of battle. A volley of handguns barked nearby; men screamed and died, their cries barely audible above the cacophony of the orcish battle-cries. He caught sight of Hertwig's standard, waving above the battle.

'Ware!' someone yelled. Another knight, his armour flecked with gore, gestured wildly and Goetz twisted in his saddle, catching a gnaw-toothed axe on the edge of his sword. His arm went numb from the force of the blow and he was forced to bring his shield around to catch a second blow.

The shield crumpled inward as the axe crashed against it. The orc who wielded it was as large a monster as Goetz had ever seen. It had a dull, dark hue to its thick hide and heavy armour decorating its muscular limbs. The beast was large enough to attack a mounted man without difficulty and as Goetz's horse shied away, the brute roared out a challenge in its own barbarous tongue.

'Come on then!' Goetz shouted back. He kneed his mount and the war-horse reared, lashing out. The orc howled as a knife-edged hoof plucked one of its bat-like ears from its head. It drove one massive shoulder into the horse's belly, toppling it onto its side. Goetz rolled from the saddle as his horse fell, losing hold of his shield. He retained his sword however and managed to block a blow that would have taken his head from his shoulders.

The orc loomed over him, its teeth bared in a grin. The edge of the axe inched downwards towards Goetz's face, despite the interposed sword blade. Muscles screaming, he drove a fist into the orc's jaw, surprising it as well as numbing his hand in the process. It had been like punching a sack of granite.

The beast stepped aside, more from shock than pain, but the hesitation was enough. Goetz swung around, chopping his sword into the orc's side. It roared and backhanded him, denting his helm and sending it flying. He fell onto his back, skull ringing.

Bellowing in agony, the orc jerked at the sword, trying to pull it free. It gave up after a moment and, bloody froth decorating its jaws, swung its axe up for a killing blow despite the presence of Goetz's sword still buried hilt-deep in its side. Before the blow could land a lance point burst through the orc's throat. It dropped its axe and grabbed at the jagged mass of wood, bending double and nearly yanking its wielder from his saddle.

'Are you just going to sit there all day, brother, or are you going to help me?' the knight cried out as Goetz looked up at him. Goetz's reply was to throw himself towards the hilt of his sword. The orc arched its back, gagging as it tried to remove the obstruction in its throat. Even now, nearly chopped in two and with a lance through the neck it was still fighting... and still more than capable of killing.

Goetz caught the hilt with his palms and shoulder and thrust forward with all of his weight. The orc's roar turned shrill as the sword resumed its path through the beast's midsection. Goetz stumbled as dark blood sprayed him. The orc fell in two directions, fists and heels thumping the ground spasmodically.

Rising, Goetz caught his horse's bridle. 'Easy, Kaspar, easy,' he murmured, knuckling the horse at the base of its jaw as it nuzzled him. He hauled himself awkwardly up into the saddle. Muscles aching, he turned to his rescuer.

'My thanks, brother,' he said, jerking on his mount's reins and turning it. The other man raised his visor and snorted. Goetz recognised the fine-boned features as those of the man who had taken offence at Berlich's comments earlier. Velk, he thought the man was called.

'Save your thanks, Talabeclander,' Velk said. 'If I'd known it was one of you lot, I might have let the brute finish you off.'

Goetz spat out a mouthful of dust and shook his head. 'I see the hospitality of the Mark is as generous as ever.'

Velk glared at him and opened his mouth to reply when a sharp voice interrupted. 'Brothers! Cease this nonsense. There are still orcs to kill.' Goetz turned and saw Wiscard, riding towards them, a blood-stained warhammer dangling loosely from his hand. Three other knights trailed after him, including Berlich, who looked as cheerful as ever despite the blood matting his beard.

As Wiscard drew close, he motioned with the hammer and said, 'Look!' Goetz followed the gesture and saw a crude standard rising above a cloud of dust. The tattered remnants of a number of banners, some from regiments native to the Empire, others from Bretonnia and one or two from places that Goetz didn't recognise, hung from the crossbeam of the standard, flapping amidst an assortment of skulls and gewgaws. As they watched, the Elector's standard, gleaming gold and purple, hurtled towards the other.

'Must be their warlord,' Berlich said, setting his horse into motion with a swift kick. 'Having fun, Brother Goetz?' he said, grinning at the younger knight.

'More than is decent, hochmeister,' Goetz said. The knights began to trot forward as a solid wedge, resting their horses for a moment. Even the strongest animal could only do so much carrying the weight of a fully armoured knight.

Berlich laughed and slapped Goetz a ringing blow on the shoulder. He looked at Wiscard. 'Didn't I tell you the boy had spirit?'

'As a matter of fact, no,' Wiscard said. 'Then, I rarely pay attention to your blathering, Tancred.'

'Blathering?' Berlich said with a guffaw. 'Do I blather, Brother Goetz?'

'Incessantly, Hochmeister Berlich,' Goetz said, recognising the game. Berlich liked to pretend he was nothing more than a common soldier, despite having more titles than fingers. The Kappelburg Komturie was a place of little truck with authority or discipline.

Berlich clutched his chest. 'Cut to the quick! And by a fellow knight… the ignominy of it all.'

'From what I know of Talabeclanders, you should have expected as much,' Velk interjected. 'Traitorous pack of killers, the lot of you.'

Berlich ignored him. 'What say we introduce ourselves to yon beastie, Wiscard you old stick?' he said, gesturing with his sword to the warlord's standard.

'My thoughts exactly,' Wiscard said. He slapped his visor down and the other knights did the same. 'Velk, Goetz, form up on me.'

As one, they charged. They crashed into the orcs from behind, bowling several over. Goetz leaned over his horse's neck, chopping down on those orcs not quick enough to get out of the way. Surprised, several of the creatures ran, and those that didn't fell soon enough.

One of the creatures, however, spun and chopped down on Velk's horse with a vicious looking double-bladed axe. The horse fell squealing and rolled over its rider, leaving him in the dust. Goetz yanked hard on the reins and sent his own horse leaping between the downed knight and his would-be slayer. 'Haro Talabecland!' he roared, shouting the battle-cry of his home province. 'Up, Talabheim!'

The orc yowled as Goetz's sword took its hands off at the wrists. His second blow cracked its skull. Velk was on his feet by then, his face tight with pain. One arm hung at an awkward angle, and he grudgingly nodded at Goetz. A moment later, his eyes widened as a massive shape loomed up out of the dust.

A stone-headed maul crashed against the armoured head of Goetz's horse, killing the animal instantly and throwing Goetz to the ground for a second time. He skidded across the rocky ground, narrowly avoiding being trampled by the other combatants. His eyes widened as he looked up at what had to be the leader of the orc horde.

The creature was far larger than the dark-skinned brute from earlier, and its skin gleamed like polished obsidian. A horned, crimson-crested helmet rode on its square head and made it look even taller as it spread its ape-like arms and bellowed. The motion and the sound caused the oddments of plate and mail that it wore to clatter loudly. With a start, Goetz realised that the beast had its standard strapped to its back, as well as a basket full of smaller, vicious looking creatures, all clad in black cloaks and hoods and armed with crude bows. Goblins, he realised, as he rolled out of the way of a spatter of arrows.

'Myrmidia's Oath,' Velk said, stumbling back. 'It's huge!'

'That just means it's easier to hit!' Berlich roared, swooping past them towards the warlord. Whooping, the hochmeister swung his sword overhand, shearing off one of the horns on the orc's helmet. The monster howled in outrage and spun much more quickly than Goetz thought possible for a creature that size.

Berlich grunted as the stone maul rose up and rang down on his shield, shattering both it and the arm it had been strapped to. Goetz watched in horror as Berlich's horse sank to its knees from the force of the impact and a second blow swept the knight from his saddle and sent him sailing. Berlich landed with a sickening thump several dozen yards away and did not move.

'No!' Goetz surged to his feet and brought his sword down on the side of the orc warlord's head, cutting a divot out of its helmet and its face. The maul swung out at him and he leapt back, ignoring the weight of his armour and the growing ache in his limbs.

'The Mark! The Mark!' Velk shouted, sounding his own province's battle-cry and stumbling towards the creature from the other side. His sword struck sparks off the orc's mail, but did little else. An almost casual jab of a titan elbow sent him tumbling.

The orc made to finish Velk off and Goetz hacked through the haft of its weapon, more through luck than intention. He swung again, slicing links from the brute's rusty suit of mail. The creature's spade-sized hands crashed against his shoulders and he was hoisted into the air. As it opened its mouth, he realised that in absence of its weapon it intended to bite his head off.

'Myrmidia make me lucky rather than stupid,' he hissed as he kicked out, driving a foot into its teeth. The blow shattered several tusks. Squirming, Goetz freed his sword-arm and stabbed clumsily at the orc's face. Most of the blows landed on its helmet, but one found a yellow eye, popping it like a blister. Yellow pus erupted from the creature's socket and it shrieked and dropped Goetz.

'Ha!' Gripping his sword with both hands, he rammed it into the creature's belly and cut upwards. The orc's shriek grew louder as Goetz dug the blade in, trying to pierce its heart. Great fists crashed down on him, snapping off a pauldron and cracking his shoulder.

Goetz ignored the pain and forced the blade in deeper, until, at last, the brute's cries faded and it went limp. He staggered back as it fell, its remaining eye glazed over and its jaws wide. One hand clawed momentarily at the earth but then splayed flat.

Somewhere a cheer went up. Goetz turned, exhausted, and raised his sword over his head. A moment later a sharp pain flared through him and he grunted. He stumbled forward, reaching towards his back.

A thin shaft had sprouted from a gap in his armour. A second shaft, and then a third and a fourth thudded home. A burning sensation erupted from the points of impact and slithered through him. He wobbled around, body going numb. His sword slid from nerveless fingers and he sank to his knees. He saw the goblins clamber out of the crumpled basket on the warlord's back. He clawed awkwardly for his sword.

Evil green faces glared at him in malicious glee as several dark shapes darted forward, crude blades drawn. As the goblins closed in, chuckling and slinking, Goetz collapsed, his world melting into fire.

Athalhold looked at the man in bemused silence. The common room of the coaching house had fallen silent, and every eye was on the disparate duo at the bar. Athalhold wore light mail and jerkin bearing the emblem of the Order of the Blazing Sun, and was far larger than the man who'd accosted him. One hand rested on the pommel of his sword and he smiled slightly.

'Repeat that, if you please,' he said. He had only arrived in the free-city of Marienburg a few hours earlier, and while he knew of the city's reputation, he hadn't expected to be confronted with the evidence of it quite so quickly.

'I said, we don't want your kind here,' the man said, smoothing his moustaches with the side of one hand. He bared his teeth at the knight. He was slender and dark-skinned, with a dancer's grace to his movements. In contrast to the knight, he was clad in fine silks and tights; in other words, every inch the stereotypical Marienburg fop.

'My kind?'

'Knights. Arrogant, jumped-up, foreign bully boys.' The man turned to the common room and swept his hands out. 'We don't need their kind here, do we? Marienburg is a free-city, isn't it?'

'The Order of the Blazing Sun goes where it is needed,' Athalhold said, paraphrasing part of the Order's creed. 'Even to free-cities.'

The glove struck him lightly across the face. It was such an unexpected gesture that Athalhold could only blink in surprise. 'You are challenged,' the fop said. 'Outside is the traditional venue. If you accept the challenge, that is.'

'Have I offended you in some way?' Athalhold said.

'No. Do you accept the challenge or not?'

Athalhold looked around, then back at the man before him. 'Why do you want to fight me?'

'I don't, particularly.'

Athalhold grunted. He had been a member of the Order for close to two decades, and a member of the Middenheim aristocracy since birth, and had been witness to and participated in many challenges. Granted, most had taken place on the field of battle, but every so often some young puppy fresh from the upper reaches of the nobility decided to test their spurs. This man, however, was neither a soldier nor an aristocrat. Athalhold took in the scars on the man's long fingers and those that decorated his cheeks. And despite his fancy clothing, the hilt of the rapier on his hip was well worn and shiny from use.

A professional then, Athalhold decided. Likely looking to improve his reputation by duelling a knight of the Empire. In other words, a waste of time. He decided to fall back on his usual response to such things. 'Go away, little man. There's no sport for you here today.' Athalhold turned away.

The hiss of a sword leaving its sheath alerted him a moment before the tip of the blade would have pinked his hand where it sat on the bar. Athalhold jerked his hand away and turned. The blade slid lightly across his cheek. Instinctively he slapped a palm to his cheek. His fingers came away wet.

The rapier tip waggled in front of his eyes like the head of a cobra, then dipped backwards over the fop's shoulder. 'Just because you refuse doesn't mean I don't get to kill you,' he said with a sneer.

Athalhold rubbed a thumb across his cheek and looked at it. Then his eyes flickered up to the duellist. 'Do you know who I am? Who I represent?'

'Of course. I challenged you didn't I?' the duellist said. 'Now, are you going to fight, or are you going to just stand there while I slice bits off you?'

Athalhold frowned. A second later, his sword sprang from its sheath and cut the air just beneath the duellist's nose. The latter danced backwards, upending a table in his haste to get clear. His rapier twirled forward, curling around the knight's blade and scratching against his jerkin. The two men broke apart and began to circle one another.

The knight was impressed despite himself. The duellist was fast and skilled, for a hired blade. More so than many professional soldiers. But Athalhold had been tested on fields of combat more dangerous than any Marienburg back-alley. He lunged suddenly, trapping his opponent's rapier with the flat of his blade and grabbing for the man's wrist. If he could disarm him–

A wooden club connected with his shoulder, momentarily numbing the attached arm. Athalhold turned and sliced through the club as it came down a second time. The burly thug who held it jerked back in surprise. Athalhold's eyes narrowed as he saw several more men advancing from out of the crowd. They carried daggers and clubs.

He looked at the duellist. 'Is this your idea of a duel?' he said.

The duellist shrugged. 'Marienburg rules,' he said, and then lunged. Athalhold swatted the blow aside and backed towards the door. While he was confident of his ability to handle the newcomers, he needed room to do it.

He backed out into the courtyard, blade extended. The men followed. Four of them, in all. The duellist leaned against the door frame, watching calmly. 'Be gentle lads. We wouldn't want people to start questioning our hospitality,' he said.

A club snapped out towards Athalhold's chest and he removed the wielder's fingers before turning and smashing his blade down on a second tough's collarbone. The other two men hesitated, and Athalhold dispatched the closest with a quick sweep, taking his leg off at the knee. The last man made a desperate leap but only succeeded in spitting himself on the knight's blade.

Using his boot heel to shove the twitching body off his sword, Athalhold turned to confront the duellist, fully expecting to find the man gone. Instead, the rapier point dug for Athalhold's face, then whipped across his forehead, releasing a curtain of red into the knight's face.

Momentarily blinded, Athalhold reacted on instinct, swinging wildly. The duellist was forced to jerk back out of reach. Athalhold scraped the blood from his face and rammed an elbow into the other man's chin. His opponent staggered and the knight swatted him on the side of the head with the flat of his sword, knocking him to the ground.

The knight stomped down on the duellist's wrist a moment later, trapping his sword-hand. Then he placed the tip of his own weapon against the hollow of the downed man's throat and said, 'Now, tell me what this was about.'

'I should have thought it was obvious,' the duellist grunted, his eyes on Athalhold's sword. 'Someone has a bone to pick with you.'

'Who?'

'How should I know? Who have you annoyed?'

'You don't even know who you're working for?' Athalhold said in amazement.

'I know who paid me,' the man said. 'You'd be surprised at how rarely that's the same thing.'

'Enlighten me.'

'Do I look like a priest?'

Athalhold didn't reply. He grunted and stepped back. 'Get out of here. You failed.'

'Maybe.' The duellist rose smoothly, then, like quicksilver, he was moving, a thin-bladed knife in one hand. It scraped across Athalhold's side as he turned and his sword flashed out, separating the duellist's head from his shoulders. There was a surprised expression on the latter's face as his head bounced away.

Athalhold touched his side, relieved to feel no pain. The knife hadn't done much more than slice through his jerkin. He straightened and his ears caught a faint hiss of air. He turned and his face moved through a variety of expressions before settling on puzzlement. The expression deepened as he reached up hesitantly to touch the point of the crossbow bolt that had suddenly sprouted from his throat. Athalhold blinked and gurgled, swaying. Then he sank to his knees and slumped forward, head bowed, his blood pooling in the spaces between the stones of the courtyard.

The crossbowman hidden on the roof of the coaching house nodded in satisfaction. He had hoped that the bravos would have accomplished things without his intervention, but the thing was done regardless, more the pity.

He pulled his cloak tighter about himself and glanced at the scraggly looking crow perched nearby. It cocked its head and one beady black eye fixed on him. 'It's done,' he murmured, stroking the puckered brand that covered the inside of his wrist. 'He's dead.' Then, 'Was it really necessary?'

The crow croaked and he flinched. A moment later it flapped scabrous wings and took to the air, leaving him alone with his regrets.

In the darkness, daemons shrieked. The old man ignored them with a courage born of experience. His spirit flew on wings of ice, high above the rocks and raging waters of the Sea of Claws. The air was thick with the ghosts of others who had made this trip and failed to return, sailor and shaman alike. The old man ignored them as well.

Ulfar Asgrimdalr had faced both ghosts and daemons in his time as his tribe's gudja and neither held any fear for him these days, though both had left scars on both his body and his soul. He had left the warmth of his body, his hall and his hearth this night for one reason only and that reason was directly below him.

It was an old duty, one held by his predecessor and his predecessor's predecessor, for as long as the sea had been wet and the ice, cold. Nevertheless, Ulfar did not regard it as one of the more pleasant responsibilities he was tasked with. It had claimed too many lives for that. Too many souls.

The island bled a sour chill into the spirit-world. It was encircled by a dome of frozen ghosts, all screaming silently and eternally bound to the rock by skeins of Dark Magic. The old man passed over the curve of the dome and tried to spy upon what went on within, but all he could see was the same black pressure that always boiled there. A sense of relief flooded him.

The daemon was still bound, still trapped. Hopefully it would remain so for as long as he lived. Let some other gudja deal with it. A younger man. Stronger. At one time, it would have been Ulfar's own blood who would be tasked with the job, but now... no, best not to think of such things. Bad memories brought real pain in the between-lands.

Satisfied, Ulfar banked and turned back towards home. A moment later a scream of agony escaped him as claws of smoke and ash tore through his wings. He tumbled through the air as his attacker harried him. He twisted, trying to return the favour, and a familiar face shoved through the filthy cloud and grinned at him. 'Too slow, Asgrimdalr,' the face hissed at him as smoky tendrils pierced his limbs. 'Too old.'

'You–' Ulfar began. The face changed, becoming an avian nightmare. A beak studded with crooked fangs bit down and Ulfar screamed again. Though neither he nor his attacker were physical, the pain was real enough. Ulfar beat withered fists against the beak, and the face dissolved into smoke. Laughter filled his head and the darkness within the dome of spirits pulsed in time.

It couldn't be! Not here! Not now!

'Hexensnacht comes, old wolf,' the thing hissed. 'The bonds you and your foul kin placed on Her weaken! She will be free to devour you all!'

Ulfar tore away from the foul smoke, hurling himself towards the clean air. Suddenly, ethereal fingers tore at his wounds, digging for the raw matter of his spirit. He flung the spectres that tried to swarm over him aside with desperate strength. To a strong man, ghosts were an inconvenience. To a weakened one, they were dangerous. But then, his opponent had known that.

A screaming phantom clutched at him, icy teeth snapping. Ulfar slapped it aside and raced for safety with every ghost in the Sea of Claws hurtling after him. If they caught him – no! He pushed the thought aside and concentrated on the path ahead. He skidded over the savage waves, his spirit shape transforming from bird to seal as he ducked beneath the water and shot towards the shore.

Instantly, he realised that he'd made a mistake as something foul and dark barrelled after him, teeth like spears crashing together. It was one of the many daemon-things that lived on the border between the Sea of Claws and the Sea of Chaos. Subsisting on the spirits of drowned men, they hunted in both worlds. If he could make it to the shore, the rune markers he had laid would protect him.

He dodged this way and that as the daemon-thing pursued him and as he drew within the protective circle of his magics, the entity gave a terrible howl and whipped away, back into the depths. His seal-shape sprang from the water even as it unravelled into diaphanous strands and sought his physical frame.

His eyes sprang open a moment later and he gasped, lurching upright out of his furs. Instinctively he clutched at himself, feeling for wounds that weren't there. Blunt fingers skidded over the protective sigils carved into his flesh and the tattoos etched where the sigils left off. He was a skinny man, all leather and sinew, with skin baked brown by the northern sun. Heart thudding in his sunken chest, he reached for his staff.

'Father?' a woman said as she ducked through the hide curtain in the doorway. She was a tall woman, young and muscular. She wore a battered hauberk under her furs and carried a naked sword in one hand. 'Father?' she said again, warily.

Ulfar coughed and gestured. She grabbed a ladle out of a nearby bucket of melting ice and extended it cautiously. Ulfar grabbed it and greedily sucked the chill slush into his mouth. Smacking his lips, he looked at her and nodded brusquely. 'It is me, Dalla. You may sheathe your blade.'

Dalla let out a sigh and sat beside him, her sword planted point down into the floor between her feet. 'When you screamed, I thought–'

Ulfar waved a hand, cutting her off. It was a depressingly common occurrence for a shaman to leave his body and for something else to return in his place. 'I am fine, I said. Where is the godi?' he snapped, grabbing his staff and using it to pull himself to his feet.

Dalla blinked. 'He's in council–'

'Come then. I must speak with him. Now.'

'Father, you can't simply interrupt him!' Dalla said, grabbing one of his stick-like arms.

'Am I not the gudja? I can interrupt whomsoever I please!' Ulfar snarled, ripping his arm free. 'Especially when I tell him what I have learned.' Slinging a wolf-skin cloak around his hunched shoulders he hobbled out into the night. Dalla followed him.

'What is it? What have you seen?'

'The end of everything, daughter. Nothing less than that,' Ulfar said.

Conrad Balk, Hochmeister of the Svunum Komturie and knight of the Order of the Blazing Sun, shivered as the chill of the sea wrapped around him. He clutched his axe more tightly and kept his eyes on the horizon. It was not meet to watch the goddess's representative when she

was about her business. Nor was it particularly conducive to a restful
night's sleep.

The first time he had seen the twitching, spasming ordeal of a trance,
he had been horrified. But age and familiarity had brought the reassurance that the priestess could not – would not – harm herself. Still, it always
raised his hackles.

Swallowing his nervousness, he draped his fingers over the head of his
axe and leaned forward, peering out of the mouth of the cavern. The mist
that clung to the surface of the Sea of Claws was as thick as stone, but Balk
knew where the southern coast of Norsca was. In his head, a map unfolded
and he saw the scars of memory. He saw the place where his predecessor Hochmeister Greisen had died; the place Greisen's own predecessor,
Kluger, had fallen; in both cases, the Norscans were to blame.

In his darker moments, Balk supposed that they would be responsible
for his own death as well. He took a breath and pushed the thought aside.
Death was unavoidable. Better to think about what could be accomplished
before that moment, whenever it came.

Better to think about what could yet be built.

A crow swooped into the cavern and hopped onto a rock near Balk. It
cocked its head and croaked. Balk nodded and stepped aside. The crow
flew past him and a few moments later he heard the priestess stand.

'Well, Lady Myrma?' he said, not turning. He knew what he would see...
a young woman, lithe and limber, shrouded in a feathered cloak with her
face covered in tribal tattoos. As she moved into the light, the tattoos briefly
seemed to writhe into a different pattern, though he knew that was impossible. Lady Myrma; the latest in a long line of priestesses, and the third by
that name known to the men of his Order.

'Dead,' she said, her youthful timbre touched with an inhuman resonance.

Balk closed his eyes and said a quick prayer. Then he said, 'How?'

'Does it matter?'

'Yes. Did he die well?' Balk said intently.

'As well as can be expected,' the priestess said, pulling the edges of her
cloak more tightly about her. She tapped two fingers against her temple.
'He felt nothing.'

Balk sighed and kissed the flat of his axe. 'Good.'

'Do not indulge in guilt, Master Balk. It is a useless thing and self-indulgent.'
She looked at him and stroked the crow that sat on her shoulder. 'Besides,
it will be forgotten soon enough. The Enemy is at our gate.'

'The–' Balk's eyes widened. 'You felt something? Learned something?'

'Felt, tasted and chased,' Myrma purred, licking her fingers. She frowned.
'Unfortunately, I did not catch him. He is cunning and cruel, that one.'

'A shame,' Balk said. He looked out at the sea and gestured with his axe.
'Well, he will be waiting on us, I suppose. Whoever he is.' He pulled the
axe back and let it rest on his shoulder. 'They all will. Goddess pity them...'

'For we will not,' Myrma said, laying a hand on his arm. 'Norsca will be burned clean in the fires of Her wrath, Master Balk. It will be your hand that sets those fires alight come the Witching Night.'

Balk hesitated. 'I still dislike that aspect of it. As nights go, that's not an auspicious one...'

'Is it not? A night where the winds of magic roar and where the gods themselves can step onto the skin of the world?' Myrma said. 'What other night could it be?'

Balk grunted and made his way towards the roughly hewn stone steps that led upwards to the komturie. The woman watched him go, her dark eyes considering. Then, as if coming to a decision, she shook her head.

'No. He is not the one, is he?'

She cocked her head, as if listening to the roar of the surf as it thundered against the rock. Beneath her feet, the bedrock of the island trembled slightly. 'No, you are right as ever, Mistress,' she said, stroking the crow. It croaked in pleasure and flapped its wings. Myrma looked at it and smiled.

'But the one is coming, eh?' Her smile split, revealing cruelly filed teeth in a carnivorous grin. 'Yes. He is coming.'

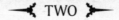

◄ TWO ►

Goetz dreamed of fire. Not a cleansing fire, but a sickly one. A witch-fire, that flickered and curled between dark trees. In the fire, something danced and howled and called his name.

He tried to ignore it, to concentrate on something else, but there was nothing. Just the darkness, the fire and the voice. It slithered into his skull and caressed his thoughts the way a miser fondled coins. Pain spiked through him and he screamed himself awake.

Sweat coated his trembling form as the priestess of Shallya dabbed at his face with a wet cloth. 'Rest easy Sir Knight,' she said. 'Rest easy. The battle is done.'

'I... what... where...?' Goetz mumbled. He was burning up. His skin felt as if it were inundated with spiders riding the curve of his bones. He hunched up on the cot, his arms wrapped around his middle. 'What happened? What happened to me?'

'You were poisoned,' the priestess said, running the cloth across his brow. 'Rest.'

Goetz slapped her hand away as a flare of pain speared through his back. Bending forwards, he clawed at the bandages on his back, ripping them away in a haze of agony. Twisting, he looked and then immediately wished he hadn't.

The coiling wounds were leaking dark pus and the flesh around them was turning the colour of rotten meat. As he watched, something black moved beneath the pus and dead flesh. Another lash of pain rippled through him and he squirmed on the cot.

'What is it?' he hissed.

'Poison,' the priestess said, her voice rougher than it had been previously. Rougher and more menacing. Goetz looked at her and bit back a scream.

Bird-like talons dug into his cheeks. He was shoved back. A scream of pain escaped him as the priestess – the thing that had been the priestess – ripped him from his cot and thrust him into the air. Feathers the colour of

522

a diseased rainbow graced the impossibly thin wrist that turned him this way and that as the thing examined him.

'Poisoned,' it croaked. 'You were poisoned.'

'N... no,' Goetz said, grabbing at the thing's face. He ripped away handfuls of feathers in a frenzy, revealing not the priestess's face but that of – who?

'You were poisoned,' the woman said, her strong face radiating a terrible peace. Goetz let the greasy feathers drift from his unresponsive hands.

He awoke with a start. Truly awoke this time, by the pain in his limbs and the ache in his middle. He staggered upright and lurched towards a chamberpot. When he'd finished, he staggered back to the bed, collapsing even as the door opened and a jolly red face peered into the chamber.

'The dream again, yes?' the owner of the face said.

'Pasqual?' Goetz said. 'What are you–'

'The hochmeister wishes to see you, young Goetz,' the other man said softly, in a liquid accent. Pasqual Caliveri was a transplant from one of the Tilean city-states, just which one no one was sure, and like Goetz, he was a knight of the Order. He wore a plain brown robe, the sigil of the Blazing Sun dangling from his neck.

The Knights of the Blazing Sun, unlike the other knightly orders that made the Empire their home, welcomed members from foreign climes. They were an inclusive brotherhood and Pasqual was only one of many. Within this komturie there were accents from Bretonnia, Tilea and Estalia as well as from Kislev and Middenheim. The only commonality was the quality of the blood. The Order of the Blazing Sun, like the other major knightly orders sanctioned within the borders of the Empire, chose their members almost exclusively from the loftier tiers of society.

Goetz's family, while noble in theory, were hardly high on the scale of the aristocracy, having originally come from Solland. He'd never been much further than the Mark himself. His father, Armin Goetz, had donated land and money to the Order to secure his son's place as a novice. It was a decision Goetz was determined he not regret.

'It was the dream, yes?' Pasqual said, reaching out a hand. Goetz batted it away.

'I don't know what you're talking about.' Goetz swung his legs off the cot. He rubbed his face again, and groaned. The freshly-healed wounds in his back pulled tight beneath the bandages as he stretched, and he winced. 'The hochmeister wants to see me?'

'I said so, yes?'

'Yes.' Goetz stood and rubbed his side. Pasqual looked at his back and clucked in concern. The Tilean was a worse mother-hen than any priestess of Shallya.

'They are still bothering you, yes?'

'No.' Goetz grunted as a soft pain flared up again and made him a liar. He rubbed the bandages and felt the small, twisting marks there. The goblin arrows had been crude, barbed things and cutting had been necessary for their removal. Gently, he probed their edges and felt for something that the doctors assured him wasn't there.

Goetz knew what he felt, however. It was there, eating through him like a particularly slow acid. There had been a fungus smeared on the arrows that had entered his flesh through the joins in his armour. Some cave-brewed poison that had entered his bloodstream in minutes and burned through his mind for days afterwards, leaving him a raving wreck. There were still splinters of those arrows imbedded in him he knew, no matter what they said. How else could the dreams be explained? 'No. I'm fine.'

'Hrmph.' Pasqual frowned, his red face disapproving. 'Ten minutes, young Goetz, yes? In the library.'

'Ten minutes.'

Pasqual swept out of the room, and Goetz rose to splash some water on his face. The reflection in the basin was that of a young man, tall and broad in all the right places with the pale, fair features of the aristocracy. His hair was shorn close to the scalp beneath his helmet, as was proper for one of his Order, and his wrists and shoulders were thick with muscle.

He genuflected to the altar to Myrmidia in the corner, making the sign of the twin-tailed comet. His eyes slid towards his armour. Next to that sat his sheathed sword. While he had been raised in the Sigmarite tradition, Myrmidia was the patron of the Order of the Blazing Sun, and had been since its founding.

The story itself was an odd one. Half anecdote and half miracle, with the undignified humour that characterised much about the Order itself. They had quite literally been created by accident. During the wars in Araby, when the Sultan's armies had invaded Estalia, a number of knights from both the Empire and Bretonnia had gone south under the Crusader's Hammer. Not many, but enough. In Magritta, a band of knights had found themselves pushed back into the grand temple of the war-goddess Myrmidia, hemmed in by the swords of the Black Scimitar Guard, and near death.

Then, like a literal bolt from the blue, the great statue of Myrmidia had toppled and buried their attackers, killing most of them and putting the rest to flight. At the time, the surviving knights had claimed it as a miracle, and pledged themselves then and there to following the path the goddess in her mercy had cleared for them.

Goetz, being something of a practical sort, doubted the event had occurred in exactly that fashion. Faith was all well and good, but a top-pling statue was usually the work of shoddy construction, rather than divine intervention. 'No offence,' he said quickly, making a bow to the altar. The small bust of the goddess seemed to smile up at him and he was reminded of the face in his dream for just a moment.

He blinked and began to dress as quickly as possible. It wouldn't do to keep the hochmeister waiting. He felt better after he buckled his armour on. It was a skin of burnished metal between the world and him; though whether he was wearing it to keep something out or something in, he couldn't say. The feeling had been with him since he could recall... uncomfortable in his own skin, that was how his father had described him. Goetz thought it was less about comfort and more about satisfaction. He was dissatisfied with his lot in life, though he couldn't say why.

The corridor outside his room was empty, but then that was no surprise. There was training to be done, and most of the komturie were likely engaged in helping with the harrying of the remainder of the orc army back up into the mountains. That was the sort of thing that he was just as happy to avoid.

'And what would old Berlich say about that, hmm?' he muttered to himself. Nothing, a traitorous part of his mind whispered, because he's resting in the crypts below this structure even as we speak. Unconsciously, his fists clenched. The old hochmeister had died from the wounds he'd suffered at the hands of the orc warlord, and when the rest of the Kappelburg knights had returned to Talabecland earlier in the week, they'd left his body to lie in state until arrangements could be made. But Goetz had come close to death many times in his short career, and it didn't frighten him.

'But it should mean something, shouldn't it?' he said out loud. He stopped and looked up at the colourful tapestry that occupied the wall of the corridor. It showed the events of the infamous (at least among members of the Order) Conference of Brass, where the sultan-sorcerer Jaffar made his dark compact with the powers of Chaos. As with all art commissioned or created by members of the Order, the known facts were stuck to with almost religious rigidity. Jaffar, rather than being daemonised, was depicted as the handsome, if rather ordinary, man he had reportedly been. Clad in colourful silks and armour wrought of the black iron favoured by the daemon-worshippers of the wastes, Jaffar stood in the centre of a ruined arena and raised his hands in awe at the sight of the daemonic throng that watched him from the stands.

Whether he had, in fact, summoned daemons to his banner was a matter of some conjecture among Imperial scholars, Goetz knew. Even the historians of the Order of the Blazing Sun weren't entirely positive that Jaffar hadn't been, in the end, simply an excellent strategist and politician.

After all, he had welded together a coalition of desert tribes and minor caliphates without any help, daemonic or otherwise. He'd turned his own small kingdom into a vigorous empire within a few short years. That's when the trouble had started. Heading north, Jaffar's army had crashed into Estalia like a thunderbolt and subsequently provoked the Crusades.

Goetz moved on. The next tapestry showed the issuing of the Edict of Magritta by the Grand Theogonist of the time, Helmut Karr. The Edict had sent a number of nascent templar-orders scurrying off to the south to join their opposite numbers from Tilea, Bretonnia and Sartosa in driving the

Arabyans from Estalia. Which they had done in the end; despite suffering
one alarming defeat after another on the way.

Goetz stopped in front of the next tapestry and genuflected, as was the
tradition. It was a highly stylised depiction of Myrmidia's Blessing – the day
the goddess had turned the tide of battle in favour of a few weary knights.

Those same knights had been looked on with suspicion after they returned,
bearing with them their new goddess. For most Imperial citizens, whether
they were poor or noble, a Southern goddess was no sort of deity. More than
one knight had been lashed to a post and sent to Myrmidia's citadel on wings
of smoke and flame by overzealous witch hunters and priests.

In 1470, the Order had gone to war with the Church of Ulric, and knights
wearing wolf-pelts had clashed with knights clad in burnished metal in the
streets of Middenheim. Political pressure had put a stop to the feud in the
end, but even today there was no komturie in the City of the White Wolf.
Not that Goetz had heard anyone complaining. He'd been to Middenheim
once, on one of his father's trips. It hadn't been pleasant.

'A long and storied tradition,' he said quietly, and it was. The only problem was that Goetz did not believe in either stories or traditions. In one
blazing moment, he'd had all claim to such illusions stripped from him.
They hadn't, as yet, come back. In a way, he hoped they never would. His
wounds from the goblin arrows had only reinforced his belief in the essen-
tial meaninglessness of the whole business.

He turned. The library doors sat at the end of the corridor. Wiscard was
waiting. He went to the doors.

The library was a grand example of its kind. Rough-hewn shelves of books
and parchments from the world over occupied much of the space in the
room. Between these shelves were smooth nooks where busts of past Grand
Masters and heroes of the Order glared out at Goetz as he passed them.

Wiscard sat at a heavy table in the centre of the room. Like Pasqual, he
wore a rough robe over a suit of ceremonial chainmail. He was just finishing a letter when Goetz stopped before his desk.

'You requested my presence, Hochmeister Wiscard?' Goetz said, after
several moments of silence. Wiscard looked up after carefully scattering
drying-sand on the letter. He blew the sand off and smiled.

'Brother Goetz. Up and walking, I see. Praise Myrmidia.' He folded the
letter and tapped it on his desk. 'Do you know what this is, brother?'

'A letter?'

Wiscard looked at him, frowning slightly. 'Yes. Quite. A letter which
recounts your actions in battle against the orcs here recently, as well as
the wounds you suffered which have kept you here in Bechafen since that
time, and away from your duties in Talabheim. Your new hochmeister, by
the way, is most eager for you to return to those duties as soon as possible.'

Goetz flinched, wondering who the new hochmeister would be.

'Granted, he will be disappointed in that regard,' another voice said.

Goetz turned, surprised. A tall figure, one he hadn't noticed before, turned from the bookshelves and fixed him with keen eyes. Goetz automatically sank to one knee, his head bowed.

'Grand Master,' he said.

Dalla had been born on a battlefield; or, more properly, a scene of slaughter. Her first blurry infant-memories had been of fire and blood. She could still smell the stink of that day deep in her nostrils. It tainted everything she had experienced since, though she felt no grudge. Indeed, she was proud. She had proven her strength from the cradle, and none could deny it.

She moved through her exercises, loosening up her limbs and thoughts. Snow crunched beneath her bare feet as she spun and twisted, bringing the sword up, around and down in an ever-more complex series of movements.

The Pattern of Steel was as much a religious rite as it was an exercise in swordplay. The Great Planner valued intricacy in all things, or so her father said. What Dalla knew from the gods would fill a helmet, and a small one at that. Still, as she thrust and chopped at imaginary foes, she kept to the Pattern, as Ulfar had taught her.

It was good, he said, to honour the gods in all things so that you avoided the risk of dishonouring them in some things. Thus, she indulged in pleasure to honour the Lover, and consecrated the blood she shed to the Blood-Wolf and left a bowl of meat to rot for the Crow-Father. In return, they left her alone. To Dalla's way of thinking, that was the best possible outcome.

She stamped forwards, crunching snow beneath her toes, and let the sword sing out. The edge bit into the wooden pole and she ripped it free and whirled, chopping the top of the pole off. 'Faaah,' she breathed out, crouching, every muscle tensed.

Behind her, something crunched across the snow. She turned and her blade stopped inches from her father's throat. Ulfar smiled and pushed the sword away with his knuckles. 'You are getting better,' he said, eyeing the pole.

Dalla said nothing. She leaned on the pommel of her sword, sweat rolling down her face and beneath her hauberk. Besides a loincloth it was all she wore, the cold being no more bother to her than it was to her father.

'You do your brother's sword proud,' he said.

'Would that he were carrying it now,' she said, snatching up a handful of snow and rubbing it over her face.

Ulfar frowned. 'That is not what I meant girl. Your mother carried that sword before him. They still sing songs about her, in the high crags. As they'll sing of you.' He took her chin in his palm and smiled. 'A shield-maiden makes for better sagas than an old gudja any day.'

'Hardly a maiden,' Dalla said with a snort. Ulfar chuckled and shook his head.

'Too much to hope for, I suppose.'

'Too much to ask,' Dalla said, baring her teeth. Like many in the tribe, she had filed them to shark-like points. Ulfar knew too well that she had used them more than once. 'What do the spirit-winds say old man?'

'They say we are drawing close to interesting times. A child of the Great Planner spins webs within webs, and we are all caught in the threads.'

'Child...?' Dalla blinked. 'Svunum?'

'Your mind is as quick as your sword, daughter,' Ulfar said. 'It stirs. On the Witching Night it will awake, unless we stop it.'

'It always stirs, since the einsark arrived.'

'This is different. It is stronger. It has eaten souls aplenty in these past years and now it grows hungrier still. For vengeance, among other things.' He smiled crookedly. 'Though they deal in treachery, they cannot abide betrayal.'

'Then they are more like men than most would care to admit,' Dalla said, raising her sword and making a slow thrust. 'The godi is looking for you.'

'Is he?'

'He is quite angry.'

'I cannot imagine why,' Ulfar said.

Dalla looked at him. 'Try harder. You summoned a council of chieftains, old man. Against his wishes. You'll be lucky he doesn't feed you to that troll he keeps in the stables.'

'I do not have to be lucky. I am right. And he knows it.'

'He is worse than an old woman,' Dalla said. Ulfar looked at her and she flushed. 'He is!'

'Eyri Goldfinger is many things,' Ulfar said. 'A woman is not one of them.'

'Well, at least your eyes haven't yet succumbed to age. I wish I could say the same about your brain, old man,' a rough voice interjected. Eyri Goldfinger was as broad as Dalla was lithe, and as squat as she was tall. Someone had once joked that Eyri's father had been a dwarf, but only once. If there had been truth to the joke, however, no one would have been surprised. Dark, small and built like an overturned cauldron, he stumped forward, his thumbs hooked into his belt, and faced down the woman he'd once tried to claim as his wife and her father. 'Calling an alvthing? Without my say-so? Are you mad?'

Ulfar shrugged. 'Desperate perhaps. But not mad.'

'One and the same I'd say!' Eyri spat. 'Calling a council of chieftains is the prerogative of the chieftains, not some wizened old–'

'Careful,' Dalla said mildly, the blade of her sword drifting towards Eyri's throat. He swatted the blade aside with the two remaining fingers and thumb on his left hand. Dalla had taken the others for what Eyri had, when deep in his cups, often referred to as her dowry.

'I'm godar. People should be careful around me. Not vice-versa!' he snapped. 'Now you've roused the Skaelingers and the Bjornlings and the Sarls – a dozen chieftains are on their way here now! Here! Now!' His voice rose an octave as he flushed crimson. 'Do you have any idea what that means?'

'Yes. They will bring men. Men we will need come the Witching Night,' Ulfar said calmly.

'Men I will have to feed! Men I will have to watch lest they filch my steading out from under me!' Eyri snarled, gesticulating. 'You may just as well have stabbed me in the gut old man. Mermedus take you, you old fool.' Eyri slumped, his round shoulders dipping. He shook his head and blew out a frustrated breath. 'Why?' he said, looking at Ulfar.

'I told you why,' Ulfar said. 'You did not listen.'

'Listen? To what? Ghost stories?'

'A warning.' Ulfar's eyes narrowed. 'She stirs.'

'She? She who?'

Ulfar said nothing. Helplessly, Eyri spun to look at Dalla. 'Tell him he's mad!'

'He's not.' It was her turn to shrug. 'You know that as well as I do.'

Eyri groaned and ran calloused hands through his braided hair. 'Of course I do! But I can't – this steading is small! Small!'

'It's about to get bigger. And noisier,' Dalla said.

Eyri shot a glare at her. 'We'll be needing to bolster the stocks.' He pointed at Dalla. 'That means you too.'

'Me?'

'I need a scout. And the Southerners don't pay as much attention to pretty lasses as they should.' He flashed a grin. 'I want a fat merchantman before the other godar arrive. Mead, ale and the like. Those Southern wines that taste of fruit or oak. You'll mark me a ship.'

Dalla laughed suddenly. 'Why didn't you say? It has been too long since I've gone avyking. Where?'

'Marienburg,' Eyri said.

Beneath the island, a ceremony was taking place. It was as old as time itself, or insofar as could be recalled. The attendants wore feathered cloaks and masks of seal-hide. They chanted softly as the initiates saw to the culling of the herd-beasts. Saw-toothed stone knives flashed through worm-pale rubbery hide and the great bulks moaned, floundered and bled out in the tidal pools.

They had been men once, the herd-beasts. Now they were flabby things, more fungus than seal and more seal than man. They made dull groans as their watery blood spilled across the rocks. Passive and dull-witted, they neither fled nor resisted, their tiny minds filled with her grace and their eyes blinded by her ever-shifting radiance. Yet one more gift she had given to Myrma and her people.

Myrma watched the slaughter of the mutants with only partial interest. She had seen the same ceremony performed so many times before, over so many long years that it had lost the ability to elicit all but the dimmest of emotions in her. Idly she looked down at her body. Nude and youthful, it held no more fascination for her than a set of borrowed clothing. The only thing that concerned her was how long it would last. There were already streaks of grey in her hair and wrinkles beneath her eyes. How long before she must find another skin?

She was not vain; youth held no more joy than age held horror. But if she were to serve her mistress ably and well, she must maintain her vigour. She plucked at the skin, feeling the looseness, and looked up, gauging the nude bodies of the initiates. They were daughters of her line, for the most part, five and six generations removed; their blood freshened with that of slaves and captives. One of them would serve her as her skin in time.

A slab of white meat was brought to her and she bit into the pink muscle. She chewed thoughtfully, letting the blood soothe the torn runnels in her throat. She waved the attendants aside. 'Feed the rest to Her children and empty the blood into a pool,' she said, indicating the upper reaches of the cavern ceiling where dim, almost wraith-like leathery shapes humped and quarrelled. She looked up, trying to differentiate between them for a moment, but it was a vain effort. They were not really here in any sense. Only partially, if that. Gripping the world's rim with ghostly talons, held in this place by the will of their mistress and by the regular blood sacrifices Myrma and her folk offered them. Hungry ghosts that howled silently in their mother's womb.

In truth, that was what it was. She looked around, letting the mingled smells of blood and salt invade her nostrils. A rocky womb, in which her people would be reborn. As she herself was reborn again and again, reinvigorated by the sacrifice of her debased kin. Though it was early days yet, she lived by the idiom of 'waste not, want not'. The initiates emptied the bodies of the herd-beasts into a stone trough, letting their brackish blood fill it. Stepping lightly, Myrma stepped into the lukewarm pool and sank down, letting the oily bloody coat her flesh. She hissed in pleasure as she felt abused muscles and cramped tendons heal and grow strong. It kept the borrowed skins she wore flexible and pliant. Cupping her hands, she scooped up the blood and drank it down in messy gulps. It tingled, bitter with the stuff of Chaos which had made the beasts what they were.

The same stuff had kept her young and had made her people strong. It had made them fierce and terrifying to the brute Norsii, upon whom they had preyed like wolves. It would make them strong again, when the time came.

As the blood filled her, so too did the voice of her mistress. The cavern shuddered gently, the rocks enfolding her with gentle strength. The island was no rock, but a protean thing, able to shift and change as needed. At one time, before the arrival of their allies, it had drifted across the sea, carrying them out of danger or into battle.

It had ever been thus. A goddess's favour for those who still followed her.

Then had come, the conclave and the great reaping. Longships, daubed in blood and protective sigils, had made landfall. As the Norsii had met her folk blade-to-blade at the behest of their warlords, the gudjii had pitted their magics against hers. Chaos winds had howled across the rocks, bursting men like overripe fruit and burning the very stones and in the end, at the behest of jealous kin, her lady had been bound in place. Trapped twice over by ungrateful powers.

Now island and goddess had both set down mighty roots and things grew in the depths. Black seed-pods nestled in the nooks and crannies of the cavern, growing ripe with the fruit of her workings. Myrma's eyes sought the pods and she let her gaze slide across the hairy sacks that would ripen and burst on the Witching Night. They were not meant for her folk. A brief moment of bitterness spiked through her exultation. No, those were for the Lady's newest followers... then; waste not, want not. She smiled crookedly and sank down to her cheeks in the blood.

Hadn't that been a surprise when it came? She could still remember the day – the brief moment of terror – as the armoured shapes of the Knights of the Blazing Sun stepped onto the island's rocky shore. They had brought strange engines with them, and their weapons were mightier still than any her people had taken in their long-ago raids. Her people had never recovered from that last great battle with the Northern dogs, and they had been able to muster only a feeble resistance to the newcomers.

She ran bloody fingers through her hair, forcing down the familiar pulse of anger that always came when she thought of that day. Their power had been broken for all time that day. Their remaining temples burned, their herd-beasts driven into the deepest depths and their people enslaved. Oh, not that they knew they were enslaving them, these knights, but she had recognised it for what it was. After all, did not the Great Schemer bind his servants tight in bonds of thought and counter-thought? So what difference then, between one sort of binding and another?

They had sought to change their thoughts, who they were. They had sought to make of her folk something much like the herd-beasts... dull, witless and helpless. She bared her teeth. But that was not to be, no. No, the changers had succumbed to changes themselves, though not the physical kind. They had been perfect. In time, she had realised why her Lady had brought them, had let them burn and pillage... they were strong. Stronger even than the Norsii. With them as the spear-point, her people could finish the Task.

She felt a thrill of excitement. After so long, it was all coming to an end. Her Lady would be free; free to rejoin the Great Game and take her place once more in the All-Pattern with her brothers and her father, the Changer and Shaper.

For her part, she would see the old wolf spitted and cured like ham.

'Ulfar,' she hissed, almost lovingly. It was a beautiful thought, and one she cherished above all others. She closed her eyes and stretched her newly reinvigorated limbs. 'Oh my Lady. Oh mighty S'Vanashi, daughter of the Great Mutator, Queen of Crows,' she murmured. 'Enfold me in your web that I might better further your design.' And slay my enemy, she thought.

All at once, as if in response, from their perches on the surrounding stalagmites the crows set up a croaking rhythm. In its harsh melody, Myrma could hear the voice of her mistress. Calling for her. Welcoming her.

'I am coming, my Lady. I am coming.' She rose from the blood, eager and dripping, and allowed the initiates to help her up. As they wrapped her in her cloak, she opened her thoughts and breathed in the harsh gases of the cavern, letting the Lady's breath fill her fully. The cavern warped and shattered like a mirror, scattering shards of reality across the expanse of the space between moments. A smell filled her nostrils, like a rookery but somehow harsher. She heard the clatter of iron feathers in the darkness and smiled in welcome as the Queen of Crows enfolded her in her mighty wings.

◀ THREE ▶

Otto Berengar, the Grand Master of the Order of the Blazing Sun, was an older man, older than Wiscard, but strongly built. He was tall and broad like Goetz himself, but with the beaky face of a Reiklander. Berengar was said to be a scholarly man, though he'd been in the forefront of every battle the Order had directly participated in.

He was by turns informal and infuriating, and many a member of the Order had been reduced to stammering confusion by the old man's sudden line of questioning at an inappropriate time. While the other knightly orders of the Empire were content to create warriors, the Grand Master of the Blazing Sun wanted something more. As such, he was less than popular among his peers, but a figure of awe to those he led.

'Grand Master,' Goetz said, on one knee.

'Oh do get up,' Berengar said irritably, snapping his fingers. 'Five heartbeats of honour is five heartbeats of thought lost. Up. Up!' Goetz rose as rapidly as his armour would allow. 'Full armour, young Goetz? Am I so frightening?' Berengar went on, motioning for Goetz to rise.

'Sir, I–' Goetz began. The Grand Master waved a hand heavy with thin scars.

'Hector Goetz. Goetz is a Solland name, I believe? Yes. Your family fled that province when the Ironclaw put it to the torch. Minor aristocrats, I believe they were. In any event, your father sells grain now. You had a brother who was promised to the Order, but who instead chose a different path. Your father sent you in his place.'

Goetz nodded dumbly, fighting to restrain the instinctive grimace that mention of his brother always brought to his face. Berengar stroked his beard. 'You are a replacement knight, Brother Goetz. But a very effective one, I am told. Thus, you will be playing replacement again.'

'Milord?'

'Never mind. Describe the flag of the Reikland, boy.'

'The–?' Goetz cleared his throat. 'An eagle rampant, Grand Master.'

'Correct. But not just any eagle… it is specifically Myrmidia's eagle. Did you know this?' Berengar said, twitching a finger like a schoolmaster.

'No, Grand Master.'

'What was the symbol of the Sudenland?' Berengar continued rapidly.

'A... ah... a blazing sun, Grand Master.' Goetz frowned. 'Also a sign of Myrmidia.'

Berengar smiled. 'Well done, boy. We'll make a scholar of you yet.' The smile grew thin. 'Some say the crown of Solland was taken by the Ironclaw and twisted to fit his barbaric brow. Others say that that crown was merely the Electoral circlet, and that the true crown was hidden away. It was said to be shaped like a sun as well, and that it was divided into twelve parts and those parts were given to twelve retainers... the Myrmidons.'

'I wasn't aware that there was a crown of Sudenla– Solland,' Goetz said.

'No. Why would you be?' Berengar's smile filled out. 'Goetz – Gohtz, in the original dialect – was the family name of one of those retainers. In a way, I suppose, your family has served the goddess since time immemorial. Interesting, eh?'

'Yes,' Goetz said noncommittally. Berengar chuckled.

'No interest in history, brother? Well, we'll fix that. What do you see, young Goetz?' the Grand Master said, rapping his knuckles against the great map spread across the far wall of the library.

'A map,' Goetz said. He peered more closely and saw a number of pins stabbed into the material of the map at odd points. Suddenly, he recalled seeing a similar map in the library of his own komturie. 'Those markers... they indicate our komturies, don't they?'

'Very good,' Berengar said as he nodded in a manner disturbingly similar to that of one of Goetz's old tutors. 'These pins are an illustration of our current strength. They are an indication of our resources and our presence.'

'You make it sound like a military campaign,' Wiscard grumbled. The Grand Master grinned like a naughty child and nodded.

'Exactly; it is a campaign, in fact. A very long, much extended, campaign.' He turned to look at the map and the grin faded. 'A campaign we are not winning...' He trailed off.

'Sir?' Goetz said.

'Pins on a map, young Goetz... that is all we are. Pins on a map,' Berengar said, shaking himself. He rapped the map again. 'Now, what does all of this tell you?'

Goetz, who had never truly paid attention to the map before, took a guess. 'Our Order has spread far.'

'Our Order has spread faster and further than any other in the Empire, though we do not brag of that fact. Fancy a guess as to why?'

Goetz opened his mouth to reply but the Grand Master interrupted him. 'It is because we are not bound by tradition. We are not servants to dogma or slaves to the chains of thought that bind our brother-orders.' Berengar held up two fingers. 'Our creed is but two-fold... We go where we are needed, and...'

'We do what must be done,' Goetz finished the creed instinctively.

'Excellent. 2478 as per the Imperial Calendar, young Goetz. Describe it to me.'

'Sir?' Goetz said.

'The year,' the Grand Master said. He gestured. 'Come, come. You know your history better than most, young Goetz. Or so I'm assured. And it is among your duties to know, after all.' He fixed Goetz with a startlingly blue stare. 'After all, if you do not know where it is that you come from, how can you ever know where to go?'

'Go?' Goetz said.

'Here. Take this,' Berengar said, tossing a book to Goetz. Behind him, the hochmeister hissed. The Grand Master chuckled. 'Oh do relax, Wiscard. Books can be replaced far more easily than the men who write them.'

Goetz looked at the book. 'Marienburg?'

'I thought you might want to brush up on the customs before you go. I know many young aristocrats take the Grand Tour of the lands outside the Empire, or which were formerly part of the Empire, but...' The Grand Master trailed off.

'I wasn't one of them,' Goetz said. Berengar sniffed.

'No?'

'No. I was learning about grain prices, milord. And bridges.'

'Bridges?' The Grand Master looked taken aback.

'I wanted to build them. Sir.' Goetz swallowed.

'Hmph. So, you've never been to Marienburg.'

'No sir,' Goetz said.

'A shame. Do you know the customs then, at least? The dialect?'

'Somewhat. I had well-travelled tutors.' Goetz flipped through the book.

'Always beneficial. There are some who say that isolation is our only protection from foreign corruption. I, personally, believe that a little foreign corruption is somewhat inoculating against the more fatal kind. Svunum.'

'Svunum?' Goetz felt like a fool, mindlessly repeating the Grand Master's words, but the old man's mind was like quicksilver, dancing from one thought to the next with seemingly little connection between them.

'An island. Our island, actually. In the Sea of Claws. A gift, in 2478, from a grateful merchant-prince. One of a council made up of the leading families of Marienburg.' Berengar grunted. 'Fifty-odd years ago, we were given the rock in payment for spilled blood. There have been three hochmeisters in that time, with the third being one Conrad Balk, a Talabheimer of some note. Have you read Siegecraft in the Time of the Three Emperors?'

'We're talking about that Balk?' Goetz said.

'Yes. Precocious boy. Very keen on the intricacies of campaign organisation. Would have made a brilliant general, I'm told.' Berengar snapped his fingers again. 'But, back to Svunum. The year 2478, boy. Show me you have a brain.'

'The Pirate Wars,' Goetz said, slightly stung as things clicked into place. 'The year the last of the Westerland enclaves were burned out.'

'There we go. Sometimes I despair of the younger generation,' the Grand Master said. 'Svunum is a rock. On that rock, we built a komturie. In time, it became something a bit more. It was given to us with the charter to defend against further naval incursions from the north. Nowadays, our brothers in Svunum mostly hunt Westerland pirates and Norscan raiders.'

'There's a difference?' Goetz said, before he could stop himself. The Grand Master chuckled, and Goetz flushed.

'Depending on who you're speaking to, but yes. For our purposes, not so much.' The Grand Master tapped the book with a finger. 'We receive yearly reports. How much income they've taken in bounties, how many knights they have and such.'

'You want me to go to Svunum,' Goetz said. The Grand Master gave him an irritated glance.

'I thought that was obvious, yes.'

'May I ask why?'

'I'm getting to that. The impatience of youth,' Berengar sighed. 'We haven't received a report from Svunum in three years. Four years ago, the brothers of our komturie in Marienburg moved to Svunum, to help bolster the defences during one of those interminable seaborne invasions from the North Lands. They tend to inflame the coasts.'

'And we've sent no one to check on them?' Goetz said.

'We have been busy, young Goetz. The recent overland Northern incursions have kept our meagre resources otherwise occupied.' Goetz frowned at the rebuke, but the Grand Master went on. 'I did send a messenger, however. Brother Athalhold, a knight of this very house.'

'And?' Goetz said.

'He died,' Wiscard grated. 'Killed in a back-alley brawl, according to witnesses.'

'How?' Goetz said automatically.

'Shot in the back.'

Goetz's hand instinctively brushed against his back. If either man saw the gesture, they gave no indication. 'Who shot him? Why?' he said, after a moment.

The Grand Master frowned. 'We don't know. You will rectify that, however.'

'Me?' Goetz said.

'You.' Berengar leaned forward. 'You acquitted yourself well I understand. In the recent set-to.'

'Not as well as I could have,' Goetz said, swallowing as the memory of his earlier dream washed across his mind's eye.

'And in the Drakwald,' Berengar said.

Goetz froze. A sudden bloom of memory paralysed him for a moment. A witch-fire flickering between dark trees and the cavorting shadows of beasts.

He smelt blood and heard the whispered promises of something that had crawled up out of the dark between worlds. The pain of the goblin-wounds flared madly and a muscle in his jaw bobbed as he clenched his teeth. 'Most of the men I led into the forest died.'

'Men die. You survived. Therefore, you accrue the collective glory,' the Grand Master said bluntly. 'Your guilt does you credit, though it is unnecessary.' His hand fell on Goetz's shoulder. The young knight could feel the weight of the Grand Master's hand even through his armour. 'It is also a cancer.'

Wiscard cleared his throat. 'Brother Pasqual tells me that you have done little but sleep since recovering from your wounds. You have not gone out, not requested leave to return to your komturie or requested a transfer to an ongoing military assignment.'

'I–' Goetz began. The Grand Master silenced him with a gesture.

'Wiscard has allowed it, because you are young. Because you are among the youngest of our Order to win your spurs and because you had, perhaps, earned a rest. You have fought hard and continuously since you took your oath. It shakes a man, to face the darkness that often. But it can only be allowed to shake him for so long.'

Goetz said nothing. Berengar searched his face and then, as if he'd found what he was looking for, turned away. 'You will leave in the morning for Marienburg. There's a river ferry heading that way. You will be on it. Warrants of travel have been obtained. You will visit the temple of Myrmidia in Marienburg and pay your respects prior to boarding whatever ship's berth you can acquire. I gather our brothers on Svunum have been lax in that area as well. Or so the abbot says.'

'And then?' Goetz said. The Grand Master turned.

'Then you will see what there is to see and report back to me. I want to know why we've had no contact with our brothers. Does our Order still hold Svunum?' His eyes held Goetz's own. 'And I want to know what happened to Brother Athalhold.'

'As you say, Grand Master.' Goetz banged his fist against his breastplate and bowed his head. The Grand Master waved the gesture away, his face irritated.

'Just come back alive, young Goetz. We've lost two whole houses, not to mention an experienced knight. I'll not lose a single man more.'

Goetz nodded and turned. He felt the Grand Master's eyes on him the entire way. He closed the library doors behind him and leaned back against them, trembling slightly. He banged his fist against his side, and winced.

Was it a test? It felt that way. He knew that men could be wounded in more ways than the physical, and that his wound was perhaps one of those. Perhaps the Grand Master knew it as well. Perhaps–

He shook his head, and pushed away from the door. It didn't matter. Marienburg then. That far from the forests, maybe his dreams would fade.

* * *

'You may as well share your opinion, Wiscard. I know you're dying to,' Berengar said as he listened to the fading boot-steps.

'I? You must have me confused with someone else. I would never think to countermand the Grand Master.' Wiscard bent over his papers, his mouth set. Berengar sighed and looked up at the ceiling, and then turned.

'Tell me what you think.' It wasn't a command. Not really. Berengar did not command so much as manoeuvre.

Wiscard grunted and looked up. 'He is ill. There's a shadow over his soul.'

'Very poetic.'

'Truth, not poetry. I have read the reports of the incident in the Drakwald. He exceeded his authority, was almost killed and faced a – a thing of Chaos,' Wiscard said.

'And defeated it,' Berengar said. 'Not many can claim that sort of victory.'

'Did he really defeat it, or did he simply survive?' Wiscard countered. 'Berlich was good at playing the fool, but he knew enough to keep the boy busy in minor skirmishes and with unimportant assignments. Until we could see–'

'See what?' Berengar interjected. 'See whether he has been – what? – tainted perhaps? Marked by the Ruinous Powers in some way? Are we Sigmarites now, to see devilry and corruption in every shadow?' He gave a snort of disgust. 'Are we followers of Ulric, to condemn one of our own for having the bad luck to meet and survive an encounter with the enemies of mankind instead of dying bravely and uselessly?'

'I merely meant that we do not know how he has been affected. Brother Pasqual says that he hasn't been sleeping.'

'Sleep is a useless vice,' Berengar said, chopping the air with a hand. 'I don't sleep. Are you implying that it's a problem?'

'Be that as it may,' Wiscard said, avoiding the question, 'He has been having nightmares.'

'Then he needs something to keep him busy. Travel is the best cure for brooding.' Berengar tapped a spot on the map. 'Speaking of brooding... your brother-hochmeister. Balk. Your opinions?'

'I told you what I thought before you sent Athalhold,' Wiscard said, resisting the urge to add to his death. From the look the Grand Master gave him, Wiscard knew that though it had been unspoken, Berengar had heard it all the same.

'Has your opinion changed?' he said.

'Balk – the Balk I knew – was over-eager. Over-zealous as well,' Wiscard said carefully. 'In many ways, the opposite of Brother Goetz. Full of faith and fury.'

'And Brother Goetz is full of... what?' Berengar said, looking back to the map. His finger traced the path Goetz was to take, stopping on the marker for Marienburg. 'Sense, I hope. Dedication and faith I have in abundance. I need a man who can think. No, not just can, will.'

'The question is; will he think the right thoughts?' Wiscard said. Berengar didn't answer. He glared at the map, as if willing it to assume sentience and speak.

He had been Grand Master for twenty years; politicking had become second nature to him. The Order had been a small thing when he had taken the reins, and under his watch it had flourished. Not just in terms of martial glory, but in other, more important ways. The Order's funds had gone into public works and into the coffers of academics and engineers and artists. As a young knight, Berengar had carried materials with which to teach children the art of writing in his saddlebag and he had never wanted for students. Civilisation was more than just weapons and grand strategies. Without those other things, it was not worth the having.

He knew his fellow Grand Masters would not agree with him. They saw the world in terms of war and survival. For them, the Empire lurched drunkenly on the edge of a precipice, and one wrong step could send it reeling into the maw of Chaos. But Berengar knew the truth – Chaos was already here. It lurked in every flagellant's mad eyes and in every witch hunter's heart. It gnawed at the roots of civilisation, reducing men to beasts. Reducing them to savages, who thought of nothing more than the next conquest, the next enemy.

The Great Enemy could not be defeated with sword and pike, however. Only with knowledge. Myrmidia was the Goddess of Knowledge, even as she was the Mistress of War.

'He wanted to build bridges, Wiscard,' he said after a moment.

'What?' Wiscard said, looking up.

Berengar shook his head and looked at the other man. 'What did you want to be, old friend? Did you dream of bridges?'

Wiscard grimaced. 'Poetry,' he said flatly.

Berengar raised an eyebrow. 'Were you any good?'

'I was horrible at it, frankly.'

'Ah. Well then, best for all concerned that you found your true calling, eh?' Berengar said, smiling.

◀ FOUR ▶

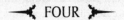

'He's a fine horse, sir,' the stable hand said, running the curry-comb over the stallion's flanks. He was a young boy, pledged to the Order fairly recently, if Goetz was any judge. 'Good chest on him.'

'I can see that,' Goetz said, scrubbing the horse's neck. He'd been given a new mount, since his old one had died during the battle with the orcs. 'You've taken good care of him,' he said. The boy beamed. Goetz had worked in the stables himself, his first few months after joining the Order. It was an often thankless job, and a bit of recognition was worth its weight in honours or ribbons. The horse whickered softly and he extended a slice of apple. The horse lipped it and crunched contentedly.

'I will ride a horse like this some day,' the boy said, bolder now that Goetz had complimented him.

'Will you?' Goetz said.

'I will be a knight,' the boy said, bending to check the horse's hooves.

'When I was your age I wanted to build bridges,' Goetz said, feeding the horse another slice of apple.

The boy looked up at him incredulously. 'Bridges?'

'Bridges. Big ones. Small ones too. The world needs more bridges, I think.' Goetz smiled as the boy stared at him as if he were insane. 'Don't you think so?'

Someone cleared their throat, saving the boy from having to answer. Goetz turned. 'Brother Velk,' he said, nodding to the other knight.

'Brother Goetz.' Velk gestured to the stablehand. 'Get out.' The boy looked at Goetz, who nodded, and then scampered out, edging carefully past Velk.

'Hector, I–' Velk began and then stopped.

Goetz smiled as Velk's face moved through a variety of ever more torturous expressions, before finally showing pity. 'We go where we are needed, brother. We do what must be done.'

'You're just making this harder,' Velk snapped. Velk had avoided him in the weeks since the battle, though whether from an Osterman's natural

540

distaste for those from Talabecland or for some other reason, Goetz couldn't say. Nor, in truth, did he particularly care.

'Sorry. Carry on making faces, by all means,' Goetz said, turning back to the horse. The animal, for its part, nudged his hand, sniffing for another bit of apple.

'I knew Athalhold,' Velk said, finally. 'He was a good man. A fine knight, despite being far too practical.' He stared down at his feet for a moment, then looked up. 'If someone killed him...'

'I'll be careful,' Goetz said.

'Athalhold was careful,' Velk said sharply. 'You have to be more than that.'

'Why the sudden concern?'

Velk made a face. 'A Velk always pays his debts, regardless of the recipient. You saved me, and it cost you. So now I'm telling you to be careful.'

'Consider the debt paid, then,' Goetz said, pushing away from the horse and facing the other knight. Velk frowned.

'The debt's clearance is mine to judge, not yours,' he said. With a final glare, he spun and stalked away across the courtyard. Goetz watched him go in bemusement, then turned back to the horse.

'Bridges are fine things,' he said, patting it on the nose. 'They're never as confusing as the people who walk across them.' The horse merely snorted in reply. Goetz sighed and left the stable.

For all his posturing, Velk had made an important point, and one Goetz would have to be blind not to recognise. Someone had killed Athalhold, that much the Grand Master had seemed certain of. The question was who? And why?

He shook his head and stopped to watch the novices beginning their afternoon training. Wearing padded armour and wielding wooden practice weapons, the boys went at each other with commendable fierceness as an elderly knight barked orders.

He wondered if he had ever been that fierce. 'Probably not,' he said out loud. The old knight glanced at him, hand half-raised in greeting, eyebrow quirked. Goetz waved at him.

As he continued to watch, a number of squires trooped out of the dormitories, their packs slung across their backs. They were young men, all on the cusp of adulthood and only a few years younger than himself. One by one, they climbed into the back of a wagon that sat near the side-gate of the komturie as a grizzled rider watched them from the back of his horse. The man wore the ornate cuirass and plumed helmet of an outrider, and the fat scar that decorated his face from brow to chin attested to a life of hard service. A brace of heavy pistols was holstered within easy reach on his saddle, and his hands rested on the wide barrel of the repeater handgun that lay across his lap.

He caught Goetz watching and raised a finger to the brim of his helmet. Goetz returned the gesture and continued on. He remembered the day he'd climbed into a similar wagon, watched over by another outrider. Perhaps even the same man, though he didn't think so.

Life as a pistolier was exciting, though the squires looked more nervous than eager. Goetz wondered if he'd looked the same, on his day of leaving. Probably so, and possibly worse. Mostly, they would be used as couriers, carrying messages from one place to another, or as road wardens, patrolling the Imperial highways. They would learn the ways of the horseman, as well as how to fight in a group.

It was also a chance for those who had neither the desire nor the ability to become fully-fledged templars of the Order to find a worthy calling. A chance to avoid the shame of being dismissed from the komturie and the Order for failing to live up to the demands placed upon them. Glancing again at the outrider, Goetz wondered whether that wouldn't have been the better choice where he himself was concerned.

He closed his eyes, imagining the look on his father's face. Wouldn't that have been a sight? Goetz smiled and shook his head. He didn't hold his father particularly accountable, or bear him any real grudge. The old man was a tree stump, rooted in place by ideas, desires and determinations that had little consideration for the same in others.

Their family was an old one, and it had old ideas and traditions. Every generation had provided a son to the Order and Myrmidia. It had apparently been a tradition among the Old Families. Twelve Sons of Sudenland, every twelve years. Myrmidia's Due, his father had called it, the Myrmidons. Even now, though Solland was long gone and the Families with it, the sons still went, and the Due was still owed and the Myrmidons were still needed. Or so his father had said. As far as Goetz knew, he was the only Myrmidon in the Order.

In the end, he could have simply said 'no'. But he hadn't, and now he was here, following the edicts of a goddess he didn't particularly believe in and the tenets of a philosophy that only broadly appealed to his sense of progress. He sighed and thumped the door frame. Across the courtyard, the wagon rolled out through the portcullis. Goetz watched it for a few moments more, and then went inside.

He left that evening without fanfare, his armour gleaming with a fresh coat of polish. Unlike the other knightly orders, the Knights of the Blazing Sun disdained the use of tabards, instead wearing plain jerkins embroidered with the Order's sigil beneath the heavy plate. It was a utilitarian garment, being more akin to what a hedge-knight or a mercenary might wear than the garment of one of the leading orders of the Empire.

Goetz, for his part, found the plainness of the thing comforting. At the end of the day, knights were soldiers. Better armed and equipped than other soldiers, true, but soldiers nonetheless. Flash was all well and good when you were on parade, but was uncomfortable the rest of the time.

He patted the bundle of armour strapped to his saddle affectionately.

Still, it was nice to have the option, should the need arise. He carried neither lance nor spear, instead relying on a small, triangular shield tethered to his saddle pommel, and the sword belted at his waist.

Lances had never been his forte, though he admitted they had their uses. Tools were tools, and sometimes you needed a certain tool for a given task. He preferred swords however. Especially this sword.

A snarling lion's head carved from ivory adorned the pommel, and the hilt was wrapped in pale leather. His father had bought it from a trader, who'd sworn up and down that the sword was elven made, though Goetz doubted it. He'd seen elven swords and they were light, needle-shaped things. This sword was a chunky thing, broad and long.

His father had gifted it to him when he'd won his spurs. A congratulatory gift Goetz had known was intended for his brother, despite his father's pre-emptive protestations to the contrary.

So many of his father's hopes and plans had relied on Stefan. Come to that, so had most of Goetz's. He smiled ruefully. It was Stefan who was to join the Order, Stefan who was to bring glory to the Goetz name, to make his father's business associates forget that the Goetz family had come penniless from a forgotten province and been reduced to tradesmen.

Stefan, Stefan, Stefan. Stefan would have done it all. Little Hector would have been free to do – what? Anything he wanted. Instead, Stefan had flung himself from one insane venture to the next, obsessing over trivia and sour bits of history, determined to make his own name, to restore the family honour, until finally he'd been swallowed up by it. He'd stolen away in the dead of night, a number of precious heirlooms in his possession, never to be seen again. Oh, there had been no token of death, no sprawled body or eyewitness account, but Goetz knew he was dead. What else could he be? Why else would he not have contacted his family or returned home?

What had the Grand Master called him? A replacement knight. Goetz frowned. There was no shame in it, he knew.

But then, neither was there especially any honour.

He kicked his horse into motion and set off at a gallop. The ferry would be leaving at sunrise, and Goetz was to be on it.

'You know what to do then?' Eyri said for the fifteenth time since they had left the coast of Norsca behind them. Dalla scraped a lock of salt-encrusted hair out of her face and gave him a hard look. He raised his maimed hand in a placatory manner and grinned. 'I'm just checking.'

'I have done this before, Goldfinger,' she said, hopping up onto the rail. The longship crested the waves as its crew plied the oars. There was a wind out, but it was low and they were in dangerous waters. She looked down into the open hold where the slaves and crew alike swung the oars to the rhythmic beat of a drum. Occasionally a whip would snake out and leave a red mark across someone's shoulder or back, encouraging them to move faster. Warriors paced the decks, geared for war, their eyes on the horizon.

Eyri followed her gaze and grimaced. 'We're running close to that blasted island.'

'Too close?' Dalla said. 'How close is too close?'

'We're not in their waters, if that's what you mean.'

'How can you tell?'

'Because we're not being peppered with arrows and rocks from those damnable galleys of theirs,' he said. 'Even if they do spot us, I still have those letters of mark from the old hochmeister...' He caught her expression. 'What?'

'They are our enemies,' she said.

'No, they are your enemies. Yours and the old man's. They are merely irritants to me,' he said. He hooked his thumbs in his belt and shook his head. 'Things were fine under the others. I paid my tolls and they let my ships be. But this new one – Balk – he's mad. Madder than any Kurgan.'

'Paid my toll,' Dalla mimicked, pitching her voice teeth-shiveringly high. Eyri glared at her and she laughed. 'You really are a woman, aren't you? What man of Miklgardr has ever paid a toll to sail the seas? Are you a lackloin? Is that why you've dressed this ship up like a hog- wallow?' She gestured to the thin planks and panels that had been loosely nailed to the hull in order to hide the distinctive lines of the longship. It wouldn't hold up under close scrutiny, but at a distance it would appear to be any other merchant vessel as opposed to a sleek raider. 'Deception is the way of the coward.'

'Careful girl,' Eyri said. 'This is my ship and I can have you pitched overboard easily enough.'

'Who here would dare?' Dalla said, glaring at the nearest warriors. To a man they shied back or looked away. She snorted in satisfaction and slapped the hilt of her sword.

Eyri shook his head in disgust. His eyes rolled upwards. 'This is what I get for having you around, isn't it? The gods are mockers.'

'Ware! Sails! Ware!' A young boy dropped from the mast onto the deck, his over-large hauberk rattling. 'Black sails, my chief!'

Eyri spun to the rail with a curse. Dalla twisted, peering towards the horizon. Black sails with a golden sun emblazoned in their centre sped towards them, and the whine of cornets and horns set her teeth on edge. Her hand found her sword-hilt, but Eyri grabbed her wrist. 'No,' he said. 'I'll not endanger this trip because you can't hold your sword.' He turned. 'Run up the flags we took from those ships last time out! Stow the oars and let the sails pull!' he bellowed. 'At a distance they might confuse us for something harmless.'

'And if they don't?' Dalla said.

Eyri grunted and patted the hatchet stuffed through his broad leather belt. 'Then we see who the gods really favour, Dalla Ulfarsdottir.'

'There's the man I almost didn't maim,' she said, smiling.

'Almost?' Eyri eyed his maimed hand.

Dalla shrugged. 'For a few moments. I was feeling sentimental, so I was.'

'Sentimental,' Eyri muttered.

'I could have killed you.'

Eyri chuckled. 'Aye, so you could have.' He turned his attention back to the approaching ships. If they could just keep the wind... He frowned and thumped his knuckles on the rail. Old Greisen had been all right, as far as Southerners went. A practical man, that one. He knew who the threats were, and he knew that a bit of piracy was inevitable. Eyri was by no means the worst captain on the Sea of Claws, and he traded more than he stole. Trade was a much more sensible undertaking than staggering through the surf with a torch in one hand and a screaming wench over his shoulder. Not that he hadn't done that in his younger days, but there was no real profit in it, not in the long term.

The world moved on, no matter how much you might want to turn it back. He bared his teeth in a humourless grin. Among the other godar, he was a bit of a black sheep. They called him a merchant and thought it was an insult. Yet they bought the good steel weapons he sold and the materials to waterproof their longships and hovels.

None of it would have been possible without the help of the einsark – the iron skins. 'Knights' the Southerners called them. Old Greisen had funded him in building his steading, had set him up. After all, why fight a man when you can buy him? Eyri had no qualms about being bought, as long as the buyer could meet his price.

Staying bought, on the other hand... now that was a trick he'd never mastered. But Greisen had deserved it. Thought he'd had himself a tame Norscan, rather than an ally. Eyri hadn't done the deed himself, but he'd arranged it, and if the einsark ever found out... He grunted and shook himself. They'd become more savage since Greisen had died. More like – well, more like Norscans.

There were new stories on the ice these days; stories of black-sailed galleys rowing up the rivers and of burned and empty villages. Of men and women chained and herded into the galleys at the point of einsark swords. He watched the sails draw closer and wondered if that doom awaited him in his future. He gripped his hatchet, but found it less than comforting.

Wouldn't it be a funny thing, if he had set this path by setting the trap that killed Greisen? Greisen had had many faults, but he was a predictable sort. Balk wasn't. Eyes like black ice and a brain to match, all cold angles and cunning schemes. He'd have made a good Norscan, would Balk. Except that he seemed to detest them with a personal loathing that Eyri found frightening. Not that he would admit to such in public.

In truth, if the old man hadn't called the alvthing, Eyri likely would have, though not on the basis of old stories about daemon-islands and witches.

There were more than enough of those in Norsca, and they held no fear for him.

But, an armed enemy, crouching on his doorstep like a snow-bear... that was a real danger. Balk hated him, he knew that. Maybe because he suspected that Eyri had got Greisen killed, or maybe just because he hated Norscans.

As he watched the black-sailed galleys skim across the waters and prayed that they wouldn't draw any closer, he wondered idly whether that hatred might not be deserved.

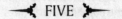

FIVE

Beasts danced beneath the dark pines of the Drakwald, pawing the soil around a crackling witch-fire and braying out abominable hymns. Mingled amongst the brute forms of the beasts were the smaller shapes of men and women. All were nude, save for unpleasant sigils daubed onto their flesh by means of primitive dyes and paints.

The shriek of crude pipes slithered beneath the trees, their rhythms carrying the gathered throng into berserk ecstasy as the dance sped up. The flames curled higher, turning an unhealthy hue, casting a weird light over the proceedings as man and beast engaged in unholy practices.

As vile as it was, however, Hector Goetz couldn't look away from the foul spectacle, no matter how much he might wish to. Crouching deep in the trees above the madness, Goetz ran his fingers across the double-tailed comet embossed on his breastplate. Then he touched the blazing sun engraved at the base of the blade laying flat across his knees.

It had only been three weeks since he'd won his spurs in a test of strength. This hunt was to be his first duty upon becoming a full knight of the Order of the Blazing Sun and he was only just now feeling the full weight of that responsibility. The men hiding around him in the forest were all that remained of his first command.

'Sir Knight?'

Goetz started at the harsh whisper, nearly jumping out of his skin. He turned slightly. 'Are they in position?' he asked the scruffy looking woodsman who had crept up behind him. The man was dressed in animal skins and rough leathers and he stank of an ointment meant to keep his scent hidden. He clutched a bow in one scarred hand.

'Every mother's son, Sir Knight,' he said, displaying rotten teeth in a fierce grin. 'Just waiting on your signal.'

Goetz licked his lips and looked back at the fire. It seemed to play tricks on his eyes, showing him first this many gathered around it, then fewer. He tasted bile in the back of his throat.

'Sir?' the woodsman said, eyes narrowed. The young knight looked back at him, then nodded jerkily.

'Kill them. All of them.'

The woodsman growled and rose to his feet, scraping the head of an arrow across the bark of a nearby tree. The specially-treated arrow burst into flame and he fired it straight up. With a shout, Goetz kicked aside the blind and rose to his feet as the assembled militia let loose with a withering rain of arrows from the darkness of the trees.

The battle was a confused mess of darting shapes and screaming voices. Goetz blundered towards the fire, sweeping his sword out with instinctive skill. He lopped off an offending sword-hand and kicked something with too many limbs away. Then something struck him across the back, nearly knocking him into the fire and slapping the air from his lungs.

Flat on his belly, Goetz tried to pull air in. He coughed as a raw, animal scent invaded the confines of his helmet. His eyes opened, and he looked up into a face out of nightmare. The beastman was an ugly thing, all muscle, fang and claw. Piecemeal armoured plates strung together with twine and less savoury things clung to its bulky frame, less protection than decoration. Horns like those of a stag curled up from its flat skull and back in on themselves. Dark eyes glared balefully at him from beneath heavy brows, and snaggle teeth snapped together in a bovine mouth, its foul breath misting in the cold air as it grunted querulously.

Using his sword as a crutch, Goetz levered himself to his knees and stifled a groan. His body felt like a bag of broken sticks. He shook his head, trying to clear it. He could hear the gentle rumble of the river nearby, somewhere past the crooked, close-set pines of the forest.

The beastman pawed the ground and snorted. Some of them, it was said, could speak. This one showed no such inclination. It lunged clumsily, swinging its crude axe towards Goetz.

Still on one knee, Goetz guided the blow aside with a twist of his wrist and countered with his own weak thrust. The beastman stumbled back with an annoyed bleat as his sword sliced a patch of rusty mail from its cuirass. It was larger than the others, larger than Goetz himself by more inches than he cared to consider. Its axe was so much hammered scrap, but no less dangerous for that.

It was strong too. Muscles like smooth stones moved under its porous, hairy hide as it swung the axe-blade up again and brought it down towards Goetz's head. He caught the blow on his sword and grunted at the weight. Equal parts adrenaline and terror helped him surge to his feet, shoving the creature back. Weapons locked, they strained against one another. Goetz blinked as the weird runes scratched into the creature's axe-blade seemed to squirm beneath his gaze. Its smell, like a slaughterhouse on a hot day, bit into his sinuses and made it hard to breathe. Goetz kicked out, catching the creature's knee. It howled and staggered, and they broke apart.

Steady on his feet now, Goetz stepped back, raising his sword. The beast-man clutched its weapon in both hands and gave a throaty snarl. Teeth bared, it bulled towards him.

Despite his guard, the edge of the axe skidded across Goetz's breast-plate, dislodging the ornaments of his Order and the ribbons of purity he wore in order to announce his status as a novice of the Order of the Blazing Sun. Sparks flew as Northern iron met Imperial steel, and Goetz found himself momentarily off balance.

The beastman was quick to capitalise. It crashed against him, clawed hand scrabbling at his helm, trying to shove his head back to expose his throat even as it flailed at him awkwardly with its axe.

Smashing the hilt of his sword against its skull, Goetz thrust his forearm against its throat and forced the snapping jaws away from him. They fell, locked together, and rolled across the ground, struggling.

Goetz lost hold of his sword, but managed to snatch the dagger from his belt. He drove it into the beastman's side, angling the blade up aiming for the heart, his old fencing teacher's admonitions ringing in his mind. The beastman squealed in pain and clawed at him. He closed his eyes and forced the blade in deeper, ignoring the crunch of bone and the hot wet foulness that gushed suddenly over his gauntlet. The creature's struggles grew weaker and weaker until they stopped completely. It expired with a whimper, its limbs flopping down with a relieving finality.

Breathing heavily, Goetz pushed the dead weight off himself and stared up at the stars dancing between the talon-like branches of the pines. The sky seemed to spin, and for a moment, just a moment, he thought he could make out a face, looking down at him. A woman's face, he thought, before he dismissed the idea as ridiculous.

Grimacing, he climbed to his feet. Dead men lay all around, their bod-ies mixed among those of the creatures they had been hunting. In the flickering witch-light, it was almost impossible to distinguish them from one another. His eyes were pulled towards the fire and what it contained.

Staggering, he moved towards it, and it seemed to curl and quiver at his approach. The stink of the weird flames grew heavier, almost solid. He caught a glimpse of bones scattered around it, and in the light of the fire he though he saw something floating within. Something that turned in its bloated womb to look at him with eyes like open wounds.

Deep in the woods, something had been born. Something horrible and beautiful. A whisper of sound caressed his ears, and a lovely voice spoke to him, making promises and predictions. A sweet smell, like sugar on ice, tickled his nose and he hesitated.

What had he been doing? What–

Behind him, something growled. Fear shot through him. He stooped for his sword, and froze as he realised that it wasn't where it had fallen.

Goetz whirled even as the beastman, bloody froth decorating its black lips, drove his own sword up through him, lifting him off his feet. Goetz screamed in pain and shock. Blood filled his mouth as the creature released the sword and he fell onto his side.

Goetz looked up, his vision already blurring. 'This – this isn't how it happened,' he said, clutching weakly at the hilt of the sword. 'Not how it happened–' The beastman loomed over him, an indistinct shadow, somehow no longer bovine but... avian? It reached down, claws caressing his face.

'Poisoned,' it snarled in a woman's voice. 'Poisoned.'

Hector Goetz woke up, covered in sweat, his heart thundering in his chest. He sat up and dug the heels of his palms into his eyes, trying to ignore the fear that gripped him. Swallowing, he looked down at his chest in something approaching panic. Other than sweat, it was barren of liquid. No blood, no wound, only bandages. He wasn't in the Drakwald. He was on a boat.

It was hard to say which was worse.

He had been given a corner of the crew's berth for his own, including a hammock that had seen better days. He'd left his horse at the ferry junction, where it would be sent back to the komturie, hopefully. He hadn't trusted the look of the crossing-master, but there was little enough he could do about it. As he brooded, a dark hand rose and thin, strong fingers tugged at the hair on his chest. 'Bad dream?' the young woman said sleepily.

'Ah – yes,' Goetz said, removing her hand and holding it. 'Hello, Francesca. I didn't realise you'd still be here,' he said lamely. Francesca sat up, dislodging the thin blanket that had covered her. She blinked and a slow smile spread across her face. She was pretty, with olive skin and eyes the colour of dark ale. Curly dark hair spilled across her bare shoulders and other, more interesting portions of her anatomy.

'Of course I'm still here,' she said teasingly. 'Why would I leave when we were having so much fun? I didn't think knights could get bad dreams, eh?' she continued slyly, reaching up to stroke his head. 'Maybe if I kiss it, it will make it better, hmm?'

'And maybe if you don't get back to your cabin before your father finds you missing, I'll wind up having to swim to Marienburg,' Goetz said. He swung his legs over the edge of the hammock and hung his head. It hadn't been a good one, as ideas went, but he found it hard to resist an interesting face. The gaff-hook scar that coiled across Francesca's cheek and the knife trails on her sides had been like a book he simply had to read.

'He wouldn't throw you off the boat,' she said, pouting slightly.

'He would if he knew what we had been doing since Altdorf,' Goetz said. 'Besides, I need to practise.' He stood, pulled on his trousers and hefted his sword, falling into the Stance of Seven Thrusts. Slowly he worked out the kinks, thrusting against imaginary enemies in the confined space. Francesca watched him for a moment, then, realising that he wasn't coming back to the hammock, she sniffed loudly and dressed. Goetz, already lost in the pattern of swordplay, didn't hear her pad out.

Mind blank, he moved from the Seven Thrusts into the Eagle's Beak and then on into the Hohenstaffen Gambit, easily compensating for the pitch and yaw of the deck beneath his feet. From the Gambit he moved easily into the Liptz Cross and let the hilt of his sword roll in his palm as he sank into a Crogan Hook with an Altdorf Curve. Behind him, something scraped against the wood of the deck.

He spun on his heel, sweeping the edge of the blade out and pulling it short at the last moment as the cabin boy stared at him in horrified fascination. Goetz twisted his wrist and turned the edge to the flat, lightly swatting the side of the boy's head. 'Don't sneak up on armed men, Wilhelm, or you might find yourself short a head.'

'I–' Eyes still on the sword, Wilhelm stammered unintelligibly. Goetz pulled the sword back and let it rest on his bare shoulder.

'Take a breath,' Goetz said, smiling.

'Th... the captain requests your pre... presence on deck, Sir Knight!' Wilhelm yelped.

Goetz repressed a flinch. This was likely going to be awkward. He forced a smile and nodded. 'I'll be up in a moment, Wilhelm. I just need to dress,' he said. The boy nodded jerkily and scampered up the stairs. 'In retrospect, it was probably a mistake to sleep with the captain's daughter,' Goetz said to himself. He looked at the hammock and chuckled. 'Fun though.'

The look of incredulity on Francesca's face when he'd responded to her flirtations had been priceless in and of itself. While some knightly orders practised the monastic discipline of celibacy, Myrmidia's followers had never been among them. Goetz dressed quickly, arming himself as well. He doubted he was in for more than a bit of play-acting, but it never hurt to be prepared. He paused as he ran his thumb over the engraved sun on his sword blade. He felt a twinge in his side and shook the feeling off.

The deck was awash with activity when he got up there. The crew – hardened rivermen all – ran back and forth, most carrying weapons. Francesca was armed, wearing a short blade belted to her narrow waist and carrying an ugly-looking knife in her hand. She blew him a kiss and he turned away. The captain was at the tiller and he waved Goetz over. 'We're passing through the fringes of the Drakwald now,' he said. 'Where the forest thins into the Cursed Marshes.' Captain Stiglitz was a big man, running to fat. A patchy blond beard clung tenaciously to his jowls and his thinning hair was swept back from his pink pate. Still, the hands that held the tiller looked strong enough to crack stones and the well-cared for handgun that rested near his foot looked deadly enough.

'The Drakwald,' Goetz said hollowly. His good mood had evaporated and he looked at the trees that clung to the shore to either side of them. Stiglitz eyed him.

'Been here before then?'

'Yes. Not this far north, but... yes.' Goetz shook himself. He nudged the handgun resting against the rail. 'Expecting trouble?'

'It's the Drakwald. What do you think?' Stiglitz said, his eyes on the river bank. 'But... attacks have been increasing, they say.' He met Goetz's eyes and nodded. 'Oh aye, the Fen-Guard have been having running battles with bands of mutants and beastmen in the Marshes, or so the gallows-patterers scream. Something has stirred them up, that's for sure.'

'Something is always stirring them up,' Goetz said. He felt a chill pass through him as he caught sight of something white flitting between the trees. Leaning over the rail, he squinted against the glare of the setting sun, trying to make it out. When he did, he bit back a startled curse.

The woman was tall, taller than any woman had a right to be. She held a long spear in one hand and carried a battered circular shield on the other. On her head was an archaic helmet and her eyes flashed like exploding stars as she met Goetz's gaze and held it the way a child might hold a struggling moth. Recognition flooded him, and with it a terror that he had not felt since childhood. Her mouth opened as in greeting, or perhaps in warning, and she stabbed her spear at the sky. The blade caught the light and Goetz ducked his head, blinking spots out of his eyes.

It was only because of that, that he avoided the swoop of the scimitar that would have removed his head from his shoulders. Jerking back with an oath, Goetz narrowly dodged the bite of the blade as it hissed through the air. The cyclopean monster that clutched it hissed in frustration and swung itself up onto the boat with one jerk of a thickly muscled arm. The colour of river mud, with a head shaped like a bird's skull save for the single burning orb that occupied the centre of its face, it was a huge brute and simian-broad, with a reptilian tail that jerked and thumped dangerously.

Someone rang the alarm bell as other creatures, beastmen and more humanlooking mutants, scrambled aboard, dripping wet. They had been waiting in the water, Goetz realised, and had climbed aboard as silently as cats. If he hadn't seen the woman, they might not have realised until it was too late. Looking past the brute that stomped towards him on splayed feet, he saw that the woman – whoever she was – had vanished as if she'd never been. Then he had no more time to think about it as the rusty scimitar swiped out again and he was duelling for his life.

The creature shrieked, exposing needle-like fangs, and brought its blade down on his with bone-crushing force. Its inhuman muscles bunched and Goetz, off balance, sank to his knees and bent backwards. It hunched over him, grunting in triumph. Goetz let himself fall back and swept his leg up, catching it in the junction of its own bandy limbs. It shrilled in agony and stumbled sideways. Goetz rolled to his feet and slashed out, carving a red trench through its brown flesh and piecemeal armour. Agonised, its knobbly tail thudded into the deck inches from him, spattering him with splinters. Goetz chopped the bulging tip of the limb off and the mutant crashed into him, carrying him back against the rail hard enough to cause his armour to creak and for bolts of pain to shoot up and down his spine.

Spade-sized hands made a go at throttling him and Goetz slugged the mutant, breaking teeth. 'Get off me, filth!' he snarled, hitting it again. It shrieked into his face and, desperate, Goetz stabbed hooked fingers into its single bulging eye. The eye burst and the mutant howled. It released him and staggered back, groping at its wounded face.

With his sword-arm unpinned, Goetz let his blade drift out and the mutant toppled, its cries cut short. He turned, scanning the deck. He caught sight of Francesca gutting a scrawny creature that was more sheep than ape with an almost gentle brush of her blade. Another crewman wielded a boar-spear with experienced precision as he impaled a croaking frog-thing with more eyes than fingers. In other places, the fight wasn't going so well... something that had a wrinkled child's face clubbed down a sailor with hairy arms and bawled out hymns in a grunting tongue. Two goat-headed beastmen tore another hapless man in half and brayed out in victory as his insides spilled across the deck. Everywhere, crewmen strained against mutants across a blood-slick deck and Goetz knew that it could go either way. He spotted Captain Stiglitz trying to hold off an axe-wielding beastman with his smoking handgun and moved to help.

As Goetz approached, the beastman, a vulture-headed monster, shoved Stiglitz down and spun, axe ready. Goetz raised his sword, only to hesitate as the beastman's bestial eyes widened comically. It squawked and stumbled back, waving its axe. Goetz took a step forward and it turned and hopped towards the rail, throwing itself overboard.

'What?' Goetz said, turning to the others. All eyes, human and mutant alike, were on him now. Slowly, as if compelled, the latter disengaged and retreated to the rails with low moans and snarls. Goetz advanced on them, but before he could reach the creatures they too fled, heaving themselves into the river with desperate abandon. Goetz stared after them in shock as the crew set up a cheer. Still befuddled, he didn't even resist when Francesca threw aside her own bloody blade and leapt into his arms, kissing him full on the lips in front of her scowling father.

Why had they run from him? Could it have been simply because he killed their chieftain or champion, assuming that was what the fiend had been? He glanced back at the mutant's body where it lay sprawled near the rail. A crow was perched on its deflated skull, one black eye cocked it Goetz's direction. It croaked and took wing a moment later, flying towards Marienburg.

The longship drifted into the harbour, watched by the keen gazes of the Marienburg Sea-Watch. Men in green livery, wearing breastplates emblazoned with the face of the sea-god Manann, stalked the docks in a professional manner, clutching halberds and crossbows. Boats full of watchmen and bureaucrats met the longship on its way to the shore and Eyri greeted the latter with an easy grin and wide arms.

'My friends! My friends! Welcome aboard!'

As he enfolded the lead official in a bone-breaking hug, Dalla stealthily slipped over the side into the water, the oilskins she was wearing wrapped around her limbs keeping out the cold of the water. It was a practice of the Marienburg Merchant's Association to count the number of Norscans in every crew and count them again as they weighed anchor. More than one seaborne invasion had come as a result of spies left behind by cagey captains. While Dalla couldn't fault them their caution, she could – and did – curse them for it all the same as the cold of the water seeped through the oilskins and tugged at her limbs. Snow she could handle, and ice, but the water was all around her. Inescapable and all-consuming.

They had lost sight of the einsark ships as they drifted into Marienburg waters. Eyri had been confident that it had simply been a patrol, seeing what they were about. Dalla wasn't so sure. If her father was correct, something was going on. Pushing the thought aside, she concentrated on swimming.

Dragging her sword and a waterproof pouch behind her with the belt of the sheath clenched between her teeth, she swam with short, easy strokes. She avoided the orange patches of water where the light of the torches and lanterns fell, keeping instead to the sides of the other vessels anchored in the docklands. Propelling herself along off the keel of a fishing trawler, she shot into the shadows beneath the docks. She coasted through the forest of wooden posts and flotsam that had been swept into the tangle.

Beneath the docks it was another world. A city of shattered wreckage and forgotten vessels. Some were still whole, moored in secret spots, waiting for owners who would never return. Marienburg was a city of spies and assassins and neither was a profession that inclined to longevity. She took a moment to scan her surroundings. There was more than wreckage beneath Marienburg's docks... mutants and worse things prowled the shallows. More than once on one of Eyri's trips she had had to fight with things with too many limbs or none at all beneath these docks.

Pulling herself up onto the upright prow of a half-sunken rowboat, she perched and stripped the wet oilskins off her arms and legs and tossed them aside. Hanging her sword across her chest, she opened the waterproof pouch and dressed swiftly. Above her, boots thudded across the wood of the dock. She froze and looked up, watching the drizzle of torchlight as it passed over the gaps between the boards.

There were more guards about than was entirely normal. Holding her sword tight against her so it wouldn't get caught, she jumped lightly from the prow to a broken spar, then from the spar to a dangling sheet of fraying fishing net. Even as she landed, a pinkish tentacle speared out of the water and wrapped itself around her leg. With barely enough time to grunt in surprise, she was yanked backwards and into the water, her elbow connecting painfully with a floating crate on the way down.

She bounced along the bottom for a moment, teeth gritted against the urge to suck in a breath. Breathing in the foul slop-waters of Marienburg would be just as fatal as falling to the lamprey teeth of the scavenger that had snagged her. It was shaped like a pink anemone, all teeth and lazily moving limbs. Something that had likely been caught in the nets of a fisherman who had drifted too close to the Sea of Chaos and got free in Marienburg waters. Pink tendrils shot towards her. She snatched her sword free of its sheath and cut through the lot. Foul-tasting blood spurted into the water, creating a cloud around her. She shoved off from the silt and pinned the squirming creature to a post with her sword. With a fire in her lungs from lack of oxygen, she grabbed the hilt in both hands and twisted savagely. She heard a sound like bells, and wondered if it was the creature squealing. Ripping her sword free, she watched it tumble down into the mud, tentacles trailing after it limply. Then, with a flash of her legs, she propelled herself to the surface.

Snagging the fishing net, she hauled herself up out of the water. Climbing to the top, she looked back down. Behind her, a fin rose from the water, navigating the bobbing detritus with ease. Clinging to the net, she watched it pass. When it had gone, she scampered up the net and pressed her palms against the rough board above. Gripping her sheathed sword, she smacked the pommel against the edge of the board. The rusty nails popped loose with a groan. She paused, waiting. Then, reaching up, she moved the board aside and shimmied up through the gap.

Crouching on the dock, she replaced the board and looked around again. The bobbing lanterns of the guards were at some distance. She rose to her feet and, leaving a trail of water behind her, padded away from the docks.

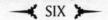

SIX

The River Talabec was a wild thing, all raging currents and cascading eddies. The river-ferry moved through a combination of current and muscle-power, propelled along by twelve-foot poles of polished wood. It was said that the river had killed more men than any invasion from the North. Regardless or not whether that was true, Goetz was glad to see the back of it.

Marienburg sat on the mouth of the river, where it entered the sea. A freistadt, it was a city independent of the Empire and it rulers, yet still in some ways a part of it. Resting on the Northern coast, Marienburg was one of the largest trading centres in the Old World. Ships from every corner of every civilised land made port here, and the narrow streets were full of languages that could be heard nowhere else and the canals were full of barges bulging with trade-goods of every description.

As Goetz paced the deck impatiently, the river-ferry joined others of its kind in a slow queue through the river-bar. The bar was composed of two square towers connected by an iron portcullis that could be lowered into the river in order to block traffic.

Goetz grimaced as he caught sight of the gibbets dangling just above the river. Bodies huddled in each, though whether they were living or dead he couldn't say. Each cage bore a crude placard stating the prisoner's crime… 'PIRACY' was the most prevalent, though one simply said 'LUST'. Crows flew back and forth between the cages, causing them to rattle and shudder. Goetz cast his eyes downward, where skiffs carrying watchmen in the liveries of the various merchant-counsellors who ruled Marienburg checked cargo manifests and passenger rolls with the bored detachment of men who hadn't seen nearly enough action in their careers.

Goetz leaned against the rail, his bundle and pack by his feet. The trip downriver had taken several days thanks to the damage the ferry had taken, as well as the need to avoid any more attacks, and Goetz hadn't slept well for the duration. In his dreams, beastmen cavorted with orcs, strange fungi burst from his pores and his skin felt slick and greasy at times. The terrified

bird-face of the beastman mingled with that of its one-eyed leader, both
of them staring at him in horror as the fungi spread into iron feathers that
flared and cut him to pieces from the inside out. Consequently he was in
a sour mood. With his shield strapped to his back, his sword on his hip
and the emblem of the Order prominently displayed across his chest, he
was hoping for as little trouble as possible from the River-Watch. Armed
men attracted undue attention in most cities, and a knight of the Empire
wasn't likely to be welcomed with open arms in Marienburg, considering the associations.

If he were being honest, there weren't many places they were welcomed.
Not unless there was fighting to be done. Goetz smiled sourly and tapped
his fingers on the rail. For all that he was dedicated to the Order, and understood its importance, Goetz knew that not all of his fellow knights shared
his disposition. Too many of them had been bred for battle and command,
rather than common sense. The other knightly orders all too often simply
reinforced that straightforward view.

Honour was what you made of it, not a thing in and of itself. It could
neither be broken, nor insulted, lacking as it did either a personality or a
physical form. That was his view anyway. Even among his own Order, he
knew that it wasn't likely to be a popular one.

'We go where we are needed,' he murmured. 'We do what must be done.'

'What?' Francesca said.

Goetz turned. 'Nothing. You look lovely,' he said automatically. Francesca snorted and rubbed the scar on her cheek.

'Liar. Father says we'll be at dock soon enough.'

'Does he – ah–?' Goetz made a helpless gesture.

Francesca chuckled throatily. 'If he didn't, he wouldn't be much of a captain, eh? Yes.' She shot a glance at her father and frowned. 'And if he knows
what's good for him, he'll hold his tongue.' She looked back at Goetz and
patted his wrist. 'I just wanted to wish you good luck. Maybe I'll see you
on the journey back to Ostermark, eh?' Feeling slightly flustered, Goetz
watched her as she moved away, her rear twitching like a cat's.

Clearing his throat, he turned back to the rail. As a second son, he hadn't
given much thought to either women or marriage, at least not in serious
terms. It was a given that he'd be married off to one well-bred daughter
of Talabheim or another. Now, as with so many things, with Stefan gone
and his pledge to the Order, there was no telling what would be expected
of him. As long as he was in the field, he could avoid it.

For that reason, as much as any other, he hadn't wanted to return to his
komturie after his nearmiss with the goblins. It would have meant avoiding
his father's well-intentioned bluster and his step-mother's subtle dealings
to see him married off to someone with a better bloodline to raise their
family a rank or two in the Game.

He sniffed. The 'Game'... in Talabheim, that meant the game of politics.

Like the other great cities of the Empire, Talabheim was a hotbed of political warfare. Claimants to thrones, positions and provinces pushed and pulled against one another with a viciousness that rats would envy. It hurt his head even thinking about it.

As the ferry neared the guard post, he straightened. Watchmen clambered aboard the ferry, their beribboned halberds making the entire process more awkward than it had to be. Goetz settled for watching the traffic. The river was a hodgepodge of tightly clustered craft. He watched as a flotilla of merchant rafts pressed tight up against the iron-bound hull of a dwarfen paddle boat and slid around it, their crews jeering at the cursing dwarfs.

Turning from the scene, he caught a bulldog-faced watchman with a halberd cradled in the crook of his arm watching him with narrow-eyed speculation. The man turned away as Goetz's eyes met his own and conferred with a compatriot. The back of Goetz's neck prickled and the ache in his back flared up, just enough to remind him it was there. A harsh croak caught his attention a moment later and he looked up.

A number of crows had alighted on the prow rail of the ferry. The one that had made the noise sat a little way away from its fellows and was a scraggly example of its kind, with sickly grey skin showing beneath ragged feathers. Goetz felt a thrill of revulsion as it hopped down onto the deck and moved towards him, head cocked. It croaked again and his fingers instinctively sought his sword. He wondered if it was the same one he'd seen perched on the mutant's body days earlier.

'I have neither bread nor seed, Brother Crow,' Goetz said. The crow eyed him for an uncomfortable moment and then took wing in a shower of mangy feathers. One drifted across Goetz's arm and he cringed unconsciously, swatting it away. When he looked up, the watchmen had disembarked when their search was over. The ferry was moving on. A sense of relief flooded him, though he knew there had been little enough reason to be concerned.

Perhaps it was simply Velk's warning coming back to haunt him. What the Grand Master had told him had made him nervous enough, but Velk had only added to his worries. Goetz kept his eyes averted as the ferry passed beneath the dangling cages and didn't look up again until the vessel docked. Somewhere in this city was an assassin... a killer with a thirst for knightly blood. The question was; how exactly did one go about the process of hunting an assassin?

Goetz had no training for such things. He was no watchman or road warden to be investigating a crime. He didn't know the first place to start. Disembarking, he caught sight of his earlier observer standing away from the crush of the crowd that milled about on the wharf. The watchman was speaking to someone and apparently gesturing at Goetz, or at least in his general direction.

'And that's not suspicious in the least,' Goetz murmured. The sound of shattering glass caught his attention. The tavern sat just across the street and on the corner. It was three stories tall and a monument to the eccentricities of Marienburg's architects. A man was propelled out onto the street by a boot to the rear as Goetz came to a halt.

Dressed finely, if a few years out of fashion, he was spindly, but handsome. He rolled across the filth of the street and scrambled upright, features white, jaw slack. The man who followed him out was dressed in dark clothing, weighed down by a plethora of implements of violence. In contrast to the deadly devices, however, was the lute he clutched in one hand.

'Hercule Portos, you are challenged. Also, your playing is horrible,' the man clutching the lute said. He swung the lute against the doorpost, wrecking the instrument. Tossing the remains aside, he drew his rapier and pointed the tip at the man in the street. 'Draw your sword, sir.'

'I... I... I have no sword,' Portos said, climbing to his feet, hands spread. 'I am no warrior! I merely sing of them!'

'You do that badly as well. How did you become so popular?' the swordsman said. 'On your feet. Someone will lend you a blade, I'm certain.' He glanced around. 'Anyone?'

No one moved. Goetz was suddenly aware that the narrow street was packed. Gulls wheeled overhead, crying loudly. Duelling, while not common where he was from, still happened and Goetz's father had joked that it was a way of pruning the dead branches of certain family trees. In Marienburg, however, it was practically a profession.

This however was more along the lines of an assassination. The swordsman's demeanour didn't suggest an excess of passion. It was clinical, even professional. Goetz was less squeamish than he had been before that night in the forest, but even so, the thought rankled. A duel was the result of passion; of honour stolen, or wrongs done. It wasn't done in the street, the way a man might kill a dog.

'A blade, damn it!' the swordsman barked.

'Let his patron give him a blade!' someone in the back of the crowd shouted.

'No, I think we'll let you do it,' the swordsman snarled, gesturing with his sword. 'Push that bastard forward or I'll gut the first three rows!' He swiped the air with his rapier and it made an evil hiss.

Goetz, almost hypnotised to this point, found his hand clenched around his own hilt. He stepped forward, drawing his own blade. The swordsman looked at him with narrow eyes.

'He can use mine,' Goetz said. He flipped his long sword around and proffered it hilt first to the still-kneeling Portos. The swordsman shook his head.

'No. He wouldn't even know how to lift it.'

He slashed out without turning, the tip of his sword slicing through a nearby rough's sword-belt. As it fell, he caught it with the flat of his own blade and sent it spinning across the street towards Portos.

'That's a better fit, I think.' He looked at the rough, who pressed back into the crowd, palms extended. He looked back at Goetz and saluted him crisply. 'Thank you anyway, Sir Knight.'

Goetz said nothing, merely nodded and turned on his heel. As he waded through the crowd, he heard the rasp of steel on leather. The crowd took in a deep breath. Goetz didn't stop.

Belatedly, he realised that he'd lost sight of the watchman and whoever he'd been talking to. He began to make his way towards where he'd last seen the duo when something jabbed his neck, eliciting a yelp of pain. Goetz spun, one hand slapping to the hilt of his sword. The crow, startled, took wing and flapped away, croaking. Goetz felt his neck and his fingers came away dappled with blood.

Dalla cursed and pressed herself back against the door frame, turning her face away from the street as the city watch patrol tromped past. Hard-eyed men in brass armour with turquoise and amethyst livery, kept their hands tight on the hafts of their halberds. Something was going on. She had been to Marienburg a few times, and never before had she seen this many patrols in the streets. These were heading somewhere in particular.

As they passed, she pushed away from the door and continued on her way. She wore a plain robe with a hood, but beneath its concealing folds there was her hauberk, much patched and cut down to fit her properly. She had her sword as well, a battered thing of crude manufacture. She would need a new one, if what her father believed was true.

If, if, if. She watched the legs of the market crowds shuffle past, and watched thieves eel among them and the alley cats filching fish from the stalls. If her father was right, all of this would soon be done. It was not a pleasant thought. She did not like the city, nor its inhabitants, but to think of that befalling them – she restrained a shudder.

She had once skirted the coast of the Chaos Wastes on a raid and seen what happened to lands that fell under the sway of such things. While her folk might worship the Great Powers, at their most rampant they could be terrible. The thing that her father's father's father had sealed within the stone of Svunum was as rampant as any of them.

It was an old story, handed down through the generations of the tribes whose gudjas had supposedly been involved. Five men of power had gone to the Island That Walked and forced it to remain in one place, and scattered the ruined tribe who lived on it like fleas. Later still, her father had led a raid onto that cursed shore and pruned the tribe back yet again, in retaliation for the raid that had taken the lives of her mother and brothers. Yet still they lingered; still they were dangerous. Such was the way of things. Fire and sword could only do so much.

In its stone cage, the daemon stirred and the land groaned in sympathy. She could see the marks of the Great Planner's followers scratched into lintel posts and in the brick of the walls, marking those houses safe for worship. To one who knew what to look for, this city was teeming with the human lice who battened on the power of such beings. No wonder the guard patrols had been increased.

There were stories back home, as well as brought by merchants and escaped slaves, of the Kurgan stirring in their blasted fastness, and lone prophets spouting nonsense. When one daemon stirred, they all did, it seemed. One tug on the Pattern, and all of the threads felt it. She bared her teeth, eliciting a yelp from a nosey matron who scurried away. That was her father's business... hers was merely to find prey for Eyri in preparation for the alvthing – the council of chieftains her father had called.

She had only seen one other alvthing in her lifetime, just prior to the raid her father had led to Svunum. A gathering of the mightiest chieftains of Southern Norsca, and their best jarls and thanes with them. A mighty conclave of heroes. She snorted. Robbers and bandits, more like. But they had done well enough, harrying the beasts who had killed her mother and brother.

Dalla slapped the sword on her hip. Perhaps, soon enough, she would get to do the same.

# SEVEN

Temples clustered together like scabs on a doomsayer. One of his father's more cherished sayings, but Goetz agreed despite that. Even in Talabheim, the temple district was a crowded one. Sigmarite chapels brushed shared stonework with the altars of Ulric and Taal. Here, in Marienburg, there were even more options for the religiously inclined. Shrines to Manann dotted even the most isolated of cul-de-sacs, and brass plates wrought in the shape of the god's face, foamy beard and all, hung everywhere.

The largest temple, and the most gaudy by far, was that of Handrich. The patron of merchants occupied a rarefied position in the city's celestial hierarchy, being beloved of the upper classes. Overly ornate and gilded to the point of being extremely dangerous on sunny days, his temple acted as a gathering spot for traders of all types and it occupied the centre of the district with the stolid arrogance of a fortress.

In comparison, the temple of Myrmidia was a slight thing. Unassuming, even, for all its size. Goetz made for the doors, noting with a moment of trepidation that a number of crows lined the archway. Glittering black eyes watched him, and he stopped in the middle of the street, suddenly struck by a flash of agony. It had been building for the last hour. A deep, savage pain, echoing outward from the place, and he knew with a sure certainty that its cause was not, as he had thought – as you hoped, part of him whispered – goblin poisons.

No, it was something worse.

He stepped back from the temple and leaned in what he hoped was a casual manner against a doorway. Eyes closed, he took several deep breaths, wishing he could breathe the pain away. It wasn't in his head, not entirely. He took his hand away from the old wound and examined it, half-expecting to see blood.

'Unclean!'

Goetz jerked his head up, startled. The yell had come from the lips of a ragged-robed flagellant who stood on a busted plinth nearby. He was wrapped in rusty chains and his bearded aesthete's face was bulging with barely contained fervour. The man rattled the cowbells attached to his chains and shrieked again. 'Unclean! Worshippers of heathen idols!'

Snarling, he speared the growing crowd with a dagger-gaze. 'Repent! Repent of your bilious ways! The only path to redemption is through Sigmar! Only Sigmar can save you from the talons of daemons, from the maws of dragons and the tusks of orcs!' He shook a fist shrouded in a rust-splotched metal gauntlet for emphasis. 'Doom rides to night-winds! The Queen of Crows stirs in her eyrie and the Children of Abomination flock to banners of flyblown meat! Unclean!' he roared, pointing a metal finger at Goetz. 'Follower of a false god!'

Goetz frowned and opened his mouth to reply when a stone spanged off his armour. Surprised, he stepped back. The crowd had turned ugly, seemingly in the space of a few moments. Above, the crows had taken flight. They croaked and rasped, making noises that were disturbingly close to laughter.

'Foreign devil!' the flagellant continued, bent over, his neck muscles bulging with the force of his screaming. 'Lapdog of wicked gods! Only Sigmar can save you! Only Sigmar! Sigmar!'

Goetz backed away as the crowd murmured and heaved, growing agitated. They had somehow got between him and the sanctuary of the temple doors. His hand dipped for his sword, but he resisted the urge. Drawing a weapon now would only provoke the crowd, and he couldn't take the chance that they'd rush him. So, instead, he began to back away down the street.

The flagellant continued to howl imprecations. A street-rough dove at Goetz. Goetz caught him across the jaw and sent him reeling back into the crowd. Somewhere in the mass of humanity, a fight broke out. Then another, and another. Mobs were fragile things. Goetz stepped into a side-street as the crowd forgot about him and focused on the half-dozen brawls going on within its own ranks. From somewhere, he heard the thin trill of one of the brass whistles the city watch used to clear the streets. He hurried down the street, not wanting to be caught in a riot. He'd witnessed the Pudding-Tax Riots in Altdorf as a boy, and it wasn't a memory he cherished.

The street opened onto a narrow passage and a curving stone walkway that scalloped over a canal. Barges laden with goods going to one of the dozen market squares in the city passed beneath it, the bargemen singing lurid songs to accompany the thud of their poles. Goetz paused at the apex of the bridge, looking back towards the temple district. The pain in his back had receded as he'd left the temple behind and that fact caused a chill of despair to prod gently at him.

What did it mean? Why now? He had gone almost two years since he'd faced that thing in the Drakwald. Almost two years since he'd plunged into a storm of witchfire and put the unclean thing growing in a sour patch on the earth to the sword. It had been the making of him; his first duty as a full knight, and almost his last.

He had led an ad hoc assemblage of militia-men and foresters into the Drakwald on the trail of what he had thought, at the time, was a band of everyday bandits. Instead, he had found himself on the hunt for a herd of beastmen and mutants. Not to mention that half of his men had turned out to be cultists, their true loyalties to the nightmare thing that the beastmen's raids were responsible for keeping fed.

In the end, he had killed it, though not before it had invaded his mind and touched his spirit in some indefinable and horrible way. He repressed an instinctive shudder. The wounds from where it had touched him had festered for weeks. He had been too in shock at first to realise it, but it had left its mark on him sure enough.

Now the dreams had begun again. Old nightmares rising through the sludge of forced forgetfulness. Maybe it was simply the hallucinogens in the goblin arrows, or perhaps it was simply an egg that had at last begun to hatch. Either way, it wasn't just pain growing in him. He smiled grimly... wouldn't it be amusing if that flagellant had been right, and he was unclean?

'No,' he said aloud, shaking himself. 'Not in the least.'

Still, the thought lingered. He had been a born sceptic, unsure of anything that he could not touch and shape with his own two hands. Killing in the name of a distant, divine being had never sat well in his stomach. Killing for any reason, really. He was no milksop or pacifist; violence was second nature to him by now. But it was an automatic thing, an instinct as opposed to a calling. An instinct he tried to deny at most opportunities. Though sometimes...

He felt eyes on him and looked up. Down the canal, a distant shape seemed to float across another footbridge. Pale and marble-hued, the woman turned to look at him, her blazing tresses spilling from beneath an archaic helmet. 'What?' he said, half to himself. She raised a hand and the sun seemed to flare. He blinked spots out of his eyes.

He felt a tug at his belt and looked down to find a gap-toothed urchin attempting to filch his dirk. The boy froze as Goetz spotted him and then gave a frenzied yank and fell back, clutching the dagger in his hands. Goetz cursed as the boy took off as fast as his skinny legs could take him. He followed as fast as he could. He'd been so preoccupied, he hadn't noticed the cutpurse. Though why the boy would want a dagger, Goetz couldn't fathom.

The chase led him away from the temple district and through a crowded market forum. Goetz followed the boy into a cul-de-sac, leaving a trail of cursing merchants and customers behind him. The youth skidded to a stop and spun, chest heaving. He couldn't have been more than six years of age, and his eyes were wide with terror. Goetz felt a pang of guilt for having been the cause of it. 'Easy,' he said, keeping his hands away from his sword. 'Easy. Give it back, and we'll say no more about it.'

'Well, you won't, at any rate,' a voice said.

The gate to the cul-de-sac slammed shut and the boy dropped the dagger and eeled past Goetz, vanishing into a gap in one wall. Goetz turned as a bevy of armed men stepped out of the shadows. They were a motley lot, with the look of hardened mercenaries. One was quite obviously a Kislevite judging by his moustaches and top knot, while another had the lean, feral look of a Tilean dock-tough. There were five in all, and they were armed to the teeth. Snatching up his dagger, Goetz straightened and let his palm fall to his sword. 'Gentlemen.'

'Gentlemen,' the Tilean repeated mockingly. His dark eyes took in Goetz's cuirass and harness and he grinned, displaying a mouthful of golden teeth. 'Those will fetch a pretty penny. Oleg was right, the fat fool.' With a start, Goetz realised that they were likely referring to the watchman who'd been paying undue attention to him earlier.

'What is this about?' Goetz said, as they spread out around him, slowly.

'Call it a tax,' said one, a pinch-faced thug dressed in stained leathers.

'A tax?' Goetz said, playing for time. There was no way out. It looked as if he were going to have to fight.

'On foreigners,' a second said, tapping his cheek with an iron-banded cudgel.

'If you fight, it will only be worse for you,' another rumbled, stroking the plaits of his beard. He wore a battered breastplate, the Imperial eagle painted on it having faded to an anaemic-looking buzzard, and had the brawny look of a Nordlander. 'I would prefer not to fight a knight of the Empire.'

'Then leave, you cod-eating brute,' the Tilean snapped, tightening his grip on the halberd he carried. 'More money for the rest of us!'

'Stop talking and take him!' the Kislevite barked, drawing twin hatchets from the silk sash around his waist. He lunged with a wild yell, chopping down even as Goetz drew his sword. Goetz slid back and whipped his sword out and around, slicing through the man's belly. As the Kislevite stumbled past, dying, Goetz moved towards the others with the sure, smooth steps of a trained fighter.

'You want a fight? Fine. Have at it!' he said, gliding towards them as violence surged up in him, washing away all questions and doubts. His sword drew sparks as it slid along the length of the pinch-faced thug's blade. Goetz beat the man's weapon down and slashed upwards, opening his thin face to the bone. As he stumbled back, clutching at his face, Goetz shouldered him into the one with the cudgel. The two went down in a tangle and Goetz drove his boot into the second man's temple. Bone cracked as his head bounced off the cobbles.

'Fastarda!' the Tilean hissed as he came in low, the wicked point of the halberd gleaming as it skidded off Goetz's breastplate. Goetz turned and slugged him and then spun to meet the big man with the plaits in his beard. The Nordlander's sword met Goetz's with a steely hiss and the two men strained against one another for a moment.

'Now's your chance to give up, if you don't want to fight,' Goetz grunted. The big man didn't reply. They stamped in a circle, moving back and forth. They broke apart and then slammed together again. Goetz set his feet and shoved, causing the big man to stumble. The latter screamed as, a moment later, a crossbow bolt sprouted from his back!

The big man sank to his knees, pawing weakly at the shaft of the bolt that had killed him. Goetz, in shock, looked up. On top of the cul-de-sac gate, a robed figure hastily reloaded a crossbow. Goetz reacted swiftly and charged forward, scooping up the Tilean's discarded halberd as he went.

Without stopping, he hurled the weapon at the crossbowman. Awkward as the halberd was, it didn't come anywhere close to its target. Nonetheless, the crossbowman gave up on his weapon and leapt down from his perch. Goetz hit the flimsy gate at a run, smashing it off its hinges even as the cloaked figure fled into the crowded street.

Thoughts of what had happened to his predecessor flashed through Goetz's head as he shoved through the crowd and he wondered if this might be the same man that had done for Athalhold. After all, how many renegade crossbowmen were there in Marienburg? Bloodied sword in hand, he followed the man through the winding streets, intent on finding out.

People scrambled out of his way and a hue and cry went up as he forced his way into the crowd choking the runnels of the street-market. The crossbowman fled on, tipping over a cart full of overripe produce as he passed. Goetz trod through it unheeding, every iota of his attention fixed on the fleeing man's back.

Unfortunately, the man was faster than he was. Much faster, and he had a head start. Growling in frustration, Goetz stopped and snatched a melon from a stand. It squished unpleasantly in his hand.

'Here now, you need to pay for that–' the fruit-monger began, stepping out from behind his counter threateningly. Goetz ignored him. He wound his arm back and then let it snap forward. The melon flew like a stone erupting from a catapult.

It caught the fleeing man in the back of the head and sent him tumbling head over heels into the gutter. Groaning, the would-be assassin began to crawl away. Goetz stalked towards him and used the tip of his sword to flick the melon out of the way as he went. 'I'm not in the habit of giving assassins second chances,' Goetz said, lifting his sword point and tapping the crossbowman's rear. The man continued to crawl. The knight stomped a foot down on his concealing robe, momentarily trapping him.

'Now my fine friend, you'll–' He paused as he heard the snap of wings and glanced up as a shadow fell across him. The crow's talons scraped the cheek-guards of his helmet and Goetz stumbled back with a curse. Mangy wings battered his face and head and a hideous croaking assailed his ears. He flailed, trying to drive the bird away.

When the crow flapped away, Goetz dropped his arms to find that the crossbowman had scrambled to his feet and made off. Cursing, Goetz started after him, but a burly form interposed itself. The fruit-monger glared up at him. 'You owe me a pretty karl, my friend,' he grunted, rubbing his finger and thumb together beneath Goetz's nose.

'What?'

'That melon came all the way from Magritta, friend. Two karls.'

'Two – it was half-rotten!' Goetz protested.

'It had character! Three karls!'

'I'm not paying three anything for a half-rotten melon I bounced off someone's head!' Goetz resisted the urge to shove the man aside and stepped back, sheathing his sword.

'Just like one of you Imperial louts. Cheating an honest merchant of a day's wage,' the fruit-monger said, glowering at Goetz. He looked around at the gathering crowd. 'You all heard him! He refused to pay!'

A grim mutter swept the crowd, and Goetz tensed, suddenly realising that he was at the centre of a situation spinning rapidly out of hand. His first instinct was to draw his sword again, but he knew that if he did that, someone would die. Several someones, and considering the ever-expanding size of the crowd, he was likely to be one of those someones. So, just as before, he firmly drew his hand away from his sword-hilt.

'I said I wasn't paying three karls,' Goetz said, laying on his best sneer. His tutors had been good for some things. 'Not for something that couldn't even stun a man for longer than a few seconds.'

'Fruit's for eating, not throwing,' the fruit-monger said.

'Same principle,' Goetz snapped. 'If it squishes on the head, it would have squished in my mouth, right?' He looked around, nodding. Unwittingly, several others did so as well. 'One, and I don't report you to the grocer's guild.' Goetz didn't even know if Marienburg had a grocer's guild, but from the look on the fruit-monger's face, they did and he had scored a telling point.

'That's highway robbery!' the man blustered, but without very much heat.

'We're not on a highway, and I'm not robbing you. One karl,' Goetz said, digging into his purse. He held up a gold coin and tossed it to the fruit-monger. The man caught it and bit it, then glared at Goetz.

'Fine. I still don't see why you had to go and waste a perfectly good melon.'

'It'll feed the rats, won't it?' Goetz said, already moving through the dispersing crowd. Slowly, he released the breath he'd been holding and looked around. His quarry was well and truly gone. Above, a crow – perhaps even the same one – eyed him from a window sill. Goetz stopped and watched it for a moment, until it took wing and flew away. He shuddered and turned his steps back towards the temple district.

* * *

The cavern faded as Myrma took a deep breath and let the strands of volcanic smoke enter her. Inside her head, the skeins of destiny unwound and extended into the silent cacophony of the Pattern of Fate. Worlds upon worlds, each more different than the last, bled into one another like a vast field of soap bubbles and darting bird-like shapes dove in an out of the bubbles, popping a few on the way.

She shivered instinctively as one of the bird-shapes headed for her, only to bank at the last second and plunge into a newborn world. The Lords of Change, some men called them. To her, they were the Sons of the Master Planner and each one carried within its shape a fragment of the Great Mutator's mighty design. Each world, each scheme and skein, birthed new additions to the Pattern, expanding the field of bubbles past the limits of her puny vision. As always, it left her reeling and frightened by its sheer complexity.

Something massive swam through the sea of too-vibrant colours towards her, great iron wings cutting silently through the pink and turquoise clouds. An avian shadow, smelling of lightning and sugar. A voice like the tolling of a dozen bells echoed wordlessly around the priestess. It was a question, though it was shaped like a wave.

'Yes,' she answered, raising her staff. 'He yet survives! He moves on, wrapping himself in our snares ever more tightly!'

Another rumble and the Queen of Crows enfolded her in a barrier of feathers, protecting her from the sight of the Pattern Unchecked. Comforted, Myrma writhed in pleasure as the tips of the feathers wrought changes in her form. Though never were they changes for changes sake. That set the Maiden of Colours apart from her kin, or so she whispered to Myrma. Change for change's sake was not true change but merely indecision, and there was nothing Old Father Fate despised more than indecision. Without decision, there could be no movement, no future.

Talons scraped along the edges of her spirit, teasing out hidden secrets. It was the toll for this communion: deep desires and forgotten fantasies, memories of lost loves and never-helds. She was always surprised by what her Lady dredged up from the depths of her past to gobble down like a sweetmeat.

'He is the one, then,' she said as the Lady held her. 'The one who will set the Great Game in motion?' A coloured mist of assent swept around her, teasing her ear drums with its delicate harmonies. She clutched her staff to herself and bent her head back, inhaling the beautiful vapour. Images of possibilities trampled down her thoughts... a city dedicated to the worship of the Pattern, with every man engaged in the contemplation of its skeins; a land purged of competing indulgences, where only one banner swayed in the cosmic wind; a land protected by black-armoured sorcerer-soldiers who worshipped at the feet of a Great and Terrible Queen of Air and Darkness, and who schemed eternally against one another. For such was the desire of any who served the Great Mutator... he who fed upon eternal change and alteration fed too upon the schemes of those positioned to cause change.

But not for the Queen of Crows the petty schemes of barbarians or the shallow ambition of pampered aristocrats. No, like a gourmand, she desired only the tastiest, most ambitious, most convoluted patterns for her feast. Minds turned towards eternal alternates, where every decision cascaded into a billion-billion possibilities.

The Great Game. Tzeentch's Game. The only game that mattered.

EIGHT

Goetz had decided to go to the watch in the end. By the time a patrol responded to the site of the ambush, the bodies had been picked clean by street-dwelling scavengers. The watchmen were singularly unhelpful, but then Goetz hadn't expected them to be. Murder in Marienburg was a commonplace occurrence and street-duels even more so.

'Crossbow is a common enough tool. Cheap manufacture,' said the watch-sergeant in charge of the small group of men who'd responded to the fight. 'By which I mean Imperial,' he added, giving Goetz a careful look.

'I'm from Talabheim,' Goetz said automatically. 'I wouldn't know.'

'Hnh.' The sergeant played with his ribbon of rank and looked down at the bodies. His men were 'scouring the streets for the assassin', which Goetz knew meant that they were standing off to the side somewhere inconspicuously, asking mild questions and carefully keeping their eyes vacant. If you wanted a long career, asking pointed questions wasn't the best way to go about it in Marienburg. 'You sure you didn't know any of them?'

'If I had, would I have killed them?' The sergeant looked at him and Goetz shook his head. 'Never mind. No, I didn't know them. Do you have a guard working for you by the name of Oleg?' Goetz said. If the 'Oleg' who had hired his attackers was also behind the crossbowman, then he might be one step closer to finding Athalhold's killer.

'Why do you ask?'

'I heard the name,' Goetz said.

'Where?'

'Does it matter?'

'If you're asking about my men, yes. Yes it matters,' the sergeant replied pugnaciously.

Goetz held up his hands in surrender. 'Forget about it, sergeant. It was of no importance, I expect.'

'Then why are you bothering my men with it, Sir Knight?' the sergeant began. His eyes widened slightly as he took in something over Goetz's shoulder. Goetz turned as the sound of hoof-beats filled the air. The horse was a slender Arabyan, with silk bows in its mane and an evil glint in its eye. Its rider was a stout man, resembling for all the world an overfed bird of paradise. Colourful livery and expensively enamelled armour competed with an over-large hat with an indecently sized feather for attention.

'I am Lieutenant Ulfgo, Sir Knight. I have come to escort you to the Prince,' the peacock said.

'Which prince?' Goetz said. 'Marienburg has a surplus, I'm given to understand.' The sergeant stifled a chuckle.

'The only one who matters,' Ulfgo said, his chubby features displaying not a twitch at the jibe. 'My Lord Aloysious Ambrosius, Lord Justicar of Marienburg and Master of the Fens.'

'Very impressive,' Goetz said. 'Why does he wish to see me?'

'You will have to ask him, Sir Knight.' Ulfgo inclined his head towards a second horse behind his, which impatiently scraped a hoof on the cobbles. 'You know how to ride, I trust?'

Goetz didn't bother to reply. Instead he swung into the saddle smoothly and jerked the reins, turning the horse around. He gestured. 'Lead the way, lieutenant, by all means.'

The ride was a swift one, taking them to the nearest canal, where a resplendent gondola awaited them. The prow had been carved into the shape of a bird's head and it had a canopy that was both garish and sublime. Armed men, wearing the livery of the Marsh-Watch, stood to attention both alongside the canal and on the gondola itself, clutching the wicked tridents that were their weapon of choice. Breastplates engraved with Manann's scowling visage and bronze full-face helms completed the image of deadly competence. From what Goetz knew of the Marsh-Watch, it was a reputation they deserved. They were as hardened a fighting force as any in the Empire, for all that their masters rarely employed them beyond the boundaries of the Cursed Marshes.

A seneschal, clad in fur and silk, stepped out from under the canopy and beckoned to Goetz with fingers dripping with jewellery. 'This way, if you please Sir Knight,' the man said in a high-pitched voice. Goetz dismounted and strode towards the gondola. As he made to board, one of the watchmen extended his trident and said, gruffly, 'No weapons.'

Goetz nodded. 'Then no discussion,' he said genially. He turned back towards the horse, his hand on the hilt of his sword. Two more watchmen stepped between him and his mount, their tridents not quite aimed at him. Goetz stopped and cocked his head. 'I've already killed five men today. Two more won't weigh any more heavily on my conscience,' he said, without menace. It never failed to surprise him how much truth was in him when he said such things. He felt a dim sadness at the prospect, but no worry. No fear.

Ulfgo leaned forward across his saddle horn, his stiff features turning a slightly darker shade. 'Remove your sword, Sir Knight. It is not your right to refuse an audience with the Lord Justicar.'

'The last time I looked, I wasn't a citizen of Marienburg. Therefore, I am hardly bound by its peculiarities,' Goetz said. 'But, since it's a mercantile sort of place, I'll haggle – my sword stays, but I'll happily peace-bind it, if you wish.'

Ulfgo made to draw his own weapon, and the watchmen levelled their tridents. Goetz sighed and shrugged. 'I tried,' he said, drawing his own sword.

'Not very hard, I must say. Enough, gentlemen. Enough.' There was a sharp clap immediately following these words and the watchmen backed off. 'I'm sure that the good knight means me no harm.' Goetz turned unhurriedly. The seneschal had backed away and a rangy man of indeterminate age had replaced him. He was clad not in silk, but in leather, with polished armour and a trident insignia emblazoned on his hauberk. One eye was covered with a large green eye-patch with a similar insignia and his hard mouth quirked in a flat smile. 'I am Aloysious Ambrosius, Sir Knight. I would be obliged if you would speak to me.'

'All you had to do was ask,' Goetz said, sheathing his sword.

'I thought I was asking. Thank you for correcting me.' Ambrosius eyed him as he stepped onto the gondola. 'Would you have really fought? No. Never mind. You would have, of course.'

'Of course,' Goetz said.

'Knights are all the same in that regard,' Ambrosius said, grinning slightly. 'At least in my experience.'

'What you know of proper knightly behaviour wouldn't fill a tankard, Ambrosius,' a voice said from within the canopy. As Ambrosius gestured for Goetz to step under it, a short shape stood, armour creaking. The man within wore armour the colour of kelp, its surface intricately engraved with aquatic motifs. Beneath it, he wore robes of a turquoise hue, which did little to hide the overall impression of a barrel that had grown legs. The scarred face glared frightfully at Goetz, and the hand that was extended in greeting was no hand at all, but instead a miniature trident, affixed to the stump of the man's wrist by a steel bracer.

'Sir Hector Goetz, of the Order of the Blazing Sun, if I might introduce you to the honourable Grand Master of the Knights of Manann, Dietrich Ogg,' Ambrosius said.

'Grand Master,' Goetz said, inclining his head in a shallow bow. The templars devoted to Manann were a strange lot, half political animal, half military organisation, they were centred in Marienburg and had been since they had been created by an edict of the merchant-princes. Religion had little to do with their day-to-day function, or so Goetz had heard. But then, that could be said of more than one knightly order, his own included.

'You Myrmidians are far too casual for my tastes,' Ogg grunted. 'I get more respect from the blasted Reiksguard!'

'That's a lie,' Ambrosius said helpfully. He sat down on a cushioned bench and draped his arms over the gondola rail as his men pushed the gondola off into the flow of the canal. 'The Reiksguard, being loyal Imperial citizens, rarely acknowledge our existence, let alone pay a visit to an order of templars that the Imperial Grand Master of the Knightly Orders doesn't recognise.' He sniffed. 'But by all means, continue to grouse.'

'I will, thank you,' Ogg said, stumping back to his bench and sitting with a clatter. He cast a baleful eye at Goetz. 'It's ours, you know.'

'He means Svunum,' Ambrosius supplied. 'Please take a seat, Sir Knight. We have much to discuss.'

'Do we?' Goetz said, sitting on the bench Ambrosius had indicated. He glanced out at the canal. Marienburg looked almost beautiful from this angle. Serene, even.

'Oh yes,' Ambrosius said, leaning forward. He shoved a finger beneath his eye-patch and scratched furiously. 'It wouldn't do to have two members of your prestigious Order laying dead in our fair streets, now would it?'

Goetz froze. Ambrosius chuckled. 'Oh yes, I took note of that. I know an assassination when I see one you might say, Sir Knight,' he said, tapping his patch. Ogg sniggered and rubbed his trident.

'We both do,' the Grand Master said, still chuckling.

'Who killed him?' Goetz said quietly.

'You'd know better than us. I'm given to understand you almost caught him,' Ambrosius said, scratching at his socket again. The gesture made Goetz's skin crawl.

'Almost being the operative word. I never saw his face.'

'A shame.' Ambrosius sighed and leaned back. He looked at Ogg. 'That would have simplified things immensely.'

'Our lot is not a simple one, Lord Justicar,' Ogg said, his tone mocking. He looked at Goetz. 'Why did Berengar really send you?' he demanded.

'To re-establish contact with our brothers on Svunum,' Goetz said carefully. Something was going on here. He could almost taste it, like the charge in the air just before a lightning storm.

'And to investigate this murder?'

Goetz said nothing. Ogg snorted and jabbed the air with his trident. 'I knew it! He's too damn clever by half!' He looked at Goetz and smiled a shark's smile. 'I know bait when I smell it. How many of you blazing bastards are in the city? Is it Knock you're reporting to? I never trusted him! Abbot my soggy-'

'As you can see, paranoia is a disease and my friend has caught it,' Ambrosius interjected. 'I doubt Dietrich here would have even allowed you off the boat. If your Grand Master hadn't offered to sell your Marienburg Komturie to us-'

'What?' Goetz said, slightly appalled. Berengar hadn't mentioned that.

'Oh, you didn't know?' Ambrosius said. 'Our esteemed paladins share the temple of Manann with the priests. We would, however, like to expand their holdings, you might say. And since your people all left and have yet to return... well.' He shrugged. 'You could see how it was an arrangement that interested us.'

'Yes,' Goetz said. He frowned, puzzled. 'Us?'

'Well... me,' Ambrosius said, smiling broadly. 'Do you know what I was before I was Lord Justicar?' He chuckled. 'A mercenary. And before that, I was a member of the most esteemed Order of the Gryphon, in Altdorf.'

'They cashiered him,' Ogg said. 'Stripped him of his lands and titles,' he continued, taking an almost perverse pleasure in recounting Ambrosius's disgrace. Goetz was slightly taken aback.

'Why?' he said, before he could stop himself.

'A woman,' Ambrosius said off-handedly.

'A man,' Ogg corrected. 'Specifically, a nephew. The Grand Master's nephew. I know, because we were picking the bodies of Altdorf swords-for-hire out of the canals for weeks after you arrived. That alone would have garnered you a commission, mind...'

'And my point was that we must not be beholden to foreign bodies or past ties,' Ambrosius said firmly. 'The Order of the Blazing Sun bears no loyalty to Marienburg. Grand Master Ogg happens to agree with me. He also agrees that Svunum can – and should – belong to the Order of Manann.'

Goetz forced himself to relax. 'Why are you telling me this?'

'I merely want you to understand your position,' Ambrosius said. 'Like as not Berengar sent you here as bait to draw out an assassin. An assassin he thinks has some connection to your Order, if I judge his mind right, the crooked devil. Or at the very least, a grudge.'

'And if so?' Goetz said, keeping his face neutral.

'And so we'd like you to succeed, thank you very much,' Ogg snapped. 'The quicker we find out who killed your man, the quicker you can get to the important bit – getting that lot of brass-plated squatters off my island!'

'I am merely to re-establish contact,' Goetz said. 'You'll have to take the rest of it up with the Grand Master.'

'Oh we will,' Ambrosius said. The gondola bumped against a mooring post. 'You, however, must be sure not to die in the meantime. I have no doubts that Berengar would lead your Order to war in our streets if he thought it was necessary. And two knights dead might convince him of that necessity. Then what, eh? Our streets full of bronze-armoured crusaders, which is the exact opposite of what we want. We're here, by the by.'

Goetz turned and saw that the ride had taken them back to the temple district. Watchmen patrolled the streets and there was no sign of the mob from before, nor of the flagellant who had roused them to action. 'Was this little talk just to warn me to be careful?' Goetz said, stepping onto the jetty.

'In a way,' Ambrosius said. 'More, I wanted to see what kind of man Berengar had sent.'

'And?'

'You certainly are a man of some type or other. I haven't decided which type yet,' the Lord Justicar said, gesturing to his men. The gondola drifted away from the jetty. 'I'm glad we had this talk.'

Goetz watched them go, hoping the puzzlement he felt wasn't showing on his face. There was more to things than what the Grand Master had told him, it seemed. He was no stranger to schemes, political or otherwise, but he felt as if he had wandered into someone else's story. Shaking his head, he moved towards the temple and stepped through the doors.

A moment later a gong sounded as the great brass-bound doors closed behind him. Strange Southern spices burned in the braziers that lined the entryway, eradicating the stink of the city beyond and putting Goetz in mind of somewhere warmer. Ceremonial bronze-tipped spear-butts thudded into the stone floor with rhythmic force.

Goetz did not look at either of the ceremonial guards, clad in their archaic armour and crimson robes. Over the robes they wore burnished breastplates with sculpted gleaming muscles. The full-face helmets they wore were engraved with prayers to Myrmidia, and crimson-dyed horsehair crests added inches to their height. 'Who comes?' one said.

'A seeker,' Goetz replied, looking straight ahead, his helmet beneath his arm, his palm resting on the pommel of his sword.

'What do you seek?' the second guard said.

'The path forward,' Goetz intoned, bowing his head.

'A seeker comes! Illuminate his path!' the first guard cried, slapping his spear blade against the long oval shield decorating his other arm. As the echoes of metal on metal faded, the ornate lanterns lining the walls flared to life, one after the other. Goetz blinked, trying to clear the sudden burst of light from his eyes.

'Impressive,' he said.

'I'm glad you think so. It was for your benefit,' a man said, shuffling down the corridor to meet him. He was broad shouldered and, Goetz suspected, bow-legged beneath his rough, homespun robes. 'We get so few official visitors that we felt a proper display was called for,' he went on, throwing back his hood to reveal a narrow face. 'You're late, by the way. I am Abbot Knock. Be welcome and may enlightenment be yours,' the man said, bowing his tonsured head. When he looked up, he was grinning. 'Now that that bit of business is out of the way... how is my old friend Berengar?'

'You know the Grand Master?' Goetz said, slightly taken aback.

'Of course! A man should know his cousin, even if he is an Imperial lickspittle.' Knock smiled, as if to show it had been a joke. Goetz blinked, suddenly aware of the resemblance between the two men. 'I trust he's well?' Knock went on as Goetz fell in step with him and they started down the corridor.

'I'm not privy to his thoughts, but he seemed healthy enough,' Goetz said hesitantly.

'For an old man, you mean?' Knock said, chuckling. 'Don't fool yourself, Sir Knight. Berengar will outlive us both, I have no doubt.' He looked at Goetz. 'You are... Goetz, yes?'

'Hector Goetz, Master Abbot,' Goetz said.

'Solland name that. 'Gohtz' or 'Steadfast' in the old tongue of the Merogen. Old name. There was a Gohtz at Hergig, you know, when Gorthor the Beastlord of foul memory tried to sack Hochland. He was a Myrmidon – one of the twelve retainers of the Electoral household. He was a knight of the Order as well.'

'Yes,' Goetz said. 'He died, as I recall.'

'All men die. You're a bit young to be a knight, I should think.' Knock smiled before Goetz could reply. 'No matter. All men look young to me.' Goetz made to protest, but Knock shushed him. 'Never mind boy. We have other things to discuss.' He looked Goetz up and down, his eyes lingering on the symbol of the Order engraved on his cuirass. 'Namely, the death of one of our brothers.'

'Athalhold,' Goetz said.

'Yes. He was to meet with me. Instead I had to go and claim his body from the brethren at the temple of Morr.'

'You almost had to do the same for me,' Goetz said.

'What?' Knock's eyes widened.

'I was attacked not far from here.' Goetz slapped his sword. 'I almost got the same surprise Athalhold did, in fact.'

Knock hesitated. 'Did you see him? Catch him?'

'Almost.' It was Goetz's turn to hesitate. 'I wasn't fast enough.'

'Hmph.' Knock led him through the temple. Its influences were plain, mimicking the circular temples of Tilea and Estalia. Smooth columns held up the roof, and the floor was tiled with oven-hardened ceramic that Goetz feared would crack with every step he took.

'I'm not even certain it was the same attacker,' Goetz said hesitantly.

'How could you be? No, the crossbow is a common enough killer's tool in Marienburg.' Knock gestured sharply. 'Still, while I have faith in many things, coincidence is not one of them.'

'The Lord Justicar seems to share your suspicions.'

'Ambrosius?' Knock said, pausing and looking at Goetz. 'You've met him?'

'Just now,' Goetz said. 'He learned of my attack and wanted to speak to me.'

'I'll bet he did. As cunning a snake as ever slithered, that one,' Knock said, running his fingers over his pate thoughtfully. 'If he's involved, there's definitely more to things than I first suspected.' He looked at Goetz. 'And more to Athalhold's death than misadventure.'

'But why would someone try to kill me? Or any knight of our Order?'

'I don't know. We could always try asking Her,' Knock said, leading Goetz into the rotunda. Goetz stopped short, his breath catching in his throat.

The statue of Myrmidia rose up through the centre of the temple, bathed in a shaft of sunlight descending from the open roof. It was small, as such statues went, but then, so was the temple, and the statue loomed in the limited space available. Goetz examined her with a boldness born of familiarity. Clad in ancient armour, one hand on a spear, the other on a shield, she was both beautiful and terrible in the way that all goddesses were. Mounted on a winged horse, she was the personification of victory.

Yet there was something else to her; something inexplicable. She looked down on Goetz with marble eyes, her expression as blank as the stone she was carved from. Briefly, he was reminded of the face that had stared down at him from the night sky in his dream and then, with a twinge of foreboding, the pale shape he'd seen on the river. Could that have been her? Was Myrmidia watching over him, even in his nightmares?

'She is beautiful, isn't She,' Knock said softly.

Goetz tore his eyes from the statue. 'All goddesses are.'

'But She is different,' Knock said, spreading his hands. 'She is ours, and we are Hers and thus Her beauty affects us in ways we cannot fathom.'

'You make Her sound like a lover,' Goetz protested.

'Not quite that poetic, perhaps.' Knock shrugged. 'Then again, maybe so. Who can say?'

Uncomfortable, Goetz turned away from the statue. 'You have a room prepared for me, I believe?'

'That we do,' Knock said. 'I'll show you to it.'

'An abbot showing around a simple knight?' Goetz said. 'People will talk.'

'This is Marienburg, lad. People are always talking. Incessantly, as a matter of fact. Can't get them to shut up. Besides, you're the first of your Order we've played host to in many a year.'

'What of the brethren of the Marienburg Komturie?' Goetz asked. 'Surely you had some contact with them? Before they left, I mean.'

'Not enough,' Knock said. He sighed. 'They were a small group, and cliquish. And when they left...' He paused.

'Yes?' Goetz encouraged.

'When they left, we were the last to know,' Knock said plainly. 'Otherwise, I would have organised the brethren here for war. We might be priests, but we are quite capable of fighting. Indeed, I fear most of the younger initiates look forward to it.' Knock peered at Goetz as they moved out of the rotunda. 'You seem as if you've seen your share of it yourself.'

'More than I cared to,' Goetz said, idly knuckling the small of his back.

'Sensible,' Knock said, clasping his hands behind his back. 'Never look for a fight, lad. Inevitably, one will come to you.' Knock shook his head. 'More is the pity.'

'The Grand Master has a different take on the matter,' Goetz said diffidently. Knock snorted.

'Of course he does! That's why he is who he is and why I am who I am.' He smiled again. 'Still, there is room enough for both of us, here beneath the sun.' He gestured upwards to the ceiling. Goetz glanced up, noting for the first time how a series of suns had been carved into the stone there.

Goetz traced the sun on his cuirass and nodded. 'Would that its light had protected Athalhold as well.'

The crow circled the temple roof, careful not to draw too close. There were only a few weak points in the spiritual armour of the place, and it would not do to land elsewhere. It had followed its prey through the twisty canal-streets of Marienburg throughout the day, watching him as he went looking for answers.

The crow knew all about answers; and questions and rhymes and schemes and other things. It knew more than a crow ought, because it was not alone in its skull. Another looked through its eyes and that other grunted impatiently as she inhaled the deep gasses of the island. Myrma squatted over the natural vent and let the gasses inundate her sinuses. She was nude, save for the crude tattoos which curled across her pale flesh like a lover's caresses.

'Well?' Balk demanded. He stood out of reach of the gasses, holding the edge of his cloak up over his nose.

'He's in the city,' she said hoarsely.

'The assassins–'

'Failed,' she said curtly. 'He is faster than the other. Younger. More alert.'

'Then use more men! Use your magic! I want him dead! If Berengar figures out what we're up to...' He trailed off and frowned. 'If it were up to the Grand Master, this island – everything we have built – would be forgotten like so much refuse. I cannot allow that to happen. I won't!'

It was less a justification than a rationalisation. In his own mind, Balk saw the knight's presence for what it almost certainly was. The Grand Master was no fool. He had allowed Greisen to build up the island's strength, but only so he could sell it to the damn merchant-princes! Fury filled Balk and the haft of his axe creaked as his grip tightened.

Myrma's eyes flickered to the axe. It was an old weapon, crafted for a chieftain of her acquaintance, back long ago before they'd been driven from their ancestral lands by the upstart Sigmar. Before he'd welded the Svanii to his own Unberogen, and scattered to the wilderness any who opposed him. The axe had not served its owner well then, when Sigmar's hammer had fallen on his skull.

Balk knew nothing of this, of course. For him, it was merely a weapon – a gift given by a grateful, if primitive people. In truth, it was one more link in a chain binding him to her Mistress's designs. Funnily enough, or perhaps not, it was his own ancestor who had first wielded that axe. One of the first chieftains of old Sudenland, or Solland, as it became known.

'Kill him,' Balk said again. 'But I want no connection to us!'

'As you wish,' the priestess said, smiling slyly. 'As you wish.' She let her mind strike out again, and she touched the brain of the thing shaped like a crow, angling it towards the sill of one cell window in particular. Its talons itched as it landed, and it eyed the scene within with avian derision. The man was a tool – a pawn, not even of the level of Balk or the others. But useful nonetheless.

There were many such in the city – tools tailor-made for Old Father Fate. Men who schemed and plotted and worshipped the Nine Unfolding Paths, venerating the Great Mutator even as they were cast aside when their usefulness dimmed. This one was not one of them, but much like them in many ways. A true believer, with a fanatic's determination.

'He is here!' Brother Oleg, initiate of the Myrmidian temple, hissed as he crouched before the shrine to the goddess that adorned one corner of his cell. 'Here! In this temple!' He paused, head cocked as if listening. 'No, I – they failed.' Then, a moment later, 'I failed.' He cast a guilty glance at the crossbow he had hastily shoved beneath his cot upon returning. He had not expected him to be so fast. The other one hadn't been that fast, had he?

He wrung his hands together until they knotted painfully. The ivory-faced statuette stared blankly at him. He'd hoped the men he'd hired would do the deed, but, just as in the case of the other, they had failed. What had he been thinking? Mere mercenaries, hardened or not, against a knight of the Order? Madness.

No. Optimism. A hope he would not have to sully his own hands with the blood of a holy brother. 'Why,' he said plaintively, half-stretching his hand towards the statue. 'Why must it be this way? This cannot be right. It cannot–'

Pain flared in his arm and he snatched his hand back, cradling it to his chest. Hissing in agony, he glared at the claw-like brand on the inside of his wrist. The mark of loyalty burned as badly as it had the day he had received it. As badly as the day the others had left the city for Svunum.

A croak startled him and he whipped around. Perched on the sill of the slender window of his cell, the crow cocked its pointed skull and fixed him with a dark gaze. A feeling of contentment flooded through him, causing the pain to fade. The crow squawked again. The Estalians said that Myrmidia might wage war with eagles, but that she spoke through crows, the cleverest of the clever birds. And more readily found on battlefields, a voice whispered in his head. He shook it aside. 'I understand,' Oleg breathed. 'But... here?'

The crow fluttered past him and perched on the statuette. It dipped its head, and Oleg stood, his hands clenching and unclenching nervously. 'Yes. Yes, I'll do it, if it can be done. And then? Then will you–'

But the bird took off before he could finish, leaving the same way it had entered. Leaving Oleg alone again. While it was terrifying to be in its – her – presence, it was somehow more frightening in her absence. Fear was a new thing for Oleg. He had had no fear of anything as a young man, but now that he was older, it gnawed at him. Fear of dying, fear of being found out by that treacherous abbot. His fingers curled, making fists.

Knock was of a kind with that fool, Berengar. That was what she had said. They were men who mouthed the Duties and paid lip-service to the goddess, but who were, in truth, merely politicians; pigs scrambling for temporal scraps.

He looked down at the mark on his wrist again. It was shaped vaguely like a feather. Like the feathers of her messengers. He stroked the brand and prepared his mind for what was to come.

There were those he could contact. Men of faith, though it was a darker faith than his own. The goddess had many weapons, and some were more horrid than others. He shuddered again. 'Goddess forgive me. We do what must be done.'

◄ NINE ►

Night fell on Marienburg, and though he was tried, Goetz found himself for once unable to sleep. The air smelt of foreign spices and rotten fish as the moon rose. It was a heady scent, and Goetz found it annoyingly pervasive. It had taken up residence in his clothes and in his hair and didn't look to be leaving anytime soon. His joints ached with the exertions of the day, and his head was full of questions. He lay on the rough cot that had been provided for him, and tried to puzzle it all out – his meeting with the Lord Justicar, the assassins, all of it.

Sweat rolled across the smooth planes of his face and neck, carving a trail down beneath the sackcloth shirt he wore. It was humid in the little cell, thanks to the marshes Marienburg sat on, and the only relief was from the sea breeze issuing through the window. He pressed his forearms to the stone and bowed his head, closing his eyes as he listened to the sounds of the city beyond.

The marks on his neck and face where the bird had attacked him were healing already though they ached almost as badly as the scars on his back. He'd learned that it wasn't unusual for the crows to do so, though he had to wonder about the timing. Something was going on, that much was obvious. Goetz was neither a witch hunter nor a spy, but he could smell a conspiracy easily enough. The question was how big was it? And what was its purpose?

Thinking dark thoughts, he went to the basin in the corner, where he splashed water on his face and chest. Water dripping down his face, he looked around. The cell was barren save for a lithograph of Myrmidia, which gazed down on him from over the basin. 'I don't suppose you'd like to illuminate me?' he said. The picture didn't answer. He didn't know whether to be grateful or not. As Goetz scraped his skin dry with his wadded-up shirt, someone knocked on the door.

'Enter,' he said, sliding into his shirt. The heavy wooden door of the cell swung inwards and admitted a young novice. Pale and stocky like most Marienburgers, the young man glanced curiously at the sword and armour in the corner before meeting Goetz's inquiring gaze.

'You asked to be woken after the final bell, brother-knight.'

'Yes, thank you, Brother Jerome,' Goetz said. Without waiting for a reply, he began to dress. The young man watched him for a while, eyeing Goetz's sword with something that might have been envy. Goetz ignored him until he slipped out. The brothers of the Myrmidian temple meant well, he was sure, but they grated on his nerves. There was nothing worse than a building full of would-be warriors with no real war to fight.

There were battles aplenty within the confusing jangle of Marienburg's almost organic streets, of course. Every minor princeling with a grudge was on the warpath six months out of a given year, looking to increase his portfolio or his influence. That discounted the so-called blood claimants to the long-vacant Barony of Westerland. Every two or three years, some minor cousin of the third sister's descendant would find foreign backing and take to the streets, looking to seat his thin-blooded rear on the throne.

In the end, it never amounted to anything. Regardless, the Myrmidians, as servants of the war-goddess, went to battle eagerly. As much so as the priests of Ulric, at any rate. But it was unsatisfying on a spiritual level to kill the same people over and over again. Half the younger novices prayed daily for another invasion from the north, and one that would reach their walls.

It all smacked of asking for trouble, from Goetz's perspective. Not a very knightly thing to think, but then, Goetz had never really wanted to be a knight. Architecture had been his passion as a boy. The shaping of stone and wood into something greater than either. He looked around the room again, noting the obvious dwarfish influence to the curve of the ceiling, and sighed. Nowadays, his studies tended more towards the construction of trebuchet and fortifications than simple habitation or decoration. Architecture was so much simpler than people. Stone held few secrets, plotted no schemes.

'I wanted to build bridges,' he said softly, meeting Myrmidia's gaze. 'But you wouldn't understand that, would you?' He scooped up his sword and drew it a few inches from its utilitarian sheath, examining the twin-tailed comet that had been stamped on the base of the blade just before he'd left Talabheim the first time. The sword had seen him through a number of battles. Steel never let down flesh. Invariably, it was the other way around. Slamming the sword back into its sheath, he buckled the belt around his waist and snatched up his helmet.

A few minutes later, after a last, long genuflection to the lithograph, Goetz made his way through the halls of the temple. Robed priests passed him, murmuring softly among themselves. They nodded to him, more out of respect to the sigils displayed prominently on his breastplate than any familiarity.

The rotunda of the temple of Myrmidia was a quiet place. Old weapons and battered, now useless, suits of armour decorated the curved walls. The latter rested in specially prepared niches, were they were cared for by the lay brothers who scoured them and anointed them in oils. The weapons and arms belonged to men who had died for civilisation in all its forms, martyrs to progress. Martyrs to the cause of order.

It gave Goetz a chill to see those cracked and empty shells with their deep brown stains and gaping rents. Not all belonged to men of the Order, some simply to adherents of the faith. There a Tilean hauberk, there an Estalian bowl helmet, and there, a mangled gauntlet, boiled in the gut acids of some breed of troll. Goetz touched his own breastplate, with its delicately engraved sun in the centre, and wondered whether or not it would ever decorate a niche like these.

His eyes were drawn to a dented helmet, its feathered crest shaved to a few pitiful quills that dipped depressingly. The date on the niche marked it as having belonged to a knight who'd fallen in battle with the Westerland pirates. In the Pirate Wars, when the merchant fleets of Marienburg had sought to eliminate the pestiferous enclaves that had, at that time, dotted the coasts of what had been Westerland and Nordland like rat-nests, the knights of the Order had supported them, sending armsmen and brother-knights alike.

Despite being mostly waged at sea, there had been land battles as well, as the Marienburgers had sought to take the pirate-towns that clustered in the marshes and wastes from their owners and put them to the torch. The Knights of the Blazing Sun had been at the forefront, there, as the only knightly order of the Empire to become involved in what was considered at the time to be the ever-independent city-state's problem and no one else's.

Standing in the temple proper, eyes closed, Goetz could almost hear the howls of the pirates as the knights thundered forwards on horseback, and the ground seemed to tremble beneath his feet. It must have seemed that the End Times had come for those doomed, sinful wretches. They had only their scurrilous captains to look to for command. But the knights had the goddess.

Goetz knelt at the feet of the statue, his sword flat across his knees. He had waited until the temple was empty to make his prayers, wanting the privacy. Eyes closed, he tried to clear his mind. Hands clasped about the blade, he brought the crosspiece to his lips and whispered a short prayer. Myrmidia, as ever, didn't bother to answer. Likely she had more important things to do. He sighed and stood.

'It is an honour to have you here, you know.'

Goetz turned. The priest was clothed as simply as the rest of his brethren, but his broad shoulders and scarred hands spoke of another life, one outside of the confines of the temple. 'It is rare that one of the men who brought her to us sets foot within these walls these days,' the priest continued.

'I had heard that they all left some time ago,' Goetz said. 'Gone to Svunum, I'm told, Brother...?'

'Oleg. Yes. Like others I could mention,' the priest said. He frowned.

'She is more than just a war-goddess, you know,' he said, gesturing to the statue. 'She is also the Patroness of Civilisation. That was what the Tileans call her. The Queen of Muses and the Mother of Invention.'

'Yes,' Goetz said, looking at the statue again. Why did the priest's name sound familiar? Where had he heard it before? Before he could puzzle it out, the shadows drifting across the marble face of Myrmidia seemed to alter it, and Goetz looked away, uncomfortable with the illusory expression he had seen there. 'Unfortunately, we of the Order are more often called upon for duties of war, rather than peace.'

'Both bring about the same thing, do they not, brother?' Oleg said, looking at Goetz intently. 'Order.' He made a fist. 'The goddess brings order.'

'I just wish that it didn't have to come at the point of a sword,' Goetz said, patting the hilt of his own. 'Still, if wishes were horses, every man would be a knight, eh brother?'

Oleg turned back to the statue of the goddess. 'Yes. I wanted to be one myself.'

'But?'

'A distinct lack of noble blood, I'm afraid,' Oleg said, smiling sadly.

Goetz shifted uncomfortably. 'I'm sorry.'

'It's hardly your fault, Sir Knight. More that of my parents, I should think.' Oleg chuckled.

'There are orders that do not require noble birth, brother,' Goetz said gently. Oleg snorted.

'Yes. But none who serve our goddess, eh?' He scratched at his wrist and gazed adoringly at the statue. 'She speaks to me, you know.'

'She speaks to all of us.'

'No!' Oleg said, his voice suddenly filled with heat. 'Not like me!'

'Brother–' Goetz blinked as realisation set in. Oleg! He recalled then why that name sounded familiar. But it couldn't be, could it?

'I'm sorry, Sir Knight. But it is the Second Duty... we do what must be done!' Oleg cried, drawing a knife from within his robe. Before Goetz could draw his sword, Oleg hurled himself upon him and they crashed to the floor, struggling.

'I didn't want to kill him!' Oleg hissed, straining to plunge the dagger into Goetz's throat. 'But she commanded it! And she must be obeyed!'

'Who?' Goetz snarled.

'Her! Myrmidia must be obeyed!' Oleg howled. Goetz drove a fist into the man's jaw, sending him sprawling. Even as he got to his feet, a shout set him spinning. Men clad in iridescent robes and brass, bird-shaped masks, lunged out of the darkness. Nine of them in all, they seemed to dance towards him with disturbing eagerness. He met the first one, his heavy blade sweeping aside the man's rapier and crashing through his screeching mask.

A sabre slashed across his arm, freeing mail links. Goetz backhanded the wielder, sending him flying and desperately parried a jabbing trident. 'Myrmidia!' he roared, hoping to wake the temple. 'Myrmidia!' He stamped on the trident and, as it dipped, cracked an elbow into its bearer's head, knocking him to the side. Goetz chopped down on the man's exposed neck, separating his head from his shoulders.

The sabre scraped against his cuirass and Goetz caught the blade with his arm, forcing it flat against his side. Turning, he ripped it from the man's hands and hacked at him, carving a canyon through his sternum. Shoving the twitching body away with his boot, he turned, countering another blow. The remaining six attackers swooped towards him en masse like a flock of birds, and they uttered weird, shrill cries as they came. Goetz fell back until he found himself pressed against Myrmidia's shield. 'Myrmidia!' he shouted again.

'Manann!' came a response and one of the remaining assassins slumped as a trident punctured his heart. Dietrich Ogg yanked his deadly prosthesis free and grinned savagely. 'Hello again, boy,' he said. Behind him, Aloysious Ambrosius parried a sword thrust and spitted his opponent with a thrust of his own, and the men of the Marsh-Watch moved forward with tridents ready. Somewhere above, an alarm bell was ringing, and the Myrmidians were spilling into the rotunda, clutching their weapons. Abbot Knock led them, a broad-bladed axe clutched in his hands.

'What in Myrmidia's name is going on here?' he roared.

'Ask Brother Oleg,' Goetz snarled. 'Where is he?'

'Brother–?' Knock paled. He turned one of the other priests. 'Find Oleg! And someone check on the seneschals!'

'Too late for them, I'm afraid,' Ambrosius said, cleaning his sword on a dead assassin's robe. 'These killed them as they entered. I am sorry, abbot,' he continued, nodding politely to Knock.

'How did you two come to be here?' Goetz said, glaring at them.

'We followed these, as a matter of fact,' Ogg said. He gestured with his trident. 'A thank you wouldn't be out of order.'

'My thanks, Grand Master,' Goetz said, after a moment. He shook his head and tried to catch his breath. 'I meant no disrespect.'

'None taken,' Ogg grunted. 'Sons of the Crow,' he said, kicking a body.

'What?' Goetz said.

'That's who they are,' Ambrosius said, sinking to his haunches and yanking a sleeve back from a limp arm. A feather-shaped brand stood out against the pale flesh. 'The Sons of the Crow. Or the Feathered Children, as they're called in Altdorf.' He stood and scratched at his eye-patch. 'They're worshippers of the Ruinous Powers. Cultists.'

'And why are they in my temple?' Knock said, staring at the bodies.

'One of your men opened the doors,' Ogg said bluntly.

'Oleg,' Goetz said, rubbing his back. He felt slightly sick as he contemplated it. 'Oleg let them in. He said that he was doing what had to be done.'

'Killing you,' Knock said slowly.

'Killing Athalhold as well,' Goetz said. 'He admitted it, as he was trying to do the same to me.' He looked up at the statue and tried to discern some sense from the pristine features that gazed blindly down at him. 'He said Myrmidia had commanded him.'

'There are cultists everywhere. At every level of our society,' Ambrosius continued. 'I'm satisfied that these were responsible for the death of your brother, and the attempts on you.'

'Because it's expedient to do so,' Goetz said dully. He looked at Ambrosius. 'You allowed them to enter. You want this whole affair swept away.'

'Yes,' Ambrosius said, meeting his gaze. 'We'll continue to look for this... Oleg, but like as not he was a secret cultist. I know these ones, they like schemes and deceits. Their plot was likely a simple one; get the Order at our throat and watch the fun.'

'You don't believe that for a moment, do you?' Goetz said.

'No. No, I think they were just as much pawns as the men you killed in that cul-de-sac, sacrificed to hide another move in someone's game.' He tapped his eye-patch. 'Regardless of the reason, it doesn't take two eyes to see that someone doesn't want you getting to Svunum.'

'Which is why it's in our best interests to see that you do,' Ogg put in. 'Beyond the obvious reasons of course.'

Goetz leaned back against the statue, a number of things falling into place. 'Athalhold... he wasn't sent to investigate anything. He was sent to deliver the order to abandon Svunum,' he said slowly. 'You think that's why he was killed.'

Ambrosius tapped the side of his nose. 'Berengar was right. You are a thinker.'

'He wanted the assassin almost as badly as we do. Killing knights can't be allowed. It gives the common man ideas,' Ogg said, jabbing at Goetz with his trident.

'Be fair. They already have ideas. But it shows them it can be done.' Ambrosius knocked his knuckles against his hip. 'Athalhold – was that his name? – was here to make your brethren leave. Only someone killed him before he got to do that. Initially, we suspected a private concern was the cause, but recent – ah – incidents...'

'Chaos,' Ogg said gruffly, rubbing his trident again. 'The fen-beasts are getting riled up. And we've got trouble in the walls as well. Strange things have been seen... not to mention these scum, painting the walls with corpse-daub and stealing beggars for midnight rites.'

'The Norscans are quiet,' Ambrosius said. 'And that's never good. Something is building, out there beyond the horizon. Interesting that it should do so now, eh?' he said, fixing Goetz with his good eye. 'Since the last sea-herd of Norscans bent on pillage crashed into our harbours, every member of your Order here has been penned up on that hunk of rock. We see their ships at a distance. Merchants trade with them. But they have abandoned the city... and perhaps more.'

'More?'

'Gunpowder. Iron. Stone. Wood. The makings of an army, a fleet. Any number of things.' Ambrosius ticked his fingers as he spoke. 'What are they building out there? Out of our waters, but close enough to – what?' He looked hard at Goetz. 'Some say it's an Imperial plot to re-take the city... a crusade for these uncertain times. We'd be quite the feather in Karl Franz's cap, eh?'

'We don't serve the Emperor,' Goetz said.

'Only when it suits you,' Ambrosius countered. 'Others say the knights are intent on invading Norsca. Laughable, but if they do, who shall bear the Northmen's rage when such an attempt inevitably fails? Marienburg.' He smiled sadly. 'I think it's somewhere inbetween those two, myself. I think that whoever is in charge out there has now decided to declare his independence from any law save his own. And I think your brother's death, and the attempts on you, is nothing but collateral damage in an attempt to ensure that no one found out about it before they – whoever they are – were ready.'

'You can't think that they had anything to do with Athalhold's murder!' Goetz said. 'Surely Oleg was acting alone, or on behalf of this cult!'

'They wouldn't be the first men to turn pirate,' Ogg said. 'Or the last.'

'They aren't men. They are knights. Servants of Myrmidia,' Goetz said flatly.

'So was Oleg,' Ambrosius said quietly. Goetz sank down. There was nothing to say. 'It's a moot point anyway,' the Lord Justicar went on. 'We'll be setting sail for Svunum soon. I've got agreement from the Council, as well as the Naval Guild and the fleet-lords.'

'You intend to take it by force,' Goetz said, his mouth suddenly very dry.

'We intend to evict your brethren by any means necessary.' Ambrosius scrubbed beneath his eye-patch. 'I'll give you a week, barring travel time, to convince them to leave peacefully. After that... well.' He shrugged apologetically. 'Hexensnacht. An inauspicious day, what with the connotations of witchcraft, but appropriate enough, I suppose if you read into such things.'

'This isn't right,' Goetz said, looking at his hands. He looked up at the ceiling, where the painted face of Myrmidia seemed to frown down at him. 'We won that island through sweat and blood.'

'And we'll take it the same way,' Ogg said firmly, scraping the tines of his trident across his breastplate.

'A week,' Ambrosius said. He nodded to Knock. 'Abbot. We'll see ourselves out. My men will remove the bodies to the temple of Morr so that these festering carcasses do not foul your temple any longer.'

Knock watched them go, his wrinkled hands curling into fists. Shaking his head, he turned back to Goetz. 'I hope Berengar knows what he's doing.'

'How can they do this?' Goetz said. He looked at the abbot. 'How can the Grand Master just give away something our brethren died for?'

'Because he is Grand Master, Hector. It is his prerogative. And in this case, a wise one.' Knock held up a hand to forestall Goetz's protest. 'We – you – are fighting a war, boy. Not a skirmish, or a battle, but a war. A war against forces which we cannot hope to defeat. But we can forestall them, until such time as they can, and will, be defeated. Berengar knows this. He knows that not every piece on the board is valuable, and that value changes based on the board and on the players. Svunum is a rock, but it is also a stepping stone. An anchor. Worth more than every man on it, and worth nothing at all. Do you see?'

'I–' Goetz began. 'No. No, I don't see it. I can't see the world that way.'

'We're playing dice with the gods themselves, boy,' Knock said, putting a hand on his shoulder. 'Pray we win this throw and all the ones that follow.'

TEN

Goetz looked up at the bearded face of Manann that glowered down at him from a spot over the archway to the immense double doors that led inside. The doors were open, indicating that the temple was open for business. The smell of fish was even stronger in the morning than it was in the evening, though the heat was less oppressive. Marienburg woke early and the clamour of the harbour rolled over this section of the city like a blanket.

He was tired, but hadn't been able to sleep. Oleg had not been found, and nothing in his cell had seemed out of place. Goetz fingered the amulet Knock had given him before he had departed. It was a simple thing, shaped like a spear-point and engraved with the Litany of Battle. No Plan Survives Contact With The Enemy. 'That's why he's called the enemy,' he said, finishing the Litany as he rubbed the ancient Tilean script. True enough, he supposed. His own plans seemed to have been co-opted by those belonging to others.

Why hadn't the Grand Master simply told him? Because he knew you'd protest. Maybe because Wiscard didn't know. Maybe no one knows except him... answers came quickly, though none seemed to fit the question perfectly. There could be many reasons that the Grand Master no longer wanted Svunum counted among the komturies of the Order; and just as many reasons for those there to want to keep it. But would they kill to do so? Kill a member of their own Order?

Consciously, Goetz knew that men killed for many reasons and if blood-relation didn't stay their hand, then why would shared allegiance? But it rankled nonetheless. 'If it's true,' he murmured, shaking the thoughts away. Perhaps Ambrosius's assertion was correct... perhaps the cult had undertaken the assassinations in order to sow confusion and chaos. Perhaps it was as simple as that. They could have waylaid messengers and stolen missives as well, especially if they had a man inside the temple of Myrmidia.

Maybe that was why Berengar wanted to dispense with the place. It was too much trouble, and too far from the Order's centre of power. It had outlived its usefulness, and the Brothers could better serve elsewhere. Still, to ask – no, to demand that they leave... Goetz sighed and clamped down on such thoughts. They served no purpose save to stall him from his duty.

Goetz stepped inside the temple, his boot heels loud on the polished pearl tiles that covered the floor. Fishing nets hung from the ceilings and he carefully brushed them aside as he made his way into the temple. Voices crashed over him like a wave as he stepped into the main rotunda. Tables carved from the bones of leviathans were scattered across the floor and, around each, men and women gathered, all talking at once. Some were merchants, others were seamen, and all were engaged in negotiations. Priests in sea-green robes threaded through the knots of argument, holding aloft smoking incense that smelt faintly of rotting seaweed.

'Brother Goetz?'

Goetz turned and looked into a face the colour of coral. A man's face, wrought from metal. A moment later a green-enamelled gauntlet raised the visor and a bearded face grinned at him. He was big and broad, with a broken nose and scars on his lips and cheeks. Also he was, fully-armoured from head to foot in the most intricately engraved suit of plate-mail that Goetz had ever seen. Goetz hesitated, then extended his hand and the man clasped his forearm.

'Erkhart Dubnitz,' the man said, still grinning. 'A humble sword-brother of the Order of Manann. I was asked to meet you and – ah – guide you through things.'

'Ogg,' Goetz said. 'He sent you to shepherd me?'

'The Grand Master is a – ah – a man who worries easily,' Dubnitz said. He pulled off his helmet, revealing a shorn scalp covered in scars.

'He's paranoid, you mean.'

'That too.' Dubnitz gestured to the crowd. 'Though, in fairness, it can be a bit confusing, if you're not used to it.'

'Yes,' Goetz said, looking around. 'You allow merchants in your temple?'

'Not my temple. His,' Dubnitz said, indicating the statue of Manann that loomed over the gathering. Manann crouched on scaly legs, balancing his weight on a trident.

'Impressive,' Goetz said.

'Not quite as nice to look at as your goddess, but we're partial to him, yes.' Dubnitz chuckled. Goetz bristled slightly, but forced a chuckle. 'This is your first time in our fair freistadt I understand?'

'Yes,' Goetz said. 'I was born in Talabheim, but this...'

'It's a cesspit, right enough,' Dubnitz said, nodding. 'But it's ours.'

'I didn't mean to imply–'

'Didn't say you did, didn't say you did!' Dubnitz swatted Goetz on the shoulder. 'Calm, brother. With a knight of Manann to guide you, you'll find your way safely to shore.'

'I place myself in your capable hands,' Goetz said, smiling despite himself.

'That's the spirit,' Dubnitz said. 'Now, I've made some preliminary introductions with a captain of my acquaintance – he's a Hochlander, but we shouldn't hold that against him.' He laughed and swatted Goetz again. For a brief, painful moment Goetz was reminded of Berlich. Dubnitz was a similar sort – loud and boisterous, with an easy manner. He led Goetz through the crowd, most of whom got out of the way quick enough. Dubnitz didn't appear to be one to slow his stride just because someone was in the way.

'I thought we might get a bite to eat first, however,' Dubnitz went on, clapping his hands to his belly. 'Bargaining on an empty stomach is the surest way to get the worst end of the deal.'

He led Goetz through the crowd, towards a long galley lined with tables groaning beneath the bounty of the seas. Great platters heaped with boiled seaweed and fish squeezed inbetween immense, intricately carved wooden bowls of chowder and stew. Goetz found his eyes drawn towards a roasting spit where a full-grown shark was rotated slowly by a priest in a sea-green robe.

'This is...' He trailed off, at a loss for words. Dubnitz nodded happily and began piling a plate high.

'Manann's bounty, brother. Eat and enjoy!'

'Is this all fresh?'

'Every day. Pickled cod?' Dubnitz said, extending the bobbing morsel to Goetz. When the latter shook his head, the big knight dropped the slimy chunk into his mouth and chewed with relish. 'I do so love pickled cod. Manann's gift to humanity.'

'Some might disagree with you there,' Goetz said, staring queasily at the other man's plate. 'Me among them.'

'Bah. You have the palate of a bumpkin,' Dubnitz said, slapping one paw on the closest table and causing it to tremble. 'A bumpkin!'

'I heard you the first time,' Goetz said. 'I prefer my food hoofed and horned rather than be-finned, is all.'

'Try some octopus. It's like a cow,' Dubnitz said, his mouth full.

'How exactly?'

'It has legs.' Dubnitz caught his look and shrugged. 'Fine. But if your growling belly interrupts our negotiations, don't blame me.'

'Your Order is a strange one, friend,' Goetz said as they moved to a table to sit. 'You open your temple to merchants, you put out a feast...'

'All in Manann's name,' Dubnitz said, plucking tiny fish bones out of his mouth. 'Besides, we have to fund our activities somehow.' He cast a mock baleful look at Goetz. 'It used to be that we hunted pirates.'

'Oh,' Goetz said, leaning back in his seat. 'Was our Order that effective then?'

'By all rights, Svunum should have been ours,' Dubnitz said, cracking open a crab shell. 'It's been a bone of contention for several generations now. Or so I'm told. I don't pay much attention to politics, I'm afraid,' he continued, unconvincingly.

'Really?'

'Fine. I do, but in this city it's a survival trait. Crab claw?'

'No thank you,' Goetz said, pushing the proffered claw away. 'And how did the men of my Order feel about that?'

'As far as I know, they barely acknowledged it. We're a small – if prosperous – order. The Merchant Council though, they had a few issues.' Dubnitz shook the crab claw. 'Imperial ties, they said. Spies for the Empire, they bellowed,' he said theatrically. 'Quietly, of course.'

'Of course,' Goetz said, leaning forward. 'Our Order bears no great loyalty to the Empire though.'

'No?' Dubnitz sucked the meat out of the claw and tossed the shell onto his plate. 'I suppose the Merchant Council didn't see it that way. And my Order certainly didn't.'

'Is that why they're planning to invade then?' Goetz said, fighting to keep the bitterness out of his voice.

'Ah. Yes, well,' Dubnitz looked embarrassed. 'That is a bit awkward. But that's why we're here, eh?' He gestured at the temple. 'To get you out there so that the awkwardness is limited to bad feelings as opposed to grievous bodily harm?'

'Yes,' Goetz said. Still frowning, he watched as an urchin in a frayed blue uniform scurried up to Dubnitz. The big man bent low and listened as the boy whispered into his ear. He stood and motioned for the boy to sit.

'Be a good lad and finish my plate for me.' He looked at Goetz. 'It looks like the Hochlander is here, brother. Would you care to speak to him?' The urchin stared at the heaped food in evident greed and Goetz chuckled.

'I suppose so. Lead on, brother.'

The Hochlander's name was Feldmeyer and he was waiting for them at a table covered in squid-like carvings. 'Captain Feldmeyer,' he snapped as Dubnitz introduced them. Feldmeyer was a screw-eyed man clad in naval motley, with scars on his face and hands. 'I didn't know I'd be playing host to one of his sort,' he continued, jerking a calloused thumb at Goetz.

'One of my sort?' Goetz said.

Feldmeyer held up a hand. 'No offence, Sir Knight.' He looked at Dubnitz. 'I have enough trouble with those on Svunum. I'm not taking one on my ship.'

'What sort of trouble?' Goetz said, leaning forward and thrusting his face towards Feldmeyer. 'Speak up man. What sort of trouble?'

Feldmeyer hesitated and then looked at Dubnitz who knocked his knuckles on the top of his helmet. 'Honesty is always the best policy, captain,' Dubnitz said.

'Trouble is all,' Feldmeyer said, sitting back with a frown.

'Is the Order's hospitality not to your liking?' Goetz said, trying for humour.

'Svunum isn't to my liking,' Feldmeyer said, yanking on his beard. 'Nothing that close to the Sea of Chaos ever did a man any good. You'd do well to remember that, Sir Knight.'

'Thank you for your concern, captain, but I'm quite certain I can handle myself,' Goetz said. 'I won't be staying long in any event.'

'You're young to be wearing that ribbon,' Feldmeyer said, gesturing to the ribbon of rank attached to Goetz's breastplate by a hardened seal of wax. The seal had been chipped in the fight in the cul-de-sac, but it still held firm.

'And you're old to be a boat captain,' Goetz said.

Feldmeyer blinked. 'It's a ship.'

'There's a difference?' Goetz said innocently. Dubnitz stifled a chuckle and Feldmeyer yanked on his beard again.

'Enough, Feldmeyer, you old pirate,' Dubnitz said, slapping a palm on the table. 'I named a price earlier. Is it still fair?'

'I suppose.' Feldmeyer made a face. 'But only because we're already going that way!' he said, making a sharp gesture. 'And I want Manann's blessings.'

'Do I look like a priest?' Dubnitz said, rising. He waved a hand at one of the green-robed men and summoned him over. Feldmeyer looked at Goetz.

'We catch the tide at sunrise, Sir Knight. If you're not there, we won't be coming back to get you,' he said.

'Have no fear, captain. I won't be late,' Goetz said.

'That's what I'm afraid of,' Feldmeyer mumbled. Goetz stood and joined Dubnitz, who stood waiting for him a little ways away.

'I want to thank you for going to the trouble...' Goetz began.

Dubnitz made a rude noise. 'It's not me, as I said. Besides, we sword-brothers need to stick together, aye?'

'Stand together or hang separately, you mean?' Goetz said, smiling crookedly. Dubnitz blinked, then gave a roar of laughter.

'Exactly! Exactly!' He caught Goetz a ringing slap on the back, nearly knocking him off his feet. 'Now, you have less than a day left in our foul little burg... what would you like to do?'

The urchin rattled his cup insistently, his blue uniform grimy and fading. Dalla grunted and waved him away sharply, pulling the edge of her hood lower over her face as she did so. She sat slumped against the wall of a dock-side tavern, watching the temple of Manann. It straddled the line between the more respectable bit of Marienburg's docklands and the rowdier areas.

Dalla made little distinction between either, finding it hard enough to process the fact that a city could be this size and still function. She was no awestruck babe, to be driven to fits of panic by the sheer number and size of the stone structures that surrounded her, but even now it was impressive. She shifted uncomfortably and pulled her already damp cloak tighter around her.

Her father had not wanted her to come, reasoning that it was too dangerous. Then, for him, life itself was too dangerous. Besides which, Dalla had her own duties to attend to... such as spying out the fattest vessels setting out across the Sea of Claws. The ones ripest for the plucking by her godi.

She spat. The godi was a vain, irritating man, but smart. Smarter than most godar, who, as a rule, seemed to think that diplomacy was what happened when you lost a battle. No, Eyri Goldfinger was smart. Cunning even, with the savvy of a salt-hardened sea wolf to temper his greed. He was greedy, no mistake there. He wanted everything the world had to offer. Even things that were manifestly not his to take.

Her grin surfaced like a shark's fin and swiftly vanished. She was the daughter of a gudja; Eyri would remember that now, and if he didn't, his missing fingers would certainly remind him. She spat to clear her mouth of the sudden taste of bile, and shifted her seat. Above her, a number of crows perched on a window, their croaking cries drifting down to her. She did not look up. Crows were the eyes of her father's enemy, even as her father used wolves and seals and, once, a fish.

Not all crows, true. But there were bound to be some here as everywhere. A particularly harsh caw caught her attention and she blinked, her vision momentarily dazzled by the sunlight glinting off polished metal.

'Einsark,' she hissed. One of them? Here? He was not clad head to toe in his gilded iron skin as the others had been, as the others always were, but he was one of them if the insignia he wore were any indication. Her hand clenched tight on the hilt of her sword and she forced herself to relax. No. Not here. Besides which, she still had a duty to perform.

But, perhaps she could kill two birds with one stone. She rose smoothly to her feet and started towards the wharf.

ELEVEN

'Not what I had in mind, exactly,' Dubnitz said, looking up at what had once been the Order of the Blazing Sun's Marienburg Komturie. Now, however, it was little more than a mausoleum, its treasures moved to the Myrmidian temple and its inhabitants gone to Svunum. Like most Myrmidian komturies, it was built circular, though not overly large, with sloping walls and a tiled roof quite unlike anything else in the Empire. Goetz knocked on the portcullis and turned.

'Don't feel that you have to accompany me,' he said. 'Besides, you'll get to see it soon enough, won't you?' Goetz said irritably.

Dubnitz snorted. 'Oh, but I do. It would look very bad indeed for two brothers of your Order to die under our noses, now wouldn't it?' Dubnitz said. He caught his helmet by the visor and struck it against the portcullis, setting it to ringing. 'A knight killed during an alley skirmish? Bad for all our reputations.'

'Worse for Athalhold, I think,' Goetz said, dropping to his haunches and removing his glove. He ran his fingers across the stones of the street, his eyes narrowed.

'Hnh. You're likely right about that, true enough. What are you doing?'

'Looking for the – ah!' Goetz stood as the portcullis gave a shriek to rival that of the sea gulls circling overhead and began to rise. Dubnitz gaped as the iron-banded doors swung in, admitting them. Goetz gestured. 'After you.'

'What the devil was that?'

'Progress. Also, a way of ensuring that we're never locked out of our own keeps.' Goetz followed Dubnitz inside. The courtyard wasn't large, though it seemed more expansive, empty as it was. 'Arabyan, I'm given to understand. A bit of artifice they learned from the dwarfs. The sluice-gates are Tilean, however,' he said, gesturing to the steel shutters that lined the interior walls of the keep.

'And those are for...?'

'Boiling oil. Naphtha. Dwarf-fire. I understand the komturies in the

595

Border Princes often let orcs into their central keeps and burn them alive as a matter of course. Best way to deal with the greenskins, really.'

'Your lot do enjoy their gewgaws, don't you?' Dubnitz said, not unkindly.

Goetz nodded. 'There's more to siegecraft than block and tackle.'

'Is that the one for throwing things or the one for hitting things?'

'Both,' Goetz said. 'We only use such things as the push-gate in cities, however. Only place the under-structure will support the pulley systems that–' He stopped as he saw Dubnitz's eyes begin to glaze over. 'Never mind.'

'It's –ah –it's not really honourable, is it?' Dubnitz said, swatting the sword on his hip. 'I mean, we burn out pirate nests readily enough, but to turn your own komturies into weapons...'

'The Second Duty,' Goetz said, shrugging. 'We do what must be done.'

'Myrmidia is a harsh one, no two ways there,' Dubnitz said, nodding to the statue that occupied a niche at the rear of the courtyard. Myrmidia at rest; her shield by her foot, her spear against her shoulder. Goetz looked at her and felt a moment of disconnect as his eyes met those of that inhumanly perfect marble face. He blinked and turned away.

'What?' he said.

'I said why did you want to come here?' Dubnitz said.

'To see what I could see,' Goetz said. 'The brothers left in a hurry. I want to know why they didn't come back.'

'And you think the answer is here?'

'No. But I wanted to get a sense of them,' Goetz said, looking at the other knight. 'A komturie is an extension of the brothers who inhabit it, by and large. It conforms to their methods and manner.'

'A house is a house is a house,' Dubnitz said.

'Not for us. Every hochmeister of the Order is expected to improve the defences and design of his komturie when he is made master. To make of it a monument to Myrmidia's influence. The latest works of literature and art and science. The latest engineering innovations.' Goetz turned in a circle. 'To let a house simply sit, silent and abandoned, is almost...'

'Heretical,' Dubnitz finished for him.

'Yes,' Goetz said. He shook his head. 'A funny word to use. Considering how often we're on the other end of it, I mean.'

'I had heard that the Grand Theogonist was on the warpath again about the 'proper conduct' of His Imperial Majesty's knightly orders.' Dubnitz snorted. 'Lucky thing we don't have to bother with the old stirpot.'

'Nor do we, in truth.' Goetz shrugged. 'If the Empire rescinds its hospitality, we'll simply move the Order elsewhere. Unlike the Reiksguard or the White Wolves, we are not tied to Imperial demesnes.' He sighed. 'Still, it'll be a black day when it comes to tha–'

The portcullis chose that moment to crash down with a roar of straining metal, causing them both to whirl in surprise. 'By Manann's scaly nethers!' Dubnitz bellowed as the echo faded. 'Did you–'

'No. And it certainly shouldn't have done it on its own.' Goetz drew his sword and looked around. 'Wait – hsst!'

'What?'

'Listen!'

Faintly, the sound of boot leather slapping against stone came to them. Goetz looked up at the walls, his eyes widening. 'Oh no.'

'What? What?' Dubnitz growled.

'The sluice-gates!' Goetz grabbed the other man's arm and shoved him towards the stairs. 'Up! We have to get up! Go!'

With a grinding of stone on metal, the steel shutters of the sluice gates began to swing open. A moment later, boiling pitch sprayed out of them in tight arcs. Goetz hissed as some splattered his legs and he shoved Dubnitz up the stairs, forcing him towards the second level of the keep.

'Why is there even still boiling pitch in there?' Dubnitz yelped as some splashed him.

'Dwarfen warming runes,' Goetz snapped. 'Work better than a cauldron any day!'

As they reached the top of the stairs, the streams of pitch abruptly shrank to a trickle and then tapered off completely. 'They must have run out,' Goetz said. 'There couldn't have been much in there to start with, not after all this time.'

The crossbow bolt skidded across the cheek-piece of his helmet and spun him around. He slammed back against the balustrade, dazed. Dubnitz spun, roaring. A second bolt caught the knight of Manann high in the shoulder, knocking him backwards. He clattered down the stairs with a sound akin to a crockery shelf going over. Goetz staggered upright, trying to spot their attacker. Across the expanse of the courtyard, a figure raced up the stairs to the next level.

'Dubnitz!' Goetz said. He looked back. The other man was on his back on the stairs, jerking at the crossbow bolt that stood at attention from the shoulder joint of his armour.

'I'm alive!' Dubnitz grunted. 'Barely a scratch! Get after him! I'm right behind you!'

Goetz darted after the assassin without further hesitation.

Oleg kicked the door to the bell tower closed and tried to catch his breath. He looked around, frowning. The bells, used to summon the knights to battle or prayer, had been silent since the brothers of the house had departed, and the engraved faces of Myrmidia glared at him from the dusty surface of each.

'It's not my fault,' he hissed, scratching at the puckered brand on his wrist. It burned like acid, and had since the previous evening when he'd failed to kill the knight. 'He's faster than the other one. Better,' he protested.

Something croaked. He swallowed and turned. The crow cocked its head and flapped its wings, its beak seemingly filled with a carnivore's teeth. But that wasn't right, was it? Birds didn't have teeth. Not normal birds at any rate.

'Myrmidia protect me,' Oleg murmured. The crow squawked and ugly black feathers rained down on him. They burned where they touched him and he shuddered away. 'I'm sorry! I'm sorry!' he said, backing away from the door and drawing his sword. He could hear the knight's boot heels thudding against the stone stairs.

The crow hopped across the bells, following him, its beady eyes watching him. He looked at the bird and said, 'What would you have me do? I can't defeat him. Once, maybe when I was younger, but not now... not here.' The crow croaked again, and the pain in his wrist intensified into something sublime.

He'd been left behind by the others when they'd gone. Left behind because he was too old, too weak to be of any help where they were going. Left behind to watch and wait and keep their trail hidden. He had done that, all of it and more. Now... now he would be rewarded for his faithful service.

'Oh. Oh yesss,' he grunted. He sank to his knees, his sword dropping from nerveless fingers. The crow flapped its wings and he crawled forward, opening his mouth. With a shudder of its feathers, the black bird thrust itself into the air and crossed the distance between them in an eye-blink. Then, in a moment of discomfort, it squeezed into Oleg's mouth and scrambled down his gullet. Oleg gagged and fell over, shuddering as the bird burrowed into him.

In moments, things moved beneath his skin, spreading outwards from the brand, growing and flaring. Bone quills pierced his flesh and he groaned. He raised his hands in supplication and tried to give thanks to the goddess for her blessing, but his skin had already pulled away from his jaws and the only sound he could make was a screech.

Goetz paused in the doorway to the bell tower, listening for the telltale sound of a crossbow's mechanism as the scream faded. He eased the door open with his sword. He'd fancied he'd heard voices, just before that plaintive howl, but who would be up here with the assassin? The door swung open with a creak. He smelt bird dung, and heard the raucous croak of a crow. Slight shapes darted among the rafters of the tower.

'Where are you? Oleg? Brother Oleg?' Goetz said, sidling around the bells. 'Why have you been trying to kill me?' There was no answer. In truth, he hadn't expected one. Goetz turned, sweeping the tower with his gaze. Nothing. Were could he have gone?

The answer occurred to him almost a half-second too late as a swordpoint drove into the wood of the tower floor and the crossbowman dropped from where he'd been crouching atop the bell mechanism. He ripped his sword free and launched a salvo of strokes at Goetz, who back-pedalled furiously.

They traded blows for a moment, moving back and forth across the floor. Then Goetz caught the weight of the man's blade on the crosspiece of his hilt and twisted, sending his opponent's weapon flying. Before the man could react, Goetz pinned him to a bell, setting it to ringing dully. The assassin gagged and clutched at the sword, pulling himself forward as his hood slipped from his face.

Goetz jerked back as a bony beak snapped shut inches from his face. A thicket of fangs jutted crookedly from the protuberance and the red eyes set on either side of the triangular head blazed with madness and agony. Irregular feathers poked through the stretched and wrinkled skin and the thing's hands were more like the talons of a bird. Its claws scraped his fingers and he released his sword with a cry of disgust.

'What are you?' Goetz said, stumbling back.

'Blessssed,' Oleg hissed, yanking his sword out of his sternum and tossing it aside with a clatter. Claws extended, it leapt for him and he thrust up an arm to protect himself. Goetz stumbled under its weight as its malformed jaws snapped shut around his vambrace, piercing the metal. He drove a blow into where a normal man would have had kidneys and it screeched, swiping at him. The claws scored his helmet and the force of the blow sent him reeling against the wall.

The creature hunched towards him, circling, its head cocked in a distinctly avian manner. Beak-jaws clacking, it sprang again. Goetz spun aside and the creature hurtled over the edge of the tower and out over the courtyard. It fell with a shriek.

Breathing heavily, Goetz peered over the edge. Clawed fingers fastened around his helmet and he was yanked unceremoniously off his feet. Goetz grabbed hold of the creature's wrist with both hands before it could release him and they hung suspended for a moment.

It held tight to the stonework of the tower with its free hand and taloned feet. The bird-like head darted down at Goetz, pecking at his hands as it hauled him closer. Whipping back and forth, Goetz snatched out at it and grabbed its lower jaw in desperation. Its teeth slammed together on his hand and he screamed.

Planting the soles of his boots against the tower, Goetz twisted his hips and strained every muscle he had, wrenching the bird-man from its perch and sending them both hurtling towards the courtyard below!

◄ TWELVE ►

As they fell, the creature squirmed closer, its snapping jaws aimed at his unprotected throat. Goetz grappled with it and tried to ignore the ground that was fast rushing up to meet them. Grabbing a handful of loose skin and feathers he yanked the creature forwards and crashed his head against its own, the metal of his helmet ringing hollowly as it met the monster's mutated bone. Then he shoved away from it, clawing desperately for any sort of purchase to arrest his fall.

His hand slapped into Dubnitz's waiting palm and the knight of Manann gave a roar. Before Goetz's full weight could settle, Dubnitz slung him up over the balustrade and against the wall of the second level in a massive display of strength.

The green-armoured knight sank to his hands and knees as Goetz fell flat, his face pressed to the cool stone, his shoulder and back numb from both impact and exertion. When Dubnitz looked up, his face was red and covered in a sheen of sweat. He made a sound like an exhausted horse and staggered to his feet. 'What in the name of Shallya's milky bosom do you call that?'

'Improvisational strategy,' Goetz groaned, sitting up. He tore off his glove and examined the hand the monster had bitten. Faint indentions beppled his palm, but the skin hadn't been broken. He breathed a silent prayer of thanks to whoever had sewn the chainmail inside his glove and then hauled himself up, using the wall for support.

'Not that,' Dubnitz grunted, rotating his shoulder experimentally. 'That,' he continued, hiking a thumb towards the courtyard. Goetz stepped to the edge and looked down. The creature looked like a broken doll discarded by a careless child. Its limbs were bent at odd angles, and it seemed deflated; emptied of all malice and ferocity.

'I don't know what that is,' he said, flexing his hand.

'It's a mutant, obviously. Some foul Chaos-thing.' Dubnitz tapped the broken-off crossbow bolt still protruding from his armour. 'Never knew one of them that could use a crossbow, however.'

'Or a sword,' Goetz said. He looked down at the body for a moment longer and then turned away. 'Speaking of swords, mine is still up there.'

Goetz led the way, ascending the stairs to the bell tower much more slowly than before. The door still hung open, but the crows were silent. Dubnitz stayed by the door as Goetz scooped up his sword. As he straightened, however, he thought he saw something. Something tall and foul, that glared at him from the shadows in the corner of the tower. Goetz froze, unable to move or speak as the form stepped towards him. Eyes like dying embers fixed on his own and something hissed inside his head.

A band of sunlight chose that moment to strike the dusty surface of the nearest bell as the latter shifted on its frame. A deep, bone rattling toll sounded, shaking Goetz from his paralysis. The face of Myrmidia, engraved on the bell, blocked out those horrible eyes and Goetz stepped back, his sword raised.

The bell swung back revealing the retreating form of a scraggly crow. It hopped to the edge of the tower and took flight without a backwards glance. Goetz watched it go, then started as Dubnitz touched his shoulder.

'Everything all right?'

'I – yes. Fine. Everything's fine,' Goetz said, sheathing his sword. 'Did you set the bells off?'

'I thought you did,' Dubnitz said, looking at the bells curiously.

Goetz didn't reply. The two men retreated back the way they had come, followed by the sounds of the bells, which gave voice to a mournful rhythm.

'Get those crates loaded!' Captain Feldmeyer of the merchant-ship Nicos bellowed. Feldmeyer was a thirty-year veteran seaman. Twelve of those years had been spent plying the coastlines of the Sea of Claws and his sun-darkened frame bore the scars to prove it.

The Sea had its secrets, and its dangers, resting as close as it did to the Sea of Chaos where the black arks sailed and worse things than kraken crawled in the deep. Feldmeyer had fought kraken before, and point-eared corsairs from Naggarond, and orcish reavers and Norscans gone raiding. His crew were a motley bunch, as diverse a lot as one could find on the Northern Seas. Tileans, Estalians, Arabyans and Bretonnians crowded the decks along with men from a variety of Imperial provinces, moving about the tasks associated with a ship setting sail. Like their captain, they were veterans.

His first mate stalked past, scarred palm resting on the handle of the club stuffed through his belt. Feldmeyer whistled and caught the man's attention. 'Has our passenger arrived yet?'

'I have, actually,' Goetz said, stepping up the gangplank, his armour in a bundle on his back. 'Permission to come aboard, captain?'

Feldmeyer nodded and made a curt gesture, waving the first mate off at the same time. 'You're late.'

'You said sunrise,' Goetz said. He squinted upwards. 'And the sun has yet to rise.'

'Metaphorical sunrise,' Feldmeyer grated.

'Ah.' Goetz set his bundle down and rested a hand on his sword. 'You don't seem happy to see me, captain. Is there some reason for that? Have I given offence somehow?'

'No. Not you,' Feldmeyer said. He spat over the side and turned away. Goetz took the opportunity to look around, noting that he himself was the recipient of any number of similar covert glances. It took him a moment to realise that they weren't looking at him so much as at his armour.

But while it was understandable that a member of one of the Empire's knightly orders might attract some small attention away from the Empire's borders, the looks he was getting were anything but curious. Rather, they were the look a man might give an adder he had just stumbled upon.

He shook his head and turned to watch as the green-robed priests from the temple of Manann began their rituals of blessing for the ship's journey. Dubnitz had explained that the Order of the Albatross, the ritual navigators of the temple, were paid a hefty sum to perform their rituals. The stink of sacred oils filled the air as urns containing ambergris and other concoctions were slopped across the deck and the sound of the deep rolling hymns of Manann, Stromfels and Mermedus filled the air.

The latter two brought a chill to Goetz's flesh, being songs of ill-omen and disaster. Holy statuary representing the three faces of the god, mounted on the three prongs of an overlarge trident. The priest who held it up was a muscular specimen, and wore a speckled breastplate emblazoned with an albatross in flight. As he paced the deck, stabbing the sea breeze with the trident, his fellows swabbed the deck with their holy oils, singing all the while.

Goetz stepped aside as oils spilled across the deck towards him and held his breath as the stink of fish paste and whale fat rolled over him. At the last, the burly priest thumped the deck with the butt of the trident three times and roared out, 'Manann! Bless this boat!'

'That's... an interesting blessing,' Goetz said tactfully.

Feldmeyer snorted. 'Manann is a god for little time with niceties.'

The priests tromped back down the gangplank a moment later and the ship set sail with the first breeze of morning. Goetz couldn't help feeling no small amount of relief. Two nights in Marienburg and he'd almost been murdered twice. Granted, the assassin was dead now, but he had a feeling that that wasn't the end of it. Ogg had demanded that he spend the night in the temple of Manann, and Abbot Knock had concurred. Oleg, or whatever – whoever – that creature had been had been disposed of by the servants of Morr, cremated in the cleansing flames of a marshland pyre, overseen by the Marsh-Watch.

'Hexensnacht' was all that Ambrosius had said to him as they watched the body crumble to ash. 'One week.' Goetz hadn't replied. He had been too preoccupied, wondering what awaited him on the island. Thinking of the attempts on his life brought him back to Svunum. In their history, they'd run up against Northern fleets more than once, being assailed by Norscan fleets at least twice in the last century. Add in the occasional attack by orc reavers or Chaos fleets come south, and Svunum had well earned a reputation for being the rock upon which many a dream of empire had broken.

An island fortress, built on a rock that straddled a major trade route. Goetz smiled at the thought. It was a common enough tactic these days, employed everywhere the Order had a presence. Each komturie was a bastion of the finest that civilisation had to offer, but they were also gatehouses, blocking or opening the way to the civilised world proper. 'Or so we like to think of ourselves,' he murmured. Now it was almost over. The Order would be forced to abandon Svunum and all that they had built;and for what? A political ploy? A move in some game that he couldn't understand?

'What was that?' Feldmeyer said, joining him at the rail. The captain was frowning. It seemed to be his default expression.

'Never mind. Something I can help you with, captain?' Goetz said.

'We make port in Svunum in two days. Be ready, for I don't intend to stay there any longer than necessary.'

Goetz turned. 'A man might think you had something against us, captain. Care to speak your mind?' Feldmeyer's frown deepened and he strode off without replying, bellowing orders to his crew. Goetz watched him for a moment. Then, shaking his head, he turned back to the ocean and quickly lost himself in its depths. Staring down, he watched the trail of foam ride along the lower half of the hull, contorting itself into a myriad of shapes. He looked up at the sails. The wind was good, insofar as he could tell.

Two days, Feldmeyer had said. Then what? He thought of Oleg again, and a slight shiver of revulsion coursed through him. Chaos was not an unfamiliar enemy. Not since that night in the Drakwald, and the sweetly singing thing that had almost devoured him. Beastmen too, he knew. The assassin had not been one of their kind, though. Had Oleg truly been a cultist, as Ambrosius said? A mutant? Was that what he was facing? Had Chaos taken Svunum? The thought sent a chill through him and the pain returned, caressing his nerve endings with delicate cats'-claws of agony. Sweat beaded on his skin despite the chill of the sea.

His wound had fully healed now. Before he'd left the city, Dubnitz had brought a priestess of Shallya to see him and she had seemed surprised that such a wound had closed so quickly. Now it was nothing but another patch of scar tissue to join the others. But the pain was still there. Still in his head. He wondered if it always would be... perhaps he was just as marked as Oleg had been. Just as 'blessed'...

Hands clenched, he looked towards the horizon. The coastline was still visible, though only barely. It was a rare seaman who didn't hug the coast to some degree. Especially this near the Sea of Chaos, where worse things than pirates lurked in the coves. The Sea of Claws was little better. Goetz had heard that there were sea serpents there.

A speck cut through the air, and a half-familiar sound tugged at the edges of his hearing. 'Hunh.' Goetz rubbed his eyes, certain he'd seen something on their trail. A bird? Seabirds certainly weren't rare, even here, though Sigmar alone knew what they looked like a few miles south, at the edges of the Sea of Chaos. He dismissed the thought and pushed back from the rail, turning his attentions elsewhere.

Dalla watched the einsark board the merchant vessel and bared her teeth. With one of them aboard, it made the tub an even worthier prize. Eyri would not be pleased that one of the Svunum-filth was there, but her father would, sure enough. If they could question him–

'Pfaugh. Counting wolves before they've sprung,' she said to herself. The vessel was heading for Svunum, and the route was an open one. They could easily intercept it, provided she delivered the message in time.

The wharf was alive with the sound of commerce as she headed for Old Jarl's shanty-hall. Jarl had been a raider in his youth, but he'd since grown accustomed to the softer, Southern life. He ran a mead hall of meagre size and splendour down near the city's shore-gate. He also sold information on cargo convoys and other ripe prizes to proper Norscans; and, in a pinch, he could get you out of the city.

Jarl's was a dilapidated structure, and it smelt like a sty, but she breathed a sigh of relief as she slipped inside. It was as crowded as always, full of drunks of every race and description, and Jarl himself loomed behind the bar, looking like an overstuffed bearskin that someone had crammed into a food-spotted doublet.

'Dalla?' he said, spotting her.

'Don't bellow so you old sea-cow,' she hissed, gesturing sharply. 'I need to borrow the cog.'

'The cog?' Jarl's frost-coloured eyebrows went up. 'Something important?'

'A pretty bit of pillage,' she said, flashing a grin. 'Nothing more. Eyri will reimburse you.'

'The day Goldfinger reimburses me is the day the dwarfs shave their beards,' Jarl snorted. 'I didn't hear of anything worthwhile leaving today. What ship?'

'None of your concern,' Dalla said, leaning over the bar. Though he out-weighed her twice over, Jarl leaned back. 'The cog?'

'In use, I'm afraid,' Jarl said.

Dalla's eyes narrowed. 'What?'

'It's in use. Some of Tassenberg's boys are looking to use the river to–'

'I need that cog, Jarl!' she snapped, interrupting him. 'Is it still here?'

'Downstairs, but–'

Dalla whirled and darted for the privy where Jarl kept the entrance to his own private wharf. She jerked it open and slugged the man squatting inside. Booting him out, she struck the hidden catch and started down the slippery, foul-smelling stone stairs.

Jarl indulged in a bit of smuggling among his other activities, and he'd chosen the location of his establishment carefully. Built over the bones of an old warehouse, it had access to both the river and the sea via an underground dock. Normally Jarl used it and the sturdy wooden cog moored there to bring in illicit merchandise, but every so often he used it to get something – or someone – out.

Ignoring the smell of the day's privy leavings that sat fuming in the nightsoil barrels set at calculated points, Dalla started down the makeshift corridor that led to the dock. She loosened her sword in its sheath as she moved.

She slowed as she heard voices. A group of street-ready toughs stood on the dock, discussing something in the flickering torchlight. Five of them in all, with the cog bobbing up and down just beyond. They were brutal looking creatures – Tassenberg's men, she recalled Jarl saying; Uli Tassenberg was one of the city's most ruthless purveyors of flesh. His men had kidnapped youths of both sexes from as far away as Cathay, though they usually stuck to those they could snatch near the river. Likely they were planning another raid now. Well, Tassenberg would just have to make do.

Dalla drew her sword and stepped out into the light. 'I'm taking the boat,' she said, loudly.

The men looked at her, then, as one, began to laugh. Before the echoes of that first burst of mirth had faded, Dalla was among them, cat-quick and deadly. Her sword was no rapier or sabre, but instead a chopping tool and as her wrists flickered and snapped it did just that. She hammered into the men with brutal efficiency, wasting neither words nor energy.

It was not unusual for women of her race to take to the sword. They were not like the frail creatures of the South, afraid to even step outside without an armed escort. By the time she was thirteen, Dalla had killed two would-be suitors and joined four raids, earning her prizes honourably. The mail she wore and the sword she carried had been among the latter.

She had fought Kurgan and orcs and even the black-armoured elves who sometimes swept the coasts looking for easy pickings. She had fought them all and won, or at least survived. The street-toughs, surprised as they were by the ferocity of her assault, were no match for her. The stones of the floor greedily inhaled the blood. Kicking the last man off her blade, she turned as Jarl stepped off the stairs. He began to curse loudly.

'How am I supposed to explain this to Tassenberg?' he sputtered, his big hands clenching in fury. 'Those were five of his best!'

'I killed them. What is to explain?' she said, cleaning her blade on her cloak. 'I'm taking the cog.'

'And if I say no?'

Dalla stopped her cleaning and fixed him with a cold stare. Jarl hesitated. He looked around at the bodies and then at her and spat. 'Fine! Take the damn cog! Get out of here! And tell Goldfinger he owes me!'

Dalla didn't bother to reply. She untied the line and dropped into the cog. With broad, easy strokes of the paddles, she set out to sea.

THIRTEEN

By the time night began to descend, they had lost sight of Marienburg entirely.

Goetz had a hard time of it, enough so that he eventually abandoned his position above decks and retreated to the berth Feldmeyer had grudgingly provided him. He had never travelled by sea before, and it wasn't an experience he was not enjoying all that much.

Swaying in his hammock, trying to get comfortable, Goetz finally had time to appreciate the full joy of ocean travel. His stomach began to protest almost as soon as he stretched out. Eyes closed, Goetz mumbled a prayer and listened to the dull thud of water pressing against the hull.

He rose after a while, unable to relax. Sitting on the edge of his hammock, he stared at his armour where it lay in a heap across his bag. Grabbing his sword, he unsheathed it and laid it across his knees. Then, he began to sharpen it. The gentle scrape of the stone across the steel helped him ignore his stomach.

'It's sharp enough, I think,' a voice slurred.

'Captain,' Goetz said. Feldmeyer swayed slightly before plopping himself down on a box of fruit. A bottle of rum hung from his fingers and as Goetz watched, he tipped it back and took a swig.

'I hate you, you know,' Feldmeyer said, as he lowered the bottle.

'I got that impression, yes,' Goetz said, bemused.

'Damn knights. Always shouting orders and swinging swords. Killing people.'

'Yes, we do indeed kill people,' Goetz said. He slid the stone down the length of his sword again. Feldmeyer squinted at him.

'Why?' he said.

Goetz opened his mouth to reply, then shook his head. He looked back down at his sword. If Feldmeyer noticed that he hadn't replied, he gave no indication. 'It's a strange place, Svunum,' he continued. 'Strange people.'

'Who? The knights?' Goetz said.

'No. The others. Not... Norscans.' Feldmeyer made a face, as if he were searching for a particular word and it was eluding him. 'I like Norscans, mostly. 'S' why I trade with them. But I don't like them on Svunum.'

'Any reason in particular?' Goetz said carefully.

'No,' Feldmeyer said petulantly. He took another swig. Goetz waited for him to continue, but he remained silent. Eventually, a savage snore alerted him to the fact the captain had fallen asleep. Goetz rose and went on deck.

The first mate, a brawny man of indeterminate origins, started towards him and Goetz gestured towards the hold. 'He's down there. Asleep.'

'Sleeping it off, more like,' the mate said, with obvious affection. He sighed. 'I am sorry he disturbed you, Sir Knight.'

Goetz shook his head. 'I'm sorry I disturbed him. As I so obviously have.'

'Not you,' the other man said. He tapped Goetz's jerkin and the stylised sun emblazoned there. 'Your Order has a bad reputation out here.'

Goetz frowned, taken aback. 'What? Why?'

'Usual reasons,' the mate said. 'Fine line between pirates, privateers, merchants and smugglers. Hard times makes for hard men. The knights on Svunum don't make as pretty a distinction as we'd all like.'

'We do what must be done,' Goetz said, automatically. The mate looked at him, his broad face showing nothing. Goetz sighed. 'Yes, fine. I get your point. What have they done besides that?'

'Every so often they'll pressgang a crew and a ship. You don't hear much about them later. Some folk think they're building a fleet. Others that they're taking slaves to build up that damn great fortress they've got.'

'You've seen it?' Goetz said. The sky was growing light on the horizon as the chill of night began to retreat. A cold mist had settled across the water, and out in the darkness, something heavy splashed. Goetz looked away.

'At a distance.' The sailor shuddered. 'I'd not want to try and storm it, that's for sure.' He fell silent. Goetz didn't press the issue. Instead, he watched as the man carefully stuffed Moot-weed into a hand-carved pipe and lit the bowl. Soon he was puffing contentedly. 'We've been running this route for six years now, and it just gets bigger every year.'

Goetz held his tongue. It wasn't unusual, given the isolation and the nature of the threats they faced. The komturies that dotted the larger towns of the Border Princes did much the same. The mate continued, puffing on his pipe, 'It's almost a city these days, from the looks of it. Not that the captain lets us go ashore. Not that I blame him, mind.'

'The islanders are dangerous then?' Goetz said.

'One way of putting it, right enough,' the man said. 'They–'

'Ware! Ware!'

Both men turned as the cry echoed from the rail. It was echoed a moment later by the voice of the lookout at the top of the main mast. 'Ware! Dragonships!'

They came out of the mist rolling over the Sea of Claws like the great leviathans of legend – dragon-prowed and armoured. Instead of fire, however, they breathed arrows. Goetz twisted out of the way as the first volley thudded home. Some of the crew screamed in pain as the arrows bit flesh and punctured bone.

Goetz raised his head and saw that there were three of the dragon-ships and they were circling the Nicos like wolves, propelled by heavy oars that slapped the water like thunder-strikes. Raiders for the most part, the Norscans clung precariously to the precious few clean stretches of land between the sea and the Far North, where the Winds of Chaos blew. More civilised than the inland cousins who had formed the backbone of every invading army from the North for the past few centuries, they were no less feared by those living on the northern coasts of the Empire. While they might not have had the taint of Chaos in their blood, they were just as savage as any beastman or marauder.

'Arm yourselves!' the mate bellowed, thrusting himself back from the rail as more arrows thudded home in the deck. 'Up you sea-dogs! Up!'

'I'll get the captain!' Goetz said, heading below-decks. Feldmeyer, however, was already on his feet, seemingly sober. He swung a pistol towards Goetz as the latter descended. Goetz froze and raised his hands.

'What is it? What's going on?' the captain snapped.

'Norscans, captain. They appear to have taken an interest in us,' Goetz said, moving past him towards his bundled armour.

Feldmeyer gaped at him. 'What? No! It can't be!'

'It is. Now if you'll excuse me, I'd like to get dressed before our guests arrive,' Goetz said, unrolling the bundle. Swiftly he began to don his armour, snapping buckles and pulling straps with experienced fingers. When he had finished, he saw that Feldmeyer had already fled onto the deck. Goetz slid his shield onto his arm and drew his sword. He extended it, admiring the play of the lantern light across the blade for just a moment. Then, dressed for war, he clambered up on deck, his sword naked in his hand and his ribbons of merit fluttering in the sea breeze.

'You'll sink like a stone in that,' Feldmeyer said upon sighting him.

'I don't plan on having to swim for it, captain. You?' Goetz said, stabbing his blade point-first into the deck. He stood calmly, hoping no one had noticed the tension in his limbs or the slight tremor in his hands. A massed battle was always somehow more frightening than any brawl or skirmish. Perhaps it was the chaotic nature of the thing... even the best strategists only had the dimmest idea of how a given battle might go. The fewer participants, the easier to control things. To end them swiftly.

'This isn't right,' Captain Feldmeyer snarled.

'More men than you have likely made that claim in these waters,' Goetz said.

'No! You don't understand... it's not raiding season,' Feldmeyer said, glaring at him. 'They shouldn't be here!' He pointed an accusing finger at the boats circling them. 'Why are they here?'

'Offhand I'd say they've come to gut us and turn us into shark bait,' Goetz said. 'Look!'

More arrows swept the deck in a desultory fashion and then there was a crunch of metal on wood as a claw-footed climbing plank extended from the closest of the boats and thudded into the rail of the ship. A moment later, two more planks latched on at different points.

'Prepare to repel boarders!' Feldmeyer roared, pulling his pistol and his cutlass both. The first of the Norscans were over the rail a moment later, clad in furs and leather and wielding broad-bladed axes. Others beat the flats of their swords against their brightly coloured wooden shields as they hopped over the rail, and bellowed out savage hymns.

Then, with a roar worthy of any sea-borne leviathan, the battle began!

Goetz moved to meet the Norscans, his sword singing out to parry a looping axe cut even as he rammed his shield into its bearer's midsection. He shoved the man over the side and jerked back as a saw-edged sword chopped into the rail, spattering him with splinters. Goetz traded blows with the Norscan for a moment, then battered the man's weapon aside and chopped through the crude hauberk he wore, crushing his ribs. As the warrior dropped, an arrow skidded across Goetz's helmet, setting his ears to ringing.

A pistol barked nearby, sending the archer spinning into the water. Feldmeyer tossed the smoking weapon aside as he met the attack of another raider with his cutlass. Goetz didn't even have time to thank him before he was lost in the melee. The deck was already slick with blood as Feldmeyer's crew fought with desperate abandon against their attackers. One of the latter, naked save for a matted loincloth of wolf skin, bounded towards Goetz, howling and frothing.

The axe he carried flashed out in seemingly random patterns, chopping the air and the deck with equal ferocity. The Norscan howled like a wolf and his eyes were wide, his neck a mass of straining veins. Goetz had heard of such men – ulfsarks. Men possessed of a battle-lust that would make an orc's look puny. They fought until there were no enemies left, or they died.

'Myrmidia!' Goetz roared, blocking a blow that would have gutted him. 'Up, Talabheim! Haro, Talabecland!' The ulfsark paused, as if puzzled by the foreign battle-cries. Then he charged forward, snarling. His axe chopped whole sections out of Goetz's shield, rendering it down into so many useless splinters that he discarded it with a curse. The berserker came again, a web of spittle drenching his jaws.

Goetz met him and, for a moment, they traded ringing blows. In a spray of steel flinders, the berserker's sword shattered as Goetz swept it aside, and the berserker dove on him, digging for his face with the jagged stump of the sword.

Goetz's sword slid up into the man's belly and surfaced from his back. The berserker jerked and gnawed the air as his spasming fists beat at Goetz.

Then, with a groan, he went limp. Goetz heaved him aside and climbed to his feet. He shook his head, trying to clear it, and turned only to reel back as a wooden shield smashed into his face. Instinctively, he lashed out, trying to drive his attacker back. Shaking his head to clear it, he took a two-handed grip on his sword and fell into a defensive stance.

The Norscan was smaller and slimmer than the others. A youth perhaps, though his eyes had the hard glint of experience to them as they glared at Goetz through the slits in his helmet. The sword in his hand was of better condition than most and it flickered over the rim of his shield with startling alacrity. The tip sliced through Goetz's ribbon of rank and it fluttered away on the wind.

Goetz, rather than stepping back, moved into the blow, letting the second thrust glide over his shoulder. His own sword pierced the centre of the shield and he shoved his opponent back. With a twist of his shoulders, Goetz ripped the shield from his opponent's arm and flung it across the deck.

They circled one another after that, weaving a complicated pattern of strike and counter-strike. For every one blow that Goetz managed, the Norscan made three. Goetz's armour rang with the other man's lunges, but so far none had found a way past it.

They fought for what seemed like hours but was, in reality, only minutes. Sweating despite the chill rolling off the sea, Goetz stepped back, lowering his sword. The Norscan took a breath and lowered his sword.

'Good fight,' he said, in a surprisingly high-pitched voice.

'No such thing,' Goetz said. The Norscan looked at him with what might have been pity. Goetz frowned, feeling his anger surge. He sprang forward, gripping his sword in both hands. He chopped down. His opponent threw himself out of the way as Goetz's blade chopped into the deck.

The Norscan's sword darted in at Goetz's exposed side and he felt warmth blossom along his ribs. Panic burned through him and Goetz grabbed his foe's wrist, pinning him in place. The flat of his sword caught the edge of the Norscan's helmet and sent it flying.

A woman glared up at him, her eyes blazing with hate. Surprised, Goetz released her sword-arm and stepped back. 'What–' Goetz began. Then, a blow caught him on the back. A second numbed his hip. He turned awkwardly, and the haft of an axe smashed into his face, sending him crashing to the deck in a daze. Before he could even attempt to rise, a foot pressed down on his throat. He looked up at the woman through bleary eyes.

'I am Dalla Ulfarsdottir, Svunum-filth! Tell your master who it was who sent you to its bosom!' she snarled, raising her sword. Blackness claimed him a moment later.

'No!'

Dalla snarled as someone grabbed her wrist and wrenched her around. A stiff blow caught her in the jaw and sent her stumbling back. After nearly tripping over the einsark's unconscious form, she regained her balance and extended her sword.

'He must die!' she snapped.

'Agreed. But not like this,' Eyri growled. 'People – our people – need to see him die,' he continued.

'There are enough here to witness it now!' Dalla snapped, gesturing to the men who had boarded the ship. Fully two-dozen Norscans stood on the blood-washed deck, their eyes riveted to the scene before them. She raised her sword and started forward. None of Eyri's crew made to stop her.

Her sword chopped down, but shivered to flinders inches from the unconscious man's skull. Dalla jerked back, her pale face crimson with rage. 'What–' The blood drained from her face as she caught sight of the elderly figure pushing through the crowd towards her.

'I seem to recall that you thought we could take him alive, daughter,' Ulfar said, poking her in the chest with his staff. 'Have you then changed your opinion?'

Dalla said nothing. Her hands curled into fists and she stepped back, allowing her father to move past her. With a grunt, the old man sank to his haunches and traced the already purpling bruise on the knight's skull with two fingers. 'His skull is cracked, but he'll recover.'

'Took a half-dozen blows to even get him off his feet,' Eyri said. 'He wears more armour than a Kurgan.' He spat a wad of phlegm onto the deck and sniffed.

'Not quite so much as that, I think,' Ulfar said. He traced the outline of the blazing sun engraved across the swooping curves of the cuirass and sighed. 'He's not from Svunum.'

'What?' Dalla said, picking up the fallen man's sword and testing its balance. 'But he wears their sign!'

'Mayhap they wear his,' Ulfar said. 'Regardless, he is not of them.'

'Perhaps he was going to join them? The others did, after all,' Eyri said, scratching his chin.

Ulfar stood with a groan and nodded tersely. 'Possibly.'

Eyri made a face. 'Don't play seer with me old man. Do you know or not?'

'We should kill him, just to be safe,' Dalla said, glaring at Eyri, who raised his hands in mock surrender. She looked at her father. 'At the very least it'll be a clean death.'

'Aye, because the manner of his passing is what's important here, isn't it?' Eyri said. 'No. I agree, he needs to die, but he needs to die where our people can gain strength from it. In the pit with the rest of the monsters.'

Ulfar looked away. 'I will not gainsay you, godi.'

'But...?' Eyri said, grinning crookedly. 'There's always a "but" with you, my faithful gudja.'

Ulfar looked at Dalla, and then up, at the rising sun. 'But nothing. Do with him as you will.'

FOURTEEN

The orc's maul crashed down on him, driving him inches into the bloody soil. Goetz gasped and floundered, unable to breathe. The maul rose up, blotting out the sun, and the orc's piggy eyes narrowed in anticipation.

'This isn't the way it happened!' Goetz coughed, rolling aside just as the maul struck the ground with a dull thump. He tried to get to his feet, but his body felt brittle and broken. Another blow caught him on the hip and he rolled across the ground, his every nerve screaming in agony. 'It's not what–'

The orc laughed and the laugh became a snarl and suddenly it was no longer an orc, but a stag-headed beastman. Goetz made to rise, but arrows sprouted from his wrists and thighs like barbed roots, holding him in place as the creature trotted forward, his own sword raised to strike. Goetz thrashed in agony and the sky above him seemed to rupture and a face peered down through the clouds–

His eyes shot wide and he looked up into the Norscan woman's grim features. She rose from beside him as he sat up to the accompaniment of the dull clinking of chains. Goetz coughed and looked around. He was below-decks somewhere, in a cramped hold. Other bodies, chained as he was, lay scattered around. He had been stripped of his armour, save for the quilted undershirt, and bound in chains.

'Where am I?' he said hoarsely. He felt sick. Nauseous. His temples were pounding like a dwarfen smithy and his limbs felt loose and weak. The old pain in his side and back flared and he winced. 'Where am I?' he said again, trying for forceful, and afraid he only got desperate.

The woman – Dalla, he recalled – said nothing. Her knuckles were white where she gripped the hilt of a sword – his sword, he realised with a start. 'That's my sword,' he said.

'Mine now,' she spat, after a moment. 'Too good for the likes of you.' Her accent was atrocious, and it took him a moment to puzzle through it. When he had, he made a face.

'Says the pirate,' he said. Her boot lashed out, catching him in the chest.

613

He slammed back against the wall and a groan escaped him. Every muscle in his body felt as if it had been dipped in acid, and his lungs struggled to pull in air. 'Perhaps I misspoke?' Goetz gasped, clutching at his chest. 'Privateer, perhaps? Would you prefer corsair?'

'We are not pirates. We are Norscan. We are the wolves of the sea, and everything in the sea is our prey,' she said, glaring at him. 'You are our prey.'

'Duly noted,' Goetz muttered. 'Any reason you chose us in particular?'

'What?' Dalla said, looking nonplussed.

'Only, it seems to me that obstacles to my goal are popping up at every turn,' Goetz continued. 'And I am not a believer in coincidences...'

'And what is your goal?' she said, sinking to her haunches and leaning against the sword, its point dug into the deck. 'Why are you here, einsark?'

'Einsark?' Goetz repeated, rolling the word around in his mouth.

She tossed her head impatiently. 'Iron-skin. Or brass-skin, in your case. Like the Kurgan or the dwarfs. You wear enough metal to crush a sane man.'

'My armour, you mean?'

'No. This–' she swatted the hauberk she wore. 'This is armour. What you wore was ridiculous.'

Goetz said nothing. He examined her through bleary eyes... she wasn't a classical beauty, not with the pale scars that cut across her cheeks and the bridge of her nose. Broad shoulders and slim muscles made her as far from the women he was used to as it was possible to get and still be of the same gender.

She drew his sword and sank to her haunches, pressing the tip of the blade against his throat. 'If I had my way, I'd–' she began, but was interrupted by a barked order from the stairs leading to the upper deck.

She rose and turned, replying in kind, her face flushing, though whether in anger or embarrassment, Goetz couldn't tell. Another Norscan stood on the stairs, his thumbs hooked into the wide, studded belt he wore over his furs. He wore a conical helmet and his dirty blond beard flared beneath it like a spade. He jerked a wide hand upwards and Dalla gesticulated with the sword, the tip coming dangerously close to Goetz's nose. Then, with what he could only guess was a curse, she stalked past the man without looking back.

The Norscan watched her go, then strode over to Goetz. He grinned down at the knight. 'She was about to kill you but good.'

Goetz blinked. 'Your accent–'

'I do a fair bit of trading along the coasts,' the Norscan said. 'Captain Eyri, that's me.' He swatted his chest with his palms. 'Or Eyri Goldfinger, around some fires. Chief Eyri, if you like.'

'Why did you attack us?' Goetz said.

Eyri eyed him speculatively, then said, 'Why not?' He shrugged. 'I'd watch yourself around Dalla, however. She hates you, brass-skin.'

'I've never met her before,' Goetz said.

'Wish I could say the same,' the Norscan said, squatting. 'Dalla is a bad one. A witch, like her skinny-shanks of a father no doubt. And she's got a temper.' He chuckled. 'Dead is dead, I say. It doesn't matter who – or how – it happens, unless there's profit to be had in the doing.'

'Why are you so concerned for my safety? I am your prisoner, am I not?'

'If Dalla kills you prematurely, I'm out no few coins,' Eyri said, rubbing his thumb and forefinger together.

Goetz felt a chill creep down his spine. 'I won't beg for my life,' he said.

The Norscan gave a roar of laughter and slapped a meaty hand against his thigh. 'Good! Or I might just let the witch-girl chop you up.' He fluffed his beard. 'You're marked for the pit as it is.'

'The pit?'

Eyri rose and beamed down at him genially. 'It's a good death, as such things go. I caught a troll a few weeks ago. That'll be a fine fight to see, I think.' Chuckling, he turned and left the hold, leaving Goetz alone with his thoughts.

After a time, he took hold of his chains and tested their weight. Gathering his legs under him, he hauled on them, trying to pull them loose from their moorings. He set his feet against the wall and pulled, his muscles burning with exertion. He rolled his arms side to side. He knew how much pressure a given mooring plate could take, especially when fixed to wood. He couldn't break the chains, or the plate, but he could – there! There was a crack of wood and the mooring plate sprang off the wall, bolts and all. Goetz fell backwards onto his rear and sat for a moment, shaking. His head swam, and he shook it viciously, trying to focus.

'Impressive. Now you come with us.' Goetz spun as Eyri stepped down into sight, followed by four men. The Norscan clapped his hands together. 'Chains make noise, you know. And this is quite a small vessel.' He smiled and gestured. 'We're only a few miles out, so you may as well come up on deck.'

His men moved forward and Goetz sprang to meet them. He swung the chains out and caught one on the side of the head, sending him staggering over the other captives. As the other three closed in, Goetz swept the chains out, driving them back. With a jerk of his wrists he sent the chains looping around one man's hand and hauled back, yanking him off balance and into his companion. Goetz dodged past them and headed for Eyri, head lowered.

The big Norscan drew a polished club from his belt and brought it down just as Goetz reached him, dropping the knight to his knees. 'You've got spirit, I'll give you that. You are worth every penny I'll get for you,' Eyri said.

Goetz staggered as he was propelled up on deck. He fell, eliciting a round of laughter from the watching Norscans. As Goetz clambered to his feet, he caught sight of Dalla watching him from the prow, her expression unreadable. He turned as he was shoved forward and saw what was waiting for him beyond the rail.

The fog began to thin even as the drummers on the aft deck began to pound on the bear-hide drums. The inlet was a semicircle of rocky shore and scabrous, malnourished scrub pine that seemed altogether more menacing than it should have.

The village crouched on the rocky shore like a dog that had been whipped one too many times. The greasy smoke of a hundred cooking fires rose and rolled out over the water, bringing with them the stink of boiled fish and bear fat. As the dragonships scuffed along the shore, Norscans leapt over the sides and grabbed the great anchor hooks that dangled from the rails, dragging them through the surf towards the shore, where others waited with mattocks.

The anchor-spikes were driven into the shore by swift blows and the ships were dragged up out of the grip of the tide. 'Welcome to Eyristaad, brass-skin,' Eyri said, baring his teeth at Goetz. 'It's as good a place as any to find your way to the halls of the gods.'

FIFTEEN

Goetz was dragged through the streets, his chains looped around the axle of a trundle-cart. Eyri stood on the cart, gesticulating and bellowing to the crowd that bellowed back in reply. He held Goetz's cuirass over his head and angled it so that it caught the sun. The noise of the crowd seemed to double and clods of earth and other, less fragrant, substances smacked into Goetz's battered frame.

Goetz ignored the pelting and crowd both. He glared at Dalla, where the warrior-woman stalked alongside the trundle-cart, her fingers dancing protectively across the hilt of his sword. He shook his head and looked around. Eyristaad was small, as towns went. Less a town, really, than a collection of villages that had merged together around the mouth to an isolated inlet. Tradesmen and merchants shouted at the crowd and one another, hawking crude wares. Stray dogs ran yapping underfoot. Even the most remote outpost of the Empire had more a veneer of civilisation than this place. Abruptly, they came to a halt. The men guarding Goetz knocked him to his knees and Eyri hopped off his cart. 'Well brass-skin, what do you think?'

'I've seen prettier pigsties,' Goetz said, trying for urbane politesse.

Eyri cuffed him. 'Be polite.' He tossed Goetz's cuirass into the mud at his feet. 'You can have it back now. Like as not, it won't do you any good.'

Goetz looked at his filth-stained cuirass and then back up at Eyri. 'What do you mean?'

'I told you, you're going in the pit.' Eyri squatted and tapped two fingers against the battered breastplate. 'It's rare we get one of your kind for an evening's entertainment. My people will want a show.'

'Give me my sword and I'll see what I can do,' Goetz said.

Eyri grunted. 'You'll take what you're given, brass-skin.' He stood and shouted an order. The crowd raised a cheer as Goetz was dragged into a wooden outbuilding. It was only when they were inside that Goetz realised that the entire structure had been built around a wide pit dug into the rock. It reminded him of the theatres in Talabheim, with raised viewing

617

platforms surrounding a circular stage. Only these platforms were crowded with jeering Norscans, rather than clapping Talabeclanders.

His handlers cuffed him and sent him sprawling, and then laughed and joked in their guttural fashion. Blows, pokes and prods sent him reeling up the rough-hewn stairs, and the hiss of a blacksnake made him lose his footing. The whip snapped a chunk out of the rail and Goetz grabbed it and pulled hard.

The whip-man howled as he was jerked forward and Goetz sent him flying through the rail to land on the floor in a crumpled heap. Spear-butts and clubs were his reward and an exquisite jewel of agony blossomed in his side as the blows connected with his newly healed wounds. He half-fell on the stairs, and the Norscans growled and groused as they jerked him up.

As he was dragged along a creaking walkway, Goetz caught a glimpse of the pit. A pack of half-starved wolves surrounded one of the pale-furred bears he had heard occupied the mountains here. The fight was a bloody one, and as he watched the bear swatted a leaping wolf from the air, breaking its neck with one powerful blow.

He was unceremoniously tossed into a wooden cell and his chains were stripped from him with efficient brutality. His cuirass was tossed in as well, to land with a clang on the floor. Goetz got to his feet just as the door was slammed shut, leaving him alone. He snatched up his breastplate and began to buckle it on as he turned from the door, eyeing the cell's interior.

It was a squalid square, with sunlight pouring in through the holes in the slats. His engineer's mind began calculating the stresses and pressures needed to force an opening.

'It won't do any gut, yes?'

Goetz turned as a heap of rags unfolded into a battered heap of a man. Another Norscan, he was small by their standards, and he looked as if he had died and been dug up soon after. Bloodshot eyes met Goetz's, and the man smiled, displaying broken teeth. 'No way out, yes?' he said, in broken Reikspiel. 'Go nowhere, yes?'

'No,' Goetz said, and began to run his hand along the wall. In the neighbouring cell, something moved. Something heavy. The adjoining wall suddenly creaked. Goetz scrambled away from it.

'No way out, yes? Ha – ha!' the Norscan wheezed.

'What is it? What's in there?' he said. The Norscan only shook his head and laughed harder. The wall creaked again. It was followed by a snort, and then a foul odour wafted through the cracks in the wood. Goetz gagged. On the other side of the wall, something gave a grumbling moan. Then the wall shuddered, as if it had been slapped by a huge hand.

Looking down, his eye caught a number of rusty brown stains on the wood. More stains ran along the wall. Blood, he was certain. 'Keep it fed, yes?' the Norscan cackled. 'Keep safe, keep it fed!'

'What?' Goetz was about turn as the Norscan slammed into him with frenzied strength. A broken chunk of bone, sharpened to a razor-edge, stroked his throat and Goetz made a desperate grab for the skinny arms. The man howled like a broke-back wolf as Goetz slung him around and planted him against the wall. The makeshift bone knife flew from the spasming hands even as cracks appeared in several of the boards that made up the wall. The thing on the other side gave a roar, and the Norscan shrieked in obvious terror.

Goetz eyed the cracks in consternation. If the creature got in here they wouldn't stand much chance. Another slap caused the floor beneath his feet to tremble. A red eye glared at him through a crack, and the slobbering sound that followed caused Goetz to shudder in revulsion. The Norscan clawed at his arms and tried to shove himself away from the wall. 'Keep it fed, keep safe! No escape, yes?' he whimpered, kicking weakly at Goetz.

Suddenly realising what the stains meant, Goetz hurled the man aside in disgust. 'Get away from me,' he snarled. The Norscan scuttled away, cowering in a heap in the corner. Goetz sank down in an opposite corner, near the door, and eyed both the madman and the wall behind which their monstrous neighbour lurked.

Outside the cell, he could hear the crowd roaring in pleasure as the bear snarled and wolves howled. As the noise reached a fevered pitch, Goetz, decision made, lunged to his feet and moved to the far wall of the cell. Through the gaps in the boards, he could see the town beyond.

'No no no no escape, yes?' the Norscan muttered, not looking at him.

'No. No escape,' Goetz said, grabbing two slats and working them loose. When he had created a gap, he shoved his way through and swung out onto the outside wall. Below him an armed guard paused to urinate in the alleyway between the pit and the next building along. Goetz grinned mirthlessly and dropped onto the man as he finished.

His weight drove the Norscan an inch into the mud of the alley, and Goetz grabbed the man's hair, shoving his face deeper into the muck. The Norscan flailed for a moment, then went still. Goetz rose, breathing heavily, and stripped the man's cloak from him. As an afterthought, he smeared mud across his cuirass, dulling it, and yanked the unconscious man's sword belt loose and draped it over his shoulder before snatching up his crude helmet.

His first thought was to find a boat, but he dismissed the idea. There was a distinctly nautical gap in his education, and leaving without looking for any survivors from the ship left a bad taste in his mouth. Moving swiftly, he pulled the helmet over his head, trying to ignore the crawling sensation that he was going to wind up with lice.

The village looked better from this side of captivity; people went about their business much the same as in Marienburg, albeit with a bit more crude humour. The women were freer with their bodies and mouths, hurling crude obscenities at children and grown men alike as the latter proved a bit too free with their hands.

He passed a stall selling skinned wolves for their meat, and a beast-master selling squalling malformed pups as their mother, a bony spike-covered brute whose ancestor might have been a wolfhound, snarled inside her cage. Mutation was rampant here, though not so much as the Sigmar-botherers of his childhood would have had him believe. Children ran and played in the muck, the same as in any city. He was forced to step aside for several of the latter.

He made it as far as the wharf before he heard the hue and the cry of his captors behind him. Cursing, he left the boats behind and moved into the shanty town. He didn't run, knowing it would only encourage pursuit. Instead he made it look as if he were searching houses, even as he kept an eye out for something that looked like a temple.

The Norscan idea of architecture lacked the sharp angles of the Imperial School of Measurement, but it made up for it with a 'bigger is better' ethic that made finding the temple of Mermedus easy work. It rose up from the shore like a pile of splintered keels and hulls, and it was both savage and impressive.

A stone carving of Mermedus, the dark mirror of Manann, rose up in front of it, crouching on its flippers. It, like its temple, was crudity manifest, but there was a raw power to it nonetheless. Mermedus had more in common with the brute-god Stromfels than with the more civilised Manann, but there was an eerie similarity. A wide mouth gaped from within a tangled beard, and shark-like rows of stone teeth protruded. The eyes lacked Manann's serenity, and were instead narrowed with predatory intensity. Mermedus clutched a wide-bladed sword and an anchor rather than a trident, and looked ready to use either to sweep aside worshippers and enemies both.

As he'd hoped, the slave-market had been set up in front of the temple, and men were being led up to the auction block in chains. More than just the unlucky crew of the Nicos were in evidence, and the crowd of customers ebbed and swelled as Goetz approached.

The slaver was an obese Norscan covered in tattoos, his thick ginger beard curled into greasy plaits. He bellowed out prices, insults and suggestions with seeming abandon as he jerked the chains and ropes that held his merchandise. There were men and women from as far away as Cathay, and even a few altogether more disturbing prizes. A Kurgan, covered in strangely-angled scars and blasphemous tattoos, roared out crude jeers at the guards who surrounded him with spears. They seemed nervous despite the chains that had been wrapped around the barbarian's thick frame.

Besides the Kurgan, there were a number of pale-haired Nordheimers, their pale faces slack with dull ferocity. Their hands and necks were trapped in wooden stocks and their feet were chained to the auction block. As Goetz watched, they yelled out oaths and cursed at their captors.

Anger boiled up in him as he drew closer, and he fought to keep his hand from his sword. Slavery of this sort was practically unknown in the Empire, especially in Talabecland, where even a peasant wouldn't hesitate to spit in a lord's eye if the opportunity presented itself. To see men chained and branded as cattle or merchandise roused a fury in him that he had rarely felt.

Forcing himself to stay calm, he looked around. There were too many people to risk a rescue. The crowd would pull him apart before he got ten steps. So what–?

He saw her a moment later, drifting through the crowd, her white limbs flashing in the grey light of the day. No one else saw her, that much he was sure of, for a woman as tall as that, as beautiful as that, would surely draw notice from a crowd as barbaric as this.

Eyes like pale flames met his and the pain in his back surged to life, coiling through his limbs and eliciting a grunt of agony. Black tears rolled down his cheeks and he resisted the urge to sink to his knees. He tore his eyes away from the goddess, ignoring the silent appeal on her lips, and crashed into a burly Norscan.

The man shoved him back with a bark. Instinct took over as pain thrummed through his mind. He swept his stolen sword out of its sheath and the crowd began to clear. Overhead, crows circled, croaking raucously. Men backed away from him, eyes wide. Someone yelled. Goetz shook his head trying to clear it.

The slaver's guards bulled their way through the crowd, clutching whips and hatchets. Goetz, barely able to see through the haze of agony consuming him, lunged for them. He killed the first with sadistic ease, gutting the man as he moved past. As the others gaped, he charged past them and up onto the auction block. The slaver growled and reached for his hatchet, but Goetz was quicker. His borrowed sword snaked out and cut through the chains that bound the Kurgan, freeing the brute. He howled joyfully and dove past Goetz onto the slaver, bearing the man down.

Goetz chopped through chains and ropes with abandon, freeing men as his head threatened to split open. Crows dove at him, their cruel beaks tapping at his stolen helmet. Flailing, he drove them back and jumped off the block.

'There!' someone shouted. Goetz spun, and saw Eyri and a group of his men running towards him. The Kurgan, having dealt with the auctioneer, headed them off, swinging a stolen sword as he howled out the praises of the Dark Gods.

A dozen spears punctured the barbarian's hairy hide, pinning him kicking and screaming to the ground. Goetz used the distraction to take the opportunity to flee. Armour and weapons rattled as Eyri's men pursued him. Not looking back, he sped away from the temple, clutching his head. The fire in his side made every step an agony, but Goetz ploughed on, crashing amidst the shanty dwellings that spread out around the temple.

Before him, the white shape of Myrmidia ran, almost tauntingly. She did not glance over her shoulder, or otherwise acknowledge his pursuit, and he plunged on after her. Above him, the crows kept pace.

The shacks and huts pressed close together, almost as if Eyristaad were seeking to entrap him in its streets. He stumbled against a wattle wall, breathing heavily. Something that might have been panic filled him. It was hard to think with the pain...

Snarling, he kicked in a door and came face-to-face with the frightened features of a child and her mother. Goetz froze, the fury draining out of him on the instant. The woman babbled in fear, a boning knife held in trembling hands as she stood between him and her child. The fear on her face was out of all proportion to his entrance. Glancing down, he realised that the mud he had covered his cuirass in had come off and that the sigil of Myrmidia blazed brightly.

The woman stared at that sigil in a terror that he found inexplicably hideous. 'I–' he began, before realising that she likely didn't speak Reikspiel. He held up his hand, and kept his sword point dipped to the ground. 'I mean you no harm,' he said. 'I know that you can't understand me, but... I don't mean to hurt you.'

The woman kept up her babble, poking the air between them with her knife, and Goetz stepped back against the door frame, hoping to avoid a confrontation. Outside, he could hear boots rattling across the rocks. He yanked off his helmet and tossed it to the woman, causing her to drop her knife. Running his hand over his sweaty scalp, he looked at the door and tightened his grip on his sword.

'I know you're in there einsark!' Eyri called out. 'Come out, or we'll come in after you. There's no escape.'

Goetz stepped outside, his sword held loosely. Eyri stood across the narrow street. The chieftain was leaning against the wall, grinning, his brawny arms crossed. A dozen men crowded the street, spear-points aimed at Goetz. 'Granted, you made the gods' own try, I have to give you that,' Eyri continued. 'Would you believe that no one has ever thought to escape that way?'

'No,' Goetz said. 'Unless your people are dimmer than has been claimed.'

'Well, fair enough,' Eyri said, pushing away from the wall and striding through his men. 'No, a lot of men try and escape. We always bring them back one way or another. It might please you to know that the odds on you have gone up. Everyone was quite impressed.'

'How nice,' Goetz said, wondering how quick he would have to be to get past the wall of spears surrounding him.

'I probably shouldn't have left you that armour. It made you bold.' Eyri was within an arm's length of Goetz and he sighed. 'Too kind for my own good, I suppose.'

'Yes, that is your problem,' Goetz said.

Eyri snorted. 'Come quietly, or come bloodily. It doesn't matter. I'd rather you conserved your strength, however. I need you healthy, you see.'

'I'm dead either way,' Goetz said.

'Wasn't it one of you Southerners who said "where there's life, there's hope"?'

'I'm not a man for philosophy,' Goetz said, gauging the distance. Eyri's eyes narrowed and he put a hand on the hatchet at his belt.

'Don't do it,' he grated.

Goetz let a grin flash across his face. 'Or what?'

Eyri paused, a perplexed look crossing his face. 'Err...'

'I hope you've invested in a nice afterlife,' Goetz said, his hand tightening on his sword-hilt. He was trapped; alone and without the prospect of aid. But he could teach these Norscans about how a Myrmidon died. Goetz tensed, preparing to lunge.

A pale hand extended over Eyri's shoulder then, fingers outstretched almost pleadingly. Goetz froze, his eyes widening. Her gaze was solemn and she gestured, and in his head, he heard the Litany of Battle recited.

'There is no trap a man cannot escape,' he said, straightening.

'What?' Eyri said.

'I give up,' Goetz said, tossing his sword down.

'You... surrender?'

'No. I'm engaging in a strategic withdrawal from the current impasse,' Goetz said, smiling crookedly. Eyri snatched up the sword and stepped back quickly as his men took Goetz's arms and bound him.

'Sounds like surrender to me,' Eyri grunted, as they stripped Goetz of his armour.

'Then your education has been sorely lacking,' Goetz said as they shoved him out of the alley. As he went, he glanced over his shoulder and saw the woman he'd frightened earlier clutching her child to her and watching him with a loathing that he could not understand.

They took him back to his cell, and he saw no more of the pale shape. He didn't know whether to be thankful or not. The agony that had enflamed his body had vanished as mysteriously as it had appeared, and his suspicions concerning it were growing stronger. He was reminded of the leash on a dog. The pain grew and flared at times when he looked to be diverging from some path he could only dimly discern. Was this the hand of Myrmidia? Or was it something else?

He was tossed back into the same cell that he had escaped from, though the exit he had made had been repaired and reinforced during his absence. His cellmate was missing, which was something of a relief.

Before he could muse farther, the cell door was jerked open and Eyri stepped inside, his thumbs tucked into his belt. 'Don't bother getting settled.'

'No?'

'No. I've decided you're too much trouble to keep around. I was planning to show you off for a special event, but well, you've ruined that.' His eyes narrowed and he glanced at the cracks in the wall. 'You've met your opponent already,' he said.

Through the open door behind him, Goetz saw several men move towards the adjoining cell with lit torches. 'He's a smart one. Not too stupid to be afraid of fire.' Eyri smiled. 'Already killed a bear, two orcs and some ugly thing we found that came down from the North and ate one of my thralls. The beast is a popular one with the crowd, if you can believe it. A merchant I know says he can get me one of those big lizards they have across the Southern Ocean for it to fight.' He cocked his head. 'You'll do until then, I suppose.'

'You expect me to fight it – whatever it is – barehanded?' Goetz said.

'Still on about your sword?' Eyri grunted. He snapped his fingers and one of his men stepped forward, tossing a sheathed blade at Goetz's feet. 'Settle for this one. Its dwarf-made. Got a good bite to it, if you get close enough to hurt the beast. Better than the one you stole from poor Orgun.' He laughed. 'Best thing about having a troll... no matter how much it gets torn up, it'll be fierce as frost for the next fight.'

Troll. The word sent a chill of fear down Goetz's spine. At least now he knew. He scooped up the sword and slid it a little ways from its sheath. It had seen hard use, that much was obvious, and there were rust-coloured stains on the hilt. 'How many men have used this same sword?' he said, glaring at Eyri.

'A dozen I'd say. None very well though.' The Norscan stepped aside as more men stepped into the room, clutching spears and shields. 'Maybe you'll do better, eh?'

Goetz was herded out onto the catwalk. The crowd around the pit seemed to have grown. Planks were extended and he was forced down one at the point of his escorts' spears. He drew the sword and tossed aside the sheath, testing its weight.

It was well-made, but the blade was too heavy. Like as not, it had been made for a dwarf though there were precious few swordsmen of note among that race. He tested the blade's edge along his forearm, slicing threads from his sleeve. It would do.

Dead wolves littered the floor of the pit, and the bear was slumped not far off, black-fletched arrows jutting from its hairy carcass. The smell was atrocious, and Goetz swallowed back the bile that burned in his throat.

'Don't worry, brass-skin, if you win, we won't stick you. The bear is for tonight's feast, just like the wolves. If you survive, you'll live to fight another day!' Eyri called down.

Goetz said nothing. A hundred faces or more glared down at him, and jeers and catcalls rained down. He had never encountered such hatred before. Such raw fury, as if he were some foul thing of Chaos. He tightened his grip on his borrowed sword and waited.

The troll did not walk down a plank. Instead, it was driven off the cat-walk by burning brands and boar-spears. It tumbled to the ground in a flailing heap. Long ungainly limbs unfolded and it shoved itself up, its wide head rocking back and forth on a deceptively spindly neck. With skin the colour of slate it almost blended into the rock floor of the pit. Immense bat-like ears unfurled and twisted on a malformed skull as Goetz's boots slid across the rocky floor.

The creature looked almost ridiculous, if you discounted the muscles that lined its limbs and the size of its jaws. The dull eyes took in the bear the wolves and the crowd and then, at the last, settled on Goetz. Worm-like lips wrinkled back from tombstone teeth as the troll caught sight of him. It snuffled the air, then gave a grunt. Goetz tensed. If the beast caught hold of him, that was it. He raised the sword even as the troll began to amble forward. The trot became a lope, the lope became a run, and then the mon-ster was hurtling towards him like a veritable avalanche. Jaws gaping, it stretched impossibly long arms towards him.

Goetz ducked, sliding under the grasping paws, and slit the beast's belly. Loops of foul-smelling intestine spilled out, tangling around the creature's stumpy legs and it staggered, whining. Goetz circled it, and darted in, hop-ing to hamstring it.

A backhanded blow caught him on the side of the chest, denting his armour and sending him skidding across the pit. He crashed into the dead bear and his sword went flying from his grip. The troll gathered up its intes-tines and hissed, swinging towards him. Knuckling the ground with its free hand, it rushed towards him in simian fashion, head swinging from side to side, jaws champing spasmodically.

Goetz climbed over the bear's bulk and grabbed the hind legs of a stiffen-ing wolf. With a grunt he heaved it up and swung it around, cracking the troll in the snout with the wolf's mangled skull. The troll stumbled off balance and Goetz threw himself towards his sword. His breastplate drew sparks from the stone as he skidded across it and his fingers wrapped around the pommel even as he felt the troll's approach. A knobbly fist crashed into the ground as he rolled aside. Desperately he chopped at the arm, hack-ing through the thick wrist. The sword quivered in his hands as it chewed through inhumanly thick bone.

The troll reared back, shrieking. Foul ichor sprayed from its stump. Goetz took the opening offered and plunged his sword to the hilt in the creature's chest, angling for where he hoped its heart was. The blade scraped bone and hot fluid coursed down Goetz's arms as he twisted the hilt, wedging the weapon in place. Coughing, he stepped back. The troll had a puzzled look on its face as it bent double, mouth opening.

Realising what was about to happen, Goetz threw himself out of the way as the troll vomited a blistering tide of bile. The substance charred the stone black where it landed, and Goetz scrambled backwards. The troll stumbled around in a circle, its one good hand pawing at the sword-hilt trapped by its already healing flesh.

Breathing heavily, his muscles aching, Goetz got to his feet. The crowd had gone silent now. Swiftly, he unbuckled his breastplate and let it hang loose in his grip. Then he scraped its edge across the ground once. Twice. Flipping it up, he grunted. It would have to do.

'Nothing for it,' he murmured. The troll shook its head and jerked on the sword again. Black blood gushed from its mouth and it fell to one knee. Unable to extricate the weapon, its struggles only caused it to wound itself further. Eventually, however, the blade would simply dissolve, courtesy of the troll's acidic internals. It might take hours or minutes.

Goetz gripped the breastplate tightly, the straps wrapped around his forearm. It was awkward, but it would do the job. If not–

'We do what must be done,' he said, taking little comfort in the mantra. Then he cried 'Myrmidia!' and charged towards the troll. As he drew within arm's reach of the beast his feet left the floor and he smashed the cuirass into the beast's face. It fell back in surprise as his weight carried it down onto its back. Lifting the breastplate over his head, he brought the edge down on the troll's throat again and again. He slammed the chunk of metal down until his shoulders were on fire and his arms screamed in agony.

The troll lay still as he finally stood. Straddling it, he looked up at the platform where Eyri stood with wide eyes and a gaping mouth. 'That for your bloody troll,' Goetz said, his voice loud in the silence.

A moment later the troll lurched up, spilling Goetz onto the floor. With his breastplate jutting from its throat and his sword from its breast, it brought a fist and a swiftly healing stump down between his legs. Goetz raised his arms and closed his eyes.

When no blow fell, Goetz cracked an eye. The troll had fallen once more, and its head lay some distance away.

'Well met, brother,' someone said. Goetz twisted, looking up. Three men in armour stood over him protectively. They wore dark furs over their armour, mud and clay had been slathered over the plates, obscuring any insignia, but their ornate helmets bespoke their origins as well as any symbol. The one who'd spoken offered his hand to Goetz. In his other hand was the dripping axe that had decapitated the troll. He chuckled as Goetz gaped at him.

'Don't look so surprised, brother. Surely you know by now that the Knights of the Blazing Sun look after their own.'

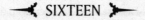

⟨ SIXTEEN ⟩

The knight removed his helmet, revealing handsome, hawk-like features. Pale blue eyes examined Goetz and then flickered to the troll. He clucked his tongue. 'Such ill-treatment of your armour, brother... what would your hochmeister say?'

'We do what we must,' Goetz said, accepting the helping hand.

'Including experimenting with non-traditional weaponry,' one of the other knights said, chuckling. 'I remember when we got stable duty for that sort of thing.'

'Times change, Brother Opchek. Circumstances as well, eh brother?' the first knight said as he pulled Goetz to his feet.

'Goetz. Hector Goetz. I – who are you?'

'Salvation come on the wing,' Opchek said, tapping a finger against the winged figurine of Myrmidia that crouched atop his helmet. 'Another tradition.'

'And a good one. I am Balk, hochmeister of the honourable komturie of Svunum. The quiet one here is Brother Taudge. And it's a lucky thing we happened to be passing by, eh?' Balk said, turning his blue eyes towards the viewing platforms. 'Ho Eyri! Who said you could kill one of our Order, eh?'

Eyri's normally ruddy face had gone pale. The Norscan stepped forward, his fists dangling at his sides. 'Who we take and what we do with them is no concern of yours, brass-skin!' he barked. 'And who said you could kill my troll, then?'

'It'll recover, more is the pity,' Balk said, kicking the head aside. The troll's eyes blinked alarmingly. 'That's more than I can say for you, however.'

'Is that a threat?' Eyri said, raising his arms. 'Here?' Along the platforms, Eyri's men raised bows.

'A warning,' Balk said, apparently unconcerned. 'We'll hang you eventually, Eyri. But not today, if you play nice.'

Eyri grimaced. Then he gestured, and the bows were lowered. 'What do you want, Balk?'

'Him,' Balk said, gesturing to Goetz.

'Take him and be damned!' Eyri snapped. 'Now leave my steading.'

627

'Gladly,' Balk said, smiling brazenly up at the Norscan. 'The smell of fish and filth is getting too much to bear anyway.'

They trooped up and out, the glares of Eyri and his men following them the entire way. 'How did you come to be here?' Goetz said as they stepped out of the pit's stifling confines and onto the street.

Balk smiled. 'At so fortuitous a moment, you mean?'

'Yes, I suppose so.'

'Pure happenstance, I assure you.' Balk gestured to the buildings around them. 'We visit every few months or so to buy slaves.'

Goetz nearly choked. 'What?'

The three knights laughed. Opchek slapped him on the shoulder. 'Don't look so dismayed, brother. We buy them and free them.'

'We go where we are needed, eh?' Balk said. He looked around. 'And we are most certainly needed here, I think.'

Eyri watched sourly as his men cleaned up the troll. Balk had been correct – it would heal, eventually. But it would be several days. He spat and turned away, stopping short as the tip of Dalla's looted sword pricked his nose.

'You had them,' she hissed. 'You had them and you let them walk out of here!'

'Aye,' Eyri said, using two fingers to carefully push the blade aside. 'What would you have had me do? Cut them down where they stood?'

'Yes!'

'No,' Ulfar said, stepping out onto the platform. He extended his staff and gently shoved his daughter to the side. 'Godi Eyri was correct to do as he did. He was thinking of his people. Of the good of Eyristaad.' Ulfar watched the men tossing bits of troll into its cell for a moment, then turned back. 'Even if he does play the fool sometimes.'

'I caught that troll fair and square I'll have you know,' Eyri said. 'People love that troll. I love that troll.'

Dalla snorted. Ulfar chuckled. 'Regardless, it was a dangerous game you played. Be glad you didn't lose more than a bit of face.'

'I can weather the loss. As long as I get to take the cost out of Balk's smug face,' Eyri said, making a fist. 'I'll call it even then.' He looked at Ulfar. 'And when are we getting to that, old man? My men are restless.'

'Soon enough,' Ulfar said. 'Once the godar have gathered here, we will speak more.' He looked up, his attention drawn to the outermost wall of the pit. A scraggly crow watched them, head cocked so that one black, shiny eye was fixed on them with unblinking intensity. Ulfar sniffed and flicked his fingers. A stiff breeze swept up dust and grit from the pit floor and flung it at the bird, driving it into the air with a squawk.

Dalla watched it flap away, her fingers clenching nervously around the hilt of her sword. Ulfar met his daughter's gaze and smiled benignly, patting her arm. Then he turned and left the platform, having said his piece. Eyri watched him go and then looked at her. 'He knows more than he's telling, your father.'

'Always,' she said. She drew her sword a little ways from its sheath before slamming it back down. 'He's wrong about this.'

'Oh?'

She looked at him. 'Don't play the innocent with me, Eyri Goldfinger.'

'Don't call me Goldfinger, Ulfarsdottir,' Eyri shot back. 'What? I suppose you'd take a few men and see that they never reached their galley, aye?'

'Maybe.' Dalla hesitated.

Eyri cocked his head. 'Or maybe you'd even have men lying in wait. Knowing, as you would, that they'd come running, the brass-skinned dogs, once their daemon-spies told them who we had.'

Dalla stared at him for a moment, then chuckled. 'I wondered why you waited as long as you did to feed him to the troll.'

Eyri tapped the side of his nose. 'I am godi for a reason, girl. Never forget that.'

'Don't call me 'girl', man,' Dalla said. 'Where?'

'Where do you think?' Eyri spread his hands and smiled.

'Truly a treacherous people,' Balk said. 'Don't you agree, Brother Goetz?'

'I'd heard the opposite, actually,' Goetz said. 'I'd heard the Northmen held personal honour in high regard.'

Opchek grunted. 'They do. They just don't think it applies to us soft Southerners, you see.' He slapped his hands together. 'That they include Kislev in that sweeping generalisation is proof of their ignorance.'

Goetz eyed the other knight's dangling mustachios and fought back a grin. 'I see.'

'I don't think you do,' Balk said genially. 'But experience is the best teacher, I've heard tell. We'll see you blooded yet, brother.'

'Where are we going?'

'We have a galley waiting,' Balk said.

'More a tub really,' Opchek said, nudging Taudge. The knight, who had not spoken the entire time, grunted softly in acknowledgement, but said nothing. Opchek made a face. 'You'll have to forgive Brother Taudge. He's under a vow of being a humourless stick.'

'Maybe I just don't think you're very funny,' Taudge said, his voice a hoarse rasp.

'Impossible,' Opchek said, winking at Goetz. Then he said, 'How did you come to be here, Brother Goetz? Just out of curiosity.'

'I was coming to see you, actually,' Goetz said, after a moment's hesitation. 'You are from the chapter house on Svunum, are you not?'

Balk stopped so abruptly that Goetz nearly crashed into him. 'Coming to see us? Why?'

Goetz stepped back, suddenly aware that he had neither weapons, nor armour. 'At the Grand Master's command,' he said.

'The–' Balk stopped. 'Why?' he demanded.

'He feared for you,' Goetz said, skirting the truth. 'It has been some time since your last report and with one thing and another...' Goetz gestured helplessly. 'He feared you might have been overrun.'

Balk eyed him for a moment and then let out a breathy chuckle. 'Of course he did. You hear that, brothers? A few messengers get waylaid and the Grand Master loses confidence in us.'

Goetz flushed. 'I wouldn't call the murder of a brother of our Order a simple matter of being waylaid, hochmeister,' he snapped.

'Murder – what?' Balk said, looking shocked.

'Oops,' Opchek interjected. He made a surreptitious gesture. 'I thought Goldfinger was being too pleasant.'

Goetz looked past Balk and saw that their path to the quay was barred by a dozen men. He recognised several of them from Eyri's vessel. Balk clucked his tongue. 'This is unfortunate.' He looked at Goetz. 'You see what I mean, brother. Treacherous.'

'Sneaky, even,' Opchek said, loosening his sword in its sheath. Taudge did the same, his grim face growing even more so.

'What is the meaning of this?' Balk said, stepping out in front of the group. He kept his hands well away from his weapons, but Goetz had little doubt that he could have them to hand quickly enough.

One of the Norscans barked something in his own tongue, and gestured with the long-handled axe he held in one hand. Balk replied in the same tongue and then looked at the others over his shoulder. 'Eyri is a sore loser. I'd wager he set this up. Be ready...'

'He's going to try and kill us in the street?' Goetz said, his hands clenching uselessly.

'No. He's going to try and make us kill him,' Opchek murmured. 'How quick on your feet are you, Brother Goetz?'

'Quick enough,' Goetz said, eyeing the closest of the Norscans.

'I hope so.'

The first clod of dung struck Taudge in the face. The knight twisted aside and clawed at his eyes, cursing virulently. More clods struck the others, sliding across their armour and leaving grimy patinas in their wake. Opchek cursed and made to start forward, but Balk held him back with a look. A crowd had gathered now; jeering, cheering Norscans, all hurling dung and curses with equal fervour.

Something hard struck Goetz in the cheek and he staggered. Another rock caught him in the small of the back and he fell against Opchek. The latter caught him and spun him around, placing his armoured form around Goetz protectively. 'Do something, Balk!' Opchek snarled.

'Just keep moving forward,' Balk said, moving towards Eyri's men steadily, his visor flipped down. 'If we attack, they'll be on us like wolves.'

Goetz suddenly realised what Eyri's plan must have been. If Balk and the others reacted in a hostile manner, the Norscans could claim they were only defending themselves when the rest of the Order came calling. A shabby fiction at best, but Eyri didn't seem altogether too concerned about such niceties.

As they pushed on through the swelling crowd, one of Eyri's warriors got too close and jammed the butt-end of his spear into Taudge's side, knocking the knight off his feet. Immediately a half-dozen Norscans fell on him, striking out with fists, clubs and knives.

'That's torn it,' Opchek barked, and drew his sword. It came free of his sheath with an evil hiss and looped out in a glittering arc. Men screamed as the blade danced across their extended arms and legs. Goetz immediately set to pulling Taudge to his feet. Balk turned back and drew his axe, blocking a blow meant for Opchek and gutting the man who'd made it.

'Nothing for it now,' Balk said. 'Kill them all.'

'I was hoping you'd say that!' Opchek said exultantly.

Getting Taudge to his feet took no small amount of effort. Besides the weight of his armour, he was solidly built. As Taudge stood, a Norscan darted towards them, roaring, an axe raised over his head. Goetz snatched the other knight's sword out of its sheath and lopped the head off the axe as it fell towards them. The Norscan looked at his beheaded weapon stupidly for a moment, then tossed the haft at Goetz and snatched for a dagger at his belt. Goetz didn't give him the opportunity to draw it. He batted the axe handle aside and sent its owner's head to join the blade in the dust.

More of Eyri's men were forcing their way through the crowd now, armoured for war. It was well-planned as ambushes went, and for the life of him, Goetz couldn't see how Balk intended to escape. He blocked a blow and thrust an elbow into his opponent's face. A hand fell on his shoulder and Goetz whirled. Iron fingers fastened on his hand.

'My sword, if you please,' Taudge said. Goetz gave him the blade and stooped to pick up a fallen one. Before he could grab one, however, Balk grabbed the crook of his arm and shoved him forward.

'Get to the docks!' the knight growled. Impossibly, the three men had cleared a path for them all through the crowd. Bodies and blood covered the ground and the survivors were drawing back. Arrows hissed off the rooftops, and Opchek chopped a number of them out of the air.

'I'll say this for them... they're determined!' the Kislevite said, laughing.

Goetz stumbled ahead of the trio, heading in the direction Balk had shoved him. A boat was waiting in the harbour, smallish and protected by a fourth knight, whose eyes widened as the group approached.

'What–' he began as Goetz stopped in front of him.

'No time! Into the boat!' Balk snapped. He jumped down off the dock into the coracle and hefted a large flag. As Goetz climbed down after him, he raised the flag and let it unfurl in the sea breeze.

Opchek slapped Goetz on the shoulder. 'Grab an oar, brother! Pull like your life depended on it!'

'Because it does,' Taudge added. Goetz grabbed one of the four oars and, despite the ache in his muscles, began to pull. The coracle slid away from the dock as their pursuers closed in.

'What good is waving a flag going to do?' Goetz said.

'You'll see,' Opchek said cheerily.

The crack of the waves slapping against the hull of the coracle was suddenly overwhelmed by a thunderous roar. Then another, and another. Five times in all, and with every belch a section of Eyristaad's waterfront disappeared in fire and death. Goetz dropped his oar and slapped his hands to his ears as he watched bodies and broken wood alike tossed into the air the way a child might toss a toy. He turned and caught sight of a long, heavily built galley sliding out of the cold fog, black sails fluttering in the breeze.

'Ha!' Balk crowed as he dropped the flag. 'Show those heathens the light of righteousness!' he roared, striking the air with his fists. More thunder rolled across the choppy surface of the sea, battering the shoreline.

'Blow them to hell more like,' Opchek said, resting his oar across his knees. 'You did us a good turn back there, brother,' he continued, looking at Goetz. 'Saving sourpuss like that.'

Taudge grunted and looked away. Goetz shrugged and then winced. 'We do what must be done,' he said, rubbing his aching shoulder.

'That we do, Brother Goetz,' Balk said, sitting down in the prow of the coracle. 'That we do.'

◄ SEVENTEEN ►

Svunum was a striking sight, even at a distance. Square stone towers rose up seemingly out of the very rock of the island, as if they had been birthed rather than built. The harbour nestled in a curve of the shore, and entrance to it was blocked by a number of great stone pylons which jutted from the water like the fangs of some immense sea-beast. A heavy chain had been threaded through the holes carved into the pylons and as Goetz watched, the chain was rendered limp and subsequently retracted out of the path of the galley.

'In the best traditions of our esteemed Order, Svunum is something of an ongoing project,' Balk said, sipping from a cup of iced fruit juice. The secrets of iced drinks had been brought back from the Crusades in Araby, along with the more material treasures used to fund the nascent Order.

Goetz and Balk sat on a raised platform on the aft deck, beneath a fur-lined awning. Balk had stripped off his armour and now sat in a thick bearskin robe on a chair made from tusks and sinew. Goetz wore a similar robe, and had it pulled tightly around him to ward off the chill.

'I can see that,' Goetz said, admiring the ingenuity that must have gone into crafting and depositing the pylons. 'Someone has read Mario Flavia's treatise on naval combat.' He gestured to the pylons as the galley slid past. 'Not to mention Hellestrome's pamphlet on ship-board artillery,' he continued, motioning to the ten slender brass-barrelled cannons that lined the rails, five to either side.

'I see the Order's standards haven't diminished since I came out here,' Balk said, chewing a sliver of ice. 'We've made a few innovations of our own as well, to be sure.'

'I'd be interested to see them,' Goetz said carefully.

'In due time, brother,' Balk said, smiling. The expression faded. 'What you said earlier... about a murdered brother...'

'Athalhold. From the Bechafen Komturie,' Goetz said. 'He was sent to – he was my predecessor in this mission.'

'The mission to check on us, you mean?' Balk said carefully.

Goetz heard the care in his words and decided to take the hint. There was no reason to antagonise his saviour with Marienburg's demands. Not yet anyway. 'Yes,' he said.

'How did he die?' Balk said, his eyes never wavering from Goetz's own.

'Murdered.'

'By who?'

Goetz hesitated. Then he said, 'Cultists. Followers of the Ruinous Powers.'

Balk sat back, almost slumping. He sighed and hung his head. When he looked up, his expression was ragged. 'Another brother gone. We will tip a goblet to him and carve his name upon a Martyr's Niche in the komturie.' He shook himself and said, 'I had no idea, brother. I thought that we were being ignored. If I had known... well.' He waved a hand. 'For now, I can but extend the courtesy of our komturie to you. Make yourself at home.'

Goetz sat back on his stool and took in the galley as an excuse to avoid Balk's haunted gaze. A long vessel, it stood in contrast to the more bulky dragonships of the Norscans despite the similarities in design. There were forty knights aboard, though only a few wore armour. The rest had stripped themselves down to their trousers as they bent forward over their oars, though their swords and shields remained near to hand.

The rail was studded with heavy iron plates, each of which bore a face that Goetz assumed was Myrmidia's, though the engraver had obviously never seen a lithograph or a statue of the goddess. Braziers filled with incense hung from the mast and from the deck railings, filling the air with a warm, calming scent.

Those knights who were not at the oars moved across the deck seeing to other duties – some stowed the guns, while others brought water to the rowers.

'I'm curious,' Goetz said, turning back to Balk after a moment. 'The Norscans seem to bear our Order a grudge.'

'That's a polite way of putting it,' Opchek said, striding up onto the deck. The big Kislevite had his helmet tucked beneath his arm and his bald head gleamed in the faint sunlight. 'They bloody hate us might be more accurate.'

Balk grunted. 'True enough, unfortunately.' He looked at Goetz speculatively. 'It's not so complicated, brother. We have had to undertake a more – ah – proactive approach to dealing with our neighbours to the North, I'm afraid.'

'Proactive?'

'Punitive,' Opchek said merrily.

Goetz frowned. 'You mean that what I saw today–'

'Was a taste of something that jumped-up pirate Goldfinger has had coming for months now,' Balk said, nodding brusquely. 'In truth, we were scouting his defences. Eyri has become much bolder than he ought to be, and I wanted to know why.'

'And did you find out?'

Balk smiled crookedly. 'No. We got a bit distracted.' Goetz flushed. Balk held up a hand to forestall his reply. 'No offence meant or blame attached, brother. But you did pick a rather busy time of year to visit us.'

'I'll make a note of that for next time,' Goetz said.

Scribes and other functionaries, clad in the livery of the Order, were waiting for them at the docks. They instantly besieged Balk, waving papers and shouting questions. Opchek took Goetz's arm and guided him out of the way.

'Come lad, let our fearless hochmeister handle this most dangerous of foeman by himself.'

'I wasn't expecting it to be so busy,' Goetz said. He continued on quickly. 'Not that it shouldn't be, but...'

'We are out on the fringes, aren't we?' Opchek said. He chuckled. 'Or so it must seem. In truth, I believe we are one of the busiest komturies in the Order.' He gestured at the ships in the small harbour. There were over a dozen vessels of various sizes – merchantmen, galleys and sloops, flying half a dozen different flags. 'We've made ourselves over into something approaching a port-of-call for the local money grubbers.'

'And what do the authorities in Marienburg make of this?' Goetz said.

Opchek laughed. 'Oh they're fit to be tied I expect!' He tapped the side of his nose. 'What are they going to do about it then, eh?' He gestured to the towers. 'We are the most heavily fortified area for miles around. We keep the trade routes open, save for when there's reason to close them.'

'And is now one of those times? Is that why the vessel I was on was taken so quickly? And so close to Svunum?' Goetz said carefully. Opchek stopped and turned, frowning.

'No. That is a different matter entirely. And one I'll thank you to hold your tongue on until such time as Hochmeister Balk chooses to illuminate you.'

Goetz raised a hand in surrender, and Opchek's smile returned. 'Besides, there are more pleasant discussions to be had. We can–'

A crow croaked, interrupting Opchek. They turned to see a slender figure standing behind them, swathed in a robe of feathers and fur, with a crow perched on its shoulder. A smooth face peered out from under the peaked hood and two dark eyes peered out of a mask of intricate tattoos to fix on Goetz.

'Ah, our hostess,' Opchek said softly. Almost reverently.

'Who?' Goetz said, confused.

'The lady of the island,' the other knight murmured, sinking to one knee. Goetz hesitated, and then followed suit. Slim hands threw back the hood and a smile curved across the woman's face. She was young, perhaps a year or two older than Goetz himself, with a curious cast to her features. The dark tattoos coiled across her cheeks and brow like a lover's fingers, and Goetz was uncomfortably reminded of the woman in his dreams, her face caressed by dark feathers.

'Myrma,' she said softly, reaching up to stroke the crow. Goetz felt a chill go through him. He turned slightly and met Opchek's gaze.

'You feel it, don't you?' the Kislevite said.

'Of course he does,' Balk said, approaching them, followed by his scribes. 'How could he not? How could any true servant of the Order not?'

'What?' Goetz said, getting to his feet. Myrma looked away, a half-smile curling across her face. 'Who is she?'

'Better to say what is she,' Balk said, inclining his head to the young woman, who returned the gesture. 'To which I answer, a blessing from the goddess on our endeavours.'

Goetz tore his eyes from Myrma. 'Endeavours?'

'Later,' Balk said. 'First, we must get you settled, brother. Our komturie is open to you, and I hope you will indulge in our hospitality.'

The crow took flight from the woman's shoulder. Goetz watched it fly, and then turned to Balk. 'Nothing would please me more,' he said.

Smoke rose into the cold air, meeting the rain as it came down, mingling into a grey sludge that coated the ruins of the wharf. Dalla rested her chin on the pommel of her sword and watched as Eyri's men searched for survivors.

'Foolishness,' her father murmured, his eyes on the sea.

'You did warn him,' Dalla said bluntly. Her fingers played across the intricately wrought hilt of the sword. It was a beautiful thing. Heavy, but somehow light at the same time. 'Is it your fault if Goldfinger is too stubborn to listen to the advice of his gudja?'

'Maybe if the gudja's advice had been less cryptic, the godi might have listened!' Eyri snarled, stalking forward with a naked sword in hand. He was covered in ash, soot and blood, and his eyes were wide and fierce.

'Sheath your sword, Goldfinger!' Dalla snapped, rising cat-like to her feet. She extended her own sword and batted Eyri's aside contemptuously. 'No man threatens my father.'

'I'll threaten who I damn well like wench!' Eyri roared, swiping at her. Their swords met and Ulfar's staff came down on them, sweeping them from their hands.

'Enough,' the old man said harshly. 'Maybe you will listen now, godi… now that you have seen what our Enemy is capable of.'

Eyri stooped to snatch up his sword. 'This was your idea of a lesson, old man?' He glared at Ulfar. 'Did my men die so you could show me what a fool I've been?'

Ulfar met his glare silently. Eventually, Eyri looked away. He made a snort and sheathed his sword. 'What now?'

'Now, you do as I asked earlier. You call a meeting of the godar. A council of war,' Ulfar said, looking off in the direction the galley had gone. 'We must prepare for the storm to come.'

As Eyri stalked off, Dalla looked at her father. 'Is it truly that bad then?'

'No.' He smiled slightly. 'It is worse.'

'Your comforting skills leave something to be desired, father,' Dalla said. Tenderly, she brushed a few specks of soot out of his beard. He batted at her hand irritably.

'That was your mother's job.'

'No. Mother's job was to take care of you, old goat,' Dalla said, grinning. The grin faded as she said, 'He fought well.'

'Who?'

'The einsark,' Dalla said. 'For a Southerner, I mean.' A note in her voice caused her father to look at her.

'Yes. His kind are born to the blade.'

'Not this blade,' Dalla said, slapping her looted sword. 'It's mine now.'

'For how long?'

'What?'

'I am reminded of a story,' Ulfar said. 'A thane of some standing gave, as a gift, a fine dwarfish blade to the maiden he wished to marry. She, in her turn, gave it back to him, though not entirely in the manner he'd intended.'

'She killed him?'

'No. Though he did learn that swords do not make proper gifts,' Ulfar said. He looked at her. Dalla blinked.

'I took this sword from him. He did not give it to me.'

'Yes.' Ulfar turned away. 'Maybe the story is not similar at all.'

Dalla was about to reply when she caught sight of the gathering crows perched on the still-smouldering remnants of the destroyed buildings. 'Father...'

'I see them. Rest easy. They are naught but ordinary scavengers,' Ulfar said, leaning on his staff. 'Our foe has turned his eyes from us for the moment.' He sighed wearily and looked up at the circling birds. 'I do not know why, but I can but hope it will last long enough for us to act...'

EIGHTEEN

Goetz was back in the Drakwald and avian furies spun around him in a black kaleidoscope, shedding rotten feathers as they tore strips from his flesh. His sword was broken and his armour was held on by ragged strips of leather, and neither did him any good. The witch-light made the trees look sickly as he spun, lashing out blindly at the bird-shapes that left ragged canyons in his battered flesh. Staggering, he tried to find escape, but there was none to be had.

Goetz stumbled and fell, sinking to his knees, blinded. Fingers gripped his chin and jerked his head up.

'You were poisoned,' Myrmidia said. 'Poisoned.'

Goetz snapped awake, covered in sweat.

'You were dreaming,' someone said.

Goetz turned sharply. The young woman called Myrma sat on a stool in the corner of the room he'd been given. She stroked the feathers that lined the edge of her robes. 'How did you get in here?' he pressed.

'I go where I am needed,' she said. She stood and left the room as silently as she had come. Goetz waited until the door had shut and then stood, shrugging into a robe. He shuddered slightly, though whether from the chill in the room or the lingering echo of his dream, he couldn't say.

He went to the window, rubbing the scars on his back as he went. Were these dreams the product of whatever poisons remained in his system? Or was it something else? He leaned against the sill and turned, looking for the lithograph of Myrmidia that should have been on the wall somewhere.

As he'd noticed last night, there was neither image nor icon anywhere to be seen. The thought made him uneasy and he turned back to the window. He could see the sea from where he stood, and he could hear the sharp snarl of the waves crashing against the rocky shoreline. Svunum was not beautiful, save in the most savagely aesthetic sense. Kleerman or Pattilo would have made much of this place, with their love of the darker end of the colour spectrum.

Still, he wasn't here to think about painters. Goetz pushed away from the window and dressed swiftly. What had been built here was far more impressive than he'd been led to believe by Grand Master Berengar. Even the Talabheim Komturie paled in comparison to this citadel.

Goetz left his room and moved through the torch-lit corridors. He wrinkled his nose at the smell of pitch emanating from the torches and moved towards the stairs, hoping to find open air. Taking them up, he moved out onto the battlements, his hands behind his back. Above, the moon rode through dark clouds. The wind whipped at him as he stepped out of the shelter of the doorway and he stumbled slightly. He rubbed his arms as the cold bit into him and he moved towards the edge.

'Couldn't sleep?'

Goetz frowned as Balk turned towards him. The hochmeister smiled thinly. 'After the beating you took, I thought you'd sleep like the dead.'

'I feel fine, hochmeister,' Goetz said, flexing his hands for emphasis. 'The girl – Myrma – was in my room.'

'Ah. You should feel honoured,' Balk said, looking out towards the sea.

'Who is she?'

'I should have thought that that would have been obvious,' Balk said, not looking at him.

Goetz let the comment go unanswered and joined him at the wall. 'I wasn't aware that this island was inhabited,' he said, recalling what the first mate onboard the Nicos had said. Balk chuckled.

'You mean that the Grand Master wasn't aware, don't you?'

Goetz said nothing. Balk glanced at him, and then went on. 'When our Order was gifted with this island, it was without the permission of its owners.'

'The merchant-princes?'

'Pfaugh,' Balk said, making a sharp gesture. 'Those money-grubbers? No. No, there were folk here then, and long before. A primitive people, but touched by grace despite that.'

'Norscans?'

'No.' Balk's face twisted slightly. 'Not Norscan. Not precisely at least. They call themselves Svanii, after the island one assumes. Quite a surprising folk. Our first meeting was an interesting one, albeit a bit bloody.'

'They fought?'

'Oh my yes. But our Order held firm. And in the end, we followed Myrmidia's teachings and brought civilisation to the savages,' Balk said, motioning to the fortress. 'They are still here and they serve our Order as faithfully as any knight.'

Goetz shook his head. 'And her?'

'Ah, there we have an interesting story,' Balk said. 'She is a priestess. I suppose that is as good a word as any.' He scratched his chin, smiling slightly. 'They worship a goddess, you see. One of the old ones, before artists, poets and philosophers made them palatable for the common herd. They call her the Young Crone, or the Maiden of Wisdom.' He tapped the side of his nose. 'A war-goddess, as well as a goddess of knowledge.'

Goetz felt a chill that had nothing to do with the wind blowing off the sea. 'Coincidence?' he said.

'Do you believe in coincidence, Brother Goetz?' Balk said, turning to him. 'Or do you believe in something greater? Why else would you have joined the Order?'

'Obligation,' Goetz said softly.

Balk looked at him. 'Faith is no burden, brother. It is the armour that defends us and the sword that pierces the darkness.' He turned back and pointed a finger at the sea. 'That darkness.'

'Norsca?'

Balk spat. 'Yes. Norsca. A weeping tumour on the shank of the world. That. That is why we are here, brother!' The hochmeister clapped his hands together. 'The Norscans are the wolves at the gates of the world, and we have been placed here to bar their entry.' He smacked a fist against the parapet. 'Chaos surges across the mountains of the Old World in ever increasing numbers, brother, their daemonic ranks swelled by the Northmen. They worship the Ruinous Powers as gods, brother! Gods! And they follow them as zealously as... as...'

'As we do Myrmidia,' Goetz said.

Balk swung around, and for a moment, Goetz thought the other man might fly at him in a rage. Then, Balk began to laugh. 'Exactly. Exactly!' he said, clapping his hands against Goetz's shoulders. 'And that, brother, is why we must be the ones to face them.' He sighed and crossed his arms. 'We can end the Long War with a single mighty stroke. And we can do it from here.'

Intrigued, Goetz said, 'Is that why the Marienburg brothers abandoned their komturie to come here?'

'In part, yes. But we have days yet,' Balk said. He moved past Goetz and headed for the stairs. 'Get some rest, brother. Tomorrow will be busy.' Goetz wanted to call to him, to stop him, but he refrained. He was a guest here, and Svunum seemed to lack that easy familiarity that so characterised his own komturie.

He couldn't blame them. He looked out over the Sea of Claws and tried to pierce the icy fog that covered it. Balk had a grudge, that much he was certain of. Justified or not, it was a bit disturbing. He wondered what had caused it... what had given birth to the raw hatred he'd seen blossom in the hochmeister's eyes when he'd spoken of Norsca?

More importantly, what had it grown into?

'Up, lad!'

The boot struck the side of Goetz's bed and he sat upright. Weak grey light came in through the windows and the sound of gulls echoed loudly off the stone. Ivan Opchek had flowing moustaches and a face like an apple. Older than Goetz, he radiated good cheer. He grinned down at Goetz and tossed a sheathed sword onto his blankets. 'This looked to be about your size, so I took the liberty of bringing it here.'

The Kislevite hooked the stool with his foot and sat down, swinging his legs up onto the bed. He tore a chunk out of the loaf of bread he held with his teeth and chewed noisily. 'Can't have you wandering around without a proper sword or armour.' He ripped the loaf in half and tossed the unchewed section to Goetz, who caught it.

'No butter?' Goetz said.

'Am I your maidservant?' Opchek leaned back and looked away as Goetz dressed and buckled on the sword. He drew it and sighted down the blade.

'Good balance,' Goetz said. 'Bit lighter than I'm used to.'

'Our weapon-smith is a bit of an artist,' Opchek said.

Goetz looked at him. 'You have a weapon-smith? Here?'

Opchek snorted. 'And an armourer and a blacksmith or three. We also grow our own vegetables and bake our own bread.' He waved his half-loaf at Goetz for emphasis. 'Isn't your own komturie self-sufficient?'

'Yes, but not quite on this scale.' Goetz sheathed the sword. 'Good bread though,' he said, taking a bite.

'The secret is in the yeast, I'm told.' Opchek hopped to his feet. 'Our ever-attentive hochmeister would like to see you.'

'Am I in trouble?'

'Depends on your definition of trouble,' Opchek said. 'He's quite taken with you.'

'He seems like a good man,' Goetz said noncommittally. He recalled the previous night, and the expression he'd seen on Balk's face. 'Dedicated.'

'As we all are,' Opchek said wryly.

'You make it sound like a bad thing.'

'Heh. I worshipped Ulric once. Wore the fur cloak and the wolf's head, damn me if I didn't,' Opchek said, stroking his moustaches. 'Dedication can lead a man down ugly paths.'

'There's a difference between duty and fanaticism,' Goetz said.

'Oh aye. Indeed there is. The question is can you tell the difference?'

'You're one to talk.' Taudge pushed himself away from a wall and joined them. 'You wouldn't know dedication if it attacked you in a dark alley.'

'Well obviously,' Opchek said, winking at Goetz. 'It being a dark alley and such.'

Taudge shook his head. 'Idiot.'

'Possibly,' Opchek said. 'Joining us on our constitutional?'

'Yes,' Taudge said tersely. Goetz was about to say something when they stepped out through the gatehouse door and he caught sight of Svunum in the morning light. He hadn't fully appreciated the sight the day before. He stood, dumbstruck.

'It's a sight to behold, is it not?' Opchek said. 'Fairly takes your breath away. Or that might just be the smell of the nightsoil containers.'

Goetz didn't reply. He looked down at the town that pressed close to the walls of the komturie with the faintest sense of unease. It was a bit like looking back into the history of the Empire. Crude huts battled for space with more modern-looking dwellings, and every man and woman went armed, as far as he could see.

The town encircled the section of the komturie that did not rest on the steep sea-cliffs, spreading out in a sickle-moon shape. It bustled with activity, and the smoke of a hundred or more cooking fires wafted up into the air, carrying with them the mingled scents of spices both familiar and otherwise. It was no primitive fishing village, but a town, full of life, noise and colour. In short, the very last thing he had expected.

'I can't believe it,' he said after a moment.

'Why not? You've seen isolated backwaters before haven't you?' Opchek said from behind him. 'This one just happens to be a bit better taken care of than most.'

'Still, to be so– so–'

'Pure,' Taudge said. The other knight had stopped nearby, hands behind his back.

Goetz looked at him. 'I was going to say large.' He ignored the other knight's glower. 'They seem to have adapted to your presence well enough. The Svanii, I mean.'

'After we killed a hundred or so of them, way back when,' Opchek said. He had picked up a chunk of driftwood in his hand and began whittling it to a point with his dagger. 'They became very quiet after that.'

'Wouldn't you?' Goetz said mildly. Opchek laughed. Taudge bestowed a disapproving gaze on both of them.

'Fools, the pair of you,' he said. He gestured to the village. 'It is a sign of Myrmidia's blessings that we were sent here, to this untainted land, to spread the word of Her coming!'

Goetz blinked. 'I wasn't aware that the goddess was going anywhere, let alone coming here,' he said.

Opchek coughed. 'What he meant to say was–'

'I think I heard him quite clearly, thank you.' Goetz ignored the Kislevite and faced Taudge. 'What do you mean, brother?'

Taudge made a face. 'I simply meant that we are bringing the light of Her to these people.'

Goetz glanced at Opchek, who looked away. He stepped back. 'You don't like me very much do you, brother?'

'It is not a matter of like or dislike,' Taudge said. 'I do not know you. And you have a quick tongue, a trait I find annoying in even those I do know.' He glared at Opchek, who made a rude noise. 'Come. See for yourself what I meant,' he said, starting down the slope towards the village.

Goetz looked at Opchek, who gestured with his driftwood. 'After you, brother. I've seen it before. And that's why I brought you out here anyway.' They started after Taudge. The knights were apparently a common enough sight and several times Opchek and, to a lesser extent, Taudge, stopped to make conversation with the locals. They were a people not entirely dissimilar to the folk of Talabecland, with the slight oddities of feature any isolated region might eventually come to favour. Dark tattoos covered what flesh was visible beneath their rough clothing, and several times Goetz found himself staring blankly at the weaving skeins of ink that crawled across a cheek or forearm. If any of the locals took offence, they didn't show it.

'They get the ink from octopuses, apparently,' Opchek said after he caught Goetz looking.

'I wasn't aware there were any such creatures in the Sea of Claws,' Goetz said.

'Neither was I until one tried to eat one of our galleys,' Opchek said. 'Big as a whale and twice as tasty, once we'd given it the business.'

'You ate it?'

'It's not exactly good farmland hereabouts.'

Goetz shook his head and turned to watch a bevy of knights, stripped to their trousers and boots, pull down a shack with equal parts of rope and virulent swearing. 'What are they doing?'

'Improving the view,' Taudge said with evident satisfaction.

'What?'

'We're in the process of rebuilding the older structures in the village as it expands. Can't have it becoming a sty like Eyristaad now can we? Or Marienburg for that matter,' Opchek said. He motioned around with his driftwood chunk. 'We'll have a suitable little city here soon enough.'

'Besides which, it gives the brethren something to do when they're not fighting,' Goetz said. 'Right?'

'Your intuition does you credit, brother,' Balk said, stepping out from a doorway. Goetz started in surprise. Balk jerked his head. 'Come, she wishes to see you.'

'Who?'

'Who do you think, brother?' Balk said, half-smiling. 'Our hostess. Now come, it wouldn't do to keep her waiting.' The hochmeister started off, leading them deeper into the village. People stepped aside for him, heads bowed. Some made the sign of Myrmidia, Goetz noticed. Thumbs hooked together and palms spread like the wings of the goddess's messenger-crows. Thinking of the birds caused him to look up. Hundreds of the birds circled above, alighting on rooftops or skimming across the street. The sound of their croaking provided a disturbing counterpoint to the sounds of routine industry.

'I know what you're thinking – why'd it have to be carrion-eaters?' Opchek said slyly, tilting his head so the others couldn't hear. 'Crows go everywhere, see? And they can get into anything. Only animal that might be better at ferreting out knowledge and secrets are rats, and even Myrmidia, bless Her name, probably can't stand those little buggers.' He sniffed. 'That's my thinking anyhow.'

'There are enough of them around,' Goetz said, still watching the birds.

'More every day. The Svanii look on it as a good omen.' Opchek shook his head. 'I don't see it myself, but as Myrmidia wills it, I suppose.'

'She will be pleased to hear that you have no objections, I'm sure,' Balk said without turning. Opchek made a face at his hochmeister's back and Goetz fought to restrain a chuckle. They stopped a few moments later before an incongruous hut that sat at the farthest edge of the village. The hut sat on a circular wooden platform which itself sat upon legs made of what looked to be repurposed ship's masts. Crows lined the roof and waddled across the platform. There was a strange smell on the air that had nothing to do with either the birds or the sea.

'It's a sort of mould that grows on some of the rocks around here. They burn it and it puts off an odd odour,' Opchek whispered. Balk lifted the tanned hide curtain that blocked off the hut's doorway and extended his hand.

'She waits within, brother,' he said.

'Try not to embarrass us,' Opchek added.

Goetz ducked his head and stepped inside. The strange smell enveloped him and he fought back a cough. Two knights, clad in their burnished plate-mail, knelt before the woman, Myrma. As Goetz watched, she lifted a crude ladle of water and poured it over them, murmuring the entire while. The water crawled across the armour and dripped down and as one the knights rose. They filed out past Goetz without a word.

'They go hunting,' she said, without waiting for him to ask. She dropped the ladle back into the bucket near her seat.

'For what?'

'Their enemies. Your enemies,' she said, smiling. She leaned back in her seat and spread her arms. She was wearing only a thin robe and Goetz suddenly felt uncomfortably cramped in the tight confines of the hut. To distract himself, he looked around. With some surprise, he suddenly realised where all the images and lithographs of Myrmidia had gone. They lined the circular walls and ceiling of the hut, plastered together like tiles. The goddess's face stared down at him from every conceivable angle.

Goetz felt suddenly light-headed and stumbled. 'Sit,' Myrma said softly. 'You are still weak.'

'I feel fine,' Goetz said, sinking down. A flare of pain cut off his protest and he grunted. He fell forward and caught himself inches from the floor. His side felt as if it were on fire.

'Yes?' she said, rising from her seat. She glided forward on bare feet and placed a hand on his side. He hissed as red blossoms of agony burst at the corners of his eyes. 'Take off your shirt.'

'I do not think–'

'You are ill. Take it off,' she said, her voice steady and warm. Goetz did as she asked, his movements awkward and stiff. The scars on his side were inflamed and as she pressed her fingertips to the edges of them, pus leaked out in thin streams. 'Poison,' she said, the word reverberating oddly in his head. The world seemed fuzzy at the edges and he shook his head, trying to clear it.

'They said there was nothing there,' he said.

'They say many things. Believe your eyes, not the words of others,' she murmured. She drew something from within her robe – a feather with a sharpened quill. Goetz couldn't stop himself from cringing slightly as she jabbed it into his wound. He wanted to pull away, but the eyes of the multitude of Myrmidia's that looked down on him seemed to hold him in place.

The quill dug into the soft scar tissue, peeling it away. More pus leaked out and the pain intensified. Goetz groaned. His vision went black at the edges and he felt himself falling forward.

Then, beneath his face, damp grass. He opened his eyes and saw the hatefully familiar glare of the witch-fire and heard the stamp of beast-hooves between the twisted trees of the Drakwald. He pushed himself up, his movements loose and slow, as if he were underwater. Automatically he reached for his sword but it wasn't there.

The fire roared up and he turned. A woman stepped out of the flames, her armour gleaming with an eerie light. 'Poisoned,' she said. 'You were poisoned.' She extended a hand and Goetz reached for it even as a storm of crows exploded out of the dark between the trees and sped around him in a cyclone of digging beaks and flashing talons. Amidst the feathers, he thought he caught a glimpse of the woman's face, before it became something else. Someone else. Goetz threw up a hand as the face expanded, passing through the black feathers even as it somehow was the feathers and then the great mouth was closing on him and he screamed.

He sat bolt upright, his breath burning in his lungs and his stomach churning. Twisting, he looked down at the poultice that had been placed on his wound and bound with strips of cloth. Myrma had resumed her seat, her robe loose where she had torn strips off to make the bandage.

Goetz staggered to his feet, sweat dripping from his face and chest. 'What did you–'

'You are ill. We will speak later. Rest now,' she said gently.

Bewildered, Goetz walked drunkenly towards the curtain and stepped out into the light of day. Balk was there to catch him as he fell.

'I told you he was going to embarrass us,' he heard Opchek say, even as consciousness fled.

NINETEEN

Goetz awoke to the smell of cooking fires and the night breeze. He had had dreams, but he could not, for the life of him, recall them. Head full of muggy, half-formed thoughts, he left his room and wandered until he came to the battlements of the komturie. The battlement was circular and composed of equal parts stone and wood. There, he found Opchek, sitting in a chair, his booted feet propped up on the stone buttress. 'The wood comes from the Drakwald. We had it shipped in special. Resists fire like nothing I've ever seen,' Opchek said, taking a swig from a jug of wine.

Goetz looked down, his skin crawling slightly as the bad memories pressed tight to the door of his mind. Angrily he shook them aside as Opchek offered him the jug. He took it and gulped a swig down before handing it back. 'The Drakwald?'

'Oh yes. Absorbs sound and vibration as well. Keeps the stone from shifting under the recoil of the cannons,' Opchek said, seemingly oblivious to Goetz's discomfort. He gestured to the trio of wide-muzzled cannons resting on a raised platform. 'We have nine of these, acquired over the past twenty years, I'm told. Beautiful, aren't they?'

'The cannons... how were they crafted?' Goetz said. 'Surely there are no engineers here?'

'Not unless you count us, no. I don't know about you, but I'm lucky if I can get a trebuchet working. And the College of Engineering is notorious about keeping their secrets, especially where these sorts of things are concerned, selfish beggars,' Opchek said. He patted one of the guns affectionately. 'No, we bought most of these with honest gold from the dwarfs. A few are from Tilea as well. The light guns we use on the galleys were bought wholesale from some bankrupt duke from across the Black Mountains.'

Goetz blinked. While such purchases weren't unheard of, the Imperial Assessor's Office frowned on the private purchase of powder weapons. 'And the Imperial authorities didn't interfere?'

'Marienburg is no longer under Imperial authority, brother. Don't you read your history books?' Opchek smiled. 'We bought them through third parties regardless. Had them shipped in pieces and reconstructed them here. And soon enough we'll be able to manufacture our own – albeit crude-copies. The Svanii, bless their savage little spirits, take to the manufacturing arts like a fish to water.' He knocked a knuckle on the cannon barrel and chuckled. 'Best idea old Greisen had. He was a clever one, always with the cunning plans. Shame the Norscans put an axe through his twisty brainpan.'

'So it wasn't Balk's idea?'

Opchek snorted. 'Conrad is a bright one, and as dedicated as the day is long, but this komturie has been a work in progress back since the Order was first gifted it sixty years ago. Balk just happens to be the one with the drive to implement some of the – ah – bolder strategies in our war-book.' Opchek sighed and looked out at the sea.

'You don't sound happy about it,' Goetz said.

Opchek looked at him. 'I'm neither happy nor unhappy, brother. I have faith in the doing, and the reasons for it and that's enough for now.'

'Didn't you tell me earlier that faith could lead you down the wrong path?' Goetz said, his tone teasing.

Opchek chuckled. 'So I did. So I did.' He leaned on the battlement and thrust his bullet-shaped head out over the water. 'It's a grand thing to be a part of a crusade.'

'Is that what it is?' Goetz said.

'Of course. The Northern Crusades, they'll call it when it's done,' Opchek said, taking in a deep lungful of sea air. 'It'll be a glorious tale, depicting how we brought civilisation to these savage climes. I'll get three stanzas, myself.'

'Will you?'

'Oh yes. Possibly four.' Opchek glanced at him slyly. 'You'll make do with one, I think. Being much younger, you understand.'

'Do you truly believe that she's the Goddess incarnate?' Goetz said suddenly. 'That Myrma is Myrmidia come again?'

Opchek paused and let out a long breath. 'The Tileans say that she came to the mortal world before, to lead them out of their darkest years. She appeared as a shepherdess and rose to command an empire second only to Sigmar's or that of the Dragon-Emperor in far Cathay in the annals of the Old World.'

'I'm not asking what the Tileans think,' Goetz said. 'I'm asking you.'

'Faith,' Opchek said, turning around. He crossed his arms and looked steadily at Goetz. 'I suppose you can be forgiven for being suspicious. You weren't here for it. For any of it.'

'Any of what?'

'This,' Opchek said, indicating the komturie. Seeing the look of confusion on Goetz's face, he smiled and went on. 'There's been a Myrma here since the beginning. You recall what Conrad told you earlier? About their goddess?'

'Yes,' Goetz said.

'Well, that's not the whole story.' Opchek hesitated, as if debating what to say next.

'What is then?' Goetz pressed.

'Sixty years ago, our Order arrived here. And the Svanii weren't shy about showing us how unwelcome we were. So we killed them in droves, in endlessly clever ways until, finally, we shattered them. And in the shattering, we discovered that they worshipped a goddess.'

'Myrmidia?'

'Then, possibly. Now, certainly,' Opchek said. 'A goddess of battle and wisdom regardless. A goddess who spoke through those blasted geyser caves, her words hidden in poison smoke and herbs. And then Kluger, the hochmeister before Greisen, met with the first Myrma–'

'The first? How many have there been?'

'Five? Six?' Opchek said. He caught Goetz's look and smiled sadly. 'It's the caves, you see. The gases.' He tapped his chest. 'They eat away at the lungs and the brain. The one Kluger met was on her last legs. She passed away as peace was made and her daughter took over. The daughters always take over.'

'What of the fathers?'

Opchek shrugged. 'Who knows? They're so inbred that I'm not sure it matters.' He snorted. 'Granted, they freshen up the bloodline with captives every so often, but it's a drop of clean water in a Marienburg canal, if you get my meaning.'

Goetz grimaced. 'I think I do, yes.'

'They drove mutants into the caves, you know,' Opchek said. 'When they cropped up, which was often, considering what sort of debris the Sea of Claws drags ashore from the Sea of Chaos, they drove them into those gas caves. We used to have mutant hunts, in my first years here. Until we killed them all.'

Goetz felt a chill at the casual way Opchek said it, though he was careful not to show it. Kislevites were known to have little sympathy for those touched by Chaos. 'What happens if they're born now?' he said.

'There are none, apparently.' Opchek shrugged. 'They haven't had a sour birth since we killed the last of the wild mutants.' He looked steadily at Goetz. 'The blessings of the goddess, Conrad says.'

'Do you believe that?'

'I believe my eyes,' Opchek said slowly, hooking his thumbs into his belt. 'I haven't seen any freakish specimens since then. Ergo, they don't exist.'

'A bit of philosophical fallacy there,' Goetz said, chuckling.

'I'm allowed, I think.' Opchek slapped him on the shoulder. 'A fluid philosophy allowed me to shuck the wolf-skin for the eagle after all.'

'I wasn't aware knights could do that,' Goetz said.

'I wasn't aware we couldn't,' Opchek said. 'Besides, it seemed the done thing after I punched the Ar-Ulric in the snout.' He grinned and rubbed his knuckles. 'The Brethren of the Wolf are a humourless bunch, unfortunately.'

'And we're full of jest and cheer?' Goetz said.

'Depends. Taudge, for instance, has a stick so far up his fundament that there are leaves growing out of his head,' Opchek said. He looked past Goetz. 'Hello Taudge.'

'Brothers,' Taudge said, frowning. 'What are you doing up here?'

'Getting some air,' Goetz said. 'I was thinking of taking a walk. Opchek was kind enough to join me. Care to come along?'

'Someone must,' Taudge said, falling in alongside them. 'If only to keep you both out of mischief.'

'How long has Balk been hochmeister?' Goetz said, as they left the keep.

Opchek looked at him sidelong. 'Any particular reason you'd like to know, brother?'

'Call it curiosity.'

'You'll have to try harder than that, my lad.' Opchek made a face. 'Did Berengar send you to check on us, or spy on us?'

It was Goetz's turn to make a face. 'Does it matter? I'm here now. You may as well answer me.'

'Ha! Fine. A year. No more,' Opchek said, holding up a finger. 'When old Greisen popped off, Balk was made hochmeister. Only one who wanted the job, honestly.'

'Others had more seniority?'

'Oh several. Me, for instance.' Opchek brushed a thumb along his moustaches.

'How did Greisen die?'

'Norscans,' Taudge said. 'They swept down out of the North in those serpent-boats of theirs and attacked our galleys. Killed a third of the brothers.'

Goetz's eyes widened slightly. 'What happened?'

Taudge glanced at him, then at Opchek. 'He doesn't listen too well, does he?'

'He's young. All those questions are blocking his ears.' Opchek laughed. 'Or maybe he'd like you to elaborate, my taciturn friend.'

Taudge glared at the other man, but went on regardless. 'Greisen was a diplomat,' he said, almost spitting the word. 'He made alliances with several packs of those mangy sea-wolves against the others. We were reduced to sea-wardens, keeping the peace among feuding pirate bands.' His eyes glazed slightly as he looked back into his memories. 'And then–'

'They betrayed us,' Balk said.

Taudge and Opchek flinched, as if caught out at some illicit activity. Goetz looked at the hochmeister, who had appeared almost as if out of nowhere. 'Why?' he said.

Balk's face was like something carved from marble. 'Because they are treacherous by nature. And savage by disposition. Hochmeister Greisen thought he could deal with them as one would deal with civilised men and, for that, they impaled his body and left it to rot on the shore, alongside a good many of our brothers.'

'And that's when you called for help,' Goetz said. 'From Marienburg.'

'We needed to teach them a lesson,' Balk said. 'We still need to teach them a lesson.' He smiled suddenly, the expression rippling across his face like cracks across ice. 'Which leads us to here. Today. And you,' he said. 'Come. I want to show you something.'

He led Goetz up onto the stone platform and gestured to the docks. 'Look.'

As with the previous day, there were a number of ships in the harbour. Only now they all flew the same flag. Gold on black, and a woman's face, wreathed in solar flame. As Goetz watched, men crawled across the ships, attaching armour plates and building what could only be gun-decks similar to the ones on the galley that had brought him here.

'What are you doing?' he said, despite already knowing the answer.

'What we must,' Balk said, smiling triumphantly. 'And what you see is just the beginning. Our fleet will stretch from horizon to horizon when we're done. But for what comes first, we only need these.'

'First?' Goetz said. 'What comes first?'

'Eyristaad,' Opchek murmured. 'Won't he be surprised, the stumpy little thief?'

Goetz looked at him and then at Balk, realisation slowly setting in. 'You were scouting his defences,' he said.

Balk turned away, his hands clasped behind his back. 'It's the perfect staging area. Whether he knows it or not, Eyri Goldfinger has built a settlement on the perfect point by which to invade Norsca. The rivers, you see,' he said, glancing at Goetz. 'We have a number of ships which can sail up those rivers as easy as an eel. And once they are armoured and armed, there will be nothing that can match them, save the daemon engines of the far north.' Balk's eyes narrowed. 'And I have it on good authority that we will be ready for them before too long.'

Goetz turned as the words left Balk's mouth. Myrma stood nearby stroking the feathers of the crow perched on her shoulder. She cocked her head and smiled and he felt a flush of heat spread through him. Instinctive wariness warred with fascination. Shaking his head he turned back. 'This – it's impossible!' he said.

'No, merely improbable.' Balk's smile faded. 'And worthwhile. Think of it brother! The North, civilised at last! Brought from heathen darkness into the light of our goddess!' His voice rose an octave. 'And then – then with the Norscans, we will sweep east, into the Chaos Wastes themselves. We will drive every daemon and daemon-worshipper off the edge of the world.' Balk chuckled. 'Oh, it will take generations, to be sure. But we do not lack for clarity of purpose, or dedication, do we brothers?' he said, looking at the others.

Taudge inclined his head and Opchek gave a hearty laugh. 'Nor do we lack for weapons and artillery!' he said, crossing his arms over his barrel chest. 'Either of which I'll take over purpose and dedication any day.'

Balk frowned, but before he could respond, Goetz said, 'Why haven't you informed the Grand Master of your plans?'

Balk's face lost its humour. 'Why? Who says I haven't? I've sent letters. Missives. A pigeon, even!' he snapped, his face flushing. 'Did Berengar ever respond? No! Not even when Greisen died!'

Goetz was tempted to take a step back in the face of such fury, but he held his ground. 'He says he has received nothing. That's why he sent Athalhold.'

Balk hesitated at the mention of the dead knight's name, but he regained the initiative quickly enough. 'He says. He says! He says one thing and sends a spy. Because that's what you are, brother... a spy,' Balk snarled, jabbing a finger at Goetz. 'And not the only one, I'd wager.'

'Hochmeister–' Opchek began, trying to interpose himself. Balk thrust out an arm and shoved him back.

'No,' Balk growled. 'Let him speak.'

'I already explained why I was coming here,' Goetz said, feeling himself growing angry. He thought of Athalhold and of the assassin, of everything that had occurred and his fists clenched. 'If I were a spy, would I announce myself?' Of course, if I weren't a spy, I'd have mentioned that the Marienburgers want you off this rock and soon, he thought, somewhat guiltily. He had been so preoccupied with what he had discovered, not to mention the injuries he had sustained, that he had failed to mention it to Balk. Now, as he paused to think about it, he wondered whether he should.

'Would he ask so many questions?' Opchek said, glaring at them both. 'And would we keep secrets from our own Order?' He made a sound like an aggravated bull. Balk's scowl switched from Goetz to Opchek. Then it faded and he laughed bitterly.

'No.'

Goetz stepped back. 'I never intended to accuse you, hochmeister,' he said. That at least was the truth. He had no evidence that Balk was involved in anything. As far as he knew, it had been the Norscans who were behind things, using catspaws to assure that the war between them and Svunum stayed private.

'Or I you,' Balk said, extending his hand. Goetz hesitated, and then they clasped forearms.

'We will block the surf with their bodies!'

A roar of assent filled the smoky hall and Dalla flinched as the wave of noise rolled over her. A dozen godar sat around the immense mammoth-bone table Eyri had scrounged up from somewhere. Ringed around the table, the followers of each man bellowed and shouted across at one another.

The alvthing was as ancient a tradition as any in Norsca. The gathering of chieftains; only able to be initiated by one of their own or a man of sufficiently high renown, such as her father. Here, each man had a voice equal to every other, and it was in such councils that the important matters were decided. When the Kurgan rode to war, it was at an alvthing that the men of the southern coasts decided whether they would follow the banners of the Aesgardr to war with the Empire across the sea. When their shared shores were invaded, it was at an alvthing that recriminations were planned.

It reminded her of nothing so much as a beach full of bull seals in the rutting season. Thalfi Utergard was the primary cause of the noise, capering across the table as he was, punching the air with his ham-sized fists, the plaits of his greasy beard slapping against his hauberk. 'Just as we did before, we will turn the sea to wine with their blood!'

'Somehow, Thalfi, I don't think they'll be falling for that trick twice,' Eyri shouted. 'Now get off my table!'

'Goldfinger is right,' another chieftain said, even as he used his staff to sweep Thalfi's feet out from under him. The big godi fell onto the table and was hauled off by his men, who snarled at his attacker like wolves. The other godi made an insulting gesture and turned to Eyri. 'As much as I hate to say it, you are right. They will be more cautious.'

'Your common sense is appreciated Lok.' Eyri rose to his feet and leaned forward on his knuckles. 'The rest of you kindly shut up.' He swept the gathering with a flinty gaze. 'You've seen what's left of my harbour, I trust.' He thumped a fist on the table. 'Well, that'll happen to each of you unless we do something about it here and now!'

'The way I understood it, you had one of theirs in a pit with that man-eating pet of yours,' another godi said. He was called Kettil Flatnose, for obvious reasons. His handsome features were marred by the offending protuberance, broken and squashed at some point and time in the past. He stood, and the Imperial coins threaded through his hair clattered as he moved. His armour was of better quality than any other man in the room, save Eyri, and he wore a torc around his throat. 'That's why they blew the helheim out of you.'

'Aye, if you hadn't provoked them we wouldn't be here now,' another chieftain piped up, rubbing an amulet shaped like a golden frog's face between his fingers. Hrothgar Olveksan, Dalla knew. The only man among the chieftains gathered here who'd been across the great ocean and seen the green and deadly land there. His people paid for their purchases with the gold of the ancients. 'You always were a troublemaker, Eyri Light-Finger–'

'Don't call me that!' Eyri hissed, his hand going to the long knife at his belt. 'I'm no thief!'

'And a liar as well,' Kettil said in his curiously nasal voice. 'Next you'll be trying to explain that you didn't mean to break my nose or that your shield got away from you.'

'Are you still going on about that?' Thalfi said. 'You ask me, he did you a favour!'

'No one asked you, oaf,' Kettil said, ignoring the other chieftain.

'Oaf? Oaf!' Thalfi said, his hand dropping to the hilt of his sword.

'Oaf,' Lok said, swatting Thalfi in the jaw with his staff. Lok was the oldest of the chieftains gathered there, and his plaited hair was as white as snow. It contrasted with his sun-darkened features. He wore heavy robes and a suit of archaic chainmail. His staff was topped with the broken and lashed pieces of an orc's skull, which made it almost as deadly a weapon as any sword.

Thalfi fell heavily, dazed and nearly senseless. His men went for their swords, but Lok's interposed themselves. Lok slammed his staff against the table. 'Oaf I call you, and oaf you are.' He looked around the hall. 'All of you, in fact. I would hear the words of Ulfar Asgrimdalr, gudja to godi Goldfinger!' he roared, sweeping his staff out to indicate Dalla and her father, where they sat out of the way. The other chieftains fell silent as her father stood.

'I thank you, Lok Helsgrim,' Ulfar said, stepping forward through the formerly raucous crowd and moving towards the table. 'I thank you and I ask that you all listen to me. I have ridden the waves of the daemon-sea and seen the ghosts that cling to the night-winds, and felt the talons of that which drives our enemies forward.' He raised his staff. 'She returns. And with Her comes an ending. Our ending, unless we strike, and strike now,' he thundered, slamming the butt of his staff on the floor. The sound was loud in the silence.

'And where is your proof?' Kettil said, sitting back in his chair. 'Our gudjas have said nothing of this to us. Our priests remain silent.'

'Your priests are whipped dogs,' Ulfar said. 'You have bent them to see only that which benefits you.'

Kettil flushed. 'And if what you say is true, would not they then have spoken of it, considering the implications?'

Hrothgar laughed nastily. 'There are only implications if we join Light-Finger in this mad enterprise.' He stood, one hand on his sword-hilt. 'Also, we all know the grudge Asgrimdalr bears the einsark. Now, as he enters his twilight, it is not so strange that he wants one more chance to claw their guts?'

Ulfar tensed. Dalla half-rose from her feet, her lips peeling back from her teeth. Without turning, Ulfar swung his free hand up and gestured for her to sit. 'Aye, they owe me weregild. As do you, Hrothgar Olveksan.'

'I? I owe you nothing old man,' Hrothgar blustered.

'Oh but you do. For did you not take tainted gold to kill the einsark commander? And like a rock rolling down hill, did that one death not result in the deaths of hundreds as the brass-skins sought vengeance? Including those of my wife and sons?'

Hrothgar stood abruptly, clawing for the hatchet shoved through his belt as Eyri went pale. Dalla was faster, however, lunging past her father. She was up on the table and across it even as the chieftain yanked his weapon clear. Her sword sang a moment later and the hatchet fell to the table with a dull thud, accompanied by a flopping hand. Hrothgar shrieked and stumbled back, clutching his gushing stump. Kettil reacted with a curse and grabbed the other man's arm and forced the pumping wound into the nearest torch flame, cauterising it with a hiss.

As Hrothgar collapsed into the arms of one of his men, Kettil turned on Dalla. 'You dare? You dare strike a godar under the roof of an alvthing?' He looked at Eyri. 'Perhaps you meant the same for us all, eh?'

'What?' Eyri stood, his face red. 'You go too far!'

'And just how did you take this steading anyway? The same way you meant to take ours I think!' Kettil snatched up Hrothgar's hatchet and gesticulated with it. 'I knew you couldn't be trusted, Light-Finger!'

'Enough,' Ulfar said. His voice was mild, but it reached every ear in the room. Kettil paused in mid-rant and swung around.

'What will it take to convince you?' Ulfar said.

'A sign from the gods themselves,' Kettil snapped. 'Nothing less than that, old man.'

'Then you will have it,' Ulfar said. He looked at Dalla, who still crouched on the table, her sword out and dripping red. 'A challenge, my daughter.'

Dalla spat at Kettil and stood. 'A challenge.'

Kettil eyed her sword and went pale. 'But–'

'You wanted a sign, Flatnose,' Lok said, smiling grimly. The old man rose. 'If you win, this alvthing concludes as it began, with nothing changed. If Dalla Ulfarsdottir wins, however, we go to war!'

Balk stirred his axe through the water that had collected between the fang-like rocks. In the ripples, he saw the images of what had been. Memories were his burden to bear, heavier even than his armour. A thrill of guilt flared through him and he fought it down.

'He fought well,' he said, after a moment. 'Precise. Efficient. He is a credit to the Order.' He looked at the priestess, squatting over her vent, her head hung low after the effort of bringing the visions to life. She looked up at him through her curtain of hair and grinned. If she noticed Balk's shudder at the sight of her teeth, she gave no sign.

'Yes,' Myrma said. 'He is blessed by the goddess, though he knows it not.'

Balk made a face and his grip on his axe tightened. She could practically see the thoughts that flashed across the surface of his mind like lightning. An almost incandescent fanaticism and lust for vengeance, coupled with a stubborn determination and iron resolve. He did his ancestors proud in that way, she knew. Such men had been instrumental in giving her people the time they needed to escape Sigmar's wrath. 'Yes,' he said. He hesitated a moment, and then said, 'Should we–?'

Myrma cocked her head and eyed him with an amusement she didn't let show on her face. 'At your command, Master Balk...'

'Wait!' he said, throwing up a hand. 'Just – just wait. Give me a moment to – to think.' He looked away. 'I need to think.'

'Of course. But–'

'I said that I need to think!' Balk roared, startling the crows that perched on the rocks. They fluttered into the air croaking and scattering feathers.

'Do you still think he is a spy? Like the other?' she needled. It pleased her no end to point out his hypocrisy, though doubtless he did not notice it. He was far too preoccupied to be so self-aware. His schemes were brittle things, like the footsteps of a calf. Easily disrupted and tripped up. Easily butchered; easily supplanted by better things, stronger things.

'Yes. No.' He shook his head, like a bull beset by a nettlesome fly. He looked at her. 'No. If Myrmidia has taken him to Her bosom, I will think no ill of him.' Of course he would think so, with his mulish devotion to the Slaughter-Woman and her glib pronouncements. Myrma fought to keep her face blank.

She rose and shrugged. 'Then do not.' She waved a hand. 'Go. Make ready for war, master.'

'But–'

'Myrmidia thirsts for the blood of our enemies.' she said, pressing her hands against his breastplate. She bent her fingers, scraping her nails down across Myrmidia's symbol, now caked with mud and oil. His armour was dulled and stained, as was the armour of every knight on this island, and the hated sigils were hidden. 'Take him with you, show him the rightness of the goddess's cause or else all that you have worked for will be endangered. What will he do, your fallen Grand Master, if he learns of our true goal... of the goddess's design?'

'Berengar,' Balk said, his face becoming grim. 'He'd wipe us out in a heartbeat; he'd bring the full weight of the Empire down on us.'

'So he will, if Goetz does not join us.' She smiled slightly and continued, 'You go where you are needed...'

'And we do what must be done. Yes.' He looked at her, his face set in grim lines. 'I will make him see.' He reached out and touched her face, almost fearfully. 'I wish it had been me. I thought it would be. I thought...' He pushed her back gently. 'Thank you for showing me what I must do, my lady.' Then he turned and stalked away, his back ramrod stiff. When he had gone she sighed and sank back onto her haunches, a grin on her lips. The island rumbled softly beneath her as the volcanic vents belched and simmered.

'Exactly as you said, Mistress,' she murmured. 'Balk is not the one, but he has brought him to us sure enough. He has brought us our Myrmidon.' She chuckled, and the crows perched in the nooks and crannies of the cavern echoed her.

She had nearly exhausted herself days earlier, ensuring that the fen-dwellers hadn't killed the knight. 'Goetz,' she said, rolling the name around on her tongue. He was marked by the Great Mutator, his body riven with poisons that were as insidious as they were undetectable.

That those poisons hadn't yet begun their fearful work on him was either a testament to his strength, or to the hand of the Father of Illusions. Her queen had whispered the secret skeins that clung to this man to her... not of destiny, but of place and position. He was a cog, shaped and placed to fill the hole of another, but ill-fitting for all of that. Plans within plans which had been dislodged by still other plans. In her mind's eye, she saw a screaming thing, writhing in a blister-burrow within the tainted heart of the Drakwald. Another child of the Lord of Labyrinths, birthed to meet the wrong man. She grinned, baring her filed teeth in an agony of ecstatic contemplation.

A push here, a pull there, and Old Father Fate wove strange circles. None of which was stranger than the one now encircling the man known as Hector Goetz.

As one, the crows set to croaking, and in their cacophony she heard a voice purring assent. Yes, Goetz was marked for great things indeed. She glanced towards the bulging pods that nestled in the corners and crevices. They seemed to flex and moan as her gaze touched them and her smile threatened to split her face as she glanced down at the piles of discarded, dwarf-forged armour that nestled at the foot of every pod. Birthed as they were from the cast-off shells of dead men, they were growing into something wonderful indeed.

TWENTY

'Invasion?' Goetz said.

'Invasion,' Balk repeated, tapping a finger against the mast. They stood on the deck of one of the black-sailed galleys preparing to launch. Balk looked out over the Sea of Claws, his face set in an easy smile. 'Specifically an invasion of the southern coast of Norsca.'

'That's a bit...' Goetz trailed off, looking around as preparations were made for casting off with the evening tide. It was a far brisker sort of affair than he had witnessed in Marienburg. The crew, composed mostly of Svanii, moved with a sharp efficiency that bespoke both unfamiliarity and eagerness.

'Grandiose?' Balk said.

'I was searching for a less insulting word. Rhetoric was among the subjects I was taught.'

'Ha! Yes.' Balk grinned. 'It is grandiose. Epic, even. Worthy of a saga or three, as the Norscans would say.'

'Why?' Goetz said. Balk had taken him into his confidence soon after their argument. The man was mercurial, his moods changing like the tides. Goetz was coming to understand why Berengar had been concerned, though he was careful not to let it show on his face.

'It needs to be done. And the goddess commands. Isn't that enough?'

Goetz said nothing. Balk went to the upper deck and sat in the chair mounted there. He pressed his fingers together and rested his chin across them as Goetz came to a halt in front of him. He frowned. 'I sense trepidation.'

'There are rumours. In Marienburg...' Goetz said.

Balk sighed and leaned back. 'Still you doubt me?'

'It's this plan I doubt,' Goetz said. 'Do you think you can hold Eyristaad? With the men you have now?'

'I could hold half the Empire with the men I have now,' Balk said primly. 'But, fine. Why not see for yourself?' He leaned forward. 'Come with us. I intend to begin as soon as we're ready to cast off. We'll put Eyristaad to the torch and build a new beginning on the ashes. Then, maybe, you'll begin to see things my way.'

Goetz nodded slowly. 'Perhaps.'

'Besides, I assume you'll be wanting a bit of repayment for the trouble they gave you,' Balk said.

'I try not to hold grudges.' Goetz watched as the Svanii laid in sail and tied off ropes with simian-like agility. With their savage tattoos and grunting language, they reminded him of nothing so much as feral children. Then he would catch sight of a weapon or a coiling scar and he would be reminded that they were anything but. Smaller and slimmer than the Norscans they were related to, they nonetheless possessed a similar brute vigour that Goetz couldn't help but be impressed by.

'The dwarfs have a saying... "cherish your grudges as your children, for both will only grow stronger with time",' Balk said.

'Not exactly something to look forward to,' Goetz said.

'Really?' Balk said, looking at him in mock surprise. 'Quite a wise folk, dwarfs.' He stood. 'Still, you take my meaning. We leave in an hour. I'd like to have your sword with us.'

Goetz watched him leave. 'Stay or go?' he mused. What would the Grand Master say? he wondered. He looked at the harbour and the galleys that populated it, and wondered what Ambrosius's fleet would think when it arrived to kick Balk's men off the island. He smiled grimly. What was it the abbot had said? 'We are playing dice with the gods,' he said. 'Is that what I'm doing?'

He went to the rail and leaned on it, looking at nothing. 'Use your brain,' he muttered. Neither Ambrosius nor Berengar for that matter had seemed to be aware that Svunum was inhabited... had the hochmeister hidden that from them? Or had Balk's predecessors merely not thought it worth mentioning?

'Not worth mentioning,' Goetz said. He watched cogs bearing Svanii warriors bob towards several of the farther galleys. Armed and eager, they shook their spears at him and he waved half-heartedly. 'Not at all, eh?'

An armed encampment. Not merely a hundred or so knights, but an armed, aggressive population, divinely motivated and well-led. It was like something out of an epic saga of the time before Sigmar.

That's likely how Balk wanted to think of it at any rate. Goetz thought of the armies said to populate the Chaos Wastes to the north and wondered at the parallels there instead. It wasn't a pleasant thought, and it stirred up memories of the bird-masked assassins who had tried to kill him in the temple of Myrmidia.

Thinking of them naturally led him to meet the gazes of the crows perched on the rail and on the ropes. The birds eyed him with disturbing intensity and his hand found the hilt of his sword. No, not his sword. His sword was still in Eyristaad.

'Balk said he needed my sword,' he said to the crow watching him from the rail. 'Only I don't have my sword, do I?'

'Perhaps you'd like to get it back, hmmm?' Goetz didn't turn as the woman slid off the rail and came to stand behind him. The crow on her shoulder fluttered its wings in agitation and she cooed softly to it before turning back to him. 'Losing a good weapon is like losing a limb.'

'I didn't realise you were there,' Goetz said, glancing at Myrma. As lovely as she was at a distance, there was something frankly unnatural about her beauty close up. It was as if her face shifted, forcing you to focus on each aspect of her features individually. As if there was more than one face there, striving to be seen.

'That is because I did not wish you to,' she said. 'You interest me.'

'And you interest me,' Goetz said.It was the truth. Though not for the reasons that a woman usually interested him. 'You speak the tongue of my people well. The brothers here educated you?'

'They educated all of my people. We have learned the arts of the sea and metal from them over several generations,' she said. She reached up and stroked the crow's beak. Its glittering eyes bored into Goetz's own, and he made a game attempt at ignoring it. It reminded him unpleasantly of the bird that had attacked him the day he'd arrived in Marienburg.

'Where I come from, Myrmidia is associated with the eagle, not the crow,' he said, more for something to say than any other reason. She wielded silence like a flail, and it scraped raw runnels in his temper.

'Eagles are great warriors. But the crow is a survivor,' she said. 'As are we.'

Something about her gaze made him nervous. 'I have not yet thanked you for what you did for me,' Goetz said, tapping his side. She smiled and inclined her head.

'It was nothing. Payment on a debt yet to be owed,' she said. Goetz was about to ask what exactly that meant, but she continued on before he had the chance. 'Your faith is like water. It has not the solidity of Balk's or the others. Why?'

'What do you know of my faith?' Goetz said, feeling slightly insulted.

She laughed and Goetz felt his flush deepen as the sound danced along his spine. 'I know it is a hard thing, and not comforting. Like the sea, it rises and falls and it is cold. Your faith does not warm you, Hector Goetz. It drags you down.' Goetz turned away. He scowled out at the sea.

'In your heart, in your soul, you do not believe,' she said. He glanced at her out of the corner of his eye and her face seemed to bulge and shift oddly. He whirled and she met his confused gaze calmly. 'Despite everything, you do not believe.'

'I believe,' he said hoarsely.

'You do not. But you will,' she said. Then she left him where he stood, gaping after her.

Gulls banked and spun through the grim grey air. Torches were lit and a hue and cry went up all across the steading as word of the challenge spread.

Eyristaad was crammed with people, each of the godar having brought a retinue worthy of their esteemed status. Those merchants who made the steading their home were pressing their wares on the newcomers with glee. The slave-market especially was doing a booming trade.

Dalla ignored all of this, preferring instead to focus on her swordplay. The gleaming blade caught what little light there was as she moved through a series of exercises she'd learned from a travelling Cathayan mercenary. Her mimicry was crude at best, but she found the movements soothing. She wondered if the einsark felt the same way when he practised. Thinking of that made her think of him.

He was a warrior, no two ways there; and a good one. There were not many men who could put a troll down with only a sword, yet he had done it. It made him... interesting. She pivoted and slashed, pushing the thought aside.

'Foolishness,' Eyri muttered, watching her. Dalla ignored him.

'Necessary,' her father corrected.

'And if she fails?'

'She won't,' Ulfar said, hunching forward as a chill wind rippled through the steading. 'She can't.'

'Cheerful as ever,' Eyri said, pulling his cloak closer about his squat form. 'Kettil is good. Better than most.'

'And I am better than that,' Dalla said, stabbing her sword point into the ground. 'Or have you forgotten?' She motioned towards his hand, with its missing fingers. Eyri frowned and looked away.

'Kettil won't be drunk. And he won't be trying for a kiss, woman.'

'You've seen me fight, Eyri. Is it concern prompting your words, or are you hoping to frighten me off?' Dalla said.

Ulfar chuckled. 'Is that it, godi? Do you yearn for failure so that you might have an excuse to let things lie?'

'I am no coward!' Eyri snapped.

'No one said you were,' Dalla said. 'Merely that you might want to shirk your responsibilities. That we do know you do.'

'Mind your tongue.'

'Mind yours,' Dalla said, yanking her sword free of the soil. Once more she admired the balance of the thing. In all ways it was an improvement over any other blade she had held. She gave a few swipes and turned as the sound of drums started up. The beat was steady and deep and the crowd fell silent as Kettil Flatnose stepped into the circle of torches. He carried a long-handled axe in one hand and a round shield on his other.

Dalla scooped up her own shield and trotted forwards to meet him. The sun was a distant promise on the horizon. She took a final, cleansing breath, and slapped the flat of her blade against her shield's rim. 'Well? Ready to get on with it, Flatnose?'

Kettil winced as she slapped her shield again. 'I'll give you one last chance, Ulfarsdottir... renounce your challenge and no man here will mock you.'

'Whereas every man will mock you, eh? No, no, I think we shall see this through, Flatnose,' Dalla said. Dirt skidded beneath her foot as she lunged, the tip of her sword scoring a line across the face of Kettil's shield. He jumped back like a scalded cat and his axe looped out. She deflected it with her shield and jabbed his leg, causing him to yelp.

He was only off balance for a moment, however. Jerking his leg back, he chopped out with his axe, cutting a divot out of her shield. Her arm ached from the force of the blow. Pretty as he was, Kettil was also a strong man and an experienced warrior. She went for his leg again, drawing blood this time. The edge of his shield dropped, punching her sword to the ground and the handle of his axe connected with her head. Stars burst in her vision and she only just avoided the next blow. She threw herself aside and scrambled to her feet as he came at her in a rush.

They traded blows for several minutes. Dalla hopped back and took a breath as he overextended himself and stumbled.

'You fight well,' he grunted, wheezing.

'For a woman?'

'For anyone,' he said. 'But it will avail you little. I am stronger.'

'We'll see,' Dalla said. She stamped forward, her sword licking out to draw a line of red across his cheek. He jerked back with a snarl and her blade gouged a line across his neck before scraping against his hauberk. She spun and chopped into the side of his shield, using the momentum of the blow to rip it off his arm. Off balance, he dropped his axe and fell.

Dalla kicked the shield off her blade and advanced. 'Surrender, Flatnose. Your people need their godi.'

'If their chieftain can't defeat a woman, even a woman as skilled as you, then he doesn't deserve the title,' Kettil said, scooping up his axe and cracking a blow against her hastily interposed shield. It cracked at the point of impact and her shoulder screamed in agony. Dalla ignored the sensation and drove forward, slamming the crumpling shield against Kettil's chest. She shoved him back into one of the torches and he went tumbling, the flames licking at him.

He tossed his axe aside to beat at the flames and she raised her sword in triumph. Before she could say anything, however, an explosion rendered all of her efforts moot.

The first was followed by a second, a third and a fourth. Wood splintered and toppled as already abused structures collapsed in the orange glow of newly born fires. Crouching to avoid flying debris, Dalla looked in incomprehension at the sea. Four black-sailed galleys drifted past the steading, their decks awash in bronze dragon-maws that belched death and ruin.

TWENTY-ONE

'Ha! That got them running!' Opchek said, pounding the rail with a fist. He, along with Goetz and a dozen others, waited to descend into the sleek boats that would take them ashore.

Goetz didn't share the other man's enthusiasm about either the destruction being wrought or the rest of it. He held tight to the hilt of his new sword and scanned the shore, almost hoping for some sign of organised resistance.

The galleys had anchored themselves parallel to the shore and presented a solid wall of armour and gun muzzles. The latter roared as swiftly as the Svanii manning them could load them and light the fuses. 'They seem quite enthusiastic,' Goetz yelled, trying to be heard over the roar of the guns.

'Considering how often the Norscans raided their shores before the Order took up residence, can you blame them? These folk cherish their feuds almost as much as the dwarfs.' Balk said, crossing the deck towards them. As with Goetz and the other knights, the hochmeister was clad in the full panoply of field-plate, with a towering helmet and a wide shield that bore the same emblem as that on the sails of the galleys.

Goetz looked up at the sails and the design on the shields that surrounded him. It was just familiar enough for the alterations to strike him as alien and strange. 'Eyes front, Hector,' Opchek said, bringing the side of his fist down on Goetz's shoulder. The big Kislevite had taken to calling him by his given name in the aftermath of his disastrous visit with Myrma. 'We're ready to go ashore.'

Awkwardly the knights clambered down the wood and rope ladders into the waiting skiffs. Each skiff could hold ten fully armoured knights as well as the same number of livery-clad Svanii, each of whom carried a hatchet, spear and shield and were already waiting for the former.

Goetz couldn't help but flinch as the cannonade continued, pounding the shoreline. Opchek grinned at him as they both settled into a crouch at the prow of the skiff. 'It'll take some getting used to, but goddess help me I do so love the smell of a good barrage.'

'I've never seen it so – so concentrated,' Goetz said, ducking as the tell-tale whistle of another round filled the air. 'I've been in battles before where it was used, but this...'

'Aye, I once fought alongside the Ironsides during one of the Countess Emmanuelle of Nuln's interminable forays into territories not her own. If we had a few of those hand-cannons, we'd be near unstoppable. As it stands, this pounding is only as good as our follow-through,' Opchek said. 'Speaking of which...'

The skiff crunched as it slammed ashore, propelled ashore by Svanii muscle. The spearmen clambered out and formed a rough line. They knelt, spears extended and shields raised. The knights stopped just behind them. There were only a few Norscans on shore, and these immediately charged forward, howling out their barbaric war-hymns at the top of their lungs.

Goetz could not fault them for their courage. It took a certain kind of bravery to charge headlong into a bristling wall of spears, and each of them possessed it in abundance. Balk, however, did not appear to share that respect.

'Spears... UP,' Balk snapped. The Svanii raised their spears and waited. The first Norscan to reach them crashed gut first into a waiting spear, unable to halt his rush in time. The second and the third ploughed past him, almost leaping over the Svanii in their eagerness to come to grips with the knights behind them.

'Leave them! They're mine!' Balk snapped, as Goetz moved forward. Balk's axe thundered home into the hairy skull of the first man to reach him and he backhanded the second with his shield, knocking him flat. The other knights reacted then, with five swords striking out to pin the Norscan to the shore. Balk whirled on his men, his eyes blazing with rage. 'I said he was mine!'

'Plenty to go around, Conrad,' Opchek said, gesturing with his sword. Out of the smoke boiling across the shore, indistinct shapes moved. Goetz turned and saw that the other two skiffs had beached themselves. Little under fifty men, facing the goddess alone knew how many.

'Crossbows would have been nice,' Goetz said as they started forward.

'A lot of things would have been nice,' Opchek said. 'A jug of wine, a bit of good Ostermark cheddar, maybe a pretty girl.' The Norscans charged onto the shore in a disorganised mass. Opchek raised his shield and glanced at Goetz. 'A lot of things.'

The Norscans slammed into them with a roar.

Dalla swung her arm, trying to work some feeling back into it. Nearby, Eyri barked orders at his men, trying to organise the steading's defenders. The other godar were doing the same, bullying their followers into warbands.

'What is going on?' Hrothgar said, looking around wildly. He was still pale from blood loss, and his stump had been bound tightly and strapped to his chest. 'What is it?'

'While we argued about seeking out trouble, it came looking for us,' Lok said. He looked at Eyri. 'My men are yours. We stand or fall together, Goldfinger.'

'Wonderful sentiments,' Kettil said. He had acquired a new shield and he tested the edge of his axe against the rim. 'Of course, it's not like we can escape, eh?'

'Escape? Who wants to escape?' Thalfi roared, raising his sword and axe. 'Let us wreath them in their own intestines!'

'We'll have to get through their armour first,' Eyri snapped. Dalla's eyes widened as she saw a group of his men coming forward, their arms straining as they held tight to the chains attached to Eyri's troll. The beast had been crammed into a suit of crude armour and it roared and jerked as they hauled it forward.

'And your plan is to use that?'

'No, I intend to give it to Balk as a token of my esteem,' Eyri said acidly. 'Get that brute going in the right direction damn you!' The latter was directed towards his men. The troll had obviously smelt the fire and the blood and it was growing far more agitated – not to mention animated – than Dalla had ever seen it. A chain whip snapped out, flensing the creature's rubbery skin.

With a berserk scream, the beast tore itself free of its handlers and charged towards the beach with a simian motion. It crashed through a lean-to, scattering squawking hens and tossing animal hide and wooden scraps in every direction.

'Troll's loose,' Dalla said unhelpfully. Eyri glared at her.

'Yes. Thank you. Shouldn't you be doing something useful?'

'I intend to,' Dalla said, slapping her sword against her shield rim. She glanced at Kettil. 'Come, Flatnose. The world's black rim calls for walkers.'

'I don't intend to die here, witch,' Kettil said, falling into step with her. His men followed suit.

'Good. Neither do I,' Dalla said, baring her teeth in a feline grin. The other chieftains joined them, striding forward with weapons in hand, their einjhar gathered about them in a protective mob. Thalfi began singing a bawdy tune, belting out the verses with more enthusiasm and volume than ability.

A flash of brass caught her eye through the smoke. Spear-points pierced the cloud of ash and embers and she shrieked in anticipation. Then, still shrieking, she began to run towards her enemies.

TWENTY-TWO

Goetz nearly fell as the rocks of the beach shifted beneath his feet. He smashed the edge of his shield into the Norscan's wide-open mouth, cutting off his war cry. As the man staggered, clutching at his bloody mouth, Goetz chopped him down. Stepping over the body, he rejoined the group as they moved up into the settlement.

'Some fun, eh?' Opchek said, shaking the blood off his sword.

'No,' Goetz said.

'Could be worse,' the Kislevite said. 'You could be dead.'

'True,' Goetz said, raising his shield even as a drizzle of arrows pounded down upon them. The entire group halted with well-trained precision and sank down, shields raised. Goetz winced as three arrows hammered into his shield, the broad head of one scraping across his vambrace. He looked at Opchek. 'Crossbows,' he said. 'Those would have come in handy.'

'The Svanii aren't what you call natural archers,' Balk said as the group rose. 'Besides, until we have a bowyer and a fletcher in residence, I'd rather not rely on anything we can't build or repair ourselves.'

'Says the man wearing dwarf-made armour,' Goetz said. Balk looked at him, his features unreadable behind his visor.

'Yes, well, we'll soon have an answer for that,' he said. Then he turned away, leaving Goetz puzzled.

'What did he–' he began, glancing at Opchek. His inquiry was interrupted by another blanket of arrows. 'The houses. They've got archers on the rooftops,' he said.

'Smart,' Opchek said. 'Someone's thinking.'

'Yes. Me. Let's go,' Goetz said, shoving his way out of the group and trudging towards the closest houses. He paused only to snatch a torch from the hand of a startled Svanii. Opchek hurried after him, positioning his shield over both their heads as they moved.

'What are you planning?' the other knight said. 'Whatever it is, it better be worth it!' he continued as an arrow glanced off his shield and scuttled down across his arm.

'Trapner's On Clearing Redoubts, page fifteen,' Goetz said, hurrying towards the closest doorway. 'Fire is the invader's closest ally.' Without slowing, Goetz kicked in the door. The driftwood cracked and split from the blow and he shouldered his way in, using his shield as a prise-bar.

'These huts are too damp to light! Not like this anyway,' Opchek said, following him inside. They could hear men running across the roof above. Goetz kicked over a clay urn full of whale oil.

'Did you know that they use this oil in lamp wicks?' he said, touching the burning end of the torch to the oil. It caught with a crackling hiss. Goetz tossed the torch to Opchek and hefted the urn, splattering the dregs of the oil all over the room. Letting the urn fall and shatter on the floor, he stepped back as the flames spread hungrily. Foul-smelling smoke spread towards them.

'Wonderful,' Opchek coughed. 'Now what?'

'Now we repeat,' Goetz said, gesturing to the sagging wall. 'It's not all stone.' Without waiting for Opchek, he charged at the wall and crashed through, scattering chunks of loose stone and dried mud. Off balance, he crashed through the next wall and fell into the hut. He was on his feet in a minute, face to face with a Norscan who had dropped through the thatch roof. Goetz slammed his shield into the startled warrior, pinning him against the wall. 'Opchek!' he called.

'Busy!' Opchek cried out as he backed through the hole Goetz had made, duelling with a gigantic swordsman. The Norscan growled and battered through Opchek's defences, and the Kislevite cursed as he lost his grip on his sword. Opchek made do, shoving the torch into the man's face and setting his beard and hair aflame. The Norscan screamed shrilly and clutched at his fiery skull. Opchek kicked him back into a set of raw-edged shelves. Urns splattered and the fire leapt from the dying man to the floor and the ceiling.

Goetz, meanwhile, jammed the edge of his shield up under his opponent's chin. With an almost apologetic grunt, he jerked the curled rim of the shield to the side, tearing a ragged hole in the man's throat. He stepped back as the body toppled forward, twitching.

'Did you sharpen that?' Opchek said incredulously. Goetz shrugged.

'You never know when you're going to have to improvise. First Litany of Battle...'

'Always be prepared, yes,' Opchek finished, shaking his head. 'Still...'

'You're obviously not familiar with Brother Helmeyer of the Talabheim Komturie,' Goetz said. He tapped the surface of his shield. 'He puts murder holes in his shields. He mounts two of those nasty little repeating crossbows the elfs like so much on the inside.' Goetz headed for the door, shaking his head. 'That's much worse, I should thi–'

The grey arm and boulder-sized fist pounded through the door, narrowly missing Goetz's head. He staggered back, eyes widening as the door was ripped from its hinges and a familiar, horrible visage leered at him. 'Troll!' he shouted.

'What?' Opchek said.

Goetz had no time to reply as fingers like boat hooks pierced the surface of his shield and wrenched him off his feet. He was slung through the wall and into the street by one whip-like motion of the monster's arm even as it splintered the support beam for the shack, bringing it down. Goetz hit the ground and bounced. When he rolled to a stop, breathing heavily, he saw the troll batter its way free of the burning wreckage of the hut as Opchek staggered to his feet. The Kislevite levered a ruined roof beam off himself only to find the troll bearing down on him.

'Out of the way!'

Opchek dove aside as Balk and Taudge and a squad of Svanii charged out from between the burning buildings. Taudge met the beast with a bellow and smooth lunge. His blade slid through the creature's belly and became snagged on something in its ponderous gut. It brought both fists down on the knight, dropping him insensate on the street.

'Off him, monster!' Opchek said, cutting at it from the side. A second later, he went down like a sack of bricks, hammered flat by the slightest swat of the creature's paw. Two Svanii died next, torn into pieces by the blood-maddened monster. Goetz and Balk went after it from either side. Goetz cursed as his sword edge met the troll's armour and skidded off in a shower of sparks. Balk had more luck, his axe whirling around to lop off one of the creature's hands.

It howled in agony and punched the hochmeister with the gouting stump, knocking him off his feet. A splayed foot thudded down inches from Balk's head as he desperately rolled aside. Goetz lunged, driving his sword home through a gap in the badly fitting armour. The troll reared back, grabbing for him. Goetz avoided the clumsy movement and twisted his blade, causing the beast to double over and vomit. The rocks sizzled and hissed as the acidic bile turned them into sludge.

Ripping his sword free, Goetz immediately brought it down on a gangly arm, severing it at the elbow. His sword rebounded off the rocks and he twisted, chopping upwards into the creature's belly, opening it in a burst of slippery flesh and foul gases. The troll screamed like an oversized child and brought its spurting wrist thudding across his head. Goetz fell to his knees, dazed.

Balk's axe flashed, splitting the troll's head in two. It groaned and slumped, body twitching. Yanking his weapon free, the hochmeister helped Goetz to his feet. 'Nicely done, brother,' Balk said, flipping up his visor.

'As you say, hochmeister,' Goetz said. 'Look out!' He drove his shoulder into Balk, knocking the other man aside. The thrown spear tore a furrow in Goetz's cheek and he pitched backwards, one hand clapped to his face.

The Norscans roared out brutal war-songs as they charged down on the group. On his back, Goetz saw that these men were more richly attired than any other Norscan he had seen. Then he caught sight of Eyri Goldfinger's squat shape and he pushed himself to his feet, eager to come to grips with his former captor.

Snatching up his sword, he dove into the melee. He parried a blow that would have finished a wounded Svanii and swept his attacker aside and out of the world. Spears dug for his blood and he chopped them to kindling. Using shield and sword, he forced himself a path through the Norscans. Weapon points blunted and chipped on his armour and their swords broke on his own when they met. The best armour that the elder race could produce met crude Northern iron, and the latter was forced to retreat.

For a moment, Goetz thought he saw a pale form sliding through the press of combat. A woman's face, sharp and beautiful turned towards him through a space between the spears and swords, her mouth open in what might have either been benediction or warning. A glowing spear gestured and Goetz's hackles prickled as he was forced around.

The movement saved his life. An axe that would have split him crown to groin bounced off the turf. Goetz struck back, gutting his attacker with a surge of desperate strength. Just as suddenly as that, he found himself in a cleared space. Bodies surrounded him, and his armour was no longer gleaming, instead coated in the excrescence of slaughter. Men pressed away from him, their eyes wide. Only one in particular held any interest for him.

The old man stood amidst the slaughter like an old tree weathering a storm. Spear-points shivered to pieces before they got too close and swords shattered on his withered shoulders. He stood calm, his face twisted in an expression of concentration. Goetz fancied that he could see the faintest pulse of an arctic-hued nimbus surrounding the shaman. With a shout, the old man lifted his staff and struck the ground. Warriors were thrown off their feet as the ground shuddered and heaved. Goetz kept his feet, but only barely.

He pushed through the melee towards the old man. If he were some sort of barbaric sorcerer, then he was far too dangerous to leave alive. Though Goetz bore him no personal malice, he had to die. As if sensing these thoughts, the old man glanced at him and Goetz felt a shock of something like recognition.

'What–?' he began. Then a spear-point darted for him and he was forced to turn aside to parry it. 'Captain Goldfinger,' he said, pointing his sword at the spear's wielder. 'Or is it Chief Goldfinger?'

'Sir Knight,' Eyri said, hesitating. 'I wondered if you'd pay us another visit.'

'Happy to oblige,' Goetz said thickly. He spat out the blood that had collected in his mouth from the wound on his cheek and started forward. 'I owe you for that rap on the head. For the crew of the Nicos, and for trying to feed me to a troll.'

'I seem to collect debts like a whorehouse collects lice,' Eyri said. He struck out, the spear in his hands piercing the battered face of Goetz's shield and driving him back a half-step. The Norscan was stronger than Goetz had given him credit for. Eyri's thick arms bulged with muscle as he shoved Goetz back another step.

Setting his feet, Goetz strained against his opponent, putting his weight behind his shield. Suddenly, Eyri stepped back, releasing his spear. Goetz stumbled forward, nearly toppling. A hatchet chopped out and he only narrowly avoided it, jumping back and losing his shield in the process. Eyri advanced, drawing a second hatchet.

'Come on then, einsark!' Eyri crowed. 'Come and take your debt!'

'I think mine takes precedence,' Balk said as he brought his axe around into Eyri's belly. The Norscan was driven into the air for a moment by the force of Balk's blow and he flopped to the beach with a limp finality. Balk stalked forward, swinging the axe up. 'It was always going to end this way, Eyri. There's only so long you can stand in the path of a goddess.'

A hurtling form caught the hochmeister in the back before he could deliver the deathblow and he staggered. A shield-rim caught him on the side of the head, shattering as it impacted with his helmet. Balk was thrown off his feet, senseless. The sound of the blow snapped Goetz out of his reverie and he charged forward. Balk's attacker spun to meet his charge and their eyes locked over their crossed swords.

'You,' Goetz said.

'You!' Dalla growled. 'Again, you!'

Goetz forced her sword aside and rammed her with his shoulder, sending her flailing backwards. 'Always me,' he said, stepping forward. 'That's my sword you have there.'

'Then come take it,' she said, scrambling up, waving the blade between them. 'Have the full measure!' She sprang forward, faster than he could track, and tried to drive the sword through his chest. Goetz tried to parry and was thrown off balance as his weapon shivered asunder at the point of impact. With a triumphant cry, Dalla capitalised on his predicament, chopping down on his exposed side. He twisted desperately and caught the descending blade with both hands. Metal rasped against metal as he halted the tip only bare inches from his chest. Straining, he pushed the weapon up. Blood ran down the insides of his gauntlets. Eyes wide, Dalla tried to force it back down.

Goetz shoved the blade aside and it sank into the ground. Rising, he drove a fist into the swordswoman's belly, knocking her down. She curled around the blow and made a whooping sound as she tried to suck air into her lungs. Goetz uprooted the blade and jabbed the tip between her eyes.

'Yield,' he said.

'I know no such word,' she spat, and made to rise. Goetz shook his head and stepped back.

'I'd rather not kill you,' he said.

Dalla uttered a wordless snarl and pulled her legs under her, preparing to spring. Goetz tensed.

The haft of the axe connected with the top of her head with a decidedly audible thump. Dalla pitched forward and didn't move. Balk grinned at Goetz. 'For shame, brother. You should know that she-wolves are more dangerous than the males.'

'I've traded blows with her twice now,' Goetz said, looking down at the unconscious woman.

'And?'

'And nothing. I can't seem to kill her,' he said.

'Didn't look like you wanted to,' Opchek said. He gestured over his shoulder. 'They're regrouping, Conrad.'

'Eyri?' Balk said, looking around.

'Gone. They've retreated, but listen...' Goetz did. Faintly, on the wind, he could hear the wail of horns.

'What is that?'

'Reinforcements. Damnation.' Balk frowned. 'There were more of them here than we figured. Why?'

'Questions for another time. We've shown our strength. Now it's time to go before they show theirs.' Opchek began shouting orders. 'Grab the wounded and then gather up the prisoners and the loot!'

'Loot?' Goetz said, hesitating. 'I thought we came for the town?'

'Call it a consolation gift. If we can't have it, we'll take what we can and burn what we can't, eh Conrad?'

'Yes,' Balk said distractedly. He was looking down at Dalla, his finger running gently across the curve of his axe. Goetz watched him and Balk, as if noticing the other knight for the first time, shook himself and said, 'Take her.'

'Why? She doesn't look like she can pull an oar,' Opchek said.

'You're making a habit out of questioning me, brother,' Balk said, letting the head of his axe tap gently against Opchek's breastplate. Opchek blanched.

'Right. Take her with us. Wonderful idea, hochmeister.'

Balk smiled serenely. 'That's better. We must maintain discipline, eh brother?' he said, looking at Goetz. 'Now... let's take a page from Brother Goetz's book and burn this sty to the ground, shall we?'

'Is he dead?' Thalfi Utergard said, looking down at Eyri. The big man was painted red from crown to sole, though none of the blood seemed to be his. There were some who said Thalfi was ulfsark, and looking at him, his fellow chieftains could believe it.

'I'm not dead,' Eyri groaned. He patted his armoured torso gingerly. 'Gromril. Won it in a game of draughts from a trader a few months ago.'

'Are you sure you're not dead?' another chieftain said warily. 'Axe might have crushed your lungs. You could be suffocating even now...'

'I'm not dead, Grettir Halfhand, no matter how much you might wish,' Eyri growled. 'Someone help me up.'

'If you're not dead, what do you need our help for?' Halfhand said. He was nearly as big as Thalfi, with a ginger-coloured spade-shaped beard that had been greased with bear fat and twisted into spikes. One hand was covered by a modified knight's gauntlet, its gleaming surface covered in hammered runes.

'Up, Goldfinger,' Lok Helsgrim said, extending his staff. Eyri grabbed it and the old man hauled him to his feet with little apparent difficulty. 'The gods were watching out for you, trickster.'

'The gods help those who help themselves,' Eyri said. He looked at Ulfar, who sat hunched on a rock nearby, watching Eyristaad burn. 'Old man, I–'

'They took her,' Ulfar said.

Eyri shook his head. 'She saved my life.'

'And she likely paid for it with her own.' Ulfar stabbed his staff into the ground and levered himself to his feet.

'I–I'm sorry,' Eyri said, sounding as if every word pained him.

'Don't be. She still lives. And while she lives, we have not lost.' Ulfar took a deep breath and turned to look at the assembled chieftains. 'We have a day until the Witching Night. One day until the force that drives the ein-sark is freed once more to tread our shores.'

'And if what you say is true, what then?' Kettil Flatnose said as a thrall tied a bandage around his bicep. 'What do you want of us, old wolf?'

'Ships and men,' Ulfar grunted. 'We will raid that hell-rock and kill every living thing on it. As we should have done before.'

'And why would this time be any more successful?' Hrothgar Olvek-san wheezed.

Ulfar turned a red gaze on the wounded chieftain who shrank back, cra-dling his bandaged stump protectively. 'My daughter won her challenge. Do any here deny that?' Ulfar said.

'None deny that,' Lok said, casting his own glare around. 'But mayhap the deed must be done carefully, eh?' He frowned. 'We need to–'

A shriek cut him off. The chieftains and their men spun as a dark blotch dropped out of the sky. The blotch spread and split, becoming a murder of crows. The crows dove upon the gathered warriors, pecking and clawing. Lok swung his staff, swatting feathered bodies out of the air.

'What in the name of Olric is this?' the old man growled.

'Our foe is taunting us!' Ulfar said. 'Look out!'

Lok howled as one of the birds fell upon him even as its form bulged and ballooned into something else. Flames crawled from its beak and envel-oped the old chieftain, consuming him in weird fires. Lok's strong form heaved and thrashed as the flames crawled across him, changing him in unutterable ways.

The other chieftains watched in horror as Lok's body expanded past the stretching point of his weathered flesh. Red, wet muscle became crusted carapace and his stern face dissolved into something at once reptilian and arachnid. Lok screamed as segmented limbs burst from his torso and then it was Hrothgar's turn to scream as those spiked, jointed limbs tore into the wounded godar, ripping him limb from limb.

'Dark Prince's Pleasure!' Kettil spat, swinging his weapon at the thing that had been Lok. 'What's happened to him?'

'It's obvious isn't it?' Eyri snapped. He looked at Ulfar. 'Can't you do something old man?'

'Nothing but put him out of his misery,' Ulfar growled.

The chieftains and their men fell on the squirming, squealing thing that had been the most respected member of their group and their weapons flashed amidst the feathered storm of crows that still squawked and spilled through the air.

Ulfar ignored the battle, his eyes seeking out the bloated shape of the fire-breathing creature that had changed Lok. It waddled along the beach like a cat caught in a sack, purple shimmering flesh showing through its feathers. Its neck bulged and it breathed more fire, this time enveloping one of Eyri's men.

The man screamed and burst apart as the flames wreathed him, his gutted form writhing like an oversized starfish. Ulfar moved swiftly, his old bones creaking in protest. His staff shot out and a cleansing cold flame consumed the mutated man, reducing him to ash. Whirling, he caught the waddling crow across the skull with the weighted tip of his staff. It flopped around alarmingly, and twisted towards him with serpentine elasticity.

Ulfar pinned the creature in place and sent his power coursing through the staff. The daemon, a minor petty thing, writhed and shrieked, its true fungous nature bursting into visibility through its shell of feather and bone. It spat coloured flames in weak spurts as he ground it into the shore. Crows clawed at him, pecking and gouging. The daemon squirmed and dissipated, its essence scattered back to the spirit-sea.

Lok – the thing that had been Lok – had sunk to one rubbery knee as Thalfi hacked at it with a broken sword, roaring a battle-song. Bilious blood spilled from the rents in its carapace, and its limbs flailed, hurling men about. It screamed out imprecations in a dozen languages, some not meant for human ears, and heaved itself up as Ulfar confronted it.

'My friend,' Ulfar said softly.

'No friend, Asgrimdalr,' a horribly familiar voice spat from between the creature's clicking mandibles. 'Only death...'

'Not mine,' Ulfar said, gripping his staff tightly. He felt tired. The creature shrugged off its attackers and reared up.

'You will die, old wolf. I will have your pelt for my cloak,' the thing said, speaking in a woman's voice now. The same voice that had taunted him with the deaths of his wife and child at the hands of the einsark. The same voice that had tormented him above the island only days before. 'I will peel your soul like scales from a fish and devour it raw.'

'Myrma,' Ulfar said. 'You have lost your beauty, queen of rocks and corpses.'

'My-?' The mutated thing hesitated and then shrieked wildly. Its hooves tore the earth as it charged towards him. Ulfar met it, shedding his frail flesh like a cloak and greeting the foul thing with fang and claw.

Clothed in the skin of a great white bear, Ulfar wrapped powerful paws around the creature and ripped it off its feet, scooping it up and crushing it to his hairy breast. Claws and spikes dug into his transformed flesh but he ignored the pain and roared. Ursine muscle flexed and the carapace splintered, spilling acidic blood across the rocks.

Savagely, he bit off the struggling thing's head and spat it out. A canny warrior pinned it to the ground with a spear. Ulfar let the body fall and spread his paws. He roared again, casting his challenge into the wind. He turned, dropping to all fours and then into his old skin. He rose, naked and wrinkled, and looked at the chieftains. None of them met his eyes and he grunted and spat a wad of phlegm and blood.

'I will have my weregild, men of Norsca. Will any here gainsay me?' he said.

As one, the godi raised their weapons and uttered a hoarse cheer. Ulfar let the sound wash over him and turned to face the sea, satisfied. 'I am coming, Myrma,' he said. 'I am coming for my daughter, mistress of curs.'

Myrma's eyes sprang open and she spat blood as the tang of the old wolf's power filled her mouth. Hawking and retching, she toppled over. She cursed and raved and clawed at the stone until she could muster the strength to rise. The years had not dimmed his might, no matter how much she might have hoped otherwise. Or perhaps she was simply growing weak.

One of her daughters helped her to her feet, and Myrma fondled her, testing the firmness of her flesh. The girl flushed, though more from fear than embarrassment. Which was as it should be. 'Tomorrow,' Myrma croaked. 'You will join Her.' The girl tried half-heartedly to pull away, but Myrma's grip was firm. Even knowing it was their lot, some still tried to resist, however token an effort it might be. It was the nature of her people to do so, to rail against fate.

She shoved the girl into the arms of her initiates and they locked their arms around her. 'Prepare her,' Myrma said, hobbling towards one of the tidal pools. She leaned heavily on her staff and glared at her reflection. Her hair was going silver, and her face was lined with what another might have called exhaustion, but which she recognised for what it was... decay. Entropy. That was the price of her power; the more she expended, the more her physical form withered. It was a small thing, as such payments went, and her mistress had seen to it that she had a ready supply of skins with which to clothe herself, but still, it was too soon.

She was more powerful than Asgrimdalr, but the old wolf had a daemon's stamina. Pickled as he was, he would take more than she dared give to kill. Still, it had been worth the effort. It had been too long since she had tasted direct battle and her fingers curled like talons as she indulged in a pleasant reverie. His strength, cracking the bones of the spawn-thing, had been delightful. The feel of his teeth – ah!

The island trembled and she pushed the pleasurable sensations aside. Her mistress was a jealous one, and would not tolerate her priestess feeding the Dark Prince. She rubbed her arms and turned away, seeking out the black pods. They clustered like barnacles now, growing larger. They would burst in a matter of hours. A day, maybe less, and they would be ripe for the Witching Night. She stroked the closest of them, feeling the warmth of its hairy shell beneath her fingers. Her toes touched the cold metal of the fertiliser and she looked down at the breastplate, with its decorative sun. A woman's face stared up at her from the within the stylised corona and she grimaced and spat.

'Out of weakness, comes strength,' she said mockingly. 'Your weakness, our strength, false goddess.'

TWENTY-THREE

As the galley slid away from the shore, Goetz watched Eyristaad burn. He held tight to his sword, happy at having regained it despite the circumstances. Somehow it didn't seem right. Conquest Goetz understood, though he rarely approved. But this – this was seemingly destruction for destruction's sake.

'Are we knights?' he murmured, feeling a pang for having started the fires in the first place.

'It's an Unberogen word, you know,' Opchek said, coming up behind him. The Kislevite was chewing on a strip of dried jerky. 'Or it was.' He offered the jerky to Goetz, who shook his head. 'Battle always makes me hungry,' Opchek went on.

'It has the opposite effect on me. What is an Unberogen word?'

'Knight. It originally meant "servant" or somesuch.' Opchek chewed and swallowed. 'Which is quite appropriate, when you think about it. We are servants, and of a higher power, no less.'

'Are we?' Goetz said.

'You doubt it?'

'Somehow I don't think Myrmidia would be in favour of burning a village full of innocents,' Goetz said, his tone turning harsh. Opchek grunted.

'Who's to say? Gods are funny things, Hector. Who can say what they want or don't want at any given time?' Opchek cocked his head. 'Besides, it was a practical military decision.'

'Was it?'

'Definitely. They'll be too busy putting out those fires to worry about following us. I don't know if you noticed, but there were more ships there than there should have been this time of year.'

'Meaning?'

'Meaning, we aren't the only ones who are up to something,' Opchek said, tapping the side of his nose. 'The Norscans are a sneaky bunch. Wouldn't be the first time one of their chieftains has whipped them into a frenzy.'

'They didn't seem that frenzied to me,' Goetz said pointedly. 'More like any Imperial peasant trying to defend his home.'

'Are you honestly comparing the citizens of your Empire with a bunch of fur-clad barbarians?' Opchek said. 'Even we Kislevites are more civilised than those savages, and we still wrestle bears!' He caught Goetz's look and continued. 'Not me, you understand. It's foolishness. Bears don't really wrestle anyway.'

'No?'

'No. They grapple,' Opchek said, spreading his arms and growling. Goetz couldn't help but smile.

'Be that as it may, my point stands, I think.'

'If you had a point, I might agree,' Opchek said. 'You're a knight, Hector. And they are your enemy. Do not do them the discourtesy of viewing them as anything less.'

'Now I believe you were a servant of the White Wolf,' Goetz said. 'That sounds like something a follower of Ulric would say.'

'A man can follow more than one god. And don't forget, Myrmidia is a war-goddess. She may have more interests than spilt blood, but she is still the Patroness of Battle.' Opchek made a fist. 'We must smash the fortifications to rebuild the city.'

'You don't have to recite the fifteenth catechism at me.' Goetz rubbed his face. His face ached from the cut that split his cheek wide, exposing his jaw. Opchek had proven to be a competent battlefield surgeon and had cleaned the wound and sewed it shut with leather. The Kislevite slapped his hand.

'Don't touch it. It'll go sour.'

'I'm going to have a scar.'

'And a handsome one at that. You're lucky it didn't peel away from the bone. Then you'd have people asking you what you're grinning about all the time.' Opchek laughed. 'I–' A scuffle interrupted him and they both turned from the rail. A trio of Svanii was dragging a prisoner up onto the deck.

The Norscan roared in fury as the Svanii threw him against the mast. He was a big man, and bare-chested. They lashed his hands and feet tight, pinning him in place. He bellowed and struggled, trying to free himself but to no avail.

One of the Svanii bowed to Balk, and proffered a knife. Balk inclined his head and waved the man off. He spoke rapidly in Svanii and the natives gave a barbaric cheer. Goetz felt a sinking sensation in his stomach as the one wielding the knife turned back to the mast-bound captive.

'What are they doing?' he said. His throat felt dry.

Opchek didn't look at him. 'Making an offering to Myrmidia.'

When the knife went in the first time, the Norscan did not scream. Instead, he spat full in the face of the closest Svanii. When the knife blade reached his ribs, he tensed, grunting in agony. At a bark from the knife-man, other Svanii crowded forward, holding the Norscan still. The knife sliced easily through muscle and meat. Bones snapped and popped wetly as eager fingers dug into the gaping wounds. Now the Norscan screamed.

'No,' Goetz said. 'No!' He grabbed the hilt of his sword and started forward. Opchek made a grab for him, but was too slow. Goetz had his sword out when Balk stepped between him and the mast, the latter's axe hanging loosely in his hand.

'No further, brother. This is a holy moment, and it cannot be interrupted.'

'Holy? This is an abomination!' Goetz sputtered. 'They're torturing him!'

'So they are. Do you think his kind haven't done worse?' Balk said softly. 'They have raped and pillaged the coasts of the Old World for centuries, putting towns and temples alike to the sword.'

Behind Balk, the Norscan's screams had risen in pitch, becoming animal squeals. Goetz made to shove the hochmeister aside. The axe came up and the flat of the blade rested on Goetz's shoulder, its edge within a razor's distance of his neck. Balk continued speaking quietly, as if Goetz hadn't interrupted them.

'They are a treacherous people, brother. Daemon-ridden and corrupt. They bathe in foetid pools that glow in the night, and make offerings to twisted idols. They venerate the mutant, the beastman and the marauder. They are not human. They are not worthy of your blood or your sacrifice.'

'I–' Goetz didn't take his eyes off Balk. The other man's face could have been carved from marble, so serene it was.

'Make no mistake, if you interfere with our allies, I will stop you,' Balk said. The axe slid forward, and the edge shaved off a few stray bristles on Goetz's cheek. 'It is a holy moment. One the goddess herself approves of... see?' he continued, gesturing.

The Norscan would have hung slack in his bonds, had not the Svanii been there to hold him upright. His back had been reduced to red ruin and his ribs had cleaved from his spine and spread away from the rest of him. Goetz felt a wave of bile rise up in his throat as one of the Svanii reached inside the dying man's back and carefully, almost gently, pulled his lungs free.

It looked, for all the world, like some great red bird. An eagle, or even a crow. Goetz turned away. The Norscan was dead, of either blood loss or suffocation. He caught a glimpse of white in the crowd. A swaying shape that moved through the men slowly, almost mournfully. Ancient eyes met his own, and the warmth of her gaze filled him with a sense of shame and regret.

'Do you see her,' Balk whispered. 'Do you see her, brother? She walks among us, to show us the way.' He sounded ecstatic, like a doomsayer crouching on a plinth in the Square of Sigmar in Altdorf, terrified and excited and certain, oh so certain.

Goetz felt no certainty. No excitement. Only a dull ache. The woman-shape wove between the men unseen, and something that might have been a spear rose and pointed at him, and he saw those eyes again, blazing brighter and brighter, making him feel smaller and smaller. The harsh croaking of crows broke him from the trance. He tore his eyes away from the now empty spot and looked back at the mast.

The crows had gathered to feast. Balk raised his axe. 'Myrmidia! Myrmidia!' The gathered knights and tribesmen echoed the cry. Goetz alone was silent. It was only a few minutes later that he realised that Balk hadn't been looking at either the dying man or the white shape when he'd spoken.

After they reached the safety of the harbour and docked, the prisoners were herded down the ramp and onto the docks in a rattle of chains. The Svanii clustering on the wharf raised a cheer. Rocks and fruit flew with abandon until Balk roared out something and the crowd began to scatter. Goetz was reminded of his own treatment at the hands of the Norscans. He didn't feel any pleasure at the thought of them now undergoing the same treatment.

The body of the sacrifice was left strapped to the mast for the crows and the gulls. Goetz resolutely ignored it, trying not to think about what he'd seen. It wasn't as easy as that, however. Pain crept through his face, making every expression an experience in agony, and with every twinge he was reminded that there was a difference between death in battle and death after the fact.

They were better than this. They had to be. Had the goddess truly approved? Was he just squeamish? He wanted a sign. Something. Anything. Something to tell him which path was the right one. What would the Grand Master do? What would he think? He watched the knights and their allies disembark, and wondered if this were a noble army of civilisation or something else.

He caught sight of the warrior-woman in the crowd of captives. Their eyes locked for a moment, and a thrill of something passed through him. She looked defiant, even now. Like a panther in a cage.

Goetz glanced back at the galley, and the body lashed to the mast. His face hardened. 'Sign enough,' he muttered. 'Thank you, my Lady.'

'You are welcome,' Myrma said, appearing at his elbow. Goetz turned to find Balk and the priestess standing behind him. The latter looked as tired and worn as any warrior. Balk slapped his gloves into his palm and smiled wearily.

'Well, brother? What say you? Do you see now why we need more men?'

'I see,' Goetz said. 'Opchek said there were more of them there than you were expecting.'

'Yes. They are gathering for war. War against us,' Myrma said, her lips tightening. Her eyes flashed, and for a moment Goetz was again struck by her resemblance to his patron goddess. But beyond that initial similarity, there was something else, some fundamental flaw in her proportions that he hadn't quite noticed until now. What was it? What was he seeing?

'Which is why you need to do as I've asked, brother,' Balk said. 'We need to bring the full force of the Order to bear on these savages.'

'I... understand,' Goetz said, keeping his face blank. 'I will compose them tonight. But in the meantime, are we capable of withstanding a siege?'

'Hopefully,' Balk said. 'Why, brother? You have a suggestion?'

'Several. Siege-craft was a specialty of mine.' Goetz hesitated. 'That is, if I'm not overstepping my bounds.'

'Ha! Hardly,' Balk said, smiling broadly. 'I look forward to it! But first–'

'The letters,' Goetz said, nodding. 'Do not worry, hochmeister. I will make them my priority.'

'Very good. Now, I must see to the dispensation of the prisoners. I have a feeling we're going to need the extra labourers. My lady?' Balk said, looking at Myrma. She did not look at him as she shook her head.

'I will stay. I wish to speak to Hector.'

A dark expression flashed across Balk's face, but then vanished as quickly as it had come. 'As you say.' He left with a swirl of his fur cloak. Goetz watched him go, and then turned to Myrma.

'Speak,' he said.

Her eyebrow quirked. 'You sound angry, Hector.'

'What I am is of no concern to you, surely,' he said. She frowned.

'Rude too.'

'What do you want?'

'To talk. To help you.' Her fingers stroked the edges of the rawhide thong that held his cheek together. He jerked his head away.

'I'm fine, thank you.'

'I helped you before, didn't I?'

'I don't know.' Goetz stepped away from her. Her hand shot out, snagging his wrist with surprising strength.

'The poison is still in you,' she said, and he felt a jolt in his side. He flinched and the leather in his face pulled tight, eliciting a grunt from him. 'You should let me help you.'

'I can manage, I think. I have letters to compose,' he said, pulling his wrist free. Without waiting for a reply he headed away from her, one hand clutching his side.

Dalla glared at the einsark as she was dragged away from the ship. He was speaking to the – no, not a woman. She knew what that creature was, even if the brass-skins appeared to be oblivious. Her father had described the hag-queen of Svunum often enough.

Lagging slightly, she watched as the knight stalked away from the hag, limping slightly. A strange sense of relief flooded her, only to be angrily shoved aside as the witch met her eyes. The woman grinned, bearing filed teeth, and Dalla turned away. Beneath her tattered hauberk, the amulets her father had crafted for her seemed to burn white-hot against her skin.

Hopefully that meant they were working. Keeping her invisible to the eyes of the hag's daemon-familiars. She rattled her chains in frustration.

There was nothing that would please her more at the moment than getting her fingers into the soft flesh beneath the hag's jaw, but such was not to be.

Instead, all she could do was hold her peace and bide her time. There would come an opportunity for escape. And when it did... she fought to keep the lupine grin off her face. It became easier when the hiss of a lash split the air. The tattooed savage garbled something at the prisoners and snapped the whip again.

Dalla hurried, not wishing to feel the sting of the whip. She saw familiar faces among the group. The raiders hadn't been picky... there were women mixed in among the old and the far too young and there were a number of warriors, most bearing wounds. One man saw her looking and grinned, baring broken teeth. She recognised him as one of Flatnose's jarls.

'Ho, Ulfarsdottir... we are swimming in a sea of dung now, eh?' he rasped. Blood leaked out from between the fingers pressed to his shoulder.

'Yes, but I intend to make for shore as soon as possible,' Dalla said. 'Are you with me?'

'Oh aye. I saw you bash Kettil... any woman who can fight like that I'll follow to Hel itself.'

Dalla snorted. 'You must follow a lot of women,' she said.

'A fair few,' the warrior grunted. 'You have a plan?'

'Not yet.'

'Best hurry. I'd hate to bleed to death before I get a chance to strangle one of these cannibals with his own tongue.' He pulled his hand away from his wound and grimaced.

They were harried away from the harbour and out past the town towards the rocky reaches of the island shore. Scrub trees and bedraggled weeds clutched at them as they were forced towards the mouth of a cave. A foul smell, like rotten eggs, emanated from it and Dalla pressed her hands to her mouth as they were herded inside.

More Svanii were waiting there, though these were not the tanned warriors who had escorted them. These were pale wraiths, covered in tattoos that looked like fish scales and they wore wooden masks shaped like beaks and feathered cloaks. They took over escort duties with a smoothness born of practice. They carried weapons crafted from what looked like volcanic glass and moved through the stinking darkness with sure-footed grace.

The captives were led down a flight of stone slab-steps. The smell grew fouler and the air tasted of sulphur. Vents in the rock belched witch-light and noxious clouds that made Dalla's eyes water. Her vision played tricks on her, and she thought she saw flat shapes hunching along the roof of the cavern.

Finally, they came to a large grotto which echoed with the roar of the sea. The thunder of waves was amplified by the shape of the cavern, and a sea breeze battled with the stink of the gases, making the air semi-breathable.

They were forced at spear-point into a pen – one of many in the grotto – constructed of bone and other, less pleasant substances. There were cages of smaller size hanging from the great fangs of rock that occupied the upper reaches of the cavern, all of them crammed with prisoners, most in some state of malnutrition.

Dalla considered making a lunge for the nearest guard, but knew that she wouldn't get far, even with help. No, she would have to wait until a better opportunity presented itself.

'As cunning as ever, my daughter.'

Dalla froze, not quite believing her ears. She opened her mouth.

'No. Do not speak. Do not draw the attentions of any that might be listening. Look up.'

She did, as casually as she was able. The dim shapes she had spied before suddenly sprang into stark focus and her blood chilled. Flat, plate-shaped multi-hued things clung to the grotto ceiling like bats. They constantly moved, shoving and jostling like puppies at the teat, their circular maws clinging to the rock as if they were leeching strength from it.

There were other shapes than just those; there were cackling pink things as well, like stretched and boiled infants capering back and forth invisibly around the pens and the captives within, reaching out to pinch at the captives with ethereal fingers. She watched a man so molested shudder, as if a chill had passed through him. Past the pink things were fungoid creatures that glided along on flat disk-like feet, trailing spurts of rainbow-hued flame. One drew too close to the pen she was caged in and she felt her amulet burn. She placed fingers to it and looked away as the thing glided past.

'The children of Old Father Fate, daughter. They are held to this place by Her whom we bound here. The Black Crow-Queen and Her mad court.' Her father's voice was soothing and she felt the fear that had filled her upon sight of the creatures fade. 'And they will be free again, come the Witching Night.'

Dalla's hands clenched. Her father's voice began to fade. 'We are coming, daughter. And we bring sword and fire.' And then he was gone. Dalla leaned against the bars of her cage, eyes closed. As her father left her, so too did the vision he had bestowed. It was almost worse not seeing the daemons. She shook her head. She had other things to worry about. She turned and her eyes met those of several of the men. The one she had spoken to earlier nodded. Slowly they drew together amidst the crowd, and Dalla began to speak in soft tones.

TWENTY-FOUR

Black sails set off in the night. Goetz watched them from the library window, a half-finished letter sitting on the desk behind him. Three slim galleys, sails unfurled to take advantage of the night-wind, sped out of the harbour.

He turned away from the window. The library was big, bigger than that in the Bechafen Komturie, incorporating as it did the accumulated knowledge of two houses. The shelves were overflowing and piles of books, stacked sloppily, hugged the bulk of the floor space. Most had the look of books that had been placed and left, if the sheen of dust was anything to go by.

Too concerned with their crusade to read, perhaps. He sat down at the desk and stared at the letter. It contained neither plea nor explanation. Instead, it was a condemnation. One likely to have heads on the block and bloody consequences. His skin crawled at the thought and he pressed his hand to his side. The pain had not abated. Nor did he think it would. Not this time.

In the Order, they were taught to think first above all else. To scrutinise, ponder and decide. The key to strategy was to consider the possible variables and create a plan of action flexible enough to accommodate random happenstance, and yet firm enough to deal decisively with the enemy. Watch and wait was how old Berlich had put it. Goetz felt a pang. He could have used his old hochmeister's advice.

He was neither novice nor naive, but still the situation confused him. There were too many elements to the thing, too many instances of seemingly random happenstance that he knew – he knew – were anything but. Every instinct he had screamed warnings at him.

Goetz looked around the library, scanning the faded bindings. Unlike in other komturie libraries there were no icons here, no representations of ancient heroes or even of the goddess herself. It wasn't just the library which was barren... for such a divinely inspired bunch, the brethren of the Svunum Komturie were not fond of displays of devotion.

Unless you counted blood sacrifice, of course. Goetz frowned. Surely the goddess did not truly demand blood; but then, how to explain what he'd seen? Had he seen anything?

He sat down and scraped his palms over his scalp, trying to think. Who was it who'd said that Sigmar's wrath was turned aside by the blood of mutants? Wasn't that simply a form of blood sacrifice? What was the difference, in the end, between the blood of one enemy and the next?

'Are the gods so picky then?' he said, his voice surprisingly loud in the silence of the library. He gripped the medallion Abbot Knock had given him and rubbed his thumb over the embossed spear and shield. The tools given to man to defend his nascent civilisation, the one to prod and the other to ward.

Was that what this was? Civilisation in the offing? In the beginning, there was fire and there was blood that was what the First Book of Sigmar said. His fingers tightened around the medallion and he turned back to the window. Something pale and grave looked back at him in place of his reflection. The face was the same as the apparition he'd seen on the beach and on the boat, and its gaze bored through his own and into his mind beyond. The mouth opened but all he heard was the cry of birds.

Goetz closed his eyes and backed away from the glass, his fists clenched. 'I don't know what you want,' he said. Then, louder, 'I don't know what you want!'

The face grew larger, expanding through the glass. It seeped through the brick, spreading like a mist. Cold crept through his limbs and he tried to turn away, but he found himself unable to move. The medallion burned on his chest and in his head he saw chained figures shoved down gangplanks and into dark holes.

He saw fire and death, and the komturie felt as if it were collapsing around him. 'You see?' a rough voice said. Goetz spun and saw the old shaman sitting not five feet away, hunched against his primitive staff, his ancient eyes locked on Goetz's own. Though he'd only seen the old man at a distance before, Goetz easily recognised him.

'I'm dreaming again,' Goetz said, forcing himself to relax.

'Are you?' the old man said.

'I must be. Otherwise you wouldn't be here.'

The old man smiled. 'As you say,' he said. 'I am Ulfar Asgrimdalr, gudja of Goldfinger, father of a wayward daughter.' He gestured to Goetz's sword, where it sat sheathed on the desk.

'Father... her?' Goetz said, slightly shocked. 'She's your daughter?'

'Every daughter has a father. Should mine be any different?' Ulfar smiled and leaned forward. 'You are brave and strong.' He frowned. 'But for how much longer, hmm?'

'What?'

The staff swung out, the tip motioning towards the scars on Goetz's side. Instinctively he looked down. A thrill of panic went through him as he saw the black lines radiating from the wound point and staining his shirt. 'Those weren't there before,' he said hoarsely. He pulled up his shirt and reached out a finger to touch the puffy flesh around the wounds, but a grunt from his visitor stopped him.

'Do not touch it,' Ulfar said.

'Why?'

'It would not be wise. What causes pain in one world, can cause death in another.'

'Death?' Goetz said. 'Who are you? Why are you here?'

'I told you who I was. As to why I am here... ah. I owe you a debt, one I am here to repay.'

'Your daughter,' Goetz said. Ulfar nodded.

'You could have slain her. Others would have.' Ulfar smiled, his strong yellow teeth surfacing in his white beard and then fading. 'Thus, I owe you, boy. And Ulfar Asgrimdalr always repays his debts.'

'And how do you intend to do so?' Goetz said warily.

'I intend to save your life. And hopefully your soul in the bargain,' Ulfar said solemnly. He cleared his throat. 'Our gods are old and hard and wild, like the wind in the great troll-peaks. They do not give, but instead take, even as we take from the soft Southerners. Our gods raid us for blood and souls and we give to them freely enough. But sometimes they want more than even we are prepared to give. Sometimes their messengers come and take and take and take and we are left empty and hollow like a drained tun of wine.' The old man shifted in his seat, and his eyelids drooped as if gravity were warring against him. They sprang open a moment later. Goetz stepped forward.

'Are you–?'

'I am fine. It is wearying to speak like this.' Ulfar took a breath and continued. 'We worship many gods, and among their number are counted aspects of those you call the Ruinous Powers, though in our tongue they are less ruinous than capricious. The Wolf-Father, the Crow-Brother, the Laughing Prince and the Shaper-of-Things, these are just some of their names and faces. They are each unto themselves a pantheon, warring and growing in high Aesgardr – the Wood Between Worlds.' He sucked on his teeth for a moment, as if the taste of the words to come were not to his liking in the least. 'They pluck champions from among us, the way a man might pluck a pup from a litter. They raise them up and dash them down. But there are others...'

'Others?' Goetz prodded. Ulfar smiled bitterly.

'Daemons,' he said, in perfect Reikspiel. Goetz could not repress an instinctive shudder as the word hung heavy in the air. Ulfar went on. 'That is what your people call them, aye?'

'Yes,' Goetz said, his mouth suddenly dry. 'That is what they are.'

'They are what they are, no more, no less,' Ulfar responded with a shrug. 'Some are worse than others.' He thumped his staff on the hard stone floor, and the echo caused Goetz's bones to quiver. 'Some are more dangerous than others. More cunning. More foul.'

'What are you trying to tell me?'

'My gods speak to me. Your goddess speaks to you.' Ulfar paused. 'And something else...' He cocked his head, as if listening. Goetz followed suit. He heard nothing. He hadn't really expected to.

'I have never heard Myrmidia,' Goetz said. Ulfar looked at him with what might have been pity.

'That does not mean she has not spoken.' He tapped an ear. 'The deaf cannot hear. That does not mean we do not speak, eh?'

Goetz got the point. Annoyance filled him. 'I think I would hear a goddess if one spoke to me!' he retorted.

'Not if someone else was speaking too loudly,' Ulfar said and thumped the floor again, more loudly this time. Goetz hissed as his body was suddenly wracked with pain. Gasping, he ripped his shirt open and stared down at the scars on his side. The pale tissue bulged and puffed like some sort of deranged fungus. Beneath his skin, something sharp and dark moved.

The tip of Ulfar's staff jabbed out, catching him in the side. Goetz fell to the floor with a scream. Blood flowed between his fingers as whatever was inside him thrashed. A black beak pierced his flesh and the scars gaped wide and the crow thrust itself out into his room, wet and foul. Goetz rolled away desperately, leaving a trail of blood behind.

The crow hopped after him, croaking. 'Poisoned,' it said, in a woman's voice. 'Poisoned.' As it drew closer, however, its voice changed, becoming deeper and harsher. 'Poisoned,' it said, talons clicking across the floor. 'Poisoned.'

'Poisoned,' Ulfar said, sweeping the bird aside with his staff. It struck the wall with bone-snapping force and tumbled to the floor, twitching. Goetz looked at Ulfar, then at the bird.

'What–' he began.

'Hush,' Ulfar said. 'Come out, come out, wherever you are, old hag.'

Before Goetz's horrified eyes, the bird's corpse twitched. Then, a number of white maggots poked through its feathered breast and wriggled into the air. The maggots extended further and further until, with a start, Goetz realised that they weren't maggots at all but fingers!

The fingers bent and tore at the feathers, spreading the wound they had emerged from, even as the bird had previously torn its way out of Goetz. The carcass flopped wide and something far too large emerged, rising up and up, its pale white head brushing against the ceiling.

'Asgrimdalr,' it said, the words slipping from between ash-black teeth and riding on a waft of carrion breath. 'I find you slinking around Her temple like an alley cur. Appropriate...'

'Myrma. Old charlataness. Troll-wife. Still hiding in the skins of your betters?' Ulfar said, standing between the thing and Goetz.

'I have many skins now. My Master, my Mistress, they give me so many to wear in Her service, in His schemes,' the thing replied, drawing its feet from within the bird one at a time with an almost dainty grace.

It looked like a woman as seen in the surface of warped glass. Too-long limbs stretched from a bloated torso and a head like a chopped mushroom bobbed on a stalk-like neck. The feet were wide and splayed, almost like flippers. Tattoos covered the entirety of its naked form, the ink almost dripping down its limbs and face. Eyes bright like balefires gleamed above a mouth full of rotten teeth. In the drift of its words was the scream of a flock of birds and every movement made a sound like the rustle of oily feathers.

Man and monster faced one another, and Goetz, bleeding like a stuck pig, could only watch helplessly. He tried to get his feet under him, but he was weak. He felt feverish and sick, and the hole in his side wasn't helping. Holding his arm tightly to his side, he began to crawl away. If he could find some weapon, any weapon...

'He is mine. They are all mine,' Myrma gurgled. 'They have heard Her song and have joined the Great Game.' Black teeth clicked and its eyes flickered to Goetz, who froze. 'He will join too.'

'The game of gods is for them alone. Not for mortals,' Ulfar barked.

'Says one who interferes,' Myrma countered, advancing. Her too-long arms shot out, grasping for the old man. Ulfar evaded the clutching talons and jabbed his staff into her stomach. The creature squealed and caught the staff, wrenching it out of Ulfar's hands. 'You'll interfere no more though!' She swung the staff up as if to crush Ulfar's skull, but suddenly in the old man's place a great white-furred bear reared back and swept out a crushing paw.

She shrieked as the paw sent her flying. But even as she flew, she changed, shedding her skin like droplets of water. Her shape twisted into that of a malformed hound and she sprang at the bear. The two beasts roared and thrashed, tearing at one another. Even as they fought, however, they both lost cohesion, becoming so much vapour. Goetz closed his eyes as the mingled vapours suddenly swept over him and when his eyes sprang open, the cacophony of birds filled his head. A murder of crows flew past the window, their dark shapes merging with the night as they shot upwards as if in pursuit of something white. Goetz took a breath and felt the chill fade.

His body hurt all over, but the agony of his wound had become a dull thing, pushed to the back of his head. The old man – Ulfar – had done something to him. He had tried to protect him from – what?

Goetz felt bile rise up in his throat as he considered what he had seen. If he believed it, then this island was lost, not just to the Order, but to humanity. He leaned over the desk and looked at the half-finished letter. How long had it been? How many days were left until the Marienburg fleet would arrive? When was Hexensnacht? Casting a glance at the window, he knew the answer to that. Both Mannslieb and Morrslieb were almost full, which meant Hexensnacht was tomorrow night, if he was any judge. The fleet was already on its way, and the blessings of Myrmidia on them.

He knew what he had to do.

He left the library and moved through the silent corridors, heading down towards the sound of the sea. There were Svanii on sentry duty in the courtyard, but when they caught sight of his arms and armour, they stepped aside respectfully.

'Master,' one said in oddly accented if passable Reikspiel, nodding. Goetz stopped and looked at the man. He was, like all the Svanii, slightly smaller than the average Imperial citizen, though much broader. Round, slightly brooding features dominated by a crudely shorn bristle of dark hair and facial tattoos that reminded Goetz of a flock of startled birds. The man blinked nervously as Goetz peered at him.

'Something we can help you with, master?' the other sentry said, smiling ingratiatingly.

'The prisoners. Where are they held?' Goetz said.

'Ah–'

'Hurry now!' Goetz barked. 'The goddess commands!'

The two men exchanged glances and then one said, 'In the sea-caves, master. With the others.'

Goetz nodded his thanks and stepped past them, wondering whether they would alert someone as to what they had seen. Possibly, though it wouldn't matter. Goetz left the komturie behind, his skin crawling with every step. Outside of the fortress-monastery's protective embrace he felt as if he were being stalked by something monstrous. The worst part was that he knew it was true now.

He could not say why he had so readily believed the old man. Everything he saw in the library could have been a sorcerous illusion easily enough. But in his gut, he knew it hadn't been. The old man had been trying to warn him. Even as, perhaps, Myrmidia herself had. Which meant what, exactly, a small part of him murmured. What of your sceptic's faith now?

He grunted and pushed aside that latter thought. This was no time to consider the philosophical ramifications of divine intervention. Before tonight was out, he was likely going to have to spill the blood of men who were his brothers.

Crows perched on the lintels and rooftops of the Svanii village, watching him as he moved through the ill-lit streets towards the wharf. There were more birds in evidence than he thought the island could support. Doubtless Balk would say it was a sign of the divine.

Balk. How much did the hochmeister know? Was he a pawn of a sorceress? Or a willing convert? The mouth of the sea-cave rose up suddenly and Goetz halted, his hand on his sword. Questions were for later. Right now, he had someone he hoped was a friend to save.

The longships slid through the mist smoothly. The oars were stowed and the drums were silent, and a spirit-summoned wind filled the sails to bursting. Eyri watched the other ships for a moment, and then turned to Ulfar.

The old man sat hunched in the prow, leaning on his staff. It never ceased to amaze Eyri that someone so powerful could look so fragile.

'What are you looking at?' Eyri muttered as he leaned against the rail beside the gudja.

'I'm not looking; I'm concentrating,' Ulfar growled. Eyri blinked and suddenly realised that the sheen on the old man's face was sweat. 'The sea is angry enough as it is.'

'I would be too, with a daemon in my belly.' Eyri grinned at Ulfar's expression. 'I do listen to the legends, old man. I know what we are heading for. The question I have is why? And don't play the concerned father.'

'I am concerned,' Ulfar said.

'But not about her. She's a tool, just like the rest of us,' Eyri said. 'I know the smell of a grudge, old man.'

Ulfar glared at him for a moment. Then the old man sighed and shook his head. 'You know the stories, yes?'

'I said I did.'

'When I was a young man, more than sixty years ago, we – I and my fellow gudjas – bound the Island That Walked to this point on the sea. We broke the power of the creatures that lived there and put a stop to their raids on our villages.'

'Islands don't walk,' Eyri said.

'This one did. It wasn't really an island. It's not an island now.' Ulfar grinned humourlessly. 'It's a corpse.'

'A corpse?' Eyri stared at him incredulously.

'Big corpse,' Ulfar clarified, holding his hands apart.

'Who died?'

'A goddess,' Ulfar said. He looked up and to the north, where the soft ever-present glow of the polar realm lit the horizon with a cursed light. Eyri followed his gaze and made a warding gesture against bad luck.

'One of them?' he said.

'S'vanashi is what our ancestors called Her. The Lady of Ten Thousand Cloaks. The Crow-Queen and the Hag-Mother. A daughter of the Great Planner, one of his flock,' Ulfar said slowly. 'Thrown down and buried beneath the sea for some crime we do not know. And beneath the sea, Her corpse slept and dreamed, and like roots growing through a barrow, she excreted an island. From the very stuff of this world, she grew herself a body that moved and spoke, and she called Her servants to Her across the great land bridge and then she taught them all that she knew.'

Eyri turned to the rail and peered into the evening mist. It was growing lighter now, as morning approached. 'Tomorrow night is the Witching Night.'

Ulfar nodded. 'They will kill all they have taken. They will soak the roots of the island in blood and it will break the bonds that bind Her in the deep dark.'

Eyri turned. 'You know that for a fact?' he said.

Ulfar shrugged. 'I know what the spirits tell me. What horrors they whisper in my ear as I dream. I know what the hag-girl Myrma thinks. Whether it is true or not, who can say? It is all naught but the laughter of the Dark Gods from where we sit, small and insignificant.'

'Comforting words.'

'They were not meant to be.' Ulfar's head jerked up. 'Look!' He pointed.

Several black shapes wheeled and banked through the misty sky. Eyri's eyes narrowed. 'Crows.'

'Kill them! Now!' Ulfar snarled.

'What–?'

'Now!'

Eyri turned and gave the order. Bowstrings twanged and two of the shapes fell limply into the sea. The others turned and began to glide away. Ulfar made a sound halfway between a whine and a growl and he spun his staff. His veins stood out on his neck as he glared up at the sky. Before the disbelieving eyes of the crew, the mist congealed into a rough shape that pursued the departing crows.

Ulfar hunched forward, stretching out his hand. His fingers curled like hooks as he rotated his wrist with bone-snapping speed. The mist closed around the crows. Eyri heard a distant croak, which cut off abruptly. Black feathers drifted down onto the deck.

'Did you get them?' he asked, turning to look at Ulfar. The old man was on his hands and knees, breathing heavily. Eyri was at his side in an instant. 'What's wrong?'

'I'm old, Goldfinger,' Ulfar said with a wheezy laugh. 'Old and tired.'

'Can you continue on?'

'Going to put me back ashore somewhere? And then where would you be, eh?' Ulfar barked. He stood with a groan. 'No. You'll need what magics I can muster before this day is out.'

'I hope you have some sort of plan, old man. Killing crows is all well and good, but we're going to need a bit more than a mist to get past their harbour defences.' Eyri gestured towards the distant shapes of the pylons which marked the entrance to Svunum's harbour. They would be on them as the day waned, and he knew there was no way they could avoid being spotted.

Ulfar merely shook his head. 'I will handle them. You will handle the landing. You will need to occupy that damnable keep as soon as possible.'

Eyri cut him off with a snort. 'I know my business old man. Besides which, I've wanted to loot that drafty pile for years now. I'll take it, no worries.' He looked back. Behind his vessel, the mist began to clear and more than a dozen longships slid out behind his, sails billowing with Ulfar's wind.

Eyri had built a small fleet of his own, and the other chieftains had brought their swiftest and sturdiest. Armed men crowded the decks of each, straining for a glimpse of the island that was the source of so many dark childhood tales. He grinned and patted the hatchet on his belt. 'We could sack all the coasts of the Empire with this fleet. I think we can take one island, daemon-possessed or not.'

The cavernous grotto echoed with the sound of barbarous music. Drums made of stretched human skin were battered with doomful rhythm to the accompaniment of the moans of the beast-things that lurked in the water-logged deep tunnels. These lurked at the edges of the grotto, grunting and excited as the depths of the island trembled with hidden explosions. Strangely hued torches lit the dripping walls as the initiates of the Crow-Queen made the ritual ablutions to the strange, face-like formations scattered about the interior of the cavern.

Raw, ragged waves slapped across the rock as the tide came in with the dull light of the distant morning. They had taken several men and women from the cages and dragged them away over the course of the evening towards a deeper grotto, where the thunder of drums was loudest.

Those drums sounded different from the ones Dalla saw. Their beat was bone-deep and it made her feel as if she had swallowed a stone. At times it overrode the sound of the closer instruments and sometimes seemed to be in rhythm with the occasional tremor that ran through the floor of the cavern. It was an evil sound, and Dalla had a suspicion that the rise in tempo had some connection to the sound of screams cut short that reached her ears, if only rarely.

She was determined not to find out, however. Dalla gestured. The man across from her – Greki, he'd said his name was – nodded and began to pull on a femur that composed part of their cage. With a grunt, he twisted it free of the leather lashings and broke it as quietly as he could.

He tossed the sharper end to her and she caught it and slid it through the back of her belt. Then, face composed, she leaned against the cage and draped her arms above her head, her chest outthrust, legs crossed. She mouthed silently to the closest guard and he stared at her. He licked his lips and looked at his fellows. None of them were paying any attention.

'Come to me, man,' she cooed. She had bedded men before, and knew what sort of look made them stupid enough to trot after her. She pressed herself against the cage and he wrapped an arm around her waist. He popped loose the chains that held the cage shut and pulled her to him, grunting endearments.

She jammed the broken femur into his neck, gouging a hole completely through his windpipe. He staggered against her. His spear clattered to the rocky floor before she could catch it and the other guards turned. One of them said something, and several of the others laughed cruelly.

Acting quickly, she hooked the spear with her foot and flipped it up into the air, catching it even as she allowed the body to tumble. Without missing a beat, she hurled the spear at the closest guard, catching him beneath the arm. He screamed and fell back against the cage. Greki, or perhaps one of the others, wrapped a brawny arm around the man's neck and snapped it.

Snagging the glass dagger from the belt of the body at her feet, she jerked the cage door wide. 'Out! Out! Out! Make for the sea!' Dalla shouted, waving her blade over her head. 'The sea you fools! The sea!' The great mass of slaves didn't listen, being far too panicked to pay attention to a lone voice. Freedom was at hand, and she was forced to press herself back against the cage as they stampeded.

A guard fought his way through the crowd and stabbed at her with a sword. She twisted aside from the blow and drove the dagger up through his chin. His eyes rolled up in his head and he fell away to be trampled into a paste by the escaping slaves, leaving her with his sword.

Greki and the other warriors clustered around her, recognising her presence if not her face. They knew a shieldmaiden when they saw one. 'What now, spear-daughter?' one of them asked, his forked beard streaked with blood. 'Should we go to the shore? See if we can steal a boat?'

'No. We have other prey,' Dalla said with a snap of her teeth. Several muttered, but they all followed as she began to make for the sounds of combat, now echoing from the great stairs that led upwards. Armed Svanii burst out from a side tunnel ahead of them and charged towards her group with eager cries. She killed the first with her stolen blade and picked up his shield. Beating the rim of the shield with her sword, she grinned at the oncoming barbarians. 'Come then, witch-men! Come and die!'

Goetz killed the two guards as quickly as he could. They had watched him warily as he approached the mouth of the sea-caves, but had not otherwise reacted until it was too late. He stared down at the tattooed bodies for a moment, wondering whether it had been the only choice. Then, steeling himself, he stepped inside.

A rush of foul air greeted him, and he raised his free hand to his mouth. He felt a rumble through the soles of his boots that travelled all the way up his spine to his skull. He felt slightly sick, though whether from his wound, the smell, or the situation, he couldn't say.

He stopped, listening to the sound of the sea which echoed through the tunnel before him. He heard something – a sharp rasp of sound. Hand on his sword, he waited. The sound grew louder; with a start, Goetz realised that it was the sound of bare feet slapping on stone. Acting quickly he stepped out of the shadows and the runner smashed into him, falling backwards. Goetz looked down, trying to make out who he had stopped.

His eyes widened. 'Captain Feldmeyer?'

'No! I'm not going back!' the Hochlander snarled, swinging a rusty length of chain at Goetz. Goetz stepped back, letting the links swoosh past him.

'Captain, how did you get here?' Goetz said, holding up his hands. The frenzied seaman didn't reply. Instead he swung his chains again. They scraped sparks off Goetz's cuirass and the knight grabbed them, yanking the other man off balance. 'Calm down,' Goetz said, driving his fist into Feldmeyer's belly. 'What's going on?'

'Escape,' Feldmeyer wheezed. His eyes were unfocused and he looked gaunt and hungry. From somewhere close by, a bell began to ring. Goetz heard voices raised in fear and anger. He smelt smoke on the breeze and he looked up as an orange haze lit up the night. 'She set the slave-pens on fire,' Feldmeyer said, crawling to his feet. 'We have to get away. While there's time!'

'Get away? From what? I thought the Norscans took you?' Goetz said. But the Hochlander was already hobbling away. Goetz watched him disappear into the darkness, and then turned back to the light. 'What's going on?' he muttered, as he started in the direction Feldmeyer had come from.

Balk had mentioned that they'd been buying slaves, hadn't he? But he'd said they were letting them go. Obviously that was a lie. Goetz's face settled into hard lines, the wound on his cheek pulling tight. It was looking more and more like Balk, and by extension his fellow knights, were willing participants in whatever was going on.

The corridor began to fill with people as he drew closer to the scene of the blaze and the stink of it grew stronger. The freed prisoners shied away from him in obvious terror as they caught sight of him. Goetz forced his way through them and they streamed away from him like fish avoiding a shark.

Columns of oily smoke threaded through the tunnel. Somewhere an alarm bell was ringing mindlessly. Goetz loosened his sword in its sheath. A figure stumbled out of the smoke and collapsed, coughing. He recognised the knight as Krauss, a Reiklander.

'Krauss?' Goetz said, rushing forward. He saw a dark stain of blood on the man's scalp and even as he reached him, a burly Norscan charged out of the smoke, lifting a chunk of stone high in both hands. Goetz's sword jumped into his hand and he sent the Norscan spinning away, trailing streamers of blood. More approached, however. They wore chains and carried improvised weapons and they panted like wolves.

'Up, brother,' Goetz said, hooking his arm under Krauss's own and tried to lever the other man to his feet. 'Up or we're dead!'

A length of doubled chain flashed out and nearly battered Goetz's sword from his hand. Awkwardly he spun the injured man out of the way and stabbed out at his attackers. They crowded around him in the close confines of the tunnel with bloodthirsty eagerness. Goetz cursed and tried to back away, while still remaining between them and Krauss.

'Myrmidia! Myrmidia!' An axe split the stalemate, chopping down through the pate of one of the Norscans. Balk wrenched his weapon free in a spray of gore and nodded grimly to Goetz. 'Well met, brother. It seems we're having a bit of a labour dispute.'

'Is that what you call it?' Goetz said. Faced with two armoured and armed knights, the gang of Norscans hesitated. Then one gave a growl worthy of a bear and they charged forward. Goetz parried a strike with a shovel and spitted the man wielding it. Balk dispatched two more, his axe gleaming crimson as it rose and fell with a precise, smooth rhythm.

'What I call it is an act of sabotage,' Balk said, flicking blood off his weapon. 'Someone set fire to the prisoner pens. They're all loose. All of them.'

'How many is that?'

Balk frowned. 'Hundreds.'

Goetz stared at the hochmeister, the sick feeling coming back. 'Hundreds?' he echoed. 'We didn't take that many prisoners before... did we?'

'Not then, no. But we have been raiding the Norscan coast for several months now,' Balk said. He didn't look at the other knight as he said it, and Goetz's heart sank. 'Mostly under cover of darkness, to preserve our anonymity, but...' He trailed off and glared at Goetz defiantly. 'We needed the labour force!'

'Slavery is against the most sacred tenets of our Order,' Goetz said.

'I didn't say they were slaves, now did I?' Balk said, turning away. 'They're impressed labourers. Prisoners of war. We planned on releasing them once we were finished.'

'But–'

'Do you want to stand here arguing about this, or do you want to help me fix this?' Balk snapped, his eyes gleaming dangerously. Goetz helped Krauss to his feet and gestured with his sword.

'After you, hochmeister.'

Balk snorted and moved into the smoke. Goetz followed and soon they were joined by other knights responding to the alarm. How they had reached the caverns so quickly, Goetz couldn't say, though his suspicion flared bright. Opchek grinned at Goetz, his features stained with soot. 'There's been battle at every turn since you joined us, Hector!'

'You sound almost pleased,' Goetz said.

'We do serve a goddess of battle, brother,' Opchek said teasingly. 'Be a shame if we didn't honour Her at every opportunity.'

'Including the slaughter of prisoners?'

Opchek blinked and looked away. He didn't reply. A few minutes later, it didn't matter. A dozen gaunt men, clad in rags and soot, charged towards them in a ragged horde. Goetz parried a shovel and tried to use the flat of his blade. The other knights weren't so forgiving. They cut down the prisoners with brutal efficiency. Goetz held his tongue. It was not an ideal situation, but if he wanted to live long enough to get to the bottom of things, he would have to paddle with the flow.

The Svanii were mobilising as well, and small groups joined up with them in threes and fours, carrying spears and shields. They spoke in their own tongue nervously, casting sidelong glances at the knights. Overhead, the crows flew through the tunnels, their eerie croaks echoing loudly above the din of battle.

'Burn them to the waterline!' Eyri roared to his crew. Men poured over the rails of the longship and onto the black-sailed galley. The knights aboard the galley had been surprised when the fleet of dragonships had ploughed out of the spell-summoned mist and crashed past them, and even more so when Eyri's men had boarded them with eager ferocity. 'Teach them that we are the wolves in these waters, not them!'

Eyri joined his men a few moments later, hurling one of his hatchets into the face of a Svanii sailor. Not pausing to free it, he merely pulled his second axe from his belt and engaged a knight. The brass-skin called out to his goddess as Eyri ducked beneath his sword-stroke and buried the hatchet in his groin.

Ripping his weapon free, Eyri kicked the dying man over the side and turned to meet the next threat. 'Kill them all! No survivors! No prisoners!' he shouted, fighting to catch his breath. His chest and belly still ached from Balk's blow, but he knew what would cure it... the knight's head on a spike. It had been a long time coming.

He had dealt with Balk fairly for far too long, frightened of the manic intensity the man had. Granted, he wouldn't take Balk's head tonight, not unless he was luckier than the old man had predicted. No, tonight was for burning that cursed island to the waterline, and to kill a few hundred of those flesh-eating savages. Maybe, just maybe, to get back the old man's she-wolf of a daughter. He owed them that much, and Eyri Goldfinger always paid his debts.

A wounded knight stumbled towards him, both hands clutching his throat. Eyri allowed him to stumble past and chopped him down. He spit on the body, and turned. The galley was slick with blood stem to stern and he wondered what sound it would make as it sank.

'Burn it!' he shouted, raising his hatchet. 'Burn this cursed boat and let the fires light our path–'

'No!' Ulfar bellowed from back aboard Eyri's own ship. 'Cease, Goldfinger! Or are you as battle-dumb as Thalfi Utergard?'

'What?' Eyri called out as he stepped over bodies and strode to the rail. 'What are you barking about old man?'

'How did you think we were going to get past the harbour guards, you fool?' Ulfar roared, slamming the butt of his staff against the deck. Eyri winced.

'Fine, but–'

'Gather the other chieftains! Now!'

It took far longer than Eyri would have liked to do so, but when the other godi were gathered on the deck of the captured galley, Ulfar explained. He swept his dark gaze across the group. 'There are cannon on those sea-towers,' he growled, motioning towards the distant pylons. 'My mist has concealed us thus far, but once we get too close to the island, the daemon's magics will scatter my own like a flock of scared birds. They will see us and–'

'Sink us,' Kettil said, looking thoughtful. 'Unless we get them first. Clever, old man.'

'There are two galleys. My men took the other. I'll sail it down their gullets,' Grettir Halfhand said, his rune-studded gauntlet creaking. It was a terrible thing, seething with blighted power and when he made a fist, red light crackled between the fingers. 'Who'll take the other?'

'I'll do it,' Eyri said. He looked at Ulfar. 'I've seen what Imperial gunpowder does when you burn a bunch at a time. I'll fire the magazine in the ship's hold and take the tower on the right while they're busy dealing with the explosion.' He looked at Halfhand, who growled in anticipation and stroked the Skulltaker's Mark branded into the flesh between his eyes. 'You take the left, eh, Halfhand?'

'Aye,' the other chieftain said. 'And the towers?'

'We turn their own devil weapons on them,' Eyri said with relish. 'Imagine what that oh-so carefully constructed harbour will look like when we do to it what they did to Eyristaad!'

Dalla took the hand that grabbed her tangled hair off at the wrist. The Svanii shrieked beneath his bird mask, but the yell was cut short as she pinned his head to the stone with a quick thrust. 'Quiet, hell-hound,' she said, pulling his sword free. She looked around. The others had fared equally well. Her companions-in-captivity had scavenged weapons from the dead guards and now they were all armed. Shaking blood off her blade she kept going. They were following the herd of escaping captives, chivying the stragglers on, arming who they could.

It was not out of kindness, but desperation that prompted her to do so. If her father were on the way with a fleet, she was determined that he would find the defences of the island as open as a whore's arms to a customer. That meant causing as much trouble as possible.

'You know what we must do?' she barked at Greki and the others.

'We burn this festering pile to the ground, aye,' Greki said, flashing his broken teeth. 'Do not worry, Ulfarsdottir, if there's one thing we know how to do, it is burn things to – ack!' He gagged as the crow swept across his face, leaving thin red trails in its wake. He cursed and clutched at his face.

'Myrmidia!' someone shouted and Dalla cursed as the torches her men carried caught the sheen of brass armour charging towards them.

'Take them!' she said, bounding to meet the knights. Her sword whistled out, crashing against a hastily raised blade. She nearly shrieked in frustration as she recognised both the blade and its wielder. 'You!'

'Oh bloody hell, get off me!' Goetz snapped, whirling her around and driving her back towards the wall of the tunnel. The two forces crashed together behind them and he bent towards her, narrowly avoiding the wad of spittle she sent his way. 'Well, this is awkward,' he said.

'I should have gutted you on the boat!' she said.

'It would have simplified things no end if you had,' Goetz said. 'I was coming to free you!' he continued hastily as she tried to kick his legs out from under him.

'Were you so eager to die then, einsark?' she hissed as she forced him around. His back connected with the wall and dust spilled down on him.

'Would you believe that your father sent me?'

'No!'

'Of course you wouldn't! That would be too easy!' Goetz snapped, his voice dripping with frustration. 'Am I going to have to kill you to get you to listen to me?'

'Yes!' she said, shoving him back with a flurry of blows. He stepped back and she broke off, her sword point dipping. Goetz steadied himself against the cavern wall and looked past her. Opchek was behind her, his sword raised.

Goetz hit her with his shoulder, sending her rolling across the floor. He made an apologetic gesture to Opchek who stared at him incredulously and followed after her, his sword drawing sparks off the wall as he made a show of attacking her.

Unencumbered by armour, she bounced to her feet and met him blade to blade, their crosspieces entangling. He was the stronger, but she was as close to berserk as he'd seen anyone not frothing at the mouth. 'I was telling the truth,' he said hoarsely. 'You must believe me!'

'So?' Dalla spat. 'I will burn this daemon-haunted island to ash and bones!'

'Good plan,' Goetz grunted. 'At last we're on the same page. When I drop my sword, run.'

'Run?' Her eyes bulged. 'I do not run!'

'Then make a strategic advance in the opposite direction!' Goetz snarled. 'Just go. Do whatever you were planning on doing, but do it quick!' He shoved her aside and stumbled intentionally into the wall. For all her disbelief, Dalla didn't hesitate. She sprang past him like a she-cat and called out to her companions. Those who could broke off from their combats and followed her, fleeing pell-mell up the tunnel and outside.

They burst past the Svanii guarding the cave mouth, Greki pausing only to behead the one who got in their way and then they were rushing towards the town. 'Some fun, shield-maiden!' he howled. 'Now a fire, hey?'

'A big fire,' Dalla shouted back. Alarms were sounding everywhere. Most of the prisoners with any sense had likely headed for the harbour or the shore. There would be enough confusion to cover what she needed to do. 'We'll burn it all!'

TWENTY-SIX

Goetz got to his feet just in time to meet Balk's fist. The hochmeister's blow sent him sprawling. 'You let her go!' he spat.

'She slipped past me,' Goetz said as Opchek stepped between them.

'We have more escapees to worry about than just that one, Conrad,' Opchek said. 'No reason to strike a brother.'

'I'll strike who I like!' Balk roared, gesticulating with his bloody axe. Opchek paled and stepped back. 'I'll strike anyone the goddess commands!' As if in agreement with Balk's scream, the island gave a bedrock-deep growl that caused the roof of the corridor to rain dust and rock chips.

'Half of them only fled into the depths,' another knight said. 'The Svanii will root them out. We can go after the others if we hurry...'

'Yes. Yes, we'll go after them,' Balk said, spinning and starting back up the corridor. 'We'll kill them here and now and damn what she says!'

'Wait, what does he mean,' Goetz said, grabbing Opchek's arm. 'What does he mean "here and now"? In contrast to what?'

'Hector, I–' Opchek pulled his arm free and shook his head. 'You haven't been here long enough. You haven't seen...'

'Seen what?' Goetz said. 'I've seen a man – a prisoner! – carved like a goose and innocents enslaved. I've seen destruction and things that no sane man would countenance in any knightly order, let alone ours! So tell me... what haven't I seen?'

Opchek's mouth opened and shut like a fish's. Before he could reply, Balk swung back around, his youthful features enflamed with rage. 'You haven't seen Her!' he said. 'I know you, Hector Goetz. I know you, though I've never seen you before this week! I know what you are!'

'Illuminate me, hochmeister,' Goetz said, fighting to stay calm. 'What am I?'

'A false knight!' Balk snapped. 'Maybe you're not a spy, but you're a traitor nonetheless...' He stopped, as if suddenly aware as to what he'd said. The other knights stared at their confrontation with a variety of expressions, ranging from surprise to anger.

'Conrad, let's not say something we'll regret...' Opchek began.

'Quiet,' Balk said and his voice was like the rasp of iron across stone. 'You have no faith,' he continued. 'No faith.'

'Better to have no faith, than the wrong kind,' Goetz said, without thinking.

'Hector!' Opchek said. 'Please, just be quiet.'

'Treason! Heresy!' Balk said, hefting his axe. 'And to think, I came to rescue you after – after...' he trailed off, going pale.

'After what?' Goetz said quietly. Part of him already knew the answer. He thought of Oleg's panicked apologies even as he'd tried his best to kill him. How do you know that they still follow Myrmidia? Ambrosius had said. 'After what, hochmeister?'

'I–' Balk began and stopped. For a moment, he looked as if he were going to be ill. Then he shook it off and said, 'When this is over, I want you off this island.'

'Are you rescinding your offer of hospitality?' Goetz said, carefully sheathing his sword.

'Yes!' Balk said. 'Go back to Berengar. Tell him that I know what he is. Tell him that Myrmidia is with us, and unless he bends knee and begs Her forgiveness, he and the rest of your false order will be ground under our heel.'

'Are you declaring war on your own brothers?' Goetz said, knowing full well that that was exactly what Balk meant. This wasn't rage talking, but cold intent. 'Are you declaring war on your own Order?'

'Not war,' Balk said. 'I'm declaring a death sentence. The goddess is on our side.' His features softened and he licked his lips. 'You're a good man. Everything you've seen... you have to understand... I know that she will welcome you. I know you will join us. Why else would she have spared you?'

'Yes. Why else?' Goetz said hollowly. Balk turned away, shaking his head, and the others followed him back above ground. Goetz watched them go. His fingers found the amulet nestled beneath his armour and he clutched it tight.

Chaos was here, and he was terrified to his very core. He recognised it now, even as he had in the Drakwald. It permeated everything, and he wondered why he hadn't seen it before. Maybe he had wanted to believe.

He looked down the tunnel. He could hear fighting down there, and the screams of the dying. How many of the escaped prisoners had gone the wrong way? What awaited them down there in the dark? He thought of what the old shaman had shown him and repressed a shudder.

'We go where we are needed, we do what must be done,' he said, his voice echoing in the silence of the tunnel. There was nothing he could do here. Not for those down there. But he could possibly save others, such as those who had already fled. Not to mention warning the Marienburg fleet, if such a thing were possible. If there was Chaos here, they had to know. 'We do what must be done,' he said again, though this time it was more in the nature of a curse.

He followed the others up the tunnel, the screams from below following him the entire way.

The galley exploded in a ball of fire, which swept around the base of the sea-tower. The knight in command gawped as he watched the flames lick upwards and felt the pylon shake. 'What in the name of the goddess...?' he said before ordering his men to see to the guns. It had been one of their galleys, he was certain of that. An accident with the powder magazine perhaps? Surely no one could have been that careless...

The trapdoor that led down to the jetty rattled as someone pounded on it. Assuming that it was the men he'd sent down to see to the galley, he was taken off guard when the Svanii he ordered to open it fell back, clutching a gashed belly.

'Anyone home?' Eyri said as he climbed into the tower, his hatchet in his hand. With a flick of his wrist he sent it spinning into the knight's unprotected head. The man only had a moment to process the sight of the spinning blade before it sank between his eyes and knocked him head over heels. Eyri had already drawn his second axe when the first of the Svanii on guard duty reacted, diving for a spear that was propped against the wall.

'Ha!' Eyri said, throwing the second hatchet and catching the savage high in the back. As the others moved towards him, he grabbed the hilt of the dead knight's sword and drew it with a flourish. 'Come and show me how you die, eaters of the dead!'

The Svanii came in a silent rush. There were three of them and they died in as many minutes. Eyri kicked a body away from the trapdoor and looked down at the men who'd helped him steer the galley into the tower. 'Up, dogs! We've got guns to aim!'

As the men clambered up, Eyri went to the centre of the room and grabbed hold of the massive wooden crank that occupied a fair amount of space. Pressing his shoulder to one of the dowl-grips, he waited until his men had joined him and they began to turn the crank. The effort set their muscles to wobbling like jelly and sweat streaked their faces in thick sheets. The mechanism gave a squeal as salt-corroded gears bit and the turret began to turn to face the interior of the harbour.

It was a good ploy, as such schemes went. Eyri had seen it in action in his youth... the clockwork towers could rotate and fire their deadly payload at ships that had breached the outer defences and thought themselves safe within the field of fire. He could still remember what it had been like as those cannons they'd thought facing the other direction had belched and torn through their dragonships and sent men hurtling into the freezing waters. Eyri had only survived that day because one of his father's warriors had thought to hook him aboard the lone surviving ship as it fled back to Norsca.

'Now it's my turn, you brass-skinned bastards,' he growled, straining the final few inches to get the turret in place. He stood and looked at the cannons. Hauling a body out of the way, he checked the gun and saw that it was ready to be loaded. Swiftly he began to explain to his men how it worked. 'Right, powder, ball, pack and light you curs. Let's get this right or I'll use your hides for sails.'

Even as he said it, the cannons in the opposite tower began to fire. A galley in the harbour was ripped asunder as one of the great balls sheared through its mast and crashed across its keel. Eyri howled like a wolf. 'Looks like old Halfhand wasn't just boasting, eh, lads? Hurry up! We can't let the old blood-drinker have all the fun!'

Dalla nearly dropped the torch as the galley anchored nearby seemed to explode. She shook splinters out of her hair and turned back to the task at hand. Her men moved through the town, setting fires and causing chaos amongst the inhabitants. Alarm bells rang throughout the town, but none of that concerned her.

Swiftly she tossed her torch through an open window and grabbed the thatch drooping over the roof opposite and hauled herself up. Climbing up to the apex of the roof, she looked out to sea and nearly let loose with a cheer as she saw the unmistakable shapes of Norscan ships sailing into the harbour, serenaded on their journey by cannon fire.

'Something interesting, maiden?' Greki said as he pulled himself up after her. Blood oozed from the cuts the crow had left on his face.

'My father comes with the might of Norsca,' she said in satisfaction. 'Now we'll show these creatures who rules here!'

'Will we?' Greki said, his voice sounding odd. 'Will we indeed?'

Dalla turned, her hackles rising. The oozing cuts on the warrior's face spread as she watched, the edges spreading and the unwounded flesh splitting like paper. Greki's eyes bulged in their sockets and turned in opposite directions as if something were forcing its way out of him. His tongue waggled from between slack lips and his skin turned blue in the light of the fire. His mouth suddenly champed spasmodically and his gnashing teeth severed his tongue. It flopped down onto the roof between them and wriggled like a worm.

'Greki?' she said.

His hand shot out, fingers moving independently of one another like the limbs of a squashed spider. They snagged in the amulets around her neck and ripped them free in one frenzied jerk. Greki's bulging eyes rotated until they were both looking at her. 'I seeee you,' he said in a woman's purring tones.

Dalla moved panther-swift, her sword slashing out to bisect him. His body staggered back, cut nearly in half. Blood spurted, stopped and became something else. Something that tried its best to snag her in its crimson, pulsing coils. Hissing in disgust she cut them free and kicked the shuffling body off the roof. Or tried to at any rate.

One of Greki's hands flailed and caught the edge of the roof. With a hor-rible ripping noise, the corpse swung itself back up and scuttled towards her on all fours. 'I see you Asgrimdalr's daughter,' it hissed. 'I see you now, and I will have you!'

'Not today, witch-thing!' Dalla said, avoiding the awkward lunge. Her sword looped out, cutting off an arm, and then a leg. The body rolled down the incline of the roof and scrabbled at the thatch in an effort to stay up. Brutally, she chopped down on the clutching fingers. The body rolled down into the street with a distinct thump.

Not waiting around to see whether that was the end of it, she leapt to the next roof. Atop the komturie, the cannons began to fire at the ships entering the harbour.

A sudden weight struck her between the shoulder blades and sent her rolling down the roof. Desperately she clutched at the thatch and dug her fingers in. The crow flapped down, landing above her. It cocked its head and croaked in what might have been amusement. Dalla snarled as more crows joined the first. First two, then three. Four. Five. All watching her with that same expression of amused contempt. As one they croaked, and Dalla felt her grip give way.

TWENTY-SEVEN

'To the sea-walls! To the walls!' Balk roared, his voice cracking as he spun his axe over his head. 'Man the wharf defences!'

'How did they even get past the harbour defences?' Taudge snarled as they ran towards the docks.

'That mist, I'll wager,' Opchek said. 'It's devil-summoned or I'm a Reiklander. No offence,' he continued, glancing at Taudge. 'The Norscans weave spells the way a maiden weaves hair!'

'Wizards would be helpful, you should note that along with the crossbows,' Goetz said as he joined them. He looked at the harbour, wondering if he could manage to get one of the boats moving by himself. Realising that it was likely futile he turned to find Taudge glaring at him.

'Why are you still here?' he said.

'I'm a knight of the Order, regardless of how you or any other might feel about me,' Goetz said blithely. And I need to get off this rock, he thought, matching Taudge glare for glare. Opchek slapped him on the back.

'I knew you'd come around!' he said. 'Glad to have you here! Isn't that right Conrad?'

Balk looked at Goetz warily, but then nodded briskly. 'We must hold them here... we need to give the komturie time to prepare, and to get the Svanii civilians to safety. Are you with us?'

'Yes,' Goetz said.

'And just in time too,' Opchek said. 'Look!'

A burning longship, shredded by cannon-fire, had beached itself near the wharf and men were wading ashore. One of them, a brutal-looking man, larger than the others, raised a blood-red banner and planted it in the shore with a single thrust. He gestured towards them with an evil-looking gauntlet and his men started forward with a throaty cry, echoed by the mutated hounds that kept pace with them.

'Oh pox, that's the Halfhand!' one of the knights said. 'What's he doing this far south?'

'Does it matter? He's here, he dies,' Taudge spat. He raised his sword.

'For Myrmidia! For Svunum!' He charged a moment later, followed by several others. Goetz looked at Balk, whose face had gone the colour of slate.

'Balk?' he said.

'For Myrmidia,' Balk rasped, raising his axe. 'Blood for the goddess!'

The two groups slammed together and confusion ensued. The noise of the battle was drowned out by the roar of the cannons and the screams of dying men. Goetz traded blows with screaming berserks, their faces scarred up with the eight-pointed mark of the Blood God.

The warrior that had been called Halfhand roared a challenge out to the knights and followed it up by punching his gauntleted hand through one knight's shield. Ripping the shield away, he crushed the unfortunate man's head with his eight-headed flail. Halfhand bellowed laughter as he pushed past the body and lashed out at Taudge, battering him from his feet. Goetz tried to reach him, but the press was too fierce. There were more than thirty warriors following the Halfhand, and only half that number of knights.

Balk, however, managed to hack a path to the chieftain in short order and he met the flail with his axe, shearing through the chains that bound the weighted balls to the bone handle. Halfhand cried out as if he had lost a limb and his armoured fist cracked down on Balk's shoulder, crumpling the ornate armour.

Balk, displaying a strength that Goetz hadn't suspected, shrugged off the blow and chopped off the offending limb. He kicked the hand into the bloody surf and swept his axe around in a figure of eight and drove it up under the warrior's cuirass. Pressing close, Balk snarled in the dying man's face and jerked the axe to the side, gutting him in a gory display. Even then, Halfhand refused to surrender, his remaining hand clawing weakly for Balk's face.

The hochmeister pushed him down and drove his spurred heel into the dying man's throat. Then he raised his axe and roared wordlessly at the Norscans, who began to fall back in disarray. Opchek snagged their banner and tossed it down contemptuously. 'Go back to your pickled fish and ugly women,' he jeered. 'This land is ours!'

'Not unless we can repeat this little victory a hundred or so more times,' Goetz said, pointing. Dozens of vessels were beaching themselves. The guns at the sea-towers were still firing and the Order's fleet had mostly been reduced to kindling. 'We have to fall back,' he said, turning to the others. 'Fall back, regroup. If we can just hold them off until tomorrow–' He stopped himself, hesitating.

'What? What's tomorrow?' Balk said, peering at him vaguely. He appeared to be enraptured by the sight of blood sliding through the sigils carved on the blade of his axe.

'We need to fall back,' Goetz said. 'We need to–'

The distant cannons roared and the wharf disintegrated beneath their feet. Goetz felt as if he had been picked up by a giant's hand and thrown back. He flew through the cloud of debris and hit the rocky surface of the island skidding into the burning streets. Every muscle screamed in agony as he landed and he found himself unable to move, pinned by burning wreckage. As smoke filled his lungs and burned his sinuses, everything went black.

'Get ashore you wolves!' Eyri roared. 'Slaughter and fire await! Blood for the Bloody-handed!' He vaulted over the side of the longship and landed in the chill surf. He waded towards shore, holding his shield and his axe up over his head.

A Svanii met him in the surf, stabbing a spear at him with a wild shriek. Eyri swatted the point aside and drove the edge of his shield into the warrior's skull, just above his eyes. The man flopped back, blood leaking from his eyes and nose. Eyri stepped over him, a hundred blood-mad sarls at his heels.

They raged up onto the shore, howling war cries and banging their weapons on their shields, trying to attract the attention of the gods. A foolish notion, in Eyri's opinion, but who was he to gainsay them? So long as they were in the eyes of the gods, he wasn't; that was enough for him.

The town was already aflame when he reached the outskirts, and he smiled, sensing the she-wolf's hand. She did like a good fire, did Dalla. He cut down another savage and waded into the fray. They would burn, loot and pillage as the old man had said they must. To force the einsark's hand in whatever game was being played.

It was a game, Eyri knew that much. A game of gods and daemons, playing dice with the souls of miklgardrs like him. Eyri grinned and chopped his axe into a howling warrior, splitting his skull. He had always been good at games. Pulling his axe free, he moved on.

There was little of value in the squalid dwellings of the islanders, but Eyri had his eyes on the fortifications that the knights had built. There were treasures there, to be sure. Treasures only a smart man could appreciate. He led his men towards the burning fortifications at a trot. He had seen the cannonballs split the defences there like a child shattering a toy.

They had left men in both towers, and as long as there was shot, they'd keep firing, even if their aim was altogether poor. Hopefully, having shattered the wharf, they'd raise the barrels as he'd showed them and start firing at the town.

Picking his way through the burning wreckage he caught sight of Half-hand's body lying half-in, half-out of the surf. The chieftain stared up at the sky blankly and Eyri saluted him. 'May the Blood God accept your skull with honour,' he murmured.

'More than will be said of you,' someone croaked. Debris shifted and a blackened, battered figure lurched upright, an axe dangling from his hand. Eyri grinned.

'Balk. Oh, I was hoping to find you out here, in the thick of things.'

'Were you? How fortuitous,' Balk said, moving unsteadily towards the group. His face was burned and covered in blood and ash. Only his eyes were untouched, and they blazed out at the world with a terrible strength. 'This has been a long time coming, Eyri.'

'You keep saying that,' Eyri said. 'And yet I'm still here.' He circled Balk warily. Even wounded, a man like Balk was dangerous.

'We'll soon fix that.' Balk moved sinuously, his axe looping out and catching Eyri's shield. He yanked it from Eyri's arm, nearly dislocating his shoulder in the process. Eyri stumbled back, surprised. Balk made for him, only stopping as Eyri's men closed in. The first warrior gave a bull-bellow as he charged Balk with a mace gripped in both hands. Balk ducked and spun, and the mace, as well as the hands that held it, flew aside. The axe changed directions and sheared off the screaming man's jaw.

'Quiet,' Balk said. 'I have things to discuss with your chieftain.' He glared at the warriors and they backed off, much to Eyri's astonishment. Balk seemed to swell as the men retreated, and Eyri had a hard time keeping him in focus. It was as if there were two bodies there, and only one of them was Conrad Balk. The other was something else entirely.

'I'll discuss them at leisure, over your body!' Eyri snarled and, mustering his courage, he slammed his hatchet down on Balk's arm. The hochmeister ripped his arm aside, taking Eyri's axe with it, and drove his own axe one-handed into Eyri's chest. The gromril stopped the bite of the blade, but not the force behind it. Eyri fell, the breath punched out of him. Something grated in his chest as he tried to crawl away. Balk was stronger than he remembered... far stronger.

The axe hissed and Eyri screamed as one of his legs spun free. Balk followed him and put a boot between his shoulder blades. 'I told you that the day would come when you would die, Eyri. You should have listened.'

Eyri coughed and tried to snatch the knife from his belt. His hand came off next and was sent sliding to join Halfhand's somewhere in the tide. He didn't even have the strength to scream as Balk rolled him over and raised the axe.

As it fell, Eyri realised that he had lost a game at last.

Dalla ran as buildings disintegrated around her. The crows followed, swooping through the smoke and flying timber with supernatural ease. It was all Dalla could do to avoid them and her limbs ached with the strain of it. She had been running for what felt like hours, and she knew that they were herding her somewhere.

But if she could give them the slip... if she could find her father...

She leapt over a contorted body and slid through a sagging door frame. The first crow followed her into the shack, croaking eagerly. She turned on her heel and chopped through the bird's neck. It flopped into the dirt and its body made strange movements, as if it were full of insects. She continued on, but was forced to stop as a blizzard of feathers engulfed her. The feathers were soft but razor-sharp and as they tore at her, the sound they made seemed to be a voice.

It laughed mockingly and she felt strong fingers caress her jaw. Then she was flying backwards. She crashed into a mound of debris and rolled awkwardly to her feet, groping for her sword. Instead of the crude Svanii blade, however, her fingers found the snarling lion-head pommel of a familiar sword. With a victorious cry, she whipped it free and swung it about her head, scattering the feathers.

Breathing softly, she looked about her. The shack was a crippled wreck, torn apart by fire and shot. The birds seemed to have abandoned the chase, though she wondered how long that would last. She looked down at the sword, then around. A burned and scarred gauntlet extruded from the debris, the fingers dangling limply. With a grunt she sank to her haunches and began to clear away the rubble, knowing what she'd find and praying that it wasn't too late.

━◄ TWENTY-EIGHT ►━

In the bright darkness of the Drakwald, things moved beneath Goetz's skin. The buboes on his side rose black and slick against his sweating flesh as a chorus of crows croaked and laughed in the trees above. Goetz groaned as he clawed at his rotting flesh. He tried to dig out the poison with his numb fingers, but the rubbery flesh resisted his efforts. A white shape faded into view and inhumanly precise fingers gripped his chin, pulling his sweating face up to meet hers.

'Myrmidia?' he rasped, tasting blood. The eyes of the goddess did not meet his as her spear-point caressed the wound on his side. He groaned as pain flared through him and he fell to his hands and knees, black bile bursting through his lips to pool in the dirt. The spear jabbed him again.

'Wake up.'

A familiar length of metal pricked Goetz's throat, snapping him into full wakefulness. He swallowed, looked up and said, 'You need to stop taking things that don't belong to you.'

'I like it,' Dalla said, resting back on her heels as she raised his sword and laid the flat of the blade across her shoulder. 'It is a good sword.'

'I would have thought that you would have been gone by now,' he said as she climbed off him. He sat up and grunted in shock as a wave of agony passed over him. His clothes were sticky and red when he whipped them aside. Though his scars remained as whole as ever, blood stained his side and the ground around him. 'It was just a dream,' he said blankly.

'It looks like blood to me,' Dalla said. 'Get up.'

'Why?'

'You ask too many questions. Get up.'

'Asking questions is the only path to wisdom,' Goetz said. 'Why are you still here?'

'To repay my debt,' she said, as if it were obvious.

'Lot of that going around,' Goetz said, pushing himself to his feet.

'What?' Dalla looked confused.

Goetz shook his head. 'Nothing. I–' He paused. A dim scratching sound reached his ears. A persistent, familiar noise. 'What was that?'

'What was what?'

'That,' Goetz said, as the scratching sound came again.

'Don't move!' Dalla said, grabbing for him. Goetz turned to tell her that he had no intention of doing so when, with a shattering crash, the roof of the ruined shack exploded downwards, showering them both with debris. Something horrible flopped into the room. Goetz recognised it as Myrma's crow... or rather, something that had once been a crow.

The bird croaked as pink flesh bulged hideously beneath black feathers. The croak became a chuckle, then a giggle and the crow hopped forward, shedding feathers and expanding in size with every step. Soon enough, the pink thing stepped out of the bird skin, kicking it aside the way a strumpet might launch a shoe. Massive hands opened and closed in apparent eagerness as it chuckled. It had arms like ropes and its face squatted inside the barrel chest, its tongue lolling between its bandy legs. Beaks opened and closed on its shoulders and its iridescent skin seemed to shift and squirm on whatever passed for its bones.

Goetz felt ill just looking at the horror as it ambled forwards, apparently unconcerned about the sword Dalla held. It giggled and shifted from one foot to the other, sidling around them. 'What does it want?' Goetz said, already knowing the answer.

'Me,' Dalla said, fear reducing her voice to a hoarse whisper. Then, as if to give lie to her assertion, the pink thing lunged, but not for the swordswoman. In a flash of pink, the spade-sized paws crashed down towards Goetz!

Goetz threw himself aside. The ache in his side screamed into full-blown agony and he hit the floor hard, curling into a ball. The creature wheeled around, its chuckles striking his ears like hammer blows.

With a loud cry Dalla chopped her sword down through one of the gangly arms, only to be left staring in shock as the wound knitted itself back together in an instant. The creature turned in a leisurely fashion and swept out a backhand that would certainly have killed her had it connected. Instead, she bent backwards and fell onto her rear.

She crab-crawled backwards, as it ambled after her. Goetz hauled himself to his feet, looking for anything that he might use as a weapon. Desperate, he flipped a chunk of the roof over and wrenched a charred chunk from one of the fallen support beams free in a burst of strength. Then, whirling it over his head, he brought it down solidly on the creature's back. It jerked forward in surprise and twisted, beaks snapping. Goetz stamped forwards, striking out at it again and again, wielding the improvised club like a sword. Splinters and ash flew as he battered the creature.

It flailed at him and he gave ground grudgingly, fending off its blows as best he was able. After another near miss he began to come to the sickening conclusion that the creature was playing with him. It chuckled and grabbed his club, striking him at the same time. He flew backwards. The thing – the daemon, he knew – advanced, its hands clenching and unclenching eagerly.

Pushing himself to his feet, his hands brushed across something hard. He glanced down and saw the amulet of Myrmidia that Abbot Knock had given him. Snatching it up, he stabbed it into one of the daemon's bulbous eyes. It reeled back with a despairing shriek that sent waves of pain radiating through his nerve endings. It clawed at the amulet which sank deeper and deeper into its skull with a bubbling hiss. Its beaks clacked in agony and it hunched over, ignoring the two humans.

'Throw me the sword!' Goetz barked. Dalla hesitated, but then did as he asked. He caught the blade and whipped it around, driving it through the creature's malformed pink body and into the stone floor below. The shriek became a piercing wail that threatened to puncture their eardrums.

Goetz shut his eyes against the pressure building in his skull, and when it abruptly faded, he was relieved to find that the daemon had vanished, leaving only a sticky residue to mark its passing. He knelt, leaning on the sword for support, and fished the amulet out of the mess. He held it up and thought of what the old shaman had said. 'I wanted a sign,' he murmured. 'I suppose I got one.'

'What are you blathering about?' Dalla said, glaring warily at the patch on the floor.

'Faith renewed,' Goetz said, hanging the amulet from his neck.

'We need to get out of here,' she said, shuffling impatiently. 'The daemon's master will know soon enough that it has been sent back.'

'I'm well aware of that. I–'

The door slammed open and sagged from its blistered hinges. Goetz made to draw his sword, but the figures that faced him convinced him otherwise. 'Hochmeister,' he said.

Balk, flanked by Opchek and Taudge, stepped into the room, his axe in hand. All three men looked as badly used as Goetz felt. 'Brother,' Balk said. 'I see you've caught our runaway. Stand aside.'

'No,' Goetz said, stepping between the trio and Dalla. The latter hissed and tensed. She was ready to spring despite the odds against her. 'No, I think not,' Goetz went on. 'I think, in fact, that we'll be leaving.'

'I told you,' Taudge snapped. 'He's besotted with the wench!'

'Well, she is quite comely,' Opchek said. He frowned. 'Hector, we won't hurt her. Just step aside.'

'I'm sorry my friend, but no,' Goetz said, slowly drawing his blade.

'She has bewitched you,' Balk said. 'Step aside.'

Goetz said nothing. He had a sense of a string being pulled taut and getting ready to snap. When it did, it was Taudge who moved first. Goetz wasn't surprised. He let Taudge's blow glide off his sword and rolled with it, driving his shoulder into the other man's chest. He shoved Taudge back into the others and then jerked his head at Dalla. 'Come on!'

She leapt over the tangle of knights nimbly and she and Goetz fled out into the street. There were men waiting for them – Svanii, armed with spears. Balk had come prepared. Goetz grabbed Dalla and spun her aside even as he threw himself at the feet of the spearmen, sending the group tumbling. Dalla snatched up a fallen spear and pierced the belly of the first man unlucky enough to get back on his feet, shoving him up and back against the far wall. The Svanii shrieked as Dalla left him where he was and made to grab another spear.

The staff came out of nowhere and struck her across the face. The swordmaiden fell and lay still. Goetz got to his feet and Myrma turned to face him, her beautiful features twisted into a furious grimace. She spat strange syllables that crawled down his spine like spiders and a coruscating talon of black-hued lightning clawed for him. Goetz threw himself aside.

'Take him,' the priestess spat. Goetz turned, but not quickly enough. The haft of Balk's axe connected with the bridge of his nose and he was knocked back into darkness.

'What about her?' Taudge said, nudging Dalla's limp form with the toe of his boot. 'Do we take her as well?'

'Why would we do that?' Balk said, directing the Svanii to pick up Goetz. 'Let her lay here and rot with the rest of the Norscan filth.'

'Speaking of Norscan filth...' Opchek gestured towards the komturie, which was seemingly aflame. The sounds of fierce fighting could be heard. 'Even with the defences we built into the inner keep, I'm not sure our brothers can hold out for very long. Not with so many of them engaged in rounding up the escapees.'

'It doesn't matter,' Myrma said, her eyes closed, her face the picture of exhaustion. 'It is too late for them to stop it. The more blood that soaks into these stones, the better.'

'Those are our brothers you are talking about!' Opchek barked. He grabbed Myrma's arm as if to whirl her around, but a blow from Balk sent him reeling. Opchek stared up at his hochmeister in disbelief. 'Conrad?'

'Sacrilege, brother,' Balk said mildly, letting the blade of his axe scrape the stone. With the fire engulfing the village and the harbour behind him, he looked positively daemonic. 'Our brothers gladly give their lives in return for the Order of the Blazing Sun's triumph. Even as you yourself swore you would. As we all would.'

'I so swore,' Opchek began. In his head, he heard the whirring of wings.

'Is your faith wavering brother? Are you losing heart?' Balk helped Opchek to his feet. 'This close to our sacred goal?' The hochmeister's voice was low and intent and it bit into Opchek's doubts like a sword blade. Opchek frowned. 'I am happy to kill the Order's enemies. But this was one of our own!' he snarled, gesturing to Goetz. 'Just like the other one.'

'I told you... the goddess commanded me!'

'Bollocks!' Opchek spat. It was Balk's turn to flush.

'I am hochmeister! I know what needs to be done!'

'Since when has assassination ever been our remit?' Opchek said.

'Since our Order turned from the path Myrmidia laid out for us!' Balk said. He grabbed Opchek's arms. 'I know you don't want to believe that brother, but it is the truth!'

Opchek shook him off. 'How do you know? Greisen never–'

'Greisen is dead. And all who followed him are dead,' Balk said harshly. He glared at the other knights, as if daring them to disagree. 'Led into a trap and butchered because they thought that they could deal in a civilised manner with the Norscans. And Berengar, damn his hide, encouraged him in that path!' Balk made a fist and shook it. 'Talk, talk , TALK! That is what Berengar wants! He wants the Order of the Blazing Sun to be the thrice-cursed Reiksguard–' Balk spat the name of the Emperor's bodyguards, 'Politicking and kowtowing to every petty lordling and bureaucrat! Myrmidia is the patroness of civilisation, yes, but also of war! And Berengar has no stomach for war. Even Greisen knew that!'

'Maybe not, but he is the Grand Master,' Opchek said. 'And now...' He trailed off, looking ill. 'We didn't have to do it. We don't have to do it!'

'But you do,' Myrma said.

'And you know this how?' Opchek said, after a moment of hesitation.

She looked at him. 'I know only what the goddess tells me. If you would but listen, she would tell you the same.' Before he could reply, she held up her arms and spread them like wings. The island gave a groan as the ground shifted and growled. Water splashed over the burning docks and the splintered decks of the wrecked ships and the komturie shuddered in the distance.

'Do you hear Her, knight? Do you dare listen?' Myrma said, raising her staff with a flourish. Opchek staggered as a piercing light blazed into being around the priestess. In its depths, the Kislevite saw a shape grow from a pinpoint to a rushing shadow. He heard the snap of wings and the face of a goddess looked down on him sadly. He fell to his knees as she reached out with her great spear – or was it a talon? – and touched the tip to his brow. She spoke in a voice at once soft and thunderous and he clapped his hands to his ears.

Balk grabbed his wrists, forcing his hands away from his head. 'Listen!' the hochmeister said, his eyes blazing with adoration. 'Listen to her!'

Opchek did, as did the others. As one, they sank to their knees, heads bowed.

'It is the Witching Night,' Myrma said in satisfaction. 'The moons have risen and our time draws close. We must begin the ritual!'

Opchek looked at the komturie, and then at the others. 'But–'

'It is your decision, brother,' Balk said softly. He put his hand on the brawny Kislevite's shoulders and pulled him to his feet. 'Come with us, and see what wonders the future holds, or join our brothers in defending our shores. Either way, you serve the Order.'

'I–' Opchek nodded jerkily. 'I'll go with you.'

'Good!' Balk smiled. The smile faded as he took in the destruction wrought on the island. 'We shall pay them back for this threefold, brothers! Myrmidia will see to it!'

'Can't come soon enough,' Taudge grunted.

As a group, they left the burning shore and descended into the sea-caves. Balk paid little heed to the bodies, though Opchek looked ill and even Taudge made a face as he caught sight of armoured corpses. More knights joined them as they moved down. Kropch, a hardy veteran of the Marien-burg Komturie, saluted Balk.

'We've rounded up most of the escapees. But we heard cannon-fire. Should we–?'

'No. The komturie was built for this purpose,' Balk said, making a cutting gesture. 'We can best serve our brothers by seeing to matters here.'

'But the Norscans have invaded,' Kropch said. 'We must toss them back!'

'We will,' Myrma snarled impatiently. She thrust her way into the group and glared at the gathered knights. Her skin sagged alarmingly on her bones and her face was pinched with weariness. 'But the night slips away from us! Myrmidia requires your strength! Will you shirk Her?'

'We go where we are needed, brothers,' Balk said.

'We do what must be done,' Kropch and the others echoed. Myrma watched them and nodded in satisfaction. There were eighteen knights gathered here. Two nines, the holy number of the Great Weaver. There was twice that number of seed-pods growing in the deep caverns, enough to match the entirety of the komturie. But for the purposes of the ritual, it would be perfect.

She glanced at the unconscious body of Goetz and a smile spread across her face. She clutched her staff as a wave of weakness spread over her. 'Too late Asgrimdalr. It is too late for you... for all of you.'

The end of the staff caught Dalla a blow on the head. 'Up, daughter. There is red work to be done.' Groggily, Dalla looked up. Ulfar looked down at her. 'Up,' he said again.

'What–?' she groaned. Every muscle felt like it was on fire.

'You live, child. I should have thought that would be obvious. Others were not so lucky.' Ulfar turned. Thalfi Utergard, squatting near the water at the edge of the wrecked dock, held up something pale and bloodless.

'I found Goldfinger's hand,' he rumbled.

'I'm pretty sure this was the rest of him,' Kettil Flatnose said, standing over a sodden heap. 'Poor cunning fool.' He looked at Ulfar. 'Halfhand is dead as well, old man. Along with Lok and Hrothgar, that's four godi, dead on this mad venture of yours.'

'Not mine,' Ulfar said, looking down at Eyri's body. Dalla, on her feet, joined him. Still queasy she looked down at the pitiful remains of Eyri Goldfinger and felt a moment of regret. It was washed away a moment later as she realised that someone was missing. 'Goetz!'

'Who?' Ulfar said, looking at her.

'The einsark! They've taken him!'

'You're concerned about one of them?' Kettil said incredulously.

'No! But why would they take him?' she said, hesitating.

Ulfar shook his head. 'He is cursed. A poison lurks in him and they will exploit it.' His knuckles turned white as he leaned against his staff. 'I did not foresee this... I had hoped... pah. We must get to those caves.'

'My men and I are ready!' Thalfi bellowed. 'And Halfhand's gauntlet with me!' He held up the grisly trophy and emptied it of its contents before sliding it onto his own hand with a squelch. The gauntlet hissed like a kettle and Thalfi grunted and flexed the brass fingers. 'Yesss.'

'Fool,' Kettil muttered. He looked at Ulfar. 'That thing is cursed.'

'What of it? This island is cursed.'

'All the more reason to leave... my boats are loaded with booty. Their fortress burns, the Svanii are without shelter... we have done this thing and done it well!' Kettil said.

'And what then?' Ulfar spun, his eyes blazing. Even Dalla stepped back, so surprising it was to see the old man actually angry. 'I have done this before, Flatnose! I have burned them to the water's edge and back and like mushrooms in night-soil they grew back and took from me what was mine!' His withered hand clenched like a claw. 'They always come back, fool. That is their nature... but not this time. This time, I will purge this place though it take the life of every sarl and every baersonling, every thane and jarl, every son of Norsca to do it!' Ulfar roared, his staff raised over his head. Both chieftains were reminded of the old man's transformation into a bear and they fell back a step.

'Father,' Dalla said.

Ulfar calmed and took her hand. 'Daughter.' He looked at the chieftains. 'Gather your men. Let the others storm the citadel. We will deliver a dagger-stroke to the beast's heart!'

'Something's on fire,' Grand Master Ogg said, lowering his spyglass. He tapped it on the rail and looked at Ambrosius. The one-eyed man rubbed the heel of his hand against his eye-patch and grinned.

'I suppose it's too much to hope that they're throwing us a welcoming feast, eh?'

'I'd say not, sir,' Dubnitz said, standing nearby. The big knight looked at his Grand Master. 'Do you think they're preparing for us, sir?'

Ogg said nothing. He swatted the rail with his trident, and looked at the fleet. It was not a large one, as far as fleets went, but it was battle-hardened and armed to the teeth. Weapons straight from the Gunnery School at Nuln lined the decks and men in green armour paced beneath sails bearing Manann's likeness.

He turned. 'No. Something is going on. Those aren't fires of welcome or siege preparation.' He met Ambrosius's eye. The Lord Justicar nodded.

'Norscans,' he said flatly. When they'd heard that the Nicos had been taken, they'd feared the worst. Ships being taken weren't an uncommon occurrence by any means, but it was all too perfect. They both assumed that Hector Goetz had met the same fate as Sir Athalhold; victim of some conspiracy none of them could see clearly. 'We may have to fight a two-pronged war, Grand Master.'

'No island is worth that,' Ogg said, frowning.

'Yet we're still heading that way, I notice,' Ambrosius said. 'Would you like to weigh anchor then? Turn the fleet around?'

'No,' Ogg said, unfolding his spyglass again. 'The wisdom of Manann says that when you see a storm, the best thing to do is sail into it and try and find the eye.' He frowned. 'Let's go find the eye of that firestorm, eh?'

TWENTY-NINE

He was back in the Drakwald. The familiarity and frequency of the dream was becoming tedious and in frustration Goetz raised his fists to the ceiling of cruel branches and said, 'What do you want of me?'

'She will not answer,' a hoarse voice intoned. 'We have seen to that.'

Goetz lowered his hands. 'Who are you?'

'A friend.' A shape shuffled out of the close-set trees, leaning heavily on a staff decorated with black feathers. The hood was thrown back, revealing a maggot-pale face that was unpleasantly familiar.

'Myrma,' Goetz said, disgust curling at the edges of his words. If she heard the tone, she gave no sign. She bared rotten teeth in what Goetz supposed was a welcoming smile and nodded. 'I knew there was something wrong with you. Even before the old man told me.'

'Aye.' Her accent was a savage thing, with a rolling brutal lilt that Goetz had trouble understanding. 'And he should know, being who he is.'

'And who is he?' Goetz said, taking a step back.

'The man who killed me, of course,' Myrma said. She threw off her cloak, revealing a body that was withered and rotting. Black blood streamed down from a cavernous sore in her side. Goetz's own wound tingled in sympathy, and he fought the urge to touch it. She, however, seemed to know what he was thinking.

'Aye. The same we are, sure as sure.' she chuckled wetly. 'Poisoned.'

'That's–' Goetz blinked. Myrma's form seemed to blur, to become slimmer. Goetz felt a rising tide of disgust threaten to overwhelm him. 'How many shapes do you have, witch?'

Myrma laughed and shook her staff. The bones hanging from the tip clattered and the sound was echoed from the trees by the croaking of crows. Goetz twisted in a circle, looking up. Every branch was bent with dark, avian shapes. Hundreds of them. Thousands, even. All of them watching him. He shuddered, his spirit going cold. He put a hand on his side, and his fingers touched wetness.

'Many,' Myrma said. 'Just skins, provided for me by my Mistress, in Her benevolence and wisdom. Daughters of daughters' blood, all of them.'

'All of them...' Goetz said. Between the trees, pale, limp shapes moved forward into the light of the witch-fire and the bile in his mouth dried up. Ragged, torn skins stumbling forward on empty feet, their eyes dark blotches on tattooed skin. There were dozens of them, their sagging features all bearing an eerie resemblance to those of Myrma. They drifted towards her and flopped down at her feet in supplication. The rotten teeth clicked together in an exultant grin as her beast-yellow eyes fastened on Goetz.

'Skin of my skin, blood of my blood. My Lady has given me mighty weirdings so that I might aid Her in Her own,' she said. 'And now... now I will give Her you.'

'Me?' Goetz said.

Myrma's lupine smile threatened to split her desiccated face. She tapped his weeping side and flung droplets of oily blood in Goetz's direction. 'You were touched, even as I was, by the stuff of the gods. It has strengthened you. Made you more durable than any other on this island.'

Involuntarily, Goetz's eyes were drawn down to his side. Blood stained his tunic. Frantically, he ripped the cloth aside and saw the black streaks growing across his skin. Pain shot through him as, above, the crows gave voice to what might have been mocking laughter.

'And in the touching, they gained hold of you,' Myrma said, making a fist with her bloody fingers. 'A raw, red door in the meat of you. Just waiting for the right key.' Her gaze dimmed. 'My skins go quickly these past years. They are not fit for my weirdings, let alone the mighty soul that inhabits this place. But you...' she smacked her lips. 'Hollowed out, you will be a fine suit of strong iron for Her spirit!'

'No!' Goetz said, staggering. The black streaks grew thicker as they spread across him in a pattern eerily reminiscent of the aura of the sun on his medallion. His wound was a black sun, spreading the cold of oblivion through him. Above, the crows took flight, rising above the trees and spinning into a maelstrom of black feathers. At the eye of the maelstrom, something looked down at Goetz, and his soul shrivelled in horror. 'No,' he said again.

'Yes!' Myrma cackled, spreading her arms and looking up in rapture at the presence above. 'With you as my armour, I shall at last break the stone chains that bind Herself! I shall rouse Her from Her mighty dreams! IA! S'vanashi! IA! Tzeentch!'

As the hideous syllables smashed through him, Goetz's eyes sprang open and he lurched forward. Strong arms gripped him and hauled him back. 'Too late for that now, brother,' Opchek said sadly. 'Too late for any of it, I'm afraid.'

Goetz shook his head, trying to clear it. He was in a cavern. He could smell the tang of salt water and a number of oddly coloured torches had been stuffed into crevices in the rock and lit. He looked at his captors; they were no longer wearing the dwarfen-wrought armour that was every knight's right. Instead they wore black suits of plate, festooned with odd sigils and features. In place of Myrmidia's sigils were those of some other god entirely, and they hurt Goetz's eyes to look upon them. The armour was the colour of tar and it gleamed with a sickly radiance in the torchlight, looking less like metal than the insides of a nut. Scattered around the cavern were great empty husks that looked like large seed-pods.

'What have you done to yourselves?' he said.

Balk stepped in front of him and used the flat of his axe to lift Goetz's chin. 'We have accepted the blessings of Myrmidia, brother. As you should have done when we gave you the chance,' he said. 'But now, now you will serve Her regardless.'

Goetz spat and tried to jerk his head away. Taudge grabbed him by the scalp and forced him to meet the hochmeister's eyes. Balk knelt and leaned on his axe. He indicated his armour with a gesture. 'She grew this armour for us, to replace that which was made by fallible human hands. It is god-forged this stuff, and it will make us Myrmidons in truth... ah, you see? I knew you were no fool,' he said, noting the look on Goetz's face. 'Myrmidon,' Balk said. He tapped his ear. 'She told me all about you, Sudenlander. They came from there you know, these folk. Svanii. The children of Myrmidia, driven into the wasteland by the machinations of the Ruinous Powers. But in you is the hope for this Order, for our goddess... I thought at one time, she might bless me in this fashion. But I see now that she has chosen you. It's fitting, in a way. Of course she would choose you. Why disrupt the chain of command when the perfect vessel just drops in your lap, after all?'

'You have no idea what you're doing,' Goetz said. 'This is wrong. All of it.'

'Yes. It is wrong. This world is wrong. It is barbaric and destructive. But we will make it orderly. Tidy, even,' Balk said, rising to his feet. 'And you will lead us, brother. You will be our figurehead. Our living standard, touched by the goddess Herself! She will remould your frail flesh into the very stuff of power.' He raised his axe and the other knights gathered in the cavern sent up a cheer that chilled Goetz to the bone.

'Take him to the altar!' Balk said. Goetz was yanked to his feet and propelled forward, towards a gross bubo of rock and dirt that rose blister-like from the stone. Around it had been heaped the discarded armour of the other knights, as well as the lithographs, icons and amulets of Myrmidia. Everything that belonged to the goddess had been tossed here, in the dirt. A web of rusty chains descended from the roof of the cavern, manacles hanging from them at odd points. The cavern walls seemed to tremble in delight as he was dragged forward.

He hadn't truly wanted to believe it. But he couldn't deny the evidence of his own eyes. Opchek and Taudge manacled his hands, the former not looking at him, the latter glaring. 'Don't do this,' Goetz said. 'This is wrong, brothers. You know it.'

'Silence,' Taudge said, backhanding him. Goetz's head rocked back and he tasted blood. He spat it out and looked up. Heaving, flat-bodied shapes clustered across the roof of the cavern, their colourful scales glinting in a hideous rainbow as they squirmed. Every so often, one would emit a screech from an unseen mouth. Goetz shuddered and cast his eyes down.

Myrma looked up at him, leaning tiredly on her staff. Her hair was threaded through with white, and her previously useful face was heavily lined and worn. Nonetheless, she smiled up at him. 'You killed my pet. Not many men could do that. You are everything She promised.'

'Who? Who promised?' Goetz snarled, pulling against his chains. Around them, the cavern trembled as if rocked by titanic laughter.

Myrma raised her arms and gestured to the cavern. 'She who protects us! She who gathered us unto Her womb and carried us away from our enemies! She who has planned for this moment from the beginning! IA! The Queen of Crows! IA! The Maiden of Colours! Come forth Lady and let him gaze upon your splendour!'

The crows took flight all at once with shrill screams. They spun around and around, faster and faster, as they had in Goetz's dream. Feathered shapes blurred into one another with a sound like snapping bones until what had been a flock was now a pulsing, floating mass. As the mass sank downwards, the island rumbled again, much louder this time. The gathered knights shifted uneasily as the Svanii worshippers threw themselves about in a crooked, flopping dance that reminded him of the movements of a wounded bird. The cavern seemed to contract as the mass of feathers and meat dropped to the ground.

Then, in the silence that followed, the mass unfolded into a horribly tall, slim shape. A hideously familiar face protruded through a mane of sticky black feathers.Slim, talon-tipped fingers reached for Goetz as the thing took a dainty step forward, looming over its followers. The marble-pale face twisted into a smile.

'My lovely boy,' Myrmidia – the thing that wore Myrmidia's face – said. Corpse-black lips peeled back from shiny obsidian teeth as she leaned forward. The sickly-sweet stink of her washed over Goetz, inundating his senses with ever-shifting odours, tastes and images. Her feathers were so black that they seemed to encompass all colours and none, and spots danced in front of his eyes as he tried to focus on them.

Bird talons caressed his face, leaving a sticky residue on the leather-bound edges of the wound on his cheek. The entity leaned close, her glittering eyes boring into his. On his chest, the amulet of Myrmidia seemed to grow warm. 'Your mind is like quicksilver,' the Queen of Crows said, in a pleasant gurgle. 'So much deception. So many thoughts.'

'What – what are you?' Goetz said, trying to twist his face away from its touch. It was a question he already knew the answer to, but something told him that he needed to keep the creature talking if he had any hope of escaping.

'I am the Queen of Crows, the Maiden of Colours, the Hand-Maiden of the Great Mutator, the She-Spider, the Whisperer in Darkness, the Love of Cats, the Sadness of Wolves, the Silence of Tigers...' It recited the names with obvious relish, letting them trip across its lips in a parody of song. 'I am the Lady of the Island, Hector Goetz. I am your goddess.'

'Not mine,' Goetz said, trying for defiance. He was afraid it only registered as petulance. The woman-thing threw back her head and laughed and as she laughed, the island shook. Her face snapped down and talons grabbed his chin. One finger rose and the leather thongs holding his cheek closed snapped and split. Blood spilled down his face and the Queen of Crows leaned forward, extending a feline tongue to lap up the blood with sinister tenderness. As its tongue made contact with him, images invaded his mind, falling across his consciousness like shards of broken glass.

...a war in heaven, as reality heaved like an angry sea...

...falling, she tried to stop her plunge, but HE had taken her wings to punish her and she fell and fell and FELL...

...the pain as she forced her blood to mix with the stuff of the sea and grow into an island...

...the Knowing that the Game was going on without her was the most exquisite torment...

Goetz jerked his head back with neck-cracking urgency. He thrashed in his chains, not fully in control of his movements. 'Daemon,' he said.

The hideously beautiful face dipped in acknowledgement, but the mouth said, 'No. Just a ghost.' Goetz shuddered again and tried to pull away. The daemon clucked pityingly and gripped the back of his head. 'Stop. Your plans are all undone, your dreams unfettered and scattered. Give in,' it said softly. 'I will ride you to heights undreamt, and in your skin, in the armour of you, I will retake my place in the Game.'

'Game?' Goetz began. He felt numb, almost pleasantly so. On his chest, the amulet was no longer warm, but hot. The numbness was flushed away by sudden, searing pain and Goetz arched in his chains. The daemon stepped back with a croak as light speared from the amulet.

'Take that off!' it snapped, flailing with one titan paw. Parts of it began to dissolve back into dirt and bird-meat and Goetz realised that this was not its real form, but merely an amalgamation created from the raw stuff of the island. The images showed him the truth... it had no flesh, no physical presence. It was just a phantom, made of decaying matter, the very stuff of its soul rotting the body it had created. 'Take it off!'

Several Svaniis scrambled forward, reaching for Goetz. Muscles straining, shoulder-blades threatening to separate, he hauled himself up and drove a kick into the face of the first to reach him. The man slipped and fell off the altar stone with a howl. Another grabbed Goetz's leg and he swung himself back, pulling the hapless Svanii with him. He shook the man off even as a shout echoed through the cavern.

A spear took the last Svanii on the altar through the chest. Goetz twisted, trying to see what was going on. The knights and their ghoulish retainers were engaged in battle with a number of shapes; with a start, he recognised them as Norscan!

Dalla darted through the press, Goetz's sword in her hand. Without looking at the daemon, she sprang onto the altar and sliced through the chains holding him aloft. He collapsed onto the stone just as Myrma scrambled towards them, jabbing her staff at Dalla like a spear.

'No! He is mine!' the sorceress squealed. Goetz swung the remnants of his bindings up and across her face. Her neck snapped with a loud crunch and she fell, her staff clattering away.

'Die and be damned,' Goetz spat, dropping the chains. He looked at Dalla. 'You took your time.'

'I was hoping they'd kill you,' she said flatly. 'I got bored.' She tossed him his sword and drew a hatchet from her belt. 'Your armour is down there.'

'Yes, but they're up here!' Goetz said, hauling her aside as one of the flat shapes from the cavern ceiling dropped from its roost and swooped towards them with a horrible shriek. Goetz's sword flashed up, shearing through the alien flesh and spattering his face and arms with corrosive droplets. A moment later it was Dalla's turn to shove him as a second Screamer dropped towards them. Her hatchet buried itself in the thing's armoured carapace and she was ripped off her feet and into the air as the thing twisted and bucked.

Goetz dropped from the altar and began shrugging into what armour he could. Crouched, he buckled on his cuirass with trembling fingers. There was a scrape of sound behind him and he managed to turn and bring his sword up just in time. Opchek's sword met his for an instant and then they broke apart.

'I'm sorry, Hector,' Opchek said, his voice echoing hollowly from within his grotesque new helm. 'Put the sword down. This can still end well...'

'No. It can't,' Goetz said, lunging forward, aiming the point of his blade for Opchek's gorget. The Kislevite backpedalled and Goetz followed, his blade licking out with startling quickness.

'You're faster than I thought!' Opchek said as Goetz's sword cut a groove in the cheek-guard of his helmet. Goetz didn't reply, merely pressing close. He beat aside Opchek's sword and scored a hit on his chest, knocking the wind out of the other knight. Opchek staggered. 'Much faster,' he wheezed.

'Stop playing with the bastard and kill him!' Taudge roared, charging into Goetz and sending him sprawling. Goetz got to his feet and faced both knights. Taudge's armour was stained with newly-spilled blood and he favoured one leg. 'I told you all this was a bad idea! Let's kill the traitor and put down this thrice-damned Norscan rabble!'

'Feel free to try,' Goetz said. He continued to back away until his foot crashed down on a battered shield. Myrmidia's face gazed serenely up at him from the embossed surface. Goetz stooped and swiftly scooped the shield up, shoving his arm through the loops even as Taudge came for him.

Goetz caught the blow on the shield and swept the other man's sword blade against the altar stone, trapping it. As Taudge gaped in shock, Goetz drove his own blade through a gap in his opponent's armour, scattering mail-links and blood over the ground behind him. Taudge fell back, sinking into a sitting position as blood spilled down his legs and pooled in his lap.

'It was supposed to make us invincible,' he said haltingly. 'She said!'

'She lied,' Goetz said, taking Taudge's head off with a backhanded swipe. Opchek stared at him in shock, but only for a moment. The Kislevite's face hardened and he charged with a roar.

Opchek beat Goetz's shield aside and aimed a chopping blow at his head. Goetz jerked back and twisted, using his momentum to send a blow of his own ringing across Opchek's helmet. The Kislevite staggered and Goetz kicked him in the side of the leg, dropping him to his knees. With brutal desperation he brought his shield down on the top of Opchek's head, driving him face-first into the rocky floor of the cavern. The Kislevite lay still. Goetz kicked his sword away just to be sure and turned, breathing heavily. Every muscle ached and his cheek was a throbbing ball of agony.

'How easily you strike your brothers.' Goetz turned. Balk sat on a nearby rock, his axe across his knees. 'How easily you shed your loyalties. I wish I could be so... fluid,' Balk said, rising to his feet.

'I'm sure Brother Athalhold will feel better knowing that you define murder as loyalty,' Goetz said.

Balk hesitated for a moment, and then continued forward. 'I did what must be done.'

'As do I,' Goetz said.

'Berengar is corrupt!' Balk said. 'He leads the Order into ruin! I will give us back our purpose! Our soul!'

'You sold your soul for a fancy suit of armour and the chance to shed blood,' Goetz snapped. He gestured at the daemon behind them. Its form continued to disintegrate as it watched the battle unfolding at its feet. 'Does that look like a goddess to you? Are you that blinded by hate that you can mistake that for this?' Goetz said, slapping the face of his shield for emphasis. Balk looked at the shield for a moment and then back up.

'I–'

'How long have you listened to it?' Goetz said. 'How long has it been filling you with – with poison?' He pointed at Balk with his sword. 'Because that's all it is... poison. It's nothing but poison. It eats you away, from the inside out until all that's left is a hollow suit of armour for it to wear.' He grabbed the amulet and thrust it at Balk. 'This! This is our goddess. She does not take, she does not conquer! She builds! She fights only to defend what exists!' Even as he said it, a strange sort of peace filled him. For the first time, in a long time, he actually believed what he was saying. 'I wanted to build bridges, Balk. What did you want to do before She called upon you? Do you even remember?'

Balk shook his head. 'I – I have always served Her.'

'Maybe once, but not any longer,' Goetz said.

'No. No, no, no. I serve Her! I am the only one who serves Her!' Balk said, shaking his head furiously. 'Myrmidia!' he snarled.

'Myrmidia!' Goetz roared in reply. Balk's axe licked out and cut a trench in the face of the shield even as Goetz's sword did the same in his opponent's buckler. They moved back and forth across the slippery rock, trading savage blows. After the axe slipped past his defences and cut a gash in his cuirass, Goetz began to realise belatedly that the hochmeister was stronger, and fresh. Also that his armour, unlike Taudge's, didn't appear to have any weaknesses.

Desperately Goetz parried the axe as it darted for his face and tried to regain momentum. But Balk was too fast and too experienced. He slammed forward, using his shield like a second blade, jabbing the edge into Goetz's thigh and belly. Breathing heavily, Goetz stumbled back. Balk paced after him with wolf-sure steps. 'The goddess guides my axe,' Balk said. 'Though I wish it was anyone else, brother. You had the potential to be the best of us. Truly blessed of the goddess.' He made a lazy swipe and, tired as he was, it was enough to knock Goetz's feet out from under him and send him crashing to the ground. 'Now you will be just one more nail in the pillar.' Balk stepped on Goetz's wrist, pinning his sword-arm. He raised his axe. 'Forgive me brother.'

'No!' Balk spun as Opchek crashed into him. The two knights reeled for a moment, until Balk shoved the other man away. 'I can't let you do this, Conrad. Not again...' the Kislevite said, his voice slurred and his eyes unfocused.

'Opchek, I grow tired of your obstinacy. Get out of my way!' Balk said.

'No!' Opchek glanced over his shoulder at Goetz. 'Get up, brother. Get out of here. I'll–'

'Die,' Balk said sadly. He whipped his axe out with fierce inevitability, chopping into the Kislevite's neck. Opchek grabbed the handle of the axe and sank to his knees, gagging. Balk tried to rip his weapon free, but to no avail. 'Stubborn until the – ah – end,' Balk grunted.

Goetz lurched up and drove his sword up through Balk's back. He forced the blade up until the tip scraped out from behind Balk's breastplate. 'Forgive me, brother,' Goetz whispered. Then he twisted, jerking the blade free. Balk staggered away, trailing red. Goetz followed him towards the water, pausing only for a glance at Opchek's body. A wave of sadness passed through him, but he let determination replace it. Balk fell onto all fours where the water met the rocks. Wheezing, he ripped his helmet off and tossed it behind him. Goetz kicked it aside as Balk fell into one of the tidal pools and rolled onto his back.

'It's done,' Goetz said.

'No,' Balk coughed. He reached pleadingly towards Goetz. 'D–do what must be done.' The hand fell. Balk closed his eyes. Goetz raised his sword and prepared to grant Balk's final request. Instead, he staggered as trails of fire were carved across his back. Gasping, he fell to his knees. The daemon loomed over him, her human features dissolving into avian hideousness. A massive paw swept him up and Goetz flailed out blindly with his sword, striking sparks off the black-iron feathers.

He found himself tumbling through the air a moment later. His back connected painfully with a stalagmite and he collapsed onto the cavern floor. The daemon stalked towards him, her massive wings unfurling even as they lost cohesion. The island bucked beneath his palms like a dying horse and there was a shrill screaming coming from every rock, nook and cranny. The vast shape staggered and seemed to plunge into the limp body of Myrma, filling it like an empty pig's bladder. With a lurch, the dead woman sat up, eyes blazing.

Her mouth opened and it was filled with night-black teeth. 'My Myrmidon...' the daemon hissed and then it laughed. Myrma's flesh blackened as she gestured and a sizzling bolt of energy leapt from her palm and crawled through the air towards Goetz.

'No.' The bolt exploded as it connected with the tip of Ulfar's staff. The old shaman staggered, but did not fall. 'Your story has gone on too long, daemon. It is time for endings.'

Myrma – the daemon – drew itself up and sighed. It plucked a hank of hair from its corrupting scalp and let it drift away. 'The Game does not end, mortal. Win or lose, it keeps going. Win or lose, we persist.'

'Persist elsewhere,' Ulfar said. He roared out a harsh flurry of syllables and frosty lightning struck the dead woman, ripping through her with ease. She staggered, but did not fall. In fact, she seemed to grow stronger; and larger. Her body began to balloon, muscle and bone changing into something else entirely.

Her head, still horribly human, shot forward at the end of a serpentine neck, her black teeth snapping together through the middle of Ulfar's staff. For a moment Ulfar stared stupefied at his shattered staff, but he recovered quickly, spitting words of power at the black shape that was doubling in size. Wings made of bloody bone snapped and nearly bowled Ulfar over.

Goetz scrambled to his feet and made to charge towards the creature, but a gesture from Ulfar stopped him. 'No! I will deal with this filth. You must shatter the ley line!'

'The–?' Goetz stared at him.

'The line of power! The root of the daemon, the connection between its corpse and this hell-island! Destroy it!' Ulfar snarled.

'Stop whispering secrets, little bird,' the daemon said, pouncing on the old man and bearing him down with bone-crushing force. It had grown into a grotesque mockery of a bipedal shape, something between reptile, bird and woman, with the lashing tail of a cat and the face of a girl. Goetz narrowly avoided a scaly backhand and backed away as the beast rose and advanced on him, talons scraping the rock. Bits of it bubbled and dropped away and its face was pinched in a mockery of human pain. 'This raiment is not enough,' it purred. 'It is not enough to contain my magnificence. My beauty burns it to cinders.'

'Rot and be damned,' Goetz said, raising his sword. Talons slashed out and he narrowly avoided a blow that would have pulped him. He came to his feet close enough to smell the conflicting sickly sweet stink of the thing and his sword passed through several metallic feathers, sending them rattling to the ground. A wide palm struck him and shoved him back, pinning him to the floor. Myrma's blistered face drew close on its long neck and her cat-like tongue tickled the wound in his cheek.

'I will enter you and wear you to the ball, my Myrmidon. I will remake you and shape you and we will shine like a star in the wa – AHRP!' The human facade burst like a pustule. The creature's head, already reforming, whipped around.

'Up boy,' Ulfar croaked, clutching his chest, the remains of his staff extended, smoke rising from the tip. 'Go where you are needed!'

'Do what must be done,' Goetz said, driving his sword into the creature's paw, freeing himself. A moment later a white-furred bear slammed into the daemon, tearing at its shifting flesh with berserk ferocity. The daemon oozed around the bear, its alien malleability allowing it to reach for Goetz with a cracking of bones and a ripping and re-knitting of warped flesh.

'Einsark! Your hand!'

Goetz looked up as Dalla swept by, her hatchet buried in the brainpan of one of the Screamers. She stretched out her hand and he caught it, even as the daemon lunged. It shrieked in frustration as he was hauled into the air and onto the broad back of the daemon-beast. 'Is this thing safe?' he asked, shouting to be heard.

'No!' Dalla shouted, laughing as she wrenched the hatchet sideways, sending the Screamer looping through the air.

'Your father – he said something about a ley line!' Goetz said, leaning close.

'A what?'

'The root of the daemon! We have to find it!'

Dalla replied by jerking the handle of her axe, sending their mount hurtling into the upside down forest of stalactites. As they sped along, more Screamers dropped from the ceiling, falling into pursuit. Their screams rattled Goetz's teeth in his jaw and he struck out at them as best as he could whenever they got too close.

'Look! There!' Dalla said, pointing towards a bulging stalactite that hung from the upper reaches of the cavern. Tendrils of sickly-hued fibres clung to it and even as Goetz watched, they flexed slightly. He remembered what the daemon had shown him and realised all at once what it was he must do.

'Get me alongside it!' he said, gesturing with his sword. 'Now!'

Dalla hauled on the hatchet-handle, sending the Screamer swooping towards the great stone mass. As they swooped past, Goetz bounded from his seat and grabbed for one of the thick bundles of matter. His fingers dug into the spongy mass and somewhere, the daemon shrilled. The island shook harder than before and a rain of stalactites thudded into the ground and sea. Men, Norscan, Svanii and knight alike screamed and died as the rocks fell.

Goetz hauled himself up towards the root of rock that held the whole mass suspended. His body shuddered with weakness, and he wanted desperately to close his eyes, just for a moment, but he bulled on. Behind him, a sound like a hundred swords being drawn split the air and a great weight landed opposite him. He turned.

The daemon bared a beak full of serrated teeth. Through her feathers, Myrma's screaming face surfaced and sank back. 'You cannot do this,' she hissed, a horribly mellifluous voice emanating from within the sculpted bird-like skull. 'You are my piece; my Myrmidon. It is not allowed,' she continued, bloody fingers crooking. The wound on his side split, and something strained to be free. Goetz howled in agony as black blood slithered up through his armour and sought his throat. More tendrils drifted out through his jerkin and sought to snag his sword-arm and his legs.

'You are almost ready, almost eaten away. You will be scoured clean and I will wear you to war with my faithless flock,' the daemon said, stretching towards him. She reached for him and he slashed at her, ripping his arm free of the black coils of his own blood, now alive and turned against him. She jerked her hand back and his sword connected with the rock. She shrieked and metal feathers drifted loose from her titan frame.

Grinning despite the pain, he said, 'Ha! Struck a nerve?', and pulled himself erect on the bulb of the stalactite. The daemon reared up on the other side, her serpentine neck swaying hypnotically.

'This is not part of the plan,' she said.

'No plan survives contact with the enemy. That's from Litany of Battle... the book of Myrmidia,' Goetz said. 'And She commands that I do what needs doing!' He swung his sword up with what remained of his strength and chopped into the thin stone ligament. The daemon screamed and lunged. But even as the tips of her claws tore his flesh, the stone snapped and she faded like a sea-mist, her stolen flesh going apart like burning paper. The stalactite hurtled downwards, carrying Goetz with it.

Desperately, he thrust his body away from the abominable organ and towards the water. The sea reached up eagerly to meet him...

THIRTY

His eyes opened as the sound of massive clockwork gears grinding together filled his head. The temple rotunda glowed with the orange light of eternal dawn and bronze and silver trees rose from beds of dark Tilean clay. A white shape stood among them, letting the delicately engraved shapes of clockwork wrens trip over her fingers.

'This isn't the Drakwald,' he said stupidly.

'How observant, my Myrmidon.'

She turned as Goetz stood. He almost immediately fell to his knees as the warm brass eyes met his own. 'Myrmidia,' he said. She did not reply; instead, the great spear she held rose, its tip pointed unerringly at him. Thick streams of black liquid spilled from his pores and collected on the polished tiles of the temple floor as he watched. The spear dipped, and the pool lengthened into a stream, spilling towards the spear-point. But before it reached it, it grew paler and paler until it was impossible to see.

The spear swung up, the flat of it brushing his chin and lifting him to his feet. The beautiful face examined his own, the eyes lingering on his ruptured cheek and the blistered scars from the troll-bile and the touch of the daemon's claws. 'I–' Goetz began.

The goddess held up a hand and leaned close. 'I trust that you can hear me now?' she said.

'Yes?' Goetz said helplessly.

'Good. We will speak more, soon, I think.' She smiled, and the world seemed to burn brighter than Goetz had ever thought possible. 'For now though... wake up.'

'What?'

'I said... wake up!'

Goetz's eyes sprang open as Dalla shook him hard enough to rattle his teeth. He sat up and groaned, his hand flying immediately to his side. Feeling nothing, not even a trace of scar tissue, let alone a hole, he looked down. His skin was unblemished, save for a dark bruise. His hand flew to his face and his fingers scraped his teeth through the hole in his cheek. He winced and hunched forward.

'Up, einsark!' Dalla said, dragging him to his feet. 'Fret about your looks later. We must go!'

'Go? What? Where?' Goetz looked around, dazed. Bodies lay scattered everywhere across the cavern, and Norscans moved among them, silencing the wounded with grim efficiency. The island gave a groan and its roots shuddered as debris rained from the ceiling. Cracks had appeared in the floor and sea water was lapping at their ankles. 'What happened? I was falling...'

'Yes. Falling and you fell, right enough,' Dalla said, pulling him along. 'And I pulled you out of the water. No easy feat with your armour weighing us down.'

'That's two I owe you, I expect,' Goetz said.

'Three, but who's counting? We–' Dalla stumbled to a stop, her face collapsing into a mask of pain. Goetz looked past her and saw Ulfar, lying broken and bloody on the ground, the water rushing around him. Goetz hurried forward and knelt by the old man. Ragged wounds covered his thin frame, and his stomach was a gaping mess. Ulfar grinned blearily at him, exposing blood-stained teeth.

'She is gone,' he said.

'Yes,' Goetz said. 'I expect so.'

'And you? Still deaf?'

'My hearing has cleared up some,' Goetz said hoarsely. 'Can you stand?'

'His guts are in the water,' Kettil Flatnose said, coming forward. He was covered in blood and the look he gave Goetz said he wouldn't mind spilling a bit more. 'He won't last the next five minutes, let alone a hike to the beach.'

'That's my father you're talking about,' Dalla snarled, shoving between Kettil and the others. 'He is strong!'

'I am dying,' Ulfar grunted. 'As is this place. It rots, now that the magic keeping it alive has fled. You must go.'

'We can carry you–' Goetz began, knowing even as he said it that it wasn't so. Moving the old man would only mean a more agonising death

'No,' Ulfar said, coughing. His eyes were unfocused and his face was knotted with pain. 'Do what you must, daughter.'

'Father...' Dalla began. She looked at Goetz, her eyes blank. Without speaking, he handed her his sword and turned, moving away to give them what privacy could be had in a crumbling cavern. To distract himself, he searched for Balk's body. It was like trying to find a needle in a pile of needles. He couldn't even recall where he'd seen it last, or whether Balk had actually been dead. He hoped so, for the Order's sake as much as anything else.

Stepping back as a rock splashed down into the water, he wondered what he was going to say. What would he tell Berengar? That his suspicions had been correct? That two entire komturies' worth of brothers had fallen to Chaos? Thinking of that made him wonder about the fate of the men above, those who had been defending the komturie. Were they still alive? Or had the Norscans overwhelmed them? Would it be better if they had? Had they all been corrupted, or simply a few? Almost sixty years on a Chaos-tainted island... could any man be called pure?

He caught sight of Opchek's body, still lying where it had fallen. The black armour had crumbled to dust and rotting meat, and the Kislevite lay bare and shrunken, his pale body looking entirely too fragile. Goetz sank to his haunches and pressed two fingers to the dead man's brow. 'Why did you save me?' he said out loud. There was no answer, for which he was grateful. There was more to the story than he'd seen, more than he'd felt. He looked at the rotting remains of the armour as the current caught it and carried it away.

Beneath his feet, the floor cracked and bucked and he stood abruptly. 'We must go. Now,' Dalla said from behind him. She held his sword down by her side and her face was drawn and tired looking. She turned away, and then turned back just as quickly. 'Thank you,' she said.

Goetz didn't know how to reply. He hurried after her as the cavern began to collapse in earnest. The surviving Norscans joined them in ones and twos, some, he noted, carrying the discarded armour of the knights of the Order. He thought of protesting, but then realised that he had little right to complain about the warriors scavenging what others had so carelessly discarded.

As they moved quickly through the tunnels towards the surface, Goetz saw the fearful movements of what he assumed were the Svanii. They did not try to attack, however. Upon reaching the surface, he saw that the komturie was ablaze and that the besiegers were retreating to their vessels, carrying armfuls of loot. From the smell on the wind, something had happened to the powder-room. Likely one of the brothers had blown it up rather than see it fall into the hands of the Norscans. In that thing, if in no other, the brothers of the Svunum Komturie had been true to the tenets of Myrmidia. Anger and despair flashed through him as he thought of the library, and all that was surely now lost. Had it been worth it? Had it been necessary?

Goetz forced the thought aside. It didn't matter now. The daemon was gone, and the island with it soon enough. The water was slowly creeping up the shoreline, engulfing the remains of the harbour. He stopped and watched a black-sailed galley sink. Something sharp pricked his neck and he turned. A burly Norscan grinned at him. 'One last bit of fun, hey?' he said.

'Step aside, Thalfi,' Dalla said, coming to stand beside Goetz. 'He aided us in the caverns.'

'And so? Nits make lice.' Thalfi stepped back and raised his sword. Goetz tensed, ready to spring aside. He was suddenly aware of just how isolated he really was now; and he was weaponless to boot.

'Thalfi is right,' Kettil said. 'Kill him, and we're done with the whole sorry lot. That is why we came on this mad venture, eh?'

'You'll have to come through me first,' Dalla said, stepping between the warriors and their prey.

'I think I'd like my sword back now,' Goetz murmured.

'I'm busy now,' Dalla replied.

'Stand aside girl. Your father led us to plunder and I'll not sully his name by killing you,' Thalfi rumbled, making to shove her aside. Dalla twisted around him and tapped the edge of her blade against his hairy throat. Thalfi froze even as his men began to move forward with angry murmurings. Kettil snorted in amusement and stepped around the tableau, his axe swinging loosely.

'You can't fight all of us,' he said to her as he moved towards Goetz.

'We don't have to,' Goetz said, stepping forward quickly and slugging the chieftain across the jaw. Shocked, Kettil stumbled to one knee. Goetz kicked him in the head a moment later and the other man fell, his eyes rolling to the white. Goetz scooped up his axe and pointed it at the converging Norscans. 'I've killed my own brothers today, as well as a daemon. What makes you think I won't butcher the lot of you and make for the mainland on a boat made out of your corpses?' he said in what he hoped was a casual tone of voice. Both Thalfi and Dalla eyed him with respect. Before anyone could reply, however, the crash of a cannon split the air.

One of the Norscan ships gave a groan as it split in two and spilled men into the water. Goetz turned and saw the face of Manann rising above the wreckage. The ships glided into the harbour, armoured men on their decks. Goetz turned back to the stunned Norscans. 'Did I not mention they were coming?' he said.

Thalfi stepped back and gave a roar of laughter. His men were already running for their boats. He saluted Goetz even as he hauled Kettil to his feet. 'Rot in Hel, brass-skin,' the big man said, grinning. He looked at Dalla. 'Coming Ulfarsdottir? We'll need every sword to fight past those yapping sea-curs...'

'I'll be along, Utergard,' Dalla said, not looking at him. She stood in front of Goetz and frowned. 'Good fight, einsark.'

'No such thing,' Goetz said, tossing Kettil's axe aside.

'Shows what you know, hey?' Dalla said. She brought her sword to her temple and saluted him. 'Olric keep you strong.'

'Myrmidia keep you smart,' Goetz said. She grinned and loped off after the others. It was only as the Norscans shoved away from shore that he realised that she still had his sword. Goetz shook his head ruefully and murmured, 'I really need to learn to hold on to things better.' Several ships from the fleet were harrying the Norscans, but not seriously... evidently, the Marienburg captains, whatever their allegiances, weren't prepared to possibly start a war with a still sizeable Norscan fleet this close to home. He felt some relief at that... after all, if they sunk the ship Dalla was on, how would he ever get his sword back.

Thinking wholly unchivalrous thoughts, he turned back as the landing party reached him. 'Ho! I told you that he was alive!' Dubnitz roared, trotting towards Goetz at the head of a group of his fellow knights. The big man looked as hale and bluff as Goetz had last seen him. 'Saw them off yourself then? Left nothing for us, have you?' The knight of Manann was clad in full plate, one hand on his sword. He took in Goetz's ravaged state and winced at the sight of his face. 'It looks like someone tried to give you a permanent grin. Does it hurt?'

'No, it feels like the caress of a courtesan,' Goetz said.

'Does it?'

'No. It hurts. Badly,' Goetz said.

'Should we be after them then, Grand Master?' Dubnitz said, turning back to Ogg as the latter drew close, Lord Justicar Ambrosius by his side and a full contingent of marines and knights with them.

'No. Let the barbarians go,' Ogg snarled. He looked around and stumped towards Goetz, his trident extended. The tips of the tines scratched across Goetz's much abused breastplate. 'What have you done to my island?'

'Nothing, though it won't be an island for much longer,' Goetz said as the ground rocked beneath their feet.

'What?'

'It's dying,' Goetz said. 'And we should probably watch it from a safe distance.'

'How can an island die?' Ogg nearly shrieked, turning in place.

'Like this, one imagines,' Ambrosius said. He looked at Goetz. 'The komturie fell to the Norscans, then?' he said carefully.

Goetz hesitated. Then, he nodded. 'They fought valiantly and broke the back of a fleet meant for Marienburg and the imperial coast,' he said. Ambrosius's good eye narrowed speculatively.

'Valiantly,' he said.

'To the last man,' Goetz said.

'Which is you, I imagine. And thus the final word on what happened here,' Ambrosius said. He nodded. 'Fine. Back to the ship! Let's let this place not collect any more souls, shall we?' An explosion from the komturie punctuated his command, and the group hurried back to its boat.

'I can't believe this! To come all this way and to be denied...' Ogg said, shaking his head. The men pushed the boat off and Goetz watched from the stern as the island trembled. Its contortions were becoming more violent now, and the water released a foul smell.

'Yes,' Goetz said, thinking of the daemon's shrieks as it faded back into whatever darkness awaited one of its kind. 'It's quite a shame.' He turned to find Ambrosius watching him. The Lord Justicar slid towards him and bent his head.

'What will you tell Berengar?' he said, his voice pitched low.

'The truth,' Goetz said. 'The brothers of Svunum met an enemy they could not defeat. And they died.' He looked at Ambrosius. 'Athalhold's death was a result of an unconnected plot, instigated by Chaos cultists. Possibly the same cultists who stirred up the Norscans and set them to invade the coasts...'

'An invasion your Order repelled, at significant cost.' Ambrosius scratched under his eye-patch and smiled thinly. 'A good story. Young men will flock to your Order at the telling, and the loss of a komturie is explained and forgiven.'

'And then the generous donation of an empty house to a penniless order of brother-knights,' Goetz said, nodding towards Ogg's fuming shape. Ambrosius's smile grew feral.

'You're learning to play the Game,' he said.

'No. Merely doing what must be done,' Goetz said.

Svunum trembled and the burning shell of the komturie finally came crashing down. Flames rose high as the island sank low. Goetz turned away, his fingers tight around the amulet of Myrmidia that hung from his neck. As they left Svunum behind, he closed his eyes and said a prayer.

Myrmidia didn't bother to answer, but Goetz knew she was listening all the same.

DEAD CALM

Josh Reynolds

When the wind died and the mist began to roll in across the Sea of Claws, Hermann Eyll knew the captain had come for his due. From the great bay window in his study, the master of Marienburg's south dock watched as every billowing sail fell limp and the wine-dark sea became as still as glass. Flags from a dozen principalities drooped as seabirds swooped and screamed, hurtling inland in one vast, raucous cloud. On the docks, men and women stopped and stared upwards, watching in wonder.

Eyll ignored the birds and instead turned to face the thin, olive-complexioned man sitting behind his grandfather's ancient claw-footed desk. 'He's coming. Just as I said, Fiducci. He's coming for his due and I'm damned if I'll pay it,' Eyll said, fear turning his tones savage. A thin man with a whip-like build and clothes of expensive cut, Eyll was every inch the merchant-prince. Pale, manicured fingers did a rap-a-tap patter on the scrimshaw butt of a pistol rising from the colourful sash about his waist, and he began to pace. 'You're certain you can deal with him?' he said.

'As certain as one can be in these – hmm – these matters,' Signor Franco Fiducci said, shoving his spectacles further up the bridge of his beak of a nose. 'Necromancy is not as exact a science as we would wish, hmm?' The little Tilean bared blackened teeth in a half-hearted smile. 'But Kemmler made careful records, and the ritual itself is not so far out of the bounds of this sort of thing, eh?' He waggled worm-pale fingers. 'A prick of the thumb and something wicked will surely come, as they say.'

Eyll grunted and eyed the necromancer. Fiducci came highly recom-mended, having performed certain services for certain people under certain conditions that could, at best, be characterised as stressful. He looked like a crow, dressed all in black and bobbing his head alarmingly as he spoke. But he was dangerous for all that. 'It's not his coming that worries me… it's what he intends to do once he gets here.'

'Ah, just so, yes, eh?' Fiducci waggled his fingers again. 'No matter. The captain is old and hard and wild like the sea itself, but Franco Fiducci is an artist of the bones, eh?' He made a tight fist, his knuckles popping unpleasantly. 'We will trim his sails back, have no fear.'

'But his powers,' Eyll said. 'My grandfather said he was a sorcerer as well as...' he trailed off and swallowed thickly, his mind shying away from the thought.

'Yes. His kind are notorious for their sorcerous abilities. He likely possesses a far greater grasp of the winds of magic than my humble self,' Fiducci said. His lips quirked in what might have been a grimace. One spidery hand splayed out possessively across a tumble of books, one of several that were stacked sloppily on the desk in haphazard piles. 'But I am a quick study, eh?'

'You'd better be, for the price I'm paying you sorcerer!' Eyll said and lunged, slamming his knuckles down on the desk hard enough to cause Fiducci to jump. 'I hired you to protect me from that – that thing and I expect you to do it!'

'Of course,' Fiducci said. 'Let it never be said that Franco Fiducci does not have his employer's best interests at heart.'

Eyll glared at him for a moment longer, and then looked away. 'Stromfels take me,' he muttered, shoulders slumping.

'I have no doubt he will, Signor Eyll. He, or one very much like him, takes us all in the end. Except for your captain, of course,' Fiducci said, stacking the books neatly. 'But I will see to that, I think, provided you get for me that which I require.'

Eyll made a face. 'I'll have them this afternoon. Tassenberg drove a hard bargain, blasted flesh-peddler,' he grunted.

'But you got them? Twelve of them?'

'Twelve of them, yes.' Eyll looked away.

'And pure?' Fiducci pressed, leering.

'Tassenberg said they would be, damn you,' Eyll growled.

'Oh no, Signor Eyll. Damn you, in fact, if they are not. Only twelve pure souls can save yours, one for each generation the captain has prowled the seas, making you and yours rich.' Fiducci smiled nastily, displaying his black teeth again. 'Your ancestor employed him as a privateer, sinking the ships of his competitors until his coffers swelled. And eleven generations since have reaped the benefits of that bargain. Now you want to weasel out of it, like a good merchant. Well, just so, Franco Fiducci will help you.' He rubbed a thumb and forefinger together. 'And then you will help Fiducci, eh?'

'Yes,' Eyll said quietly.

'Good.' The necromancer rose to his feet. 'I must go and prepare. And you must gather our materials.'

Eyll watched Fiducci leave, his fingertips tracing the patterns carved into the handle of his pistol. Like everything else in his possession, it was a hand-me-down from better times. He imagined putting a bullet in the little necromancer's back, and then just as quickly dismissed the thought. Like pity, petty satisfaction was something he could ill afford at the moment.

Striding to the bell-rope dangling in the corner near the door, he gave it a yank, summoning a servant.

It was time to collect the captain's due.

'Don't move,' Erkhart Dubnitz growled. Water trickled from the docks above and ran down the piscine designs engraved on his sea-green armour. Sword in hand, he reached for the back of the priestess's green robe. 'Just... don't... move.'

'Why?' Esme Goodweather, novice of the temple of Manann, said from between suddenly clenched teeth. Young and slim, she was a striking physical contrast to the bluff, broad knight reaching for the hood of her robe. Above her head, she could hear the clatter of iron-shod wheels and the babble of voices as Marienburg went about its business, unaware of what went on below their feet on the unterdock.

The unterdock was an open secret... an artificial world beneath the massive docklands that occupied Marienburg's northern coast. Built in an ad hoc fashion by generations of smugglers, merchants, pirates and beggars, the rickety wooden walkways spread like a massive spider's web beneath the docklands, cutting between the shallows and the surface. Stairs, ladders, fishing nets and overturned dinghies occupied the spaces between wooden planks, and formed natural landmarks. The air was muggy and thick with sea-salt. Barnacles clustered in patches like moss and things moved beneath the water. Things Goodweather didn't particularly like to think about.

'Because it's watching you,' Dubnitz said.

'What's watching me?' Goodweather gulped.

'Don't worry about it. Go limp,' Dubnitz said. He grabbed a handful of her robe and yanked her backwards. Something sprang out of the shadows that collected beneath the dock and Dubnitz sent the priestess tumbling unchivalrously to the soggy wood of the unterdock as he lunged forward to meet it. It was an ugly something, all iridescent scales and teeth, like a cross between a frog, alligator and shark. Dubnitz bellowed out a bawdy hymn to Manann as his sword sliced through the gaping mouth, shattering teeth and spraying the water with stinking blood. The creature squealed and crashed into a tangled bed of flotsam and fishing net. It twisted and leapt onto Dubnitz, its claws scrabbling at his armour. Roaring, Dubnitz head-butted it and the bulbous bearded metal face of Manann that served as his visor sank into the malformed flesh, causing the beast to flop backwards into the dark water. It croaked and tried to rise. Dubnitz pinned it in place a moment later with an awkward two-handed thrust.

Giving the sword a vicious twist, he jerked it free and kicked the spasming creature into the water. 'Back to Manann, you blubbery fiend,' he grunted, lifting his visor to watch it sink.

'What was that?' Goodweather snarled, clutching the trident icon that hung from her neck. 'What was that thing?'

'One of Stromfel's children,' Dubnitz said. He grabbed a handful of the priestess's sleeve and cleaned his sword. 'The Chaos-things breed like roaches down here and no two of them are the same, besides the teeth and the bad attitudes. Incidentally, that's why you're here, isn't it, to ward these buggers off?'

Goodweather jerked her sleeve free of Dubnitz' grip and grimaced as the barb struck home. 'Yes. It just surprised me.' She hesitated. 'I've – ah –I've never seen one of them before.'

'Well, now you have,' Dubnitz grinned. 'Who did you annoy to get sent down here on this little expedition then?'

'No one,' she said, looking around suspiciously as if waiting to see what else might leap out.

'It must have been someone.' Dubnitz scraped blood off of his cuirass and flung it aside. 'No matter, I suppose. You'll get used to the Shallows soon enough...' He looked past her at the motley gang of sewerjacks clustered behind them. Made up of condemned prisoners, mercenaries and disgraced watchmen, the sewerjacks patrolled the unterdock as well as the sewers and under-canals of Marienburg. These looked particularly shamefaced as Dubnitz glared at them. 'You lot, on the other hand should already be bloody used to them!' he snarled and several of the 'jacks flinched and edged back from the big knight. 'By Manann's scaly nether-regions, are you professionals or mewling infants? How did you miss that thing?'

'Nobody talks to Big Pudge like that!' one of the 'jacks growled. Big and bald, Pudge shoved his way through his compatriots, nearly knocking one or two of them off into the water as he forced his way nose-to-nose with Dubnitz. 'Nobody calls Pudge a baby!'

'Right. Noted. In fact, you're far too ugly to be a baby. Maybe you're an orc instead, eh?' Dubnitz barked, his beard bristling. A fist the size of a cooked ham swung out, but Dubnitz ducked his head and the blow caromed off of his helmet. Pudge yelped and stepped back. Dubnitz stomped on his instep and shoved him off the wooden walkway into the grimy water. The man howled and thrashed in the water.

'Stop screaming. It'll only attract more of the beasties,' Dubnitz said, sinking awkwardly to his haunches. He cast a glare at the other 'jacks. 'I hope someone thought to bring a rope. Otherwise I'm leaving him.'

As the 'jacks hauled their fellow up, Dubnitz joined Goodweather. 'Every day is an adventure,' he said, smiling.

'I'll take your word for it,' Goodweather said, pulling her robes tighter about herself. 'I hate this.'

'Probably shouldn't have gotten yourself sent down here then, eh?'

'It wasn't my fault!' she snapped. 'And besides, you're one to talk you great oaf!' She glared at him. 'Aren't you down here because of that stunt you pulled with an uncooked octopus and a drunken goat?'

'Lies and calumny,' Dubnitz said, flushing. 'That goat was hardly drunk.' He hesitated. 'You – ah – you heard about that then?'

'The whole temple district heard about it! Ogg makes enough noise for three men twice his size!' Goodweather said, her distaste evident in her tone.

Dubnitz couldn't find the heart to fault her for it. Grand Master Ogg, leader of the Order of Manann, was an acquired taste. The bad-tempered, trident-handed Ogg was famous in Marienburg both for his bull-headed bravery and his political paranoia. His knights were fast becoming figures of familiarity in the households of the mighty of the city; he rented his warriors out as advisors, bodyguards and celebratory decorations alike, and it was said that whatever they heard, so too did he.

Granted, not everyone approved of Ogg's expansionism. Dubnitz had no feelings either way. He chuckled. 'He did, didn't he? I'm hardly old Oggie's favourite fish at the moment, eh?'

Goodweather snorted and looked away. 'You deserve to be down here with these cut-throats,' she said, gesturing surreptitiously towards the sewerjacks as they took turns kicking the water out of Big Pudge's lungs.

'And you don't?'

'No,' she muttered.

'Ha!' Dubnitz shook his head. 'Girl, you wouldn't be down here if you didn't deserve it for some reason. For now though, lets concentrate on why we're here... where are they?'

Goodweather sank smoothly onto her haunches and pulled a handful of seashells and shark's teeth out of one of the pouches dangling from her harness. Like all members of the Order of the Albatross she wore a tarjack's harness over her robes, with dozens of pouches and reliquaries tied to it, as well as a hooked knife carved from the tooth of some unpleasant deep-sea leviathan and a handful of silver bells. She scattered the shells and teeth across the dock. All of the teeth pointed in the same direction. 'soutch dock,' she said, looking up.

'Hmp. The Eel's territory,' Dubnitz said, stroking his beard. 'He's a touchy one is Prince Eyll. We'll have to tread lightly.'

'Surely our remit extends past his,' Goodweather said, collecting her shells and stuffing them back in her pouch.

Dubnitz looked at her and grunted. 'In theory.' He sighed. 'In practice, on the other hand...' He clapped his hands together, the metal of his gauntlets clattering loudly. 'Well, nothing for it but to do it. Form up you pack of half-drowned rats!' he said, directing the latter towards the 'jacks. 'On your feet Pudge, you orc-stain. All of you, get to trotting. soutch dock! On the double!'

The group moved quickly and quietly, save for the creaking of hauberks and the rattle of weapons. The 'jacks, for all their slovenliness, were professionals and they knew their job. At the moment, that happened to be the interception of a shipment of human chattel being delivered by Uli

Tassenberg's men to a buyer on the docklands. Tassenberg was the boldest purveyor of human flesh in Marienburg, taking captives to the water wherever it flowed. They said he could get any hue of flesh or size or build, guaranteed. It was one of the current Lord Justicar's pet-peeves. Aloysious Ambrosius, the Marsh-Warden and supreme judicial champion of Marienburg, had few bees in his bonnet, but slavery was one of them. The one-eyed former knight hated the practice with a loathing most people reserved for mutants or orcs.

Dubnitz was against slavery as well, in a general sort of way. He had never been one and had no intention of becoming one, but felt that it was a relatively simple state of affairs to change, man or woman, if you really wanted to do so. Simply kill the bugger holding the other end of the chain. No man, no problem. In this case, the man was Tassenberg.

'I grew up with him, you know,' he said out loud. Goodweather, following behind him, looked up.

'What?'

'Tassenberg the Slaver. I grew up with him. Fat little bastard, even then. Hard too. We boiled horse-hide and made leather and glue like the other orphans in the Tannery.' Marienburg was like an apple riddled with brown patches, and of those patches the Tannery was one of the worst. Located in the maze of streets that played host to the city's tanneries, it was a squalid, foul-smelling territory and the gangs of mule-skinners and cat's meat-men who made it their home were as dangerous as any dock-tough or river-rat. And now that he was powerful, Tassenberg made it his fortress. 'Me and Uli and Ferkheimer the Mad and Otto Schelp, the Sewer-Wolf. Gods yes, got out as quick as I could too.'

'I thought you to be of noble birth to be a knight,' Goodweather said.

'Who says I'm not?' Dubnitz said. 'Maybe I was switched at birth, eh?' She looked at him, not quite knowing how to respond. Dubnitz gave a belly-rattling guffaw of laughter and clapped his hands. 'Or maybe Ogg, bless his crusty little heart, wanted fighters first and fops second. He was no nobleman himself. Just a merchant seaman with a love of politics and esoteric Tilean pornography.'

'What?' Goodweather said again, her eyes widening in disgust.

'Of course one has little to do with the other,' Dubnitz went on, swinging an arm out. 'At least in Ogg's case. No, he picked the roughest, toughest, saltiest rogues he could find to form the core of the most holy and violent Order of Manann. And isn't that what knighthood is about, really? Hitting people so hard that blood comes out of their ears? Of course it is!'

Out in the darkness of the unterdock, something shrieked. Dubnitz roared back. Silence fell. Goodweather scrabbled for the net of bells that hung from her hip and raised it, giving it a shake. There was the sound of something heavy splashing in the darkness of the Shallows. Then it faded.

'Handy,' Dubnitz said.

'Shouldn't you try to be more quiet, perhaps?' Goodweather said, lowering the bells. Several of the sewerjacks made noises of agreement.

'Being quiet only attracts 'em, the buggers,' Dubnitz said. 'They equate creeping with weakness, so I'd hurry up the pace if I were you.' He strode on, one hand on his sword. The group followed at a slightly increased pace.

Behind him, Eyll sensed his bodyguards shifting. One of them tapped him on the shoulder and murmured, 'They're here, my lord.' The two men were the best money could buy. Both were professional killers, skilled with the rapier and the dirk and honed to the peak of excellence in a hundred street-brawls and duels. He touched his pistol where it rested in his sash reflexively, reminding himself that he wasn't helpless himself. He looked and saw a skiff sliding through the debris of the Shallows towards the unterdock, a hooded lantern marking its dim path through the thick, corpse-white mist.

Seeing the mist, Eyll felt a clammy chill squeeze his backbone with tender fingers. It had permeated the docklands, curling around ships and buildings alike, seeping into the canals and into cellars and hidden jetties. Despite the cool, he felt beads of sweat pop to life on his face. Somewhere out there, in the mist, a daemon waited to take his soul. A daemon with red eyes and teeth like knives and... fiercely, he shook himself.

Fiducci had assured him that he could bind the captain. Bind and break him. It. And once that was done, what? Eyll, like any man of his position, had a mind like quicksilver when it came to ambition. Once bound, what could a monster like the captain be turned to? Maybe his ancestor had had the right idea, to use the daemon to break and batter the fleets of his rivals. That was how the Eylls had made the soutch dock the power that it was today. But what could it become in the future?

'Let them know we're here,' he said, fear momentarily buried beneath eagerness. One of his men held up a lantern and twisted the shutter-cap, sending the signal. The skiff approached and an anchor chain was looped around a wooden post. Five men climbed up onto the dock. One of them, a rangy Norscan, waved cheerily.

'Hello Eel,' he rumbled. 'We brought your wares.'

Eyll ignored the nickname and looked at the skiff. A number of huddled forms occupied the centre of the boat, chained together, their heads obscured by burlap sacks. 'Where did you get them from?' Eyll said, trying to ignore the stifled sobs. It was harder than he'd thought.

'Does it matter?'

'Would I have asked otherwise?' he said. It didn't really matter. But he felt he needed to know, for some indefinable reason. If he was spilling their blood to save his own, he owed it to them to at least know where they had come from.

The Norscan snorted. 'Here and there,' he said. 'Do you have the money?'

Eyll dropped a handful of coins into the Norscan's hand. The blond brute gave a gap-toothed grin and bit down on one. 'It's good,' he said and looked at his fellows. Eyll grimaced.

'Of course it's good.'

'Only Tassenberg says maybe not always, huhm?' the Norscan grunted. 'Uli says maybe you tell us why you need these, hey?' The Norscan swept his wolfish gaze across Eyll and his bodyguards, sizing them up boldly. 'Can't be selling to undesirables, Uli says.'

'Undesirables?' Eyll said. 'I'm a Prince of the Dock!'

'Blood don't mean dung,' the Norscan said. 'Not to Tassenberg. Got to have standards. Can't be selling valuable wares to daemon-lovers or sorcerers. Bad for business. Lot of girls,' the Norscan continued, smiling. The coins had disappeared into his filthy hauberk and he fondled the hand-axe on his belt. 'Why you need so many Eel? Maybe a party? Or something else?'

'What?' Eyll looked at the cut-throat. 'It's none of his concern. And certainly none of yours, oaf!'

'Oh, but it is,' the Norscan said, pulling his hatchet and gesturing offhandedly. 'Tell us, Eel.'

'Don't call me Eel,' Eyll said. 'In fact, do not speak to me until spoken to. I am the Master of the soutch docks and you will show me–'

The Norscan's fist shot out, and Eyll's nose popped like an overripe cherry. He fell back into the arms of his bodyguards, his hands clawing at his face. The Norscan grinned. 'And Tassenberg is the Master of Men, Eel. What he wants to know, you tell him, hey?' The other cut-throats moved forward, drawing weapons. 'Tassenberg heard you hired Fiducci the bone-fondler. He heard you're planning something. Tassenberg wants to know what's going on,' he continued, stepping closer.

Eyll blindly fumbled at the pistol thrust through his sash. 'Don't come a step closer!' he snarled thickly, aiming the weapon at the Norscan.

The big man hesitated, his eyes narrowing. 'Only got one shot, hey?' he said, after a minute. 'Best make it count, Eel.' He raised the hatchet.

'There they are. And with their fingers right in the pie,' Dubnitz muttered as he watched the skiff dock and Tassenberg's men clamber onto the jetty to speak with their customers. He waved Goodweather back. 'You keep those bells handy. If this gets bloody, the beasts will be on us in a frenzy. The rest of you, fan out. Horst, Molke, get those crossbows ready. Tarpe, Pudge, the rest of you... follow me. But be careful. This blasted mist is as thick as mud.'

'Wait, what are you doing?' Goodweather said, as Dubnitz made ready to step out of the shadows.

'Arresting them. The quicker we do this, the quicker we get back up to the clean air and the quicker I can go to lunch. Fighting that beastie got my belly growling,' he said, patting his stomach.

'Listen, this mist... it's not natural!' Goodweather hissed, grabbing his wrist. 'It feels wrong.'

'Handle it then,' Dubnitz said, gently pulling his arm loose. 'That's why you're down here. And I'm here to arrest those buggers there.' So saying, he thrust himself out into full view of the group gathered at the other end of the walkway and smashed a fist into his cuirass with a loud clang. The group of criminals spun, stunned. 'Hoy! You're done! Nicked! Nabbed! Give up and we won't hit you too much!' Dubnitz bellowed at the top of his voice.

A pistol snarled and one of Tassenberg's men pitched backwards with a howl. Dubnitz reached the clustered criminals a moment later, the 'jacks just behind him. His sword swung out and crashed against a rapier as a man armed with the tools of a duellist intercepted him. The man was fast, dancing around the big knight, the tip of the rapier carving its signature in Dubnitz's exposed flesh. Roaring, he managed to catch hold of the blade and jerked the swordsman off balance. He punched him in the face with the cross-piece of his sword and then gutted him with a casual swipe, kicking the body aside a moment later. 'What part of "you're under arrest" don't you people understand?' he snarled.

He made a grab for the pistol-man, whose terrified features struck him as familiar in the moment before one of Tassenberg's men struck at him with a halberd. Dubnitz sank to one knee and blocked the strike, then twisted, forcing himself up and his sword down through his opponent's skull. 'Don't run! I hate running!' he said, as the pistol-man began to flee towards a nearby set of stairs. If he got to the upper level, Dubnitz knew he would lose him in the confusion of the docklands.

Behind him, he heard weapons rattling and a man screamed. The mist was thigh-high and swirling around them like serpents. Dubnitz ploughed through it and made a lunging grab for the fleeing man's cloak. He snagged it and jerked the man around. He gave an oath as recognition hit him like a brick. 'You!'

Hermann Eyll snatched the dirk out of his belt and made a desperate stab. The blade broke on Dubnitz's armour and the knight drove a knee into the other man's codpiece. The prince collapsed with a shrill scream. Dubnitz grabbed the back of his collar. 'Oh, Ogg will just love this, won't he? And the Lord Justicar too!'

'No!' Eyll wheezed, clawing weakly at the iron grip that held him. Dubnitz grimaced.

'Yes. You're for the yardarm jig, I'm afraid, milord.'

'A dance of inestimable amusement, I'm given to understand, providing you're not the one performing it,' a chipper voice interjected. Dubnitz looked up. At the top of the stairs, a black-clad little form grinned at him.

'Fiducci!' Dubnitz rasped.

'Hello, Erkhart. And, alas, goodbye,' Fiducci said as he raised a peculiarly shaped bosun's whistle to his thin lips. As the echo of its unpleasant trill faded, the abominable sound of heavy, slippery bodies splashing out of the mist filled the air.

* * *

'Oh no,' Goodweather said, rising to her feet, her bells hanging forgotten in her hand. The two crossbowmen looked at her nervously. The rising mist had made it impossible for them to get a shot off and now one of them said, 'What's that sound? Is it the beasties?'

'It's all of the beasties,' Goodweather muttered, the hairs on the back of her neck prickling unpleasantly, though whether from the dank touch of the sorcerous mist or the sound of flabby bodies splashing closer. She peered through the mist, trying to spot the man in black she'd caught sight of just a moment earlier. The sound of the whistle had alerted her immediately to the danger. Goodweather was by no means the most experienced member of the Order of the Albatross, nor was she the most popular. Women and boats didn't mix, or that was the assumption in some quarters. In truth she could haul sail with the best of them, and knew the stars like the freckles on her own hips. And she damn well knew the sound of one of Kadon's Whistles and what it meant.

Carved long ago by the infamous beastmancer at the behest of one of the first merchant-princes, the whistles could summon or disperse the nastiest inhabitant of Manann's realm. Sharks, whales, sea-wyrms and other things fell under the power of the whistle. So too, evidently, did Stromfel's Children. As far as she knew, they were also all locked up in the temple of Manann. How someone had gotten their hands on one of them was a mystery to her, and for another time at that. Right now, survival was the priority.

Cursing, she raised her bells and dug in her pouches for sea-salt. Flinging the latter out in wide curves, she was rewarded by an immediate withering of the mist around her. Whatever was causing it didn't like the touch of the Blessed Salts, no two ways there.

'What are you doing?' one of the 'jacks said. 'What's going on?'

'Quiet!' Goodweather snapped. She pulled a handful of seagull feathers out next and flung them up, hoping she wasn't going to see what she knew she would. A stiff sea-breeze hissed through the Shallows, shoving the mist aside and revealing a horde of tumbling, savage bodies. Some of them looked like otters or eels, while others looked like sharks and octopi. They heaved and squirmed through the water, forcing their way past the wrecks and small reefs of netting and barnacles towards the far end of the walkway, where Dubnitz and the others struggled. Goodweather froze for a moment, struck dumb by the horror. Bulbous eyes rotated behind filmy membranes and something that was like a frog and a fish and lion scrambled up onto the dock and scuttled towards them, jaws snapping. The crossbowmen screamed and fired as one. The beast snapped forward, jackknifing as the bolts thudded home. It slid across the wet wood towards them, thrashing in its death throes. More of the beasts began to follow its course however.

'Stay close!' Goodweather said, and then saw that it was no use. Both men were already turning to flee. She ignored their final moments and concentrated on keeping herself from joining them. 'Manann bless and keep me from the beasts of the sea,' she whispered, scattering salt around her and grabbing for her shark's teeth. The creatures were of Stromfels, and the priests of Manann had long since devised methods for keeping such monstrous afterbirths in check. Squeezing the teeth in her hand hard enough to draw stripes of blood from her palm, she shook them and threw them into the water, hoping that she wasn't too late.

Even as something that was more jellyfish than cormorant flapped squishily towards her, a red shape tore it into wet rags. Two more shapes joined the first and the phantom shapes of long-dead sharks spun lazily through the air around her, their ghostly teeth reducing even the boldest of the mutant beasts to ruin. She hurried towards Dubnitz and the others, blood dripping steadily from her hand. The spell wouldn't last long, and there was safety in numbers. Or so she hoped.

As the knight of Manann was bowled over by one of the Shallows-beasts, Eyll found himself hauled to his feet by Fiducci. The necromancer flashed his black teeth and laughed wildly. 'It works! It works!'

'What works? What did you do?' Eyll sputtered, yanking himself free of the little man's surprisingly strong grip.

'It is the answer to your prayers, Signor Eyll,' Fiducci said. 'But only if we have the bait. Where are they?'

'In the – the skiff!' Eyll yelped, turning. The slaver's skiff rocked in the water as the beasts thundered past it, drawn by the whistle up onto the walkway. For the moment, they were ignoring it, but that wouldn't last long. 'Make them go away! We have to get to that skiff!' he shouted, grabbing two handfuls of Fiducci's robe.

In reply, Fiducci blew hard on the whistle. The roiling mass of beasts split and fell back as the necromancer began to walk down the steps, Eyll close behind. 'Did you know that armoured buffoon who attacked me?' he said, looking around for the knight. 'Who was he? He seemed to know you...'

'Dubnitz,' Fiducci said, giving the whistle another toot. 'Erkhart Dubnitz. He tried to hang me for practicing my art. Can you imagine? I was only doing as my clients asked, and the girl's parents were so happy to have her back, when all was said and done. What's a few maggots between family, eh?'

Eyll shuddered. His eyes were riveted on the beasts as they thrashed over and gnawed on the bodies of Tassenberg's men and the sewerjacks. Eyll's surviving bodyguard had vaulted into the skiff, obviously realising that the beasts were ignoring it. He watched them approach wild-eyed, his rapier extended.

'Good man, Stromm,' Eyll said as he dropped down into the skiff.

The man nodded jerkily. A moment later, his head disappeared down the gullet of the frog-thing that rose out of the water and grabbed hold of the skiff. Eyll screamed and fell backwards. The monster reached for the closest of the girls, its talons puncturing the poor wretch's chest like a knife through a water-skin. With a triumphant croak it began to pull the whole lot overboard, the chains that bound them inextricably together rattling. Eyll grabbed on from the other end and a momentary battle of tug-of-war ensued. Then, something red and horrible reduced the monster to squealing wreckage. Eyll gaped up at the spectral sharks as they dove and curled through the air.

Fiducci dropped into the boat and felt for the dead girl's pulse. 'Fie! Dead!'

'She's the last, bone-licker,' a voice growled. Fiducci and Eyll looked up. Dubnitz stood above them, his sword extended, his helmet missing, his armour covered in deep scratches and dents. 'The last one ever.'

Fiducci reacted like a striking snake, grabbing Eyll and pressing a blade he produced from his sleeve to his employer's throat. 'Drop the sword or the Signor dies!'

Dubnitz hesitated, and that was long enough. Eyll elbowed Fiducci back and swung his pistol up. He had reloaded on the walk, and the weapon barked. The knight staggered back, a wash of red suddenly covering his face. Fiducci howled with glee and blew on his whistle. Monstrous shapes closed on the reeling knight, diving upon him hard enough to splinter the weakened wood of the walkway. The struggling knot of man and monsters plunged down into the dark water, causing the skiff to bob alarmingly.

Eyll twisted, shoving the smoking barrel of the pistol beneath Fiducci's nose. 'Are you mad?'

'Eccentric, possibly,' the necromancer said. 'Grab an oar, Signor. We must go! Now, before there are any more interrup–'

A hand rose out of the frothing water and fastened on the edge of the skiff. Eyll scrambled back, thinking for a moment that it was the knight. But as he moved, he caught sight of more shapes, swimming forward in the mist. The chill on his soul returned, and suddenly, the struggling monsters behind him did not seem as bad as he'd first thought.

The dead man heaved himself up, his puffy, blackened flesh encrusted with algae and barnacles. Mutely, he glared at Eyll. 'The... bargain... has... come... due,' the corpse said, in a voice like oil sloshing in a lantern. A rotting hand reached for him. Fiducci interposed himself, teeth bared. Uttering several gurgling syllables, he tapped two fingers to the corpse's head. It's unseeing eyes rolled up in their sockets and it slumped back into the water.

'He's found me!' Eyll shrieked. 'He's come for me!'

'Of course he has,' Fiducci said, wiping his fingers against his robes. He made a face and looked at the dead girl. 'We will need to be clever, yes? Grab an oar!' More zombies made their way through the water even as the two men got the skiff moving. Bloated hands reached for them, plucking at the oars and their arms as they made their getaway into the ever-thickening mist.

* * *

Dubnitz hit the bottom of the Shallows and silt exploded upwards, blinding him. He'd instinctively taken a breath before hitting the water, but it wasn't going to save him, he knew. Claws scraped at him and he jabbed an elbow into a hideous face, shattering saw-edged teeth. With painful slowness, he chopped out with his sword, trying to drive off the rubbery forms of his assailants. His armour, a boon on land, was anything but beneath the water. It made his limbs feel as if they were wrapped in anchor chains. He struggled to disengage from the beasts now chewing on his limbs before his lungs exploded. It would be humiliating to drown in less water than filled a rich man's tub.

Then, there was a flash of crimson and a wafting cloud of blood sprang into being around him. Waving it aside, he saw spinning ethereal shapes drive off his attackers and fade away into nothing. And beyond them he saw... what? Lungs burning, he peered closer, trying to make out the dim, dark figures plodding through the water away and out into the harbour. Finally, unable to stay down any longer, he thrust himself up. The water splashed against his cheeks and throat as he surfaced, and he clawed at the supports of the walkway, trying to haul himself up.

'Give me your hand!'

Dubnitz looked up at Goodweather. 'I'm too heavy,' he gasped.

'Just give me your hand, oaf!'

He did so, his gauntlet slapping into her hand. With a groan, she helped him clamber back up onto the wooden walkway. Stromfel's Children had departed as swiftly as they'd come, leaving behind only bodies and the stink of blood and death on the close air. 'Are they...?' Dubnitz said.

'All of them,' Goodweather said grimly, rubbing at a scrape on her face. Her robes were torn in a dozen places and blood and ichor stained them. Her hands too were bloody, and they trembled noticeably. 'We're the only survivors. Other than–'

'Fiducci,' Dubnitz growled and thumped the walkway with a fist. 'That foul little bog-stench.'

'Fiducci?' Goodweather said.

'A necromancer. And a bad one. Why was he here? Why in the name of Manann's drooping tail would he need a skiff full of women?' He raised his hand as Goodweather made to speak. 'Never mind. I know why.' He growled again and pushed himself to his feet. 'Did you see them?'

'See who?'

'Fiducci's little friends,' Dubnitz said harshly. 'In the water. Dead men by the dozens. Walking along as if they were out for a stroll.'

'The water-logged dead...' Goodweather whispered, her face going pale.

'We have to get after them,' Dubnitz said, looking around. He spotted the steps and pointed. 'He came from up there. And I'd bet fifty Karls he's heading to the soutch dock.'

'The soutch dock? Why?' Goodweather said.

'Because of who's with him,' Dubnitz said grimly. Stepping over the bodies of the dead, they made their way to the stairs and then up. There were access points to the docks above strewn throughout the unterdock. Forcing the wooden cover aside, Dubnitz gagged as more of the foul-smelling mist poured down onto him and spilled down the stairs. 'Gods below, it smells even worse than it did before!'

'It's growing stronger,' Goodweather said, through the torn strip of robe she'd pressed to her nose and mouth.

'What is? What is it?'

'An abomination,' the priestess said curtly as Dubnitz helped her topside. The mist had settled between the structures and buildings of the docklands, obscuring the sight of the few people still about their business. Dubnitz heard the rattle of armour and saw a troop of watchmen hurry past, their faces tight with fear.

'Something's going on,' he said. In the distance, from the direction of the soutch dock, he saw the mist turn orange. He sniffed. 'Smoke.' Then, an instant later, an alarm bell began to ring loudly and desperately. He heard the shouts and knew in an instant what it was. 'Fire... come on!' he said, hurrying after the watchmen. The knight and the priestess moved as quickly as they were able through the dense mingling of the smoke and the mist. The crackle of flames filled their ears, and people lurched through the mist, fleeing.

Moaning, someone stumbled against Goodweather, knocking her off of her feet. She fell back onto her rear and looked up at a ruined face. Fleshless jaws worked mushily as the dead man reached for her. Dubnitz's sword sang out, decapitating the zombie. 'He's dead!' she said as she climbed to her feet.

'If he wasn't before, he is now,' Dubnitz said. He used his sword to point towards the harbour. 'Hear that? It's not just the fire. There's a fight going on out there!'

'Should we get help? Alert the watch?'

'No time. Besides, they'll figure it out soon enough!' Dubnitz growled, taking a tighter grip on his sword. 'Got anything in that bag of tricks that can clear this blasted fog?'

'I can try,' she said, reaching for more gull feathers. Out of the swirling whiteness, awkward shapes shambled. Dubnitz stepped forward, both hands wrapped around his sword's hilt.

'Hurry it up!' he said as the first ambulatory corpse came into view. A rusty cutlass struck out at him and Dubnitz batted it aside and took its wielder's arm off at the shoulder. The dead man gave no sign he'd noticed and simply reached for the knight with his remaining hand. Dubnitz took that one off as well, and then bisected the stubborn zombie. As the two halves thumped onto the wood, the second and third closed in, followed by the fourth, fifth and fifteenth. More and more of them shambled out of the mist, their blind eyes glowing with an eerie light.

'Where are they all coming from?' Goodweather said as she let a handful of feathers loose. Out here, closer to the clean sea, the breeze was far stronger then before and it flushed the mist back out from between the closest structures. What it revealed gave her her answer. There were dozens of the dead things staggering into the docklands from the sea. Not just dead men, either. There were the shapes of drowned horses and fenbeasts, Shallows-monsters, fish, eels, sharks and porpoises. A rotting octopus, missing most of its limbs, hauled itself across the dock, its eyes like poached eggs. They climbed up out of the water and across the docks, jetties and wharfs, striking out at whomever or whatever they came across.

'By Manann's foamy locks,' Dubnitz breathed, his sword point dipping. 'This isn't Fiducci's handiwork. It can't be.'

'It's not,' Goodweather said, pointing towards the harbour. 'Love of the Sea-Lord... it's not!'

'They're all over! Swarming like ants!' the bosun shrilled, ringing the alarm bell. There were more than a dozen ships becalmed in the harbour, and on each of them, the crews were setting up a clamour. Torches were lit and men grabbed for weapons. Cutlasses, boarding hooks and other implements of defence found their way into sweaty palms as every eye watched the mist, which had begun to roil like a hurricane-tossed sea. For hours, neither wind nor tide had touched the keel of any ship in the harbour. Yet now, something was happening. Dead things thrashed in the sea, and boathooks were deployed to shove off the rotting, climbing things that sought to board every ship, including the Nordland merchant vessel that was the closest to this newest disturbance.

When it happened, it happened so gently, so quietly, that no man on the deck noticed until it was too late to do anything beyond stare in slack-jawed awe at the apparition sliding out of the all-consuming mist. With neither wind nor oar to propel it, the ship cut through the water like a shark's fin. Its hull sagged from the weight of the barnacles that clung to it, and its sails were tattered wisps, the bare memory of once vibrant-coloured cloth. As it glided forward, the water seemed to shudder back from its warped prow, where the skull of some great leviathan had been lashed to the wood by heavy lengths of rusted chain.

It came on with no sound to mark its passage, and it neither slowed nor veered off as it approached the becalmed vessel. At the last moment, the quicker-witted among the crew gathered their senses enough to dive over the side and take their chances in the maelstrom the harbour had become. The others could only stare stupidly as the juggernaut bore down on them and then, with a terrible snapping and splintering of wood, the larger vessel split the smaller in two! The merchant vessel sank and the newcomer surged on, approaching the soutch dock like the hand of some vengeful god. Ancient cannon, crusted over with the filth of the sea, barked out a savage hymn and the soutch dock bucked beneath the onslaught. Docks ruptured and shattered. Bodies were thrown into the air like ragdolls and ships were burst at the waterline.

Eyll watched it all with a horrified fascination. His empire... everything his family had built... was gone in a flash. As burning body parts and wood rained down around him, he looked down at his hand, now bound tightly in a handkerchief of Cathyan silk which was thoroughly ruined by the blood seeping through it. He curled his fingers tight around it. 'I-I can't do this...' he moaned, watching another ship rise up on an explosion and sink.

'If you want to survive, you must!' Fiducci said. They stood on the dock, the eleven living women and the one dead behind them. Fiducci had cast a glamour upon them, and they were as listless as the dead things wandering nearby, including the one who truly was dead. Fiducci had animated her, so that her lolling corpse squirmed beside the others. 'It is a bold gamble, but it will work, and with a bit of luck, your family will again have the services of the captain!'

'And you?' Eyll said, still staring at the oncoming ship. 'You have yet to say what it is you want.' He glanced at the necromancer. Fiducci shrugged.

'If we survive, I'll make my price known eh?' He gestured to the pistol in Eyll's sash. 'Did you load the bullet I prepared?'

'Yes. Are you sure this will work?'

'Not in the least,' Fiducci said. 'But one can hope, eh?'

The death-ship slowed as it approached the dock and a pitted anchor dropped with a dull splash. Beneath the water the beasts that lurked in the shallows fled the shadow of the ship. Seaweeds and scummy algae turned brown and dead where the shadow fell, and those fish unlucky enough to be unable to avoid its clutches drifted upwards, belly up. Ancient chains squealed like hogs at the slaughter as lifeboats were lowered into the water. Everything was quiet, save for the sound of buildings burning and distant screams.

The captain had returned to harbour at last, and all of Marienburg held its breath. Eyll shuddered uncontrollably as below him, he felt the thud of the prow of the first lifeboat as it connected with the dock. Fiducci stiffened. 'He's here, Signor,' he whispered. Eyll glanced at the necromancer, and his heart sank. The little man's confidence seemed to have been washed away, and he sagged, his fingers intertwined as if in prayer.

Zombies climbed up onto the dock. These were in better condition than the others, and they carried weapons as if they still remembered in some fashion how to use them. Eyll's fingers stretched towards the butt of his pistol. 'Do something,' he hissed. Fiducci didn't reply. Eyll spun, and he gave a horrified groan as he realised that the little man was gone.

'Have I kept you waiting then, young Eel?' said a voice as deep and as horrible as the catacombs that now contained his family. 'Forgive me.'

A tomb-cold hand caught Eyll's own, pinning it in place as he turned and instinctively tried to draw the pistol. The cold crept up his arm and his eyes started from their sockets as he looked up at a face out of childhood nightmares. A spear-point nose, wide-flanged and quivering jutted pinkly from the sickly grey flesh of a beast-face. Teeth that were like triangular arrow-points both pierced and passed over worm-like lips, dappling the scabby thorn-bush beard with black blood. Eyes like wind-tossed torches held his own in a poisonous grip. He could feel tendrils of ancient scents and bad memories slithering through his brain as the eyes bored into him. A flat, tar-coloured tongue slid out through the thicket of teeth and waggled in the air as a fart of laughter made Eyll's legs go limp.

'Now, now. No need for that, little Eel. The captain won't hurt you, no,' the apparition hissed. 'Not when you've brought him a repast fit for an admiral, my yes.' The hell-eyes swivelled towards the shadows, where the offerings huddled.

'I-I...' Eyll began hesitantly. His mind groped for the words Fiducci had taught him. 'I want to pay my debt!' he blurted. The eyes swung back, freezing his tongue in place.

'Your many times great-grandfather and I had a bargain, young Eel, my yes. And such a bargain it was too. The oldest bargain. Blood for gold. Blood for the sea's bounty, every glittering morsel. But why would you want to end that bargain? Didn't I give him enough?' The cunning beast-eyes glowed like lamps.

'I want to pay my debt,' Eyll croaked again, wanting to look away but unable to do so. A chalk-coloured hand rose out from beneath the rotting cloak, and something glittered between the spidery fingers. Eyll's mouth went dry and he automatically stuck out his hand. Heavy coins plopped wetly one by one into his hand.

'There are older wrecks beneath the sea by far than Sigmar's petty kingdom.' Shark teeth snapped together. 'Good yellow gold from the Vampire Coast or the far seas that sweep the beaches of Tilea or Ind. All men love gold, young Eel. Just as I love other things...' The gurgling voice fell to a purr and Eyll shuddered. Clutching the gold to him, he made a motion to the chained women, who were beginning to come out of their stupor. One of them screamed, until a mossy hand clamped tight over her mouth. The zombies clustered around the women, pawing at them idly. He looked down at the gold again and swallowed the rush of bile that burned in his throat. 'Twelve souls. That's what the books said,' he said.

The captain laughed. 'Ha. Yes. Twelve innocent souls for one black one.' A moment later, black words dripped from his gnawed lips and there was a sudden rush of effluvium – a foul stink like Eyll imagined that the ocean's bottom must smell of. Bloated faces glared mindlessly at Eyll and then at the prisoners. 'Twelve pure souls for twelve generations of service, aye. Yesss. Let us have 'em, lads,' the captain said, shifting slightly. In the moonlight, Eyll caught a glimpse of tattered finery and rusted armour coated in barnacles and other things, some of which moved in an unpleasant fashion. 'Twelve good and true, my yes. I–' The captain broke off and spun suddenly, his cloak snapping wetly. Eyll heard him sniff and he cringed as the captain clawed at him with a narrow gaze. 'What is that I smell, young Eel? Got rot in the pork, have you?'

'No. No! No!' Panic tore through Eyll like a knife.

The captain seemed to ripple and bend like shadows beneath the surf. One moment he was there and the next... gone. Hastily, Eyll dropped the coins and tore the pistol from his sash. He cocked it with the edge of his bandaged palm and winced. The zombies hesitated, as if unsure of what to do. The captain reappeared next to one of the women... the dead one, Eyll realised with sickening dread.

'What's this? What's this?' The horrible eyes pinned Eyll. 'This one's no good, young Eel. Gone all overripe she has.' Teeth snapped together. 'Trying to flimflam me, are you?'

Eyll levelled his pistol. 'Just trying to survive, really,' he said weakly, and fired.

Dubnitz beheaded another zombie and charged towards Eyll and the thing that had come off the monstrous ship. His breath rasped hot in his chest as he ran full tilt, battering aside the dead in his haste to reach the living. Behind him, Goodweather hurried to keep up, her ragged robes tangling around her legs. As soon as he saw the creature, he knew what it was, if not who. Dubnitz had fought its kind before, with Ogg and the others, on a Sartosian expedition.

He cursed as Eyll fired at it, knowing it would be no good. The black manta-shape of the vampire lunged over the heads of the chained women and flowed through the soupy air towards Eyll. 'Free the women!' Dubnitz shouted at Goodweather. 'I'll handle the rest!'

Before the priestess could reply, Dubnitz had barrelled into the slinking shadow-shape and knocked it sprawling. Eyll gawped at him, the smoking pistol hanging forgotten in his hand. 'You? But you're–?'

'Still planning to arrest you!' Dubnitz snarled, backhanding the prince and sending him sprawling. 'But not just yet.' The zombies moved forward, weapons raised. Dubnitz tore into them, hacking them to pieces even as he bellowed a rough seaman's prayer. But even as the last of them slumped, fingers like bale-hooks sank into the back of his gorget and he was summarily jerked from his feet. He was thrown hard into a pile of crates, which shattered and covered him in fish.

'Come to challenge the captain, have you?' the vampire growled. Talons flexed and then, with a wet chuckle, it drew the cutlass hanging from its hip. The blade was big and worn, but not rusty in the least. 'Come on then,' it challenged.

Dubnitz crawled to his feet, head ringing from the force of his landing. Black blood dripped sluggishly down the creature's face from a circular hole in its temple. Evidently Eyll had left his mark. The vampire touched the wound and snarled loud enough to rattle Goetz's teeth. He stomped forward and the cutlass sprang to meet him. Every parry and reply stung his arms to the root. The vampire was far stronger an opponent than Dubnitz was used to, and it well knew how to use its strength. Also, the mist seemed to curl and tighten about his limbs, hindering his movement.

'The captain has spread red waters from here to Ind, little warrior,' the vampire said. 'He has butchered elven corsairs and broke the hump-backs of sea-beasts. You think you can stand against him?'

'That depends, are you him?' Dubnitz muttered through gritted teeth. He had only just blocked a blow that would have taken his head off and now he strained against the uncompromising weight of the vampire's fell blade. Snarling, the vampire jerked its sword to the side, pulling the knight off balance and punched him in the chest, sending him skidding back across the dock.

Dubnitz rolled to a stop with a clatter and gingerly felt at the fist-shaped dent in his cuirass. Breathing heavily, he pushed himself up and glanced around, looking for Goodweather. The mist, however, was too thick for him to spot anything but the loping shape of his opponent, trotting forward unhurriedly, black tongue caressing the tips of his dagger teeth.

'You fight well for a landlubber,' the vampire said. 'You'd make a fine bosun, strong lad like you.'

'Flattery won't save you,' Dubnitz wheezed, bringing his sword up. The vampire laughed and darted forward so swiftly that Dubnitz couldn't track him. The cutlass blade stopped inches from his face and the knight staggered back in surprise as the vampire suddenly dropped the weapon and clapped both hands to its skull. It shrieked and Dubnitz's ears throbbed.

'Scream all you want, captain,' Fiducci said, stepping out of the mist, holding up a strange sigil composed of writhing shapes. 'It will avail you nothing. Not with a shard of warpstone embedded in that corrupt brain of yours. And not when I hold this!'

'What-what-what?' the captain croaked. Green and black serum flowed down the vampire's craggy face as its fingers clawed at the wound in its skull.

'A little something I picked up in the East. Old Kemmler created it, according to its former owner. Made it to control your kind, which, apparently, it does. It harmonises with the warpstone, you see, creating a bond between this and thee,' the necromancer chuckled. 'You're mine, captain.'

'I think you mean mine,' Eyll said, stepping out of the fog, his pistol cocked. His jaw was purpling already from Dubnitz's blow. 'Forgetting yourself, Signor Fiducci?'

'I never forget myself, Signor Eyll. Merely my employer, once our business is concluded,' Fiducci said. He smiled nastily. 'You asked me what price I would demand. Well, there it is... the captain.'

'You promised me–' Eyll began.

'I promised you that I would save you from the captain. And I have. But I said nothing about myself,' Fiducci said. He pulled the sigil close. 'captain, be so kind as to tender my resignation, eh?'

The vampire whirled and with a frustrated snarl, dove upon Eyll. Eyll fired his pistol and then fell beneath the pouncing shape, which reduced him to a ruinous mess in mere moments. Above the sounds of bones snapping and flesh tearing, Fiducci howled with laughter. The necromancer danced a little jig, stopping only when his eyes settled on Dubnitz, who glared at him.

'You are annoyingly persistent, Erkhart,' Fiducci said. 'Like a wart that keeps coming back.'

Dubnitz straightened, trying to keep an eye on both the necromancer and the vampire. 'I won't pretend to know what was going on here, but I'm guessing it's another of your little schemes, corpse-eater.' He gestured with his sword. 'And I'll be damned if I let you get away with it.'

'Damned if you do, damned if you don't,' Fiducci giggled. 'Oh, captain...'

Dubnitz threw himself to the side as the vampire dove for him, its talons scraping grooves along his back. Rolling to his feet, he caromed off of another stack of crates and spun, hoping to land a blow. The vampire seemed to ooze around the edge of the sword and then its claws were at his throat and he felt himself being bent backwards. His gorget was ripped free and tossed aside, baring his throat to the greedy lamprey mouth that descended moments later.

The vampire stopped as an immense shadow spread across them. Fiducci's giggles died away into stunned silence as the wide crest of water rose above them and then summarily slammed down! Dubnitz was torn from the vampire's grip and tossed back up against a wall as the wave covered that section of the soutch dock and dissolved into puddles and foam.

Sputtering, Fiducci clawed around in the water. 'Where is it? Where–'

'Looking for this, are you?' the captain hissed, hefting the sigil in one talon. As Dubnitz pulled himself erect, the vampire crushed the device as easily as another man might crumple paper. 'Control me, would you? Better to attempt to control the tides.'

Fiducci fell onto his backside and began to splash away as the hulking shape of the vampire stalked towards him, clawed fingers flexing in eagerness.

'I know your kind, necromancer... remoras, clinging to king sharks. Thought you'd twist this sacred debt to your benefit, eh? Thought you'd make the captain your play-pretty, your cabin boy, eh? I'll give you a taste of the lash...'

As Dubnitz retrieved his sword, he saw Fiducci's hand dart into his robes and felt a sinking sensation in his gut as he realised just what the little man was after. 'No!' he said, darting forward. The vampire, between him and Fiducci, turned and caught him, wrenching him into the air.

'I'll settle our account first then, shall I?' the captain gurgled, eyes blazing. Behind him, Fiducci stuffed the scrimshaw whistle between his lips and blew a wet melody. Dubnitz, desperate, thrust his fingers into the leaking wound in the vampire's skull. The creature shrieked and released him, and Dubnitz dropped heavily to the dock. He could feel the wood trembling and hear the smashing of great bodies through the Shallows. The wood cracked and burst abruptly as a number of horrible shapes thrust their way up in response to Fiducci's summons.

Cutlass in hand again, the captain swung it as the first of Stromfel's Children dove for the vampire, wide mouth gaping. The vampire cleaved the thing in two and met the next, matching it snarl for snarl. Dubnitz barely reclaimed his own sword in time to fend off his own attackers. As they fought, Fiducci blew on the whistle again and again, until the becalmed harbour waters fairly boiled with heaving piscine nightmares. Where only moments before the sea had given up its dead, it now gave forth every monstrosity that stirred in the deep silt. Krakens with clashing beaks and frenzied sharks made mad war on the floating dead and the monstrous offspring of the storm-god. Alarm bells sang out as the docks came under attack.

Dubnitz stabbed something with entirely too many flippers and stepped past it, reaching for Fiducci, who seemed enraptured by the chaos he had caused. Dubnitz grabbed the necromancer around the back of the neck and flung him to the ground. 'You! Send them back!' he snapped.

'I think not! If Franco Fiducci is to be thwarted, the city itself shall pay!' the necromancer yowled. 'And you with it!' He yanked a dagger from his robes and stabbed wildly at Dubnitz.

The knight caught his arm and bent it back, forcing Fiducci to drop the blade. Driving his sword into the dock, he made a grab for Fiducci's other hand, where the whistle lurked. 'Give me that!'

'Get off of me you oaf!' Fiducci shrilled, struggling. The whistle slipped out of his grasp and Dubnitz batted it aside, into the thick of the confusion. Fiducci screamed and scrambled after it even as the shark-shape of the captain cleaved its way towards them.

'I'll have my due one way or another, necromancer!' the captain roared.

Dubnitz jerked his sword up and the cutlass scraped sparks the length of the interposed blade. Berserk, the vampire slashed at him, all pretence of humanity now gone from its form and feature. It hammered at him as if seeking to pound him flat, and he was in no shape to prevent it. It was only stubbornness keeping him upright and even that was fast fading.

'Dubnitz!'

He looked down as something skittered across the dock and saw a medallion emblazoned with Manann's sigil. He gave a furious shove, pushing the captain back long enough to clear enough room for him to snatch the medallion up. As the vampire swooped down on him again, he shoved the sigil into its face. The captain screeched and stumbled back, covering its eyes. Dubnitz's flush of victory faded quickly; he could only keep the beast at bay so long.

The trill of a whistle cut the air. Large shapes blundered out of the mist like hounds on the scent, and Dubnitz tensed, preparing for the attack. Only it was not be. The Shallows-beasts leapt on the captain, one after another, dogpiling the vampire beneath a mound of mutated flesh. The captain's angry shriek was cut abruptly short as the dock gave way in a fashion reminiscent of Dubnitz's earlier plunge.

Dubnitz hurried to the edge of the hole, his whole body aching. The captain glared up at him, jaws working, bloody foam bubbling from between ragged lips. A jagged spear of wood had been shoved up through the vampire's back and out through its chest. A claw stretched out towards Dubnitz with hateful intent and then sagged as the hell-light faded from the creature's eyes. The body slumped and began to dissolve like seaweed in the morning tide. Dubnitz sank back and sat down, his body shuddering with exhaustion and not a little relief.

'I'll have my medallion back now, if you please,' Goodweather said. The priestess picked her way carefully through the debris. Dubnitz looked at her wearily.

'The women?'

'Safe with the watchmen. Are you unhurt?'

'Yes. Yourself?'

'As well as can be expected,' she said, taking her medallion back and hanging it around her neck. 'My intervention appears to have been timely.'

'It's becoming a habit with you,' Dubnitz said. 'That wave–'

'You're welcome.' Goodweather opened her hand and showed him the whistle. 'And this will go back in the vault where it belongs.'

'I don't see Fiducci anywhere. I suppose it's too much to ask that the little rat got eaten by one of his own monsters...' Dubnitz sighed and stood. The mist was beginning to clear with the captain's demise and the fires were being put out. 'How in the name of Manann's trident am I going to explain any of this to Ogg?'

'I'm sure you'll think of something. As long as it's better than your explanation about the goat and the octopus,' Goodweather said, scattering salt over the bodies of the dead and beginning the rites of her order.

Dubnitz laughed, and the sound was echoed by the cries of the returning seabirds. The birds swooped and dove and followed the retreating mist back out to sea, as the wind picked up once more and the calm faded at last.

STROMFEL'S TEETH

Josh Reynolds

It was the afternoon of the eve of Mitterfruhl and the sound that rose from the streets was as deep and as black as the ocean bottom. Those who heard it first, mistook it for thunder. For the voice of the storm that had rolled in moments earlier from the Sea of Claws. The sound stalked beneath the celebratory ringing of the city's bells like a sea-beast through the shallows and tore the holiday cheer from the hearts of every citizen who heard it. And as the last, dull echoes drifted out to sea, Marienburg erupted in blood and terror.

Near the docklands, hooves struck sparks from rain-slick cobbles as the evening market crowd screamed and parted. A grocer flew into the air, conducting a lazy somersault, trailing red the entire way. A matron was slapped from Manann's realm to Morr's by a flick of inhuman claws. Something pearly grey and wet-skinned swam through the sea of humanity like a sword through flesh, leaving mangled wreckage in its wake. Saw-edged teeth slammed home on an outthrust arm, tearing and masticating.

The hooves thundered on, like an oncoming wave. Black, dead eyes rolled in tight sockets and the thing turned to face its pursuers as they burst out of the drover's way, their mounts lathered and snorting. Steam rolled off of the animals in the rain. The horses were clad in emerald and turquoise barding and carrying men in heavy armour of similar hues. The knights carried tridents and their armour was engraved with piscine designs. At their head, a bulldog figure leaned over his horse's neck and roared, 'There's the bugger!'

Manann take me if he's not a master of the obvious, Erkhart Dubnitz thought. The broad-shouldered knight grinned behind his visor as he looked at the stocky shape of Dietrich Ogg, Grandmaster of the most humble, and violent, Order of Manann galloping next to him. Ogg would spit him on a hook and use him for bait if he made such a crack out loud. Ogg's temper wasn't the best even when he hadn't been pulled from a warm feast-hall to ride through a storm in full armour, in pursuit of something with entirely too many teeth.

'Speaking of which,' Dubnitz muttered as the creature rose to its full

height, gill slits flaring and its wedge-shaped head swinging around. It wore
the tattered trousers of a sailor, now stretched and torn. It had the form of
a man, though much distorted by muscle, but its head was utterly inhuman. As it spread its arms, the horses skidded to a stop, issuing alarmed
neighs as their hooves splashed in the rainwater.

The knights had pursued the thing from the red ruins of a tavern deep
in Marienburg's bowels, and it had left a trail of death through the Nar-
rows as it made its way towards the North Dock. Monsters of one sort or
another weren't uncommon in Marienburg; things with too many limbs
or too few clustered beneath the docklands like barnacles and there were
stories of rats of unusual size in the sewers. Not to mention those one-eyed
devils in the marshes.

But this was something else again. It stood in the rain, barrel torso heaving,
as if it were having trouble breathing. To Dubnitz, it looked as if someone
had sewn a shark onto a bear and then beaten it until it got angry.

'Manann's scaly nethers, Dubnitz,' one of the knights breathed as he
fought to control his agitated mount. 'He's a big one!' Dubnitz glanced at
him. Gunter was young. A merchant's second son, his dreams of adventure
in the great wide world had been sewn up tight and kicked out of reach by
a handsome donation to the Order from his father. Still, once he'd come
out of his pout, the boy had taken to the spurs quickly enough.

'Bigger they are, Gunter,' Dubnitz said, absently dropping his fist between
his horse's ears. The animal snorted and calmed. Dubnitz flipped up his
visor and peered at the creature that waited for them at the other end of
the market square. 'Is that thing wearing trousers?'

'I do believe it is,' another knight said, cradling his trident in the crook
of his arm as he lit a scrimshaw pipe. He sucked thoughtfully on the stem.
'You don't suppose it's a modest beastie, do you?'

'If it is, it's doing a bad job of it, Ernst,' Dubnitz snorted. 'I can see it's–'

'Silence in the ranks.' Ogg gestured towards the creature with the small
trident that occupied the stump of his left hand. 'If you're quite finished
mooning over it, would someone go and whack its bloody ugly head off?'
he snarled, his pudgy features bathed in rain, torchlight and sweat. 'There's
a Mitterfruhl feast I'd like to get back to, thank you very much.'

The half-dozen knights all looked at one another surreptitiously. One of
the first rules you learned in the Order was never, ever, under any circumstances, volunteer for anything. Unfortunately, some took longer to learn
that lesson than others.

'Right, one spitted shark coming up,' Gunter said, kicking his horse into
motion before Dubnitz could stop him. The too-wide mouth gaped as the
young knight drew close. It lunged and tackled his horse, wrapping grey
arms around its neck and chest. As Gunter gave a yell and jabbed at it
with its trident, the creature turned, yanking the whinnying horse off its
feet and smashing both it and its hapless rider into the hard cobbles in

a crash of metal. Black talons snatched at the tangled knight's head. The ornate helmet burst, as did the skull within.

'Manann gather his poor, stupid soul,' Dubnitz snarled, slapping his visor down. He'd liked the lad. He dug his spurs into his horse's flanks. The creature tore Gunter's corpse free of the thrashing horse and swung it about before hurling it at the others. Horses reared as the body hit the street. The shark-thing did not pause, but dove on towards Ogg, jaws wide.

The Grandmaster tried to sidestep the creature, but the square was too crowded and it was too quick. It was on him a moment later, its talons tangled in his horse's barding. The jaws champed at him and Ogg cried out.

Dubnitz jerked his horse's reins, causing his mount to bump against Ogg's and both horses stumbled. The shark-thing lost its grip and rolled beneath the stamping hooves. The other knights had gotten over their shock and they closed in, hemming the creature in from all sides.

Tridents plunged towards it, driving it back before it could rise. It retreated, still silent; its eyes were empty of everything save raw, wild hunger. Its blunt snout rose and it audibly sniffed the salty air. Then it spun about and began to lope away.

'It's heading for the sea. Cut it off,' Ogg said.

'I'll do more than that,' Dubnitz said, urging his horse into a gallop. The crowded streets were rapidly emptying as the creature raced on. It had fallen onto all fours, its heavily muscled limbs pumping. It shouldered aside a fruit wagon and toppled a night soil cart, spilling dung across the street. Dubnitz cocked back his arm, hefting his trident as his horse leapt over the fallen cart. 'Manann guide my aim,' he muttered, blinking rain out of his eyes. With a grunt, he hurled the trident, catching the creature in the back. It stumbled and caromed off a wall. It twisted around, snapping at the weapon that had suddenly sprouted from its back.

Dubnitz circled it and his horse snorted and shied as the thing snapped blindly at it. The shark-thing shook its head and darted forward. Dubnitz's horse reared and he was almost thrown from the saddle. The knight reached out and grabbed the haft of his trident, hoping to pin the creature down. Instead, he was ripped off his horse as the creature began to thrash.

Dubnitz hit the ground hard, his armour scraping on the cobbles. A clawed foot stomped down, nearly doing for his head the way it had done for poor Gunter's. Dubnitz rolled awkwardly to his feet even as the shark-thing loomed over him. Foul breath washed over him and he swept his sword from its sheath in a wild, wide arc. Blood sprayed the far side of the street and the monster staggered, clutching at its split, hopefully useless jaw. Dubnitz didn't give it a chance to recover. He sprang past it and grabbed for the trident, kicking it in the back of its leg as he did so.

It toppled with a wheeze. He shoved on the trident, knocking the thing flat. It squirmed beneath him, gnawing at the cobbles. A sharp elbow hit his cuirass hard enough to put a dent in it. Dubnitz staggered, wheezing. The creature yanked itself off the street and whirled towards him. He swung his sword at it, but it caught his wrist in an unyielding grip. He dug his free hand into its throat, but it didn't seem to notice, so intent was it on getting its teeth into him. Its weight drove him back and began to bend him double as it leaned against him. It stank of the deep places of the sea.

Dubnitz glared through the eye-slits in his faceplate, meeting the thing's eyes. For an instant, just an instant, he thought he caught sight of something in them other than hunger. Then its bloody, shattered jaws spread wide and it bent its head towards him.

A moment later, its skull ruptured like an overripe fruit, splattering him with cold blood. He tore himself free of its grip and let the body slump. As it fell, it revealed a tall, one-eyed man who thrust a smoking Hochland hunting rifle into the hands of one of the soldiers behind him. The latter were clad in the uniforms of the Marsh Watch, and bore the insignia of Manann's golden trident on their uniforms.

'Dubnitz,' the one-eyed man said, stripping off his gloves as he approached the body of the shark-thing. One of the men accompanying him trotted close behind with an upraised shield to keep the rain off of his master. Dubnitz stood and saluted with his sword.

'Lord Justicar,' Dubnitz said. 'It is, as ever, a delight and a joy to see you.'

Aloysious Ambrosius, Master of the Marsh Watch and Lord Justicar of Marienburg, grunted and squatted, looking at the dead creature. Dubnitz turned as Ogg and the other knights rode up. Ogg's face went through a number of contortions as he caught sight of Ambrosius before settling on what he likely thought was an expression of pleasure. 'Aloysious,' Ogg grated.

'Dietrich. Lovely weather we're having,' Ambrosius said as he examined the creature.

'At least it's not raining cuttlefish again,' Ogg said. 'What are you doing?'

Ambrosius didn't answer. 'What have we here?' he said as he reached beneath the creature and jerked loose something small. Holding it up to the rain to clean the blood off, it was revealed to be a shark's tooth on a thin cord.

'A shark with a shark-tooth amulet,' Dubnitz said. 'That's not odd at all, is it?'

'Coincidence is the bugbear of lazy minds,' Ambrosius said, rising to his feet. He rubbed his eye-patch with the heel of his hand. 'One of these things just attacked me in the opera house, Dietrich.'

'And it escaped?' Ogg demanded. He turned in his saddle. 'Mount up! We'll–'

'Calm down,' Ambrosius snorted. 'Of course it didn't escape; I dispatched it. Cost me a cape of fine Cathayan silk though,' he added regretfully. 'And it ruined my evening.'

'Manann forfend,' Dubnitz said. Ogg and Ambrosius looked at him. The latter snorted and kicked the creature's body.

'Indeed. I–'

The sound was as deep and as solid as a punch to the gut, and it interrupted the Lord Justicar just as effectively. The first toll shuddered through those gathered in the square and lumbered on towards the docks. Dubnitz staggered, feeling ill. It tolled again, and the street seemed to shiver. Distant screams erupted, and an alarm bell began to ring. 'What was that?' Dubnitz said, looking around. More alarm bells began to sound, ranging from the silvery peal of the fire bell on the Street of Mercy to the deep, grim boom of the Mourners' Bell in the Garden of Morr near the Marsh Gate. And then, finally, the long, low melodious sound of the ship's bell mounted above the doors of Manann's own temple.

'It's the Tide Bell,' Ogg said. His eyes were wide with dismay. 'Erkhart, Ernst, get going. The rest of you, pair off in squads and ride for the other temples.'

'I just got my pipe lit!' Ernst complained as he dumped the contents of his pipe on the street and stuffed it back within his saddle.

'Isn't that always the way of it?' Dubnitz said as he climbed back into the saddle. Moments later he and Ernst were riding hard for the Temple of Manann. Smoke from dozens of fires rolled through the city streets, and the rain beat it down into a slushy scum of ash. People ran through the streets, fleeing in panic. The celebratory mood of Mitterfruhl had turned into terrified anarchy.

'Pity about Gunter,' Ernst said as they forced their horses through a choked square. 'Lad had real promise, I thought.'

'Promise is no proof against teeth and claws,' Dubnitz said sourly. 'Or against bad wagers. Did you know he still owed me five Karls?'

'Owed–' Ernst began as his eyes widened in sudden realization. 'By Manann's sea cucumber, that little rat owed me as well!' He began to curse virulently. Dubnitz nodded sympathetically.

'Do you think his family might cover his debts?' Ernst said hopefully a moment later.

'One thing at a time,' Dubnitz said, pointing.

The square before the Temple of Manann was packed with a heaving crowd. It was an undeniably angry heaving crowd at that and it pressed close about the doors of the temple. Several pale-faced temple guards stood between the crowd and the doors, their tridents locked to form a makeshift barrier. 'This looks bad,' Ernst said, gripping his own trident more tightly.

'Get between those guards and the crowd,' Dubnitz said, kicking his horse into motion. He swatted about him with the flat of his trident, causing the fringe of the crowd to contract. People were yelling and screaming in a mingled cacophony of fear and anger. In times of trouble, people looked to their gods, but such a mob had been too quick to form. There was something other than blind panic at work here.

'Get back or get trampled,' he roared as he nudged his horse into the current of curses, boils and rude gestures. 'Don't make me come down there.' Probing hands went for his legs and his saddle and he gave a portly fishmonger a jab with the business end of his trident. 'This horse is church property, get off.'

As his horse spun, lashing out with its back-hooves, Dubnitz caught sight of several priests of the sea-god standing on the marble steps of the temple, watching in consternation. Only one of them was a familiar face. 'Goodweather,' Dubnitz bellowed, 'Fancy seeing you here!'

The young woman, slim and dark, blinked in surprise as she caught sight of Dubnitz. She gave a half-hearted wave as Dubnitz urged his horse closer to the line of temple guards. 'Goodweather, can't you summon one of those winds of yours, or how about something nastier?' Dubnitz said, leaning over in his saddle.

'What are you doing here, Erkhart?' she hissed, gathering up her robes and stalking down the steps. 'I thought I told you to–'

'What? Stay away from a temple dedicated to my patron god?' Dubnitz said in mock disbelief. 'And just because of a simple misunderstanding,' he continued.

'Is that what you call it?' Goodweather snapped, glaring at him. Dubnitz flipped up his visor.

'Of course,' he said, beaming at her. 'It was dark. Mistakes were made.'

Her fingers curled into claws. 'Mistakes,' she repeated darkly.

'Yes. I thought she was you, obviously. Forgive me?' he said, leaning down towards her. Her punch, when it came, nearly knocked him off his horse. She hopped back as he righted himself, clutching her hand and cursing. He rubbed his jaw. 'Is that a no?'

'Yes,' she snarled.

'Yes you forgive me, or yes it's a no?' Dubnitz said.

'We don't need your help!' Goodweather said.

'Looks to me like you do,' Dubnitz said, looking back at the crowd. The faces of the crowd were studies in frustration, fear and anger. Most of them were just scared. Some of them were trouble-makers looking to make whatever was going on worse. And others... his eyes narrowed as he caught sight of a particular, peculiar figure, standing on an overturned cart and gesticulating in a frenzied fashion.

The man was all ribs and shoulders, with coarse clothing and a dozen shark-tooth necklaces clattering around his scrawny neck. Strange tattoos covered his puckered, tough looking skin and warning bells went off in Dubnitz's head. 'Oh that's not right,' he muttered. He turned back to the fuming Goodweather. 'See that skinny fellow on the cart there, Goodweather? What do you make of him?' he said.

Before she could reply, someone hurled a cobblestone into the head of one of the temple guards. The man's head snapped back and he toppled like a felled tree. Dubnitz cursed and jerked around in his saddle as Goodweather rushed towards the fallen man.

'If you're finished fraternising, Erkhart, I could use some bloody help!' Ernst shouted, flailing about with his trident. His horse snorted as a human wave surged up around him, hands grabbing and improvised weapons stabbing, hacking or thumping. The crowd, unpleasant looking before, had turned ugly in a matter of moments. More cobblestones flew, accompanied by dung, bricks and several contradictory political slogans. Someone somewhere was beating a drum in time to the sound of the Tide Bell ringing. Dubnitz rode to the aid of his fellow-knight, but as he cut through the crowd, his horse gave a terrified snort and reared up.

The sickening sound tolled again, rattling his teeth in his jaw and causing the world to spin before his eyes. His stomach felt like it had the first time he had ever climbed to a crow's nest, as if it were full and falling all at the same time. His horse reared again, screaming and lashing out at something he couldn't see.

He heard cries of fright and saw bodies tumble past, trailing blood through the rain. A familiar smell bit into his sinuses and he forced his horse to drop down, revealing the hideous shape that was blossoming before him. The man was no different from any other; he had the look of a sailor or a sea-jack. He screamed and thrashed, his ballooning limbs snapping out to swat aside anyone who got too close. His eyes met Dubnitz's and he reached out with fingers that looked like overcooked sausages.

'Huh-help muh-meeee...' he whined. His words spiralled up into a wordless shriek as pink flesh turned grey as twitching limbs wobbled in an unpleasant fashion. Bones cracked, splintered and re-knit even as the flesh on them puffed up and split and the face, once human, tore in half to reveal a great triangular maw full of razor teeth.

'Gods below,' Dubnitz hissed. The creature, obviously in agony, thrashed about as it tore too-tight clothing off. It was the spitting image of the monster from earlier; possibly uglier, in fact, if it was possible. Before it could realise he was there, he stabbed down at its roiling flesh with his trident. The prongs sank into the mutating meat and the trident was jerked from his grip as the creature whipped around. Talons fastened on his horse's snout and a single, savage jerk snapped the animal's neck and nearly decapitated it.

Dubnitz roared as he was forced to drop out of the saddle. He hit the street and immediately found himself being trampled upon by fleeing people. Luckily, his armour kept the damage to a minimum and he soon forced himself to his feet, just in time to meet the monster's awkward, flopping charge. Moving quickly in full armour was difficult, but a strong desire not to be disembowelled lent him speed. He stumbled aside as the creature bounded past him, pouncing on a luckless man. The creature's victim screamed just once before the shark-thing bit his head off in a single wide-mouthed bite. Dubnitz waited for the nearest bystanders to clear out of the way and then drew his sword.

The shark-thing stuffed the rest of the body into its maw, chewing noisily. Its black eyes scanned the crowd like those of the animal it resembled; there was no glee there, no sadistic pleasure, nothing to imply that the thing gained any enjoyment from its actions. It had no impetus but cold, pure hunger.

Dubnitz advanced towards it, sword held out before him. It turned, slurping a twitching foot down its gullet. Dubnitz grimaced and then blinked as he caught sight of a shark's-tooth necklace dangling from its bulbous throat, the material of the necklace itself biting into the thing's gray skin. He wanted to look around, to see if the skinny man with his many necklaces was capering about somewhere, but he didn't dare take his eyes off the monster.

It gazed at him hungrily and started forward, picking up speed as it came. Dubnitz ducked under a wild sweep of its claws and his sword drew a red line across its barrel chest. The creature gave no indication that it felt any pain as it dropped a fist on him, knocking him to one knee. It snagged a fleeing woman as Dubnitz fought the catch his breath and took a leisurely bite out of her neck.

'Monster,' Dubnitz snarled. He lunged and the beast flung the woman's body at him, sending him stumbling. It jumped at him with a quickness that belied its size and its claws sank into his armour.

'Hold fast, Erkhart,' Ernst shouted, galloping towards Dubnitz and his opponent. The other knight threw his trident, catching the shark-thing in its thigh. It shoved Dubnitz aside and turned, yanking the weapon loose in a spray of blood. As Ernst rode past, chopping down on it with his sword, it slapped him out of the saddle with the trident. Ernst crashed into the street and lay unmoving. The creature stalked towards him, still clutching the trident.

Dubnitz rushed towards it and drove his sword between its shoulder-blades. It shuddered and threw its arms wide. He threw himself against the hilt, forcing the blade in deeper, hoping to shatter its spine or pierce something vital. It hunched over, chomping at the air. He was nearly pulled off of his feet, but he drove a boot into the small of its back and ripped his sword free. The shark-thing turned and grabbed for him. He backpedalled and chopped into its wrist. The blade cut halfway through its limb and stopped. It whipped its arm aside, pulling his sword out of his grip and stabbing at him with the trident. The tines scraped off of his cuirass and he tripped over his own feet, landing heavily.

Coughing blood, the creature raised the trident over him. It dove towards his head and his palms slapped together around the outer tines. Jerking his head to the side, he guided the points into the street and kicked at the creature's belly. It was like kicking a wall, but it rocked back, off balance. Desperate, he grabbed the head of the trident and snatched it out of the creature's slack grip. Spinning the weapon around, he jammed it into the creature's belly. It loomed over him, jaws snapping, and began to pull itself down the length of the trident.

'Dubnitz, get the necklace!' Goodweather screamed from somewhere just out of sight. 'Get the necklace you great oaf!'

He lunged for the necklace and hooked it with a finger even as the thing's saw-edged teeth scraped his visor. Dubnitz ripped it free and the creature convulsed as if he'd removed a limb. It bucked and thrashed and he rolled it off of him with a grunt of disgust. It curled around the trident and its heels thudded into the street as steam began to boil off of it, carrying a strange stench into the air.

Dubnitz watched in horrified fascination as the creature began to shrink back to human proportions. It sloughed off the corrupted grey hide, revealing bloody pink flesh beneath. The man gasped and gazed at him blankly. His wounds had not disappeared and as Dubnitz sank down beside him, he coughed, muttered and went still. He didn't look much like a cultist; then, they never did.

Still, he had asked for help. What cultist or mutant would do that? The knight closed the corpse's staring eyes and stood as Goodweather moved quickly towards Ernst's splayed form. Moving towards her, Dubnitz said, 'Is he...?'

'No. Just had his lights put out is all,' she said, looking at him over her shoulder. 'More than I can say for some.' Dubnitz looked around. The square was now host to a scene of carnage – bodies laid heaped here and there, mostly the result of the crowd's panic at the creature's initial appearance. The survivors had cleared out quick enough, and the other priests were endeavouring to help those that they could, while the temple guard looked on warily. The air stank of smoke and blood, despite the rain washing both away. Alarm bells were still ringing, and he could hear the crackle of fire and the clash of weapons. The latter was likely the Dock Watch or Ambrosius's Marsh Watch snapping into action with all the speed an underpaid, unenthusiastic autocratic body could muster.

He looked back at Goodweather. She was an altogether more pleasant sight. Women weren't a common fixture in the Grand Temple of Manann. Thus, Goodweather was, in many ways, an uncommon woman. She knew the holy sea-shanties backwards and forwards, even the rude bits most priests left out. And she had a punch like a mule.

'We've sent for the priestesses of Shallya, but they're in the same situation we were,' Goodweather said, wiping her hands on her robes and standing. 'There're mobs at every temple. What,' she said, noticing the look on his face.

Dubnitz coughed and shook his head. 'We might want to send runners and warn them to be on the look-out for more individuals wearing these little beauties,' Dubnitz said, letting the shark's tooth necklace dangle from his fingers. 'How did you know, by the way?'

'I guessed,' she said with a shrug.

'Dubnitz blinked. 'What?'

'In the stories, it's always the amulet. Or the crown, or the glove or the ring, some out of place innocuous thing,' she said, turning back towards the temple. She gestured to two of the guards. 'Pick him up,' she said, motioning to Ernst. They hastened to obey.

'Well, regardless of your astonishing disregard for my safety, you were right,' Dubnitz said, hurrying after her. 'The question is, why?'

'Stories are stories for a reason,' she said. She stopped and looked at him. 'There's something moving in the city. It's in the air and the water; it's in the rain, Erkhart,' she said, holding out a hand. The rain filled her palm and gleamed greasily before she dumped it onto the street. 'It's moving through Marienburg, just out of sight and sense.'

'Like a shark in the shallows,' Dubnitz said, holding up the necklace and eyeing it.

'Are you trying to be funny?' she snapped.

'No,' he said. He bounced the shark's tooth on his palm. It felt warm. He turned, prompted by some instinct. 'Hunh,' he said.

'What?' Goodweather said.

'I wonder what happened to our friend with a neck full of necklaces just like this one, the skinny wastrel on the cart. I suppose it's too much to hope he got trampled.' He looked at her. 'Did you see him?'

'No, I was distracted by the monster,' she said tersely. 'Give me that!' She snatched the necklace out of his hands. A moment later she grunted and almost dropped it.

'What?' Dubnitz said.

'Stromfels,' she hissed, turning the tooth over to reveal a curiously shaped scratch in the surface. The tooth seemed to squirm in the rain, and Dubnitz felt a prickling, crawling sensation in his gut.

'Oh bugger,' he said. Stromfels... the god of pirates, storms and sharks. Every sailor's least favourite things. The worship of the shark-god had long been outlawed in Marienburg, thought furtive sects still worshipped him in badly lit back rooms and isolated tributaries out in the marshes. It was a name that every follower of Manann, devout or otherwise, knew well. Stromfels was the bogeyman... the dark of the deep sea and the doom that waited down below the white-capped waves. 'Was he just some deranged cultist then? Daemon-possessed?' he said, his mouth suddenly dry. He looked back towards the body of the man who'd been a shark. Was that what it had been? He thought again of the confused, despairing look in the man's eyes and shuddered.

'If he was, then he was not alone,' someone said. Dubnitz turned and his eyes went cross as he stared down the tip of a sword. On the blade dangled a half-dozen more necklaces like the one Goodweather held. Most of them were bloody. Dubnitz looked up.

'Lord Justicar,' he said. 'Ah, I ¬– that is to say, we–'

'I see,' Ambrosius said, leaning across the pommel of his saddle, his sword blade resting on his forearm. Dots of blood marred his cheek and armour. His horse whickered softly and stamped a hoof dangerously close to Dubnitz's instep. Past the animal's rump, Dubnitz saw members of the Marsh Watch, mostly looking worse for wear, moving through the carnage of the temple square, arresting those who weren't dead or dying. Ambrosius tilted his blade, spilling the necklaces into Goodweather's hands. 'We have reports of more of the creatures, though we've only managed to kill a few. Their numbers are increasing. I am alarmed by this,' he said calmly. 'Ogg and the others are protecting the other temples in the district, as well as certain other, ah, strategically important areas.' That meant they'd be guarding the richest and most influential members of Marienburg society, Dubnitz knew. Even in the midst of a crisis, Ambrosius was keenly aware of which side his bread was buttered on.

Goodweather looked at the pile of teeth in her cupped palms and her face took on a slightly queasy look. Dubnitz looked up at the Lord Justicar. 'That's a lot of monsters,' he said.

'One is more than this city needs,' Ambrosius said grimly.

'Mitterfruhl,' Goodweather said suddenly. The two men looked at her. She made a face. 'Mitterfruhl – the beginning of the rainy season–is a day sacred to Stromfels. Traditionally, it's when his worshippers made their sacrifices.' She looked up. 'Storms were a sign of Stromfels's pleasure.'

Thunder grumbled and the grey sky looked swollen and ill as Dubnitz looked up at it. 'Sacrifices,' he said. 'As in more than one, you mean.'

'Stromfels is a hungry god,' Goodweather said. 'He is as hungry as the ocean and twice as wild.'

'Very poetic,' Ambrosius said, sheathing his sword. 'These amulets then are... what? Signs of his favour?'

'That poor bastard didn't seem very favoured to me,' Dubnitz said, nodding towards the body of the former shark-man. Several more of Goodweather's fellow priests surrounded the body and were engaged in a purification ritual involving sea-salt and crushed seagull bones. 'More surprised really,' he murmured.

'What?' Goodweather said, looking annoyed.

He looked again at the necklaces. 'They're all the same, aren't they?' he said.

'What are you getting at, Dubnitz?' Ambrosius said.

'They're all the same!' Dubnitz said, gesturing to the teeth. He grabbed one of the amulets and pulled the cord tight. 'Look at this.'

'It's made of horse hair,' Goodweather said, looking puzzled.

'Not what it's made of but how it was made,' Dubnitz said. 'I grew up in the Tannery, remember?' Located in the maze of streets that played host to the city's tanneries, the Tannery was a squalid, foul-smelling territory and the gangs of mule-skinners and cat's meat-men who made it their home were as dangerous as any dock-tough or river-rat. 'Weave-men have particular ways of making cords. It's like a signature of sorts.'

'And these all have the same signature,' Goodweather said, examining the others. She looked at him in shock. 'Manann carry me, but your head might be useful for something other than balance.'

'Now do you forgive me?' he said. She glared at him but didn't reply. Dubnitz looked at Ambrosius. 'These were all made by the same person,' he said.

'I gathered, thank you,' Ambrosius said. 'The question would be, who?'

'No idea,' Dubnitz said, grinning. 'But I know how to find out.' Dubnitz pointed towards one of the large marble statues of Manann that stood watch around the temple square. 'If anyone will know where these are coming from it's that little mud-puppy,' he said, indicating the boy who was crouched on the statue and watching the goings-on in the square. His blue coat was unbuttoned, likely because the brass buttons had been pawned. A ragged sash was wrapped around his waist, with a rust-dotted sailing knife thrust through it. Bare feet and fingers clung to Manann's marble beard, despite the rain.

The blue-coats were omnipresent on the streets of Marienburg, especially when there was trouble afoot. If there was a riot or a festival or a brawl, they'd be there, on the fringes. People no longer even noticed them. Whether orphaned or abandoned, they all wore the same blue-dyed coats given to them by the priests who ran the Tar Street workhouses, and they all scampered through the streets like miniature northern savages, yelping and howling when those houses emptied for the evening.

'What would a street-cur know about Stromfels?' Ambrosius said.

'Likely a surprising amount,' Dubnitz said, tapping the side of his nose. 'You wouldn't believe what people let slip around little shell-like ears.' Without waiting for a reply, Dubnitz strode towards the statue. When he reached it, he looked up at the boy. 'Renaldo, you little snake. Get down here. I need to talk to you.'

'Talk to me from down there, steel-fish,' Renaldo said, sticking out his tongue. Renaldo was a regular face in the Temple of Manann. Dubnitz knew he begged alms from the merchants and picked the pockets of drunken seamen in the square. He'd boxed the boy's ears more than once for trying the latter on Dubnitz himself.

Dubnitz grunted. 'I have a job for you, you ungrateful little eel.'

'Does it pay in food or fancies?' Renaldo said, shimmying along Manann's outthrust arm. He hung upside down from the extended trident, his dark eyes narrowed cunningly.

'Both. Either,' Dubnitz said. He let the shark's tooth amulet dangle from his fingers. The effect on Renaldo was immediate. The boy hissed like the stray cat he resembled and scooted back up the statue. Dubnitz blinked. 'That was unexpected. Renaldo, get back here!'

'I ain't taking that, steel-fish! I saw what those things do!'

'And what's that?' Dubnitz pressed, circling the statue in pursuit of the boy.

'They're cursed!' Renaldo barked.

'Yes, well, I need to know where they're coming from,' Dubnitz said. 'You don't have to fondle the damn thing, just tell me where they're coming from!'

'Ikel!' Renaldo crowed, eyeing Dubnitz suspiciously from behind Manann's crown.

'What's an Ikel?' Dubnitz said.

'It's not a what, steel-fish, it's a who,' Renaldo said. He stood on Manann's shoulder and leaned against the statue's head. 'Ikel the marsh-man. He came into the Tannery about a week ago. He's been shilling those teeth in the Beggar's Market. Oleg the blind beggar tried to filch a few and Ikel cut him a sharp smile over his kidneys.'

'Wouldn't be the first time Oleg had to digest a bit of steel,' Dubnitz grunted. 'The Beggar's Market, you say?' A thought occurred to him. 'What's Ikel look like? Is he an inked-up gentleman, perchance?'

'Like a squid shat on him,' Renaldo said, nodding.

'Wonderful,' Dubnitz said. 'Best scarper Renaldo, lest the Marsh Watch get hold of you.' Dubnitz watched the boy slide away into the growing dusk and turned back to Ambrosius and Goodweather. 'Beggar's Market,' he called out, tossing the amulet up and catching it. 'Fellow called Ikel.'

'You have a way with children,' Goodweather said.

'I'm something of a hero to the downtrodden, yes,' Dubnitz said, puffing out his chest.

'Be that as it may, is the boy's information good?' Ambrosius demanded. 'Can we trust it?'

'As much as anything heard on the streets,' Dubnitz said, tossing the necklace back to Goodweather. 'I think Ikel was here earlier. Watching the festivities.'

Ambrosius's eye narrowed. 'Hnf. Priestess Goodweather?'

'Stromfels is an enemy of Manann,' Goodweather said, dumping the necklaces into the pouch on her belt. 'Our missionaries in the marshes and in the north have been attacked before.'

Ambrosius sighed. 'Fine. You two will go to the Beggar's Market. Find this Ikel. Take him into custody.' He looked at Dubnitz. 'That means I want him alive, Dubnitz.'

'But of course, Lord Justicar,' Dubnitz said, banging a fist against his cuirass smartly.

'You want me to go with him?' Goodweather said, her tone implying that she hadn't heard Ambrosius correctly.

'You have worked together before, yes?' Ambrosius said, pulling on his horse's reins and turning about. 'Far be it from me to break up a successful partnership. Get me Ikel.'

'But–' Goodweather began, following Ambrosius.

'And do hurry,' Ambrosius said, ignoring the priestess.

'But-but–' Goodweather said, watching Ambrosius ride away.

Dubnitz coughed into his fist. Goodweather turned and glared at him. 'What?' Dubnitz said.

'Let's just be about this,' Goodweather snarled.

Luckily, the Tannery was close to the docklands. Marienburg was in a tumult. The streets were packed with people fleeing in one direction or another; some sought the safety of the temples while others huddled in taverns and shops. Though the shark-things were few, the rumours of them were flying thick through the canal-streets. Looters were mistaken for daemon-worshippers and the armoured knights of the Order of Manann for the black-iron clad warriors of the north. Mobs of panic-stricken citizens burned the buildings of their neighbours as old grudges blossomed into violence. Through it all, the rain pounded down like the tears of Marienburg's many gods.

Several times Dubnitz was forced to fend off the attentions of the opportunistic and terror-maddened. His sword was heavy with blood as he forced Goodweather through the throngs clogging the streets. However, those throngs thinned as they entered the Tannery, eventually disappearing entirely.

The Beggar's Market occupied a natural meeting point between several side streets in the Tannery. The stink of boiling fat and rotting meat was thick on the wet air. The streets were empty of life, save the scrabbling of rats in the gutters. Something crashed in the distance. Dubnitz wondered if another of the shark-things was loose somewhere. Ambrosius had said as much. The thought made his muscles tense. The haze of still-burning fires danced above the rooftops like a false dawn.

'I shouldn't be here,' Goodweather said. She had her hood pulled low, and the symbol of Manann was displayed prominently on her chest. 'I should be at the temple. There are things to be done.'

'Are they more important than countering the machinations of the minions of the shark-god?' Dubnitz said, his palm resting on his sword hilt. Drying blood dotted his armour, hiding the piscine designs beneath red splashes.

'Minions,' Goodweather repeated, looking at him.

'What would you call them?' Dubnitz said.

Goodweather merely shook her head and looked around. Empty stalls lined the walls of the buildings on either side of the street. On any other night, rain or not, those stalls would be crammed with men and women selling their wares. The Beggar's Market was almost a parody of the great mercantile squares that occupied other parts of Marienburg. Here was where the poor came to buy and sell their pitiful wares; they were doing neither tonight.

'How do we tell which stall we're looking for? And where is everyone?' Goodweather said.

'As to the latter, I can only guess. But as to the former... there!' He pointed. The shark's jaws were larger than any beast Dubnitz had had the misfortune to meet in the sea or otherwise. They spread wide on a rough cut wooden post mounted over a dingy stall. 'They're not a subtle folk, these worshippers of the shark-god.'

'No,' Goodweather said grimly. 'Stromfels is as subtle as the oncoming storm.'

'And as remorseless,' Dubnitz said. 'That explains that. The people of the Tannery have always had a nose for trouble. They go to ground like rats when trouble rears its head.' He held up a hand. 'Hsst...we're being watched,' he said softly. Goodweather twitched and looked around, her fingers sliding towards the knife on her belt.

'Why didn't the Lord Justicar send any men with us?' she muttered. The knife in her hand was hooked and serrated, the blade engraved with the name of Manann.

'Probably because he had none to spare, Goodweather,' Dubnitz said, his eyes flickering across the street. 'The whole city is going up in flames and inundated with monsters. Finding one man, no matter how important, isn't high on his list of priorities.'

'There's no guarantee that Ikel is even here!' Goodweather snapped, looking around warily.

'So who's watching us then, hmm?' Dubnitz said. The two of them had moved back to back instinctively. The rain had picked up, coming down now in semi-opaque sheets. Thunder snarled and then, the deep tolling rolled through Dubnitz's bones. Goodweather gasped and clutched at her chest. The puddles of water collecting on the street rippled and the rain wavered into weird shapes.

Shapes rose suddenly from the street, clad in rags and trash, their faces masked by blackened peat bags. Swords, axes and clubs were gripped tight in grimy hands. In silence, they rushed towards the duo. Dubnitz drew his sword and chopped upwards into an attacker's skull in one smooth motion, cutting the man in two from chin to pate. He turned as another, carrying a rusty billhook, leapt wildly at Goodweather. The priestess flung out a hand, and a fistful of fish-scales drifted towards her attacker. The flimsy, tiny scales pierced the man's chest, arms and face like tiny arrows, leaving blisters and burns in their wake. The man screamed and fell, clawing at himself. Goodweather swept her hooked knife out and cut his throat with one economic bend of her elbow.

Dubnitz shoved her aside as an axe dropped towards her head. He caught the blade on his own, and sparks dripped into his face as the two weapons slid across one another with a squeal. He kicked out and was rewarded with the sound of snapping bone. The axe-man fell, and Dubnitz caught him on the back of the neck with his sword. The head rolled loose into the gutter.

There was a scream from behind him and as he turned he saw a cultist stagger, clawing at the billhook sticking up from his back. Goodweather put a boot and jerked the confiscated weapon loose. Dubnitz inclined his head and she gave him a sharp nod. Then, her eyes widened and she hurled the billhook.

Dubnitz cursed and fell backwards. The billhook scraped across his cuirass as it caught his attacker in the throat, dropping the man into a heap. 'Nice throw,' he said, straightening up and turning towards her.

'Not really,' she said, as the last of their attackers pressed the edge of his notched cutlass to her throat meaningfully.

'Drop your sword,' the man growled, his voice muffled by his mask.

'No,' Dubnitz said, starting forward.

'I'll kill her,' the other said.

'He'll kill me,' Goodweather added.

'No he won't,' Dubnitz said, drawing closer, the rain pattering across his armour.

'He won't?' Goodweather said.

'I will!' the cultist said.

'You won't,' Dubnitz said. 'Because if you do kill her, I'll hurt you for it.'

'I do not fear death,' the cultist said.

'I didn't say anything about death. I said I'd hurt you. And I will. I will personally oversee your sentence in the Temple of Manann. I will put the Question to you again and again, until you are nothing more than shark-chum. Your every moment will be an eternity of agony, my friend, and I will not let it end,' Dubnitz said mildly. He stopped and extended his sword. 'It's your choice, of course.'

The cultist shoved aside Goodweather with a cry and launched himself at Dubnitz. Dubnitz beat aside the cutlass with an almost gentle gesture and spun around, swatting the man on the back of the head with the flat of his blade. The cultist dropped onto the water-logged street like a pole-axed ox. Dubnitz looked at Goodweather, who was rubbing her throat. 'Are you all right?'

'Yes. Nice speech,' she said.

'I meant every word,' he said softly.

'Of course you meant it. You always mean what you say, when you say it. That's the problem, Erkhart,' Goodweather said. Dubnitz fell silent. He occupied himself with jerking the cultist to his feet and shaking him into sensibility.

'Up,' Dubnitz barked. The man groaned and Dubnitz prodded him with the tip of his sword. 'Where's Ikel? Did he know we were coming?'

The cultist didn't answer, shaking his head. Dubnitz lifted the man's chin with his sword. 'Talk, or I'll begin carving the Litanies of the Sea on you, friend. And my friend here has enough salt to do the job properly.'

'Erkhart...' Goodweather began.

'I know what I'm doing,' Dubnitz said, glancing at her. She shook her head.

'So do I. Hold him,' she said. As Dubnitz swung the weakly struggling cultist around, Goodweather scooped up two handfuls of rainwater. She murmured into her cupped hands, and the water bubbled in a strange fashion as she placed it beneath the cultist's nose. Steam rose from the water. 'Take off his mask,' she said. Dubnitz complied. The cultist was a pale faced, pop-eyed man, with strange ritualistic scars on his cheeks and forehead. The steam wavered in the rain and then plunged up into his nose and eyes. The cultist shuddered and gurgled.

The hairs on the back of Dubnitz's neck rose as the body in his grip went slack. 'What are you–' he began. Goodweather silenced him with a look.

Finally, she stepped back. 'Release him.'

Dubnitz did, and gladly. The prayers of the servants of Manann were a strange, wild thing and though he served the god, Dubnitz knew that there were mysteries that he would never be privy to. The cultist jerked back and forth, gurgling. 'Lead us to Ikel,' Goodweather said, her face slick with rain and sweat. Her eyes showed the strain of what she was doing. The cultist spun and staggered, like a marionette. Then, with a moan, he stumbled off.

'Let's go,' Goodweather said hoarsely. Dubnitz followed her.

'What did you do to him?'

'A simple trick, though I've never tried it with anything larger than a seagull,' she said. She rubbed her head. 'As long as the steam stays in him, he'll do as we say. Manann will compel him. But once it escapes...'

'Hopefully he'll get us to where we need to go then,' Dubnitz said.

The cultist led them on a crooked, circuitous route through the Tannery. As they entered a badly lit cul-de-sac, the deep, black tolling happened again, and it made Dubnitz's head feel as if it were fit to burst. Goodweather grabbed her head and nearly sank to her knees. Prayers to Manann burst from her lips in desperate speed. The cultist shuddered to a stop as it happened, steam rising from his ears, mouth and nose. The street seemed to be submerged beneath murky water and vast, terrifying shapes slid between the buildings, swimming from shadow to shadow.

Dubnitz opened his mouth to speak, and bubbles flowed into the air around his head. The rain had become something else entirely. His limbs felt sluggish and leaden and as the echoes of the deep boom faded, and those immense, terrible shapes shot past and over him into the city faster than any bird, the world snapped back to normality.

Goodweather clutched at her amulet, her thumbs pressed tight to the trident symbol of Manann. She looked at him, her face pale and her eyes wide with horror. Dubnitz knew that his own face was likely the mirror image of hers, but he shook it off.

The cultist lay limp on the street, his body contorted and rigid. Dubnitz didn't have to examine him to know he was dead. 'I think we've found the place,' he rasped.

The store front had seen better years. It was shabby even by the standards of the Tannery and it smelled of rotting fish. A number of the latter had been nailed to the lintel, their blank eyes staring out at the street. It was only by looking carefully that Dubnitz could tell that the fish had been nailed up in the shape of Stromfels's symbol. He felt cold and sick and he hesitated before the door.

'We could go back. We could get help,' Goodweather said from behind him.

'And what would happen between now and then, eh?' Dubnitz growled, all humour gone. He looked up into the rain. There was a feeling on the air, like sailors got just before that first storm-tossed wave crested the bow and caused the boat to dip alarmingly. 'Those bells – whatever they are – are becoming stronger. You felt it as well as I did.'

'We're at the eye of the storm,' Goodweather said. She gingerly touched one of the fish and then drew her fingers back as if they'd been burned. She looked at him. 'Erkhart...'

'I know,' he said. Then he lifted a boot and kicked the door in. Sword at the ready, he shouldered his way in. Rain dripped down through the sagging ceiling and ran in rusty runnels across the mouldy wooden planks of the floor. There was a vile smell, like a pig left too long on the butcher's block in the summer air. 'You'd think there'd be more guards,' he said quietly.

Goodweather stepped past him. She pulled a gull feather from her pouch and released it. A cool breeze, smelling of the clean sea, took it and carried it through the shop towards the back of the room. The feather dropped to the floor and spun gently in a small circle. Dubnitz stood over it, his eyes narrowed. He dropped to his haunches and, with his sword-point he traced the edges of a trapdoor out in the thin skin of mould that covered the floor.

Carefully, he levered it open with his blade, revealing an unpleasant looking set of stairs. A foul stink wafted upwards-he smelled blood, and stale water. He looked at Goodweather. 'Ladies first,' he said.

'Manann's sword before Manann's shield,' she said piously.

'Bloody dark down there,' he said.

'Isn't it?' she said. Dubnitz sighed and started down. The smooth stone of the foundations were wet to the touch, sweating with the stuff of the canals which criss-crossed the city. No place in Marienburg was more than a few feet from the water, whether it was fresh or salt, canal, marsh or sea. The city floated on moist foundations, the stones eroded century by century. Dubnitz paused at the curve of the stairs. Weak torchlight illuminated the bottom steps and he could hear the steady slap-slap of water against stone. Some places in the Tannery had underground docks, for moving illicit goods into the marshes or deep wells that provided water.

Goodweather pressed against his back. He continued down. Goodweather gasped as they caught sight of the first body. The man lay sprawled in the corner across from the steps. His hands were curled around the handle of the knife buried to the hilt in his belly. He was not alone. A dozen more bodies filled the oddly angled confines of the cellar. More than a dozen, in fact. Bodies were heaped upon bodies, all with self-inflicted wounds and all surrounding the deep well of scummy water that occupied the centre of the cellar.

In fact only three living forms occupied the cellar as Dubnitz and Goodweather reached it. A man easily recognizable as Ikel was one and the other two were soon of no consequence. As Dubnitz stepped forward, the two cultists stabbed each other and fell in a heap.

As they fell, the strange, fang-like shard of black stone that thrust out of the dark water of the pool shuddered and vibrated with a hideous bell-like peal of noise. It was thunderous in the confines of the cellar, causing the stones to grind against one another. The water swirled suddenly with a number of water-spouts and Dubnitz shielded his face as shadowy immensities burst free of the pool as the bell-noise pounded at his bones and eardrums. The shadow-things shot upwards, passing through the upper floor and away as the echoes of the bell faded.

Blinking through the pain of the sound, Dubnitz focused on Ikel, who smiled at him in apparent recognition. The cultist grinned, revealing crudely filed teeth. 'You're too late,' he said. 'Stromfels's teeth dig deep into the meat of Manann's realm. The King of Sharks will have his Mitterfruhl feast.'

'Looks like he'll be doing it sans guests,' Dubnitz said, kicking a body. Ikel chuckled.

'Blood must enter the water to bring the sharks,' the cultist said.

Dubnitz caught Goodweather's eye. Her face was as stiff as those of the corpses that lay around them. 'They needed a sacrifice.'

'Blood calls to beasts,' Ikel cackled, rattling the shark's teeth necklaces he wore. 'We gave them away freely. Good luck charms we called them, and aye, so they are... Stromfels's luck!' Dubnitz saw that the black stone was studded with such teeth. Indeed they almost seemed to be growing from the rock like barnacles. Hundreds, thousands of sharp shark's teeth poked through the slick surface of the stone and the sight of them made his flesh prickle.

'What?' he said.

'The necklaces,' Goodweather breathed. Her voice was full of horror and loathing. 'The teeth are parts of Stromfels, parts of his power, even as this symbol I wear is Manann's.'

The realization hit Dubnitz like a fist. 'Then everyone wearing one of those...'

'They belong to Stromfels now!' Ikel yelped. 'They are Stromfels. Or they will be. It takes blood, so much blood...' Dubnitz froze, remembering the great shadows he had seen. Moving like sharks through the streets. Had they been seeking the wearers of the necklaces? Were they daemons hunting hosts to use to feed and ravage the city of the sea-god?

'What was the point?' Dubnitz said, tearing his eyes from the stone and moving closer to Ikel, who sidled aside, his fingers tapping on the hilt of the knife thrust through his belt.

'Careful Erkhart,' Goodweather said. 'Don't let him do it.'

'Don't let him do what?' Dubnitz snapped.

'Don't let him kill himself. If he kills himself, the sacrifice will be completed,' Goodweather said. 'And those who haven't been transformed yet will be.'

'Silence,' Ikel snapped. 'Manann has no voice here. This is Stromfels's place. Stromfels's temple!' He gestured wildly at the black stone. 'His teeth pierce the veil of Manann's flesh, opening the way for us... for all of us!'

'To do what then?' Dubnitz said harshly, his eyes on the knife in Ikel's belt. If he could keep him talking...

'To feed the god,' Ikel said. 'Stromfels is as hungry as the ocean, and like the ocean he must be fed.' He drew the knife. 'His children burst through the veil and feed on the unworthy. And it is our honour to help them.' Ikel lifted the knife to his throat. 'It is my honour–'

'No!' Goodweather shouted, flinging her own blade. It slid across Ikel's wrist and he yelped and dropped his knife. Goodweather leapt on him, robes flapping. 'Erkhart, get the stone,' she said.

'And do what with it?' Dubnitz roared, plunging into the water. It closed about his legs greedily, and his limbs went immediately numb, nearly causing him to fall. Things brushed against his knees and he nearly fell forward into the stone. He caught himself at the last minute, his hands shooting out against the stone. Impossibly, the metal and thick leather of his gauntlets gave way before the teeth like thin paper and Dubnitz snarled in pain. He jerked his throbbing hands back. His palms bled freely.

Goodweather, struggling with Ikel, shouted, 'Get it out of the water. Hurry!'

Dubnitz looked at her and then at the stone. It gleamed nastily and he hesitated to touch it again. But, not knowing what else to do, he sank down into the water, digging for its base. His blood coloured the water as his fingers were shredded. Pain ran wild up his forearms and sparks bounced at the edges of his vision. It felt like his hands were being chewed.

'Dubnitz, hurry!' Goodweather called from behind him.

With a groan, Dubnitz lifted the stone. His chest and shoulders swelled and his feet slid beneath the water as he ripped it free of the pool. Fangs fastened into his thigh as some unseen something coiled about his legs. He stamped blindly, and a powerful blow crashed into his back, nearly knocking him over. He staggered forward, still holding the stone aloft. It seemed to grow heavier, its weight doubling and tripling. His arms trembled as he fought to reach the edge of the pool.

In his head, he heard the slash of a shark's fin through eternal waters and the thunder of a great, gluttonous heart. His lungs were full of water and the smell of his blood spread across the spirit-sea that held Stromfels and his progeny. Shadow-things spun around him, darting at the edges of his vision and fear cut through him like a knife. 'Manann help me,' he muttered. For the first time in his life, the prayer was a sincere one.

He caught a glimpse of movement, and saw Goodweather on her back among the bodies, Ikel straddling her, his filed teeth darting for her throat. Dubnitz, reacting on instinct, bellowed and hurled the stone at the cultist. It caught Ikel in the head and shoulders and he fell without a sound, the black stone settling on him with an almost hungry squelching sound. Despite the blood, there was no toll of sound. No shadow-things springing from the water's depths to rampage through his city. Nothing, save a disappointed silence.

The waters of the pool thrashed suddenly and then went still. The oppressive feeling of the cellar faded slowly, as if whatever presence had been causing it were receding. Dubnitz collapsed, half in and half out of the water. He coughed and looked at Goodweather, who got to her feet slowly. 'Did it work?' he said, pulling himself out of the water.

'I don't know,' she said, looking around. 'I think so.'

'You think so? You seemed bloody certain when you were ordering me in there!' Dubnitz growled, trying to get to his feet and failing. His hands and legs were covered in blood and the shredded remnants of his armour.

She helped him sit up. 'It seemed like the thing to do.'

'Seemed like the...' Dubnitz gaped at her. 'Are you saying you guessed?'

'I suppose I did, yes,' Goodweather said hesitantly.

Dubnitz began to laugh, softly at first, and then great, echoing guffaws. Goodweather joined him and the sound of their mingled laughter drove the last lingering shadows back into the depths.

LORDS OF THE MARSH

Josh Reynolds

'I was drunk,' Erkhart Dubnitz said, stepping back to avoid the rapier's tip. The deck of the *Fenrunner* rolled beneath his feet and the rail of the river-barge connected with his hips. He held up his big hands, palm out, trying to look simultaneously innocent and contrite. As a true son of the Most Holy Templar Order of Manann, Dubnitz was equally bad at both, and his expression slid more easily into one of slightly panicked guilt. He wasn't frightened, but he was worried. It had been miscalculation on his part. It had been enjoyable, but, in retrospect, unwise.

'That's no excuse for despoiling my sister, you-you lout!' Sternhope Sark barked. The Averlander wore what passed for finery in Averheim, but his rapier was real enough and sharp. The tip of the blade scratched across the enamelled sea-green surface of Dubnitz's cuirass, marring Manann's face with a thin scar. Dubnitz's gauntleted hand snapped shut on the blade and jerked it and Sark's arm forward. The rapier's tip bit into the rail and Dubnitz's other fist came down on the flat of the blade where it met the crosspiece, snapping the thin metal.

'Whoops,' Dubnitz said, flinging the broken blade into the Reik. There was a heavy mist on the river, and it seemed to reach up and clutch for the rail as Dubnitz turned back to Sark. 'How clumsy of me, I do apologise.' There was a murmur of laughter from the nearby crew, and they gathered to watch. There was little to do on a barge, and any entertainment was good entertainment.

Sark gawped at him for a moment. Then, with a hiss, he struck at Dubnitz's face with the broken end of the blade. Dubnitz grabbed Sark's wrists and wrestled him around, trapping the smaller man between him and the rail. Dubnitz's forehead connected briefly with Sark's and the latter's limbs went noodle-limp. Dubnitz grunted as a thin trickle of blood ran down from his brow, across his cheek and into his beard. Averlanders were a prickly lot when they were sober, in his experience. They were worse than Reiklanders, in their way, but he couldn't fault the young man's determination.

'And I'd hardly call what I did despoliation,' Dubnitz said, grabbing the young man's coat to keep him on his feet. 'It was more a peaceful transfer of military aid, if anything.'

'Are all Marienburgers so bad at euphemisms, Erkhart?'

Dubnitz turned and glanced at the woman who had pushed through the throng of sailors who had gathered to watch the confrontation. There was a resemblance about the cheeks to the young man he held, which, given that they were siblings, was no surprise. Sascha Sark was dressed in the latest Nuln had to offer for the upper-class out-of-doors woman, with an exquisitely carved iron and wood hunting crossbow held braced against the ample swell of her hip. She was flanked by two bodyguards, the best money could buy.

'We're a simple folk, Sascha. Unsophisticated, even,' Dubnitz said. 'Granted, we also manage to keep our private affairs private.' The light cast over the deck by the lanterns mounted on the mast and swoop of the rail was becoming muted by the evening mist rising from the river. The mist crept across the deck sliding between the feet of those gathered. Something about it pricked at his instincts, but he dismissed it, being more concerned with the matter at hand.

'We're on a boat, Erkhart,' Sascha said glibly.

'We weren't on a boat in Nuln, Sascha. In fact, I seem to recall a very soft bed and–' Dubnitz began, momentarily lost in a bouquet of pleasurable memories. It hadn't been his idea, but then, he'd never been one to say 'no' to a lady.

'Fiend,' Sark mumbled, grabbing at Dubnitz. The mist was creeping up his slumped form and Dubnitz waved it away. It had the smell of the Reik on it, which was unpleasant enough, but there was something else just beneath it... the stink of standing water or old stone perhaps.

'Knight,' Dubnitz corrected, still looking at Sascha. 'Why did you tell him?'

'Why did you bed me?' she countered.

Dubnitz snorted. 'Fine, but you could have waited, perhaps, until after the order's business with your family was concluded.' The business in question was trained warhorses, specifically the Order of Manann's lack of them and the Sark family's possession of some of the finest horseflesh in the Old World. Dubnitz had been sent by Grandmaster Ogg to sweet-talk the horse merchants into opening up a business relationship with the order, which he'd done. 'More or less,' he muttered. The mist reared up before him and he had a momentary impression of a striking serpent. He blew the tendril into swirling threads. It was thicker than normal for this time of year.

'What was that?' Sascha said.

'Nothing, my lady,' Dubnitz said, beaming. 'I trust that this won't sour our burgeoning relationship.' The Sarks had insisted on sending representatives to Marienburg to meet with Ogg and the Masters of the Order. Of those representatives, he found Sascha to be the most convivial for obvious reasons. Her brother, he thought, was mostly along to glower at the proper points during the negotiations.

Sascha laughed. It wasn't a polite laugh, or a girlish laugh. It was crude and bursting with innuendo. Dubnitz suddenly recalled that it had been that laugh that had led him to his current predicament. 'I meant in regards to the horses my humble and pious order requires if we are to serve the good folk as Manann, in all of his foamy wisdom, intended.'

'You're thugs in armour, Erkhart, nothing more.' Which was true, as far as it went; the order was a work-in-progress, as Ogg liked to state. It was a halfway professional fighting force, composed of the best of the worst, and dedicated, roughly, to spreading the word of the god of the seas. 'Nonetheless, we are happy enough to sell you horses, should my brother agree.' Sascha gestured to her brother, smiling prettily.

Dubnitz looked down at the semi-conscious young man and sighed. 'Wonderful.'

Sascha was a cunning one. After several weeks in her close company, Dubnitz had become grudgingly aware that there was a very good reason that it was she who had been sent. He wasn't afraid to admit that she had had him wrapped around her finger within an hour of their first meeting. In Nuln, he had done his level best to abuse his hosts' hospitality in several tried and true methods, and one or two that he hadn't even considered, before Sascha had suggested them. It was a game that Dubnitz knew how to play. However, it was disconcerting to discover that his opponent was even better at playing it than he was.

Ogg should really have sent someone else, someone more... pious.

'I don't suppose I could convince you to tell him that he slipped?' he said hopefully.

Before Sascha could reply, there was a crunch. It was a loud sound, and the faces of the sailors turned ashen as the boat shuddered. Dubnitz knew that sound. The bottom of the river boat had struck something. An alarm bell began to ring, the sound of it muffled by the thick blanket of mist that had settled on the boat.

'What was that?' Sascha said.

'It sounds like we've run afoul of something,' Dubnitz said. He peered over the rail. Something splashed, out past the rail. Then something else, there were more splashes and a number of thumps. The mist boiled up over the rail like a billowing curtain. He squinted, thinking he'd seen lights flickering in the mist. Suddenly wary, Dubnitz reached for the sword sheathed on his hip. Sark struggled in his grip and he released the merchant, shoving him towards his sister. 'Sascha, get your brother back to your cabin and stay there.'

'What is it?' Sascha said. Her bodyguards tensed, looking around. Like him, they had sensed something wrong. Both men were veterans of Nuln's infamous Blacklegs regiment, and as swordsmen, only Dubnitz was their equal. They had enough battlefield experience to know when something went wrong.

'Maybe nothing,' Dubnitz said, trying to see through the mist. He could barely make out a shape near the waterline. They had struck something. He saw skeletal trees looming through the mist and the shore was covered in the thick grasses that marked the Cursed Marshes. The Reik was separated from the darker waters of the marsh only by the thickly clustered hummocks and boils of earth and soggy stretches of semi-dry land that the marshes consisted of.

As always, whenever he passed through these narrow waterways, his mind conjured any number of ways in which the trip could go wrong. Now the worst had apparently happened. But not as the result of random happenstance, he suspected. He loosened his sword in its sheath. There were so many stories about the Cursed Marshes that it was hard to know what to be afraid of. It was the haunt of mutants, Chaos-worshippers, goblins and less physical threats. Ghosts clung to forgotten structures and swamp-goblins ambushed Marsh-Watch patrols every full moon.

But this was something different.

'Erkhart, what is it?' Sascha said again. The mist seemed to swallow the sound of her voice.

'Stay back,' Dubnitz began. His eyes narrowed and then widened.

'Lady Sark, you should go back to your cabin,' one of the bodyguards said, grabbing for her arm. She cast a hot glare at him and he sighed and stepped back.

'Sarks do no cower in cabins, Helmut,' she snapped.

'What is it? What do you see?' Sark demanded, throwing his own glare at Dubnitz. His previous ire had been washed aside by concern. Hot-headed the boy might be, but Averlanders were a practical lot at the bone.

'Nothing, but that doesn't mean...' Dubnitz trailed off. His eyes were tearing up from the strain of trying to see through the mist, and he blinked. Something was moving out there. All he saw were hints and vague bubbles of movement, swelling in the mist. He heard thumps and scrapes and his gaze travelled down, where the soup of the mist clutched at the hull.

Something rose to the surface. Sharp and stiff, it cut into the wood with a dull noise. Dubnitz blinked. Was that–?

More sharp things stabbed the hull. Something metal swooped past him and chopped into the rail – a grappling hook. Dubnitz stepped back with an oath.

'What is it?' Sascha said, her voice rising.

'Get back!' Dubnitz snapped.

Faces pierced the mist, grinning like wolves. Sabres, cutlasses, spears and axes followed as their attackers gave vent to blood-curdling cries. Dubnitz jerked back as a spear skidded off his pauldron and danced across his earlobe, sending a rush of warmth down the inside of his gorget. He cursed and chopped down, splitting the spear. Its wielder stumbled, off balance, and Dubnitz opened his throat to the bone.

But even as the one fell, more replaced him. Dubnitz was forced back from the rail. 'Pirates,' someone yelled. ''Ware, pirates,' the cry bounced from crewman to crewman. In these parts, piracy wasn't confined to the open ocean. Much trade was moved along the Reik, and where there were valuables there were men who would look to take such for themselves. Still, for pirates to have gotten this close to a fully-crewed barge was astonishing. The river-jackals were normally more cautious, laying breakwater chains and playing wrecker on rougher waters. Perhaps the mist had made them ambitious.

'Take the big one first!' a pirate barked, swinging a club towards Dubnitz's head. Dubnitz caught the blow on his vambrace and the club cracked. As the pirate gawped, Dubnitz split his skull, crown to chin. He kicked the dead man in the midsection and jerked his sword free. More blades and clubs and spears sought him and he grabbed the dying man and flung him into a knot of his attackers. 'Manann,' he bellowed, lashing out with his sword.

'Stromfels,' someone shouted in reply, invoking the god of pirates and storms. The mist cleared and a broad shape stepped forward, sword extended, gold teeth glinting in the torchlight. He was around Dubnitz's size, though rangier, with years of hard-living stamped on his face. At his gesture, the pirates retreated.

Dubnitz stiffened, his eyes narrowing in recognition of both the face and the voice. 'Fulmeyer,' he growled. 'I heard that the Reiklanders had stretched your neck.'

'If it isn't my old friend Dubnitz,' the pirate said. 'Still stringing up honest river-men?'

'Who is this devil?' Sark demanded, his hands clutching emptily for the rapier Dubnitz had broken. The two groups faced each other tensely, the pirates on one side, the crew on the other and only the mist separating them, like a thin curtain caught in a breeze.

'A dead man,' Dubnitz said tersely.

'Quintus Fulmeyer, at your service,' Fulmeyer said, spreading his arms. 'Some call me the Marsh-Hound, but none do it twice.' His dark eyes narrowed. 'Dubnitz here tried to have me hung.'

'Several times,' Dubnitz said, tightening his grip on his sword. 'I should have just done it myself.'

Fulmeyer laughed. 'Maybe you should have at that. Fancy running into you here,' he said. 'The gods truly are kind.' Fulmeyer was one of those thorns that you never realised was in your side until it began to hurt. He was a pirate's pirate, and Dubnitz dearly hated pirates, especially ones with the temerity to avoid Manann's justice on three separate occasions.

'They are indeed,' Dubnitz said, starting forward. Fulmeyer stepped back and raised his blade.

'I have more than twenty men, Dubnitz. And you've no troop of mounted knights to aid you this time. Just some poxy sailors and a handful of toffs,'

Fulmeyer said. 'Surrender, as we'd rather not kill any we don't have to. We have you fair and square,' the pirate barked. 'No need for this to turn bloody.'

Dubnitz was about to comment, but before he could so much as open his mouth, a crossbow suddenly went tung and a bolt spiralled through the mist towards Fulmeyer, who squawked and fell back. The bolt narrowly missed his hunched form. Dubnitz glanced back at Sascha, who was already reloading her crossbow. 'What was that?' he said incredulously.

'You Marienburgers talk too much,' Sascha said, lifting her reloaded crossbow. Before Dubnitz could reply, the pirates surged forward with a full-throated roar. The fight was brutal, and swift. The *Fenrunner* had a small crew, and the pirates outnumbered them two to one. Nonetheless, the former fought like born brawlers. Sascha's bodyguards took a terrible toll also.

But the pirates had other, unnatural advantages on their side. Dubnitz's skin crawled as the mist seemed to thicken and grip at him, as if to aid the pirates. Coils of wet air snagged his sword-arm, slowing his blows and causing him to stumble. Too, the dank smell of it invaded his head, causing his vision to blur and his lungs to seize. Was it sorcery, he wondered. It wouldn't be the first time he had faced a daemon-spawned mist, after all.

Thoughts of that brought a longing for absent companions. He wished Goodweather were here with him. The priestess of Manann's prayers could easily have dispersed the mist, which seemed possessed of an almost malign will. And that will was bent towards hampering the increasingly desperate efforts of the defenders of the river boat. Fulmeyer had never displayed any mystical acumen in their previous encounters, however. This was something new... something dangerous. Perhaps the pirate had hired a hedge-mage or some grave-robbing necromancer to help him. Such criminal activities were well within the Marsh-Hound's purview.

Dubnitz cursed as he saw one of Sascha's bodyguards stumble, as if something had pulled on his ankle. A moment later, Fulmeyer brained him with his sword, dropping the ex-soldier to the deck, blood running from his eyes and ears. The other bodyguard gave a coughing roar and swooped to the attack, but Fulmeyer merely stepped back into the mist, avoiding the wild blow.

In his place, a quintet of spears shot from all sides, impaling the hapless warrior. The mist cleared slightly as the pirates jerked their weapons free. Dubnitz was on them a moment later, charging across the blood-slick deck with an agility born of experience. Two of the five fell before the others retreated, leaving Dubnitz surrounded by a muffling wall of mist.

'Sascha,' he called out. 'Sark,' he tried. No answer from either. The alarm bell had fallen silent. The sounds of combat had faded. Dubnitz's skin crawled. There was a hint of distant noise, like heavy bodies moving through the water.

'It's over, Dubnitz,' Fulmeyer's voice said, from close by. 'Drop your sword.'

'Or what, you'll kill me?' Dubnitz said, his eyes scanning the mist. Were the Sarks still alive? If not, Ogg would kill him.

'We'll do that anyway, it's more a question of the way of it,' Fulmeyer said.

Dubnitz licked his lips, and tried to pierce the swirling mist. He didn't like the sound of that. He cleared his throat. 'If you want my sword, Marsh-Hound... come and take it.'

Feet scraped on the deck. A cutlass chopped into the back of his cuirass, shredding a strap and sending a flare of pain shooting through his back and chest. Dubnitz stumbled forward, his chest striking the rail. He pushed himself around and his sword slashed through the curling mist, releasing a spray of red. A scream faded to a gurgle.

'You'll have to do better than that,' Dubnitz said, breathing heavily.

Two men emerged from the mist with twin yells. Dubnitz's sword cut the head from one's hand-axe and finished its arc buried in the second man's side. Dubnitz jerked the dying man around and threw him into his fellow. The moment's distraction enabled him to deal with the survivor.

Boathooks burst past the falling body of the second man, thumping into his chest. His armour was thick enough that the hooks did little damage. But the rail wasn't as sturdy. Wood cracked and then Dubnitz was falling backwards. His vision lurched as vertigo conquered his thoughts for several terrified moments and then the mist swallowed him. A moment later, the Reik did the same.

The water was cold as he sank into its embrace. He could taste mud and foulness as he clawed vainly for the surface. His body felt as if it were being crushed in a giant's fist. His vision blurred as the dark water burned his eyes and seared his sinuses as it sought out his nostrils, ear canals and mouth.

Knights of the order learned early on how to swim in armour. It was a survival skill, when most of your business was done on the decks of ships. But the river had its own ideas. He felt the bottom of the Reik beneath his feet, and mud billowed up around him. His lungs began to burn. He couldn't see.

Men who were unarmoured and excellent swimmers had drowned in the shallowest areas of the Reik. It was murderous, as bodies of water went. Part of him thought that maybe, just maybe, he should simply acquiesce to fate. Nonetheless, he began to walk. His body throbbed with weakness, but he pushed on, until he saw a ripple of orange light above and he shoved himself upwards, reaching. His face split the surface of the water and he swallowed a gulp of air even as the weight of his armour pulled him back down.

He shoved his panic aside. The river bank wasn't far, not if the boat had run aground, and surely Manann, bless his scaly nethers, wouldn't let one of his chosen warriors drown. As the claws of oxygen deprivation squeezed his mind into an ever-shrinking black ball, Dubnitz forced himself forward, fighting against weight and the current's pull, using his sword as an anchor against the latter.

Something dark spread above him agonising moments later, and things like bony fingers scratched his face and armour and he grabbed at them. The soft solidity of waterlogged wood met his palm and he reached out with sudden hope. His thoughts were sputtering like a candle flame in a wind as he heaved himself up out of the water with the help of the tangled roots of the fallen tree. The tree rested in a bend in the river and it had been newly felled. The boat had struck it, and torn out its hull.

As his vision cleared, Dubnitz saw that the source of light he'd seen from below was the *Fenrunner*. It had been set ablaze, likely after being picked clean. His heart sank. But just as quickly as it had come, the black mood was swept away by adrenaline. Several shapes moved on the shore, searching through what could only be the *Fenrunner*'s cargo. The pirates had dumped it on shore, by the looks of it.

A born pragmatist, Dubnitz reviewed his choices as he clung to the tree. He could attempt to make his way back to Marienburg and return with a force of knights or even Ambrosius's Marsh-Watch. Granted, if he returned to Marienburg without the Sarks, Ogg would gut him like a fish and Ogg was more frightening than any mist-borne daemon or savage pirate.

There was little for it. Once more, Erkhart Dubnitz was forced by circumstance to play hero. It was not a role he relished, but it beat the alternative.

Carefully, and as quietly as he could, Dubnitz eased himself along the roots, pulling himself towards the dubious safety of shore. The Cursed Marshes weren't dry land by any stretch of the imagination, being more akin to a scum of slime mould atop the water, but it was safer to be above the mould than below it. Water dripped in runnels down his sea-green armour as he pulled himself up into the light of the burning boat. No one had spotted him yet.

The main body of the pirates were nowhere in sight, leaving only the three scavengers he saw. Stragglers, then, Dubnitz decided. He squinted. The mist was gone as well. There was no sign of the surviving crew or the Sarks, though they could still be aboard the boat. The stink of burning flesh was heavy on the air, weighing it down. He looked at the fire, a swell of mingled emotions rolling through him.

'Roll it towards the fire,' one of the pirates said, kicking a crate and interrupting Dubnitz's ruminations. He was big and bearded, with eyes like ugly coals. 'Fulmeyer wants what's left burned while they take the prisoners to the stones.' There was a certain shuddering emphasis placed on that last word that piqued Dubnitz's curiosity. Even more importantly, the Sarks were likely still alive. Fulmeyer had an eye for prisoners. Ransoms had been his game early and often.

'Seems a shame,' another said, fondling a bolt of Cathayan silk. 'Was a time when we'd have taken the boat and everything with it,' he added.

'Better times,' added the third.

'Shut your mouths,' said the first. 'We've made our bargain now, and it was a good one.'

'Fulmeyer made the bargain, not us,' the third pirate said, frowning. 'We can leave.'

'And see that mist creeping in my wake? You don't play foul with the lords of the marsh and get away with it,' the first retorted, shaking his head.

'So you say.'

'Are you calling me a liar?' the pirate snapped, reaching for the dagger sheathed on his hip.

Dubnitz didn't allow the other to reply. He rose to his feet, shedding water, and swept his sword out, chopping through the third pirate's neck. The man gurgled and slumped. Before the second could do more than gape, Dubnitz ripped the sword free and plunged it into his chest, where it became lodged in bone. The first man howled and leapt, his dagger seeking Dubnitz's guts.

The knight grabbed the man about the middle and flung him over his hip, into the water. Dropping to his knees in the shallows, Dubnitz held the struggling pirate under the water for a moment. Then he dragged him up.

'Where are the others?' he asked the sputtering, gasping man casually.

'G-go t-to-' the pirate croaked.

'Wrong answer,' Dubnitz said cheerfully. He forced the struggling pirate back under water. Fingers clawed at his pauldrons and cuirass. As the bubbles began to lessen, Dubnitz pulled him back up. 'Where did they go?'

'I-into the m-marshes,' the pirate wheezed.

'Can you show me where?'

'No!'

'Pity,' Dubnitz said, making to press the man back under the water.

'No! Wait!' the pirate gasped.

'Friend, I'll be honest, I'm in a foul mood, and I'm all for consigning your soul to Manann's realm. Play silly beggars with me, and I'll do just that.' Dubnitz stood, pulling the pirate up with him. 'But you help me find Fulmeyer, and maybe you live to do the yardarm jig.'

'Not much of a choice,' the pirate rasped.

'Better than you deserve.' Dubnitz shook him slightly. The Order of Manann had a special hatred of pirates, worshipping, as they did, a god of the seas and rivers. Dubnitz had hung more than his fair share, and it was one of the few of the order's activities that he had anything approaching a professional interest in.

'I'll lead you to them,' the pirate said, his eyes closing.

His name was Schafer, and he was a Stirlander by birth but a water-man by choice. He'd been a crewman on a trade skiff for a number of years before he'd grown bored, slit the mate's throat and taken off with the pay chest. Once he'd drunk the contents of the chest away, he'd signed on with Fulmeyer.

All of this he related unasked and slightly defensively. Dubnitz could have told him that he'd heard worse, but didn't feel like wasting the breath to reassure a man he fully intended to hang. Instead, he tried to steer the conversation into more productive waters as they made their way through the marsh. 'What stones were you referring to earlier?' Dubnitz said.

Schafer looked back at him. The pirate was bound tight by a set of thin chains that Dubnitz had scavenged from what was left of the 's cargo. 'What?'

'The stones, the ones you said Fulmeyer was taking the prisoners to.'

Schafer frowned. 'They're just stones. There are lots of stones in the marshes.'

Dubnitz fell silent. That was true, as far as it went. There were stones aplenty in the marshes, piled higher than nature intended. The Cursed Marshes had an ancient history, pre-dating men by a margin that was wider than Dubnitz was comfortable with. He looked around. The trees had thinned as they left the river behind. The ground was spongy beneath their feet, and water filled their tracks as they walked. The air was thick with damp and the sun was hidden behind a grey miasmic curtain.

The water was high here, spilling over the roots of crooked trees and boles of sagging earth. Schafer had said that the pirates used skiffs to manoeuvre through the swamp. Dubnitz wished he had one, but he'd have to settle for foot pursuit.

He blinked stinging beads of sweat out of his eyes. The heat was always surprising. Even in winter, the dark waters of the marsh held in the heat of rot and decay. But edging towards summer as it was now, it was nigh unbearable. Sweat rolled down, causing his skin to itch beneath his armour, which was caked in filth and rusting already. Schafer seemed hardly bothered, but then the pirate was probably used to the heat.

They travelled in silence for a time, Dubnitz moving as quickly as he could in his armour.

'What do you do with prisoners?' Dubnitz asked. 'Is it ransom?'

Schafer was silent. His heavy shoulders hunched forward as if he were thinking of something unpleasant. His jerkin was stained with sweat. Dubnitz narrowed his eyes and jerked the chain, nearly pulling Schafer off of his feet. 'I asked you a question.'

Schafer glared up at him, but behind the anger, there was fear. Not of him, Dubnitz knew. His eyes widened slightly, and Dubnitz spun, hand on his sword hilt. A low fog clung to the path behind, caressing the trees and sliding across the ground. He caught a hint of movement, but heard nothing and saw no shape. He tensed, filled with a sudden, unreasoning fear.

'What was that?' he said, turning back to Schafer.

The pirate licked his lips, but didn't answer. Dubnitz considered striking him. Instead, he shoved him forward. 'Keep going, friend; and you'd better not be leading me into a trap.'

Schafer stubbornly refused to answer any more of Dubnitz's questions as they made their way deeper into the marshes. But his manner became more furtive as they went. Finally Dubnitz jerked him to a halt and said, 'If you find this place so frightening, why in Manann's name would Fulmeyer seek sanctuary here?'

Schafer stared at him. 'No one said anything about sanctuary,' he said softly.

'Then where are they going?' Dubnitz demanded, drawing his sword. He pressed the tip to the pirate's throat.

Schafer spat. He looked away. 'They're paying the toll.'

'What toll?' Dubnitz said. He pressed on the sword. A bead of blood spilled down Schafer's unshaven throat. 'What are you talking about?' A sudden thought bobbed to the surface of Dubnitz's mind. 'Who are the lords of the marsh?' he said, recalling Schafer's earlier words.

'You'll see soon enough,' Schafer spat. 'They're watching us now. We ain't safe here. Nobody's safe, except Fulmeyer, and those with Fulmeyer. And even they ain't as safe as they like to pretend, damn him.' Schafer made a sound that was half whine and half growl. 'Damn him!' he said again.

'Who's watching us? More pirates, perhaps? Is Fulmeyer working for someone?'

Schafer laughed harshly, but didn't answer. It was getting dark, and the evening mist was rising from the water. Beneath the surface of the water, faint lights shimmered, and Dubnitz shivered slightly. The brightest minds of the best universities stated that the ghost-lights of the Cursed Marsh were nothing more than trapped gases. This close, however, Dubnitz lacked such certainties.

He had scavenged a lantern and wicks from the cargo, as well as the chain that bound Schafer, and he lit it as the darkness closed in. Schafer seemed content to stay close, and the pirate's eyes darted back and forth like those of a frightened rabbit. 'We should stop,' he said. 'We should stay here until morning.'

'No,' Dubnitz said. 'We go on.'

'I can't find my way in the dark,' Schafer protested.

'You had better figure it out,' Dubnitz said, tapping his sword.

'You're mad. If you knew–' he stopped himself abruptly.

'If I knew what, more about these lords you seem so afraid of?' Dubnitz said. The mist was rolling across the ground. Something splashed in the water. Schafer started. Dubnitz held the lantern higher, but the mist swallowed the light. 'What are they? Not men, by the way you're acting...'

Schafer laughed shrilly. 'No, not men, but you can ask them what they are yourself!'

Large shapes moved in the mist. The soggy soil squashed under heavy treads. Dubnitz swung the lantern about, but he could see nothing. There were sounds just past the edge of the lantern's light and he caught a glance at what might have been scaly skin.

'Here he is!' Schafer was yelling. 'Take him! Take him, not me!'

'Quiet,' Dubnitz growled. He could feel something watching them. Lights that might have been eyes or marsh gas blinked in and out of sight in the mist. He had his sword half-drawn. The shapes he saw did not evoke familiarity on any level. They were not men or beasts or trees. He could not say what they were.

Abruptly, Schafer lurched forward with a despairing wail. He crashed into Dubnitz, knocking him off balance. Dubnitz stumbled forward, and crashed into something solid. Pain burst through him and he dropped the lantern. Luckily, it didn't burst. Hastily, he staggered to his feet and snatched it up, catching sight of what he'd run into.

The stone had been shaped at some point and time in the past. Not by human hands, or even those of a member of the elder races, but by something else. Dubnitz examined it as the mist congealed around him. Strange shapes had been carved into the stone, prompting faint memories of the crude trinkets he'd seen in the possession of one of his brother-knights who'd visited a wet little fog-shrouded island to the west. The shapes were man-like in their proportions, but they hinted at something far larger, and more horrible. He saw what might have been representations of standing stones, and what could only have been bodies dangling from them, like some prehistoric gallows.

Whatever the symbols represented, they provoked a feeling of disgust in Dubnitz, and he rose slowly to his feet, his sword out. Schafer had vanished. Dubnitz cursed and raised the lantern. The pirate couldn't have gotten far, not with the chains on him. As the mist swirled, he saw more stones. Moving towards them, he again heard the sound of distant splashing, as if something were moving with him.

Schafer screamed.

Dubnitz charged into the mist. The pirate's body laid a-sprawl at the foot of a large example of one of the stones. A dark blotch marked where the pirate had seemingly run headlong into the stone. It was only when he drew closer that Dubnitz realised that the blotch was far too high up on the stone for that to have occurred. Schafer was dead regardless, his skull crushed like an eggshell.

Dubnitz froze, listening. Through the blanket of the mist, he heard the slap of wood on water. The skiffs! Forgetting Schafer, he started forward, splashing into the water. It sucked at his legs and for a moment, he regretted his decision to not wait until morning. There was no telling what he would stumble on in the darkness, even with the lantern.

Forcing himself to be cautious, he slowed. The trees clustered thickly, their mossy branches scraping gently on his armour and across his scalp as he moved. As he walked, he had the impression of large things keeping pace. The lantern's light flickered and sputtered, as if the wick had grown wet. Dubnitz shook it, but it gave a despairing poof and went out, plunging him into darkness. But only for a moment, as the night was pierced by dancing motes of ghost-green light, that swept almost playfully across his path.

Discarding the useless lantern, he followed the motes and soon learned that they were sparks, rising from the strange flames, the colour of emeralds, which crawled up a number of stones, casting weird shadows across the mist-covered water. Dubnitz hesitated. He knew magic when he saw it, and the tales of popular bards to the contrary, there was little a man, no matter how pure of heart or strong of arm, could do against magic.

The trees had thinned, leaving the water to the stones and the strange grasses which grew around them. There was no moon, but the scene was illuminated well enough by the bale-fires burning on the stones and the mist seemed to absorb and amplify those weird lights. It was almost as bright as day, though not nearly as comforting.

There were a trio of low-hulled skiffs ahead, bobbing gently in the water. There were more than a dozen armed men spread among them and a huddled group Dubnitz took to be the prisoners. On the lead skiff, the steersman stood and let his pole rise. Fulmeyer rose to his feet and stood on the prow. He pulled a strange object from his belt and raised it to his lips. The other two skiffs stopped as Fulmeyer stood.

The horn was small, as horns went. It was curled tight on itself, like a ram's horn, and bore no decoration save for certain familiar markings. Fulmeyer blew a single, bleating note and the flames on the stones seemed to blaze more brightly. He blew another, and the mist began to thicken and rise. Dubnitz, in his hiding spot, froze. Fear slithered through him; it was an ancient fear, bred into his bones and mixed into his blood. Childhood nightmares bristled in the caves of his mind. 'The lords of the marsh,' he murmured. Who, or what, held that title?

'Where have you brought us?' Sascha snapped, her voice carrying across the oppressive silence of the marsh. 'My father will hear of this! He is a personal friend of the Elector of Averland!'

'Is he now?' Fulmeyer didn't sound impressed. Dubnitz restrained a chuckle.

'He will have you fed to bears!'

'That's a new one by me. Remind me to stay away from Averland,' Fulmeyer said, and several of his men chortled appreciatively. 'You're in no position to demand anything,' he added, grinning, his gold teeth glinting in the light of the bale-fire as he grabbed Sascha's chin and tilted her head up. She spat in his face and Fulmeyer slapped her, an oath escaping his lips.

Sark shot to his feet and lunged for the pirate. The others fell on him, beating him down as Fulmeyer chuckled. Dubnitz grimaced and looked away.

Across the water, the mist rose and spread like an ocean wave, cresting over the trees and then just as quickly falling to reveal – what? They were stones, but not solitary ones. Instead, they were towers of heaped stone, rising from solid islets in the mere like the grave markers of giants.

They looked flimsy and ill-stacked, but somehow more solid than even the best-built manor house of Marienburg's aristocracy. Moss and mould grew on them, coating the dull black and brown and grey in sheaths of green and yellow, and on them, and in them and between them, dim shapes moved, as if summoned by Fulmeyer's horn.

On the skiff, Sark was struggling as Fulmeyer jerked Sascha to her feet and shoved her into the prow. Fulmeyer jerked her head back by her hair and shouted something that the mist swallowed. As he called out, several pirates climbed down from the skiffs, dragging the prisoners with them.

'They're paying the toll.' That was what Schafer had said. But paying it to what? Dubnitz hesitated. The mist was coalescing like a thing alive, and vague, titan shapes seemed to move within it as the echoes of the horn faded. It looked as if he were going to get the answer to his question. The mist was dispersing. He could see the heaps of stone more clearly, noting the profusion of strange dark stains which marred the rocks at the upper levels.

Something about those stains set his stomach to roiling. They looked far too similar to the splash of Schafer's blood he'd seen on the marker stone earlier. The fear grew in Dubnitz's gut. He could slip away now. No one would know. He was no hero, to die of shame. A fight you couldn't win wasn't glorious, it was foolish.

'Then again, I'm already here. Besides, fortune favours the bold,' he muttered. With a shout, Dubnitz shot to his feet and ran towards the closest of the pirates, drawing his sword as he drew close. The man spun around, his jaw dropping. Dubnitz's sword sprang from its sheath and cut a furrow through the pirate's chest and face.

Even as the first pirate fell, Dubnitz waded into the others. Surprise and speed were enormous advantages, if you were audacious enough to take advantage of them. Unfortunately, even the smallest thing could take that advantage away. His sword swept up, chopping into a tattooed chest. He cursed as the blade became lodged in a breastbone. Dubnitz jerked at the sword and planted his foot on the twitching body, trying to jerk it loose.

Despite his predicament, however, the remaining pirates weren't attacking. Dubnitz gave a grunt and finally freed his sword. Water splashed behind him. 'Erkhart,' Sascha screamed, struggling with her captors.

Dubnitz turned. A smell, like old deep, wet places, washed over him. A single cyclopean eye burned into his wide ones, and a leathery beak split in what could only be called a smile, revealing dagger-fangs. It shed the mist like water, and its scaly flesh was stretched over inhuman muscle beneath ancient bronze armour that did little to conceal its contorted shape. The armour was engraved with looping patterns that hurt Dubnitz's eyes to look at. A stone maul, dripping with filthy water, rose, clutched in the thing's two large hands.

'Manann preserve me,' Dubnitz whispered, as certain stories of his childhood suddenly rose to the fore of his fragmented thoughts, stories of terrible marsh-demons, driven into the mists by Sigmar and Marius the Fenwolf, in a time of legends before Marienburg was anything more than a dream.

The maul rose and fell with a monstrous finality and Dubnitz only just dove aside as the weapon set up a splash of water. He turned and a club-headed tail crashed against his side, driving him to one knee. The thing circled him on bowed legs, its heavy shape sending rough ripples through the water. The leathery snout wrinkled and a sound like water gurgling over rocks escaped from between its teeth.

'What the devil are you then?' he hissed.

Things that might have been words dripped from between its tusks, bludgeoning his ears. If it had answered his question, he couldn't say. Nor did it seem particularly important. Dubnitz shoved himself to his feet using his sword. More creatures had joined the first, the mist clinging to them like some vast, communal cloak. They watched him and the first moved forward, raising its maul. Dubnitz extended his sword and stepped back.

There were dozens of them, perhaps even hundreds. Where had they all come from?

'The mist,' Fulmeyer called out, as if reading his mind. 'They live in the mist. That's where they went when Sigmar and Marius put them to the sword. A good hiding place, if I do say so myself.'

'You'd know all about hiding,' Dubnitz muttered.

'If you put the blade down, they'll make it quick. They're not as bad as some,' Fulmeyer said. The pirate captain had one foot cocked up on the prow of the skiff, and leaned across his knee, the horn dangling from his hand. Dubnitz glanced over his shoulder.

'When did you begin worshipping daemons, Fulmeyer? I always thought you were an honest rogue...' he grated.

Fulmeyer gave a bitter laugh. 'I've always had an eye for opportunity, me, you know that Dubnitz.' His face fell. 'Of course, sometimes opportunity finds you, rather than the other way around.'

'What foul hole did you find this particular opportunity in?' Dubnitz said. The creatures splashed around him, never drawing too close. He wondered if one of them had done for Schafer.

'Here, actually,' Fulmeyer said conversationally. He'd always liked to talk, had the Marsh-Hound and Dubnitz intended to keep him barking away until he could figure out how he was going to salvage the situation. 'I was looking for sanctuary from the damned Altdorf River Patrol. I found it, and allies with it.'

'Allies, is it?' Dubnitz said. 'I didn't see them helping you take the *Fenrunner*.'

'Didn't you?' Fulmeyer said. He waved the horn. 'Then you're blind as well as stupid. I said they live in the mist, didn't I, and it does as they ask.

And they do as I ask...'

'And in return, you give them what – human sacrifices?'

Fulmeyer's glee dissipated. 'Better them than us,' he snarled. 'Everything has a price!'

'Ah, the rallying cry of every half-baked cultist,' Dubnitz said. 'A match made in darkness, to be sure, Marsh-Hound. You get to loot to your black heart's content, and all you have to do is turn the innocent over to inhuman monstrosities.'

'I pay the toll required, Dubnitz. And it's your bad luck that tonight's toll is you,' Fulmeyer said, gesturing. The pirates formed up around the skiff, their weapons prodding at Dubnitz, keeping him from coming too close. They did not look so much triumphant as terrified. They had pulled Sascha and her brother off of the skiff and thrust them into the water. With curses and oaths, they shoved them and the other survivors of the *Fenrunner* towards Dubnitz.

'I said it before – drop your sword, Dubnitz. Go quiet like, and they'll be gentle. As gentle as they get...' Fulmeyer said. Dubnitz ignored him, checking on the others. There was only a quartet of the *Fenrunner*'s crew remaining, and two of them were the worse for wear. Sascha and her brother seemed healthy enough, despite their terror.

'You're late, Erkhart,' Sascha said, her voice tight.

'A horse would have come in handy,' Dubnitz said.

'Get us out of this, and you'll have more horses than you can stable,' Sark said, his face pale.

Dubnitz didn't reply. He glanced at the pirates. There were more than a dozen of them, but they looked ready to bolt. Fulmeyer's protestations to the contrary, his men weren't entirely comfortable with their 'allies.'

'Everyone stays together,' Dubnitz said. The creatures appeared to be growing impatient and several were splashing forward, their club-tails lashing.

'Maybe we should run,' Sascha said, clutching at his arm.

'I don't think we'd make it very far,' Dubnitz muttered.

As if it had overheard them, one of the creatures gave out a great cry and the others followed suit, slapping the water with their tails and stamping their feet. At the sight, one of the sailors sidled away from the bulk of the group, his face tense and pale with fear.

'Don't,' Dubnitz said. The sailor didn't listen. He turned and began to splash away, uttering prayers to Taal, Manann, and Sigmar as he ran. The mist seemed to solidify in front of the fleeing man and then the shape of one of the creatures lunged from it, incredibly swift. Talons fastened almost gently about the man's head, cutting off his scream. The creature lifted the struggling man and the other things set up another howl.

'Damn it let him go!' Dubnitz roared, lunging forward. He had little hope of helping the sailor, but he'd be damned if he wasn't going to try. His sword chopped into the rubbery limb and the thing shrieked, more in surprise than pain. It flung its arm out, knocking Dubnitz off his feet.

The stone maul wielded by the first of the beasts he'd encountered smashed down, spraying him with water and nearly mashing his head to paste. It drove him back, away from the one he'd attacked, swinging its maul out in short and brutal arcs. It didn't seem to want to kill him so much as prevent him from interfering with whatever its companion was doing.

'Erkhart, be careful!' Sascha shouted, her brother holding her back.

'What does it look like I'm doing?' he yelled back. The maul dropped, nearly crushing his foot. Reacting swiftly, he stepped on the haft and half-threw himself forward, his sword slashing wildly at the glaring, single eye. The creature reared back and the sword barely missed its snout. It jerked the maul out from under him, tumbling him into the water with ease.

A massive three-toed foot slammed down on his chest, pinning him in the water. The creature looked down at him, and there was something that might have been respect in its eye. It gestured with its weapon.

The other creature loped towards the tumble of stone with its captive. It climbed up the stones, displaying none of the awkwardness its ungainly form would imply. As it reached the top, something bent and hidden within thick, sodden animal hides crawled out of the rocks to meet it. Despite the concealing skins, Dubnitz could tell that it was of the same race as the others, though wizened and perhaps crippled. It leaned on a staff and croaked something at the other. The sailor's screams were muffled by the beast holding him.

The bent beast scooped up what looked like a length of crudely woven rope and set a noose around the writhing, whining sailor's neck. Then, with a gurgling roar, the first creature sent the sailor tumbling from the stone. The rope pulled taut and the sailor smashed headfirst into the stone, leaving a new stain to join the old ones that Dubnitz had noted earlier.

The creatures howled, clawing at the air or gesticulating with their weapons. The one holding Dubnitz down stepped back, letting him climb slowly to his feet. Rubbing his aching chest, he backed away. The body of the sailor twisted in the muggy breeze, and its heels drummed on the stone.

Behind Dubnitz, Sascha gasped and turned away, leaning against her brother. 'Stay close, all of you,' Dubnitz barked as he rejoined the others. He swallowed thickly and put himself between them and the beasts that squatted, waiting.

Why weren't they attacking? What were they waiting for?

'Going to fight them all, Dubnitz?' Fulmeyer called out, half-tauntingly, half-admiringly. 'That doesn't work. I know.'

'Talk your way out of that noose as well, did you?' Dubnitz shouted back. 'A trade was it?'

'And if it was? Is my life – our lives – worth any less than these fine, fancy folk?' Fulmeyer said.

'Yes, it is,' Dubnitz said bluntly. 'You're noose-bound, human hangman or otherwise, if I have anything to say about it.'

'Good thing you don't, then,' Fulmeyer said, laughing harshly. 'The lords of the marsh will do for you!'

As the pirate cackled, the creature that had first confronted Dubnitz gestured with its maul and gave a querulous croak. Fulmeyer stopped laughing. More of the creatures emerged from the mist, appearing on the other side of the pirates' skiff. Fulmeyer half-lifted the horn, and the creature bellowed. On the high stones, the wizened monster raised its staff and shrieked. The pirate flinched, like a beaten dog. Dubnitz grinned. 'Will they now? Somehow, I think you spoke too soon, Fulmeyer.'

Dubnitz had seen enough to know that form and ritual were everything where sacrifices were concerned. If the creatures had bothered to bargain with Fulmeyer, they would abide by the rules they had laid down. It seemed that they wanted their sacrifices delivered to them, not just dumped on the doorstep.

Fulmeyer swallowed and hopped off the skiff. He drew his sword as he splashed forward, and gestured with the hand that held the horn. 'Take them,' he snarled, and his men moved forward, grimly intent, more than one of them darting a nervous glance at their monstrous allies. Dubnitz realised that he had been wrong earlier. It wasn't an alliance; the river-pirates were simply hunting dogs and now they were being whipped to the kill.

Fulmeyer and a large, tattooed Nordlander closed on Dubnitz. 'Don't kill him,' Fulmeyer growled. 'They wouldn't like that. Just get that sword out of his hand.' He grinned in a feral fashion. 'In fact, take the hand as well.'

The Nordlander roared and lunged, his boat-axe swooping down. He was bigger than Dubnitz, and wore a rust-riddled sleeveless suit of mail. Dubnitz lunged forward, and the axe blade skirted down the side of his cuirass at an angle, shaving the metal and creating an ache in Dubnitz's chest. He smashed the pommel of his sword into the Nordlander's face, busting teeth. The big man reeled with a moan and Dubnitz cut his leg out from under him. The Nordlander fell with a scream and Dubnitz stepped over him, moving towards Fulmeyer.

More pirates closed in, leaving their captives unattended. Armed and in a foul mood, Dubnitz looked more dangerous than a pack of terrified sailors. Fulmeyer barked orders, trying to regain control of the situation, but to no avail. Dubnitz swept his sword out in a wide arc, spilling red into the water. A pirate screamed and sank, clutching at his ruined hand. The heavy blade in the knight's hand was little more than a cleaver with a pointed end; Dubnitz had grown to manhood in Marienburg's tannery district, chopping through the muscle and bone of abattoir animals.

The pirates fell back after a few fraught moments, leaving the dead and dying in their wake. The creatures set up a cry and the mist seemed to vibrate with the frustration inherent in that sound. Fulmeyer's eyes bulged and he half-lifted the horn.

'Go on,' Dubnitz wheezed. Sweat coated his face and his shoulders twitched with strain. His sword blade dipped towards the water. 'Blow it, Fulmeyer. Send them back. Break your damnable bargain.'

Fulmeyer's face hardened. 'It ain't that simple.'

'No, it never is,' Dubnitz said. His armour felt as if it had grown heavier. He looked up. The darkness at the edge of the mist had faded, turning from purple to pink. One of the creatures snarled something unintelligible and pointed a talon at Fulmeyer, who flinched and waved his sword.

'I'll do it, damn your eye! Our bargain stands!' the pirate screamed. He charged awkwardly through the water towards Dubnitz. 'Take him, you marsh-dogs! Take him or we're all for having our brains dashed on those cursed stones! Take him before cock-crow!' His sword rattled off of Dubnitz's own hastily interposed blade. Several other pirates surged towards them, their obvious panic sharpening their faces to vulpine ferocity.

The creatures seemed to gather close, their heavy shapes moving towards the others. Dubnitz booted Fulmeyer in the belly and spun around. 'Run!' he roared. 'All of you run!'

The sailors needed no prompting. They broke and fled, thrashing towards the skiff, the hale helping the wounded. Sascha, however, snatched up an axe from one of the dead pirates and promptly brained the closest of his still-breathing compatriots. Her brother punched another and jerked the stumbling man's blade from its sheath. Dubnitz cursed. 'Get to the boat you fools,' he snarled, grabbing a pirate's shirt and jerking the man forward so that their skulls connected.

'Not without you!' Sascha said waving her axe as her brother gutted a pirate.

'I'll be right behind you,' Dubnitz said.

'Then there's no reason to hurry, is there?' Sark said, driving a pirate back with a swift slash of his purloined blade.

'You Averlanders are a stubborn bunch,' Dubnitz said. The creatures were moving towards the skiff now. Before, they had been content to watch, but now they had been prodded into motion – why? Why the sudden urgency, Dubnitz wondered as he blocked a blow that would have sent him to his knees. Why were the pirates suddenly so desperate? 'Cock-crow,' Dubnitz said suddenly.

'What?' Sascha said.

'Morning is coming! That's why they're so impatient!' Dubnitz said. 'If we can just hold on until morning...'

'I don't think they're going to let us!' Sark yelped. He staggered back as one of the creatures grabbed for him. Sascha screamed. Dubnitz turned and saw her backpedalling from a scaly shape that loomed over her. Before he could go to her, Fulmeyer stepped between them, his eyes wild. The pirate hacked at him with berserk abandon. Dubnitz was forced back, his arm and shoulder throbbing with fatigue-ache as he blocked the wild blows.

'I'm not going into the mist!' Fulmeyer howled. 'Not me, you hear?'

'I hear,' Dubnitz grunted, as he caught another blow. His eyes found the horn, clutched in Fulmeyer's manic grip. With a twist of his wrist, he sent the pirate's sword sliding from his grip and rammed his shoulder into the other man's chest. Fulmeyer staggered, and Dubnitz grabbed the horn, yanking it out of Fulmeyer's hand.

'No!' the pirate screamed.

Dubnitz didn't waste breath replying. Instead, he put the horn to his lips and blew. The note shivered out and the effect was nigh-immediate. The mist seemed to harden, as if frozen, and then it collapsed like a curtain that has had its straps cut. It sank and retreated, like the tide going out. The strange rock formations wavered like heat mirages and faded as the mist writhed past them. The rising sun glared down, its gaze suddenly no longer obscured by the daemon-sent mist.

As one, the creatures gave out a great cry. There was despair in that sound, and a resigned rage. They began to stagger away, covering their bulbous eyes and heads as well as they could. A foul-smelling smoke rose from those not quick enough to reach the mist and their screams caused every man's heart to shudder. Only one didn't retreat – the first, the beast clutching its stone-headed maul like a talisman. It rose over Sascha, reaching for her. It didn't intend to return to the mists without one sacrifice, at least. She screamed and raised her axe.

'Ho beast! That's not the one you want,' Dubnitz bellowed. Its triangular head whipped around. Dubnitz grabbed Fulmeyer and propelled him into the water near the beast. The pirate screamed and tried to run, but the maul flicked out, and bones turned to splinters and he fell, his legs rendered into ruined sacks. He coughed and whined and splashed as the creature stood over him, considering. Its eye found Dubnitz again.

'Go on, take him you one-eyed son of a frog,' Dubnitz said. His limbs trembled from his exertions and he wanted nothing more than to fall down. But he forced himself to stay upright. He extended his sword. 'Take what you're given, and go.'

The creature's eye flashed with something that might have been a look of promise, and then it reached down and grabbed Fulmeyer by his scalp. The pirates who hadn't fled found themselves in much the same predicament. Scaly, abnormally long arms shot from the retreating mist and grabbed ankles, elbows, heads and arms, jerking the terrified pirates into the mist they had earlier so eagerly sheltered in.

The creature hefted Fulmeyer, whose shrieks had dwindled to moans, and pointed at Dubnitz with its maul. Smoke billowed from its heavy shape as it held his gaze for a moment, and then it turned and stalked after its fellows, its club tail sending waves slopping against the side of the skiff.

Dubnitz watched it go, and when it had vanished and the mist had gone, he raised the horn and brought his sword down on it, shattering it.

'Erkhart–' Sascha began.

'Get on the skiff,' Dubnitz said hollowly. 'We need to be far away from here by nightfall.' Sascha and her brother got aboard the skiff, and Dubnitz followed slowly, looking back warily. The creatures might not come after them, but he couldn't take that chance. He felt ill and tired. He hadn't had a choice, and he wouldn't weep for Fulmeyer and his crew, but it sat badly with him nonetheless. They had earned their ending, but he wished that he hadn't been the one to deliver it in such a fashion.

Even pirates deserved better than that.

In the fading drifts of mist, Dubnitz thought he could see dim forms struggling, and hear distant screams and the thump of skulls on stone. Then he could hear nothing but the sounds of the Cursed Marshes, and the splash of the pole into the water as the skiff began its journey back towards the clean waters of the Reik.

DEAD MAN'S PARTY

Josh Reynolds

It was Spring Tide, and Marienburg was awash in revelry of both the sublime and more boisterous sort. Poles bearing caged seagulls were hoisted aloft as the celebration unfolded. Cornets and other instruments were played, mostly badly, by over-enthusiastic revellers. Buckets of seawater were sloshed about on the unwary as priests and pilgrims bellowed out the more profane hymns to Manann, popular among sailors.

Steel spheres containing handfuls of incense and hot coals were draped from every available protrusion, and clouds of exotic spices drifted across the streets, battling for dominance with the normal urban stew of the canals. Children threw dried flakes of seaweed and coral into the waters of the Central Canal as the great altar-barge of Manann hove to, the high priest roaring his praises and shaking his gull-pole until the bird's raucous squawks threatened to drown out his own.

Every citizen was either in the streets or in the taverns, or heading from one to the other. Or so it seemed to Erkhart Dubnitz, knight of the Most Holy Order of Manann-in-Marienburg, as he stiff-armed a red-faced drunk into the canal in order to clear a path for his charge. 'Right this way, Meneer Lomax,' he said obsequiously, bowing and sweeping an armour-plated arm out just in time to catch a bucket-bearing priest in the belly. The seawater sloshed across the cobbles and Dubnitz's charge chuckled.

'At least the stones are getting a good scouring, hey?' Bernard Lomax said, rheumy eyes taking in the celebration with a weary air as he leaned on his narwhal-horn cane. He was dressed archaically, in the fashion of his youth, and his clothes showed signs of having been repaired, rather than replaced. Lomax was old, and age weighed heavily on his thin form. He had the heft of a Nehekharan mummy in his twilight years but none of the joie de vivre, as the Bretonnian saying went.

'Are you enjoying yourself, Meneer Lomax?' Piet Van Taal said. Like Dubnitz, Piet was a knight of the most holy, and only occasionally violent, Order of Manann. In contrast to Dubnitz's barrel-chested heft, he was a lean whip of a man with the stamp of one of the lower rungs of

Marienburg's aristocracy on his features. Like Dubnitz, he wore a coat of chainmail beneath an emerald surcoat bearing the trident-and-crown emblem of Manann, god of the seas.

'Who can enjoy themselves with the stench and the noise?' Lomax said, coughing into a clenched fist. 'Is this what you do for fun?'

'Not quite, no,' Dubnitz said quickly. 'Normally our carousing takes place indoors, away from the hurly-burly.' He spun and punched a celebrant who'd been about to place a wreath of eel-skins and shark fins around his neck.

'That sounds good,' Lomax said, watching the wreath clatter across the cobbles.

Piet looked at Dubnitz over the top of Lomax's head and mouthed, 'The Scalded Gull?'

Dubnitz nodded. He laid a leather gauntlet on Lomax's shoulder. 'Right this way, Meneer Lomax. We'll have you quaffing in no time.'

'Are you taking me to a dive? Is it filthy?'

'The filthiest,' Dubnitz assured him.

'Will there be loose women?'

'The loosest,' Piet said.

'It sounds delightful,' Lomax murmured, clasping his trembling hands together. 'Lead on Sir Knights! I have a half-century's worth of abstinence to make up for.'

The knights led him through the crowd into the back alleys that stretched out from the Central Canal, where the noise of the Spring Tide celebration grew muted and the natural odoriferousness of Marienburg reasserted itself. The Scalded Gull clung to a little-used stable on Fishhook Lane like an unsightly growth. It was an overlarge shed, with wide windows and a door that was less an obstacle than a curtain. It wasn't crowded, for which Dubnitz muttered a silent prayer of thanks to Manann.

The barman grunted an unintelligible greeting and Dubnitz raised three fingers and gestured to a table in the back corner that sat beneath the hide of giant rat that had been stretched across the wall and nailed in place. Lomax looked curiously at the hide as they sat. 'What is it?'

'It thought it was a man,' Dubnitz said. 'Now it's a conversation piece. We cleaned out a nest of the pestiferous beasts a few years back in the area, now all of the local swill-sellers let the Order drink for free.'

The drinks arrived and the two knights emptied their mugs in moments, slamming them down almost simultaneously. Lomax blinked at the speed. He hesitated, his fingers gripping his own mug as he looked into the foam as if it hid secrets. Then he jerked it convulsively to his lips and knocked it back. Dubnitz waved his hand, signalling for another round. Lomax went momentarily cross-eyed and coughed. 'It has been some time since I had anything stronger than turnip juice,' he said. He licked his lips. 'I quite liked it.'

'Glad to hear it,' Dubnitz said, and he was. He examined the old man. Lomax was a man of means. He was also a miser with money to spare. Money which he'd promised to the Order of Manann, money which they desperately needed, if the hollow echoing sound of the tithe coffers was anything to go by. All Lomax had asked in return was one night, just one night of carousing and stupidity, to make up for a lifetime of thrift and denial, because misers like Lomax didn't make charitable donations without strings attached.

It wasn't that strange a request, all things considered. Lomax's ascetic life hadn't been by choice so much as by necessity. A man without pleasures or vices was a hard man to trap. The life of a dyspeptic shut-in had kept old Lomax toddling along through two generations of greedy grasping relatives who chafed at the tightness of Lomax's purse strings and weren't shy about trying to cut, burn or poison their way into said purse. Those same relatives had set up a howl that would have sent invading Norscans scurrying back to their boats when they found out that Lomax was leaving his substantial fortune to the Order of Manann.

It was more out of spite than religious epiphany, Dubnitz knew. Lomax was doing the next best thing to taking it with him, and because greedy relatives didn't like it when miserly relations loudly announced their intention to change their will and leave the bulk of their substantial fiduciary assets to an up-and-coming order of humble templars, there would be some attempt to stop it.

Thus, strings. A night of sybaritic pleasure, one full night, and then the new will took effect at cockcrow. All the Order had to do was give their new patron the best night of his life. Grandmaster Ogg was filled with a joy that he could barely contain and had ordered his most masterful carousers to take things in hand. Dubnitz and Piet set to it with a will, the former theorizing that Lomax, long having gone without, might mistake quantity for quality, and make the night's work quick and easy.

By the eighth mug of rotgut, Lomax was cackling and clapping as a Strigany dancing girl spun and shook across the tabletop. The Scalded Gull had grown loud since they'd arrived as celebrants filtered into the alleys from the party outside. Dubnitz watched bleary-eyed as pickpockets plied their trade through the dense crowd and the dancing girl's ferret-faced kin did the same to the pickpockets. Then, as Lomax started shouting a bawdy tune he'd known in his boyhood, Dubnitz spotted the assassin.

He was a dock-snake, one of the lean, lethal savages who ascribed to no union or guild and who roamed from berth to berth, unloading and loading vessels for under-the-table pay. A hooked fish-knife sprouted from one sinewy hand as he slithered through the crowd, his eyes locked on Lomax with the feral intensity of a starving wharf rat.

Dubnitz roared and shot awkwardly to his feet. Alcohol fumes clouded the edges of his vision. The dock-snake stumbled back as the dancing girl screamed and the crowd began to roll back like ripples spreading from a stone dropped in a rain barrel. Piet, still in his seat, was looking around blearily as he groped blindly for his sword.

Dubnitz's sword sprang from its sheath in a crooked arc, slicing air rather than flesh as it passed just in front of the dock-snake's nose. The man sprang past him, one bare foot hooking the table edge as he propelled himself up and at Lomax, who had tipped his head back and was raising a mug all unawares. Dubnitz spun and grabbed the back of the would-be killer's trousers and, with a roll of his shoulders, sent the dock-snake hurtling backwards into the wall behind the bar with bone-breaking force.

And then, as the echoes of that crash faded, it all went to hell. People screamed. The dancing girl leapt off the table in a splash of silks and a rattle of bangles. Dubnitz spun in a circle, seeking enemies even as he noted that it was taking Lomax a long time to gulp his ale.

'Dubnitz,' Piet said. 'Did something just happen?'

'Someone tried to kill Lomax,' Dubnitz mumbled. The room swayed around him.

'Did you stop them?'

'Yes,' Dubnitz said.

'Are you sure? He looks dead. Is he dead?' Piet said, gesturing sloppily towards the crossbow bolt that had sprouted from the bottom of Lomax's mug. The point of said bolt had passed through the mug and between Lomax's open jaws, piercing the soft tissues of his sinuses on its trek into his brain.

Dubnitz looked blearily over his shoulder. He blinked owlishly and belched. 'I'd say it's a definite possibility,' he said, stumbling over 'possibility'.

'Are we sure he's dead?'

Dubnitz kicked the body, toppling over in the process. From the floor, he said, 'Almost positively, yes.'

'We're dead,' Piet muttered, shaking his head.

'I thought he was the one who was dead,' Dubnitz said, as he heaved himself to his feet.

'Ogg is going to kill us.'

'Bound to happen,' Dubnitz said cheerfully, squinting around at the empty tavern. The evening crowd had chosen discretion over curiosity and fled. The Scalded Gull was empty of life, though the sounds of the Spring Tide celebration still curled through the open windows. 'Don't sober up on me now, Piet, it'll only end in tears.'

Piet cursed and tried to stand, but he only succeeded in windmilling his arms and causing his chair to groan in protest. 'What are we going to do? Lomax is dead!'

'Says who?' Dubnitz said, spreading his arms. 'Tavern's empty, Piet.'

'He's got an arrow sticking out of his head!'

'So we pull it out,' Dubnitz said mildly, striding to the bar and reaching under it. He pulled out a bottle and eyed it, then pulled the stopper with his teeth and knocked back a slug. Wiping his mouth with the back of his hand he stomped back towards the table. 'Have some good Sartosian red and calm down,' he said, tossing the bottle to Piet, who caught it awkwardly.

'I don't think more alcohol is the solution here,' Piet said, taking a long drink.

'Can't hurt,' Dubnitz muttered, taking hold of the end of the bolt transfixing the dead man's head to the back wall of the tavern. He had been tilting his head back for a swig from his mug when the bolt had perforated his palate and nailed him and his mug to the wall. Dubnitz worked the bolt free with a grunt and squinted at it. 'Pretty sure he's dead,' he said.

'I thought we'd established that,' Piet said gloomily.

Dubnitz didn't reply. He carefully pulled the dead man's head back down. The eyes had rolled to the white and a trickle of blood seeped from one nostril, but other than that, there was little sign of what had killed him. Unless you got a good luck in his mouth or at the top of his head, Lomax could have simply been dead drunk, as opposed to just plain dead.

'I'm sorry old man,' Dubnitz murmured, closing Lomax's eyes. 'We promised you a night out to celebrate your generosity and what did you get for it but a bolt to the brainpan. Maybe you should have given the money to the Cult of Morr instead.'

'What are we going to do?' Piet said mournfully, staring into the bottle, which he'd managed to half-empty in impressive time. 'Grandmaster Ogg is going to pickle us like herring.' He looked blearily at Dubnitz. 'I don't want to be pickled.'

'We won't get pickled,' Dubnitz said, peering at Lomax's body speculatively. He turned, swaying slightly, and sighted down the crossbow bolt. He found the open window of the tavern and said, 'Aha!'

'Aha?' Piet said, blinking.

'The window,' Dubnitz said, stumbling towards the window. He stuck his head out and peered at the wall of the stables opposite. The night-stew that passed for fresh air in Marienburg slapped his face, sobering him slightly. 'The arrow came from outside.'

'Brilliant deduction,' Piet said, shoving himself to his feet. 'Sam Warble himself couldn't have done it better. Are you sure your name isn't Zavant Konniger? We're going to get pickled!'

'Stop saying pickled. Ogg will jelly us, if anything. Man loves his jellied eels.' Dubnitz absently scratched his chin with the crossbow bolt, then thought of poison, stared at the bolt and swallowed thickly. 'What time is it, Piet?'

'How should I know? Time to find warmer waters,' Piet said, taking another swig from the bottle. 'If we ride out now, we can be halfway to Altdorf in a few days.'

'Don't put the saddle on the horse just yet,' Dubnitz said and snatched the bottle from him and knocked back the rest of it in one gulp. He tossed the bottle out of the window and strode back towards the bar. 'I've got a cunning plan.' He grabbed a broom and number of rags from behind the bar and several more bottles. He used his foot to roll a small keg of Averland Bear's Milk towards the table.

'This isn't going to work,' Piet said as Dubnitz pulled Lomax's corpse upright by its shirt-front.

'Of course it will,' Dubnitz said, yanking the cork out of a bottle of wine with his teeth and pouring the contents over the body. 'If he smells like a brewery exploded, no one will give him a second look. And all we need to do is keep him moving until the will goes into effect.'

'This is madness,' Piet said as he draped the dead man's arm over his shoulders. 'We should alert the watch. Captain Schnell, over at the Three Penny Bridge watch station, is a friend of mine.'

Dubnitz shook his head. 'I owe Schnell money. Besides, this is Marienburg, and we've done worse,' Dubnitz said, doing the same with Lomax's other arm. 'Besides, it's all for a good cause, Piet. We're seeing that Lomax's last request is carried out.' The body slumped between them, feet dragging. 'We need twine.'

'Twine,' Piet muttered, looking around. 'Why do we need twine?'

'Well, to keep him walking, obviously,' Dubnitz said. 'It doesn't have to be twine. See if you can get this broomstick down his trousers.'

'Couldn't we just sit here quietly with a few drinks?' Piet implored.

'People need to see him up and about,' Dubnitz said. 'It is our duty, for the Order and for Manann. Now, in his name find some twine or a broom or... here.' Dubnitz grabbed up a chair and broke it on the floor, depositing the bulk of Lomax's weight onto Piet. Taking the pieces of the chair, he stuffed them down the back of Lomax's trousers and into his boots, stiffening his legs. Then he swiftly tied Lomax's ankles to Piet's and his own.

'With him between us, we should be able to manage it,' Dubnitz said, draping Lomax's arm back over him. Awkwardly, he snatched the broom from Piet's hands and jammed it down the back of Lomax's jerkin and down into one leg of his trousers. Then he handed a rag to Piet and jerked Lomax's head up. 'Now, tie his head to the back of the broom.'

'People are going to notice!' Piet protested.

'Not with his hat on they won't,' Dubnitz said assuredly. 'Trust me, I've done this before.'

'When?' Piet demanded.

'I'm not at liberty to say. A woman's honour was involved. The situation was very uncomfortable for everyone concerned,' Dubnitz said, stuffing Lomax's fallen hat on his head. Lomax hung between them, not quite sagging. His head tilted down slightly, and he looked – and smelled – drunk.

'Now what do we do?' Piet said.

'Now we carouse as we've never caroused before,' Dubnitz said. He snatched up Lomax's cane and spun it with the dexterity of a professional alcoholic.

They shuffled towards the door, Piet first and then Dubnitz, walking Lomax's corpse between them. As they exited the tavern, a sound from above caused them to look up. A body, dressed in battered leathers, rolled off of the stable roof and thumped into the alleyway. A moment later, a crossbow followed, shattering as it struck the ground. Dubnitz stretched out Lomax's cane and prodded the fallen man.

'He's dead too,' he said.

'I hope so,' Piet said. 'That's Giuseppe Giancarlo, the Miragliano Murderist!'

'How can you tell?' Dubnitz said, rolling the body over to reveal its mauled face and chest. The man, whatever his identity, looked as if he'd walked face first into an exploding cannon.

'Only man I know whoever lavished that much affection on his crossbow,' Piet said, nudging the broken crossbow with his boot. Dubnitz saw that it had been inlaid with silver and the stock was ornately engraved.

'Didn't do him much good,' Dubnitz said, peering up. 'I suppose we know now who shot Lom– I mean, shot at Lomax.' Giving in to ghoulish impulse, he grabbed the back of Lomax's head and made it nod. Piet blanched.

'Don't do that,' he said.

'He doesn't mind.'

'It's blasphemous!'

Dubnitz snorted and looked at the body again. 'Of course, now we're left with the question of who killed your friend Giuseppe.'

The sound of soft sandals scraping the cobbles caused the two knights to swing around to the darkened end of the alleyway, their burden causing them to almost overbalance. 'I think we're about to find out,' Piet said.

The Arabyan was the first to step forward. He was wreathed in black robes and he stopped and leaned on his scimitar. 'I want Lomax,' he said, fluffing his curled beard. A discreet cough caused him to pause, and he turned slightly. 'We want Lomax, Mock Duck and I,' he corrected. The Cathayan slid forward to join him, pistols strung from his narrow frame like holy talismans. He drew one and cocked it, aiming it at Dubnitz. His dark eyes found the body of Giuseppe and narrowed. He looked at the Arabyan, who frowned. 'Which one of you killed Giuseppe?'

Dubnitz and Piet both held up their hands. 'Not us,' Dubnitz said. 'I assumed it was you.'

The Arabyan blinked. Then, he coughed. Something bright protruded from his throat. He reached up with a trembling finger and touched it. Then, with a gurgle, he toppled forward, revealing the wavy-bladed dagger jutting from the back of his neck. The Cathayan spun, drawing a second pistol. He leapt into the darkness, his pistols roaring. More pistol shots sounded, and then, silence.

'We should go,' Piet said.

'I concur,' Dubnitz said. 'Make for the alley mouth–'

The shapes were shadows within the darkness at first, blotches of black. As they eased into the torchlight, metal gleamed. Brass masks, wrought in the shape of a daemon's grinning leer, peered out of ragged cowls. Gauntleted hands emerged from voluminous sleeves, clutching wavy-bladed daggers. There were three of them.

'Well, there's a sight I hoped never to see,' Dubnitz hissed.

'The Murder-Brothers of Khaine,' Piet whispered, the colour draining from his face. The murder-brothers, sometimes known as the massacre-monks or the slaughter-priests, were the pre-eminent assassins in Marienburg. Devoted to Khaine, god of murder, they lathered an unhealthy amount of religious fervour onto even the simplest back-alley killing.

'We're lucky it's not all twelve of them,' Dubnitz said, extending Lomax's cane. Tiles crashed down from the roof, shattering on the ground. Dubnitz's eyes flickered upwards and he caught sight of furtive movement. 'Spoke too soon,' he added.

'Oh gods,' Piet said hoarsely. 'They're all around us.'

'Back away slowly,' Dubnitz said. 'If we can get to the mouth of the alley–'

'Give us the merchant, dogs of Manann,' one of the murder-brothers croaked, his voice distorted by the contours of his mask. 'Khaine has no interest in your hearts today.'

'Glad to hear it, but as you can see, our friend here can barely stand without us, so–' Dubnitz said, tapping Lomax's chest with the cane.

There was a rush of feet and a wavy dagger speared out of the darkness to the side. Piet snarled and drew his sword, the motion swinging Dubnitz around to face two more of the murder-brothers as they sprang for him. He lashed out with the cane, catching the tips of both blades in the carved grooves that lined the cane and twisted his wrist, jerking the knives from their wielders' hands. His metal shod boot came down on a sandaled foot and an assassin yelped. The cane slashed out. Narwhal horn was almost as hard as iron, and a brass mask crumpled.

Piet's sword chopped out, separating a cowled head from hunched shoulders and then they were galumphing towards the mouth of the alleyway, the hounds of Khaine in hot pursuit. As they ran, Dubnitz was reminded of the three-legged races he'd participated in as a boy, and of the Tannery rats which had pursued the racers along the course. He'd hated it then, and time hadn't dulled the feeling. Sound and the smell of the canals washed over them as they burst out into the throng. People laughed and jeered and wept. Men draped in flags stumbled past on stilts carved to look like ships' masts. Clowns clad in paper seaweed gambolled past. Dubnitz, Piet and the corpse between them fit right in to the madness of Spring Tide.

As they awkwardly shoved into the morass of drunken revelry, Dubnitz craned his neck. 'I think we lost them!' Adrenaline had burned away the last dregs of drunkenness that had made their current predicament seem like a good plan. Thinking on it, Dubnitz wondered if it might not have been better to simply hide the body somewhere until the next morning.

'Knife,' Piet hissed.

'What?'

'Knife,' Piet snarled, flailing his hand. Dubnitz looked down and saw a wavy-bladed dagger jutting from Lomax's belly.

'Whoops,' Dubnitz said, plucking it out and tossing it into the gutter. The wound wasn't deep, but it was dark. Dubnitz snatched a bottle of something equally dark and strong smelling from the hands of a woman balancing a trained seagull on her nose and splashed it on the wound. Then he knocked back a drink and handed it to Piet, coughing.

'Are there really twelve of them,' Piet said, taking a drink.

'Supposedly,' Dubnitz said, scanning the crowd. All of the nearby taverns would be cramped and reeking messes, with no room to move, if it came to that, which it likely would, as the murder-cultists of Khaine were nothing if not persistent. 'Keep your eyes peeled, Piet.'

'No worries on that score. I won't be closing them again until we're done with this farce,' Piet hissed. 'This is an idiotic plan, Dubnitz. We were almost killed back there!'

'Ish-is thath-that-Bernie?' a voice roared before Dubnitz could reply. 'Hey! It's old Penny-Pinch him-himshelf!' A fat hand, bedecked with rings of varying degrees of vulgarity, grabbed Lomax's shoulder and tried to turn him. Momentarily panicked, Dubnitz and Piet flailed about, their balance off. They righted themselves and turned as the fat merchant stumbled back, blinking blearily. The man's chubby features brightened as he blew at the feather that drooped from his shapeless hat out of his face. 'It is you!' he said, slurring his words. He ignored Dubnitz and Piet and poked Lomax in the chest. 'I shaid to myshelf, I said, 'Rupol-Rudolpho, that can't be Bernie Lomax, because he hates parties! But it is you and–' he sniffed Lomax and reeled back extravagantly. 'And whooh! You've been at it!'

Dubnitz grabbed Lomax's hand and stretched it out to swat playfully at the drunken merchant's shoulder even as he grabbed the back of Lomax's head and made it nod. Piet glared at him, but Dubnitz jerked his head towards the merchant and shrugged.

The merchant blinked again. 'Shay, Bernie you look sort of peaked. I know thish wonnerful cure– ack!' He reached up to swat his neck and Dubnitz saw a tiny feathered dart pop free of his third chin and bounce into his palm. The man blinked a third time, his eyes out of synch. 'Down I go,' he said mournfully, sinking to the street, where he was swiftly swallowed up by the crowd. Dubnitz heard a 'tink' and saw another dart rattle off of his cuirass, leaving a tiny trail of fluid in its wake.

'Time to go,' he said, using Lomax's cane to open a path. Piet staggered after him with a strangled curse.

'What happened?' the other knight barked. 'What was that?'

'Poison dart!' Dubnitz replied. 'They use them in the Southlands, I'm told.'

'I thought the Khaine-lovers only used knives!'

'They do,' Dubnitz said. 'That was someone else.'

'How many assassins did Lomax's relatives hire?' Piet nearly shouted.

'My guess would be all of them,' Dubnitz said. 'Duck!'

'What?' Piet said as Dubnitz sank down. Piet, unprepared, was jerked directly into the path of a blow from a pair of iron-shod knuckles. He swayed and tripped over his own feet, pulling Lomax down and forcing Dubnitz to stand. Dubnitz twisted, lashing out with the cane to strike the scar-faced bruiser who'd lunged from the crowd. The weighted knob of the cane bounced off the big man's brow, and the latter staggered, shaking his head like a fly-stung ox.

'Get him, Bull!' a smaller, thinner man dressed in a stylish outfit that had seen better months shouted. 'I'll get Lomax.' The little man had a thin moustache in the style of Estalian duellists and a dagger sprouted from his hand as he dove towards his prey.

'Piet,' Dubnitz said, thwacking the big man again. 'Shake it off Piet! Duty calls!'

Piet, jaw already purpling, reached out with his free hand, grabbing the little assassin's wrist and slamming it against Lomax's knee. 'Middenheim! Get this fool!' the little man yelled, struggling with Piet. A thick rope dropped over Piet's free hand with alacrity, and he was jerked around. A lanky Middenheimer who was dressed in wolf skins and wielding a hunting lasso, pulled on the rope, pulling Piet towards him. He frowned as the bonds holding Piet to Lomax and Dubnitz held. 'He's stuck, Danzig!' he shouted.

'Not for long,' Danzig snarled, another knife appearing in his hand as if by magic. Dubnitz gave the big man another whack with the cane and the ivory shattered on his broad head, revealing a hidden blade. Dubnitz's eyes widened and then he whirled, parrying the little man's blow. Danzig stared in shock and then back-pedalled as Dubnitz swiped at him. Dubnitz jabbed the tip of the blade just beneath Danzig's chin. 'Fancy Danzig, as I live and breathe,' Dubnitz said. 'And this must be Bull Murkowski and Middenheim Oscar, who's from Talabheim, if I remember correctly.'

'Erkhart,' Middenheim said, still holding Piet's arm trapped in his lasso.

'If I recall correctly, there's a warrant out for all three of you,' Dubnitz said. The crowd swirled around their island of deadly calm. If anyone noticed the five men and the corpse, no one gave any sign. Fire-eaters belched nearby, filling the air with heat and the smell of sulphur.

'Just give us the merchant, Dubnitz,' Danzig growled.

'He hit me,' Bull grunted, rubbing his face.

'I did, and several times at that,' Dubnitz said, nodding. 'And I'll do worse than that if you three jackals don't scarper.' He hugged Lomax's stiffening body close. 'Bernard Lomax is under the protection of the Order of Manann.'

'You–' Danzig began. Whatever he'd been about to say was cut off abruptly by a wave of boiling heat as a tongue of flame shot between them. All of them turned to see a fire-eater gesture with his fire-stick. Then he let loose with another belch of fire. Middenheim cursed as his lasso curled and fried, snapping and sending him tumbling. Piet, free, grabbed for his sword.

'Dubnitz,' he snapped. Dubnitz turned from the fire-eater to see the black shapes of the murder-brothers of Khaine prowling through the crowd like sharks.

'Them again,' Dubnitz said. 'They're like a bloody rash.'

The fire-eater had been joined by a tumbler, clad in silk and humorous pantaloons. The tumbler bobbed and bounced and sent a slipper-clad foot elegantly crunching into Bull's dumb features. The big man backed away, puzzled, as the tumbler continued to kick, punch and prod him. 'Lomax is ours Danzig,' a man clad in a Tilean carnival mask said, levelling a repeating pistol that was so intricately engineered that it qualified as a work of art. The pistol burped and Danzig scrambled away, hands raised as the cobbles beneath his feet were chewed to dust by the pistol.

'We're going to be killed by jugglers!' Piet said. 'I don't want to be killed by jugglers!'

Dubnitz didn't reply. The repeating pistol was swinging towards him, smoke curling from the barrel. The eyes behind the carnival mask were dark and eager. Then, abruptly, they widened. Carnival-mask slumped, a wavy-bladed dagger jutting from his back. A murder-brother vaulted over him, plucking the dagger free as he did so. Dubnitz lunged, spitting the cultist on Lomax's sword-cane. The move pulled Piet and Lomax out of the path of the fire-eater, who unleashed a titanic flume of heat. A nearby drunkard burst into flame and suddenly the crowd noticed the pandemonium going on in their midst.

Screams mingled with music and prayers as the crowd thrashed in sudden panic. People fell into the canal. Others scrambled for the safety of doorways or open windows. Dubnitz jerked the sword-cane free of the murder-cultist's chest and narrowly parried a thrust harpoon. A man with the look of a Norscan whale-hunter jabbed the harpoon again, trying to pin Dubnitz to the cobbles. 'Piet, I need some help here!' Dubnitz shouted.

'You're not the only one,' Piet said. He'd lost his sword, and now held a broken cobblestone, which he brought across the jaw of a mime that drew too close with a satisfying crunch. 'I hate mimes.'

'Was that mime an assassin?' Dubnitz grunted, the tip of the harpoon nearing his face.

'I have no idea,' Piet said, bouncing the cobble on his palm before throwing it at the fire-eater, who unleashed another plume of flame. The cobble bounced off the man's tattooed skull and he instinctively took a breath, inhaling the fire he should have been spewing. The fire-eater's screams were cut short as he was cooked inside out.

'Bad show, monsieur,' a purple clad Bretonnian snarled, driving his foot into Piet's armoured chest. Off-balance, he fell, dragging Lomax and Dubnitz with him. 'The ancient art of mummery is sacred,' the Bretonnian continued, as the two knights flailed helplessly, trying to get to their feet. Lomax's dead weight, however, made that difficult. 'It seems I, Bartok of Bastonne, master of the mystical art of the Athel-Loren war-dance, am granted the honour of collecting the bounty on Monsieur Lomax.' Bartok blinked. 'Why are the three of you tied together?'

The harpooner jabbed at Dubnitz while the Bretonnian spoke, and the knight, having lost Lomax's cane, grabbed the harpoon as it stabbed at him. With a convulsive shove he rammed the handle into its wielder's face, busting lips and freeing teeth. As the harpooner reeled, Dubnitz swung the harpoon at the Bretonnian who was preparing to launch a kick at Lomax's wobbling head. The haft of the harpoon caught the assassin on the knee, and he fell with a cry. As he hit the ground, Dubnitz hit him again and again, battering the master of the mystical art of the Athel-Loren war-dance into bloody unconsciousness.

'Piet, let's go, up and at them, can't spend all evening in the gutter,' Dubnitz roared, using the harpoon to pull himself to his feet and to simultaneously drag Piet up. Lomax bobbed between them like a cork on water. The body was already going stiff and further hampering their movements.

'I want to go home now,' Piet said, punching an Estalian knife-man wearing too much green and yellow to be wholly sane. The Estalian staggered back into the crowd and was trampled by yelling drunks.

'The night's young yet,' Dubnitz said. A murder-cultist darted from the screaming, pushing, crowd, twin daggers raised high. Two miniature crossbow bolts caught him and sent him spinning into the canal. A killer in a featureless helm and a red hauberk calmly reloaded the small crossbows attached to his armoured forearms as he stood on the bundle-board of an abandoned wagon. 'On second thought, you're right, it's time to go!'

The Spring Tide crowd around the central canal had thinned as the realization that attempted murder was being committed on a grand scale set in. Outside of the immediate area, however, the party was still in full swing. Dubnitz and Piet lurched towards the crowd. Crossbows twanged and Piet glanced over his shoulder, cursing. 'He's got arrows in him,' he said.

'He's got more than that,' Dubnitz said. 'I think the harpoon nicked him; he's leaking all over my armour.' He snagged a flagon of ale from a tipsy bawd bellowing out a hymn to Manann and knocked it back. 'Piet, this wasn't one of your better ideas I must say,' he said, slopping foam on the street.

'My idea,' Piet nearly shrieked, glaring at him. 'I– pigeon!'

'I think you mean "duck",' Dubnitz said. Piet dove for the ground, yanking Lomax and Dubnitz atop him as a pigeon hurtled through the space occupied by their heads only seconds previously. The pigeon struck the sign of a tavern and exploded in a ball of fire and feathers. Dubnitz gazed at the charred spot that marked the unfortunate avian's final impact and said in shock, 'By Manann's scaly nethers that was a Herstel-Wenckler pigeon bomb.'

'It's a swarm!' Piet yowled, trying to crawl away, his armour clattering. Dubnitz, on his side atop Lomax's corpse, stared up in horror at the feathered shapes descending towards him like verminous avenging angels. Only a fool or a madman would release pigeon bombs into streets this closely packed.

'Death by pigeon,' he murmured, suddenly calm as he faced his imminent doom. 'Who'd have thought such a thing possible in these civilised times?'

'Shut up and help me run,' Piet screamed, shoving Dubnitz off. Lomax flopping between them, the two knights stumble-ran into the safety of the crowd as the first pigeons struck the street and fire erupted. Dubnitz's foot skidded as he stepped in a cuttlefish. The high priest of the Cult of Manann was flinging the creatures from his altar-barge as it passed along the canal.

'Get to the barge!' Dubnitz said, forcing them a path to the canal with the harpoon.

'But–' Piet began.

'Go, go, go,' Dubnitz said, bashing a set of stilts aside and sending a man dressed as an Arabyan schooner staggering into a low hanging sign. He sensed more than saw the assassins following them. Lomax's relatives had seemingly spent their inheritance before they'd even gotten it. Every killer in Marienburg was after them and some few from farther afield.

'Dubnitz, to your left,' Piet said.

Dubnitz twisted as a man wearing a bronze mask crafted in the shape of a snarling tiger's head lunged out of the crowd, clawed gauntlets scraping off Dubnitz's chainmail sleeve. He thrust the harpoon between the assassin's legs, tripping him up. But even as he fell, a hard-faced killer wielding a notched axe took his place, chopping at Dubnitz. Dubnitz swatted him with the harpoon and as the axe-man stepped back, a pigeon alighted on his shoulder. He had time for a single expression of panic before the pigeon bomb blew him into gory bits. Dubnitz blinked blood out of his eyes as overhead, Cathayan fireworks went off, lighting up the night sky. Somewhere, the great Tidal Bell in the Temple of Manann was ringing.

'Hear that? It's almost morning,' Piet said. 'We made it, I can't believe we–'

The crowd thinned at the edge of the canal. They had gotten ahead of the barge, but not of the assassins.

'Bernard Lomax, you are marked for death,' an oily duellist said, gesturing with his rapier. 'Meet it manfully.'

'Give us the merchant and you can go free,' a sinister halfling with a dagger spinning between his pudgy fingers said. Around he and the duellist, a half-dozen other would-be bounty killers had eased forward. Like as not, half of them hadn't even been hired to do the deed and were simply opportunists. Dubnitz could hear sword fights breaking out throughout the crowd as other assassins, too far back to join the fun, turned on one another either in frustration or optimism.

'I'd be happy to,' Dubnitz said, keeping the harpoon extended. 'And I will, as soon as you tell me which of you lot was throwing the pigeons.'

'What pigeons?' one of a pair of twin beauties wearing little more than scars and armour said. She and her companion looked up. 'Oh,' the other one said softly.

All eyes swivelled upwards as flapping sounds filled the air. Dozens of pigeons swooped over the street, beady eyes looking for perches. 'Pigeons; thousands of them,' Piet muttered.

'Run!' Dubnitz said, stumbling forward.

Bird droppings and explosions rocked the street and a body pin-wheeled through the air. The explosions weren't large, but then, neither were halflings, Dubnitz reflected as he loped towards the canal with Piet. Those assassins not caught in the airborne conflagration hurried after them.

Piet was muttering prayers to Manann as he ran. Dubnitz simply cursed, letting flow a shower of creative invective. He cursed Lomax and his relatives, Ogg and his grandiose designs, and Marienburg with its proliferation of professional murderists. He'd always suspected he'd die at the end of a hired blade, the victim of a jealous husband or scorned woman. Possibly a city official with a grudge, or an old enemy, free of prison, or even Grandmaster Ogg, once he figured out what Dubnitz had done with his missing hand. In fairness, it made a lovely candelabrum and the Duchess had been quite appreciative, but Ogg wouldn't understand. He had no sense of proportion, that man.

But, mostly, Dubnitz cursed Manann, because once again the sea god had given him no luck but bad. Even as he settled into a quiet, snarling rhythm of curses, however, the holy altar-barge of Manann hove into view ahead of him and cuttlefish slapped the stone, hurled by the high priest. 'Haha! There it is Piet! Get to the barge! It's our only chance,' Dubnitz said, trying to hurry them along.

'The barge? But–' Piet began.

'No time for buts, Piet,' Dubnitz said. The stones were slick near the canal and he had to stop himself from falling head over heels. 'It's the barge or the blades.'

'Maybe we should think about this,' Piet said.

'What sort of knight are you? Just jump,' Dubnitz shouted, grabbing a handful of Lomax's jerkin and leaping. Piet, despite his protestations, jumped along with him. The barge wasn't far from the edge of the canal, being as wide a craft as the temple could afford.

A moment of vertigo stretched across eternity before Dubnitz's foot found the edge of the barge. The altar attendants reached out automatically to grab the knights as they swayed back and forth on the edge of the deck. Dubnitz and Piet staggered forward, nearly knocking over the votive candles and sending an iron pot of blessed seawater spilling across the deck. Priests slipped and slid as the water sloshed around their feet. The high priest turned, mouth open in mid-bellow. His hands were full of cuttlefish and words of benediction died on his lips. He looked at Dubnitz, who grinned sheepishly. 'Bless a trio of pilgrims, your supremacy?' he asked.

'Aren't you one of Ogg's bully-boys?' the high priest said, flinging a cuttlefish over his shoulder. 'You are! You're Dubnitz, the one who let that goat–'

'May I present Bernard Lomax, your excellency,' Dubnitz interjected. 'He is a humble merchant and follower of His Most Salty Majesty, Manann.' He glanced at Lomax's dangling head. 'He's overcome with emotion, your benevolence.'

The high priest waved a hand in front of his nose. 'He's overcome with something, I'd say.' He squinted. 'Is that a–?'

'What dagger?' Piet said, hastily plucking the errant blade out of Lomax's back and flinging it over the side of the barge.

'Are those crossbow bolts?'

'You know how it gets during Spring Tide, your most tidal excellency,' Dubnitz said swiftly. 'People go wild. They let their hair down. Sometimes crossbows are involved.'

'Are you sure he's–' the high priest began dubiously.

'Oh Mighty Manann, Bless Us Your Servants!' Dubnitz bellowed, falling to his knees and causing the barge to rock as Piet and Lomax followed suit. The latter's stiffening limbs and joints gave forth a plaintive series of cracks and pops as abused ligaments split. 'He's too afraid to ask it of you himself, your saintliness,' Dubnitz said, cracking one eye open. 'Could you bless him, perhaps? Let the crowd see that he has your favour?'

'I–'

'Oh Mighty Manann, Absolve Us of the Sins of Dry Land!' Dubnitz shouted, gesturing wildly, making sure to jerk one of Lomax's hands so that it flopped beseechingly at the high priest's robe. The crowd was cheering now, every eye on the barge. Seagulls squawked and horns blew. The high priest leaned close.

'What are you up to, Dubnitz?' he said.

'I assure you, it's for the greater glory of Manann, your pristine parsimoniousness,' Dubnitz said. The high priest frowned, but straightened and raised his hands in benediction.

'I expect we'll be getting a nice donation this week from the Order,' he muttered before launching into the words of Manann's Blessing. The noise of the crowd surged in volume, hammering at the ears of those aboard the barge. It was only by the slightest of chances that Dubnitz heard the whine of a bullet. He leapt to his feet, yanking Piet and Lomax up. The bullet punched into Lomax's back and sent them stumbling forward, into the high priest, who squawked in sudden fear as the corpse lurched into him.

A triumphant assassin leapt to his feet on a ledge overlooking the canal, the Hochland long rifle held over his head as he let out a yell. Dubnitz swept the harpoon's blade through his bindings, freeing himself from Lomax and then sent the harpoon hurtling towards the assassin. 'Imperial assassin!' he roared. 'He tried to kill the high priest!'

The assassin fell from his perch with a yell as he twisted to avoid the harpoon. Rifle and assassin both tumbled into the canal as the crowd gave a howl like an angry beast. Dubnitz spun and pointed at a familiar black-clad shape. The murder-cultists of Khaine had been following the barge at a distance, picking off their competition with the patience of stalking tigers. 'More assassins,' he shouted, and the crowd drew back, suddenly exposing the brass-masked killers, who looked around in confusion. Then, as one, the revellers fell on the killers, dragging them under as surely as the waters of the canal had swallowed the rifleman. Fierce as the murder-cultists were, they were no match for an entire city's worth of fists and feet putting the boot in. Black-clad shapes sank beneath the press, battered into insensibility by the Spring Tide celebrants.

'A fine display of the old Marienburg fighting spirit,' Dubnitz said, hands on his hips. 'By which I mean filching their valuables while they're bleeding on the street.'

'If you're finished congratulating yourself, I could use some help,' Piet snarled.

Dubnitz turned to see the other knight fumbling with Lomax's body, which was tangled in the high priest's robes. Dubnitz scampered over. 'One moment your excellency, help is on the way,' he said, surreptitiously unknotting the bindings that held Piet tied to Lomax. Dubnitz hauled Lomax's abused corpse off of the high priest and pulled it into an embrace. 'Bernie! By Manann's beard, no!' he said, adding a wail for good measure as he shook the body. Lomax's head flopped back and forth, his neck having been broken at some point and time. 'He's been shot!' Before the high priest could scoot away, Dubnitz grabbed his hand. 'Take his hand, excellency, take it and comfort him as he goes to Manann's realm!' He grabbed Lomax's limp hand and slapped it atop the high priest's. The latter blanched and tried to pull away, but Dubnitz held on, his face the picture of tortured melancholy. 'Shot, your mercifulness, shot while saving you from a killer!

'I thought he was–' the high priest began.

Dubnitz rode over him, shouting, 'He has given his life for you! For

Marienburg! Comfort him as he...' He paused, watching the horizon. 'As he – hold on,' he said, counting the strokes of the Tide Bell in his head. 'Wait for it – yes, there we go – comfort him as he dies, oh great sage of the Free City!'

The high priest, uncertainty writ on his features, mumbled something as spontaneous weeping broke out amongst those elements of the crowd not busy kicking in the faces of the murder-cultists. Dubnitz shoved the high priest aside and pulled Lomax into another embrace, tears spilling into his beard as he blubbered heroically. Word of mouth was a fine thing, and street corner patterers were already carrying the word of Lomax's heroic sacrifice across the city, Dubnitz wagered.

The entire city had witnessed Lomax die at cockcrow, and there'd be no contesting of the will by his relatives, not when the manner of his death was known. A hero of the city, dying to rescue the high priest of Manann, and donating his worldly wealth to the templars devoted to said god. 'Sometimes, I suspect the gods love me,' Dubnitz said as he blubbered. 'Do you ever get that feeling, Piet?'

Piet dropped to one knee beside him, a hand placed comfortingly on his shoulder. 'You're a horror, Erkhart. A literal horror,' he muttered.

'Yes, but what I am not is pickled,' Dubnitz said. 'And neither are you, so stop complaining. It all worked out for the best. Now, would you say it's cockcrow yet?'

Piet sighed and nodded. 'I think we're in the clear.'

'Ah well, Manann giveth and he taketh away, drift into his bosom, be at peace and such, et cetera and so forth,' Dubnitz said, dropping the body and rising abruptly to his feet. He clapped his hands together and looked around. The rising sun caused the scum on the surface of the canal to sparkle prettily. 'So... who's for breakfast?'

BERNHEIMER'S GUN

Josh Reynolds

'Faster, you spavined nag! Faster,' Erkhart Dubnitz, knight of the most holy (and violent) Order of Manann, roared as, hunched low over the neck of his warhorse, he raced in pursuit of the stolen coach. A number of his brothers followed him, shouting similar sulphurous encouragements to their own horses as they galloped through the cramped and twisted streets of Marienburg.

A vegetable stall seemed to appear out of nowhere, and Dubnitz howled curses as his mount burst through it with enthusiasm, squashing radishes beneath its iron-shod hooves and savaging lettuce with its yellow teeth as the vendor was sent sprawling in the gutter. The man's virulent curses pursued Dubnitz like arrows.

'Feel better?' Dubnitz snapped, clubbing his horse between the ears with a mailed fist. The animal flicked its ears, but otherwise gave no sign that it had felt the blow. 'Got that out of your system, now?' he snarled, digging his spurs into the horse's heaving flanks even as he plucked a leaf of lettuce from the sea-shell shaped elbow joint of his armour. 'Go faster, beast!'

The coach was just ahead. It squeezed through a narrow side-street, scraping paint off of its sides as the wheels sparked from the cobbles. The curtain on the back window was yanked aside and someone fired a crossbow awkwardly through it. Dubnitz cursed again and twisted clumsily in his saddle as the bolt struck one of his ornately engraved squid-shaped pauldrons and nearly tore it from his cuirass. With a growl, he snapped the reins and bent as low as possible over his horse's neck, hoping to make himself a smaller target. Given his size, he knew that was a faint hope at best. Dubnitz was what the charitable-minded might call 'barrel-chested'; though in his case, it was less a barrel and more a keg, and on better days full of alcohol and Manann's bounty, spiced and roasted to preference.

Unfortunately, today was not one of the better days. *Today is a day for the annoyances of full armour and mad riding, swords and spear-rattling,* Dubnitz thought sourly. And all because of one poxy turn-coat engineer. Mikal Bernheimer was his name, and he'd come running down the Reik all the way from the Imperial Gunnery School in Nuln, with a satchel full of plans and a head full of secrets, or so he claimed. Bernheimer had arrived begging sanctuary, but someone didn't want him to have it. Somehow, he'd been snaffled from the city watch while the High Council dithered over what to do with him, and bundled into a purloined coach by a tiny band of cut-throats and sell-swords who were even now haring off to Manann alone knew where. Dubnitz suspected that it was the docklands. In Marienburg, it always came down to the docks, one way or another.

The order had been roused to the hunt easily enough, as Grandmaster Ogg had bullied his way into a permanent invitation from the High Council, and he and a number of his knights, including Dubnitz, had been present during the kidnapping. Ogg had only haggled with the High Council for a few minutes before letting his armoured hounds slip their leashes.

Dietrich Ogg was famous in Marienburg both for his bull-headed bellicosity and the unsubtle nature of his political scheming. The knights of the order were fast becoming familiar figures in the households of the mighty of the city; he rented his warriors out as advisors, bodyguards and celebratory decorations alike, and it was said that whatever they heard, so too did he. Granted, mostly what they heard was 'I could have sworn we had more wine in the cellars' as they walked away whistling, bottles stuffed down their cuirasses. There were certain perks to knighthood, after all.

The coach burst out of the side-street and nearly rolled over, smashing against a wall before crashing back down onto all four wheels. The crowd of merchants, street-hawkers, crusty jugglers and wide-eyed gawkers scattered like a flock of fen-quail as the coach careened through them. In the wider thoroughfare, Dubnitz was able to pull up alongside the coach and reach for the thin trident sheathed along the side of his saddle. He considered using it on the team of horses pulling the coach, but discarded the idea. No sense in wasting good horseflesh if he didn't have to. Instead, he stabbed the trident at the coach's rear wheel, trying to slow it, but the coach was moving too fast. The trident ripped from his hand and he was nearly yanked from his horse.

Swaying in his saddle, Dubnitz's flailing hand caught hold of one of the ornamental stanchions that lined the frame of the carriage, and, seizing the moment, he hauled himself onto the side of the carriage with a thump. The iron stanchion, shaped like a grinning sea-nymph, nearly came away in his hand, but he awkwardly dragged himself onto the top of the coach, his sea-green enamelled armour rattling. His horse, as well-trained as the order's animals went, came to a stop as soon as his weight left the saddle and took the opportunity to finish munching its filched lettuce, watching the coach continue on with equine equanimity.

The coach was of the bigger variety and had enough room for three men on the top, plus baggage. Dubnitz carefully got his feet under him as the coach rattled and swayed across the uneven cobbles. If he could get to the driver, he'd stand a chance of stopping it, but he'd have to be careful – one wrong move could send him sailing off the coach. As Dubnitz crawled forward, the driver turned to face him, his eyes bulging comically.

The driver was unkempt and wearing a battered breastplate emblazoned with an anchor and crown, much like the kind worn by the marines of the merchant-fleets. Oaths and spittle spattered down from his lips into his bramble beard and he cried, 'Cap'n, we been boarded!'

Dubnitz jerked to the side as a length of sword blade punctured the roof of the coach with almost-lethal accuracy. He barely managed to hold on to the roof, narrowly avoiding being hurled off. The sword was withdrawn and the door on the opposite side of the coach was kicked open, allowing a man to clamber out. He wore no helm, allowing his stringy hair to flutter around his face, but as he hauled himself onto the roof, sword in hand, Dubnitz's eyes widened in recognition as his opponent's artificial leg thudded down. It was crafted from a scrimshawed length of driftwood, balanced by a carved paw, into which a trio of toe-bones had been set like claws. The knee-joint was hidden behind a chunk of brass, beaten into the shape of a crude skull.

'Oh bugger,' Dubnitz said. 'I should have just killed the horses.'

'Erkhart,' the other man growled in recognition, steadying himself on the roof of the swaying coach with the ease of a man used to the pitch and yaw of a storm-tossed ship. 'I heard you'd given up honest graft for a career as one of Ogg's swabs, but I hardly credited it.'

'Hello Edvard, I'll tell the Grandmaster you said hello,' Dubnitz said, fighting his way to his feet, his hand reaching for the hilt of his sword. 'I should have realised that your merry band of salty gallows-thieves were the only ones greedy and stupid enough to annoy the High Council.'

Edvard Van der Kraal, captain of the free company known as Manann's Blades, smiled cruelly. 'Stupid, is it? This little job will guarantee us a berth on any ship in the Manaanspoort.' His artificial leg squeaked and his sword plunged towards Dubnitz. The latter drew his blade and blocked the blow with more force than finesse and was forced to dig a hand into the top of the coach to maintain his balance.

'Only if you succeed,' Dubnitz growled. He thrust his blade out and Van der Kraal drove it aside almost contemptuously. Dubnitz grimaced. He wasn't one to avoid a fight – indeed, some of his most cherished memories involved fights of one sort or another, usually followed by feasting or... other entertainments – but Van der Kraal was as deadly a man as they came, and in Marienburg they came plenty deadly. The mercenary was a salt-blooded killer, with iron filings for eyes and a heart colder than a Norscan winter. Even worse, he'd taken an irrational dislike to Dubnitz due to an entirely innocent misunderstanding, completely out of the latter's control.

'Brave words for a body bound for the tannery,' Van der Kraal growled, lashing out again.

They traded clumsy blows as the coach rattled on, neither man able to put much force into his blow for fear of knocking himself off, as well as his opponent. Every bump or jerk of the coach was a missed blow or a near-fatal one, adding an element of chance to the whole business that Dubnitz found increasingly unpleasant.

'Never could stomach a heaving deck, could you?' Van der Kraal taunted. 'Your time on land has made you soft, Erkhart.'

'Compared to you, Edvard, a stone in the Sea of Claws is soft,' Dubnitz said. 'Lucky for me, your men aren't made of as such stern stuff as yourself.'

He caught Van der Kraal's blade on his own, even as he plucked the thin, Tilean stiletto from its sheath on his belt and sent it sailing into the back of the driver's neck. Both men goggled as the driver slumped sideways and toppled from the coach, causing the horses pulling it to go suddenly wild. Dubnitz looked at Van der Kraal. 'I can't believe that worked,' he said, somewhat nonplussed.

The coach, driver-less, swept on. The horses began to pick up speed, heedless of what was happening to their burden. The coach smashed from side to side, striking walls and stalls and bouncing from one end of a street to the next. Neither Dubnitz nor his opponent had much time for fighting, as both put all of their efforts into trying to hold on.

Suddenly, the coach burst out from the narrow street it had been on and into the docklands. Crates were thrown aside and cages of poultry and exotic animals smashed, freeing chickens and ocelots by the score as sailors, dock workers and men of the Harbour Watch fled out of its path with shouts and curses.

Dubnitz glanced at Van der Kraal and saw that the other man was distracted by the rapidly approaching docks. 'I think this is your stop,' he said, twisting around to drive his boot into the mercenary's belly. Van der Kraal went flying and Dubnitz was alone on the coach. Acting as quickly as he dared, he clambered towards the buckboard to where the reins had become entangled in the mouth of a carven grotesquery mounted on the front of the coach.

A bump sent Dubnitz tumbling face-first onto the buckboard and he clawed blindly for the reins. He caught them and heaved himself upright, bracing his feet against the edge of the board and hauling back on the reins with every ounce of strength he possessed in his stocky frame. The horses snorted in protest and their hooves rattled on the docks as they skidded to a halt only a half-moment away from the quay's edge and the briny waters of the sea. Breathing heavily, sweat running down his face into his beard, Dubnitz looked back at the coach.

A loaded crossbow was pointing straight at him, aimed over the top of an open door. The mercenary holding it grinned and said, 'Much obliged.'

Dubnitz grabbed the head of the bolt before the mercenary could pull the trigger and ripped it loose from the runnel. The man gaped at him stupidly, and then toppled over backwards as Dubnitz's armoured fist caught him square in the nose a moment later. 'You're welcome,' Dubnitz said, dropping off the buckboard to the ground.

He peered into the coach. A lean, aesthetic-looking man, all elbows, knees and nose, was crammed into the far corner of the coach, a heavy engineer's satchel cradled against his chest, and a pair of Bretonnian *pince-nez* askew on his face. 'Ah–ah–ah,' he said, his mouth trying to form words that wouldn't come.

'Good afternoon,' Dubnitz said, grinning. 'Mikal Bernheimer, is it? How are you enjoying Marienburg so far?'

Bernheimer's eyes widened and Dubnitz stiffened as the flat of a sword blade fell lightly on his shoulder, its edge far too close to his neck for comfort. He clawed for his sword before he realised he'd lost it during the coach ride. He sighed. 'Hello again, Edvard,' he said.

'You kicked me off the coach,' Van der Kraal said.

'I did? How clumsy of me. Must have been an accident,' Dubnitz said, turning around slowly. The sword blade moved with him, pricking the hollow of his throat. 'Care to get me my sword so that we can pick up where we left off?' Van der Kraal looked at him as if he were an idiot. 'No? Never mind, I just thought I'd give it a try.'

'You always were an amusing sort, Erkhart,' Van der Kraal said.

'How's Elisa, then?' Dubnitz said mildly. It was a dangerous gambit, but he needed to play for time. If the others arrived, Van der Kraal would have no reason to kill him. Icy as he was, he didn't shed blood for the love of it, especially when there was no profit in it.

'She's fine,' Van der Kraal grunted. He stepped back. His face had an angry cast to it, which Dubnitz had expected. Mentioning Elisa was like poking a wolf-seal with a stick.

'Still pining for me?' he asked.

'No,' Van der Kraal said.

'Pining for you?' Dubnitz said.

'No,' Van der Kraal snapped. His eyes narrowed. 'She's married. To a milliner,' he added, sourly.

'A milliner,' Dubnitz said in disbelief.

'Yes,' Van der Kraal growled. 'A milliner – a very wealthy milliner – and I would like to get on with this, so step aside Erkhart. Bernheimer is coming with me.'

'I don't think so,' Dubnitz said, looking past Van der Kraal. The mercenary frowned and turned slightly as a number of mounted knights thundered onto the docks, tridents levelled. Dubnitz reached up and used two fingers to gently push the sword aside. Van der Kraal frowned and stepped back. He lowered his sword as a number of tridents were aimed in his general direction, but didn't drop it. He wasn't intimidated in the least. Dubnitz had once seen Van der Kraal stare down a crew of Norscan raiders, so this wasn't too surprising.

What was surprising was the sound of a number of crossbows being made ready to fire. Dubnitz looked around and spotted the new arrivals creeping through the obstacle course of busted casks, broken crates and unhappy chickens – crossbows aimed and swords and halberds ready. They were a nasty looking lot, but then they would have to be, to join the Manann's Blades. Van der Kraal smirked. 'Did you really think I wouldn't have my lads waiting on the docks for me?'

'The question is, do you think you have enough lads for the job?' Dubnitz said, crossing his arms.

'They have crossbows,' Van der Kraal said.

'Not many, from what I can see. And how quickly can they load them?' Dubnitz said.

Van der Kraal frowned. But before he could reply, a third ring of bared blades and armoured bodies were added to the proceedings with a clash of metal and the wail of a marsh-horn, which made the hairs on Dubnitz's neck prickle. It was an eerie sound, meant to travel across the vast, damp emptiness of the marshes that sat to either side of the city. The men of the Marienburg Marsh Watch were a disciplined bunch, and as rough and unpleasant in their way as Van der Kraal's rowdies. They wore well-cared for cuirasses over leather jacks and had heavy, conical helms on their heads. They carried weapons that had seen much use against pirates and smugglers as well as other, more unpleasant enemies. They surrounded the men of the Manann's Blades with brisk efficiency, and levelled their heavy gisarmes. The mercenaries looked prepared to fight, but their captain held up a hand, forestalling any sudden combative impulses his men might have been feeling.

Van der Kraal cursed as a pair of horsemen nudged their way through the gathered knights. One was Grandmaster Ogg, his stocky form clad in full armour, and his prosthetic trident-hand tapping against his thigh in an irritated fashion. The other was far less armoured, and yet far more terrifying. Aloysious Ambrosius, Marsh Warden and the closest thing Marienburg had to a Lord Justicar, was a lean, one-eyed man, dressed finely if not ostentatiously. The patch that covered his missing eye was embroidered with the trident and crown symbol of the Marsh Watch and the same sigil decorated his polished cuirass.

The rumour was that Ambrosius had once been a member of knightly order himself in the Empire, before certain personal peccadilloes had seen him cashiered and sent running for Marienburg, a bevy of bounty hunters and professional duellists hot on his heels. In his first week in the city he had seen Ambrosius lose an eye, gain a position as head of the Marsh Watch and kill almost a dozen men. Since that time, the Marsh Watch, once an underfunded and badly equipped joke of an organization, had grown to rival the Black Caps, as the City Watch was sometimes known, and the River Watch in influence over city affairs. Marienburg was a city of ever-shifting political tides, and Ambrosius was as fine a navigator as those dark waters had ever seen.

'Well, here we are,' Ambrosius said. Knights and mercenaries alike eyed one another nervously. 'You are well, *Herr* Bernheimer?' Ambrosius asked, looking at the little man. 'Nothing rattled loose in that valuable mind of yours, I trust?'

'Ah–I– no, milord,' Bernheimer said, looking nervous. Dubnitz didn't blame him.

'Good,' Ambrosius said. He glanced at Dubnitz. 'Ah, Dubnitz,' he murmured, 'somehow, I felt certain that you would be leading the charge. You are a credit to your order.'

Dubnitz blinked. It hadn't sounded like an insult, but with Ambrosius you could never be too sure. Before he could reply, he caught a look from Ogg and shut his mouth. The Grandmaster sniffed and said, 'What about the mercenary?'

'What about him?' Ambrosius said. He glanced at Van der Kraal. 'One assumes that it will be next to impossible to get you to divulge the identity of your employer in this matter?' Van der Kraal grunted, and Ambrosius smiled thinly. 'As I thought,' he said. 'I trust that your dues to the Guild of Military Contractors have been paid to date?'

Dubnitz hadn't thought it possible, but Van der Kraal's expression grew even stonier. The mercenary nodded tersely. Ambrosius's smile widened and he made a 'run along' gesture. 'Good, good, be off with you then. I am given to understand that there's a river caravan riding the tide east come the morning, and that they are looking for men to guard them. Something you would perhaps be interested in, eh?'

Dubnitz could almost hear Van der Kraal's teeth grinding. The mercenary nodded shallowly. It was tantamount to a temporary banishment, but it was better than being hung, or left in the tide-cages for the gulls and crabs. Without a word, he sheathed his blade, gave Dubnitz one final glare, and then stumped away. His men followed more slowly, warily watching for any sign of pursuit.

'I can't believe you're letting them go,' Ogg said. 'Van der Kraal has been due a good neck stretching for a while now.'

'As have a number of your knights, Dietrich,' Ambrosius said. 'But I think that we can both agree that they are more useful alive than dead, eh?' He looked at Dubnitz as he said it, and Dubnitz assumed his best look of utter innocence. Ambrosius looked again at Bernheimer. 'Herr Bernheimer, you will forthwith be placed under my personal protection. The High Council is... chastened by this unfortunate affair, and has graciously allowed the Marsh Watch to step in and lend aid to our brethren in the City Watch.'

I'll bet they are, Dubnitz thought, *and I'll bet the City Watch is glad to be rid of him to boot. I wouldn't wish such a task on my worst enemy.* Ambrosius looked at him again, as if he'd heard Dubnitz's thoughts, and swung down out of his saddle. One long arm fell across Dubnitz's shoulders and the knight found himself being pulled away from the crowd. Ambrosius smiled at him. 'Erkhart, Erkhart, Erkhart. You are a useful man. Did you know that? You have an innate capacity for innovation and drive to succeed, which is impressively pugnacious, if I do say so myself.'

'Thank you,' Dubnitz said warily. He began surreptitiously scanning for potential escape routes.

'I refer specifically, of course, to that business with the zombies and the unfortunate Prince Eyll. Oh, and the matter of the cursed shark teeth last Mitterfruhl. Dietrich assures me that you have displayed a ruthless cunning on numerous other occasions as well, such as the curiously public demise of Bernard Lomax this past Spring Tide. Such qualities are why he offered you a position in the order, rather than leaving you in the cages with the rest of the scum.'

Dubnitz wasn't entirely sure how to reply. Ambrosius released him and gestured towards Bernheimer. 'Look at him, Dubnitz. Tell me what you see.'

'Someone who could use a few more good meals, maybe a bit of a lie-down,' Dubnitz said.

'No. What you see there is... *potential.*' Ambrosius kicked idly at a chicken as it ran between them, clucking loudly. 'Quite simply, we need him. We need his expertise,' he continued. 'Marienburg has many merits, but engineering has never been one of them. The art of the gun and cannon is one little practised here. Our cousins to the east guard their secrets jealously, and what artillery and handguns we possess were obtained through illicit and altogether difficult means. If this city is to maintain its independence, we must have an edge.'

'So why not bargain with the dwarfs ourselves?' Dubnitz asked, plucking an apple out of a broken crate and rolling it around on his palm before taking a loud, wet bite. Chewing, he continued, 'The little buggers love gold, and we've got plenty of that.'

'Have you ever haggled with a dwarf?' Ambrosius said. 'Merchant families of good standing have spent entire *generations* bargaining with the dwarfs for what few crumbs we now possess. Also our esteemed Imperial cousins have expended treasure and blood to ensure that our relations with the mountain folk are strained at best. While the dwarfs do not make much of a distinction between our peoples, Karl Franz's Empire cannot afford to allow us to become a blackpowder society.'

'Not really a fan of it myself,' Dubnitz said. 'A handgun will punch through armour as if it were paper.' He patted his cuirass. 'I'm fond of my armour.'

'Your opinion is noted,' Ambrosius said, in a tone that implied that it had been discarded as well. Dubnitz nearly choked on his apple and cursed his tongue for wagging so freely. The only reason he still had it was that Ambrosius thought he was amusing.

'Bernheimer claims to have the secret to blackpowder manufacturing, and to have designed a gun – cannon – which is second to none currently in use by our neighbours. That's why the High Council even deigned to consider his request. Renegade engineers are more trouble than they're worth, and our cousins in the Empire spare no expense in hunting down such escapees.'

'But is Bernheimer worth it?' Dubnitz asked, looking doubtfully at the little man where he sat disconsolately on the edge of the coach, his satchel clutched to his chest. He looked like a noodle that had been left in the pot too long. If he was as valuable as all that, no wonder someone had hired Van der Kraal to get him back.

Ambrosius nodded. 'His knowledge will be combined with that of the artisans working on the city's flotilla of landships, to improve their design and to improve their armament with his oh-so special gun,' he said. Dubnitz grimaced. The landships were mobile fortresses of oak and iron, shaped like sailing vessels but mounted upon massive wheels and powered not by wind or oars, but by experimental boilers that, as yet, had a tendency to explode unexpectedly. The landships had been Ambrosius's pet project for a while now. He'd managed to somehow talk a number of the city's wealthiest burghers into opening up their vast coffers to pay for the blasted things. And now, apparently, he wanted to add cannons to them on top of the exploding boilers.

'His old masters won't like that very much,' Dubnitz said warily.

'I should say not, as evidenced by this little escapade,' Ambrosius said. 'I was ready for it, this time. I knew it would only be a matter of time until the City Watch allowed Bernheimer to slip through their grasp. I knew and planned accordingly.'

Dubnitz frowned. 'You wanted him to be taken,' he said. What better way to impress upon the High Council the inefficiency of the Black Caps than to have a number of them publically slaughtered and their charge kidnapped?

Ambrosius inclined his head. 'Did I say that? Of course not, but he was and here we are.'

'We,' Dubnitz repeated. There was a sinking feeling in his gut. Ambrosius smiled, and the feeling got worse.

'Yes, quite. I argued from the first that there was only one body of men capable of protecting our new engineer from those who would seek to deny our city his skills.' Ambrosius's smile grew even wider and Dubnitz swallowed hard.

'The Order of Manann,' he said hesitantly.

Ambrosius's grin was positively vulpine as he clapped his hands on Dubnitz's shoulders. 'The Order of Manann and their best knight,' he said.

'Grandmaster Ogg, you mean,' Dubnitz assayed.

'Not quite.'

'Oh,' Dubnitz said.

'I have every confidence that you will keep him healthy and safe for me – for us – Sir Dubnitz. I cannot bear to consider otherwise,' Ambrosius said. Dubnitz had seen less terrifying smiles on sharks. Ambrosius turned and said, loudly, 'Dietrich you are to be commended on the courage of your knights!'

'I am?' Ogg said, looking confused.

'He is?' Dubnitz said, trailing after Ambrosius as they rejoined the others.

'Quite,' Ambrosius said, climbing back up onto his horse. 'I will send several of my clerks around, to aid Herr Bernheimer in getting acquainted with his new duties. Duties he is no doubt eager to take up, now that this excitement is over with.'

Bernheimer perked up. An odd glint came into his eyes as he stood up. 'Oh aye, my lord, I am quite enthused with the prospect of starting afresh here, in this mighty citadel of possibility!' His smile was disjointed, like a crack in polished glass. 'I shall craft such artifice as shall raise the art of war to heights undreamt of in this fallen age!' He hugged his satchel to his chest, and Dubnitz wondered if the man who'd invented the pigeon-bomb had had the same look on his face as he'd sent his first lethal payload skyward. Probably, he decided; all engineers were mad, to some extent. Of course, who was maddest – the mad man, or the man who had to guard him?

'Manann carry me safely to shore,' Dubnitz muttered.

'Uncork, Van der Kraal,' Uli Tassenberg said, eyeing the mercenary captain over the rim of his cup. His heavy bulk was parked behind an ornately engraved table, covered in sprawling piscine designs and sturdily anchored to the cabin floor. 'You're still getting paid.'

The sun was setting, casting a watery orange light over the ships anchored in the harbours of the Suiddock. Captain Van der Kraal had returned to the private yacht where his employer was waiting, albeit reluctantly. Now he stood in the cabin of Tassenberg's pleasure yacht, matching the latter's amused gaze with a glare of defiance. Tassenberg had a reputation for rewarding failure in a fairly permanent fashion, and his guards had taken Van der Kraal's sword.

If there were any man in Marienburg more frightening than the Marsh Warden, it was Tassenberg the Slaver. He'd boiled horse-hide and made leather and glue like the other orphans in the Tannery. Marienburg was like an apple riddled with brown patches, and of those patches the Tannery was one of the worst. Located in the maze of streets that played host to the city's tanneries, it was a squalid, foul-smelling territory and the gangs of mule-skinners and cat's meat-men who made it their home were as dangerous as any dock-tough or river-rat. And now that he was powerful, Tassenberg had made it his fortress.

From the Tannery, he purveyed human flesh all over Marienburg, taking captives to the water wherever it flowed. They said he could get any hue of flesh or size or build, guaranteed. If you needed concubines or doxies, he could get you fifty before the sun had set; if you needed men or beasts for the fighting pits, he could have them in a fortnight, less if they didn't need to be blooded, though he drew the line at rats of any size, unusual or otherwise – Tassenberg hated rats. If you were a recruiter, looking for a hardy crew, Tassenberg's men could have you a full complement before the morning tide. More than one man of Van der Kraal's acquaintance had gone missing after incurring a debt with Tassenberg.

'We failed,' Van der Kraal said, eyeing Tassenberg warily.

'So? It's not my money,' Tassenberg said. His chubby, florid face rippled in a toothy grin.

'No, it's his,' Van der Kraal said, looking at the cabin's third occupant. The man was big, bigger than the low ceiling of the cabin could comfortably accommodate, and the cowled cloak he wore only made him seem larger still. An untouched goblet of wine sat before him, and one large, blunt-fingered hand rested on the hilt of the massive, archaic blade that served as a buffer between him and the two Marienburgers. 'I don't like taking money from men who don't show me their faces,' the mercenary continued.

The big man didn't react. Tassenberg chuckled. 'No, but you'll take it all the same, Van der Kraal, and you'll pay your bully-boys and go somewhere nice for a few weeks, eh?'

'Funny, the Marsh Warden said the same thing,' the mercenary said, snatching up the sack of coins and hefting it. 'Seems a shame to miss whatever is going on,' he added. Tassenberg was about to reply when the big man shifted abruptly in his seat. His knuckles popped audibly as his fingers curled around the sheathed blade. Eyes like dull, dark stones fixed Van der Kraal with a stare that was simultaneously bland and menacing.

The mercenary hesitated. Then, with a sigh, he nodded. 'Ah well, the lads need a rest anyway. Thank you kindly, *Meneer* Tassenberg. If you ever require my services...'

'I know exactly where to find you,' Tassenberg said. He watched the mercenary troop back out to the deck, where Tassenberg's men would escort him off the yacht with all due haste. The High Council had eyes everywhere. He took a noisy gulp from his goblet and refilled it from the flagon on the table. 'He was probably followed. That's the only reason that one-eyed thief-catcher would let him walk away.'

The big man tensed slightly. Tassenberg chuckled. 'Easy does it, *Mein Herr*. I have my most trusted blade prowling those docks, hunting for Ambrosius's little spies. Otto will deal with any prying eyes or ears never fear.'

'You had best hope so, slaver,' the big man rumbled.

Tassenberg smirked. 'Have you ever heard the saying about flies, honey and vinegar, Herr Bruckner? No? No, I don't suppose you have. Not Countess Emmanuelle's headsman. Straight ahead, chop-chop-chop, that's how you do it in Nuln, eh?'

'Still your tongue before I rip it out by the roots, fat man,' Theodore Bruckner growled, his dull eyes flashing as he thrust his hood back from his craggy face. Long hair and thick, braided moustaches covered his head and obscured his face, save for his hooked nose and odd eyes. 'I do not suffer mockery.'

'Unless it's the countess doing the mocking, eh,' Tassenberg said. 'The stories I've heard about her. Whatever happened to her brother, eh? Was it as bad as the gossipmongers say?' When Bruckner didn't answer, Tassenberg shrugged and smiled. 'Never mind. Business associates should stick to business and not try and make small talk.'

'Do you think he knows that he was played false? That we never wanted him to bring Bernheimer to us, successfully?' Bruckner said.

'Possibly; he's a cunning one, that Van der Kraal. But he won't care. And he served his purpose – now those wet hens in the High Council will think Bernheimer is valuable. The best way to convince a rich man he wants something is to try and take it from him. Out of curiosity, how would he have gotten away, had Van der Kraal managed it?'

Bruckner smiled slightly. 'He's... resourceful.' He didn't elaborate further.

Tassenberg licked his lips. 'My men are ready, for when he's done it's done. When should it be?'

'A few days, at most. He's assured me that he will concoct the proper signal. Can you get him out of the city?' Bruckner said, running his fingers across the plain leather sheath of his sword.

'Easily,' Tassenberg said. 'I'll send Otto, and a few of my best cut-throats. It'll look like a coincidence, I assure you. Especially given that it's in the eastern docklands. It'll look like just another shot fired across the bows of a rival of mine.'

Bruckner grunted. 'It doesn't bother you, betraying your people this way?'

'I'm not betraying *my* people,' Tassenberg said expansively. 'I'm betraying my enemies – men and women who would see me hung or left in the tide-cages for my supposed crimes. Besides, a bit of sabotage is only politics, after all. And I've got other things to worry about than *politics*.' He spat the last word, his joviality evaporating momentarily.

It was Bruckner's turn to smile, albeit thinly. 'Yes, you do.'

Tassenberg looked at him. His eyes narrowed speculatively. 'What have you heard?'

'The Master of Shadows still controls the eastern docks, does he not? He – whoever he is – has as much a stranglehold over his section of this detestable city as you do over yours.' Bruckner said it matter-of-factly. 'My agents approached him about arranging this matter first. The one who found him was sent back to Nuln via the Reik on five different boats.'

'Yes, he is a mean bugger, that one,' Tassenberg said. 'Not sociable, like me. Not a man of the people, you could say.' He patted his belly. 'A man willing to enter into profitable arrangements without bias,' he continued, 'and on that note, when do I get my guns, headsman?'

'When Bernheimer is back aboard this yacht, slaver,' Bruckner said. 'And not before.'

'Fine, fine,' Tassenberg chuckled, waving a hand in surrender. 'I'm a patient man, me. After all, I've waited this long to bring the light of gunfire to the shadows of the eastern docks, I can wait a few days more. Besides, I can count on Otto to cause plenty of collateral damage when he pays them a visit.' He grinned and lifted the flagon. 'Wine?'

The shipyards of the eastern docklands occupied a structure that had once been a massive temple, though whether to Manann, Stromfels or even Mermedus not even the scholar-priests of the Order of the Albatross could say. It had been built upon a natural quay, formed from stone, densely packed soil and mud at some time in the distant past that had settled into a sort of trident shape. The first men to inhabit that area had raised a temple, though whether at their recognizance or at the behest of the ancient devils which had once inhabited the misty coastlines and marshes was a mystery. The temple was a vast space and open to the elements, consisting of oddly spaced stone formations that some scholars insisted aligned perfectly with the stars at certain times of the year, including Mitterfruhl.

During the construction of the shipyards in the time of Magnus the Pious, the temple had been used as the skeleton of what was to come. Now, the sky had been blocked out by great ribs of pitch-hardened wood connected by huge expanses of overlapped netting. Anchor chains had been wrapped around the antediluvian stones, and icons and symbols of Manann had been tied to the links. Smaller jetties and quays made from wood jutted from the crook of each curve of the trident, and crews of artisans and craftsman were hard at work at projects stationed at each. Priests of Manann were also present and in great numbers, moving amongst the crews and casting ladles of salt water across the unfinished vessels in order to bless them.

Dubnitz took a deep breath and clapped his hands against his cuirass. 'Breathe it in, my friends,' he said loudly, his voice carrying easily over the rattle of hammers, the hiss of saws and the shouts of workers. 'Industry,' he said, flinging out his hands, as if to grasp the entirety of the shipyards.

'Industry smells an awful lot like tar,' one of the two knights accompanying Dubnitz said, tamping down tobacco into the bowl of his scrimshaw pipe. Ernst Rohmer was an older man, with a seamed face and a build almost as heavy as Dubnitz.

'It's also quite loud,' added the other, a lean whip of a man with the stamp of one of the lower rungs of Marienburg's aristocracy on his features. Piet van Taal had his helmet under one arm and his palm resting nervously on the squid-shaped pommel of his blade. 'I've been in battles that were less noisy.'

'Two,' Ernst said, holding up two fingers. 'You've been in two battles.'

'And this is louder than both of them,' Piet said.

'That's because both of them involved less than thirty men, and took place almost entirely in ill-lit courtyards,' Dubnitz said. 'Crowd control isn't the same thing as waging war, young Piet.'

'Depends on the crowd,' Piet retorted.

Dubnitz chuckled. Gulls wheeled overhead, or waddled across the nets above, squawking raucously as the morning sun blazed down on the shallow quays where the first trio of what many were hoping would be Marienburg's answer to the Empire's infamous steam-tanks were being assembled by every available hand. Marienburg's craftsmen had developed a quick assembly-line method of manufacture that stood in contrast to the artisans of the Empire or Bretonnia. Each of the merchant houses had their own method, but all were standardised to some degree, out of necessity. There were only so many shipyards, after all, and time was money. The faster a ship could be built, the faster it could be plying the waters, whatever its purpose. When a new, faster, better method of construction was discovered by a group of craftsmen, it was quickly duplicated by all the rest. Occasionally, this led to sporadic outbreaks of violence in the shipyards, as rival crews sabotaged or stole from one another, but, in Dubnitz's opinion, a bit of blood now and then helped keep the wheels of commerce turning.

A shout caught his attention. Bernheimer was scrambling across the hull of one of the landships, hooked into a barnacle scraper's harness, shouting instructions to the coterie of artisans and workers who had gathered around him at the behest of Ambrosius's clerks.

There were three of the landships – one almost completed, and the other two in various stages of construction. They were as large as any galleon or grain-ship, with hulls that would have put the walls of a border-fort to shame and masts as thick as a giant's legs. At the top of each mast, rather than a sail, was a reinforced crow's nest.

Each vessel was the result of months of planning and months of construction – whole crews from the shipyards had been pressed into service, working day and night to see to their completion. The massive, iron-banded wheels alone had required a week apiece to get right, if the gossipmongers were right. Carpenters and wood-workers from the length and breadth of the Old World had been lured to Marienburg with the promise of open coffers to ensure that the behemoths were structurally sound as well as imposing. Blacksmiths, armourers and builders had been employed to craft the heavily armoured parapet-style towers that occupied the fore and aft decks, and to attach the hundreds of iron plates that guarded the joins and hull.

The three knights watched the proceedings from a safe distance. 'I don't trust anyone that enthusiastic,' Piet muttered, watching as Bernheimer swatted wildly at an overly aggressive gull with a set of rolled up plans.

'I don't trust anyone who meddles with explosives,' Ernst said, puffing on his pipe.

'I don't trust anyone,' Dubnitz said, smiling.

The other two knights looked at him, as if waiting for him to add a clarifier. Dubnitz looked at them. 'What?'

Piet sighed. 'Have I thanked you yet, Erkhart, for including me in this?'

'Aye, very generous of you,' Ernst muttered. He eyed Dubnitz. 'This is about the five karls I owe you, isn't it?'

'Possibly,' Dubnitz said, crossing his arms. Ogg had offered him his pick of his fellow knights to help him look to Bernheimer's safety, and he'd chosen Ernst and Piet before either of them had had a chance to sneak out of the chapterhouse. One of the first things you learned after joining the order was to never, ever, volunteer for anything, especially if someone mentioned free food. It would only end in tears. Once they'd been caught and cornered, both men had grudgingly agreed. He'd been in tight spots with both of them before, and he knew they were born survivors and quick thinkers. Qualities that might prove useful, he suspected. Besides which, Ernst owed him money, and Piet was, in Dubnitz's opinion, born to take arrows meant for better men.

Bernheimer had retired late that first night and every night since, after jabbering the ears off Ambrosius's clerks. Marienburg had its own corps of engineers, but they were hardly of a class with a graduate of Nuln's Gunnery School. Bernheimer claimed to have learned his skills at the feet of the infamous Jubal Falk himself, the Powder-Master and Castellan-Engineer of Nuln. His notes, calculations and designs seemed to bear that out – at least according to Ambrosius's people.

In the three days since Bernheimer had been rescued from the Manann's Blades, things had gotten very busy in the shipyards. The experimental gunworks that Ambrosius had founded and funded several months before had been put at Bernheimer's disposal and subsequently set to work crafting the gun he had designed even as he had visited the alchemists' guild to see to the preparation of his particular mix of black powder. Now, he was overseeing the installation of swivel-mounts and reinforced powder caches, as well as seemingly redesigning the hulls of the landships for maximum efficiency.

Or so he claimed. As with all engineers, or at least all those of Dubnitz's limited acquaintance, Bernheimer loved to talk, and ideas and concepts spilled from him like a storm-swollen flood – it was difficult to tell, at any given moment, exactly what he was on about. Then again, maybe that was the point.

'Did you say something?' Ernst said.

Dubnitz gave a start, and then shook his head.

'Merely thinking out loud,' he said.

'I was wondering what that rude noise was,' a woman said.

Dubnitz flinched. The voice was familiar and the tone even more so. His eyes rolled heavenwards.

'Manann spare me your storms,' he murmured as he turned to face the newcomer, a jovial grin plastered to his face. 'Esme, you're looking well!'

Like all members of the Order of the Albatross, Esme Goodweather wore a tarjack's harness over her robes, with dozens of pouches and reliquaries tied to it, as well as a hooked knife carved from the tooth of some unpleasant deep-sea leviathan and a handful of silver bells. Dubnitz had seen her use that knife to unpleasant effects more than once, and as she looked at him, she fingered the hilt speculatively. 'So are you, Erkhart. Unfortunately,' she said.

'You're still upset,' he said.

'What was your first clue?'

'How many times must I apologize? It was dark! Anyone could have made that mistake!' He looked helplessly at his fellow knights.

Piet threw up his hands and stepped back. Ernst looked away, whistling genially. Dubnitz growled. *Cowards,* he thought. 'Besides it's been almost a year – you can't possibly be still holding a grudge?'

'It has been a year,' Goodweather said agreeably.

Dubnitz relaxed.

'Since the first one,' she continued.

Dubnitz tensed up again.

'Ah,' he said.

'Why are you here, Erkhart? Does it have something to do with that annoying little man yelling at everyone about firing trajectories and hull fractures?' Goodweather said. 'Is that why you and your rusty friends are here?'

'We're here at the behest of the Marsh Warden,' Dubnitz said, 'to see that "the annoying little man" as you call him, comes to no harm.' He leaned forward. 'And why are you here, then? Did you miss me that much?'

'Hardly,' Goodweather said. She gestured towards a ship in the shallows, where several other priests and priestesses were splashing the decks with Manann's sacred bilge. 'I'm here on temple business. There are boats that need blessing.' She frowned. 'But I saw you, and I thought of that business last Mitterfruhl, and decided to see what trouble the tide was bringing in.'

'You make me sound like your personal bird of ill-omen,' Dubnitz protested. 'And here I am, being civic-minded and a good Marienburger. You wound me, Goodweather.'

'If only,' she said.

Dubnitz grinned. 'Be honest. You're still on the outs with the temple authorities after you punched the high priest for getting fresh on the altar-barge, and you were hoping I'd blab something interesting, weren't you? A bit of such and such for the delicate shell-like ears of Manann's own, as to what the High Council is up to?'

Goodweather shrugged. 'And if I am? Information is as good as currency in this city, you know that.' She leaned close. 'What's going on? Who is he?'

'Did you really have to dump him into the canal during Summer Tide, and in front of the orphans to boot? What sort of example is that setting for the wee tykes?' Dubnitz said, ignoring the question. Goodweather opened her mouth to reply, when Piet said, 'What is he doing?'

'What?' Dubnitz turned around. Bernheimer was gesticulating wildly and berating the crowd of clerks and engineers who surrounded him on the deck of a landship. He was shaking one of the bulky, powder-charged Cathayan signal-rockets that many of Marienburg's warships carried, as if for emphasis. They were useful devices, rather like oversized fireworks, and they were usually colour-coded, each colour marking a different order.

'If he's not careful, that thing is going to go off,' Ernst said, tapping the bowl of his pipe on his vambrace.

The signal-rocket went off with a spiralling shriek, scattering sparks across the deck and the crowd gathered there. The rocket punched through the netting above, scattering gulls, and corkscrewed up into the sky, where it exploded in a blossom of bright red.

'Well that's lovely,' Piet said, shading his eyes.

Dubnitz, however, wasn't looking at the burst of colour and fire. Instead, he watched the gulls. Those that hadn't scattered when the rocket passed through the netting suddenly took wing, as if alerted to some further danger.

The explosion rocked the shipyard a moment later. Geysers of water, burning wood and dislodged stone spurted into the air, sending those men who hadn't been knocked sprawling by the force of the explosion scurrying for cover. Dubnitz instinctively placed himself between Goodweather and the debris that scythed through the air. Piet fell over with a curse, and Ernst was forced to steady himself against a stone.

'What in Manann's name was that?' Goodweather yelped, covering her head.

'Someone blew up a powder-keg,' Dubnitz said. 'You can smell the sulphur from here. They've blown a hole under the shipyard!' He glanced over his shoulder, trying to see through the voluminous cloud of smoke and dust that now spread through the shipyard. He cursed as he spotted several shapes hurrying through it. The first one to bull through the smoke into full view was an ogre, as big and hungry-looking as any of its kind: it was clad in the outsize burnoose and turban of an Arabayan corsair and wielding a tulwar with a blade roughly the size of Dubnitz's leg. The blade slashed out and slapped a staggering priest into the air, sending his body spinning into the water.

Behind the ogre came a number of muscular individuals who bore the stamp of the fighting-pits on their scarred faces, as well as a bevy of colourful bravos who wouldn't have looked out of place in a bloody riot whether it was taking place in Miragliano or Altdorf, and a halfling whose short, broad form was festooned liberally with pistols. As Dubnitz watched, she drew one and snapped off a shot, plucking a hapless sailor from his feet.

'I knew it! I knew it was all going to go to pot,' Dubnitz said, rising to his feet. He tore his blade from its sheath as a shave-pated and iron muzzled pit-fighter charged towards him through the spreading smoke, flail swinging. He side-stepped his attacker and gutted the man. As the body of the pit-fighter hit the planks, he snatched up the flail and used it to bash aside a spear that dug for his vitals, before chopping down on its wielder's head with his sword. He grunted and jerked the blade free of the dead man's skull. Dubnitz looked down at the two men, and saw a strange, but familiar, brand on the flesh of both. 'Ha, of course,' he muttered, 'as if this couldn't get worse.' That was Tassenberg the Slaver's mark. Every slaver had one, and Tassenberg's was shaped like a twisted horse-shoe – a bit of humour from a boy who'd grown up in the Tannery. Dubnitz sighed. At least it wasn't the Master of Shadows. He looked at the two knights. 'Get up, both of you. It's time to earn our pay.' He glanced at Goodweather. 'And you – find some cover.'

'What about you?' Goodweather said.

'Me? I've got some red work to attend to,' Dubnitz said, grinning. With that, he strode into the smoke, flail in one hand and sword in the other. Alarm bells were ringing and men were shouting, but no one seemed to be putting up a concentrated defence against the attackers. Not that the latter seemed to be after anything in particular. Attacks like this weren't uncommon, especially given that Tassenberg didn't control the docklands, and wasn't friendly with those of his ilk who did, but why now? Did it have something to do with Bernheimer?

The thought wasn't a pleasant one. Tassenberg was dangerous enough – if he got his hands on the armaments that Bernheimer had purportedly designed, he'd set the city aflame in his desire to stamp out his rivals. Marienburg was a place of precarious balance; the powerful pushed and pulled against one another, and the city sailed on riding the currents. This included the hundreds of criminal enterprises that flowered in the nooks and crannies of the city like mould, but fools like Tassenberg didn't see it that way. They wanted the whole pie to themselves, and didn't care a fig that it was poison. They instigated massacres, when a simple murder would serve.

Dubnitz chopped and hewed with the skill of a natural woodsman. He was a fair swordsman, but it was his strength and speed that gave him his edge, and he was well-aware of it. In the hack and slash of shipboard combat, finesse and skill were less useful than muscle and endurance. It was the same here. A street-fight was no place for the knightly arts. It was a place for getting the bastard down as quickly as possible and putting the boot in as many times as you could, before you moved onto the next one.

Ernst and Piet had followed him, swords in hand. They moved steadily towards the landship where they'd last seen Bernheimer, and Dubnitz cursed himself silently. One of them should have been beside the man at all times. He twitched his wrist and sent the flail snapping out to block a stabbing sword. Ernst caught the swordsman in the side and chopped into him hard enough to lift him off of his feet. Piet punched a bravo, rocking him back a moment before he lopped off his sword-hand and left him bleeding and screaming on the quay.

Side-by-side, the three knights formed a deadly wedge; armoured as they were, albeit not in full-plate, they were more than a match for the thin blades and knives of the majority of the gutter-trash who'd boiled up out of the hole the explosion had made in the quay. Most of the attackers gave the three knights a wide berth, but those who didn't soon regretted their decision.

Leaving a trail of bodies in their wake, they reached the landship quickly, but not quickly enough. The landship was aflame, and the workers were either dead or scattered. For a moment, Dubnitz feared that Bernheimer was among them when he caught sight of the engineer hanging over the shoulder of the ogre he'd noticed earlier like a side of beef. The ogre roared and swatted anyone aside who got in his way as he fought his way back towards the epicentre of the smoke.

'Manann's scaly nethers, they've got our new engineer!' Piet said.

'Well, let's go get him back, shall we?' Dubnitz snarled, hurrying after the ogre. He wasn't looking forward to fighting the brute, but if they didn't, they'd be for the tide-cages once it became known they'd let Bernheimer be taken, if Ambrosius – or Ogg, for that matter – didn't simply have them executed out of hand. A Kislevite, stripped to the waist and moustaches and scalplock flowing, bounded out of the smoke, bellowing a war cry as he brought a heavy sabre down on Dubnitz's shoulder, scoring the armour and knocking him to one knee. Dubnitz grabbed his opponent's facial hair and jerked the man forward so that their skulls cracked together. The Kislevite staggered and Dubnitz slammed into him, bull-rushing him back into a pile of lumber. He smashed his opponent in the throat with his vambrace and kneed him in the groin, leaving him gagging and gasping. 'Get to Bernheimer,' Dubnitz shouted, trying to catch Ernst's attention as the latter cut the legs out from under a Norscan who'd moved to stop them.

Ernst turned and made to reply when a large, heavy hand shot out of the smoke and wrapped around his head. Before either knight could react, Ernst was yanked from his feet and then slammed face-first into the ground hard enough to crack the stone and, by the sound of it, bone as well. The ogre let Ernst fall – whether he was dead or merely unconscious, Dubnitz couldn't say – and stepped over him, tulwar sweeping out. Dubnitz hopped back, cursing. Bernheimer was nowhere in sight.

'Crack your bones,' the ogre slobbered, lumbering forward. 'Suck the marrow.'

'Sounds delightful, but I'm afraid I must decline,' Dubnitz said, avoiding a second blow. He'd had the misfortune to fight ogres before. The brutes were far stronger than any human opponent, and one blow from that tul-war would cut him in two, armour or none. He circled the ogre, lashing out quickly to cut at the back of one of its tree trunk-like legs. The beast whirled with a bellow and nearly took his arm off at the shoulder. The ogre reached out with its free hand and fingers like bilge hooks crashed against his shoulder. Metal buckled slightly as it dragged him closer and the tulwar dropped towards him with lethal finality. Dubnitz managed to interpose his blade, but just barely, and the tulwar wasn't stopped, so much as slowed. The tangled blades descended towards his face.

Then, there was a smell like standing water in a slaughterhouse and the ogre screamed in agony. It hurled Dubnitz aside and staggered. A num-ber of red, snapping shapes, like clouds of blood in the water, circled the brute, tearing at it with spectral teeth. The phantom sharks were as insub-stantial as a morning mist, but as deadly as their physical counterparts, and the ogre clawed blindly at them as its tulwar fell to the ground. Its howls were cut off a moment later as one of the sharks swallowed its head. The ogre gave a shudder and toppled over, missing its head and a good deal of the meat from its bones.

Goodweather stood behind it, her hand extended, palm up, display-ing a number of shark's teeth. They steamed faintly. 'Still alive, Erkhart?' she asked.

'Bruised but breathing,' Dubnitz grunted, pushing himself to his feet. 'I can't say the same for poor Ernst, however.' He looked at her. 'Thank you, by the way.'

'We all serve Manann, from the highest to the lowest,' she said, kneeling beside Ernst. Gingerly, she pried off his helmet and pressed two fingers to his throat. 'Pulse is weak, but it's there. He might live, if we get him to the Sisters of Mercy in time.' She stood and shouted at a knot of nearby priests. Stretcher-bearers were already being organised for the wounded. The priesthood of Manann were as feckless and corrupt as the next highly organised bureaucracy, but they came through in a pinch, Dubnitz was forced to admit.

Piet joined them, blood caked in the crevices and runnels of his armour. 'You need to see this,' he said, his eyes flickering to Ernst and then away. Dubnitz followed him through the slowly clearing smoke. 'They cleared out after Bernheimer got filched,' the younger knight said. 'Just stopped fight-ing and started running, the bastards.' He gestured. 'I chased them to here.'

It was quite clearly the epicentre of the explosion that had rocked the shipyard. A round, ragged divot gouged out of the solid stone and wood of the quay, large enough to lose a cart and horse in. Smoke still billowed up from within it, and the air stank of sulphur and scorched wood.

'I knew it,' Dubnitz said. Weariness crept over him, and he rubbed his face. 'Bugger this for a game of sailors.' He sank to his haunches and peered through the smoke, down into the hole. 'I knew it. They came up through the *unterdock*, like sewer-rats coming up a privy-hole.'

The unterdock was a secret place that everyone in Marienburg knew about – proof that nothing remained hidden in the city of merchants for too long, and also that nobody in Marienburg knew what 'secret' meant, really. It was an artificial world beneath the massive docklands that occupied the bulk of Marienburg's coastline. Built in an *ad hoc* fashion by generations of smugglers, merchants, pirates and beggars, the rickety wooden walkways spread like a massive spider's web beneath the docklands, starting in the north and spreading slowly but surely over the centuries to the other three cardinal points. It cut between the shallows and the surface, like a wedge of fossilized peas in an Ostland pasty. Stairs, ladders, fishing nets and overturned dinghies occupied the spaces between wooden planks, and formed natural landmarks. The air was muggy and thick with sea-salt. Barnacles clustered in patches like moss and things moved beneath the dark, sludgy water.

'I'm surprised they didn't set the air down there on fire,' Piet said, in disgust.

'They probably did. But it's not like that sort care about casualties, do they?' Dubnitz glanced up at Piet. 'I hope you brought your waders.'

'We're not going down there?' Piet said, aghast.

'They have the engineer,' Dubnitz said, rising to his feet. It wasn't a long drop. Hopefully they wouldn't go right through the rotted planking and into the drink.

'Dubnitz – wait – I'm coming with you,' Goodweather called, hurrying towards them. She had snatched up a sword from somewhere, and held it balanced on her shoulder. Dubnitz turned and held up a hand.

'As much as I'd rather have another old hand at the under-routes with me as opposed to a man who gets the urps when the privy overflows...' He cut a look at Piet, who made a rude gesture, 'I need you to alert the Marsh Warden and Grandmaster Ogg as to what's happened.' He turned and barked an order to a nearby sailor, and scurried away.

Her eyes narrowed. She opened her mouth, as if to argue, but then nodded sharply. She put a hand on his arm. 'Try not to die,' she said. The sailor he'd sent away scrambled back, carrying a bilge-lantern. Dubnitz took it and slapped it into Piet's arms

'I make no promises,' Dubnitz said. He clapped his hand over hers, trapping it momentarily. 'Best hurry, though,' he added. 'I'm only a fan of stacked odds when they're on my side.' He released her hand and turned, jostling Piet towards the hole. 'Come on Piet, down we go!'

They clambered down and moved carefully through the depths, the light cast from Piet's lantern revealing the path before them. 'Which way do we go?' Piet asked, looking about nervously.

'If memory serves, there's a way out, into the docklands, just south of here,' Dubnitz said. 'That'll be the quickest way out, and they'll be in a hurry, I imagine. Come on.'

The unterdock groaned and sighed like a living thing around them as the tides and the breeze from above caused the structure to expand and contract slightly. Walking through it reminded Dubnitz of moving across a ship's deck during a summer storm – not altogether difficult, but unpleasant all the same. Water dripped from above them, and the air was heavy with dampness. Things splashed in the darkness, causing Piet to start more than once, but Dubnitz ignored the sounds. He'd been assigned to sewer-jack duty more than once for various infractions, and he knew that, for the most part, the mutated beasts that swam the black waters of the unterdock avoided armed men.

The other knight glanced at him. 'You know, I could have alerted the Grandmaster,' Piet said.

Dubnitz grunted. 'You mean before or after he finished gutting you for dereliction of duty?'

Piet paled. 'Yes, I suppose you're right. Much safer down here,' he said, shaking his head.

Tassenberg patted the panting messenger-boy on the head and then cuffed him with an open fist, sending him scrambling. 'There we go. See? No problems, headsman. Otto is on his way, your engineer safely in hand.'

Bruckner grunted and crossed his arms. He stood on the deck of Tassenberg's yacht and surveyed the ships that clustered in the eastern harbors of Marienburg. There were hundreds of vessels, from an equal number of ports, carrying men from every nation, all flooding into Marienburg to conduct their business. Gulls wheeled over the harbour in vast, croaking clouds, and the bells rang, and over it all, a thick column of black smoke that twisted up into the air. They'd heard the explosion from where they were, and Tassenberg had laughed and clapped with joy. Bruckner had merely watched.

Bruckner was not a man for the subtle arts of the saboteur or agent provocateur. He was, as his title proclaimed, a headsman. He reaped lives, brutally, efficiently and without concern for rank, creed or gender. He had taken the heads of ladies' maids and manor-house lords alike at the behest of Countess Emmanuelle von Liebewitz, and it was only at her earnest request that he was here now overseeing this task. He would have preferred, on the whole, to have come at the head of an army, instead of relying on the dubious skills of a creature like Tassenberg to get him into and out of the city.

But it was important that no one, least of all the electors of the Empire, knew about this. At the moment, Nuln maintained a long-held and cherished monopoly on blackpowder weapons and trained artillery crews, and it was that monopoly that enabled Nuln to remain free of interference from imperial authorities. But the monopoly could not be maintained, if someone else – Marienburg, say – began to sell blackpowder weapons as well. Thus, the countess's spymasters and the castellan-engineer had come up with a way of sabotaging the freistadt's burgeoning blackpowder efforts. It needed to be done, of that Bruckner had no doubt. Nonetheless, skullduggery put a bad taste in his mouth. Better to simply take heads.

'Your efficiency does you credit, slaver,' Bruckner said, leaning forward over the rail. He peered towards the raised section of dock nearby, where an aperture composed of heavy chunks of wood, akin to those used in mines to bolster a tunnel-mouth, opened out onto the water. 'They'll come out there, then?' he said.

'Yes,' Tassenberg said, joining him. 'It's the quickest route out of the unterdock. It's all about the speed now, I'm afraid. Little time for subtlety,' he continued.

'That was subtle?'

'Subtle for Otto,' Tassenberg clarified. 'He's a good lad, but he lacks restraint. Besides, I told him to have fun with it.' He grinned. 'By the time the authorities react in force, we'll be sliding through the Reik-Gate, and right past those fools in the River Watch. I've got most of the current shift on my payroll, so we shouldn't have any problems.' He smacked the rail with a plump hand. 'And this boat is meant for river-travel. I use it to procure certain – ah – speciality items from up north.'

'I noticed the cages in the hold,' Bruckner said. His voice held no clue as to whether he approved or not. Tassenberg peered at him for a moment and then shrugged.

'Always be prepared, that's my motto,' he said.

'And are you prepared for pursuit?'

'Otto can handle himself,' Tassenberg said. Bruckner looked at him. Tassenberg stepped back. 'I have close to thirty men on this tub. All armed and perfectly ready to spill blood in our defence, headsman, not that you need defending,' he added quickly.

Bruckner shifted slightly. 'I will feel better when we are away from this garbage heap.'

'Marienburg's not that bad. Our sewers work, and we've got lovely local cuisine.' Tassenberg paused and added, 'If you like fish.'

'I don't,' Bruckner said.

'Yes, well.'

Bruckner stared at the aperture, willing Tassenberg's man to appear. The sooner that he was out of this city and could get back to doing what he did best the better, rather than skulking about on a criminal's yacht.

* * *

The pistol shot took a bite out of the plank next to Piet's face, spraying him with splinters. The knight cursed and staggered back. Dubnitz grabbed him and pulled him into cover behind a heavy stone support. 'What in the name of all the devils of the deep was that?' Piet snarled.

'I think they've realised we were following them,' Dubnitz said. He peered around the edge of the stone and could just make out the watery orange light of the gloaming. They were near the exit. He could hear water slapping against hulls and signal bells.

'That's the way, Bella my girl,' someone snarled loudly. 'Kill him! It's open season on armoured bastards!'

Dubnitz recognized that voice. 'Otto,' he growled.

'Who's Otto?' Piet asked, peering at him.

'Otto Schelp, the Manann be-damned Sewer-Wolf, that's who!'

'Uli Tassenberg's pet killer,' Piet muttered. 'Wonderful.' Everyone who dealt with the less savoury elements of Marienburg society knew the Sewer-Wolf, even if they didn't know his name. The lean, grey-faced killer was the subject of bawdy ale-house legends and mothers used stories of his exploits to frighten their children. Schelp had carved a red, wet hole into the city's heart, ensconcing himself forever amongst such luminaries as Mad Chipley, van Markowitz the Devil-Dog, and the Face-Eater of Fish Pie Street.

Another flurry of pistol shots punched slivers from the column they were hiding behind. Dubnitz recalled the halfling he'd seen at the shipyards and cursed. 'They're somewhere up ahead of us.' He drew his blade. 'Watch yourself, Piet. They're trying to keep our heads down, likely while somebody–'

The men rose from the water to either side of the boardwalk the two knights stood on, and thrust at them with tridents and bilge-hooks. Whether the men had been waiting, or whether they had taken to the water with the first shot, Dubnitz couldn't say. He swatted aside a trident and chopped down, cutting the head off and leaving its wielder to fall backwards into the water. He had no time to check on Piet. A bilge-hook skittered across his side and his arm clamped down, trapping it. He twisted, ripping it from its owner's hands, and rammed his sword into the man's chest. The blade became lodged in bone, and Dubnitz was forced to let it go as he heard feet drum on the planking behind them. While they'd been distracted, the rest of the gang had crept up on them. He swung the bilge-hook about, narrowly blocking a blade that chopped down at him.

'Hello Erkhart,' the swordsman barked. 'Fancy meeting you here!' Otto Schelp grinned widely at Dubnitz, his grey face pinched and oily beneath a bowl of stiff, pale hair. He wore black leathers that were shiny with grease, and his sword was smudged with soot in order to dull the blade. He hacked at Dubnitz, forcing him back through sheer enthusiasm. 'Tassenberg will pay me a bonus for bringing him your head! You broke his heart the day you left the Tannery.'

'I broke his head, you mean,' Dubnitz said, twisting the bilge-hook and driving its butt into Schelp's belly. 'I broke yours as well, as I recall, Otto.'

Schelp stumbled back, wheezing as Dubnitz swung the blade of the bilge-hook at his head, but he ducked aside, weasel-quick, and brought his blade down, snapping the bilge-hook in half.

Schelp snarled and slashed at him. Dubnitz fell, and rolled over the body of the man he killed earlier, using his momentum to wrench the blade free. Dubnitz rose to his feet and locked blades with Schelp. The thin man was fast, and deadly. He always had been, even when they'd been boys in the Tannery together, with Fat Uli Tassenberg and Crazy Rat-Eating Edwin. But Dubnitz had been better than Schelp when they were boys, and he was better now too. The Sewer-Wolf was used to killing unaware sewer-jacks and the out-of-shape guards of the River Watch. Dubnitz stamped down on Schelp's foot, bones snapping as he howled. Dubnitz punched him in the throat and Schelp wobbled, clutching at his throat with his free hand, his face going blue. 'Your problem, Otto, was that you were always too dumb to cheat,' Dubnitz said, beating his blade aside and launching out a kick at Otto's belly.

Schelp flew backwards and smashed through the rail of the boardwalk, plummeting down into the stew of sludgy waters. Dubnitz waited for him to resurface, then, when he didn't, he turned to check on Piet. 'You – ah – you have a bit of brain on your helmet there,' he said, after a moment. Piet stood in the centre of a ring of carnage, breathing heavily. His sword-arm was red from blade tip to elbow and his armour was coated in the detritus of slaughter.

Piet plucked the offending lump of grey tissue from his visor and said, 'Thank you.'

Dubnitz shook himself and started forward. 'Let's go get our engineer.'

The two knights stalked forward. As the sun set, a thick mist was rising from the water, filling the unterdock. He heard the splash of oars, and realized that Schelp had been trying to delay them. He spotted a row boat tied to a slight-looking jetty, abandoned by the remainder of Otto's crew. He dropped off the dock into the boat and snatched up an oar, tossing it to Piet. 'Grab an oar, Piet.'

'It's just my opinion, but one engineer isn't worth all of this effort,' Piet groused as Dubnitz hacked through the line that held the boat to the dock. 'It's a sad day when a knight has to row his own boat.'

'Stop complaining. This is what you signed up for,' Dubnitz said, as they began to row.

'No, I signed up for the easy women and free beer,' Piet snapped. 'A man doesn't become a knight if he's looking to do all of this work.'

Dubnitz grunted. He didn't disagree, but now wasn't the time. 'If we don't get that engineer back, work will be the least of your worries. Ambrosius will make us his personal projects.'

Piet bent forward. 'Let's row faster,' he said.

Their boat slid out of the unterdock and onto the Reik. The mist was thicker now, and it was almost impossible to see ahead of them. The mist enveloped them, muffling the sounds of the harbour. Dubnitz knew that their quarry had to be rowing towards a ship; like as not, it was the same ship that Van der Kraal had been trying to get Bernheimer to earlier.

'Are we just going to row around until we find them?' Piet hissed.

'I'll admit I didn't think that far ahead,' Dubnitz replied softly.

'I can't even see where we're going!'

'Trust in Manann, Piet. He's never steered me wrong,' Dubnitz said piously. The mist had been stirred ahead of them, and he could just make out the shape of a large ship, growing larger as they drew closer. Suddenly, he spotted another row boat, and saw that it was pressed up against the large ship. Someone had tossed down a ladder, and men were shimmying up it. The halfling with the pistols was still on the boat, as well as another man. Dubnitz gathered his legs under him and passed his oar back to Piet. 'Keep rowing,' he said.

'What?'

'Keep rowing!' Dubnitz bellowed, drawing his sword as the prow of their boat smacked into the side of the other. Dubnitz leapt onto the other boat, his sword whistling out. The cut-throat fell back into the water, trailing blood. The halfling gaped at him and clawed for one of her pistols and Dubnitz booted her over the side. 'Come on Piet!' he said, lunging for the ladder. Piet stumbled after him, and they clambered up the ladder towards the deck rail above.

They cleared the rail, surprising those on the deck. Bernheimer was standing among them, surrounded by armed men. The engineer seemed unhurt, so far. Dubnitz planted an elbow in a man's stomach and heaved him over the side as Piet joined him, his blade looping out to open the neck of another. They marched forward, scattering crew and bravos before them, until they reached the knot around Bernheimer. Dubnitz recognized a face in the crowd that faced them. 'Well, well, well,' he said. 'I should have known that where Otto went, Fat Uli wouldn't be far behind.'

'Erkhart,' Tassenberg growled. 'Don't call me fat.' The slaver had his thumbs hooked into his wide leather belt and his chubby face twisted in an expression of malice. 'I haven't seen you in a dog's age, Erkhart.' A large man stood behind him, faintly familiar to Dubnitz.

'Who are these fools?' the big man rumbled.

'Oh, where are my manners? Theodore Bruckner, meet Erkhart Dubnitz, of the Order of Manann, and whoever his friend is,' Tassenberg said.

Dubnitz froze.

'Did – did he just say that that's the Headsman of Nuln?' Piet muttered.

'Yes,' Dubnitz said. He looked at Tassenberg. 'What's this then? Selling out our fair city, Fat Uli?'

'I told you not to call me that,' Tassenberg said, his smile slipping slightly.

'Come here, Bernheimer, we're getting out of here,' Dubnitz said, extending a hand to the engineer. Bernheimer blinked and extended his hand. A small pistol popped into his palm, springing from a mechanism hidden in his sleeve, and fired. Piet made a tiny sound, and looked down at the neat hole in his cuirass.

'Oh,' Piet said. Then he toppled forward, as Bernheimer hopped backwards. Dubnitz gave a roar and lunged, even as Piet fell. But Bruckner was quicker – impossibly quick, for a man of his size – and his big blade sprang from its sheath and skidded across Dubnitz's ribs hard enough to send him sailing backwards against the deck rail, his sword spinning from his hand. Dubnitz tried to push himself to his feet, but a flare of pain tore through him, and he looked down to see blood pulsing down his side. Somehow Bruckner's blade had punched through his armour and into his flesh. Dubnitz slid down, clutching at the wound. The mist coiled across the deck, damp and thick, making it hard to see.

'You call yourself a knight?' Bruckner asked. 'You're a street-thug in armour. I have fought knights, Marienburger. You are nothing. Like this pest-hole of a city, you are a pale copy of your betters.'

'Good old Erkhart has always had something of an inflated opinion of himself,' Tassenberg said, giving Piet a kick. 'The whole order is a joke. Pantomime knights, rousted out of grog-shops and the tide-cages to put on a show for the punters. Think just because they've got themselves a fancy new chapterhouse that they can conduct themselves like their betters.' He looked down at Dubnitz and smiled. 'You never should have left the Tannery, Erkhart.'

'Why?' Dubnitz grated, glaring at the engineer.

'Why what... why did I shoot that oaf, or why did I come to Marienburg?' Bernheimer asked, stuffing the pistol back up his sleeve. 'It doesn't matter. It's the same answer to both questions. It was my duty, and one I happily performed.' He looked at Bruckner. 'It went exactly as you said.'

'Of course it did.' Bruckner planted his sword in the deck and leaned on the cross-piece. The mist roiled about him, and he waved a hand irritably. Dubnitz thought he heard a splash, but the thought vanished in another wave of pain.

'I did as you requested. It was child's play,' Bernheimer said. 'The first time they fire my guns, they'll explode, and Marienburg's attempts at duplicating our steam-tanks will be reduced to burnt and broken hulls. And the powder mixtures I "created" for them will crack the housing of any cannon they're used in. The secrets of the Gunnery School will remain with Nuln and Nuln alone.'

Bruckner nodded slowly. He looked at Dubnitz, his dark eyes glittering with satisfaction. 'Excellent. The countess, not to mention the castellan-engineer, will be pleased.'

'We've got your engineer. We'll weigh anchor and you'll be back in Imperial territory before the next cock-crow, headsman,' Tassenberg said. 'By Stromfels's scaly rear, I'll sail you all the way back to Nuln, if you like. That way I can collect my guns in person, eh?' He grinned down at Dubnitz again. 'You always were a disappointment to me, Erkhart. You would have made a wonderful criminal, had you stuck with it.'

'Just... like Otto, you mean?' Dubnitz gasped. The mist had grown thicker. He heard another splash, and then something that might have been a thump of wood against wood.

Tassenberg's smile vanished, and he drove a boot into Dubnitz's side. The sudden burst of pain caused him to exhale in agony. 'I'm going to enjoy wrapping you in irons and dropping you over the side, Erkhart.'

'A statement so common in this city as to be utterly without merit, I believe,' a familiar voice said. Men cursed and spun, reaching for weapons. Aloysious Ambrosius sat on the rail, an intricately engraved and painstakingly crafted pistol in one hand. He aimed it in a general fashion. 'Isn't that so, Sir Dubnitz?'

'He is no knight,' Bruckner snarled.

'No? Well neither am I, these days. And neither are you, headsman.'

'How did you get on this boat?' Tassenberg snapped. 'I'm a private citizen, Ambrosius. You can't just sneak aboard my private vessel for your own amusement!'

'Of course I can,' Ambrosius said. 'You're a private citizen harbouring agents of a foreign and hostile power, Meneer Tassenberg. You appear to have assaulted two members of the most holy Order of Manann in Marienburg. Either of those would be enough to see to your incarceration.' He uncocked his pistol and shoved it back into the sash about his waist. 'Not to mention giving aid to the aforementioned agents in sabotaging the military infrastructure of Marienburg.' He removed his gloves. 'I am quite disappointed in you, Herr Bernheimer, I must say.' Ambrosius slapped his gloves into his palm. 'Did you truly think I had my clerks following you about to help you? I might only have one eye, gentlemen, but I can still see well enough. Your "modifications" to our armaments were noted, logged and tested. I'm confident that our own engineers will be able to make them safe enough for our use. And you, of course, will help.' He smiled at Bernheimer.

Bernheimer spluttered. Bruckner stepped past him, blade raised, its edge still wet with Dubnitz's blood. 'Your overconfidence was always your least attractive trait, Aloysious,' the big man said.

'And those ghastly moustaches make you look like some flea-ridden Norscan, Theodore. Still – it was a cunning little gambit, and those idiots in the High Council would have snapped the bait up, greedy creatures that they are, under different circumstances.' Ambrosius shoved back the edge of his cloak and rested his hand on the pommel of his blade. 'For instance, you should never have gone to a bloated creature like Tassenberg when the Master of Shadows turned you down. You insulted him.' He sniffed and looked at Tassenberg, who blanched and reached for his own blade. 'So he, being a conscientious citizen of our little freistadt, passed along word of your undertaking to me.'

'Not that you needed it,' Bruckner said, raising his blade slightly.

'No, Herr Bernheimer is a cunning saboteur but as liars go, well, he is but an amateur.'

Ambrosius glanced at Dubnitz, who had pulled himself upright against the deck rail. The Marsh Warden's good eye narrowed slightly. Then his full attention was on Bruckner, and he drew his own blade, which looked ridiculously small and light compared to his opponent.

'Marienburg is a city of plotters and schemers, Theodore. It has to be, to survive. Your scheme was not the first and will not be the last to threaten our independence from Karl Franz's Empire. But today – ah, today we remain free.' He paused. 'Then, perhaps this was never about that. Perhaps you simply missed me.'

Bruckner growled audibly and took a step forward, his face flushing.

'No, of course not,' Ambrosius purred, as if Bruckner had spoken. 'Nothing as sentimental as that, I suspect. No, this is about money. It always comes down to money. Nuln makes a hefty profit on its powder and shot, does it not? But it will make less, if Marienburg gets into the game. Money rules everything around us.' He made a come-hither gesture. 'So let's see who has wasted theirs this time.'

Dubnitz swept the deck with a bleary gaze as Ambrosius spoke. Piet was lying still and quiet in his own blood, where Bruckner had left him. Anger flared within him. This hadn't been about independence or sovereignty. Ambrosius was right – it was about money. It always came down to money and murder in Marienburg. He wanted nothing more than to bury his sword in the headsman's back.

Even as he thought it, Ambrosius and Bruckner slid towards one another with a particular grace that trained swordsmen display. All eyes on the deck were riveted on the duel. Every man-jack of Tassenberg's crew was distracted by the clash. Bruckner had the advantage in size, reach and ferocity, but somehow Ambrosius refused to be split in two. Dubnitz wondered, as he stretched a blood-slick gauntlet towards his sword, whether this was merely the latest in a long series of skirmishes between the two. They spun and slashed at one another, causing the mist to billow and froth about them. Dubnitz peered past them, and saw shapes moving in the thick, grey morass and, for a moment, a fearful memory gripped him of another mist and the things within it, but then he caught sight of a trident and he knew what it was. 'Good girl,' he hissed and groped for his sword.

One of Tassenberg's men turned, alerted by the scrape of metal on wood. His mouth opened and he raised his own blade as Dubnitz's fingers closed on the hilt. He shoved himself up with desperate speed and swept his

sword, opening the man's belly. Then, with an awkward heave, he was up
on unsteady legs, one hand clamped to the hole in his side and his blade
slashing across the back of another man's neck. He thrust himself forward,
bulling into the crowd around Tassenberg, using his bulk to send them
sprawling, and in the case of one, pitching the man over the rail.

Tassenberg turned with a yelp as Dubnitz staggered into him and bore
him to the deck. He felt the slaver's blade dig into his mail, but it failed
to pierce it and he hunched forward, pressing the edge of his blade to the
other man's throat. He looked up at the remaining men. 'Drop your weapons, or I cut Fat Uli's throat.'

'You wouldn't,' Tassenberg gasped. 'You're a bloody knight!'

'No, I'm not,' Dubnitz said, glaring down at him. 'Remember? I'm a pantomime knight, a thug in armour. I'm good old Erkhart, Uli, and you know
I've cut more than one throat in my time.'

'Drop them. Drop them!' Tassenberg shrieked.

Weapons clattered onto the deck. The mist began to clear, revealing men
of the Marsh Watch standing on the deck, tridents levelled. And among
them, Goodweather stood, the mist clinging to her arms like silk ribbons.
She nodded to Dubnitz as he shoved himself to his feet, still holding tight
to Tassenberg. The crime-lord gave a snarl like a cornered alley-cur and
suddenly threw himself over the rail, tearing free of Dubnitz's grip. Before
anyone could stop him, he was gone. Dubnitz longed to chase after him, but
there was still the matter of the headsman. He turned slowly, still clutching his side.

Across the deck, Ambrosius and Bruckner still traded blows. As Dubnitz
watched, the bigger man beat his opponent down with a sudden blow and
raised his blade over his head for a two-handed blow. Ambrosius's hand
flashed to his sash and he plucked his pistol free and cocked it. Bruckner froze.

'I never could beat you, Theo,' Ambrosius said, almost gently. 'Not in a
fair fight, at any rate.'

'You have no honour,' Bruckner growled, lowering his blade.

'That makes two of us,' Ambrosius said, getting to his feet.

'I am a representative of a sovereign power,' Bruckner said, slamming
his blade into its sheath.

'So you are,' Ambrosius said. 'And you'll be treated as such.' He looked
at Dubnitz. 'Sir Dubnitz, I am simply overjoyed to see you alive.'

'I was hoping you'd show up,' Dubnitz said. He went to Piet, even as
Goodweather sank down beside him. 'Is he–?'

Piet coughed. 'What stomped on me?' he croaked.

Goodweather quickly cut the straps on his cuirass and pulled it aside.
She reached into his jerkin and Piet winced. 'Looks like his armour slowed
it down enough so that it only lodged in the muscle in his chest. He'll live.
What about you?

'This? Pah. Barely a scratch,' Dubnitz said, pressing his hand tight against his side. He looked up as Ambrosius's shadow fell across him. 'Tassenberg got away,' he said.

'So he did. Good.' Ambrosius said. 'Fat Uli keeps the others of his ilk on their toes. If we stretched his neck, someone new would take his place in a fortnight, and I already have my people in Tassenberg's organization. Besides, I'm given to understand that the Master of Shadows wants a word with him.'

Dubnitz shuddered. Fat Uli was going to have to swim fast to avoid that particular shark. 'And what about Bernheimer?' he said.

Ambrosius tilted his head and turned slightly. Two of his men had Bernheimer in a tight grip. The murderous engineer looked as if he'd deflated. 'We'll keep him, I think. He did place himself under our authority. And we can get more use out of him now. It's not like he can go home, after all. Isn't that right, Theodore?'

Bruckner stiffened where he stood, encircled by tridents. He said nothing, but his expression spoke volumes. Ambrosius smiled. 'As I thought,' he said. 'No, better he stays here and shares his vast knowledge with us. We'll pay you well, Herr Bernheimer. Better, I expect, than Nuln ever has.'

'You used us, didn't you?' Dubnitz said. 'To find out where Bruckner was? You knew they'd come for him again, and you used us to flush them out.'

'The first time they came for him was a ruse,' Ambrosius corrected. 'But yes, I did. I used you as my hound, even as I will use Bernheimer to improve our weaponry, and make us equal to any Imperial province, and just like I'll use Bruckner to wring concessions from our fair sister-city Nuln. As I will use any tool at my disposal to keep this city from sinking into the mire,' he said, smiling. There was no warmth in the expression. 'Try not to die on your way to the Sisters of Mercy, Sir Dubnitz. I have a feeling that the next few months are going to get very interesting.'

Dubnitz winced and glanced at the redness seeping between his fingers. 'That's what I'm afraid of,' he murmured.

ABOUT THE AUTHORS

Dan Abnett has written over fifty novels, including *Anarch*, the latest instalment in the acclaimed Gaunt's Ghosts series. He has also written the Ravenor and Eisenhorn books, the most recent of which is *The Magos*. For the Horus Heresy, he is the author of *Horus Rising*, *Legion*, *The Unremembered Empire*, *Know No Fear* and *Prospero Burns*, the last two of which were both *New York Times* bestsellers. He also scripted *Macragge's Honour*, the first Horus Heresy graphic novel, as well as numerous audio dramas and short stories set in the Warhammer 40,000 and Warhammer universes. He lives and works in Maidstone, Kent.

Nik Vincent is the author of the Gaunt's Ghosts short story 'Viduity' in *Sabbat Crusade*, and 'Cell' in *Sabbat Worlds*, which focused on the Imperial resistance on a Chaos-held world. She also co-wrote, with Dan Abnett, the novels *Gilead's Blood* and *Gilead's Curse*. She has written a number of short stories focusing on the Iron Snakes Space Marines, including 'The Third Wise Man' and 'The Fissure'.

James Wallis started his first magazine at fourteen. Since then he has been a TV presenter, world-record holder, games designer, political firebrand, auctioneer, convention organiser and internet commentator, and has written for publications from the *Sunday Times* to the *Fortean Times*. He launched the magazine *Bizzare* and *Crazynet*, and his books have been translated into eight languages. He lives in London where he lectures in games design and interactive narrative.

Richard Williams was born in Nottingham and is the author of the Warhammer 40,000 novels *Imperial Glory* and *Relentless*, featuring the Imperial Guard and the Imperial Navy respectively, the Warhammer novel *Reiksguard*, and various short stories including 'Orphans of the Kraken'. He also penned the Black Library background book *Liber Chaotica Khorne*. He is a theatre director, tabletop game designer and game design podcast co-host.

Josh Reynolds is the author of the Horus Heresy Primarchs novel *Fulgrim: The Palatine Phoenix*, and two audio dramas featuring the Blackshields: *The False War* and *The Red Fief*. His Warhammer 40,000 work includes *Lukas the Trickster* and the Fabius Bile novels *Primogenitor* and *Clonelord*. He has written many stories set in the Age of Sigmar, including the novels *Shadespire: The Mirrored City*, *Soul Wars*, *Eight Lamentations: Spear of Shadows*, the Hallowed Knights novels *Plague Garden* and *Black Pyramid*, and *Nagash: The Undying King*. His tales of the Warhammer old world include *The Return of Nagash* and *The Lord of the End Times*, and two Gotrek & Felix novels. He lives and works in Sheffield.

WARRIORS OF THE CHAOS WASTES
by C L Werner

Many horrors stalk the blasted wastes at the top of the world. Mortals and daemons alike wage war – and in this volume are three tales of such monstrous, god-touched warriors.